AUTOCOURSE

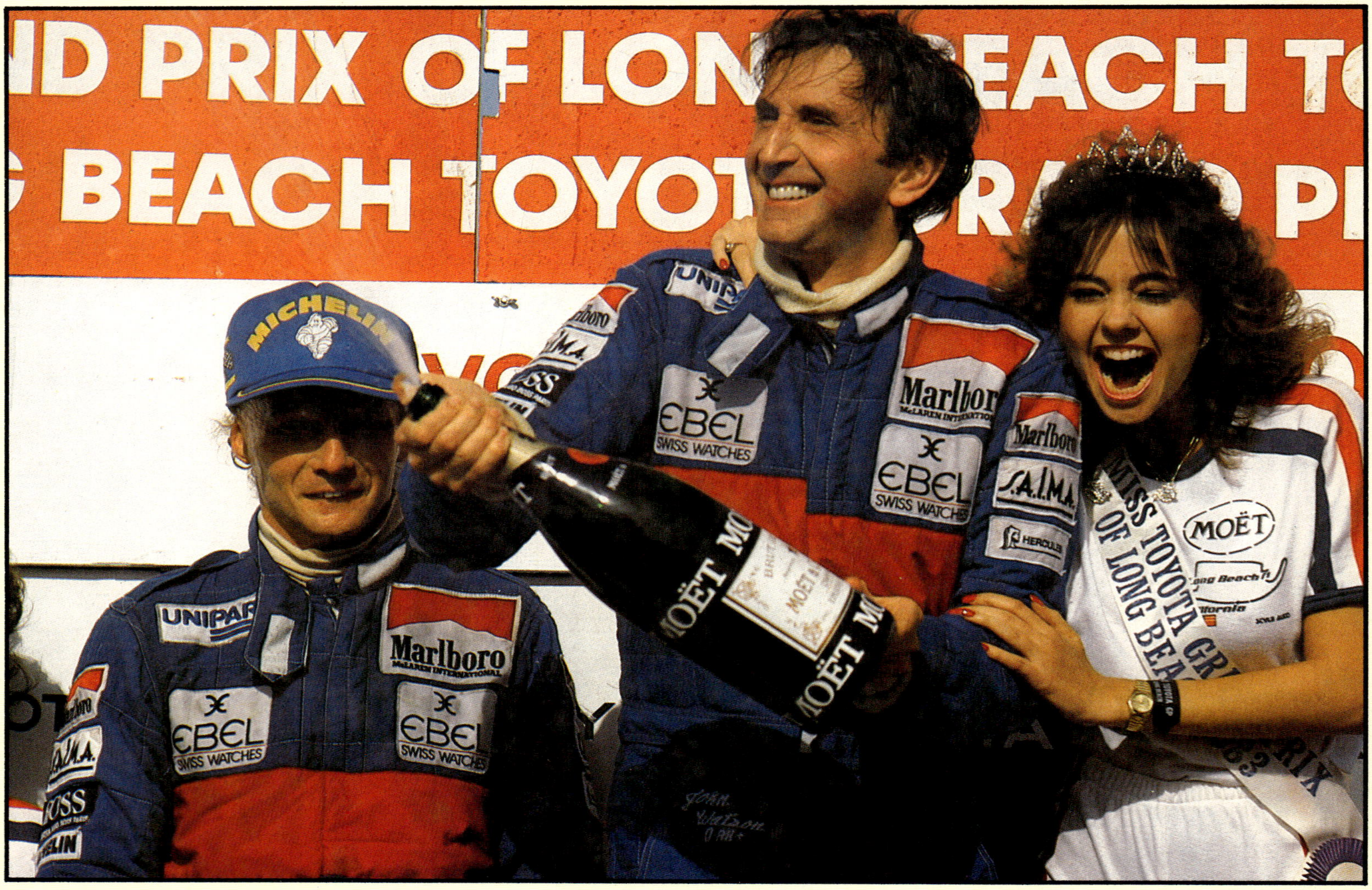

Publisher: Richard Poulter
Editor: Maurice Hamilton
Assistant Publisher: Liz Wagstaff
Publishing Assistant: Hilary Foakes
Editorial Secretary: Nicky Harrop
Design and Production: Jim Bamber
Lap Charts: Angela Poulter
Results and Statistics: John Taylor
French Editor: José Rosinski
United States Editor: Gordon Kirby
Chief Photographer: Nigel Snowdon

AUTOCOURSE is published by Hazleton Publishing
3 Richmond Hill, Richmond, Surrey TW10 6RE
Printed in Holland by drukkerij de Lange/van Leer b.v., Deventer
Typesetting by C. Leggett & Son Ltd, Mitcham, Surrey, England

ISBN 0 905138 25 2

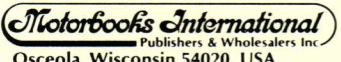

John Watson celebrates his victory at Long Beach *(above)*.
Photo: John Colley

United States distribution by

Motorbooks International
Publishers & Wholesalers Inc
Osceola, Wisconsin 54020, USA

UK distribution by

EP Publishing Limited

Bradford Road,
East Ardsley,
Wakefield,
West Yorkshire WF3 2JN

The photograph on the dust jacket is by Paul-Henri Cahier and depicts the 1983 World Champion, Nelson Piquet, in his Parmalat Brabham BT52B-BMW during the European Grand Prix at Brands Hatch.

Contents

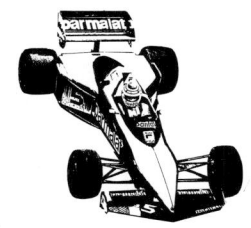

Photographs in *Autocourse* 1983-84 have been contributed by:
Bernard Asset
Jeff Bloxham
Peter Burn
Diana Burnett
Paul Henri Cahier
Mark Clifford
John Colley
D.P.P.I.
Bruce Grant-Braham
Maurice Hamilton
Robert Harmeyer Jnr
David Hutson
Jeff Hutchinson, International Press Agency
Michael Keppel, Formula One Photographic
Charles Knight, Motofoto
Mike Levasheff
Don Morley
Jad Sherif, International Press Agency
Nigel Snowdon
Keith Sutton
John Townsend
David Winter
Andrew Whyte

ACKNOWLEDGEMENTS

The Editor of *Autocourse* wishes to thank the following for their assistance in compiling the 1983-84 edition:
Canada: Canadian Automobile Sports Club. France: Automobiles Ligier, Danny Hindenock, Renault Sport, Jean Sage. Germany: BMW GmbH, Dieter Stappert. Great Britain: Arrows Racing Team, ATS Engineering, John Barnard, Cosworth Engineering, Mike Doodson, Brian Hart, Tony Jardine, Edgar Jessop, Brian Lisles, McLaren International, March Grand Prix, Motor Racing Developments, Spirit Racing, Tony Southgate, Team Lotus, Theodore Racing, Toleman Motorsport, Tyrrell Racing Organisation, Dave Wass, John Wickham, Williams Grand Prix Engineering. Italy: Pierluigi Corbari, Euroracing, Ferrari SpA SEFAC, Giorgio Piola, Brenda Vernor. Switzerland: Kaspar Arnet, Olivetti/Longines. United States of America: Championship Auto Racing Teams, Daytona International Speedway, International Motor Sports Association, NASCAR News Bureau, Sports Car Club of America, United States Auto Club.

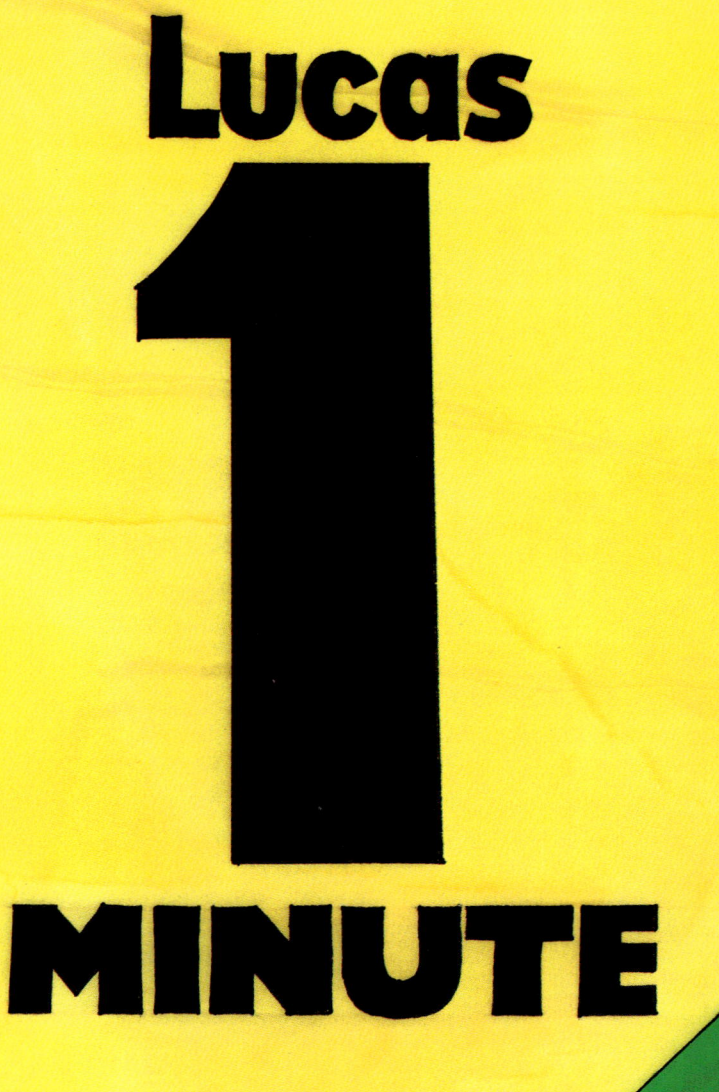

Lucas
1
MINUTE

FROM THE START
OF ANOTHER SUCCESS

Over the years Lucas equipped cars have been driven to more championship victories, simply because they have performed with total reliability throughout the season.

This illustrious record has been achieved by our technical support, monitoring and constant development of Lucas competition equipment which has attained a level of reliability unsurpassed in motor sport today. To pass this support on to the competitive motorist there is a nationwide network of dealers known as the "Lucas Special Section". To find your nearest dealer phone: 021-236 5050, Lucas Electrical Limited, Rallysport, Great Hampton Street, Birmingham B18 6AU.

You'll be in good company with today's champions, Jonathan Palmer, European Formula 2 Champion using Lucas Petrol Injection and continued successes in Formula 1, European Formula 3 and USA Formula Super Vee Championships.

Lucas Electrical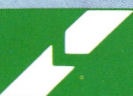

"For those destined to go further"

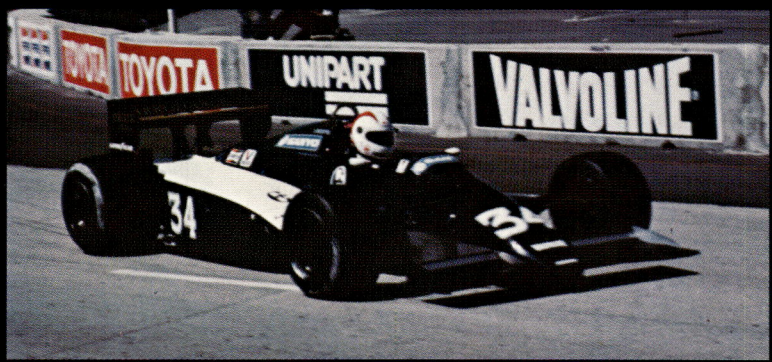
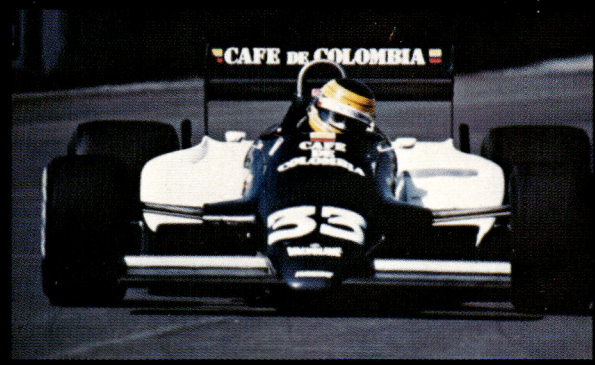
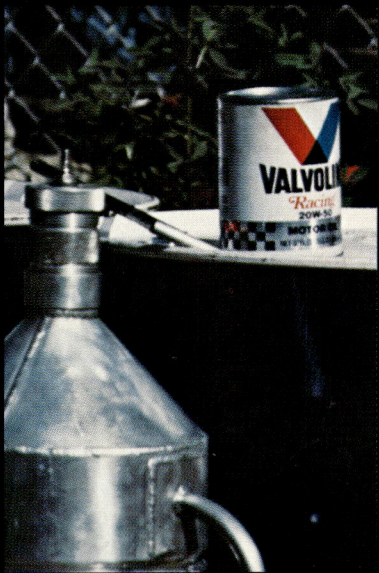
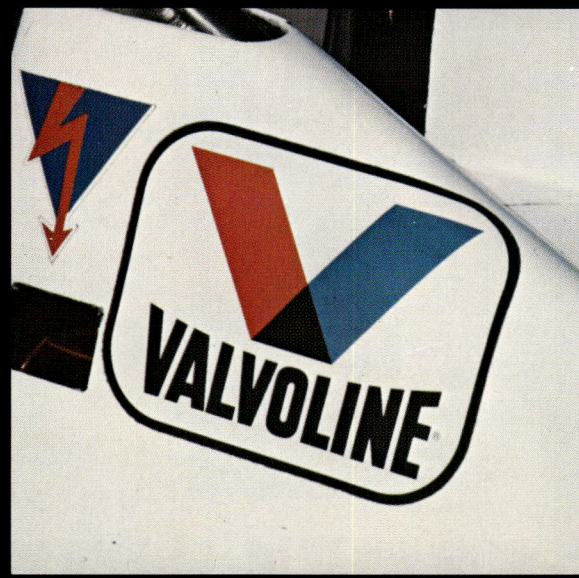
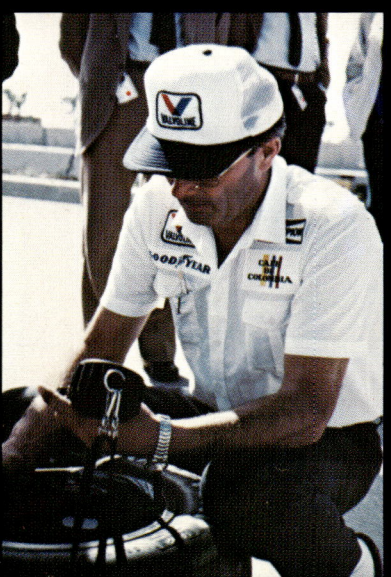
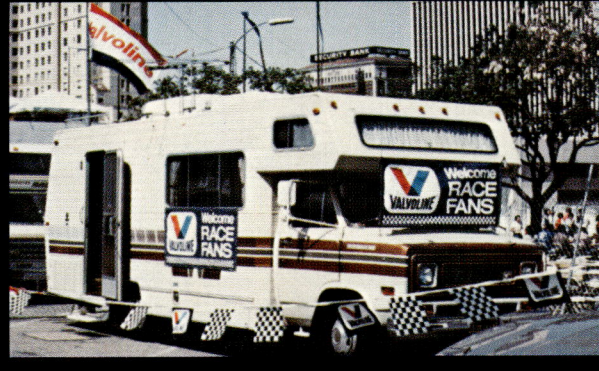
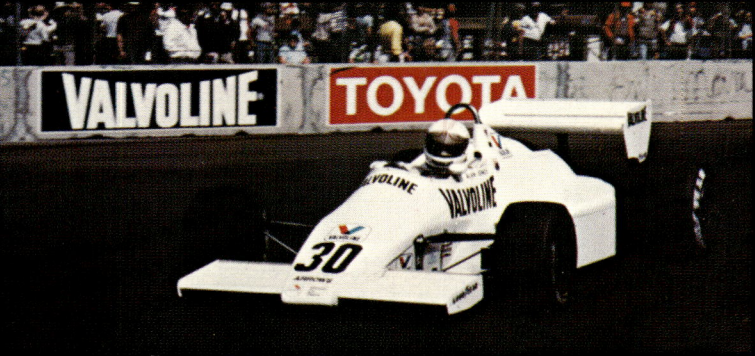

VALVOLINE. Seen in the Best Places.

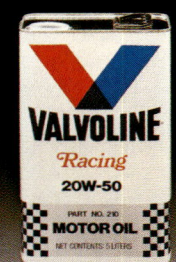

On the Grand Prix Formula One circuit, there is one motor oil that is dominant in dependable engine protection. Valvoline® Racing Motor Oil.

Formula One teams the world over have long recognized Valvoline as a leading motor oil. Because Valvoline

protects Grand Prix engines from the tremendous heat and friction of racing.

And, for everyday stop-and-go driving, Valvoline® Motor Oil protects your engine the same way it protects the most expensive racing engines in the world.

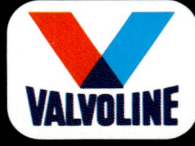 **Valvoline Motor Oil**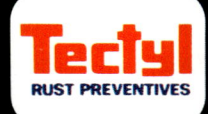
RACE PROVED FOR EVERYDAY DRIVING.

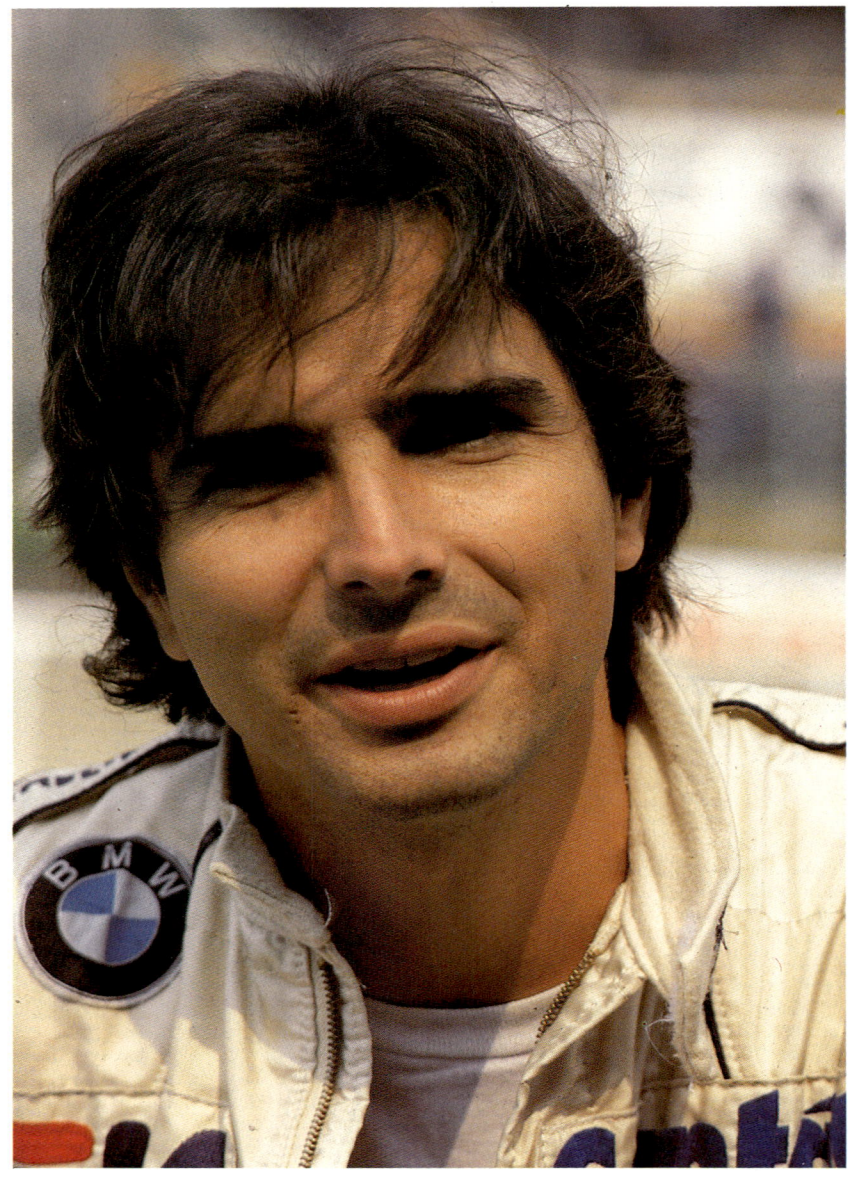

Foreword

by Nelson Piquet

Most of my friends will be amused to see that I have written my second Autocourse foreword because they know that I don't read very many books. But I do know that it is a privilege to be asked to write this, and I promise to try to read some of the things which my journalist friends have written this year.

I want to put on record my appreciation to the Brabham team for making the best car of the year. I knew as soon as I drove it that we had a good chance of winning the championship, and it was only some unpredictable little problems which kept everyone in suspense until the last race at Kyalami. The contribution of BMW has been equally fantastic; they must be congratulated on becoming the first makers of a turbo engine to become F1 champions.

Nelson Piquet

Winners –

The winning smiles on the opposite page are an appropriate summary of the 1983 Grand Prix season. The dissention which pervaded the sport during the previous years disappeared, from the surface at least, and *Autocourse* has the pleasant duty of recording events in what has been a troublefree and pivotal year for Formula 1.

If history is a signpost to the future, then Imola 1982 marked the change in direction which led towards the more agreeable climate enjoyed during this past season. The divide between FOCA and FISA may have reached gaping proportions in 1982, but at least the ground rules were established; FOCA held the purse strings and FISA made the rules. And, to that end, the most fundamental and far-reaching change for 1983 has been the return to sensible cars.

Ground effect, the simple phrase which described a complex phenomenon, was wiped out, and with it went stiff suspensions and cars which favoured the brave rather than the skilful. The 'flat bottom' rule of November 1982 may have been straightforward in concept but it did create a massive amount of work for the teams to carry out in time for the first race of the season. Yet, the fact that the rule change was accepted with equanimity and good grace – without recourse to boycotts and wingeing – was the most heartening aspect. Perhaps sanity did prevail after all; perhaps people really did care about the future of the sport and the image it presented.

Along the way, FOCA had come to accept the inevitable; turbos were here to stay. That once powerful organisation began to weaken when the teams with muscle began to fall in line with the manufacturers and this, of course, has been the most significant switch. If the Imola aftermath helped shape the guidelines for the administration of Grand Prix racing, then Colin Chapman's declaration in August 1982 that he would use Renault engines signalled just what form Grand Prix racing would take.

From seven turbos on the grid at the final race of 1982, to 17 at Kyalami one year later, Formula 1 has gone down the path pioneered by Renault in 1977. The fact that the French company did not win the championship while the going was good, while the majority of teams were clinging resolutely to the Ford-Cosworth, means their task will be even more difficult in 1984, particularly in view of the rapid progress made by TAG-Porsche and Honda, new arrivals during the past year.

While there may be objections to the increasing presence of manufacturers in Formula 1, the British Brabham team, no more than 40-strong, demonstrated clearly that millions of dollars and unlimited manpower are no substitute for a compact, purpose-made racing organisation headed by a design genius. Our Formula 1 Review by Alan Henry, and the examination of technical developments by Doug Nye, map out the intense struggle for a championship which ran until the very last lap of the final race.

There were boring races, of course, but when they were good, they were very good and the close friendship between the principal championship contenders, Nelson Piquet and Alain Prost, merely underlined the sense of well-being in the formula.

Piquet, profiled by Mike Doodson on page 30, demonstrated all the deftness and poise which a champion should possess – at the wheel. By his own admission, Nelson's work out of the cockpit will fall short of the energetic example set by Keke Rosberg. It was appropriate that Keke should make such a fine ambassador (and a lot of money!) in the year which marked the 10th anniversary of Jackie Stewart's retirement. The fact that the Scot has been permitted to remain at the forefront of motor racing promotion is not only a tribute to his professional approach and business acumen, but it is also an indictment against the behaviour and attitudes of his successors. Nigel Roebuck, in an exclusive interview for *Autocourse*, talks to JYS on page 76 and extracts some fortright observations.

Stewart has never been one to forget the importance of the paying spectator and FOCA and FISA would do well to take a leaf out of Jackie's book. Agreed, steps were taken to keep the arguments and disagreements behind closed doors but, in the meantime, the fundamental requirements of the spectators were frequently ignored. Television, you see, means more to FOCA than the unruly mob cluttering the roads to the circuit as they queue to pay anything from £15 to £80 per head. Never mind, if we make Silverstone a fine example of how to mollycoddle the drivers and keep the public at bay, then maybe the interfering enthusiasts will go away.

Yet FOCA seem to win both ways. Televised Grand Prix racing became ever more popular and attendance figures indicated that the crowd will keep coming back for more – perhaps to the detriment of Formula 2 and Formula 3, reviewed by Ian Phillips and David Tremayne. Endurance Racing did not progress as anticipated but, as Quentin Spurring relates on page 228, that was largely because Group C's enormous potential was diluted by problems of its own making. The European Touring Car Championship showed a healthy revival thanks mainly to the splendid news that Jaguar made a return to motor sport in an official capacity and, this year, we have allocated space for a review by Andrew Whyte of this important season. American racing had its ups and downs but CART continued to grow in stature as the corner stone of a broad spectrum of racing which Gordon Kirby has examined in depth, starting on page 218.

A switch of emphasis in the United States (some would say a blank refusal to accept FOCA's excessive financial demands) means one of the more regrettable losses will be that of Long Beach as a Grand Prix venue, although there was little remorse when Las Vegas opted for CART rather than Formula 1.

There were 15 Grands Prix in 1983 and, at 14 of them, pit stops were usually carried out with exemplary precision. Denis Jenkinson describes the background and preparation for a phenomenon which became a necessary tactic, one which has been banned in 1984. Scheduled stops for fuel and tyres provided an interesting diversion but, the danger aside, they had no place in Formula 1 and we are happy to report that the predicted holocaust in the pits did not happen.

We are also gratified to be able to present you with a Grand Prix season which can claim no serious accidents. In fact, hardly any accidents at all, the only injury being sustained by Bruno Giacomelli when he fell off Rosberg's car while hitching a ride to the pits at Montreal! A season, then, of many winners and few losers.

October 1983   Maurice Hamilton
                                                  Dorking
                                                  Surrey

and very few losers

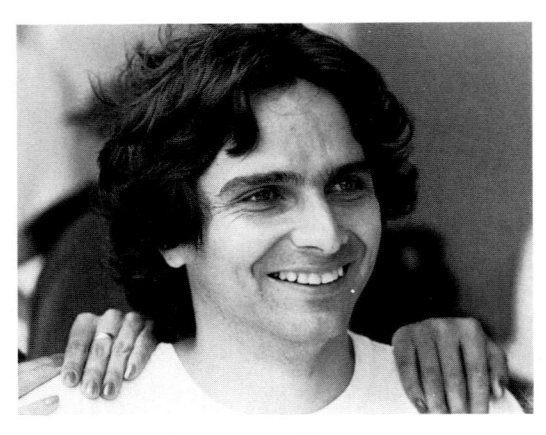
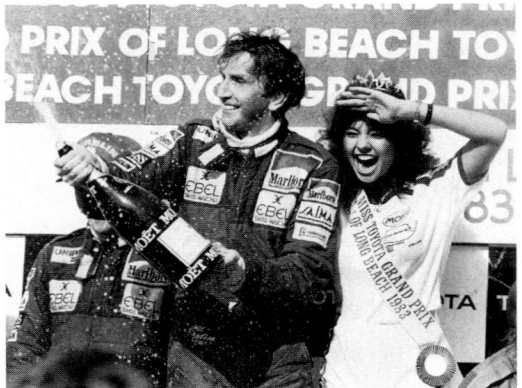
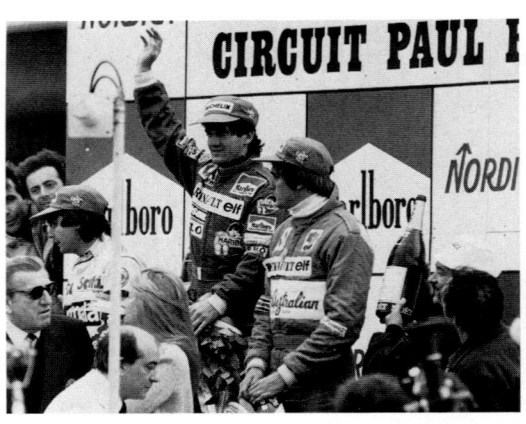
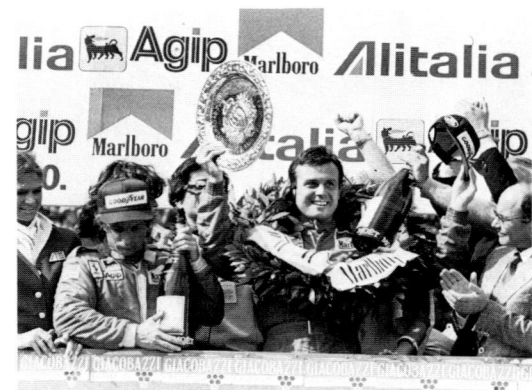
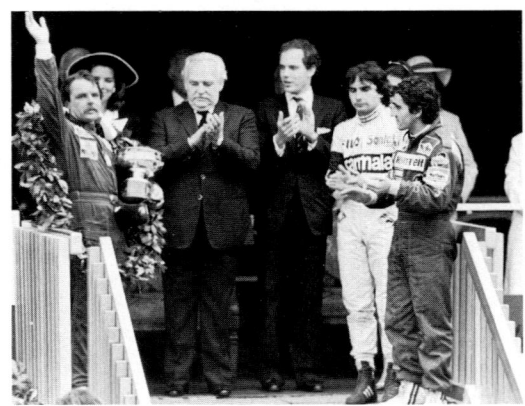
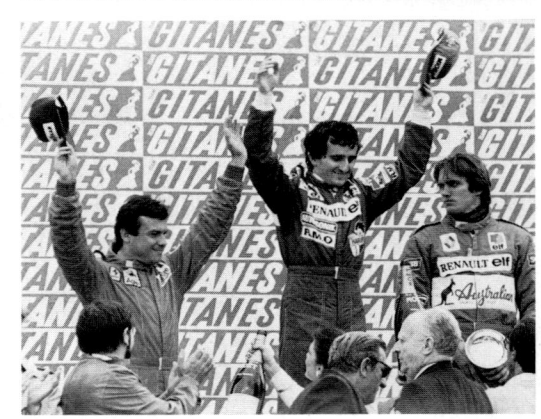
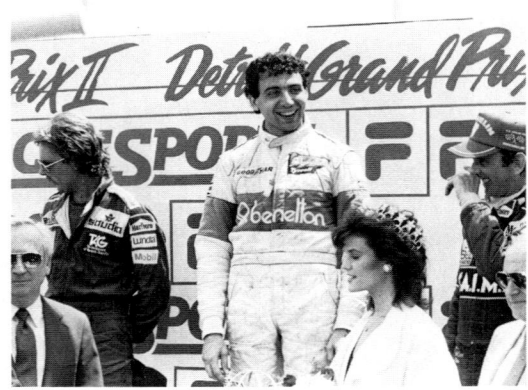
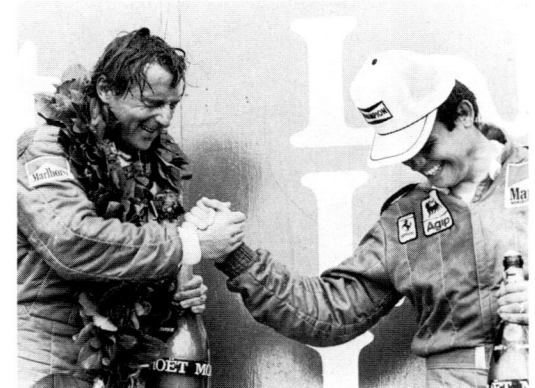
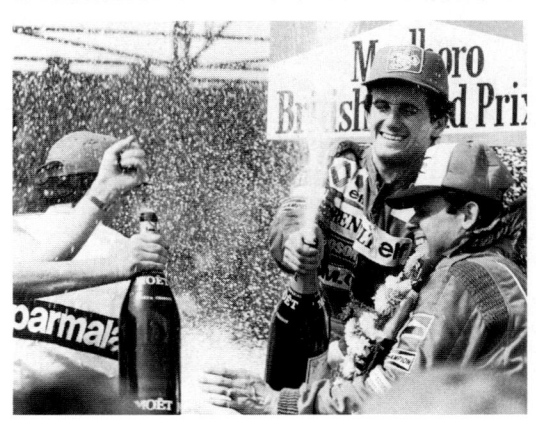
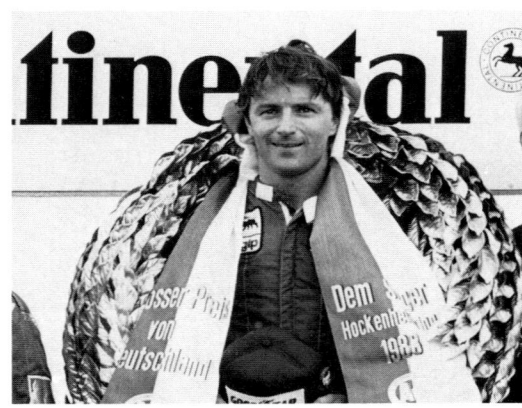
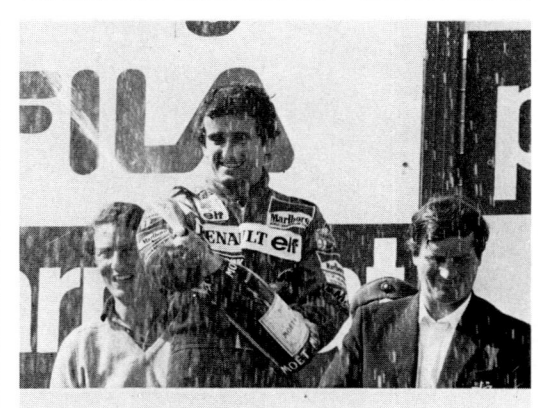
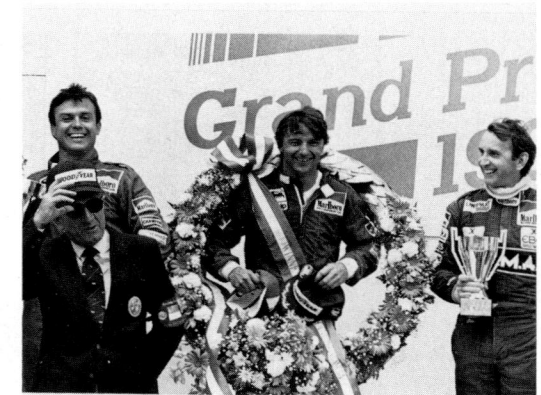
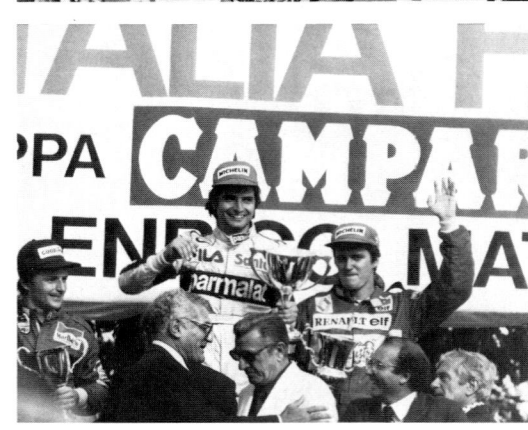
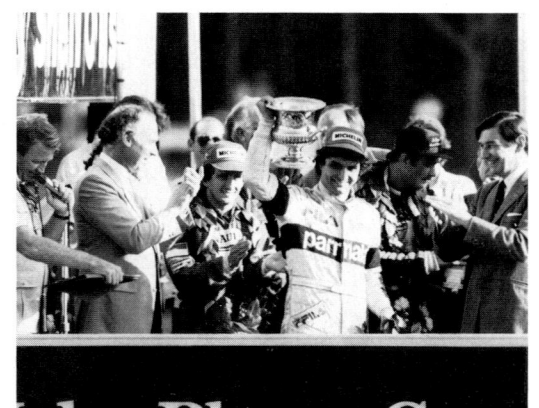
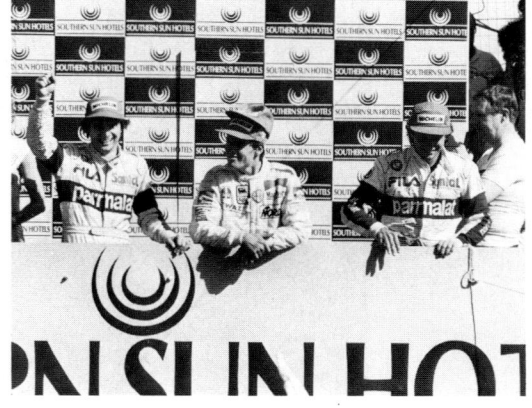

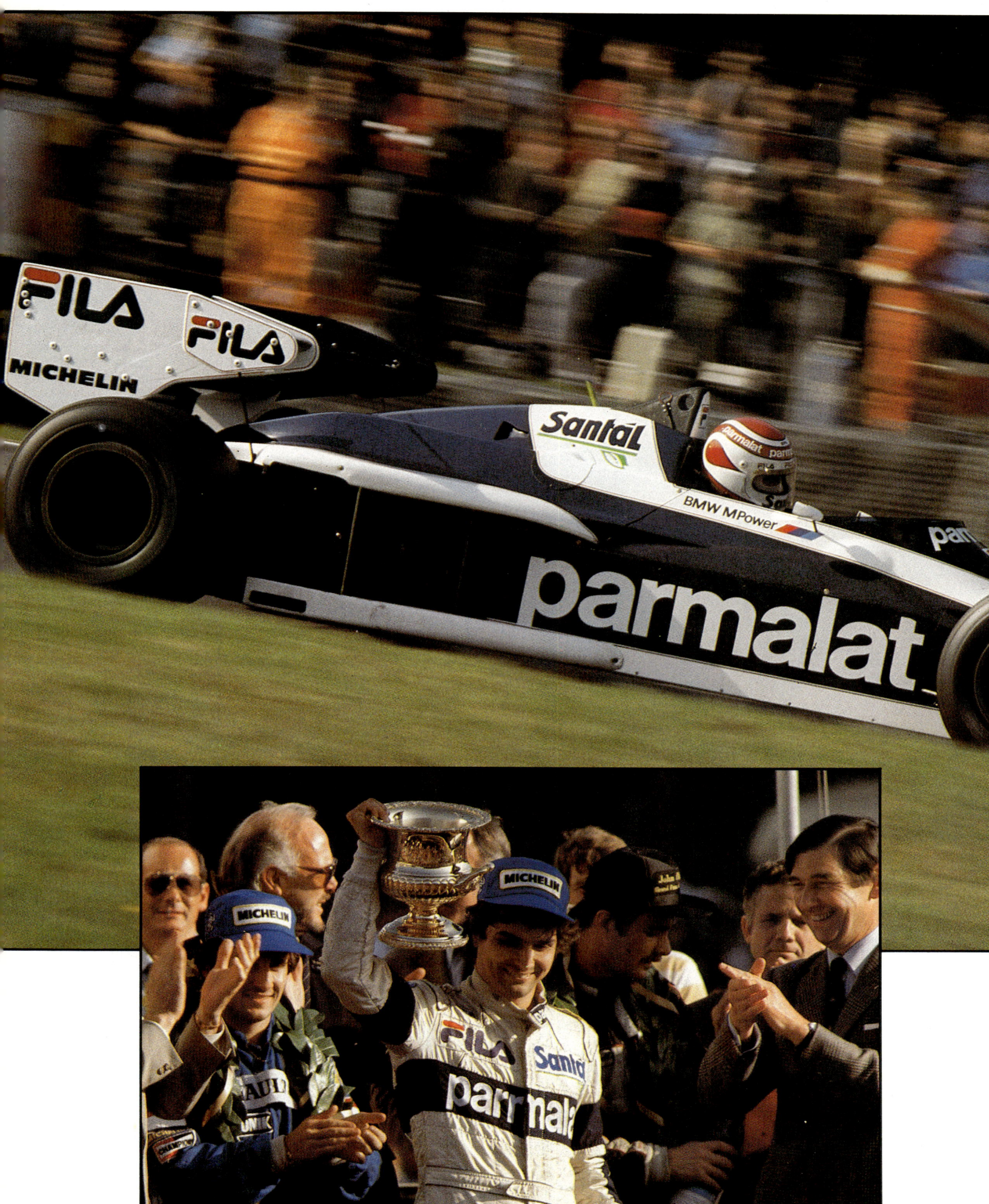

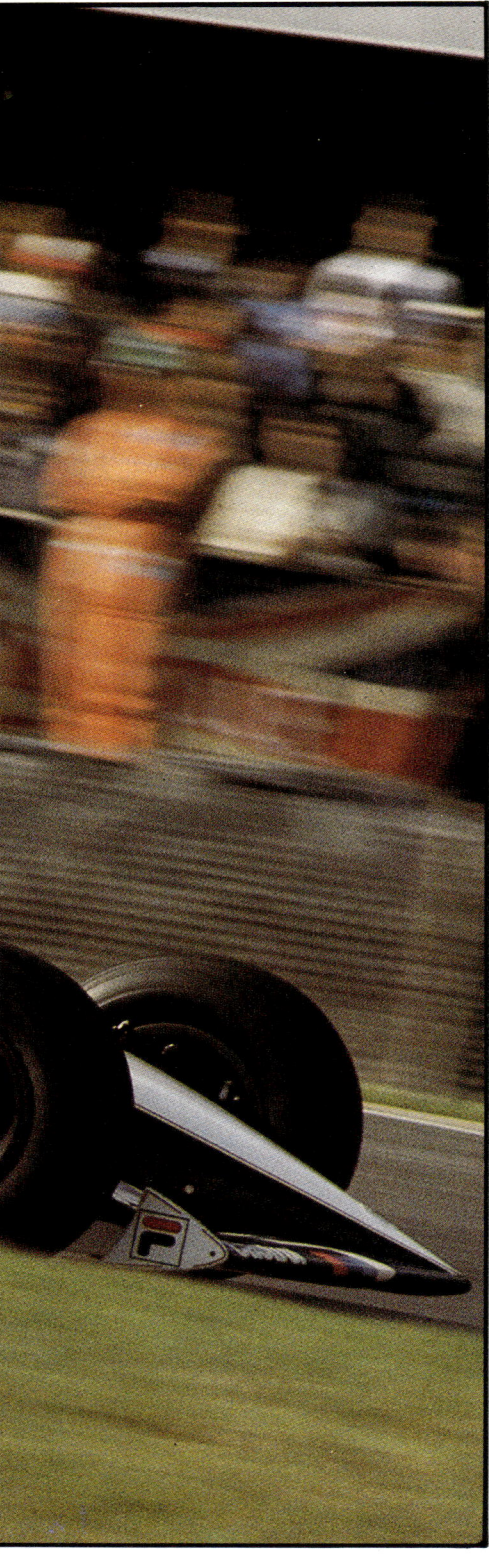

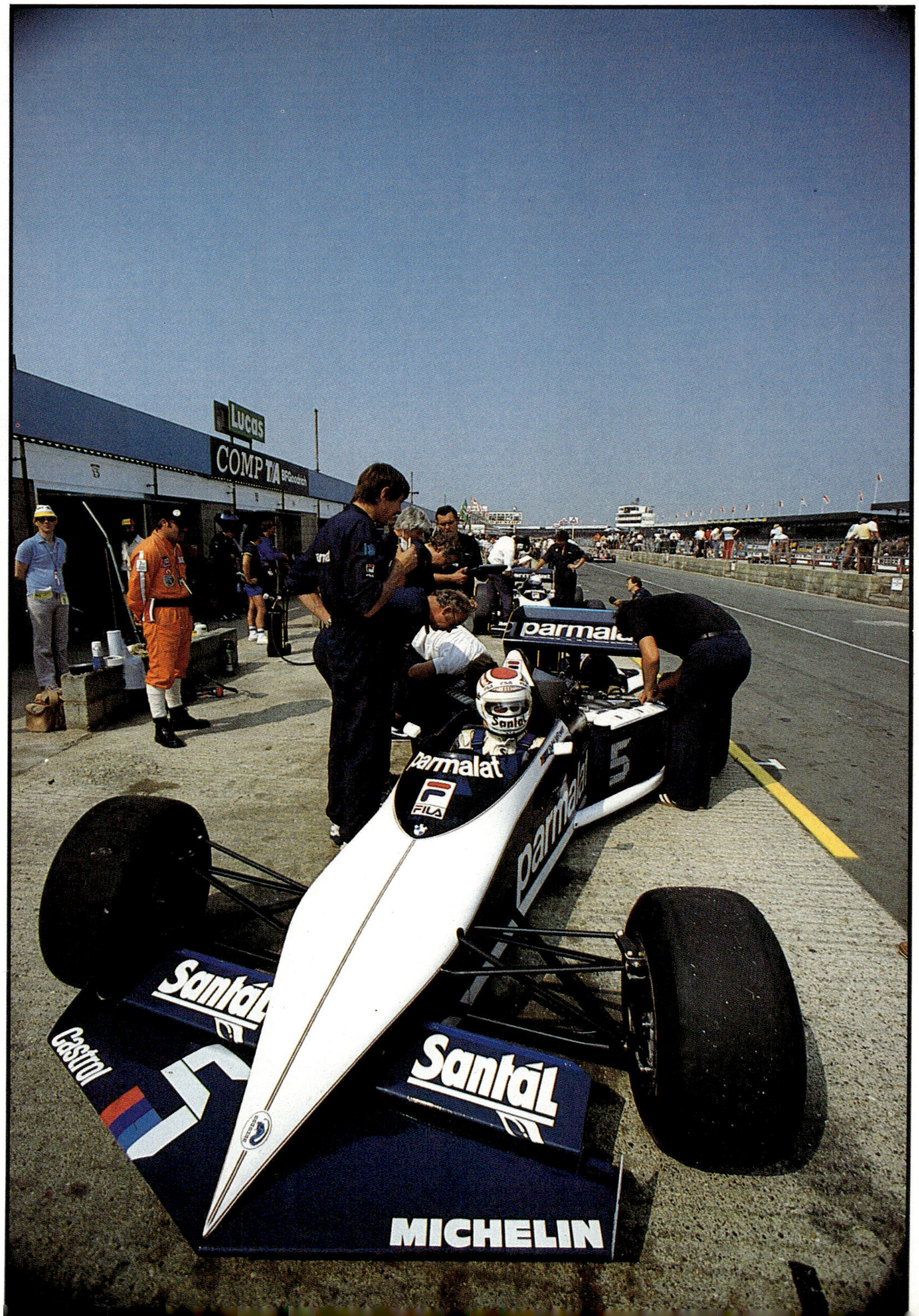

Nelson Piquet, one of
the leading runners on
Michelin tyres, helped
the French company to
win nine Grands Prix
during the season.
Photo: Nigel Snowdon and
(right) Bernard Asset

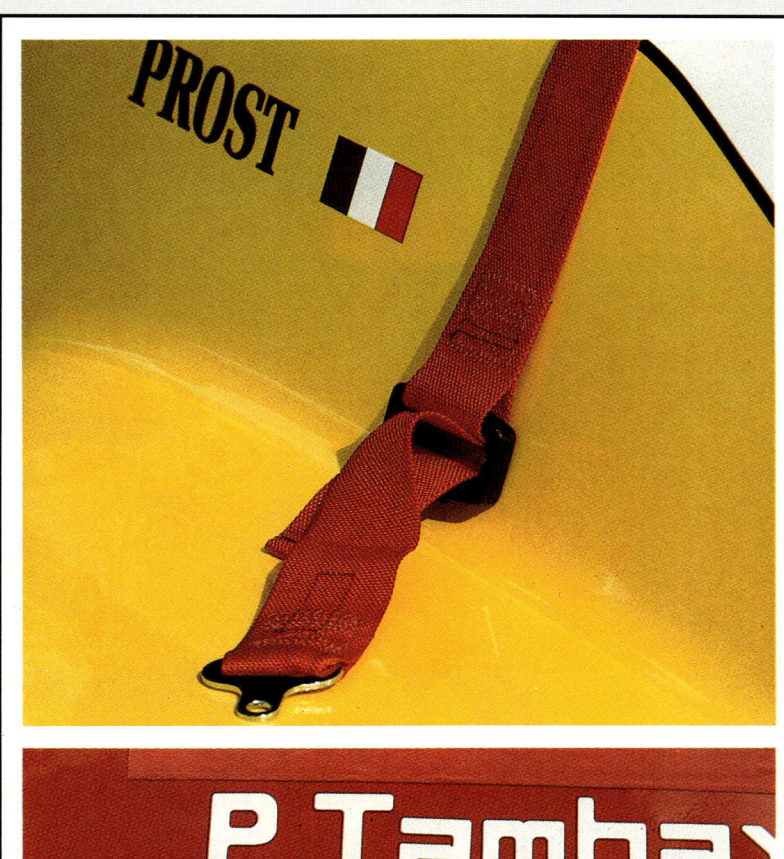
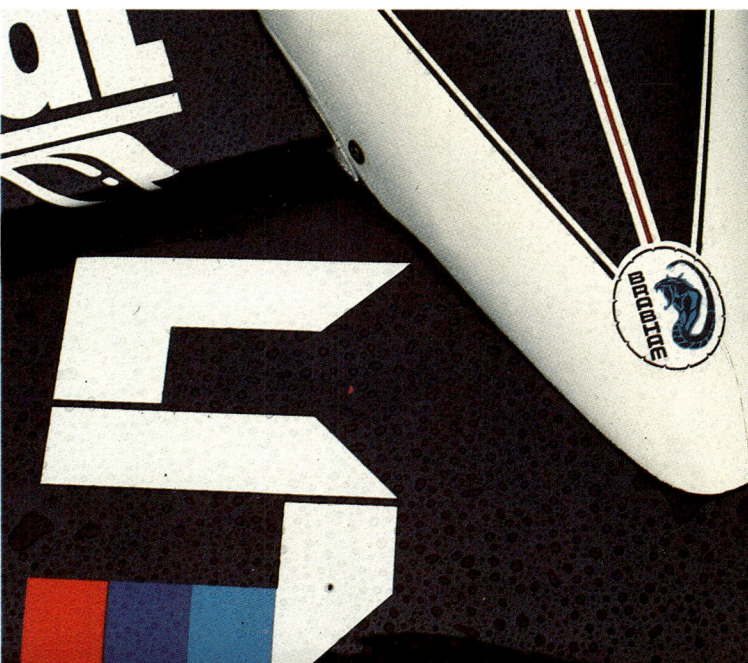
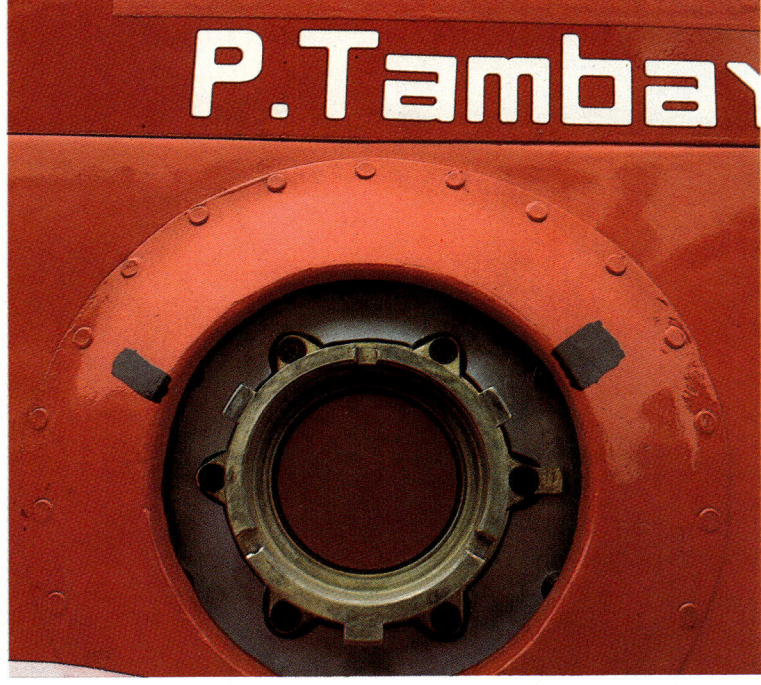
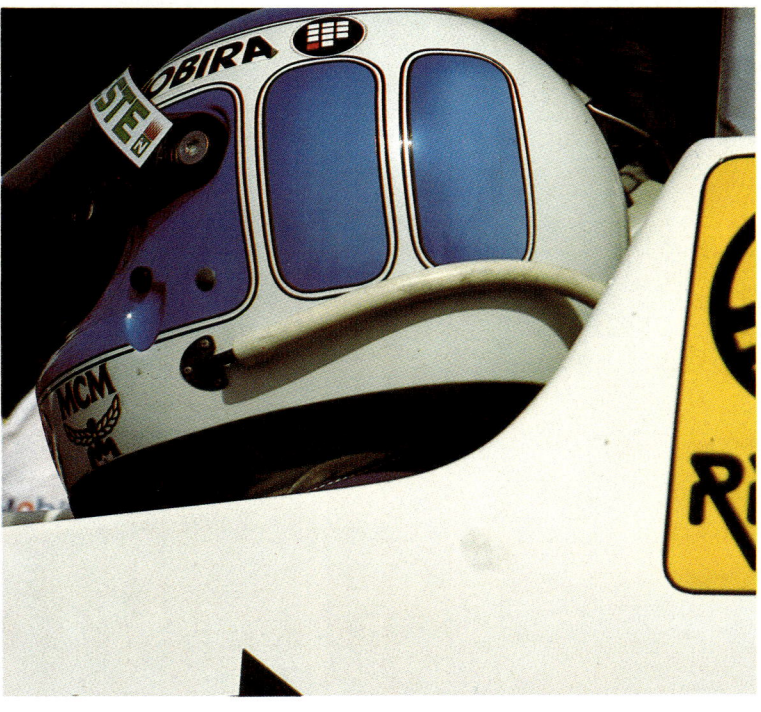

Photos by Paul Henri Cahier

TOP TEN

1 Nelson Piquet
2 Alain Prost
3 Patrick Tambay
4 René Arnoux
5 Keke Rosberg
6 John Watson
7 Eddie Cheever
8 Derek Warwick
9 Niki Lauda
10 Andrea de Cesaris

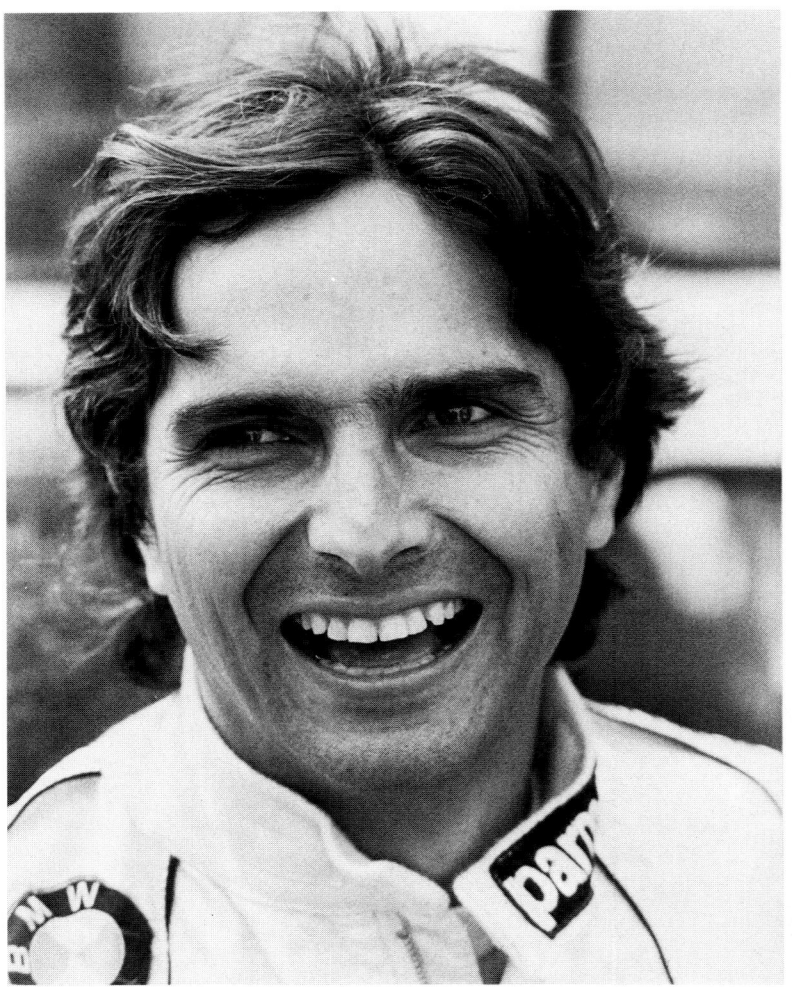

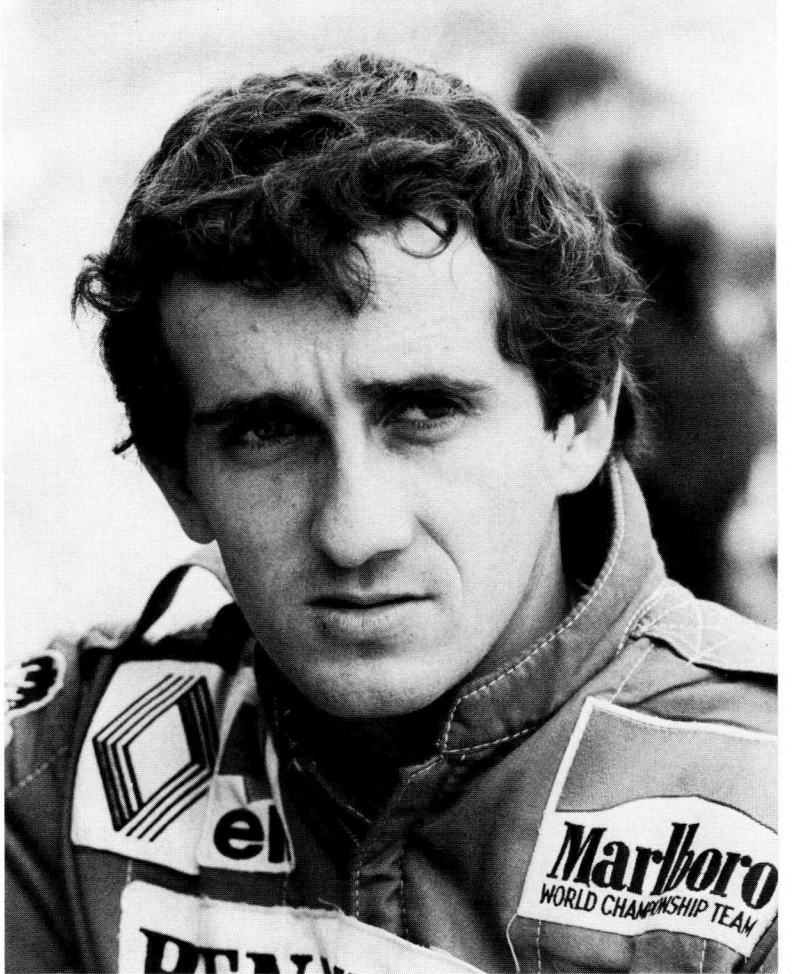

1 Nelson Piquet

At Rio, he made it look easy – just as he would at Monza, Brands Hatch and Kyalami. In between, however, we were able to judge why Nelson Piquet was, quite simply, the outstanding driver of the year. Victory first time out with the BT52 in Brazil merely flattered to deceive. At Paul Ricard, he had to show immense bravery and resolution to finish second with a car which was twice as difficult to drive. Then at Monaco, a street circuit he detests, Nelson finished second again thanks to a patient and intelligent drive. And so it went on. Wherever the circuit, whatever the problem, Nelson Piquet could be relied on to provide the perfect mixture of speed and mechanical sympathy, aggression and composure. He was let down by circumstances beyond his control on at least six occasions; by a driving error, just once. Yet he maintained a calm, philosophical approach and the fact that it was the driver who consoled the team, rather than the other way round, demonstrated that the chemistry was right for Piquet to become World Champion. In 1981, he won almost by default. In 1983, he was the class of the field; a driver approaching his peak.

2 Alain Prost

It is easy to point to the Zandvoort incident and say that a driving error cost Alain Prost the championship. That is an over-simplification, rather like saying Piquet won the championship because he had a good car. Perhaps Prost did allow the personal feud with Arnoux to cloud his judgement and force an attempt at what should have been a legitimate passing manoeuvre at Zandvoort but that should not detract from a season which has seen Prost become even smoother and more intelligent as a driver. There were times, such as Silverstone and Spa, when he simply destroyed the opposition without putting a wheel so much as an inch out of line. And in Austria, he refused to be ruffled by what others might have regarded as a poor grid position, preferring instead to turn on a brilliant display of judgement, tactics and crisp aggression. Zandvoort aside, his driving has been as exemplary as it has been monotonous to watch. With four races to run, he had managed to bring his car home in the points more times than any other driver but, in the end, unreliability struck again. Perhaps he should have aimed at outright wins rather than driving for points. Piquet, the man he pushed off at Zandvoort, summed up the end result best when he said it was not Prost who had lost the championship – but Renault.

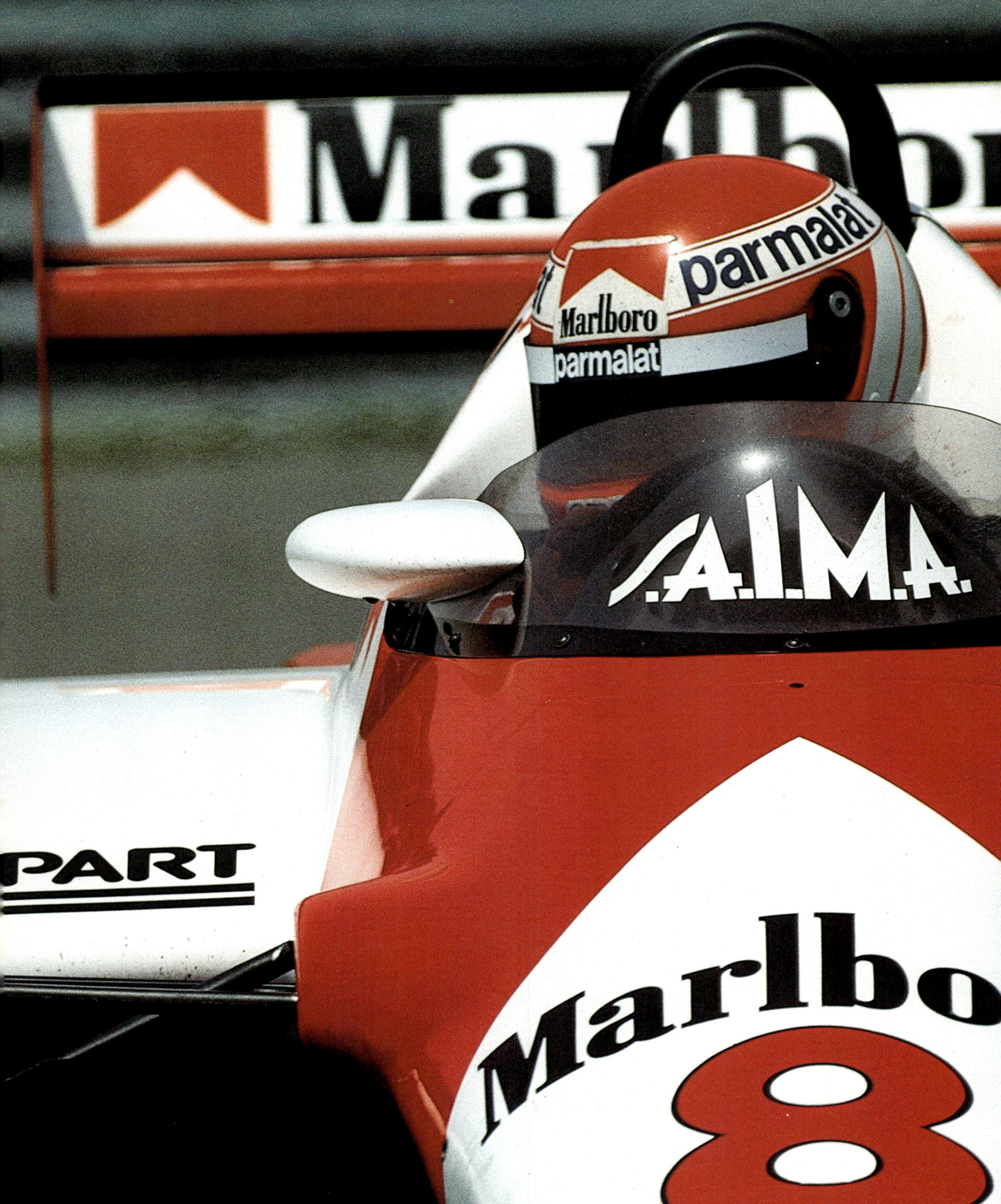

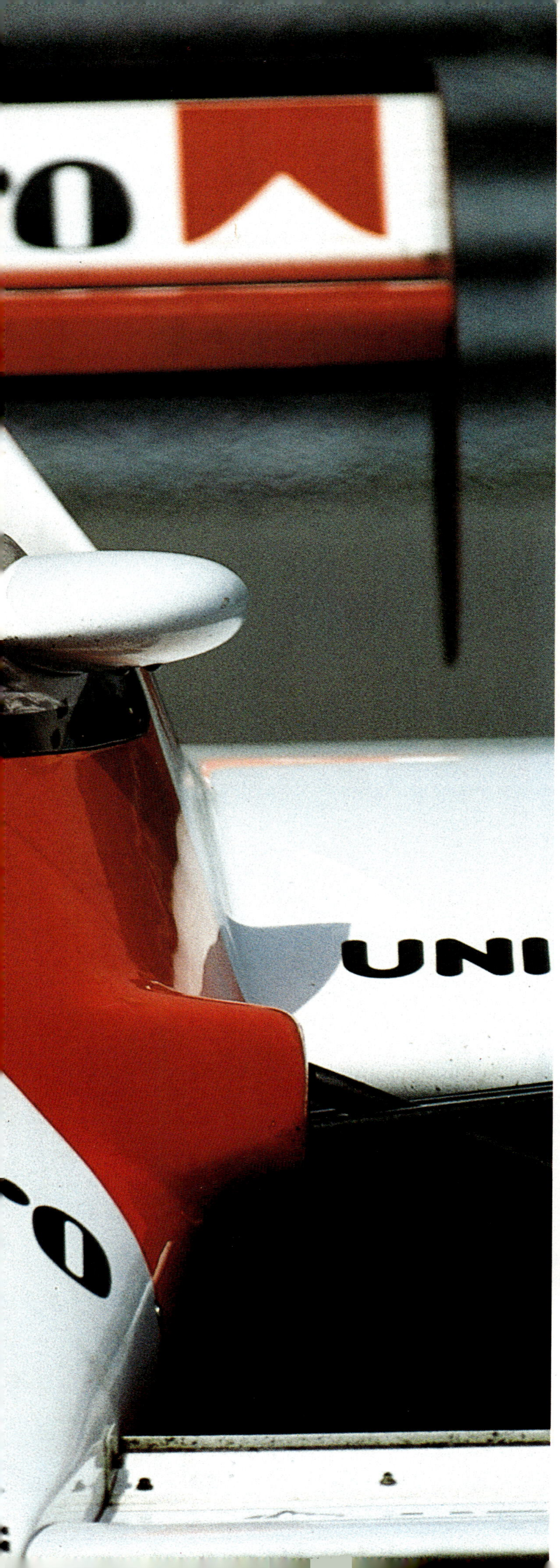

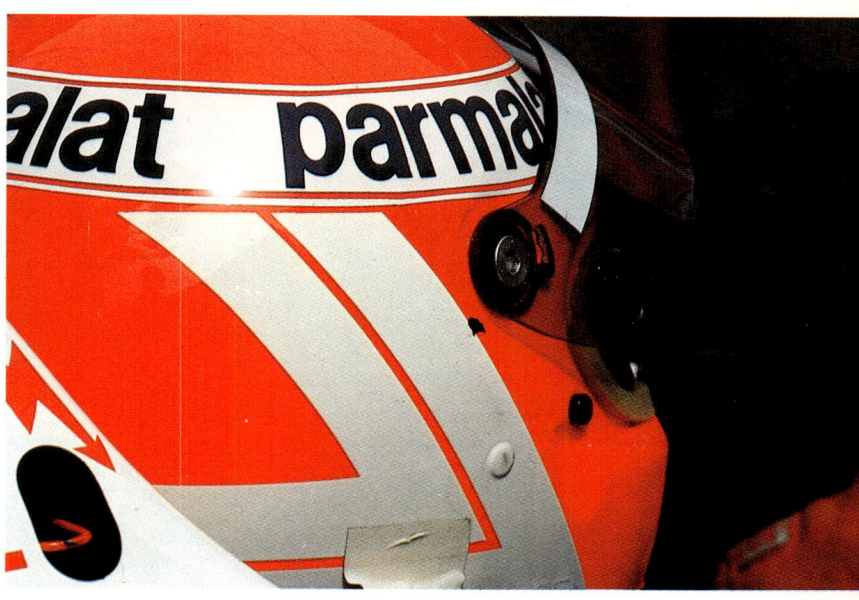

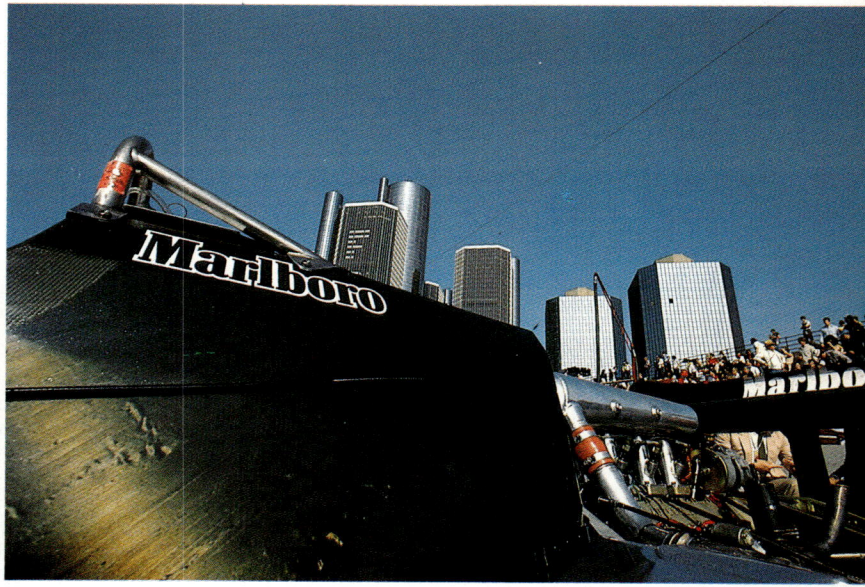

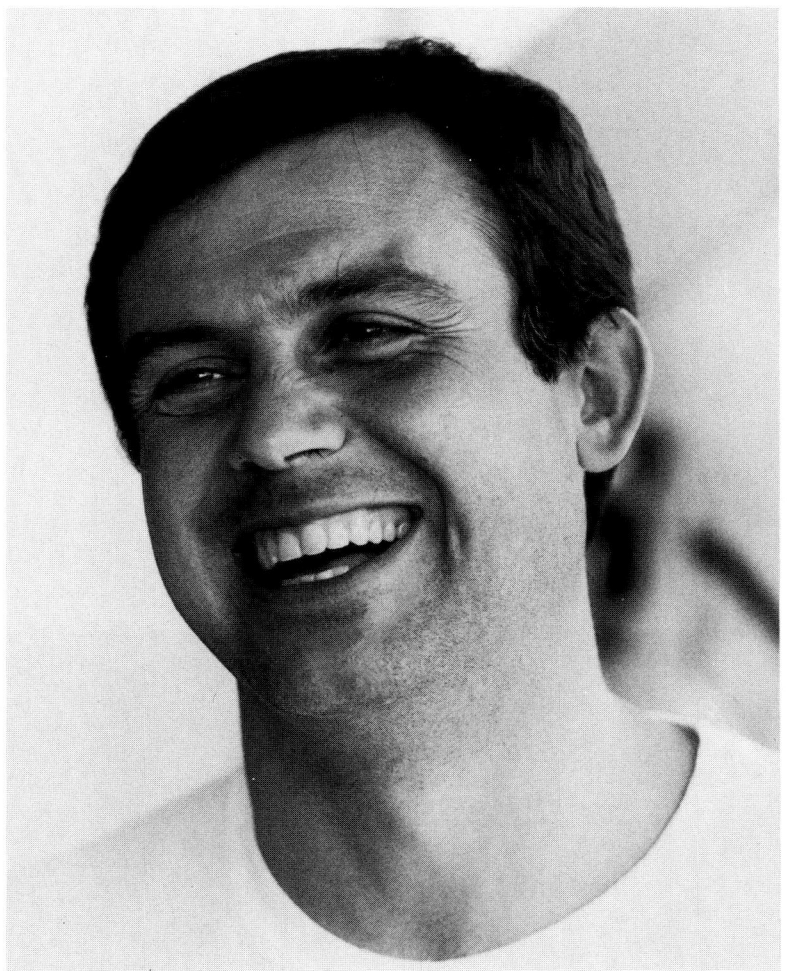

Patrick Tambay

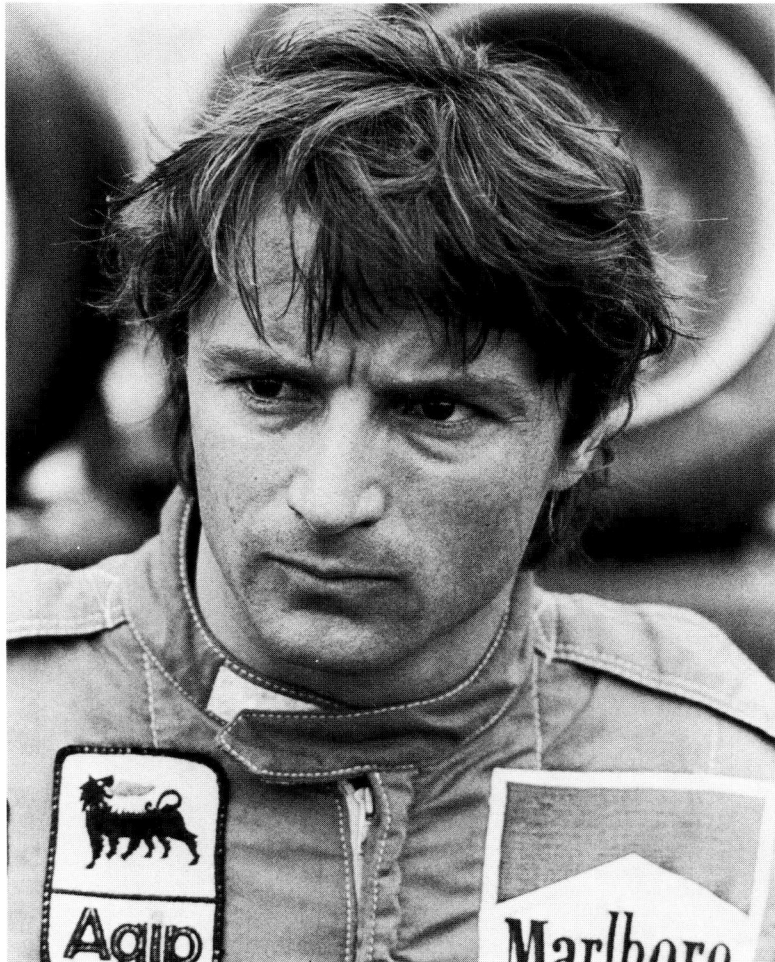

René Arnoux

3 Patrick Tambay

Patrick Tambay's consistency was expected but his sheer pace surprised even his most ardent supporters. The ability to respect his equipment during races was anticipated but the speed to out-qualify Arnoux eight to seven was an indication of Tambay's all-round talent. Smooth and stylish, the Frenchman more than justified the faith shown in him by Ferrari at the end of the previous year and it is a pity that the results would make him appear inferior to Arnoux. It should be remembered, however, that he was well-placed for wins in Germany and Austria when his car let him down. The incident with Rosberg at Long Beach put paid to more points – but, then, so did errors on the starting grids at Detroit and Zandvoort. That aside, Tambay's testing ability, coupled with his intelligent driving, make him one of the most accomplished drivers racing today. Indeed, his reputation is now such that it has not been tarnished by the arbitrary and unreasonable dismissal from Ferrari.

4 René Arnoux

René Arnoux won three Grands Prix and, on each occasion, he thoroughly deserved his nine points – even at Zandvoort where his relentless drive after an appalling practice made up for the disappointment after dominating in Detroit. That said, his aggression and flair were accompanied by an untidy, kerb-bashing style. And, when the equipment was less than perfect, he seemed to lack the sympathy and delicacy to nurse it through the races; Silverstone being a good example of that as he wore out his tyres while Tambay treated his with respect *and* went faster. Arnoux will always be a potential winner provided his car is competitive and it remains to be seen what state Ferrari will be in now that Tambay, responsible for most of the development in 1983, has been moved on.

5 Keke Rosberg

Keke Rosberg is the fastest driver in the business. It's a fact that few would dispute – which must have made it all the more galling for Rosberg to find himself handicapped by Cosworth power during a year when the turbos finally swept the normally aspirated teams

aside. Yet his competitiveness, the urge to give nothing less than his personal best, was never blunted. Rosberg put the Williams FW08C into places and angles where it had no right to be. From running on the limit with tyres almost falling apart during a non-championship race at Brands Hatch to clinging on in the seemingly hopeless chase of the turbos at Spa, Rosberg displayed an indefatigable spirit. His driving may still lack refinement but who would criticise the skill and daring demonstrated during those stunning opening laps at Monaco? And then, at the end of the season, to quietly admit he had not been fully fit since May . . . Rosberg may have driven like a hooligan at Long Beach but that was made acceptable by an otherwise superlative year.

6 John Watson

It was the usual story. During practice, John Watson would fiddle about and fail to throw himself into an on-the-limit lap unless the car was perfect. Then, in the race, he would drive with all the commitment, confidence, skill and aggression you could wish for. His victory at Long Beach was slightly misleading. It was an opportunist's win, extremely well taken, but it was the Dutch Grand Prix which highlighted Watson's vast natural talent. The truth is, however, that he needed to be goaded into such a stunning display and, in some respects, he made a rod for his own back. It made you wonder what he had been doing for the rest of the year; his drive at Zandvoort was that exceptional.

7 Eddie Cheever

If you take Prost as Eddie Cheever's yardstick, then the American did not have a particularly good season. There is no doubt that he is hard on his car and a lack of experience in setting up the Renault affected his performances, with particular regard to tyre choice. Cheever's detractors will say he could not make his tyres last but that is an unfair observation since he is compared with a driver who possesses an exceptionally sensitive and delicate touch. No one doubts Cheever's continual and insatiable urge to take himself and his car to the limit but, to gain a more accurate insight, his practice times in the wet at such diverging places as

Monaco, Spa and Hockenheim say even more than joint sixth place and 22 points in the championship.

8 Derek Warwick

It was unfortunate that Derek Warwick's only major mistake of the season should also have been his most public error. Until he rammed the back of Surer's Arrows, Warwick had finally been able to show just what a fine racer he is by failing to submit to the pressure exerted by Prost and Piquet. His commendable loyalty to the hard-working Toleman team meant Warwick often had to use his race craft and temperament to make up for disrupted practice sessions and inadequate tyres. But, like his Formula 3 season in 1978, Warwick's performances in 1983 hinted that he may still be one of the few drivers capable of running competitively with Piquet. And you can't offer higher praise than that.

9 Niki Lauda

Racing a Cosworth car with a full tank did not hold Niki Lauda's full attention mid-season and hopeless performances, such as a spin into retirement at Montreal, detracted from some outstanding drives. Silverstone, Hockenheim and the Österreichring proved that the sharpness and skill were still present as the Austrian set himself in a class of his own. The late arrival of the TAG turbo aroused Lauda's ability to unravel the most awkward and complicated problem and a splendid drive at Kyalami was a portent of what we can expect in 1984.

10 Andrea de Cesaris

The fact that Andrea de Cesaris has even been considered, never mind selected, for the Top Ten says much for the vast improvement shown by the Italian. He has always been quick, of course, but in 1983 it seemed at long last he was willing to curb his impatience slightly without losing any of his flair. Yes, there were 'red mist' moments but his drive at Spa was immaculate. The Alfa Romeo turbo was frequently a difficult car to control but de Cesaris tamed it at Francorchamps in a manner which belied the crazy, impetuous acts which had been a part of his previous two seasons of Formula 1.

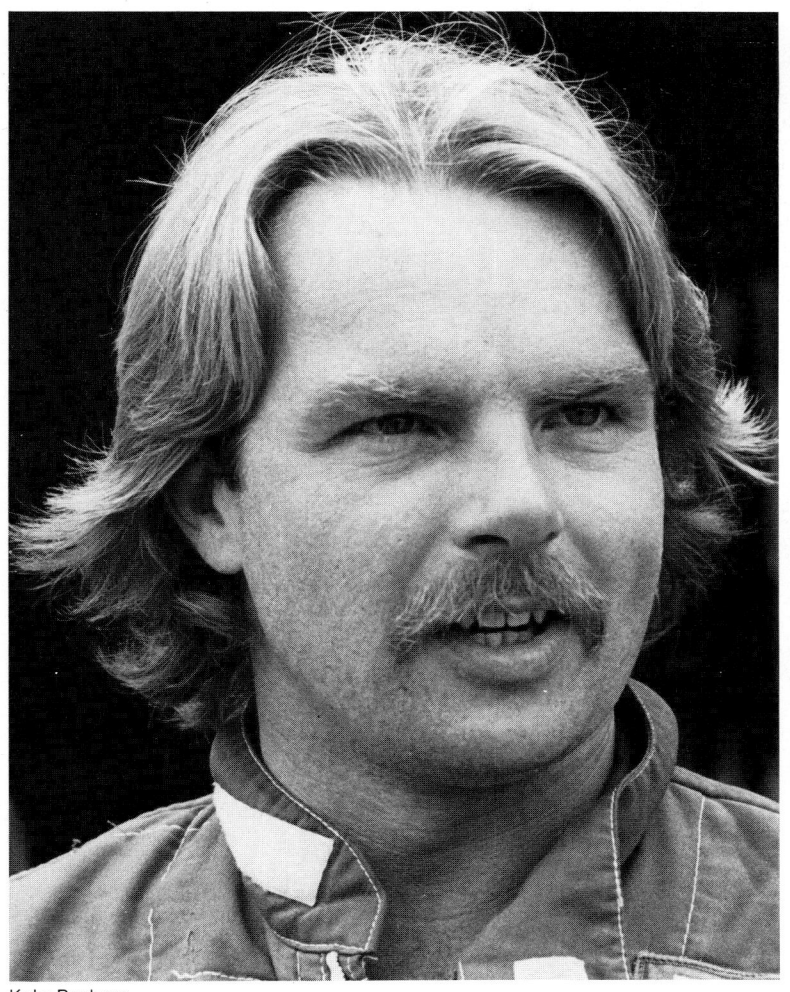

Keke Rosberg

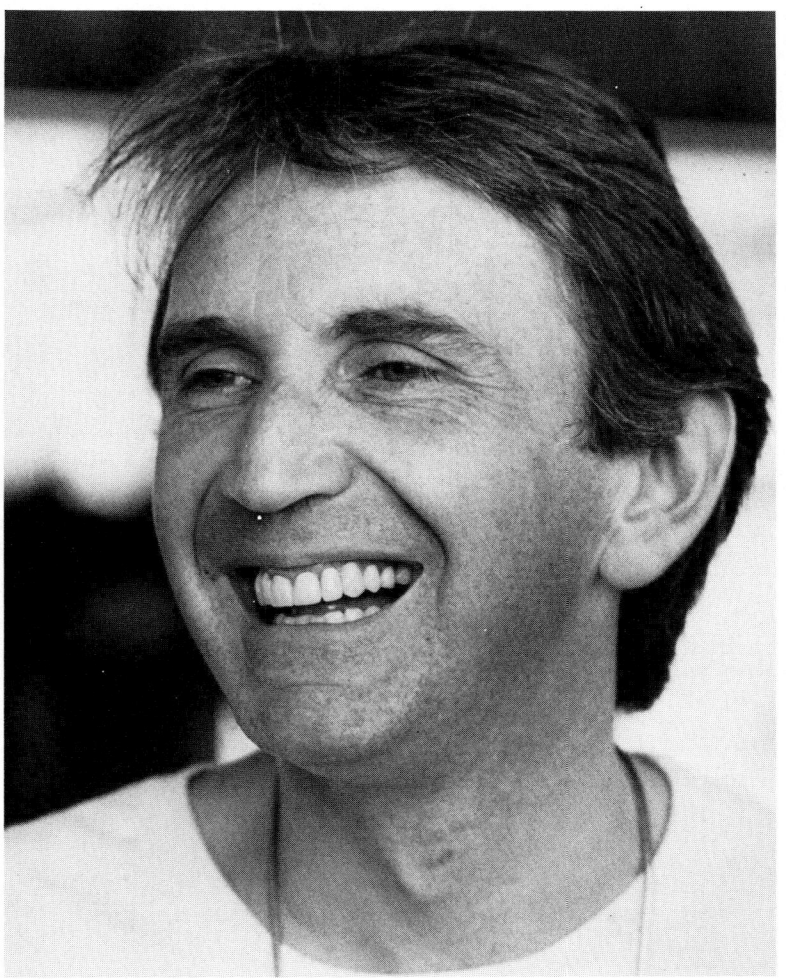

John Watson

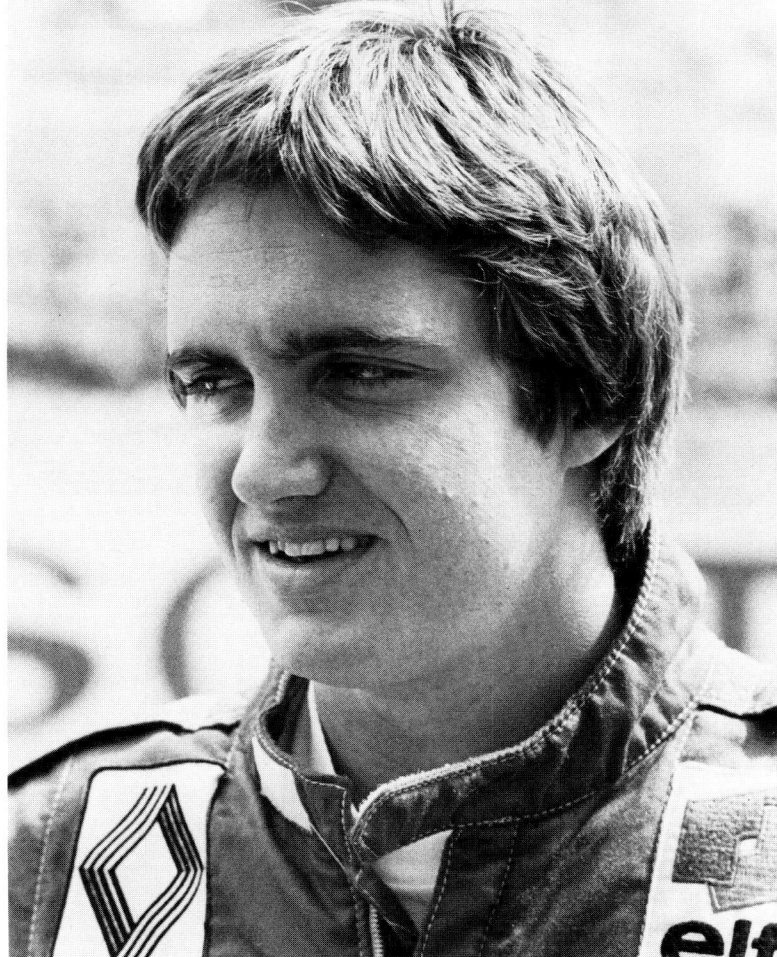

Eddie Cheever

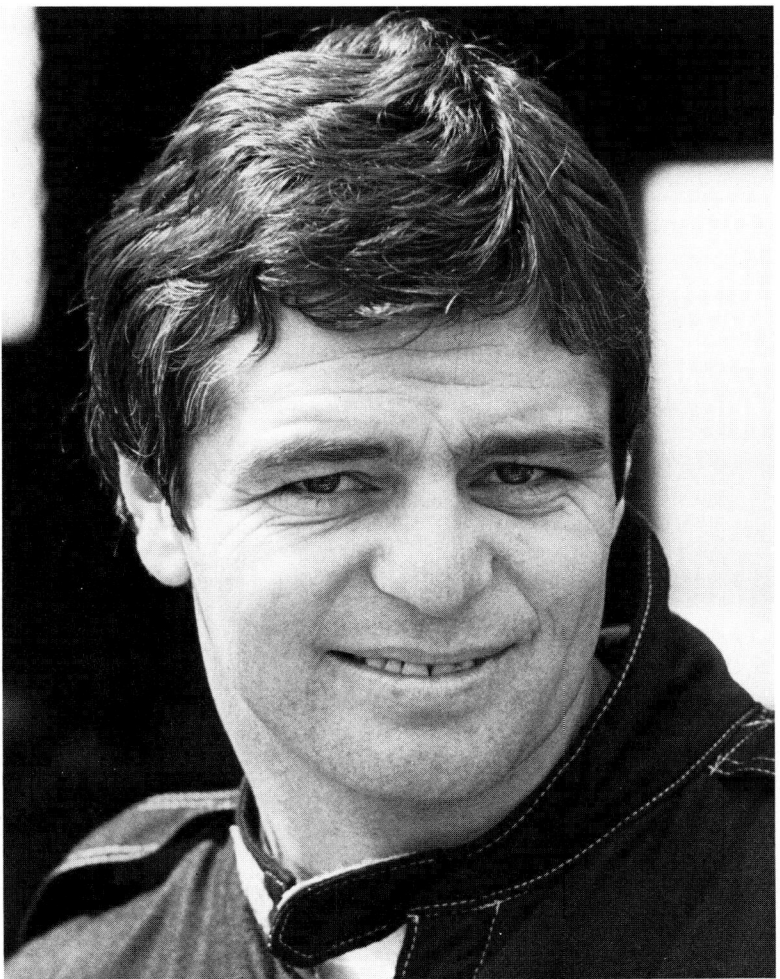

Derek Warwick

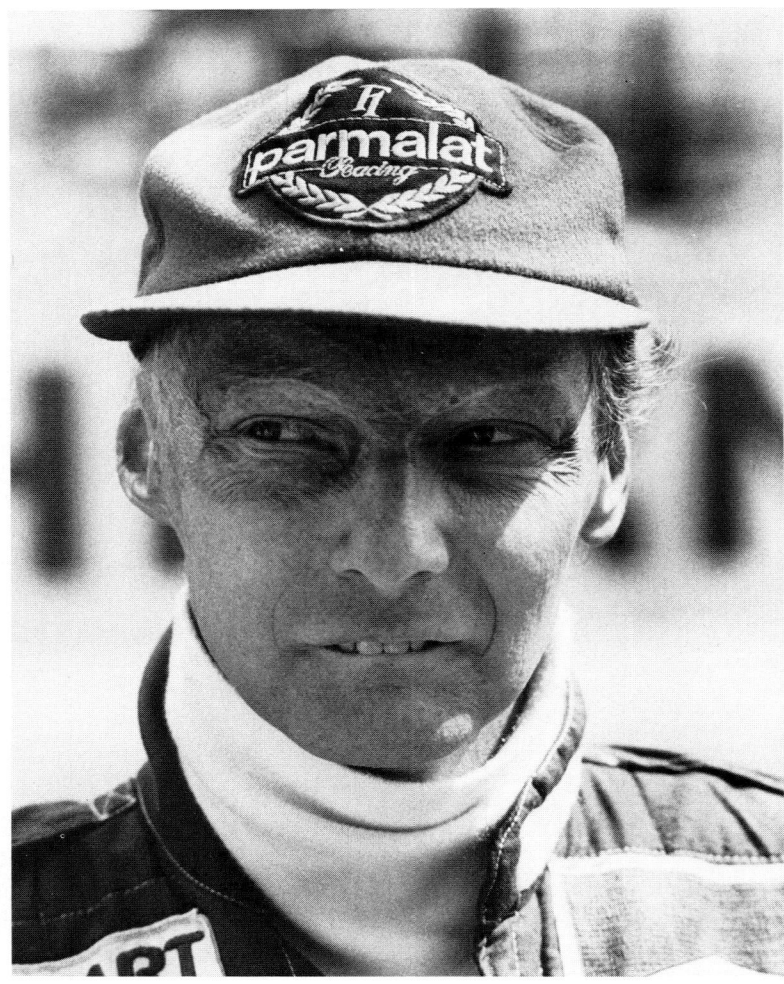

Niki Lauda

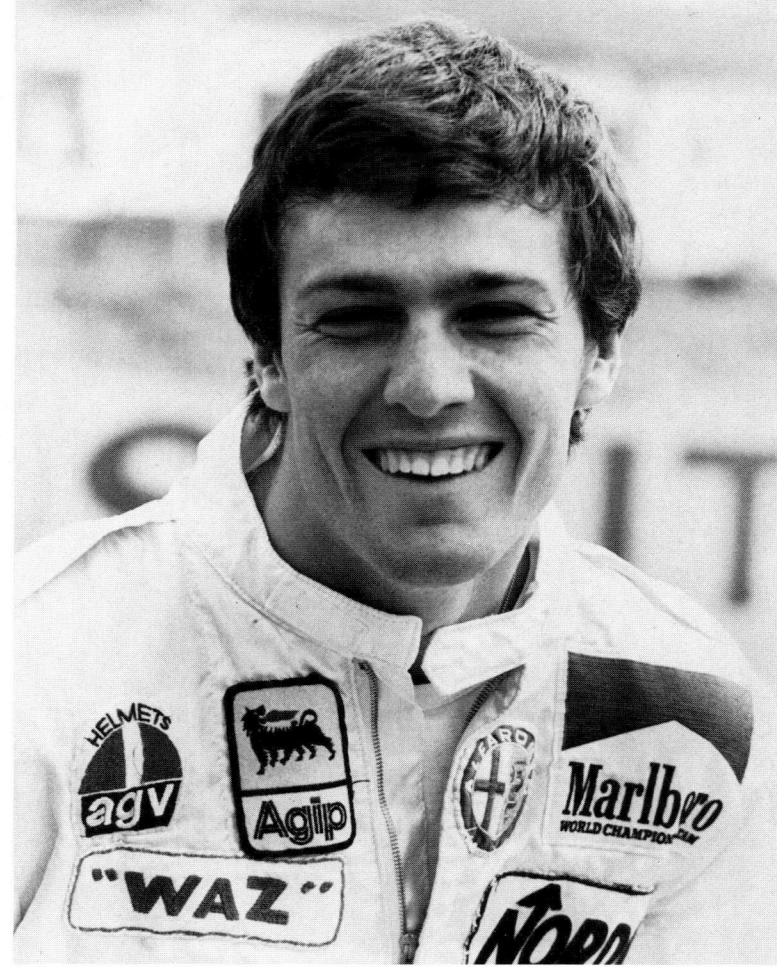

Andrea de Cesaris

For de Cesaris, read Alboreto, Patrese, de Angelis or Mansell; all four were worthy of consideration.

Michele Alboreto, number eight in the Top Ten last year, has been a disappointment. Perhaps we expected too much after his rapid rise to prominence. His natural ability remains but, somehow, he has lacked the urge and flair seen before. Admittedly, many of the retirements were not his fault and he *was* running a Cosworth car. However, his win at Detroit notwithstanding, we expected him to run at the top of the normally aspirated division – but Rosberg was in a different league. And some of Michele's moves while struggling mid-field served as a reminder that he remains comparatively inexperienced.

Riccardo Patrese's stylish run at Kyalami, his careful use of the boost control, showed just what he had been capable of all season. Yet it took the threat of dismissal from Brabham to make the Italian drive with half of the composure and intelligence shown by his team-mate. Patrese's speed is not questioned but Imola proved he remains prone to dreadful errors of judgement.

Elio de Angelis and Nigel Mansell represented the two extremes of the Grand Prix driver spectrum: one, a gifted artist constantly in need of motivation; the other, a hard-working, immensely determined and brave charger. When he ran (the word 'raced' here would be entirely inappropriate) the Lotus 93T, de Angelis may as well have gone home after his usual brilliant lap in practice. Indeed, at Imola, he did just that during the race. The 94T rekindled his interests, Brands Hatch practice being the epitomy of his talent; the race, an example of his impetuousity. Mansell needed every ounce of his resilience while struggling with the 92-Cosworth and its trick suspension. Having worked hard for one point in Detroit, it was clear that the Englishman would make the most of the 94T when it arrived at Silverstone. For de Angelis, the car needed to be on the front row, or thereabouts. For Mansell, the slightest whiff of a competitive run was all he needed – and the charge at Silverstone in a virtually unknown car is a fine example of that. Then there was Austria: Mansell third fastest in practice, de Angelis 12th. That said much about the Lotus drivers.

Working through the remainder of the entry list, the second Williams was driven by Jacques Laffite and the Frenchman had a mixed season. After a shaky start, Jacques almost won at Long Beach and kept that momentum going until he reached the faster circuits later in the season. Here, his smooth, late-braking style was in complete contrast to the flamboyant Rosberg way of making the Williams/Cosworth/Goodyear package work and, unfortunately for Jacques, his year will be remembered for the non-qualifications at the end rather than the more appropriate performances at the beginning. Never underestimate Laffite; his style should be ideal for the FW09-Honda.

Danny Sullivan settled into Formula 1 very quickly with steady, mature drives – but he failed to progress much further. The highlight of his year with Tyrrell was second place at the Race of Champions and that drive gave a fair indication of what was to come. Sullivan did everything right – but passed very few cars. Manfred Winkelhock, on the other hand, really went to work in the ATS-BMW. He may not have been smooth, but no one questioned either his courage or his reflexes. The pity is that reliability problems with such a potent car did not allow him to prove just what he could do during an entire race distance.

Of the various RAM-March drivers, Eliseo Salazar and Kenny Acheson were the most regular incumbents in a team which suffered through receiving the worst of a bunch of tyres which were often not acceptable on a turbo, never mind a Cosworth car. Salazar lost heart (and sponsorship) after shunting at Monaco while Acheson, taking the brave decision to jump in at the deep end where few thought he would come up for air, never mind swim, persevered and finally earned the chance to show he could act sensibly in elevated company.

Mauro Baldi, at times as exuberant as de Cesaris, lacked the flair of his team-mate and rarely did anything worthy of note; a major disappointment in the light of his promising drives the previous year. Jean-Pierre Jarier, still a driver of great skill, had the opportunity to win at Long Beach – and blew it. Enough has been said about his behaviour in Austria and, apart from a good run at Silverstone, he became

no more than a disinterested mid-field runner in a mediocre car. Raul Boesel, given that he had the worst of a poor selection of equipment, tried hard and was never far off his team-mate's pace. And, when he had the Ligier team to himself, he set second fastest lap at the Race of Champions. It was clear that a promising talent, never mind a healthy budget, has been frittered away.

Marc Surer's season fell into two halves; Before Boutsen and After Boutsen. The Swiss driver started off with spectacular displays of car control and enthusiasm and brought his Arrows home consistently, often in the points. His practice laps at Spa and Detroit were superb and, even though he continued in this vein, he was gradually overshadowed as Thierry Boutsen found his feet. Undoubtedly the 'Rookie of the Year', the Belgian was overawed by no one and his ability to learn circuits quickly was uncanny. A fine test driver into the bargain, Boutsen possesses a promising future. The pity is that he has edged such a fine driver as Surer into the sidelines.

Considering the Osella drivers managed only 16 races between them (and finished just once!), it is difficult to form an opinion. Those who watched Corrado Fabi in Formula 2 speak highly of his talent and it is unfortunate that he did not get the chance to progress in Formula 1. One of the most promising teams in terms of driver talent (if not sponsorship and preparation), was Theodore. Roberto Guerrero used his flair and enthusiasm at circuits both slow and fast; Johnny Cecotto, a newcomer to Formula 1, adapted very quickly and showed a cool, laid-back approach worthy of moulding by a top class team.

Occasionally, Bruno Giacomelli shook himself into life and produced flashes of exceptional form (Montreal and the Österreichring) but generally he did not respond well as the Toleman team attempted to turn their fortunes around. Stefan Johansson, on the other hand, drove his heart out all the time, rain or shine, misfire or no misfire. The Swede's talent is remarkable, his thirst for driving, for racing, unquenchable. Given a full season with a competitive car there is every chance that he will one day jump to the opposite end of this Top Ten review.

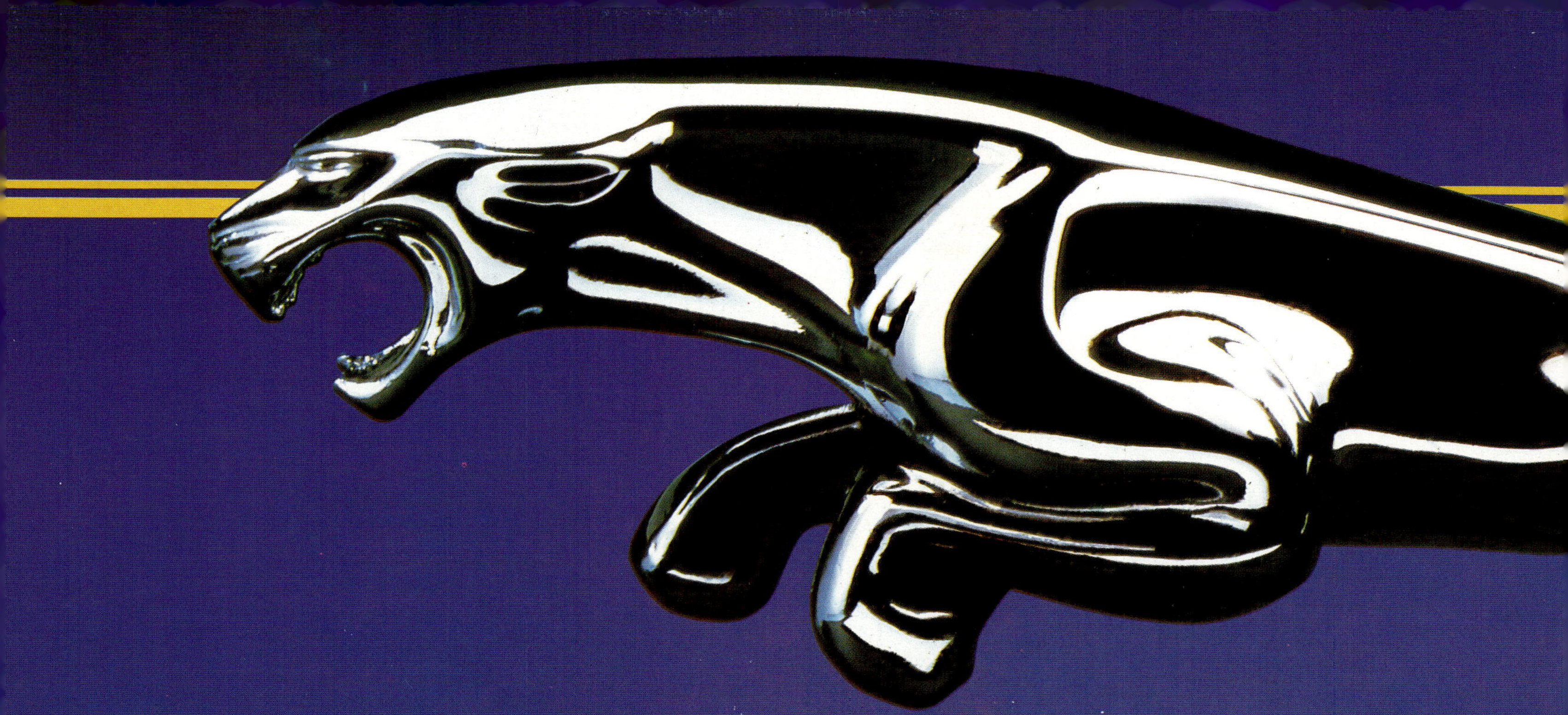

The lege

Jaguar have always made cars that fire the imagination, stir the senses, command attention; cars that possess the legendary power to move you with a combination of performance, refinement, roadholding

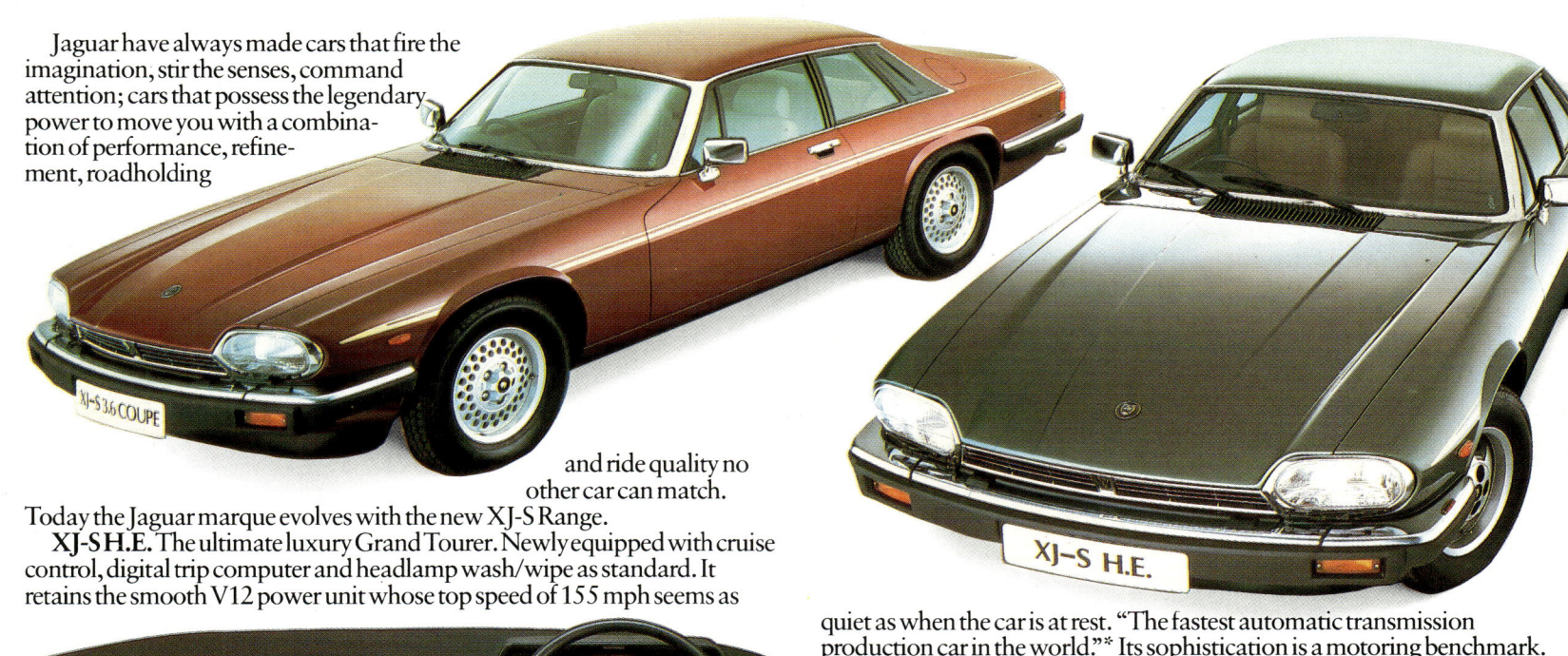

and ride quality no other car can match.

Today the Jaguar marque evolves with the new XJ-S Range.

XJ-S H.E. The ultimate luxury Grand Tourer. Newly equipped with cruise control, digital trip computer and headlamp wash/wipe as standard. It retains the smooth V12 power unit whose top speed of 155 mph seems as quiet as when the car is at rest. "The fastest automatic transmission production car in the world."* Its sophistication is a motoring benchmark.

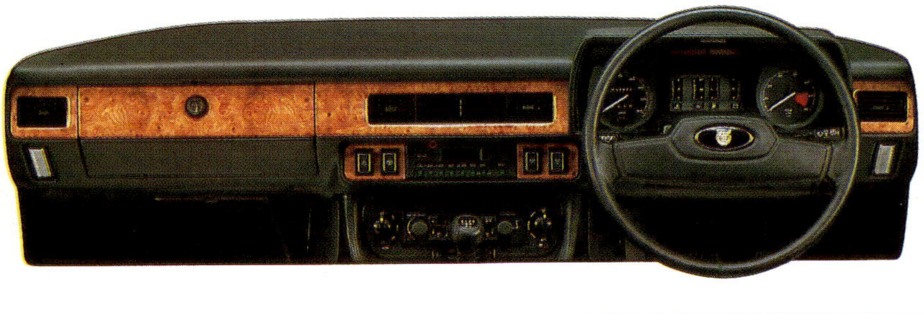

Alongside the XJ-S H.E., and with the new generation Jaguar engine making its first appearance, now come the XJ-S 3.6 Coupe and XJ-SC 3.6 Cabriolet.

XJ-S 3.6 Coupe. Now, even more the driver's Jaguar — the first real alternative to the automatic XJ-S H.E. With its new 3.6 litre 24 valve 6 cylinder DOHC engine, coupled with a 5-speed manual Getrag gearbox, a dynamic, responsive, performance-oriented excitement becomes yours for the taking.

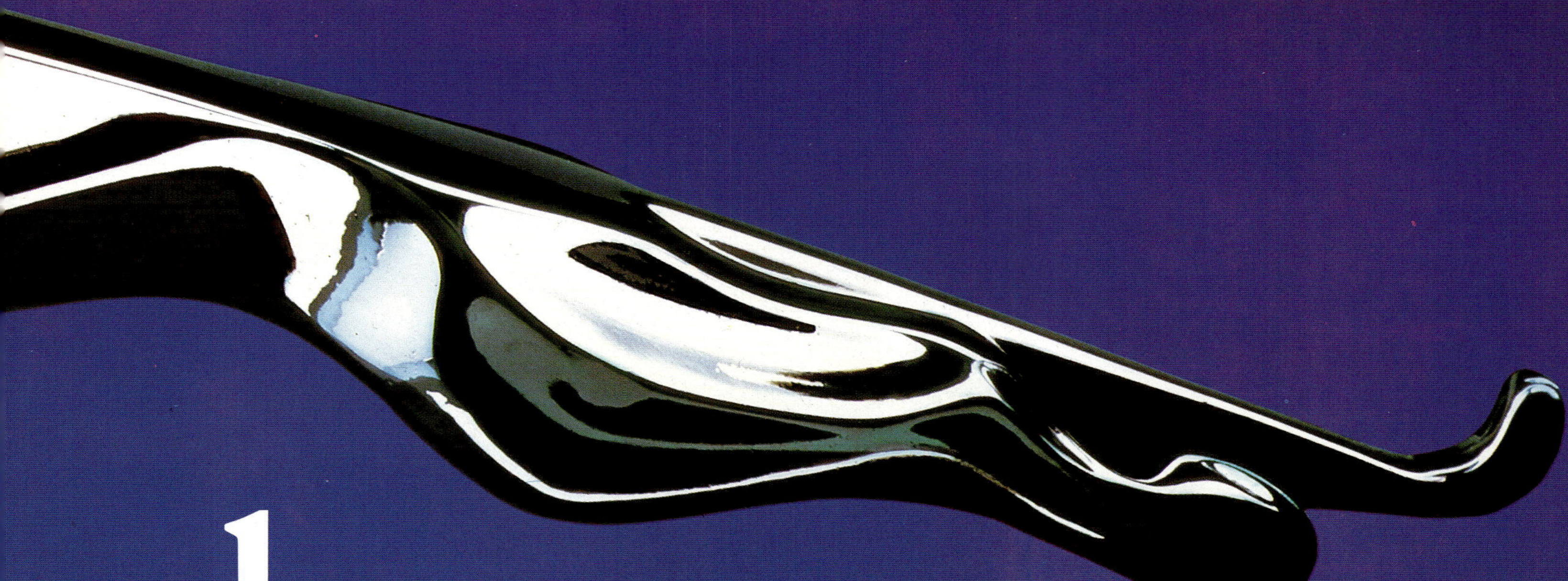

nd grows

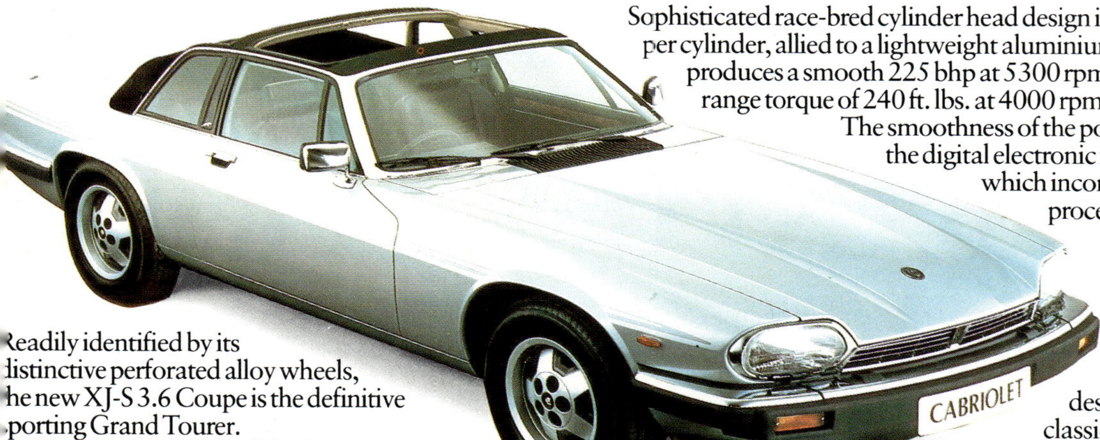

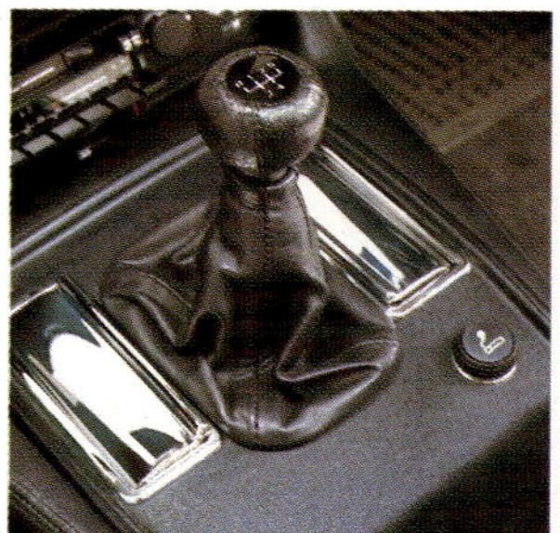

Readily identified by its distinctive perforated alloy wheels, the new XJ-S 3.6 Coupe is the definitive sporting Grand Tourer.

XJ-SC 3.6 Cabriolet. The first 2-seater open top Jaguar for years. Sporty. Individual. Eye-catching. Powered by the same engine and with the same transmission as the XJ-S 3.6 Coupe. All the exhilaration of the Jaguar roadster is available once again. Its certain exclusivity will make it a difficult car to acquire.

New 3.6 24 valve, 6 cylinder, twin overhead camshaft engine. Evolutionary engineering from the most consistently respected engineering team in the automotive industry makes this a major event by any reckoning. The introduction of this new engine encapsulates over 30 years of knowledge and practical experience, it reflects Jaguar's unsurpassed grasp of modern engineering trends at the highest levels of quality and performance. As a result it provides Jaguar's new cars with even higher levels of efficiency.

'State of the art' automotive technology, rigorous testing and build quality ensure the highest standards of durability.

Sophisticated race-bred cylinder head design incorporating 4 valves per cylinder, allied to a lightweight aluminium alloy block, produces a smooth 225 bhp at 5300 rpm, and excellent mid-range torque of 240 ft. lbs. at 4000 rpm.

The smoothness of the power unit owes much to the digital electronic fuel injection system which incorporates a micro processor control unit.

Matchless levels of luxury. The new XJ-S Range offers levels of luxury, comfort and refinement for which Jaguar are world renowned. The finest leathers, matched perfectly seat by seat. Burr elm veneers designed into each car in the great tradition of the classic cabinet maker. Deep pile carpets. Reclining, ergonomically-designed front seats and advanced safety features already well ahead of all governmental demands. Clear, concise, intelligently laid-out instruments.

Logically-located, easy-to-use controls. Air conditioning that automatically maintains the perfect temperature within the car regardless of the climate outside. Even the in-car entertainment system gives greater levels of sheer enjoyment.

The New XJ-S Jaguars. The long-striding, high performance range that surpasses all others. Everything you'd expect of a legend.

XJ-S 3.6 Coupe £19,249.00. XJ-S 3.6 Cabriolet £20,756.00. XJ-S H.E. £21,753.00.
XJ-S 3.6 Coupe and Cabriolet models illustrated are fitted with headlamp wash/wipe as an optional extra. Prices based upon manufacturer's RRP and correct at time of going to press, include seat belts, car tax and VAT. (Delivery, road tax and number plates extra.)
For full details please contact your Jaguar specialist for a test drive.   *Sunday Times, October 1981.

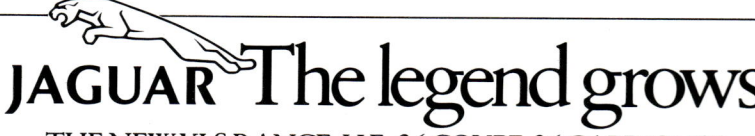

JAGUAR The legend grows

THE NEW XJ-S RANGE: H.E., 3.6 COUPE, 3.6 CABRIOLET

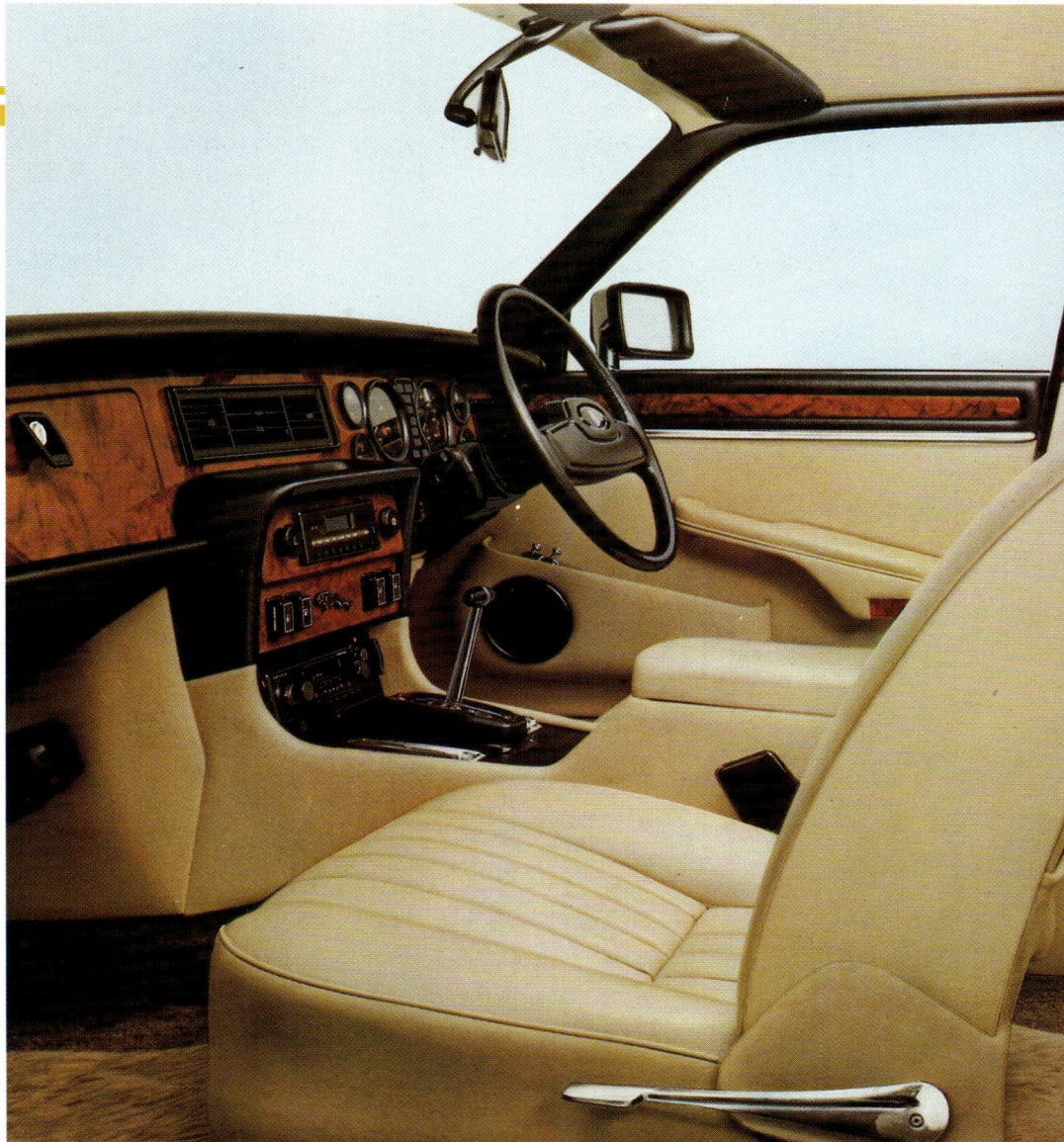

Jaguar's legendary reputation for effortless performance, supreme ride comfort and remarkable — some would say uncanny — silence is admirably reflected in the 1984 model Jaguar Series III Saloons.

Today's XJ6 3.4, XJ6 4.2 and the Jaguar Sovereign 4.2 and Sovereign H.E. models offer a level of performance and value without equal.

The looks are as sleek as ever; the famous 6 cylinder XK engines just as powerful. No other car makes driving so relaxed and easy, so satisfying and enjoyable. No other driving experience can prepare you for actually sitting behind the wheel of a Jaguar.

Take a closer look at the sumptuous interior of the new Jaguar Sovereign 4.2

The luxury that b

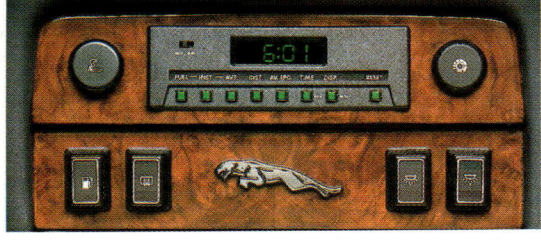

and you'll see a study in refinement — the like of which has only ever before been found with the Daimler marque.

The standard equipment reads like a list of expensive extras.

Finest quality leather hides, carefully matched for colour and grain are much in evidence.

Beautifully complemented by the superb burr walnut veneer trim to the fascia, door cappings and centre switch panel, and by colour co-ordinated, deep-pile carpeting.

A subtle and elegant combination.

The centre console has been ergonomically designed and fitted with a digital trip computer to provide a continuous visual check on average speed, fuel consumption and time.

The steering column is adjustable for comfort. The front seats are fully reclining and have adjustable lumbar support and electric height adjustment. The rear seats

have head restraints, reading lamps and inertia-reel seat belts.

A fully integrated automatic air-conditioning system is standard.

Tinted windows, remote-control door mirrors, radio antenna and central door locking are all electronically-operated for

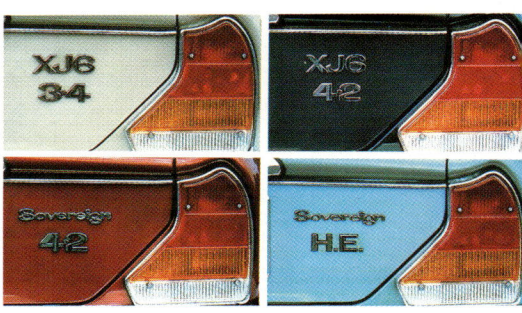

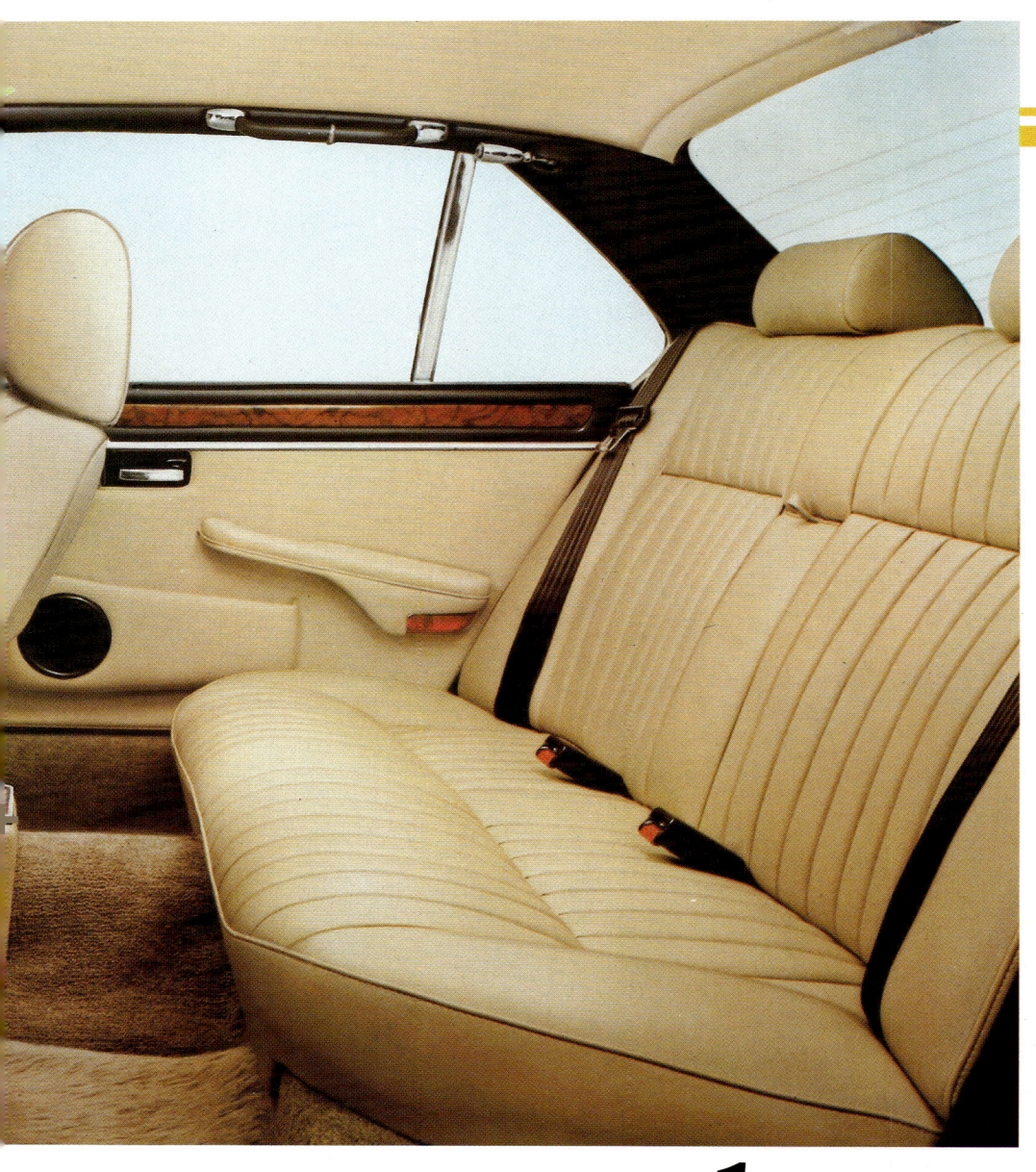

And a level of refinement that meets, more fully, the demands of today's Jaguar driver.

Many of the unique qualities of the Jaguar Sovereign 4.2 are to be found in the other 1984 model year Jaguar saloons. All share the same generous dimensions for their five-seater interiors. All display the same superb engineering, astonishing road holding, smoothness of ride and outstanding value for money.

Prices are from less than £14,000 to a little under £21,000 depending on individual specification.

Today such value may seem legendary, but it is as real as our luxury.

ecomes a legend

safety and convenience.
The 4-speaker stereo/

Jaguar 3.4 £13,991.00. Jaguar 4.2 £15,997.00.
Jaguar Sovereign 4.2 £18,495.00. Jaguar Sovereign H.E. £20,955.00.
Prices based upon manufacturer's RRP and correct at time of going to press, include seat belts, car tax and VAT. (Delivery, road tax and number plates extra.) For full details please contact your Jaguar specialist for a test drive.
Cars illustrated are Jaguar Sovereigns.

cassette system sounds simply superb, unless of course you choose to enjoy one of the most outstanding of Jaguar's built-in qualities: the blissful, restful silence.

A range of appointments lavish by any standards: but offered as standard on the Jaguar Sovereign 4.2.

The kind of added refinement that makes a Jaguar a Jaguar.

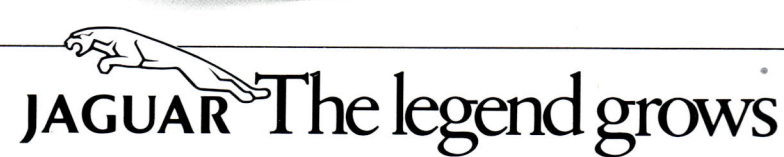

JAGUAR The legend grows

THE 1984 SALOON RANGE: XJ6 3.4, XJ6 4.2, JAGUAR SOVEREIGN 4.2 & SOVEREIGN H.E.

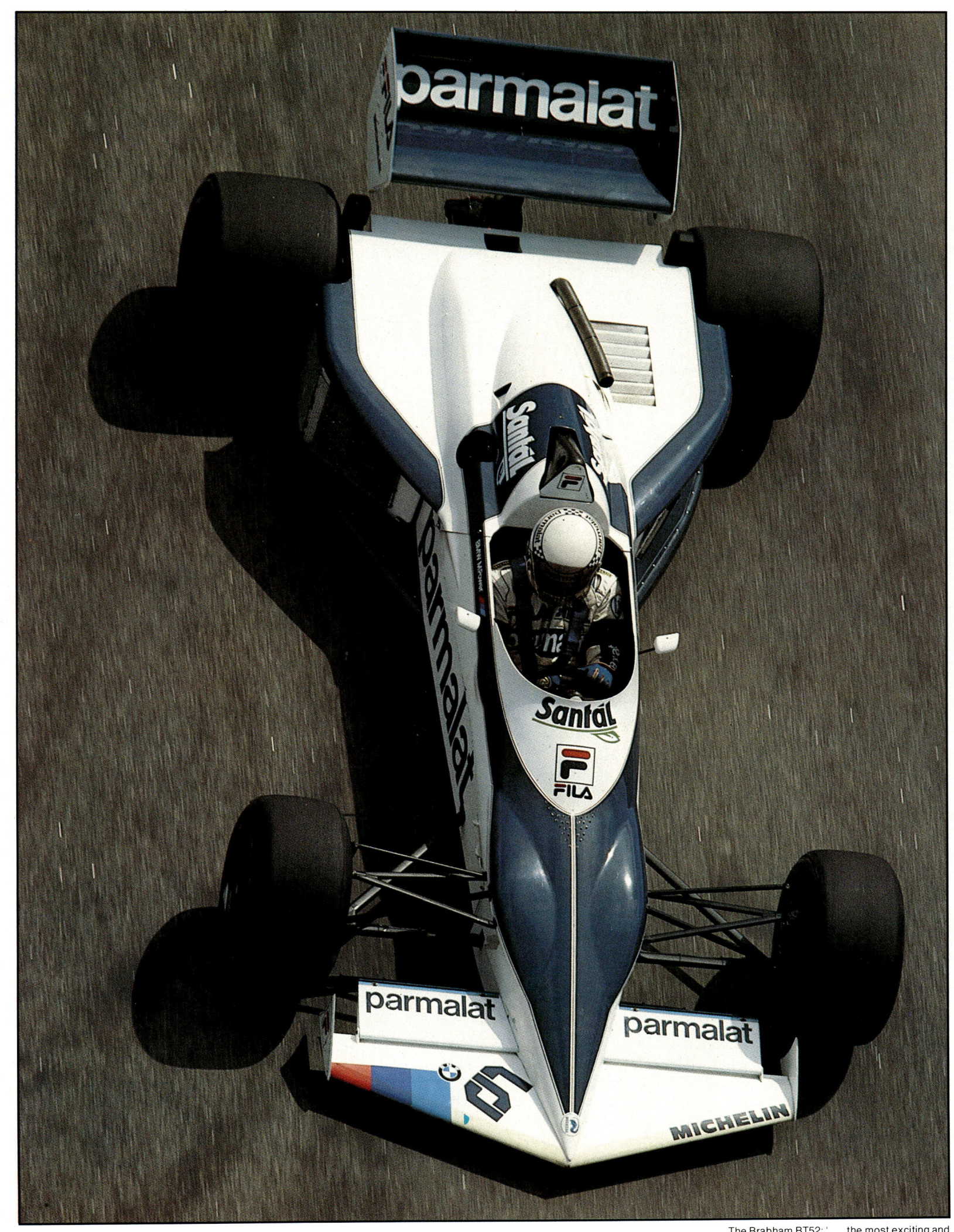

The Brabham BT52: '. . . the most exciting and
attractive car of the season . . .'
Photo: Charles Knight

FORMULA 1 emerged from the eye of the storm in 1983, leaving the rancour and turbulence which had characterised its progress for much of the previous season to fade into perspective on the pages of the Grand Prix history books. After the anti-turbo lobby's excesses in 1982 had almost ripped the sport asunder, everybody in the business seemed suddenly struck by the cold wind of reality. Whatever the ideological differences remaining between those who initiated the turbo revolution, and those who opposed it tooth-and-nail, both sides seemed to realise that they couldn't afford another major public clash. The patience of many sponsors, some race organisers and even some teams, had been stretched to breaking point, particularly over the famed Imola boycott, the off-circuit legal actions and the general lack of credibility which the sport seemed determined to heap upon itself. In 1983 it was time for everybody to shape up, and shut up.

However, there were a few rumblings of discontent still punctuating the technical scene, lurking like distant rolls of thunder after a major tropical storm has passed. Having lost the anti-turbo battle once and for all, the supporters of the 3-litre normally aspirated brigade launched a last-ditch, rear guard action against forced induction: at the British Grand Prix, Ken Tyrrell protested the water injection systems employed by Ferrari and Renault on the basis that they introduced a power boosting additive to the petrol and as such were ostensibly in breach of the technical regulations. This raised an immensely complex issue which even the FISA Court of Appeal eventually decided it was ill-equipped to pass judgement on, so the matter was eventually handed over to an eminent professor at Vienna University for further consideration. However, FISA has indicated that, whatever the outcome of any further deliberations on the matter, the final verdict will in no way affect the outcome of the World Championship. In other words, no points will be taken away from either Ferrari or Renault.

Away from the Court Room, the racing has been splendid, taken as a whole. The decision to impose a set of regulations which required flat bottomed cars for 1983 may well have been met with protestations of horror by many teams at the end of the previous season, but within a few races even the most hardened sceptics grudgingly acknowledged that it was a change for the better. We were spared the sight of rock hard racing chassis jinking their precarious way round the circuits of the world, pummelling their drivers who strained every nerve end in their bodies to keep control. The cars of 1983 were more progressive and pleasurable to handle, although the quickening of progress on the turbocharged engine development front meant that lap times hardly dropped at all for the front runners, a fact which prompted some critics to stand back smugly and remark, "there, the change in regulations has hardly made any difference at all." But the real test was to think just how dramatically lap speeds would have risen if that turbo power increase had been allowed to go hand-in-hand with continuing ground effect. The mind boggles!

As far as the battle for the World Championship was concerned, 1983 was the season in which the relentless advance of the 1½-litre turbocharged engines could be stemmed no longer by the 3-litre cars. With the minimum weight limit dropping to 540kg at the start of the year, several teams nurtured the hope that a Cosworth car might *just* be able to pull it off for one more year, but there was really no way. Williams came closest, quickly twigging that the mathematics of the fuel-stop formula, "pioneered" by Brabham in the summer of 1982, would work just as strongly in their favour as for a turbocharged machine. In the opening race of the season, Keke Rosberg's FW08C proved stunningly quick at Rio after adopting the half tank, soft rubber approach to the race, and only gave best on the road to Nelson Piquet's striking new Brabham BT52-BMW. In fact, if it hadn't been for Keke's disqualification following an alleged push-start, Williams would have held on in the lead of the Constructors' Championship for the first half of the season. Like McLaren and Tyrrell, the only other Cosworth teams to win a race, Williams was obliged to take the 3-litre route in 1983 primarily because he was late joining the turbo bandwagon. This uncharacteristic failure to keep pace with the prevailing F1 trend was largely the result of Frank's reluctance to stand in a queue behind any other team when it came to the supply of turbocharged engines, but he looks forward to 1984 with exclusive Honda turbo power so the wait has probably been worthwhile. McLaren was just marking time, waiting for its TAG-financed, Porsche-built V6, while Tyrrell stayed with Cosworth and whistled to keep his spirits up because he had no choice . . .

In order to be competitive one needed a decent turbocharged engine and a slick pit stop routine, so it was no surprise when the World Championship contest settled down into a battle between Alain Prost's Renault RE40, Nelson Piquet's Brabham BT52B and the Ferrari 126s of René Arnoux and Patrick Tambay. And that fact says everything about the destiny of the Constructors' Championship, of course: while the outcome of the drivers' contest teetered on the brink right up until the final race of the season, Maranello comfortably clinched its second straight Constructors' Championship by the simple and long-practised expedient of making certain that both its entries were capable of finishing in the top six – regularly.

This splendid record of reliability rightly paid off for Ferrari – and must have left Renault wincing in frustration. Equipped with a brand new carbon fibre composite chassis, the RE40, and with Alain Prost spearheading the team's challenge for the third straight season, Renault managed to fumble it again. A crucial driving error at Zandvoort, which eliminated both his own car and Nelson Piquet's Brabham BT52B, cost Prost the driver's title, but it was Renault's inability to field two competitive and reliable cars that deprived them of the Constructors' laurels. After René Arnoux's departure to Ferrari, amiable American Eddie Cheever was drafted into the number two spot alongside Prost. But while Alain's RE40 proved splendidly reliable, Cheever got a bad deal out of his relationship with Renault: when his car ran reliably he proved an able number two, but he was let down by mechanical problems far too frequently. At the end of the season Renault decided to dispense with his services, deciding that he hadn't been quick enough to support Prost. However, considering that he was brought into the team in the first place as a *number two*, following the chaotic lack of discipline between Prost and Arnoux the previous season, it seemed rather hard to dismiss him for, in effect, doing exactly the job he was paid for. If Cheever can be deemed to have failed, it was Renault's unreliability that spoilt his reputation, not his driving prowess.

Ferrari began the year with an air of cautious optimism, worried about tyre wear problems with their 126C2B. However, the much-touted René Arnoux had now joined the smooth, efficient Patrick Tambay on the driving strength and a good season was in prospect. So it proved, but the real surprise was the way in which Tambay comfortably eclipsed Arnoux for the first half of the year. René simply couldn't come to terms with test and development work and it was inevitably Patrick who set up the cars, and his splendid victory at Imola gave him an early psychological advantage over his fellow countryman. The advent of the Harvey Postlethwaite designed carbon fibre composite 126C3, which took first and second places on the grid for its first race at Silverstone, kept Ferrari firmly in contention for the entire season, but by then Arnoux had got into the swing of things and had already notched up a splendid victory in Canada at the wheel of the C2B.

Coincidentally, things began to go wrong for Tambay, and while he lost potential wins at Hockenheim and Osterreichring due to mechanical failure, Arnoux emerged from those two events with 15pts to his credit, including a win in Germany. He followed this up with a lucky victory at Zandvoort and, suddenly, Tambay's position within the team was at risk. With what amounted to tragi-comic bad timing, the incomprehensible machinations of Ferrari racing politics had committed the team to taking Michele Alboreto for 1984, this obligation being assumed in the middle of the season and almost certainly at Arnoux's expense. But when René started bagging race victories and Patrick hit his unlucky streak, Tambay inadvertently became the sacrificial lamb. Before the end of the season he was told that he would be replaced by Alboreto in 1984, leaving the Italian to partner the politically tactful Arnoux. To say that Ferrari backed itself into a draft position would be to understate how most observers regard this complicated sequence of events: but at the end of the day, Maranello was World Champion car constructor yet again, lending credence to those misty-eyed romantics who mutter "there you are you see, *anybody* can win in a Ferrari!"

Over at Brabham, the ever innovative Gordon Murray produced probably the most exciting and attractive car of the season, the dart-shaped Brabham BT52. Powered by the four cylinder BMW turbocharged engine, Nelson Piquet opened the season on a high note with a convincing victory in the Brazilian GP, but a series of mechanical misfortunes

Racing takes priority; politics put in perspective

by Alan Henry, Grand Prix Correspondent, *Motoring News*

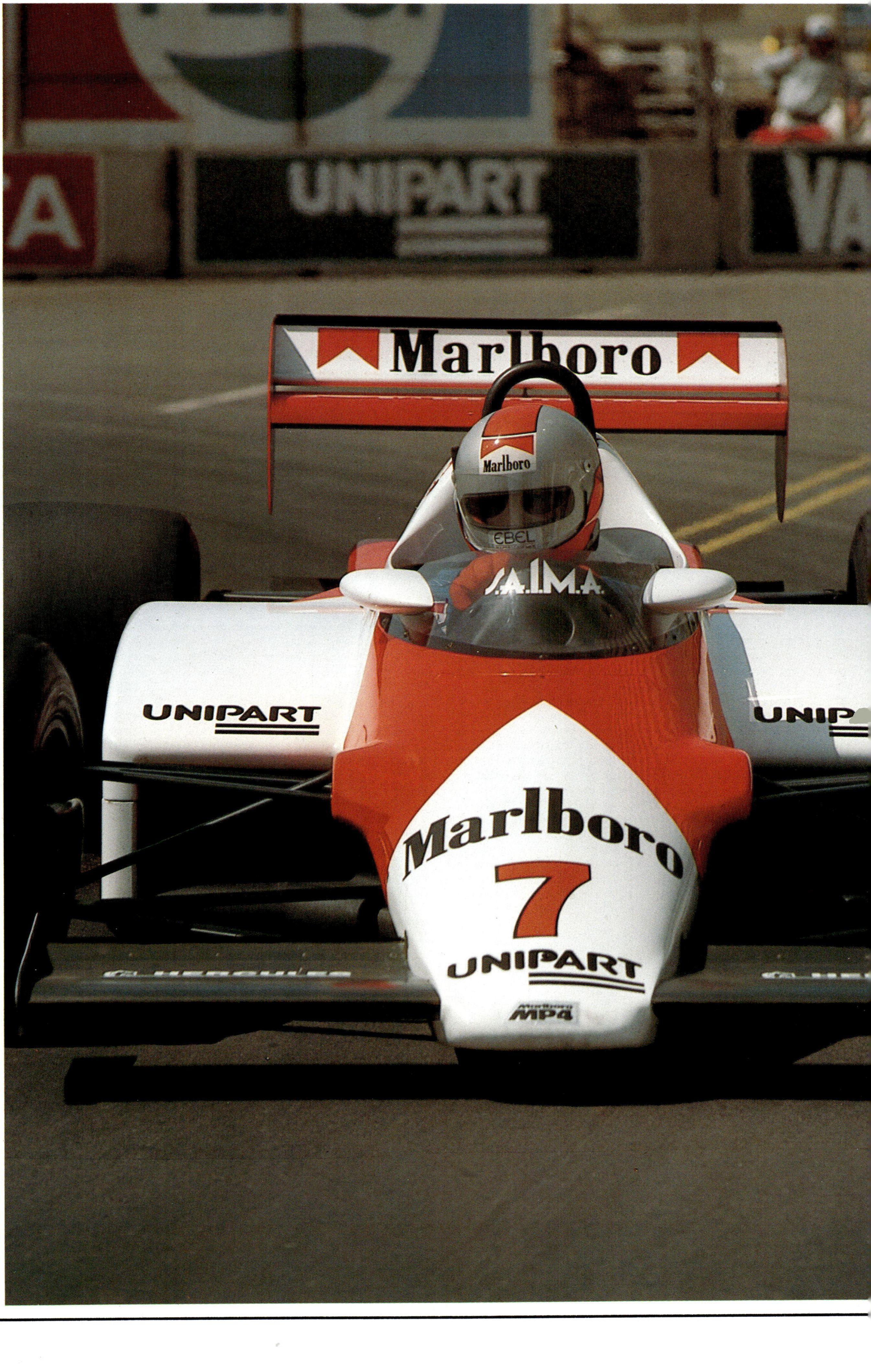
UNIPART
Marlboro
Marlboro
EBEL
S.A.I.M.A.
UNIPART
Marlboro
7
UNIPART
Marlboro
MP4

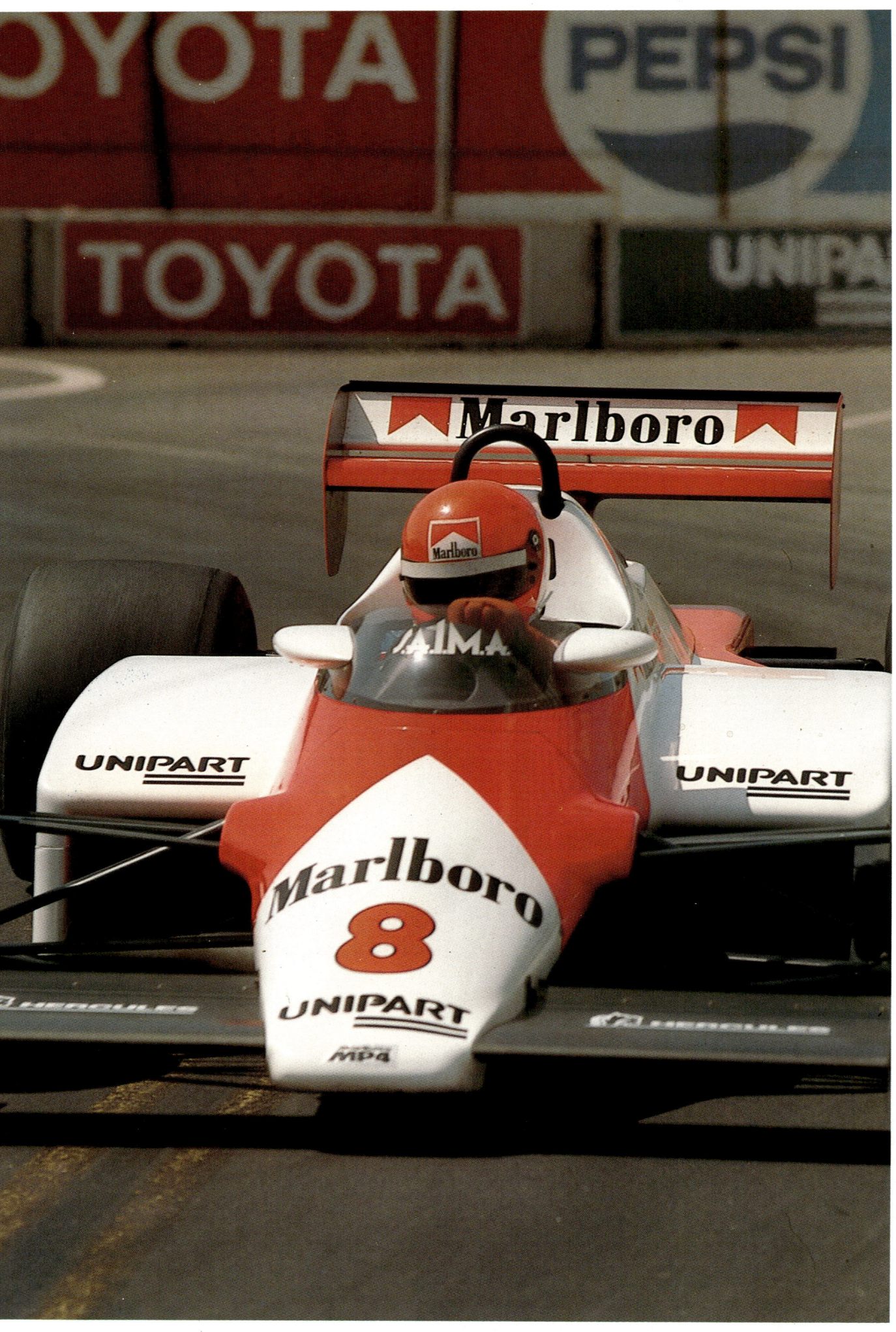

The Unipart McLarens of John Watson and Niki Lauda caused a major upset at Long Beach by finishing first and second in the second round of the championship.
Photo: Nigel Snowdon

and sheer bad luck kept him out of the winner's circle again until September, when he won the Italian GP at Monza. The Brabham mechanics' prowess at pit stops proved to be one of the most impressive aspects of team work and it's therefore somewhat ironic that Piquet was deprived of one particularly convincing victory in the one race that the Brabham, against all predictions, was going to run through non-stop. At Detroit, Piquet had the race in the bag until a rear tyre picked up a puncture less than ten laps from the finish, handing Michele Alboreto's Tyrrell a lucky victory on a plate.

Of course, Brabham suffered in the same fashion as Renault, for Riccardo Patrese seldom brought his BT52B through to the finish, his high failure rate stemming from a mixture of sheer bad luck and lack of mechanical sympathy on the part of the man in the cockpit. Now, at the end of the day, one really had to think hard to decide who was the best driver of the year. In the writer's book it was definitely Nelson. He demonstrated the brilliance we already knew he possessed, but tempered it with a calm personal approach to his racing and an ever-increasing degree of mechanical sympathy which has earned him the respect of his team's designer. When the chips were down, he seemed more aggressive than the smooth, cool Prost; more predictable than the tempestuous Arnoux and simply quicker than the stylish Tambay. Other potential candidates that should be considered, of course, include the mercurial Keke Rosberg, whose Monaco victory reminded us of his sheer star quality, and, possibly, McLaren drivers Lauda and Watson. Beyond that limited selection, shortage of experience, car problems and other peripheral factors preclude the mention of others – although there are several who will, almost certainly, fall into this elite category in years to come.

Rather than considering the other turbo teams at this point, let's just cover the other three winners: Williams, McLaren and Tyrrell. Of the three, Keke Rosberg's victory for Williams at Monaco was by far the most impressive demonstration, the team gambling on slicks from the start, successfully banking on the fact that further rain would hold off. In fact, when his Goodyears allowed, Rosberg was spectacularly quick, frequently hanging onto the tail of the turbo brigade and invariably snatching a point or two at the end of the race. Watson's victory for McLaren at Long Beach was a totally unpredictable success, strongly against the team's early season trend which saw them unable to get the best out of their Michelin rubber. Later in the season both Lauda and Watson put together some impressive results shortly before the Cosworth-engined McLarens were passed over in favour of the new TAG turbos, but Michele Alboreto's triumph for Tyrrell at Detroit proved to be a solitary success. Smooth and neat, Alboreto is an undeniably competent driver, but never looked anything particularly special at any time in 1983. Time, however, may well prove that assessment to be wide of the mark, but I'll stick by it anyway!

McLaren and Williams eventually showed their turbo hands before the end of the season, although

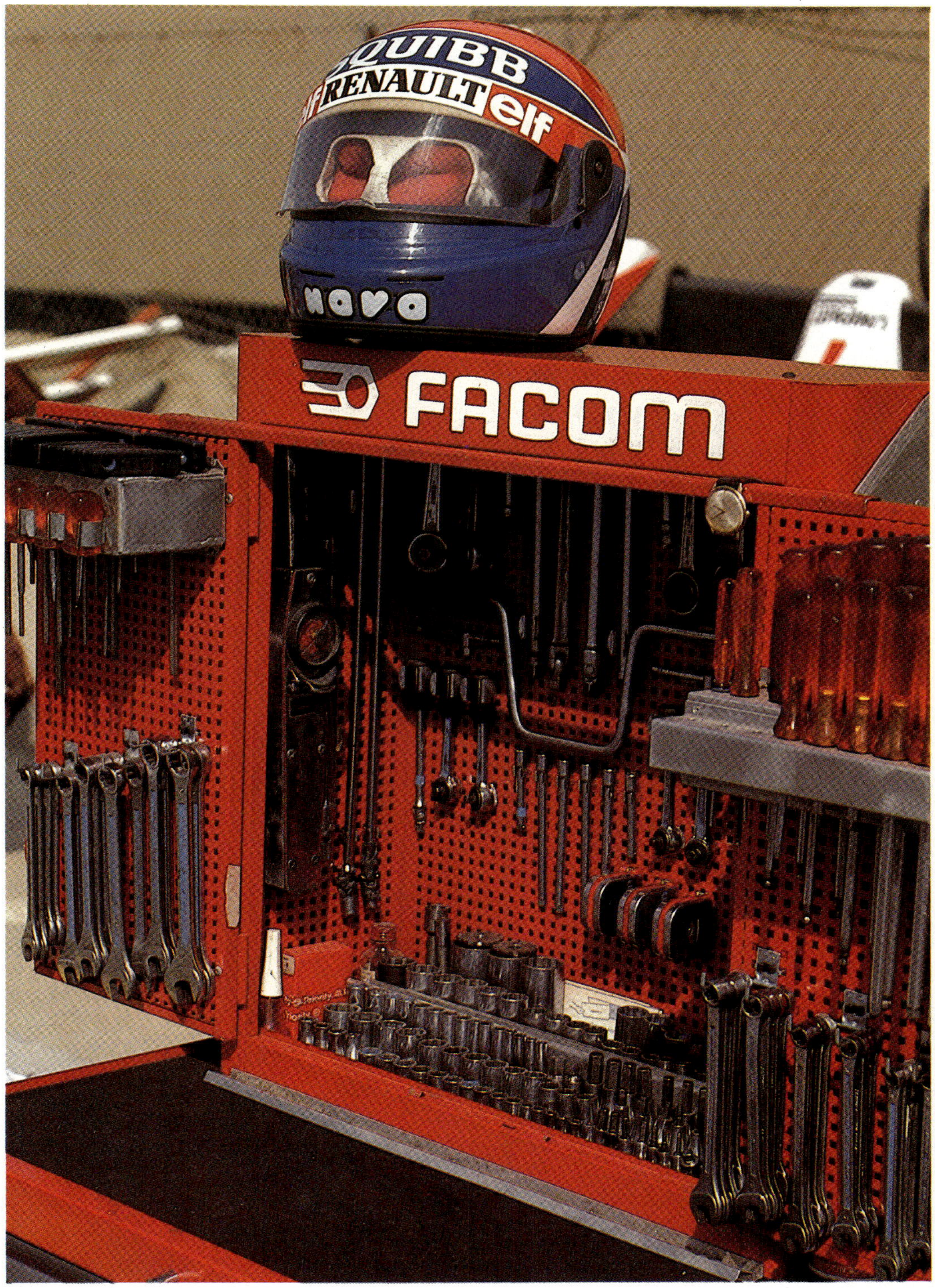

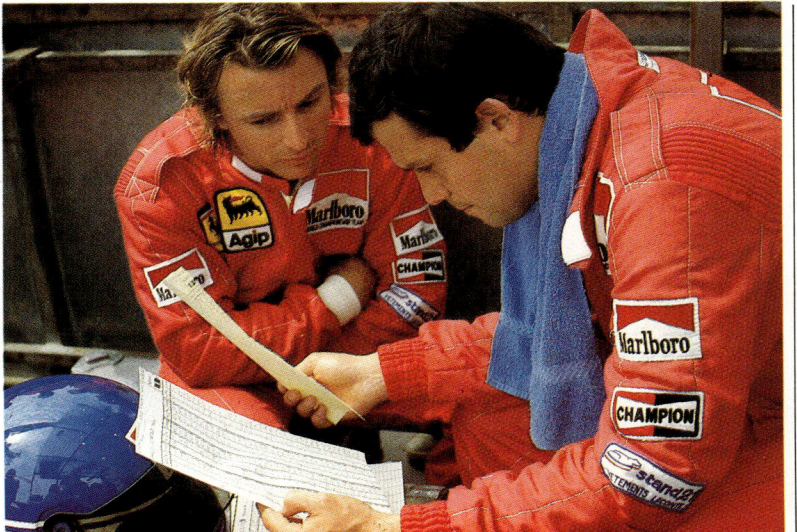

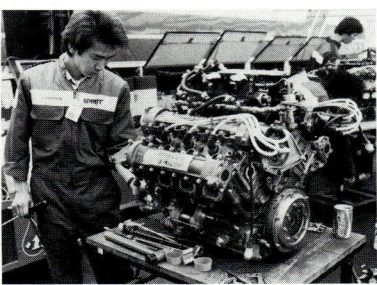

'. . . it was Renault's unreliability which spoiled Eddie Cheever's reputation, not his driving prowess . . .' (above).
Photo: Mike Levasheff
'. . . the real surprise was the way in which Tambay comfortably eclipsed Arnoux for the first half of the year . . .' (left).
Photo: Bernard Asset
The arrival of another major manufacturer. Honda reappeared on the Formula 1 scene with a V6 turbo to power Stefan Johansson's Spirit (below).

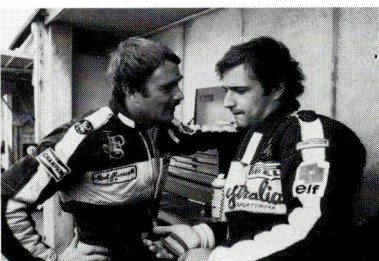

Nigel Mansell '. . . gritty driving efforts . . .' and Elio de Angelis '. . . actually gave up on one occasion . . .' made progress once the Lotus 93T had been replaced by the 94T (above). M. Balestre reminds us that politics and politicians played a secondary role during 1983 (right).
Photo: John Townsend

both were "pilot" efforts in preparation for a full-scale onslaught in 1984. The compact and obviously powerful TAG/Porsche unit obviously has a great deal of promise, but political considerations meant that McLaren designer John Barnard was obliged to hurry the new MP41E, very much an interim design, into action before the end of the season. Ideally, McLaren would have liked to defer the new engine's debut until next season, by which time a totally new chassis would have been available, but it still arrived on the scene in time for this year's Dutch Grand Prix. It made what might best be described as an unobtrusive debut and chassis problems in the remaining races of the year meant that neither Lauda nor Watson were able to realise much of its long-term potential.

Williams waited until Kyalami before wheeling out their Honda V6 turbo engined FW09, their task eased by the fact that at least the Japanese engine had been given its F1 "shake down" by the fledgling Spirit team in half a dozen races. Tyrrell finished the season with no specific turbo plans yet made public, apart from the grudging acknowledgement that "if you can't beat them, join them . . . and that's what I'll be doing next year!" To that end, the new Tyrrell 012 was designed with a long-term turbo engined application in mind.

Of those other teams who campaigned turbocharged engines throughout 1983, Lotus probably had the most turbulent time of all. Apart from the fact that they started the season reeling under the impact of Colin Chapman's sudden death, it quickly became obvious that the new 93T, designed specifically to accommodate the Renault V6 engine, was hopelessly overweight and ungainly. This fact quickly dawned on team driver Elio de Angelis, who promptly lost all his enthusiasm for the project and actually gave up on one inglorious occasion at Imola. However, Elio's Lotus career has always displayed a curious roller-coaster quality, both from the point of view of his track performance and his in-house popularity, so it was no surprise when he bobbed up as a contender again towards the end of the season. By that time, of course, the new Gerard Ducarouge-designed 94T had transformed the team's potential and, despite wrestling with the vagaries and inconsistencies of Pirelli radial rubber, the general feeling was that progress was being made by the end of the year. Nigel Mansell's gritty driving efforts at the wheel of the second 94T netted the team three good finishes in the points, even though his future seemed seriously in doubt by the end of the year.

Alfa Romeo's thirsty V8 turbo made its race debut at the start of 1983, but a combination of circumstances kept Andrea de Cesaris and Mauro Baldi out of the winner's circle. The engine staged regular mechanical rebellions against high doses of turbo boost during qualifying sessions and displayed patchy, unpredictable form when it came to the races. The feather in de Cesaris's cap was undoubtedly at Spa where he was the class of the field until a fumbled pit stop delayed him and engine failure finally stopped the 183T. Apart from that, and good runs to second place at Hockenheim and Kyalami, the young Italian continued to punctuate his racing progress with stupid

lapses of attention and concentration. Generally, Alfa Romeo's season, now administered for the sake of tactful appearances by Gianpaulo Pavanello's Euroracing concern, proved to be no worse and no better than those which had gone before.

After two seasons of struggling to qualify, 1983 was the year in which the Toleman team finally gained respectability as established members of the F1 community. Although they didn't confirm their sponsorship programme until relatively late in the day, Derek Warwick began to string together a series of very impressive performances, all of which tended to confirm the fleeting displays of talent he'd shown during '81 and '82. Unfortunately, the Toleman's Achilles heel turned out to be the turbochargers fitted to the otherwise supremely reliable Hart 415T engine. Because Brian Hart's small specialist organisation lacked affiliation to a major car manufacturer, he was unable to cajole the KKK turbocharger people to supply him with their products, as employed on Ferrari, Renault, BMW and Porsche F1 engines. Eventually he abandoned his American-made Garret turbochargers in favour of new units purpose-built by the British Holset company – after which the Toleman reliability record was transformed. Unfortunately, lack of finance had precluded Hart from developing sophisticated electronic engine management systems or water injection, and this limited budget also meant that the team was unable to risk blowing engines apart on high-boost qualifying runs. It may be that Toleman peaked about six months later than they ought to have done, but at least they started finishing in the points which, to the hard working team members, represented success as sweet as any Grand Prix triumph.

Amongst the supporting cast there was only one more turbo runner, ATS. Gunter Schmid's team had done a deal to use BMW engines in a single car entry for the ebullient Manfred Winkelhock and, although they didn't have much in the way of success, the ATS challenge looked far more professional and serious than it has done in previous years. Gustav Brunner pencilled a neat looking carbon fibre composite chassis and Manfred was unlucky, at the end of the day, to wind up without any Championship points.

Those who missed the turbo boat included Ligier, Arrows, March, Osella and Theodore. Without any shadow of a doubt, Ligier's season was the worst since he arrived on the F1 scene. The JS21 was rarely competitive, even on tight circuits, and while Jean-Pierre Jarier showed his customary intermittent flair on some occasions, his team-mate Raul Boesel must have been wondering why he ever persuaded his sponsors to fork out for a season with the French organisation. It was a waste of time for the Brazilian and any vestige of a promising reputation he may have once had lay in ruins. Ligier scored no Championship points at all . . .

Over at Arrows, the Dave Wass-designed Williams lookalike A6 was a neat and attractive little car, but apart from the odd good performance in the first few races of the season Marc Surer and Thierry Boutsen were left to struggle against the tide. Both men are extremely competent drivers and Boutsen's arrival on

the F1 scene set something of a standard for Cosworth-powered newcomers. Both deserve something better in the future, as do Theodore's pair of lads, Roberto Guerrero and Johnny Cecotto. Most people acknowledge that Stefan Johansson's talent also deserves a proper, full-time F1 chance, but problems with machinery at Osella and March make it difficult to judge the quality of Corrado Fabi and Kenny Acheson.

In 1984 it seems virtually certain that the already agreed regulations banning pit stops will be initiated, despite an energetic lobby to have this decision further deferred by a couple of teams who would like to retain the obvious performance benefits on track that accrue as a result of these stops. Coupled with a reduction in fuel tank capacity from 250 to 220 litres, it's hoped that this trend will contribute to a levelling off of engine power and result in no significant increase in lap speeds. However, there is great difficulty agreeing long-term engine regulations within F1 and there is every indication that the 1½ litre turbocharged regime, perhaps restricted in some yet-to-be defined fashion, will be with us for several seasons to come. However, those who think that the further reduction in fuel capacity allied to lack of pit stops will lead to a fleeting Indian Summer for the Cosworth DFV are probably out of touch with reality.

From a commercial point of view, Formula 1's popularity seems boundless, but there are the first signs that the Grand Prix game may not be the bottomless financial pit that some people believe it is. The first worrying brake has been applied in North America, for although Detroit stands firm in the calendar and Dallas promises to be a new fixture, Long Beach and Las Vegas each cried "enough". These organisers decided that the enormous cost of buying the FOCA package just wasn't justified and that CART offered significantly more spectator appeal and substantially less financial outlay. New York has yet to happen, Dijon also fell off the calendar and a second Grand Prix was organised for Brands Hatch in order to take up the slack.

It's quite clear that television is the prime consideration in the commercial minds that control F1's destiny, even to the exclusion of press interest and on-the-day spectator considerations. However, on the circuits themselves, the whole emphasis of Formula 1 is unobtrusively changing. Over the past twenty years the bias has been very much in favour of the drivers' World Championship with the Constructors' contest, often fought out between a group of "special builders", taking a back seat in the public eye. With a surplus of capable drivers on the market and enormous commitment from manufacturers such as Renault, Alfa Romeo, Fiat (Ferrari), BMW and Honda, the number-one attraction may well become the cars over the next few years. The personality cult within F1 may be coming to the end of its particular road as the mighty motor industry monoliths slug it out in this very public, televised arena. I don't suggest that this is either good or bad. I just suggest that this is the direction in which events are taking us.

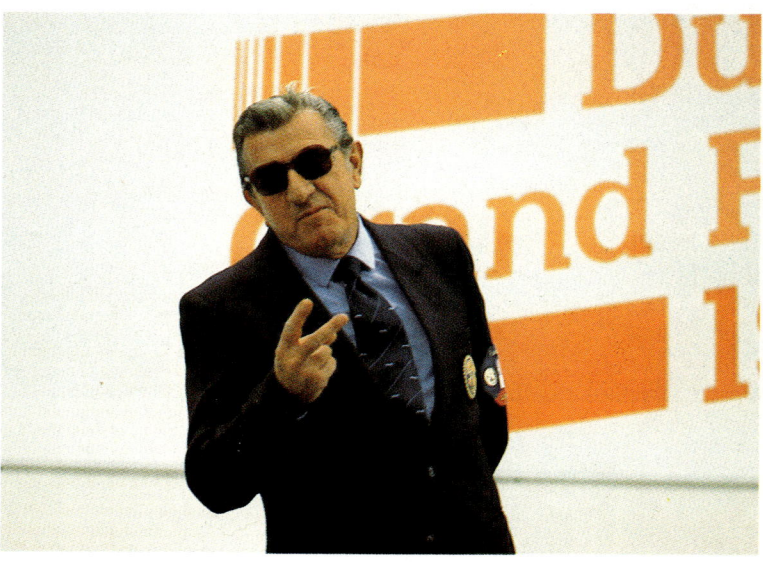

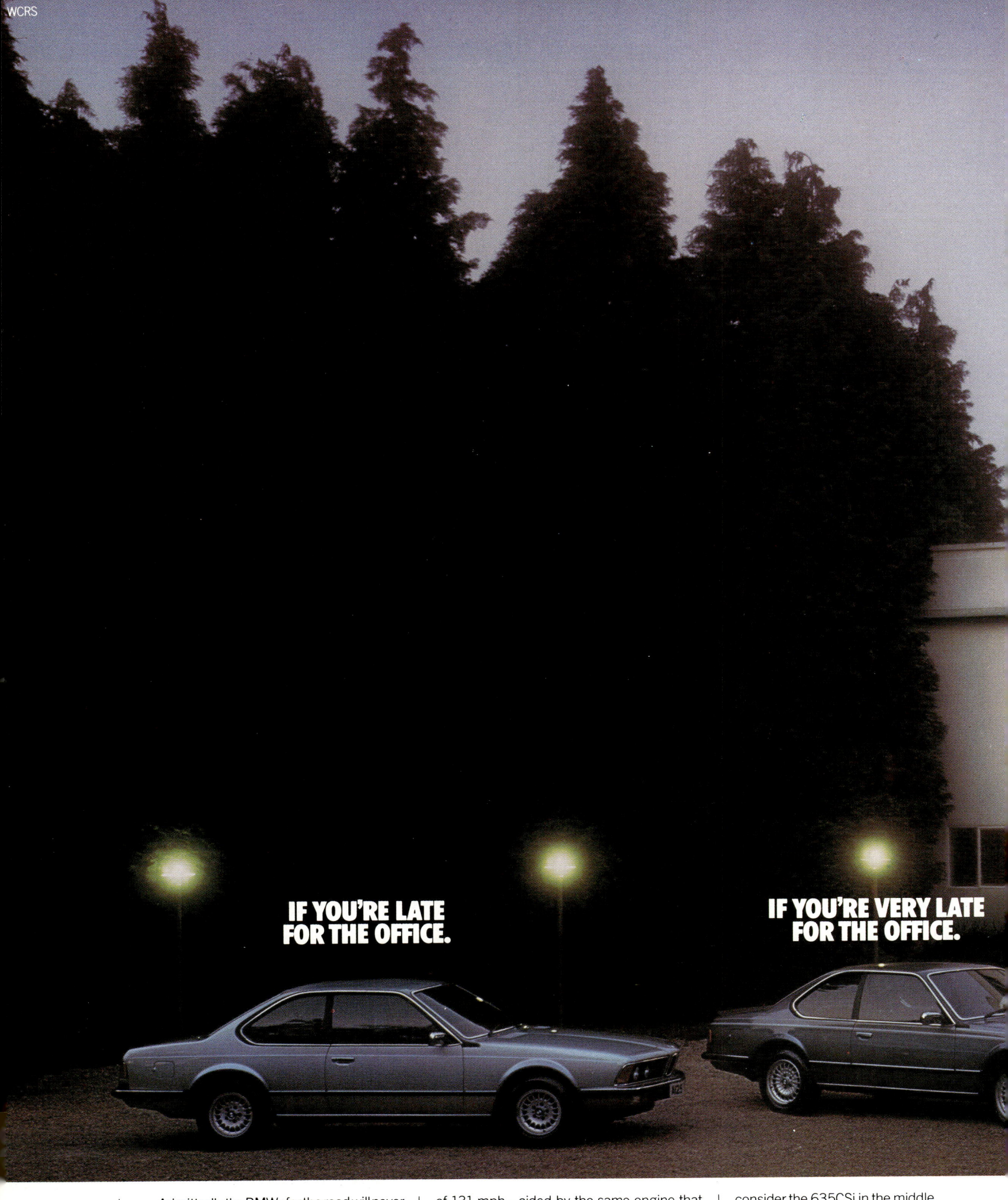

IF YOU'RE LATE
FOR THE OFFICE.

IF YOU'RE VERY LATE
FOR THE OFFICE.

Admittedly the BMWs for the road will never be quite as fast as a BMW for the track.
Which is not to say they're exactly slow.
The 628CSi on the left, for example, is capable of 131 mph – aided by the same engine that brought victory to a BMW driver in last year's European Touring Car Championships.
Should you want something livelier still, consider the 635CSi in the middle.
It reaches 60 mph in 6.9 seconds, and wil cruise on effortlessly up to 142 mph.
If you happen to own a racetrack you migh

DOE FUEL CONSUMPTION FIGURES FOR THE 635CSi FOUR SPEED AUTOMATIC: URBAN: 19.1 MPG (14.8L/100KM), 56MPH: 41.5 MPG (6.8L/100KM), 75 MPH: 32.5 MPG (8.7L/100KM). PERFORMANCE FIGURES SOURCE
INCLUSIVE DELIVERY CHARGE INCORPORATING BMW EMERGENCY SERVICE AND INITIAL SERVICES: £185 + VAT. FOR A BMW 6 SERIES INFORMATION FILE, PLEASE WRITE TO: BMW INFORMATION

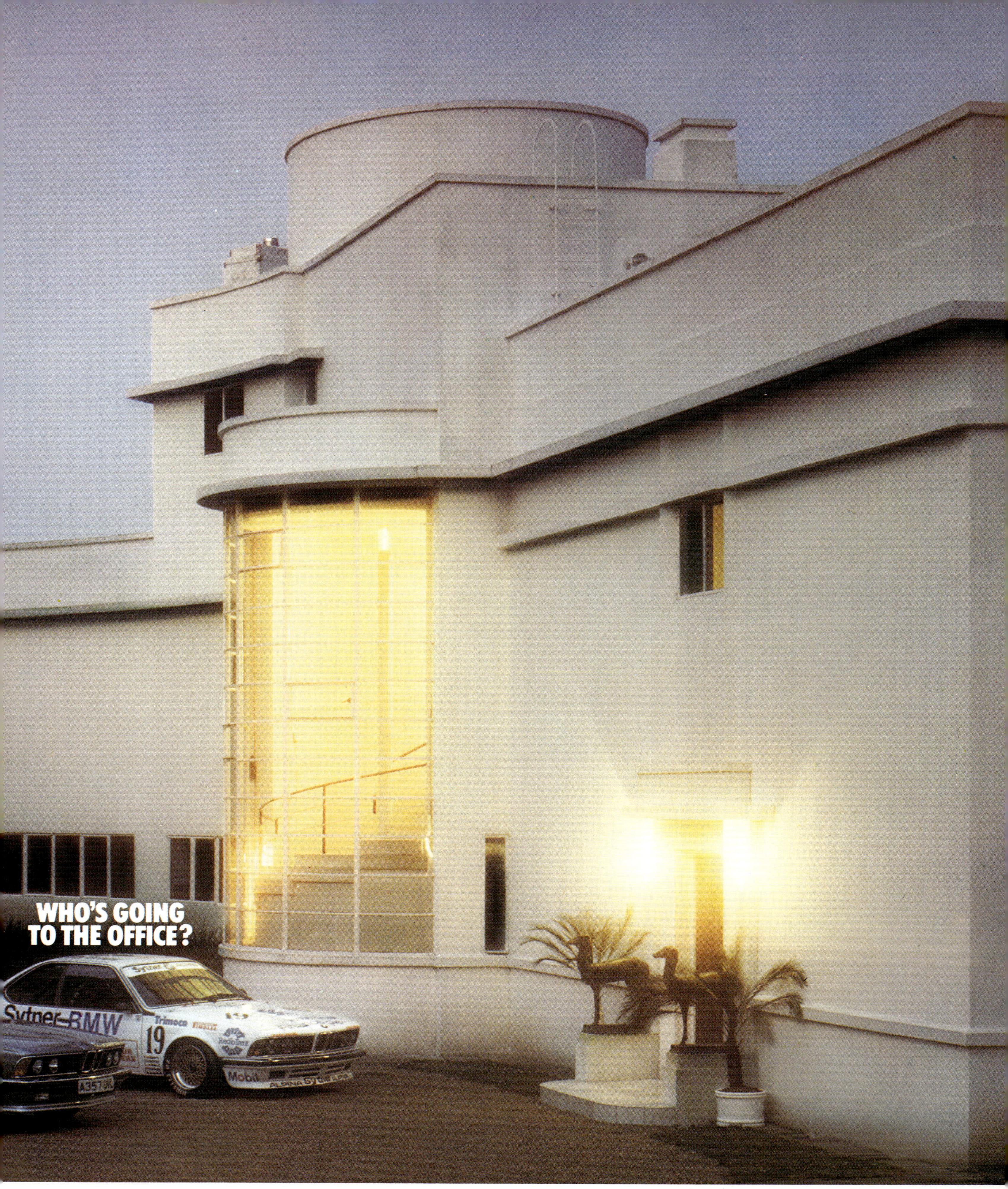

WHO'S GOING TO THE OFFICE?

prefer the racing version. For those that don't the 635CSi offers a minor compensation: a surprisingly frugal 24.7 mpg overall.

And how much do you pay for this rare combination of performance, economy and (let's be honest) sheer unashamed luxury?

£18,710 for the 628CSi. A cool £23,995 for the 635CSi. And sorry, but for those looking to buy the complete set, the racing car is not for sale.

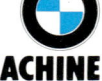

THE ULTIMATE DRIVING MACHINE

Repeat performance

by Mike Doodson, English Editor, *Grand Prix International*

Before the South African GP everything seemed to point to Alain Prost as the new world champion, France's first in the 33-year history of the title. His Renault had carried him to masterly, dominating victories at Ricard, Spa, Österreichring and Silverstone. Only once (at Monza) had the yellow French car – so recently the butt of paddock jokes – let him down. Prost himself had driven splendidly, a champion in the making, with only one (now notorious) mistake at Zandvoort counting against him. Despite Nelson Piquet's back-to-back victories at Monza and Brands Hatch, Prost still had a two-point lead.

Why then was Piquet being singled out in every pre-Kyalami poll as the likely champion? Inevitably, sentiment had something to do with it: even those who say that there's precious little left that can be described as sporting in modern Formula 1 resent the "at any price" arrival of Renault in Grand Prix racing. All teams have their faults, but Renault is the only one that doesn't have an identifiable human being as its owner and founder. For all its useful PR and well-organised "meet the drivers" lunches, Renault remains an anonymous spectre, the French nation racing as an adjunct to advertising. Renault races to increase sales, not (like the Ferraris, Ligiers and, yes, even the Ecclestones) for the sheer hell of it.

There was an element of "needle" in this final confrontation, too, for had it not been Ecclestone who led the so-called "garagistes" in their revolt against the major constructors over aerodynamic aids two years ago? Had not Ecclestone consistently spoken out against the cost escalation inevitable with the turbocharged engine? Imagine the loss of face for Renault after their much-vaunted seven years of turbo pioneering if Ecclestone's Brabham-BMW should be the first turbo-powered F1 car to carry a driver to a world championship.

Questioned after Brands Hatch, Prost and Piquet sounded non-committal about their prospects. It was, perhaps, easier to believe Piquet when he said that he didn't really care about what happened, for Prost had made himself unavailable for comment and didn't join the charter flight to South Africa. "I shall treat it like just another race," said Piquet. "Alain must be favourite because he has two points lead. But I have a better car . . ."

Nelson had joined the charter section of the regular UTA flight to Johannesburg at Nice. In his faded jeans, white socks and penny loafers you wouldn't have picked him out as a celebrity, but he turned left into the First Class compartment with Sylvia Tamsma, his German/Dutch girlfriend, and settled down to try and sleep away the hours aloft.

In the back of the same flight, at the invitation of Renault and Elf, was a contingent of French pressmen geared up to report Prost's forthcoming triumph. Two years ago, previewing the start of the 1982 season, one of those writers had headlined his story in the influential daily paper *L'Equipe* "Renault: This Year . . . or Never." This time the Régie itself had daringly anticipated success for Prost in a flag-waving poster campaign in support for its "champion" (the word used on the posters) when their star had been leading the championship by 14 points. In a major interview, Renault chief Gerard Larrousse had asserted that "we deserve to win the championship."

By the afternoon of October 14, less than 24 hours before the final showdown, there was more than just sentiment and an ill-advised poster campaign counting against Renault and Prost. Qualifying at Kyalami had underlined something that was already apparent at the two preceding races and had become glaringly obvious here: Piquet's Brabham was superior to the Renault not only on top speed (an advantage of 12 km/h according to most of the teams with timing equipment) but it was also handling more nimbly in

important corners like the Leeukop rising right-hander which leads on to the straight.

Suddenly, French hopes rested on Patrick Tambay, whose Ferrari had proven slightly faster than Piquet in qualifying. A victory by Tambay might prevent Piquet from getting the three points he needed to pass and beat Prost. Nevertheless, most people knew that Piquet would have been on pole if he hadn't ruined his qualifying Michelins on Saturday with, first, an untypical spin and then a couple of missed gearshifts on the Brabham's intricate six-speed gearbox. The betting on Tambay widened as the weather on Saturday got hotter: his Goodyear tyres would be marginal today, and the man from Cannes was destined to take a noble but comparatively unimportant role in the race itself.

That race, of course, belonged to Brabham and to BMW, whose engines have made such progress throughout the year. Piquet could have won it, but he chose not to. Instead, with everything under control, including Prost, he made an early pit stop for fuel and tyres. His well-drilled crew, equipped with new wheel guns to replace the tired-out equipment that had failed at Brands Hatch, got him back into the race in under 10 seconds. He rejoined it still in the lead on lap 29, ahead of team mate Riccardo Patrese. Prost had already been demoted to 4th place by Niki Lauda's much-improved McLaren-TAG/Porsche: five laps later, when he pulled into the pits, the Renault challenge was over. While his mechanics went through the motions of changing tyres the erstwhile championship leader unbuckled his belts and disappeared into the cool of his garage. His only chance of taking the title now rested on the possibility of Piquet's car crashing or breaking.

There were a few worried faces in the Brabham pit during the remaining laps as Piquet turned down the boost, waved Patrese through to win the race and, finally, dropped behind the Alfa of Andrea de Cesaris to take a leisurely 3rd place. Watching from the pit wall had been a subdued Alain Prost, who ambled along pit lane as the Brabham mechanics prepared to greet Nelson. Sportsman that he is, Prost offered his heartfelt greetings to Bernie Ecclestone. Soon afterwards the Brabham and Renault mechanics were swapping shirts as a memory of a season which – at least on the personal level – has been marked by close but never vindictive competition.

The same spirit was evident from the interview which Nelson gave to Murray Walker of the BBC after the victory celebrations were over. This was a wonderful piece of television, for Nelson showed himself to be fluent and thoughtful in front of the cameras, a far better subject that you care to name. "Alain, I must say, is a very good and sensible driver. I cannot say I'm happy that he lost and I won . . . but I'm sorry for him. He made one mistake all year, at Zandvoort, but I also made one mistake (a stalled start), at Imola. I don't think he lost the championship, though: I think Renault lost it . . ."

In the final analysis, and regardless of the Renault decision that put Prost in the executioner's tumbril on his return to Paris two days later, Piquet was right. Renault's racing team had mounted a remarkable campaign in 1983, producing a car that was quick enough to win races and reliable enough to take advantage of the more advanced Brabham when it faltered. The only quality which they lacked was the ability to respond to the surge of work which Chessington and Munich put into their chassis/engine combination at the end of the year. When the going gets tough, say our transatlantic friends, the tough get going. It was Brabham, not Renault, who got going at Monza, Brands Hatch and Kyalami.

So Nelson Piquet became world champion for the

second time in his career, equalling the achievement of his countryman Emerson Fittipaldi and putting himself into the same class of driver as Niki Lauda, his former mentor. No one can challenge his right to the title, for he won three races (Rio, Monza and Brands Hatch) with apparent ease and would also have taken Kyalami if caution hadn't required him to sacrifice it in favour of a finish. He would have taken Detroit, too, but for a stupid puncture.

Two years ago, after he had won his first title at Las Vegas, Nelson said that he wanted to win the championship again. "I'm enjoying this job too much to want to retire," he said: "I want to carry on racing for another ten years."

His second title hasn't dulled this ambition at all. Reminded of his "ten year" pledge before practice had even started at Kyalami, he said he hadn't changed his mind. "I still have another nine years in front of me, don't I? Yes, sure I want to win more titles. This is the only profession that I know . . ."

He also gets a huge amount of enjoyment out of racing. "There is nothing, *not one thing*," he emphasises, "as good as beating somebody you respect and winning a Grand Prix. I sometimes piss in my pants on the slowing down lap: it is a feeling which you cannot imagine."

For this, the work that gives him so much pleasure, he gets paid handsomely. Unusually, for a sportsman, he admits it. But he refuses point-blank to do any of the promotions that many other drivers agree to do, claiming that outside work burns out a drvier before his time. "Look, I make a *lot* of money already. If you go to do all this publicity you're lucky if you make 20 or 25 per cent more. It's not worth the work and the bullshit. I mean, the money is very, very good. Of course, some people are never satisfied, they always want more. Me, I'm satisfied with what I have."

The money buys him simple pleasures like the superb 18-metre boat which he keeps in Monte Carlo. It's an Akhir powered by a pair of twin-turbo two-stroke Detroit V12 diesels, each producing around 750 horsepower. A crew of two looks after the thing full-time, so that whenever he and Sylvia want to do so they can take off for Sardinia at 28 knots.

The boat is his escape, and he does a lot of escaping. "I think the mistake which people like Prost make is to let people know where they can find you. That's what I call 'pressure', and the best thing you can do is to disappear. Dieter (Stappert, BMW Motorsport chief) tried to find me all week before we came here, and he couldn't. The first thing I do is not to answer the telephone: I just call the factory once a week to make sure that the test programme hasn't been changed."

The apartment which Nelson shares with Sylvia is a modest 2-bedroom place on the 16th floor of a Monte Carlo high-rise. There is garage space for his beloved three-year-old Mercedes 500 SEL and for most of his other four cars, but only very close friends – and definitely no journalists – are invited to stay. To begin with, when their relationship started three years ago, Sylvia was not widely appreciated, but she has shown since then how good she is for Nelson; he needs an organiser who can compensate for his self-confessed laziness. He says that there is no question of marriage (both have failed marriages behind them), but the boat – for example – is in her name, and she likes to buy tasteful, expensive jewellery. Nelson doesn't care what others may think about her: "when she is at home," he says, "she is an *angel* . . ."

Friendships are divided into two categories: the Brazilian ones (i.e. the only *genuine* friends), and the others. He insists that the link-up with Prost and his family just before Monza was exaggerated by the press. "Alain phoned me because he was in Monaco on business, so I invited him to stay on the boat instead of in a hotel. We just had a nice time together."

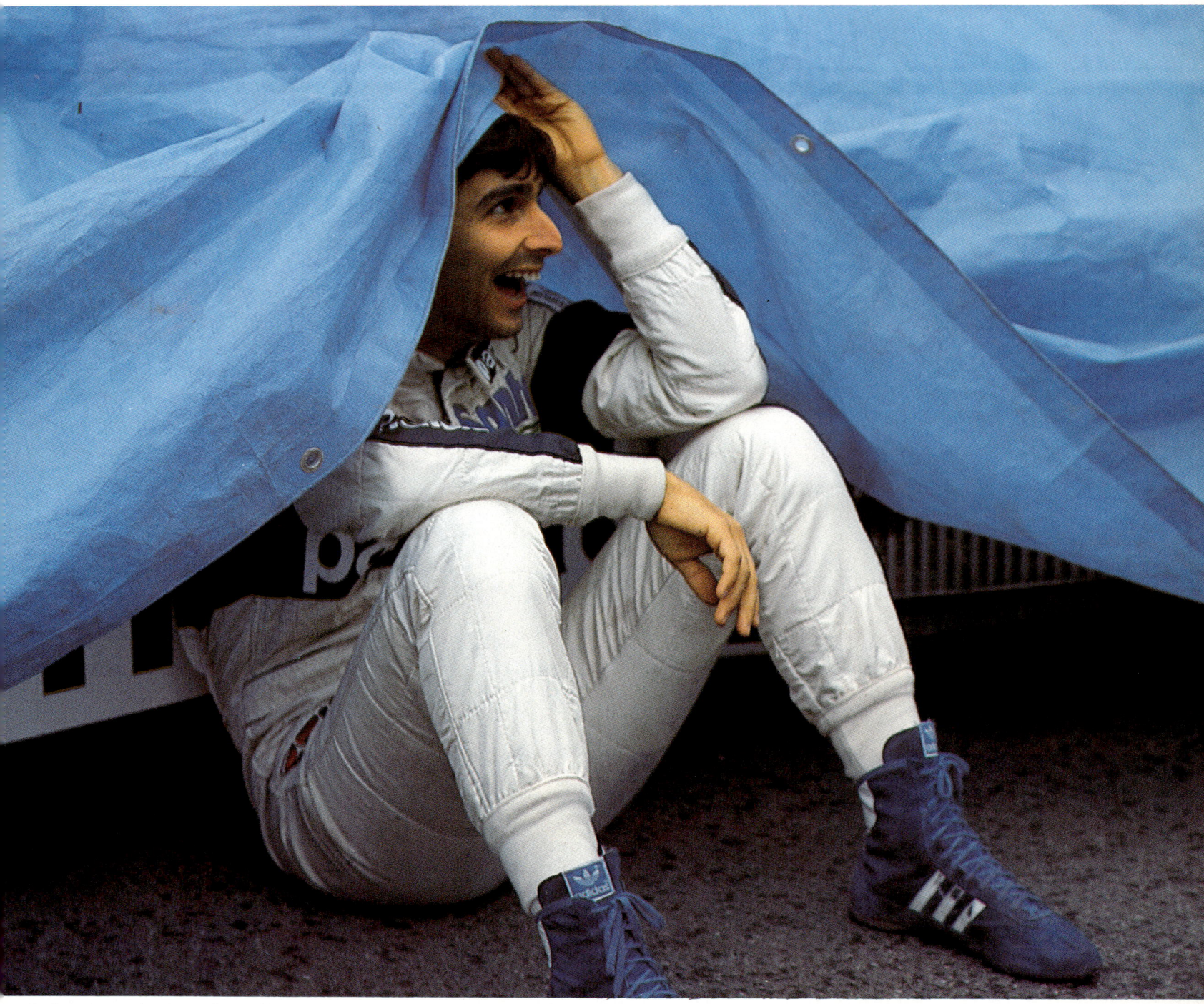

Nelson has resisted excellent offers to leave the Brabham team. He likes working with Murray and with the good-natured bunch of spanner-wielding geniuses who call themselves Brabham mechanics. "I can say I am a good friend of the Brabham mechanics because I can talk to them on the same level. But the most important thing I can say is that I trust them. You must not have to worry if the throttle is going to stick or a wheel fall off: imagine making a pit stop in under 10 seconds, like we did in practice at Brands Hatch, and wondering if they put all the wheels on tight. In five years I had only one or two problems that affected the safety of the car. That's fantastic."

Relations with Ecclestone are perhaps less solid. Before signing for 1984 Nelson demanded a measure of what he called "respect." Did he get it? "We made our agreement and I think he understands me better now. It's not so difficult to negotiate with him, but sometimes it is difficult to *live* with him. I have to live with him, though, because he takes such good care of the team, and the team is my tool for working with. If you make a balance, it is very good."

Who, I asked, had persuaded BMW to design and make the super qualifying engines which had made such a difference, beginning at Zandvoort, in the team's 1983 fortunes? "Oh, everyone did," he responded. "I don't think before that Paul (Rosche)

believed that Ferrari had special engines just for qualifying with extra boost. When he realised that they did, then he started to work, and now we are on the same level, maybe even better. In the last three races I have been almost playing with them, turning the boost down and controlling the races the way I want."

That, ironically, is not the way that this simple but enormously gifted Brazilian likes to win. He says that his most satisfying victory of the year was in Brazil, where he overcame a host of troubles to win in front of an appreciative home crowd with a car that was still a novelty that had given all sorts of trouble during practice.

But power threatens to become the key to success in the future of Formula 1, just as aerodynamics had been the vital element in 1979/82. But power is no good if the driver doesn't have the instinct to know when to use it, as a look at the results of Piquet's team-mate will show. Engine development was the most note-worthy technical element of the 1983 Grand Prix season, but without the commitment of Nelson Piquet, his devotion to test and development, and above all his innate mechanical sympathy, he has shown that driver ability still counts for something.

He wants to win the championship another couple of times. After 1983, who would dare to wager against his ability to do just that?

Nelson Piquet's relaxed and happy attitude during 1983 helped the Brazilian mature into an outstanding all-round driver.
Photo: John Townsend

31

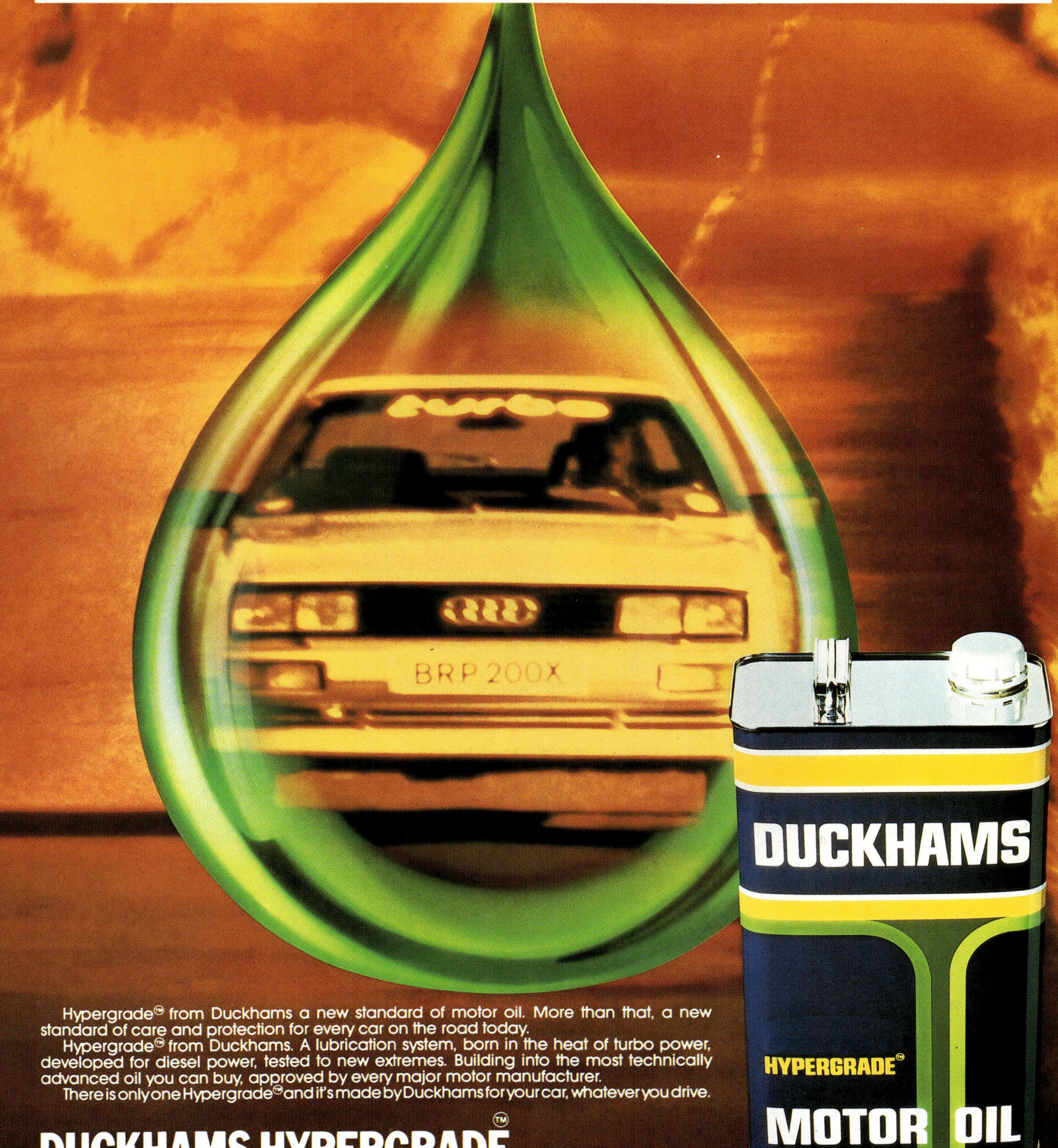

1983 Formula 1 car specifications

Full details of every car which took part in World Championship events

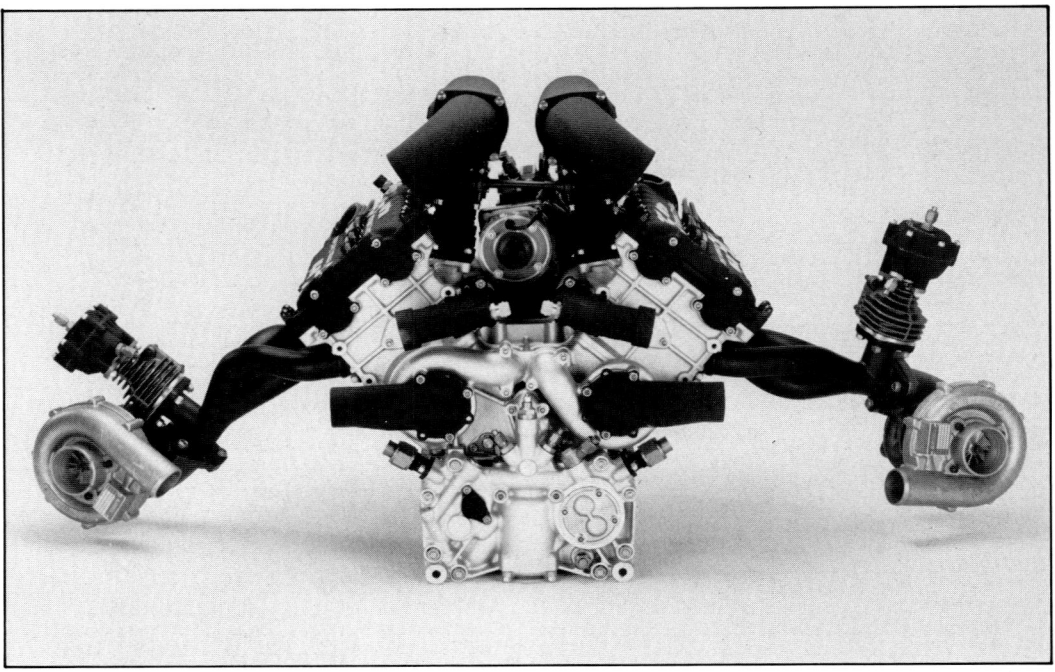

Porsche indirectly entered the Formula 1 arena, designing and constructing a V6 turbo for TAG and McLaren.

Ferrari won the Constructors' Championship for the second year in succession, and the sixth time in nine years, thanks to Tambay and Arnoux taking points 17 times from 30 starts.

Ferrari made a slow start but jumped to the top of the championship in May by scoring heavily at Imola. Renault then gathered momentum at Monaco and Spa-Francorchamps and overtook the Italian team. A win for Arnoux in Montreal meant the two teams were neck-and-neck but Renault eased ahead once more at Silverstone. Positions were reversed at Hockenheim but Prost's win in Austria gave Renault a three-point advantage. Ferrari's clean sweep in Holland ended the deadlock and their lead was such that Renault were unable to catch up even though both Ferraris retired from the last two races.

After leading initially, Brabham-BMW did not figure in the championship thanks to the team effectively scoring points with just one car and Piquet's late rally merely succeeded in consolidating third place.

The engines

Seven turbocharged engines were seen during 1983, Honda and TAG (Porsche) racing for the first time and joining Renault, Alfa Romeo, Ferrari, BMW and Hart. Turbos led all of the 16 races (including one non-championship event) and won 12 of them, Brabham-BMW, Renault and Ferrari taking four each, compared to eight turbo victories in total during 1982.

The Euroracing team represented Alfa Romeo and raced the Alfa turbo V8 for the first time, finishing second on two occasions. The Hart turbo scored points for the first time and BMW supplied their M12/13 engine to ATS as well as Brabham. Porsche designed

and constructed the TAG V6 turbo which was raced by McLaren during the last four races. Williams scored points first time out with the Honda V6, the Japanese turbo having appeared earlier in the season in a Spirit chassis. Renault supplied their turbo to Lotus, the French V6 taking four pole positions and setting four fastest laps. BMW took two pole positions and five fastest laps compared to eight pole positions and four

fastest laps for Ferrari.

The Ford-Cosworth DFV (and its latest derivative, the DFY), now in its 17th season, scored its 155th and, probably, its final Grand Prix win. The other normally aspirated engine, the Alfa Romeo 1260, was used in the second half of the season by Osella. The Matra V12 was no longer supplied to Ligier, the French team switching back to the Ford-Cosworth.

	Ferrari 126C Turbo	BMW M12/13 Turbo	Hart 415T Turbo	TAG P01 (TTE P01) Turbo	Renault EF1 Monaco	Alfa Romeo 890T
No. of cylinders	V6	4-in line	4-in line	V6	V6	V8
Bore and stroke	81 mm × 48·4 mm	89·2 mm × 60 mm	88 m × 61·5 mm	51 mm	86 mm × 42·8 mm	74 mm × 43·5 mm
Capacity	1496·43cc	1500cc	1496 cc	1499 cc	1492 cc	1496 cc
Compression ratio	6·5:1	6·7:1	6·7:1	7·0:1	7:1	7:1
Maximum power	620 bhp	640 bhp	580 bhp at 1·8 bar boost	700 bhp	650 bhp	640 bhp
Maximum rpm	11,500	11,000	10,750	11,500	12,000	11,500
Valve sizes	–	35·8 mm - Inlet	35·56 mm - Inlet	–	–	–
		30·3 mm - Exhaust	30·48 mm - Exhaust			
Valve lift	–	–	10·66 mm	–	–	–
Valve timing	–	–	102°	–	–	–
Block material	Aluminium	Cast iron	Aluminium	Aluminium Alloy	Cast iron	Aluminium
Pistons and rings	Mahle/Goetze	Mahle/Goetze	Mahle/Goetze	Mahle/ATE or Goetze	Mahle/Goetze	Mahle
Bearings	Vandervell/Clevite	Glyco	Vandervell	Glyco	Glyco	
Fuel injection	Lucas/Ferrari	Bosch	Lucas	Bosch Motronic MS3	Kugelfischer electronic	Alfa Romeo/Spica
Ignition system	Marelli	Bosch	Lucas	Bosch Motronic MS3	Marelli	Marelli Dinoplex
Turbocharger(s)	2 × KKK	KKK	Holset	2 × KKK	2 × KKK	2 × Alfa Romeo/Sylo
Weight (less intercooler)	148 kg	160 kg	290 lb	150 kg	375 lb/170 kg	140 kg

	Alfa Romeo 1260	Honda RA163-E	Ford-Cosworth DFV (Stage 1)	Ford-Cosworth DFV (Short Stroke)	Ford-Cosworth DFY
No. of cylinders	V12	V6	V8 (90°)	V8 (90°)	V8 (90°)
Bore and stroke	78·5 mm × 51·5 mm	–	85·6 mm × 64·8 mm	90·0 mm × 58·8 mm	90 mm × 58·8 mm
Capacity	2995 cc	1500 cc	2993cc	2994cc	2994cc
Compression ratio	11·5:1	–	12·2:1	12·2:1	12·3:1
Maximum power	540 bhp	600 bhp	495 bhp	510 bhp	510 bhp
Maximum rpm	12,300	–	11,000	11,000	11,000
Valve sizes	30 mm × 2	–	34·50 mm - Inlet	36·06 mm - Inlet	–
	25 mm × 2		29·97 mm - Exhaust	31·75 mm - Exhaust	
Valve lift	9 mm	–	10·41 mm - Exhaust	11·00 mm - Inlet	–
				10·41 mm - Exhaust	
Valve timing	50-70/70-50	–	102°	102°	102°
Block material	Aluminium	Cast-Iron	LM 25 Aluminium Alloy	LM 25 Aluminium Alloy	LM 25 Aluminium Alloy
Pistons and rings	Mahle	–	Cosworth/Goetze	Cosworth/Goetze	Cosworth/Goetze
Bearings	Clevite	–	Vandervell	Vandervell	Vandervell
Fuel injection	Lucas	Honda	Lucas	Lucas	Lucas
Ignition system	Marelli Dinoplex	Honda Kikaki	Lucas/Contactless	Lucas/Contactless	Lucas/Contactless
Turbocharger(s)	–	2 × KKK	–		
Weight (less intercooler)	–	–	330 lb/150 kg	320 lb/145 kg	300 lb/136 kg

Formula 1 car specifications

	Alfa Romeo 183T	Arrows A6-Cosworth	ATS D6-BMW
Sponsor(s)	Marlboro/Nordica	Various	ATS Wheels
Designer(s)	–	Dave Wass/Jim Filmer	Gustav Brunner
Team Manager(s)	Gianpaulo Pavanello/Giancarlo Casoli	Alan Rees	Gunter Schmid
Chief Mechanic(s)	–	Dave Luckett	Roy Topp
No of chassis built	6	5	3
ENGINE			
Type	Alfa Romeo V8 Turbo	Ford-Cosworth DFV	BMW M12/13
Fuel and oil	Agip	Valvoline	Shell
Sparking plugs	Champion	Champion	Bosch
TRANSMISSION			
Gearbox/speeds	Alfa Romeo (5)	Arrows/Hewland (5)	ATS/Hewland (5)
Drive-shafts	Alfa Romeo	Arrows	ATS/Löbro
Clutch	Borg & Beck	Borg & Beck	Borg & Beck
CHASSIS			
Front suspension	Top rocker arms, lower wishbones, inboard springs	Double wishbones, pull rods, inboard springs	Double wishbones, pull rods, inboard springs
Rear suspension	Top rocker arms, lower wishbones, inboard springs	Top rocker arms, lower wishbones, inboard springs	Double wishbones, pull rods, inboard springs
Suspension dampers	Koni	Koni	Koni
Wheel diameter	13 in front / 13 in rear	13 in front / 13 in rear	13 in front / 15 in rear
Wheel rim widths	12 in front / 16·5 in rear	11 in front / 16 in rear	11 in front / 16 in rear
Tyres	Michelin	Goodyear	Goodyear
Brakes	Lockheed	Lockheed	Lockheed
Brake pads	Ferodo	Ferodo	Ferodo
Steering	Alfa Romeo	Knight/Arrows	ATS/Knight
Radiator(s)	Serck	Serck/Sofica	Behr
Fuel tank	Aerotec	Aerotec	Marstons/ATL
Battery	Marelli	YUASA	YUASA
Instruments	Veglia	VDO	VDO/Smiths
DIMENSIONS			
Wheelbase	107 in/2720 mm	106 in/2692 mm	104 in/2642 mm
Track	71·6 in/1820 mm front / 66·1 in/1680 mm rear	72 in/1829 mm front / 62 in/1575 mm rear	69 in/1753 mm front / 64 in/1626 mm rear
Gearbox weight	110 lb/50 kg	95 lb/43 kg	110 lb/50 kg
Chassis weight (tub)	66 lb/30 kg	75 lb/34 kg	60 lb/27 kg
Formula weight	1212·5 lb/550 kg	1191 lb/540 kg	1191 lb/540 kg
Fuel capacity	48·4 gall/220 litres	42 gall/191 litres	50 gall/227 litres
Fuel consumption	–	5·0-5·8 mpg/49-57 litres/100 km	4 mpg/68 litres/100 km

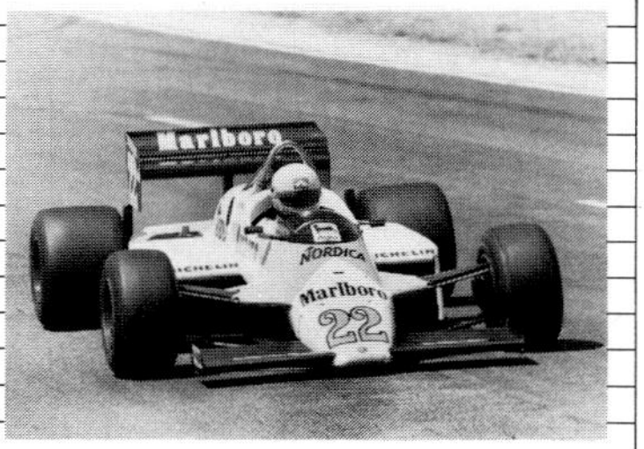

Alfa Romeo 183T

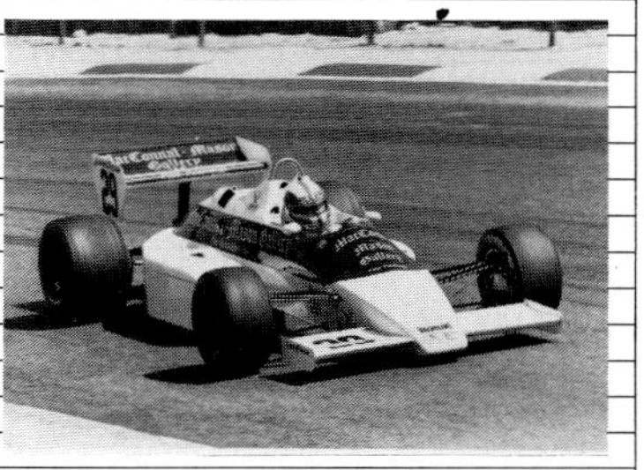

Arrows A6

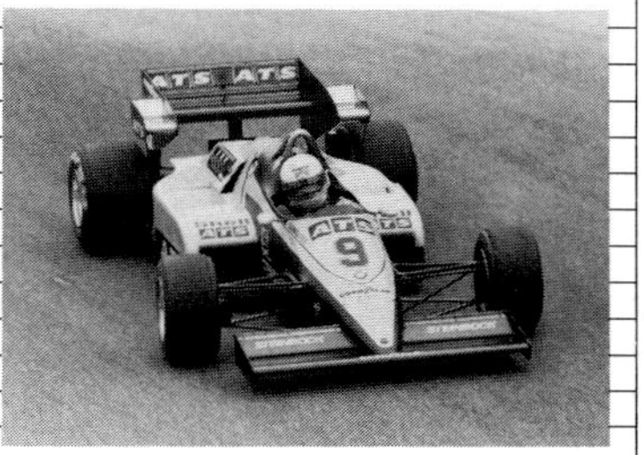

ATS D6

	Brabham BT52/BT52B-BMW	Ferrari 126C2/B	Ferrari 126C3
Sponsor(s)	Parmalat/Fila	Fiat/Agip/Goodyear	Fiat/Agip/Goodyear
Designer(s)	Gordon Murray/David North	Ferrari	Ferrari
Team Manager(s)	Herbie Blash/Bernard Ecclestone	Enzo Ferrari	Enzo Ferrari
Chief Mechanic(s)	Charlie Whiting	Bellentani/Scaramelli	Bellentani/Scaramelli
No of chassis built	6	5	5
ENGINE			
Type	BMS M12/13 Turbo	126/C	126/C
Fuel and oil	-/Castrol	Agip	Agip
Sparking plugs	Bosch	Champion	Champion
TRANSMISSION			
Gearbox/speeds	Hewland/Brabham/Weisman/Alfa/Getrag (5/6)	Ferrari	Ferrari
Drive-shafts	Brabham	Löbro/Ferrari	Löbro/Ferrari
Clutch	Borg & Beck	Borg & Beck	Borg & Beck
CHASSIS			
Front suspension	Double wishbones, pushrods,	Double wishbones, pull rods, inboard springs	Double wishbones, pull rods, inboard springs
Rear suspension	Double wishbones, pushrods,	Double wishbones, pull rods, inboard springs	Double wishbones, pull rods, inboard springs
Suspension dampers	Koni	Koni/De Carbon	Koni/De Carbon
Wheel diameter	13 in front / 13 in rear	13 in/15 in front / 13 in/15 in rear	13 in/15 in front / 13 in/15 in rear
Wheel rim widths	11·5 in front / 16·5 in rear	10 in/12 in front / 16 in rear	10 in/12 in front / 16 in rear
Tyres	Michelin	Goodyear	Goodyear
Brakes	Hitco/Brabham/Girling/AP	Brembo	Brembo
Brake pads	Hitco/Ferodo	Ferodo	Ferodo
Steering	Brabham rack and pinion	Ferrari	Ferrari
Radiator(s)	Behr	Behr/Valeo/IPRA	Behr/Valeo/IPRA
Fuel tank	ATL	Pirelli	Pirelli
Battery	YUASA	Varley	Varley
Instruments	VDO	Borletti	Borletti
DIMENSIONS			
Wheelbase	112 in	104·6 in/2657 mm	102·4 in/2600 mm
Track	69 in/1753 mm front / 64 in/1626 mm rear	70 in/1780 mm front / 64·7 in/1644 mm rear	70·5 in/1790 mm front / 64·7 in/1644 mm rear
Gearbox weight	105 lb/48 kg	102·5 lb/46·5 kg	102·5 lb/46·5 kg
Chassis weight (tub)	92 lb/41·7 kg	92·6 lb/42·0 kg	92·6 lb/42·0 kg
Formula weight	1191 lb/540 kg	1252 lb/568 kg	1217 lb/552 kg
Fuel capacity	42 gall/191 litres	52·8 gall/240 litres	52·8 gall/240 litres
Fuel consumption	–	–	–

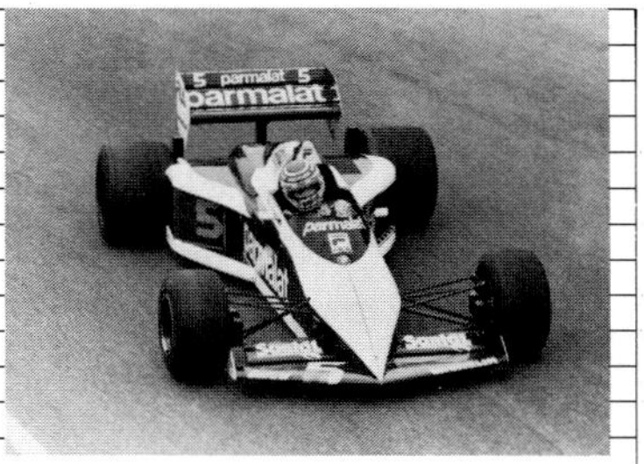

Brabham BT52B

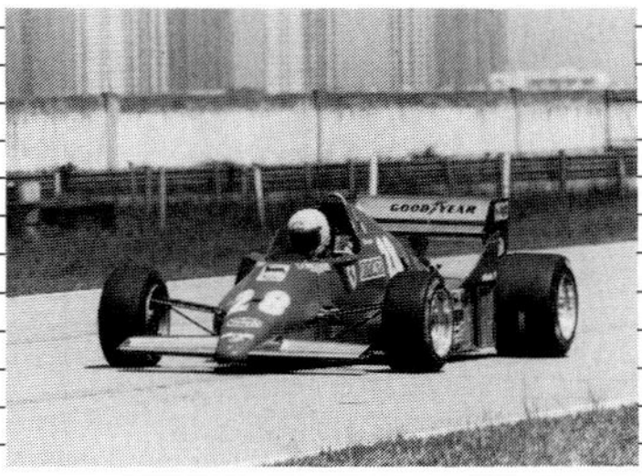

Ferrari 126C2

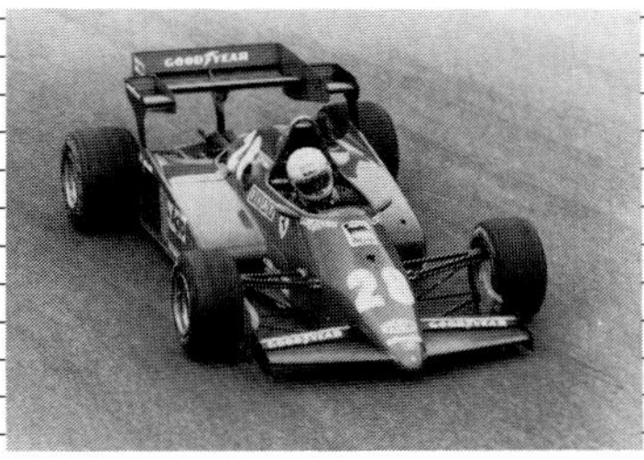

Ferrari 126C3

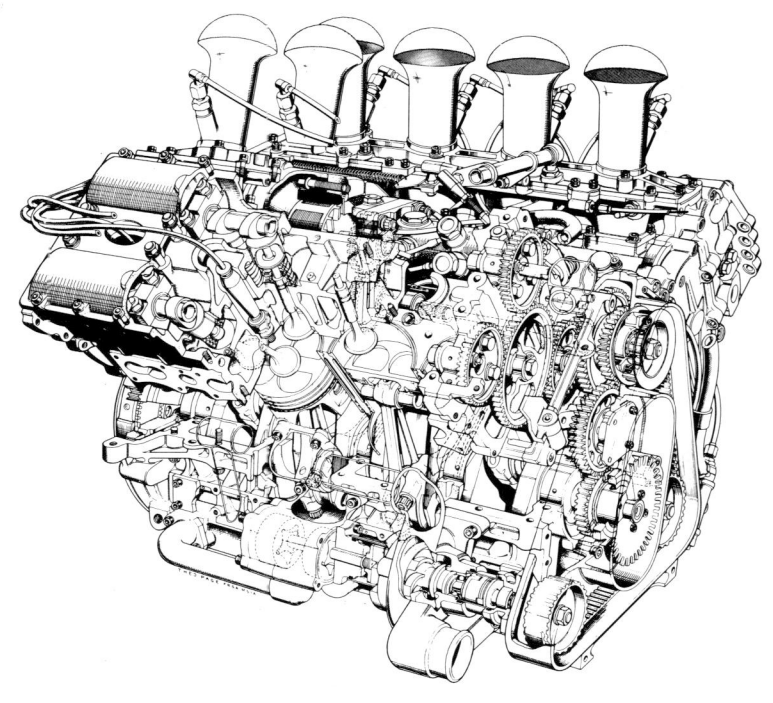

Formula 1 car specifications

	Ligier JS21-Cosworth	Lotus 92-Cosworth	Lotus 93T-Renault	
Sponsor(s)	Gitanes/Embratur/Cafe du Bresil/Elf	John Player & Sons	John Player & Sons	
Designer(s)	Michel Beaujon/Claude Galopin	Martin Ogilvie	Colin Chapman/Martin Ogilvie	
Team Manager(s)	Guy Ligier/Danny Hindenoch	Peter Warr	Peter Warr	
Chief Mechanic(s)	Jean Claude Guenard/Daniel Vizier	Bob Dance	Bob Dance	
No of chassis built	4	2	2	
ENGINE				
Type	Ford Cosworth DFV and DFV (Short stroke)	Ford-Cosworth DFV and DFV (Short stroke)	Renault EF1	
Fuel and oil	Elf	Elf	Elf	
Sparking plugs	Champion	Champion	Champion	
TRANSMISSION				
Gearbox/speeds	Hewland (5)	Lotus/Hewland (5)	Lotus/Hewland (5)	
Drive-shafts	Citroen	Löbro	Löbro	
Clutch	Borg & Beck	Borg & Beck	AP/Borg & Beck	
CHASSIS				Ligier JS21
Front suspension	Upper and lower wishbones, pull rods	Double wishbones, pull rods, inboard springs	Double wishbones, pull rods, inboard springs	
Rear suspension	Upper and lower wishbones, pull rods	Top rocker arms, lower wishbones, inboard springs	Lower wishbones, top rockers, inboard springs	
Suspension dampers	Citroen	Koni	Koni	
Wheel diameter	13 in front	15 in front	15 in front	
	13 in rear	13 in/15 in rear	13 in/15 in rear	
Wheel rim widths	11 in front	11 in front	11 in front	
	16 in rear	16·5 in/17 in rear	16·5 in rear	
Tyres	Michelin	Pirelli	Pirelli	Lotus 92
Brakes	Brembo	Girling (front), Lockheed (rear)	AP/Lockheed	
Brake pads	Ferodo	Ferodo	Ferodo	
Steering	Ligier	Lotus/Knight	Lotus/Knight	
Radiator(s)	IPRA	IPRA	Secan	
Fuel tank	ATL	ATL	ATL	
Battery	Tudor	YUASA	YUASA	
Instruments	Contactless	Contactless	Contactless Tacho/Poinsot Boost Gauge	
DIMENSIONS				
Wheelbase	103·5 in/2630 mm	110 in/2794 mm	106 in/2692 mm	
Track	70·4 in/1788 mm front	68·89 in/1750 mm front	70·9 in/1800 mm front	
	63 in/1600 mm rear	62·36 in/1584 mm rear	63 in/1600 mm rear	
Gearbox weight	119 lb/54 kg	98 lb/44·45 kg	98 lb/44·45 kg	
Chassis weight (tub)	88 lb/40 kg	75 lb/34 kg	75 lb/34 kg	
Formula weight	1212 lb/550 kg	1191 lb/540 kg	1191 lb/540 kg	Lotus 93T
Fuel capacity	46 gall/210 litres	42 gall/191 litres	55 gall/250 litres	
Fuel consumption	5·7 mpg/50 litres/100 km	5·4 mpg/52·25 litres/100 km	4-5 mpg/57-68 litres/100 km	

	Lotus 94T-Renault	March RAM 01-Cosworth	McLaren MP4/1C-Cosworth	
Sponsor(s)	John Player & Sons	Rizla/Newsweek/Copec/RMC	Marlboro/SAIMA/Unipart/Michelin/ Ebel/Boss/Hercules	
Designer(s)	Gerard Decarouge	Dave Kelly	John Barnard	
Team Manager(s)	Peter Warr	Mick Ralph	Ron Dennis	
Chief Mechanic(s)	Bob Dance	Ray Boulter	Dave Ryan	
No of chassis built	3	3	8	
ENGINE				
Type	Renault EF1	Ford-Cosworth DFV	Ford-Cosworth DFV (Short stroke)	
Fuel and oil	Elf	Valvoline	Unipart oil	
Sparking plugs	Champion	Champion	Unipart	
TRANSMISSION				
Gearbox/speeds	Lotus/Hewland (5)	Hewland (5/6)	Hewland/McLaren (5)	
Drive-shafts	Löbro/Lotus	RAM Automotive	McLaren	
Clutch	AP/Borg & Beck	Borg & Beck	Borg & Beck	
CHASSIS				Lotus 94T
Front suspension	Lower wishbones, top rockers, inboard springs	Upper and lower wishbones, pull rods, inboard springs	Push rod operating inboard auxiliary rockers, lower wishbones, inboard springs	
Rear suspension	Double wishbones, pull rods, inboard springs	Upper and lower wishbones, pull rods, inboard springs	Top rocker arms, lower wishbones, inboard springs	
Suspension dampers	Koni	Koni	Bilstein	
Wheel diameter	15 in front	15 in front	13 in front	
	13 in rear	13 in rear	13 in rear	
Wheel rim widths	11 in front	11 in front	11 in front	
	16·5 in rear	16 in rear	16 in rear	
Tyres	Pirelli	Pirelli	Michelin	
Brakes	Girling/Lockheed	Lockheed	SEP/AP or AP	March RAM 01
Brake pads	Ferodo	Ferodo	SEP or Ferodo	
Steering	Lotus/Knight	RAM Automotive	McLaren	
Radiator(s)	Secan	Behr	McLaren/Behr	
Fuel tank	ATL	Premier	ATL	
Battery	YUASA	National	YUASA	
Instruments	Contactless Tacho/Poinsot Boost Gauge	Tacho/Lucas	Contactless/VDO	
DIMENSIONS				
Wheelbase	106 in/2692 mm	106 in/2692 mm	105·8 in/2687 mm	
Track	70·9 in/1800 mm front	70·5 in/1791 mm front	71·5 in/1816 mm front	
	68·1 in/1730 mm rear	63·25 in-65·75 in/1607 mm- 1670 mm rear	66·0 in/1676 mm rear	
Gearbox weight	95 lb/43 kg	–	125 lb/57 kg	
Chassis weight (tub)	75 lb/34 kg	85 lb/38·6 kg	78 lbs/35·5 kg	
Formula weight	1191 lb/540 kg	1188 lb/540 kg	1191 lb/540 kg	McLaren MP4/1C
Fuel capacity	40 gall/182 litres	40 gall/181 litres	39·5 gall/179·5 litres	
Fuel consumption	4-5 mpg/57-68 litres/100 km	5·6 mpg/50 litres/100 km	5·3 mpg/53 litres/100 km (average)	

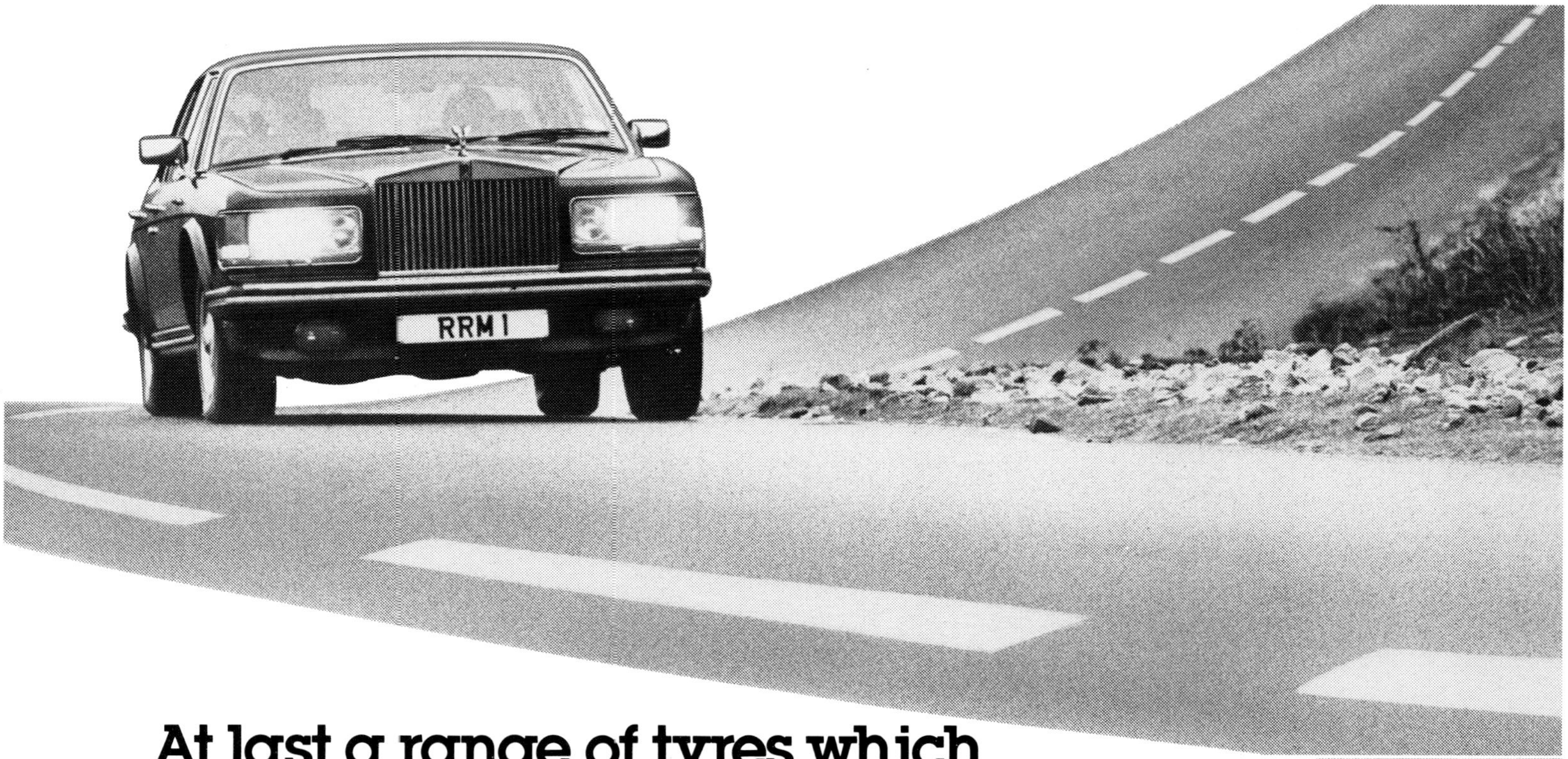

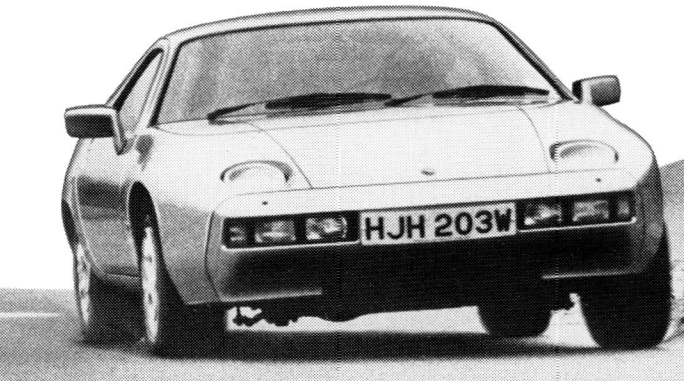

At last a range of tyres which recognises that 2½ tons of Rolls corners differently from 1½ tons of Porsche.

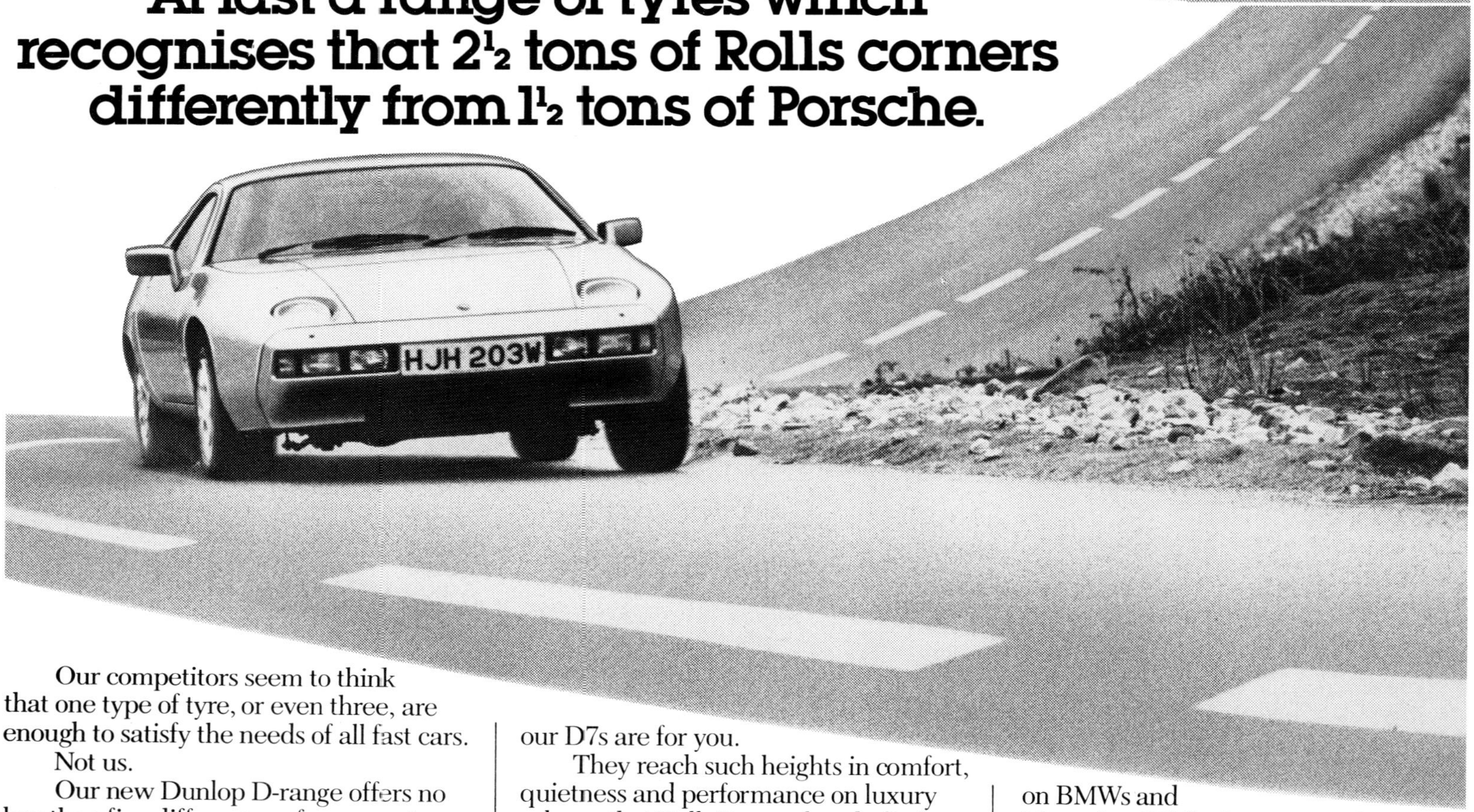

Our competitors seem to think that one type of tyre, or even three, are enough to satisfy the needs of all fast cars.

Not us.

Our new Dunlop D-range offers no less than five different performance tyres.

Each one designed with emphasis on specific performance aspects.

The D4s for example are made exclusively for those machines that are built to take corners at 120 mph. Like the Porsche 928 and the BMW M1.

They're twice as wide as they are deep.

And they'll keep more of their computer designed tread on the road in a tight corner than any other tyre made.

If however, you're more concerned with not upsetting the cocktail cabinet than imitating Emerson Fittipaldi, then our D7s are for you.

They reach such heights in comfort, quietness and performance on luxury saloons that Rolls Royce already fit them as standard on their new models.

The difference between the two is the D3.

They're made for the latest generation of fast sports saloons like the Audi 80 and the new Ford Escort XR3.

They give a smoothness of ride never before obtainable on extra wide tyres.

Their steel breakers have a nylon wrap which shrinks at running temperature minimising tread movement and maximising cornering capability.

The D6 is just as silently impressive on BMWs and Mercedes. While the D2 matches the crisp handling requirements of executive saloons like the Rover 2600 and Peugeot 505.

All in all, you'll find there's a tyre in the new Dunlop D-range that's better designed for your car than your present ones. Simply because it was specifically designed for your car.

And not for someone else's.

The new D-range of performance tyres.
⊘DUNLOP

Formula 1 car specifications

	McLaren MP4/1E-TAG	Osella FA1D-Cosworth	Osella FA1E-Alfa Romeo	
Sponsor(s)	Marlboro/SAIMA/Unipart/Michelin/Ebel/Boss/Hercules	Kelemata	Kelemata	
Designer(s)	John Barnard	Enzo Osella/Giuseppe Peirotta	Tony Southgate	
Team Manager(s)	Ron Dennis	Enzo Osella	Enzo Osella	
Chief Mechanic(s)	Dave Ryan	—	—	
No of chassis built	4	3	2	
ENGINE				
Type	TAG Turbo P01 (TTE P01)	Ford-Cosworth DFV	Alfa Romeo 1260	
Fuel and oil	Elf/Unipart turbo oil	Agip	Agip	
Sparking plugs	Bosch	Champion	Champion	McLaren MP4/1E
TRANSMISSION				
Gearbox/speeds	Hewland/McLaren (5)	Hewland/Osella (5)	Alfa Romeo	
Drive-shafts	McLaren	Osella	Alfa Romeo	
Clutch	Borg & Beck	AP	AP	
CHASSIS				
Front suspension	Push rod operating inboard auxiliary rockers, lower wishbones, inboard springs	Top rocker arms, lower wishbones, inboard springs	Double wishbones, push rods, inboard springs	
Rear suspension	Top rocker arms, lower wishbones, inboard springs	Top rocker arms, lower wishbones, inboard springs	Top rocker arms, lower wishbones, inboard springs	
Suspension dampers	Bilstein	Koni	Sachs (front), Koni (rear)	
Wheel diameter	13 in front / 13 in rear	13 in front / 13 in rear	13 in front / 13 in rear	
Wheel rim widths	11 in front / 16 in rear	11·5 in front / 16 in rear	11·5 in front / 16 in rear	Osella FA1D
Tyres	Michelin	Michelin	Michelin	
Brakes	SEP/AP or AP	Brembo	Brembo (front), Lockheed (rear)	
Brake pads	SEP or Ferodo	Ferodo	Ferodo	
Steering	McLaren	Osella	Osella/Knight	
Radiator(s)	McLaren/Unipart	IPRA	IPRA	
Fuel tank	ATL	Pirelli	Pirelli	
Battery	YUASA	Magneti Marelli	Magneti Marelli	
Instruments	Motometer/VDO	—	—	
DIMENSIONS				
Wheelbase	105·8 in/2687 mm	106 in/2692 mm	109 in/2769 mm	
Track	71·5 in/1816 mm front / 66·0 in/1676 mm rear	68 in/1727 mm front / 65 in/1651 mm rear	70 in/1778 mm front / 65 in/1651 mm rear	
Gearbox weight	125 lb/57 kg	126 lb/57 kg	—	
Chassis weight (tub)	79 lbs/57·5 kg	110 lb/50 kg	85 lb/38·6 kg	
Formula weight	1191 lb/540 kg	1279 lb/580 kg	1201 lb/545 kg	
Fuel capacity	39·5 gall/179·5 litres	—	48 gall/218 litres	
Fuel consumption	approx 3·9 mpg/68 litres/100 km	—	—	Osella FA1E

	Renault RE30C	Renault RE40	Spirit 201-Honda	
Sponsor(s)	—	Elf	Honda/Marlboro	
Designer(s)	Renault Sport	Renault Sport	Gordon Coppuck/John Baldwin	
Team Manager(s)	Gerard Larrousse/Jean Sage	Gerard Larrousse/Jean Sage	John Wickham	
Chief Mechanic(s)	Daniel Champion	Daniel Champion	—	
No of chassis built	3	7	1 (Converted from F2 car)	
ENGINE				
Type	Renault EF1 Monaco	Renault EF1 Monaco	Honda RA163-E	
Fuel and oil	Elf	Elf	Shell	
Sparking plugs	Champion	Champion	NGK	
TRANSMISSION				
Gearbox/speeds	Renault/Hewland (5)	Renault/Hewland (5)	Hewland	
Drive-shafts	Glaenzer	Glaenzer	Spirit	
Clutch	Borg & Beck	Borg & Beck	Borg & Beck	Renault RE30C
CHASSIS				
Front suspension	Top rocker arms, lower wishbones, inboard springs	Top rocker arms, lower wishbones, inboard springs	Top rocker arms, lower wishbones, inboard springs	
Rear suspension	Top rocker arms, lower wishbones, inboard springs	Double wishbones, pull rods, inboard springs	Top rocker arms, lower wishbones, inboard springs	
Suspension dampers	De Carbon	De Carbon	Koni	
Wheel diameter	13 in front / 13 in rear	13 in front / 13 in rear	13 in/15 in front / 13 in/15 in rear	
Wheel rim widths	11·5 in front / 16·5 in rear	11·5 in front / 16·5 in rear	11 in front / 15 in/16 in rear	
Tyres	Michelin	Michelin	Goodyear	
Brakes	Lockheed	Lockheed	Lockheed	
Brake pads	Ferodo	Ferodo	Ferodo	Renault RE40
Steering	Renault	Renault	Spirit	
Radiator(s)	Secan	Secan	Serck	
Fuel tank	Superflexit	Superflexit	Marston and Premier	
Battery	Marelli	Marelli	YUASA	
Instruments	Poinsot/Contactless	Poinsot/Contactless	Smiths	
DIMENSIONS				
Wheelbase	107·48 in/2730 mm	107·48 in/2730 mm	100 in/2540 mm	
Track	68·5 in/1740 mm front / 64·2 in/1630 mm rear	68·5 in/1740 mm front / 64·2 in/1630 mm rear	69 in/1753 mm front / 64 in/1626 mm rear	
Gearbox weight	110 lb/50 kg	110 lb/50 kg	110 lb/50 kg	
Chassis weight (tub)	92·59 lb/42 kg	81·57 lb/37 kg	78 lb/35 kg	
Formula weight	1278 lb/580 kg	1197 lb/543 kg	1301 lb/590 kg	
Fuel capacity	52·8 gall/240 litres	—	27·5 gall/125 litres	
Fuel consumption	—	—	—	

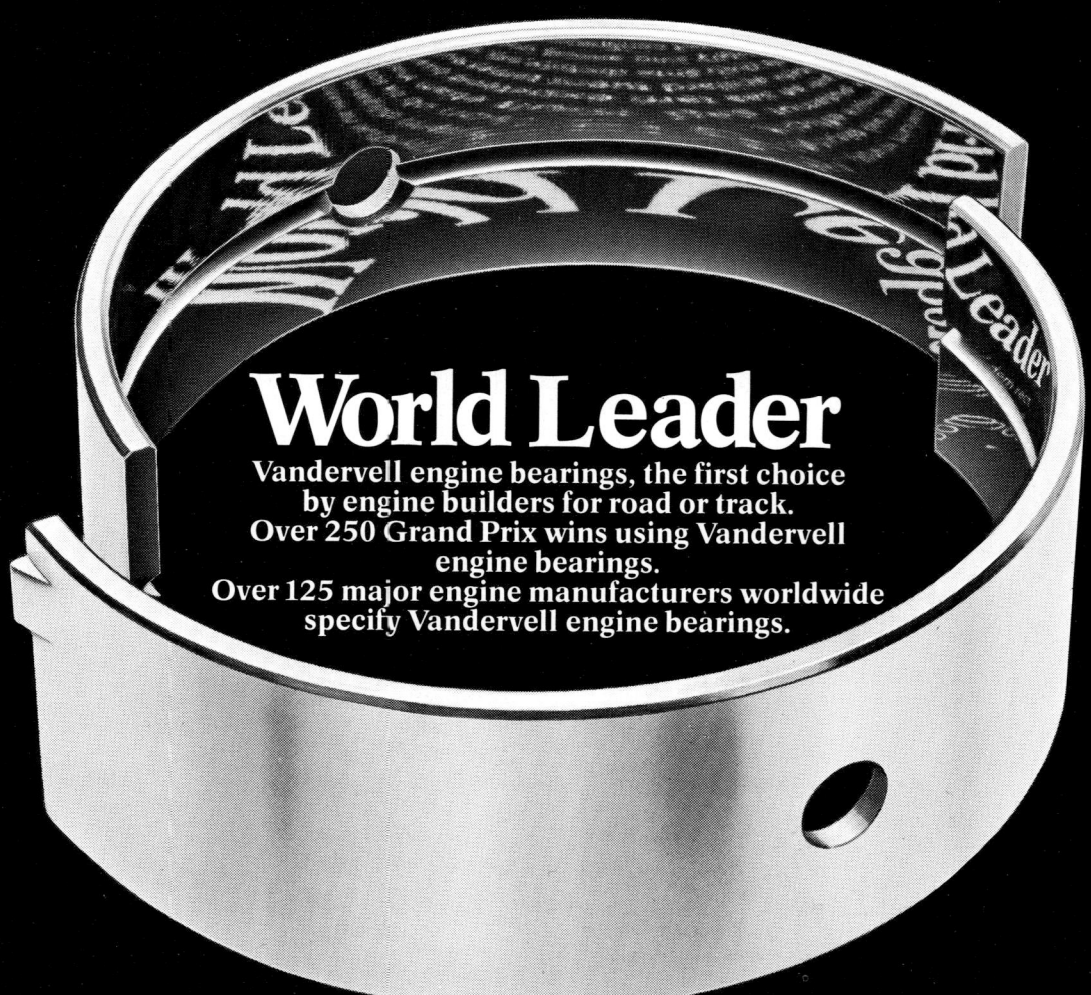
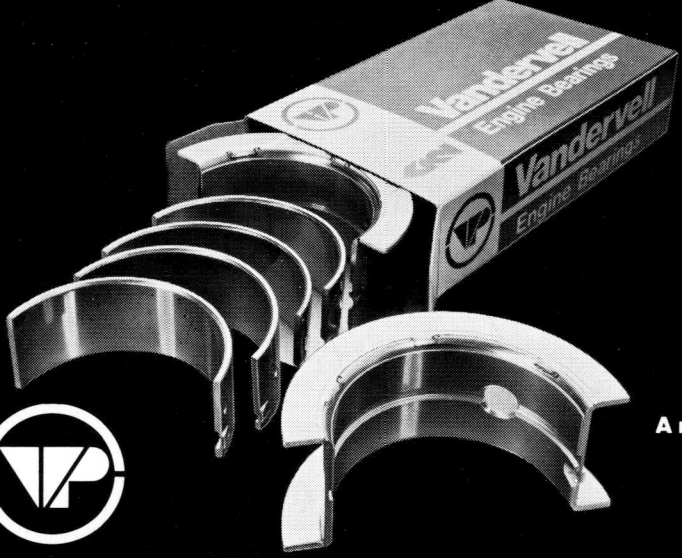
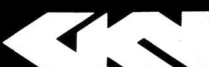

Formula 1 car specifications

	Spirit 201C-Honda	Theodore N183-Cosworth	Toleman TG183B-Hart	
Sponsor(s)	Honda/Marlboro	Cafe de Colombia/Segafreddo	Candy/Magirius	
Designer(s)	Gordon Coppuck/John Baldwin	Nigel Bennett	Rory Byrne/John Gentry	
Team Manager(s)	John Wickham	Jo Ramirez/Morris Nunn	Roger Silman	
Chief Mechanic(s)	–	T Gibbons	John Mardle	
No of chassis built	1	3	5	
ENGINE				
Type	Honda RA163-E	Ford-Cosworth DFV	Hart 415T	
Fuel and oil	Shell	-/Valvoline	BP	
Sparking plugs	NGK	Champion	Champion	
TRANSMISSION				
Gearbox/speeds	Hewland	Hewland	Toleman/Hewland (5)	
Drive-shafts	Spirit	Theodore	Toleman	
Clutch	Borg & Beck	Borg & Beck	Borg & Beck	
CHASSIS				
Front suspension	Top rocker arms, lower wishbones, inboard springs	Top rocker arms, lower wishbones, inboard springs	Upper and lower wishbones, tension link operated inboard springs	
Rear suspension	Top rocker arms, lower wishbones, inboard springs	Top rocker arms, lower wishbones, inboard springs	Upper and lower wishbones, tension link operated inboard springs	Spirit 201/C
Suspension dampers	Koni	Koni	Koni	
Wheel diameter	13 in/15 in front	13 in front	15 in front	
	13 in/15 in rear	13 in rear	13 in rear	
Wheel rim widths	11 in front	11 in front	11 in front	
	15 in/16 in rear	16 in rear	16·5 in rear	
Tyres	Goodyear	Goodyear	Pirelli	
Brakes	Lockheed	Lockheed	Lockheed	
Brake pads	Ferodo	Ferodo	Ferodo	Theodore N183
Steering	Spirit	Jack Knight	Toleman/Knight	
Radiator(s)	Serck	Porsche/Theodore	Behr	
Fuel tank	Marston and Premier	Premier	Marston	
Battery	YUASA	Cosworth	Saft	
Instruments	Smiths	Lucas	Smiths	
DIMENSIONS				
Wheelbase	104 in/2642 mm	106 in/2692 mm	106 in/2692 mm	
Track	69 in/1753 mm front	69 in/1753 mm front	72·75 in/1848 mm front	
	64 in/1626 mm rear	64 in/1640 mm rear	66·75 in/1695 mm rear	
Gearbox weight	110 lb/50 kg	–	110 lbs/50 kg	
Chassis weight (tub)	75 lb/34 kg	88 lb/40 kg	74 lbs/33·6 kg	
Formula weight	1279 lb/580 kg	1201 lb/545 kg	1190 lbs/540 kg	
Fuel capacity	28·6 gall/130 litres	39 gall/177 litres	50 gall/227·5 litres	
Fuel consumption	–	5-6 mpg/47-57 litres/100 km	3·8-4·2 mpg/55-61 litres/100 km	Toleman TG183B

	Tyrrell 011-Cosworth	Tyrrell 012-Cosworth	Williams FW08C-Cosworth	Williams FW09-Honda	
Sponsor(s)	Benetton	Benetton	TAG/Denim/ICI/Saudia Airlines/ Mobil	TAG/Denim/ICI/Saudia Airlines/Mobil	
Designer(s)	Maurice Phillippe/Brian Lisles	Maurice Phillippe/Brian Lisles	Patrick Head	Patrick Head	
Team Manager(s)	Ken Tyrrell	Ken Tyrrell	Frank Williams/Peter Collins	Frank Williams/Peter Collins	
Chief Mechanic(s)	Roger Hill	Roger Hill	Alan Challis	Alan Challis	
No of chassis built	6	2	7	2	
ENGINE					
Type	Ford-Cosworth DFV & DFY	Ford-Cosworth DFY	Ford-Cosworth DFV	Honda RA163-E	
Fuel and oil	-/Valvoline	-/Valvoline	Mobil	Mobil	
Sparking plugs	Champion	Champion	Champion	Champion	
TRANSMISSION					
Gearbox/speeds	Tyrrell/Hewland (5)	Tyrrell/Hewland (5)	Williams/Hewland FGB (6)	Williams/Hewland (6)	
Drive-shafts	Tyrrell	Tyrrell	Williams/Löbro	Williams/Löbro	
Clutch	Borg & Beck	Borg & Beck	Borg & Beck	Borg & Beck	
CHASSIS					Tyrrell 012
Front suspension	Pull rod, upper and lower wishbones	Pull rod, upper and lower wishbones	Upper and lower wishbones, pull rods, inboard spring/dampers	Upper & lower wishbones, pull rods, inboard spring/dampers	
Rear suspension	Rocker arm, lower wishbones,	Pull rod, upper and lower wishbones,	Top rocker arms, lower wishbones, inboard spring/dampers	Top rocker arms, lower wishbones, inboard spring/dampers	
Suspension dampers	Koni	Koni	Koni	Koni	
Wheel diameter	13 in/15 in front	13 in/15 in front	13 in/15 in front	13 in/15 in front	
	13 in/15 in rear	13 in/15 in rear	13 in/15 in rear	13 in/15 in rear	
Wheel rim widths	11 in front	11 in front	11 in front	11 in front	
	16 in rear	16 in rear	15 in/16 in rear	16 in rear	
Tyres	Goodyear	Goodyear	Goodyear	Goodyear	
Brakes	Lockheed	Lockheed	Lockheed	Lockheed	
Brake pads	Ferodo	Ferodo	Ferodo	Ferodo	Williams FW08C
Steering	Tyrrell/Knight	Tyrrell	Williams/Knight	Williams/Knight	
Radiator(s)	Serck/Setrab	Serck/Setrab	Williams/Behr	Williams/Behr	
Fuel tank	ATL	ATL	ATL	ATL	
Battery	Radio Spares	Radio Spares	Panasonic	Panasonic	
Instruments	Smiths/Contactless	Smiths/Contactless	Contactless/VDO	Nippon Denso/VDO	
DIMENSIONS					
Wheelbase	107 in/2720 mm	104 in/2642 mm	102 in/2591 mm	105 in/2667 mm	
Track	68 in-71 in/1727 mm- 1803 mm front	65 in-68 in/1651 mm- 1727 mm front	71 in/1803 mm front	71 in/1803 mm front	
	61 in-65 in/1549 mm- 1651 mm rear	58 in-62 in/1473 mm- 1575 mm rear	63 in/1600 mm rear	64 in/1626 mm rear	
Gearbox weight	112 lb/51 kg	112 lb/51 kg	110 lb/50 kg	110 lb/50 kg	
Chassis weight (tub)	80 lb/36 kg	75 lb/34 kg	90 lb/41 kg	80 lb/36 kg	Williams FW09
Formula weight	1191 lb/540 kg	1191 lb/540 kg	1190 lb/540 kg	1190 lb/540 kg	
Fuel capacity	39 gall/177 litres	39 gall/177 litres	40 gall/182 litres	48 gall/220 litres	
Fuel consumption	5-6 mpg/47-57 litres/100 km	5-6 mpg/47-57 litres/100 km	5-6 mpg/47-57 litres/100 km	4·4·5 mpg/52-58 litres/100 km	

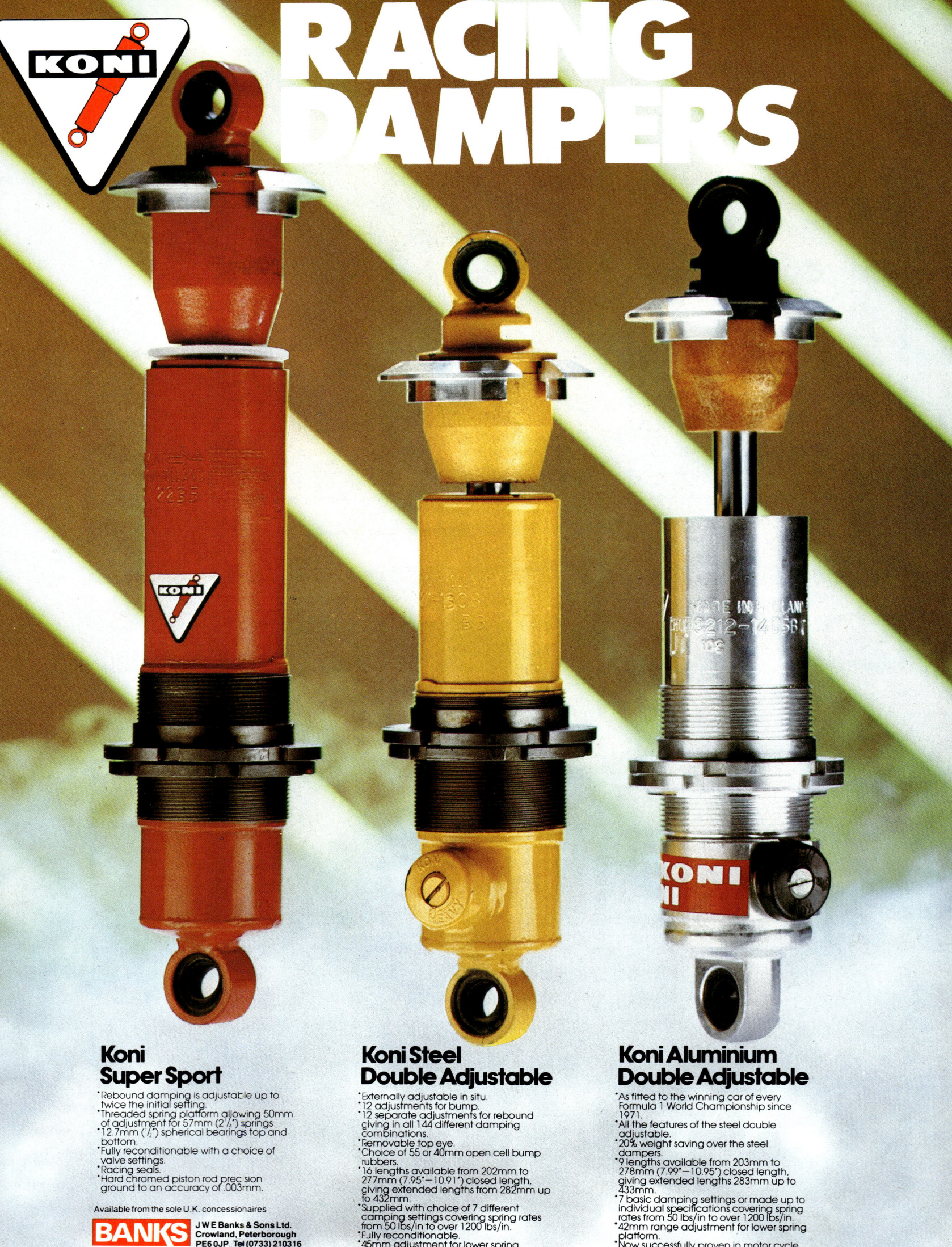

RACING DAMPERS

Koni Super Sport

- Rebound damping is adjustable up to twice the initial setting.
- Threaded spring platform allowing 50mm of adjustment for 57mm (2¼") springs
- 12.7mm (½") spherical bearings top and bottom.
- Fully reconditionable with a choice of valve settings.
- Racing seals.
- Hard chromed piston rod precision ground to an accuracy of .003mm.

Available from the sole U.K. concessionaires

BANKS J W E Banks & Sons Ltd.
Crowland, Peterborough
PE6 0JP Tel (0733) 210316
Telex 32533

Koni Steel Double Adjustable

- Externally adjustable in situ.
- 12 adjustments for bump.
- 12 separate adjustments for rebound giving in all 144 different damping combinations.
- Removable top eye.
- Choice of 55 or 40mm open cell bump rubbers.
- 16 lengths available from 202mm to 277mm (7.95"–10.91") closed length, giving extended lengths from 282mm up to 432mm.
- Supplied with choice of 7 different damping settings covering spring rates from 50 lbs/in to over 1200 lbs/in.
- Fully reconditionable.
- 45mm adjustment for lower spring platform.

Koni Aluminium Double Adjustable

- As fitted to the winning car of every Formula 1 World Championship since 1971.
- All the features of the steel double adjustable.
- 20% weight saving over the steel dampers.
- 9 lengths available from 203mm to 278mm (7.99"–10.95") closed length, giving extended lengths 283mm up to 433mm.
- 7 basic damping settings or made up to individual specifications covering spring rates from 50 lbs/in to over 1200 lbs/in.
- 42mm range adjustment for lower spring platform.
- Now successfully proven in motor cycle racing.

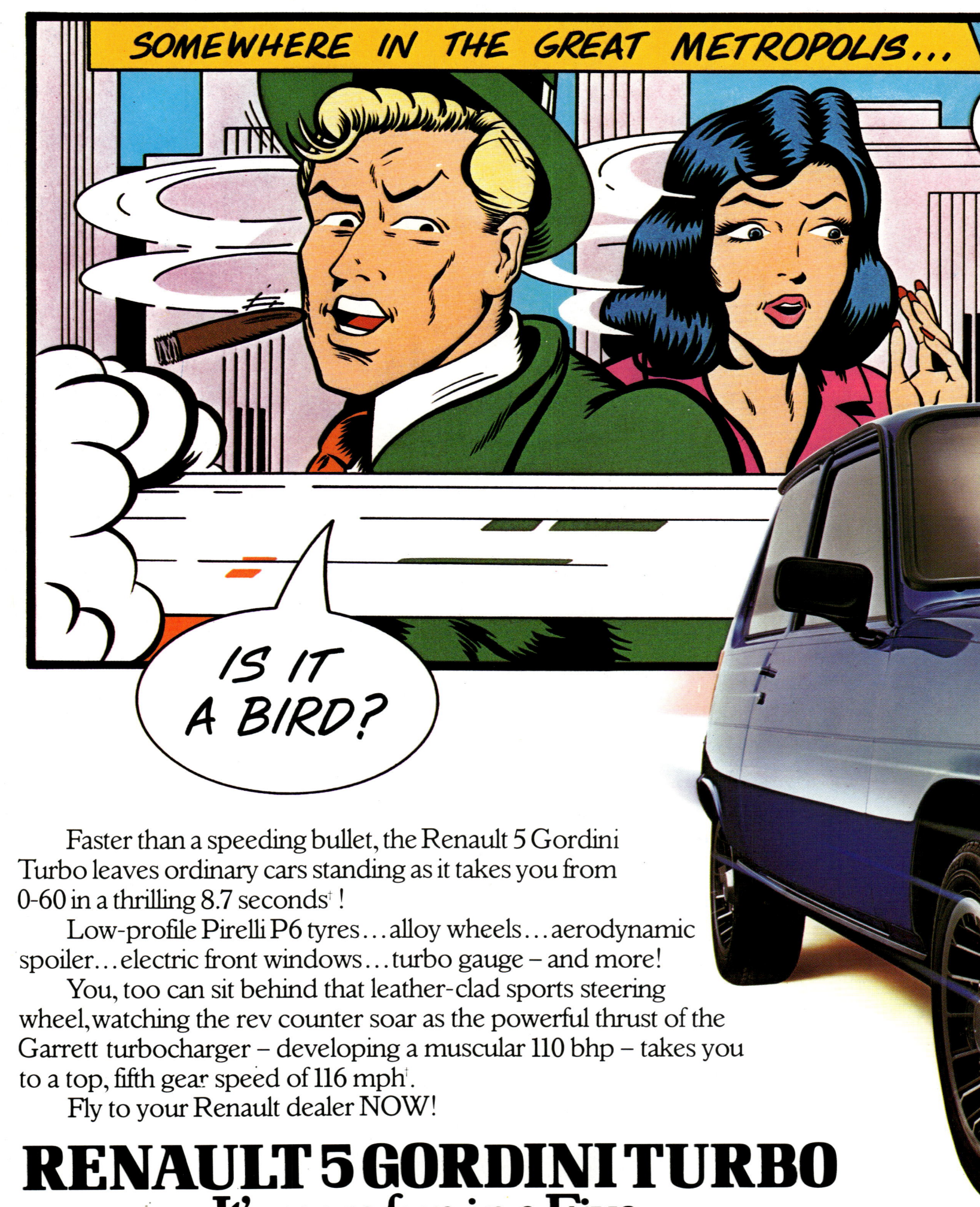

Faster than a speeding bullet, the Renault 5 Gordini Turbo leaves ordinary cars standing as it takes you from 0-60 in a thrilling 8.7 seconds† !

Low-profile Pirelli P6 tyres…alloy wheels…aerodynamic spoiler…electric front windows…turbo gauge – and more!

You, too can sit behind that leather-clad sports steering wheel, watching the rev counter soar as the powerful thrust of the Garrett turbocharger – developing a muscular 110 bhp – takes you to a top, fifth gear speed of 116 mph† .

Fly to your Renault dealer NOW!

RENAULT 5 GORDINI TURBO
It's more fun in a Five.

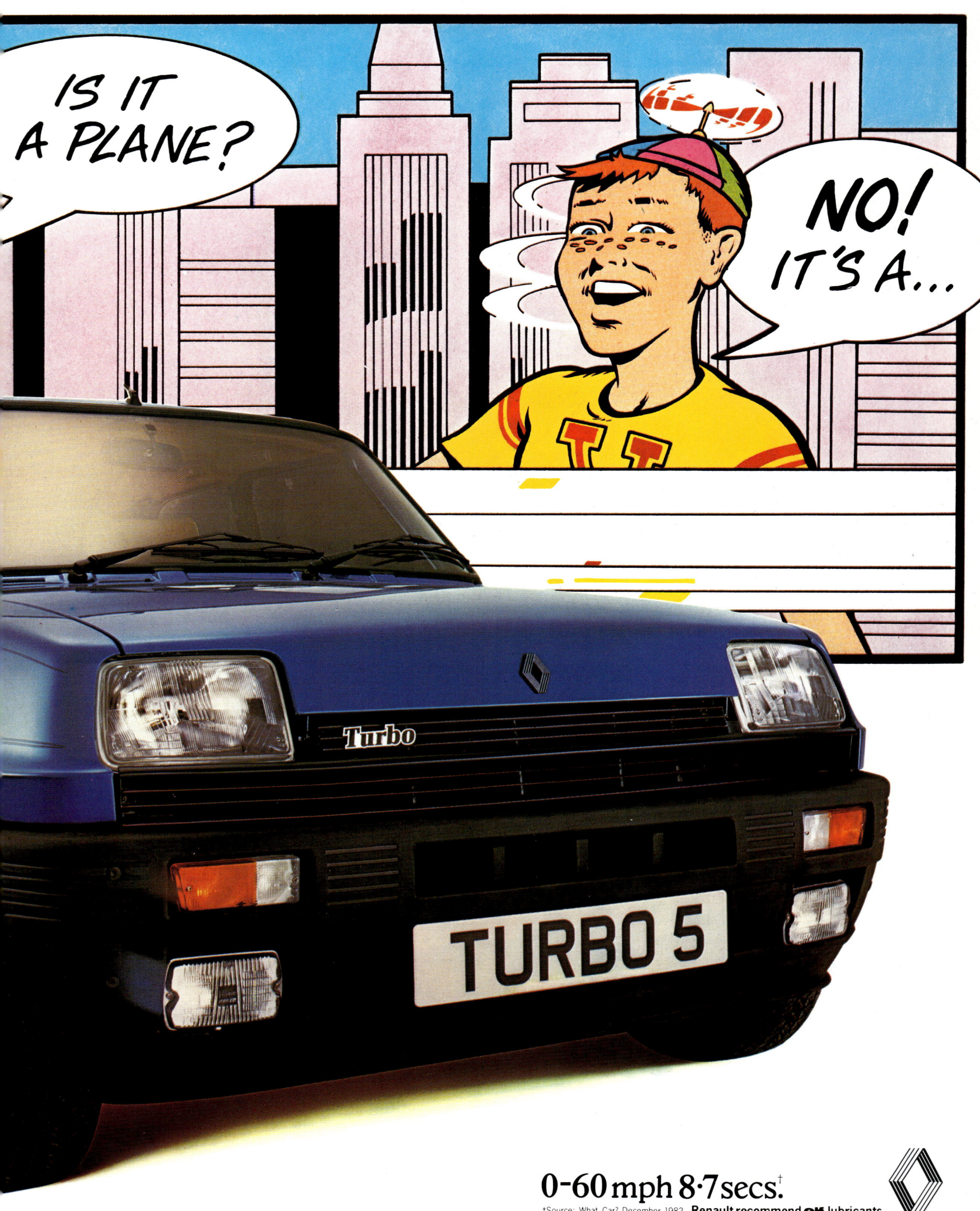

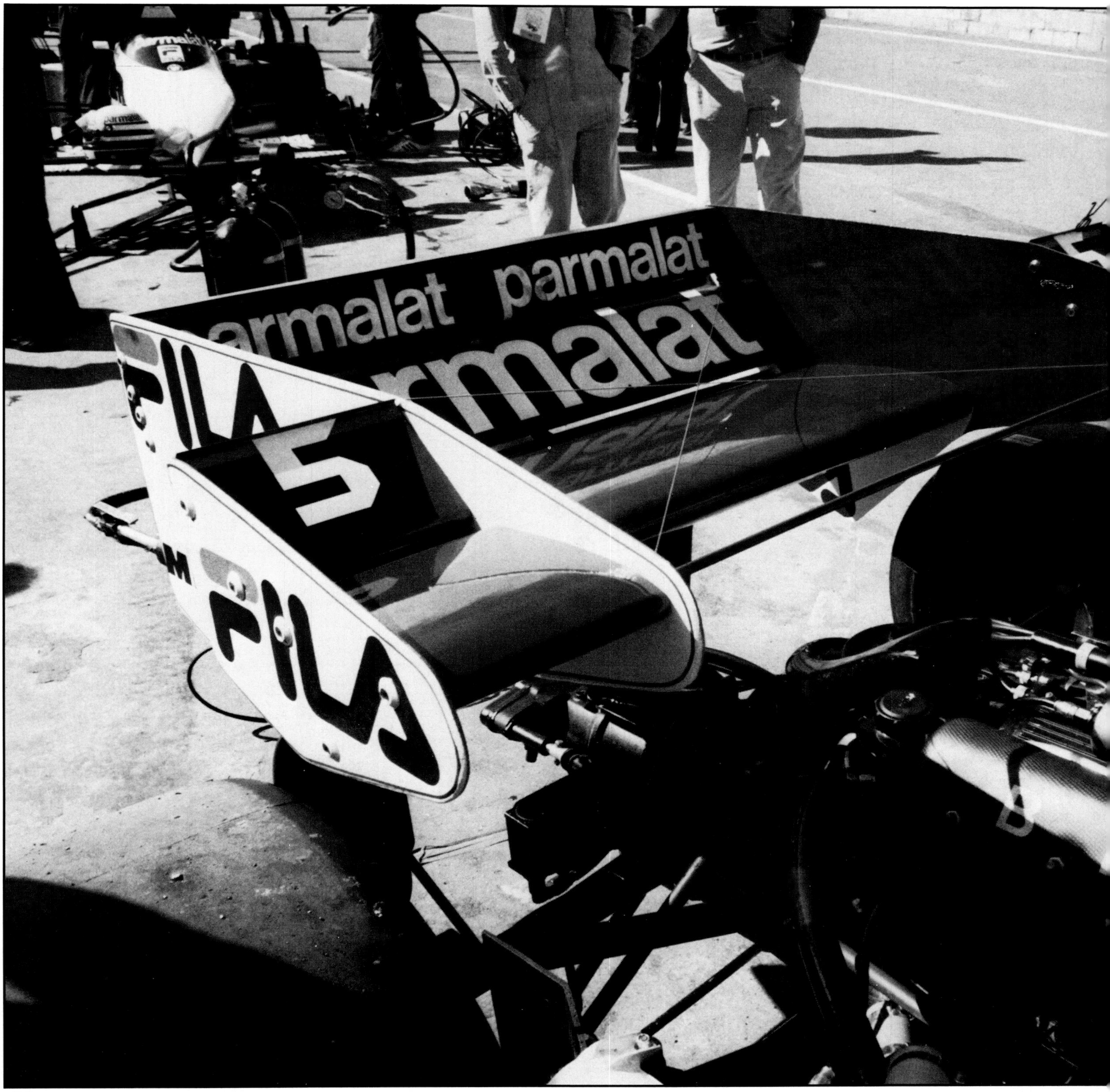

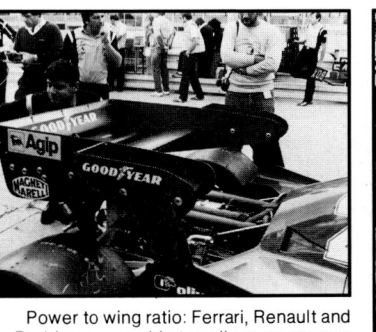
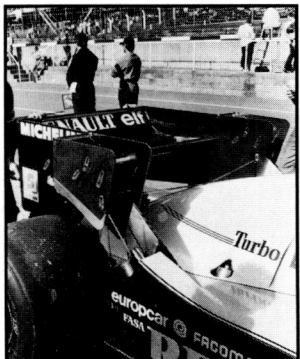

Power to wing ratio: Ferrari, Renault and Brabham were able to pull enormous rear wings, gaining vital down-force without a significant increase in drag.

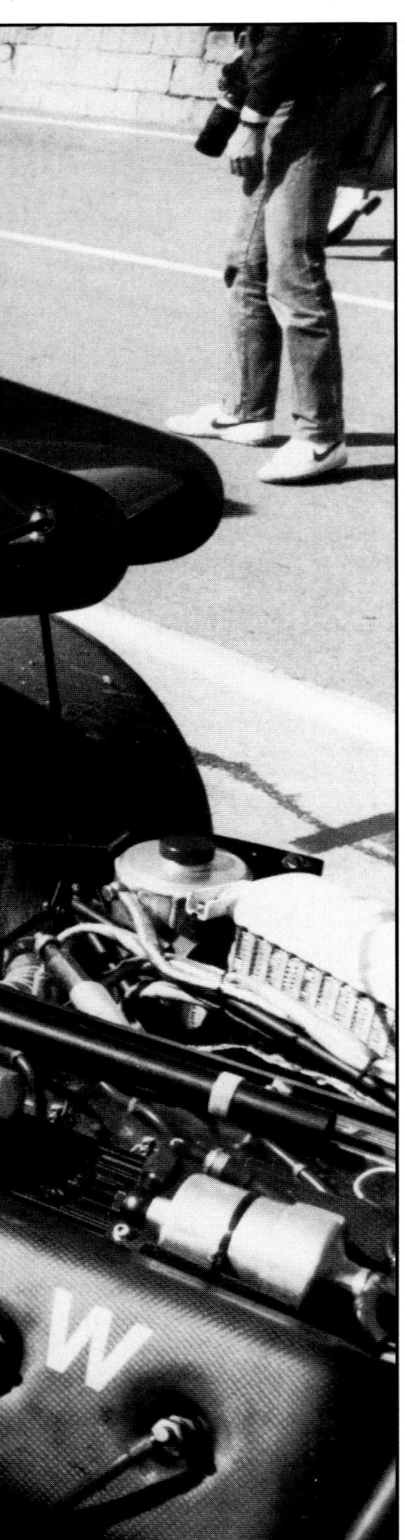

November 3, 1982, was when it all happened. The FISA Formula 1 Commission met in Paris and agreed radical rule changes to take effect from the very next race – the opening round of the 1983 World Championship.

Any supposedly sacrosanct 'stability' agreements designed to prevent short-notice rule changes were torn-up in the name of safety. Constructors had previously proposed stepped changes; new wing and weight limit measures for 1983, and more sweeping restrictions for '84. They would include a final ban on aerodynamic skirts and a flat-bottom rule to kill ground-effects under-wing forms.

Cornering speeds had soared and featured in several of 1982's nastier incidents. Circuit owners were frightened rigid, and the Circuit and Safety Commission reported some circuit licences would have to be withheld for '83 if cornering speeds were not cut.

Against this background FISA's drastic action is justified. Imagine what an American lawyer – on a share of the damages won – might make of a liability claim if a car had gone into the crowd at Long Beach or Detroit, ". . . because identified modifications to improve safety had been postponed one year . . .". It's enough to make strong men tremble. One can only feel for those exposed in Formula 1 government. And that's a novel sensation . . .

Consequently the flat-bottom regs took instant effect. In practice they sealed the eclipse of the atmospherically-aspirated 3-litre F1 engine as we know it, and assured virtual supremacy to the new-wave of 1500cc turbocharged units. Now it was a question of which teams had the spare power to pull large high-drag wing forms through the air. Once the second half of the season began, with its string of high-speed 'power circuits' grouped together, it was no contest between the 3-litre unblown cars with 500 plus bhp, and the 1500 turbos with well over 600.

So 1983 became an extraordinary water-shed season of Grand Prix racing in which the turbos at last stamped on the years of normally-aspirated engine domination by Cosworth-Ford's lustrous V8 and the glorious Ferrari flat-12. The slender-bodied cigar-shaped racing car made its return, and pit-stops became an integral – pivotal – part of the action for the first time since the 'fifties. For some teams tyres became an even more significant factor in success or failure. Water-injection played its part in assuring turbo dominance, and in nuts and bolts terms the racing was fascinating as 'proper' motor manufacturers became locked together once more in head-on combat. Some said they put the 'Grand' back in GP racing. In terms of burgeoning technical interest that has to be true.

Six teams won GPs during the season. Here's how they shaped-up . . .

FERRARI

The Italian team planned defence of their 1982 Constructors' Championship around a highly-developed 126C3 design intended to replace the successful – but fated – 'C2. Mauro Forghieri's engine group developed with AGIP their water-injection system in search of more power. This proved a contentious issue. Compressing a gas – as in a turbocharger system – heats it up. Hot gas is less dense than cold, so it is normal for racing engineers to use an intercooler (gas/air or water radiator) to lower the temperature of their compressed charge on its way from turbo to engine. With water injection, evaporation of the water within the incoming charge cools it still further. Density increases, charge capacity is enhanced. The more you can put in, the more power you get out. By slashing the temperature build-up inevitable with boost compression, water injection permits higher boost to be sustained. Really substantial power gains result.

Ferrari and Renault would run the system, but BMW doubted its legality, mindful of the F1 regulation banning fuel additives and regarding water as just that. Ferrari and Renault counter-claimed it was not used as an 'additive', merely as a 'coolant'. It was a question of 'primary function', and Formula 1 has trodden that route before – with the fascinating Brabham fan car of 1978. Perhaps significantly, 'primary function' is a phrase excised from current regs. Major manufacturers have some clout after all.

Apart from such controversy, Ferrari had built-up an interim test-hack 'C3 using a hacked-around 'C2 aluminium-honeycomb (not a prototype carbon-composite) tub before the rule-changes were confirmed. It used the longitudinal ground-effects-orientated transaxle developed in '82. In Fiorano tests it proved "an absolute *Bomba!*" according to Ferrari's English chassis designer Dr Harvey Postlethwaite. After the rule change the car was dismantled, parts strewn through the stores.

The medium-term strategic decision was taken to modify the existing honeycomb 'C2s to flat-bottom spec, while the 126C3 was totally rethought and redrawn around an all-new carbon-composite moulded monocoque. The first half of '83 saw Ferrari racing modified 'C2s while Harvey's latest 'C3 was developed.

Through 1982 Ferrari had adopted new technology to produce the honeycomb 'C2s. At Christmas they moved into their purpose-built new HQ, partly on the old works car-park across the road from the main Maranello factory. There they installed all the autoclaves, ovens and other specialised kit demanded by carbon-composite manufacture, and began learning how to use it.

Early in the season Arnoux suffered unreliability, later it was Tambay, and Ferrari could not match their awesome reliability of '82. Cock-ups included an ignition wire dropping off to rob Arnoux of nine points in Detroit, where Tambay non-started due to vapour-locks in his engine's water injection. His two later engine failures wrecked his cause. After running strongly elsewhere, apparent finger trouble at Brands Hatch saw a dismal drop in fortunes.

Even so, the interim 'C2 slaughtered the field in Montreal and Ferrari's immediate problem with the new carbon-composite 'C3 was to make it adequately better – i.e., capable of victory by a clear lap.

The 126C3 – known in the Ferrari drawing office's thick ledger as the *Tipo* 632 – became a front-row car almost everywhere, as of right. It proved at least as good as any in the team dared hope. An initial aerodynamic problem caused poor cooling, especially of the oil, but it was soon corrected.

By Monza-time four 'C3s were running, chassis '066' to '069'. Unlike 1982 not one was lost through accidents. The old *trasversale* gearbox was preferred with the passing of ground-effects demands. It also helped give the required length for optimum wing

continued on page 48

Power to Wing Ratio

by Doug Nye

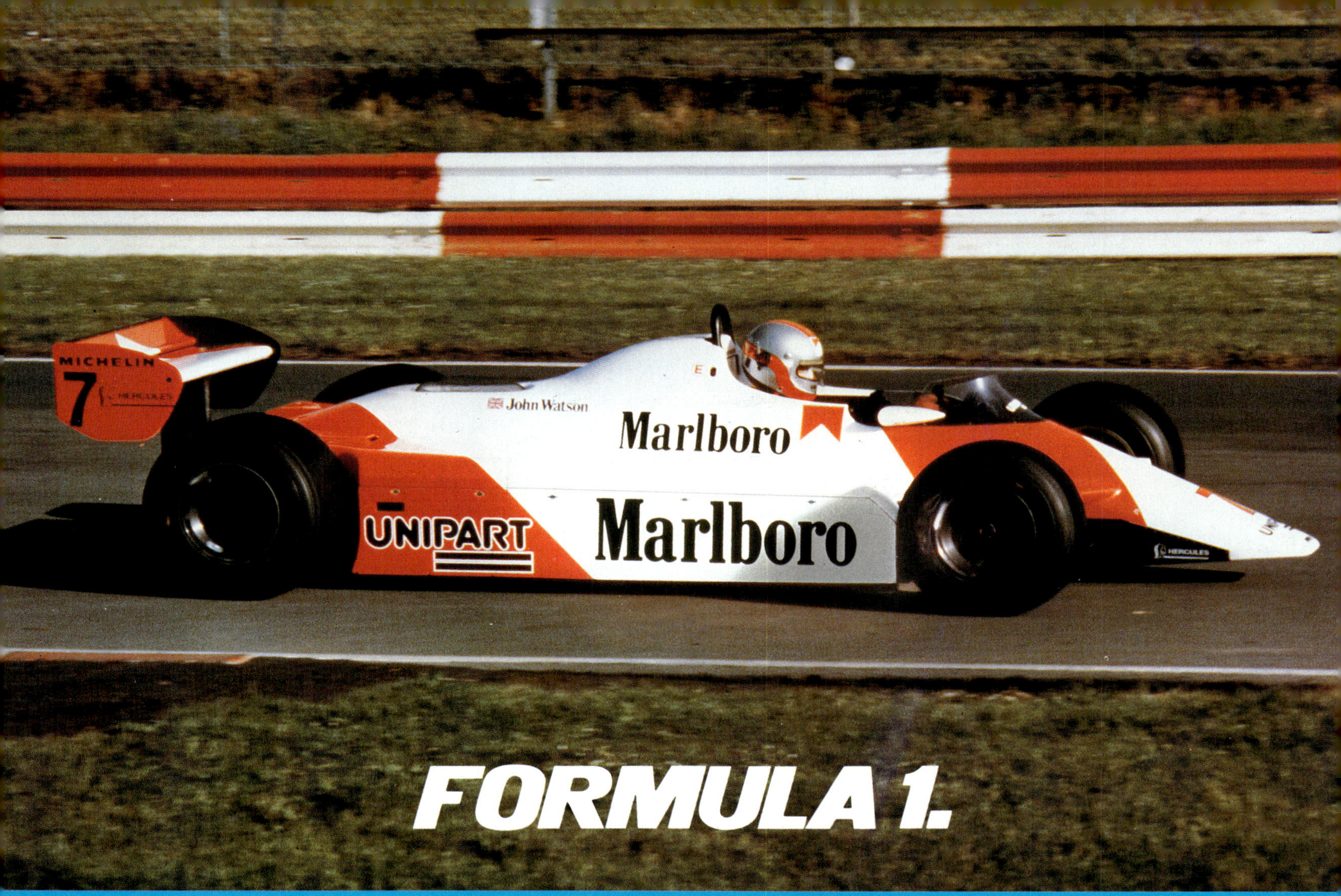
MICHELIN
7
John Watson
Marlboro
UNIPART
Marlboro
FORMULA 1.

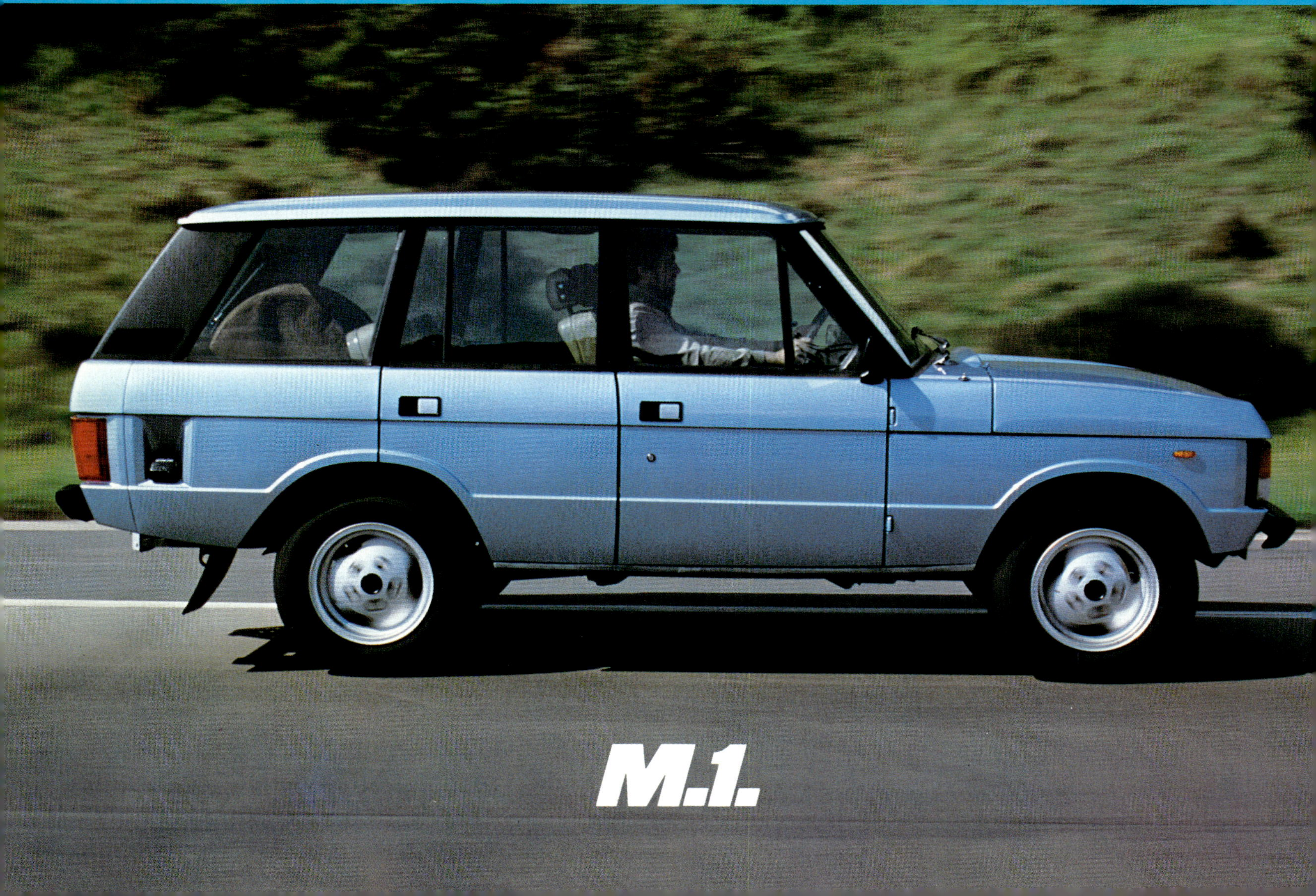
M.1.

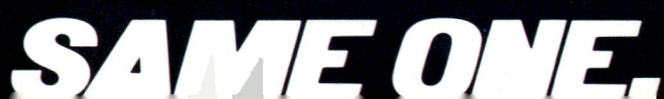
SAME ONE.

overhang requirements. Sadly reliability took an uncharacteristic dump at Österreichring, where sheared teeth on fourth gear cost Arnoux victory.

The original '3s ran 'C2 rear suspension until Monza, where geometry changes appeared. The aim was to cure inside-edge tyre consumption, and vibration. Goodyear had an often difficult year, troubling most notably Ferrari and Williams. The Ferraris went better the slower the circuit and cooler the conditions, losing that edge on faster, hotter courses. Until Zandvoort they felt they had the strongest engine, but "then BMW made a significant step forward . . .". Notwithstanding, Ferrari's two cars scored sufficient points to defend their cherished Constructors' Championship successfully.

RENAULT

One Renault Sport team member mused ruefully "If the 1982 races 'ad been five laps less we would 'ave been World Champion". The team's killer that season was the pump motor in their digitally-controlled fuel injection. It had to survive down in the heat and vibration of the engine vee, and didn't. They tried alternatives, unsuccessfully, until finally issuing a custom specification to a specialist sub-contractor who tailor-made just what they wanted. It was used in the last race of '82 and ran reliably through this past season.

Renault had twin goals for '83 – adequate reliability, and more power. They achieved both, in some degree. Bernard Dudot's technical team set about new weaponry. Michel Tetu pencilled his RE40 carbon-composite chassis, but Renault decided an interim flat-bottom RE30C would do for the opening races; time had been short and everybody would be starting this flat-bottom era equal. Brabham proved the fallacy of that thought. The RE40 programme was accelerated.

Engine man Jean-Pierre Boudy wrung more power from their ageing iron-block 90-degree V6. Most turbo teams use what turbocharger parts the German KKK company are happy to supply, which means proprietary production parts available off the shelf. They won't custom-build F1 specials – unless you are TAG Turbo-Porsche. At Zandvoort, Jean Sage of Renault and Forghieri of Ferrari stared aghast at the new German V6's tailor-made 'Kapa-Kapa-Kapa' turbos. A portent perhaps?

Boudy adopted bigger turbo casings and wheels for his 1983 V6, and developed his own water-injection pack to use their extra boost. Back in the '60s McLaren used their works Minivan to prove strutted wings. In the winter of 1982-'83 Boudy of Renault developed water-injection on his company Renault 18 . . .

Three interim RE30Cs ran at Rio and proved inadequate. The prototype RE40 appeared at Long Beach. The logistics of running two different types of car caused Sage deep grief, while electrical problems wrecked the new car's debut. It was new, it was carbon-composite; "we just couldn't find a good earth . . ."

Renault did brilliantly to claw back their lost time and momentum. They got a grip until Zandvoort and by the penultimate race Prost was all but assured of the World Championship. Six RE40s had been built, the prototype retired to static test and mock-up duties.

Prost's engine suffered significantly at Imola, Montreal and Monza. The team had problems with inconsistent performance quality after engine rebuilds. The 700rpm rev loss from the normal 11,000 to only 10,300 at Imola was never explained, the strip-down report confessing everything seemed OK. At Monza there was no mystery. "The temperature gauge regulating turbo heat build-up was faulty when fitted". The turbos overheated and the wheels were damaged, losing boost.

They ran three regular wing forms, adding a fourth "barn-door, like Ferrari's", at Brands Hatch.

If Renault had been able to complete the RE40s and test them as rapidly as Brabham did with their BT52s, the first flat-bottomed World Championship for seven years might have been settled sooner. It was ironic that the team should again miss out on the Constructors' title where both team cars score points – for Cheever's run of misfortune cost the largest motor manufacturer in Formula 1 dear indeed . . .

BRABHAM

"We keep catching ourselves out", Gordon Murray reflected, "We convince ourselves that this is the obvious way to go, this is what everybody will be doing so we go flat out to match them. And when we get to the first race everybody else has settled for the easy option, and we're out there on our own, and already worn out by the effort . . ."

By November 3, 1982 and the flat-bottom regulations' confirmation, Motor Racing Developments Ltd could already look back on a half-season's experience of pit-stop strategy. Their BT50-BMWs used conservative aluminium monocoques basically to the same design which had done duty with Alfa Romeo V12 and Cosworth DFV and V8s in so many previous years. It was time for a new beginning.

The BT50C had been a 'pit-stop' BT50, and Gordon Murray and his right-hand man David North had completed the design of a developed BT51 ground-effects car for '83 with an all-new tub, the proven BT50 rear end, small pit-stop fuel tank and relying upon a stop to survive the longer, thirstier races. The project included an all-new transmission to accommodate the turbo BMW 4-cylinder's immense torque and power.

Come November 3 and an all-new approach was dictated. It was a completely different game, and rather than compromise with a fudged-up flat-bottom conversion kit, the Chessington design team went for broke and started again from scratch. The MRD build crew are arguably the world's best in this situation, and they rose to the challenge, for the umpteenth time . . .

The result was what Gordon describes as "probably our most consistent season since '74-'75. We haven't been uncompetitive anywhere, unless in the race we've run too little power or chosen the wrong tyres. One satisfying thing was that after laughing at us in '82 when our cars often didn't last as far as the scheduled pit-stop, everybody scrambled to follow us into the pit-stop routine this year. It's been fun developing the new car, too, but the low points have been the stupid disappointments, like losing the lead with a puncture near the end, or a fuel fire near the end, or the driver falling off the road within sight of the finish . . ."

Early on, the gearbox proved a major weakness. US transmission engineer Pete Weismann assisted in beefing it up until it became a survivor. In Rio the rear radiator concentration on the BT52s cooked their rear dampers. Rearranged ducting fixed that. The team's

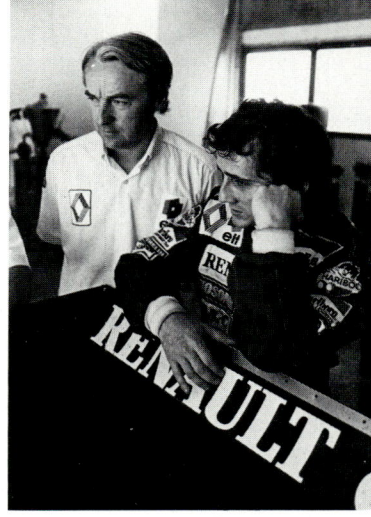

Gerard Larrousse and Alain Prost – problems with inconsistent engine performances after rebuilds.
Gordon Murray: ". . . we kept catching ourselves out . . ." The Brabham team had their most consistent season since 1974/75 (below).
Photo: Bernard Asset

continued on page 52

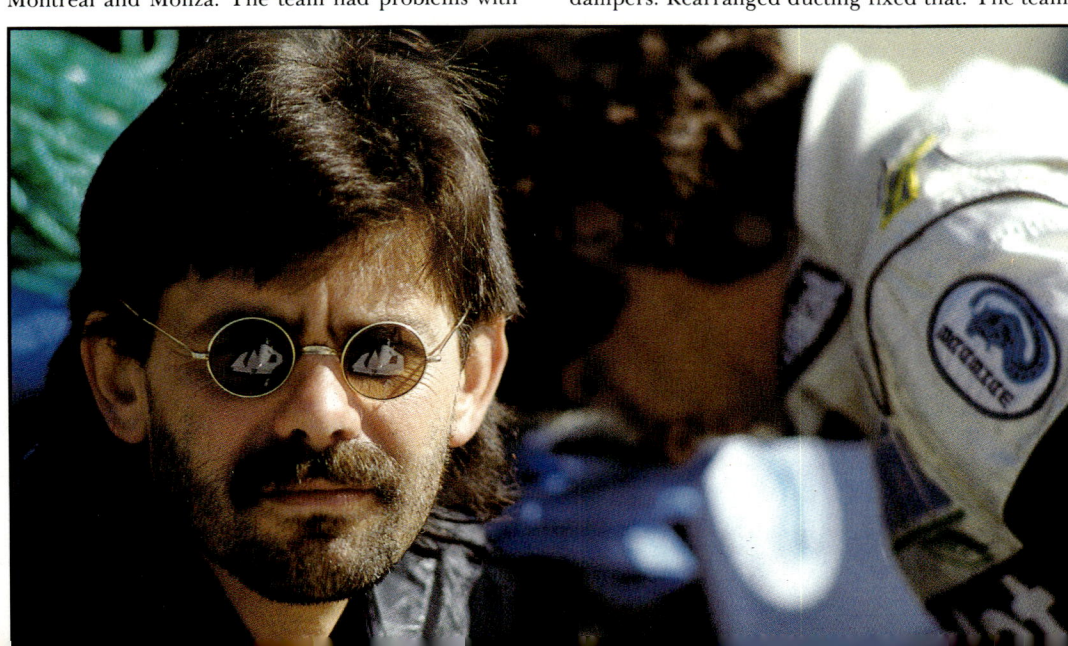

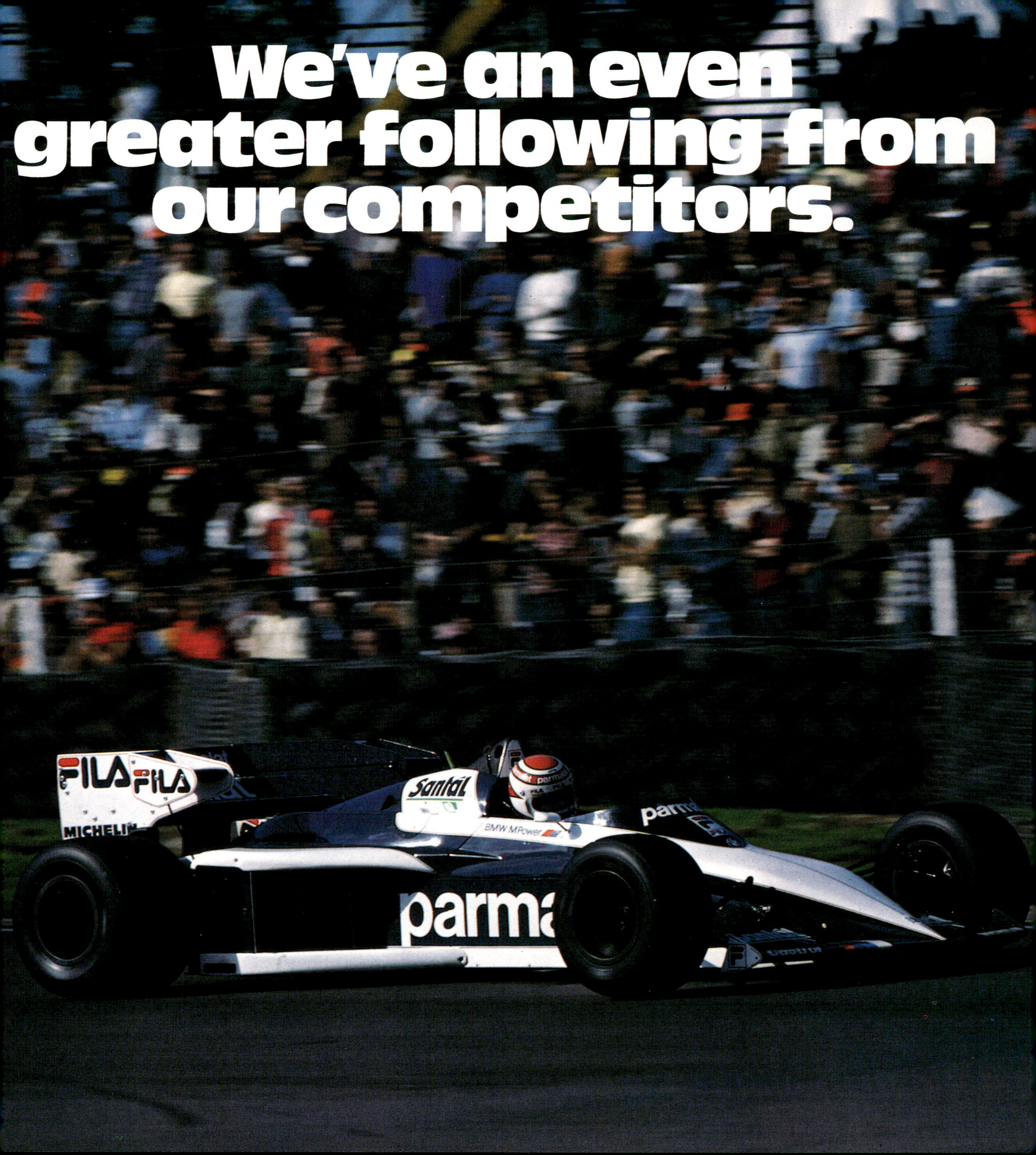

We've an even greater following from our competitors.

When Nelson Piquet raced to a great finish in the South African Grand Prix, he not only clinched the Formula 1 World Championship. He also demonstrated yet again Michelin's world-beating performance.

Jonathan Palmer enjoyed the same kind of success; taking the Formula 2 European Championship in his Michelin-shod Ralt-Honda.

And the Formula 3 European Championships were dominated by Michelin drivers.

In fact, we've left our competitors little option but to follow in our tracks, in every area of motorsport.

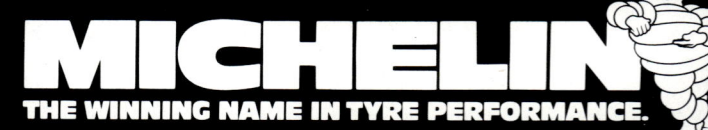

MICHELIN
THE WINNING NAME IN TYRE PERFORMANCE.

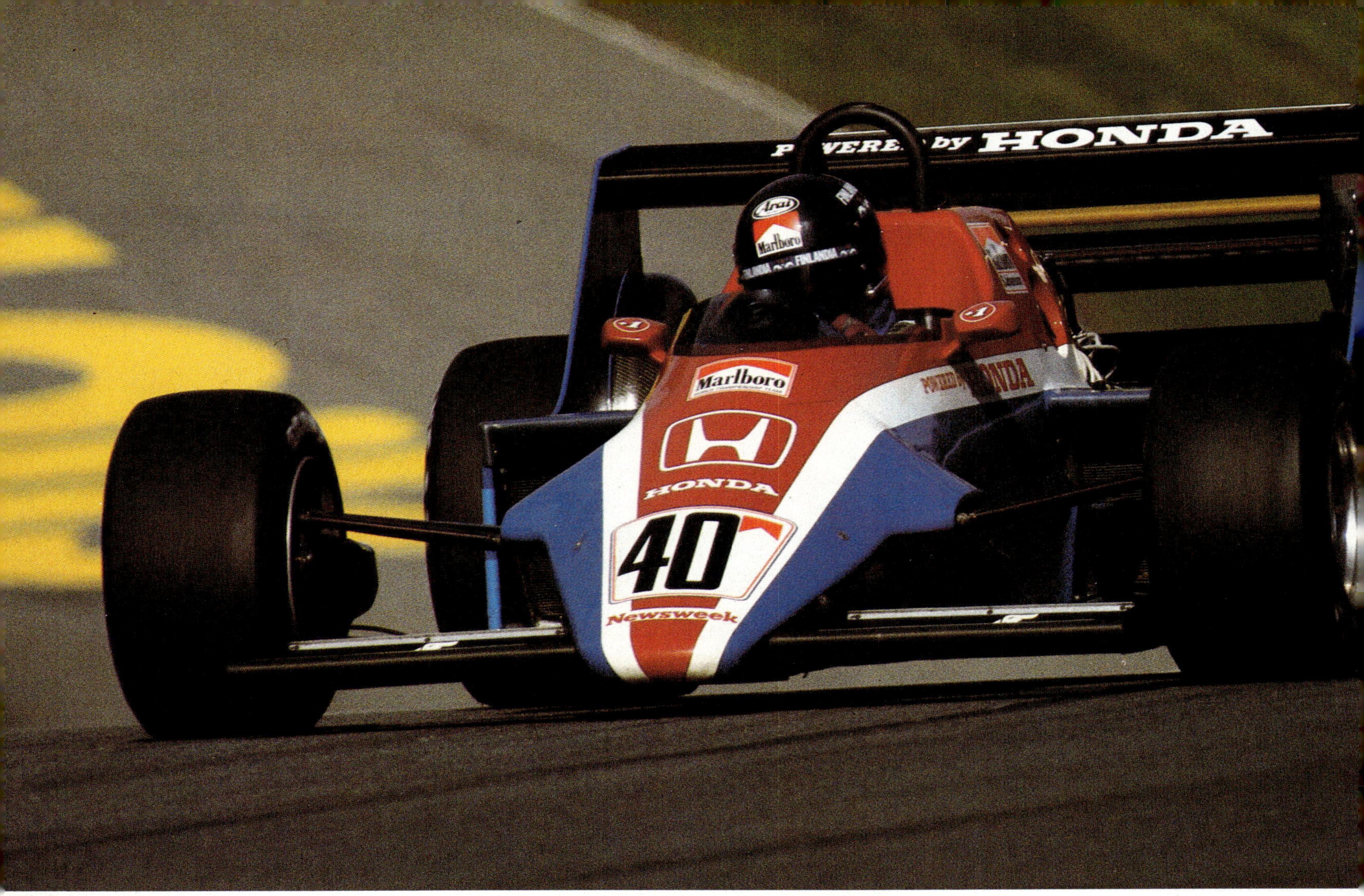
HONDA
Marlboro
HONDA
40
Newsweek

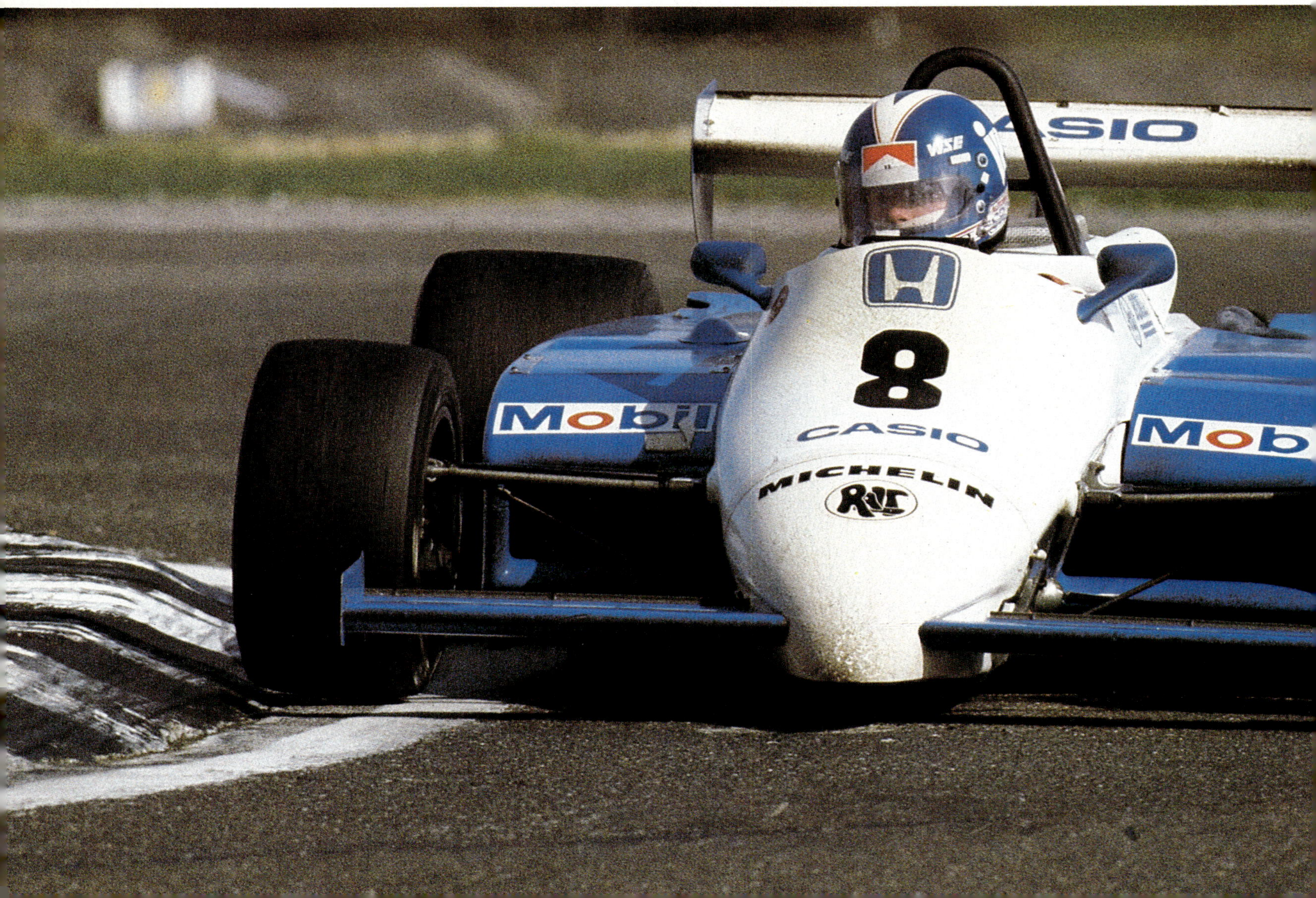
CASIO
Mobil
8
CASIO
MICHELIN
Mob

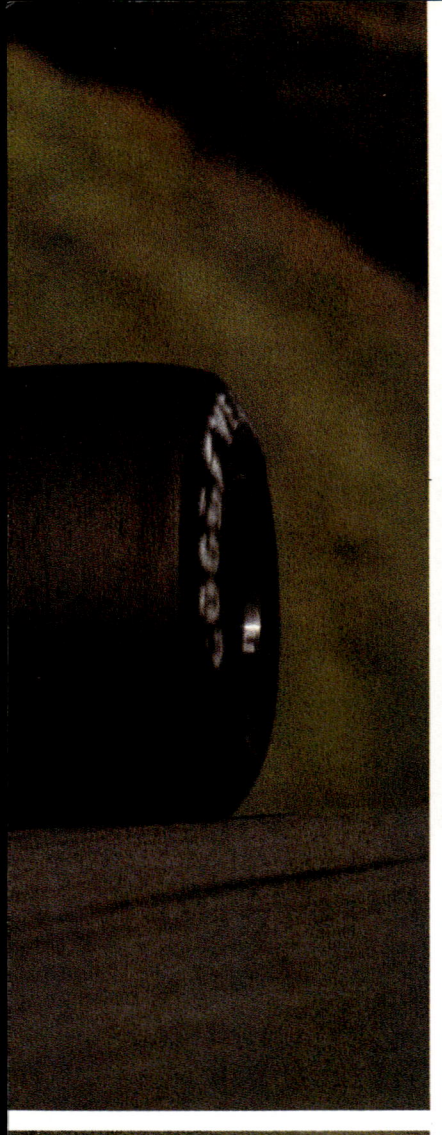
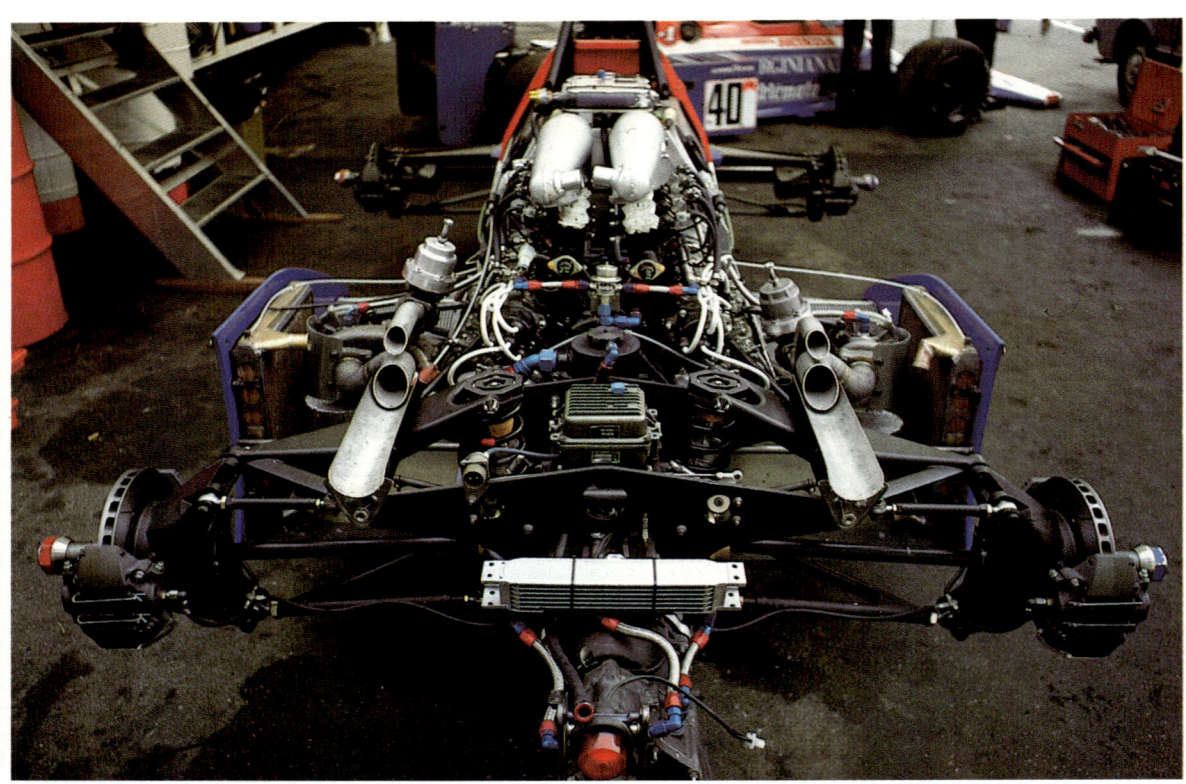

POWERED by

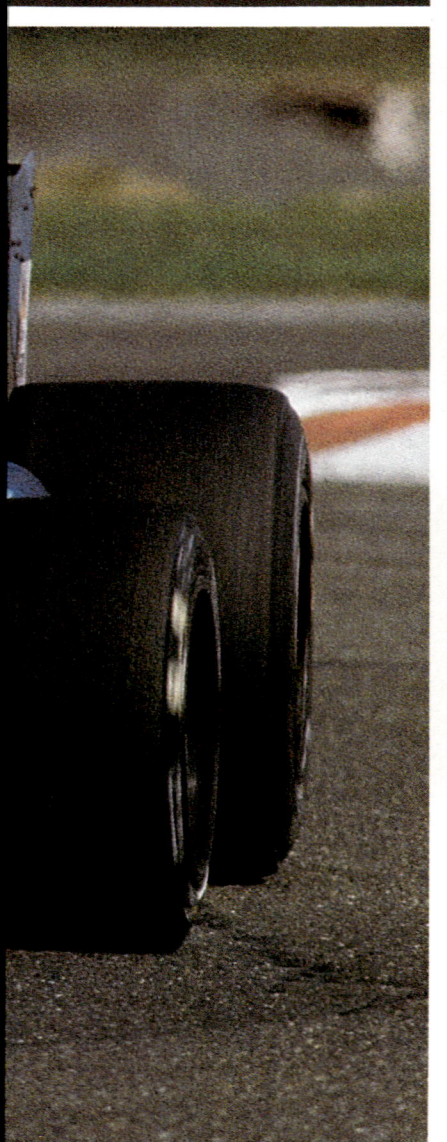
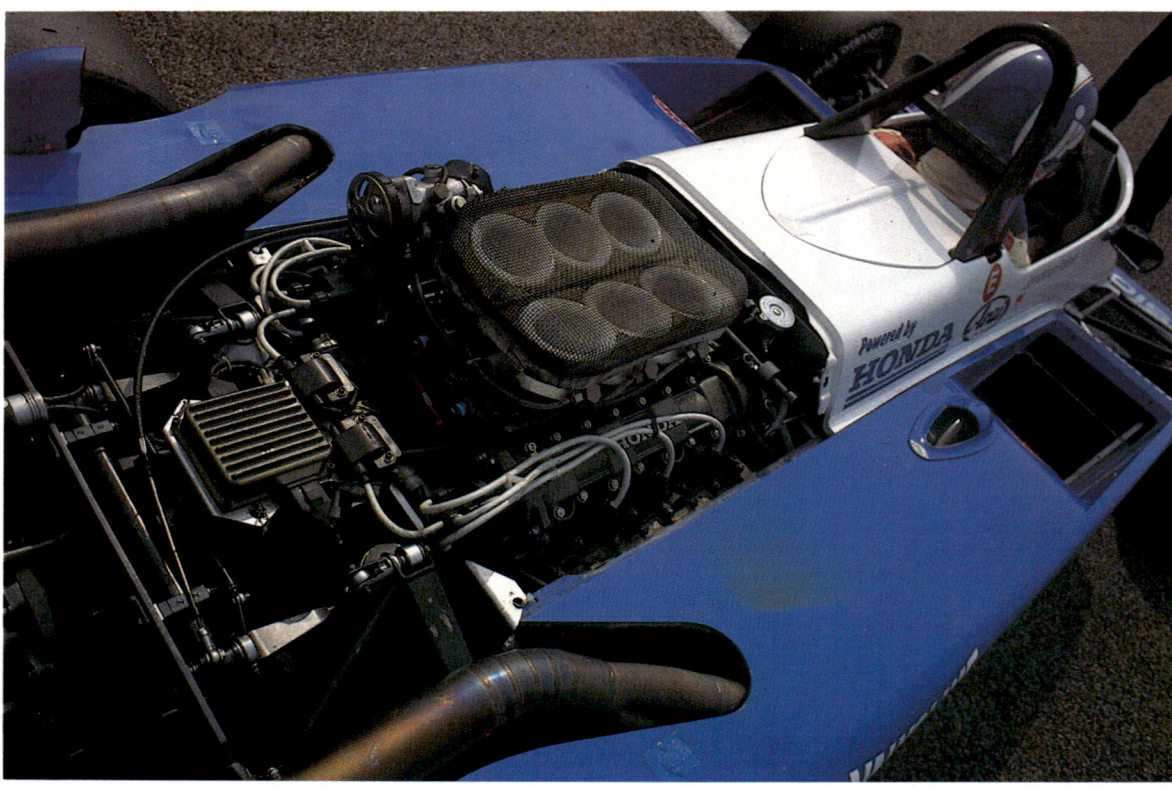

HONDA

only testing pre-Rio had been at Brands, in freezing cold. BMW's engine section under Paul Rosche progressed in leaps and bounds, the compact little 4-cylinder with its efficient electro-mechanical management system really coming on song around Zandvoort.

With 42-43 gallons fuel capacity, the BT52s could only attack the street races confidently non-stop. They were planned from inception as pit-stop cars, with onboard pneumatic jacks, and quick-change wheel fixings amongst other features. Maximum onboard fuel tankage was limited to 250-litres for '83, and now diminishes to 220-litres for '84 as a fuel efficiency measure. The pit-stop strategy allows teams to exceed 250-litres total race-distance consumption if necessary, and that allows them higher boost pressures and higher power than running non-stop. Lighter startline weight, the use of softer compound short-range tyres and two bites at tyre choice 'on the day' are other pit stop pluses. Peripherally, it made for extra excitement on the telly, and placed team mechanics even more at the centre of the action.

Brabham used six BT52s, and during the mid-season calendar gap developed them into BT52B form with myriad detail changes to the aluminium outer/carbon-fibre inner panelled tub to improve rigidity and save weight. Changes included the insertion of lightweight bulkheads. New bodywork for the '52B smoothed the original's front-suspension blisters and also subtly revised their underbody form. The early-season dark-blue on white livery was reversed to emphasise the Parmalat sponsor's logo.

Apart from blown engines on occasion, the more irritating failures were Piquet's throttle parting at Long Beach where Patrese's distributor drive broke. Nelson's Hockenheim fire was probably the most galling – and potentially title-losing – of them all. BMW used a production in-line fuel filter up on the cam-cover. This one's pressing had to be unusually thin at one point. It split, gushed fuel and the droplets were ignited by turbo over-run flame. Hopes literally went up in smoke. Better times were ahead . . .

WILLIAMS

Three teams won with Cosworth-Ford power; Williams, McLaren and Tyrrell. Early in the year Williams showed the 3-litre cars the way. On the faster circuits later in the year, McLaren went ahead. Without sufficient power to haul huge wings through the air in compensation for their lost underwing downloads, the 3-litre brigade had one hand tied behind its back. On the faster circuits it had to trade off lift (download) against drag. Only the tightest street circuits came close to levelling matters.

Williams made their prototype FW08C flat-bottom spec car in December '82 and it changed very little from original form throughout the '83 season. Williams' experiments are tested out of the public gaze at their in-house wind tunnel. Patrick Head: "We manage to test and reject all the hair-brained schemes in private . . ."

Essentially the FW08Cs began life using 1982 tubs – conservative aluminium-honeycomb nacelles – with extended nose-box protection grafted on per the new regulations. These early tubs retained the attachment inserts originally required for the old side pods and ground-effects underwings. New tubs built specifically for '83 used integral nose box structures and lacked the old attachment points. Production of FW08s in 1982 ran to number 6, which tested in C-spec at Willow Springs and Rio before Laffite ripped its bottom out. It was rebuilt as team spare, later becoming the test hack. Chassis 7 and 8 became regular cars for Rosberg and Laffite, with 9 as spare post-Long Beach. Chassis 10 and 11 were completed but not required; one serving as a show car, the other team reserve racer.

One major development programme gave the team a six-speed Hewland-based transmission. The idea was that if Keke or Jacques could latch onto a turbo car's tail through the corners, he could peak out in fifth and then have another gear to hold it – just, possibly, maybe – before the end of the straight.

The car was quite good wherever they could run a lot of wing, "but it was pretty mediocre elsewhere" which means on the faster courses. Tyres were dominant, the Goodyear's bias-belted radials gave heartache because without turbo power the team could not afford the aerodynamic load to prevent them "going doughnut-shaped" at high speed. This condition throws out the tread centre under centrifugal force, diminishing its contact patch with the road. In cornering that patch would chase from one side of the tyre to the other, causing local heating.

Towards the end of the year Laffite's form gave serious cause for concern, although prospects looked more rosy for '84 with the Honda turbo engine agreement. Initial testing was handicapped by rain and the language barrier, but the new world of turbocharged Formula 1 was proving "almost frighteningly quick" in comparison to what had been going on . . .

McLAREN

John Barnard opted for what externally was very little change to his successful MP4/1 series of carbon-composite cars. The prototype and trend-setting "Marlboro-Project 4/1" had been moulded for the Woking team by Hercules Incorporated of Salt Lake City in 1980. The design was altered in detail for chassis 2, adjusted modestly in chassis 3 and the subsequent five tubs were essentially identical. Only the '83 driver protection footbox extension dictated notable change.

With the TAG Turbo-Porsche V6 in the offing, John opted to alter the existing cars as little as possible. He retained the proven 1981/82 rear end package for his Cosworth-engined flat-bottom MP4/1Cs, and waisted-in their planform abaft the radiator housings either side while retaining much of their original ground-effects look. Turbo installation requirements deterred him from taking the slimline route.

"We have great experience of the large plan-area car. I still think we have one of the best lift/drag ratios amongst current cars. People say how sensitive it must be to ride-height and suspension rate changes, and both are significant in setting it up, but that didn't prove too much of a problem . . ."

Unfortunately, Michelin tyres did prove a problem early-on, being tailored largely to turbo requirements with Renault and Brabham. Robbed of ground-effect downloads and lacking the power to pull big wings or load the rear tyres at least to turbo standards, the minimum weight-limit McLarens had a tortured time trying to put sufficient heat into their tyres to make them work adequately.

The cars shone at Rio but in practice at Long Beach both Watson and Lauda could only say "It just doesn't feel like a racing car, it doesn't do anything with precision" and they qualified 22-23. John and his crew had tried everything to make the cars heat their tyres. For race morning they returned both cars to pre-race factory set-up: "There wasn't any magic or some smart-Alec tweaking which made the cars work on race day. We just returned them to the settings they'd been given for the flight out there. What made the difference was simply that the weather brightened on race day, it was warmer, and our car/tyre combination clicked . . .". The result was that sensational 1-2 finish from near the back of the grid, but already John was bending François Dupasquier's ear at Michelin.

He wanted a restructured type of tyre in which internal movement would serve to heat up the casing compound without relying purely on external work against the road to do the job. The prototypes arrived at Monaco too late to save McLaren's bacon. They missed first practice, second practice was wet and both cars non-qualified. It was the team's nadir.

At Imola they had watched aghast as scudding cloud cover saw track surface temperatures bobbing up and down like a ping-pong ball on a fairground fountain. They jokingly predicted when the sun went in, that their cars would lose a second lap in the shade. And they did, as the tyres cooled . . . and that after they had been the quickest Cosworths at Ricard.

At Spa they ran with the Williams until the Didcot cars pit-stopped, the McLarens didn't and they couldn't live with the green-and-white cars thereafter. Consequently, in mid-season McLaren began pit-stopping, and did it well, using pneumatic trolley jacks of their own design.

Behind Barnard's back, a workshop experiment in

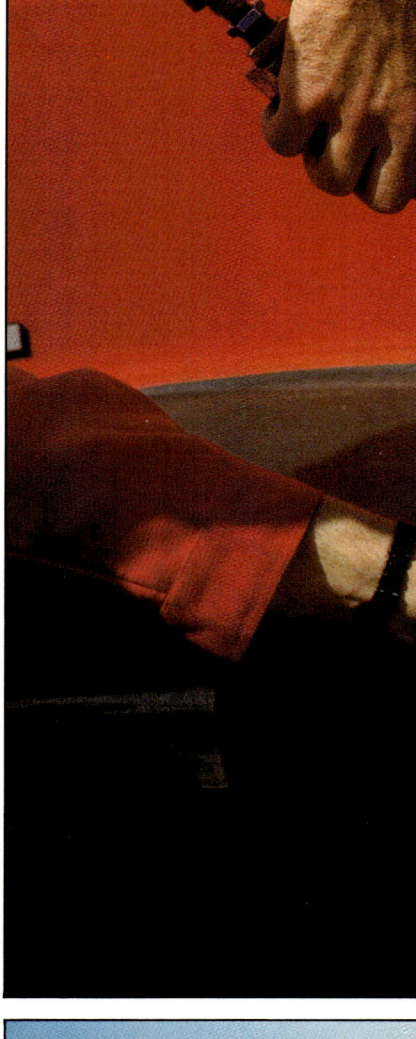

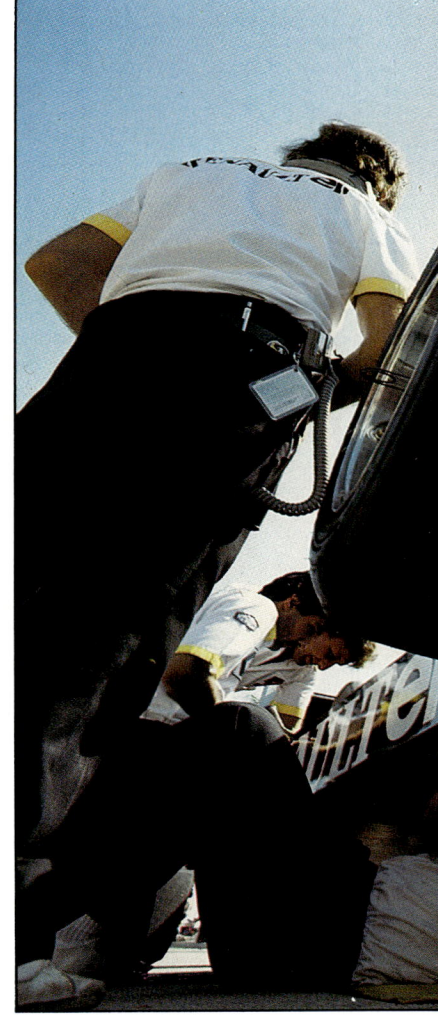

Carbon fibre brakes, a common sight in Formula 1, were to prove less suitable when McLaren switched from the Cosworth to the TAG turbo. The flat-bottomed regulations took immediate effect; Prost's Renault at Long Beach. The French team used a water injection system developed with the help of Jean-Pierre Boudy's Renault 18!

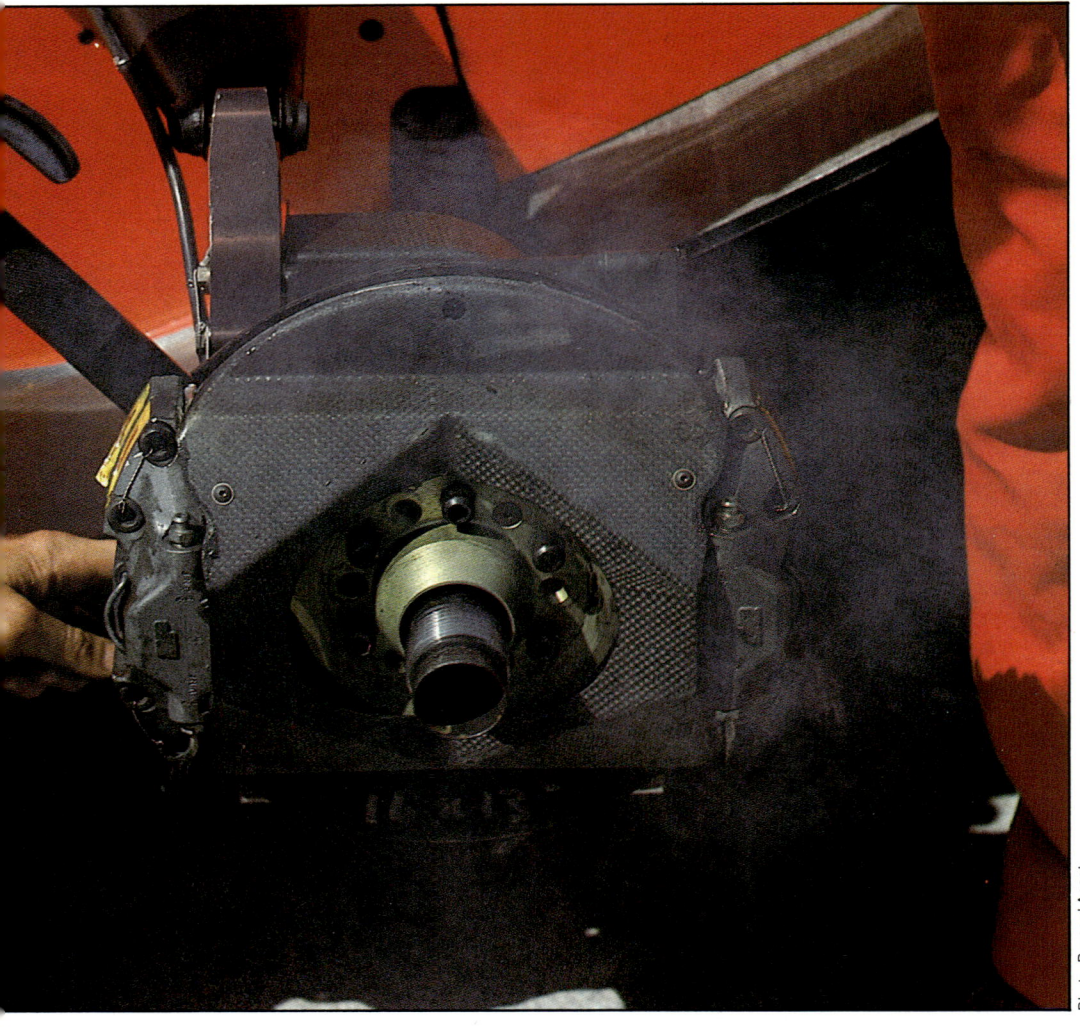

Photo: Bernard Asset

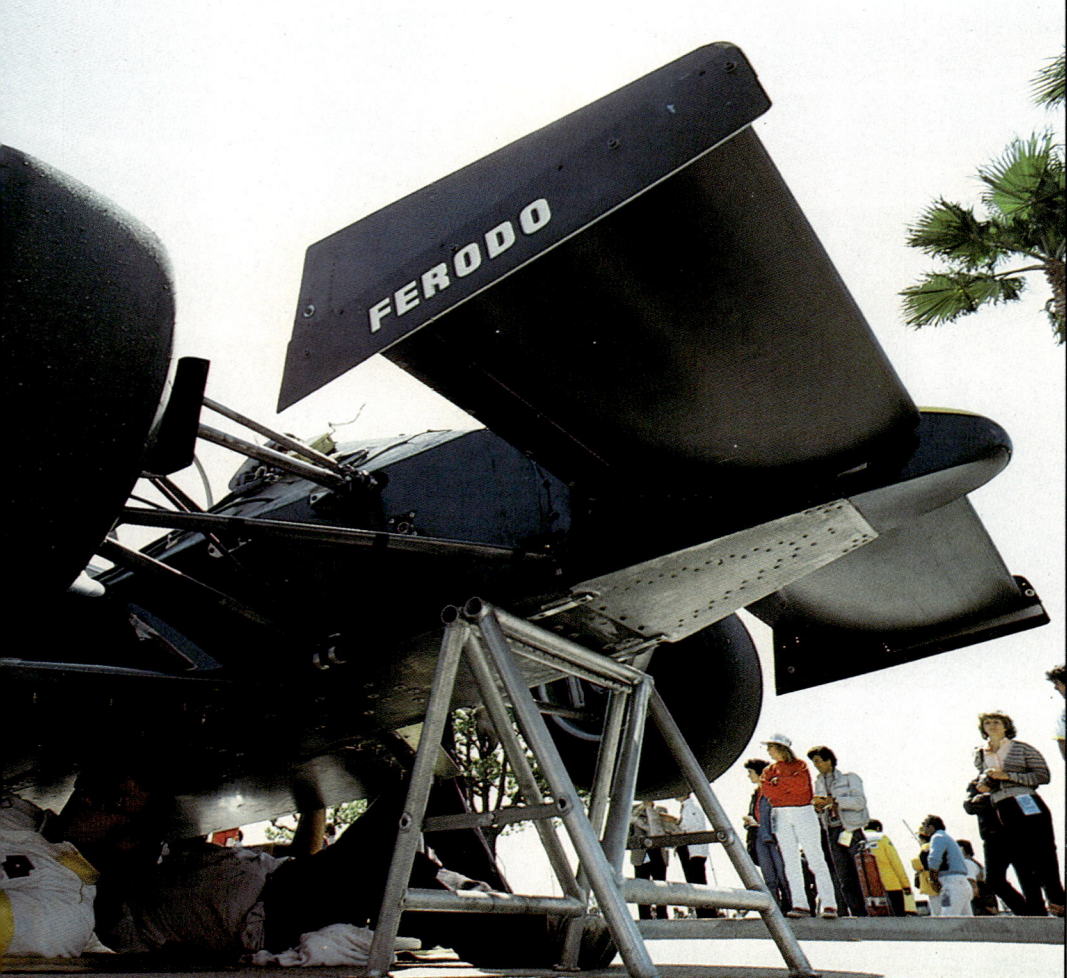

Photo: Mark Clifford

speeding refuelling by raising flow pressure went 'orribly wrong. New tub 8 was blown apart by surging air-pressure as the feed tank emptied, and turbulent fuel obstructed the air-vent outlet in the tub . . . Dangerous business, pressure refuelling . . .

The turbo MP4/1D test hack using the oldest carbon-composite tub showed promise, but the interim MP4/1E-TAG V6 raced at the end of the season was a sponsor-pleasing project which caused some aggravation at the works, where one faction saw it as deflecting time and effort from the vital all-new MP4/2 turbocar project for '84. Still race-test miles on the V6 engine can prove valuable, and McLaren's final outings with Cosworth DFY power at Silverstone, Hockenheim, Österreichring and Zandvoort (where Watson drove one of the races of his life) confirmed them as the best 3-litre late-season.

TYRRELL

By mid-season '83 it was obvious that Cosworth's long, long reign as the dominant force in Formula 1 engineering was drawing to its noble close. By that time some 387 F1 engines had been produced in the Northampton works, and this year had seen 30 built, probably more than ever before. Major thrust went into the new short-stroke DFY, whose dimensions of 90mm bore x 58.8mm stroke compare with the standard DFV's 85.6mm x 64.8mm. Two different DFY variants were built. Both were very different from the preceding DFV. They used different blocks, heads, cranks, pistons, liners and cams, different fuel system, and more. Interested teams had a choice. They could either take the short-term quicker-delivery DFY as it stood in the winter, or wait a few months for the definitive DFY with totally redesigned, externally restyled heads, with different-angled valves, new throttle-slides, manifolds, etc.

Only Tyrrell took the longer-term option, with ten DFYs, McLaren bought six, Williams and Ligier three each and Lotus a couple, while Williams relied essentially upon reliable DFVs.

Maurice Phillippe of Tyrrell based his '83 flat-bottoms initially – like Ferrari – upon existing '011' tubs, while a smaller more penetrative '012' emerged later in the season, being intended as a longer-term turbo car for '84. They campaigned four '011's, and two '012s' had appeared before season's end, losing Alboreto's '011' after his tangle with Johansson in Austria which distorted the Tyrrell tub's underside far more seriously than the Italian's apparently heavier testing shunt earlier in the year at Spa. The prototype '011/1' was cut-up during the season as a wind-tunnel test hack, with cut-out centre sections to allow it to telescope for research purposes . . .

With flat-bottom aerodynamics slashing total download by some two-thirds compared to 1982 ground-effects values, and the atmospherically-aspirated engine's inability to haul big wings without dramatic cost in straight-line speed, Maurice considers: "We lost our old advantage over the turbos in terms of pick-up out of the corners where they used to experience throttle lag or restricted traction, and since we could only afford to run perhaps two-thirds of their download we also lost our old advantage on the wet, where they can now pull a big sail of a wing and cut through the water. By the second half of the season the Cosworth was farther behind than ever before, but at least we picked-up the win in Detroit . . ."

With in total perhaps 60 per cent less downforce to react, 1983 saw the return of suspension movement. Where 1982 spec F1 suspensions would move mere fractions bump to droop they now move whole inches. In driving terms the cars slide more easily, and are certainly more comfortable and enjoyable to drive. A major difference in tyre demand marked the season, as, relieved of those monstrous aerodynamic download-ings which demanded tyre sidewall deflection as virtually the only real spring in the system, we are now back towards mid-'70s technology. Harder compounds had to be used to resist more scrub as the cars tended to slide and spin their wheels, but tyre sidewalls and construction were thinner, lighter now than had been the case.

It was a season of immense change, a pivotal season in the history of Grand Prix racing, and one which future enthusiasts and maybe the occasional historian will savour . . . The King is dead, long live the King – but which of the turbos will succeed, if succeed they will . . .

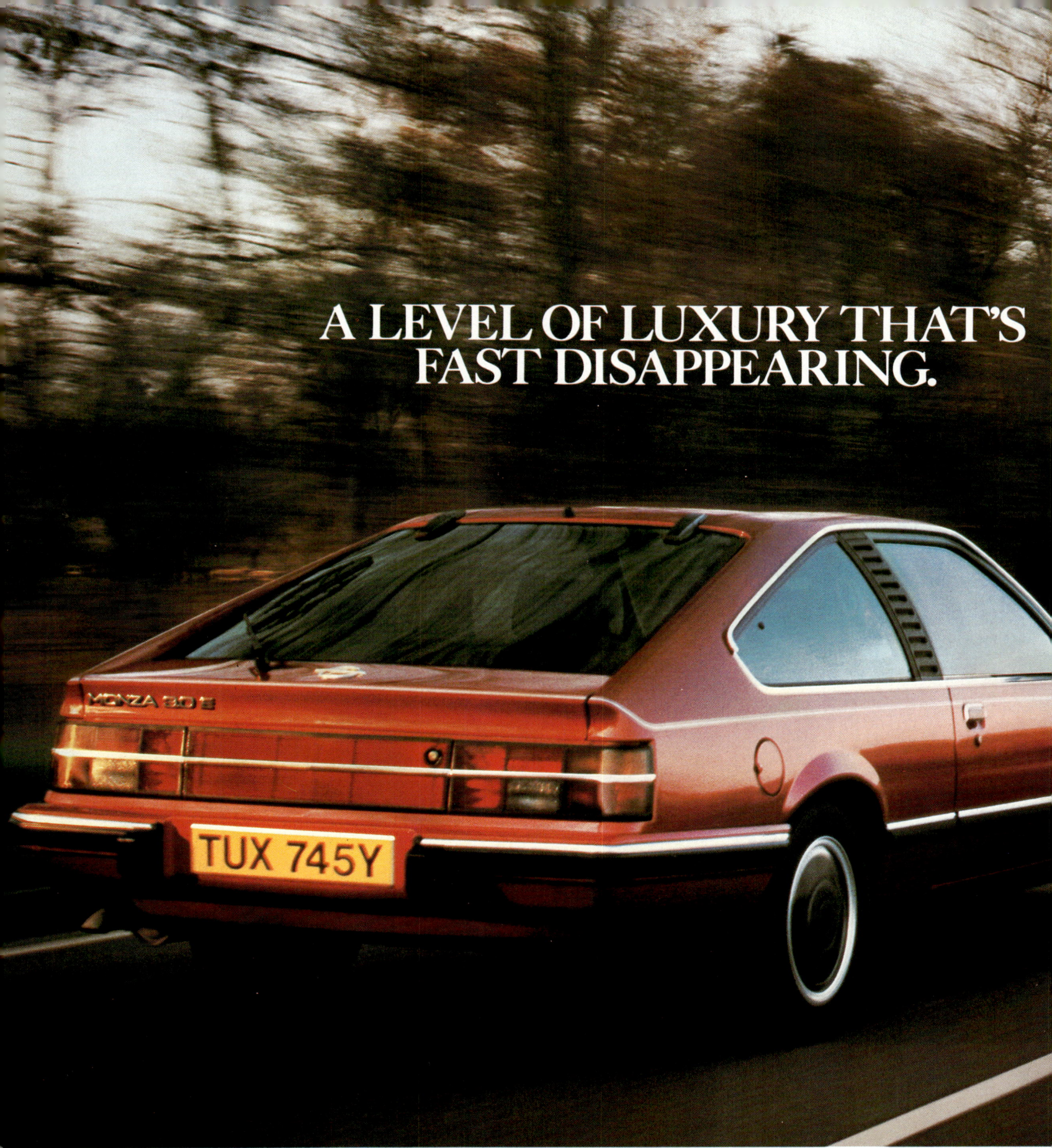

A LEVEL OF LUXURY THAT'S FAST DISAPPEARING.

The Monza's three litre, 6 cylinder fuel injected engine has been refined to take you smoothly from 0-60 mph in 8.2 seconds.*

With its exhilarating 180 hp matched to a 5 speed gearbox you could reach a top speed of 133 mph – if only the law would allow it.

With Monza's uprated suspension and limited slip differential, 'Motor' magazine commented "so easy is it now to drive the car very quickly, yet smoothly through twisty lanes, even in a typical English drizzle, that it is almost as if it had four wheel drive."

*FROM MOTOR MAGAZINE. 5-SPEED MANUAL TRANSMISSION STANDARD. AUTOMATIC TRANSMISSION IS A NO-COST OPTION.

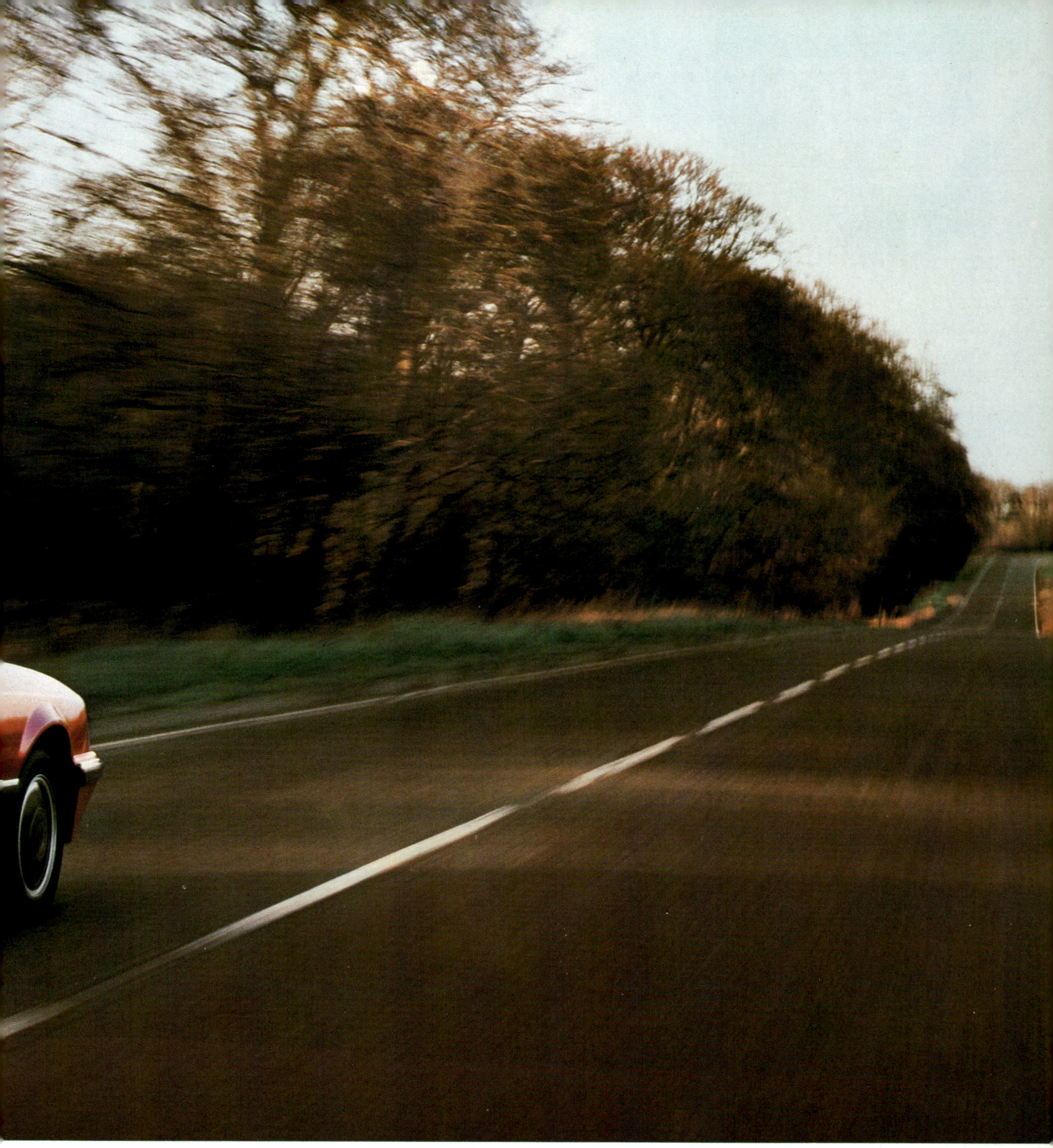

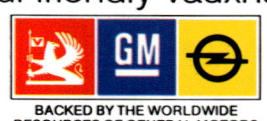

As if this kind of performance isn't luxury in itself, the Monza is lavishly equipped. Standard items include: electrically operated and heated door mirrors, headlamp wash-wipe, a steel sun-roof, built-in fog lamps, central door locking, electric windows and stereo radio cassette. All in all, at £13,501, the Monza is a rare luxury. Catch up with it at your friendly Vauxhall-Opel dealer.

BACKED BY THE WORLDWIDE RESOURCES OF GENERAL MOTORS

VAUXHALL-OPEL
BETTER. BY DESIGN.

A GRAND PRIX REPLICA FOR THE ROAD

Yamaha lead the world in two-stroke motorcycle development and if anyone ever had any doubt on that point, let them check out the sensational Yamaha RD500LC.

It's the fastest, most powerful, road-going 'five hundred' ever built, thanks to a specification that directly parallels the factory racer used by Kenny Roberts to win six World Championship Grands Prix in 1983.

We've deviated from the racer specification only where we felt changes would enhance the RD500LC as a road machine. As a result, no-one has ever built a road machine so close in technical basis to a current Grand Prix winner.

Quite frankly, we don't expect that anyone else ever will.

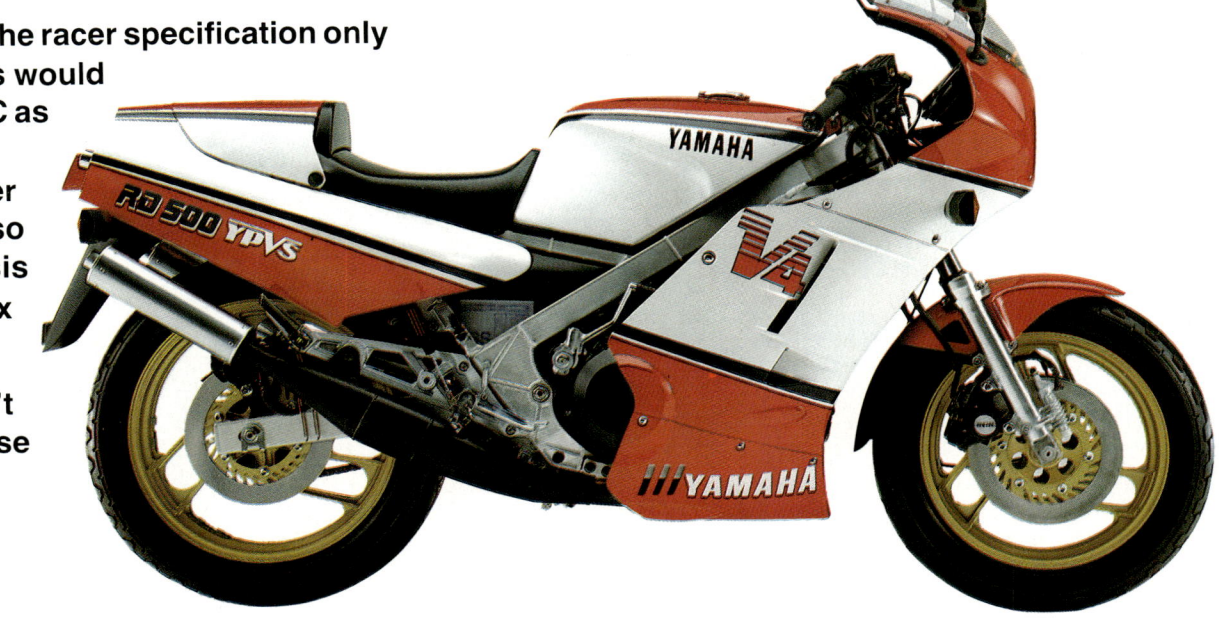

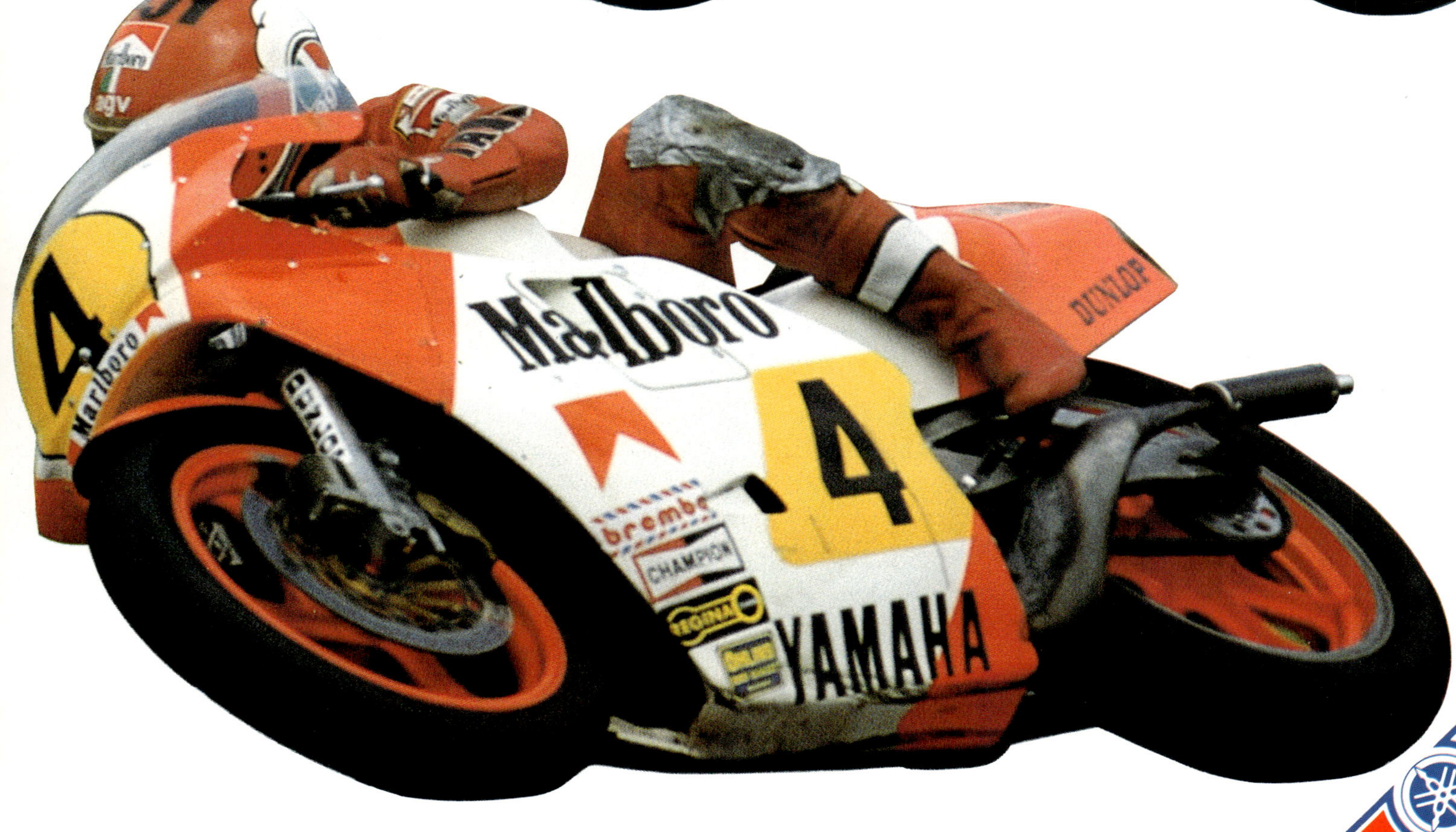

1983 Formula 1 Drivers' Statistics

During 1983, 37 drivers from 17 countries participated in the season's 16 Formula 1 races (including one non-championship event). They were seen in 16 different makes of car powered by eight makes of engine.

René Arnoux, Nigel Mansell, Keke Rosberg and Danny Sullivan took part in all 16 races. Nelson Piquet scored points 10 times, Alain Prost and Patrick Tambay nine, René Arnoux eight and Keke Rosberg seven. Tambay and Arnoux won four pole positions each and Prost took three while Piquet recorded fastest lap on four occasions.

In 1982, 40 drivers from 17 countries took part in the season's 16 Grands Prix (there were no non-championship races).

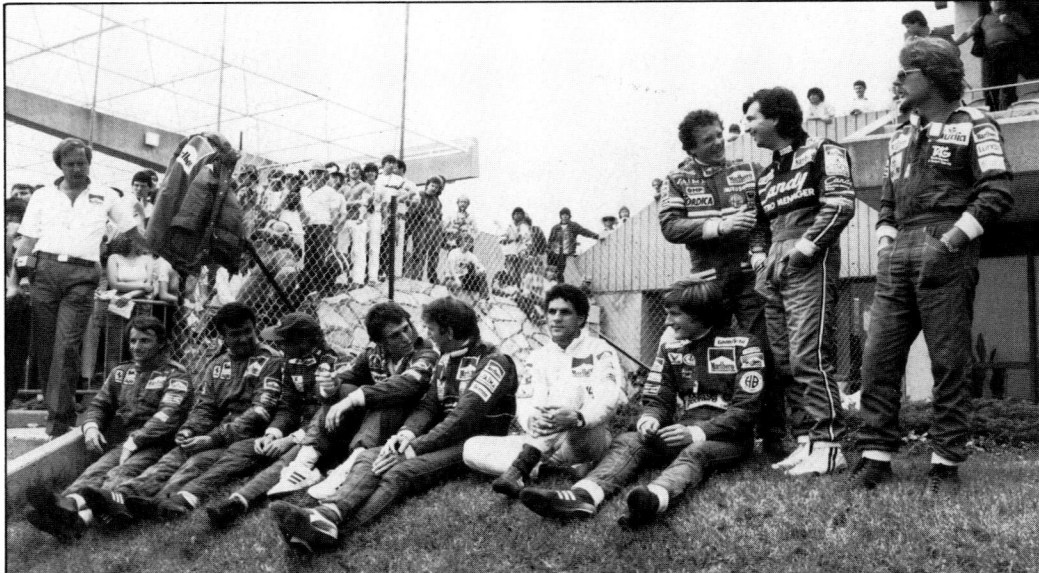

Driver	Nat	Date of Birth	Car	Rio de Janeiro	Long Beach	Paul Ricard	Imola	Monte Carlo	Spa-Francorchamps	Detroit	Montreal	Silverstone	Hockenheim	Österreichring	Zandvoort	Monza	Brands Hatch	Kyalami	World Championship Points	No. of Grands Prix started	1st	2nd	3rd	No. of Grand Prix pole positions	Race of Champions
Kenneth Acheson	GB	27/11/57	RAM March-Cosworth	–	–	–	–	–	–	–	–	NQ	NQ	NQ	NQ	NQ	NQ	12	0	1	–	–	–	–	–
Michele Alboreto	I	23/12/56	Tyrrell-Cosworth	R	9	8	R	R	*14	1	8	13	R	R	6	R	R	R	10	41	2	–	1	–	–
Elio de Angelis	I	26/3/58	Lotus-Cosworth Lotus-Renault	(13)	R	R	R	R	9	R	R	R	R	R	R	R	5	R	R	2	70	1	1	–	1	–
René Arnoux	F	4/7/48	Ferrari	10	3	7	3	R	R	R	1	5	1	2	1	2	9	R	49	79	7	7	4	18	R
Mauro Baldi	I	31/1/54	Alfa Romeo	R	R	R	*10	6	R	12	10	7	R	R	5	R	R	R	3	26	–	–	–	–	–
Raul Boesel	BR	4/12/57	Ligier-Cosworth	R	7	R	9	R	13	10	R	R	R	NQ	10	NQ	15	NC	0	23	–	–	–	–	5
Thierry Boutsen	B	13/7/57	Arrows-Cosworth	–	–	–	–	–	R	7	7	15	9	13	*14	R	11	9	0	10	–	–	–	–	–
Johnny Cecotto	YV	25/1/56	Theodore-Cosworth	14	6	11	R	NPQ	10	R	R	NQ	11	NQ	NQ	12	W	–	1	9	–	–	–	–	–
Andrea de Cesaris	I	31/5/59	Alfa Romeo	DNS	R	12	R	R	R	R	R	8	2	R	R	R	4	2	15	46	–	2	1	1	–
Eddie Cheever	USA	10/1/58	Renault	R	R	3	R	R	3	R	2	R	R	4	R	3	10	6	22	54	–	2	5	–	–
Corrado Fabi	I	12/4/61	Osella-Cosworth Osella-Alfa Romeo	R	NQ	R	R	NQ	R	NQ	R	NQ	NQ	10	*11	R	NQ	R	0	9	–	–	–	–	–
Piercarlo Ghinzani	I	16/1/52	Osella-Cosworth Osella-Alfa Romeo	NQ	NQ	NQ	NQ	NQ	NQ	R	NQ	R	R	11	NQ	R	R	R	0	7	–	–	–	–	–
Bruno Giacomelli	I	10/9/52	Toleman-Hart	R	R	*13	R	NQ	8	9	R	R	R	R	13	7	6	R	1	69	–	–	1	1	–
Roberto Guerrero	COL	16/11/58	Theodore-Cosworth	NC	R	R	R	NPQ	R	NC	R	16	R	R	12	13	12	–	0	21	–	–	–	–	7
Brian Henton	GB	19/9/46	Theodore-Cosworth	–	–	–	–	–	–	–	–	–	–	–	–	–	–	–	–	19	–	–	–	–	4
Jean-Pierre Jarier	F	10/7/46	Ligier-Cosworth	R	R	9	R	R	R	R	R	10	8	7	R	9	R	10	0	133	–	–	3	3	–
Alan Jones	AUS	2/11/46	Arrows-Cosworth	–	R	–	–	–	–	–	–	–	–	–	–	–	–	–	0	87	12	7	5	6	3
Stefan Johansson	S	8/9/56	Spirit-Honda	–	–	–	–	–	–	–	–	R	R	12	7	R	14	–	0	6	–	–	–	–	R
Jacques Laffite	F	21/11/43	Williams-Cosworth Williams-Honda	4	4	6	7	R	6	5	R	12	6	R	R	NQ	NQ	R	11	136	6	8	14	7	–
Niki Lauda	A	22/2/49	McLaren-Cosworth McLaren-TAG	3	2	R	R	NQ	R	R	R	6	(5)	6	R	R	R	*11	12	141	19	16	9	24	–
Nigel Mansell	GB	8/8/54	Lotus-Cosworth Lotus-Renault	12	12	R	*12	R	R	6	R	4	R	5	R	8	3	NC	10	44	–	–	3	–	R
Jonathan Palmer	GB	7/11/56	Williams-Cosworth	–	–	–	–	–	–	–	–	–	–	–	–	–	13	–	0	1	–	–	–	–	–
Riccardo Patrese	I	17/4/54	Brabham-BMW	R	*10	R	R	R	R	R	R	R	3	R	9	R	7	1	13	95	2	4	3	2	–
Nelson Piquet	BR	17/8/52	Brabham-BMW	1	R	2	R	2	4	4	R	2	*13	3	R	1	1	3	59	78	10	7	6	8	–
Alain Prost	F	24/2/55	Renault	7	11	1	2	3	1	8	5	1	4	1	R	R	2	R	57	57	9	6	2	10	–
Hector Rebaque	MEX	5/2/56	Brabham-BMW	–	–	–	–	–	–	–	–	–	–	–	–	–	–	–	–	41	–	–	–	–	R
Keke Rosberg	SF	6/12/48	Williams-Cosworth Williams-Honda	(2)	R	5	4	1	5	2	4	11	10	8	R	11	R	5	27	65	2	4	3	2	1
Eliseo Salazar	RCH	14/11/54	RAM March-Cosworth	15	R	NQ	NQ	NQ	NQ	–	–	–	–	–	–	–	–	–	0	24	–	–	–	–	–
Jean-Louis Schlesser	F	2/10/52	RAM March-Cosworth	–	–	NQ	–	–	–	–	–	–	–	–	–	–	–	–	0	0	–	–	–	–	6
Chico Serra	BR	3/2/57	Arrows-Cosworth	9	–	R	8	7	–	–	–	–	–	–	–	–	–	–	0	18	–	–	–	–	R
Danny Sullivan	USA	9/3/50	Tyrrell-Cosworth	11	8	R	R	5	12	R	(9)	14	12	R	R	R	R	7	2	15	–	–	–	–	2
Marc Surer	CH	18/9/51	Arrows-Cosworth	6	5	10	6	R	11	11	R	17	7	R	8	10	R	8	4	50	–	–	–	–	–
Patrick Tambay	F	25/6/49	Ferrari	5	R	4	1	4	2	R	3	3	R	R	2	4	R	R	40	70	2	3	3	4	–
Jacques Villeneuve	CDN	4/11/55	RAM March-Cosworth	–	–	–	–	–	–	NQ	–	–	–	–	–	–	–	–	0	0	–	–	–	–	–
Derek Warwick	GB	27/8/54	Toleman-Hart	8	R	R	R	R	7	R	R	R	R	R	4	6	5	4	9	27	–	–	–	–	–
John Watson	GB	4/5/46	McLaren-Cosworth McLaren-TAG	R	1	R	5	NQ	R	3	6	9	5	9	3	R	R	D	22	151	5	6	9	2	R
Manfred Winkelhock	D	6/10/51	ATS-BMW	16	R	R	11	R	R	R	9	R	NQ	R	D	R	8	R	0	27	–	–	–	–	–

* Retired but classified as a finisher. DNP = Did not practise.
DNS = Qualified, did not start. NC = Running at finish, not classified. NQ = Did not qualify. NPQ = Failed to pre-qualify. R = Retired.
W = Entry withdrawn. (D) = Disqualified.

Grand Prix Super Grid

by John Taylor

By adding together the length of all 15 circuits used in this year's Grand Prix World Championship, we arrive at a circuit with a length of 45·825 miles/73·748 kms. If we then add together the best practice times of each of the 23 drivers who achieved a practice time in each event, we arrive at a hypothetical grid for the season.

Patrick Tambay (Ferrari 126C2-B/126C3)
22m 34·176s, 121·823 mph/196·055 km/h

René Arnoux (Ferrari 126C2-B/126C3)
22m 33·563s, 121·878 mph/196·143 km/h

Nelson Piquet (Brabham BT52/BT52B)
22m 41·363s, 121·180 mph/195·020 km/h

Alain Prost (Renault RE30C/RE40)
22m 38·762s, 121·499 mph/195·533 km/h

Eddie Cheever (Renault RE30C/RE40)
22m 53·525s, 120·107 mph/193·293 km/h

Riccardo Patrese (Brabham BT52/BT52B)
22m 50·359s, 120·385 mph/193·740 km/h

Elio de Angelis (Lotus 93T/94T)
23m 01·099s, 119·448 mph/192·232 km/h

Andrea de Cesaris (Alfa Romeo 183T)
22m 56·756s, 119·825 mph/192·839 km/h

Mauro Baldi (Alfa Romeo 183T)
23m 13·496s, 118·386 mph/190·523 km/h

Derek Warwick (Toleman TG183B)
23m 08·514s, 118·810 mph/191·206 km/h

Bruno Giacomelli (Toleman TG183B)
23m 16·734s, 118·111 mph/190·081 km/h

Keke Rosberg (Williams FW08C/FW09)
23m 14·976s, 118·260 mph/190·321 km/h

Niki Lauda (McLaren MP4/1C/MP4/1E)
23m 26·205s, 117·316 mph/188·801 km/h

Nigel Mansell (Lotus 92/93T/94T)
23m 18·782s, 117·938 mph/189·802 km/h

Jacques Laffite (Williams FW08C/FW09)
23m 34·731s, 116·609 mph/187·664 km/h

Michele Alboreto (Tyrrell 011/012)
23m 33·218s, 116·734 mph/187·865 km/h

John Watson (McLaren MP4/1C/MP4/1E)
23m 35·170s, 116·573 mph/187·606 km/h

Marc Surer (Arrows A6)
23m 34·950s, 116·591 mph/187·635 km/h

Danny Sullivan (Tyrrell 011/012)
23m 46·121s, 115·677 mph/186·164 km/h

Jean-Pierre Jarier (Ligier JS21)
23m 39·639s, 116·206 mph/187·015 km/h

Corrado Fabi (Osella FA1D/FA1E)
24m 08·666s, 113·877 mph/183·267 km/h

Raul Boesel (Ligier JS21)
23m 56·571s, 114·836 mph/184·810 km/h

Piercarlo Ghinzani (Osella FA1D/FA1E)
24m 15·514s, 113·341 mph/182·404 km/h

Points per start

		Starts	Points	Average (year)	Average (career)
1	Nelson Piquet	15	59	3·933	2·385
2	Alain Prost	15	57	3·800	2·439
3	René Arnoux	15	49	3·267	1·696
4	Patrick Tambay	15	40	2·667	1·129
5	Keke Rosberg	15	27	1·800	1·167
6	John Watson	14	22	1·571	1·119
7	Eddie Cheever	15	22	1·467	0·870
8	Andrea de Cesaris	14	15	1·071	0·457
9	Riccardo Patrese	15	13	0·867	0·691
10	Niki Lauda	14	12	0·857	2·372
11	Jacques Laffite	13	11	0·846	1·419
12	Nigel Mansell	15	10	0·667	0·581
	Michele Alboreto	15	10	0·667	0·854
14	Derek Warwick	15	9	0·600	0·333
15	Marc Surer	15	4	0·267	0·220
16	Mauro Baldi	15	3	0·200	0·192
17	Danny Sullivan	15	2	0·133	0·133
	Elio de Angelis	15	2	0·133	0·775
19	Johnny Cecotto	9	1	0·111	0·111
20	Bruno Giacomelli	14	1	0·071	0·271

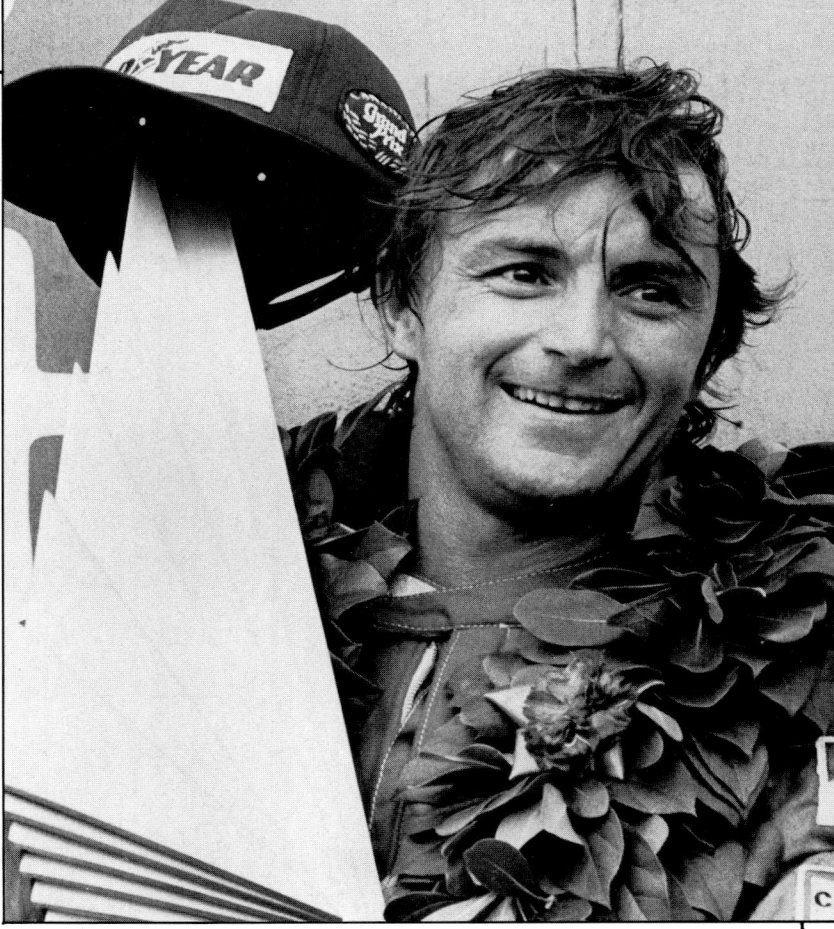

René Arnoux: winner of the 'Super Pole'.

1983 World Championship – Top Four Drivers: Race Statistics

	Wins (season)	Wins (career)	Poles (season)	Poles (career)	F. Laps (season)	F. Laps (career)
Nelson Piquet	3	10	1	8	4	10
Alain Prost	4	9	3	10	3	7
René Arnoux	3	7	4	18	2	10
Patrick Tambay	1	2	4	4	1	1

	Laps completed	Miles (to nearest mile)	Kms (to nearest km)
Nelson Piquet	810	2414	3885
Alain Prost	836	2468	3972
René Arnoux	751	2280	3669
Patrick Tambay	743	2201	3542

	Laps led	Miles (to nearest mile)	Kms (to nearest km)
Nelson Piquet	326 (34·68%)	953	1534
Alain Prost	112 (11·91%)	396	637
René Arnoux	178 (18·94%)	553	890
Patrick Tambay	92 (9·79%)	270	435

Total laps/miles/kms in season 940 laps/2761 miles/4443 kms

The season's running total – how the points were accumulated.

	Nelson Piquet	Alain Prost	René Arnoux	Patrick Tambay
Jacarepagua	9	–	–	2
Long Beach	– (9)	– (–)	4 (4)	– (2)
Paul Ricard	6 (15)	9 (9)	– (4)	3 (5)
Imola	– (15)	6 (15)	4 (8)	9 (14)
Monte Carlo	6 (21)	4 (19)	– (8)	3 (17)
Spa	3 (24)	9 (28)	– (8)	6 (23)
Detroit	3 (27)	– (28)	– (8)	– (23)
Montreal	– (27)	2 (30)	9 (17)	4 (27)
Silverstone	6 (33)	9 (39)	2 (19)	4 (31)
Hockenheim	– (33)	3 (42)	9 (28)	– (31)
Österreichring	4 (37)	9 (51)	6 (34)	– (31)
Zandvoort	– (37)	– (51)	9 (43)	6 (37)
Monza	9 (46)	– (51)	6 (49)	3 (40)
Brands Hatch	9 (55)	6 (57)	– (49)	– (40)
Kyalami	4 (59)	– (57)	– (49)	– (40)

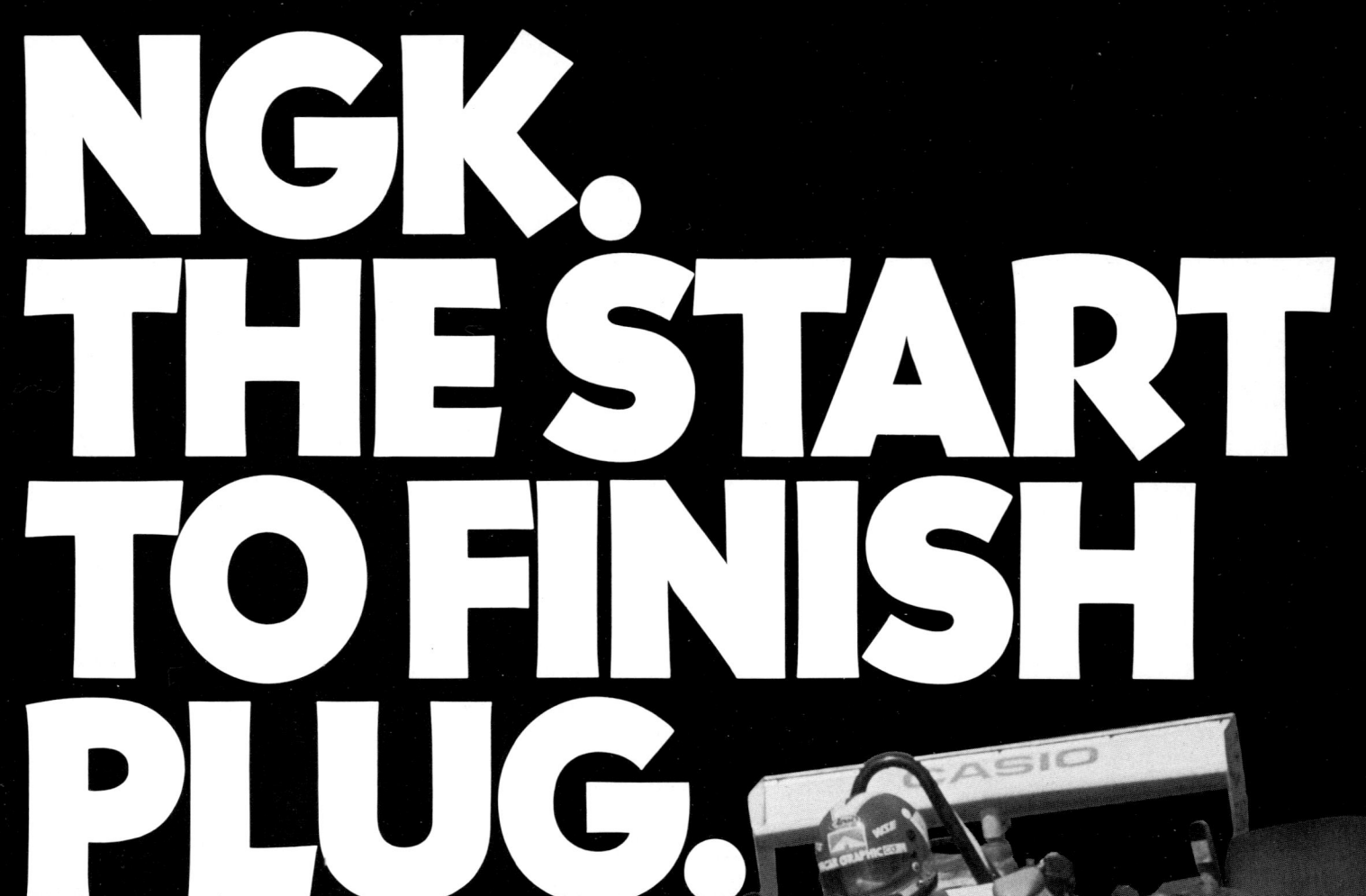

Perhaps the most interesting aspect of the 1983 season has been the comparatively small number of chassis written off during a year when the cars became more sensible and controllable. Williams, for example, built two FW08C chassis which were never used; Brabham managed their championship year with five BT52s and lost just one; Renault made seven RE40s and Ferrari, after a frantic build programme in 1982, completed just five new cars. McLaren, meanwhile, have still used no more than eight MP4s since 1981!

1983 saw the introduction of the 'flat bottom' regulations and teams either constructed new cars immediately or adapted their 1982 chassis while working on the latest design. Apart from the usual mysteries surrounding Alfa Romeo, the chassis movements have been reasonably straightforward and, once again, we would like to express our gratitude to Denis Jenkinson of *Motor Sport* and the various team managers and mechanics who helped to piece together the following facts:

Alfa Romeo

Based their 1983 car on the 182T prototype seen at Monza in 1982. (Note: details below are suspect and should be treated purely as a guide).

183T

01 182T prototype revised to suit latest regulations. Spare car at Rio, Long Beach, Ricard, Imola, Monaco, Spa, Detroit and Montreal.

02 New for de Cesaris at Rio. For de Cesaris at Long Beach, Ricard, Imola, Monaco, Spa, Detroit and Montreal. For Baldi at Monza. Spare car at Brands Hatch. For Baldi at Kyalami.

03 New for Baldi at Rio. For Baldi at Long Beach where, apparently, it was written off during the race. 03 reappeared, however, at Silverstone for de Cesaris. For de Cesaris at Hockenheim, Österreichring, Zandvoort, Monza and Kyalami.

04 New for Baldi at Ricard. For Baldi at Imola, Monaco, Spa, Detroit, Montreal, Silverstone, Hockenheim, Österreichring, Zandvoort and Brands Hatch.

05 New at Silverstone as spare car. Spare car at Hockenheim, Österreichring, Zandvoort, Monza and Kyalami. For de Cesaris at Brands Hatch.

Arrows

Started the season with two new **A6s** and converted 1982 A5.

1 Chassis A5 (1) updated to A6 specification. Used by Jones during testing at Willow Springs, California. Spare car at Long Beach, Ricard (raced by Serra), Imola, Monaco, Spa (raced by Surer), Detroit and Montreal. Not seen again. For Serra at Race of Champions. Not seen again.

2 New for Surer at Rio. For Jones at Long Beach. For Surer at Ricard, Imola and Monaco (crashed during race and repaired). Spare car at Silverstone, Hockenheim. Österreichring, Zandvoort, Monza, Brands Hatch and Kyalami.

3 New for Serra at Rio. For Surer at Long Beach. For Jones at Race of Champions. For Serra at Ricard (crashed during practice and repaired), Imola and Monaco. For Boutsen at Spa, Detroit and Montreal. Chassis stripped and tub taken to Österreichring.

4 New for Surer at Spa. For Surer at Detroit, Montreal, Silverstone, Hockenheim, Österreichring, Zandvoort, Monza, Brands Hatch and Kyalami.

5 New for Boutsen at Silverstone. For Boutsen at Hockenheim, Österreichring, Zandvoort, Monza, Brands Hatch and Kyalami.

ATS

Switched from Cosworth to BMW turbo engines. Began the season with a new car, the **D6.**

01 New for Winkelhock at Rio. For Winkelhock at Long Beach (crashed and repaired) and Ricard. Spare car at Imola (raced by Winkelhock), Monaco, Spa, Detroit and Montreal. Became Research and Development car.

02 New for Winkelhock at Imola. For Winkelhock at Monaco, Spa, Detroit and Montreal. Spare car at Silverstone, Hockenheim, Österreichring (raced by Winkelhock), Zandvoort, (raced by Winkelhock), Monza (raced by Winkelhock), Brands Hatch and Kyalami.

03 New for Winkelhock at Silverstone. For Winkelhock at Hockenheim, Österreichring, Zandvoort, Monza, Brands Hatch and Kyalami.

Brabham

Plans for the BT51 were well advanced when the sudden change to the regulations at the end of 1982 caused Brabham to design and build a completely new car, the **BT52.** Three were made ready for the first race of the season.

1 Spare car at Rio and Long Beach. For Rebaque at Race of Champions. Spare car at Ricard (raced by Piquet), Imola, Monaco, Spa and Detroit (raced by Patrese). For Patrese at Montreal. Uprated to B-spec. Spare car at Österreichring, Zandvoort, Monza, Brands Hatch (raced by Patrese) and Kyalami.

2 New for Patrese at Rio. For Patrese at Long Beach and Ricard. Became test car; written off by Piquet during test session at Brands Hatch on 31 August.

3 New for Piquet at Rio. For Piquet at Long Beach, Ricard, Imola, Monaco, Spa, Detroit and Montreal. Uprated to B-specification. Spare car at Silverstone and Hockenheim (raced by Piquet and destroyed by fire).

4 New for Patrese at Imola. For Patrese at Monaco, Spa and Detroit. Spare car at Montreal. Not seen again; used for show purposes.

BT52B

5 New car to B-spec for Piquet at Silverstone. For Piquet at Hockenheim, Österreichring, Zandvoort, Monza, Brands Hatch and Kyalami.

6 New car to B-spec for Patrese at Silverstone. For Patrese at Hockenheim, Österreichring, Zandvoort, Monza, Brands Hatch and Kyalami.

Ferrari

Rebuilt 1982 cars, **126C2B** (063) and (064), to 1983 specification and completed two new cars, (065) and (066), for first race. Carbon fibre composite car, the 126C3, completed mid-season.

062 Spare car at Ricard (raced by Tambay), Imola and Monaco. For

Arnoux at Spa. Not seen again.

063 For Tambay at Rio and Long Beach. For Arnoux at Race of Champions. Spare car for Tambay at Monaco. Spare car at Spa, Detroit and Montreal. Not seen again.

064 For Arnoux at Rio, Long Beach, Ricard, Imola, Monaco, Detroit and Montreal. Spare car for Arnoux at Silverstone and Hockenheim. Not seen again.

065 Spare car at Rio and Long Beach. For Tambay at Ricard, Imola, Monaco, Spa, Detroit and Montreal. Spare car for Tambay at Silverstone and Hockenheim. Spare car at Österreichring. Spare car for Tambay at Zandvoort. Not seen again.

126C3

066 New for Arnoux at Silverstone. For Arnoux at Hockenheim. Spare car for Tambay at Österreichring. Spare car at Zandvoort (raced by Arnoux). Spare car at Monza (raced by Arnoux). For Arnoux at Brands Hatch and Kyalami.

067 New for Tambay at Silverstone. For Tambay at Hockenheim, Österreichring and Zandvoort. Spare car for Tambay at Monza and Brands Hatch.

068 New for Arnoux at Österreichring. For Arnoux at Zandvoort and Monza. Spare car for Arnoux at Brands Hatch. Spare car at Kyalami.

069 New for Tambay at Monza. For Tambay at Brands Hatch ahd Kyalami.

Ligier

Matra V12 engines no longer available and Ligier no longer associated with Talbot. Built new car, the **JS21,** to accept Ford-Cosworth engines and began season with two monocoques converted from 1982 spec.

01 Purely a test hack used during preliminary trials.

02 Modified from JS19. Spare car at Rio, Long Beach, Ricard, Imola, Monaco, Spa (raced by Boesel), Detroit, Montreal, Silverstone, Hockenheim (crashed during practice by Boesel and repaired), Zandvoort, Monza and Brands Hatch.

03 Modified from JS19. For Boesel at Rio, Long Beach, Race of Champions, Ricard, Imola, Monaco, Spa, Detroit, Montreal, Silverstone, Hockenheim, Österreichring, Zandvoort, Monza, Brands Hatch and Kyalami.

04 New for Jarier at Rio. For Jarier at Long Beach, Ricard, Imola, Monaco, Spa, Detroit, Montreal, Silverstone, Hockenheim, Österreichring, Zandvoort, Monza, Brands Hatch and Kyalami.

Lotus

While waiting for sufficient Renault engines to become available, Lotus prepared two Cosworth cars bearing the 92 type number, but based on chassis used in 1982. The first Renault-powered car, designated 93T, was eventually replaced by a new design, the 94T.

92

5 Converted to 1983 specification. Spare car at Rio and Long Beach. Spare car for Mansell at Ricard, Imola, Monaco, Spa, Detroit, and Montreal. Not seen again.

10 Converted to 1983 specification. For Mansell at Rio, Long Beach, Ricard, Imola, Monaco, Spa, Detroit and Montreal. Not seen again.

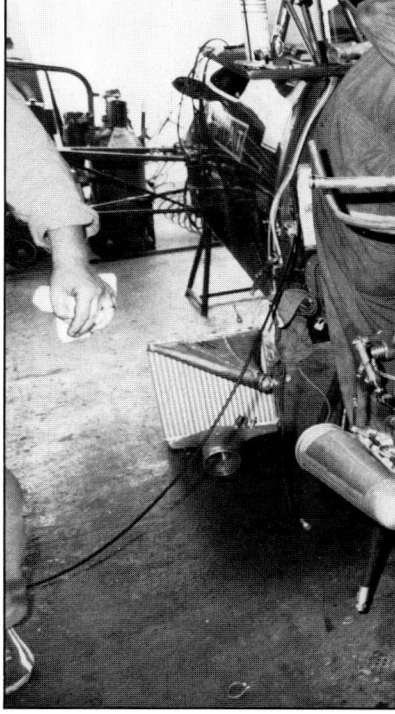

93T

1 New for de Angelis at Rio. For de Angelis at Long Beach, Ricard, Imola, Monaco, Spa, Detroit and Montreal. Spare car for de Angelis at Silverstone. Spare car at Hockenheim (raced by Mansell) and Österreichring. Not seen again.

2 New for Mansell at Race of Champions. Spare car for de Angelis at Ricard, Imola (raced by de Angelis), Monaco, Spa, Detroit and Montreal. Spare car for Mansell at Silverstone. Not seen again.

94T

1 New for de Angelis at Silverstone. For de Angelis at Hockenheim and Österreichring. Spare car at Zandvoort and Monza. (Raced by de Angelis). For de Angelis at Brands Hatch and Kyalami.

2 New for Mansell at Silverstone. For Mansell at Hockenheim, Österreichring, Zandvoort, Monza, Brands Hatch and Kyalami.

3 New for de Angelis at Zandvoort. For de Angelis at Monza (raced by Mansell). Spare car at Brands Hatch (crashed by de Angelis during practice) and Kyalami (raced by de Angelis).

McLaren

Continued to work with original MP4 chassis, uprating the 1982 MP4/1B cars to MP4/1C to comply with the new regulations. Used the Ford-Cosworth engine until the TAG (Porsche) turbo was ready to race in MP4/1E form — again, using converted MP4 chassis.

MP4/1C

2 For Watson at Race of Champions, Hockenheim, Österreichring and Zandvoort. Spare car at Monza and Brands Hatch.

4 Had been used for filming and show work but brought back into service as spare car at Hockenheim, Österreichring and Zandvoort.

5 Spare car at Rio, Long Beach, Ricard, Imola, Monaco and Spa. Converted to accept TAG turbo.

6 For Watson at Rio, Long Beach, Ricard and Imola. Spare car at Detroit, Montreal and Silverstone. Converted to accept TAG turbo.

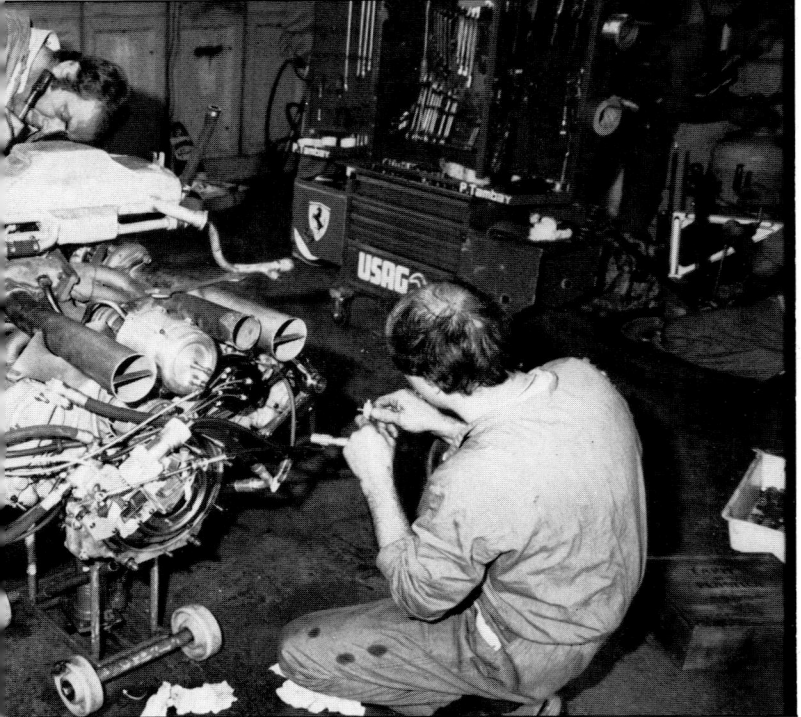

7 For Lauda at Rio, Long Beach, Ricard, Imola, Monaco, Spa, Detroit, Montreal, Silverstone, Hockenheim and Österreichring. Converted to accept TAG turbo.

8 New for Watson at Monaco. For Watson at Spa, Detroit, Montreal, and Silverstone. Destroyed in accident at factory while testing refuelling equipment.

MP4/1D

1 Original MP4 chassis used purely as test hack for TAG turbo engine.

MP4/1E

5 In paddock at Zandvoort, but not completed. For Watson at Monza, Brands Hatch and Kyalami.

6 For Lauda at Zandvoort, Monza, Brands Hatch and Kyalami.

7 Spare car at Kyalami (raced by Watson).

Osella

Uprated 1982 **FA1D** chassis and renumbered them. Built new FA1E to accept Alfa Romeo V12 mid-season.

001 For Fabi at Rio, Long Beach, Ricard, Imola, Monaco, Spa, Detroit and Montreal. Not seen again.

002 For Ghinzani at Rio, Long Beach and Ricard. Spare car at Imola, Monaco, Spa. Detroit and Montreal. Not seen again.

FA1E

001 A Cosworth chassis converted to accept Alfa Romeo V12 as interim measure. For Ghinzani at Imola, Monaco, Spa, Detroit and Montreal. Spare car at Silverstone, Hockenheim, Österreichring and Monza.

002 New for Fabi at Silverstone (raced by Ghinzani). For Fabi at Hockenheim, Österreichring, Zandvoort, Monza, Brands Hatch and Kyalami.

003 New for Ghinzani at Silverstone. For Ghinzani at Hockenheim, Österreichring, Zandvoort, Monza, Brands Hatch and Kyalami.

RAM March

RAM Automotive, retaining the March name, built a new car, the **RAM 01**, for the start of the season.

01 New for Salazar at Rio. For Salazar at Long Beach. Spare car at Ricard. Car disassembled; monocoque on hand at Imola.

02 New for Schlesser at Race of Champions. For Schlesser at Ricard. Spare car at Imola and Monaco. For Salazar at Spa. Spare car at Montreal, Silverstone, Hockenheim and Österreichring. Not seen again.

03 New for Salazar at Ricard. For Salazar at Imola and Monaco (crashed during practice). Repaired in the paddock at Spa. For Villeneuve at Montreal. For Acheson at Silverstone, Hockenheim, Österreichring, Zandvoort, Monza, Brands Hatch and Kyalami.

Renault

Rebuilt one 1982 RE30B to C-spec to comply with 'flat bottom' regulations and built two new **RE30C** chassis as interim measure while waiting for completion of RE40.

10 Spare car at Rio and Long Beach. Not seen again.

11 New for Cheever at Rio. For Cheever at Long Beach. Not seen again.

12 New for Prost at Rio. Spare car at Long Beach (raced by Cheever). Not seen again.

RE40

00 New for Prost at Long Beach. Spare car at Ricard. Became test and development car.

01 New for Prost at Ricard. Spare car at Imola, Monaco, Spa, Detroit and Montreal (raced by Prost). Not seen again.

02 New for Cheever at Ricard. For Cheever at Imola, Monaco, Spa, Detroit and Montreal. Not seen again.

03 New for Prost at Imola. For Prost at Monaco, Spa, Detroit and Montreal. Spare car at Silverstone, Hockenheim (raced by Prost), Österreichring, Zandvoort Monza (raced by Prost), Brands Hatch and Kyalami.

04 New for Cheever at Silverstone. For Cheever at Hockenheim, Österreichring, Zandvoort, Monza, Brands Hatch and Kyalami.

05 New for Prost at Silverstone. For Prost at Hockenheim, Österreichr-

ing, Zandvoort, Brands Hatch and Kyalami.

06 New for Prost at Monza. Spare car for Prost at Kyalami.

Spirit

Switched to Grand Prix racing by converting Formula 2 chassis 201 (4) to accept Honda V6 turbo. From lessons learnt during testing and at the Race of Champions, further developments on another F2 chassis – 201 (6) – led to a 'C' version and, by Monza, Spirit had produced their first pukka Formula 1 car, the 101.

(Note: 201 (5) sold to Jo Gartner for Formula 2 use during 1983.)

201 (4) For Johansson at Race of Champions. Spare car at Silverstone (raced by Johansson), Hockenheim, Österreichring (raced by Johansson), Zandvoort, Monza (raced by Johansson) and Brands Hatch (raced by Johansson).

201C (6) New for Johansson at Silverstone. For Johansson at Hockenheim, Österreichring, Zandvoort, Monza and Brands Hatch.

101 (1) Completed in paddock at Monza but not used. Spare car at Brands Hatch.

Theodore

The Theodore and Ensign teams combined at the beginning of 1983, using the former's name and the latter's cars. The Ensign type and chassis numbers were continued, the uprated cars becoming **N183** versions of the original N181.

16 Uprated 1982 car. Available at Ricard for spare parts only. Spare car at Imola. For Guerrero at Monaco, Spa, Detroit, Montreal and Silverstone. Spare car at Hockenheim, Österreichring, Zandvoort and Monza.

17 Construction of monocoque had been started during 1982. For Guerrero at Rio, Long Beach, Race of Champions, Ricard and Imola (crashed during race). Taken to Spa but repairs not completed. Spare car at Detroit, Montreal, and Silverstone, For Guerrero at Hockenheim, Österreichring, Zandvoort and Monza. Spare car for Guerrero at Brands Hatch.

18 New for Cecotto at Rio. For Cecotto at Long Beach. For Henton at Race of Champions. For Cecotto at Ricard, Imola, Monaco, Spa, Detroit, Montreal, Silverstone, Hockenheim, Österreichring, Zandvoort and Monza. For Guerrero at Brands Hatch.

Toleman

Toleman's 1983 car, the TG183, was designed and running in time for the final races of the 1982 season. The regulation change meant a revision to B-spec for the first race of 1983.

TG183B

01 Original car updated. For Giacomelli at Rio and Long Beach. Spare car at Ricard, Imola (raced by Warwick), Monaco, Spa, Detroit and Montreal. Not seen again.

02 New for Warwick at Rio. For Warwick at Long Beach, Ricard, Imola, Monaco, Spa, Detroit and Montreal. Spare car at Silverstone, Hockenheim, Österreichring, Zandvoort, Monza, Brands Hatch and Kyalami.

03 Completed in readiness for Ricard but crashed by Warwick

during testing. Rebuilt for Giacomelli at Ricard. For Giacomelli at Imola, Monaco, Spa, Detroit, Montreal, Silverstone, Hockenheim, Österreichring, Zandvoort, Monza, Brands Hatch and Kyalami.

04 New for Warwick at Silverstone. For Warwick at Hockenheim, Österreichring, Zandvoort, Monza, Brands Hatch and Kyalami (crashed by Warwick during testing but repaired).

Tyrrell

Rebuilt and modified **011** chassis used during 1982.

2 For Sullivan at Rio, Long Beach and Race of Champions. Spare car at Ricard. Damaged by Alboreto during testing at Spa. Not seen again.

4 For Alboreto at Ricard, Imola, Monaco, Spa, Detroit, Montreal, Silverstone, Hockenheim and Österreichring (damaged by Alboreto during race).

5 Spare car at Rio and Long Beach. For Sullivan at Ricard, Imola, Monaco, Spa, Detroit and Montreal. Spare car at Silverstone. For Sullivan at Hockenheim, Österreichring, Zandvoort and Monza.

6 For Alboreto at Rio and Long Beach. Stripped and rebuilt as spare car at Imola, Monaco, Spa, Detroit and Montreal. For Sullivan at Silverstone. Spare car at Hockenheim, Österreichring, Zandvoort, Monza, Brands Hatch and Kyalami.

012 introduced at Österreichring.

1 New at the Österreichring and used briefly during practice by Alboreto. For Alboreto at Zandvoort, Monza and Brands Hatch (raced by Sullivan). For Sullivan at Kyalami.

2 New for Sullivan at Brands Hatch (raced by Alboreto). For Alboreto at Kyalami.

Williams

Redesigned 1982 FW08 to suit new regulations. One 1982 car updated and two new chassis completed for Rio. Cars known as **FW08C** (FW08B being six-wheeler project abandoned after change to regulations). FW09-Honda introduced at end of season.

6 Spare car at Rio and Long Beach. For Rosberg at Race of Champions. Became test car and used by Palmer as race car at Brands Hatch.

7 New for Rosberg at Rio. For Rosberg at Long Beach, Ricard, Imola, Monaco, Spa, Detroit, Montreal, Silverstone, Hockenheim, Österreichring, Zandvoort, Monza and Brands Hatch (crashed by Rosberg during practice). Sold to Rosberg.

8 New for Laffite at Rio. For Laffite at Long Beach, Ricard, Imola, Monaco, Spa, Detroit, Montreal, Silverstone, Hockenheim, Österreichring, Zandvoort, Monza and Brands Hatch.

9 New at Ricard as spare car. Spare car at Imola, Monaco, Spa, Detroit, Montreal, Silverstone, Hockenheim, Österreichring, Zandvoort, Monza, Brands Hatch (raced by Rosberg) and Kyalami.

2 Brought to Brands Hatch as additional spare car following Rosberg's accident during practice.

10 and **11** Chassis completed but not required.

FW09 introduced at Kyalami.

1 For Rosberg at Kyalami.

2 For Laffite at Kyalami (crashed by Laffite during race).

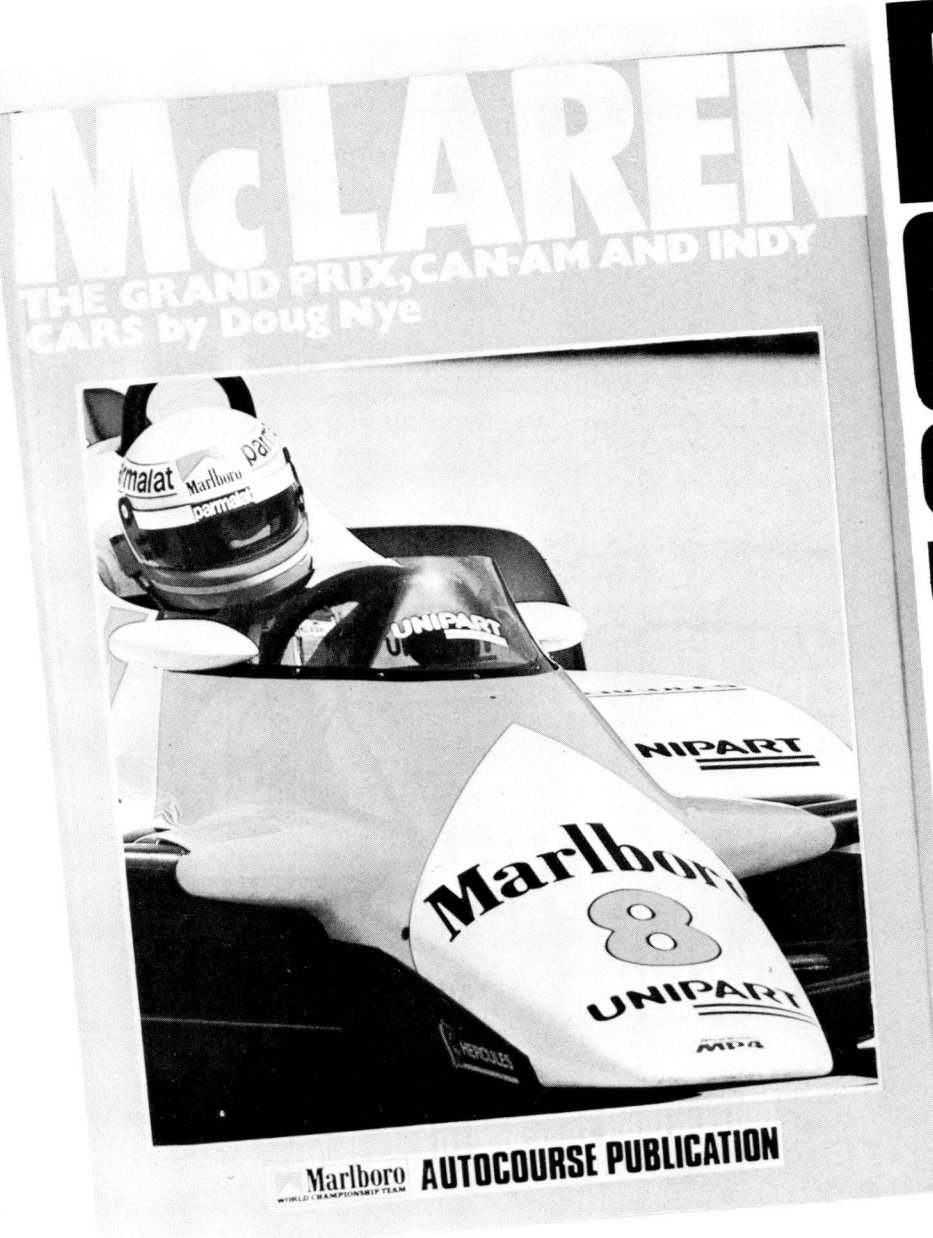

The season of 1983 Formula 1 racing will undoubtedly go down in history as the season of pit stops. Not untoward and unexpected pit stops to rectify trouble, but planned and calculated stops by more than half the starters in most of the Grand Prix races. Years ago routine pit stops for more fuel and new tyres were the normal order of things, especially in the days of alcohol-burning engines doing 1½ miles to the gallon and tyres that could not last the 300 mile race distances, and at all times the pits, or "boxes" as the French call them, have been an important part of the Grand Prix racing circuit. If they were not used for replenishment they were always available for quick repairs during a race, from changing a sparking plug to mending an oil pipe.

When Grand Prix racing was watered down in 1952 and 1953 with an engine limit of 2 litres without supercharging, refuelling stops began to die out and up to the end of the alcohol fuel era which finished at the end of 1957 they were to be avoided if possible. The new rules in 1958 which forced engine designers to use straight petrol, coupled with a reduction in race lengths, saw the end of pit stops for refuelling and new tyres and any car seen heading for the pits was clearly in trouble and out of contention. Indeed, in 1961 the Dutch Grand Prix was run at Zandvoort with a field of fifteen cars, none of which made use of the pits, all the cars running through non-stop and nobody having any mechanical trouble, which was an unprecedented situation.

The "mickey-mouse" Formula of 1961-65 which put a 1½ litre limit on engines, with no supercharging and no special fuels encouraged non-stop races even more so, and wheels were fixed on with five nuts because no-one visualized changing tyres during a race and some cars actually did three races on a set of Dunlops. The pits were merely signalling bases where a car headed for only if it was about to retire due to mechanical failure. The normal situation was that if you didn't keep running you had little hope of figuring in the results, so even inadvertent pit stops were anathema. The whole world of Formula 1 became so used to short races run non-stop that pit stops were something the newcomers knew nothing about. In the 1966 Formula for 3 litre cars or supercharged 1½ litre cars, everyone went for economical 3 litre engines and it was not until Goodyear and Firestone brought new technology into racing tyres with different tyres for different conditions that the possibility of the pits being used during a race arose again. In the early days of wet and dry tyres there were some comical scenes in the pit lane as teams learnt about changing wheels quickly. Anyone who had maintained an interest in long-distance racing never lost the art of pit stops, for they were regular happenings in 24 hour races and 1000 kilometer races. The Scuderia Ferrari benefitted from sports car knowledge when it came to changing from wet weather tyres to dry weather tyres during a Grand Prix. Pit stops were still to be avoided if possible, but most teams were fairly well prepared for emergency stops. One thing that the tyre revolution brought back was the quickly detachable wheel and a lot of progress was made in the design of single-nut wheel fixings.

In 1982 Gordon Murray and the Brabham team

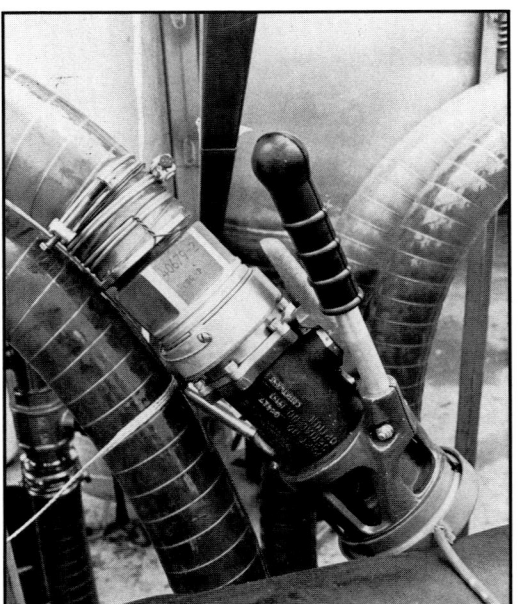

re-introduced a strategy that Maserati had used in the 1957 German Grand Prix on the Nürburgring. Without letting anyone know, the Maserati team started Fangio's 250F Maserati with only half a tank of fuel and the plan was to stop at half-distance, refuel and fit new rear tyres. With a tail tank holding 58 gallons of fuel the advantage in weight and handling with it only half full was enormous compared to rival cars starting with a full tank. In addition, in those days a pair of rear tyres just about lasted the race distance, and the final laps were a bit marginal. By fitting new tyres at the half-way point it meant that Fangio could drive really hard at a time when rivals' tyres were getting a bit worn, and he could drive hard to the finish. The strategy worked perfectly and when he stopped at the pits his rivals thought he was in trouble. By the time they realized what was happening and signalled their drivers Fangio was well and truly on his way, making up more than the time lost in stopping at the pits. His two main rivals had gone by while he was at the pits, but he caught and passed them easily before the end of the race. It was one of the classic races of all time, success coming through the surprise element and some inspired driving by the World Champion.

At the British Grand Prix at Brands Hatch in 1982 the Brabham team planned to start Nelson Piquet with half a tank of petrol and on relatively soft tyres that would be at their best for half the race distance. The pit stop would see another half tank full of petrol put in and a new set of tyres fitted and the calculation was that the advantage gained in the early part of the race might be lost while the car was at the pits, but it could be regained in the second half of the race as Piquet would be on new tyres specially selected for the second half. It was even possible that Piquet could gain so much advantage in the first half, with less weight and better tyres, that he could make the pit stop and rejoin the race within the time gained, which was in the order of 30 to 40 seconds, allowing 15 seconds for the stop and 20 to 25 seconds for slowing down and coming into the pit lane and accelerating out and back up to race speed. Rival cars would be starting with twice the weight of petrol and harder tyres which would have to last the full race distance, so they would have no hope of keeping up with the Brabham and even if they went by while it was stationary at the pits, they would be

Pit Stops: A split-second spectacle

by Denis Jenkinson, Grand Prix Correspondent, *Motor Sport*

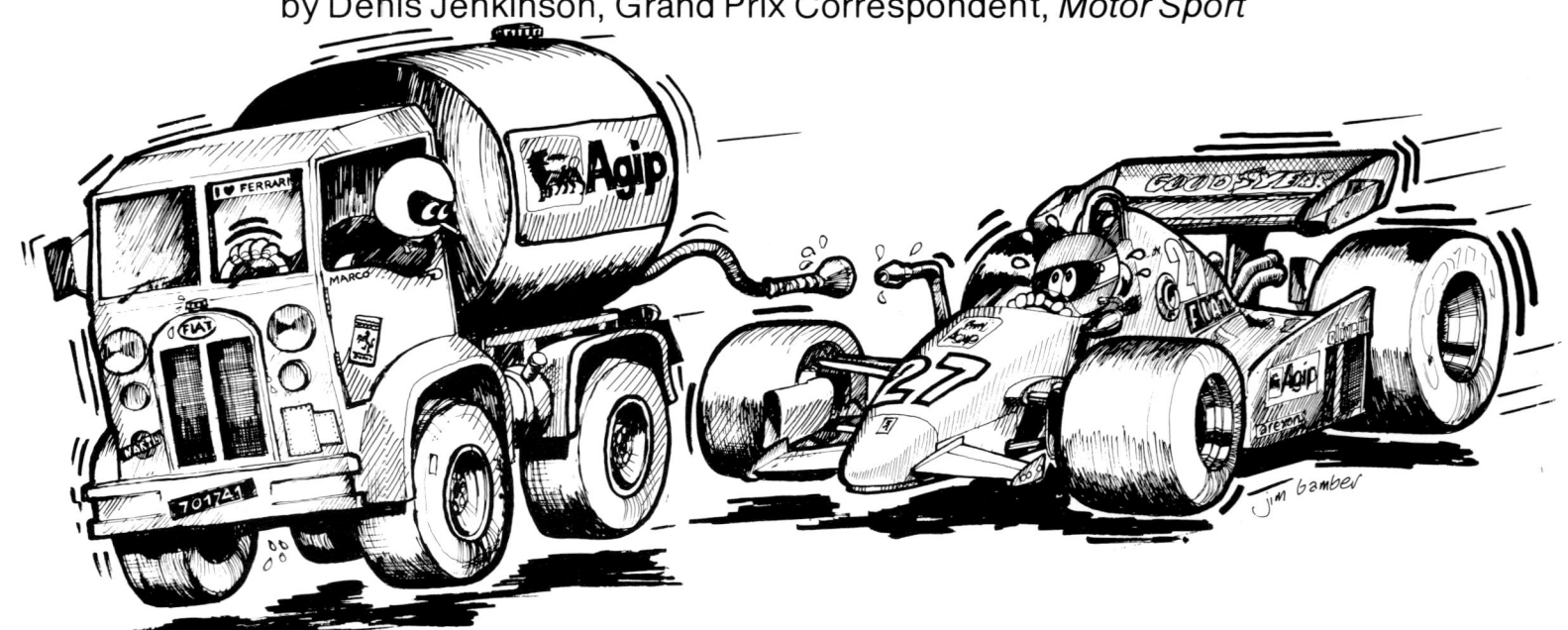

heading into the second half of the race with tyres that were wearing down and losing grip, whereas the Brabham could restart with new tyres which could go a lot faster right through to the finish. It was a very interesting situation.

Murray did not approach this idea lightheartedly; he studied Indianapolis pit-stops and NASCAR pit stops closely and sent two of his key mechanics to the Indy 500 mile race to watch things closely and to study equipment and methods used by the Americans to save split seconds during their mandatory pit stops. He drilled his teams of mechanics to a razor sharp efficiency and spent a lot of thought on time-and-motion study and the use of a video-recorder to perfect techniques. They practised in secret in the workshop and when they first tried a practice run at a circuit they surprised the onlookers with their speed and efficiency. The changing of all four wheels and putting in about 25 gallons of petrol was easily done in around 14 seconds. Their attempts to put the whole idea into practice in a race were frustrated by unreliability with their BMW turbo-charged engines, for the engines kept breaking before Piquet could get to the half-way point of a race and many people wrote the whole idea off as a silly gimmick, or they forgot about it. The overall Brabham plan was to do it with both cars, Nelson Piquet and Riccardo Patrese, and in the Austrian GP everyone suddenly sat up and took notice. Although Piquet ran into trouble early on, Patrese pulled out an impressive lead, stopped at the pits, refuelled and changed tyres and was back in the race just as the second place man came into view. The Murray calculations had worked perfectly and Patrese had the race in the bag, but unfortunately total success still eluded them for the BMW engine blew up shortly after the pit stop.

From that point on everyone took Murray's idea seriously and one-by-one the other big teams began to do sums and decided that it was a good idea. Even some of the teams who do little more than make up the end of the field began to plan organised pit stops on the Murray principle, though it was difficult to see why. The result has been that in 1983 Brabham, Williams, McLaren, ATS, Lotus, Renault, Alfa Romeo, Ligier, Ferrari and Toleman have all been running their races in two-halves with a pit stop for petrol and tyres around the mid-way point. There were some pretty hilarious practice runs carried out by some of the teams while they were learning the techniques and everyone was aiming for a time of around 14 seconds, but Brabham were honing their act and aiming for a sub-ten second stop. One team doing a dummy run in the pit lane at one Grand Prix became hopelessly muddled and by the time the stop had reached 45 seconds they had lost control of the situation and abandoned the whole thing in complete chaos. By mid-season everyone had become so proficient at the business that little was being lost or gained, though the stops have introduced an unknown factor into Formula 1 racing, in-as-much-as a bungled pit stop could affect the outcome of a race. Nobody was likely to win a race by a good pit stop but they might well lose one by reason of a bad pit stop. At most races the order of the first half-dozen cars is the same after they have all made their routine stops as it was before, as a bungled stop is the exception rather than the rule, though times can vary from 10 seconds to 15 seconds for the car to be stationary. Apart from the performance gained by less weight and softer tyres the strategy means that fuel consumption is not so critical.

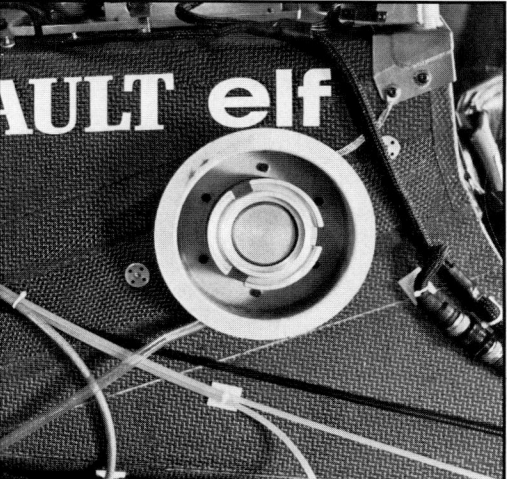

Tank capacities are restricted to 250 litres and as fuel consumption equates to power output with a turbo-charged engine and power output equates to boost pressure it means that the engineers can run higher boost pressures with greater power output and not have to worry so much about consumption. If 250 litres was marginal for getting through a race, you could start with 130 litres and take on another 130 litres half way through, to give the effect of extra tankage, which would not be allowed normally.

Each team had its own ideas on pit stop equipment and most followed the Brabham lead, but the basic system of operation was the same for all. There was no restriction on the number of mechanics employed so the usual thing was to have one at each end of the car with a quick-lift jack, one to put the petrol in, one to control the venting of the tank, two to each wheel and a controller ahead of the car. This added up to thirteen people round the car as a minimum, and practical space considerations did not encourage any more. Other team members stood by in readiness, or to retrieve the wheels and tyres that were taken off, or support the flexible fuel hose, while engineers tended to be close by just in case any problems arose. The controller, who was usually a chief mechanic or a team engineer, stood at the point where the nose of the car should be when it stopped. He held a board for the driver to aim at and this was sometimes in the team colours, or bearing the car number or the word STOP or BRAKE. The Renault team's board had the car number, 15 on one side and 16 on the other, for Prost and Cheever, respectively, and beneath each number the imprint of a large bare foot, to indicate "foot on the brake pedal". Ferrari used a polystyrene marker board that the nose of the car could actually bump into without causing any damage. Stopping at the exact spot was vitally important and there were cases of drivers misjudging their braking and over-shooting and Lauda was disqualified for reversing back to his pit in Hockenheim after over-shooting. Even a foot or two of misjudgement could waste time because it meant that all the waiting mechanics had to reposition themselves before they could start work. To enable the driver to stop accurately, the teams stuck coloured tape on the pit lane surface to indicate the line into the pit area and four "boxes" were marked on the ground

continued on page 68

. . . it was no fun standing by at the ready in two layers of fire-proof clothing under a blazing hot sun and then have your car break down two laps before it was due in

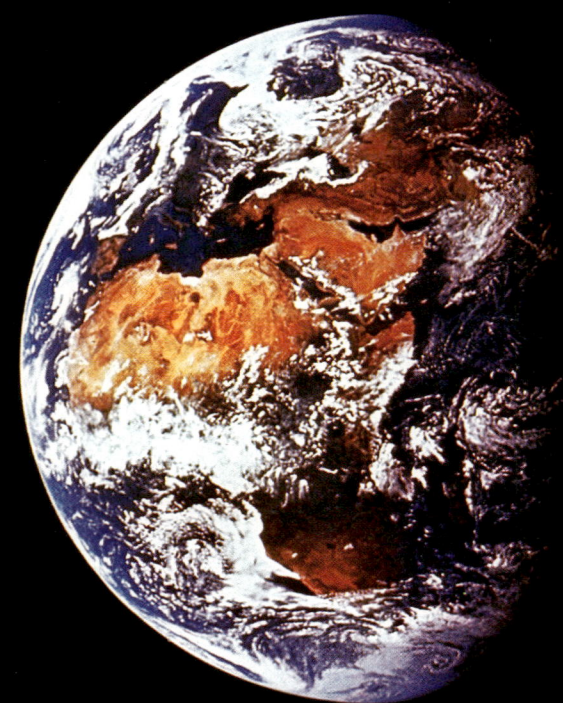

'The earth was made so vast
that you may travel its open spaces.'

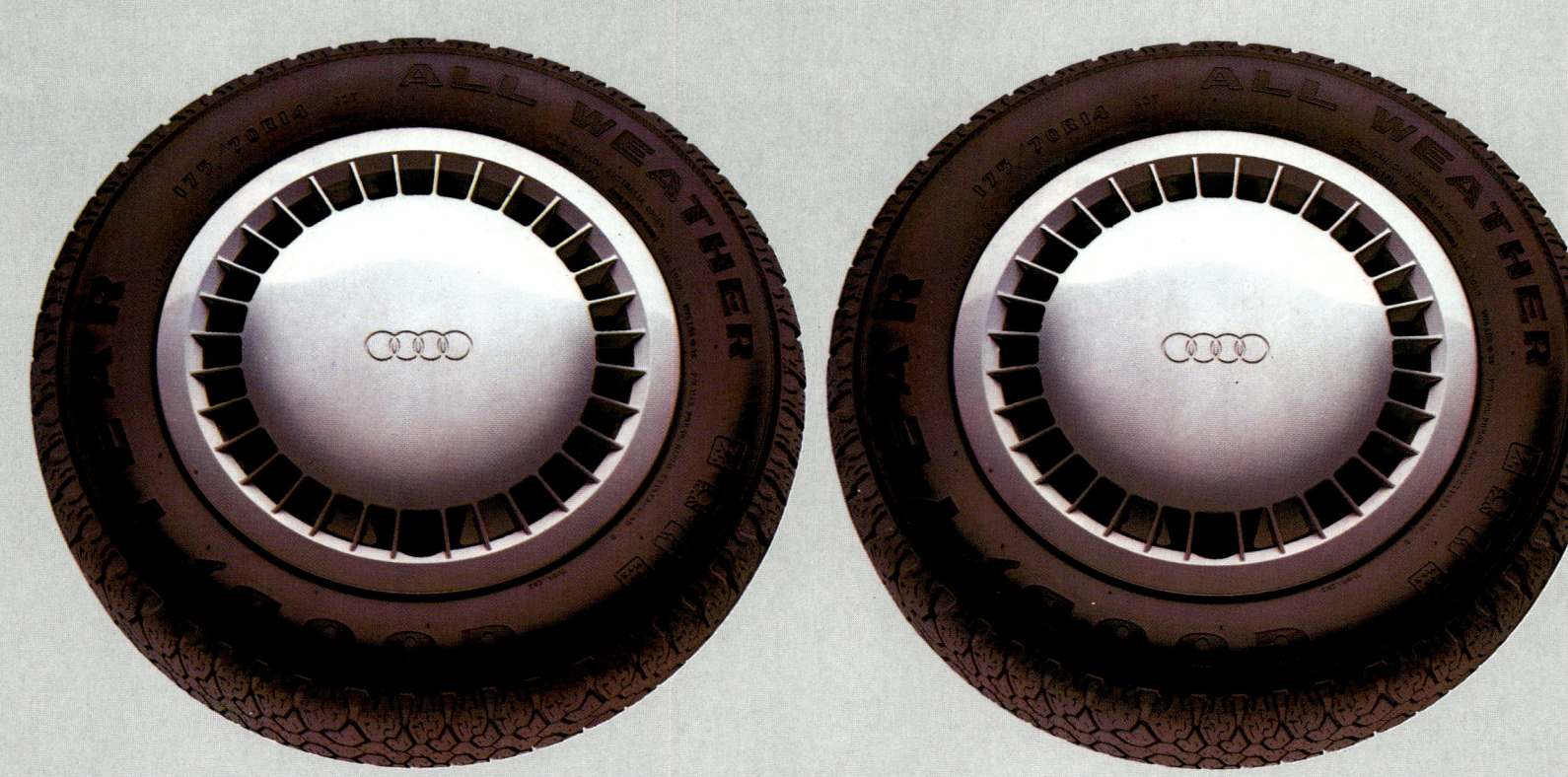

You use them all
why not use the

The very first cars in the world had 2-wheel-drive. And that basically is the way it's been ever since.

Odd, when you consider that almost everything else about a car has evolved beyond recognition. Especially when you realise the advantages 4-wheel-drive gives you.

The engine can spread its power to all 4 corners of the vehicle.

This is what gave the Land Rover the degree of grip across fields and rivers that made it famous.

And Audi, who pioneered front-wheel-drive fifty years ago, are now pioneering permanent 4-wheel-drive for high perform-ance cars.

The first car to feature this was the Audi Quattro.

The car that has taken almost every Rally Championship going.

Now, Audi are using the same system for the Audi 80 Quattro.

When you drive the car it feels more stable. In the dry and in the wet. Around corners, on ice.

Everywhere.

One motoring journalist described i

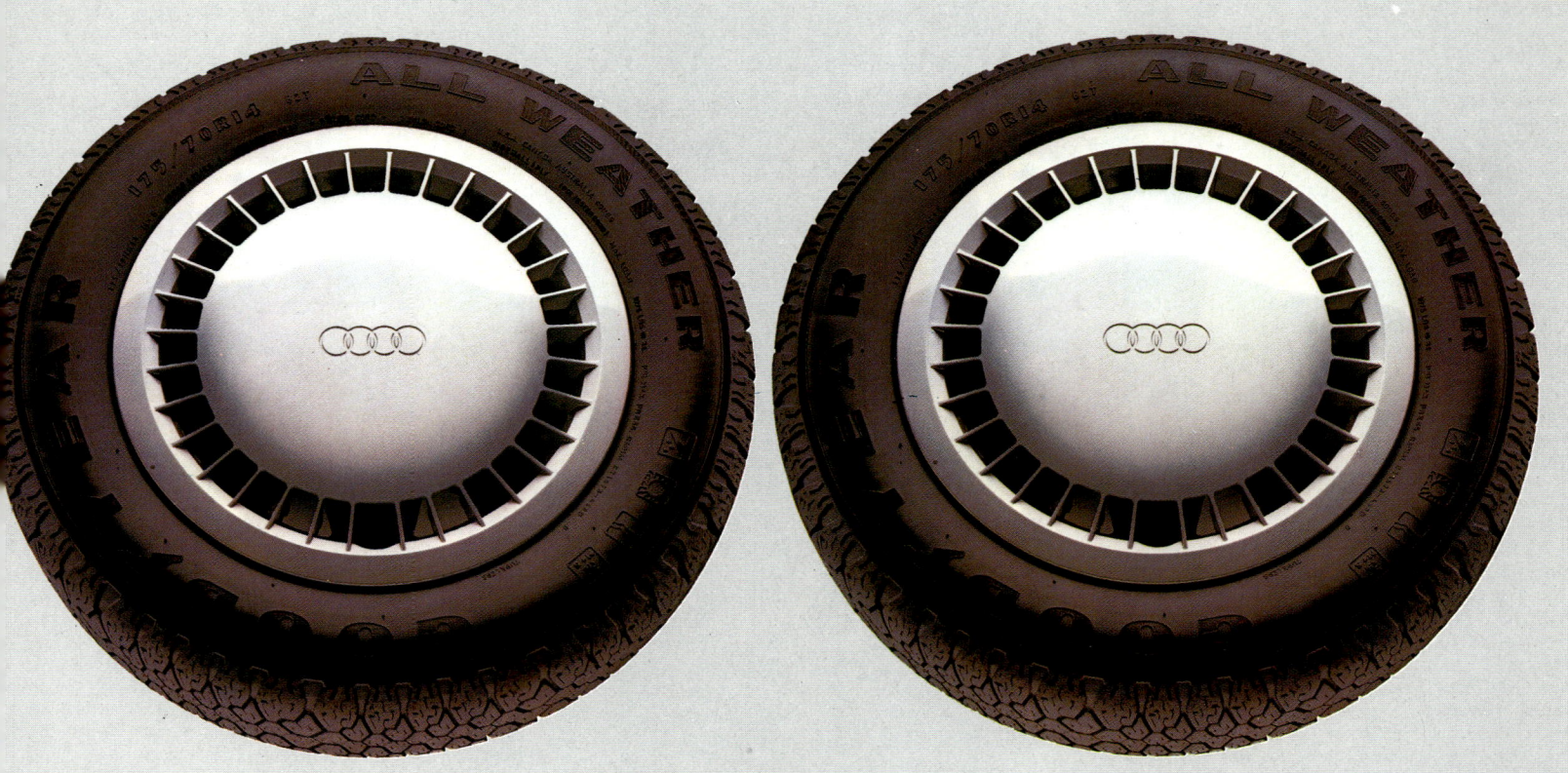

o brake your car,
m all to drive it?

as feeling 'welded to the road'.

Quite an achievement when you realise it's powered by a fuel-injected 2.2 itre engine producing 136 bhp. It reaches 60 mph in 7.5* seconds and has a top peed of 120 mph.

Of course, the Audi 80 Quattro oesn't make you invincible. Careless or thoughtless driving will still cause ccidents.

What it will do, is greatly reduce the chance of being caught out by black ice, f aquaplaning, of drifting out on a corner hat's being taken too fast.

It gives you, quite literally, twice the grip of a comparable 2-wheel-drive car.

Fortunately it's not twice the price. The Audi 80 Quattro sells for £11,474 ■

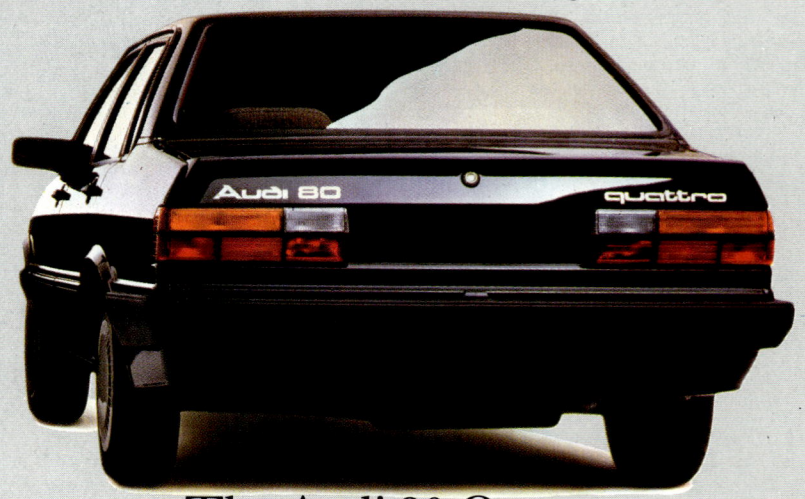

The Audi 80 Quattro

SOURCE: CAR MAGAZINE: BROCHURES FROM AUDI MARKETING: V.A.G (UNITED KINGDOM) LTD, YEOMANS DRIVE, BLAKELANDS, MILTON KEYNES MK14 5AN. TEL: (0908) 679121. EXPORT AND FLEET SALES, 95 BAKER STREET, LONDON W1M 1FB. TEL: 01-486 8411.

into which the wheels would fit if the driver was 'spot-on' line. When Brabham first employed this pit-stop routine they carefully marked out the pit road with sticky tape and the incoming line. While they were not looking, some wag applied more tape to the ground taking the incoming line sharply to the left, across the pit road and up and over the pit wall and back onto the track! With eleven teams marking out the line they wanted their drivers to take, the pit road was a sea of multi-coloured lines and, not surprisingly, a driver has been known to follow the wrong line and miss his own pit.

Standing by each wheel box marked on the ground were two mechanics, one with a compressed air operated wheel-nut spanner like a large hand-drill, and one holding a new wheel and tyre. On the pit side of the car stood the mechanic with the refuelling hose-pipe and on the other side, a mechanic with a similar hose running behind him into a collector tank. When the car stopped, the four mechanics with the pneumatic hammers removed the wheel nuts and took off the old wheels, while the number two mechanic put the new one on and the first mechanic then tightened the nut. When the job was done they leapt back with arms held high. As the nuts were being undone, the car was jacked up by the mechanics at the front and rear and as soon as all four pairs of wheel mechanics had their arms raised, the car was dropped off the jacks and the jacks were pulled out of the way. Meanwhile, the refuelling mechanics had fixed their bayonet-fitting hose fillers to the tank fillers and as the petrol rushed into the tank from one side, the air and petrol vapour in the tank escaped out of the other side and into the collector tank. As soon as the filling operation was complete, both mechanics unclipped their hoses and leapt well back and that was the signal for the controller to step aside which was the signal for the driver to let in the clutch and get back into the race.

A lot of consideration was given to the safety and well-being of the mechanics working on the car during a stop and everyone was conscious of the fire risk with petrol under high pressure, so they all wore fire-proof underwear and overalls, fire proof balaclavas and full face crash helmets with fire-proof visors, and of course, fire-proof gloves. This sort of equipment was absolutely essential for the two mechanics operating the refuelling hoses, but also made sense for the wheel-changing mechanics for they were concentrating 100% on their job and if a fire did start they would never know until they were engulfed by flame. The mechanics who operated the wheel-nut spanners equipped themselves with plastic knee pads, strapped to their legs, so that they could fling themselves at their job, which entailed at least one knee being on the ground, without fear of damage. While it may have been glamorous and satisfying to be part of the pit-stop team it was no fun standing by at the ready in two layers of fire-proof clothing under a blazing hot sun and then have your car break down two laps before it was due in.

The driver had a strict routine to follow, preplanned with his engineers before the start of the race and he had to remember a number of things. If, for example, it had been planned to make the pit stop on lap 35, then the team signallers gave the driver a "count down" as he went by. This varied with the teams, Ferrari giving a 3, 2, 1 and Brabham giving a 5, 4, 3, 2, 1 "count down". As the driver continued to race on the 'coming in' lap, for he may have been nose-to-tail or even wheel-to-wheel with a rival car that was not stopping, he had to remember to approach the last corner of the lap at a different speed and often on a different line, and he aimed to arrive in the pit lane as quickly as possible, but not too quick. He had to pick out his guide line, aim the nose of the car at it and judge his braking to perfection, for a car that slid right past the pit with all the wheels locked up was of no interest to anyone in the pit stop game. Having stopped, the driver had to do a number of things; he had to keep his foot on the brake pedal to prevent the wheels turning as the mechanics undid the nuts, and with the side of his foot he operated the accelerator pedal to prevent the engine stalling. Depending on the type of engine, he kept it running at 5000 or 6000 rpm or even more, while the lucky Ferrari drivers did not have to touch the throttle pedal as the Maranello

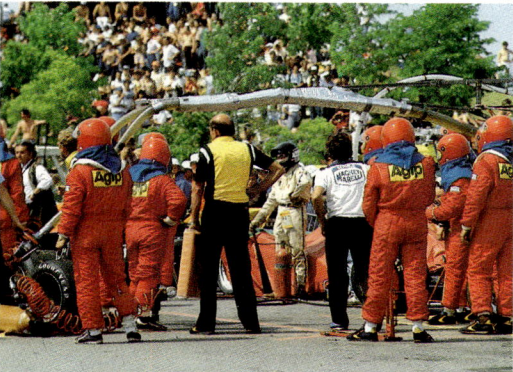
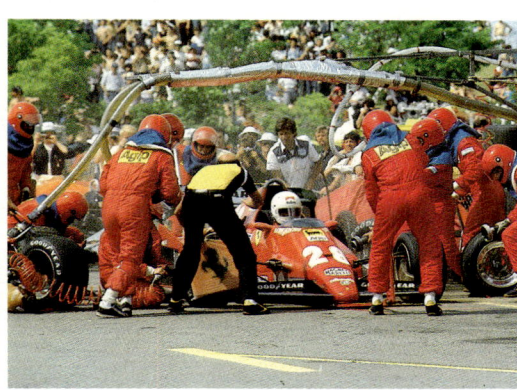
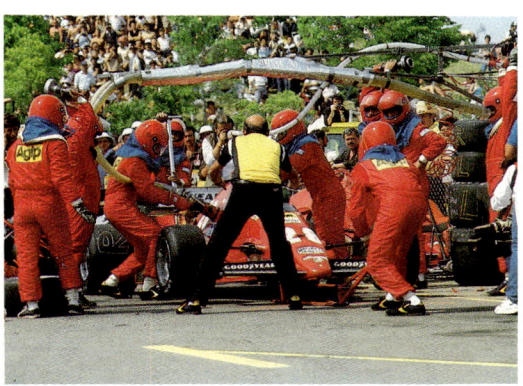
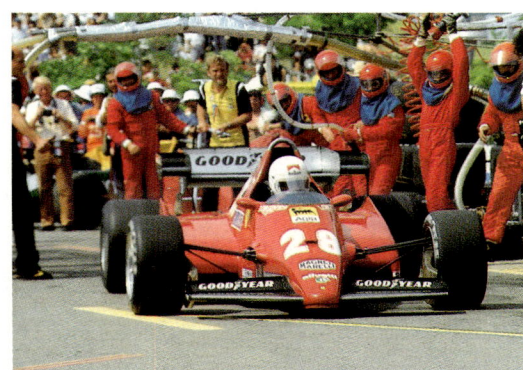

Pit stops made an excellent spectacle for television but did little for the spectators at the track. Arnoux's leading Ferrari is dealt with at Montreal.
Photos: Mike Levasheff

turbo-charged V6 was happy to be left idling at tick-over speed, even when everything was very hot. Each engine and car had its own characteristics which decided what the driver did with his right foot apart from keeping the brakes on. As he came to rest, the driver moved the gear lever into neutral as a general rule, though there were some who left bottom gear engaged and kept their left foot on the clutch pedal, but this practice could damage the clutch or overheat it. As there were only 10 to 12 seconds involved in these stops, as soon as he had come to rest in neutral, he had to be ready to engage first gear again, ready for the off and this he aimed to do as he felt the car

dropping off the jack. Many good pit stops were spoilt by the driver being late in getting back into first gear. Everyone had leapt away from the car and it didn't move! You then saw that the driver was still fumbling to engage first gear. The whole time the car was at the pit, the driver kept his eyes on the team controller for he was the key man and his movement backwards or sideways was the signal for "GO". The driver then had to do the best standing start sprint that he could and rejoin the track as quickly as possible, but this part of the manoeuvre was often dictated by the layout of the pits. It was not over yet for the driver for new tyres were going to handle and perform differently to the worn ones he had been racing on just before he stopped.

When Brabham started the pit stop game they were using Goodyear cross-ply tyres and they found it an advantage to warm up the new tyres in a hot air cupboard just before the pit stop. Depending on the ambient temperature of the day Ferrari continued to do this with their Goodyears, but Brabham changed to Michelin for 1983 and found that pre-heating the French radial tyres was not necessary. Renault and McLaren were also on Michelin tyres and found the same thing. Reading the input given to you by the tyres as you corner, to know how near the limit of adhesion you are is one of the mystical properties required by a good racing driver, and while some can evaluate the tyres very quickly others are relatively slow. This was shown up by the lap times immediately before and after a pit stop and the most remarkable was Nelson Piquet, for his very first lap after his stop was invariably as quick as those he was doing before he stopped. He openly admitted that what he was doing was "risky" but quickly added "you have to take risks if you are going to win". He reckoned to "feel" the tyres on the first two corners after leaving the pits and from then on he was back on the limit. He laughed as he said "if I make a misjudgement of the information the tyres give me in those two corners I could have a big accident". Other drivers were less sensitive, more cautious and positively careful, estimates of "knowing the new tyres" varying from one to two and a half laps. One driver was convinced his tyres had taken three laps to reach working temperature after his stop, yet his lap time showed that his first of the three was his fastest! The perceptive driver watched his front tyres change colour under cornering loads and could read the pattern, while others drove blindly until "Blisters" appear on the shoulders of the tyres and then it was too late, the damage was done.

Back in the pits the mechanics could pack everything up if they only had one car in the race, but if there were two, then they prepared to receive the second one. The usual thing was to have a petrol container and refuelling hoses for each individual car and these varied from galvanised steel beer barrels as used in pubs where the beer comes up from below by pressurisation, to purpose-built steel tanks mounted on vast portable trolleys. Teams such as Brabham or Williams used beer barrels painted in the team colours and pressurised them from air bottles, the pressure varying from 15 psi to 60 psi depending on the ideas of the engineers. The regulation beer barrels were safe to 100 psi and one team made an iron-clad test-rig in the workshop and pumped a barrel up to 120 psi without it exploding, though they did admit that it "bulged a bit". Everyone used some form of industrial or aircraft bayonet locking filler cap in which the petrol would not flow until the hose fixing was turned and locked in place and similarly, the moment the hose end was turned to unlock the valve in the filler cut off the flow. It was the same with the vent pipe the other side and while some teams vented into a tank sitting on the ground, others, like Toleman routed their vent hose back over the car and into a rubber fuel tank in a container at the back of the pit. At Indianapolis a press-on filler connection is in use, but unless it is absolutely square-on you could get leakage, and while a small leak of methanol fuel is not serious, no-one in Formula One was prepared to risk a leak of highly volatile petrol. The Indy type of filler might save one second, but the risk was not worth it.

In all the other operations involved in pit stops it was essential to avoid what Gordon Murray calls the *continued on page 72*

Two names that take Porsche to the limit.

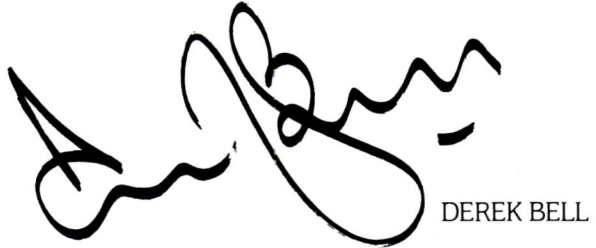

DEREK BELL

Currently, Guild of Motoring Writers Driver of the Year.

Three times winner of Le Mans and many other endurance races.

The type of performance and potential that Porsche demand.

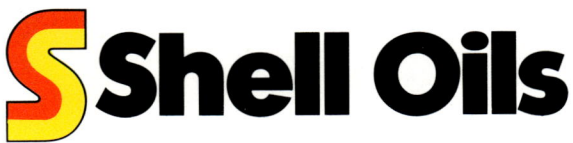

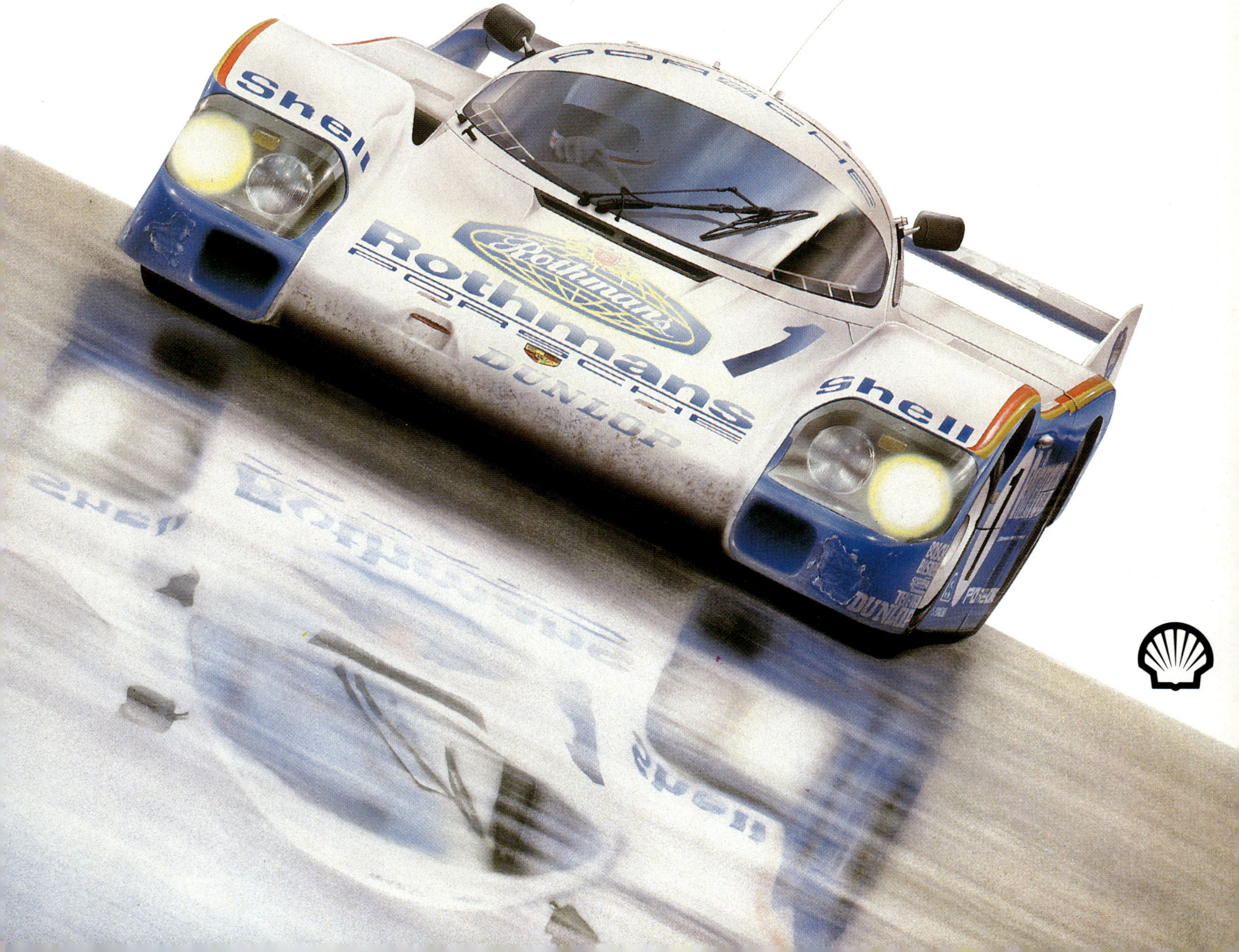

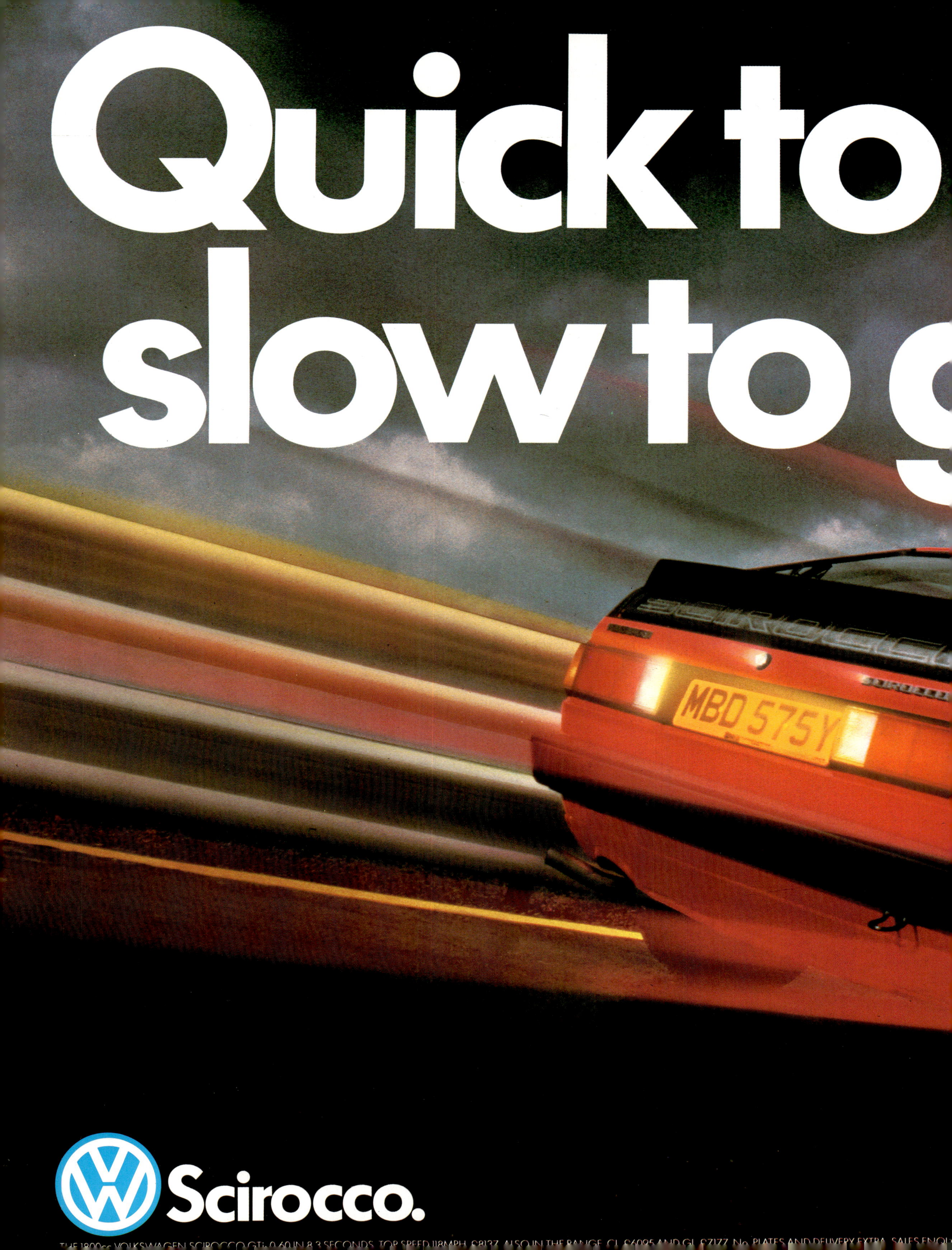

Quick to slow to g

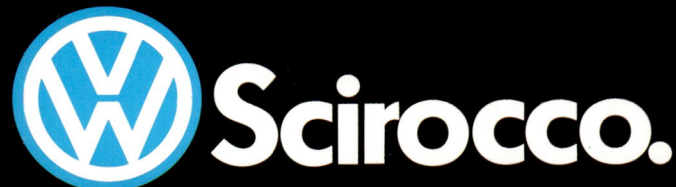

Scirocco.

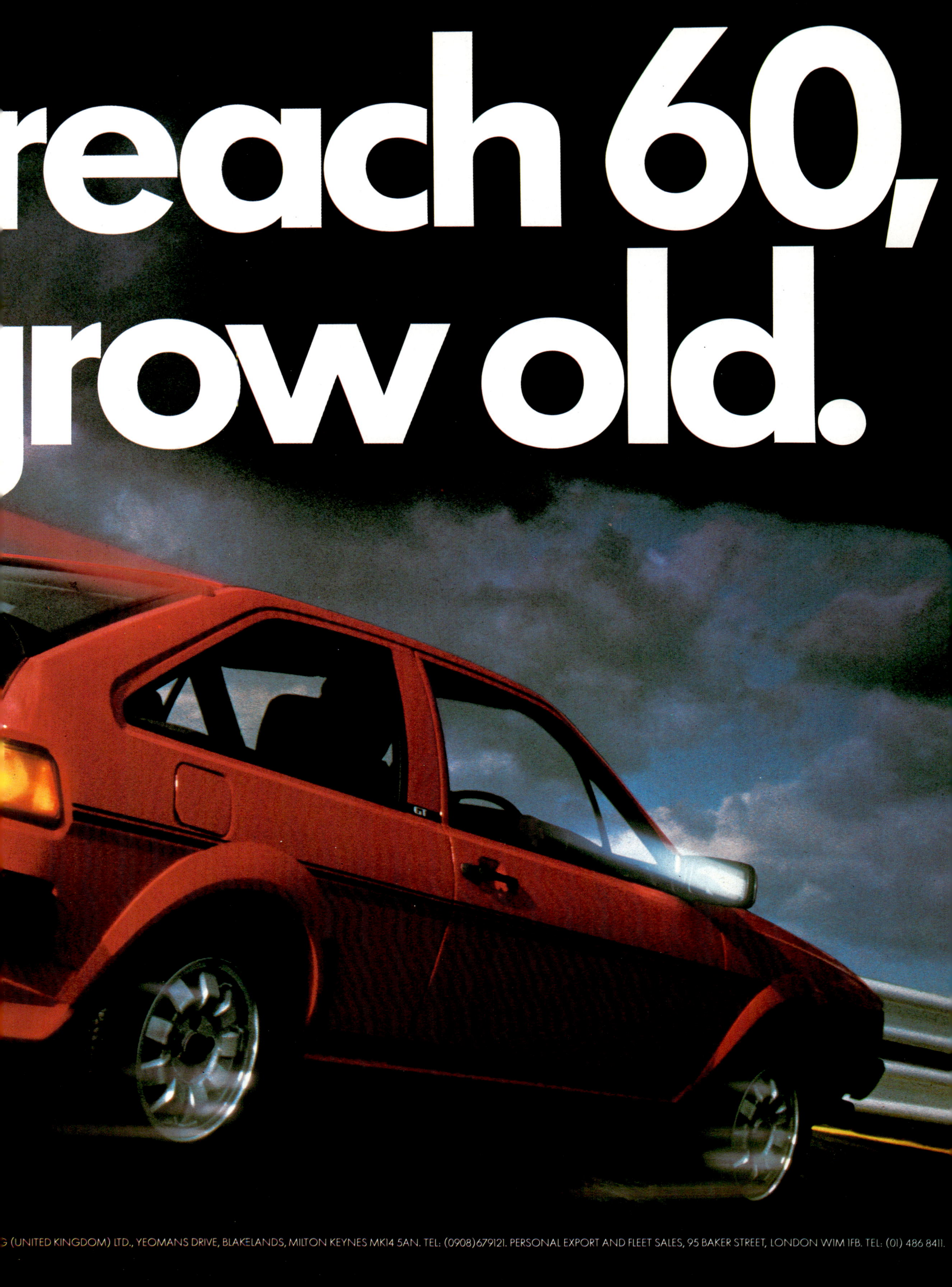

reach 60,
grow old.

G (UNITED KINGDOM) LTD., YEOMANS DRIVE, BLAKELANDS, MILTON KEYNES MK14 5AN. TEL: (0908)679121. PERSONAL EXPORT AND FLEET SALES, 95 BAKER STREET, LONDON W1M 1FB. TEL: (01) 486 8411.

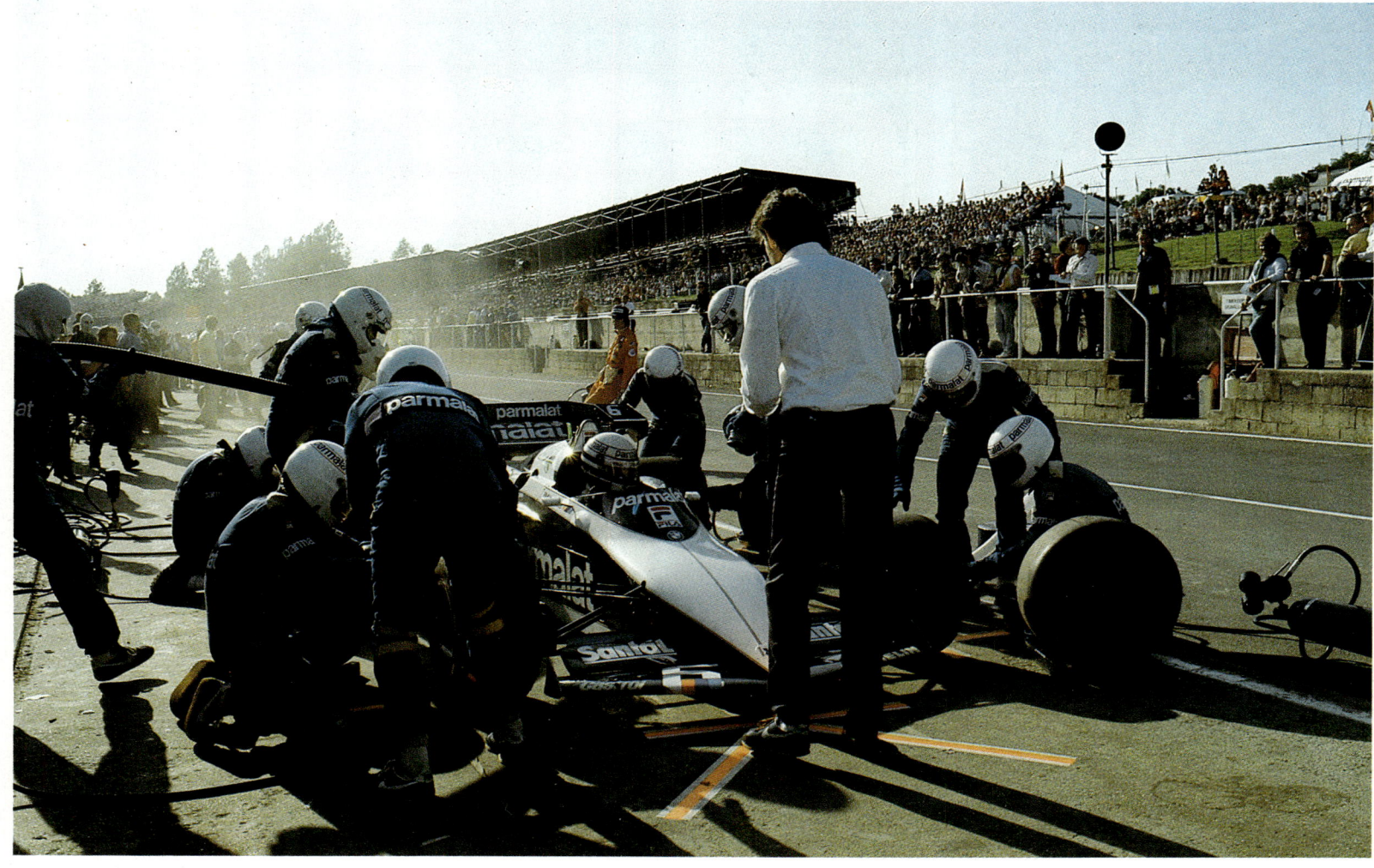

"fumble factor" and one operation that was vital was the removal and replacement of the wheel nut. Murray perfected a system of special wheel nuts that were fixed to the wheel, so each wheel had its own nut. Everyone used a single nut fixing, but sizes varied from the small inch-diameter ones used by Lotus to the 5 inch diameter ones used by Ferrari. If you were not prepared to go to the trouble and expense of making special captive nuts for each wheel then you tried to ensure that time was not wasted in putting the nut back on. Ferrari used a big taper 'lead' on the hub before the threaded portion and others used some form of rubber O-ring to retain the nut in the pneumatic hammer-gun. Lotus machined a groove in the nut itself to take the rubber ring which the hammer-gun hexagon then gripped, while Toleman fitted an O-ring into the gun hexagon. Some teams experimented with the second mechanic having a new nut at the ready so that they could let the old one roll away and slap on the new one, but without doubt Murray's captive nut was the best solution. Apart from eliminating the risk of a dropped nut or a fumbled fitting it meant that as soon as the new wheel was on the drive-pegs the nut was lined up with the thread ready for tightening. The nut held in the gun system demanded that it was offered up squarely and accurately before pressing the trigger to tighten it. A standard practice in Formula 1 is for all wheel nuts to be coloured coded, blue for left and red for right.

Jacking the car up when it stops was a fairly straight forward business and most teams used their normal quick-action lever jacks, the one at the front having a flat pad that lifted the car under the front of the monocoque, while at the rear the usual thing was to have a lever jack which engaged on a hook at the back of the gearbox. Actual operation of those two jacks could be a little tricky and the two mechanics had to work as a team for it was all too easy for them to get out of syncronization and work against each other. If the front jack worked on a parallelogram lever system then the car had to move forward slightly as it rose, in which case the rear jack needed to have wheels on it and be a long-handled simple lever affair and the forward movement of a few inches could be absorbed

by the wheels. It was no use having parallelogram movement jacks at each end, otherwise the two jacks would fight each other. The neatest arrangement of all was the Brabham system of built-in pneumatic jacks; these were small telescopic units operated by air pressure and there was a single unit in the nose of the car, attached to the front bulkhead just to the right of the brake master-cylinders, and one on each side at the rear attached to honey-comb material panelling just inboard of each rear wheel level with the rearmost extremity of the tyre. The three jacks were coupled by flexible piping and the feed line ran to a socket mounted above the gearbox, to the right of the rear aerofoil mounting. The mechanic operating the system merely plugged in an air-line from a compressed-air bottle, pressed the trigger release and the three telescopic jacks lifted the car two or three inches clear of the ground. When all the mechanics working on the wheels had finished their job he released the air pressure, the telescopic jacks withdrew and dropped the car back onto the ground.

There were some embarrassing moments in the early experimental days of these air jacks during testing sessions, when one would suffer a malfunction and only one corner at the rear would go up or only the front one would work. The worst time was when they were being used to change wheels during a normal practice session, not a pit-stop practice, and while the mechanics went away to get some more wheels, leaving the wheel-less car on its three jacks, something went wrong and the car sat down on its belly! Since their use in pit-stops they have worked perfectly and the system was typical of Murray's approach to the problem and team-owner Ecclestone's dictum of "if we are going to do something we will do it properly and spare no expense." Results have consistently shown the Brabham team to be the pit masters at routine pit stops, with times of just over 10 seconds and one actually well under 10 seconds, while practice runs in the workshop with everything cool and without the fever of race day have seen times as low as 8½ seconds to change all four wheels and put 20 gallons of petrol in.

It did not take long under actual race conditions to realize that the limiting factor on time was the speed at

Gordon Murray re-introduced planned pit stops to Formula 1 in 1982. The Brabham team went on to set the standards throughout 1983, their slick professional routine whittling down the time taken to refuel and change tyres from 14 to under 10 seconds. Murray supervises Patrese's pit stop at Brands Hatch.
Photo: Diana Burnett

which you could pump in the petrol, for study of video-films of pit stops often showed that the wheel mechanics finished their job in 10 seconds and it was taking another 2½ seconds for the refuelling mechanics to finish their work. Once more the Brabham team led the way and after analysing the petrol flow system and pressurisation they changed their strategy. There was no reasonable way of reducing the time taken to put in, say 25 gallons, so the alternative was to reduce the time by putting less petrol in and this was accommodated in the overall race pattern by starting with a bit more than half a tank full, and leaving the pit stop until well past half race-distance, so that not so much petrol was needed to complete the race.

As would be expected all the top teams soon perfected the pit-stop art and in general figures there was little to choose between Brabham, Williams, McLaren, Renault, Lotus or Ferrari but Brabham, who instigated the idea, maintained a slight edge over everyone else. At some races you could look at the race order before anyone did a pit stop and then again after they had all been in, and you would not detect any difference, even in the gaps between the cars. While not being a decisive factor in Grand Prix races, the planned pit stop brought in an interesting new factor and provided added interest for television viewers. The number of spectators who witnessed the stops at a circuit were minimal, though they all saw the results and effects. At the Italian Grand Prix at Monza Nelson Piquet was the last driver to make a routine stop and the Brabham work and strategy operated to perfection for he was in the lead the whole time that everyone else was making their stops and when he made his, the Brabham mechanics had him away in 10.15 seconds and he was back in the race before the second place Ferrari was even in sight of the pits.

Every Formula 1 racing driver has one on the end of his left foot.

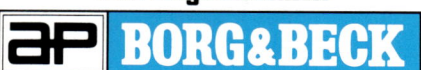

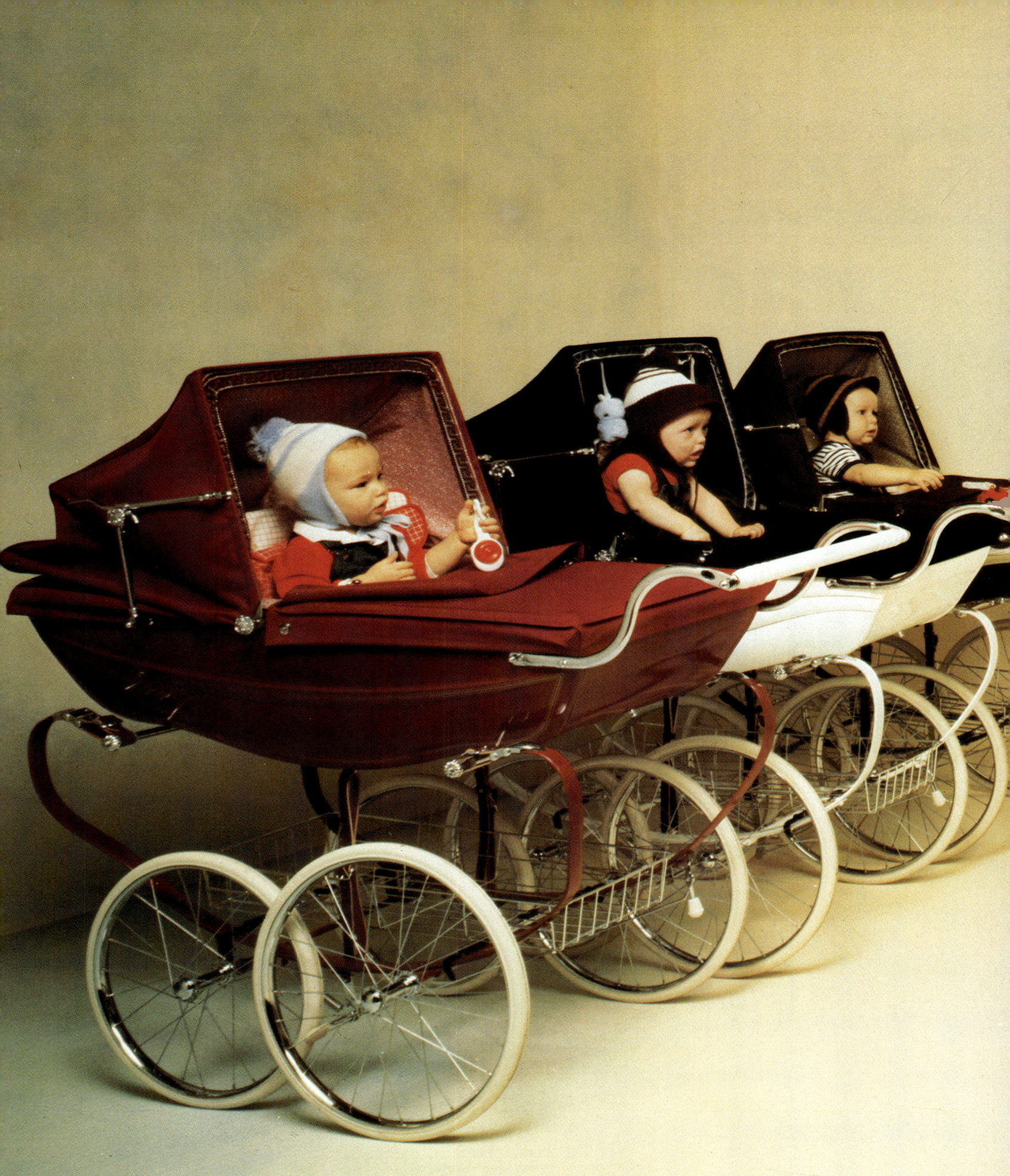

When Stirling Moss was very very young, we realised he had the potential to become a top Grand Prix driver.

So we gave him a little bit of a push.

We also noticed the same kind of potential in drivers such as Nelson Piquet and Derek Warwick.

Now there are more young hopefuls showing promise, including Britain's latest Grand Prix prospects.

We've always been able to spot a future champion.

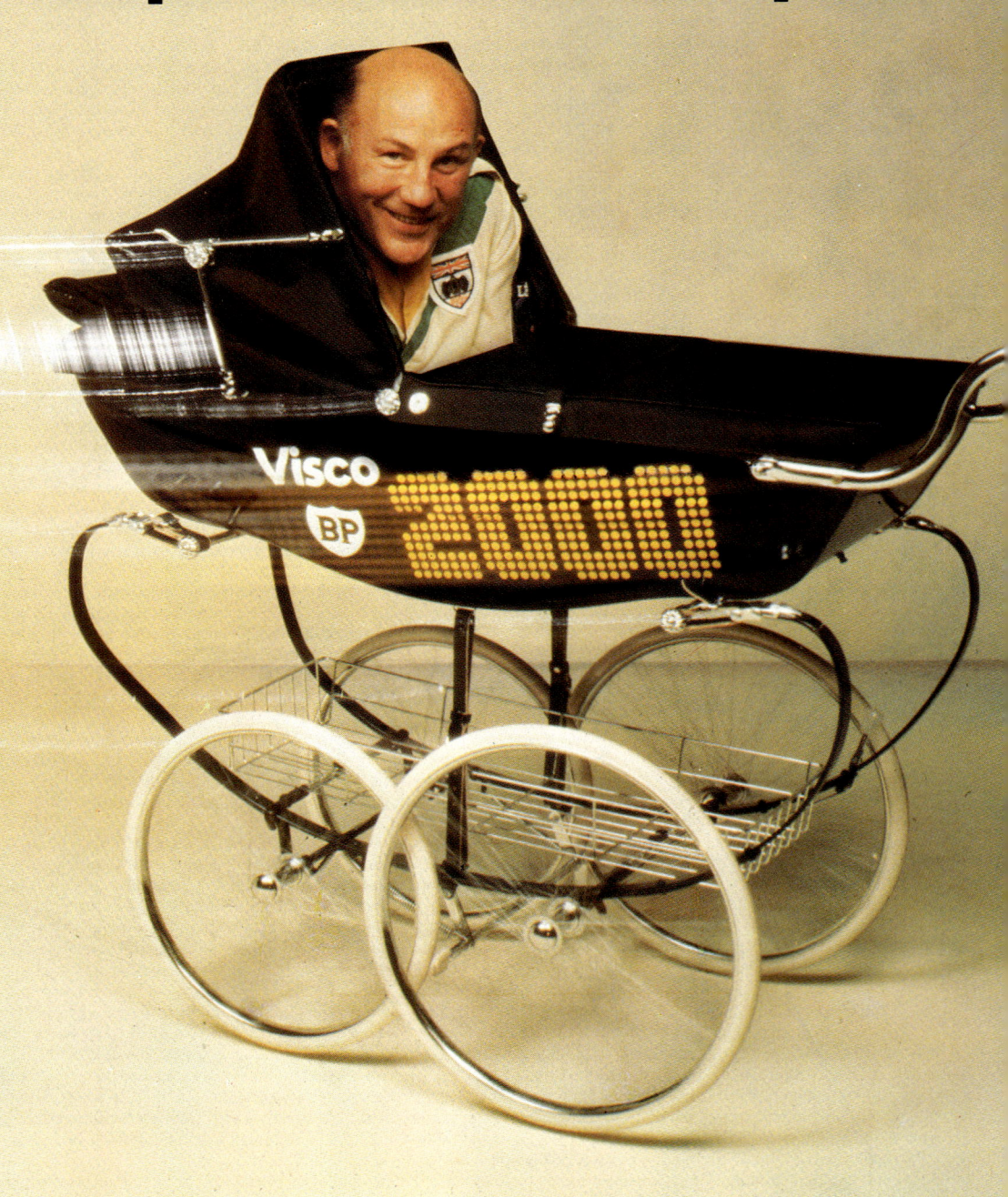

And we aim to keep these young drivers on the right tracks by giving them early backing and sponsorship.

They'll be doing us a few good turns by testing and researching our lubricants. And as long as we don't rest on our laurels, we should see a few sterling performances in Formula 1 racing over the next few years.

In the ten years since Jackie Stewart retired from racing, the three-times World Champion has remained a familiar figure in the pit lane, his jaunty walk and shrewd observations as much a part of Formula 1 in 1983 as they were when he worked his way towards 27 Grand Prix victories. In an exclusive feature, JYS talks to **Nigel Roebuck**, Grand Prix Correspondent of *Autosport*, and gives his usual forthright comments on the changing face of Grand Prix racing during the past decade.

"There are times," says Jackie Stewart, "when I wonder if I ever drove a racing car. And there are other times when it seems like only yesterday I was getting confused by gear ratios, suspension settings and other people going faster. A decade may seem like a long, long time, but for me it seems to have passed in a flash . . ."

It is, astonishingly, ten years since we saw Stewart on a starting grid, watched him strut – always on the balls of his feet, Moss-style – down a pit lane, pause by a blue car, push back fashionably long hair and don the spotless white helmet with tartan band. It is ten years since we witnessed the inevitably perfect start, assertiveness into the first corner, confident lead at the end of lap one.

If I have a single memory of Stewart's racing career, it would have to be the British Grand Prix of 1973, his final appearance in this country. As they approached Becketts on the first lap, Ronnie Peterson had the Lotus 72 in the lead, with JYS behind. Not a moment too soon the black car braked for the corner – but the blue one appeared not to. Down the inside came the Tyrrell, neatly through and away. And Ronnie, disbelieving, could only shake his head. Thirty seconds into a race Jackie had the cool and confidence to pull a stunt like that . . .

"I believe that God gives all race drivers – at Grand Prix level, anyway – a gift, in greater or lesser degrees. But there's so much more to it than just knowing how to work pedals and steer a wheel. You need the right mental attitude to channel your talent properly, get the most from it. It's terribly bad to be up or down. You must be neutral, because emotions are the most dangerous and damaging elements a driver can face. If I was good at anything, it was eliminating emotions, which is why I was always fairly sharp and together in the early stages of a race."

At the end of that 1973 season, which brought his third World Championship, Stewart announced his retirement. He was just a few months past his 34th birthday, at the height of his driving powers, and most were shaken by his decision. Everyone knew you retired when you were too old or too slow, but Jackie started something of a trend, since followed – often unsuccessfully – by others.

"When I stopped, I think it showed that you could do it early. After all, everyone *wants* to retire from driving racing cars. The only alternatives are dying in one or reaching a point where no one asks you to drive one, so of course everyone wants to retire. But the time must be right. I've had no withdrawal symptoms at all because the time *was* right for me, but if you do it too early then it becomes a burden in your life.

"Niki Lauda retired too early, and came back. Alan Jones did the same, and he's since dabbled with it. Jody Scheckter also stopped too soon, and I believe he's got a hankering to drive again – although probably not in Formula 1. I think the only guy after me who got out at the right time was James Hunt. He did the right thing because the danger aspect was really starting to get to him, and he had the courage to admit it.

"I think maybe one of the reasons why I've had no regrets is that my business life stimulates me as much as my driving did. Believe me, there *is* life after motor racing! One way and another, though, it did provide the springboard for most of my work today, and I still love coming to races. Jody, you see, hates doing that. He gets bored, and I get the feeling that he can't really picture himself at a race – except as a race driver. When I'm there, I'm totally divorced from that. Either I'm commentating or working for a sponsor or just simply enjoying myself. I went to Austria, for example, on holiday with my two sons, and I had a great time, hanging around and seeing friends and keeping up with the gossip. And the fact that Jody's not really interested in that suggests to me that he didn't really

get the driving out of his system."

Through that easy Dumbarton drawl, laced with mid-Adlantic phraseology, Stewart's words are always sharp and perceptive. In 1974, the year after his retirement from the cockpit, he attended nearly all the races, and after practice would announce, through Elf, his prediction for Sunday afternoon. Often his forecast seemed curious, but he was nearly always right. At the Nürburgring, for example, he tipped Clay Regazzoni for the only time that season. And Gianclaudio led from start to finish – for the only time that season . . .

Consider his words in April 1979. Gilles Villeneuve had won the last two Grands Prix, with Ferrari team mate Scheckter second in each, yet – "I think Ferrari will be World Champions this year, and I think in the end it will be Scheckter. Gilles, I think, is not quite ready to be World Champion, but Jody is. He's not a totally dominant winner at this time, like Gilles, but he's got the chemistry to make things happen. He won't do as much leading as Gilles, not by a long way, but over the season I think he'll score more points . . ." And the season was a mirror of those words.

Stewart's perspicacity, allied to a willingness always to say what he thinks, means that his opinions are eagerly sought, even when he is not directly involved with a particular topic or controversy.

"There's no doubt," he says, "that the present generation of drivers feel there is more pressure today than ever before. But that is only because, while they were coming along and in their early years of Formula

"emotions are the most dangerous and damaging elements a driver can face"

1, there was very little testing and development work. In terms of tyre development, the sport had stagnated. Now, from 1970 to 1973 we were testing every bit as much as they are today. The tyre war was very vibrant at that time. We would go to Kyalami for a couple of weeks – and we'd do two Grand Prix distances each day! There would be nine mechanics, two chassis and nine engines!

"So I don't go along with this 'pressure' bit today. It is only that there has been nothing to compare it with for 10 years. The teams got themselves into a position where they didn't need to test so much. Those sessions were *very* expensive, and as soon as the tyre companies stopped paying for them they stopped – apart from Ferrari, that is."

Jackie's opinions on the great drivers of the last decade are typically forthright. In evaluating driving talent, his terms of reference are clear: it is all-important to make the best of your ability, to translate it into success . . .

"I don't believe in bad luck, that's the first thing. I believe in *good* luck, but not bad. People who get known for having 'bad luck' are usually those who produce circumstances which don't eliminate 'bad luck', and Chris Amon was the supreme example of that. A nice guy with enormous natural talent, but very disorganised, and that got in the way of success for him. He had tremendous ability – yet never won a Grand Prix. Remember Clermont Ferrand in 1972? He was leaving us behind, and would have *walked* the race, but he got a puncture. That circuit was always peppered with very sharp stones, and I concentrated everywhere on driving *inside* the line, to keep away from them. I certainly didn't drive a brilliant race that day – but I did win it, and I don't consider he lost it through 'bad luck'.

"In natural car control and ability, Ronnie Peterson got a very high marking, but in my opinion he wasn't a *complete* driver. I admired Ronnie's driving very much, the seat-of-the-pants thing, but beyond that there was a lack of mental application which stopped him from winning more Grands Prix. And that was also true of Gilles Villeneuve.

"More than anyone else, Gilles reminded me of Jochen Rindt. But during Jochen's last year and a half he matured mentally to the point that he got the best out of his ability. I don't think Gilles ever reached that point, but he might well have done if he'd been given more time. I think his natural ability to drive a race car was almost unbounded – sheer unadulterated spirit

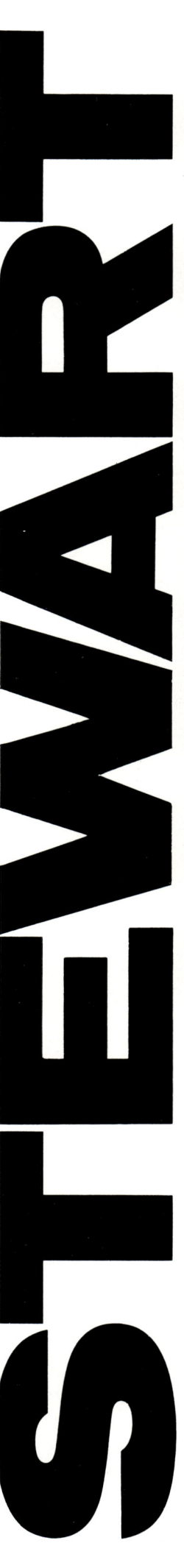

The familiar sight of a white helmet with the tartan band poking out of the cockpit of a blue Tyrrell-Ford.
Photo: Nigel Snowdon

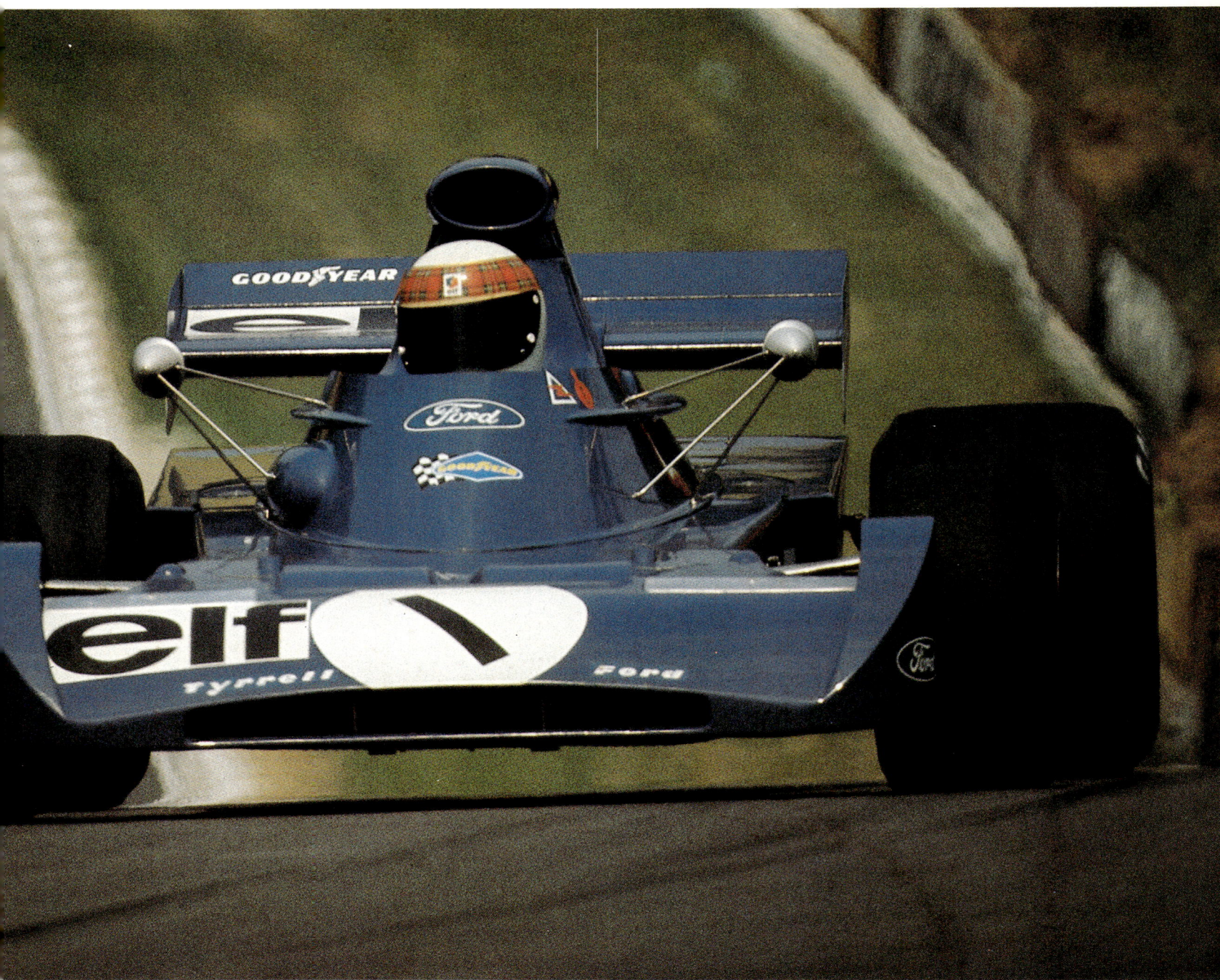

and feel. He was a great car control artist – and 'artist' is the right word in his case – but I think his talent was abstract. I will never understand, for example, why he would try to get those wrecks back to the pits. To me, that showed a lack of logic. How can he not have *known* that his race was over for the day – with a rear wheel hanging off?

"Now I understand well why Gilles was revered, and always will be. He was so exciting, wasn't he? It was the same with Ronnie and Jochen – but none of them won anything like the number of races their talent warranted. In his last season Jochen was less exciting to watch – but he started winning. I think maybe there has to be a trade-off . . ."

It comes as no surprise that Stewart particularly admires those drivers whose approach to the business is similar to his own. "Niki Lauda, in my opinion, brought to the World Championship the right kind of driving – smooth, clean, very clinical, the kind of talent I would have been proud to have. A lot of people say no, they like to see a man drive with his heart rather than his head, and certainly those are the drivers who are remembered as heroes. But don't tell me Fangio wasn't clinical about the way he went racing, or Jimmy Clark. The successful ones are *always* clinical."

Stewart's considerable admiration for Lauda stems partly from the Austrian's strength of character. "That came through in several ways: first, he turned Ferrari around, got them to do things his way. That's never easy to do at Maranello, because the Commendatore has his own ideas, and he *is* the Emperor and he *has*

won more races than anyone else. Ferrari has outlasted every other racing organisation over the years, but it's not a place for the faint of heart.

"Second, Niki's return at Monza, after his Nürburgring accident, was the most courageous thing I have ever witnessed in sport. He was by no means completely healed, and had no right to be driving there. That raised him significantly in my estimation – as did his decision to pull out in Japan soon afterwards.

"It was that, of course, that allowed James Hunt to capture the World Championship. In his day James was a talented and forceful driver, although his championship was not a classic one. For a while, though, the combination of Lauda and Hunt was an intoxicating mix.

"Now what of the others? I liked the attitude of Alan Jones, who was forceful *and* intelligent in a car. When I'm at a race I like to go out to corners, and I think I know what I'm looking for. I recall the British Grand Prix in 1979, where I watched at Stowe. Silverstone is very quick, and very few people drive at the limit there. Alan impressed me a lot. I think his natural ability was high.

"Carlos Reutemann was too much on and off. If he felt like it, he was superb, but often you could forget he was in a race. His temperament was far too emotional, and that stopped him from being great. And although Mario Andretti had very high natural ability, he compromised it by being over-aggressive. A little more calmness – especially during the early laps – would have brought him much more success.

"I think it is sad that the world will not remember Emerson Fittipaldi nearly as well as it should. He had great natural skill and excellent mental attitude, but there isn't a man alive who can keep himself super-competitive when the machinery is off the pace year after year. I believe he would have brought more honour to Brazil by winning more races and World Championships than by driving Brazilian cars carrying a Brazilian flag . . ."

As Jackie says, it remains his pleasure to go to the races, and when talking of today's drivers his basic terms of reference remain in force. There are those who make the most of themselves, and those who do not.

"Piquet and Prost impress me particularly. If you look at either of them just before a race, you'll see that they're perfectly calm, not excited, not depressed. And that's how you must be. They both know how to make the best of their ability, and they drive very intelligently. Piquet, when he needs to, has the discipline to turn down the boost, accept that he has a problem and isn't going to win today. And Prost, as we saw in Austria when he got after Arnoux, can turn on all the aggression you could want. Both of them have this ability to win by the simplest means possible, and that to me is a sign of real class. For me they're the best of the moment.

"Arnoux, on the other hand, is very hyper. Eyes can tell you a lot about a racing driver, and if you look at his you'll see that they dart around constantly. That

continued on page 82

77

Goodyear reve[their Formu[

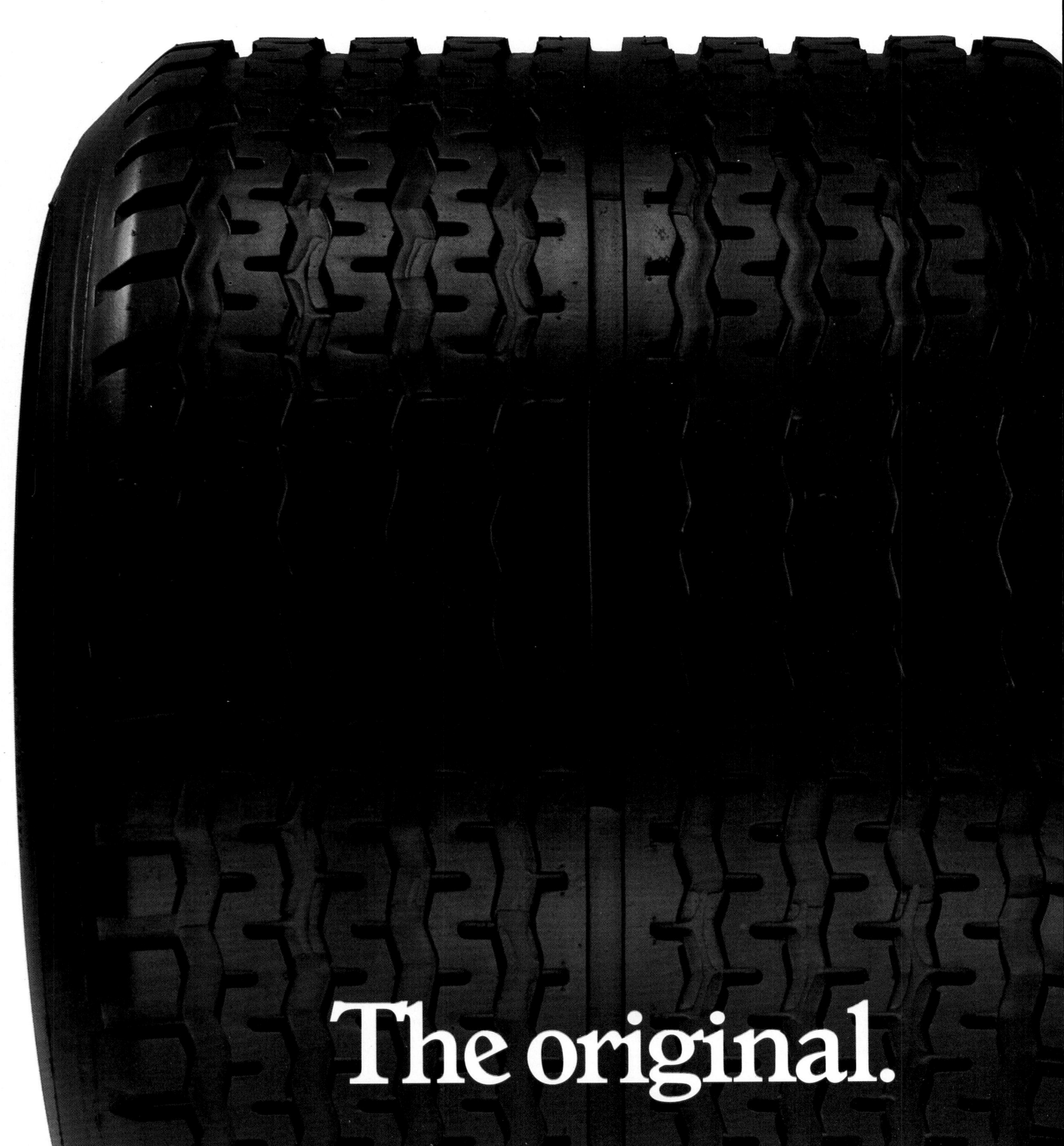

The original.

l a close copy of a l rain tyre.

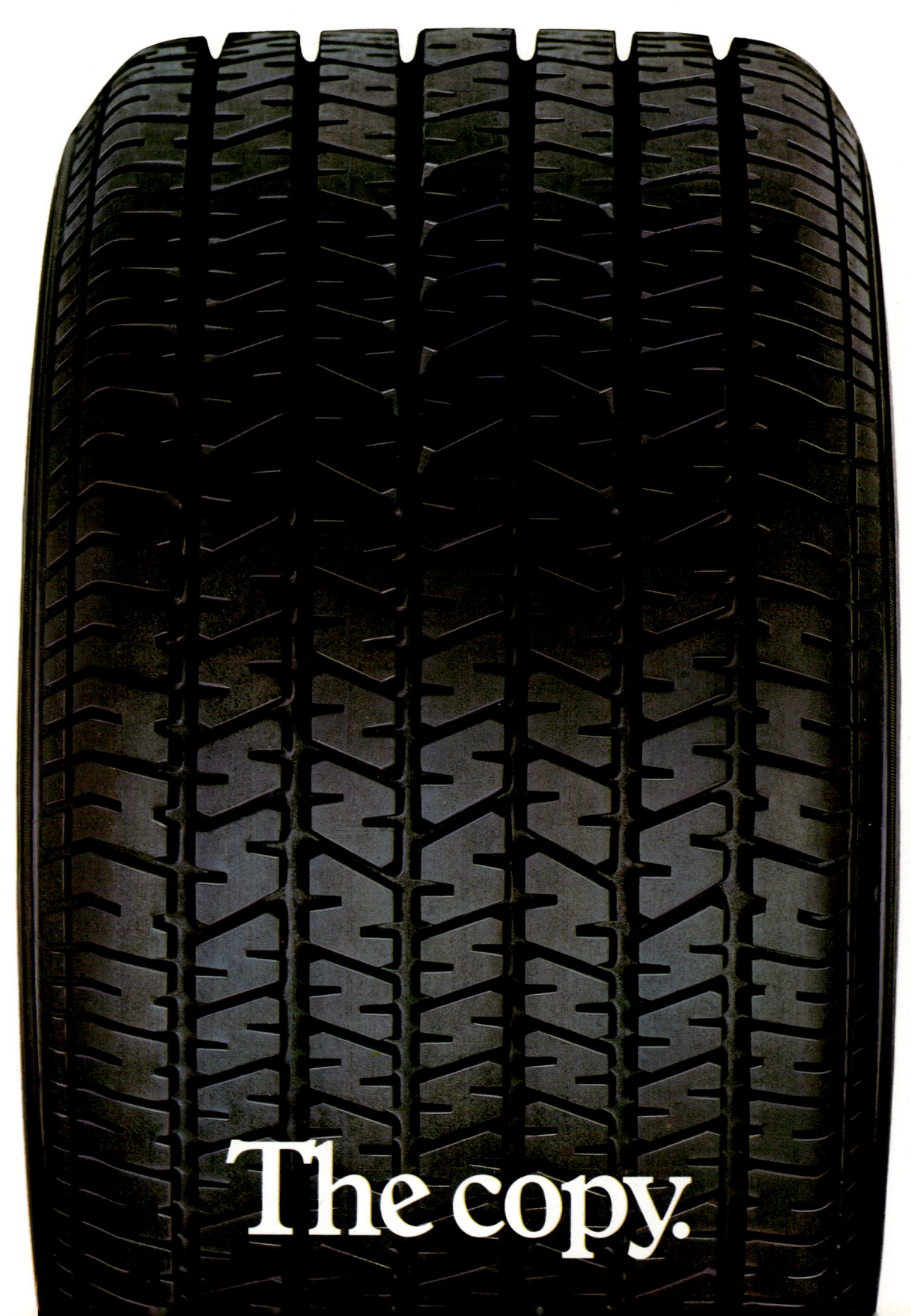

The copy.

It's the Goodyea

There is often a family resemblance between our tyres for the road and our tyres for the track.

But rarely have two been so closely related.

The most obvious similarities between the NCT and our wet racing tyre is in the tread pattern.

The straight circumferential grooves. The open shoulder rain channels.

They are features that help the tyre cut through surface water and disperse it quickly.

Reducing the risk of aquaplaning and ensuring maximum grip.

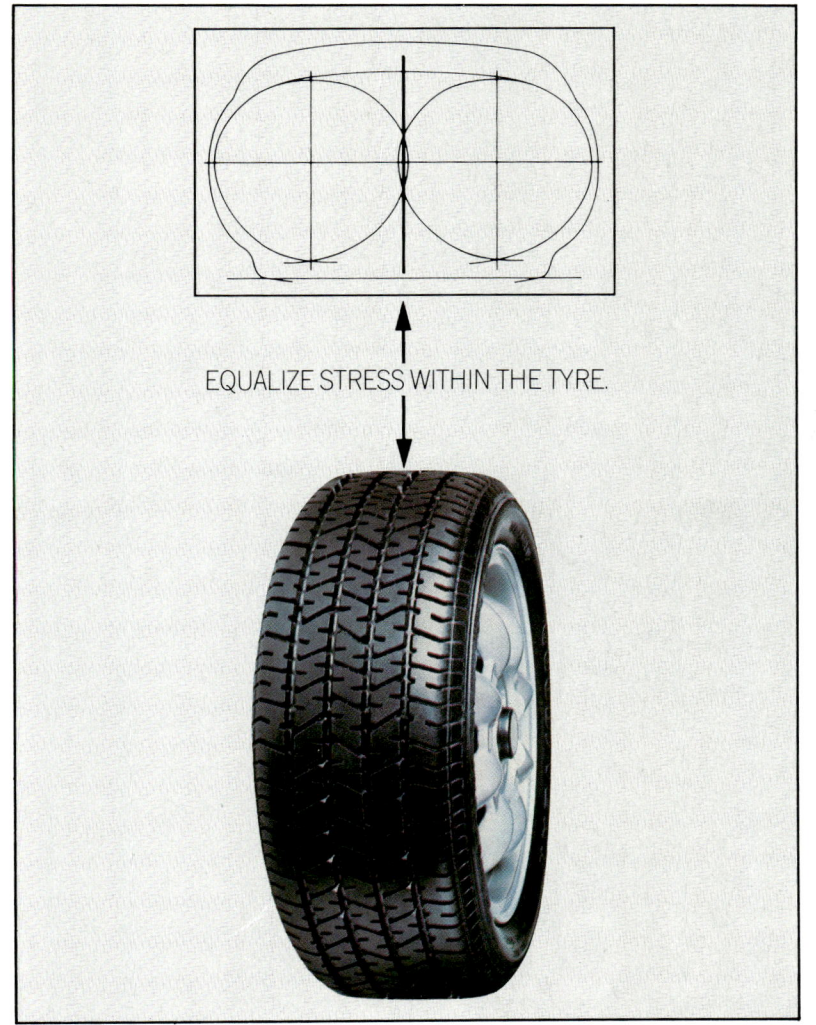

EQUALIZE STRESS WITHIN THE TYRE.

But the whole carcass of the NCT owes a debt to our Formula 1 tyres.

It is twice the width of many standard road tyres. And like our racing tyres it has smooth short sidewalls to ensure agile response.

Although NCT tyres are relatively new, the NCT concept is not.

The letters stand for Neutral Contour

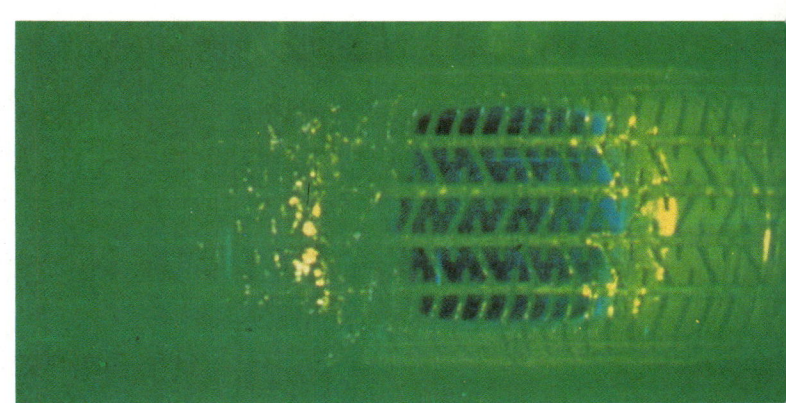

STATIC: 100% GRIP.

Technology, a concept which was developed 50 years ago, by Charles Purdey a Goodyear mathematician.

It is only recently that computer software has enabled the full use of his theory in radial tyre construction.

NCT road tyre.

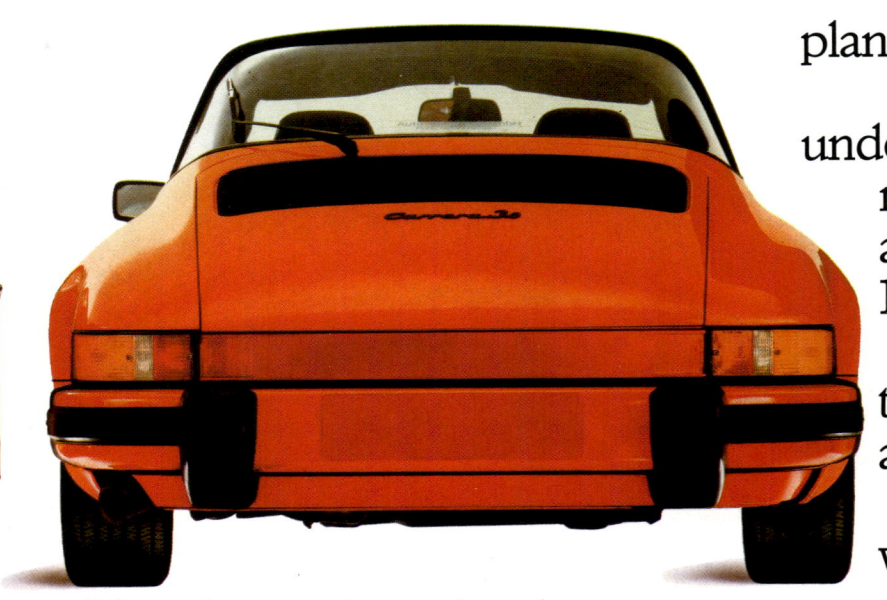

The theory is a simple one. It states that the best combination of ride and handling is obtained when stress is equalised within the tyre carcass.

The Goodyear NCT has proved on the road what Purdey proved on paper.

Our engineers tested the NCT against a standard profile radial tyre under strictly controlled conditions.

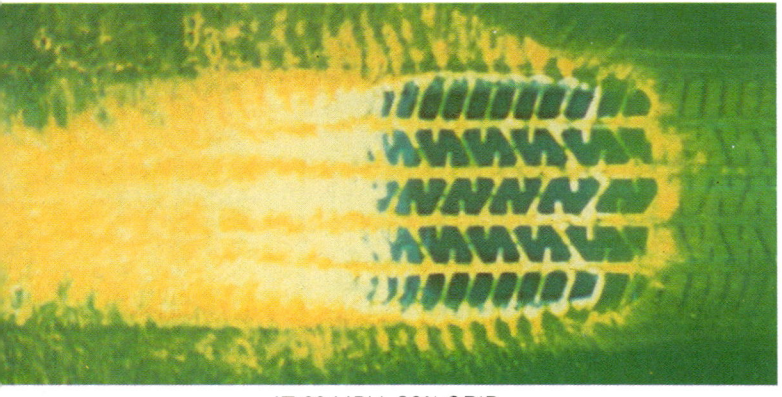

AT 62 MPH: 80% GRIP.

Its superiority was complete. A 5% improvement during overtaking manoeuvres. A 12% improvement in stability during Slalom tests. And a full 20% improvement in roadholding on wet, curved roads.

Finally, the resistance to aquaplaning was measured.

Using our unique glass plate underground photography system, we recorded the tyre's grip in the wet at 62 mph taking photographs at 10,000 frames a second.

This test result was perhaps the most impressive of all. The NCT achieved a remarkable 80% grip.

But we are not the only people who are impressed with the NCT.

Jackie Stewart who helped test it, took time out to praise both its road-holding and its ride.

Motor manufacturers have been equally enthusiastic.

As a result most of the world's high performance cars are now available with NCT as original equipment.

Still more can be equipped with NCT as replacement tyres or as part of a wheel and tyre package.

If you would like details of the NCT range and information on their fitment to your car, drop a line to Advertising Department.

The address is Goodyear Tyre & Rubber Co. (GB) Ltd., Bushbury, Wolverhampton, West Midlands WV10 6DH.

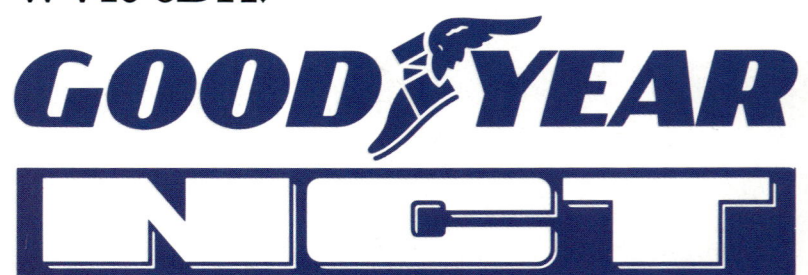

GOOD YEAR

NCT

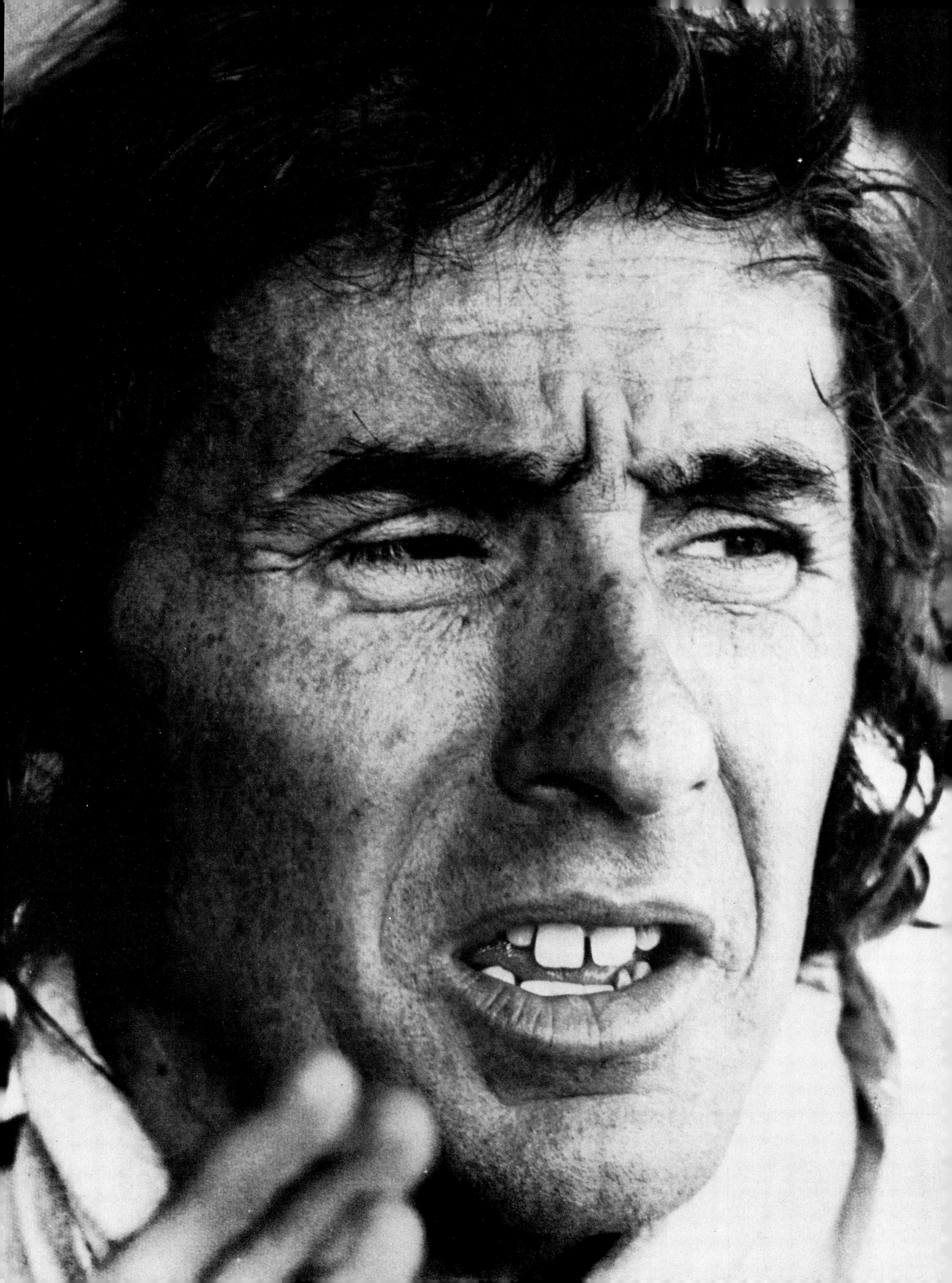

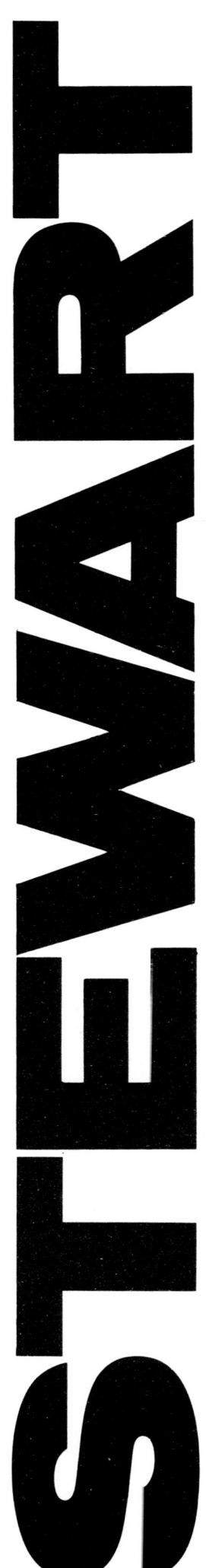

means that he's very sharp and responsive to change, but I think it also means he is in a nervous condition.

"The last World Championship contender this year, of course, has been Tambay, and I've been surprised by him. I admit that in the past I never saw him as a force to be reckoned with, but being with Ferrari transformed him. He's been consistently quick to the point that I'm very impressed."

When one looks at the great driving partnerships of the past – Andretti and Peterson, Scheckter and Villeneuve – one notes today a certain absence of respect and integrity between team members. In 1982 there were the controversies between Villeneuve and Pironi, and Prost and Arnoux, where team orders were ignored.

"Certainly," says Stewart, "I never had worries of that kind with a man like François Cevert. Apart from anything else, the Tyrrell team was always highly disciplined. I flew home with Gilles Villeneuve that day at Imola, and he was *livid* at what had happened. The World Championship was incidental to Gilles. What he wanted was to beat my record, to win more races than me. He told me that evening, and he was stunned by what had happened at Imola."

So what has given rise to this lack of respect between drivers today? Jackie's theories on the subject are fascinating.

"One of the reasons, I think, is that there is no acknowledged leader, no particular man to shoot at. If there had been someone like that last year, Prost and Arnoux would have been preoccupied with beating *him*, for instance, rather than getting into problems between themselves. In years gone by there was Fangio, then Moss, Clark, me maybe and Lauda. There was a man to beat. Hunt, for example, was out to beat Lauda, not the other way round. At the moment, though, no natural leader has emerged.

"I also think that the ground effect phenomenon altered the way drivers think. Ground effect cars removed a great deal of the talent factor – bravery counted for more than precision and finesse. And I happen to believe that, of the people who had good ground effect cars, only Alan Jones and Nelson Piquet extracted the last ounce from them. When the car is the controlling factor, suddenly nobody thinks that anybody else is better than him. The ground effect era artificially closed up the gaps in driver talent – and there was no Nürburgring on which a great driver could minimise the shortcomings of his car by sheer ability . . ."

Appropriately enough, Stewart's 27th and last Grand Prix victory came at this track with which he had a love-hate relationship throughout his career. "In my mind I still have all the braking distances and gear changes to take me round the 'Ring – surely the only way I have ever lapped it without a mistake! Each apex clipped, each exit clean . . .

"Oh my goodness, wasn't it ridiculous? In its heyday the place had 187 corners, with at least 13 places where you left the ground. The guy who says he loved the 'Ring is either a liar or he wasn't going fast enough! It's the kind of thing you say on a January evening in front of a fire . . . but it gave you a feeling of achievement like nowhere else."

Consider hypothetically a Grand Prix on the 'old' Nürburgring today. Who would be on pole position, and who would win? "Piquet or Prost would win the race," comes the prompt reply, "but neither would be on pole. That, I reckon, would go to Keke Rosberg or Arnoux."

Looking at Stewart's own career, most would suggest that his greatest victory was the 1968 German Grand Prix, run in atrocious conditions of rain and mist. Jackie himself is not so sure, however.

"We're back on this trade-off thing. I think if you're *really* fast, you have to give something away, be it attention to detail, planning your moves or whatever. You can't have everything working at ten-tenths. I gave away speed sometimes, I know it. The more I drove, the less quick I had to go, I found. Towards the end I had very few kamikaze efforts, but I think Monza in '73 – in my next-to-last race – was maybe my best ever.

"Monza, you see, was so easy. It's very easy to use natural talent and flair at a place like the 'Ring or Clermont-Ferrand or Spa, but *anybody* can drive fast at Monza! Therefore, to gain ground on someone – unless you have a big power advantage – is more difficult at Monza than at the 'Ring. At Monza you

need to be clinical and clean, technically perfect, because otherwise you scrub off speed and you're slow. That race in the wet at the 'Ring was a seat-of-the-pants drive, but catching up after the stop at Monza was different, dictated entirely by my head, and that drive was as good as I ever did. That's the secret: let the car do the work, don't fight it, don't scrub off its speed . . ."

Jackie says that he was burned out when he retired, had been driving himself too hard for too long. And he felt also that he needed a change in his life. To that end he had worked strenuously to lay foundations for his post-driving career. Ten years since the last chequered flag he remains a busy man, still more instantly 'recognisable' to the general public than any of today's Grand Prix drivers. And this, he feels, is a sad reflection on them.

"Really they shouldn't be allowing me to do this! After all, I've been away from the game a long time, but I probably earn as much as most of the top drivers. Sponsors pay a lot of money these days, and it's not just for driving. For that sort of cash, they're entitled to expect quite a bit of off-track PR work from their drivers, but often they don't get it. As I've said, Piquet and Prost are the two best in the cockpit, to my mind, but I don't think either does enough out of a car. Nelson in particular doesn't want to know about

"I do think the drivers today generally have a lack of awareness of the public"

anything but driving, which is fine – but we can't afford to have many like that. They have a responsibility to the sport, and to its future. As an ambassador for the sport, Patrick Tambay is easily the best, I think.

"In the same way, I can see why the public hates 'the motorhome syndrome', which has changed a lot since my day. Yes, it was a bit undignified to have to change in the back of the transporter and so on, but I do think the drivers today generally have a lack of awareness of the public. Probably you need to strike a balance between being approachable – and being remote enough to remain a hero figure to them. At present, though, the public rarely sees a driver out of his car, and that's very bad. FOCA has done a lot of good things in this business, but this is one aspect that has been severely neglected. In the States, of course, it's completely different – over there the stars are almost too accessible, and because of that they cease, in a way, to be stars. There has to be a happy medium there somewhere."

Stewart's strong links with Ford Motor Company ensure that he spends a great deal of time in the USA. Although he is involved with Ford in connection with road, rather than race, cars, he knows the American racing scene very thoroughly. Ford is one of his 'blue chip' contracts, the others being Goodyear, ABC TV, the Midland Bank, Moët et Chandon and Rolex. And there are, of course, many other smaller interests. Companies once involved with Jackie tend to stay that way on a long-term basis, and a conversation with someone like François Guiter of Elf (major sponsors of the Tyrrell team during Stewart's driving career) soon explains this. Forgetting his superlative ability in a race car, the Scot's professionalism and friendliness made him the ideal to carry a company name. He knows how to behave, when to be serious, when to be irreverent, what to wear, how to promote a product, an image, an idea. Guiter smilingly acknowledges that his company's association with JYS costs a great deal of money, but unhesitatingly adds that it was worth every franc.

"I like that American saying, 'there are no free lunches'. You drive and you earn good money. You have your boat and perhaps your private 'plane and your place in the sun, and you don't want to give them up. You want to carry on with that standard of living – and also you want something to do, to keep you from getting bored. I love my life. I look around my place in Switzerland, and I don't want to change anything. A lot of people don't agree with me, with my way of doing things. But I tell you what," Jackie concludes, "my formula works . . ."

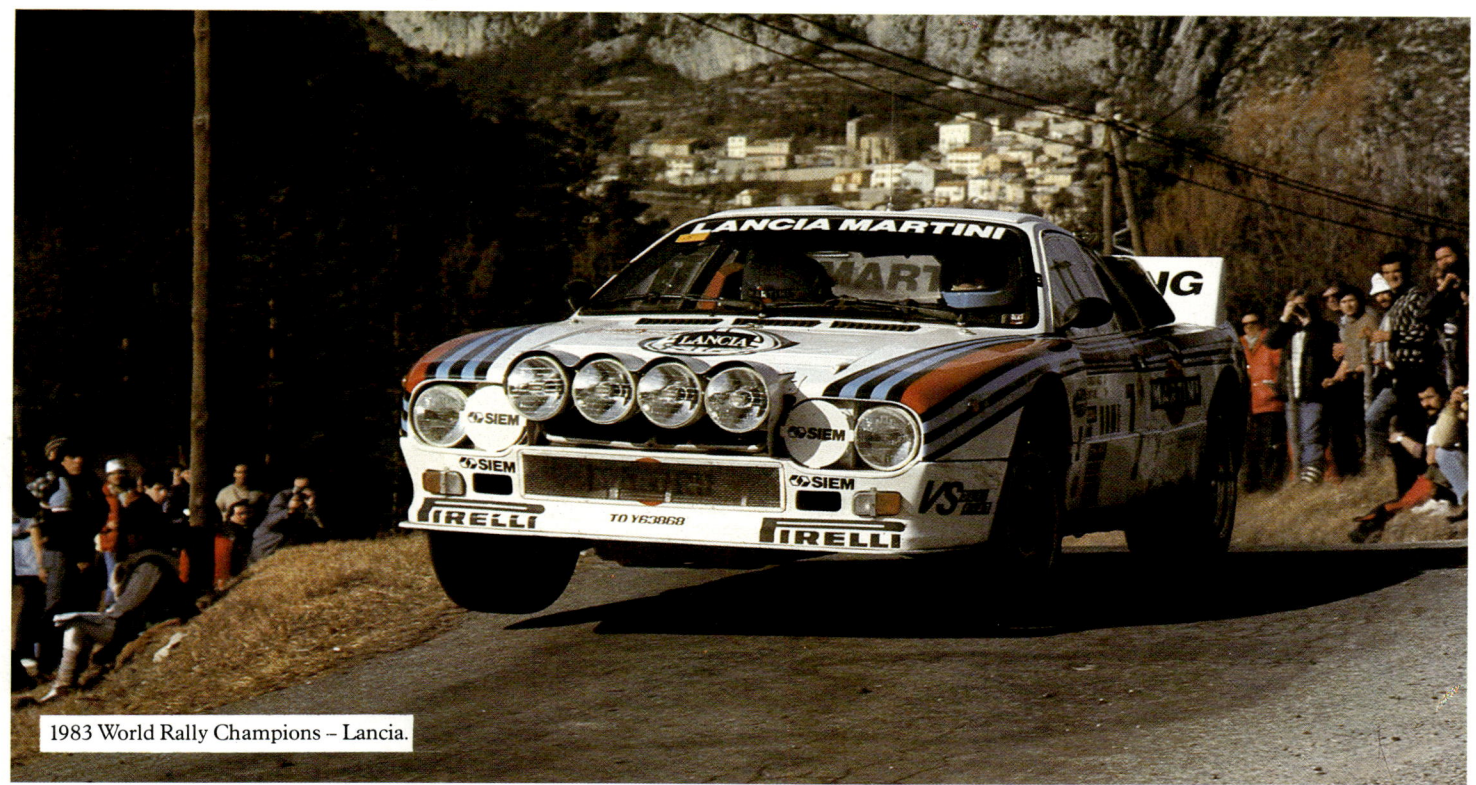

1983 World Rally Champions – Lancia.

WHEN THE CHAMPIONS GO RACING THEY GO WITH CHAMPION.

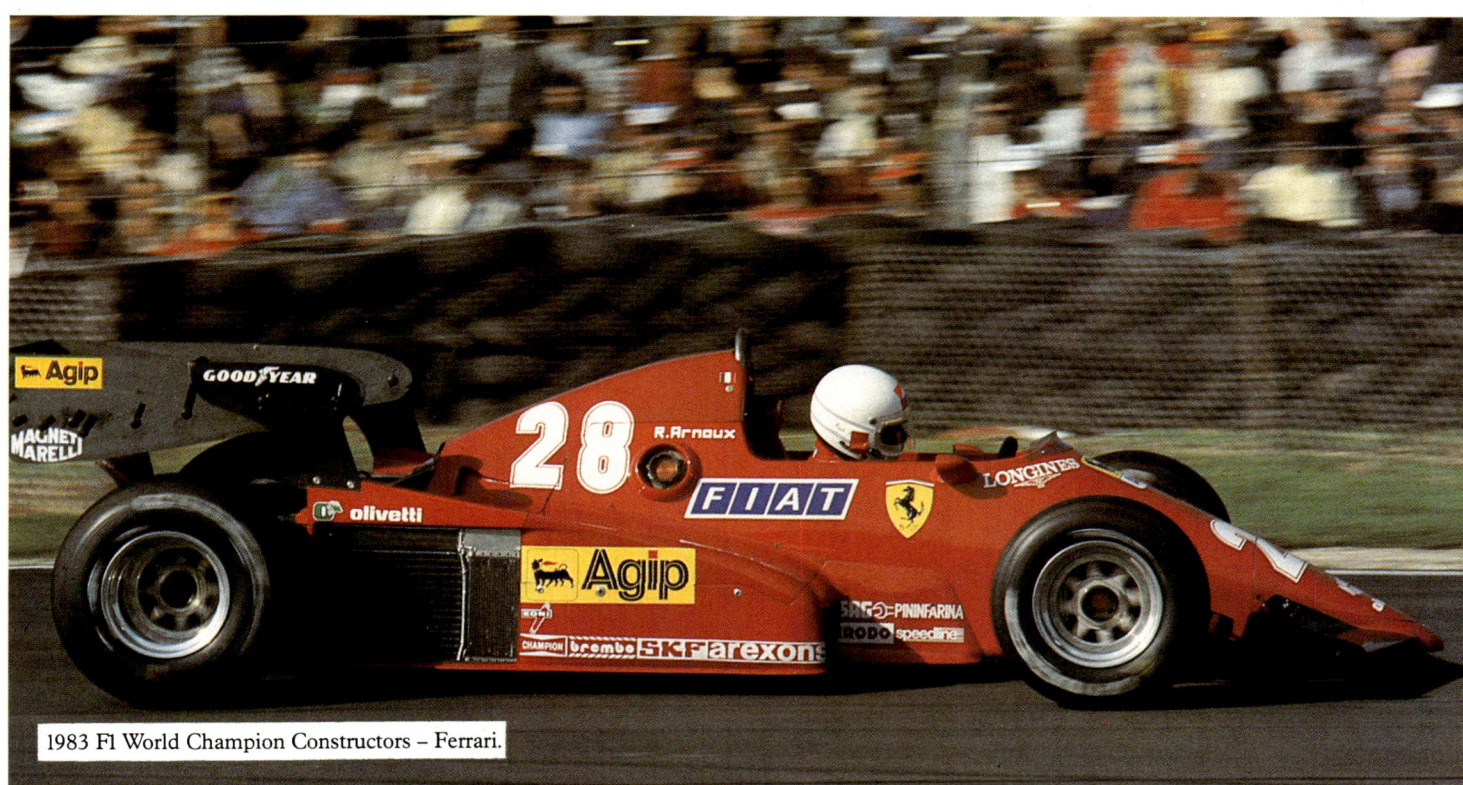

1983 F1 World Champion Constructors – Ferrari.

Like the manufacturers of most standard family saloons the men who make racing and rally cars put their faith in Champion technology. And the reason is Champion's unmatched record of performance.

And what Champion experts learn from motorsport is engineered into the Champion plugs you fit in your car.

So for your regular tune-up, take a tip from the men who make the most famous performance machines.

Fit a new set of Champions!

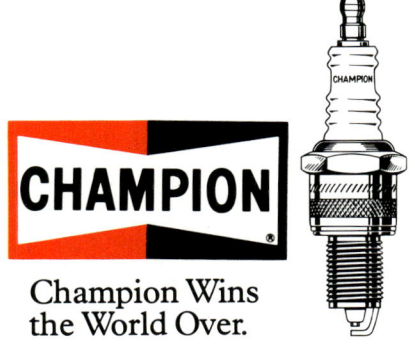

CHAMPION

Champion Wins
the World Over.

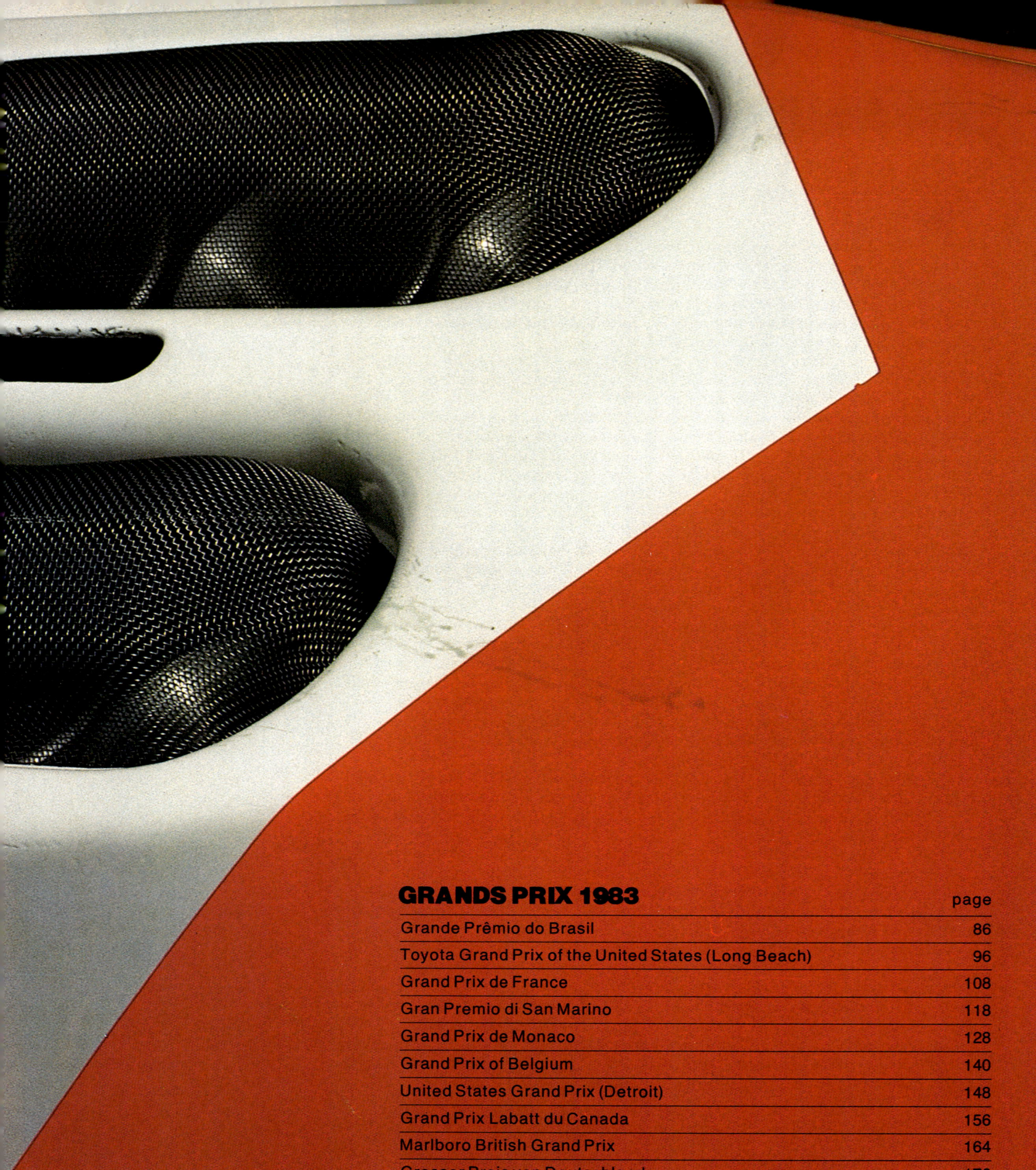

GRANDE PRÊMIO DO BRASIL

If everything went well, they decided, Gordon Murray should have a break for a few days. He would go to Hawaii, join George Harrison, relax, take in a bit of sun and generally unwind after four months of non-stop activity at the Brabham factory. But only if everything went according to plan during the Brazilian Grand Prix. And that, in the aftermath of a sudden and far-reaching rule change at the end of 1982, seemed highly unlikely.

New regulations, brought into force on November 3, had meant a complete re-think for designers. In an attempt to severely restrict ground effects, the rules called for cars with flat bottoms and no side-skirts. There were other minor changes too but the desired effect was a reduction in cornering speeds.

An immediate effect at Brabham was the junking of BT51. Murray's plans were well in hand for the development of the 1982 BT50-BMW but events on November 3 changed all that. A careful but speedy scrutiny of the rule book saw Murray formulate plans to make the most of the revisions and yet have a new car – three new cars – ready for first practice in Rio de Janeiro on March 11. Three elegant blue and white BT52s were the result.

Further along the pit lane at Jacarepaguá, other teams wheeled out their interpretations. Some had the radiators ahead of the front wheels; others had the cooling equipment just behind the front suspension. Some, like Brabham, mounted the hardwear at the rear. There were new cars alongside cars from 1982 converted to the latest specification. Some had joined the turbocharged ranks; others had remained faithful to the Ford-Cosworth DFV. Never had a season started with such uncertainty.

Yet, at the end of practice, the 'Old Firm' of Keke Rosberg and a converted Williams FW08-Cosworth had taken pole against what few odds there were. Behind sat seven turbos followed by Niki Lauda's McLaren-Cosworth, some 1.5 seconds slower than the reigning World Champion – and one second slower than the new Brabham BT52 of Nelson Piquet.

Rosberg, gambling for the first time on starting with half a tank of fuel and soft tyres, shot into the lead but Piquet, using the same tactic, was soon on the tail of the Williams, moving ahead after seven laps. Keke was still in touch as he rushed into the pits on lap 28.

In went the fuel, on went the tyres – and out came the fuel, seeping gently around loose bolts on the fuel filler neck. A flash fire had Rosberg out of the cockpit in twice the time it took the vigilant mechanics to extinguish the blaze. Patrick Head, laying a firm hand on his driver's shoulder, had Rosberg back in the car immediately and on his way to a brilliant charge back to second place.

Twelve laps later, Piquet was in the pits, the Brabham team responding with practised brilliance to allow Nelson back onto the track and into the lead. His challengers had faded. A gathering threat from John Watson ended when a fine, thrusting drive through the field by the McLaren driver was brought to a halt by a seized engine. A rear tyre vibration on Alain Prost's Renault allowed the consistent Lauda to move into third place ahead of Jacques Laffite, the Frenchman having an otherwise undistinguished first outing in the Williams. Patrick Tambay took fifth place in the Ferrari turbo while Marc Surer worked hard to give the unsponsored Arrows team a worthy point for sixth place.

It had been an absorbing race; the new cars had been exciting to watch; the drivers were happy. It was too good to last.

As Frank Williams headed for the airport, the Stewards disqualified Rosberg for receiving a push start during his pit stop. It was important to note, however, that there was no question of a protest, the organisers merely uncovering a dubious section of the rule book which would give Frank Williams adequate grounds for an appeal.

Brabham, meanwhile, were overwhelmed at the ease of this victory. It was agreed that Nelson had scarcely been under pressure during the second half of the race but such an observation would not stop Gordon Murray from stepping onto the first plane to Hawaii.

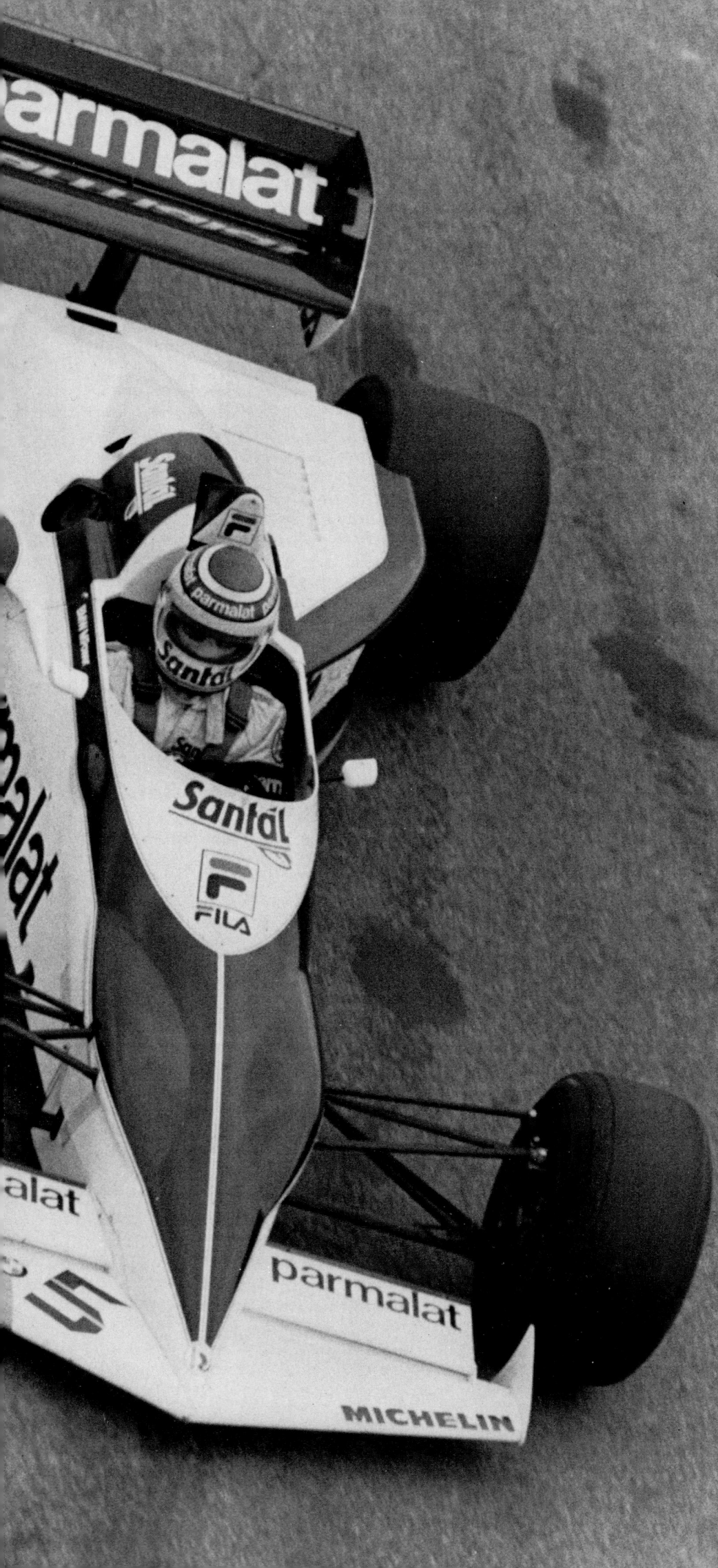

Quick, straight out of the box. Nelson Piquet scored an excellent win for the striking Brabham BT52-BMW, unveiled in Munich seven days before practice began in Rio.

ENTRY AND PRACTICE

South Africa was the first casualty of the new technical regulations. Scheduled originally for February 12, the opening round of the championship was postponed to give the teams time to prepare their cars. Rio inherited the first Grand Prix of the year and, as a result, the Jacarepaguá circuit became the focal point as the designers' ideas were put to the test before Christmas and in late February.

The first results were startling. Setting the pace became the privilege of Toleman, a team more accustomed to the opposite end of the time sheet. Rory Byrne's interpretation saw radiators mounted at the front with the undersides scooped to help promote downforce where permissible. The rules also said nothing about creating ground effect around the engine and gearbox and Toleman, like most teams, had incorporated undertrays sweeping upwards through the rear suspension. It was not a good looking car by any means but Brian Hart and his small workforce had improved the intercooling on the 415T and Warwick was delighted with the package. "It was a joy to drive," he said, with the genuine enthusiasm of a man who had forgotten how good racing cars could be.

Practice, however, was another story; Toleman's weekend was dogged with misfortune. Roger Silman, the team manager, received nasty stab-wounds while fending off thugs attempting to rob his girlfriend not a few yards from the front of their hotel in Rio. A mechanic twisted his ankle playing golf although the anticipated aggravation over a 'double' rear wing failed to materialise when scrutineers were unable to find any contravention of the rules. Fourth place for Warwick on Friday seemed reasonable considering he had messed up one lap on his first set of qualifiers and the turbo boost pressure dropped when an inlet pipe failed while he was on his second set. Pole position, they said, would be no problem on Saturday.

The first hint of trouble came during the untimed session when Warwick ground to a halt out on the circuit. Thinking it might be electrical, there was fresh optimism when the engine was eventually fired up for the final session. A sudden, dramatic engine failure during Warwick's best lap yet told the team otherwise. It later transpired that, during the morning, the engine had begun to run lean which, in turn, had damaged a piston. There was little consolation to be gained from Bruno Giacomelli's performance. Within a few minutes of Warwick's smoky departure, the Italian driver's engine failed following a change of turbo after the morning session. The boost had rocketed off the clock and Bruno, overcome by the sudden surge of power, had pressed on, unaware that the correct procedure was to shut off under such circumstances. Had the engine held together, it would have been a phenomenal lap by all accounts . . .

The talk before the season started was, of course, all about turbos. *This* time, the normally aspirated engine would be left behind and, indeed, during the first official session on Friday afternoon, it seemed we would have a Renault/Ferrari front row. Then, with typical precision, the Williams team sent Keke Rosberg out in the spare car and he stunned the pit lane with a lap of 1m 34.526s, good enough to stand for pole during a slightly slower practice session the following day. "It's a nice feeling to take pole after hearing all that turbo bullshit," said a typically confident Rosberg. What's more, he compounded his case by adding that his tyres had started to go off during that lap.

What was the Williams secret? Was there a special tweak on the car? Did Frank have a better engine? Neither, in fact. The car was a modified version of the successful FW08. The side-pods were shorter; the radiators mounted further back and the front and rear suspension was new. The rear wing had a horizontal mounting similar to the aerofoil on FW06 but, beyond

87

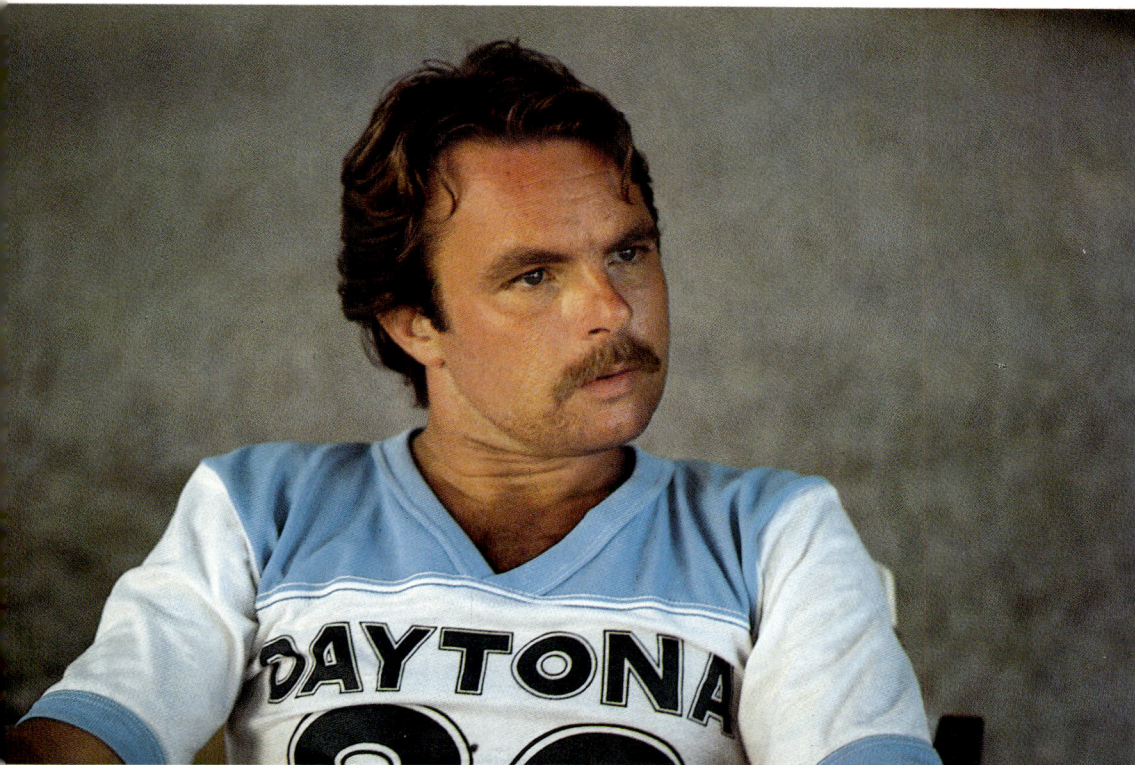

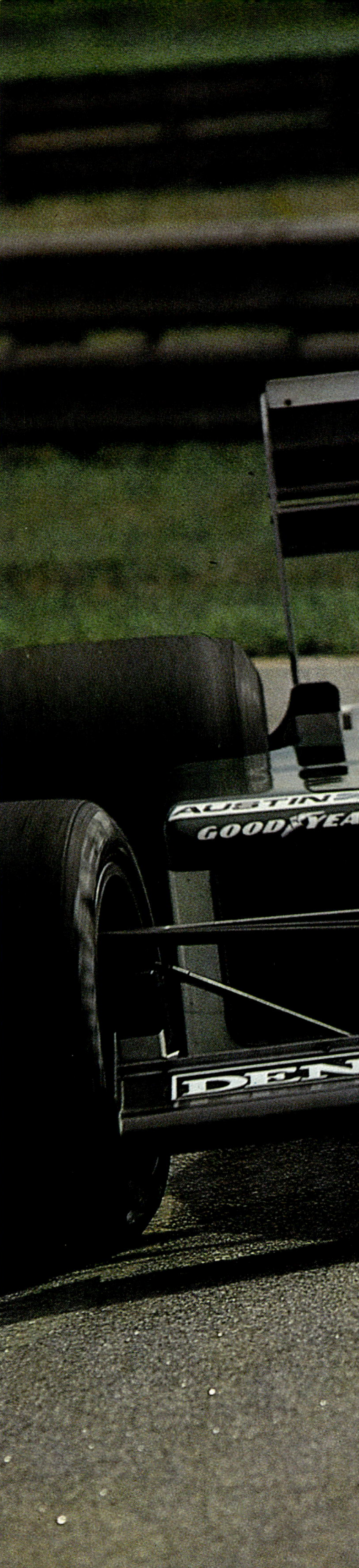

that, there were few changes. At least, there was nothing radical to suggest a reason for Keke's time. No, the surprise had been caused by nothing more than shrewd Williams thinking. Anxious not to show their hand too soon, the team had ignored the pit wall and set up a separate timing point at the first corner after the pits. The team's watches told them all they needed to know while the official timing gave a false impression – until it really mattered.

Such subterfuge was not necessary with Jacques Laffite. Apart from suffering from a touch of 'flu, Laffite was far from happy. He was unable to set the car to his liking and, when given the opportunity to use Keke's spare car (the one which had gained pole) on Saturday afternoon, Jacques came close to despair when he found the FW08C had too much oversteer for his liking and his final time was over three seconds slower than his team-mate. To make matters worse, he was even slower than both cars belonging to his old team, Ligier.

Alain Prost, on the other hand, was confident that he could beat Rosberg during his run on the second set of qualifiers but a busy track and awkward traffic meant Alain had to settle for the outside of the front row. Eddie Cheever had similar problems and actually hit Eliseo Salazar's March on Saturday. Traffic had been a problem for the American on Friday, along with a loose plug lead just as he was going for a quick time on his second set of qualifiers.

Considering the lack of testing for the new Brabhams, Nelson Piquet's time, good enough to push Warwick off the second row during the closing minutes of practice, was a tribute to the team as well as Nelson's tenacity. They had not been without their problems. Apart from Michelin's inability to produce a qualifying tyre significantly superior to their race rubber, the team had been troubled by transmission problems, the gearbox side-plate bearings showing a weakness which precluded the drivers from using full boost during practice. Furthermore, a heat build up from the turbocharger affected the left-rear damper, which did nothing for the handling! Patrese was forced to use the spare car on Saturday but, even so, his time from the previous day was good enough for the fourth row. Bernie Ecclestone, meanwhile, had been told by doctors to take a rest, the Brabham boss having overtaxed himself with the additional burden of promoting the race.

The Ferrari team were under considerable stress as well; their new cars based on the monocoques of the 1982 126C2 giving cause for concern in both the engine and handling departments. The high temperatures highlighted problems caused by having the heat exchangers mounted close to the ground and that was

---

November 1982:

Formula 1 Commission meeting in Paris agrees to sweeping changes for Grand Prix racing: side-skirts banned; cars to have flat bottoms; minimum weight limit reduced from 580 to 540kgs; stringent new methods of policing weight limit during practice and after race; engine stability until end of 1985; fuel tankage to be cut from 250 to 220 litres in 1984.

Williams withdraw legal action over Rosberg's disqualification from Brazilian Grand Prix.

Spirit-Honda turbo F1 car runs for first time.

December:

Colin Chapman dies of heart attack.

January 1983:

Walter Röhrl (Lancia Rally) wins Monte Carlo Rally.

February:

Lotus-Renault 93T unveiled.

A J Foyt and Darrell Waltrip drive Nimrod Aston Martin at Daytona 24-hour race.

March:

Alan Jones plans to return to Formula 1 with Arrows.

Jaguar announce works support for TWR Jaguar XJSs in European Touring Car Championship.

Ford cancel Group C programme for C100.

---

serious enough to have pressure gauges fitted in the cockpit to enable the drivers to keep a check on temperatures. There was very little traction to be had on race rubber although full boost and qualifiers helped push Patrick Tambay onto the second row. René Arnoux joined Warwick on the third row with Saturday's time, the Frenchman having been stuck out on the circuit after spinning during the first qualifying session.

Ferrari, though, were concerned about finding a decent set-up and a tyre which would last the race. McLaren's problems were the exact opposite. The Michelins were useless during qualifying and Niki Lauda spent most of his time working on a full tank/race tyre configuration. Lauda, of course, had done the majority of the testing while the McLaren management and John Watson continued a lengthy haggle over contracts which was not resolved until two weeks before the race. As a result, Watson had to

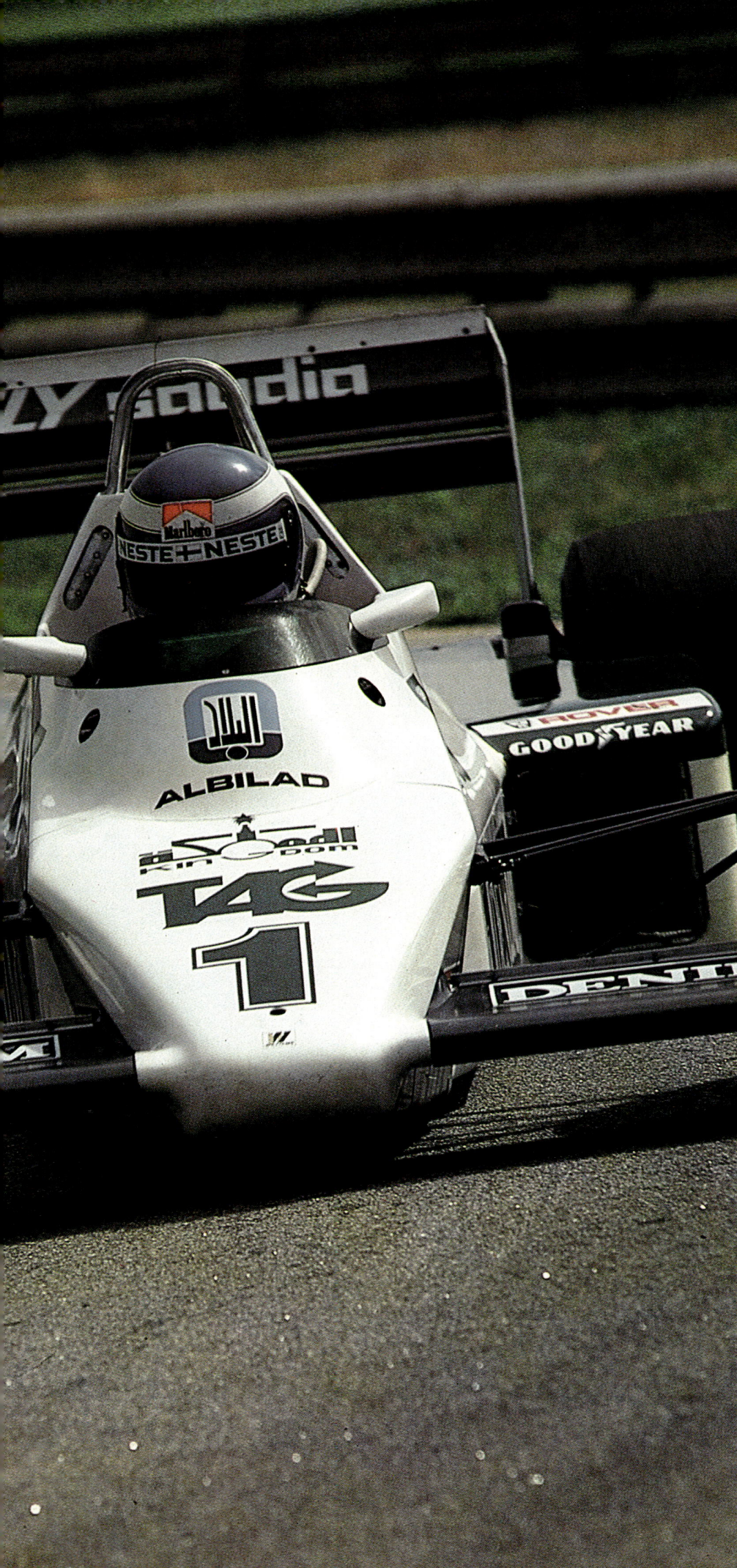

accept his car set up to Lauda's requirements and the
Ulsterman spent all of practice working back to a base
line from which he could set the car to his liking. By the
time he had done that, practice was over. Watson was
on row eight.

Major changes at Alfa Romeo seemed to have borne
fruit during winter testing. The racing team had been
handed over to Paolo Pavanello's Euroracing concern
and their main preoccupation had been to make the
V8 turbo, seen during practice at the Italian Grand
Prix the year before, work satisfactorily. The chassis
used at Monza was modified and two new cars had
been built for the season, Mauro Baldi joining Andrea
de Cesaris. Baldi seemed to enjoy the turbo power at
Rio as he pushed the 183T onto the fifth row but his
progress only made matters worse for de Cesaris who
had a terrible time with various problems including a
number of blown turbos. Then, to round off a fraught
practice, Andrea was excluded from the meeting after
failing to stop when requested and have his car
weighed.

The Tyrrell team had been testing in Brazil and that
had been made possible by the acquisition of
much-needed sponsorship from Benetton. The cars,
developments of the 011 model with which Michele
Alboreto had won the last Grand Prix of 1982, had set
encouraging times during testing but Alboreto was
struggling to reproduce that form when it really
mattered. Engine trouble on Friday meant he was
forced to use the spare car but the Italian was back in
his usual chassis for the final session and into 11th
place on the grid. His new team-mate, Danny Sullivan,
found it difficult to make the most of the one-lap
qualifiers, but the American managed to qualify for
his first Grand Prix.

The Citroen-based hydraulic suspension system
fitted to the Ligiers did not work as well as early tests
had indicated and the revamped team had to contend
with overheating problems on the purposeful JS21.
Jean-Pierre Jarier tried a double rear wing on
Saturday morning in a bid to improve traction but
nothing conclusive was proved since metering unit
trouble kept the laps to a minimum. Jarier qualified in
12th place while Raul Boesel complained of understeer on his way to 17th fastest time.

Ligier may have rung the changes in every direction
but, by comparison, Lotus appeared to be throwing
every possible obstacle in their path. For a start, the
English team, now without the brilliant Chapman, had
switched from Goodyear to Pirelli. In addition, they
had to contend with a Renault turbo 93T for Elio de
Angelis and a Ford-Cosworth powered 92 for Nigel
Mansell. To add to the confusion, Mansell's car was
fitted with hydraulic suspension although, on Friday,
both drivers were forced to use the spare car – an
updated flat-bottomed Lotus 91! Elio had a host of
problems but was managing to put a fast lap in when
he came across Rosberg cruising back to the pits. The
result; an irate Italian and 13th fastest time. Mansell
had a similar problem with Marc Surer although, this
time, the Lotus almost went off the track in avoidance.

A place halfway up the grid marked a considerable
improvement for Roberto Guerrero in the Theodore
(née Ensign) thanks to the merger between the two
teams which would give the Colombian driver a
well-deserved opportunity to show his talent. There
had been problems with understeer and a flat spot on
the engine on Friday but these were minor problems
compared to the difficulties surrounding the Ensign
team the previous year. And, to add to their state of
well-being, Johnny Cecotto managed to qualify the
second Theodore with commendable ease considering
this was his first Grand Prix and his experience with
the car had been limited to about 40 laps during
testing. The former 750cc motorcycle champion took
things in his stride, particularly when a wheel came off

New for 1983

WILLIAMS
Began the season with a modified version of the FW08. Plans for a six-wheeled FW08B were rendered useless by a change in the regulations. Jacques Laffite replaced Derek Daly. Denim joined existing sponsors.

TYRRELL
Benetton entered Grand Prix racing to give Tyrrell a healthy budget for the first time in two years. 1982 cars modified. Danny Sullivan made Formula 1 debut.

BRABHAM
Complete change, technically, with new cars and a switch from Goodyear to Michelin. Piquet and Patrese remain but Fila became major sponsor.

McLAREN
Few changes initially. A modified version of 1982 MP4B-Cosworth for Watson and Lauda with future plans based on TAG-Porsche turbo under development at Weissach. Teddy Mayer and Tyler Alexander leave team in management reshuffle.

ATS
Produce a new carbon monocoque to accept a switch from Ford-Cosworth to BMW turbo. Goodyear replace Michelin.

LOTUS
Turned upside down by the sudden death of Colin Chapman on December 16, 1982. Peter Warr assumed command of changes on every front: de Angelis to use a Renault turbo in a new chassis; Mansell drives a Ford-Cosworth engine in a chassis featuring computer-controlled hydraulic suspension. Both cars running Pirelli radials instead of Goodyear cross-plies.

RENAULT
Eddie Cheever replaced René Arnoux. A new car, RE40, tested but not used in Brazil, Prost and Cheever racing modified 1982 RE30s.

MARCH
Eliseo Salazar rejoined to drive a new car running on Pirelli.

ALFA ROMEO
Alfa Romeo handed the running of their team to Euroracing with the effort centred around the V8 turbo. Mauro Baldi replaced Bruno Giacomelli.

LIGIER
A major reshuffle. Talbot withdraw support; Laffite and Cheever replaced by Jean-Pierre Jarier and Raul Boesel; Matra V12 abandoned leaving Ligier to return to Ford-Cosworth. Plans to run Renault turbo engines dropped.

FERRARI
Spent the winter on a busy test programme with modified 1982 cars. René Arnoux joined Patrick Tambay.

ARROWS
A new car but no sponsor. Alan Jones's name linked with Arrows for future races but Chico Serra drove alongside Marc Surer in Brazil. Moved from Pirelli to Goodyear.

OSELLA
Tony Southgate designed new car for promising novices Corrado Fabi and Piercarlo Ghinzani.

THEODORE
Financial constraints forced Theodore and Ensign to combine, the 1983 Theodore based on the 1982 Ensign monocoque. Johnny Cecotto joined Formula 1 to race with Roberto Guerrero, Ensign's regular driver in 1982.

TOLEMAN
A radical new car for Derek Warwick and Bruno Giacomelli, the former Alfa Romeo driver replacing Teo Fabi who had moved to CART racing. A new air-to-air intercooler for the Hart turbo and the return of sponsorship from Candy.

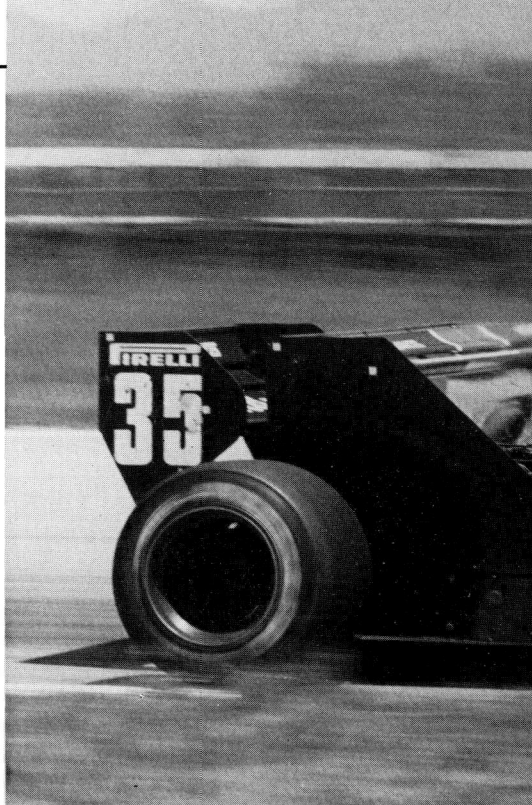

KILOGRAMMES WERE THE TALKING point of the paddock in Rio. In an attempt to monitor the weights of cars more closely, FISA drew up a system to be used during timed practice and after the race. A selection procedure involving one in four cars saw drivers being directed onto scales as they entered the pit lane during practice. A reading was taken with the driver on board and his 'official' weight was then deducted.

The car should not contravene the 540kg minimum weight limit. If it did – or the driver refused to stop when requested – then the penalty was exclusion from the meeting. Similarly, cars were weighed with the drivers on board immediately after the race. This year, however, nothing could be 'topped up' prior to weighing – a practice which had caused such a furore previously.

The drivers were weighed before practice and the readings taken were to be their official weights during the first half of the season. Even though the minimum weight limit had been reduced from 580 to 540kg, it was clear that the Cosworth teams were capable of building cars under the limit. While lightweight practice specials were likely to be caught out by the system, there was an advantage to be had in making sure your driver was as light as possible at the official weigh-in. Thus, there would be scope for him to be slightly heavier during practice and, correspondingly, the car could be that much lighter. There were mutterings about flimsy overalls and lightweight helmets as drivers took to the scales although such advantages would have been minimal.

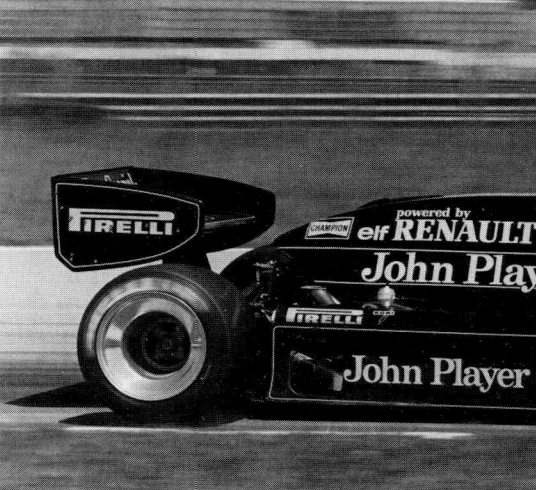

The list of weights shows a remarkable difference of almost 20 kgs between the heaviest, Cheever, and the slender Laffite.

Eddie Cheever	80.8 kgs
Patrick Tambay	80.4
Nigel Mansell	80.0
Jean-Pierre Jarier	77.8
Chico Serra	77.4
John Watson	77.2
Elio de Angelis	77.0
Riccardo Patrese	76.8
Eliseo Salazar	76.6
Derek Warwick	75.8
Manfred Winkelhock	75.6
Piercarlo Ghinzani	75.4
Bruno Giacomelli	73.0
Andrea de Cesaris	72.8
Raul Boesel	72.4
Danny Sullivan	72.2
Niki Lauda	71.2
Michele Alboreto	70.8
Corrado Fabi	70.8
Johnny Cecotto	70.4
Mauro Baldi	68.0
Keke Rosberg	67.8
René Arnoux	67.2
Marc Surer	67.2
Nelson Piquet	67.0
Roberto Guerrero	66.6
Alain Prost	65.4
Jacques Laffite	61.6

FISA showed their intention of implementing the new regulations by excluding Andrea de Cesaris from the meeting when the Italian ignored a request to stop during practice. It was an unfortunate incident since foul play was not suspected, the Alfa Romeo driver having been in and out of the pits with engine problems. The Alfa Romeo had been weighed once and, when he returned to the track to complete one more slow lap, the random check selected his car once again! De Cesaris was in no mood for wasting further time and he drove straight to his pit. The anguished team realised their driver's error and accepted the punishment with equanimity.

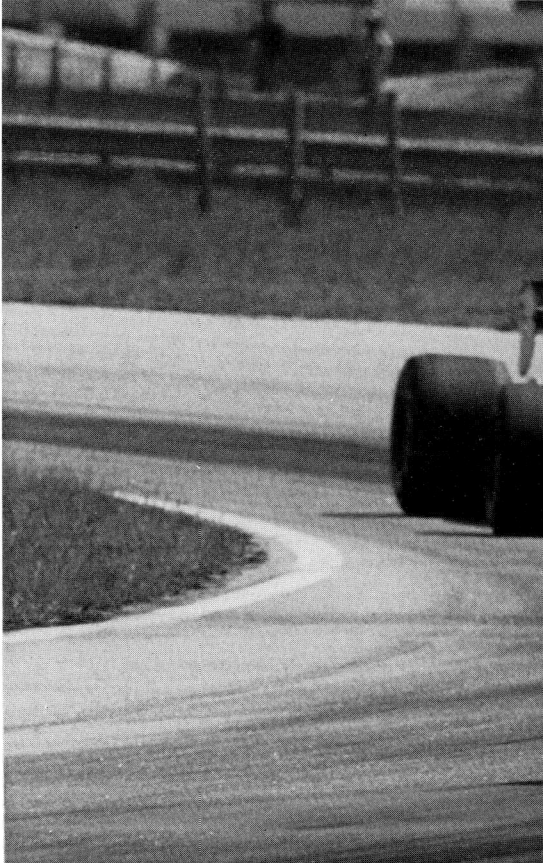

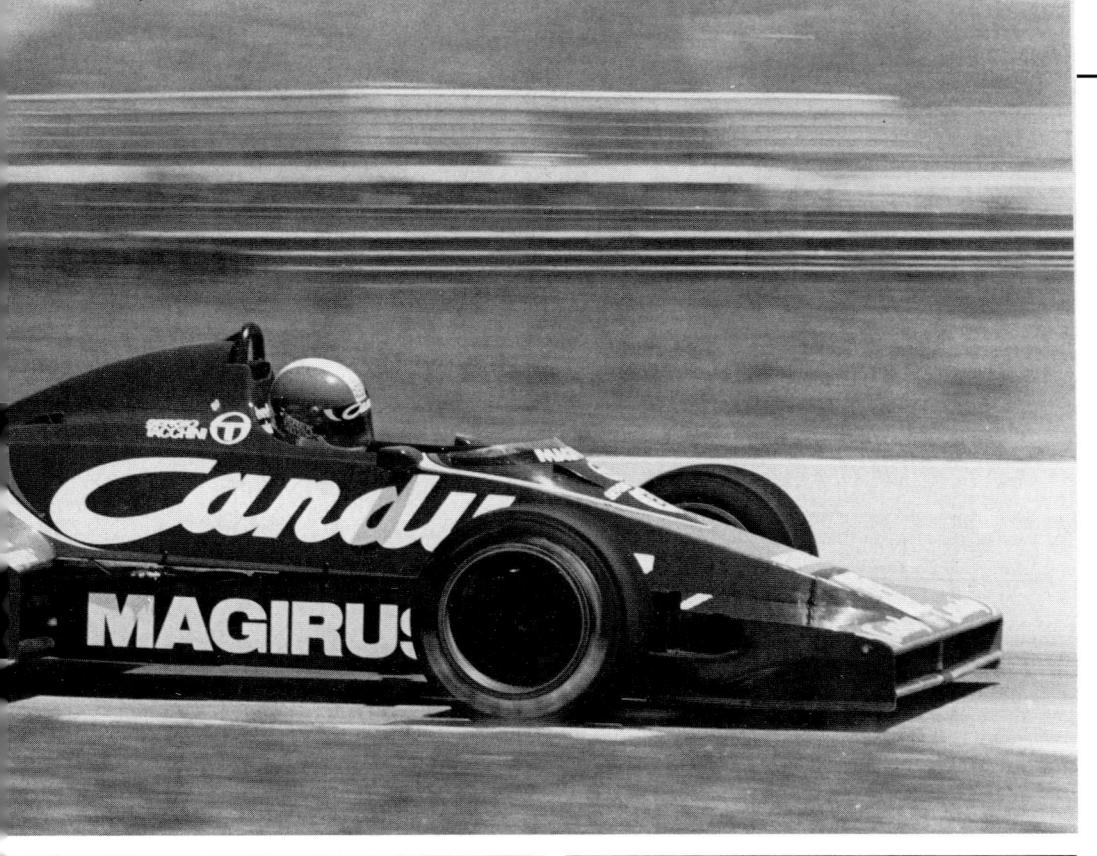

Derek Warwick set the pre-season testing pace although practice and the race were fraught with difficulties for the Toleman team. Rory Byrne's interpretation of the latest regulations produced the TG183B, featuring radiators mounted at the front with the undersides sculptured to generate ground effect where permissable.

on Saturday morning and his engine was 400 revs down during the final practice session.

Arrows had produced a new A6 in time for practice at Rio but the lack of testing was to hold up progress when, for example, the springs were found to be too stiff for the latest generation car from Milton Keynes. The first day was spent setting up the car, which was fortunate for Marc Surer since the Swiss driver was stricken by a stomach bug and in no mood for fast laps. Considering he hadn't driven a Formula 1 car since December, 20th fastest time was a good effort. Chico Serra, keen to make the most of a drive which seemed likely to be usurped by Alan Jones at a later date, was hampered by engine trouble on Friday morning and he was lucky to make the grid on Saturday after narrowly missing the Mansell/Surer incident.

Joining Serra on the penultimate row was Corrado Fabi, the European Formula 2 Champion having joined Osella to drive the Tony Southgate designed car which needed handling problems sorted out. Piercarlo Ghinzani, driving the second Osella, was pushed off the grid in the closing minutes of practice by Manfred Winkelhock, a host of engine problems with the ATS-BMW restricting the German driver to a handful of laps and giving the team little time to run qualifiers on their impressive new car with its carbon fibre chassis. March had teething problems with their new Dave Kelly designed car and Eliseo Salazar only made the grid thanks to the exclusion of the unfortunate de Cesaris.

RACE

There had been a considerable amount of stabbing at calculators in the Brabham and Williams teams as the management worked out fuel consumption and the practicalities of pit stops. Thinking the BMW engine's fuel consumption had been improved since 1982, the Brabham team hadn't bothered to cart all of their pit stop equipment to Brazil, but Gordon Murray was soon wishing they had once he saw the result of his calculations. A pit stop would be necessary and the team prepared to make do with their manual jacks and the refuelling gear they had available. Williams concluded they would have an advantage of two seconds per lap by starting with half a tank of fuel and soft 'C' tyres and, since Keke Rosberg was on pole and the advantage would add up to more than a minute during the first half of a race, then it was worth the gamble of a pit stop. With such short notice, the Williams team had little time to work on such an important routine, but the decision was made none the less.

Decisions about whether to stop or not would have

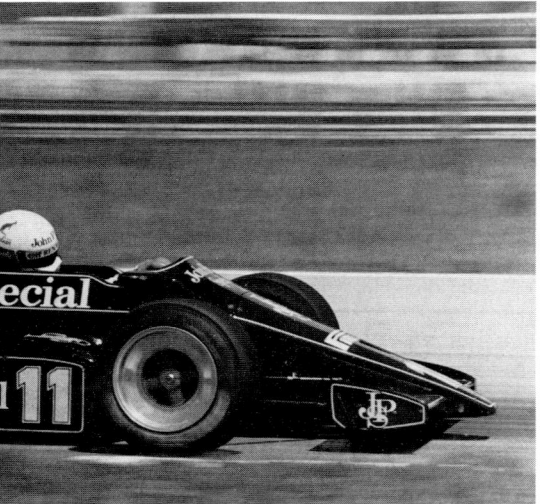

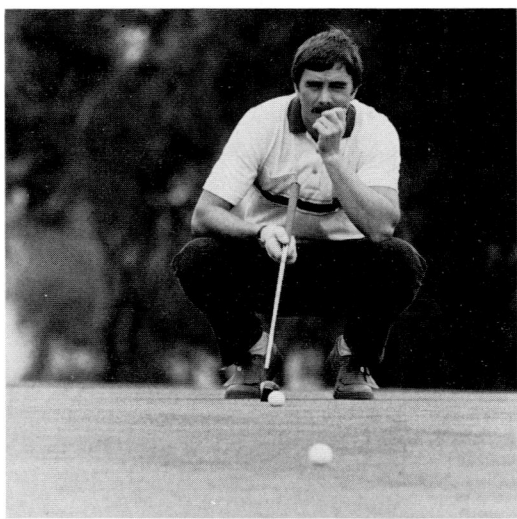

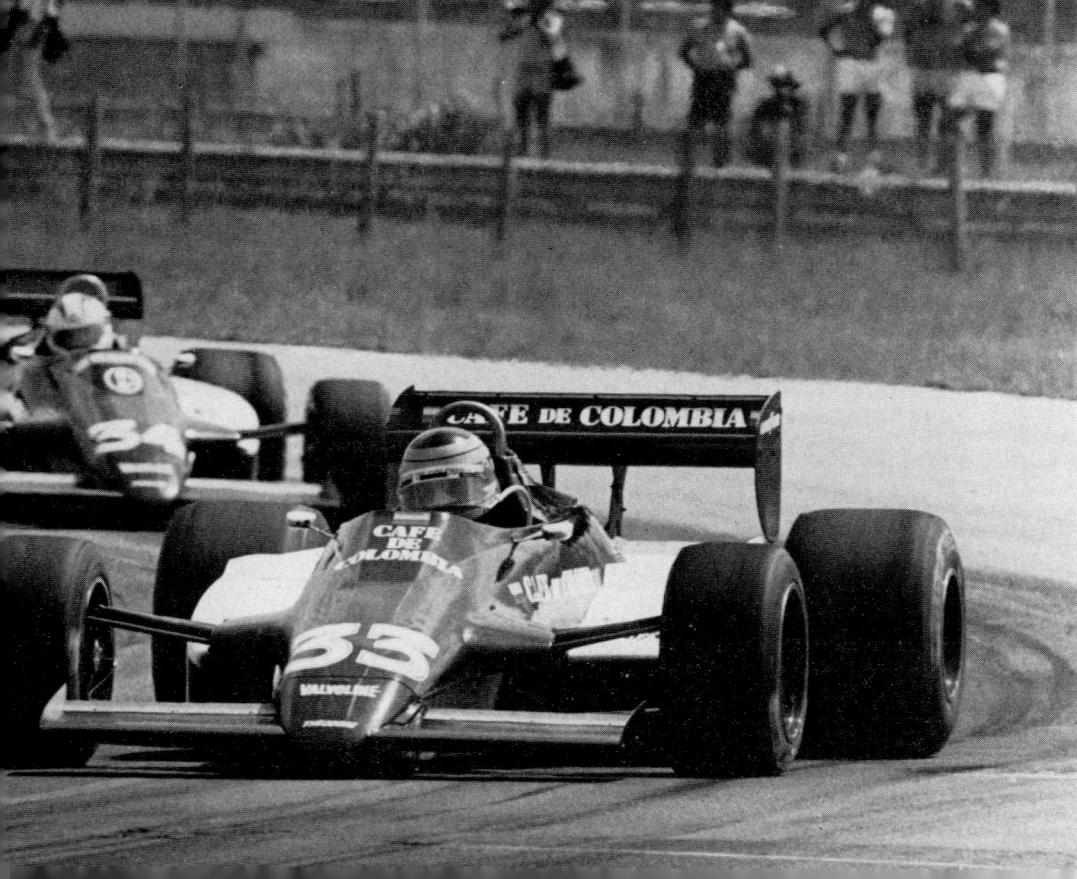

The revamped Lotus team had a difficult time in Rio. Elio de Angelis started the race from the pit lane in the spare Cosworth car only to be excluded from the results since he had practised and qualified in the Renault-engined Lotus 93T (pictured).
Nigel Mansell struggled through practice and the race with the computer-controlled 'active' suspension on his 92-Cosworth. To add to the confusion, Lotus had switched from Goodyear to Pirelli.
The merger between Ensign and Theodore, plus the arrival of Johnny Cecotto in Formula 1, breathed new life into both teams. Roberto Guerrero (leading) and the former motor cycle champion qualified comfortably and ran competitively until sidelined by brake calliper problems.

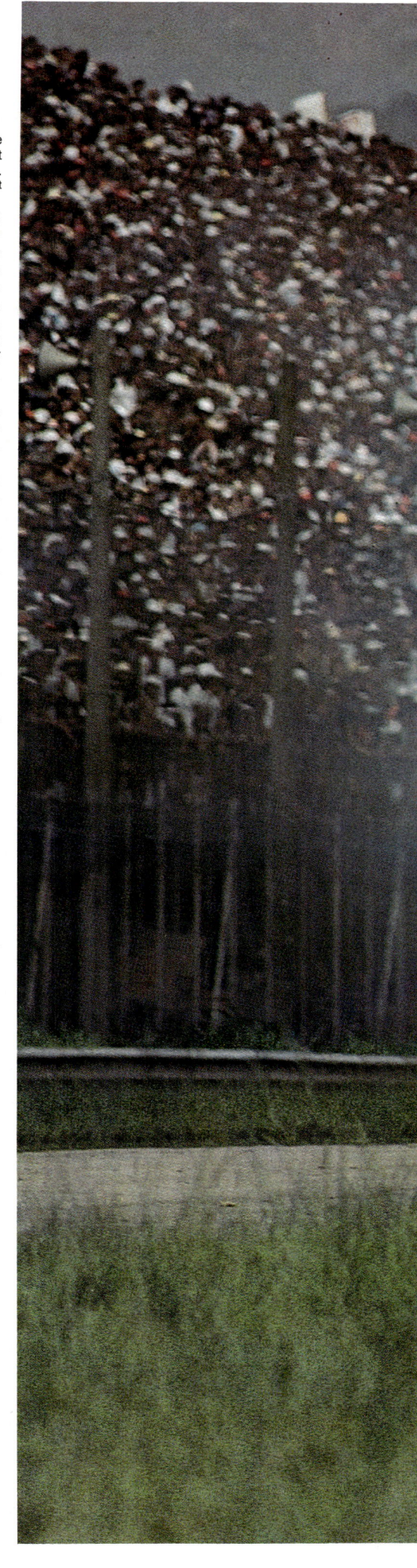

Renault started the season badly, Eddie Cheever suffering a turbo failure as Alain Prost dropped down the field to finish seventh.
Photo: Charles Knight

been a luxury for the hard-pressed Lotus team and their .weekend took a further turn for the worse during the warm-up lap when de Angelis's engine began to smoke ominously. By the time he had reached the end of the lap, a broken turbo had been diagnosed and the Italian was hastily crammed into the spare Cosworth car so that he could take the start from the pit lane.

Rosberg's lightweight advantage really told at the start, the Cosworth the equal of Prost's turbo power as the Williams surged into the lead and began to pull away at an alarming rate. Piquet was already looking for a way past the Renault with Patrese in close attendance, followed by the Ferraris of Tambay and Arnoux with Cheever darting around in their slipstream. Lauda then led a tight knot of cars including Watson, Jarier, Guerrero, Cecotto, Sullivan and the rest. In the space of a few miles, Alboreto and Baldi had touched, the Tyrrell driver coming away with a damaged oil cooler which would eventually mean retirement once the team had persuaded their driver to come in before the engine failed.

It didn't take Piquet long to slip ahead of Prost, Patrese trying to join his team-mate before being smartly cut off by the Renault. Riccardo was third not long after and it soon became evident that Piquet had the legs of Rosberg as he closed the three-second gap within a few laps. A blind man could have told you that the Brazilian was in the lead on lap seven; the crowd screaming hysterically as their man began to pull out an immediate advantage. Patrese was poised to do the same but the Brabham suddenly began to drop back, a broken exhaust pipe at a point near the turbo causing a sudden drop in power and retirement after 20 laps.

Piquet had pulled out a gap of five seconds on Rosberg, but of more importance, perhaps, was a gap of 33 seconds on John Watson, who had worked his way through the field with a most positive drive. By lap ten he had split the Ferraris although Arnoux was destined to drop from seventh place with a severe tyre vibration caused by the Goodyears moving on their rims as they tried to cope with the turbo power. René was demoted by a furious battle between Baldi and Warwick, soon to be joined by Lauda. Having found the Alfa Romeo difficult to pass, Warwick stood aside and let Lauda through to see if the McLaren driver could do better. It took the Austrian two laps to work out his move and, when Warwick tried to follow, the Toleman and the Alfa Romeo touched, leaving Baldi stalled in the middle of the track with deranged suspension. The Toleman's front suspension took a considerable knock but at least Warwick was able to continue, which was just as well since the Toleman team had already lost Giacomelli, the Italian's engine having lost boost and a handling problem then spinning Bruno into retirement.

Watson was into his stride now, finding the other drivers "slow through the corners" as he moved into fourth place behind Prost. The Frenchman would be more difficult to pass thanks to a combination of turbo power and intelligent driving but Watson took third place with a brilliant feint to the right followed by a dive inside the Renault under braking for a left-hander. Prost was bothered by a tyre vibration and Cheever had chosen too hard a compound on his Renault. The American made a pit stop for fresh tyres after slipping from seventh to 11th place but he was soon to retire with a broken turbo.

After 25 laps, Piquet led Rosberg by 12 seconds with Watson a further 27 seconds behind the Williams. Prost was next with Lauda challenging the Ferrari of Tambay for fifth place. Warwick was seventh, the Toleman under pressure from Marc Surer's Arrows, the Swiss driver feeling much better than during practice and driving with great enthusiasm. Unfortunately, that enthusiasm, coupled with a car which was

having braking problems, saw Surer leave the road briefly and drop back behind Laffite. An unhappy Arnoux was down in tenth place and about to be passed by Johnny Cecotto although a fine debut by the Theodore driver was soon to be spoiled by a pit stop to attend to a badly assembled brake calliper – an identical problem having sent Guerrero into the pits a few laps earlier. Fabi had retired his Osella with engine trouble and the Ligiers were to stop within a few laps of each other; Jarier with a broken wheel bearing and Boesel with electrical trouble.

On the completion of lap 28, Rosberg made for the pits, the mechanics pouncing on the car to change tyres and add fuel. Everything went smoothly until fuel began to seep through bolt holes at the filler neck, causing a flash fire which looked much worse than it actually was. Alert mechanics soon had the flames extinguished – but not before Rosberg had unclipped his belts and begun to vacate the cockpit. He was soon persuaded that everything was under control but, by the time he had been strapped into the car, over a minute had been lost. He returned to the track in ninth place, the Williams having been push started . . .

Piquet had 36 seconds in hand over Watson when the McLaren stopped suddenly with a broken engine on lap 34. Six laps later and the Brabham was in the pits, the 16.4-second stop being a model of efficiency – correct equipment or not. Nelson returned to the track to find he had a 55-second gap over Lauda once the McLaren had moved ahead of Prost. Any hopes of Lauda giving chase were lost, however, when he found his Michelins had lost their edge.

Piquet could have handled such a handicap with ease and, to prove how unflustered he was, the Brazilian wound down the boost to such an extent that the BMW sounded off-song and about to expire. Much to the chagrin of the Williams team, however, the Brabham kept going and victory for Nelson was secure even though Rosberg was doing amazing things with his Williams as he slashed through the field and into second place with ten laps to run.

Lauda took third and Jacques Laffite putting in an impressive run to move into fourth place ahead of Tambay in the closing stages. Marc Surer made a desperate bid to push the Ferrari back to sixth place at the last corner but the Arrows team had to be satisfied with one point at the end of a tenacious drive. Prost was bitterly disappointed to struggle home in seventh place and the Toleman team were equally dismayed with their car's performance, the understeer becoming so bad that Warwick had to dip the clutch in order to negotiate slow corners. Chico Serra, after a lengthy battle with Arnoux, had managed to slip ahead of the Ferrari while the pair were being lapped by Rosberg. Danny Sullivan drove sensibly to finish 11th while the Lotus team struggled to fill the next two places, Mansell having stopped for tyres and lost 400rpm on the straights thanks to running a large rear wing in the hope of finding grip. De Angelis had an impossible task with the spare Lotus but at least he finished ahead of Salazar who spent the latter stages of the race baulking the faster cars after stopping his March for fresh tyres. Manfred Winkelhock was four laps behind after a pit stop to rectify fuel feed problems on the ill-handling ATS-BMW.

The other BMW-engined car ran like clockwork, Nelson taking a victory which more than made up for his exclusion the previous year. As in 1982, Rosberg crossed the line in second place but, as in 1982, the Finnish driver was subsequently excluded, this time for receiving a push start. De Angelis was also excluded because, according to the Stewards, he had switched from a Renault-engined car to the Cosworth; a strange decision by the organisers considering de Angelis had driven the spare car during practice. In both cases, the teams appealed.

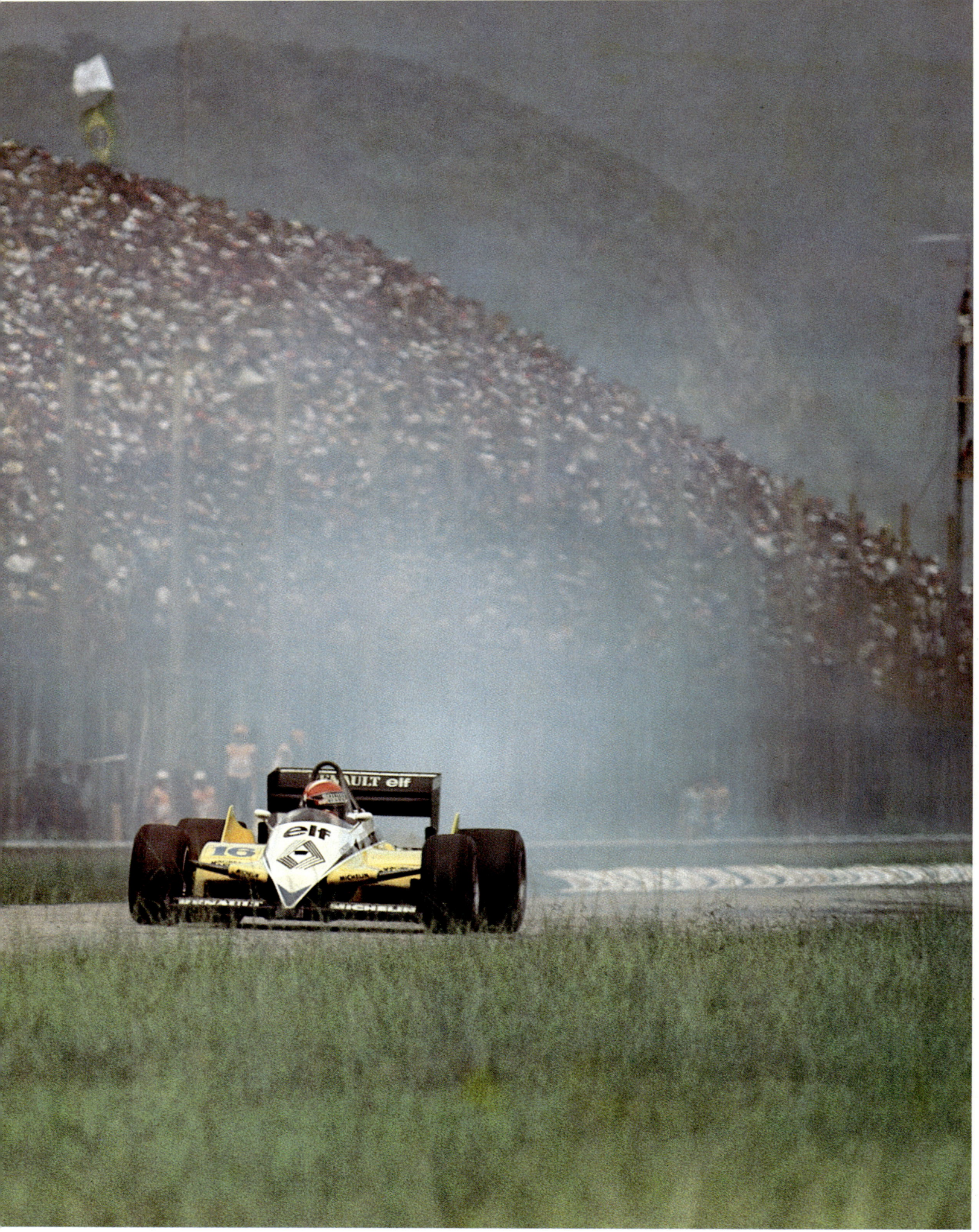

Entries and practice times

No.	Driver	Nat	Car	Tyre	Engine	Entrant	Practice 1	Practice 2
1	Keke Rosberg	SF	Saudia WILLIAMS FW08C	G	Ford Cosworth DFV	TAG Williams Team	**1m 34·526s**	1m 35·226s
2	Jacques Laffite	F	Saudia WILLIAMS FW08C	G	Ford Cosworth DFV	TAG Williams Team	**1m 38·234s**	1m 38·725s
3	Michele Alboreto	I	Benetton TYRRELL 011	G	Ford Cosworth DFV	Benetton Tyrrell Team	1m 38·747s	**1m 36·291s**
4	Danny Sullivan	USA	Benetton TYRRELL 011	G	Ford Cosworth DFV	Benetton Tyrrell Team	1m 39·697s	**1m 38·686s**
5	Nelson Piquet	BR	Parmalat BRABHAM BT52	M	BMW M12/13	Fila Sport	1m 35·815s	**1m 35·114s**
6	Riccardo Patrese	I	Parmalat BRABHAM BT52	M	BMW M12/13	Fila Sport	**1m 35·958s**	1m 36·827s
7	John Watson	GB	Marlboro McLaren MP4/1C	M	Ford Cosworth DFV	Marlboro McLaren International	1m 37·844s	**1m 36·977s**
8	Niki Lauda	A	Marlboro McLAREN MP4/1C	M	Ford Cosworth DFV	Marlboro McLaren International	**1m 36·054s**	1m 36·906s
9	Manfred Winkelhock	D	ATS D6	G	BMW M12/13	Team ATS	1m 42·292s	**1m 41·153s**
11	Elio de Angelis	I	John Player Special LOTUS 93T	P	Renault EF1	John Player Team Lotus	1m 40·056s*	**1m 36·454s**
12	Nigel Mansell	GB	John Player Special LOTUS 92	P	Ford Cosworth DFV	John Player Team Lotus	1m 42·098s	**1m 39·154s**
15	Alain Prost	F	Elf RENAULT RE 30C	M	Renault EF1	Equipe Renault Elf	**1m 34·672s**	1m 34·873s
16	Eddie Cheever	USA	Elf RENAULT RE 30C	M	Renault EF1	Equipe Renault Elf	1m 37·005s	**1m 36·051s**
17	Eliseo Salazar	RCH	MARCH-RAM 01	P	Ford Cosworth DFV	RAM Automotive Team March	1m 44·357s	**1m 41·478s**
22	Andrea de Cesaris	I	Marlboro ALFA ROMEO 183T	M	Alfa Romeo 183T	Marlboro Team Alfa Romeo	Time disallowed	
23	Mauro Baldi	I	Marlboro ALFA ROMEO 183T	M	Alfa Romeo 183T	Marlboro Team Alfa Romeo	**1m 36·126s**	1m 36·652s
25	Jean-Pierre Jarier	F	Gitanes LIGIER JS21	M	Ford Cosworth DFV	Equipe Ligier Gitanes	1m 36·828s	**1m 36·393s**
26	Raul Boesel	BR	Gitanes LIGIER JS21	M	Ford Cosworth DFV	Equipe Ligier Gitanes	1m 38·741s	**1m 37·729s**
27	Patrick Tambay	F	Fiat FERRARI 126C2/B	G	Ferrari 126C	Scuderia Ferrari SpA SEFAC	1m 34·993s	**1m 34·758s**
28	René Arnoux	F	Fiat FERRARI 126C2/B	G	Ferrari 126C	Scuderia Ferrari SpA SEFAC	1m 36·390s	**1m 35·547s**
29	Marc Surer	CH	ARROWS A6	G	Ford Cosworth DFV	Arrows Racing Team	1m 40·255s	**1m 38·468s**
30	Chico Serra	BR	ARROWS A6	G	Ford Cosworth DFV	Arrows Racing Team	1m 41·472s	**1m 39·965s**
31	Corrado Fabi	I	OSELLA FA1D	M	Ford Cosworth DFV	Osella Squadra Corse	1m 41·316s	**1m 40·309s**
32	Piercarlo Ghinzani	I	OSELLA FA1D	M	Ford Cosworth DFV	Osella Squadra Corse	1m 46·964s	1m 42·267s
33	Roberto Guerrero	COL	THEODORE N183	G	Ford Cosworth DFV	Theodore Racing Team	1m 37·237s	**1m 36·694s**
34	Johnny Cecotto	YV	THEODORE N183	G	Ford Cosworth DFV	Theodore Racing Team	**1m 38·378s**	1m 39·178s
35	Derek Warwick	GB	Candy TOLEMAN TG183B	P	Hart 415T	Candy Toleman Motorsport	**1m 35·206s**	—
36	Bruno Giacomelli	I	Candy TOLEMAN TG183B	P	Hart 415T	Candy Toleman Motorsport	**1m 36·747s**	—

Friday morning and Saturday morning practice sessions not officially recorded.

G – Goodyear, M – Michelin, P – Pirelli.

Fri pm Hot, dry
Sat pm Hot, dry
* Time recorded in Lotus 92-Cosworth

Starting grid

	1 ROSBERG (1m 34·526s) Williams
15 PROST (1m 34·672s) Renault	
	27 TAMBAY (1m 34·758s) Ferrari
5 PIQUET (1m 35·114s) Brabham	
	35 WARWICK (1m 35·206s) Toleman
28 ARNOUX (1m 35·547s) Ferrari	
	6 PATRESE (1m 35·958s) Brabham
16 CHEEVER (1m 36·051s) Renault	
	8 LAUDA (1m 36·054s) McLaren
23 BALDI (1m 36·126s) Alfa Romeo	
	3 ALBORETO (1m 36·291s) Tyrrell
25 JARIER (1m 36·393s) Ligier	
	11 DE ANGELIS (1m 36·454s) Lotus
33 GUERRERO (1m 36·694s) Theodore	
	36 GIACOMELLI (1m 36·747s) Toleman
7 WATSON (1m 36·977s) McLaren	
	26 BOESEL (1m 37·729s) Ligier
2 LAFFITE (1m 38·234s) Williams	
	34 CECOTTO (1m 38·378s) Theodore
29 SURER (1m 38·468s) Arrows	
	4 SULLIVAN (1m 38·686s) Tyrrell
12 MANSELL (1m 39·154s) Lotus	
	30 SERRA (1m 39·965s) Arrows
31 FABI (1m 40·309s) Osella	
	9 WINKELHOCK (1m 41·153s) ATS
17 SALAZAR (1m 41·478s) March RAM	

Did not start:
22 de Cesaris (Alfa Romeo), time disallowed, driver excluded
32 Ghinzani (Osella), 1m 42·267s, failed to qualify

Results and retirements

Place	Driver	Car	Laps	Time and Speed (mph/km/h)/Retirement	
1	Nelson Piquet	Brabham-BMW t/c 4	63	1h 48m 27·731s	108·926/175·3
2	*Keke Rosberg	Williams-Cosworth V8	63	1h 48m 48·362s	108·615/174·8
3	Niki Lauda	McLaren-Cosworth V8	63	1h 49m 19·614s	108·056/173·9
4	Jacques Laffite	Williams-Cosworth V8	63	1h 49m 41·682s	107·745/173·4
5	Patrick Tambay	Ferrari t/c V6	63	1h 49m 45·848s	107·683/173·3
6	Marc Surer	Arrows-Cosworth V8	63	1h 49m 45·938s	107·683/173·3
7	Alain Prost	Renault t/c V6	62		
8	Derek Warwick	Toleman-Hart t/c 4	62		
9	Chico Serra	Arrows-Cosworth V8	62		
10	René Arnoux	Ferrari t/c V6	62		
11	Danny Sullivan	Tyrrell-Cosworth V8	62		
12	Nigel Mansell	Lotus-Cosworth V8	61		
	*Elio de Angelis	Lotus-Cosworth V8	60		
14	Johnny Cecotto	Theodore-Cosworth V8	60		
15	Eliseo Salazar	March RAM-Cosworth V8	59		
16	Manfred Winkelhock	ATS-BMW t/c 4	59		
	Roberto Guerrero	Theodore-Cosworth V8	53	Running, not classified	
	Eddie Cheever	Renault t/c V6	41	Broken turbo	
	John Watson	McLaren-Cosworth V8	34	Engine	
	Raul Boesel	Ligier-Cosworth V8	25	Electrics	
	Mauro Baldi	Alfa Romeo t/c V8	23	Collision damage; front suspension	
	Jean-Pierre Jarier	Ligier-Cosworth V8	22	Rear suspension	
	Riccardo Patrese	Brabham-BMW t/c 4	19	Broken exhaust	
	Corrado Fabi	Osella-Cosworth V8	17	Engine	
	Bruno Giacomelli	Toleman-Hart t/c 4	16	Spun off	
	Michele Alboreto	Tyrrell-Cosworth V8	7	Incident with Baldi/damaged oil cooler	

Fastest lap: Piquet, on lap 4, 1m 39·829s, 112·733mph/181·426km/h.
Lap record: Nelson Piquet (F1 Brabham BT49D-Cosworth DFV), 1m 36·582s, 116·523mph/187·525km/h (1982).

* Disqualified

Past winners

Year	Driver	Nat	Car	Circuit	Distance miles/km	Speed mph/km/h
1972*	Carlos Reutemann	RA	3·0 Brabham BT34-Ford	Interlagos	183·01/294·53	112·89/181·68
1973	Emerson Fittipaldi	BR	3·0 JPS/Lotus 72-Ford	Interlagos	197·85/318·42	114·23/183·83
1974	Emerson Fittipaldi	BR	3·0 McLaren M23-Ford	Interlagos	158·28/254·73	112·23/180·62
1975	Carlos Pace	BR	3·0 Brabham BT44B-Ford	Interlagos	197·85/318·42	113·40/182·50
1976	Niki Lauda	A	3·0 Ferrari 312T/76	Interlagos	197·85/318·42	112·76/181·47
1977	Carlos Reutemann	RA	3·0 Ferrari 312T-2/77	Interlagos	197·85/318·42	112·92/181·73
1978	Carlos Reutemann	RA	3·0 Ferrari 312T-2/78	Rio de Janeiro	196·95/316·95	107·43/172·89
1979	Jacques Laffite	F	3·0 Ligier JS11-Ford	Interlagos	197·85/318·42	117·23/188·67
1980	René Arnoux	F	1·5 Renault RS t/c	Interlagos	195·70/314·95	117·40/188·93
1981	Carlos Reutemann	RA	3·0 Williams FWO7C-Ford	Rio de Janeiro	193·82/311·92	96·59/155·45
1982	Alain Prost	F	1·5 Renault RE t/c	Rio de Janeiro	196·95/316·95	112·97/181·80
1983	Nelson Piquet	BR	1·5 Brabahm BT52-BMW t/c	Rio de Janeiro	196·95/316·95	108·93/175·30

*Non-championship

Circuit data

Autodromo Internacional do Rio de Janeiro, Baixada de Jacarepaguá
Circuit length: 3·126 miles/5·031 km
Race distance: 63 laps, 196·945 miles/316·953 km
Race weather: Hot, dry.

Fastest laps

Driver	Time	Lap
Nelson Piquet	1m 39·829s	4
Riccardo Patrese	1m 40·512s	4
Keke Rosberg	1m 40·523s	3
Niki Lauda	1m 41·163s	16
John Watson	1m 41·547s	20
Eddie Cheever	1m 41·951s	22
Jacques Laffite	1m 42·343s	49
Alain Prost	1m 42·636s	4
Marc Surer	1m 42·657s	22
Roberto Guerrero	1m 42·849s	49
Patrick Tambay	1m 42·940s	36
Derek Warwick	1m 43·037s	44
Nigel Mansell	1m 43·159s	41
Jean-Pierre Jarier	1m 43·193s	4
Johnny Cecotto	1m 43·241s	48
Michele Alboreto	1m 43·304s	4
René Arnoux	1m 43·426s	5
Mauro Baldi	1m 43·514s	3
Chico Serra	1m 43·900s	58
Raul Boesel	1m 44·027s	6
Bruno Giacomelli	1m 44·178s	3
Elio de Angelis	1m 44·367s	7
Corrado Fabi	1m 44·476s	12
Danny Sullivan	1m 44·697s	16
Manfred Winkelhock	1m 45·355s	46
Eliseo Salazar	1m 45·681s	42

Points

WORLD CHAMPIONSHIP OF DRIVERS
1	Nelson Piquet	9 pts
2	Niki Lauda	4
3	Jacques Laffite	3
4	Patrick Tambay	2
5	Marc Surer	1

CONSTRUCTORS' CUP
1	Brabham	9 pts
2	McLaren	4
3	Williams	3
4	Ferrari	2
5	Arrows	1

Lap chart

1st LAP ORDER	1	2	3	4	5	6	7	8	9	10	11	12	13	14	15	16	17	18	19	20	21	22	23	24	25	26	27	28	29	30	31	32	33	34	35	36	37
1 K. Rosberg	1	1	1	1	1	1	5	5	5	5	5	5	5	5	5	5	5	5	5	5	5	5	5	5	5	5	5	5	5	5	5	5	5	5	5	5	5
15 A. Prost	15	5	5	5	5	5	1	1	1	1	1	1	1	1	1	1	1	1	1	1	1	1	1	1	1	1	(1)	7	7	7	7	7	7	15	15	15	
5 N. Piquet	5	15	6	6	6	6	6	6	6	6	6	6	15	15	15	15	7	7	7	7	7	7	7	7	7	7	7	15	15	15	15	15	15	8	8	8	
6 P. Patrese	6	6	15	15	15	15	15	15	15	15	15	15	6	7	7	7	15	15	15	15	15	15	15	15	15	15	27	27	27	27	27	8	27	27	27		
27 R. Tambay	27	27	27	27	27	27	27	27	7	7	7	7	7	6	6	27	27	27	27	27	27	27	27	27	27	8	8	8	8	8	27	1	1	1			
28 R. Arnoux	28	28	28	28	28	28	28	28	7	7	27	27	27	27	6	23	23	23	23	23	23	8	8	8	8	8	35	35	35	35	35	35	35	35			
16 E. Cheever	16	16	16	16	16	16	7	7	28	28	28	28	28	23	23	23	35	35	35	8	8	35	35	35	35	35	2	2	2	2	1	2	2	2			
35 D. Warwick	35	23	23	23	23	7	16	23	23	23	23	23	35	35	35	8	8	8	8	35	35	29	29	29	29	2	2	29	29	1	1	2	29	29			
23 M. Baldi	23	35	7	7	7	23	23	16	16	35	35	35	35	28	8	8	6	28	28	28	29	2	2	2	2	29	29	1	1	1	29	29	29	34	34	34	
8 N. Lauda	8	7	35	35	35	35	35	35	35	16	16	16	16	8	28	28	28	16	29	29	2	2	28	28	28	34	34	34	34	34	34	34	34	28	28	28	
7 J. Watson	7	8	8	8	8	8	25	25	25	25	25	25	8	16	16	16	16	29	16	2	28	28	34	34	34	28	28	28	28	28	28	28	30	30	30		
25 J. P. Jarier	25	25	25	25	25	25	8	8	8	8	8	8	25	25	25	29	29	2	25	34	34	26	30	30	30	30	30	30	30	30	30	16	16	16			
33 R. Guerrero	33	29	29	29	29	29	29	29	29	29	29	29	29	25	2	25	34	26	26	30	30	4	4	4	16	16	16	16	16	4	4	4					
29 M. Surer	29	33	33	33	33	33	33	33	33	33	33	33	33	(33)	2	34	34	26	30	30	4	12	12	16	4	4	4	4	12	12	12						
34 J. Cecotto	34	34	34	34	34	34	34	34	34	34	34	2	4	12	12	(26)	16	16	12	12	12	(12)	12	12	12	9	9	9									
4 D. Sullivan	4	4	4	4	2	2	2	2	2	2	2	4	34	34	34	26	30	30	(16)	12	16	16	16	9	9	9	11	11	9	9	11	11					
2 J. Laffite	2	2	2	2	26	26	26	26	26	26	26	26	26	26	26	30	4	4	4	(25)	16	(23)	9	9	11	11	11	11	11	11	11	17	17	(17)			
26 R. Boesel	26	26	26	26	4	4	4	4	4	30	30	30	30	30	4	12	12	16	(25)	11	11	17	17	17	17	17	17	17	33	33	33						
36 B. Giacomelli	36	36	36	36	36	30	30	30	30	4	4	36	36	36	36	12	(6)	9	9	(25)	11	17	17	33	33	33	33	33	33								
30 C. Serra	30	30	30	30	30	36	36	36	36	36	36	36	4	4	4	(31)	9	17	17	11	11	33	33														
12 N. Mansell	12	12	12	12	3	3	12	12	12	12	12	12	12	12	9	17	(6)	11	17	17	33																
31 C. Fabi	31	9	3	3	12	12	(3)	9	9	9	9	31	31	31	31	(31)	17	11	11	33	33	33															
9 M. Winkelhock	9	17	9	9	9	9	31	31	31	31	9	9	9	9	9	11	33	33																			
17 E. Salazar	17	3	17	17	31	31	31	17	17	17	17	17	17	17	17	17	(33)																				
3 M. Alboreto	3	31	31	31	17	17	17	11	11	11	11	11	11	11	11	11																					
11 E. De Angelis	11	11	11	11	11	11	11	11						−1 lap																							

38	39	40	41	42	43	44	45	46	47	48	49	50	51	52	53	54	55	56	57	58	59	60	61	62	63
5	5	(5)	5	5	5	5	5	5	5	5	5	5	5	5	5	5	5	5	5	5	5	5	5	5	5
15	15	15	15	8	8	8	8	8	8	8	8	8	8	1	1	1	1	1	1	1	1	1	1	1	1
8	8	8	15	15	15	15	15	1	1	1	1	1	1	8	8	8	8	8	8	8	8	8	8	8	8
27	27	27	27	27	1	1	1	15	15	15	15	15	15	27	27	27	27	27	27	2	2	2	2	2	2
1	1	1	1	1	27	27	27	27	27	27	27	27	27	15	15	15	15	2	2	2	27	27	27	27	27
35	35	35	35	29	29	29	29	29	29	29	29	29	29	29	29	29	15	29	29	29	29	29	29	29	29
2	29	29	29	35	35	35	2	2	2	2	2	2	2	2	2	2	29	15	15	15	15	15	15		15
29	2	2	2	2	2	2	35	35	35	35	35	35	35	35	35	35	35	35	35	35	35	35	35		
34	28	28	28	28	28	28	28	28	28	28	28	28	28	28	28	28	30	30	30	30	30	30			
28	34	30	30	30	30	30	30	30	30	30	30	30	30	30	30	30	28	28	28	28	28	28			
30	30	16	(16)	4	4	4	4	4	4	4	4	4	4	4	4	4	4	4	4	4	4	4			
16	16	(34)	4	12	12	12	12	12	12	12	12	12	12	12	12	12	12	12	12						
4	4	4	(9)	11	11	11	11	11	9	9	11	11	34	34	34	34	34	11	11						
12	12	12	9	9	9	9	9	9	11	11	9	34	11	11	11	11	11	34	34						
9	9	9	11	34	34	34	34	34	34	34	34	9	9	9	17	17	17	17							
11	11	11	34	17	17	17	17	17	17	17	17	17	17	17	9	9	9	9							
17	17	17	17	33	33	33	33	33	33	33	33	33	33	33											
33	33	33	33																						

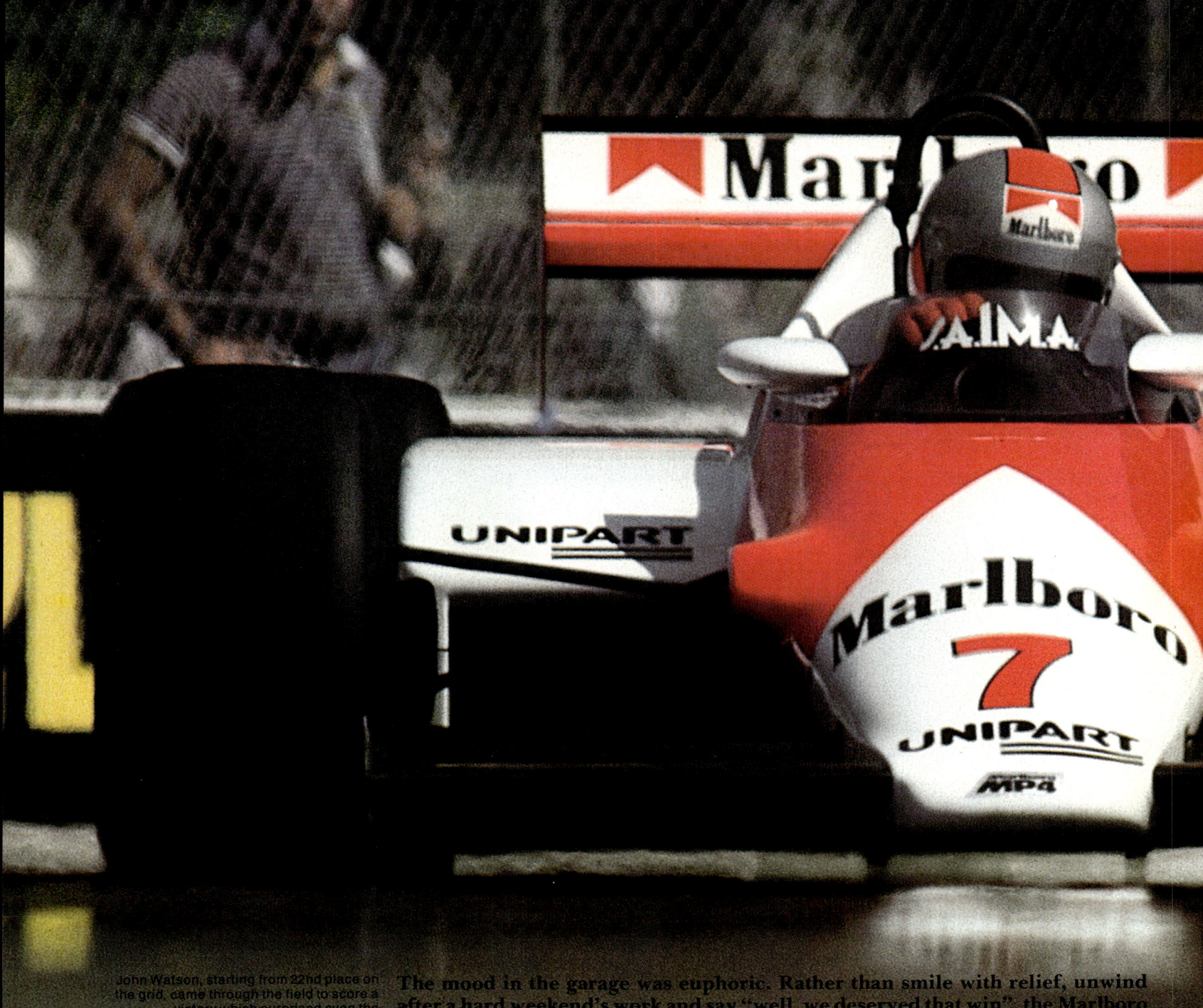

The mood in the garage was euphoric. Rather than smile with relief, unwind after a hard weekend's work and say "well, we deserved that win", the Marlboro McLaren mechanics grinned foolishly at each other, glanced at the laurels once again — and grinned some more. They had won races before, of course, although it had been 15 years since the team had scored a one-two. But that wasn't the point. This time, they had done it from the back of the grid.

"Bloody ridiculous," said one. "Incredible," said another. "Wattie, the old sod," began a third, "he just . . . well, I dunno . . ." and his voice tailed off as he looked at John Barnard for an explanation. The McLaren designer shrugged his shoulders and fingered the rear wing of the winning MP4/1C as he thought about the atmosphere in that very compound 24 hours earlier.

They had been, to put it mildly, in trouble. John Watson and Niki Lauda had come through practice complaining of no grip, of understeer, of no progress having been made. 22nd and 23rd positions on the grid said that, never mind the forlorn look on Watson's face as walked alone from the pits to the garage.

Now he was the centre of attention in the Press Room; relaxed, fit, radiant — and stunned. "Don't ask me how I did it," he said of his fifth Grand Prix victory. "I mean, you don't expect to win from back there. I believe there was a bit of trouble at the front which might have helped us."

There had been more than a "bit of trouble". It started on the green light, in fact, when Keke Rosberg clouted the front wheel of René Arnoux's car as he tried to squeeze through the Ferrari front row. Moments later, he executed a 360-degree spin while trying to take the lead from Patrick Tambay. 26 laps later the two cars came together well and truly; Tambay retiring; the Saudia Williams stopping a few yards further on, after disputing the next corner with Jacques

96

TOYOTA GRAND PRIX OF THE UNITED STATES (LONG BEACH)

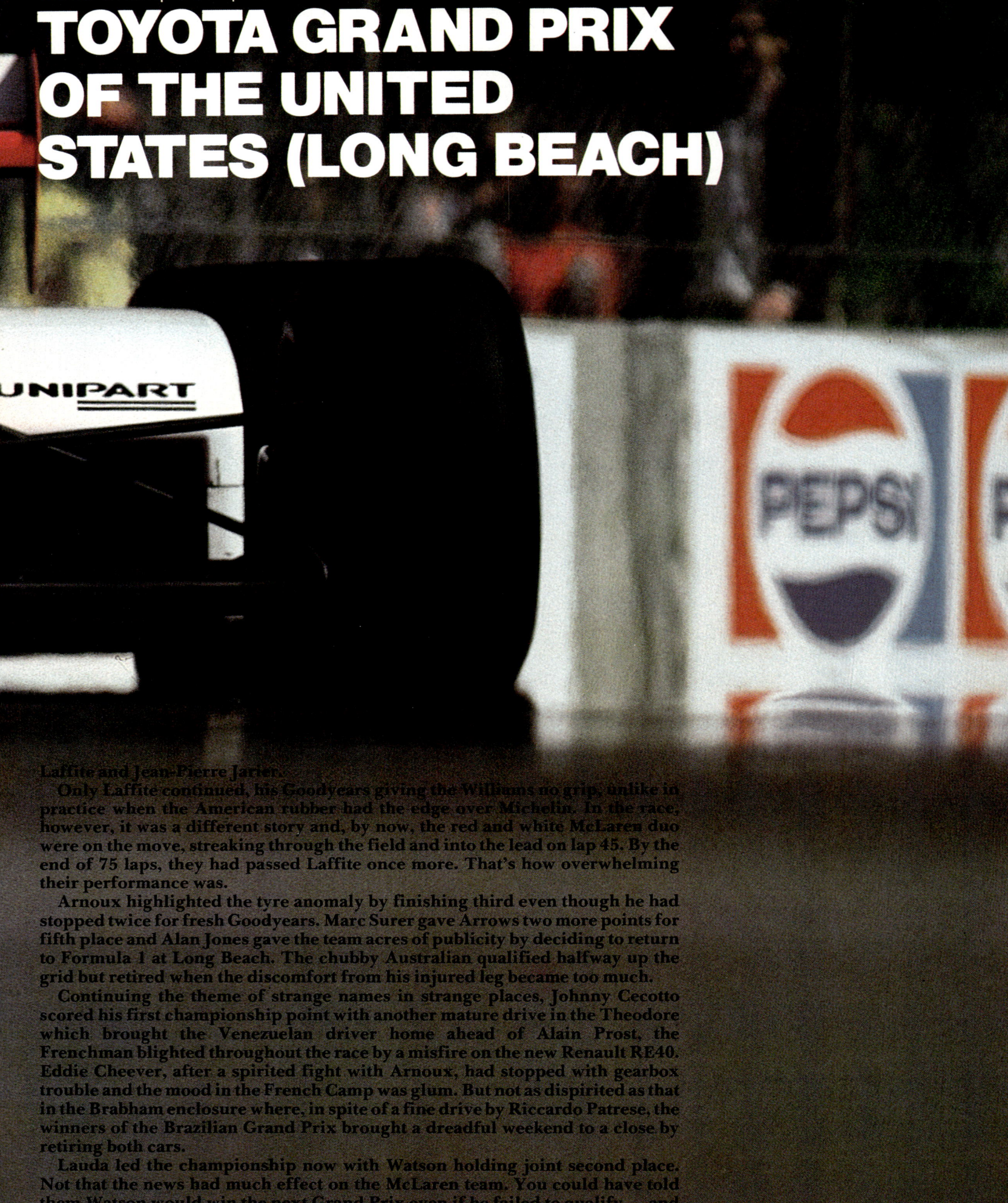

Laffite and Jean-Pierre Jarier.

Only Laffite continued, his Goodyears giving the Williams no grip, unlike in practice when the American rubber had the edge over Michelin. In the race, however, it was a different story and, by now, the red and white McLaren duo were on the move, streaking through the field and into the lead on lap 45. By the end of 75 laps, they had passed Laffite once more. That's how overwhelming their performance was.

Arnoux highlighted the tyre anomaly by finishing third even though he had stopped twice for fresh Goodyears. Marc Surer gave Arrows two more points for fifth place and Alan Jones gave the team acres of publicity by deciding to return to Formula 1 at Long Beach. The chubby Australian qualified halfway up the grid but retired when the discomfort from his injured leg became too much.

Continuing the theme of strange names in strange places, Johnny Cecotto scored his first championship point with another mature drive in the Theodore which brought the Venezuelan driver home ahead of Alain Prost, the Frenchman blighted throughout the race by a misfire on the new Renault RE40. Eddie Cheever, after a spirited fight with Arnoux, had stopped with gearbox trouble and the mood in the French Camp was glum. But not as dispirited as that in the Brabham enclosure where, in spite of a fine drive by Riccardo Patrese, the winners of the Brazilian Grand Prix brought a dreadful weekend to a close by retiring both cars.

Lauda led the championship now with Watson holding joint second place. Not that the news had much effect on the McLaren team. You could have told them Watson would win the next Grand Prix even if he failed to qualify — and they would have believed it!

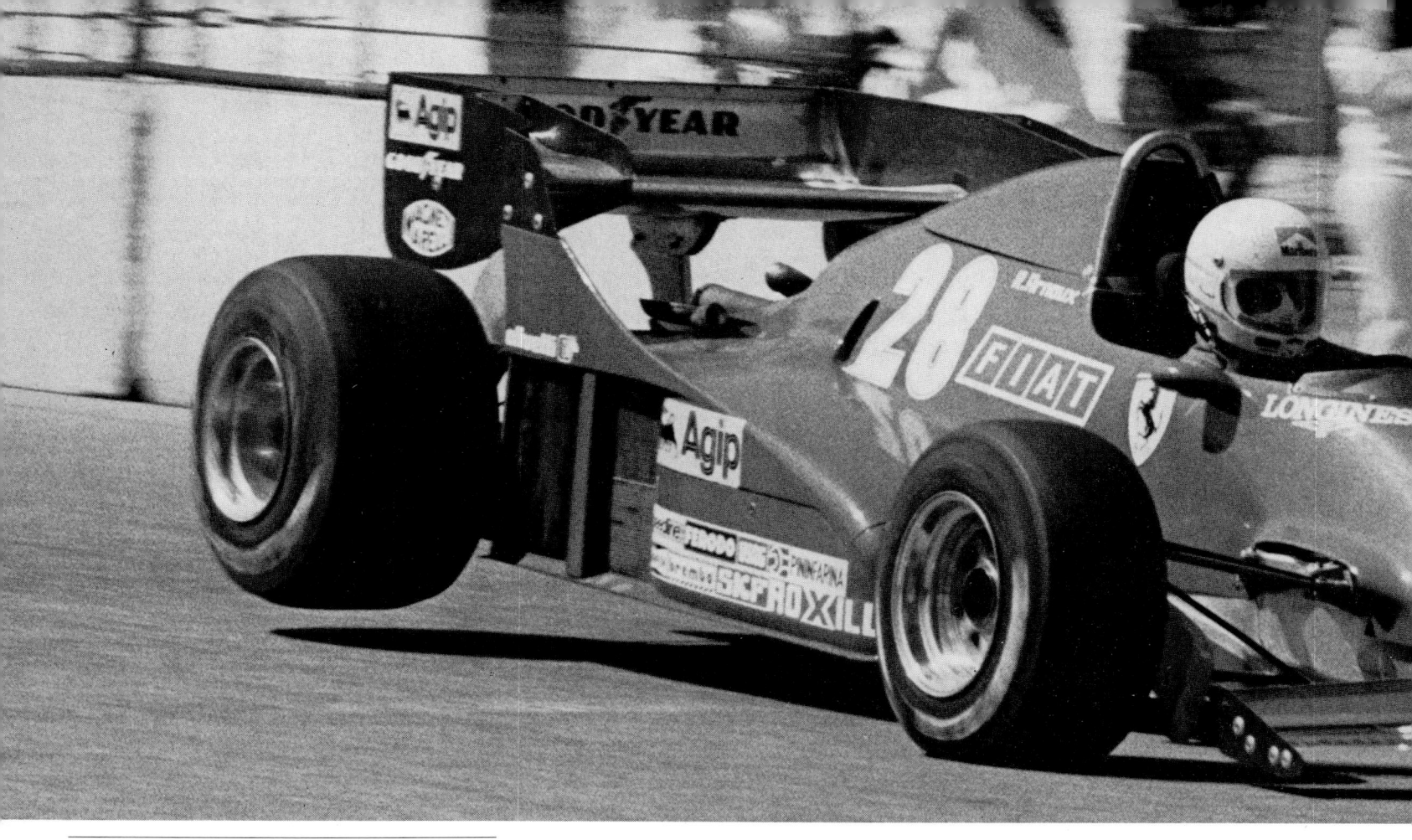

ENTRY AND PRACTICE

The rain, which had dogged the Royal Tour of California a few weeks before, left its mark on the Grand Prix. A subsidence in the road surface at the foot of the steep Linden Avenue Hill had left a dip in the track which was barely discernable to the eye. American road cars simply took the bump in their usual wallowing stride but, once the stiffly sprung Grand Prix cars crossed the point in question at around 150mph, the bump became a launching pad just as drivers were about to get on the brakes for the tight second gear corner which followed. It made for spectacular viewing although the majority of drivers didn't quite see it that way.

Sparks were flying, not only on the track, but in the pit lane. Within a few laps, Derek Warwick's Toleman had limped in with broken rear suspension. The top right wishbone had given way and a quick inspection revealed the left side to be bent. Bruno Giacomelli's car was going the same way and the team decided it was pointless to continue. They would take no further part, they said, unless something was done. Derek Ongaro was dispatched to the offending section of track and, after a few minutes spectating, the FISA Safety Inspector agreed the drivers had a reasonable grievance even though some cars, notably the Tyrrells, were riding the bump with nonchalant ease.

The organisers' reaction was swift and effective. By the time practice had finished on Friday afternoon, a squad of men were ready to cut and fill the dip with 36 cubic yards of quick-setting concrete. By Saturday morning, the complaints and the dip had been smoothed over.

Friday practice, therefore, meant little. The teams had, in effect, Saturday morning to sort their cars in time for the final hour and, from the outset, it was the Ferrari team which set the pace. Or, to be more precise, it was the Ferrari team and Goodyear which set the pace – a curious situation since the combination had been struggling at Rio two weeks previously. But this was Long Beach, a street circuit with no fast corners to overtax the tyres. They were still searching for traction, of course, and to that end Ferrari produced a development of the rear wing which saw extensions from the leading edge join the rear of the side-pods. Arnoux had been quickest on Friday, the beady-eyed little Frenchman pressing on with scant regard for the bump. A broken gearbox on Saturday morning meant he lost valuable time and was unable to

improve in the afternoon. He would have kept pole had it not been for a most polished and relaxed lap from Patrick Tambay who lost out on Friday with a misfire on his race car. For the final session, though, all was well and Tambay was enthusiastic about the balance of the car and the performance of the Goodyear qualifiers.

The benefit to be gained from those qualifiers over the race tyres continued to be something of a pleasant surprise to Jacques Laffite who was more accustomed to the inconsistent Michelins. Wiping out the disappointment of his practice performance in Rio, Laffite was a splendid fourth fastest behind his team-mate Rosberg. As ever, the Williams team had mapped out a busy programme of tests to be carried out but the problems with the bump on Friday meant the work had to be crammed into the Saturday morning practice. Running larger front wings, Rosberg's car underwent a complete change of set-up on Friday night and the improvement, while failing to eradicate completely time-consuming understeer, meant some very spectacular opposite lock motoring from the World Champion.

Elio de Angelis produced a similar performance to take fifth place on the grid although, in this instance, the spectacle was provided by a chassis which was not equal to the power of the Renault turbo. John Player Team Lotus had altered the weight distribution of the 93T by lengthening the wheelbase which, coupled with revised rear suspension and the presence in the pit lane of Tony Rudd, Director of Engineering at Lotus, added up to a car which was a considerable improvement. Pirelli qualifiers helped, too, even though the team were not placing much hope on the race rubber. The niceties of fine suspension tuning to specific tyre compounds were beyond Nigel Mansell, the Englishman continuing an unequal struggle with the Cosworth-powered 92 and its active suspension. The computer, if anything, proved too active when confronted by strange messages from the wheels as the car crashed onto the track after tackling the bump on Friday. Mansell was simply a passenger as he attempted to keep the darting car pointing in a straight line and things were not much better on Saturday, 13th place being the reward for much physical effort.

Considering they had missed the best part of Friday practice, it was something of a surprise to see the Toleman of Derek Warwick set second fastest time during the unofficial session on Saturday morning. He

then set a time good enough for sixth place on his first set of qualifiers but made the mistake of asking for a change to the car before venturing out on this second set. None the less, it was an impressive time for all that. Bruno Giacomelli was not so fortunate, his engine losing boost pressure at a vital moment and relegating the Italian to 14th place on the grid.

The move to have the bump taken out on Friday night was not well received by Ken Tyrrell. As mentioned previously, the green Benetton cars glided over an obstacle which Tyrrell considered one of the natural hazards of a street circuit. His cars could cope with it so why make a change simply because others could not ride the bump? It would make about as much sense, he continued, if he were to ask for a chicane in the middle of the straight at Ricard on the grounds that it didn't suit his Cosworth car. . . .

There were few takers for this course of discussion and Michele Alboreto simply got on with the job, the Italian producing his usual flowing style which was interrupted by a spin on Saturday morning. Everything was in order for the final session and Michele took seventh place, his team-mate, Danny Sullivan, surprising many with a fast, if not so neat, lap to claim ninth place, a shade under half-a-second slower than Alboreto.

Unhappy with the fall in competitiveness of their RE30C in Rio, the Renault-Elf team rushed through plans to bring one RE40 to Long Beach. Alain Prost drove the car at Willow Springs where, apart from a fuel injection pump requiring attention, everything went according to plan. Come official practice, however, and it was a different story, Prost's progress blighted by a misfire on Saturday afternoon. Then there was oversteer and poor Michelin qualifiers to worry about. Eddie Cheever was not much happier with a performance which, on paper at least, did not seem to merit the attention the American driver had been receiving from the local media. Eddie put a number of minor problems out of his mind in the final session and hurled the Renault into 15th place. The bumps then got the better of him and Cheever glanced a wall and pushed the left-front wheel into the monocoque. He would use the spare car for the race.

Jean-Pierre Jarier, his Ligier's suspension coping admirably with the circuit, soon discovered that the Michelin race tyres were actually a better bet than the so-called qualifiers and the Frenchman took a confident tenth place. His tyres were then handed over to

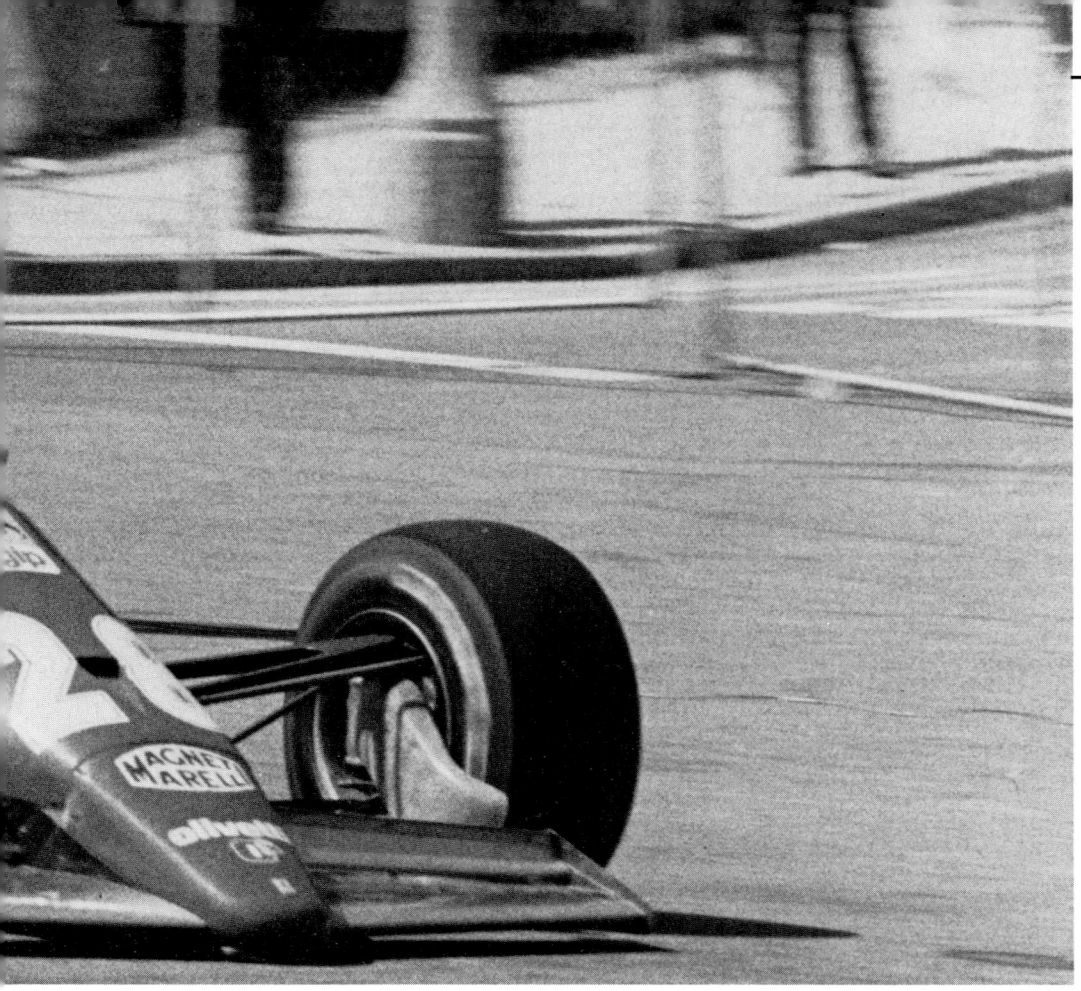

René Arnoux comes in to land at the 'bump', the Ferrari driver setting fastest time on Friday. He finished third in spite of two stops for tyres *(left)*.
Mister Cool. Sporting a tee-shirt picturing his daughter, Patrick Tambay relaxes in the pits. The Ferrari driver took an equally cool pole position *(below)*.
Danny Sullivan showed fine form, qualifying two places behind Alboreto. The American driver held sixth place initially but dropped back with severe tyre vibrations *(bottom)*.

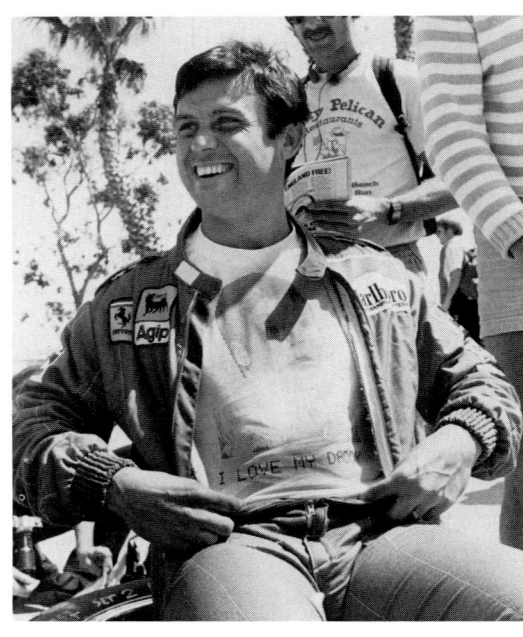

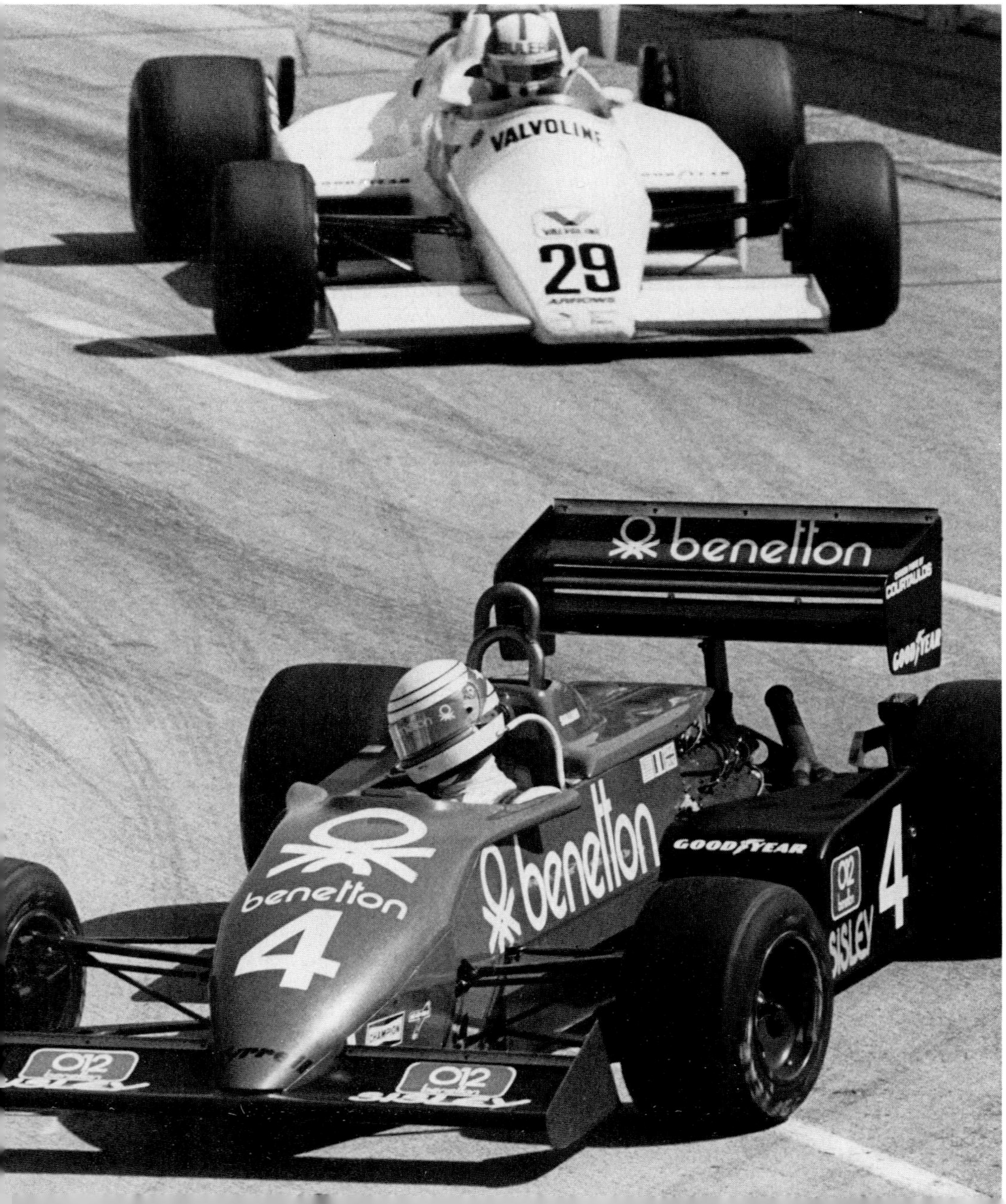

Raul Boesel but it was not explained to the Brazilian that the rubber would be at its best after a gradual warm-up during the course of several laps. He qualified in 26th place with Friday's time after clutch trouble with his race car had forced Boesel to use the spare chassis for the final session.

"I think we changed more springs on Friday than we did through the whole of 1982!" That exasperated comment from a Brabham mechanic summed up the desperate measures taken by the team as they tried to work a reasonable temperature into their Michelins. An air scoop had been inserted in the left side-pod to cool the shock absorber which had given trouble in Rio and, likewise, attention had been paid to the gearbox, but that was minor surgery in the overall ailment of a car which simply would not handle on qualifiers. McLaren were in similar trouble, the team changing the set-up of both cars completely on Friday night – but to no avail. There was even a three-piece rear wing to increase downforce but the McLaren/Michelin combination which had dominated Long Beach the year before were no more than also-rans during practice. Race tyres provided more grip so at least Brabham and McLaren had learnt something about their prospects for Sunday. In the meantime, Riccardo Patrese came off best with 11th fastest time, the other three drivers languishing at the back of the grid.

The Arrows pit, normally free from the squads of pressmen who regularly invaded teams such as Williams and Ferrari, was the centre of attention. Following a test at Willows Springs, Alan Jones decided he was fit enough to make his return to Grand Prix racing at Long Beach. Overweight and unfit thanks to the leg injury sustained the previous January when he fell from a horse, Jones nevertheless showed that he had lost none of his determination by qualifying in 12th place – and this in a car which was not tailored for the chunky Australian. Marc Surer's Arrows was back in 16th place, the Swiss driver having lost most of Friday with a seized gearbox on his race car and engine trouble when he took over the spare chassis.

Roberto Guerrero, one of the smoothest drivers on the track, complained of understeer and was pleasantly surprised when credited with eighth fastest time on Saturday. He was annoyed, however, when the organisers subsequently decided that the bodywork on his Theodore was a couple of centimetres too wide and, as a result, he would have to accept his Friday time

and 18th place on the grid. It was unfortunate since the side-pod had become distorted in the heat of Rio and the team had pointed it out at scrutineering. There was no obvious advantage to be had and the car had been passed. Now it was illegal and the organisers would not be moved. 18th place it would be – just behind the other Theodore of Johnny Cecotto. The Venezuelan driver spoiled an impressive practice by shaving the wall too close on the straight, a wheel catching the edge of a concrete block where it protruded slightly, causing minor damage.

Marlboro Alfa Romeo had made few changes since Rio but it was changed times for the pole position team of 1982. Neither Andrea de Cesaris nor Mauro Baldi looked at home as they tried to coax the turbos through the streets, both drivers having disagreements with the concrete walls as well as the usual Michelin complaints of understeer and no grip. For good measure, de Cesaris had turbo trouble on Saturday afternoon, the Alfa Romeo coming to a halt with the rear end on fire. Andrea was 19th fastest; Baldi 21st. Manfred Winkelhock was another driver to have trouble with the walls, the ATS driver qualifying in 24th place ahead of Eliseo Salazar's March. Both the ATS and the RAM car had revised suspension for Long Beach but a weight-saving programme for Corrado Fabi's Osella made little difference, the Italian failing to qualify along with his team-mate, Piercarlo Ghinzani.

RACE

Following their débâcle during practice, the McLaren team made a stab at finding a decent set-up for the race during the warm-up on Sunday morning. Judging by the times, they were unsuccessful, Lauda and Watson over one second slower than the fastest man, Rosberg. The team had thrown every conceivable Michelin they could lay their hands on at the cars but few firm conclusions had been reached. It was felt that the new 419 compound would be the one to have but Watson was not so sure. He decided on the same compound he had used at Detroit the previous year, which was a happy compromise all round since the 419s were in short supply and Lauda preferred them. Not that it would make much difference. At this point in the proceedings, it seemed McLaren might score one or two points, assuming the others ran into trouble, of course.

And, for the first lap at least, it seemed Keke Rosberg was working for McLaren International. Tambay was hesitant at the start and Rosberg, keen to be free of the turbos, swerved left, aiming for the gap between the two Ferraris. Not lifting his right foot for a second, Rosberg slid sideways and made sharp contact with Arnoux's right-front wheel. By now Tambay had gathered steam and took the lead as the pack left the grid. Rosberg was climbing all over the red car and, as they crossed the site of the 'bump' and hit the brakes for the right-hander which followed, the Williams made a lunge for the inside line. The uneven surface unsettled the car and, before he knew it, the back brakes had locked, sending Rosberg into a terrifying spin in front of 24 tightly packed cars! By a stroke of good fortune, coupled with quick reflexes, the Williams finished the gyration by pointing in the right direction, Rosberg continuing on his way having lost just one place – to Jacques Laffite! Alboreto was fourth with Arnoux, having got over the assault at the start, in fifth place ahead of Sullivan and Patrese. Alain Prost was next but destined to slip down the field when a misfire returned even though the team had installed a fresh engine for the race. Cheever was next with Jarier in tenth place and pulling away from Warwick. The Toleman was soon passed by Surer in the Arrows and Warwick's race would last 11 laps before the tread pulled away from a rear tyre, causing the Toleman to crash heavily.

De Angelis had made a bad start and was coming under pressure from Jones while Mansell made the first of many pit stops for tyres as early as lap four. By now, the field was one short since Winkelhock had survived a nasty accident when his ATS turned sharp left under braking at the end of the straight.

It didn't take Rosberg long to displace Laffite and the Williams was soon on the tail of Tambay's Ferrari once more. Sullivan lost ground as Patrese, Cheever and Jarier moved ahead but the Renault's impressive drive lasted until the end of lap 18 when Eddie peeled into the pits for tyres. Unfortunately, he found the Renault mechanics busy searching for the cause of Prost's misfire and the American was waved back out again.

Up at the front, the race was developing nicely as the Williams pair began to put pressure on Tambay. Alboreto had joined them and Jarier, making the most

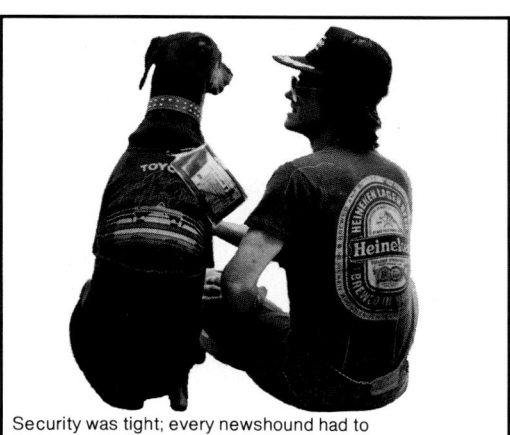

Security was tight; every newshound had to show his credentials.

of Michelins which were perfect for the race, had dealt with Patrese and was soon on the tail of the Tyrrell. Sensing that he had the upper hand for once, Jarier became impatient and a late-braking move inside Alboreto saw the two cars touch and take to the escape road. Jarier continued unabated but the Italian driver made for the pits where mechanics changed all four tyres while replacing a steering arm. Patrese had slipped through into fourth place but the hard charging Jarier claimed it back as they closed on the battle for the lead.

Tambay had chosen 'B' compound all round and was keen to conserve his tyres as he carefully dictated the pace in spite of the mounting pressure behind. On lap 26, he slid wide briefly at the exit of the left-hander leading onto the short straight before the hairpin. Rosberg, anxious to seize any opportunity, took a run at the inside line, the Williams darting and weaving on the edge of adhesion as Keke left his braking very late. Clearly, Tambay wasn't expecting this for the Frenchman had taken his normal line and, as he turned into the corner, his right-rear wheel ran over Rosberg's left-front, the Ferrari leaping into the air before crashing down onto the track, its engine stalled. As Tambay waved his arms in warning, Rosberg selected first gear and continued, his adrenalin pumping furiously. As he accelerated towards the next corner, a right-hander, he found Jacques Laffite racing alongside with an excited Jarier snapping at their heels. This, after all, was still the battle for the lead. Keke felt Jacques should give way since he, Rosberg, was the quicker of the two but it soon became clear that Laffite was just as keen to win this race. The two cars touched as they reached the braking area, a move which seemed to catch Jarier by surprise for he promptly ran into the back of Rosberg, the Williams

pulling off into retirement. Jarier continued but he, too, was forced to stop not long after. Within the space of a few seconds, the entire complex of the race had changed completely. Jacques Laffite was now in the lead.

Patrese was second, a fine performance considering the handling of his Brabham, and Marc Surer was third although this would be brief since the handling of the Arrows had started to deteriorate as the fuel load lightened. Increasing understeer meant Surer had to back off to save his tyres and the white Arrows soon gave way to – Lauda and Watson!

Almost unnoticed, the McLarens had marched through the field. Unnoticed, that is, by all but the McLaren team. From the very early stages, John Barnard was aware that his drivers were lapping as quickly as the leaders and it was obvious that a place in the points might be on the cards. Now, with the leaders having wiped themselves out, a finish in the points was certain although the team had yet to think in terms of a win. Mind you, their passage had been eased slightly by problems further down the field; Giacomelli calling at the pits for tyres, stalling his engine and finding the battery unequal to the task of re-starting the engine; Baldi had touched a wall, pitted for a new tyre and returned only to make a proper job of it by coming into heavy contact with the wall; Guerrero lost fourth and fifth gears and saw no point in continuing while de Angelis gave up when the team ran out of tyres, the 93T having been into the pits twice for fresh Pirellis. Jones, too, had had his moment with the waiting concrete, a brush with the wall sending the Arrows into the pits for a new steering arm. He was back a lap later for further adjustments and, after lapping at the tail of the field, Jones finally called it day, the pins in his thigh rubbing against the monocoque. As Jones pointed out, when you are that far behind, you feel pain more than when you are running in the points. . . .

For a while, it seemed Jacques Laffite would score nine points since Patrese looked unlikely to challenge and the McLaren onslaught was some 25 seconds in arrears. Lap 33, and Watson took Lauda with a precise move. The Austrian didn't exactly invite the Ulsterman to pass but it was clear that John had the better tyres as he began to pull away. The Brabham team passed on the news of Watson's advance and Patrese began to close on Laffite, the Frenchman unable to respond since his choice of a softer 'C' compound on the left-rear was causing the car to slide too much.

By lap 42, the McLarens had the Brabham in sight and, with the red and white reflections looming large in his mirrors, Patrese increased the pressure on Laffite. In an attempt to take the lead under braking at the end of Shoreline Drive, the Brabham driver missed his braking point and took to the escape road. Somehow, Watson failed to notice this and, when the McLaren moved ahead of the Williams on lap 45, Watson did not realise he was leading the race!

With Lauda slipping into second place, there was no denying McLaren, barring some mechanical misfortune. For a while, Lauda slowed considerably and the team prepared for a tyre change. Then, without warning, Lauda picked up speed again, his erratic progress being the result of cramp in one leg. Patrese made a proper job of passing Laffite on lap 52 and into fifth place came Johnny Cecotto, the Theodore driver showing surprising maturity throughout. Unfortunately, gearbox trouble meant he was having to hold the car in gear occasionally and he was soon overhauled by a fierce battle between Arnoux and Cheever. Both drivers had been into the pits for tyres (the Ferrari on two occasions) and the sight of a Renault was like a red rag to a bull as far as Arnoux was concerned. Keen to put one over on his old team, René attacked Cheever with vigour, the two drivers swapping places in a clean, lively battle.

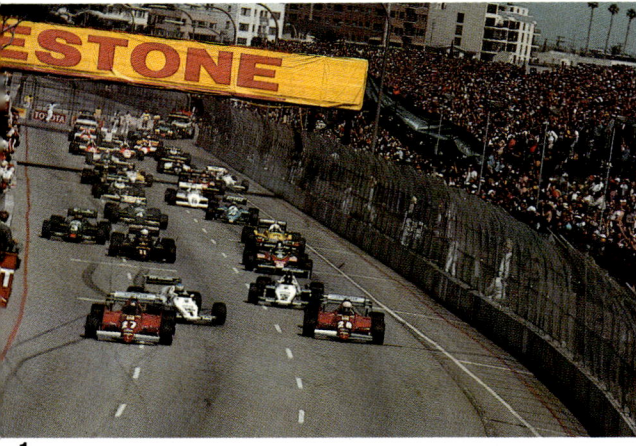

1

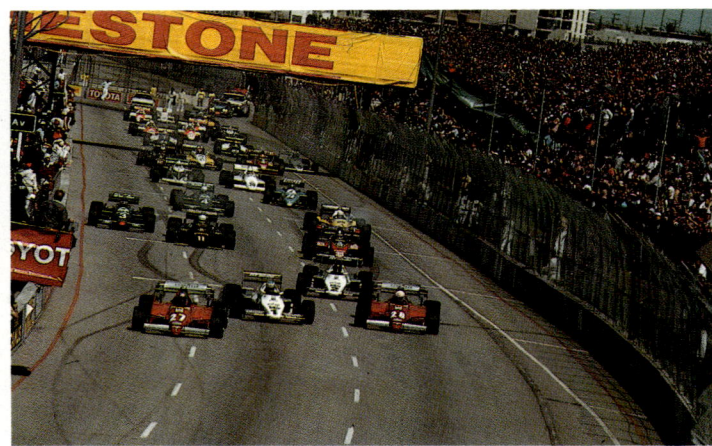

2

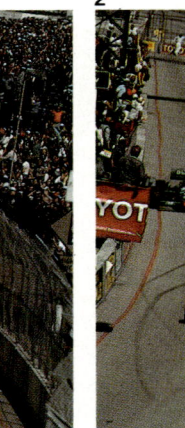

3

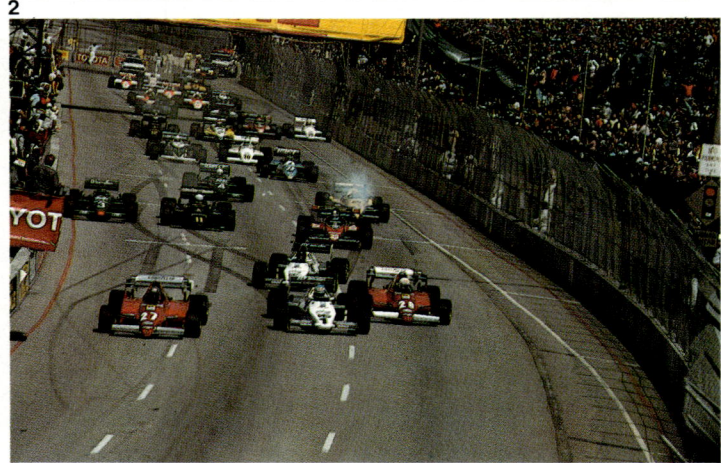

4

Photos: Mike Levasheff

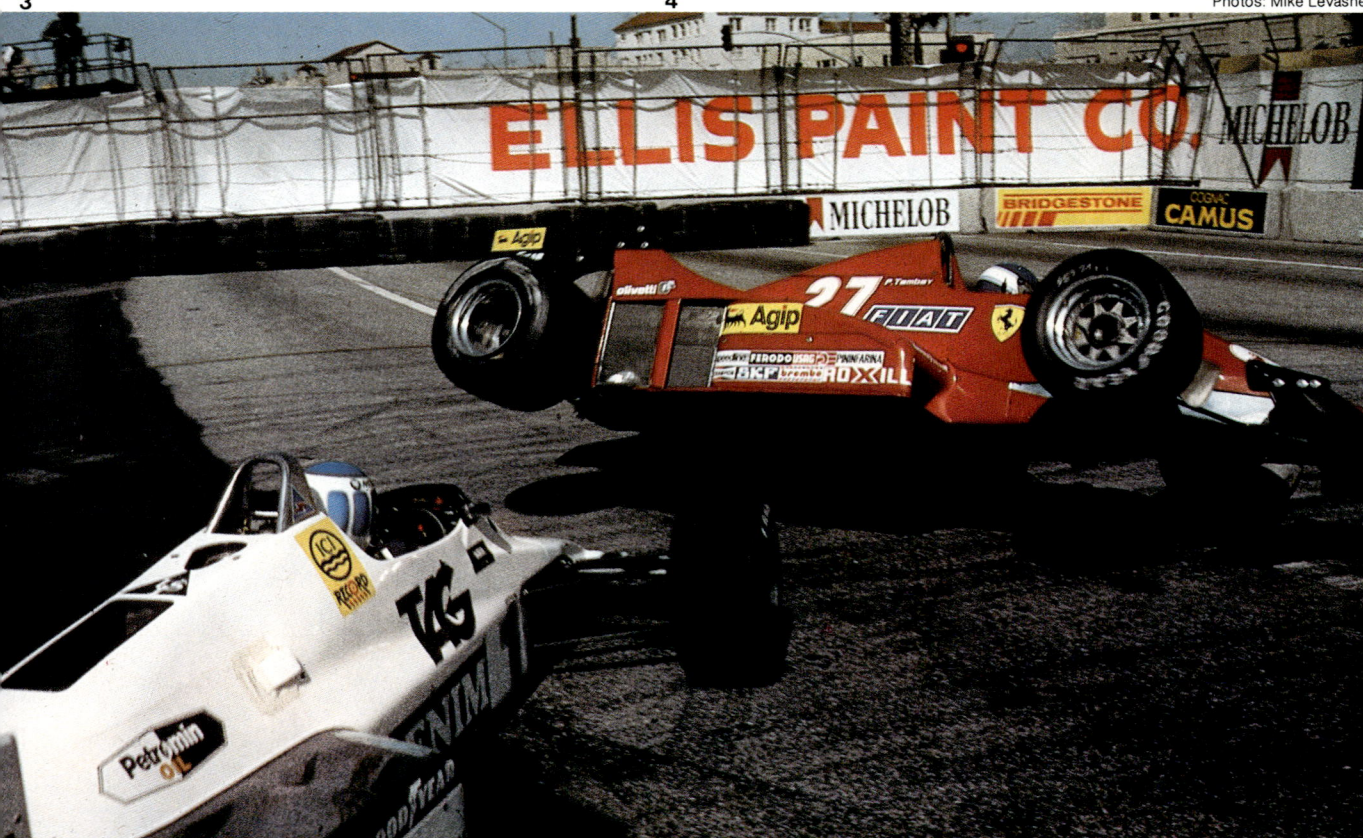

Photo: Bernard Asset

. . . not lifting his right foot for a second, Rosberg slid sideways and made sharp contact with Arnoux's right-front wheel. By now Tambay had gathered steam and took the lead as the pack left the grid.

Tambay had chosen 'B' compound all round and was keen to conserve his tyres as he carefully dictated the pace in spite of the mounting pressure behind. On lap 26, he slid wide briefly at the exit of the left-hander leading onto the short straight before the hairpin. Rosberg, anxious to seize any opportunity, took a run at the inside line, the Williams darting and weaving on the edge of adhesion as Keke left his braking very late. Clearly, Tambay wasn't expecting this for the Frenchman had taken his normal line and, as he turned into the corner, his right-rear wheel ran over Rosberg's left-front, the Ferrari leaping into the air before crashing down onto the track, its engine stalled. As Tambay waved his arms in warning, Rosberg selected first gear and continued, his adrenalin pumping furiously. . .

DESPITE A SELF-CONFESSED WEIGHT PROBLEM AND A slight limp, Alan Jones made an impressive return to Grand Prix racing at Long Beach.

When you have won the World Championship and driven for teams such as Williams, however, anything else becomes Second Division and amateur by comparison. Racing for fun wasn't such a laugh after all; the professional in Jones wanted to get out and *win*. He decided if he felt that strongly, then he may as well do the job properly and take up Grand Prix racing once again.

Not even a broken femur in his left leg, caused by a fall from a horse in January, dimmed that enthusiasm The 'silly season' was almost at an end, of course, and the top line seats had been taken by top line drivers. A call from Jackie Oliver of Arrows to Jones's hospital bed provided the answer.

Here was a useful little team peopled by team managers, designers and mechanics whom Jones knew and respected from his days racing for Shadow. They needed a driver; they needed a sponsor. He needed the opportunity to put some Formula 1 miles under his belt, discover if he was fit enough and decide whether he liked the latest Grand Prix cars. Along the way, his presence might attract a sponsor to Arrows. But, in the meantime, there would be no pressure to go out and win immediately.

A test drive at Willow Springs answered most of the questions. Within a few laps, he was sliding the white car around the dusty Californian track, thoroughly enjoying the experience; glad to be back. The two 3½in pins in his thigh were rubbing against the monocoque but it was nothing a couple of hammer blows (to the tub!) would not sort out. Apart from overalls and helmet devoid of sponsorship, nothing had changed. He would attempt to qualify at Long Beach in two day's time.

And qualify he did – in 12th place, half-a-second faster than Marc Surer, the team's regular driver. The car wasn't exactly made to fit a walking advert for Fosters Lager but, in the race, he ran

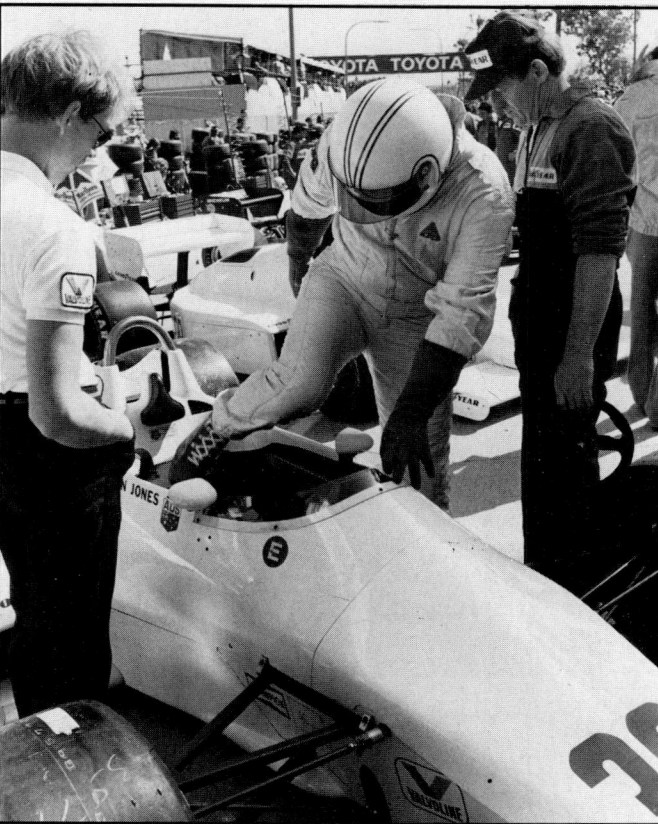

Space to sell. Jones, his helmet and overalls stripped of sponsorship, climbs into the plain white Arrows to make an impressive comeback.

competitively until contact with a wall forced a pit stop. He returned to the track but, by now, he was far enough behind for the pain from his hip to determine a circumspect retirement not long after. But the point had been made. Overweight (by some 40lbs) and limping. Alan Jones was back.

THE 1983 LONG BEACH GRAND PRIX WAS THE LAST for Formula 1 cars for at least three years. Perhaps it was an appropriate point for Chris Pook to sign a deal with CART since further changes to the circuit had robbed the track of much of the character for which it had become popular.

Pook, the expatriate Englishman who had dreamed up the idea of bringing motor racing to the streets of Long Beach for the first time in 1975, had sold the project on the grounds that it would brighten the image of a down-at-heel, shabby suburb of Los Angeles. 'Long Beach. A City Alive' became the catch-phrase and, judging by the massive rebuilding programme, Pook had succeeded.

The construction of a hotel (that was the official reason although other forces were at work behind the scenes) saw the loss of the uphill Pine Avenue, the dash along Ocean Boulevard and the spectacular plunge down Linden Avenue. Instead, the cars turned right at the bottom of Pine Avenue and picked their way through some absurdly tight corners before blasting under the Convention Centre and rejoining the old circuit at the foot of Linden Avenue. (It was at this point where the 'bump' caused chaos during practice).

The pits were relocated on the unused carriageway of Shoreline Drive, the camber and the sweeping curve causing difficulties for mechanics and pit signallers alike. These were minor problems; the sort of hazards associated with a street circuit.

Pook argued that Formula 1 had become too expensive by quoting costs of $3.5m for F1 compared to $2.5m for CART. Bernie Ecclestone replied that cost had nothing to do with it. Pook, he said, had fallen out with CBS and, as a result, a professional television package – so vital to FOCA's existence – could not be guaranteed.

Either way, it meant the passing of a most popular Grand Prix.

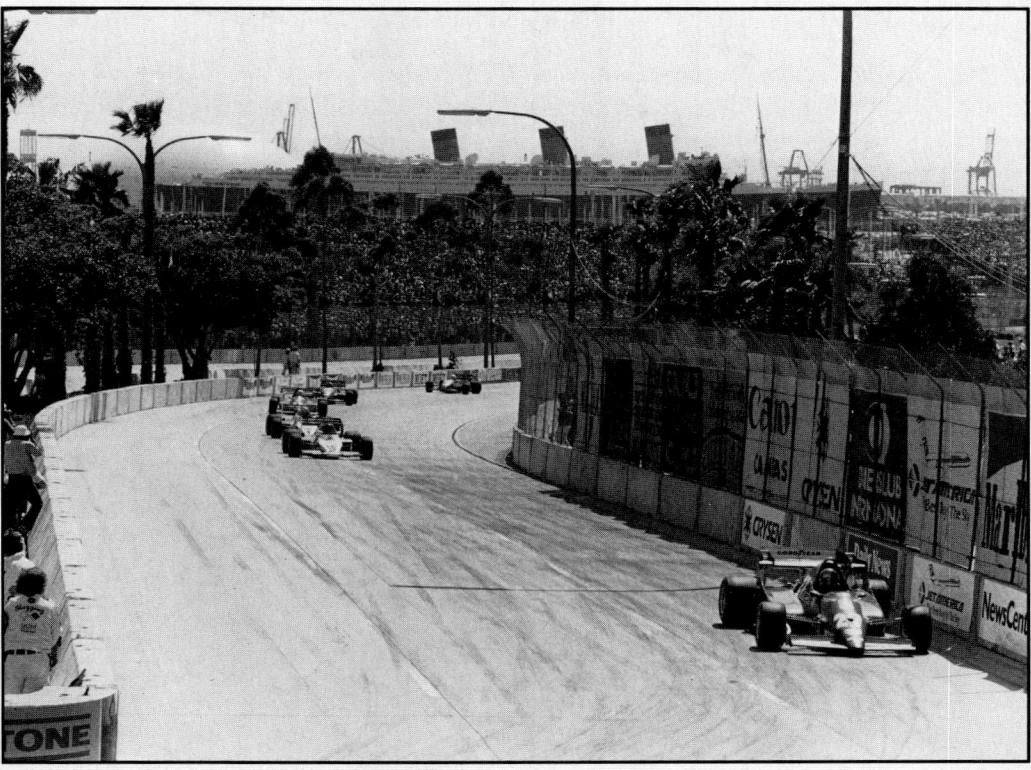

The end of a familiar landmark in Grand Prix racing? Tambay leads the field during the opening lap.

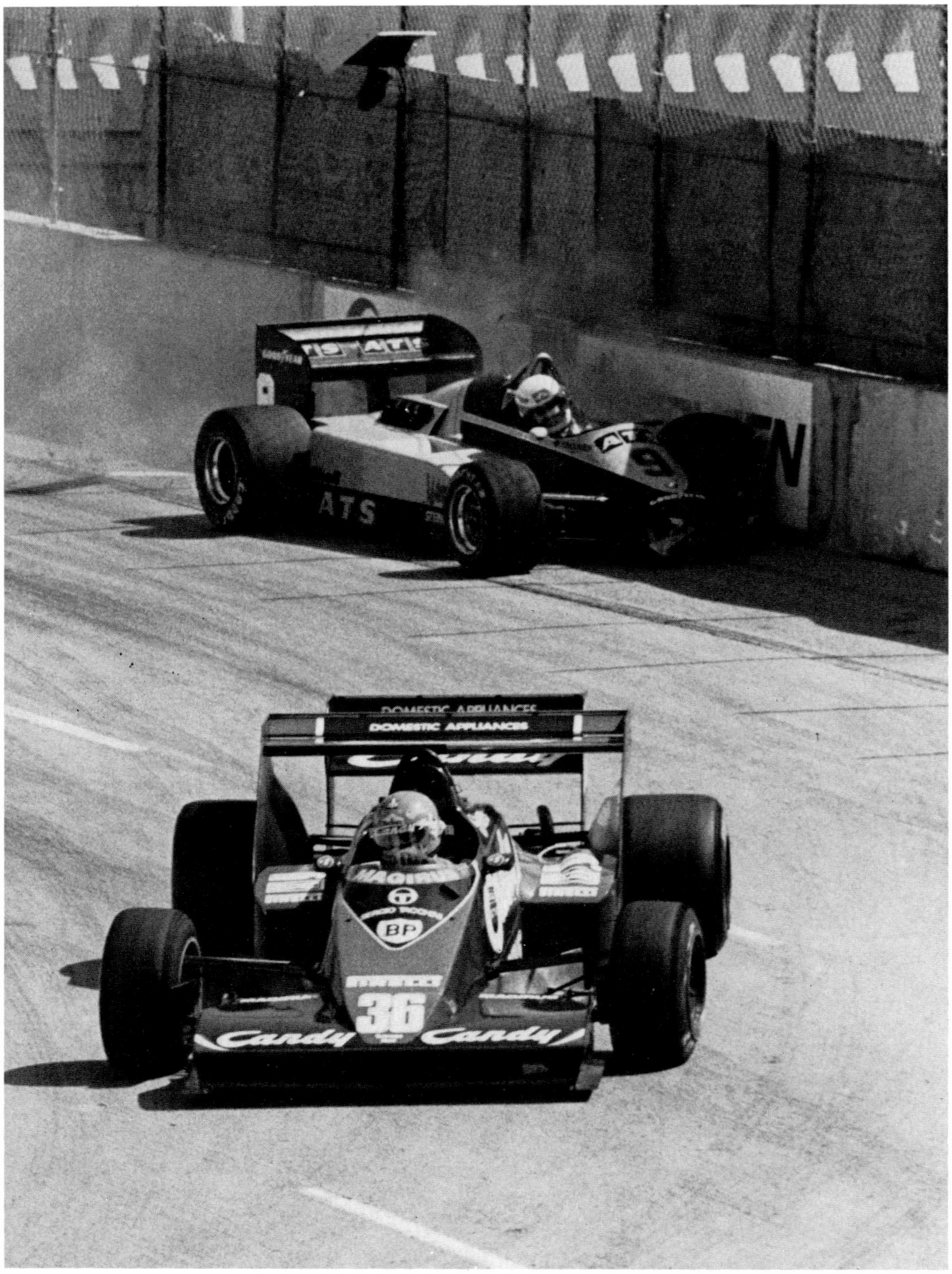

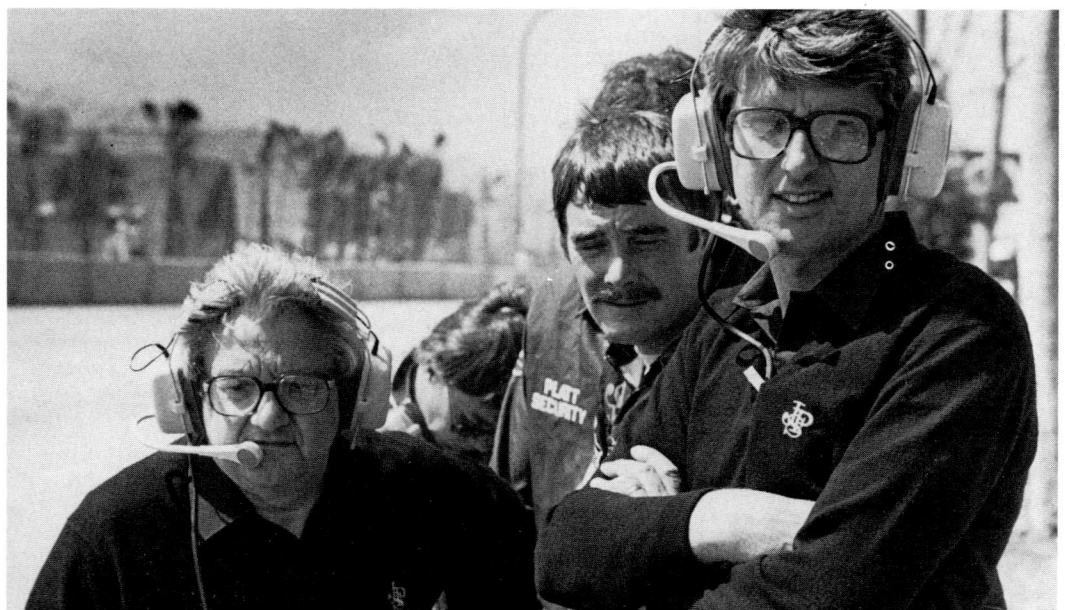

Winkelhock's race was brief, the German driver's ATS turning into the wall under braking at the end of Shoreline Drive. Giacomelli takes the corner but the Toleman driver was to suffer from tyre and, eventually, battery trouble.

The rash of pit stops had made lap charting a nightmare for those perched on the pit wall, since the cars were in view for a short period as they swept round the curve in the track. The Williams lap chart failed to indicate that Patrese was in second place and ahead of Laffite. Neither did it tell them that the Arnoux/Cheever battle was about to threaten their man. Thus Laffite, thinking he had something like 40 seconds in hand over the next car, was struggling with the drink supply pipe to his helmet and thinking about other things when the Renault and the Ferrari almost bundled him off the track and demoted the Williams to sixth place in one hit! He was soon back in fifth place, however, for Cheever's fine drive came to an end when the gearbox broke on lap 68. There was to be disappointment, too, for Patrese when the distributor broke and left the Italian to crawl disconsolately into the pits. His team-mate had retired not long before, the throttle linkage giving trouble and eventually sticking open. De Cesaris had stopped with gearbox trouble and the remainder of the field were limping home; Sullivan with a tyre vibration so bad that he could scarcely read his pit signals and was unable to fend off Boesel as the Ligier moved into seventh place behind Cecotto on the last lap.

Watson's heart skipped a beat when he felt a vibration similar to the one which had preceded an engine failure in Brazil. But on this occasion, it was no more than a tyre moving on the rim and the McLaren sailed home to an astonishing victory. They plucked him from the car and escorted him to the rostrum where dolly birds with big mouths left lipstick marks on his cheek. Then they played the National Anthem – 'Soldier Boys'. The fact that it was the National Anthem of the Republic of Ireland didn't seem to matter. After all, a win for the Ulsterman hadn't figured in the organisers' victory ceremony plans a few hours earlier. Not even the McLaren team thought they would win this one.

MARCH:

March Engineering complete their 1000th car.

Caesars Palace to hold CART race on October 8; Grand Prix in doubt.

McLaren International deny rumours that they are to replace Watson with Jones.

Tony Rudd (left), Director of Engineering at Lotus and former race engineer with BRM, returned to the pit lane to help Peter Warr and his team sort out their many problems. De Angelis qualified in fifth place with the 93T turbo while Mansell (pictured) struggled with the hydraulic suspension on his 92-Cosworth. Both drivers were defeated by a lack of suitable race tyres.

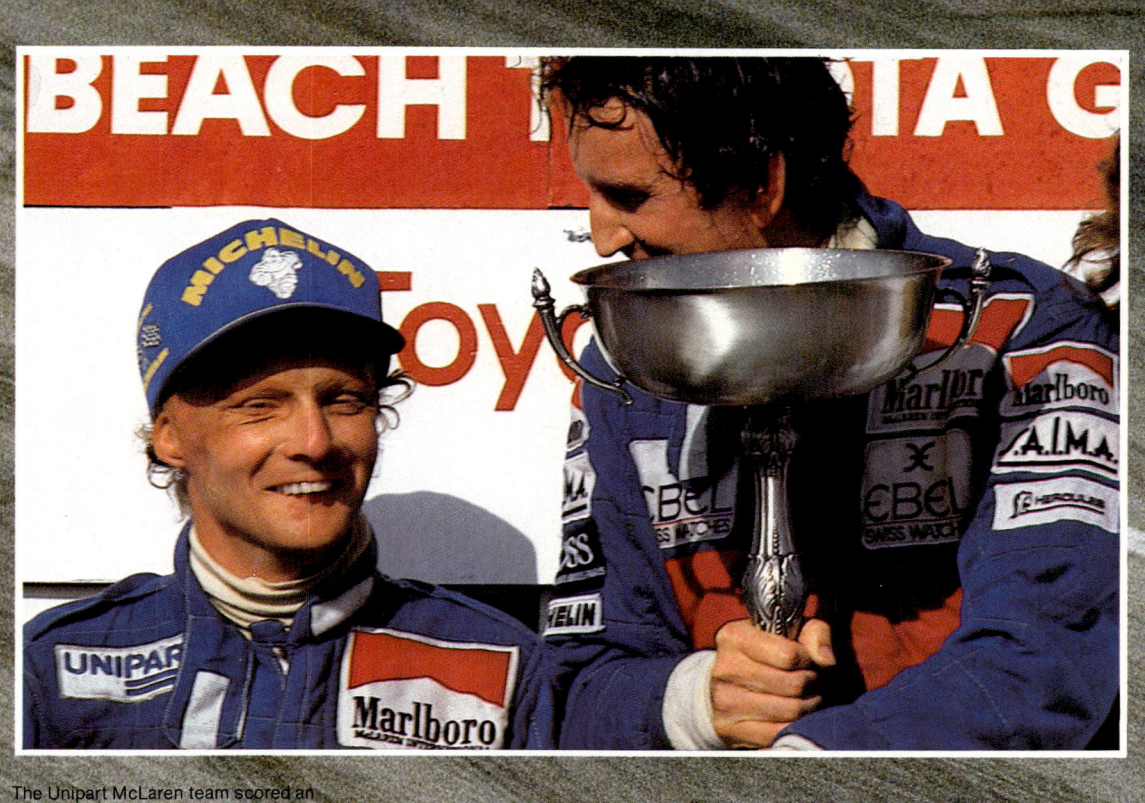

The Unipart McLaren team scored an unexpected result at Long Beach. Niki Lauda and John Watson marched through the field, the Ulsterman overtaking his team-mate to win his fifth Grand Prix.
Photos: Nigel Snowdon
John Townsend (inset)

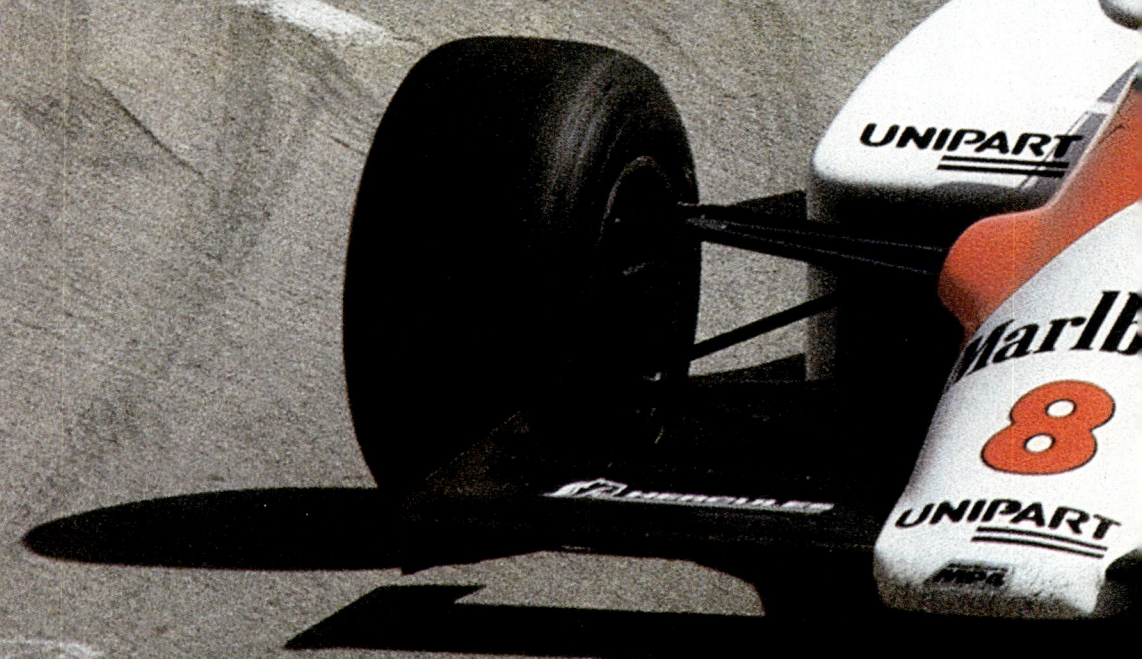

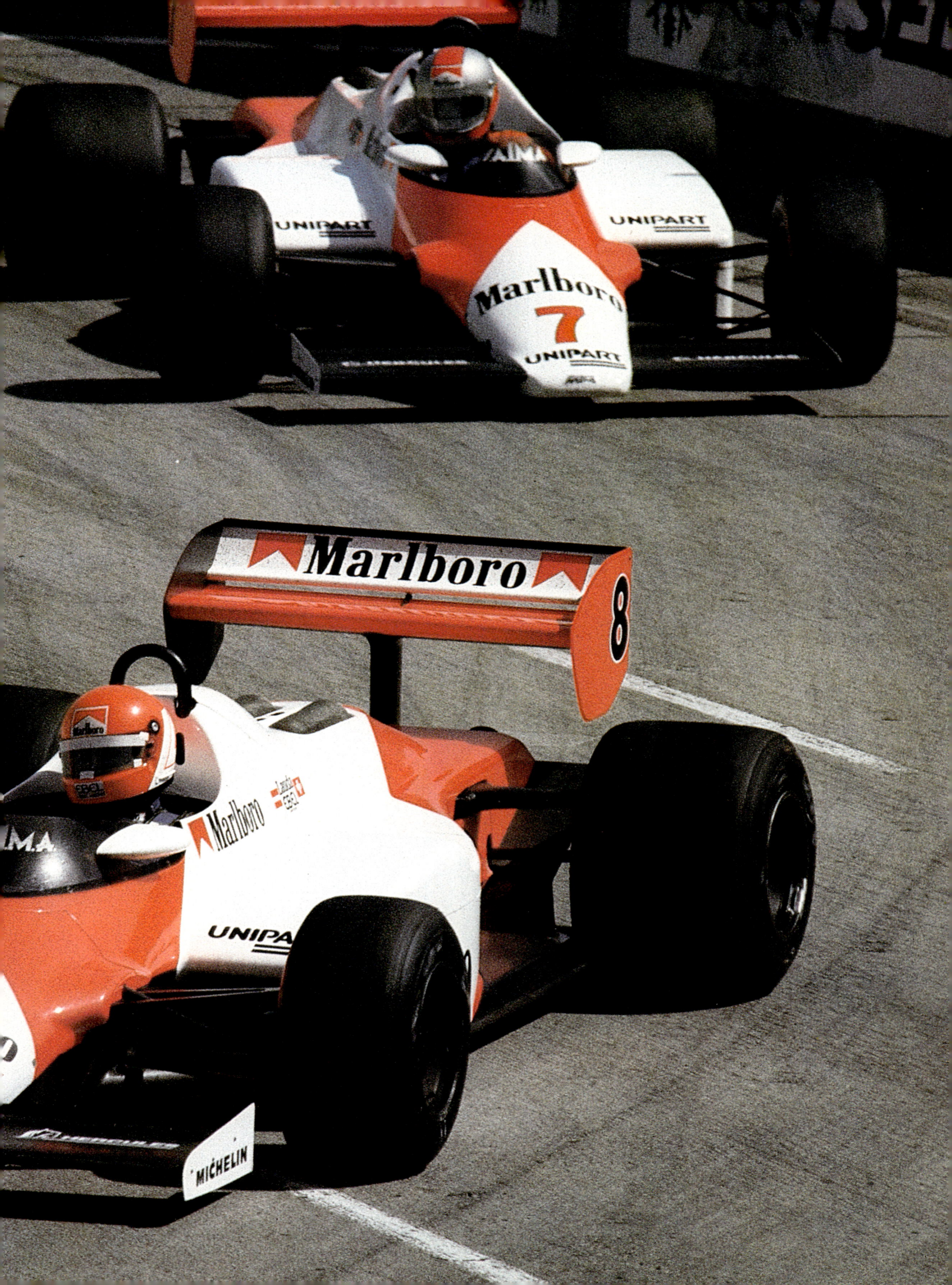

Entries and practice times

No.	Driver	Nat	Car	Tyre	Engine	Entrant	Practice 1	Practice 2
1	Keke Rosberg	SF	Saudia WILLIAMS FW08C	G	Ford Cosworth DFV	TAG Williams Team	1m 29·577s	**1m 27·145s**
2	Jacques Laffite	F	Saudia WILLIAMS FW08C	G	Ford Cosworth DFV	TAG Williams Team	1m 30·529s	**1m 27·818s**
3	Michele Alboreto	I	Benetton TYRRELL 011	G	Ford Cosworth DFV	Benetton Tyrrell Team	1m 29·066s	**1m 28·425s**
4	Danny Sullivan	USA	Benetton TYRRELL 011	G	Ford Cosworth DFV	Benetton Tyrrell Team	1m 31·271s	**1m 28·833s**
5	Nelson Piquet	BR	Parmalat BRABHAM BT52	M	BMW M12/13	Fila Sport	1m 30·173s	**1m 30·034s**
6	Riccardo Patrese	I	Parmalat BRABHAM BT52	M	BMW M12/13	Fila Sport	**1m 28·958s**	1m 29·467s
7	John Watson	GB	Marlboro McLAREN MP4/1C	M	Ford Cosworth DFV	Marlboro McLaren International	1m 32·439s	**1m 30·100s**
8	Niki Lauda	A	Marlboro McLAREN MP4/1C	M	Ford Cosworth DFV	Marlboro McLaren International	1m 30·262s	**1m 30·188s**
9	Manfred Winkelhock	D	ATS D6	G	BMW M12/13	Team ATS	1m 31·599s	**1m 30·220s**
11	Elio de Angelis	I	John Player Special LOTUS 93T	P	Renault EF1	John Player Team Lotus	1m 31·624s	**1m 27·982s**
12	Nigel Mansell	GB	John Player Special LOTUS 92	P	Ford Cosworth DFV	John Player Team Lotus	1m 31·728s	**1m 29·167s**
15	Alain Prost	F	Elf RENAULT RE40	M	Renault EF1	Equipe Renault Elf	**1m 28·558s**	1m 29·765s
16	Eddie Cheever	USA	Elf RENAULT RE30	M	Renault EF1	Equipe Renault Elf	1m 30·597s	**1m 29·422s**
17	Eliseo Salazar	RCH	MARCH-RAM 01	P	Ford Cosworth DFV	RAM Automotive Team March	1m 32·597s	**1m 31·126s**
22	Andrea de Cesaris	I	Marlboro ALFA ROMEO 183T	M	Alfa Romeo 183T	Marlboro Team Alfa Romeo	1m 33·336s	**1m 29·603s**
23	Mauro Baldi	I	Marlboro ALFA ROMEO 183T	M	Alfa Romeo 183T	Marlboro Team Alfa Romeo	1m 31·924s	**1m 30·070s**
25	Jean-Pierre Jarier	F	Gitanes LIGIER JS21	M	Ford Cosworth DFV	Equipe Ligier Gitanes	1m 29·600s	**1m 28·913s**
26	Raul Boesel	BR	Gitanes LIGIER JS21	M	Ford Cosworth DFV	Equipe Ligier Gitanes	**1m 31·759s**	1m 31·765s
27	Patrick Tambay	F	Fiat FERRARI 126C2/B	G	Ferrari 126C	Scuderia Ferrari SpA SEFAC	1m 28·598s	**1m 26·117s**
28	René Arnoux	F	Fiat FERRARI 126C2/B	G	Ferrari 126C	Scuderia Ferrari SpA SEFAC	**1m 26·935s**	1m 27·628s
29	Marc Surer	CH	ARROWS A6	G	Ford Cosworth DFV	Arrows Racing Team	1m 30·067s	**1m 29·521s**
30	Alan Jones	AUS	ARROWS A6	G	Ford Cosworth DFV	Arrows Racing Team	1m 30·451s	**1m 29·112s**
31	Corrado Fabi	I	OSELLA FA1D	M	Ford Cosworth DFV	Osella Squadra Corse	1m 33·896s	**1m 31·901s**
32	Piercarlo Ghinzani	I	OSELLA FA1D	M	Ford Cosworth DFV	Osella Squadra Corse	—	**1m 32·182s**
33	Roberto Guerrero	COL	THEODORE N183	G	Ford Cosworth DFV	Theodore Racing Team	**1m 29·585s**	1m 28·528s*
34	Johnny Cecotto	YV	THEODORE N183	G	Ford Cosworth DFV	Theodore Racing Team	**1m 29·559s**	1m 30·258s
35	Derek Warwick	GB	Candy TOLEMAN TG183B	P	Hart 415T	Candy Toleman Motorsport	—	**1m 28·130s**
36	Bruno Giacomelli	I	Candy TOLEMAN TG183B	P	Hart 415T	Candy Toleman Motorsport	—	**1m 29·266s**

Friday morning and Saturday morning practice sessions not officially recorded.

G – Goodyear, M – Michelin, P – Pirelli.

* time disallowed
Fri pm Sat pm
Hot, dry Hot, dry

Starting grid

27 TAMBAY (1m 26·117s)
Ferrari

28 ARNOUX (1m 26·935s)
Ferrari

1 ROSBERG (1m 27·145s)
Williams

2 LAFFITE (1m 27·818s)
Williams

11 DE ANGELIS (1m 27·982s)
Lotus

35 WARWICK (1m 28·130s)
Toleman

3 ALBORETO (1m 28·425s)
Tyrrell

15 PROST (1m 28·558s)
Renault

4 SULLIVAN (1m 28·833s)
Tyrrell

25 JARIER (1m 28·913s)
Ligier

6 PATRESE (1m 28·958s)
Brabham

30 JONES (1m 29·112s)
Arrows

12 MANSELL (1m 29·167s)
Lotus

36 GIACOMELLI (1m 29·266s)
Toleman

16 CHEEVER (1m 29·422s)
Renault

29 SURER (1m 29·521s)
Arrows

34 CECOTTO (1m 29·559s)
Theodore

33 GUERRERO (1m 29·585s)
Theodore

22 DE CESARIS (1m 29·603s)
Alfa Romeo

5 PIQUET (1m 30·034s)
Brabham

23 BALDI (1m 30·070s)
Alfa Romeo

7 WATSON (1m 30·100s)
McLaren

8 LAUDA (1m 30·188s)
McLaren

9 WINKELHOCK (1m 30·220s)
ATS

17 SALAZAR (1m 31·126s)
March

26 BOESEL (1m 31·759s)
Ligier

Did not start:
31 Fabi (Osella), 1m 31·901s, did not qualify
32 Ghinzani (Osella), 1m 32·182s, did not qualify

Results and retirements

Place	Driver	Car	Laps	Time and Speed (mph/km/h)/Retirement	
1	John Watson	McLaren-Cosworth V8	75	1h 53m 34·889s	80·6/129·75
2	Niki Lauda	McLaren-Cosworth V8	75	1h 54m 02·882s	80·3/129·23
3	René Arnoux	Ferrari t/c V6	75	1h 54m 48·527s	79·8/128·42
4	Jacques Laffite	Williams-Cosworth V8	74		
5	Marc Surer	Arrows-Cosworth V8	74		
6	Johnny Cecotto	Theodore-Cosworth V8	74		
7	Raul Boesel	Ligier-Cosworth V8	73		
8	Danny Sullivan	Tyrrell-Cosworth V8	73		
9	Michele Alboreto	Tyrrell-Cosworth V8	73		
10	Riccardo Patrese	Brabham-BMW t/c 4	72	Distributor	
11	Alain Prost	Renault t/c V6	72		
12	Nigel Mansell	Lotus-Cosworth V8	72		
	Eddie Cheever	Renault t/c V6	67	Gearbox	
	Alan Jones	Arrows-Cosworth V8	58	Driver discomfort	
	Nelson Piquet	Brabham-BMW t/c 4	51	Broken throttle asembly	
	Andrea de Cesaris	Alfa Romeo t/c V8	48	Gearbox	
	Elio de Angelis	Lotus-Renault t/c V6	29	Tyres	
	Roberto Guerrero	Theodore-Cosworth V8	27	Gearbox	
	Jean-Pierre Jarier	Ligier-Cosworth V8	26	Accident with Rosberg	
	Bruno Giacomelli	Toleman-Hart t/c 4	26	Battery/could not re-start after pit stop	
	Mauro Baldi	Alfa Romeo t/c V8	26	Accident	
	Patrick Tambay	Ferrari t/c V6	25	Accident with Rosberg	
	Keke Rosberg	Williams-Cosworth V8	25	Accident with Jarier	
	Eliseo Salazar	March RAM-Cosworth V8	25	Gear linkage	
	Derek Warwick	Toleman-Hart t/c 4	11	Tyre failure/accident	
	Manfred Winkelhock	ATS-BMW t/c 4	3	Accident	

Fastest lap: Lauda, on lap 42, 1m 28·33s, 82·9389mph/133·4769km/h (record for revised 2·035 mile/3·275 km circuit).
Previous lap record (2·13 mile/3·428 km circuit): Niki Lauda (F1 McLaren MP4B-Cosworth DFV), 1m 30·831s, 84·42mph/135·861km/h.

Past winners

Year	Driver	Nat	Car	Circuit	Distance miles/km	Speed mph/km/h
1975*	Brian Redman	GB	5·0 Lola T332-Chevrolet	Long Beach	101·00/162·54	86·32/138·92
1976	Clay Regazzoni	CH	3·0 Ferrari 312T/76	Long Beach	161·60/260·07	85·57/137·71
1977	Mario Andretti	USA	3·0 JPS/Lotus 78-Ford	Long Beach	161·60/260·07	86·89/139·84
1978	Carlos Reutemann	RA	3·0 Ferrari 312T-3/78	Long Beach	162·61/261·70	87·10/140·17
1979	Gilles Villeneuve	CDN	3·0 Ferrari 312T-4	Long Beach	162·61/261·70	87·81/141·32
1980	Nelson Piquet	BR	3·0 Brabham BT49-Ford	Long Beach	162·61/261·70	88·47/142·38
1981	Alan Jones	AUS	3·0 Williams FWO7C-Ford	Long Beach	162·61/261·70	87·60/140·98
1982	Niki Lauda	A	3·0 McLaren MP4B-Ford	Long Beach	160·81/258·81	81·40/131·00
1983	John Watson	GB	3·0 McLaren MP4/1C-Ford	Long Beach	152·62/245·62	80·60/129·75

*Formula 5000 Long Beach Grand Prix

Circuit data

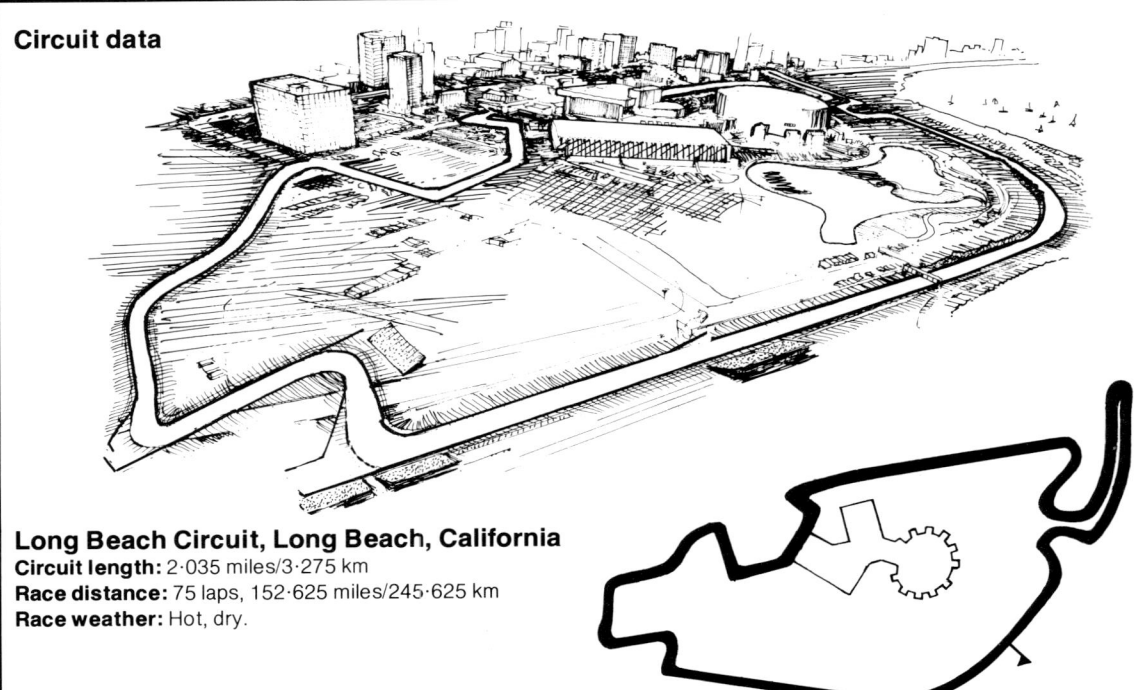

Long Beach Circuit, Long Beach, California
Circuit length: 2·035 miles/3·275 km
Race distance: 75 laps, 152·625 miles/245·625 km
Race weather: Hot, dry.

Fastest laps

Driver	Time	Lap
Niki Lauda	1m 28·330s	42
René Arnoux	1m 28·370s	62
John Watson	1m 28·652s	41
Alain Prost	1m 28·717s	67
Michele Alboreto	1m 29·032s	70
Jean-Pierre Jarier	1m 29·264s	8
Riccardo Patrese	1m 29·718s	40
Eddie Cheever	1m 30·104s	40
Jacques Laffite	1m 30·163s	40
Nelson Piquet	1m 30·256s	41
Keke Rosberg	1m 30·256s	4
Alan Jones	1m 30·261s	27
Patrick Tambay	1m 30·370s	12
Danny Sullivan	1m 30·372s	11
Johnny Cecotto	1m 30·382s	40
Marc Surer	1m 30·617s	18
Roberto Guerrero	1m 30·645s	8
Derek Warwick	1m 30·771s	10
Raul Boesel	1m 31·263s	41
Andrea de Cesaris	1m 31·280s	6
Elio de Angelis	1m 31·344s	27
Nigel Mansell	1m 31·883s	22
Mauro Baldi	1m 32·185s	19
Eliseo Salazar	1m 32·506s	22
Bruno Giacomelli	1m 33·512s	5
Manfred Winkelhock	1m 33·792s	3

Points

WORLD CHAMPIONSHIP OF DRIVERS

1	Niki Lauda	10 pts
2 =	Nelson Piquet	9
2 =	John Watson	9
4	Jacques Laffite	6
5	René Arnoux	4
6	Marc Surer	3
7	Patrick Tambay	2
8	Johnny Cecotto	1

CONSTRUCTORS' CUP

1	McLaren	19 pts
2	Brabham	9
3 =	Williams	6
3 =	Ferrari	6
5	Arrows	3
6	Theodore	1

Lap chart

		1	2	3	4	5	6	7	8	9	10	11	12	13	14	15	16	17	18	19	20	21	22	23	24	25	26	27	28	29	30	31	32	33	34	35	36	37
27	P. Tambay	27	27	27	27	27	27	27	27	27	27	27	27	27	27	27	27	27	27	27	27	27	27	27	27	27	27	2	2	2	2	2	2	2	2	2	2	2
2	J. Laffite	2	1	1	1	1	1	1	1	1	1	1	1	1	1	1	1	1	1	1	1	1	1	1	1	1	(25)	6	6	6	6	6	6	6	6	6	6	6
1	K. Rosberg	1	2	2	2	2	2	2	2	2	2	2	2	2	2	2	2	2	2	2	2	2	2	2	2	2	6	29	8	8	8	8	8	7	7	7	7	7
3	M. Alboreto	3	3	3	3	3	3	3	3	3	3	3	3	3	3	3	3	3	3	3	3	3	3	3	(3)	6	6	25	4	8	7	7	7	7	8	8	8	8
28	R. Arnoux	28	28	28	28	28	28	28	28	28	28	28	28	16	16	6	6	6	6	6	25	25	25	25	25	6	29	7	29	29	29	29	34	34	34	34	34	34
4	D. Sullivan	4	6	6	6	6	6	6	6	6	6	6	6	6	6	6	16	16	16	25	25	6	6	(3)	16	4	8	4	4	4	34	34	29	29	29	28	28	28
6	R. Patrese	6	4	15	15	15	16	16	16	16	16	16	16	25	25	25	25	28	28	28	28	28	28	28	29	7	34	34	34	4	4	28	28	28	29	29	29	
15	A. Prost	15	15	16	16	16	15	25	25	25	25	25	28	28	28	28	(16)	4	4	4	16	16	4	8	34	28	28	28	28	4	4	4	4	4	4	4	4	4
16	E. Cheever	16	16	4	4	4	4	4	4	4	4	4	4	4	4	4	29	29	29	4	4	30	7	28	5	5	5	5	5	5	16	16	16	16	16	16	16	
25	J. P. Jarier	25	25	25	25	25	25	29	29	29	29	29	29	29	29	29	29	29	16	16	30	30	29	(30)	5	16	16	16	16	16	5	5	5	5	5			
35	D. Warwick	35	29	29	29	29	29	15	15	35	35	35	30	30	30	30	30	30	30	30	29	29	8	34	16	22	22	22	22	22	22	26	22	22	22			
29	M. Surer	29	35	35	35	35	35	35	15	30	30	30	15	15	15	15	8	8	8	8	8	8	(28)	22	26	26	26	26	26	26	22	26	26	26				
11	E. De Angelis	11	11	11	11	11	11	30	30	15	15	15	11	11	11	8	7	7	7	7	7	7	34	5	26	(33)	12	(12)	12	12	12	12	12	12				
30	A. Jones	30	30	30	30	30	30	11	11	11	11	11	33	33	33	11	11	33	33	33	33	33	33	16	33	12	11	(11)	3	3	3	3	3	3				
12	N. Mansell	12	12	12	(12)	22	22	22	22	22	22	33	8	8	8	7	33	34	34	34	34	34	5	33	12	11	3	15	15	15	15	15	15	15				
23	M. Baldi	23	23	23	23	23	34	34	34	33	33	34	34	7	7	33	34	(11)	5	5	5	5	5	22	22	(36)	3	15	15	30	30	30	30	30				
34	J. Cecotto	34	22	22	22	34	33	33	33	34	34	8	7	34	34	(15)	5	22	22	22	22	22	26	26	11	15	30	30										
22	A. De Cesaris	22	34	34	34	33	8	8	8	8	8	7	22	22	22	5	22	26	26	26	26	26	12	12	23	30												
33	R. Guerrero	33	33	33	33	8	23	7	7	7	7	22	5	5	5	5	22	26	12	12	12	12	12	17	(17)	3												
7	J. Watson	7	7	7	8	7	7	23	5	5	5	5	26	26	26	26	26	12	36	36	17	17	17	36	(30)													
36	B. Giacomelli	36	8	8	7	5	5	5	23	23	23	26	12	12	12	12	12	36	17	17	36	36	36	11	11	15												
8	N. Lauda	8	5	5	5	12	12	12	12	26	26	12	36	36	36	36	36	17	11	11	11	11	11	23	23													
5	N. Piquet	5	36	36	36	36	36	36	26	12	12	36	17	17	17	17	23	23	23	23	23	23	3	3														
9	M. Winkelhock	9	9	26	26	26	26	36	36	36	17	23	23	23	23	15	15	15	15	15	15	15	15															
26	R. Boesel	26	26	26	17	17	17	17	17	17	(23)																											
17	E. Salazar	17	17	17																																		

38	39	40	41	42	43	44	45	46	47	48	49	50	51	52	53	54	55	56	57	58	59	60	61	62	63	64	65	66	67	68	69	70	71	72	73	74	75
2	2	2	2	2	2	2	7	7	7	7	7	7	7	7	7	7	7	7	7	7	7	7	7	7	7	7	7	7	7	7	7	7	7	7	7	7	7
6	6	6	6	6	6	7	8	8	8	8	8	8	8	8	8	8	8	8	8	8	8	8	8	8	8	8	8	8	8	8	8	8	8	8	8	8	8
7	7	7	7	7	7	8	2	2	2	2	2	2	6	5	6	6	6	6	6	6	6	6	6	6	6	6	6	6	6	6	6	6	28	28	28	28	28
8	8	8	8	8	8	6	6	6	6	6	6	2	2	2	2	2	2	2	2	2	2	2	2	2	2	28	28	28	28	28	2	2	2				
34	34	34	34	34	34	34	34	34	34	34	34	34	34	34	34	16	16	16	16	16	16	16	16	16	16	16	16	2	2	2	29	29	29				
28	28	28	28	28	28	28	29	16	16	16	16	16	16	34	34	28	28	28	28	28	28	28	28	28	2	29	29	29	29	6	34	34					
29	29	29	29	29	16	29	16	29	29	29	29	29	23	29	29	28	28	34	29	29	29	29	29	29	34	34	34	34	34	26							
16	16	16	16	16	16	16	(28)	4	4	4	28	28	28	28	23	28	28	29	34	34	34	34	34	34	4	4											
4	4	4	4	4	4	4	4	5	5	28	4	(5)	4	4	4	4	4	4	4	4	4	4	26	26	26	26	4										
5	5	5	5	5	5	5	28	28	5	5	4	26	26	26	26	(26)	26	26	26	26	26	26	3	3	3	3											
22	22	22	22	22	26	26	26	26	26	26	26	3	3	3	3	3	3	3	3	3	15	15	15	15													
26	26	26	26	26	22	(22)	12	12	12	12	3	12	12	12	12	12	12	12	15	15	15	15	15	15	12	12	12	12									
12	12	12	12	12	12	3	3	3	3	12	(12)	15	15	15	15	15	15	12	12	12	12	12	12														
3	3	3	3	3	3	22	22	15	15	15	30	30	30	30	30	(30)																					
15	15	15	15	15	15	15	15	(22)	30	30	30																										
30	30	30	30	30	30	30	30	30																													

GRAND PRIX DE FRANCE

"We're in good shape now, I mean that." Eddie Cheever zipped up his yellow Renault-Elf jacket against the rising wind at Paul Ricard on race morning. Tapping his feet and wriggling in his chair, anxious to start the race, the American went on to explain about the development his team had undertaken at this, their most important Grand Prix.

It was no ordinary programme reaching a final, well-reasoned conclusion during practice. On the contrary, it had been a busy two days thanks to major changes in the set-up of the RE40s. And the work had paid off handsomely; Alain Prost's pole by a margin of two seconds went some way to justifying that.

Cheever felt he could have been closer to his team-mate had he not been forced to use the spare car during the final session. As it was, he would start from the front of the grid for the first time although he continued to punch the palm of his hand in mild frustration. Minutes later, the mechanics arrived in the Renault compound for lunch – or was it breakfast? Springing to his feet, Cheever greeted each man with the traditional handshake, shouting to the chef in French as he did so, instructing him to feed the troops well for he wanted the mechanics fit and ready for a quick pit stop.

The chef must have obliged for Cheever was in and out in 17.59s; not bad for the team's first attempt. Pit stops were in vogue at Ricard, Ferrari and Renault joining Williams and Brabham, and each went without a major hitch; without the holocaust which everyone had feared.

Prost, however, made an error which could have been disastrous but which, in the event, did not alter the outcome and merely underlined Renault's superiority. Forgetting to keep his foot on the brake pedal and costing the man at the right-rear several seconds as he struggled to tighten the wheel nut, Prost still managed to rejoin in the lead and cruise to a victory which belied the problems which seemed to plague Renault everywhere but in France.

Matching Renault in power but not in handling, Nelson Piquet took second place for Parmalat Brabham and BMW while Cheever came home third, having nursed a tyre problem during the first half of the race. After two days of problems which pushed the normally affable Patrick Tambay to breaking point, the Ferrari driver did well to give Goodyear fourth place. The American rubber was inferior to Michelin, a handicap which the Saudia Williams team did not need since they were already burdened with normally aspirated engines. None the less, Keke Rosberg and Jacques Laffite drove their hearts out, fifth and sixth places being their reward in the fruitless chase of the turbos.

Marlboro McLaren would have made more of their Michelins had Niki Lauda and John Watson (running the Cosworth DFY engines for the first time) not suffered a seized wheel bearing and a throttle linkage problem. It was just the sort of niggling unreliability which usually afflicted Renault anywhere but at Ricard or Dijon. 1983 was no exception. Cheever had been right; they were in good shape.

ENTRY AND PRACTICE

Gerard Larrousse and Jean Sage had a lot on their minds as they flew home from Long Beach. The French Grand Prix was next and, clearly, they needed to have three RE40s available since the 30 series was no longer capable of giving the victory they desperately needed at home. The factory at Viry Chatillon would produce the goods in time but there was the additional worry of the curious misfire which bothered Prost in California. A complete chassis was put on the test-bed and no trace of the misfire could be found. Neither did it reappear during Michelin tests, which was good. Not so good was poor handling and the team decided to make radical changes for Ricard; spring rates were altered, wing angles increased and so on. They started practice, therefore, with an unknown quantity at the circuit where they test most frequently!

Any worries were unfounded, Prost and Cheever being among the quickest throughout practice. There were few serious problems, Prost losing time while running on his second set of qualifiers on Friday when he was forced to spin the car to avoid Raul Boesel. The Brazilian driver presented himself in the Renault pit not long after to offer his profuse apologies, which Prost accepted. He had few worries since the next day he was to stun the pit lane by turning up the boost and finding a clear track to set a time some two seconds better than the next man – who happened to be Eddie Cheever!

The American, never having run the RE40 on qualifiers before, lost revs towards the end of practice on Friday but worse was to follow the next day. A broken valve spring meant Cheever had to switch to the spare car which was not set up to his liking but he nevertheless managed to make it a yellow and white front row even though he was rather disappointed with his time.

Brabham and BMW between them had put in a vast amount of work before reaching Ricard. The cars sported stronger final drive units and modified front wings while the BMW engineers had been forced to strip and modify the entire batch of engines scheduled for Ricard when a faulty run of valves had been discovered during testing a few days before. Once on the track, the cars showed shattered straight line speed but their handling through the fast corners was terrifying to behold, Piquet and Patrese requiring all their bravery at the fifth gear (or, sixth gear in Brabham's case) left-right sweep after the pits. It was the Italian who set the best time despite a rough engine while a similar problem for Nelson meant he was in and out of the T-car and down in sixth place. To add to his troubles, the Brazilian had his rear wing fly off; not a new problem in itself although the reason was novel, the spare car shedding its exhaust pipe and the build up of heat actually causing the carbon fibre wing support to melt.

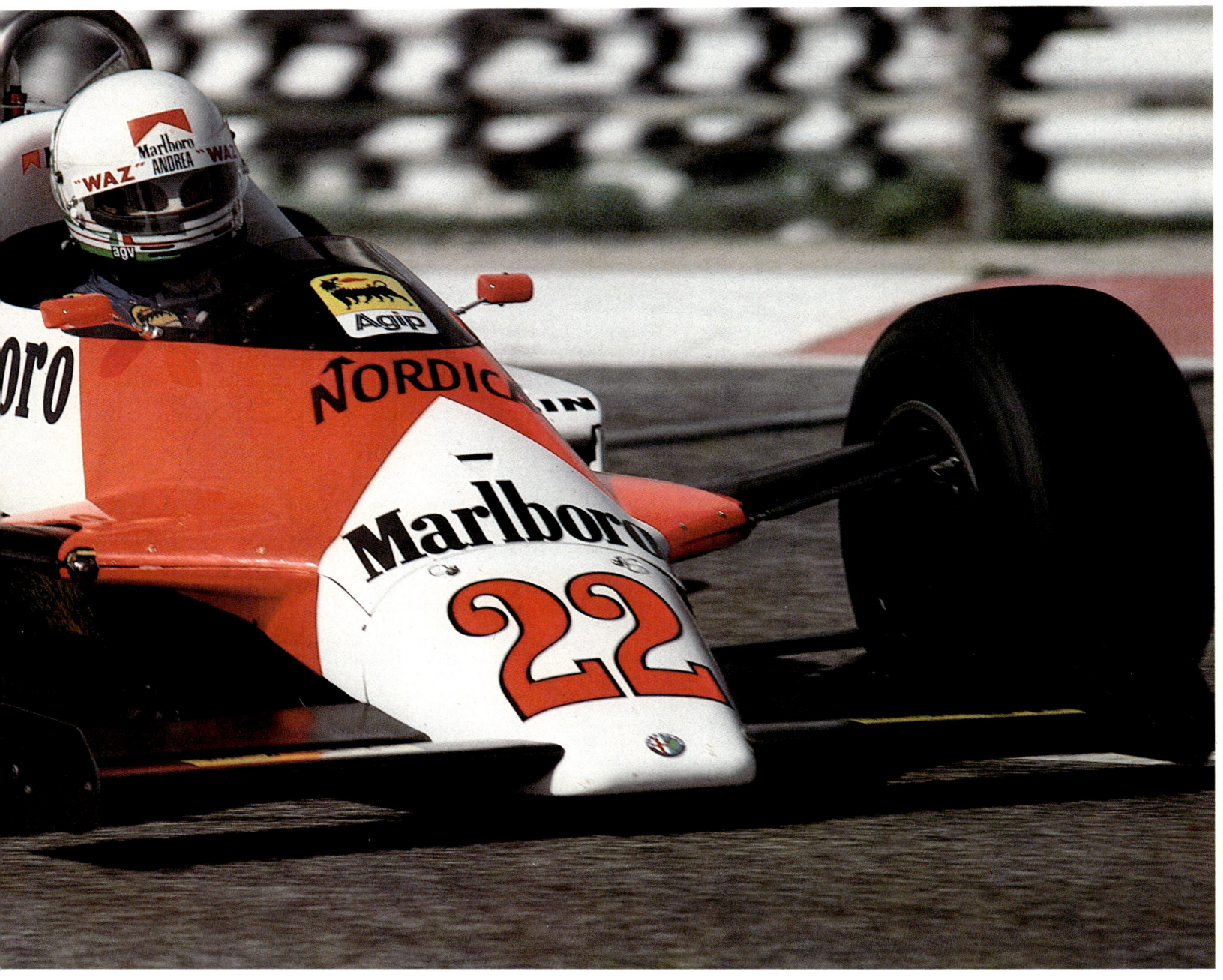

Andrea de Cesaris produced an encouraging performance in the Alfa Romeo Turbo in spite of gearbox problems.
Photo: David Winter

"Have you seen our Space Shuttle?" asked Tambay, nodding his head towards the mobile refuelling equipment present in the Ferrari pit for the first time. The French driver was in a good mood before practice began but things were to change during the course of the next two days when the entire Ferrari misfortune seemed to fall on his shoulders. René Arnoux, meanwhile, sailed through practice, his only problem being a turbo fire just after he had set a time good enough for fourth place on Saturday afternoon. As he trundled into the pits with the turbo smoking, Tambay was fuming gently, another turbo having failed, this time in the T-car. The day before, Patrick seemed to spend his time walking back to the pits as an electrical problem caused the engine to cut out constantly. Then, on Saturday morning, the race car pumped out all its coolant. So he climbed into the T-car once more – and suffered his third turbo failure. He was in 11th place, and very unhappy to be there.

John Player Team Lotus had mixed feelings about Elio de Angelis's fifth place. He had got there with a touch of bravery and a little help from improved Pirelli qualifiers although the team knew that the race tyres would be a different story. Elio had two 93Ts on hand (a second chassis having been finished in time for Mansell to scare himself silly at the Race of Champions the previous weekend). A discreet Lotus crew would only say there had been an assembly fault in the suspension somewhere). Certainly, the car didn't look such a handful although de Angelis had to work hard. He wasn't helped by the front edge of a side-pod coming loose on Friday afternoon although rapid work by the mechanics changed two turbos in time for the final session after a misfire in the morning. The heavy hydraulic suspension had been removed from Nigel Mansell's 92-Cosworth and the English driver, along with Lauda and Watson, was given a new Cosworth DFY for the first time on Saturday. Like the

McLaren drivers, Mansell commented that there was little difference apart from a little more power mid-range. It felt like a very good DFV – and even the best DFV was no match for turbos at Ricard.

One of the best turbos, in fact, had been the Alfa Romeo 183T. The Italian cars, apart from having copious power (without the benefit of turned up boost, the V8s not taking too kindly to that), were very impressive through the fast sweeps and Andrea de Cesaris set fastest time on Friday. Not long after practice had finished it was announced that de Cesaris's time would be discounted following the discovery of an empty fire extinguisher bottle on his car during post-practice scrutineering. It had been alleged that this appalling practice had been carried out by other teams in the interests of saving weight during qualifying but fire extinguisher bottles had never been checked – until Friday. It was odd that they should choose car 22 alone for this check and rumours

abounded of politics within Alfa Romeo; a tip-off and the framing of Gerard Ducarouge (who, subsequently, was sacked). De Cesaris said he had set the extinguisher off accidentally; Ducarouge said foul play was out of the question since, if that was the case, they would have had adequate time to replace the empty extinguisher before scrutineering. The Stewards could find no trace of the bottle having been used and the times were discounted. On Saturday, gearbox problems (caused by the drivers breaking teeth off the dog rings while trying to cope with turbo lag on the down-shifts) meant de Cesaris and Mauro Baldi were seventh and eighth respectively.

Candy Toleman had been busy building a new car (intended for Bruno Giacomelli) only for Derek Warwick to crash the TG183B during testing. It was repaired in time for official practice, which was just as well, for Warwick had need of it on Friday afternoon. The day had started off on an optimistic note, Warwick setting second fastest time in the morning. Then, on his very first lap in the official session, the car ground to a halt out on the circuit, victim of a broken drive to the fuel pump. Warwick legged it back to the pits and returned to the car with replacement parts which he then found had been incorrectly wired. He returned to the pits once more and, with the T-car unready for fast lappery, Warwick was forced to use Bruno's car which was tailored for the smaller driver. Everything was repaired in time for the final session but Warwick found the large rear wing, necessary to geneate heat in the Pirellis, was costing 500rpm on the important back straight. He was ninth fastest with Giacomelli taking 13th place, the slowest turbo.

ATS had managed to repair Manfred Winkelhock's car after Long Beach and the German driver made good use of the BMW power as he hurled the car into 10th place, a puncture during his final run on qualifiers spoiling his chances of improving on Friday's time. In contrast to Winkelhock sawing at the wheel at the merest hint of a corner, the McLaren drivers sailed serenely by, both Lauda and Watson taking the curves after the pits with their right foot hard on the throttle. Making the most of their Michelins, they were easily the quickest Cosworth runners and finished practice in 12th and 14th places, ready to make the most of any problems the turbos might have.

Just as commendable was the performance of Michele Alboreto on his Goodyears. The Italian driver felt unwell throughout practice, as did his DFV on Saturday morning which meant Michele had to use the spare car for a while and was unable to improve on his time from the previous day. Danny Sullivan did improve on Saturday once the engine, which had seen such good service at Brands Hatch (Sullivan finishing a close second to Rosberg), had been replaced, but he was back in 24th place none the less.

Goodyear were clearly in trouble at Ricard when Keke Rosberg could manage no better than 16th place, just behind Alboreto's Benetton Tyrrell. Apart from a handling problem in the fast corners, the Williams driver was unable to put the power down coming out of the corners in the same way as, say, McLaren and Michelin. In typical fashion, however, the team decided not to flog round and round looking for 15th instead of 16th place on the grid; their policy being to concentrate on a competitive set-up for the race. Laffite in 19th place, was three-tenths slower, not a happy situation for a Frenchman at home.

Johnny Cecotto was the quickest Theodore, both drivers expressing satisfaction with the handling of their cars in the fast corners although Roberto Guerrero felt the team had spent too long trying different settings, the result being sudden understeer on the medium speed corners at a time when he was trying to set a fast time. Ligier, by contrast, were good on the slow corners but the Gitanes cars looked dreadful as they bounced through the fifth gear sections. Jean-Pierre Jarier, frustrated by the shortage of the latest Michelin qualifiers which had been made available to Brabham, Renault and McLaren, was 20th with Raul Boesel taking a place on the back row alongside Chico Serra's Arrows. The Brazilian had been given a drive once more following Alan Jones's decision not to take any further part with Arrows until the team raised the necessary finance. It was a decision he probably didn't regret when news filtered back to the pits of a nasty accident to Serra during the final session. The left-rear tyre had come off the rim just as Chico negotiated the fast flick after the pits, the Arrows sliding onto a kerb and flipping over as it came to a sudden halt in the catch-fencing. Serra was unharmed and bravely ventured out in the spare car not long after. It was understandable, though, when he feathered the throttle each time on the approach to the corner. Fortunately, Friday's time was good enough to keep him in the race; Marc Surer qualifying in 21st place.

Corrado Fabi qualified his Osella under the watchful eye of the car's designer, Tony Southgate, but his team-mate, Piercarlo Ghinzani, failed to make the grid, as did the RAM-March team, Jean-Louis Schlesser, having made his Formula 1 debut at Brands Hatch, joining Eliseo Salazar at Ricard.

RACE

The warm-up on race morning confirmed the worst fears of the Cosworth teams. Heading the list was Alain Prost, the Renault clearly handling as well on half a tank of fuel as it did on a couple of gallons and four qualifiers. The French team would make a pit stop for the first time, as would Ferrari once they had sorted out a turbo problem on René Arnoux's car. Following much deliberation, Williams decided to stop both cars and, accordingly, chose 'B' compound all round, unlike Ferrari who dithered between that and the harder 'A' recommended by Goodyear. In the end, Tambay opted for 'B's and, unwisely as it would turn out, Arnoux made a similar decision. Tyrrell, on the other hand, felt they would get away with the softer 'C' compound all round. There was no question, of course, that Brabham would not stop but there was relief in the pit lane when the volatile Alfa Romeo team decided to keep their pit stop plans for another day. None the less, with four teams refuelling, there was a distinctly edgy feeling in the pits and the organisers made the wise move of banning everyone, with the exception of mechanics, from the pit lane. For once, the grid at Paul Ricard was reasonably clear as the cars took up their positions.

After three miles spent zig-zagging heat into their tyres, the cars returned from the final parade lap to make a reasonably clean start. Prost got it right but Cheever spun his wheels and looked to his left as Patrese made ground and moved into second place within the first few yards. Further back, de Cesaris missed second gear and was almost rammed by Baldi while Watson and Lauda fanned out to their right, keen to take any advantage of a tardy start by the turbos. Watson, in fact, got past Lauda and was climbing all over Baldi as they filed through *L'ecole* but a hesitation from the Alfa turbo meant the Ulsterman had little option but to thump the back of the Alfa Romeo and smash his nose-cone. Baldi spun onto the dirt but was able to drive slowly to the pits behind Watson, both cars continuing not long after. For Watson, though, it would be a short race. On lap four, a faulty throttle assembly caused the Cosworth DFY to hesitate and cut out once more and Watson, hearing the harsh mechanical rattling from over his shoulder, assumed the engine had blown, switched off and coasted to a halt. Subsequent inspection was to show the engine in perfect working order and suitable for practice at Imola two weeks later.

By lap three, Prost had opened a three-second gap while Cheever had taken Patrese with a brave move at the fast *Verrerie*. Piquet was fourth and Tambay took fifth place from his team-mate as Arnoux began to doubt the wisdom of starting on the softer tyres. De Angelis was next but the Lotus was soon to come under pressure from Rosberg, the World Champion having dealt with Warwick as he revelled in a superbly set-up chassis and a strong engine. After a brief tussle, the Williams driver eventually overcame the turbo power with a brilliant late-braking move on lap five just as Warwick slipped to tenth place behind Winkelhock's spectacular ATS. De Cesaris and Laffite were soon on the tail of the Toleman, the pair slipping ahead as Warwick began to feel the effects of a water pipe leaking its contents onto the left-rear tyre. He wasn't to know this, of course, and, convinced he had a puncture, Warwick pulled into the pits on lap 13. The mechanics could find nothing amiss but changed all four tyres as a matter of course. The water from the split pipe was collecting in the undertray to the engine and, as the Toleman accelerated away, the tell-tale signs of coolant on the pit road were the first indication that something more serious was amiss. Warwick was to find out soon enough, the Toleman stopping two laps later out on the circuit with overheating.

There was plenty of activity up and down the field as the Cosworth/turbo battles were fought out, the normally aspirated engines lagging breathlessly on the straights while their drivers more than made up for the deficiency on the twisting sections and under braking. Rosberg had taken sixth place from Arnoux and de Angelis had dropped to tenth place behind Winkelhock and de Cesaris. The Lotus driver was struggling with Pirellis which had lost their grip and the black and gold car was receiving close attention from Laffite and Lauda. Jacques made it by with little difficulty but the McLaren had a fraught time as the Renault engine powered de Angelis back in front once more on the straights. Lauda eventually put enough daylight between himself and the Italian to keep the Lotus at bay but, ironically, all that hard work was for nothing since the Lotus was to stop not long after when the electrics to the fuel injection packed up. The V6 died and, as Elio flicked switches on and off in a bid to coax the engine back to life, he suddenly found himself approaching the chicane whereupon he promptly locked his front brakes before coasting to a halt at the side of the track.

That was the end of the race for the Lotus team as Mansell had long since retired, the victim of an unusual accident before the start of the race. While chatting to Crew Chief Bob Dance in the pits, the noise of engines drowned a warning from mechanics as they rolled the spare car, fitted with the heavy steel setting-up wheels, into the garage. One of the wheels rolled over Mansell's left foot, injuring his toes but the English driver decided to start the race after receiving attention and a pain-killing spray. His optimism was unfounded, however, and Mansell retired after six laps. It should be added that his Pirelli tyres had passed their best, even at that early stage, and there was the chance that the driver, renowned for his bravery, might not have noticed the pain quite so much had he been in a more competitive position. . . .

That privilege belonged to Renault and Brabham today. Prost was holding an eight-second gap over Cheever when Piquet, having passed his team-mate, began to close on the number two Renault, the Brabham moving ahead on lap 17. Cheever was in no danger from Patrese, however, for the Italian driver was to have an unhappy birthday when he rolled to a halt in the pits, his water radiator dry. On the same lap, Johnny Cecotto brought his Theodore in to change what the team later described as a "rogue set of tyres", the Venezuelan continuing, having lost several places. His team-mate was holding a strong mid-field position but Guerrero was soon to retire with a broken valve two laps after Danny Sullivan rolled to a smoky halt in front of the pits. At first glance, it seemed the engine had blown but the cause, in fact, was an exploding clutch which broke the flywheel and damaged an oil pipe; hence the clouds of smoke from the hot exhausts of the Tyrrell.

So, with Patrese in retirement, doubts began to creep in over turbo reliability. The Renaults, though, appeared to be running strongly and Piquet, unable to make any impression on Prost, could only hope for a mechanical failure or a fumbled pit stop. And, considering this would be the first time the French crew had performed under pressure, the latter seemed to be the most likely.

The stops began on lap 24, Arnoux rushing under the bridge and almost knocking over the Renault team as they waited for Cheever. Arnoux was dispatched in 15.7s; Cheever in 17.59s and it was clear that both teams were well-rehearsed. Rosberg was next but all his heroic work out on the track was blown away when there was difficulty fitting the left-front wheel and the Williams was detained for 26.1s.

The leaders droned by for another lap and then Prost headed for the pit lane, his heart beating as he tried to remember the part he had to play in this important stop. Everything went well initially but the turbo, set with a weak tick-over, stalled and Prost, in his haste to dab the throttle, forgot to keep his right foot on the brake pedal as well; the result being frantic signals from the mechanic at the right-rear as he tried in vain to tighten the wheel nut. Daniel Champion, controlling operations at the front of the car, soon got

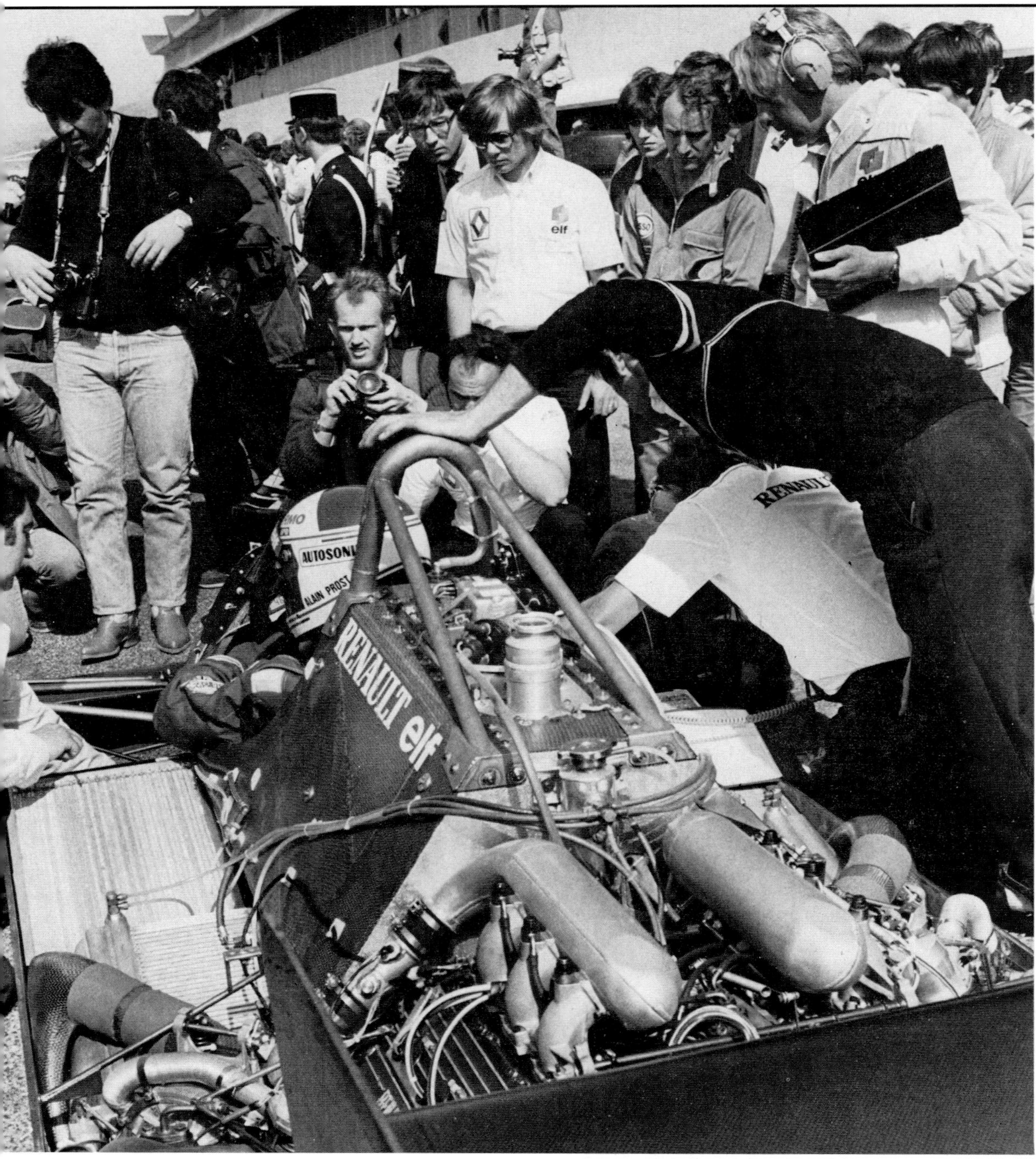

Under pressure to do well at home, Renault made major changes to their RE40s. Alain Prost took pole and an unchallenged win.

Eddie Cheever claimed a place on the front row for the first time but lost second place to Piquet in the early laps.

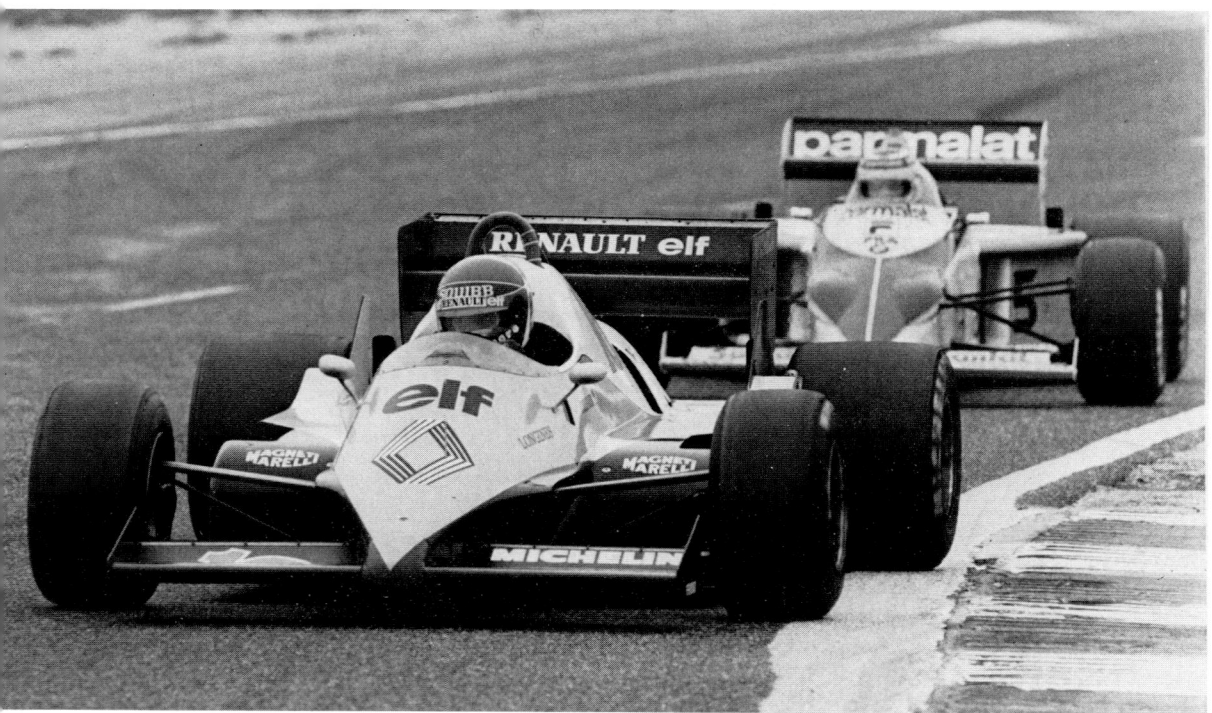

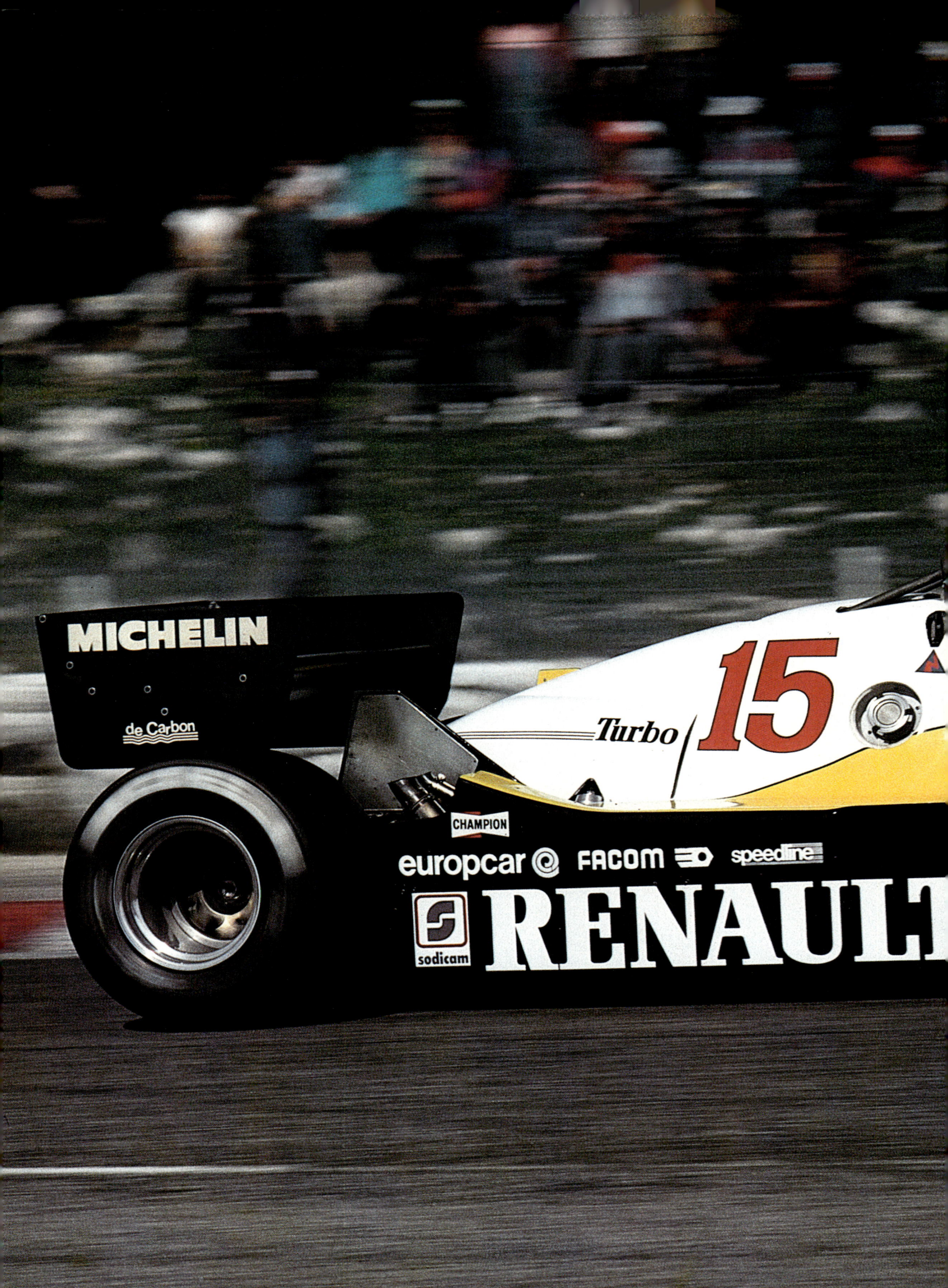

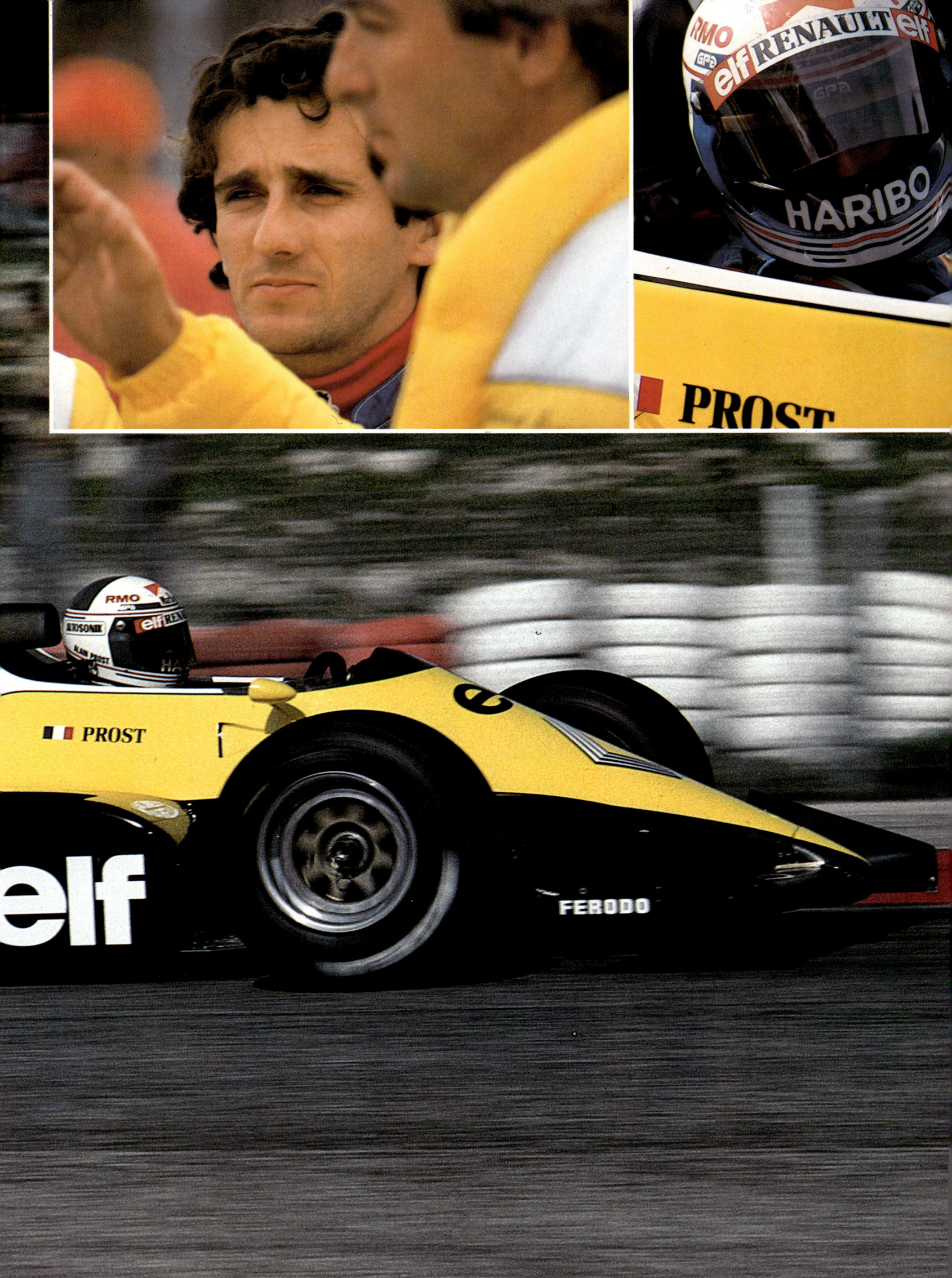

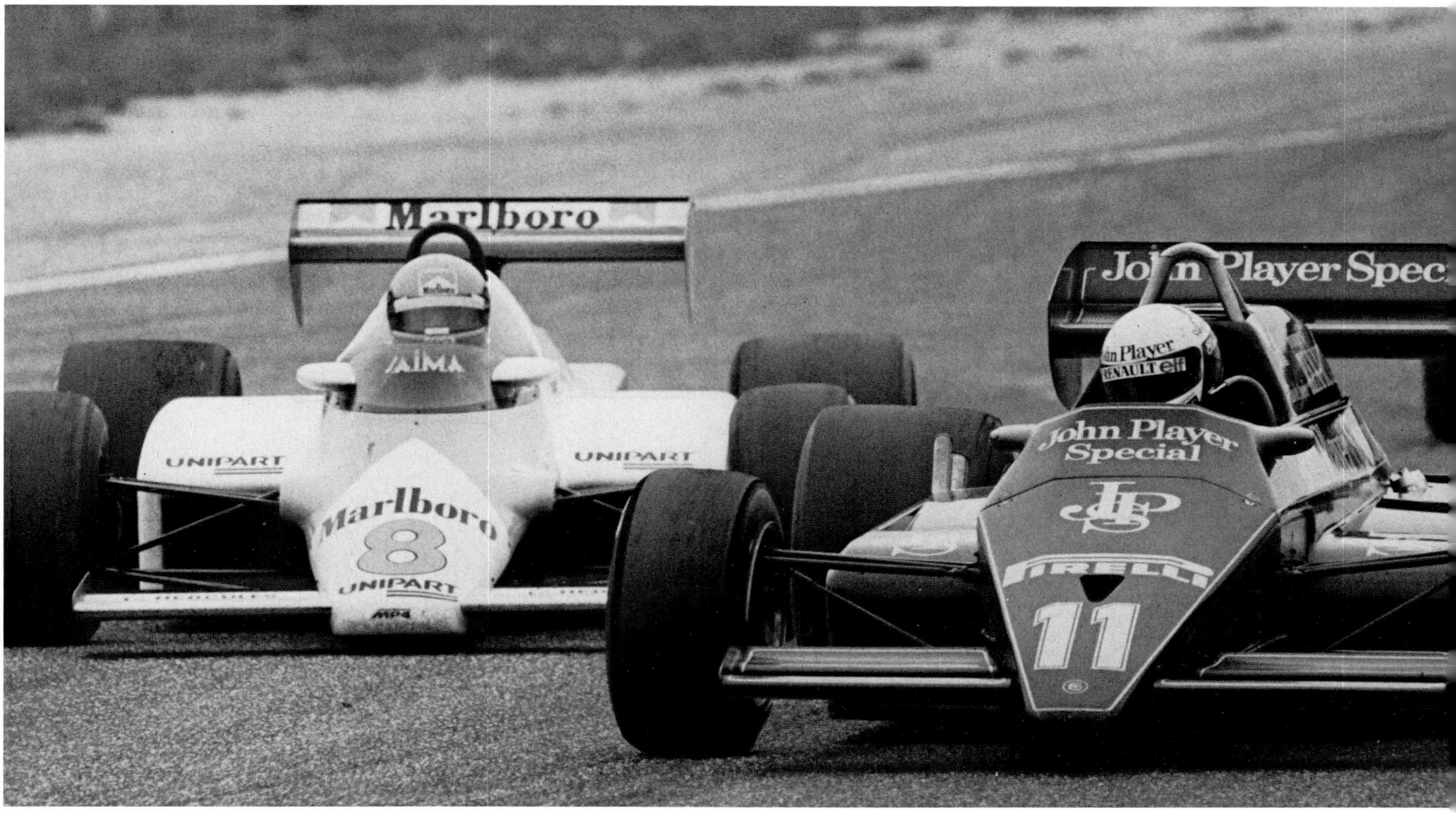

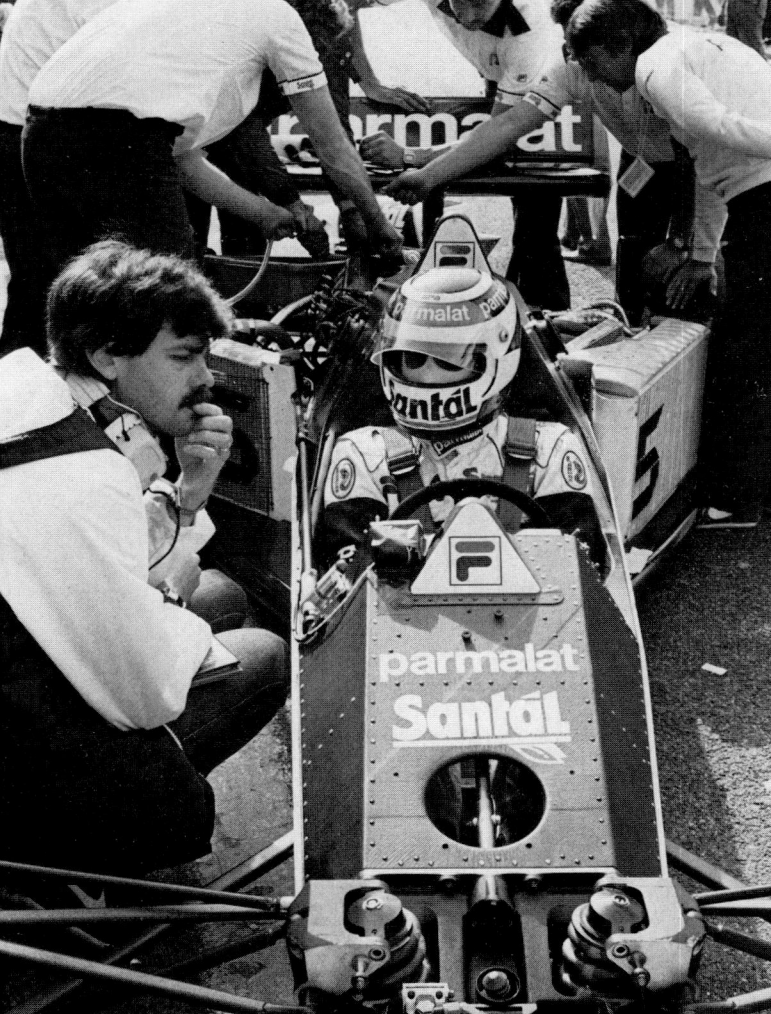

Previous pages:
Alain Prost and Gerard Larrousse worked hard to ensure a victory for Renault in France. Prost set the pace throughout and Eddie Cheever gave Renault four more points for third place.
Photos: John Townsend
Keith Sutton and Diana Burnett (insets)

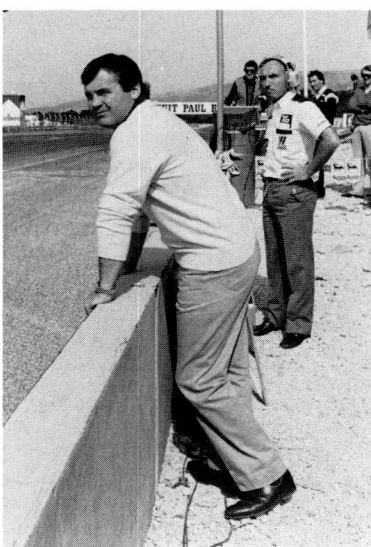

"I'll just stand in the Williams pit for a while and put Keke off his stroke. . . ." Alan Jones decided to wait for adequate sponsorship to arrive at Arrows before continuing his comeback.

Nigel Mansell, Niki Lauda and John Watson used the latest Ford-Cosworth engine, the DFY, during practice and the race. According to the drivers, there was little advantage to be had. Gordon Murray and Nelson Piquet overcame any number of problems during practice to take six points (far right).

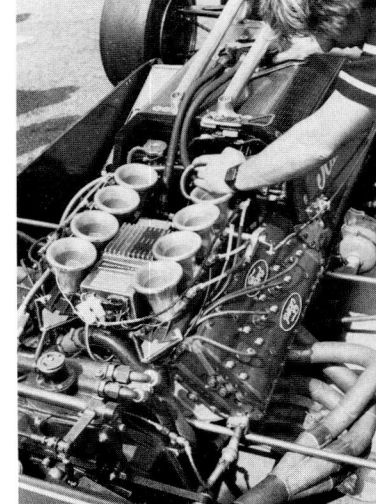
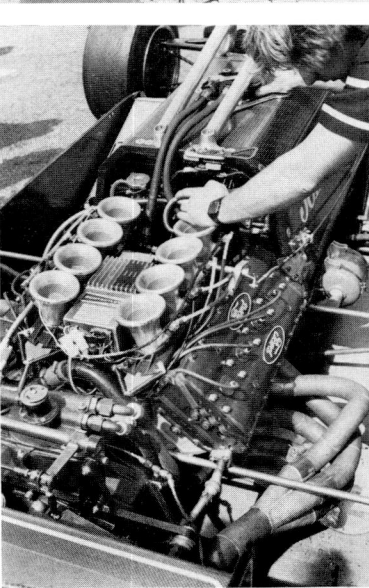

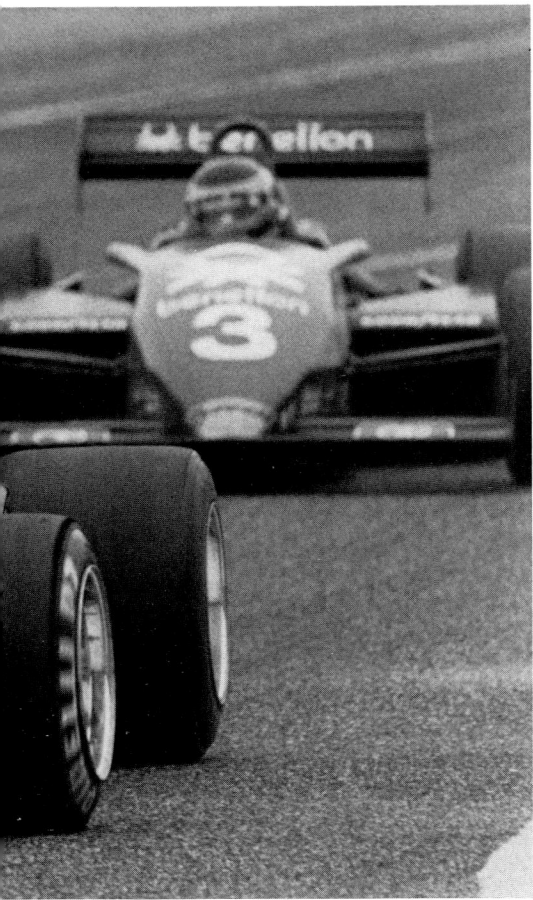

Turbos ruled at Ricard – much to the frustration of the Cosworth runners. Niki Lauda, uncharacteristically out of shape, tries to outbrake de Angelis's Lotus-Renault. Alboreto watches with interest.

the message through to Prost but, by then, the seconds were ticking away and the Renault eventually left the pits after 24.2s.

Piquet, of course, had taken the lead and it remained to be seen how damaging Prost's stop had been. Three laps later we were to get the answer as the white Brabham made for the pits, the mechanics responding in their usual manner tarnished only by the expansion tank tipping on its side and allowing fuel to flow onto the pit lane. Fortunately there was no harm done and Piquet was on his way in 16.1s. But it was not enough, the Brabham rejoining soon after Prost had started his 33rd lap. There was a gap of around 15s and it would remain that way as Piquet,

APRIL:
Keke Rosberg (Williams FW08C-Cosworth) wins Race of Champions at Brands Hatch.
Spirit-Honda V6 turbo makes debut at Brands Hatch.

WHEN BRABHAM DEVELOPED A HIGHLY-POLISHED PIT stop routine in 1982, it was greeted with scepticism. Rarely did an advantage accrue since the drivers were usually spectating by the half-way point in the race. But, when it did work – as in Brazil 1983 – the benefit was obvious and other teams gave serious consideration to this latest tactic.

Brabham had been partially forced into making pit stops by marginal fuel consumption but it soon became clear that the advantage of starting with half a tank of fuel and softer tyres more than made up for the 25 seconds or so which were lost during the halt.

Williams made a stop in Brazil and, while the flash fire had nothing to do with the actual refuelling routine, it merely heightened the growing concern over safety in the pits. A meeting prior to the Race of Champions at Brands Hatch failed to reach agreement on an immediate ban. The practice would be illegal in 1984 but it was felt than an immediate ban would penalise Brabham heavily since their car had been designed with pit stops in mind. Bernie Ecclestone, not surprisingly, was in favour of pit stops, saying it was good for television and the spectators. Other constructors spoke of a holocaust in the pits.

At Paul Ricard, then, Ferrari and Renault joined Brabham and Williams while Alfa Romeo and Lotus were known to be considering the ploy. The organisers responded by clearing the pit lane of everyone bar essential personnel during the race. It worked well – as did the pit stops – but, at the end of the day, it was difficult to draw a positive conclusion.

Race positions had been the same before and after the stops although you needed an accurate lap chart to tell you so. Apart from the dangers of refuelling under pressure from not only air bottles but also the vital seconds ticking away, there were spectators to think about. Unless they had a view of the pit lane, there seemed little point in pit stops which merely served to confuse and could lose a driver the race through no fault of his own. That sort of penalty, it was widely felt, should be reserved for the team effort associated with endurance racing and not Grand Prix 'sprints'.

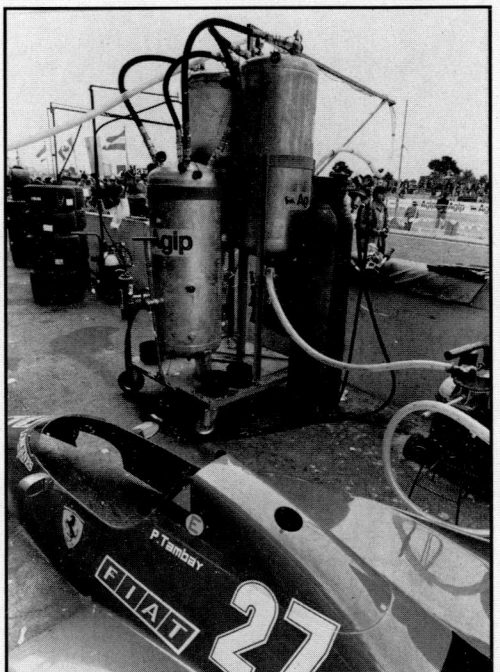

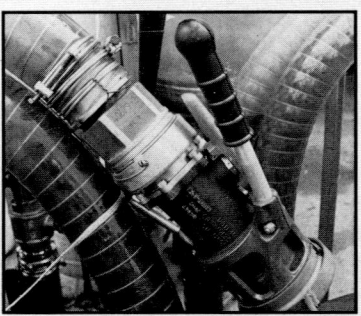

Ferrari spent over £10,000 on sophisticated refuelling equipment, complete with aircraft-type couplings.

struggling with increasing understeer, resigned himself to second place.

He was fortunate to be there since, just before his pit stop, the Brazilian narrowly avoided a nasty moment between Winkelhock and Baldi on the pit straight. The Alfa Romeo driver was making up ground after his pit stop to replace a rear tyre damaged in the Watson incident. Winkelhock had continued to make good progress even though his exhaust pipe had broken and the ATS had begun to understeer but, just as he was passing the pits, a severe vibration from the rear of the car caused alarm and the German driver pulled over to the side of the track. It was to be rather a rash move, for Baldi was almost alongside with Piquet and Rosberg in close attendance. To Baldi's horror, the ATS kept coming, forcing the Alfa Romeo onto the dirt and into a wild spin, Baldi coming to a halt after the rear of the car had struck the barrier a mighty blow. The pursuing Piquet and Rosberg, peppered with flying stones, were otherwise unscathed. Baldi was not so fortunate and the rear of his car caught fire for good measure but that was soon doused once the marshals had found an extinguisher which worked. Winkelhock, meanwhile, crept quietly round to the pits where he added his name to the growing list of retirements, Serra having stopped with engine trouble and Lauda losing sixth place when a wheel bearing seized. It was unfortunate since the McLaren, although short of grip as the gathering wind blew grit onto the track, would have been well placed in the light of pit stops by the Williams team. Rosberg had fallen behind Laffite and the positions remained that way after the Frenchman's stop. This was because a decision had been taken not to change Laffite's tyres following close inspection of Rosberg's reasonably intact Goodyears. Jacques was soon on the pace but it didn't take Rosberg long to move ahead and claim fifth place.

Thus, the first six cars had stopped – and the positions were exactly as before and were to remain that way until the end. The retirements continued, Corrado Fabi leading Raul Boesel's Ligier until both stopped with engine trouble. Bruno Giacomelli stripped fifth gear on his Toleman and the resulting noise was so bad that the Italian driver didn't think to try another gear before abandoning his car out on the circuit. Giacomelli had covered enough ground to be classified 13th and last with de Cesaris taking 12th place after a pit stop to attend to another bout of gearbox trouble. Nevertheless, the Italian driver was heartened by a troublefree run with the turbo.

Renault's past experience had shown just what could go wrong with turbos and the catalogue of disasters ran through Alain Prost's mind as he made his solitary way to the chequered flag. With his stomach tied in knots, he completed the final lap, his nerve-ends super-sensitive to every vibration, every tremor. This time the car did not miss a beat and the Frenchman punched his fists in the air, more in relief than aggression, as he took the flag. After such a dreadful practice, Piquet and Brabham were very satisfied with second place while Cheever was happy – but not deliriously so – with third. Tambay acknowledged the wave from the Ferrari pit as he took fourth, while fifth and sixth places for Williams were about right against such terrible odds. Rosberg had entertained with some brilliant on-the-limit driving and Jacques Laffite limped home with his left rear tyre rapidly loosing air. Another lap and he might not have made it.

The Renaults, by contrast, could have motored all day. Yet first and third had only been good enough to put them into third place in the Constructors' Championship. That was a more adequate reflection of their performance in the season thus far, even though, as Cheever had promised, they were in good shape at Paul Ricard.

Grand Prix de France, April 17/statistics

Entries and practice times

No.	Driver	Nat	Car	Tyre	Engine	Entrant	Practice 1	Practice 2
1	Keke Rosberg	SF	Saudia WILLIAMS FW08C	G	Ford Cosworth DFV	TAG Williams Team	**1m 42·450s**	1m 42·551s
2	Jacques Laffite	F	Saudia WILLIAMS FW08C	G	Ford Cosworth DFV	TAG Williams Team	1m 43·295s	**1m 42·678s**
3	Michele Alboreto	I	Benetton TYRRELL 011	G	Ford Cosworth DFV	Benetton Tyrrell Team	**1m 42·177s**	1m 43·317s
4	Danny Sullivan	USA	Benetton TYRRELL 011	G	Ford Cosworth DFV	Benetton Tyrrell Team	1m 44·317s	**1m 43·654s**
5	Nelson Piquet	BR	Parmalat BRABHAM BT52	M	BMW M12/13	Fila Sport	**1m 39·601s**	1m 39·746s
6	Riccardo Patrese	I	Parmalat BRABHAM BT52	M	BMW M12/13	Fila Sport	1m 41·095s	**1m 39·104s**
7	John Watson	GB	Marlboro McLAREN MP4/1C	M	Ford Cosworth DFV/DFY	Marlboro McLaren International	**1m 41·838s**	1m 42·448s
8	Niki Lauda	A	Marlboro McLAREN MP4/1C	M	Ford Cosworth DFV/DFY	Marlboro McLaren International	**1m 41·065s**	1m 41·492s
9	Manfred Winkelhock	D	ATS D6	G	BMW M12/13	Team ATS	**1m 40·233s**	1m 44·987s
11	Elio de Angelis	I	John Player Special LOTUS 93T	P	Renault EF1	John Player Team Lotus	**1m 39·512s**	1m 39·312s
12	Nigel Mansell	GB	John Player Special LOTUS 92	P	Ford Cosworth DFV/DFY	John Player Team Lotus	1m 43·320s	**1m 42·650s**
15	Alain Prost	F	Elf RENAULT RE40	M	Renault EF1	Equipe Renault Elf	1m 38·358s	**1m 36·672s**
16	Eddie Cheever	USA	Elf RENAULT RE40	M	Renault EF1	Equipe Renault Elf	**1m 38·980s**	1m 39·785s
17	Eliseo Salazar	RCH	MARCH-RAM 01	P	Ford Cosworth DFV	RAM Automotive Team March	1m 45·073s	2m 02·335s
18	Jean-Louis Schlesser	F	MARCH-RAM 01	P	Ford Cosworth DFV	RAM Automotive Team March	1m 45·866s	1m 46·102s
22	Andrea de Cesaris	I	Marlboro ALFA ROMEO 183T	M	Alfa Romeo 183T	Marlboro Team Alfa Romeo	1m 38·099s*	**1m 39·611s**
23	Mauro Baldi	I	Marlboro ALFA ROMEO 183T	M	Alfa Romeo 183T	Marlboro Team Alfa Romeo	1m 41·215s	**1m 39·618s**
25	Jean-Pierre Jarier	F	Gitanes LIGIER JS21	M	Ford Cosworth DFV	Equipe Ligier Gitanes	1m 42·808s	**1m 42·737s**
26	Raul Boesel	BR	Gitanes LIGIER JS21	M	Ford Cosworth DFV	Equipe Ligier Gitanes	**1m 44·470s**	1m 44·905s
27	Patrick Tambay	F	Fiat FERRARI 126C2/B	G	Ferrari 126C	Scuderia Ferrari SpA SEFAC	**1m 40·393s**	1m 40·488s
28	René Arnoux	F	Fiat FERRARI 126C2/B	G	Ferrari 126C	Scuderia Ferrari SpA SEFAC	1m 40·027s	**1m 39·115s**
29	Marc Surer	CH	ARROWS A6	G	Ford Cosworth DFV	Arrows Racing Team	**1m 42·962s**	1m 44·346s
30	Chico Serra	BR	ARROWS A6	G	Ford Cosworth DFV	Arrows Racing Team	**1m 44·778s**	1m 45·859s
31	Corrado Fabi	I	OSELLA FA1D	M	Ford Cosworth DFV	Osella Squadra Corse	1m 45·638s	**1m 43·411s**
32	Piercarlo Ghinzani	I	OSELLA FA1D	M	Ford Cosworth DFV	Osella Squadra Corse	1m 46·541s	**1m 45·812s**
33	Roberto Guerrero	COL	THEODORE N183	G	Ford Cosworth DFV	Theodore Racing Team	**1m 43·367s**	1m 43·602s
34	Johnny Cecotto	YV	THEODORE N183	G	Ford Cosworth DFV	Theodore Racing Team	1m 43·552s	**1m 42·615s**
35	Derek Warwick	GB	Candy TOLEMAN TG183B	P	Hart 415T	Candy Toleman Motorsport	1m 43·038s	**1m 39·881s**
36	Bruno Giacomelli	I	Candy TOLEMAN TG183B	P	Hart 415T	Candy Toleman Motorsport	1m 42·219s	**1m 41·775s**

Friday morning and Saturday morning practice sessions not officially recorded.

G – Goodyear, M – Michelin, P – Pirelli.

Fri pm Warm, dry,
Sat pm Warm, dry
* Time disallowed

Starting grid

15 PROST (1m 36·672s)
Renault

    16 CHEEVER (1m 38·980s)
    Renault

6 PATRESE (1m 39·104s)
Brabham

    28 ARNOUX (1m 39·115s)
    Ferrari

11 DE ANGELIS (1m 39·312s)
Lotus

    5 PIQUET (1m 39·601s)
    Brabham

22 DE CESARIS (1m 39·611s)
Alfa Romeo

    23 BALDI (1m 39·618s)
    Alfa Romeo

35 WARWICK (1m 39·881s)
Toleman

    9 WINKELHOCK (1m 40·233s)
    ATS

27 TAMBAY (1m 40·393s)
Ferrari

    8 LAUDA (1m 41·065s)
    McLaren

36 GIACOMELLI (1m 41·775s)
Toleman

    7 WATSON (1m 41·838s)
    McLaren

3 ALBORETO (1m 42·177s)
Tyrrell

    1 ROSBERG (1m 42·450s)
    Williams

34 CECOTTO (1m 42·615s)
Theodore

    12 MANSELL (1m 42·650s)
    Lotus

2 LAFFITE (1m 42·678s)
Williams

    25 JARIER (1m 42·737s)
    Ligier

29 SURER (1m 42·962s)
Arrows

    33 GUERRERO (1m 43·367s)
    Theodore

31 FABI (1m 43·411s)
Osella

    4 SULLIVAN (1m 43·654s)
    Tyrrell

26 BOESEL (1m 44·470s)
Ligier

    30 SERRA (1m 44·778s)
    Arrows

Did not start:
17 Salazar (March-RAM), 1m 45·073s, did not qualify
32 Ghinzani (Osella), 1m 45·812s, did not qualify
18 Schlesser (March-RAM), 1m 45·866s, did not qualify

Results and retirements

Place	Driver	Car	Laps	Time and Speed (mph/km/h)/Retirement	
1	Alain Prost	Renault t/c V6	54	1h 34m 13·913s	124·191/199·866
2	Nelson Piquet	Brabham-BMW t/c 4	54	1h 34m 43·633s	123·466/198·7
3	Eddie Cheever	Renault t/c V6	54	1h 34m 54·145s	123·280/198·4
4	Patrick Tambay	Ferrari t/c V6	54	1h 35m 20·793s	122·658/197·4
5	Keke Rosberg	Williams-Cosworth V8	53		
6	Jacques Laffite	Williams-Cosworth V8	53		
7	René Arnoux	Ferrari t/c V6	53		
8	Michele Alboreto	Tyrrell-Cosworth V8	53		
9	Jean-Pierre Jarier	Ligier-Cosworth V8	53		
10	Marc Surer	Arrows-Cosworth V8	53		
11	Johnny Cecotto	Theodore-Cosworth V8	52		
12	Andrea de Cesaris	Alfa Romeo t/c V8	50		
13	Bruno Giacomelli	Toleman-Hart t/c 4	49	Gearbox	
	Raul Boesel	Ligier-Cosworth V8	47	Engine	
	Corrado Fabi	Osella-Cosworth V8	36	Engine	
	Manfred Winkelhock	ATS-BMW t/c 4	36	Engine/exhaust pipe	
	Niki Lauda	McLaren-Cosworth V8	29	Wheel bearing	
	Mauro Baldi	Alfa Romeo t/c V8	28	Accident with Winkelhock	
	Chico Serra	Arrows-Cosworth V8	26	Gearbox	
	Roberto Guerrero	Theodore-Cosworth V8	23	Engine	
	Danny Sullivan	Tyrrell-Cosworth V8	21	Clutch	
	Elio de Angelis	Lotus-Renault t/c V6	20	Electrics	
	Riccardo Patrese	Brabham-BMW t/c 4	19	Engine/overheating	
	Derek Warwick	Toleman-Hart t/c 4	14	Engine/split water pipe	
	Nigel Mansell	Lotus-Cosworth V8	6	Driver injury/handling	
	John Watson	McLaren-Cosworth V8	3	Throttle linkage	

Fastest lap: Prost, on lap 34, 1m 42·695s, 126·555mph/203·671km/h.
Lap record: Riccardo Patrese (F1 Brabham BT50-BMW t/c), 1m 40·075s, 129·868mph/209·003km/h (1982).

Past winners

Year	Driver	Nat	Car	Circuit	Distance miles/km	Speed mph/km/h
1906	Frenc Szisz	H	13·0 Renault	Circuit de la Sarthe	769·35/1238·16	62·88/101·20
1907	Felice Nazzaro	I	15·3 Fiat	Circuit de la Seine-Inférieure	478·38/ 769·88	70·61/113·64
1908	Christian Lautenschlager	D	12·8 Mercedes	Circuit de la Seine-Inférieure	478·38/ 769·88	69·05/111·13
1912	Georges Boillot	F	7·6 Peugeot	Circuit de la Sarthe	956·76/1539·76	68·51/110·26
1913	Georges Boillot	F	5·7 Peugeot	Circuit de Picardie	569·80/ 917·01	72·12/116·06
1914	Christian Lautenschlager	D	4·5 Mercedes	Circuit de Lyon	467·66/ 752·62	65·56/105·52
1921	Jimmy Murphy	USA	3·0 Duesenberg	Circuit de la Sarthe	321·78/ 517·86	78·11/125·70
1922	Felice Nazzaro	I	2·0 Fiat 804	Strasbourg	498·84/ 802·80	79·33/127·67
1923	Henry Segrave	GB	2·0 Sunbeam	Tours	496·51/ 799·05	75·36/121·27
1924	Giuseppe Campari	I	2·0 Alfa Romeo P2 s/c	Circuit de Lyon	503·36/ 810·08	70·97/114·21
1925	Robert Benoist/ Albert Divo	F	2·0 Delage s/c	Montlhéry	621·37/1000·00	69·73/112·21
1926	Jules Goux	F	1·5 Bugatti T39A s/c	Miramas	310·69/ 500·00	68·16/109·69
1927	Robert Benoist	F	1·5 Delage s/c	Montlhéry	382·82/ 600·00	78·30/126·01
1928	"Williams"	GB	2·3 Bugatti T35C s/c	Comminges	163·42/ 263·00	66·39/106·85
1929	"Williams"	GB	2·3 Bugatti T35B s/c	Circuit de la Sarthe	376·13/ 605·32	82·66/133·03
1930	Phillippe Etancelin	F	2·3 Bugatti T35B s/c	Pau	245·99/ 395·88	90·37/145·45
1931	Louis Chiron/ Achille Varzi	F	2·3 Bugatti T51 s/c	Montlhéry	782·20/1258·83	78·22/125·88
1932	Tazio Nuvolari	I	2·7 Alfa Romeo P3 s/c	Reims-Gueux	461·58/ 742·84	92·32/148·57
1933	Giuseppe Campari	I	3·0 Maserati 8C s/c	Montlhéry	310·69/ 500·00	81·49/131·14
1934	Louis Chiron	F	2·9 Alfa Romeo P3 s/c	Montlhéry	310·69/ 500·00	85·05/136·88
1935	Rudi Caracciola	D	4·0 Mercedes-Benz W25 s/c	Montlhéry	310·69/ 500·00	77·40/124·57
1936	Jean-Pierre Wimille/ Raymond Sommer	F	3·3 Bugatti T35S	Montlhéry	621·37/1000·00	77·85/125·29
1937	Louis Chiron	F	4·0 Talbot	Montlhéry	310·69/ 500·00	82·47/132·73
1938	Manfred von Brauchitsch	D	3·0 Mercedes-Benz W154 s/c	Reims-Gueux	310·78/ 500·16	101·13/162·76
1939	Hermann Müller	D	3·0 Auto Union D-type s/c	Reims-Gueux	247·66/ 398·57	105·25/169·38
1947	Louis Chiron	F	4·5 Lago-Talbot	Lyon-Parilly	317·09/ 510·30	78·08/125·66
1948	Jean-Pierre Wimille	F	1·5 Alfa Romeo 158 s/c	Reims-Gueux	310·81/ 500·20	102·96/165·70
1949	Charles Pozzi	F	2·5 Delahaye	Comminges	314·41/ 506·00	88·14/141·84
1950	Juan Manuel Fangio	RA	1·5 Alfa Romeo 158 s/c	Reims-Gueux	310·81/ 500·20	104·84/168·72
1951	Luigi Fagioli/ Juan Manuel Fangio	I RA	1·5 Alfa Romeo 159 s/c	Reims-Gueux	373·94/ 601·80	110·97/178·59
1952	Alberto Ascari	I	2·0 Ferrari 500	Rouen-les-Essarts	240·39/ 386·88	80·13/128·96
1953	Mike Hawthorn	GB	2·0 Ferrari 500	Reims	314·56/ 506·23	113·64/182·89
1954	Juan Manuel Fangio	RA	2·5 Mercedes-Benz W196	Reims	314·64/ 506·36	115·97/186·64
1956	Peter Collins	GB	2·5 Lancia-Ferrari D50	Reims	314·64/ 506·36	122·29/196·80

Lap chart

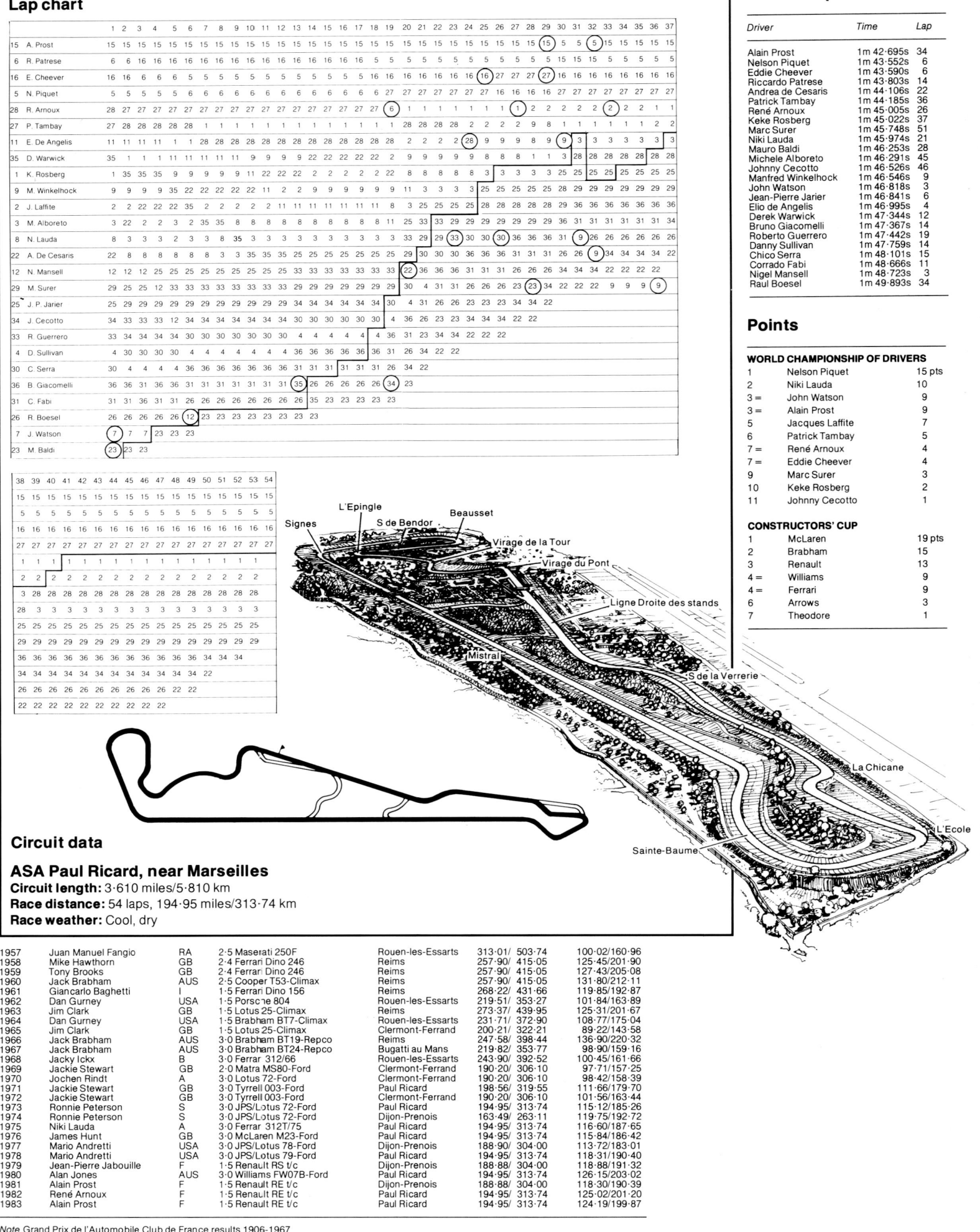

Laps 1–37

		1	2	3	4	5	6	7	8	9	10	11	12	13	14	15	16	17	18	19	20	21	22	23	24	25	26	27	28	29	30	31	32	33	34	35	36	37
15	A. Prost	15	15	15	15	15	15	15	15	15	15	15	15	15	15	15	15	15	15	15	15	15	15	15	15	15	15	(15)	5	5	(5)	15	15	15	15	15	15	15
6	R. Patrese	6	6	16	16	16	16	16	16	16	16	16	16	16	16	16	16	16	16	16	5	5	5	5	5	5	5	5	5	15	5	5	5	5	5	5	5	5
16	E. Cheever	16	16	6	6	6	5	5	5	5	5	5	5	5	5	5	5	16	16	16	16	16	16	(16)	27	27	27	(27)	16	16	16	16	16	16	16	16	16	16
5	N. Piquet	5	5	5	5	5	6	6	6	6	6	6	6	6	6	6	6	6	6	6	6	27	27	27	27	27	27	16	16	16	27	27	27	27	27	27	27	27
28	R. Arnoux	28	27	27	27	27	27	27	27	27	27	27	27	27	27	27	27	(6)	1	1	1	1	1	1	(1)	2	2	2	2	(2)	2	2	1	1				
27	P. Tambay	27	28	28	28	28	28	1	1	1	1	1	1	1	1	1	1	1	28	28	28	28	2	2	2	9	8	1	1	1	1	1	1	1	2	2		
11	E. De Angelis	11	11	11	11	1	1	28	28	28	28	28	28	28	28	28	28	28	2	2	2	(28)	9	9	9	8	9	(9)	3	3	3	3	3	3	3	3	3	3
35	D. Warwick	35	1	1	1	11	11	11	11	11	9	9	9	9	22	22	22	22	9	9	9	9	8	8	1	1	3	28	28	28	28	28	28	28	28			
1	K. Rosberg	1	35	35	35	9	9	9	9	11	22	22	22	22	2	2	2	2	22	22	8	3	3	3	3	25	25	25	25	25	25	25	25	25				
9	M. Winkelhock	9	9	9	9	35	22	22	22	22	22	11	2	2	9	9	9	9	11	3	3	3	25	25	25	28	29	29	29	29	29	29	29	29	29	29	29	29
2	J. Laffite	2	2	22	22	22	35	2	2	2	2	11	11	11	11	11	11	11	8	3	25	25	25	28	28	28	28	28	29	36	36	36	36	36	36	36	36	36
3	M. Alboreto	3	22	2	2	3	2	35	35	8	8	8	8	8	8	8	8	8	11	25	33	33	29	29	29	29	29	29	36	31	31	31	31	31	31	31	31	34
8	N. Lauda	8	3	3	3	2	3	3	8	35	3	3	3	3	3	3	3	3	33	29	29	(33)	30	30	(30)	36	36	36	31	9	26	26	26	26	26			
22	A. De Cesaris	22	8	8	8	8	8	3	3	35	35	25	25	25	25	25	25	25	29	30	30	36	36	36	31	31	31	26	26	(9)	34	34	34	34	22			
12	N. Mansell	12	12	12	25	25	25	25	25	25	25	25	33	33	33	33	33	33	(22)	36	36	36	31	31	31	26	26	26	34	34	34	22	22	22	22			
29	M. Surer	29	25	25	12	33	33	33	33	33	33	33	29	29	29	29	29	29	30	4	31	31	26	26	26	23	(23)	34	22	22	22	9	9	9	(9)			
25	J. P. Jarier	25	29	29	29	29	29	29	29	29	29	29	34	34	34	34	34	30	4	31	26	26	23	23	23	34	34	22										
34	J. Cecotto	34	33	33	33	12	34	34	34	34	34	34	30	30	30	30	30	4	36	26	23	23	34	34	34	22	22											
33	R. Guerrero	33	34	34	34	34	30	30	30	30	30	30	4	4	4	4	4	36	31	23	34	34	22	22														
4	D. Sullivan	4	30	30	30	30	4	4	4	4	4	4	36	36	36	36	36	31	26	34	22	22																
30	C. Serra	30	4	4	4	4	36	36	36	36	36	36	31	31	31	31	31	26	34	22																		
36	B. Giacomelli	36	36	31	36	36	31	31	31	31	31	31	(35)	26	26	26	26	(34)	23																			
31	C. Fabi	31	31	36	31	31	26	26	26	26	26	26	26	35	23	23	23	23																				
26	R. Boesel	26	26	26	26	26	(12)	23	23	23	23	23	23	23	23																							
7	J. Watson	(7)	7	7	23	23	23																															
23	M. Baldi	(23)	23	23																																		

Laps 38–54

	38	39	40	41	42	43	44	45	46	47	48	49	50	51	52	53	54
	15	15	15	15	15	15	15	15	15	15	15	15	15	15	15	15	15
	5	5	5	5	5	5	5	5	5	5	5	5	5	5	5	5	5
	16	16	16	16	16	16	16	16	16	16	16	16	16	16	16	16	16
	27	27	27	27	27	27	27	27	27	27	27	27	27	27	27	27	27
	1	1	1	1	1	1	1	1	1	1	1	1	1	1	1		
	2	2	2	2	2	2	2	2	2	2	2	2	2	2	2		
	3	28	28	28	28	28	28	28	28	28	28	28	28	28	28		
	28	3	3	3	3	3	3	3	3	3	3	3	3	3			
	25	25	25	25	25	25	25	25	25	25	25	25	25				
	29	29	29	29	29	29	29	29	29	29	29	29	29				
	36	36	36	36	36	36	36	36	36	36	36	34	34				
	34	34	34	34	34	34	34	34	34	34	34	34	22				
	26	26	26	26	26	26	26	26	26	26	22						
	22	22	22	22	22	22	22	22	22	22							

Fastest laps

Driver	Time	Lap
Alain Prost	1m 42·695s	34
Nelson Piquet	1m 43·552s	6
Eddie Cheever	1m 43·590s	6
Riccardo Patrese	1m 43·803s	14
Andrea de Cesaris	1m 44·106s	22
Patrick Tambay	1m 44·185s	36
René Arnoux	1m 45·005s	26
Keke Rosberg	1m 45·022s	37
Marc Surer	1m 45·748s	51
Niki Lauda	1m 45·974s	21
Mauro Baldi	1m 46·253s	28
Michele Alboreto	1m 46·291s	45
Johnny Cecotto	1m 46·526s	46
Manfred Winkelhock	1m 46·546s	9
John Watson	1m 46·818s	3
Jean-Pierre Jarier	1m 46·841s	6
Elio de Angelis	1m 46·995s	4
Derek Warwick	1m 47·344s	12
Bruno Giacomelli	1m 47·367s	14
Roberto Guerrero	1m 47·442s	19
Danny Sullivan	1m 47·759s	14
Chico Serra	1m 48·101s	15
Corrado Fabi	1m 48·666s	11
Nigel Mansell	1m 48·723s	3
Raul Boesel	1m 49·893s	34

Points

WORLD CHAMPIONSHIP OF DRIVERS

1	Nelson Piquet	15 pts
2	Niki Lauda	10
3 =	John Watson	9
3 =	Alain Prost	9
5	Jacques Laffite	7
6	Patrick Tambay	5
7 =	René Arnoux	4
7 =	Eddie Cheever	4
9	Marc Surer	3
10	Keke Rosberg	2
11	Johnny Cecotto	1

CONSTRUCTORS' CUP

1	McLaren	19 pts
2	Brabham	15
3	Renault	13
4 =	Williams	9
4 =	Ferrari	9
6	Arrows	3
7	Theodore	1

Circuit data

ASA Paul Ricard, near Marseilles

Circuit length: 3·610 miles/5·810 km
Race distance: 54 laps, 194·95 miles/313·74 km
Race weather: Cool, dry

1957	Juan Manuel Fangio	RA	2·5 Maserati 250F	Rouen-les-Essarts	313·01/ 503·74	100·02/160·96
1958	Mike Hawthorn	GB	2·4 Ferrari Dino 246	Reims	257·90/ 415·05	125·45/201·90
1959	Tony Brooks	GB	2·4 Ferrari Dino 246	Reims	257·90/ 415·05	127·43/205·08
1960	Jack Brabham	AUS	2·5 Cooper T53-Climax	Reims	257·90/ 415·05	131·80/212·11
1961	Giancarlo Baghetti	I	1·5 Ferrari Dino 156	Reims	268·22/ 431·66	119·85/192·87
1962	Dan Gurney	USA	1·5 Porsche 804	Rouen-les-Essarts	219·51/ 353·27	101·84/163·89
1963	Jim Clark	GB	1·5 Lotus 25-Climax	Reims	273·37/ 439·95	125·31/201·67
1964	Dan Gurney	USA	1·5 Brabham BT7-Climax	Rouen-les-Essarts	231·71/ 372·90	108·77/175·04
1965	Jim Clark	GB	1·5 Lotus 25-Climax	Clermont-Ferrand	200·21/ 322·21	89·22/143·58
1966	Jack Brabham	AUS	3·0 Brabham BT19-Repco	Reims	247·58/ 398·44	136·90/220·32
1967	Jack Brabham	AUS	3·0 Brabham BT24-Repco	Bugatti au Mans	219·82/ 353·77	98·90/159·16
1968	Jacky Ickx	B	3·0 Ferrar 312/66	Rouen-les-Essarts	243·90/ 392·52	100·45/161·66
1969	Jackie Stewart	GB	2·0 Matra MS80-Ford	Clermont-Ferrand	190·20/ 306·10	97·71/157·25
1970	Jochen Rindt	A	3·0 Lotus 72-Ford	Clermont-Ferrand	190·20/ 306·10	98·42/158·39
1971	Jackie Stewart	GB	3·0 Tyrrell 003-Ford	Paul Ricard	198·56/ 319·55	111·66/179·70
1972	Jackie Stewart	GB	3·0 Tyrrell 003-Ford	Clermont-Ferrand	190·20/ 306·10	101·56/163·44
1973	Ronnie Peterson	S	3·0 JPS/Lotus 72-Ford	Paul Ricard	194·95/ 313·74	115·12/185·26
1974	Ronnie Peterson	S	3·0 JPS/Lotus 72-Ford	Dijon-Prenois	163·49/ 263·11	119·75/192·72
1975	Niki Lauda	A	3·0 Ferrar 312T/75	Paul Ricard	194·95/ 313·74	116·60/187·65
1976	James Hunt	GB	3·0 McLaren M23-Ford	Paul Ricard	194·95/ 313·74	115·84/186·42
1977	Mario Andretti	USA	3·0 JPS/Lotus 78-Ford	Dijon-Prenois	188·90/ 304·00	113·72/183·01
1978	Mario Andretti	USA	3·0 JPS/Lotus 79-Ford	Paul Ricard	194·95/ 313·74	118·31/190·40
1979	Jean-Pierre Jabouille	F	1·5 Renault RS t/c	Dijon-Prenois	188·88/ 304·00	118·88/191·32
1980	Alan Jones	AUS	3·0 Williams FW07B-Ford	Paul Ricard	194·95/ 313·74	126·15/203·02
1981	Alain Prost	F	1·5 Renault RE t/c	Dijon-Prenois	188·88/ 304·00	118·30/190·39
1982	René Arnoux	F	1·5 Renault RE t/c	Paul Ricard	194·95/ 313·74	125·02/201·20
1983	Alain Prost	F	1·5 Renault RE t/c	Paul Ricard	194·95/ 313·74	124·19/199·87

Note Grand Prix de l'Automobile Club de France results 1906-1967

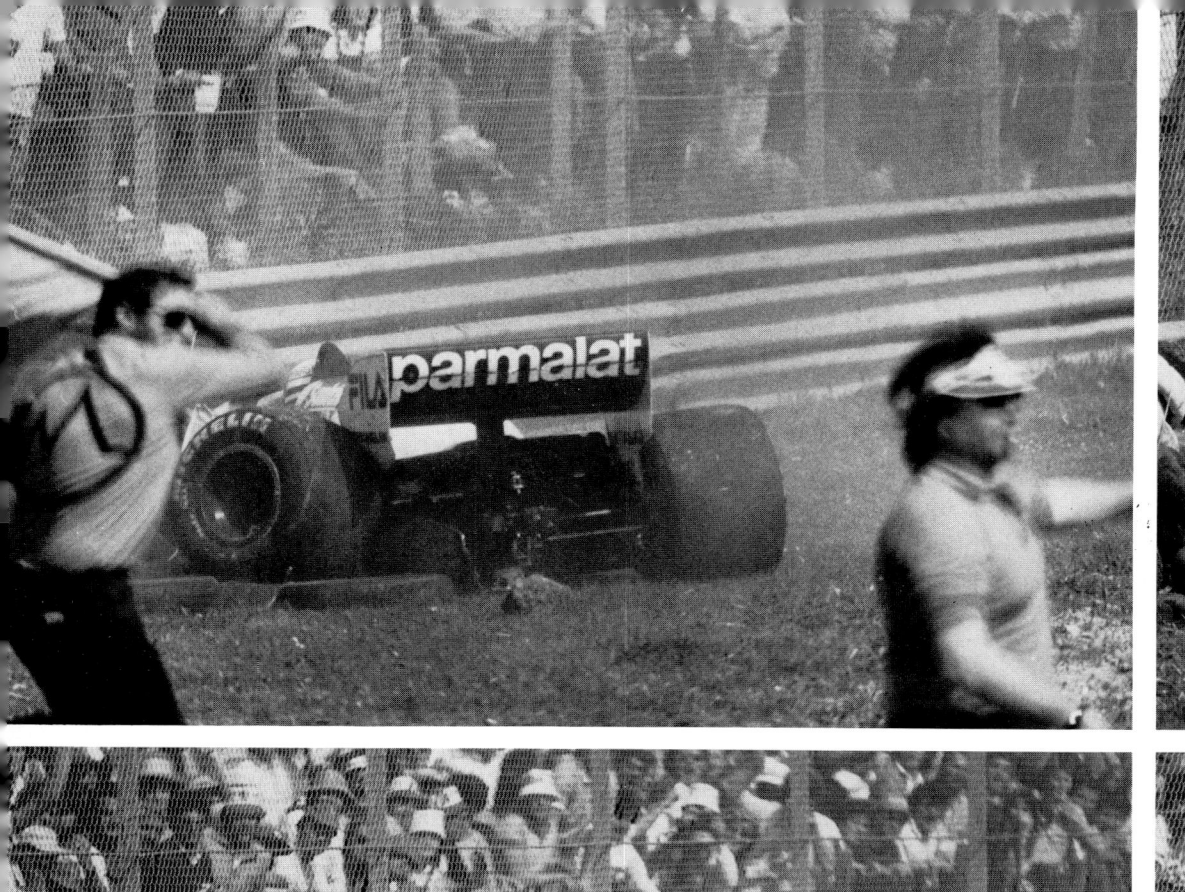
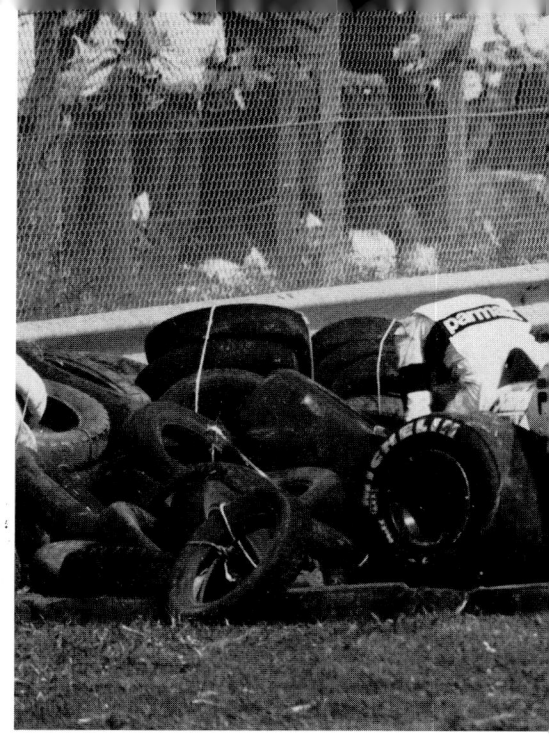
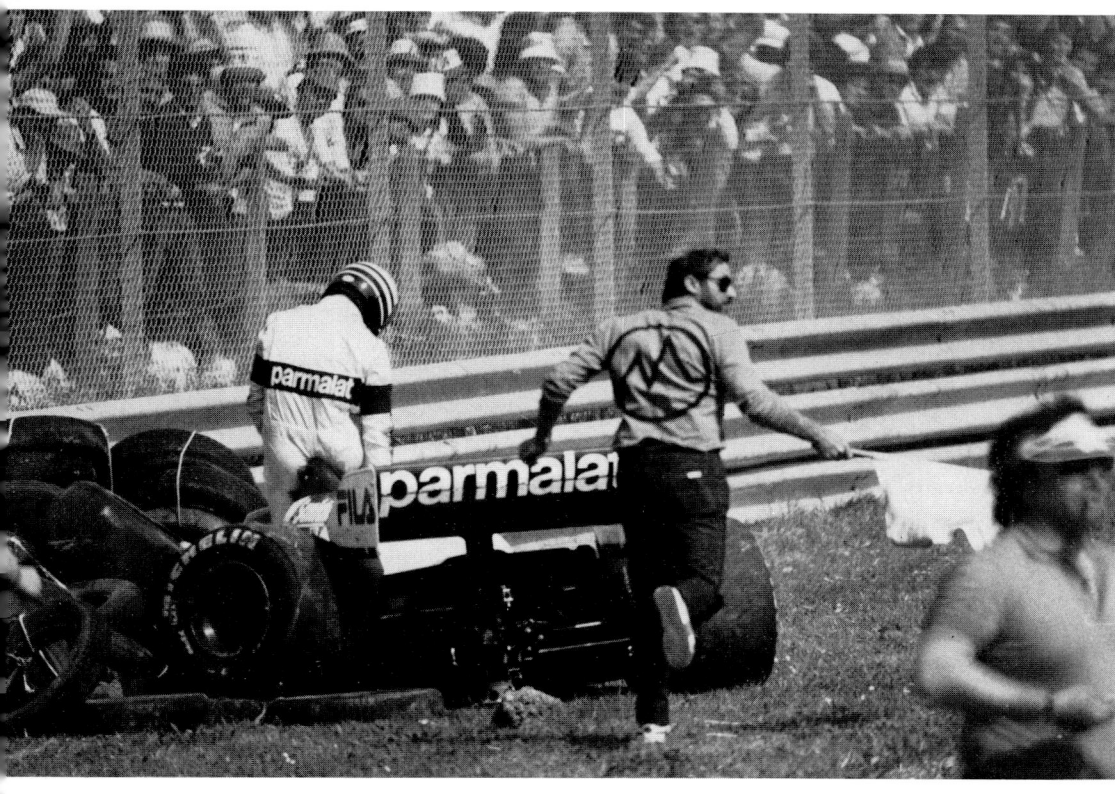
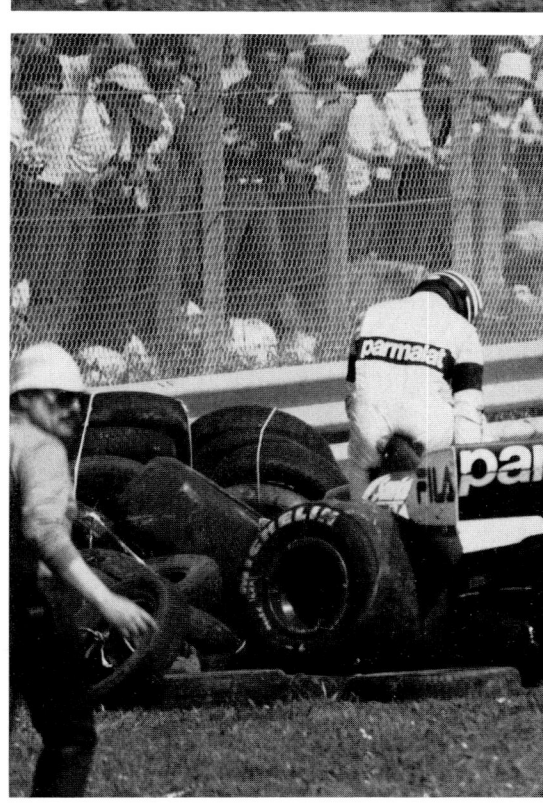
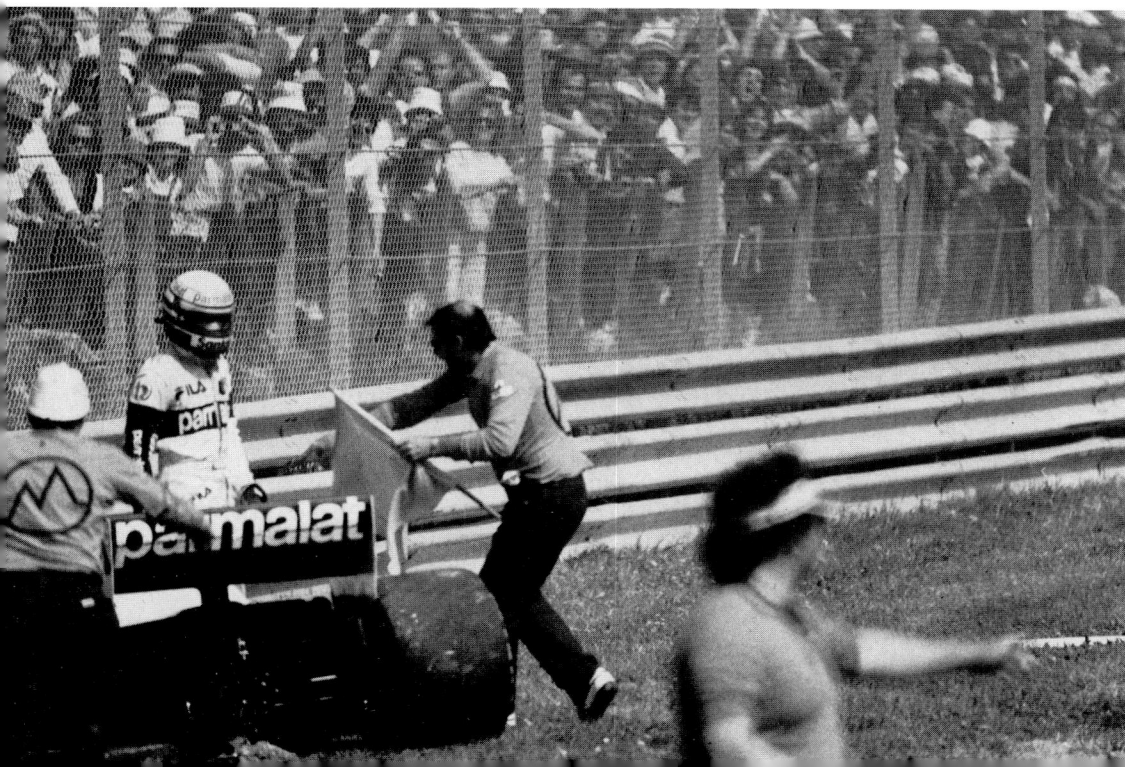
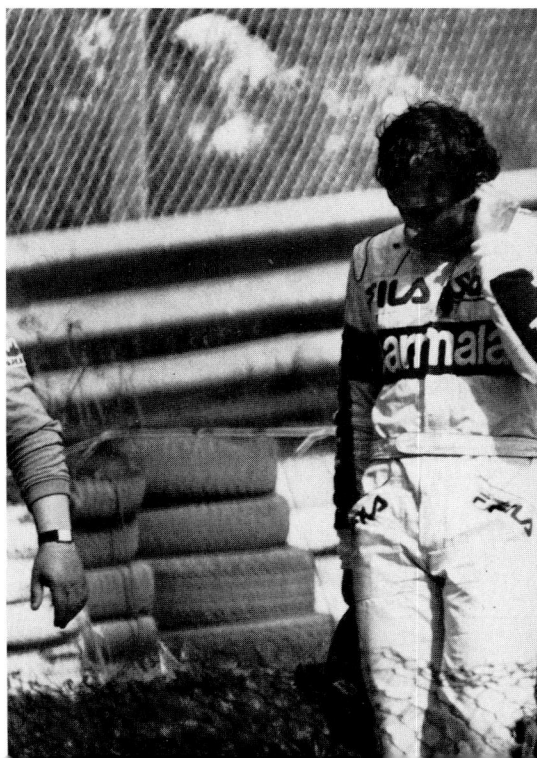

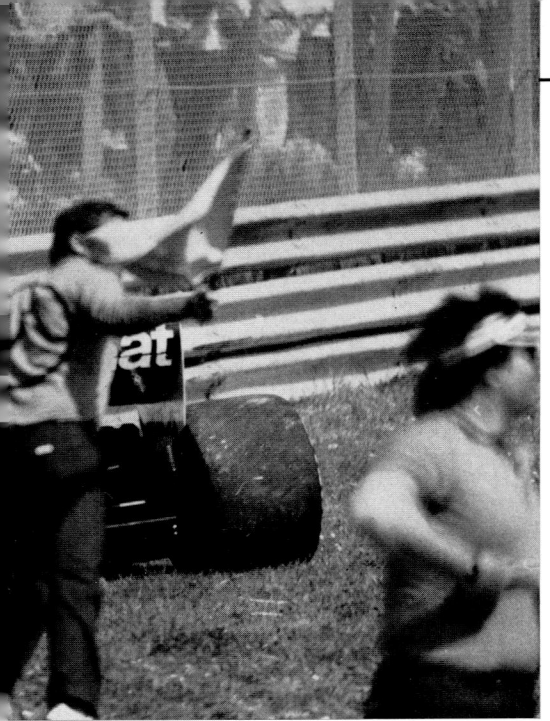

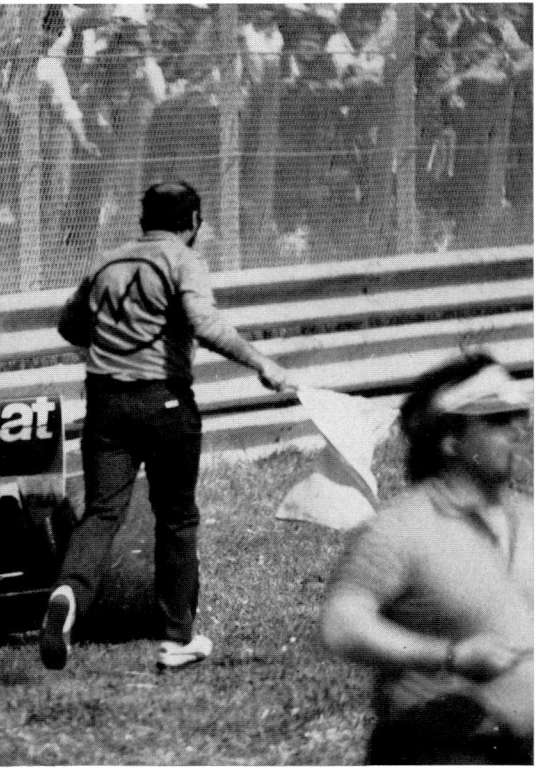

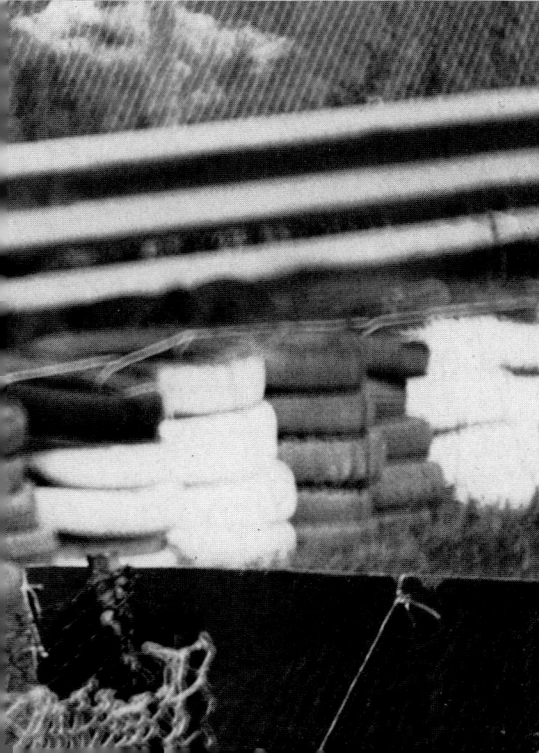

GRAN PREMIO DI SAN MARINO

Ferrari number 27 won at Imola and that, as far as the Italians were concerned, was all that mattered. Never mind that Patrick Tambay had been driving it; forget that an Italian had lost the lead with five laps to go. Number 27 had won the San Marino Grand Prix — just as Gilles Villeneuve said it should have done a year before. For the Tifosi, it was a matter of honour and Tambay's first win of the season brought an emotional weekend to a heady climax.

The 1982 San Marino Grand Prix had been the last time Villeneuve had performed before his adoring crowd and, almost a year since his fatal accident in Belgium, the memories of the man had not dimmed. Pictures and banners revering Gilles were hung on the fences. Of more significance, perhaps, was the number of Canadian flags fluttering in the enclosures; a sign of the crowd's rare attachment to a non-Italian driving for Ferrari.

They have little time for local drivers who have not been chosen to race for the Prancing Horse. Take Riccardo Patrese for example. From as early as lap six it was clear the Brabham-BMW was in perfect shape when Patrese took the lead from René Arnoux's Ferrari. Using copious power coupled with excellent traction, Patrese controlled the race as he pleased until making a stop for fuel and tyres.

Then, chaos ensued as Patrese overshot his pit and an airline broke as a mechanic struggled to reach the car. But, it seemed, not even a lengthy stop and a return to track in second place would deny Patrese victory. The Brabham soon reeled in Tambay's Ferrari and the Frenchman, hampered by an engine misfire, could offer no resistance as Patrese retook the lead to the thinly disguised dismay of the crowd.

Seconds later, they were beside themselves with joy. Patrese, misjudging the crumbling track surface, had understeered into a tyre barrier. Car 27 was back in the lead.

Arnoux, having dropped behind Tambay thanks to a tyre problem earlier on, underlined the treacherous nature of the track by spinning at the same corner but with less disastrous results, the Ferrari driver recovering to finish third. Alain Prost, happy to be fourth at one point since he was without fourth gear, could not believe his luck as he droned past Arnoux and Patrese to an easy six points.

The story so far had been about turbos — which was a surprise since the Cosworth runners had hoped for a more competitive showing at Imola following the turbo walk-over at Paul Ricard. But rapid turbo development and the ability to run large amounts of rear wing meant the Cosworth cars were merely left to pick up the points cast aside by the turbos occupying the first 10 places on the grid.

Nelson Piquet, sharing the front row with Arnoux, had been confident of victory but those expectations lasted a matter of feet, the Brabham driver stalling on the line and retiring eventually with engine trouble. Cheever retired his Renault with a blown engine and, as might be expected, it was Keke Rosberg who was ready to collect three points for a distant fourth place. John Watson, starting his McLaren at the back of the grid once more, took fifth place through perseverance more than anything else while Marc Surer, fractionally slower than Rosberg during practice, gave Arrows another point for sixth place.

These battles for the minor placings were merely a side-show when compared to the progress of Ferrari number 27. Tambay's win, according to the passionate Italians, was not merely deserved; it was ordained.

Riccardo Patrese and the Brabham-BMW proved to be the fastest combination on race day but the Italian threw away the lead by misjudging his pit stop. He regained control with five laps to go – and promptly crashed.

ENTRY AND PRACTICE

The advent of qualifying tyres, and the limitations placed on their use, had made the official practice sessions almost a weary procession: a couple of warm-up laps; two, maybe three fast laps; into the pits and on with the second set of qualifiers; the procedure on the track repeated once more. And that would be that. If someone bettered your time, there was no opportunity to reply. Paradoxically, the need for super-competitiveness through sticky tyres had taken the needle out of practice. At Imola, however, circumstances contrived to make the final hour a memorable one, the top turbo teams being within striking distance of each other and their drivers taking to the track at different times. And the whole scenario was acted out before a partisan audience whipped into a frenzy by a voluble commentator.

The man with the microphone had them on their feet from the start when René Arnoux took to the track and reasserted his overnight pole by improving to 1m 33.007s. No sooner had the Ferrari returned to the pits than Nelson Piquet crossed the line to register 1m 32.784s but he was soon followed by Patrick Tambay, the Frenchman now much happier with his car following engine problems on Friday. Looking for consistency rather than one, barn-storming lap, Tambay had chosen to use the harder qualifying tyre which Goodyear had made available and he soon had the crowd on their feet once more with a lap of 1m 32.603s. It had been a typically neat and tidy lap but the strain had been too much for the engine, the Ferrari returning to the pits with a blue haze issuing from the V6.

Riccardo Patrese, meanwhile, could only manage 1m 32.969s; an excellent time but not good enough in this exalted company, for the Renaults were ready to have their turn. Running a new chassis, Alain Prost cut a lap of 1m 32.401s despite clipping a kerb but Cheever was unable to join in the fun since he had made a wrong decision regarding the settings on his car and could not hope to compete with the wholesale improvements being made elsewhere.

A quick glance at the times thus far told Nelson Piquet exactly what he had to do on his last set of qualifiers and the Brabham driver, revelling in a car which had undergone serious testing at Spa and Snetterton, set 1m 32.148s on his first flying lap. He went even better next time round to record 1m 31.964s just as his tyres were going off. No one, surely, could beat that? The crowd sat down once more and looked anxiously at the Ferrari pit. Tambay was out in the spare car so their hopes were pinned on Arnoux as the last set of Michelins were bolted onto the Ferrari. It was just the sort of occasion which René enjoyed. Hunched forward in the cockpit, beady eyes peering through the large opening in his dirty white helmet, Arnoux completed two warm-up laps before breaking the timing beam at 1m 31.238s. The man with the microphone went to work. The home team had scored the winning goal.

Prost's efforts on his second set, 1m 32.138s, would have been good enough for third place had Tambay not turned in a superb lap at the last minute to set 1m 32.150s, almost good enough to make it a Ferrari front row. Despite Tambay's problems with an engine which would not pull properly on Friday, it was clear that the new, lighter and more rigid rear suspension was working satisfactorily, both Ferraris appearing with massive rear wings and huge brake ducts. Brabham had made few major changes, the test sessions simply improving the handling and giving much better traction out of the corners. Patrese had a new chassis at his disposal, his only trouble being a down-on-power engine and a drive-shaft failure. Prost had also been given a new chassis and it proved trouble-free

throughout practice. Cheever was not so happy with his decision to cure an oversteer problem aerodynamically but at least he knew the cure and was content with a place on the third row.

While the Big Three slugged it out at the front of the grid, elsewhere it had become clear that, during practice at least, the turbos with their large rear wings held sway over the Cosworths. Proof of that was provided by Manfred Winkelhock, the extremely brave German fighting oversteer and forcing his new ATS-BMW over the kerbs and into seventh place. This latest chassis, the second in the 1983 line, was reported to be 25 kilos lighter than the original. Refuelling nozzles were also evident although pit stops would be kept for a later date. Alfa Romeo, on the other hand, were preparing to incorporate refuelling in their plans for the first time despite the fact that the team had sacked Gerard Ducarouge after the débâcle at Ricard. It was becoming a regular occurrence for Andrea de Cesaris to set the fastest time during unofficial practice but, when it really mattered, the Italian was slowed by a turbo failure on Friday afternoon. There was a second failure on Saturday morning, the Alfa Romeo catching fire briefly. Repairs were carried out in time for the

---

APRIL:
Rolf Stommelen killed driving Porsche 935 in IMSA race at Riverside.

Gerard Ducarouge fired by Euroracing.

---

final session but Andrea was unable to better eighth fastest time in the light of the furious activity at the front of the grid. Mauro Baldi had to make do with Friday's time, good enough for tenth place overall, when he suffered another turbo problem on Saturday.

Pirelli, keen to score better results at home, had been busy producing 13in diameter rear tyres and slightly wider fronts. Elio de Angelis was reluctant to comment on any improvement in performance (which probably meant the increase was minimal), the Italian generally unhappy with the lack of traction from his Lotus 93 turbo. Nigel Mansell was not much better off with his Cosworth car when a troublesome clutch refused to free properly and gave the English driver a nasty fright during practice on Saturday. The four-tier rear wing, first seen at the Race of Champions, was tried by both drivers although de Angelis soon discarded it.

If final proof were needed, then Keke Rosberg's place on row six showed all too clearly that a non-turbo stood little chance when running to the 1983 regulations – even at a circuit such as Imola. The World Champion, complaining about a problem with the turn-in capabilities of the Williams, was as spectacular as ever while Jacques Laffite was even more frustrated with 16th time. The Frenchman was displeased with the handling of his car throughout practice and it was all too much for Jacques when the random selection process chose to have his car weighed for a second time on Saturday afternoon. Laffite showed his displeasure by screwing up and throwing away the piece of paper which notified the team of the car's weight!

Vying with Rosberg for the honour of leading 'Division Two' was Marc Surer, the Arrows driver revelling in the forgiving handling of the A6. Apart from shorter underwings to help cool the gearbox, the cars were unchanged save for sponsorship identification from Marilena sports wear. Chico Serra's car had been repaired following the shunt at Ricard and the Brazilian qualified comfortably in 20th place. Michele Alboreto said he liked Imola, a preference made clear by his enthusiastic handling of the Tyrrell. He was not so pleased, however, when Jean-Pierre Jarier failed to look in his mirrors and almost bundled the Italian off

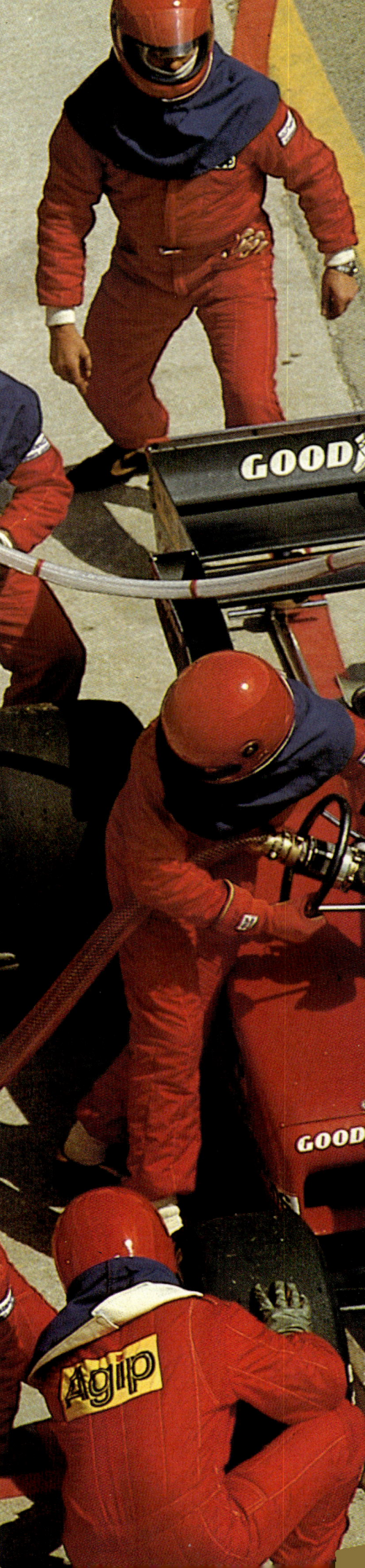

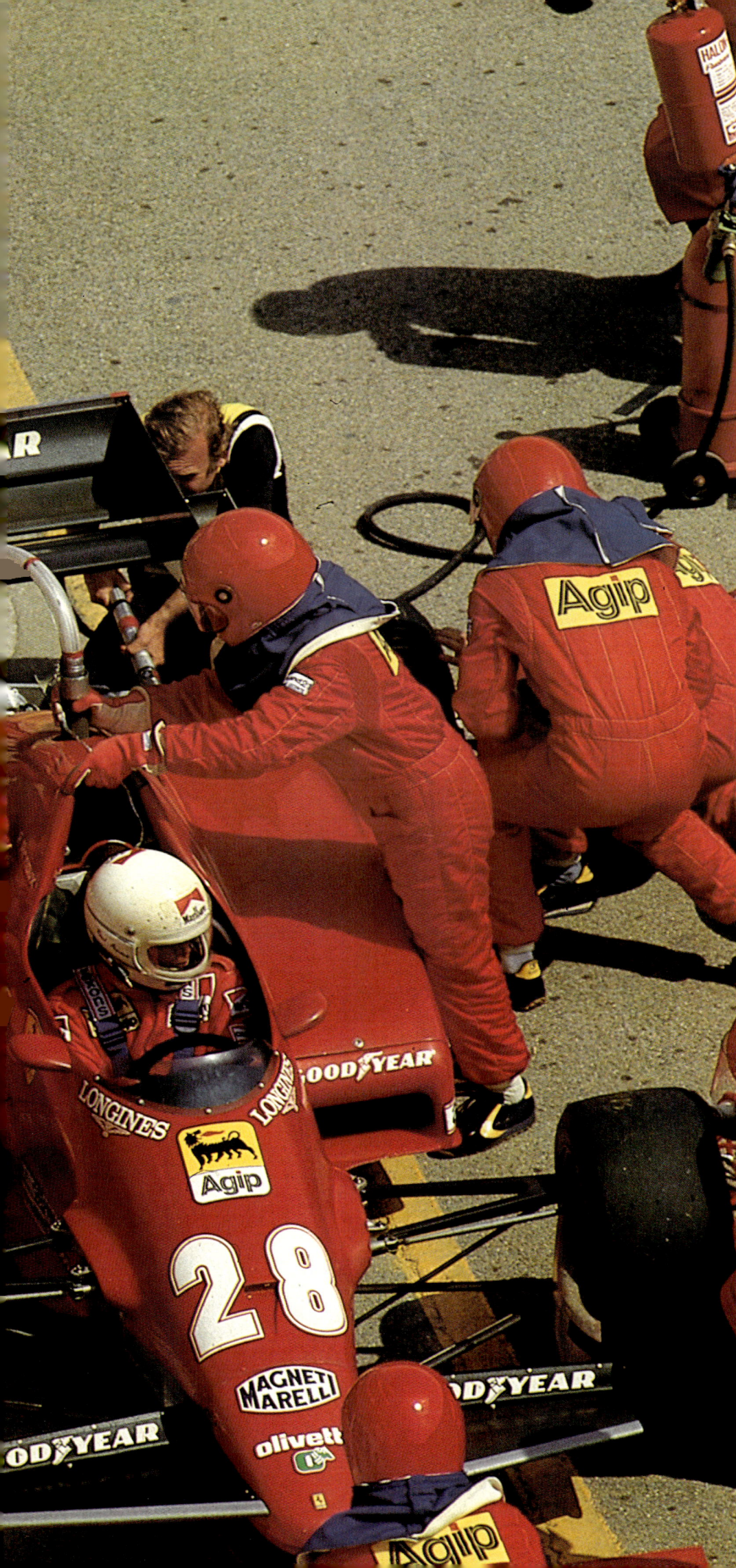

The Ferrari mechanics go to work on René Arnoux's Ferrari, the French driver having led for the first few laps. He eventually spun during the closing stages and finished third.
Photo: Bernard Asset

the track on Friday morning but, otherwise, Alboreto's practice was reasonably trouble-free, apart from a blown engine on Saturday morning. Danny Sullivan, making his first visit to Imola, did well to qualify in 22nd place, eight-tenths slower than his team-mate.

The Toleman team arrived in Imola in an optimistic frame of mind following a productive test session at the circuit but, once practice was over, the atmosphere was filled with gloom. Derek Warwick had a new Hart development engine with two plugs per cylinder and, while he was able to report an increase of 400rpm at the end of the straight, a misfire below 9000rpm restricted the workable rev-band somewhat. But that was just the beginning of their troubles. Warwick had set 10th fastest time on Friday and, after practice, it was discovered that the engine had been wired incorrectly. A rewiring job that evening only made matters worse, the car grinding to a halt with no electrics during the unofficial session on Saturday morning. Bruno Giacomelli, meanwhile, had blown the engine on his car and the spare car was wheeled out for both drivers to use during the afternoon. Warwick managed only two laps before the differential broke. Giacomelli, fortunately, had set a time good enough for 17th place on Friday; Warwick slipped to 14th.

At least Toleman could pin-point the cause of their problems. McLaren, by contrast, were mystified by the sudden decrease in performance once they fitted qualifying tyres. According to John Barnard and his drivers, there was nothing particularly wrong with the cars; the MP4/1Cs felt good but the combination of rubber on the track and an increase in ambient temperature during qualifying meant no grip – and 18th place for Lauda; 24th for Watson. With their track record, however, the race might be a different matter.

Much the same sentiments were expressed about Jean-Pierre Jarier in the Ligier; much the same excuses were offered too, the French cars finding difficulty in coping with the hard Michelins. Jarier was 19th; Boesel 25th. Joining them were the Theodores of Roberto Guerrero and Johnny Cecotto with Corrado Fabi taking the final place on the grid for Osella. His team-mate, Piercarlo Ghinzani, failed to qualify after completing what amounted to shake-down laps for the latest Osella with its Alfa Romeo V12 and rear suspension identical to the Alfa 182. With the 12-cylinder engine bolted onto a 1982 chassis, but with radiators mounted at the rear and raked back in a similar manner to the Brabham BT52, the Osella brought a welcome return of the lusty sound although the combination never looked like qualifying. Eliseo Salazar also missed the cut, the Chilean driver being the only representative for RAM-March following Jean-Louis Schlesser's decision not to continue with the team in view of their uncompetitiveness. John Macdonald, on the other hand, said the Frenchman was not driving because he had not paid his bills. Either way, he was unlikely to have qualified.

RACE

By the time the cars took to the circuit for their half-hour warm-up, the spectator enclosures were packed to capacity. With a Ferrari on pole, the crowd were in high spirits although, underneath their good humour lay an eerie mood, the passionate – some would say macabre – Italian habit of venerating deceased racing drivers manifesting itself with an overwhelming array of Villeneuve posters and slogans. "Gilles, Tambay: two hearts and one number, 27" said one. "Ferrari, win for Gilles" said another. For some time now, Patrick Tambay had been aware of the responsibility of stepping into car number 27 but the pressure increased in the cauldron of emotion at Imola. Then just for good measure, painted on his grid position – the same slot from which Gilles started

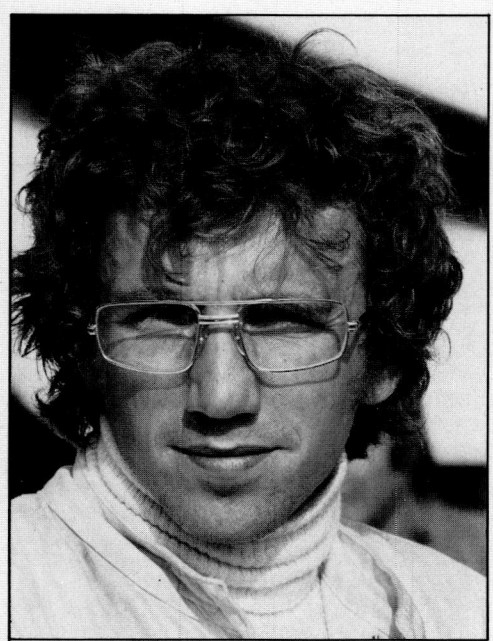

Rolf Stommelen: killed at the wheel of a 'replica' Porsche 935 during the IMSA GT Championship race at Riverside on April 24.

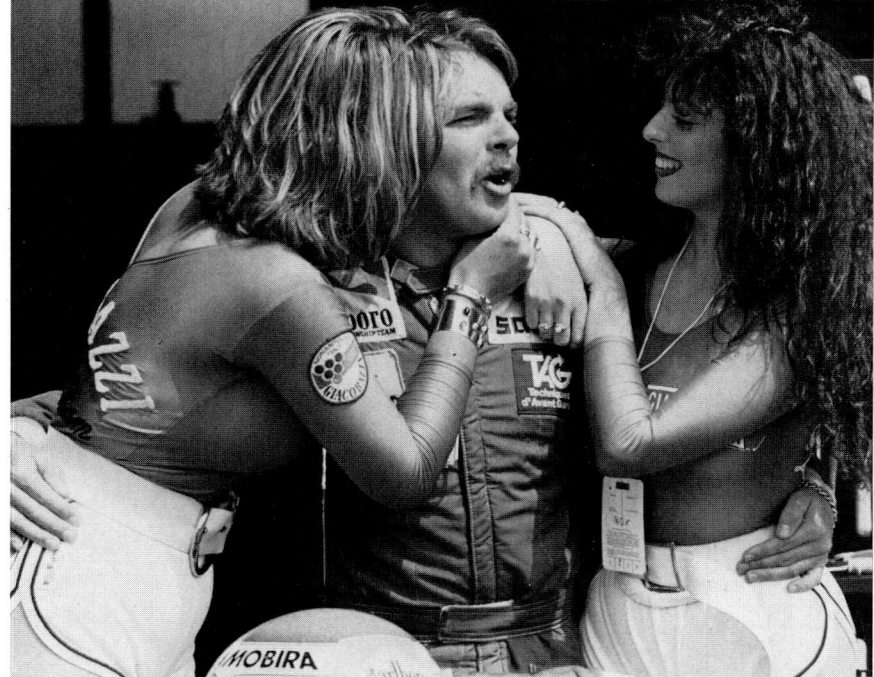
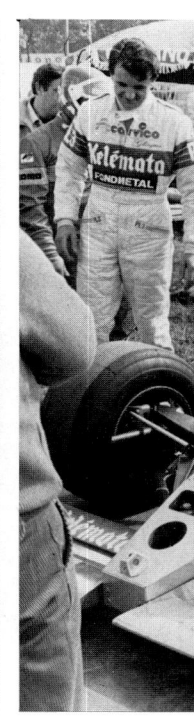

Rolf Stommelen

THE 1975 SPANISH GRAND PRIX AT BARCELONA WAS both the high point and the nadir of his Formula 1 career. Leading a Grand Prix for the first time, Rolf Stommelen was driving impeccably. His Embassy-Hill was handling perfectly and the German was having no difficulty withstanding the pressure exerted by Carlos Pace's Brabham-Cosworth on the most demanding of circuits. At last Stommelen had the opportunity to show he could make the grade; a fact which he had already proved beyond doubt in sportscar racing.

Then the carbon fibre support to the rear wing broke and the car flew over the guardrail, killing four onlookers in a restricted area. Stommelen suffered broken legs. a broken foot, arm and fingers. He made a brave return to Formula 1 not long after. But Grand Prix racing had moved on: the Spanish Grand Prix was history.

Reluctantly, he returned eventually to sportscars and carried on with the same success which he had enjoyed almost from the beginning of his career in a private Porsche. Stommelen and the Stuggart firm had been linked professionally in 1967, the combination winning the Targa Florio and, during the following seasons, Rolf won almost every major endurance race although victory at Le Mans always eluded him.

Throughout, his progress was marked by performances of great skill and remarkable bravery. He smashed the lap record at Le Mans driving the awesome Porsche 917 on narrow tyres; he finished fifth at the Nürburgring in a 936 – driving for half the race on the ignition switch after the throttle cable had jammed open. And the track was wet at the time. . . .

For Stommelen, such obstacles were there to be overcome; his first single-seater drive was another example. Racing in the Formula 2 class in the 1969 German Grand Prix, Stommelen's determination to finish was such that he brought his Winkelmann Lotus 59B across the line – even though it had caught fire long before the end of the final lap.

Formula 1 offers followed, Stommelen joining Brabham in 1970, third place in Austria that year being his best result in a Grand Prix career which saw the modest, bespectacled man from Cologne drive for seven teams in 52 Grands Prix. It may have been a rather uncoordinated and fruitless association, but it was certainly an underrated one.

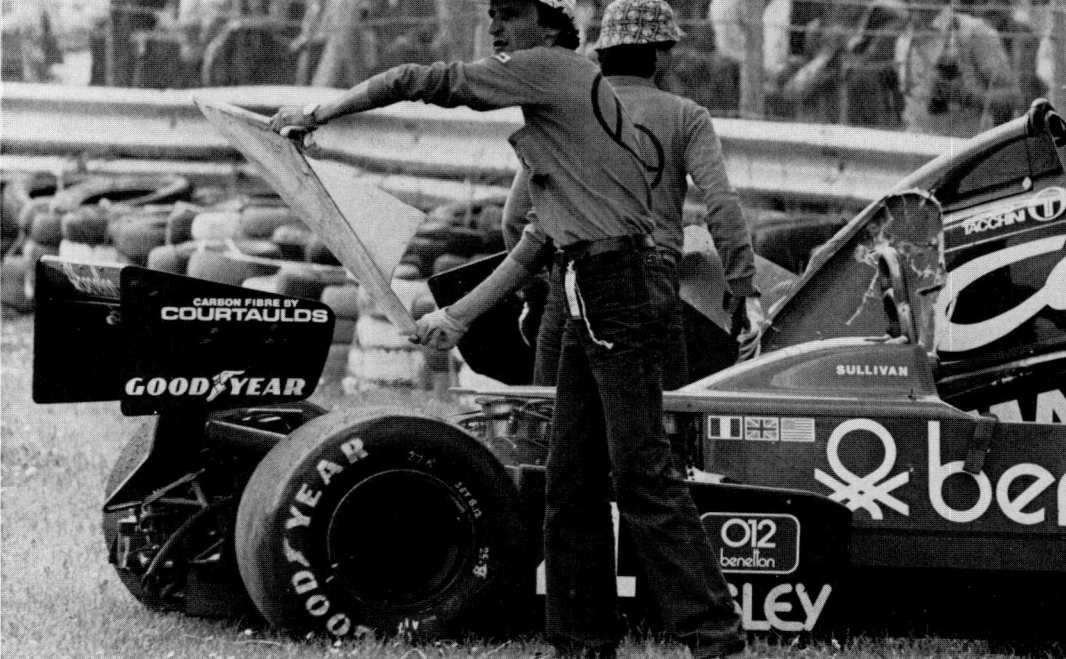

"We Cosworth drivers need a bit of a boost." Keke Rosberg makes up for the frustration of having ten turbos ahead of him on the grid *(top)*.

his last Grand Prix – was a red and white maple leaf.

Tambay had been fourth quickest in the warm-up, with Cheever fastest, happier with his car than he had been all weekend. Piquet was fifth, very confident indeed, while the McLaren team's spirits were considerably revived by eighth and ninth fastest times. Furthermore, heavy clouds had rolled across the circuit during the lunch break which indicated the temperatures might favour a typical Watson and Lauda charge from the back of the grid. Not so confident were ATS, Manfred Winkelhock reluctantly stepping into the spare car after a fuel leak had been discovered on the new chassis.

As the cars rolled onto the starting grid, there was no doubt in anyone's mind that Arnoux would be unable to resist the urge to take a commanding lead. But, as for keeping his tyres in one piece . . .

The sensible money was on Piquet with Tambay finishing a circumspect second but such speculation was shot to pieces within seconds of the green light. Piquet, anxious not to break the transmission, gave too few revs and the Brabham moved about one metre and then stalled. With the remaining 25 cars well and truly on the move, visions of Montreal 1982 came to mind as, first, de Cesaris narrowly missed the Brabham and then Watson, now in third gear, avoided the stricken car at the last minute.

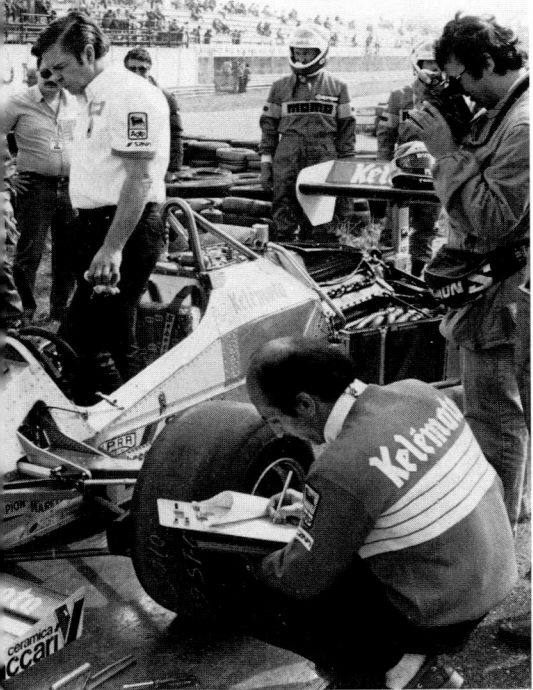

Piercarlo Ghinzani failed in his first attempt to qualify an Osella fitted with an Alfa Romeo V12 engine *(left)*.
Danny Sullivan unintentionally parked his Tyrrell in a space already occupied by Derek Warwick's Toleman; both victims of the treacherous surface *(below)*.

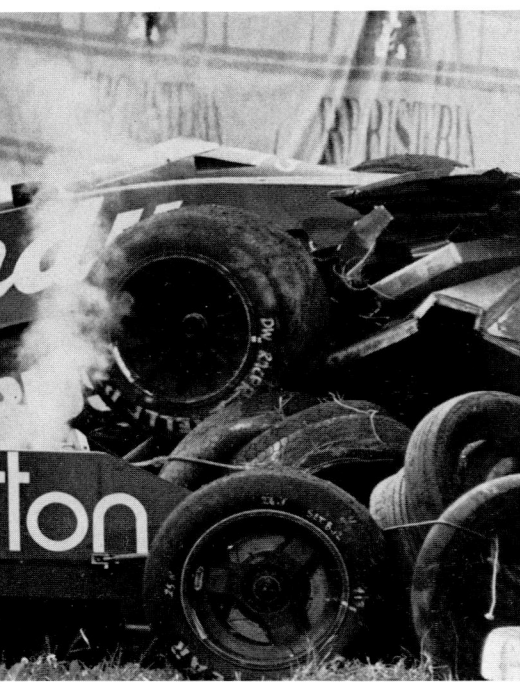

Arnoux, as expected, had taken the lead with Tambay in pursuit but it was soon apparent that Patrese had the speed to deal with them at just about every point on the circuit. By lap three, he was into second place, and three laps later, he neatly outbraked Arnoux for the lead. Tambay continued in third place, keen to consolidate his good start but anxious to settle into the smooth rhythm which would not overtax his tyres. Prost was putting pressure on the Ferrari while de Cesaris had opened a gap over Rosberg who had managed to pass Baldi's Alfa Romeo. Elio de Angelis was eighth, which was a fine effort considering the Italian had been forced to take over the spare Lotus at the last minute when his engine blew on the warm-up lap. Furthermore, he was running with a full tank since the T-car was not equipped with refuelling nozzles.

Lauda held ninth place and was easing away slightly from a close contest between Alboreto, Laffite and Mansell. Working quickly through the field were Watson and Piquet, the latter having received a push start long after the field had left the grid. The Brabham moved into 14th place at the expense of Surer, the Arrows making a pit stop to replace a punctured rear tyre, the result of a brush with Alboreto on the first lap. A rear rocker arm on the Tyrrell had bent and, on lap nine, it collapsed, sending

Alboreto into a spin and retirement. His team-mate, meanwhile, had been involved in a controversial incident with Guerrero as the Theodore driver, having lost a place to the Tyrrell, tried to tow his way back in front. As he moved alongside on the fastest part of the circuit, Guerrero suddenly found the American driver squeezing the Theodore off the track, the result being a huge spin and heavy contact with the guard rail. Guerrero was unharmed but furious, the Colombian lodging a protest over the incident. Sullivan, for his part, said he knew nothing about it.

The field was dwindling rapidly for Cheever had retired at the end of lap two with a blown engine, the oil from the V6 spraying Cecotto and causing the Venezuelan to believe it was brake fluid from his Theodore. A quick pit stop confirmed that everything was in order but he retired not long after with a spin at *Acque Minerali*. The track was beginning to break up in places, a fact confirmed rather surprisingly by Niki Lauda when the Austrian locked his brakes and slid into a tyre barrier.

Keeping clear of such hazards, Patrese maintained his lead, driving with great fluency and controlling the gap to Arnoux. Tambay had pulled away from Prost who was now 18 seconds clear of de Cesaris, the Alfa having an easy time since Rosberg, predictably the fastest Cosworth, was in a lonely sixth place, 16 seconds ahead of de Angelis.

The first change to the leader board came at the end of lap 20 when Arnoux, his tyres losing their edge, made for the pits to take on fuel and fresh rubber in 16s. He rejoined in fifth place – behind Andrea de Cesaris. There was further activity in the pit lane when Bruno Giacomelli brought his Toleman to a halt. The mechanics leapt on the car, changing four tyres and adding five gallons of fuel before realising their man was, in fact, undoing his belts and vacating the cockpit. A rear suspension bolt had gone missing and the Toleman was retired. Bruno's Mercedes 500SEL had been stolen the night before and this was more than he could take. At the same time, Corrado Fabi was to make it a bad day for young Italian drivers by spinning his Osella into retirement.

On lap 27, Prost and de Cesaris made their stops, the Renault getting away in 16.4 seconds after a slight problem with the left-rear wheel. De Cesaris was detained much longer, however, when the Alfa Romeo driver somehow contrived to miss his awaiting pit crew. On realising his error, Andrea selected reverse and raced backwards at high speed, the V8 bouncing off the rev-limiter! By the time he had completed his stop and returned, de Cesaris was in sixth place behind Rosberg and receiving close attention from Piquet, the Brabham having moved through the field in a most impressive way.

Back in the pits, there was more activity as Mansell came in and the Lotus crew carried out their routine for the first time, the gravity-feed refuelling taking just 16.4 seconds. Rosberg was next for a slick halt lasting 14.1s and attention turned to the Brabham and Ferrari pits as the leaders prepared to make their stops.

Tambay was first and an exceptionally fast stop fell apart when the crew had difficulty with the right-front wheel. None the less, he was away in 15.0s without losing his second place. Then, on lap 34, Patrese arrived in the pit lane. The entire performance got off to a bad start when Riccardo pulled up some three or four feet past his designated mark. With the routine measured in inches and seconds, there was a fair amount of scrambling as the mechanics took a couple of paces to the side and set about their tasks. Everything ran smoothly until the airline straining to feed the hammer at the right-rear popped off the end of the gun. The result was a stop of 23.5s and a return to the track in second place, 10.6s behind Tambay.

Warwick, meanwhile, had disappeared from the lap chart, his Toleman finishing the race on top of a tyre barrier after Derek had moved off line by a matter of inches and allowed the accumulated grit and stones to pull the car off the track. Ten laps later, Sullivan made exactly the same mistake, the Tyrrell ramming the Toleman for good measure.

With 20 laps to go, Patrese had closed the gap to 7.9 seconds and Tambay was unable to respond thanks to a misfire all the way through *Tamburello*. Arnoux had begun to fall back in third place since he was under no threat from Prost, the Renault V6 having lost 800rpm, which did not help a handling problem. De Cesaris, having lost fifth place to Piquet, regained it when the Brabham made an incredibly quick stop of just 11.2s on lap 36 but, as luck would have it, not only did everything run smoothly for the wrong car, Piquet was destined to retire six laps later with a broken valve. Rosberg, now a lap down, continued to drive with great vigour even though he was a long way clear of Watson, the McLaren struggling for grip now that the sun had come out and receiving attention from Jarier's Ligier. That battle would end on lap 40 when the Frenchman pulled into the pits with engine trouble, leaving Laffite to take ninth place. Tenth should have belonged to de Angelis but the Italian, now disillusioned because he wasn't winning, pulled into the pits to retire. Complaints about handling and tyres were not well-received by the hard-working team.

With ten laps to go, the crowd were becoming agitated. Patrese had closed the gap on Tambay and, by lap 52 they were circulating nose-to-tail. Sensing Tambay's engine problem, Patrese chose his moment and had no trouble in taking the lead on lap 55, Tambay, remembering Long Beach, offering little resistance and comforting himself with the thought of six points. The tail of the Brabham flicked out of line as Patrese accelerated out of *Tosa*, an Italian leading a Grand Prix in Italy; not that you would have known it, judging by the muted reaction from the grandstands. Down the hill towards *Acque Minerali*, Patrese pulled away. Down through the six-speed box, into the right, then the left, back on the power, lining up for the right which follows. Too much power! On the loose; understeer; onto the grass; into the tyres. Out of the lead; out of the race. The man with the microphone imparted the news. Pandemonium.

Seconds later, more confusion as René Arnoux makes a similar mistake, the Ferrari spinning harmlessly. But it takes time for the Frenchman to regain the track – by which time Alain Prost, with a down-on-power engine, understeer and no fourth gear, moves into second place. Tambay, 50s ahead, is secure. Prost, six points better off, is delighted.

Arnoux takes third place while fourth and fifth for Rosberg and Watson provide some reward for tenacious drives. Similarly, Marc Surer's gutsy drive brought sixth place but the drama continued until the end, Mauro Baldi bringing his Alfa Romeo to a smoky halt on the very last lap while Nigel Mansell was lucky to survive a terrifying accident four laps from the end. Just as he was negotiating the 170mph *Curva Villeneuve*, the four-tier rear wing parted company with the car, sending the Lotus into a violent spin, Mansell coming to rest by rolling backwards into the barrier.

Tambay punched the air joyfully as he took the flag and began his slowing down lap. As he reached *Acque Minerali*, the engine stuttered. Out of fuel! In an instant, the fans were over the fence, pulling the hapless driver from his car and carrying him aloft. A course car came to the rescue and, not long after, the dishevelled winner was back in the pits.

Eyes shining, there was a satisfied glow to his face. It was as though an enormous burden had been lifted from his shoulders. Car 27 had won. A debt had been repaid.

Keke Rosberg rushes past the splendid Imola
scenery, the Cosworth-powered Williams no
match for the turbos.
Photo: Bernard Asset

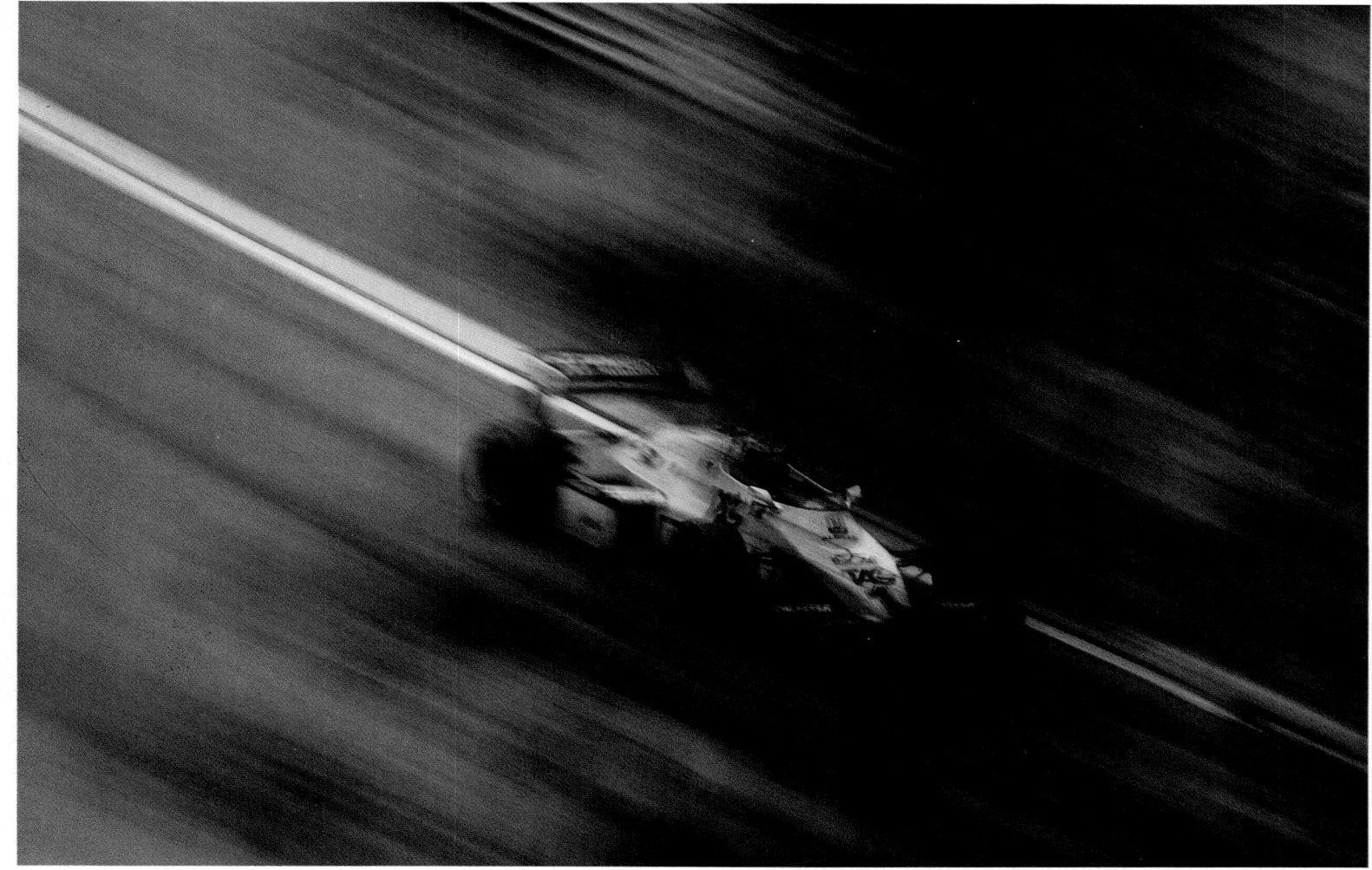

**". . . rapid turbo
development and the
ability to run large
amounts of rear wing
meant the Cosworth
cars were merely left
to pick up the points
cast aside by the
turbos . . ."**

Patrick Tambay drove a clean, crisp race, the Ferrari driver looking after his tyres throughout, the only problem being an engine misfire. The Frenchman, however, was not to be denied a victory which was thoroughly deserved in the eyes of the partisan crowd.
Photo: John Townsend

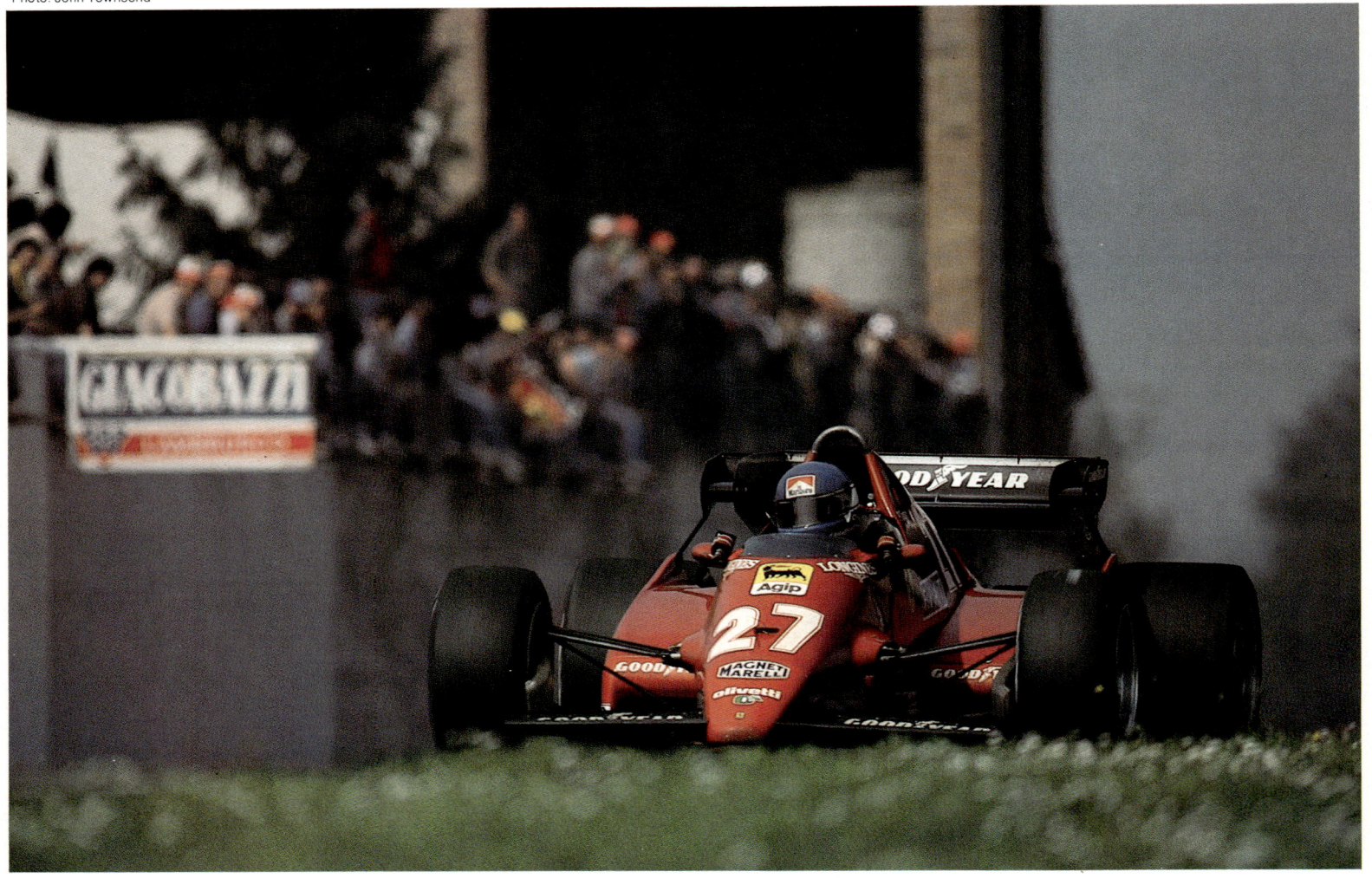

"Eyes shining, there was a satisfied glow to his face. It was as though an enormous burden had been lifted from his shoulders. Car 27 had won. A debt had been repaid."

Entries and practice times

No.	Driver	Nat	Car	Tyre	Engine	Entrant	Practice 1	Practice 2
1	Keke Rosberg	SF	Saudia WILLIAMS FW08C	G	Ford Cosworth DFV	TAG Williams Team	1m 36·145s	**1m 35·086s**
2	Jacques Laffite	F	Saudia WILLIAMS FW08C	G	Ford Cosworth DFV	TAG Williams Team	1m 36·630s	1m 35·707s
3	Michele Alboreto	I	Benetton TYRRELL 011	G	Ford Cosworth DFV	Benetton Tyrrell Team	1m 35·988s	1m 35·525s
4	Danny Sullivan	USA	Benetton TYRRELL 011	G	Ford Cosworth DFV	Benetton Tyrrell Team	1m 37·320s	1m 36·359s
5	Nelson Piquet	BR	Parmalat BRABHAM BT52	M	BMW M12/13	Fila Sport	1m 33·542s	**1m 31·964s**
6	Riccardo Patrese	I	Parmalat BRABHAM BT52	M	BMW M12/13	Fila Sport	1m 36·243s	1m 32·969s
7	John Watson	GB	Marlboro McLAREN MP4/1C	M	Ford Cosworth DFV/DFY	Marlboro McLaren International	1m 37·847s	1m 36·652s
8	Niki Lauda	A	Marlboro McLAREN MP4/1C	M	Ford Cosworth DFV/DFY	Marlboro McLaren International	1m 38·089s	1m 36·099s
9	Manfred Winkelhock	D	ATS D6	G	BMW M12/13	Team ATS	1m 35·010s	1m 33·470s
11	Elio de Angelis	I	John Player Special LOTUS 93T	P	Renault EF1	John Player Team Lotus	1m 35·091s	1m 34·332s
12	Nigel Mansell	GB	John Player Special LOTUS 92	P	Ford Cosworth DFV/DFY	John Player Team Lotus	1m 36·391s	1m 35·703s
15	Alain Prost	F	Elf RENAULT RE40	M	Renault EF1	Equipe Renault Elf	1m 33·653s	1m 32·138s
16	Eddie Cheever	USA	Elf RENAULT RE40	M	Renault EF1	Equipe Renault Elf	1m 33·888s	1m 33·450s
17	Eliseo Salazar	RCH	MARCH-RAM 01	P	Ford Cosworth DFV	RAM Automotive Team March	1m 38·691s	1m 38·097s
22	Andrea de Cesaris	I	Marlboro ALFA ROMEO 183T	M	Alfa Romeo 183T	Marlboro Team Alfa Romeo	1m 34·345s	1m 33·528s
23	Mauro Baldi	I	Marlboro ALFA ROMEO 183T	M	Alfa Romeo 183T	Marlboro Team Alfa Romeo	**1m 35·000s**	1m 36·620s
25	Jean-Pierre Jarier	F	Gitanes LIGIER JS21	M	Ford Cosworth DFV	Equipe Ligier Gitanes	1m 37·547s	1m 36·116s
26	Raul Boesel	BR	Gitanes LIGIER JS21	M	Ford Cosworth DFV	Equipe Ligier Gitanes	1m 39·435s	1m 37·322s
27	Patrick Tambay	F	Fiat FERRARI 126C2/B	G	Ferrari 126C	Scuderia Ferrari SpA SEFAC	1m 34·221s	1m 31·967s
28	René Arnoux	F	Fiat FERRARI 126C2/B	G	Ferrari 126C	Scuderia Ferrari SpA SEFAC	1m 33·419s	1m 31·238s
29	Marc Surer	CH	ARROWS A6	G	Ford Cosworth DFV	Arrows Racing Team	1m 35·723s	1m 35·411s
30	Chico Serra	BR	ARROWS A6	G	Ford Cosworth DFV	Arrows Racing Team	1m 37·337s	1m 36·258s
31	Corrado Fabi	I	OSELLA FA1D	M	Ford Cosworth DFV	Osella Squadra Corse	1m 37·952s	1m 37·711s
32	Piercarlo Ghinzani	I	OSELLA FA1E	M	Alfa Romeo 1260	Osella Squadra Corse	1m 39·248s	1m 38·873s
33	Roberto Guerrero	COL	THEODORE N183	G	Ford Cosworth DFV	Theodore Racing Team	1m 36·792s	1m 36·324s
34	Johnny Cecotto	YV	THEODORE N183	G	Ford Cosworth DFV	Theodore Racing Team	1m 37·554s	1m 36·638s
35	Derek Warwick	GB	Candy TOLEMAN TG183B	P	Hart 415T	Candy Toleman Motorsport	**1m 35·676s**	1m 36·881s
36	Bruno Giacomelli	I	Candy TOLEMAN TG183B	P	Hart 415T	Candy Toleman Motorsport	**1m 35·969s**	—

Friday morning and Saturday morning practice sessions not officially recorded.

G – Goodyear, M – Michelin, P – Pirelli.

Fri pm
Warm, dry

Sat pm
Warm, dry

Starting grid

28 ARNOUX (1m 31·238s)
Ferrari

    5 PIQUET (1m 31·964s)
    Brabham

27 TAMBAY (1m 31·967s)
Ferrari

    15 PROST (1m 32·138s)
    Renault

6 PATRESE (1m 32·969s)
Brabham

    16 CHEEVER (1m 33·450s)
    Renault

9 WINKELHOCK (1m 33·470s)
ATS

    22 DE CESARIS (1m 33·528s)
    Alfa Romeo

11 DE ANGELIS (1m 34·332s)
Lotus

    23 BALDI (1m 35·000s)
    Alfa Romeo

1 ROSBERG (1m 35·086s)
Williams

    29 SURER (1m 35·411s)
    Arrows

3 ALBORETO (1m 35·525s)
Tyrrell

    35 WARWICK (1m 35·676s)
    Toleman

12 MANSELL (1m 35·703s)
Lotus

    2 LAFFITE (1m 35·707s)
    Williams

36 GIACOMELLI (1m 35·969s)
Alfa Romeo

    8 LAUDA (1m 36·099s)
    McLaren

25 JARIER (1m 36·116s)
Ligier

    30 SERRA (1m 36·258s)
    Arrows

33 GUERRERO (1m 36·324s)
Theodore

    4 SULLIVAN (1m 36·359s)
    Tyrrell

34 CECOTTO (1m 36·638s)
Theodore

    7 WATSON (1m 36·652s)
    McLaren

26 BOESEL (1m 37·322s)
Ligier

    31 FABI (1m 37·711s)
    Osella

Did not start:
17 Salazar (March-RAM), 1m 38·097s, did not qualify
32 Ghinzani (Osella), 1m 38·873s, did not qualify

Results and retirements

Place	Driver	Car	Laps	Time and Speed (mph/km/h)/Retirement	
1	Patrick Tambay	Ferrari t/c V6	60	1h 37m 52·460s	115·251/185·480
2	Alain Prost	Renault t/c V6	60	1h 38m 41·241s	114·270/183·9
3	René Arnoux	Ferrari t/c V6	59		
4	Keke Rosberg	Williams-Cosworth V8	59		
5	John Watson	McLaren-Cosworth V8	59		
6	Marc Surer	Arrows-Cosworth V8	59		
7	Jacques Laffite	Williams-Cosworth V8	59		
8	Chico Serra	Arrows-Cosworth V8	58		
9	Raul Boesel	Ligier-Cosworth V8	58		
10	Mauro Baldi	Alfa Romeo t/c V8	57	Engine	
11	Manfred Winkelhock	ATS-BMW t/c 4	57		
12	Nigel Mansell	Lotus-Cosworth V8	56	Accident/rear wing failure	
	Riccardo Patrese	Brabham-BMW t/c 4	54	Accident	
	Andrea de Cesaris	Alfa Romeo t/c V8	46	Distributor	
	Elio de Angelis	Lotus-Renault t/c V6	44	Handling/driver gave up	
	Nelson Piquet	Brabham-BMW t/c 4	42	Engine	
	Jean-Pierre Jarier	Ligier-Cosworth V8	40	Holed Radiator	
	Danny Sullivan	Tyrrell-Cosworth V8	37	Accident	
	Derek Warwick	Toleman-Hart t/c 4	27	Accident	
	Corrado Fabi	Osella-Cosworth V8	20	Accident	
	Bruno Giacomelli	Toleman-Hart t/c 4	21	Rear suspension	
	Niki Lauda	McLaren-Cosworth V8	11	Accident	
	Johnny Cecotto	Theodore-Cosworth V8	11	Accident damage	
	Michele Alboreto	Tyrrell-Cosworth V8	10	Accident/rear suspension	
	Roberto Guerrero	Theodore-Cosworth V8	3	Accident/incident with Sullivan	
	Eddie Cheever	Renault t/c V6	2	Turbo	

Fastest lap: Patrese on lap 47, 1m 34·437s, 119·383mph/192·128km/h (record).
Previous lap record: Didier Pironi (F1 Ferrari 126C2 t/c V6), 1m 35·036s, 118·630mph/190·917km/h (1982).

Past winners

Year	Driver	Nat	Car	Circuit	Distance miles/km	Speed mph/km/h
1981	Nelson Piquet	BR	3·0 Brabham BT49C-Ford	Imola	187·90/302·40	101·20/162·87
1982	Didier Pironi	F	1·5 Ferrari 126C2 t/c V6	Imola	187·90/302·40	116·63/187·70
1983	Patrick Tambay	F	1·5 Ferrari 126C2/B t/c V6	Imola	187·90/302·40	115·25/185·48

Circuit data
Autodromo Dino Ferrari, Imola

Circuit length: 3·132 miles/5·040 km
Race distance: 60 laps, 187·90 miles/302·40 km
Race weather: Warm, dry.

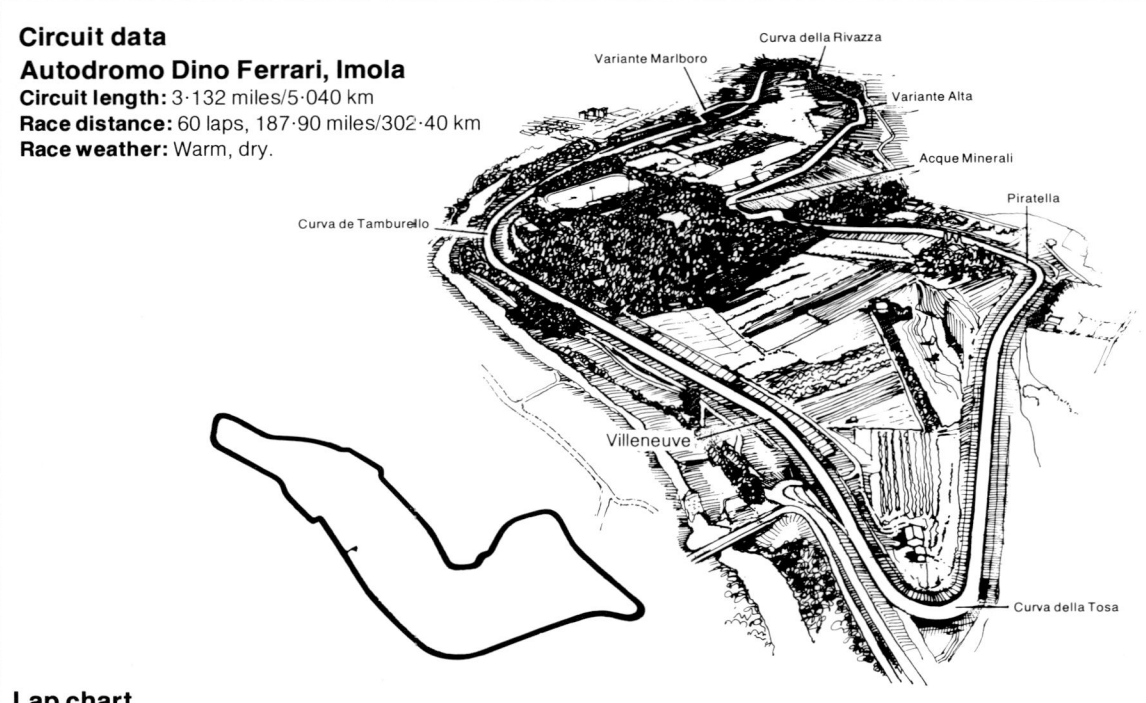

Map labels: Curva della Rivazza · Variante Marlboro · Variante Alta · Acque Minerali · Piratella · Curva de Tamburello · Villeneuve · Curva della Tosa

Fastest laps

Driver	Time	Lap
Riccardo Patrese	1m 34·437s	47
Patrick Tambay	1m 35·516s	47
Nelson Piquet	1m 36·306s	33
René Arnoux	1m 36·423s	35
Alain Prost	1m 36·833s	13
Andrea de Cesaris	1m 37·214s	24
Marc Surer	1m 37·718s	45
Keke Rosberg	1m 37·836s	45
Jean-Pierre Jarier	1m 38·026s	33
Mauro Baldi	1m 38·063s	51
Chico Serra	1m 38·366s	44
John Watson	1m 38·380s	53
Jacques Laffite	1m 38·463s	27
Nigel Mansell	1m 38·466s	24
Elio de Angelis	1m 38·615s	14
Niki Lauda	1m 38·641s	10
Derek Warwick	1m 39·069s	27
Michele Alboreto	1m 39·438s	8
Raul Boesel	1m 39·480s	51
Danny Sullivan	1m 39·685s	21
Corrado Fabi	1m 39·692s	19
Manfred Winkelhock	1m 39·903s	50
Bruno Giacomelli	1m 39·917s	16
Johnny Cecotto	1m 41·961s	10
Roberto Guerrero	1m 44·305s	3
Eddie Cheever	1m 51·645s	1

Points

WORLD CHAMPIONSHIP OF DRIVERS

1 =	Nelson Piquet	15 pts
1 =	Alain Prost	15
3	Patrick Tambay	14
4	John Watson	11
5	Niki Lauda	10
6	René Arnoux	8
7	Jacques Laffite	7
8	Keke Rosberg	5
9 =	Eddie Cheever	4
9 =	Marc Surer	4
11	Johnny Cecotto	1

CONSTRUCTORS' CUP

1	Ferrari	22 pts
2	McLaren	21
3	Renault	19
4	Brabham	15
5	Williams	12
6	Arrows	4
7	Theodore	1

Lap chart

Laps 1–37

Driver	Positions (laps 1 → 37)
28 R. Arnoux	28 28 28 28 28 6 6 6 6 6 6 6 6 6 6 6 6 6 6 6 6 6 6 6 6 6 6 6 6 6 6 6 6 6 (6) 27 27 27
27 P. Tambay	27 27 6 6 6 28 28 28 28 28 28 28 28 28 28 28 28 28 28 27 27 27 27 27 27 27 27 27 27 (27) 27 27 6 6 6
6 R. Patrese	6 6 27 27 27 27 27 27 27 27 27 27 27 27 27 27 27 27 (28) 15 15 15 15 15 15 (15) 28 28 28 28 28 28 28 28 28 28
15 A. Prost	15 15 15 15 15 15 15 15 15 15 15 15 15 15 15 15 15 15 15 22 22 22 22 22 22 28 15 15 15 15 15 15 15 15 15 15 15
22 A. De Cesaris	22 22 22 22 22 22 22 22 22 22 22 22 22 22 22 22 22 22 28 28 28 28 28 28 (22) 1 1 (1) 5 5 5 5 5 (5) 22
9 M. Winkelhock	9 9 23 23 23 1 1 1 1 1 1 1 1 1 1 1 1 1 1 1 1 1 1 1 1 22 22 22 22 22 22 22 22 22 5
11 E. De Angelis	11 23 1 1 1 23 23 23 23 23 23 23 23 23 11 11 11 11 11 11 11 11 11 5 5 11 11 5 5 5 5 5 1 1 2 2 1 1 1
16 E. Cheever	16 1 9 11 11 11 11 11 11 11 11 11 11 11 11 11 11 11 11 23 23 23 23 5 5 11 11 11 11 11 23 2 1 (2) 11 11
23 M. Baldi	23 11 11 9 8 8 8 8 8 8 (8) 2 2 2 2 2 5 5 5 23 23 23 23 23 23 23 23 23 2 11 11 11 7 7
1 K. Rosberg	1 12 12 8 3 3 3 3 3 2 7 5 5 5 5 2 7 7 7 7 7 7 7 2 2 2 2 11 (23) 7 7 7 25 25
12 N. Mansell	12 8 8 3 2 2 2 2 2 (3) 7 5 7 7 7 7 7 12 12 12 12 2 2 2 2 7 7 7 7 7 25 25 25
8 N. Lauda	8 3 3 2 12 12 12 12 12 12 12 12 12 12 12 12 12 2 2 2 2 12 12 12 12 12 (12) 25 25 25 23 23 23 23 23
3 M. Alboreto	3 2 2 12 9 29 7 7 7 7 5 35 35 35 35 35 35 35 35 35 35 35 35 25 25 25 25 30 30 30 30 30 30 30 30
35 D. Warwick	35 35 29 29 29 7 29 9 5 5 35 30 30 30 30 30 30 30 30 30 30 25 25 35 35 (35) 30 30 4 4 4 4 4 4 (4)
2 J. Laffite	2 29 35 7 7 9 35 5 35 35 9 36 36 36 36 36 36 25 25 25 25 30 30 30 30 4 4 12 12 12 29 29 29 29
29 M. Surer	29 30 7 35 35 35 9 35 (29) 9 30 4 4 25 25 25 25 4 4 4 4 4 4 4 4 26 26 26 26 9 12 26 26 26
30 C. Serra	30 7 30 30 30 4 4 4 9 30 36 25 25 4 4 4 4 31 31 (31) (36) 26 26 26 26 26 26 29 29 29 26 12 12 12
33 R. Guerrero	33 33 4 4 4 30 5 9 4 4 4 31 31 31 31 31 36 36 36 26 29 29 29 29 29 29 9 9 9 9 9 9 9 9 9
7 T. Watson	7 4 (33) 36 36 36 30 30 30 36 25 26 26 26 26 26 26 (26) 26 29 9 9 9 9 9
4 D. Sullivan	4 36 26 26 26 5 36 36 26 31 9 9 9 (9) 9 9 9 9 9
26 R. Boesel	26 26 36 25 5 26 26 26 25 26 29 29 29 29 29 29 29
36 B. Giacomelli	36 25 25 5 25 25 25 25 31 29
25 J. P. Jarier	25 31 31 31 31 31 31 31 31 29 (34)
31 C. Fabi	31 5 5 34 34 34 34 34 34 34
34 T. Cecotto	34 (34) 34
5 N. Piquet	5 (16)

Laps 38–60

Driver	Positions (laps 38 → 60)
28 R. Arnoux	27 27 27 27 27 27 27 27 27 27 27 27 27 27 27 27 27 27 27 27 27 27 27
27 P. Tambay	6 6 6 6 6 6 6 6 6 6 6 6 6 6 6 15 15 15 15 15 15 15 15
6 R. Patrese	28 28 28 28 28 28 28 28 28 28 28 28 28 28 (28) 28 28 28 28 28
15 A. Prost	15 15 15 15 15 15 15 15 15 15 15 15 15 15 15 1 1 1 1 1
22 A. De Cesaris	22 22 22 22 22 22 22 (22) 1 1 1 1 1 1 1 1 1 1 1 1 1 1 1
9 M. Winkelhock	5 5 5 5 (1) 1 1 1 7 7 7 7 7 7 7 23 23 23 29 29
11 E. De Angelis	1 1 1 1 7 7 7 7 2 23 23 23 23 23 23 29 29 29 2 2
16 E. Cheever	7 7 7 7 (5) 2 2 2 2 23 2 29 29 29 29 29 2 2 2 30
23 M. Baldi	25 25 2 2 2 23 23 23 23 29 29 2 2 2 2 2 30 30 30 26
1 K. Rosberg	(11) 2 (25) 11 23 30 30 30 30 30 30 30 30 30 30 30 30 26 26 26
12 N. Mansell	2 11 11 23 30 11 29 29 29 26 26 26 26 26 26 9 9 9
8 N. Lauda	23 23 23 30 11 29 (11) 26 26 9 9 9 9 9 9 12 12
3 M. Alboreto	30 30 30 29 29 26 26 (12) 12 12 12 12 12 12 12
35 D. Warwick	29 29 29 26 26 12 12 9 9
2 J. Laffite	26 26 26 12 12 9 9
29 M. Surer	12 12 12 9 9
30 C. Serra	9 9 9

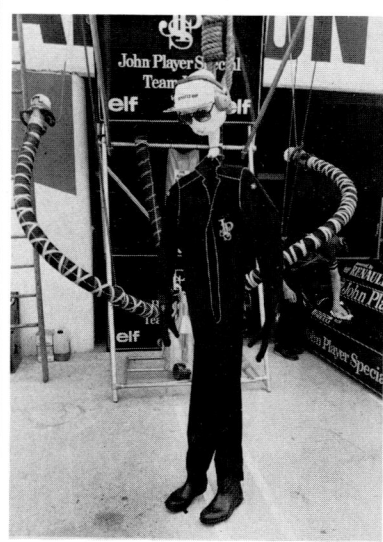

Certain members of the Lotus crew felt this way about Elio de Angelis when the Italian driver lost heart during the race. Lotus used their gravity refuelling gear for the first time on Nigel Mansell's car but the English driver retired spectacularly when the rear wing flew off as he negotiated the 170mph Villeneuve curve.

GRAND PRIX DE MONACO

Frank Williams stood in front of his car and held up four fingers. 'The first four are on wets,' he said, jerking his thumb over his shoulder at the front of the grid. Keke Rosberg, strapped into the cockpit of the FW08C, merely nodded. Patrick Head, leaning against the left-rear slick on the Williams, peered between the trees at the leaden sky and grimaced. Frank, for his part, glanced at the wet tyres stacked on the trolley nearby – and then walked away. The most important decision of the weekend had just been made.

For the Saudia Williams team, indeed, it was the *only* decision to make. Yes, it had been raining for the best part of the morning but now it had eased to a light drizzle. Rosberg had completed two warm-up laps; enough to confirm that there was a surprising amount of grip – even on slicks. And now the turbo drivers, anxious not to be hampered by wheelspin, were playing into their hands by fitting wets. If it rained, Williams would be soundly thrashed. Of course, if they fitted wets, they would still be beaten. But, if the rain held off, then Rosberg would merely wait until the line dried and take the lead as the pit stops for slicks began.

In the event, he didn't have to wait that long. The turbos made slow, circumspect starts – and Rosberg was second by the time they reached Ste. Devote. By the end of the lap, he was in the lead! There followed a most brilliant display of car control as the Williams driver actually pulled away on the still-damp track and, by the time the pit stops had begun, he was 15 seconds to the good. Not letting up for an instant, Rosberg wanted to make the most of a rare opportunity to take nine points from the turbos and, despite a misfire and badly blistered hands, that's just what he did.

Nelson Piquet, another to start on wets, brought his Parmalat Brabham into second place with Alain Prost quietly tucking away another four points even though his Renault-Elf had been in gearbox trouble. Earlier, Prost and Piquet had fought unsuccessfully with Derek Warwick, the Candy Toleman team taking the decision to start the Englishman on slicks. By the time the leaders had completed their pit stops, Warwick was running strongly in fourth place, the Brabham and Renault unable to find a way through as Warwick, in turn, put pressure on Marc Surer in the Arrows. Unfortunately, a stirring battle was to be resolved when Warwick hit the back of the Arrows under braking for Ste. Devote.

With gearbox trouble on the TAG Williams costing Jacques Laffite a comfortable second place not long after, the typically long list of retirements at Monaco helped Patrick Tambay take fourth place and allowed Danny Sullivan to score his first two championship points for fifth in the Benetton Tyrrell.

Mauro Baldi's Marlboro Alfa Romeo was sixth after a stop for slicks and Chico Serra was the final finisher in the Arrows – all of which made the Marlboro McLaren team's failure to qualify even more agonising. Here was a race where Niki Lauda and John Watson almost certainly would have scored points. They had been in trouble during practice on Thursday and rain on Saturday meant they had no opportunity to claim a place on the grid. Ironically, it was the same fickle weather which was to ensure a drive worthy of a World Champion the following afternoon.

ENTRY AND PRACTICE

While Williams and others laid their final plans at 9 am on Thursday morning for two days of practice, the 1983 Monaco Grand Prix was already over for the Theodore team. Forced to join Toleman and RAM March in pre-qualifying for the right to make up the 26 cars in official practice, Roberto Guerrero and Johnny Cecotto experienced a thoroughly frustrating and demoralising hour.

Following the serious damage inflicted on Guerrero's race car at Imola, Theodore had built up the spare chassis although there had been no opportunity for the Colombian driver to try it before the start of practice at 8 am. An initial problem with fifth gear was

soon rectified but four laps later, a universal joint broke as Guerrero climbed the hill towards Casino. With no spare available, he walked back to the pits in the hope that he would be given a run in Cecotto's car, but those hopes were dashed when the Venezuelan driver walked in to report that he had crashed in the tunnel. The South Americans had no choice but to watch their names sink to the bottom of the list as lap times improved. Mind you, it was a close run thing for Derek Warwick, the Toleman driver using all three cars before scraping in, four tenths ahead of Cecotto. It had been a bad start for Warwick. A turbo had failed on his race car but a switch to the spare led to a series of problems caused by a collapsed inlet tract. Then a front rose joint broke and, since Bruno Giacomelli had

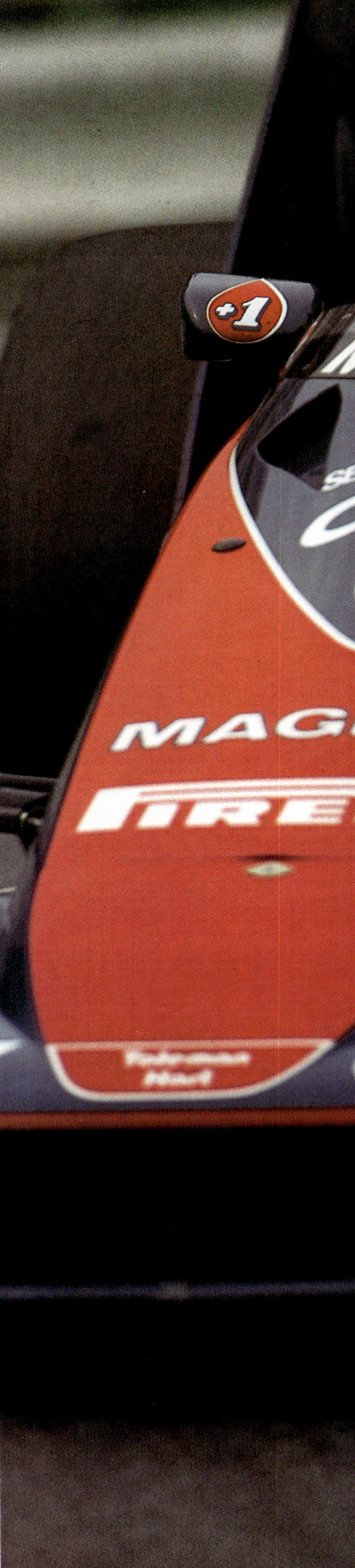

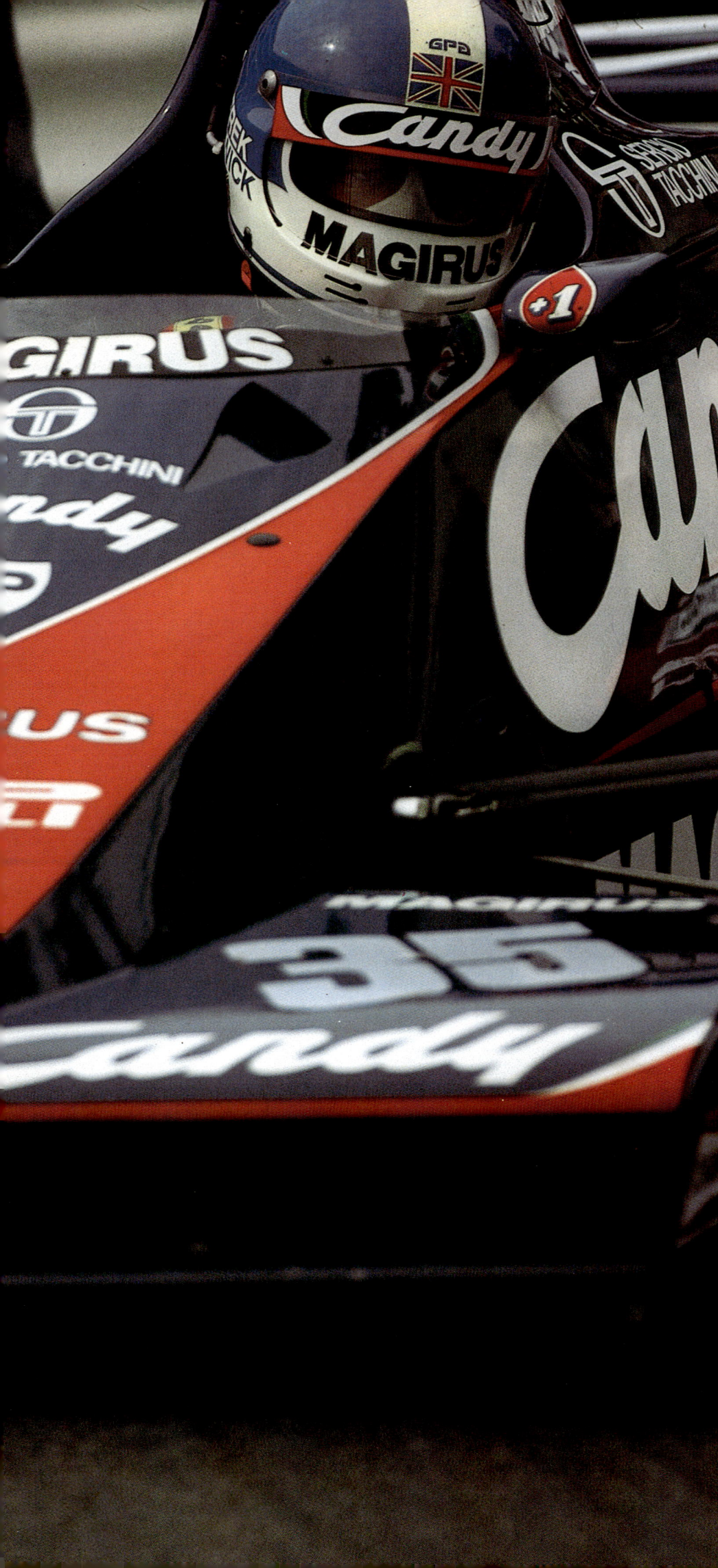

Derek Warwick drove superbly but retired his
Toleman after hitting the back of Marc Surer's
Arrows while disputing third place.
Photo: David Winter

qualified comfortably, Warwick climbed into the
Italian's car and managed to set his time despite the
fact that an underwing had collapsed. And official
practice hadn't even started. . . .

Compared with pre-qualifying, however, a minor
problem with the boost during timed practice in the
afternoon was not so serious, Warwick setting tenth
fastest time. And that, as it would turn out, would be
his position on the grid; rain on Saturday afternoon
rendering the final practice session meaningless.

So, although we were not to know it at the time,
events between 1 and 2 pm on Thursday were to be all
important as Alain Prost set fastest time in the Renault.
There had been several changes to the RE40s, the
most noticeable being a revised exhaust system, the
pipes exiting beneath longer underwings rather than
poking through the top-rear edge of the side-pod.
This, said Renault, was to help reduce tyre temperatures. Others were more sceptical and there were
mutterings about the creation of ground effect by an
illegal means. For the time being, however, Prost had
taken pole with a deceptively smooth lap once a
problem with a faulty rev-counter had been sorted out.
Eddie Cheever, by contrast, was most spectacular as he
hurled the Renault with great confidence through the
quick corners. It was the first and second gear corners,
however, which were to cause the American the
greatest difficulty as he continued his learning process
with the turbo. Cheever was third fastest, the two
Renaults split by René Arnoux who, for a while,
appeared to have secured another pole thanks to one
of his brilliant, banzai laps. Ferrari had four cars on
hand, the drivers swapping chassis at regular intervals.
For once there were few problems during practice
and, on Thursday, Patrick Tambay took fourth place
with a lap over one second slower than his team-mate.

Losing out to Tambay by less than one hundredth of
a second was Keke Rosberg, the World Champion
setting Monte Carlo alight with some breath-taking
laps as he pitched the little Williams into the corners as
though it were a Formula 3 car. Monaco represented
one of the few opportunities for a Cosworth car to
keep in touch with the turbos and, judging by his
urgency at the wheel, Rosberg meant to make the most
of it. Jacques Laffite backed him up with eighth fastest
time, the Frenchman discarding a new, slimline disc
brake after practice on Thursday morning. In an
almost desperate attempt to keep up with his
team-mate, Jacques brushed the barrier at the
swimming pool in the afternoon but, fortunately,
damage was confined to the wheel rims. Rosberg, on
the other hand, hardly put a foot wrong – which was
surprising in view of exaggerated reports of the Finn
suffering from hepatitis, a most debilitating illness.
Rosberg had complained of feeling tired for several
weeks and there was no doubt he had contracted a
virus of some sort – although you would scarcely have
known it watching him at work.

During the weeks preceding Monaco, there had
been much talk about the ban on refuelling, imposed
in Monte Carlo because a long-standing rule did not
permit the storage of petrol in the pits. Hardest hit
would be Brabham, the fuel consumption of the BMW
turbo indicating a marginal race if Piquet and Patrese
were forced to run non-stop. Bernie Ecclestone used
all his powers of persuasion, claiming at one stage that
the race could not be considered a round of the
championship if facilities were not of the required
standard, but to no avail. Following their difficulties
on the streets of Long Beach, the team did well to put
Nelson Piquet on the third row, Gordon Murray
reckoning that the Brazilian would have gone even
quicker had he not been held up by traffic while
running full boost on his second set of qualifiers.
Riccardo Patrese was not so happy, the Italian taking
17th place with the T-car after the carbon fibre airbox

129

had blown off the injection system and stranded his race car out on the circuit.

Andrea de Cesaris was in seventh place, the Alfa Romeo driver complaining of problems with throttle lag at low revs. He was in more serious difficulties on Saturday morning, however, the Alfa Romeo hitting the guard rail near the tunnel. Mauro Baldi was 13th. Tests at the Michelin track at Clermont Ferrand helped Ligier conclude that the hydraulic suspension system would be suitable for Monte Carlo and all three cars were equipped accordingly. Jean-Pierre Jarier was most enthusiastic about ninth fastest time on Thursday, the Frenchman saying that the car turned into the corners with great precision. Traction was good too, helped, no doubt by a massive double rear wing generating downforce and temperature in the Michelins. Raul Boesel underlined the worth of the new arrangement by taking 18th place even though he hit a barrier and bent a wishbone.

Modified front suspension gave the Tyrrell of Michele Alboreto a shorter wheelbase in a bid to rid the car of understeer. The ploy was not particularly successful although the Italian managed to set third fastest time on Thursday morning. He was unable to equal that, however, traffic causing problems when the watches were running officially in the afternoon and Michele had to make do with 11th fastest time. Danny Sullivan just scraped into 20th place ahead of Giacomelli and the American was one of the few drivers relieved to see rain on Saturday; there was no question that the McLarens would have eased Danny into the role of spectator – but more of that later.

Arrows turned up with their neat little cars smartly decked out in the colours of Barclay cigarettes and Marc Surer proved just how efficient the A6 was by taking 12th place with Serra qualifying comfortably in 15th position. Dave Wass had produced a three-piece rear wing in the interests of greater downforce but the Lotus team required much more than that if they were to remain anywhere near competitive. Nigel Mansell was in 14th place although his time in the morning session would have moved the JPS 92-Cosworth onto the next row. He went even better on Saturday morning with a time good enough for the second row – and this with the session interrupted by an electrical short circuit under the driver's seat! Pirelli had continued the quest to improve their tyres although Elio de Angelis had other problems, the Italian claiming that his 93T was getting out of shape on the straight! He had two turbo failures which did nothing to improve his mood on Thursday morning but, nevertheless, he made the grid in 19th place.

ATS tried a revised inlet manifold on their BMW turbo on Thursday, the brave Manfred Winkelhock barely keeping up with his car as he set 16th fastest time. They reverted to the standard set-up for Saturday and Manfred was much happier; so happy, in fact, that he set the fastest time in the morning with a lap good enough for third place on the grid. Then it rained 30 minutes before the final session was due to start. Winkelhock and Mansell were very unhappy about the weather but their disappointment was nothing compared to the gloom rising from the McLaren pit. At least the ATS and the Lotus had qualified. . . .

It was becoming a familiar story and, had it been anywhere but Monaco with its 20-car limit, McLaren's miseries would have been accepted as normal, Lauda in 22nd place, Watson in 23rd. Indeed, they had won Long Beach after similar problems during practice. Once again, it was a question of working a reasonable temperature into the qualifying tyres. The word was put about that the Michelin qualifiers were designed specifically for the turbos with their large amounts of downforce but there was more to it than that. Ligier were ninth and 18th, for instance. John Barnard felt the cars were not loading the tyres sufficiently although tests the week before at Clermont Ferrand had come up with a more suitable compound and construction for the McLaren. The problem was, they could not be produced in sufficient quantities for Thursday so the team had to wait until Saturday morning. Sure enough, changes to the car linked with the latest tyres had Lauda and Watson improving by over two seconds a lap and seriously contemplating places in the middle of the grid. But not even the might of Marlboro or the persuasive powers of Ron Dennis could change the weather. . . .

Joining the McLaren men in their wet and weary trudge back to the paddock were Giacomelli, Eliseo Salazar and the Osella team of Corrado Fabi and Piercarlo Ghinzani. Ghinzani was the slowest even though 37 kilogrammes had been shaved off the Alfa Romeo-engined car. RAM March had taken the trouble to arrange a test drive of their car by Nelson Piquet at Snetterton, the Brazilian reporting that there was nothing basically wrong with the chassis. Salazar sailed through pre-qualifying but then wrote off the front-left corner against the barrier at the exit of the chicane later in the day. John Macdonald was not best pleased. But then he had been through it all before. McLaren, by contrast, were stunned and it took Niki Lauda to sum up their weekend in his usual concise manner: 'Thursday – shit: Friday – nice weather, no practice; Saturday – rain. Thank you gentlemen. Good afternoon."

RACE

The new merged with the old as the Formula 1 teams wheeled their cars and equipment into the pit lane, mechanics carefully manoeuvring their vans among the priceless historic sports cars which had just been raced with considerable enthusiasm. Even though the rain which had greeted race day had eased by 10 a.m., the pits soon echoed to the stammer of air guns as teams rehearsed rapid tyre changes. By the time the warm-up had commenced, the track was dry, Tambay setting the pace, with Patrese and Arnoux over half-a-second slower than the Ferrari. Drama was confined to Alfa Romeo and Toleman, the Italians changing an engine on de Cesaris's car while the British rectified a turbo failure for Warwick.

Throughout the morning, the heady climax unique to Monte Carlo gathered momentum but the drivers and team managers had no time for such niceties. Rain had returned and the heavy grey clouds covering the Turini showed no signs of breaking. By the time the cars had left the pits for their warm-up lap, the track was wet although the rain had stopped. Practically all the drivers tried slicks and Rosberg, surprised at the amount of grip to be had, completed an extra lap just to make sure.

Then the grid went silent. The poseurs, carefully staying within range of the mobile television camera, mingled with the teams as the psyching began. Spots of rain began to fall; there was no blue to be seen in the sky. Both Renault drivers were on wet tyres already. With four minutes to go, Ferrari joined them. The spots of rain continued to fall on Rosberg's visor but the team remained resolute; slicks were the only choice. Marc Surer felt the same about his chances. So did Alboreto and Sullivan. Warwick and de Angelis were the only turbo runners to take the gamble although Tambay, keen to do likewise, had been overruled – a curious decision since their man had actually volunteered and it seemed logical to split the option.

Any doubts about Rosberg keeping pace with the turbos during the opening laps were answered within the first few yards of the race. As the Renault and Ferrari drivers treated their turbo power with respect on the greasy surface, Rosberg, whose grid position was on a dry piece of track below the trees, made a perfect start and, to his delight, the Williams driver found a clear path opening before him. By *Ste. Devote*, Rosberg was second, beaten only by Prost.

Arnoux had made a bad start to fall behind Cheever and Tambay while Mansell, having made the surprising choice of starting on wets, was keen to make the most of his advantage while it lasted. Taking to the pavement at *Mirabeau*, he forced his way ahead of Serra and chased after Alboreto. As the Tyrrell and Lotus left *Tabac*, Alboreto spun his rear wheels briefly and Mansell looked to the inside on the approach to the swimming pool. Unfortunately, Alboreto recovered quickly and the two cars touched, the Tyrrell spinning sideways before being rammed amidships by the Lotus. With barely one lap completed, the Monaco retirement list had been opened.

Rosberg had no intention of adding his name to the list, yet his handling of the Williams during the opening laps fairly set the adrenalin pumping. Selecting a dry line, he powered past Prost at the end of lap one and, five laps later, he had a lead of 12 seconds. It was a truly brilliant display. By now, the rain had stopped and it was obvious that slicks were the tyre for the occasion. Piquet came in at the end of lap four, by which time Arnoux had worked his way (by means of some rather desperate driving as he barged past Cheever) into third place. Fourth had become the property of Jacques Laffite, the Frenchman moving up another place in a move which resulted in Arnoux's Ferrari clouting the barrier before *Portier*.

The left-rear rim and tyre were badly damaged but Arnoux attempted to slither and slide his way back to the pits at a pace which was hardly in keeping with his problem. Bits of tyre and metal flew in all directions, the Ferrari grinding to a halt just before the pit lane. Fortunately, Ferrari occupied the first pit and the mechanics set about repairing the damage once the battered car had been pushed in. Arnoux did leave the pits once more – only to park the Ferrari soon after when damage to the electrical system caused the engine to die.

All this activity, of course, meant poor Tambay had to wait until at least lap 10 before the pit could be cleared to allow his stop for slicks; another poor piece of management by the Italian team.

Elsewhere, misjudgements on the track were whittling the field rapidly. Manfred Winkelhock had been stuck behind Raul Boesel's Ligier, the ATS driver not anxious to pass unless an opportunity presented itself. Going through the tunnel on lap four, the Ligier stepped sideways and slid to the outside of the track thus giving Winkelhock the chance to pull alongside. What happened next depends on who you talked to, but both cars touched long before the braking area for the chicane. Each driver claimed the other had driven into him. Either way, they were spectators now, the two

MAY:
Corning Glass, an American company, buys the Watkins Glen circuit for $1.6m.

FIA Court of Appeal rejects appeal by Williams against the disqualification of Keke Rosberg from second place in the Brazilian Grand Prix.

KEKE ROSBERG'S WIN AT MONACO COULD NOT HAVE been more opportune for the TAG Williams team. Spirits were low following the dismissal a few days before of the team's appeal against Rosberg's disqualification from the Brazilian Grand Prix. The World Champion lost six points for second place when it was decided that the push start, received during a pit stop, was illegal.

Article 14 of the Formula 1 'Standard Regulations for the Events' in the FIA Sporting Code covered 'General Safety Discipline' and Clause 7 stated that "Every time a car stops, be it voluntary or not, the engine must be started by the starter. The use of an external power source is allowed only in the pits and on the dummy starting grid."

The problem, as ever, arose because of the lack of a precise definition. What was an 'external power source'? Nowhere in the rules was it defined and most teams assumed that push starts by mechanics could be classified as an 'external power source'.

Furthermore, Rosberg had received a push start on the dummy grid at Brands Hatch and Dijon the previous year and yet nothing had been said. In addition, rule changes at the end of 1982 made on board starters optional rather than mandatory. Clearly, the Williams team had a strong case.

The FIA Court of Appeal, in their wisdom, decided otherwise. They also announced a clarification of the phrase 'external power source' explaining that it should be "mechanical, electrical or by compressed air". They did not explain what a team should do with the "mechanical, electrical or compressed air" power source if the car was not fitted with an on board starter.

The FIA announced that second place would remain vacant but the decision to take away six points from Williams because of another problem with the slack wording in the regulations was exceptionally harsh and out of keeping with the offence.

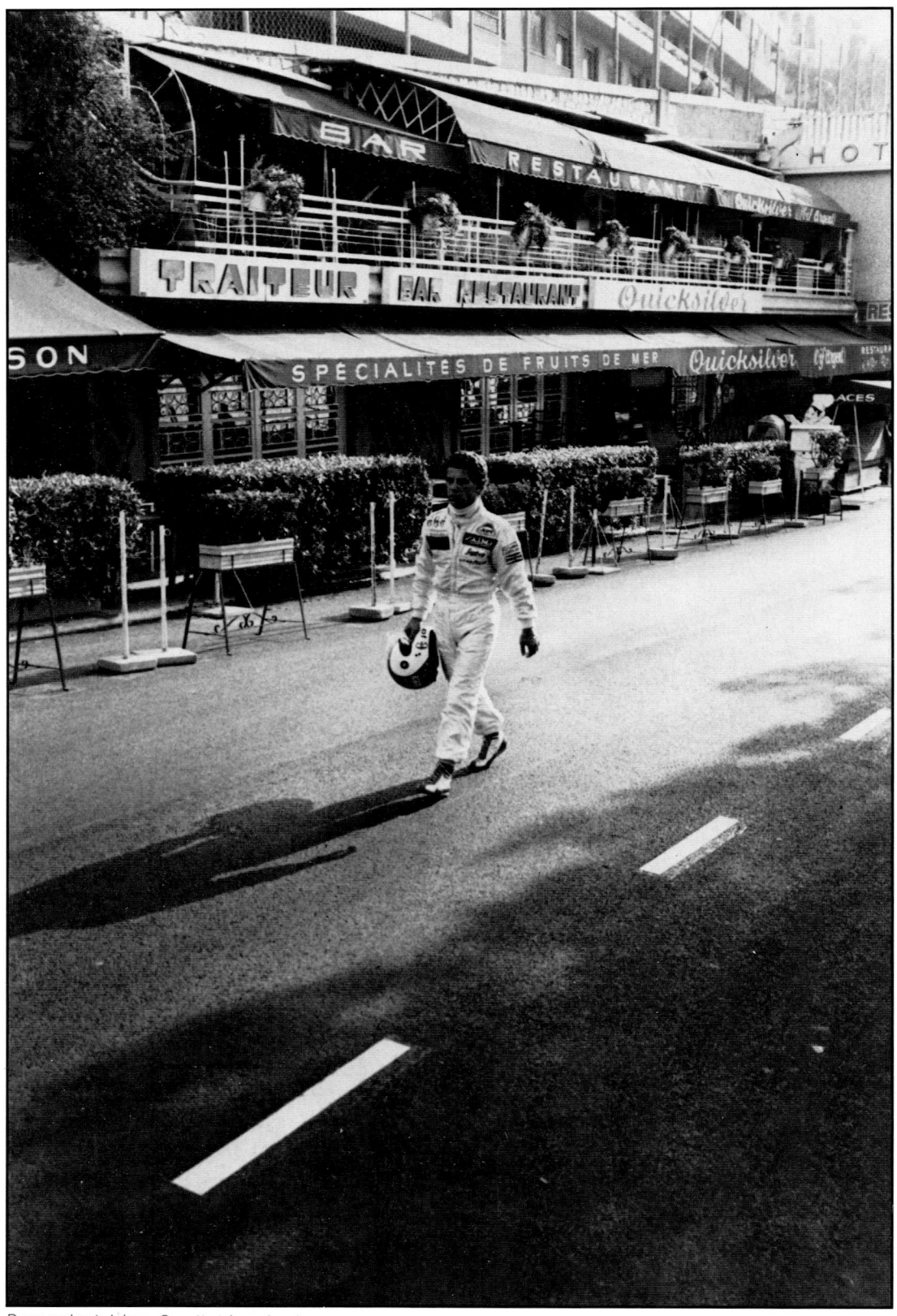

Down and out. Johnny Cecotto takes a lonely
walk back to the pits at 8.30 a.m. on Thursday to
inform the Theodore team that he has just
crashed his car in the tunnel during
pre-qualifying.

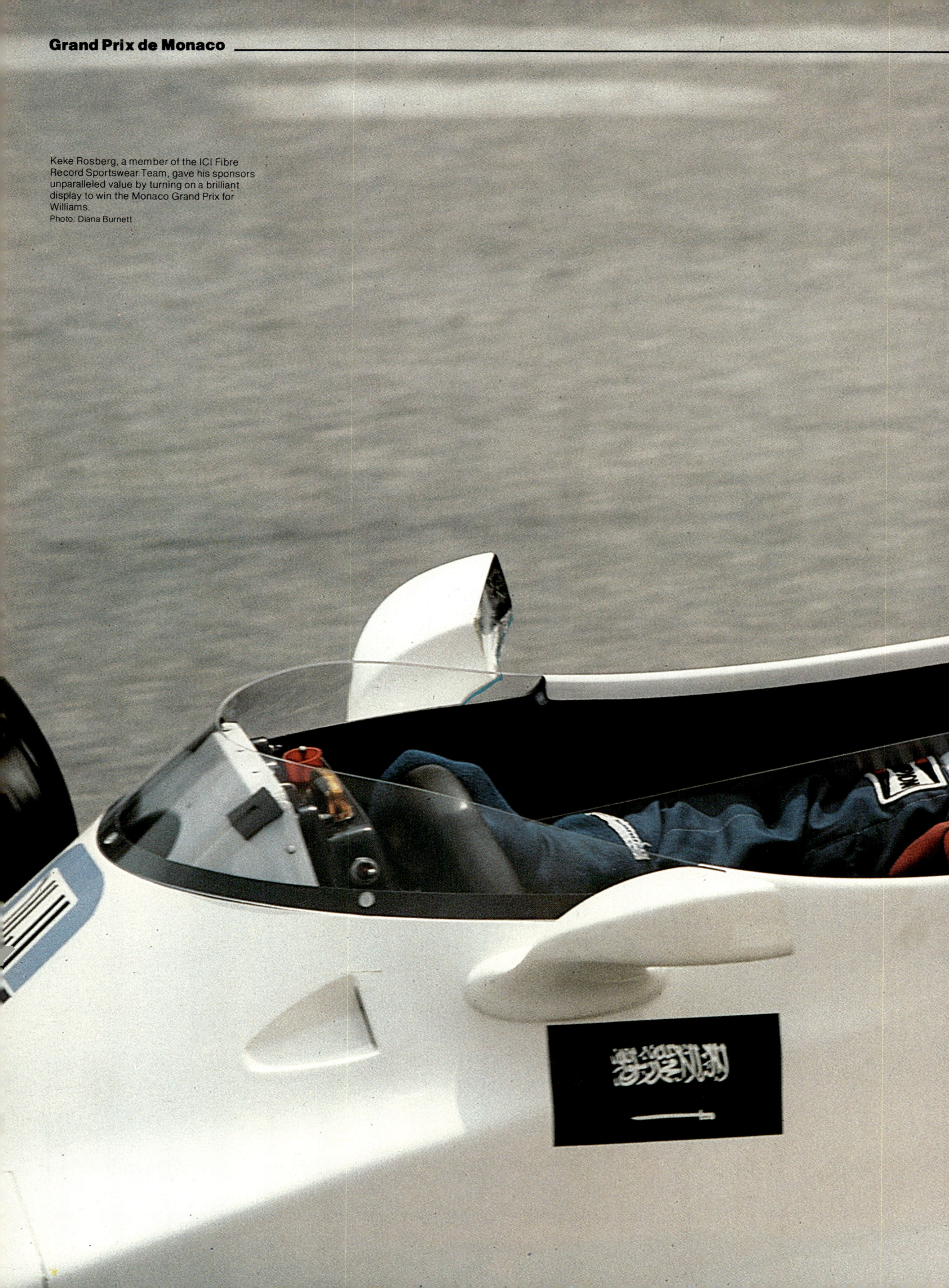

Keke Rosberg, a member of the ICI Fibre
Record Sportswear Team, gave his sponsors
unparalleled value by turning on a brilliant
display to win the Monaco Grand Prix for
Williams.
Photo: Diana Burnett

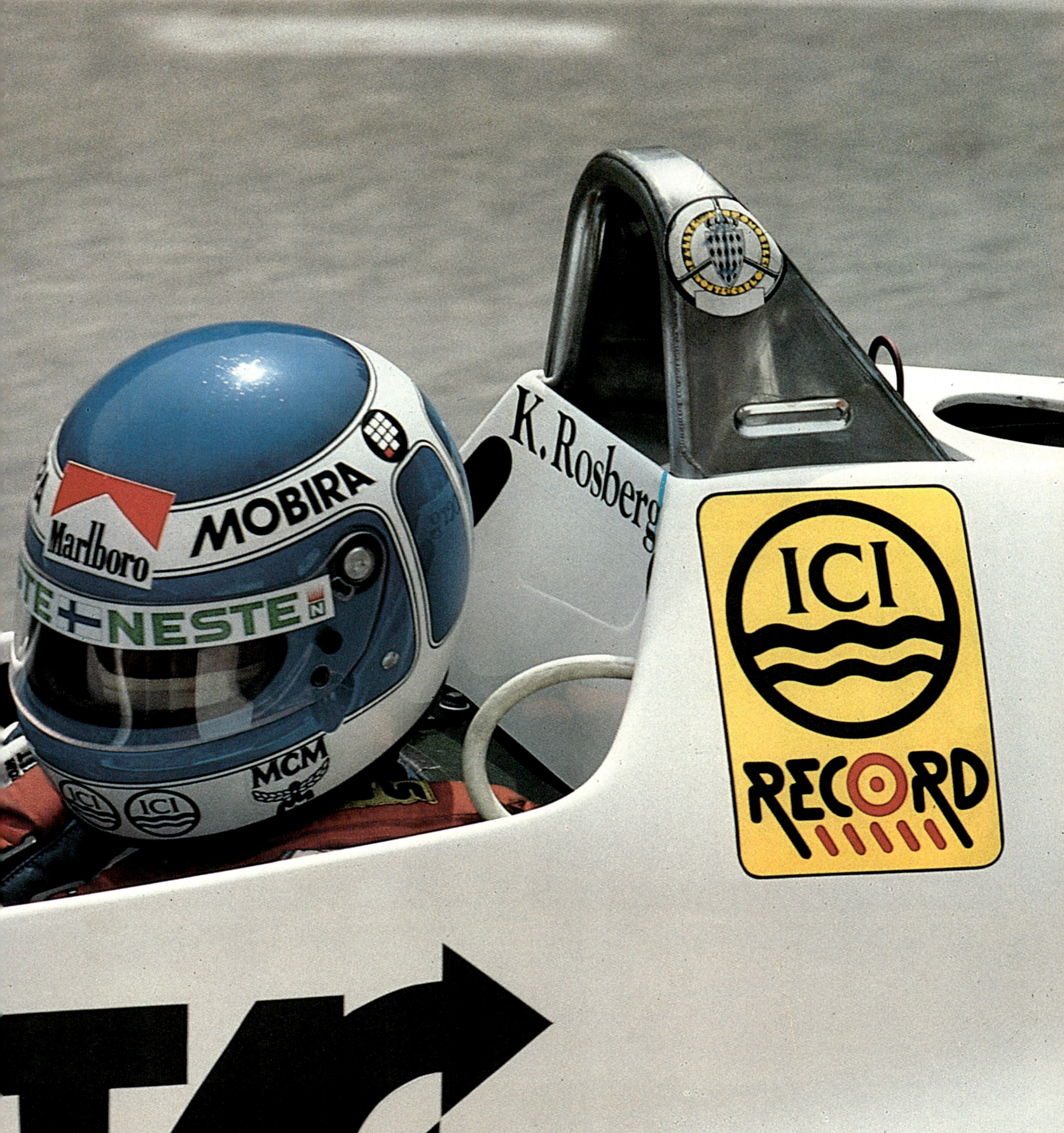

After their problems on the streets of Long Beach, Gordon Murray and Nelson Piquet did well to work the BT52 onto the third row of the grid and into second place at the finish despite gearbox problems *(below left)*.

McLaren may have had problems with inadequate temperatures in their Michelins but Ligier qualified both cars by running large wings at the rear and negative camber at the front. Jean-Pierre Jarier leaves Casino Square before retiring *(below)*.

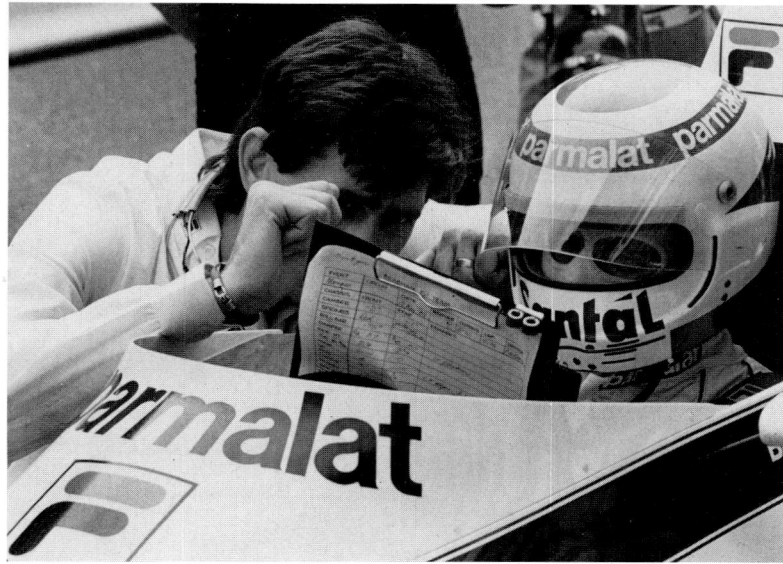

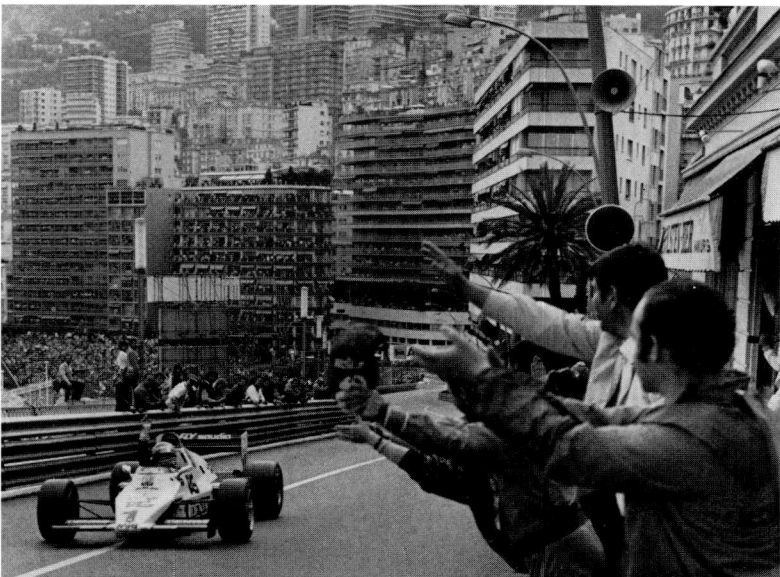

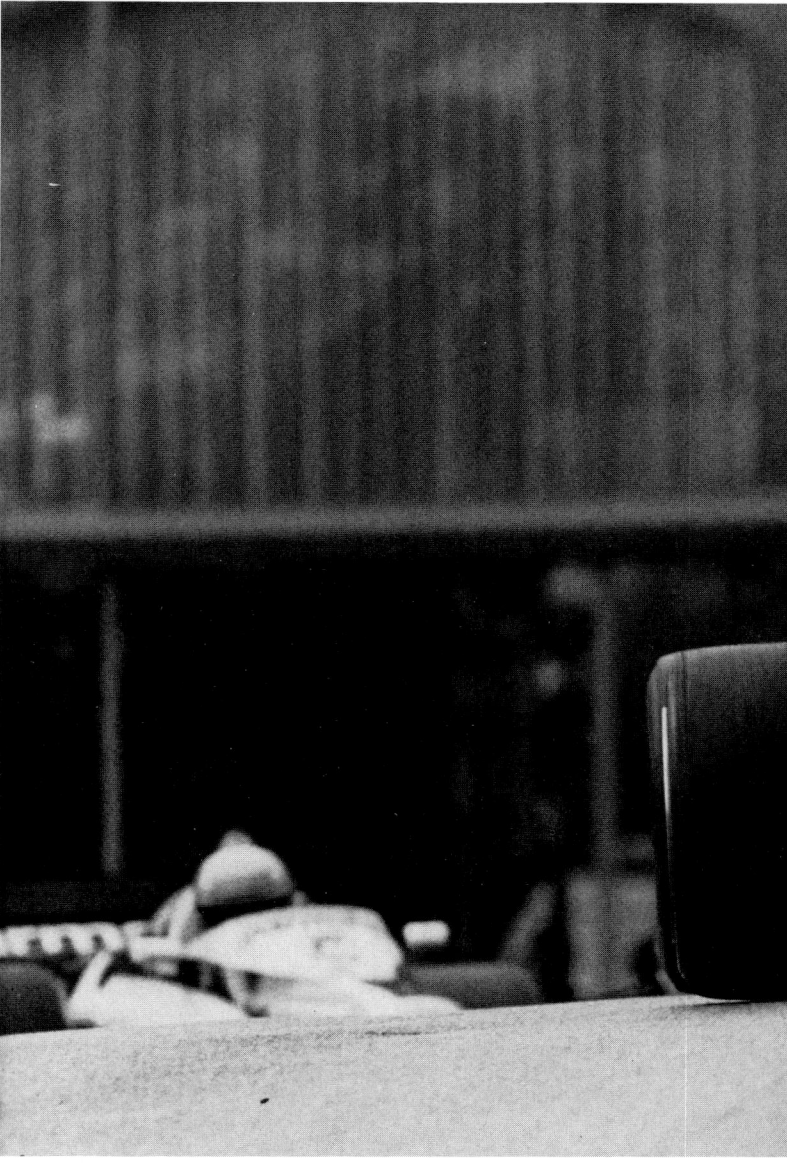

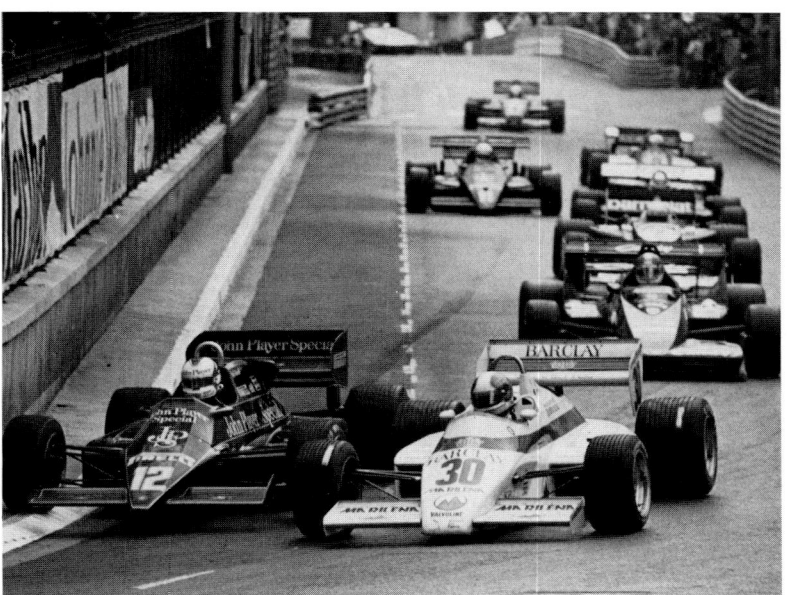

On top of the world. Keke Rosberg receives well-earned applause at Rosie's Bar after a brilliant drive on Sunday afternoon *(above left)*. As the back of the field streams into Mirabeau on the opening lap, Mansell, keen to make the most of his wet Pirellis on a rapidly drying track, forces his way past the Arrows of Serra. Warwick (slicks), Patrese (wets), Boesel (wets), de Angelis (slicks) and Winkelhock (wets) follow while Sullivan (slicks) brings up the rear. Mansell retired halfway round the lap after colliding with Alboreto's Tyrrell; Serra drove smoothly to finish seventh and last; Warwick collided with Surer; Patrese retired with mechanical trouble; Boesel and Winkelhock collided and de Angelis broke a driveshaft – leaving the way clear for Sullivan to finish in fifth place *(left)*.

The flat bottom rule and the reduction in ground effects meant brakes were no longer subjected to short but exceptionally heavy usage. AP produced a lighter and thinner disc during the early part of the season; Williams tried them on Laffite's car during the first unofficial session. The Lotus mechanics made sure the high-spirited traditions of Monaco were adhered to at the Tip Top bar during a birthday celebration *(far right)*.

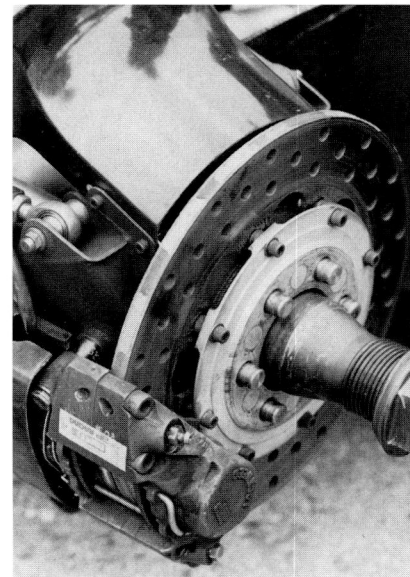

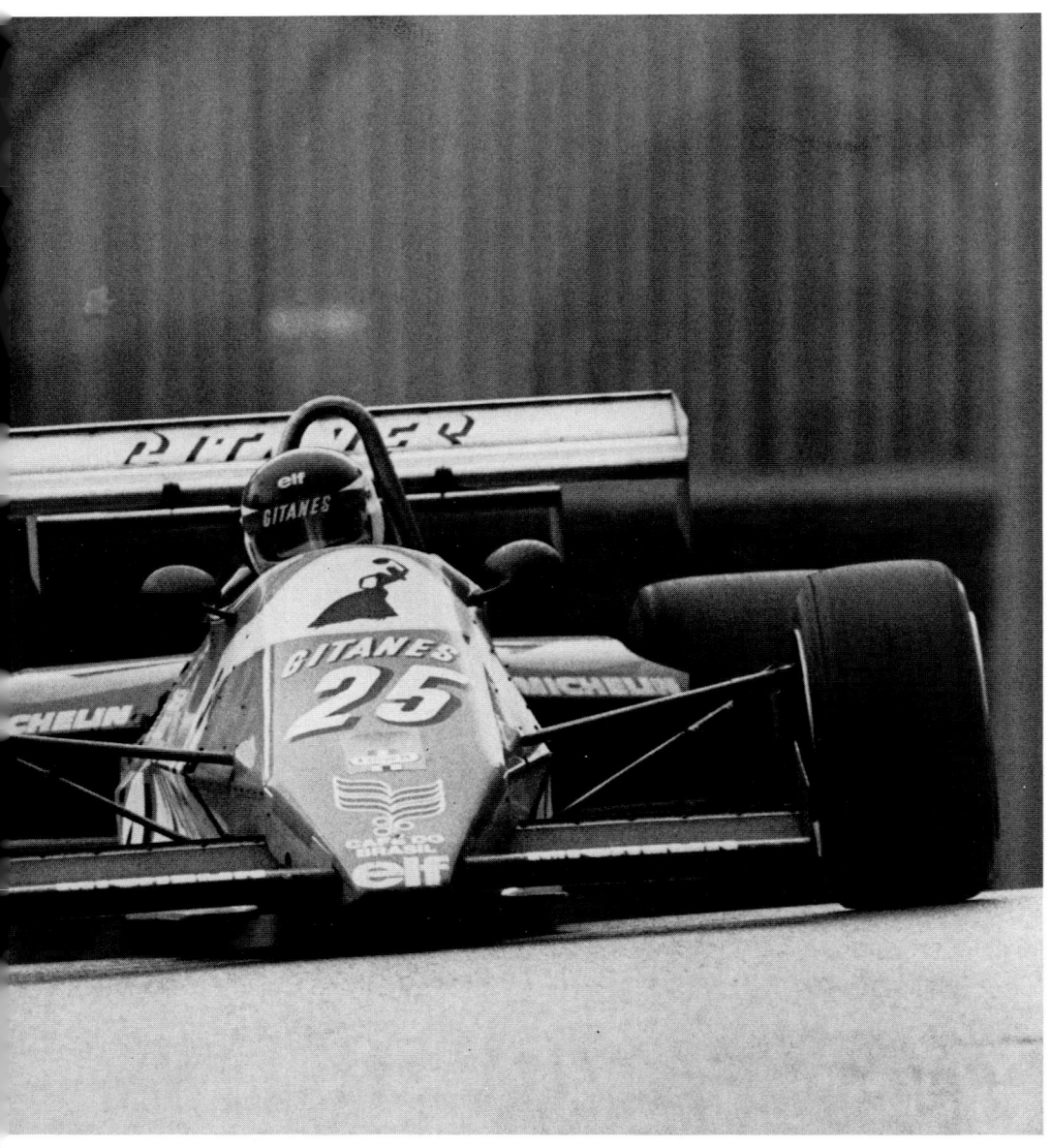

men squaring up to each other – fortunately out of range of the television cameras.

TV screens were filled, instead, with the astonishing progress of Rosberg as the Williams driver and his team-mate pulled out a commanding lead. The turbos had made their pit stops and, as the race settled down again, it became clear we had an absorbing battle in prospect. Surer and Warwick had made the most of their decision to start on slicks by moving into third and fourth places, 45 seconds behind Laffite. Prost and Piquet were closing rapidly on the Toleman with Cheever giving chase, having moved up to seventh place when de Angelis stopped for tyres. Jarier was next followed by Patrese with Tambay in tenth place. Sullivan, last at the end of lap one, had taken heed of stern advice from Ken Tyrrell and driven carefully, the American already picking up places at the expense of others as Baldi and Serra made stops for slicks and de Cesaris retired his Alfa Romeo with gearbox trouble.

The Renault mechanics had made a guess at finding a quick compromise setting for Prost's car during his pit stop – but they had guessed wrong. Now he was finding difficulty in selecting fourth gear and, after a few laps holding off Piquet, the Frenchman was powerless to resist as the Brabham made a daring move into fifth place in the tunnel. Quickly, Nelson closed on Warwick and the spectators were treated to a fine battle as the two drivers revived memories of their disputes in Formula 3. Each showed a healthy respect for the other's capabilities, Piquet challenging at *Mirabeau* and *Portier*; Warwick responding with a positive and clean defence of his position.

By lap 28, Cheever had caught his team leader, the two swapping places, allowing Cheever to launch an immediate attack on Piquet shortly before an electrical failure caused the American's engine to cut without warning. Cheever was left to pick his way on foot along the rocks by the swimming pool.

The battle between Warwick and Piquet brought them closer to Surer and, for several laps, the three cars circulated nose-to-tail. On lap 49, they came up to lap Danny Sullivan but, before they could reach the Tyrrell, Surer slid onto the kerbs at the entrance to the pit straight. Warwick was not desperate to pass since he figured it was not worth taking any risks at Monaco but he did take the opportunity to harry the Swiss driver by moving to his left as they approached the braking area for *Ste. Devote*. Unfortunately he got too close and Surer, seeing the blue car in his mirror, moved over. In an instant, the Toleman had hit the rear of the Arrows, Surer spinning into the barrier and retirement. Warwick, furious with himself, limped back to the pits but the front suspension was too badly damaged to allow him to continue.

The wily Piquet had seen the accident coming and somehow managed to thread his way through the mêlée and into third place. Laffite was around 40 seconds to the good but he then lost a comfortable second place on lap 54 when the Williams pulled into the pits with a stripped third gear, the damage done by a missed gearchange as he accelerated past the pits not long before.

With Rosberg over a minute ahead of the Brabham, the result seemed a foregone conclusion. However, it was apparent that the World Champion was not slackening his pace. Rosberg may have been tiring, his hands may have been badly blistered by kick-back from the steering but any thoughts of easing up had been annulled by an alarming tendency for the engine to cut out occasionally, one such incident at the swimming pool having caused Keke to almost hit the barrier as he jump-started the engine back to life with the clutch! Ease up? Not a chance.

Rosberg wanted as large a margin as possible in case of further trouble. He was not amused, therefore,

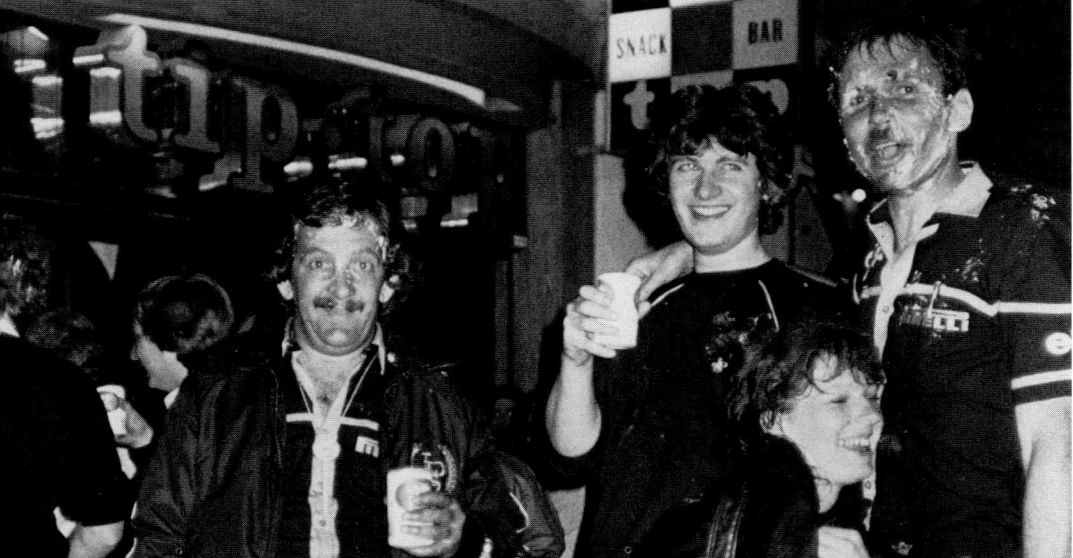

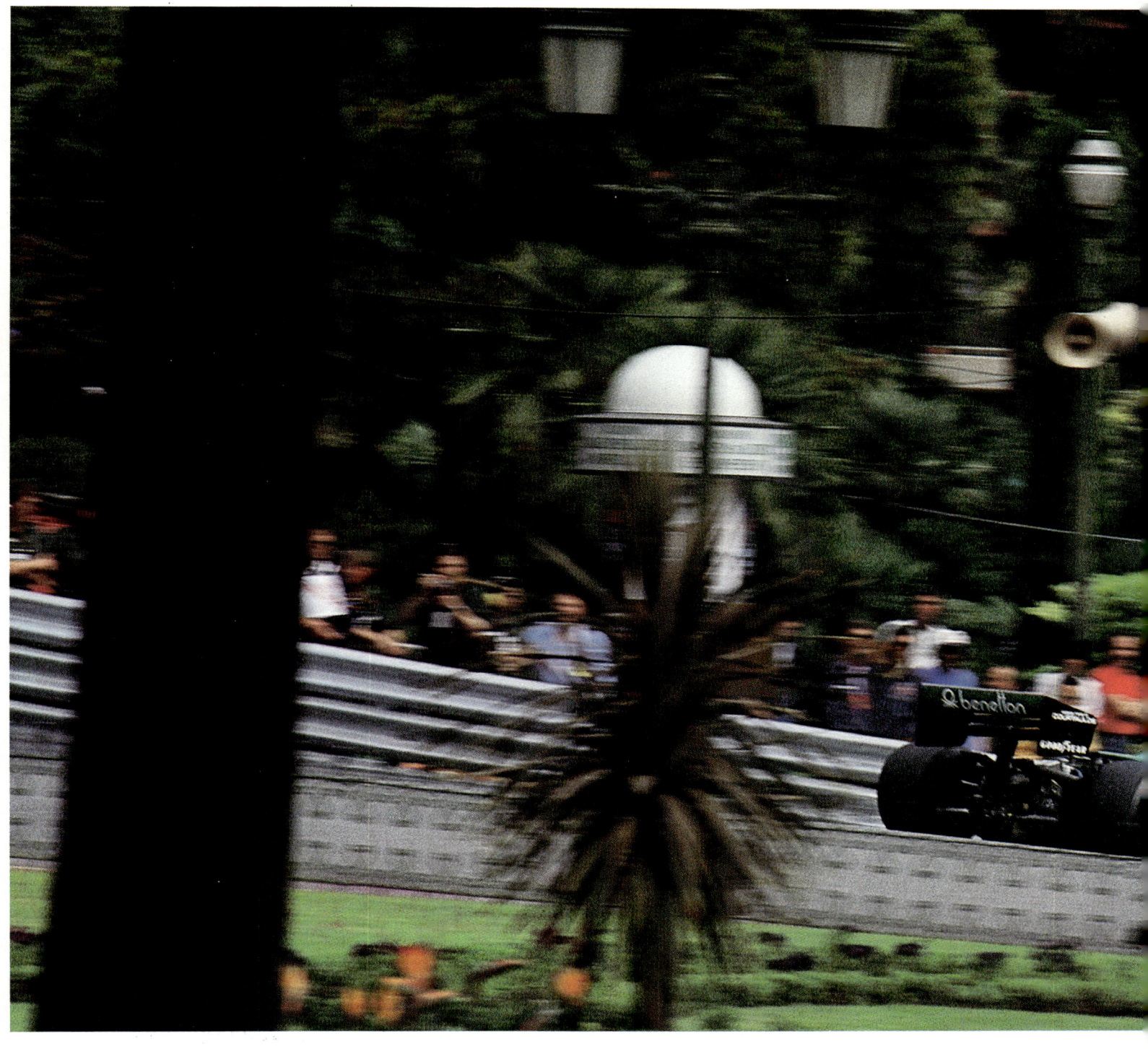

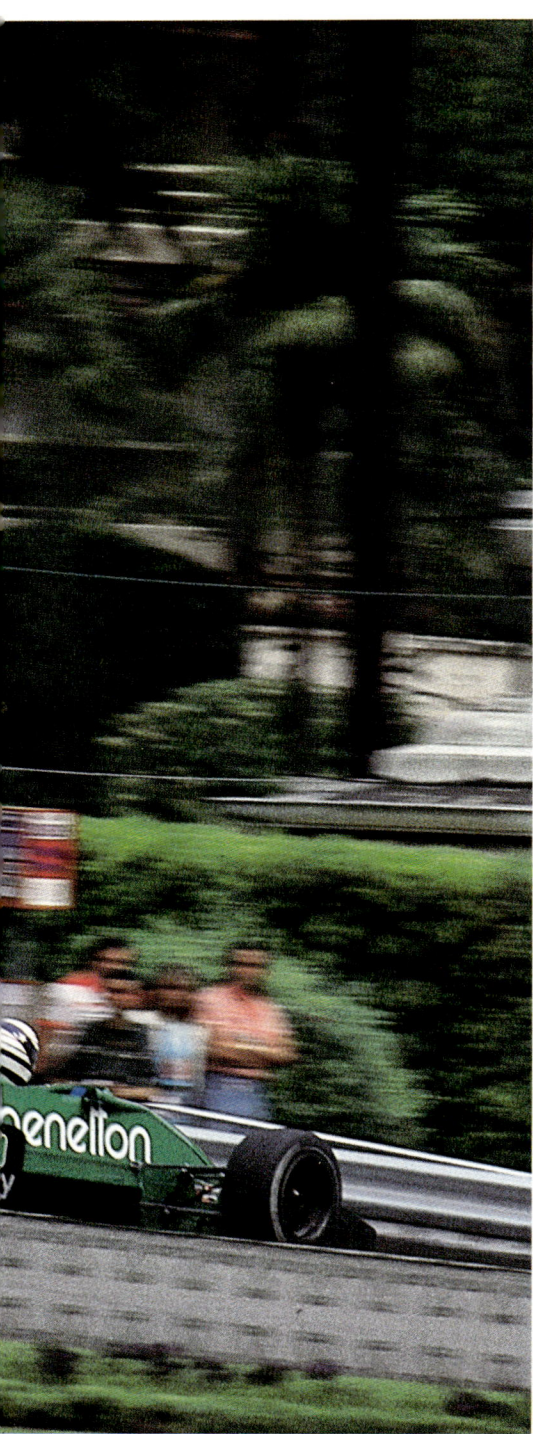

Danny Sullivan exits Casino Square on his way to Mirabeau. A sensible drive allowed the Tyrrell driver to benefit from the misfortunes of others and score his first championship points for fifth place.
Photo: Bernard Asset

when his progress was impeded by Sullivan as the Williams tried to lap the Tyrrell for the second time. The American was now in sixth place and, with Patrese struggling in fifth position, Sullivan did not feel obliged to stop and wave the leader through. Patrick Head, on the other hand, felt Sullivan should have more respect and he marched down to the Tyrrell pit and said as much. Ken Tyrrell refused to cooperate with an instruction to his driver, retorting that perhaps Williams should tell their man to get on with his job and pass the Tyrrell! Head was not amused.

Matters were partially resolved on lap 62 when Patrese called at the pits, an engine misfire leading him to believe that the Brabham was running out of fuel. A couple of gallons were added, Patrese rejoining to find that the engine misfire was persisting and, on lap 64, the BMW died, Patrese inadvertently coming to rest against the barrier as he buried his head in the cockpit and flicked switches on and off in a vain attempt to coax the engine back to life.

Sullivan was fifth and Baldi moved into sixth place while Serra, after a steady drive, took seventh and last position when de Angelis retired, the Lotus snapping a driveshaft as he attempted to accelerate out of the pits following another tyre change. Ahead of Sullivan, Patrick Tambay nursed his Ferrari along in fourth place, the 126C2 not handling nicely since part of the rear wing assembly had broken off. Prost was very happy to be third considering his gearbox problems while Piquet set fastest lap on lap 69 as he pressed on relentlessly and cut the gap to Rosberg.

It would have been a travesty had anyone other than Keke Rosberg won this race, the Finn having turned in a virtuoso display worthy of a World Champion. Soaked in sweat from head to foot, Keke received his trophy from Prince Rainier and we had to remind ourselves that this was only the second time during his Grand Prix career that the Finn had taken the winner's laurels.

For Williams, it was victory number 17 and, down by the trees on *Boulevard Albert 1er*, Frank was savouring the moment. 'It was an opportunity to put one over on the turbos," he said with relish. "The only gamble we took was it could have been a wet race – in which case we would have had no chance. . . .". A few yards away in the pit lane, Patrick Head held out his hands, palms upwards, and shouted at Williams: "Frank! It's starting to rain!" With that, the two men grinned broadly as the heavens opened.

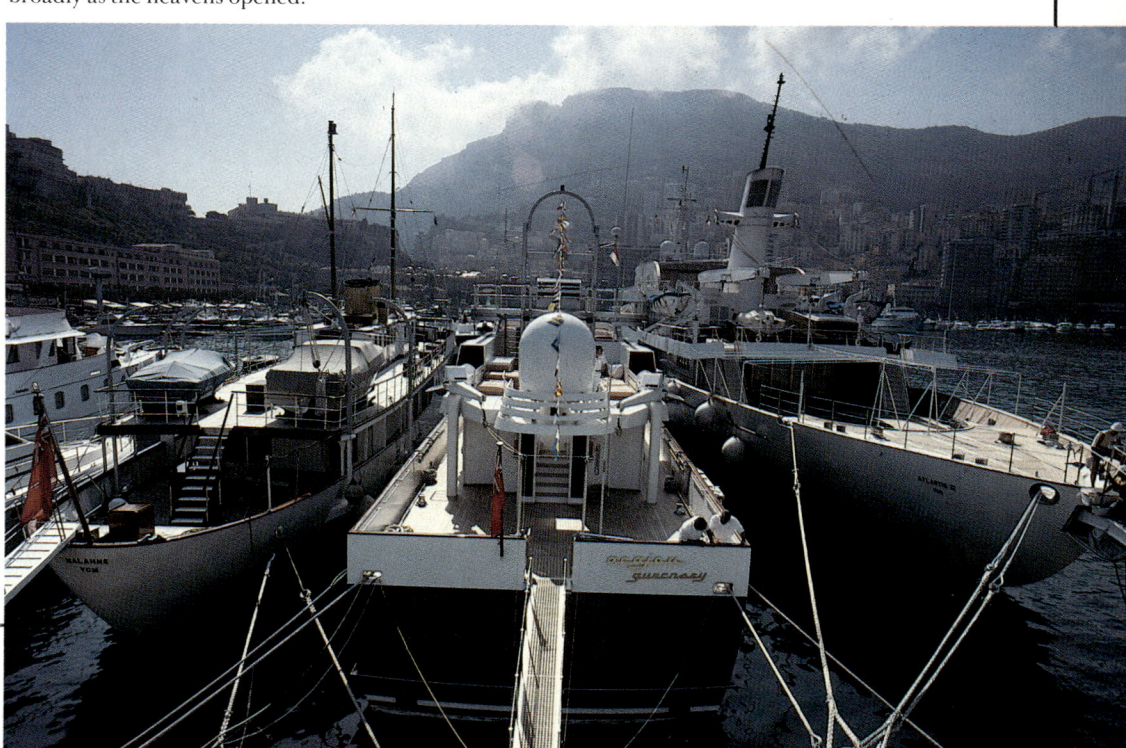

Storm clouds gather on the Turini; rain on Saturday meant the McLaren team failed to qualify.
Photo: Nigel Snowdon

Grand Prix de Monaco, May 15/statistics

Entries and practice times

No.	Driver	Nat	Car	Tyre	Engine	Entrant	Practice 1	Practice 2
1	Keke Rosberg	SF	Saudia WILLIAMS FW08C	G	Ford Cosworth DFV	TAG Williams Team	**1m 26·307s**	1m 52·030s
2	Jacques Laffite	F	Saudia WILLIAMS FW08C	G	Ford Cosworth DFV	TAG Williams Team	**1m 27·726s**	1m 53·580s
3	Michele Alboreto	I	Benetton TYRRELL 011	G	Ford Cosworth DFV/DFY	Benetton Tyrrell Team	**1m 28·256s**	2m 00·969s
4	Danny Sullivan	USA	Benetton TYRRELL 011	G	Ford Cosworth DFV	Benetton Tyrrell Team	**1m 29·530s**	2m 09·076s
5	Nelson Piquet	BR	Parmalat BRABHAM BT52	M	BMW M12/13	Fila Sport	**1m 27·273s**	1m 56·736s
6	Riccardo Patrese	I	Parmalat BRABHAM BT52	M	BMW M12/13	Fila Sport	**1m 29·200s**	
7	John Watson	GB	Marlboro McLAREN MP4/1C	M	Ford Cosworth DFV/DFY	Marlboro McLaren International	**1m 30·283s**	1m 53·772s
8	Niki Lauda	A	Marlboro McLAREN MP4/1C	M	Ford Cosworth DFV/DFY	Marlboro McLaren International	**1m 29·898s**	1m 52·448s
9	Manfred Winkelhock	D	ATS D6	G	BMW M12/13	Team ATS	**1m 28·975s**	2m 01·178s
11	Elio de Angelis	I	John Player Special LOTUS 93T	P	Renault EF1	John Player Team Lotus	**1m 29·518s**	1m 56·762s
12	Nigel Mansell	GB	John Player Special LOTUS 92	P	Ford Cosworth DFV/DFY	John Player Team Lotus	**1m 28·721s**	1m 56·560s
15	Alain Prost	F	Elf RENAULT RE40	M	Renault EF1	Equipe Renault Elf	**1m 24·840s**	1m 52·845s
16	Eddie Cheever	USA	Elf RENAULT RE40	M	Renault EF1	Equipe Renault Elf	**1m 26·279s**	1m 52·434s
17	Eliseo Salazar	RCH	MARCH-RAM 01	P	Ford Cosworth DFV	RAM Automotive Team March	**1m 31·229s**	
22	Andrea de Cesaris	I	Marlboro ALFA ROMEO 183T	M	Alfa Romeo 183T	Marlboro Team Alfa Romeo	**1m 27·680s**	1m 54·335s
23	Mauro Baldi	I	Marlboro ALFA ROMEO 183T	M	Alfa Romeo 183T	Marlboro Team Alfa Romeo	**1m 28·639s**	1m 56·398s
25	Jean-Pierre Jarier	F	Gitanes LIGIER JS21	M	Ford Cosworth DFV	Equipe Ligier Gitanes	**1m 27·906s**	1m 55·986s
26	Raul Boesel	BR	Gitanes LIGIER JS21	M	Ford Cosworth DFV	Equipe Ligier Gitanes	**1m 29·222s**	1m 59·110s
27	Patrick Tambay	F	Fiat FERRARI 126C2/B	G	Ferrari 126C	Scuderia Ferrari SpA SEFAC	**1m 26·298s**	1m 53·987s
28	René Arnoux	F	Fiat FERRARI 126C2/B	G	Ferrari 126C	Scuderia Ferrari SpA SEFAC	**1m 25·182s**	1m 52·183s
29	Marc Surer	CH	ARROWS A6	G	Ford Cosworth DFV	Arrows Racing Team	**1m 28·346s**	1m 56·836s
30	Chico Serra	BR	ARROWS A6	G	Ford Cosworth DFV	Arrows Racing Team	**1m 28·784s**	
31	Corrado Fabi	I	OSELLA FA1D	M	Ford Cosworth DFV	Osella Squadra Corse	**1m 30·495s**	
32	Piercarlo Ghinzani	I	OSELLA FA1E	M	Alfa Romeo 1260	Osella Squadra Corse	**1m 35·572s**	
33	Roberto Guerrero	COL	THEODORE N183	G	Ford Cosworth DFV	Theodore Racing Team	Failed to pre-qualify	
34	Johnny Cecotto	YV	THEODORE N183	G	Ford Cosworth DFV	Theodore Racing Team	Failed to pre-qualify	
35	Derek Warwick	GB	Candy TOLEMAN TG183B	P	Hart 415T	Candy Toleman Motorsport	**1m 28·017s**	
36	Bruno Giacomelli	I	Candy TOLEMAN TG183B	P	Hart 415T	Candy Toleman Motorsport	**1m 29·552s**	

Thursday morning and Saturday morning practice sessions not officially recorded.

G – Goodyear, M – Michelin, P – Pirelli.

Thur pm	Sat pm
Warm, dry	Wet, cool

Starting grid

28 ARNOUX (1m 25·182s)
Ferrari

15 PROST (1m 24·840s)
Renault

27 TAMBAY (1m 26·298s)
Ferrari

16 CHEEVER (1m 26·279s)
Renault

5 PIQUET (1m 27·273s)
Brabham

1 ROSBERG (1m 26·307s)
Williams

2 LAFFITE (1m 27·726s)
Williams

22 DE CESARIS (1m 27·680s)
Alfa Romeo

35 WARWICK (1m 28·017s)
Toleman

25 JARIER (1m 27·906s)
Ligier

29 SURER (1m 28·346s)
Arrows

3 ALBORETO (1m 28·256s)
Tyrrell

12 MANSELL (1m 28·721s)
Lotus

23 BALDI (1m 28·639s)
Alfa Romeo

9 WINKELHOCK (1m 28·975s)
ATS

30 SERRA (1m 28·784s)
Arrows

26 BOESEL (1m 29·222s)
Ligier

6 PATRESE (1m 29·200s)
Brabham

4 SULLIVAN (1m 29·530s)
Tyrrell

11 DE ANGELIS (1m 29·518s)
Lotus

Did not start:
36 Giacomelli (Toleman), 1m 29·552s, did not qualify
8 Lauda (McLaren), 1m 29·898s, did not qualify
7 Watson (McLaren), 1m 30·283s, did not qualify
31 Fabi (Osella), 1m 30·495s, did not qualify
17 Salazar (RAM March), 1m 31·229s, did not qualify
34 Cecotto (Theodore), 1m 33·817s, failed to pre-qualify
32 Ghinzani (Osella), 1m 35·572s, did not qualify
33 Guerrero (Theodore), 1m 38·389s, failed to pre-qualify

Results and retirements

Place	Driver	Car	Laps	Time and Speed (mph/km/h)/Retirement	
1	Keke Rosberg	Williams-Cosworth V8	76	1h 56m 38·121s	129·586/80·521
2	Nelson Piquet	Brabham-BMW t/c 4	76	1h 56m 56·596s	129·1/80·219
3	Alain Prost	Renault t/c V6	76	1h 57m 09·487s	128·9/80·095
4	Patrick Tambay	Ferrari t/c V6	76	1h 57m 42·418s	128·3/79·722
5	Danny Sullivan	Tyrrell-Cosworth V8	74		
6	Mauro Baldi	Alfa Romeo t/c V6	74		
7	Chico Serra	Arrows-Cosworth V8	74		
	Riccardo Patrese	Brabham-BMW t/c 4	64	Electrics	
	Jacques Laffite	Williams-Cosworth V8	54	Gearbox	
	Derek Warwick	Toleman-Hart t/c 4	50	Accident with Surer	
	Elio de Angelis	Lotus-Renault t/c V6	50	Driveshaft	
	Marc Surer	Arrows-Cosworth V8	49	Accident with Warwick	
	Jean-Pierre Jarier	Ligier-Cosworth V8	33	Hydraulic suspension pump	
	Eddie Cheever	Renault t/c V6	30	Engine cut out/electrics	
	Andrea de Cesaris	Alfa Romeo t/c V8	14	Gearbox	
	René Arnoux	Ferrari t/c V6	6	Accident damage/hit barrier	
	Raul Boesel	Ligier-Cosworth V8	3	Accident with Winkelhock	
	Manfred Winkelhock	ATS-BMW t/c 4	3	Accident with Boesel	
	Michele Alboreto	Tyrrell-Cosworth V8	0	Accident with Mansell	
	Nigel Mansell	Lotus-Cosworth V8	0	Accident with Alboreto	

Fastest lap: Piquet on lap 69, 1m 27·283s, 84·881mph/136·603km/h.
Lap record: Riccardo Patrese (F1 Arrows A3-Cosworth DFV), 1m 26·058s, 86·089mph/138·548km/h (1980).

Past winners

Year	Driver	Nat	Car	Circuit	Distance miles/km	Speed mph/km/h
1929	"W. Williams"	GB	2·3 Bugatti T35B s/c	Monte Carlo	197·60/318·01	49·83/80·19
1930	René Dreyfus	F	2·3 Bugatti T35B s/c	Monte Carlo	197·60/318·01	53·63/86·32
1931	Louis Chiron	F	2·3 Bugatti T52 s/c	Monte Carlo	197·60/318·01	54·10/87·06
1932	Tazio Nuvolari	I	2·3 Alfa Romeo Monza s/c	Monte Carlo	197·60/318·01	55·81/89·82
1933	Achille Varzi	I	2·3 Bugati T51 s/c	Monte Carlo	197·60/318·01	57·05/91·81
1934	Guy Moll	DZ	2·9 Alfa Romeo P3 s/c	Monte Carlo	197·60/318·01	56·05/90·20
1935	Luigi Fagioli	I	4·0 Mercedes-Benz W25 s/c	Monte Carlo	197·60/318·01	58·16/93·61
1936	Rudi Caracciola	D	4·7 Mercedes-Benz W25 s/c	Monte Carlo	197·60/318·01	51·69/83·20
1937	Manfred von Brauchitsch	D	5·7 Mercedes-Benz W125 s/c	Monte Carlo	197·60/318·01	63·26/101·82
1948	Giuseppe Farina	I	1·5 Maserati 4CLT s/c	Monte Carlo	197·60/318·01	59·74/96·15
1950	Juan Manuel Fangio	RA	1·5 Alfa Romeo 158 s/c	Monte Carlo	197·60/318·01	61·33/98·70
1952*	Vittorio Marzotto	I	2·7 Ferrari 225MM	Monte Carlo	195·42/314·50	58·20/93·66
1955	Maurice Trintignant	F	2·5 Ferrari 625	Monte Carlo	195·42/314·50	65·81/105·91
1956	Stirling Moss	GB	2·5 Maserati 250F	Monte Carlo	195·42/314·50	64·94/104·51
1957	Juan Manuel Fangio	RA	2·5 Maserati 250F	Monte Carlo	205·19/330·22	64·72/104·16
1958	Maurice Trintignant	F	2·0 Cooper T45-Climax	Monte Carlo	195·42/314·50	67·99/109·41
1959	Jack Brabham	AUS	2·5 Cooper T51-Climax	Monte Carlo	195·42/314·50	66·71/107·36
1960	Stirling Moss	GB	2·5 Lotus 18-Climax	Monte Carlo	195·42/314·50	67·48/108·60
1961	Stirling Moss	GB	1·5 Lotus 18-Climax	Monte Carlo	195·42/314·50	70·70/113·79
1962	Bruce McLaren	NZ	1·5 Cooper T60-Climax	Monte Carlo	195·42/314·50	70·46/113·40
1963	Graham Hill	GB	1·5 BRM P57	Monte Carlo	195·42/314·50	72·43/116·56
1964	Graham Hill	GB	1·5 BRM P261	Monte Carlo	195·42/314·50	72·64/116·91
1965	Graham Hill	GB	1·5 BRM P261	Monte Carlo	195·42/314·50	74·34/119·64
1966	Jackie Stewart	GB	1·9 BRM P261	Monte Carlo	195·42/314·50	76·51/123·14
1967	Denny Hulme	NZ	3·0 Brabham BT20-Repco	Monte Carlo	195·42/314·50	75·90/122·14
1968	Graham Hill	GB	3·0 Lotus 49B-Ford	Monte Carlo	156·34/251·60	77·82/125·24
1969	Graham Hill	GB	3·0 Lotus 49B-Ford	Monte Carlo	156·34/251·60	80·18/129·04
1970	Jochen Rindt	A	3·0 Lotus 49C-Ford	Monte Carlo	156·34/251·60	81·85/131·72
1971	Jackie Stewart	GB	3·0 Tyrrell 003-Ford	Monte Carlo	156·34/251·60	83·49/134·36
1972	Jean-Pierre Beltoise	F	3·0 BRM P160B	Monte Carlo	156·34/251·60	63·85/102·75
1973	Jackie Stewart	GB	3·0 Tyrrell 006-Ford	Monte Carlo	158·87/255·68	80·96/130·29
1974	Ronnie Peterson	S	3·0 JPS/Lotus 72-Ford	Monte Carlo	158·87/255·68	80·74/129·94
1975	Niki Lauda	A	3·0 Ferrari 312T/75	Monte Carlo	152·76/245·84	75·53/121·55
1976	Niki Lauda	A	3·0 Ferrari 312T-2/76	Monte Carlo	160·52/258·34	80·36/129·32
1977	Jody Scheckter	ZA	3·0 Wolf WR1-Ford	Monte Carlo	156·41/251·71	79·61/128·12
1978	Patrick Depailler	F	3·0 Tyrrell 008-Ford	Monte Carlo	154·35/248·40	80·36/129·33
1979	Jody Scheckter	ZA	3·0 Ferrari 312T-4	Monte Carlo	156·41/251·71	81·34/130·90
1980	Carlos Reutemann	RA	3·0 Williams FW07B-Ford	Monte Carlo	156·41/251·71	81·20/130·68
1981	Gilles Villeneuve	CDN	1·5 Ferrari 126CK	Monte Carlo	156·41/251·71	82·04/132·03
1982	Riccardo Patrese	I	3·0 Brabham BT49D-Ford	Monte Carlo	156·41/251·71	82·21/132·30
1983	Keke Rosberg	SF	3·0 Williams FW08C-Ford	Monte Carlo	156·41/251·71	80·52/129·59

*Non-championship (sports cars)

Circuit data

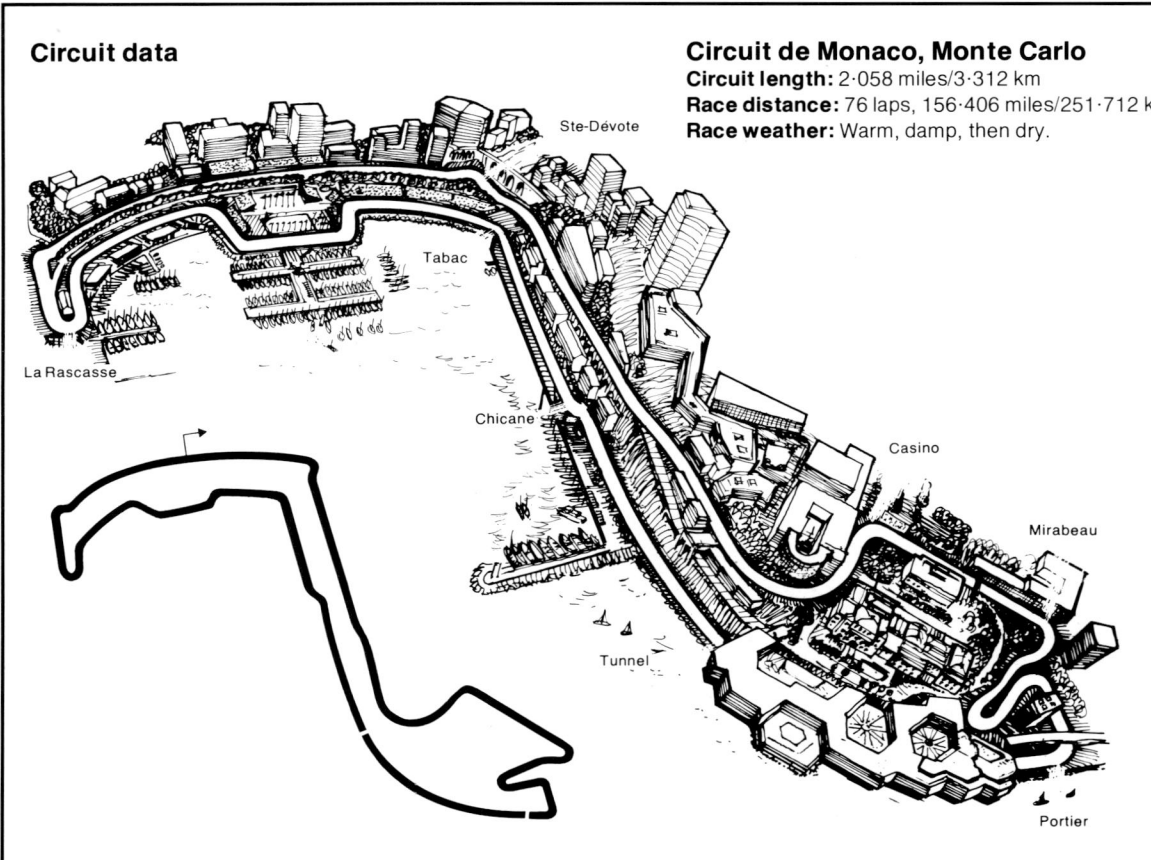

Ste-Dévote
Tabac
La Rascasse
Chicane
Casino
Mirabeau
Tunnel
Portier

Circuit de Monaco, Monte Carlo
Circuit length: 2·058 miles/3·312 km
Race distance: 76 laps, 156·406 miles/251·712 km
Race weather: Warm, damp, then dry.

Fastest laps

Driver	Time	Lap
Nelson Piquet	1m 27·283s	69
Alain Prost	1m 27·645s	60
Patrick Tambay	1m 27·911s	55
Riccardo Patrese	1m 27·922s	48
Derek Warwick	1m 28·655s	39
Jacques Laffite	1m 28·705s	49
Eddie Cheever	1m 28·719s	21
Keke Rosberg	1m 29·124s	49
Marc Surer	1m 29·159s	41
Mauro Baldi	1m 29·757s	43
Elio de Angelis	1m 30·159s	39
Chico Serra	1m 30·160s	46
Jean-Pierre Jarier	1m 30·635s	17
Danny Sullivan	1m 30·772s	46
Andrea de Cesaris	1m 32·633s	13
René Arnoux	1m 44·184s	4
Manfred Winkelhock	1m 51·607s	3
Raul Boesel	1m 52·126s	3

Points

WORLD CHAMPIONSHIP OF DRIVERS

1	Nelson Piquet	21 pts
2	Alain Prost	19
3	Patrick Tambay	17
4	Keke Rosberg	14
5	John Watson	11
6	Niki Lauda	10
7	René Arnoux	8
8	Jacques Laffite	7
9 =	Eddie Cheever	4
9 =	Marc Surer	4
11	Danny Sullivan	2
12 =	Johnny Cecotto	1
12 =	Mauro Baldi	1

CONSTRUCTORS' CUP

1	Ferrari	25 pts
2	Renault	23
3 =	McLaren	21
3 =	Brabham	21
3 =	Williams	21
6	Arrows	4
7	Tyrrell	2
8 =	Theodore	1
8 =	Alfa Romeo	1

Lap chart

		1	2	3	4	5	6	7	8	9	10	11	12	13	14	15	16	17	18	19	20	21	22	23	24	25	26	27	28	29	30	31	32	33	34	35	36	37
15	A. Prost	15	1	1	1	1	1	1	1	1	1	1	1	1	1	1	1	1	1	1	1	1	1	1	1	1	1	1	1	1	1	1	1	1	1	1	1	1
1	K. Rosberg	1	15	15	15	15	(15)	2	2	2	2	2	2	2	2	2	2	2	2	2	2	2	2	2	2	2	2	2	2	2	2	2	2	2	2	2	2	2
16	E. Cheever	16	16	16	(28)	2	2	27	27	29	29	29	29	29	29	29	29	29	29	29	29	29	29	29	29	29	29	29	29	29	29	29	29	29	29	29	29	29
28	R. Arnoux	28	28	28	2	2	16	27	29	29	35	35	35	35	35	35	35	35	35	35	35	35	35	35	35	35	35	35	35	35	35	35	35	35	35	35	35	35
27	P. Tambay	27	27	27	16	16	27	(16)	35	15	15	15	15	15	15	15	15	15	15	15	5	5	5	5	5	5	5	5	5	5	5	5	5	5	5	5	5	5
22	A. De Cesaris	22	22	2	27	27	29	29	35	15	11	11	5	5	5	5	5	5	5	5	15	15	15	15	15	16	16	16	15	15	15	15	15	15
2	J. Laffite	2	2	22	22	22	22	35	15	11	5	5	11	11	11	11	11	11	16	16	16	16	16	16	16	16	15	15	15	6	6	6	6	6	6	6
25	J. P. Jarier	25	25	25	25	29	35	22	11	5	(27)	16	16	16	16	16	16	16	(11)	6	6	6	6	6	6	6	6	6	6	27	27	27	27	27	27	27
5	N. Piquet	5	5	5	29	25	(25)	11	5	23	16	25	25	25	25	25	25	6	27	27	27	27	27	27	27	27	27	27	25	25	(25)	4	4	4	4
23	M. Baldi	23	23	29	(5)	35	11	23	23	30	25	6	6	6	6	6	6	27	25	25	25	25	25	25	25	25	25	4	4	4	23	23	23	23
30	C. Serra	30	29	23	35	23	23	30	4	23	27	27	27	27	27	27	25	4	4	4	4	4	4	4	4	23	23	23	11	11	11	11
29	M. Surer	29	30	35	23	30	30	5	4	16	6	4	4 ·	4	4	4	4	11	11	11	11	11	11	11	11	(11)	23	23	11	11	11	30	30	30	30
35	D. Warwick	35	35	30	30	11	5	4	(22)	25	30	22	22	22	(22)	23	23	23	23	23	23	23	23	23	23	23	11	11	30	30	30
6	R. Patrese	6	6	6	6	5	4	25	25	6	4	(23)	23	23	23	30	30	30	30	30	30	30	30	30	30	30	30	30	30
26	R. Boesel	26	26	26	11	(6)	6	6	6	22	22	(30)	30	30	30
9	M. Winkelhock	9	9	9	4	4	28
11	E. De Angelis	11	11	11
4	D. Sullivan	4	4	4

38	39	40	41	42	43	44	45	46	47	48	49	50	51	52	53	54	55	56	57	58	59	60	61	62	63	64	65	66	67	68	69	70	71	72	73	74	75	76
1	1	1	1	1	1	1	1	1	1	1	1	1	1	1	1	1	1	1	1	1	1	1	1	1	1	1	1	1	1	1	1	1	1	1	1	1	1	1
2	2	2	2	2	2	2	2	2	2	2	2	2	2	2	2	(2)	5	5	5	5	5	5	5	5	5	5	5	5	5	5	5	5	5	5	5	5	5	5
29	29	29	29	29	29	29	29	29	29	29	29	5	5	5	15	15	15	15	15	15	15	15	15	15	15	15	15	15	15	15	15	.15	15	15	15	15	15
35	35	35	35	35	35	35	35	35	35	35	35	15	15	15	15	15	6	6	6	6	6	27	27	27	27	27	27	27	27	27	27	27	27	27	27	27
5	5	5	5	5	5	5	5	5	5	5	5	6	6	6	6	6	27	27	27	27	27	6	(6)	6	6	4	4	4	4	4	4	4	4
15	15	15	15	15	15	15	15	15	15	15	15	27	27	27	27	4	4	4	4	4	4	4	4	23	23	23	23	23	23	23	23
6	6	6	6	6	6	6	6	6	6	6	6	(35)	4	4	4	23	23	23	23	23	23	23	23	30	30	30	30	30	30	30	30
27	27	27	27	27	27	27	27	27	27	27	27	4	23	23	23	30	30	30	30	30	30	30	30
4	4	4	4	4	4	4	4	4	4	4	23	30	30	30
23	23	23	23	23	23	23	23	23	23	23	30
11	11	11	11	11	11	11	11	11	11	11	30	(11)
30	30	30	30	30	30	30	30	30	30	30	11

The return to Spa-Francorchamps was greeted with enthusiasm – even though it rained during practice. Alain Prost, the eventual winner, points the yellow and red nose of his Renault through La Source.
Photos: International Press Agency and Paul Henri Cahier

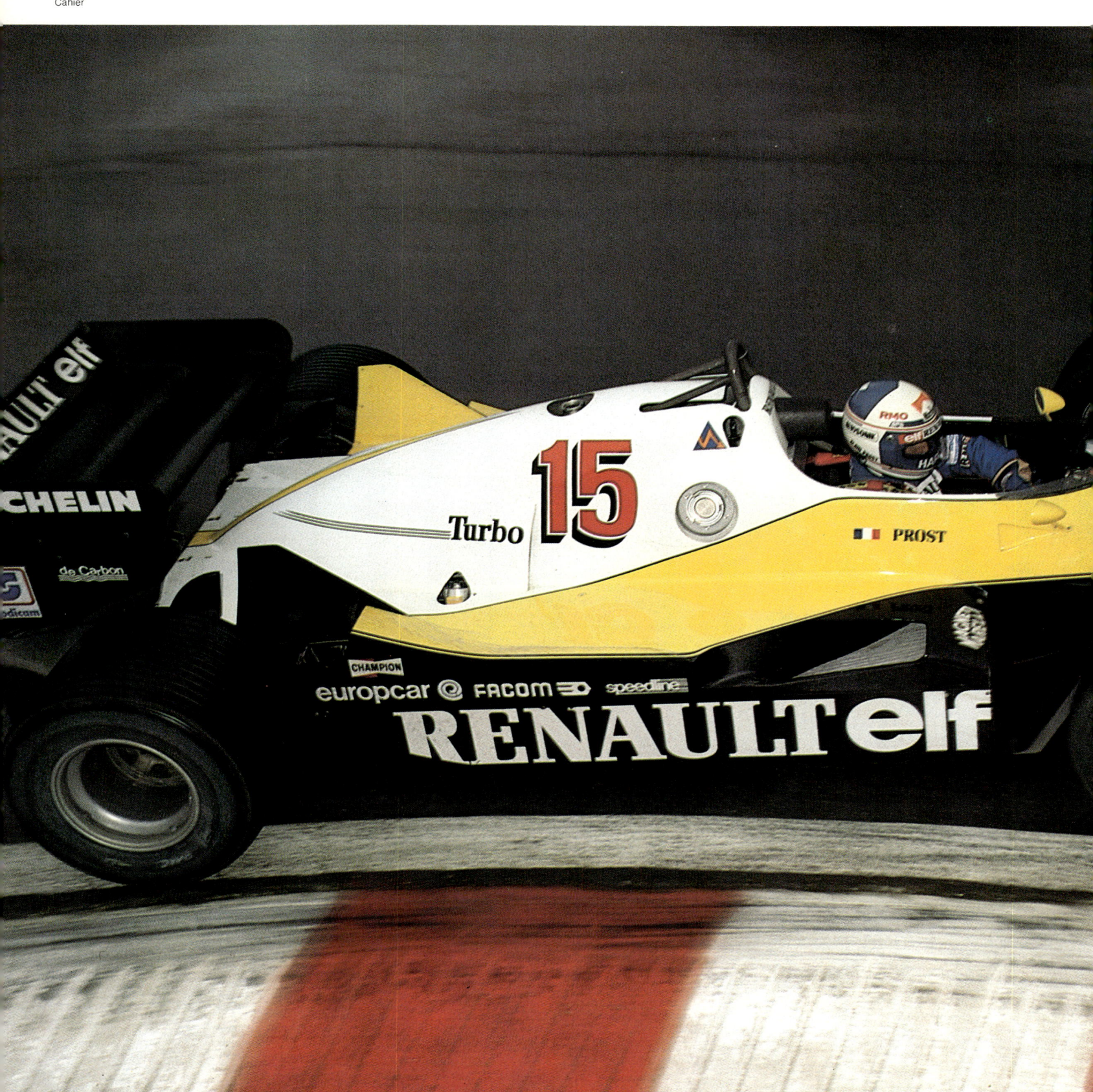

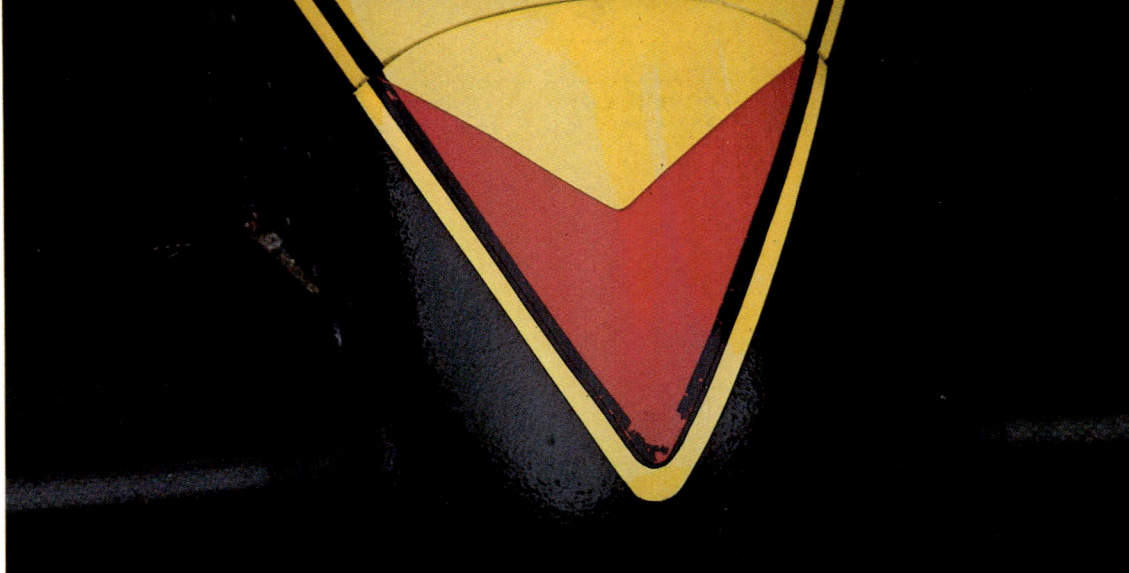

GRAND PRIX OF BELGIUM

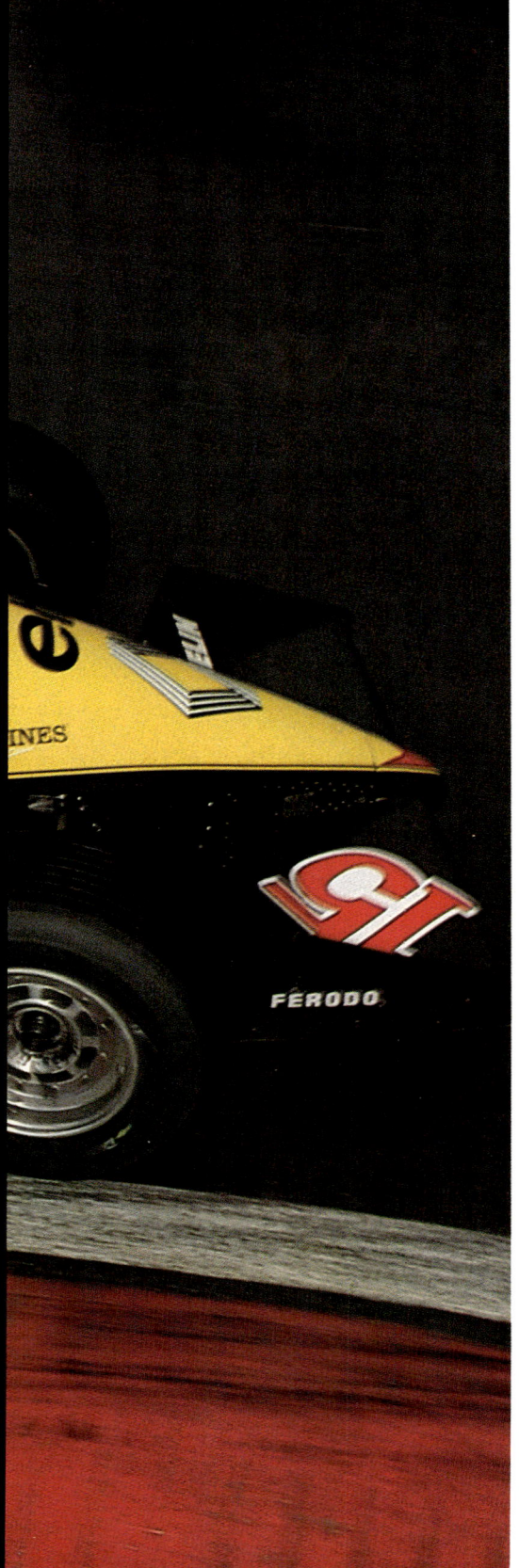

The fact that Alain Prost won the Belgian Grand Prix and regained the lead of the World Championship was almost incidental. It was not so much how he did it, as *where* he did it.

After an absence of 13 years, Formula 1 returned to the Spa-Francorchamps track and that was the talking point of the weekend — indeed, the season so far. Grand Prix racing of the Eighties had a new yardstick. It was fast, spectacular, daunting — and the drivers, to a man, loved it. Perhaps they were ready to accept the challenge, coming, as it did, seven days after the parade at Monaco but there was no doubt that the spectre of the old 8.7-mile road circuit had been banished. Worries about safety gave way to inward glows of satisfaction.

The revised 4.3-mile track included a beautifully engineered section swooping down from Les Combes to rejoin at Blanchimont, thus cutting off Burnenville, Masta and Stavelot; names now consigned to another era.

Yet La Source, the tingling Eau Rouge and the impressive climb through Raidillion remained. So, too, did the essential character of Spa-Francorchamps with its magnificent Ardennes backdrop. And with it came the weather.

On Saturday, it rained, leaving Alain Prost to take pole position with a time from Friday but, in typical fickle fashion, the sun returned for the race. There was nothing unexpected about Prost's win, however, even though the Renault-Elf driver had to give best to Andrea de Cesaris's Marlboro Alfa Romeo during the first half of the 40-lap race. The Italian had made a brilliant start to squeeze between Prost and Patrick Tambay's Ferrari and he controlled the race easily until his pit stop. A frustrating delay cost de Cesaris the lead but any hopes of his first finish in the points this season were lost when his fuel injection failed 15 laps from the finish.

Prost stroked home, his job made easier by more transmission trouble for Nelson Piquet's Parmalat Brabham-BMW as the Brazilian lost fifth gear and fell from second to fourth place in the closing stages. Tambay finished second and Eddie Cheever scored his best result to date by recovering from a poor start to take third place and give Renault a five point lead in the Constructors' Championship.

It was expected that Spa should be a turbo circuit and, equally, it was no surprise to see the Saudia Williams team lead the Cosworth cars; consistency rather than sheer pace giving Keke Rosberg and Jacques Laffite fifth and sixth places. The Candy Tolemans of Derek Warwick and Bruno Giacomelli ran reliably for once to finish seventh and eighth and, for a while, it seemed they might move into the points for the first time as the result of a rash of protests at the end of the race. Trouble had arisen at the start when Marc Surer stalled his Arrows with a broken gearbox and other drivers near the back of the grid appeared to be in distress. Derek Ongaro, having activated the red light, delayed the start by flashing the yellow light in the prescribed manner but, by then, de Cesaris and Prost had stormed off the line.

The entire field was forced to complete another warm-up and then a parade lap, the race length being reduced eventually by two laps. In the confusion, Renault took fuel onto the grid and after the race it was alleged that their cars had been illegally topped up. There were mutterings about the exhaust system on the Renaults and the French team made mention of the fact that Williams had not returned their cars to Parc Fermé immediately after the race. Protests were lodged but eventually withdrawn and the return of the Belgian Grand Prix to its spiritual home passed off without incident.

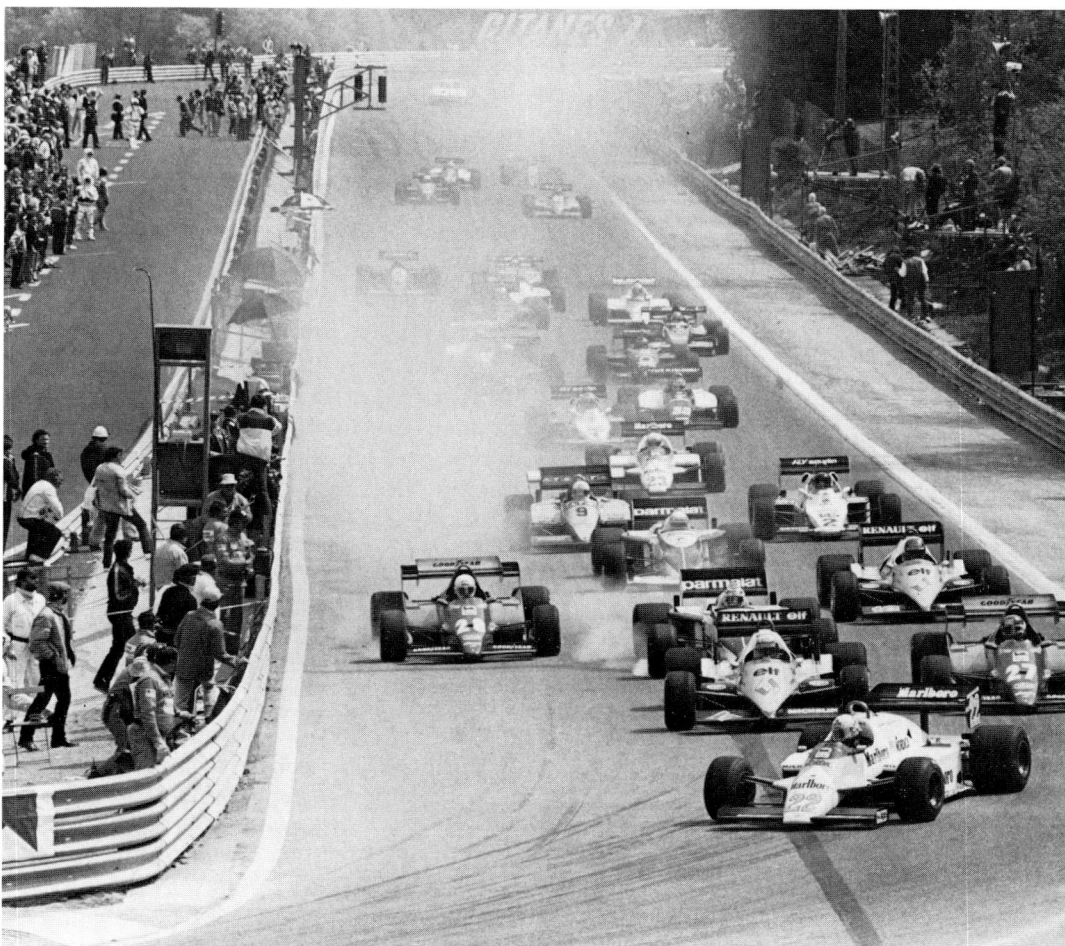

Got it right – again. A brilliant start from the second row by Andrea de Cesaris gave the Alfa Romeo the lead into La Source. Prost and Tambay follow while Piquet locks a front brake and Arnoux looks to the inside and the start at a move which forced Cheever (on Piquet's left) to run wide. Further back, Rosberg moves to his left to begin a successful run round the outside of Baldi's Alfa Romeo (23).

ENTRY AND PRACTICE

The revised circuit had been completed some years before and used for Formula 2 and Endurance racing but the prospect of a return of Formula 1 meant a complete redesign of the paddock and the construction of new pits on the approach to *La Source*. The work was more or less completed although the teams had a fair amount of delicate manoeuvring before their trucks and motor homes could be accommodated. The garages met with the mechanics' approval even if the long walk to the back of the paddock for tyres caused more than a little hardship for the 'wheel men'.

Despite the handicaps, the teams were ready, as ever, at 10 a.m., the drivers keen to get to grips with the circuit. Andrea de Cesaris set the pace during the unofficial session, new turbines in the turbo compressors continuing to give a noticeable increase in reliability, but the Alfa was eased into third place in the afternoon.

With rain due to fall during the final official session on Saturday, Alain Prost unwittingly took what would become pole position on Friday with a lap which he described as "less than perfect." By this he meant the handling was a compromise for such a long circuit, the Frenchman finding it necessary to have his RE40 bottom at *Eau Rouge* in order to have the handling just right for the more important fourth and fifth gear corners on the new section. None the less, the Renault looked reasonably stable at *Eau Rouge* compared to Tambay's Ferrari, the red car cocking wheels at all angles as it rode the bumps and changed direction under power. Patrick was not too concerned, for the 126C2/B felt fine elsewhere as his time, just one hundredth of a second slower than Prost, proved. The large rear wings had been replaced and modifications to the fuel injection system meant less engine trouble for Ferrari than before. Indeed, René Arnoux had a relatively trouble-free time even though he was over a second slower and a couple of places behind Tambay.

Splitting the two Ferraris were de Cesaris and Nelson Piquet, the Alfa Romeo driver disappointed at losing pole now that the increased engine reliability allowed a high boost for practice. He was more fortunate than his team-mate, Mauro Baldi, who blew an engine after just three high boost laps and doubtless would have been able to improve on 12th place had it not rained the following day.

Piquet's practice got off to a bad start when an engine failed on Friday morning. He then completed a few laps in the spare car only to have the transmission break and strand him out on the circuit. He therefore had little time to set the car up and fourth fastest time, one second off pole, was not a bad effort considering the car looked a handful compared to, say, the Alfa Romeo. Riccardo Patrese was sixth after a troublefree run in the dry, both Brabhams playing little part in the wet session on Saturday.

Manfred Winkelhock, on the other hand, was itching to have a go in the rain but, much to the German driver's annoyance, his ATS-BMW broke a turbo and the spare car had an electrical problem. The day before, Manfred had terrified observers as he flung the yellow and black car into seventh place to share the fourth row with Eddie Cheever. The American driver had been greatly disappointed when his V6 refused to pull cleanly on Friday and he was unable to approach the times set during testing. While the Renault may have been disappointing in the dry, Cheever was outstanding in the wet as he reeled off a string of laps comfortably quicker than Keke Rosberg.

The World Champion, of course, was nothing short of sensational, wet or dry. Struggling to make up a power deficiency and time-consuming understeer, he pushed the Williams round Spa on the limit and, on

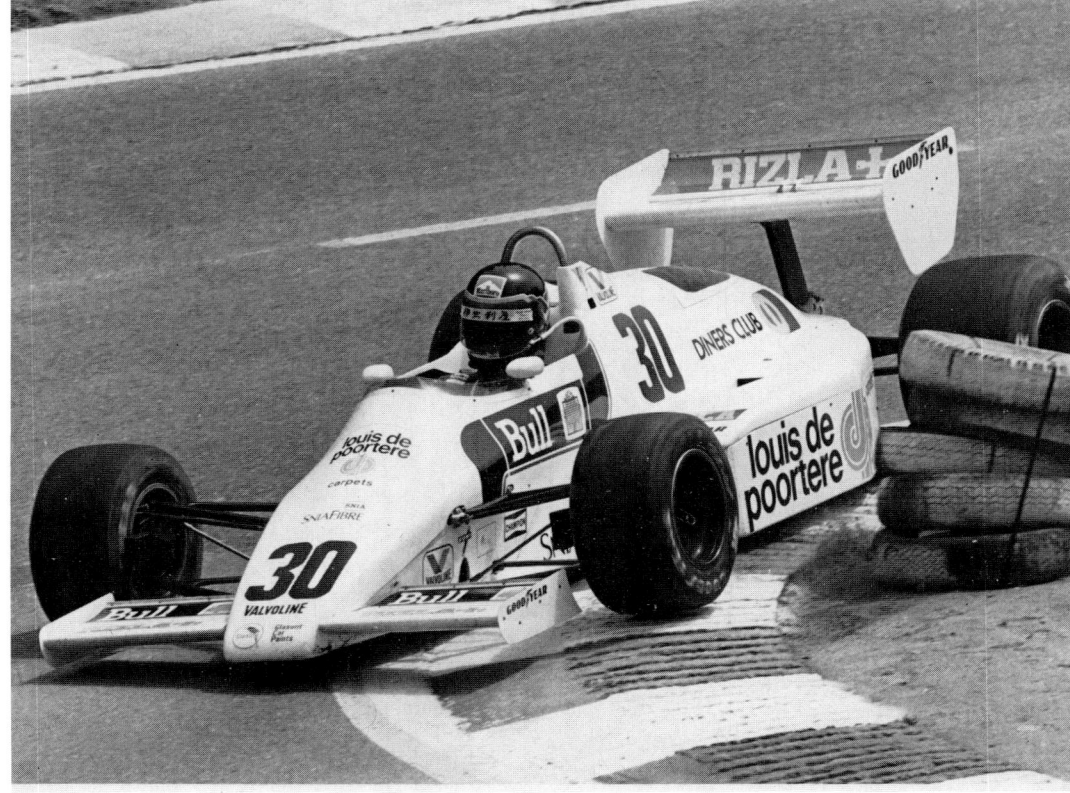

Thierry Boutsen, making his Grand Prix debut with Arrows, qualified comfortably but retired after a few laps with a broken rear rocker arm (below left).
Nelson Piquet was set to take second place when his Brabham-BMW suffered transmission trouble once more, the Brazilian losing fifth gear and two places to Patrick Tambay (following) and Eddie Cheever (below).

May:
Ligier announce plans to use Renault turbo engines with sponsorship from Antar in 1984.
Johnny Rutherford crashes Patrick Racing Wildcat Mk9 and breaks right ankle during qualifying at Indy.

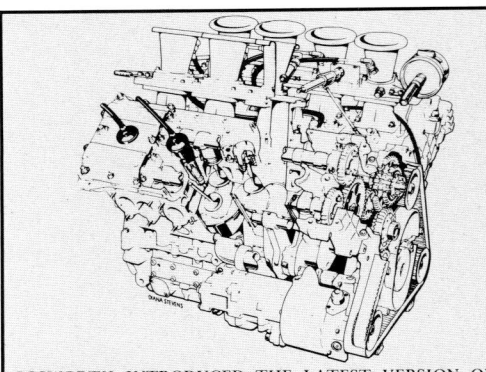

one occasion, called upon an old trick used by Stirling Moss at Reims to improve his grid time. With the timing line situated by the old pits on the downhill run to *Eau Rouge*, Rosberg took to the escape road at the previous corner, *La Source*. There, he waited for the right moment before smoking back onto the track, the Williams driver almost in third gear at a point where he would have been engaging second had he negotiated *La Source* in the normal way. He took ninth place, just ahead of the impressive Marc Surer.

Like Williams, the Arrows team were running single calliper rear brakes but, unlike their rival Cosworth team, the Arrows were found to be well balanced, Surer pitching the A6 into *La Source* like a rally car and powering it through with finger-tip control. Thierry Boutsen, after months of negotiations, at last found his way into a Formula 1 cockpit, his Arrows decked in sponsorship from various sources. The young Belgian was immediately at home although he found difficulty in making the most of his qualifiers. Even so, 18th place on the grid was extremely respectable.

At the fast, fourth gear corners at least, Jacques Laffite was one of the smoothest drivers, the Williams almost, but not quite, breaking into oversteer while tucking neatly to the apex. However, Jacques was far from happy with the understeer on second gear corners even though his problems were mild compared to those of Elio de Angelis in the John Player Lotus 93T. The large black car handled like a truck, bumping and bucking into sudden, vicious oversteer as the Italian used the horsepower from the Renault turbo to push him into 13th place. His hard work resulted in a broken front upright after hitting a kerb on Friday afternoon although the handling deficiencies were equalized by the rain on Saturday and Elio set fourth fastest time. Nigel Mansell was just half a second slower in the Cosworth 92 but the competitiveness of the field was such that the English driver was six places further back and rather concerned about a mysterious vibration from the rear of the car.

The special demands of the Belgian circuit suited

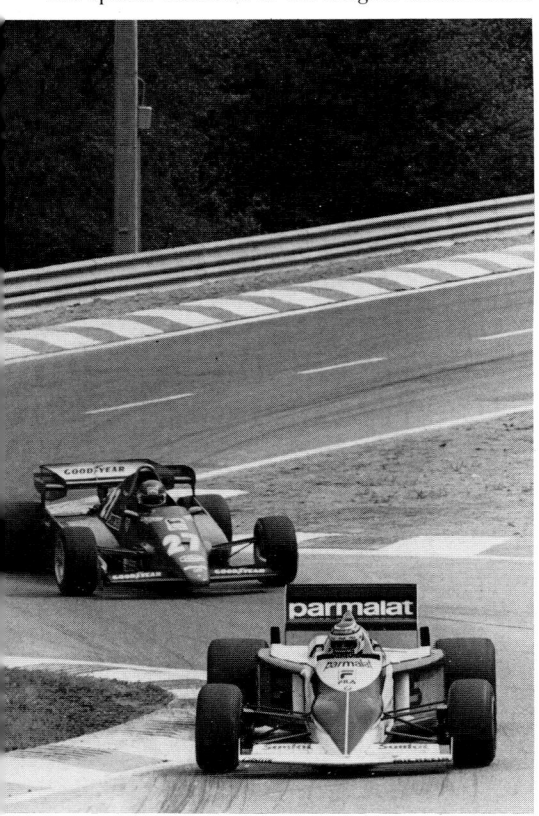

some drivers more than others and a case in point was Roberto Guerrero, the Colombian positively revelling in the challenge and whisking the Theodore round with a time good enough for the middle of the grid. Johnny Cecotto was not so happy following an incident in the morning session as the Venezuelan rushed into *Eau Rouge* just as a Brabham and Ligier were leaving the pits. The Ligier pulled out to pass the Brabham and forced Cecotto to take avoiding action, the result of which was a spin into the guard rail and damage to the front of the Theodore. A justifiably irate Cecotto, thinking the culprit was Boesel, made his way back to the pits and told the bemused South American he was not fit to ride a bicycle. Shortly afterwards, he learned the guilty party had, in fact, been Jarier!

Of more immediate importance, however, were the repairs to his car since the team did not have a spare ready to run. Cecotto had to sit out the timed practice until Guerrero had finished in order that the nose assembly could be taken off the Colombian's car and fitted to Johnny's. He qualified 25th, eleven places behind his team-mate.

The Marlboro McLaren team had been busy attempting to find a cure for their tyre problems, the result being revisions to the rear suspension and uprights on the spare car. The side plates to the rear wing joined the rear of the underwings and Lauda tried this configuration with little success, the Austrian taking 15th place and Watson 20th. Toleman, on the other hand, had called a halt to their development as they made an effort to build reliability into their cars – although you wouldn't have known it during practice. Bruno Giacomelli lost an engine on Friday morning and, when he had completed just two laps in the spare car, the clutch broke. That meant no car for Derek Warwick when his turbo failed. In the timed session, Warwick found he had lost about 700 revs with the twin-plug engine and his time was slower than a lap on race tyres and half tank of fuel in the morning. Furthermore, his Pirelli qualifying tyres barely lasted the lap, the Englishman starting his timed lap from the pit lane exit at *La Source* only to find that his tyres had gone off by the time he reached the chicane before the pits. Warwick managed 22nd place while an engine change for Giacomelli was ready half-way through the session and he was able to record 16th fastest time.

It was unusual to find Michele Alboreto in 17th place but the Italian's practice had been consumed by small adjustments as the Benetton Tyrrell team became accustomed to the latest Ford-Cosworth DFY, a second stage development with a revised head. There were mixture problems and, by the time they were cured, there was little opportunity to get the handling right and Michele managed just one satisfactory lap on qualifying tyres. Danny Sullivan took 23rd place.

Michele had disgraced himself during testing by crashing at *Eau Rouge* in a moment of over-enthusiasm. The team learnt little as a result – but it was more than Ligier had learnt since the French team had given such a valuable opportunity a miss. It showed as Jarier and Boesel fought with the Citroen-based hydraulic suspension, the cars hopelessly out of tune with the demands of the circuit, Jarier taking 21st place, Boesel scraping onto the back row. Apart from the removal of the large rear wings and the addition of refuelling equipment, the Ligiers were little changed.

Corrado Fabi qualified the Osella-Cosworth once more but Piercarlo Ghinzani looked ill at ease in the Alfa Romeo-engined example and joined Eliseo Salazar as a non-starter. The RAM March had a narrow track rear suspension but the Chilean driver was hopelessly off the pace and his future with the team seemed in doubt since his sponsorship depended on him at least qualifying; something which he had just failed to do for the fourth race in succession.

COSWORTH INTRODUCED THE LATEST VERSION OF the Ford-Cosworth DFY at Spa-Francorchamps, a project which the Northamptonshire company embarked on in 1982 following FISA's declaration of a proposed restoration of the equivalence between normally aspirated 3-litre engines and 1.5-litre turbos in 1985.

The work of Mario Illien, a Swiss engineer employed at Cosworth since 1979, the latest DFY featured a new cylinder head design distinguished from the outside by narrower cam boxes integral with the head casting. The revised bore and stroke, introduced on the 'first stage' DFY at Paul Ricard, meant a lowering of the roof of the combustion chamber to maintain the 12.3-to-1 compression ratio. This was achieved by decreasing the angle between the opposed valves. Instead of being arranged symmetrically at 16 deg each side of the cylinder axis, the inlets were at 10 deg and the exhausts at 12½ deg, making the included angle 22½ instead of 32 deg.

Integral cam carriers saved weight in the cylinder heads and Cosworth claimed substantial improvements in the power delivery across the rev band. The step in the torque curve which caused a sudden surge at 6,500 rpm had been eliminated and the overall improvement in efficiency provided more power and torque for a negligible increase in fuel consumption.

Michele Alboreto used the DFY during practice but a fresh engine, installed in the Tyrrell for the race, failed during the warm-up and the Italian driver raced a 'first stage' unit instead.

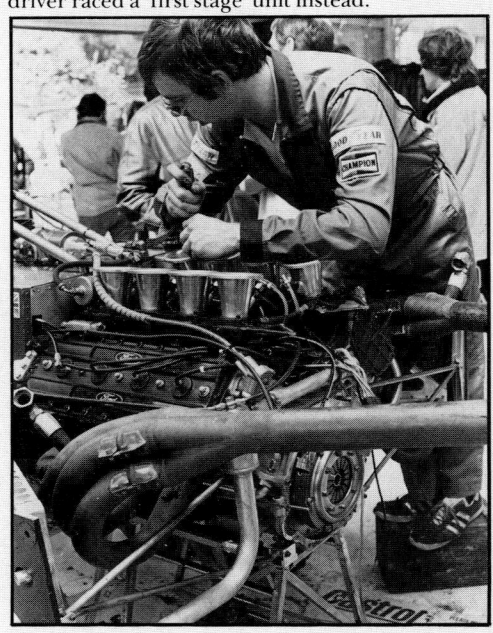

143

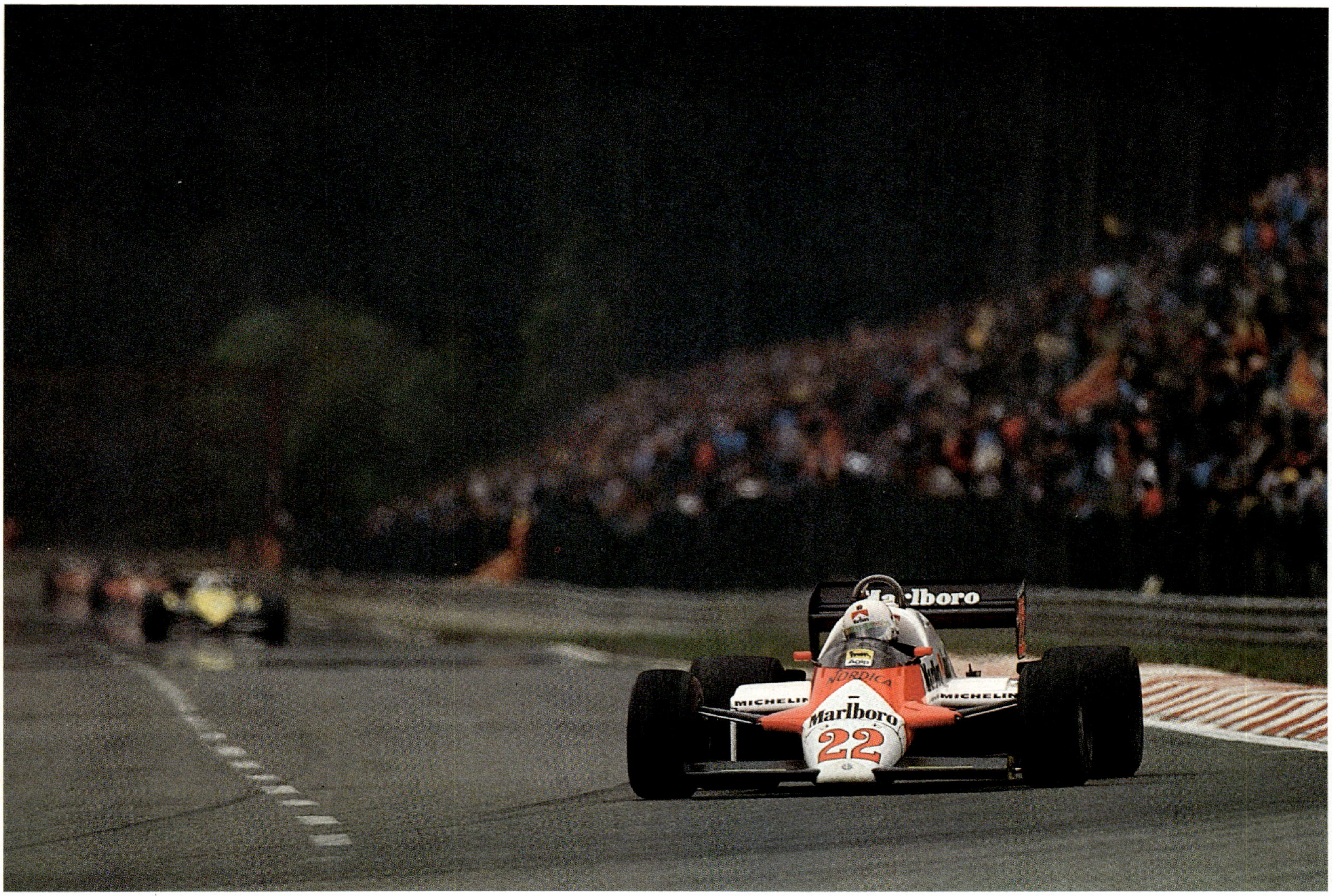

RACE

There had been gloomy prognostications from certain quarters at the end of the wet practice on Saturday. Lauda and Laffite, among others, said they would not be happy about racing if it rained as heavily as it had done during the latter part of the day. The rivers of water running across the track made conditions extremely dangerous, never mind the fact that the pine trees tended to hold the spray, making visibility extremely hazardous while following another car.

In the event, a cloudy start to the day gave way to sunshine as the warm-up began and it was clear that the turbos would be in a position to use their power; a fact much regretted by Keke Rosberg who, it was said, had hoped for a downpour!

Derek Warwick had other things on his mind when a turbo failure put him into the spare car (which was on wet settings) for the remainder of the session although a replacement was ready in time for the race. Similarly, a fuel pump problem for Jacques Laffite was rectified while the Tyrrell mechanics worked like beavers to replace a brand new DFY which had blown on Alboreto's car.

The 26 cars left the pits and made their way to the grid, Rosberg, Arnoux, Boesel and Laffite slipping back through the pit lane to complete an extra lap. The new position for the start meant the back few rows of the grid disappeared round the left-hander before the pits but, anticipating this, the organisers had installed Derek Ongaro and an additional set of starting lights halfway down the grid. Which was just as well – otherwise the start might have been even more chaotic than it actually turned out.

Trouble began when Marc Surer stripped first gear after a full-blooded practice start and stalled his car. The red light had just come on and, almost immediately, Laffite and de Angelis were waving their arms in the air along with Surer. Realising the stricken cars were close together and the potential source of a dangerous bottleneck, Ongaro brought the

emergency procedure into play and operated the flashing yellow light. This meant, 'start delayed; remain in grid positions and await further instructions.' Unfortunately, de Cesaris and Prost had other ideas, the pair storming off the grid as soon as they saw the red light go out.

The Alfa Romeo, which had rushed through from the second row, and the Renault stormed through *Eau Rouge* while the rest of the field followed at a leisurely pace. Surer's Arrows, meanwhile, was pushed into the pit lane and the Swiss prepared to start in the spare car.

As the cars returned to the grid, it was clear they would need to do another 4.3-mile parade lap and confusion arose over the race distance which, said the rules, would be reduced one lap per false start. Matters were complicated further when mechanics started climbing over the barrier, the Renault and Ferrari teams taking fuel onto the grid. Marco Piccinini of Ferrari was horrified; he knew the rules forbade refuelling on the track and he urged his men not to add petrol to the red cars. The Renault mechanics took their fuel to the cars but, according to Jean Sage, none was added. Later, one or two rivals were to suggest that refuelling had, in fact, taken place. Either way, it was not necessary since the organisers announced that two laps would be deducted from the race distance to cover the abortive lap, triggered off by Prost and de Cesaris, and the parade lap which was about to take place.

All was well second time round and, once again, de Cesaris pulled off another amazing start, the Alfa Romeo finding a way through a seemingly impossible gap between Prost and Tambay to lead the field through *La Source*. Piquet locked his brakes and an ensuing bumping of wheels with Arnoux meant the Ferrari and Brabham forced Cheever to run wide and lightly damage a wheel.

By the time they had completed the first lap, de Cesaris had opened a lead of two lengths from Prost and the two Ferraris, led by Tambay. Piquet was fifth ahead of Winkelhock and the Williams pair, Rosberg and Laffite, while an irate Cheever was back in ninth

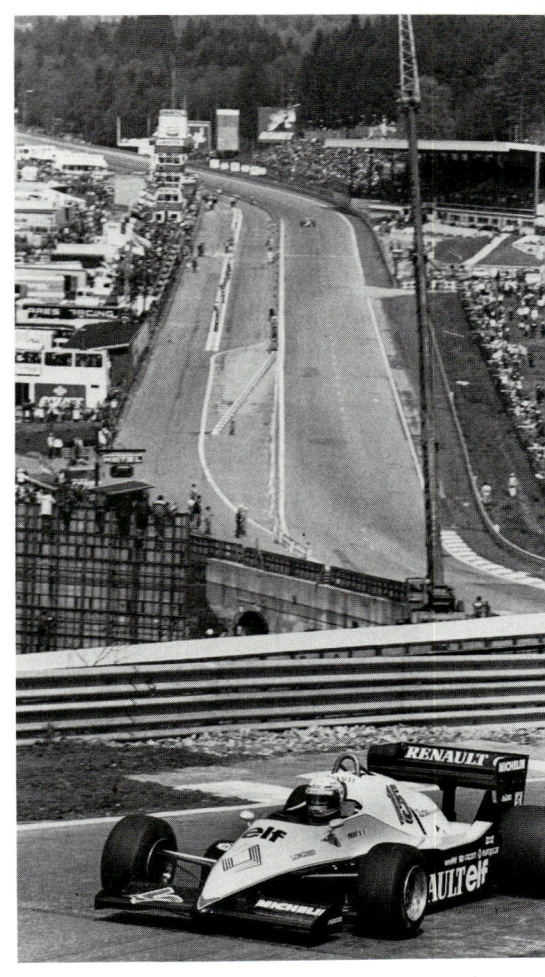

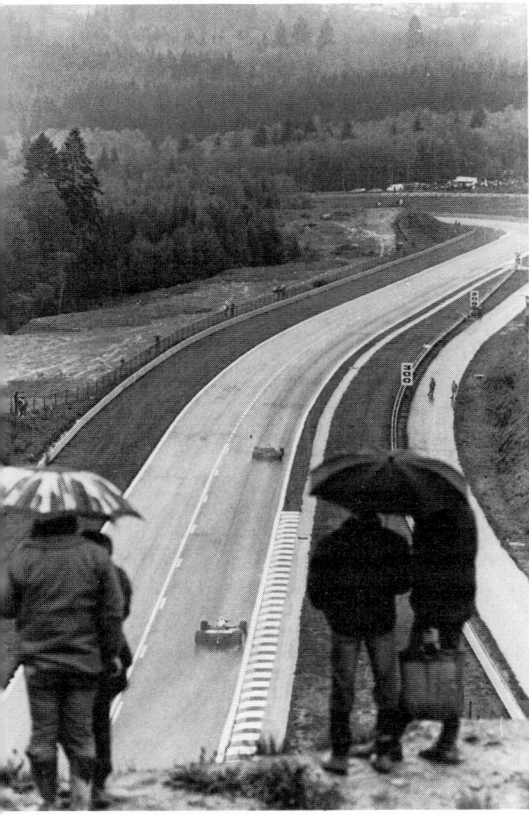

place. Baldi was tenth but soon to retire with a broken throttle assembly – or so the official reason said. The Alfa Romeo team failed to explain how their car had managed to drive into the pits with little difficulty. Already out was a very disappointed Riccardo Patrese, the Brabham stopping on the climb to *Les Combes* with a broken conrod.

De Cesaris, driving calmly and quickly under great pressure, opened the gap further while Prost had to contend with close attention from the two Ferraris. Piquet was a couple of seconds behind and being chased hard by Winkelhock who, in turn, was unable to shake off a most determined Rosberg. Cheever had got past Laffite and the Williams was comfortably ahead of de Angelis and a furious battle for 11th place. Still revelling in the challenge of Spa, Guerrero was holding off Lauda, Giacomelli and Warwick while further back, Alboreto and Watson were running in close company and about to be joined by Jarier who was making an impressive charge from the back of the field.

Earlier, Watson had been receiving attention from Thierry Boutsen once the Belgian driver had worked his way past Mansell's Lotus but a broken rear rocker arm soon had the Arrows driver in the pits. At first, Boutsen thought the problem might be tyres but one more lap on fresh rubber confirmed the problem to be more serious and he retired on lap five.

By lap nine, de Cesaris had pulled out a lead of five seconds while Prost had been unable to shake himself free from Tambay since the Renault was planning to stop at a comparatively late stage in the race and was therefore carrying more fuel in the early laps. Further back, Arnoux felt his engine was beginning to lose its edge and the French driver began using the kerbs in an effort to keep in touch with his team-mate, and, at the same time, stay out of reach of Piquet and Winkelhock.

Through nothing short of sheer bravado, Rosberg was managing to keep the ATS in sight even though

the Williams was losing out to BMW horsepower on the long climb to *Les Combes*. Cheever, suffering from oversteer, was making little impression while Laffite still managed to remain clear of the furious battle led by de Angelis and Guerrero. Watson was keeping pace with Alboreto but, for a couple of laps, the canny Ulsterman had been infuriating Jarier by keeping the Ligier out of 16th place.

Leaving the chicane at the end of lap nine, Watson had slightly less traction than Jarier and the Ligier was glued to the McLaren's gearbox as the pair raced onto the pit straight, Watson moving to the right to take the line for *La Source*. Jarier's momentum took him alongside on Watson's left and the pair reached the braking area side-by-side. Watson, of course, was on the inside but Jarier kept a tight line and the right-rear wheel of the Ligier smashed into Watson's left front. Both drivers retired instantly.

Lap 10 and a change to the lap chart came about when Warwick, having passed his team-mate not long before, shot ahead of Lauda and Guerrero. The Toleman driver had reckoned the Theodore and the McLaren were holding each other up and, by hanging back slightly and taking a flat-out run through *Eau Rouge*, Warwick was able to power ahead of a surprised Lauda and Guerrero on the run up to *Les Combes* and take 11th place. Two laps later and he was ahead of de Angelis, the Toleman inheriting ninth place not long after when Winkelhock made for the pits to have a broken fuel injector pipe replaced.

Piquet took fourth place from Arnoux by running round the outside of the Ferrari as they approached *Eau Rouge* on lap 17 and, two laps later, Arnoux stopped for fuel and tyres. On the way into the pit lane, he passed the Alfa Romeo mechanics as they made a mess of de Cesaris's stop by bungling the wheel change at the left-rear, a move which would effectively cost Andrea his well-earned lead.

On lap 20, Rosberg, Cheever and Giacomelli came in, the Renault's stop being the only one which was entirely trouble-free. Rosberg was delayed slightly as Cheever made his exit and it took two or three laps for the Goodyears to warm up sufficiently to Rosberg's liking. But there was worse trouble down at the Toleman pit. The mechanics found the fuel nozzle would not open the intake valve and, after a quick shuffle, Giacomelli was given the fuel destined for Warwick. Thus, when Warwick came in two laps later, they tried again with Giacomelli's fuel line but the same thing happened. The tyres had been changed and Warwick was sent out again while the team tried to figure out what was wrong with the nozzle. (It was discovered later than the nozzle was slightly out of shape caused, possibly, by someone dropping it). The mechanics had to work quickly for Warwick had very little fuel remaining and he was called in again on lap 25. This time, the fuel went in successfully but, by now, Warwick had lost three places.

The remaining pit stops went off without incident and the mishap in the Alfa Romeo pit meant Prost now led the Italian by 10 seconds. There had been tell-tale puffs of blue smoke from the Alfa as de Cesaris hurried away from the pits and, sure enough, a fine drive from Andrea came to an end when the Alfa Romeo crawled to a halt with engine trouble on lap 25.

Earlier, Guerrero and Arnoux had stopped with similar problems; Fabi had retired with broken suspension after a steady run and Winkelhock had been very fortunate to walk away from a high speed accident when the right-rear wheel parted company with his car in the middle of the fast, fourth gear left-hander.

With Prost now controlling a 27-second gap over Piquet, the result seemed a foregone conclusion since the Renault was handling perfectly on the same fuel load as everyone else and a tyre vibration, caused by

blistering, had disappeared with the fitting of his second set of Michelins. Tambay had lost time while his Goodyears warmed up but the Ferrari driver held third place ahead of Cheever who was now lapping as quickly as Prost following the stop for fresh tyres. Rosberg continued to put on an inspired show in fifth place, well clear of Laffite who, after his pit stop, now had to contend with Lauda, the McLaren having raced without stopping. However, that battle was to end on lap 34 when Lauda crawled into the pits with a broken valve sprayed over an inlet trumpet on his Cosworth. Thus, Giacomelli and Warwick moved into seventh and eighth places ahead of de Angelis, now the sole surviving Lotus after Mansell had ended a frustrating struggle at the back of the field when the shaft driving the gearbox oil pump had broken.

Gear selection trouble was also on Piquet's mind as the race entered its final stages, the Brazilian eventually losing fifth. He could cope everywhere but on the climb to *Les Combes* and he could only watch helplessly as first Tambay and then Cheever steamed by to rob the Brabham driver of three championship points.

Alboreto was another driver to be in gearbox trouble, a ball bearing having worked its way into the selector forks causing the gears to come and go without warning. A call in the pits proved worthless, the mechanics sending Michele on his way in the hope that he might struggle to the finish.

Prost was in no such difficulty, the Renault reeling off the final laps at a reduced pace, the mechanics hardly daring to wave as he passed the pits for the last time and made his way to the finish line which was on the hill after *La Source*. Twenty-three seconds later, Tambay crossed the line with Cheever following in third place and the frustrated Piquet a few lengths behind. Rosberg and Laffite deserved the final three points and both Williams drivers pulled over and stopped once they had taken the flag; the fuel load was marginal enough to suggest they might not be able to complete the slowing down lap!

Warwick took seventh place from his team-mate on the last lap when Giacomelli, driving flat out in pursuit of Laffite, spun his Toleman but was able to continue and finish eighth. In fact, he was lucky to finish at all since, having been forced to take on the fuel designated for Warwick a couple of laps later, Giacomelli returned to the pits with his tank almost empty. Warwick, on the other hand, had been given Bruno's fuel and had eight gallons to spare at the finish!

De Angelis was ninth while Cecotto brought his Theodore into 10th place after Alboreto had dropped back to finish 14th and last behind Surer (a disappointed 11th after such a promising practice), Sullivan and Boesel. For a while after the race had finished, there was the thought that they all might move up a couple of places in the light of a wave of protests. Brabham and Williams lodged protests over refuelling on the grid by Renault and Ferrari although they were withdrawn. Renault were fined $5,000 for taking fuel onto the track and, at one point, there was talk of Renault protesting Williams for not taking their cars to Parc Fermé within the allotted time.

Of more serious consequence, however, were reports of a protest by Brabham against the exhaust system on the Renaults. It was alleged an aerodynamic advantage was to be had by the exhaust gases energising the boundary layer of air under the car's underwing in order to reduce turbulence. The organisers announced later that "all protests have been withdrawn" and, although there was doubt that Brabham had actually made a protest, the results were confirmed.

Grand Prix racing had returned to Spa Francorchamps and, for the time being at least, all was well with the world.

Entries and practice times

No.	Driver	Nat	Car	Tyre	Engine	Entrant	Practice 1	Practice 2
1	Keke Rosberg	SF	Saudia WILLIAMS FW08C	G	Ford Cosworth DFV	TAG Williams Team	**2m 07·975s**	2m 30·151s
2	Jacques Laffite	F	Saudia WILLIAMS FW08C	G	Ford Cosworth DFV	TAG Williams Team	**2m 09·153s**	3m 20·872s
3	Michele Alboreto	I	Benetton TYRRELL 011	G	Ford Cosworth DFV/DFY	Benetton Tyrrell Team	**2m 09·739s**	2m 31·533s
4	Danny Sullivan	USA	Benetton TYRRELL 011	G	Ford Cosworth DFV/DFY	Benetton Tyrrell Team	**2m 11·683s**	2m 38·284s
5	Nelson Piquet	BR	Parmalat BRABHAM BT52	M	BMW M12/13	Fila Sport	**2m 05·628s**	3m 01·465s
6	Riccardo Patrese	I	Parmalat BRABHAM BT52	M	BMW M12/13	Fila Sport	**2m 06·137s**	3m 01·358s
7	John Watson	GB	Marlboro McLAREN MP4/1C	M	Ford Cosworth DFV/DFY	Marlboro McLaren International	**2m 10·318s**	—
8	Niki Lauda	A	Marlboro McLAREN MP4/1C	M	Ford Cosworth DFV/DFY	Marlboro McLaren International	**2m 09·475s**	3m 00·356s
9	Manfred Winkelhock	D	ATS D6	G	BMW M12/13	Team ATS	**2m 06·264s**	2m 44·663s
11	Elio de Angelis	I	John Player Special LOTUS 93T	P	Renault EF1	John Player Team Lotus	**2m 09·310s**	2m 30·478s
12	Nigel Mansell	GB	John Player Special LOTUS 92	P	Ford Cosworth DFV/DFY	John Player Team Lotus	**2m 09·924s**	—
15	Alain Prost	F	Elf RENAULT RE40	M	Renault EF1	Equipe Renault Elf	**2m 04·615s**	2m 34·212s
16	Eddie Cheever	USA	Elf RENAULT RE40	M	Renault EF1	Equipe Renault Elf	**2m 07·294s**	2m 25·700s
17	Eliseo Salazar	RCH	MARCH-RAM 01	P	Ford Cosworth DFV	RAM Automotive Team March	**2m 18·696s**	—
22	Andrea de Cesaris	I	Marlboro ALFA ROMEO 183T	M	Alfa Romeo 183T	Marlboro Team Alfa Romeo	**2m 04·840s**	—
23	Mauro Baldi	I	Marlboro ALFA ROMEO 183T	M	Alfa Romeo 183T	Marlboro Team Alfa Romeo	**2m 09·225s**	—
25	Jean-Pierre Jarier	F	Gitanes LIGIER JS21	M	Ford Cosworth DFV	Equipe Ligier Gitanes	**2m 11·354s**	2m 49·311s
26	Raul Boesel	BR	Gitanes LIGIER JS21	M	Ford Cosworth DFV	Equipe Ligier Gitanes	**2m 12·310s**	2m 34·659s
27	Patrick Tambay	F	Fiat FERRARI 126C2/B	G	Ferrari 126C	Scuderia Ferrari SpA SEFAC	**2m 04·626s**	2m 35·056s
28	René Arnoux	F	Fiat FERRARI 126C2/B	G	Ferrari 126C	Scuderia Ferrari SpA SEFAC	**2m 05·737s**	2m 30·961s
29	Marc Surer	CH	ARROWS A6	G	Ford Cosworth DFV	Arrows Racing Team	**2m 08·587s**	2m 35·016s
30	Thierry Boutsen	B	ARROWS A6	G	Ford Cosworth DFV	Arrows Racing Team	**2m 09·876s**	2m 35·832s
31	Corrado Fabi	I	OSELLA FA1D	M	Ford Cosworth DFV	Osella Squadra Corse	**2m 11·734s**	2m 41·895s
32	Piercarlo Ghinzani	I	OSELLA FA1E	M	Alfa Romeo 1260	Osella Squadra Corse	**2m 13·738s**	—
33	Roberto Guerrero	COL	THEODORE N183	G	Ford Cosworth DFV	Theodore Racing Team	**2m 09·322s**	2m 31·077s
34	Johnny Cecotto	YV	THEODORE N183	G	Ford Cosworth DFV	Theodore Racing Team	**2m 11·860s**	2m 43·780s
35	Derek Warwick	GB	Candy TOLEMAN TG183B	P	Hart 415T	Candy Toleman Motorsport	**2m 11·474s**	2m 30·477s
36	Bruno Giacomelli	I	Candy TOLEMAN TG183B	P	Hart 415T	Candy Toleman Motorsport	**2m 09·706s**	2m 35·556s

	Fri pm Warm, dry
	Sat pm Cool, wet

Friday morning and Saturday morning practice sessions not officially recorded.

G – Goodyear, M – Michelin, P – Pirelli.

Starting grid

15 PROST (2m 04·615s)
Renault

27 TAMBAY (2m 04·626s)
Ferrari

22 DE CESARIS (2m 04·840s)
Alfa Romeo

5 PIQUET (2m 05·628s)
Brabham

28 ARNOUX (2m 05·737s)
Ferrari

6 PATRESE (2m 06·137s)
Brabham

9 WINKELHOCK (2m 06·264s)
ATS

16 CHEEVER (2m 07·294s)
Renault

1 ROSBERG (2m 07·975s)
Williams

*29 SURER (2m 08·587s)
Arrows

2 LAFFITE (2m 09·153s)
Williams

23 BALDI (2m 09·225s)
Alfa Romeo

11 DE ANGELIS (2m 09·310s)
Lotus

33 GUERRERO (2m 09·322s)
Theodore

8 LAUDA (2m 09·475s)
McLaren

36 GIACOMELLI (2m 09·706s)
Toleman

3 ALBORETO (2m 09·739s)
Tyrrell

30 BOUTSEN (2m 09·876s)
Arrows

12 MANSELL (2m 09·924s)
Lotus

7 WATSON (2m 10·318s)
McLaren

25 JARIER (2m 11·354s)
Ligier

35 WARWICK (2m 11·474s)
Toleman

4 SULLIVAN (2m 11·683s)
Tyrrell

31 FABI (2m 11·734s)
Osella

34 CECOTTO (2m 11·860s)
Theodore

26 BOESEL (2m 12·310s)
Ligier

* Started from pit lane in spare car
Did not start:
32 Ghinzani (Osella), 2m 13·738s, did not qualify
17 Salazar (RAM March), 2m 18·696s, did not qualify

Results and retirements

Place	Driver	Car	Laps	Time and Speed (mph/km/h)/Retirement
1	Alain Prost	Renault t/c V6	40	1h 27m 11·502s	119·135/191·729
2	Patrick Tambay	Ferrari t/c V6	40	1h 27m 34·684s	118·619/190·9
3	Eddie Cheever	Renault t/c V6	40	1h 27m 51·371s	118·247/190·3
4	Nelson Piquet	Brabham-BMW t/c 4	40	1h 27m 53·797s	118·185/190·2
5	Keke Rosberg	Williams-Cosworth V8	40	1h 28m 01·982s	117·998/189·9
6	Jacques Laffite	Williams-Cosworth V8	40	1h 28m 44·016s	117·066/188·4
7	Derek Warwick	Toleman-Hart t/c 4	40	1h 29m 10·041s	116·507/187·5
8	Bruno Giacomelli	Toleman-Hart t/c 4	40	1h 29m 49·775s	115·637/186·1
9	Elio de Angelis	Lotus-Renault t/c V6	39	
10	Johnny Cecotto	Theodore-Cosworth V8	39	
11	Marc Surer	Arrows-Cosworth V8	39	
12	Danny Sullivan	Tyrrell-Cosworth V8	39	
13	Raul Boesel	Ligier-Cosworth V8	39	
14	Michele Alboreto	Tyrrell-Cosworth V8	38	
	Niki Lauda	McLaren-Cosworth V8	33	Engine
	Nigel Mansell	Lotus-Cosworth V8	30	Gearbox
	Andrea de Cesaris	Alfa Romeo t/c V8	25	Engine
	Roberto Guerrero	Theodore-Cosworth V8	23	Engine
	René Arnoux	Ferrari t/c V6	22	Engine
	Corrado Fabi	Osella-Cosworth V8	19	Rear suspension
	Manfred Winkelhock	ATS-BMW t/c 4	18	Rear wheel came off
	John Watson	McLaren-Cosworth V8	8	Accident with Jarier
	Jean-Pierre Jarier	Ligier-Cosworth V8	8	Accident with Watson
	Thierry Boutsen	Arrows-Cosworth V8	4	Rear suspension
	Mauro Baldi	Alfa Romeo t/c V8	3	Throttle linkage
	Riccardo Patrese	Brabham-BMW t/c 4	0	Engine

Fastest lap: de Cesaris, on lap 17, 2m 07·493s, 121·923mph/196·217km/h (record).
Previous lap record: Michele Alboreto/Piercarlo Ghinzani (Gp6 Lancia-Martini 1.4 t/c), 2m 21·18s, 110·46mph/177·77km/h (1982).

Past winners

Year	Driver	Nat	Car	Circuit	Distance miles/km	Speed mph/km/h
1925	Antonio Ascari	I	2·0 Alfa Romeo P2 s/c	Francorchamps	501·63/807·29	74·44/119·80
1930	Louis Chiron	F	2·0 Bugatti T35C s/c	Francorchamps	371·58/598·00	72·12/116·08
1931	"W. Williams"/	GB				
	Caberto Conelli		2·3 Bugatti T51 s/c	Francorchamps	820·46/1320·40	82·05/132·04
1933	Tazio Nuvolari	I	3·0 Maserati 8CM s/c	Francorchamps	369·59/594·80	89·27/143·66
1934	René Drefus	F	3·3 Bugatti T59 s/c	Francorchamps	369·59/594·80	89·95/139·94
1935	Rudi Caracciola	D	4·0 Mercedes-Benz W25 s/c	Francorchamps	314·15/505·57	97·91/157·57
1937	Rudolf Hasse	D	6·0 Auto Union C-Type s/c	Francorchamps	314·15/505·57	104·11/167·56
1939	Hermann Lang	D	3·0 Mercedes-Benz W163 s/c	Francorchamps	314·15/505·57	94·43/151·97
1946	Eugene Chaboud	F	3·5 Delahaye	Brussels	73·10/117·64	64·73/104·18
1947	Jean-Pierre Wimille	B	1·5 Alfa Romeo 158 s/c	Francorchamps	315·34/507·49	95·32/153·40
1949	Louis Rosier	F	4·5 Lago-Talbot	Francorchamps	315·34/507·49	96·99/156·09
1950	Juan Manuel Fangio	RA	1·5 Alfa Romeo 158 s/c	Francorchamps	307·08/494·20	110·04/177·09
1951	Giuseppe Farina	I	1·5 Alfa Romeo 159 s/c	Francorchamps	315·85/508·31	114·32/183·99
1952	Alberto Ascari	I	2·0 Ferrari 500	Francorchamps	315·85/508·31	103·13/165·96
1953	Alberto Ascari	I	2·0 Ferrari 500	Francorchamps	315·85/508·31	112·47/181·00
1954	Juan Manuel Fangio	RA	2·5 Maserati 250F	Francorchamps	315·85/508·31	115·06/185·17
1955	Juan Manuel Fangio	RA	2·5 Mercedes-Benz W196	Francorchamps	315·85/508·31	118·83/191·24
1956	Peter Collins	GB	2·5 Lancia-Ferrari D50	Francorchamps	315·85/508·31	118·44/190·61
1958	Tony Brooks	GB	2·5 Vanwall	Francorchamps	210·27/338·40	129·92/209·09
1960	Jack Brabham	AUS	2·5 Cooper T53-Climax	Francorchamps	315·41/507·60	133·63/215·06
1961	Phil Hill	USA	1·5 Ferrari Dino 156	Francorchamps	262·84/423·00	128·15/206·24
1962	Jim Clark	GB	1·5 Lotus 25-Climax	Francorchamps	280·36/451·19	131·90/212·27
1963	Jim Clark	GB	1·5 Lotus 25-Climax	Francorchamps	280·36/451·19	114·10/183·63
1964	Jim Clark	GB	1·5 Lotus 25-Climax	Francorchamps	280·36/451·19	132·79/213·71
1965	Jim Clark	GB	1·5 Lotus 33-Climax	Francorchamps	280·36/451·19	117·16/188·55
1966	John Surtees	GB	3·0 Ferrari 312/66	Francorchamps	245·32/394·80	113·93/183·36
1967	Dan Gurney	USA	3·0 Eagle T1G-Gurney-Weslake	Francorchamps	245·32/394·80	145·99/234·95
1968	Bruce McLaren	NZ	3·0 McLaren M7A-Ford	Francorchamps	245·32/394·80	147·14/236·80
1970	Pedro Rodriguez	MEX	3·0 BRM P153	Francorchamps	245·32/394·80	149·97/241·36
1972	Emerson Fittipaldi	BR	3·0 JPS/Lotus 72-Ford	Nivelles-Baulers	196·69/316·54	113·35/182·42
1973	Jackie Stewart	GB	3·0 Tyrrell 006-Ford	Zolder	183·55/295·39	107·74/173·38
1974	Emerson Fittipaldi	BR	3·0 McLaren M23-Ford	Nivelles-Baulers	196·69/316·54	113·10/182·02
1975	Niki Lauda	A	3·0 Ferrari 312T	Zolder	185·38/298·34	107·05/172·28
1976	Niki Lauda	A	3·0 Ferrari 312T/76	Zolder	185·38/298·34	108·11/173·98
1977	Gunnar Nilsson	S	3·0 JPS/Lotus 78-Ford	Zolder	185·38/298·34	96·64/155·53
1978	Mario Andretti	USA	3·0 JPS/Lotus 79-Ford	Zolder	185·38/298·34	111·38/179·24
1979	Jody Scheckter	ZA	3·0 Ferrari 312T-4	Zolder	185·38/298·34	111·24/179·02
1980	Didier Pironi	F	3·0 Ligier JS11/15-Ford	Zolder	190·66/306·86	115·82/186·40
1981	Carlos Reutemann	RA	3·0 Williams FW07C-Ford	Zolder	143·01/230·15	112·12/180·44
1982	John Watson	GB	3·0 McLaren MP4B-Ford	Zolder	185·38/298·34	116·19/187·00
1983	Alain Prost	F	1·5 Renault RE40 t/c	Francorchamps	173·13/278·62	119·14/191·73

Circuit data

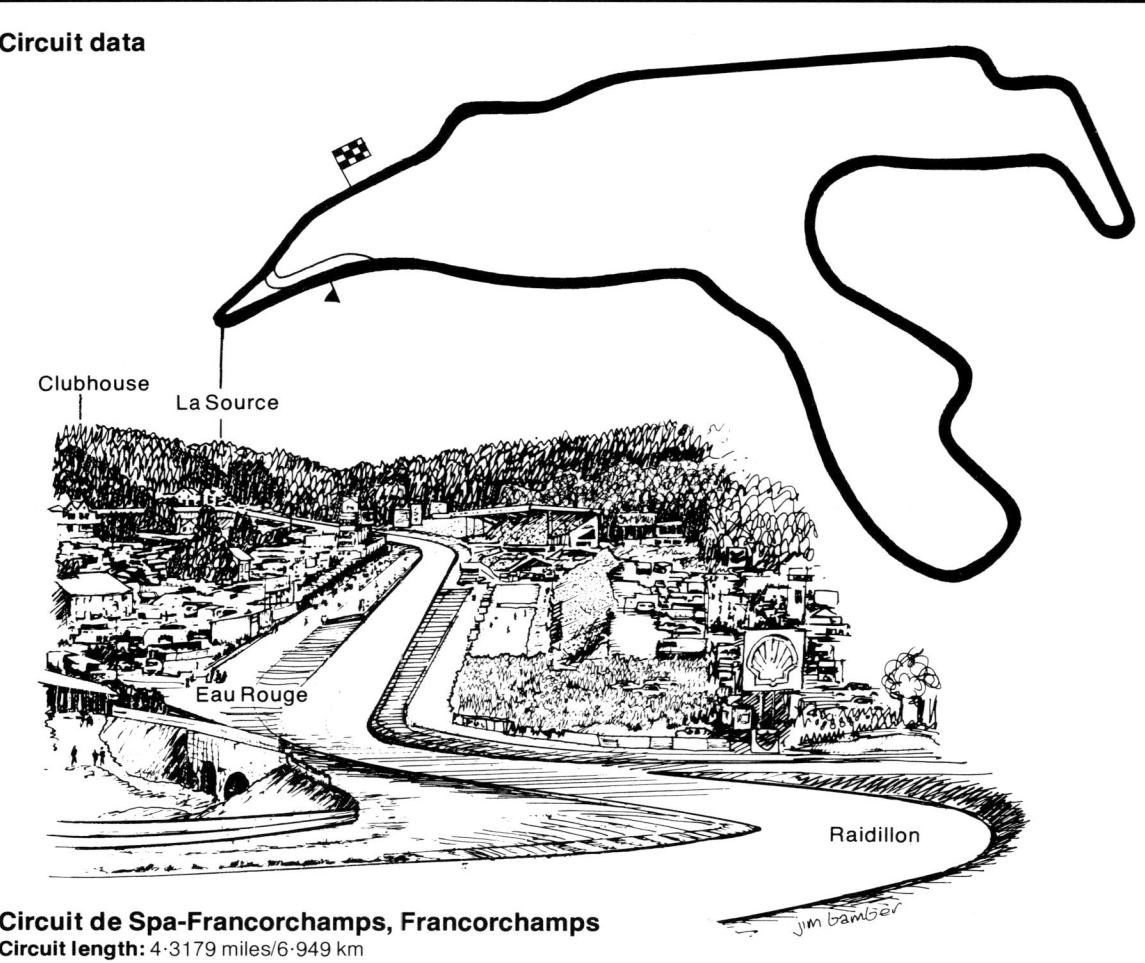

Clubhouse
La Source
Eau Rouge
Raidillon

jim bamber

Circuit de Spa-Francorchamps, Francorchamps
Circuit length: 4·3179 miles/6·949 km
Race distance: 40 laps + ·662 km, 173·127 miles/278·622 km
Race weather: Warm, dry

Note: Startline and pits located ·662 km before finishing/timing line. Cars retiring in the pits have not completed that lap and are shown purely for reference

Fastest laps

Driver	Time	Lap
Andrea de Cesaris	2m 07·493s	17
Alain Prost	2m 07·787s	20
Nelson Piquet	2m 08·081s	32
Eddie Cheever	2m 08·332s	22
Bruno Giacomelli	2m 08·941s	16
Patrick Tambay	2m 09·031s	14
Derek Warwick	2m 09·224s	17
Keke Rosberg	2m 09·631s	19
René Arnoux	2m 09·639s	18
Manfred Winkelhock	2m 10·109s	4
Jacques Laffite	2m 10·402s	16
Elio de Angelis	2m 10·643s	14
Niki Lauda	2m 10·899s	29
Mauro Baldi	2m 11·569s	3
Roberto Guerrero	2m 12·327s	23
Johnny Cecotto	2m 12·520s	15
Michele Alboreto	2m 12·630s	20
Nigel Mansell	2m 12·665s	17
Corrado Fabi	2m 13·029s	19
Marc Surer	2m 13·364s	15
Jean-Pierre Jarier	2m 13·521s	5
John Watson	2m 13·640s	6
Danny Sullivan	2m 13·863s	18
Thierry Boutsen	2m 14·040s	2
Raul Boesel	2m 15·269s	29

Points

WORLD CHAMPIONSHIP OF DRIVERS

1	Alain Prost	28 pts
2	Nelson Piquet	24
3	Patrick Tambay	23
4	Keke Rosberg	16
5	John Watson	11
6	Niki Lauda	10
7 =	René Arnoux	8
7 =	Jacques Laffite	8
7 =	Eddie Cheever	8
10	Marc Surer	4
11	Danny Sullivan	2
12 =	Johnny Cecotto	1
12 =	Mauro Baldi	1

CONSTRUCTORS' CUP

1	Renault	36 pts
2	Ferrari	31
3 =	Brabham	24
3 =	Williams	24
5	McLaren	21
6	Arrows	4
7	Tyrrell	2
8 =	Theodore	1
8 =	Alfa Romeo	1

Lap chart

No.	Driver	1	2	3	4	5	6	7	8	9	10	11	12	13	14	15	16	17	18	19	20	21	22	23	24	25	26	27	28	29	30	31	32	33	34	35	36	37	38	39	40
22	A. De Cesaris	22	22	22	22	22	22	22	22	22	22	22	22	22	22	22	22	22	15	15	15	15	5	15	15	15	15	15	15	15	15	15	15	15	15	15	15	15	15	15	15
15	A. Prost	15	15	15	15	15	15	15	15	15	15	15	15	15	15	15	15	15	27	27	5	5	(15)	22	22	5	5	5	5	5	5	5	5	5	27	27	27	27	27	27	27
27	P. Tambay	27	27	27	27	27	27	27	27	27	27	27	27	27	27	27	27	27	5	5	22	22	22	(5)	5	27	27	27	27	27	27	27	27	5	5	5	5	5	16	16	16
28	R. Arnoux	28	28	28	28	28	28	28	28	28	28	28	28	28	28	28	5	5	1	22	(27)	27	27	27	27	16	16	16	16	16	16	16	16	16	16	16	16	16	5	5	5
5	N. Piquet	5	5	5	5	5	5	5	5	5	5	5	5	5	5	5	28	28	16	28	28	28	16	16	16	1	1	1	1	1	1	1	1	1	1	1	1	1	1	1	1
9	M. Winkelhock	9	9	9	9	9	9	9	9	9	9	9	1	1	1	1	1	1	1	(22)	(16)	16	16	1	1	1	2	2	2	2	2	2	2	2	2	2	2	2	2	2	2
1	K. Rosberg	1	1	1	1	1	1	1	1	1	1	1	1	16	16	16	16	16	16	16	(28)	2	2	1	2	2	2	8	8	8	8	8	8	36	36	36	36	36	36	36	35
2	J. Laffite	2	2	2	2	16	16	16	16	16	16	16	2	2	2	2	2	2	2	(1)	35	(2)	8	8	8	36	36	36	36	36	36	36	36	35	35	35	35	35	35	35	36
16	E. Cheever	16	16	16	16	2	2	2	2	2	2	2	35	35	35	35	35	35	35	35	35	1	8	33	35	36	3	3	3	11	11	11	35	35	11	11	11	11	11	11	11
23	M. Baldi	23	23	23	11	11	11	11	11	11	11	11	11	11	11	11	36	36	36	36	36	8	8	33	35	36	3	34	11	11	3	35	35	11	11	34	34	34	34	34	34
11	E. De Angelis	11	11	11	33	33	33	33	33	33	35	35	36	36	36	11	11	11	8	8	33	33	(35)	36	3	34	11	34	35	3	3	34	34	29	29	29	29	29	29	29	29
33	R. Guerrero	33	33	33	8	8	8	3	8	8	33	8	8	8	8	8	8	8	33	33	3	3	3	3	34	11	35	35	34	34	34	34	3	3	4	4	4	4	4	4	4
3	M. Alboreto	3	8	8	36	36	36	33	36	35	8	36	33	33	33	33	33	33	3	3	34	34	34	34	11	(35)	29	29	29	29	29	29	29	29	(3)	26	26	26	26	26	26
8	N. Lauda	8	3	36	35	35	35	35	35	36	36	33	3	3	3	3	3	3	34	34	(36)	36	36	11	29	29	4	4	4	4	4	4	4	4	4	26	3	3	3	3	
36	B. Giacomelli	36	36	35	3	3	3	3	3	3	3	3	34	34	34	34	34	34	(11)	11	11	11	11	29	4	4	12	12	12	12	12	12	26	26	26	(8)					
7	J. Watson	7	7	3	7	7	7	7	7	34	34	34	29	29	29	29	29	29	29	29	29	29	4	12	12	26	26	26	26	26	(12)										
35	D. Warwick	35	35	7	25	25	25	25	25	29	29	29	4	4	4	4	4	4	4	4	12	12	12	(12)	26	26															
12	N. Mansell	12	30	30	34	34	34	34	34	4	4	4	31	31	31	31	12	12	12	12	4	4	4	26																	
30	T. Boutsen	30	25	25	4	4	4	4	4	31	31	31	12	12	12	12	26	26	26	26	26	26	26																		
25	J. P. Jarier	25	34	34	31	29	29	29	29	12	12	12	26	26	26	26	26	(31)	31	31	31	31																			
4	D. Sullivan	4	4	4	29	31	31	31	31	26	26	26	(9)	9	9	9	9	9	9																						
34	J. Cecotto	34	31	31	26	26	26	26	12																																
31	C. Fabi	31	26	29	12	12	12	12	26																																
26	R. Boesel	26	29	26	(30)	(30)																																			
29	M. Surer	29	12	12	(23)																																				

UNITED STATES GRAND PRIX (DETROIT)

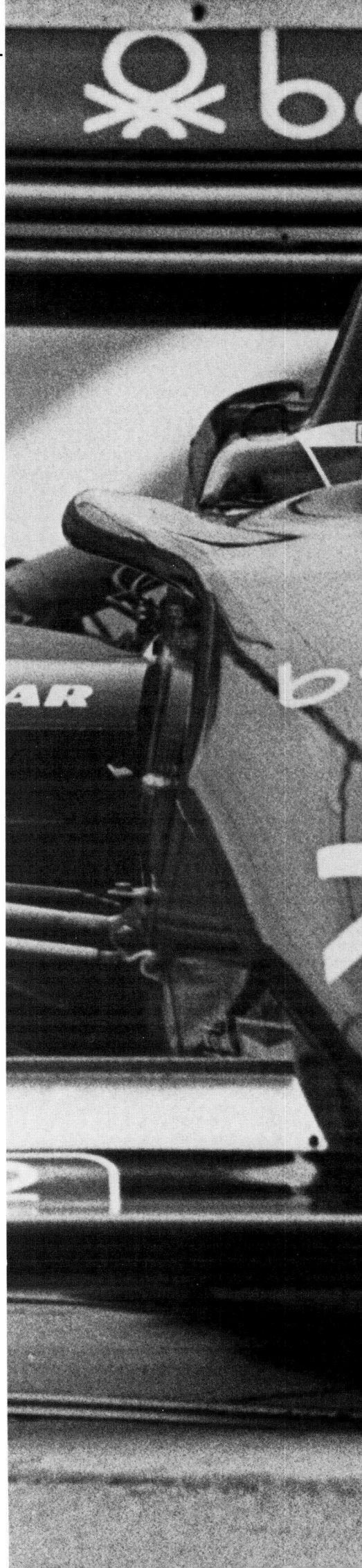

It was a motor racing deal which didn't involve money; just good, old-fashioned gratitude and diplomacy. The blue and white decal on the nose of the Tyrrell was a means of saying 'thank-you' to Ford after a 15-year association which had seen Ken Tyrrell win 32 Grands Prix with the Ford-Cosworth V8. Now he wanted to pay his last respects.

They were, after all, on the doorstep of Ford's World Headquarters. Donald Petersen, Executive Vice-President, was in the pits. So was Edsel Ford II; Michael Kranefuss, the racing boss, worldwide; Stuart Turner, Director of European Motor Sports; Harold Poling, Marketing Manager. Even Ford's television spokesman and former Tyrrell employee, Jackie Stewart, was there.

Behind them, the windows on 24 floors of a Renaissance Centre tower were blacked out to spell the name of a company which had spent £100,000 in 1966 to fund the DFV – and had enjoyed rather disproportionate publicity ever since.

But, according to Tyrrell, Detroit would probably represent the last circuit on which a Ford-Cosworth could win a Grand Prix. So it was appropriate to ask Benetton's permission to break their exclusive sponsorship deal and allow Tyrrell to carry the Ford logo.

Benetton agreed. And Michele Alboreto won the Detroit Grand Prix: 155 victories for the Ford-Cosworth; nine points, the first of the season for Alboreto. Everyone in the Tyrrell pit was happy.

A few yards away, the Brabham chief mechanic stalked across the pit lane and angrily kicked a Michelin tyre.

"Doesn't it make you sick," he fumed. "A bloody puncture. We could have won this."

And he was right. But for a rear tyre deflating with 10 laps remaining, Nelson Piquet would have moved to the top of the World Championship with a beautifully engineered victory, the Parmalat Brabham team having fooled everybody by planning to run non-stop. As it was, a rapid tyre change had Nelson back in time to finish fourth and, while that might have been disappointing for Brabham, fortune did smile on their championship hopes since the top three places had been filled by drivers who did not pose a direct threat.

With Alain Prost finishing an unhappy eighth, his Renault-Elf lacking grip and a nose-wing, and Patrick Tambay stalling on the line, it was left to Keke Rosberg to finish second and consolidate his fourth place in the championship. John Watson finished third, the Marlboro McLaren team struggling even more than Saudia Williams during a practice which had almost been washed out on the first day.

Watson's grid position was not unexpected, just as it was becoming no surprise to find René Arnoux on pole. The Ferrari driver pulled out a commanding lead once he had dealt with Piquet but the chances of an assured win were wiped out by an electrical failure on lap 31.

With Riccardo Patrese retiring his Brabham with brake trouble, Eddie Cheever stopping with a broken distributor on his Renault and Andrea de Cesaris (Alfa Romeo) and Derek Warwick (Toleman-Hart) retiring, the turbo challenge wilted and left Cosworth cars to fill five of the first six places; Jacques Laffite taking fifth for Williams and Nigel Mansell scoring the first point of the season for Lotus by finishing sixth. Just for good measure, another Cosworth car, the Arrows of Thierry Boutsen, finished seventh and Watson set fastest lap.

But more important, perhaps, was the fact that Alboreto's win meant victory first time out for the latest Ford-Cosworth DFY engine. And Tyrrell's gratitude to Ford was there for all to see.

Good old fashioned gratitude and diplomacy. Michele Alboreto's Tyrrell carried this Ford sticker as a token of appreciation for the contribution over the years from Walter Hayes and the Ford Motor Company. Ford executives were on hand to watch Tyrrell give the Ford-Cosworth DFY it's first win.

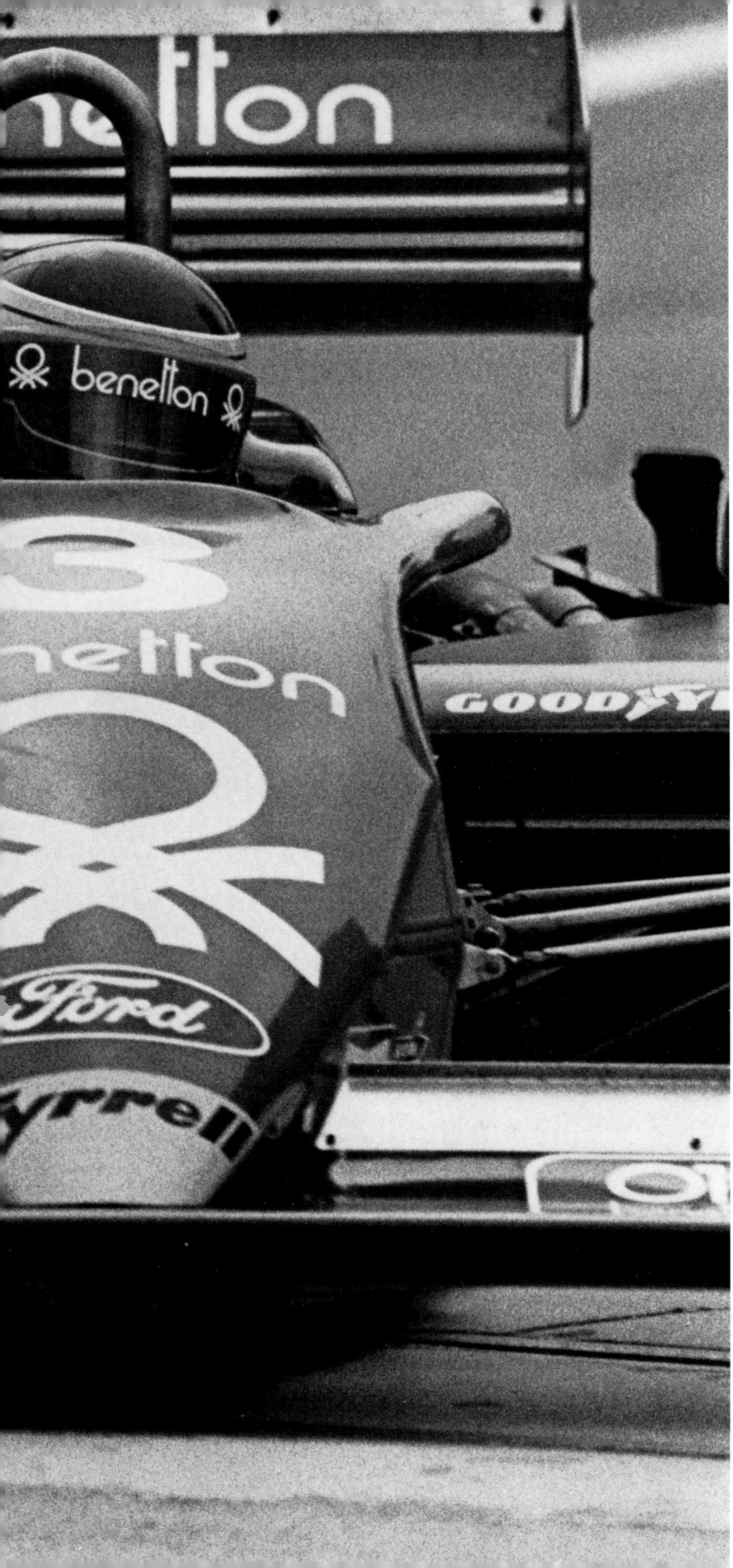

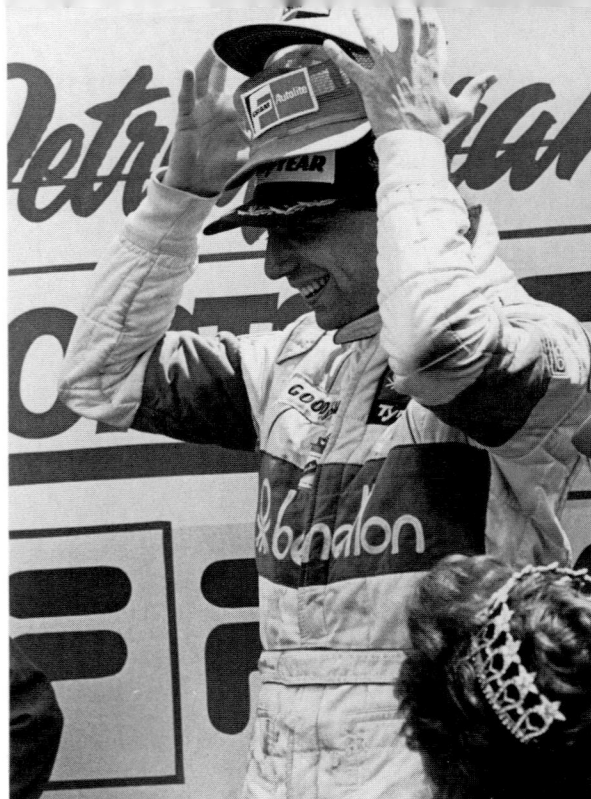

Man of many hats, but few championship points
– until Detroit. A well-judged, if slightly
fortunate, win for Michele Alboreto gave the
Italian his first points of the season.

ENTRY AND PRACTICE

Judging by the local press, the people of Detroit were rather annoyed about Grand Prix racing's response to the first Detroit Grand Prix in 1982. It was clear the city had bitten off more than it could chew but, in 1983, it was equally clear they had been ready to learn from their mistakes. The track had been the subject of much criticism but subtle improvements saw the bypassing of the tricky first-gear hairpin at the East end of the circuit. The chicane before the pits had been eased and, more important, the entry to the pit lane had been moved to a safer position. In excess of 70 manholes had been covered over and this year there were few complaints about the bumps although, in fairness to Detroit, the fact that the cars now had suspension movement again did help smooth the drivers' ride.

The start of practice may have been delayed by 50 minutes while the organisers sealed off the course but such a hold-up was acceptable in the light of the fiasco the previous year. Once the green light had been given, rain began to fall intermittently throughout the untimed session, a fact which was not well received by the mechanics who were forced to toil in a pit area which did not provide any cover. Open pits may be acceptable in the sunny climes of California but to place the long-suffering mechanics at the mercy of the Michigan rainy season was asking for trouble. To make matters worse, the heavens opened throughout the timed practice session in the afternoon. . . .

Torrents of water streamed across the track at several points, the cars creating bow waves and resembling boats on the nearby Detroit river. It was no surprise to see Keke Rosberg set the fastest time in the afternoon, the Williams driver treating the bedraggled crowd to a superb display of car control even though his best lap represented an average of just 69.5mph. His team-mate, Jacques Laffite, had the most serious incident of the afternoon, the FW08C losing grip as the Frenchman accelerated onto the pit straight. In an instant, the Williams had thumped the concrete wall although, remarkably, damage to the car was slight. The unflappable Jacques merely climbed out, vaulted the pit wall and walked away. Several luminaries spun, Tambay and Prost losing nose wings in the process, while Guerrero, Mansell, Patrese and Cecotto managed to avoid the waiting concrete. Indeed, the most potentially hazardous incident of the day occurred to a CBS television man when he fell several feet from his camera perch. Happily, he was merely shaken and bruised.

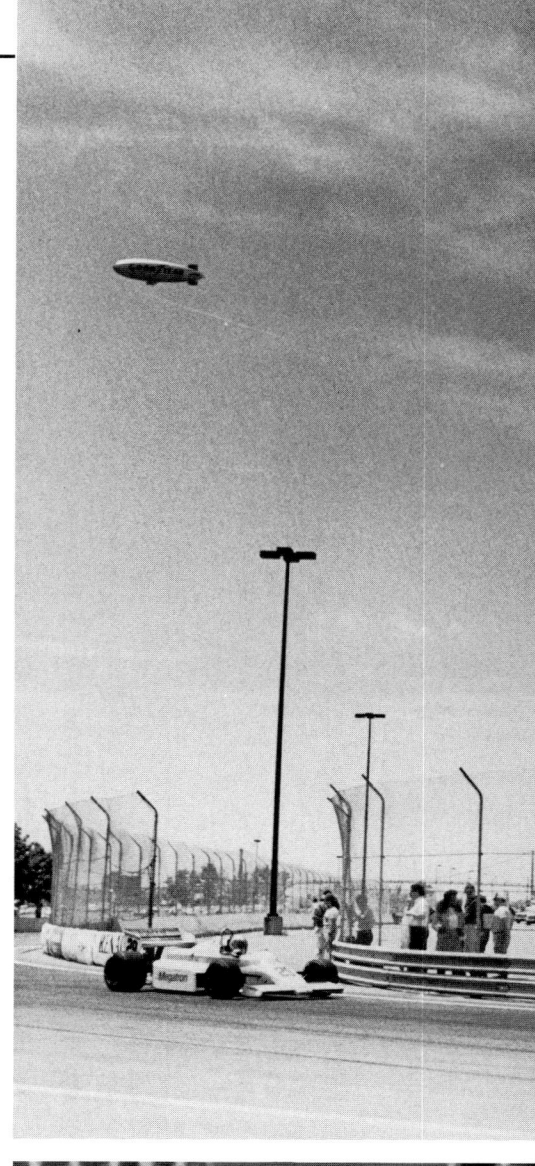

Michele Alboreto and Marc Surer set the Cosworth pace during practice but the Arrows driver was caught behind Tambay's stalled Ferrari at the start.
René Arnoux looks inside Nelson Piquet's Brabham-BMW as they approach the braking area at the end of the pit straight. The Ferrari moved into the lead not long after, but retired with an electrical problem at half-distance. Piquet regained the lead and fooled the opposition by running non-stop, a tactic foiled ultimately by a puncture which dropped the Brabham to fourth place in the closing laps.

It remained overcast for the untimed session on Saturday morning, Piquet setting the fastest time ahead of Alboreto, Prost and de Angelis (who, incidentally, had been quickest in the damp unofficial session the previous day). The teams had been forced to cram Friday's work into the 90-minute session as they struggled to find a decent set-up for the important timed session at 1 p.m.

Watson and Lauda were the first to take to the track, followed by Piquet while others played a waiting game, saving their qualifying tyres for a clear track later in the session. It was to prove a disastrous mistake. By 1.10 p.m., the sun had come out and the track, instead of gathering pace, became slower by the minute as the heat brought moisture in the tarmac to the surface.

Not one to hang around under any circumstances, René Arnoux had been out early, the Ferrari driver clipping a barrier just after setting a time which would be good enough for pole. By 1.10 p.m., the first three places on the grid had been established no matter how hard the rest of the field tried throughout the remainder of the session and, to prove the point, Arnoux was two seconds slower on his second set of qualifiers.

There had been few changes to the Ferrari since Spa-Francorchamps due, largely, to the team concentrating on production of the new C3 in time for Silverstone. Tambay set third fastest time within his first three laps of practice and yet his time was over a second slower than Piquet. The Brazilian had been happy to see a dry track since the BMW turbo power had proved an embarrassment in the wet. Nelson set his time almost immediately, which was fortunate since an engine misfire was to interrupt his progress later in the day. A leaking fuel tank during the morning meant Riccardo Patrese had little opportunity to set his car up in the dry conditions and the Italian driver had to make do with 15th place just behind the Lotus-Cosworth of Nigel Mansell.

The Englishman was kicking himself for having waited so long in the pits since he had been seventh fastest during the morning session even though the Lotus 92 tended to jump out of fourth gear occasionally. Mansell's car sported the double rear wing seen previously on Elio de Angelis's Lotus-Renault and, for this race, the Italian's car had been fitted with tougher lower wishbones. The addition of stiffer Pirellis and a fair amount of boost from the turbo pushed Elio onto the second row with a time set on his first flying lap. Needless to say, it was recorded within the first 15 minutes of practice.

The one outstanding exception to that rule, however, was Marc Surer who set fifth fastest time on his second set of qualifiers. Apart from being the fastest Cosworth, Surer's performance was a sure indication of the suitability of the neat Arrows A6 when it came to the sudden changes of direction required by the 90-degree corners at Detroit. The team had concentrated on making the front tyres work properly and Surer used a narrow front during qualifying. Thierry Boutsen underlined the potential of the Arrows by taking 10th place, the third fastest Cosworth, an excellent performance by any standards.

From the outset, it seemed likely that the Benetton Tyrrell team would set the Cosworth pace, Michele Alboreto running as quickly and confidently as he had when he won in Las Vegas at the end of 1982. Now, of course, he had the latest Ford-Cosworth DFY at his disposal and the improved torque at low revs was to prove ideal for Detroit, the Italian joining Surer on the third row while Danny Sullivan was a comfortable qualifier in 16th place.

Not so happy were the Renault team, Alain Prost complaining of poor balance and grip, the RE40 switching from understeer to oversteer for no apparent reason. The team made matters worse by

waiting for the track to improve and Eddie Cheever realised their mistake when he found wheelspin in fourth and fifth gear; the American was seventh while Prost languished in 13th place, his worst grid position since Long Beach 1981.

The Marlboro Alfa Romeo team remained most secretive about what was believed to be revised heads on the V8 engine used by Andrea de Cesaris during practice. Slight alterations to the front and rear suspension could not help Andrea repeat the form shown at Spa but the Italian qualified in eighth place while Mauro Baldi was a disappointing 25th in spite of setting his time early in the session. Derek Warwick was equally unhappy with ninth place, the Candy Toleman driver reporting that the car felt fine but, somehow, he was unable to build up the rhythm necessary for the succession of tight corners. Bruno Giacomelli was down in 17th place after being forced to use the T-car following a suspected valve problem with the Hart turbo in his race chassis.

At Spa-Francorchamps, Roberto Guerrero had said how much he enjoyed the challenge of the fast track. Two weeks later in Detroit, he was saying the same thing about the precision required by the street circuit, the Colombian proving his point by taking 11th place alongside Keke Rosberg. The second Theodore was on the back row, Johnny Cecotto setting his time in the T-car after damaging the rear suspension of his regular car against a wall during the morning session. Williams had repaired Laffite's car but they paid the price of running harder tyres during the early part of the session. Rosberg, suffering from a head cold, also paid for being saturated on Friday, the World Champion commenting that his car felt reasonable – but it was just plain slow.

If Williams had a problem, it was lack of traction, something which the McLaren team knew all about as they struggled to make their Michelins work once more. Like Williams, John Watson and Niki Lauda reserved their qualifying tyres for late in the session and they were mystified to find they had set faster times on race rubber, Lauda taking 18th place while Watson was back in his now customary position near the back of the grid. At least on this occasion McLaren were not embarrassed by the Ligier-Michelin-Cosworth package setting a faster pace, Jean-Pierre Jarier and Raul Boesel suffering from a lack of grip and the absence of engineer Herve Guilpin, at home making a start on drawings for the 1984 Ligier-Renault.

It had been a clear for some time, of course, that turbocharged engines were the only way to go, a fact demonstrated clearly by the rise in competitiveness of the ATS team since the arrival of their BMW turbo at the beginning of the season. It was surprising, therefore, to find Manfred Winkelhock on the 11th row although his grid position was partially explained by an oil line breaking on his race car, forcing the German to use a heavily revised T-car for most of timed practice. Apart from shorter side-pods, the spare chassis had a new heat exchanger and lower location for the turbo and exhaust system. A hard charge through the field seemed assured. Piercarlo Ghinzani, on the other hand, was certain to drive with reasonable care having managed to qualify the Osella fitted with the V12 Alfa Romeo, the FA1E benefitting from a new oil system. The withdrawal of the RAM March team due to driver/sponsorship problems meant Corrado Fabi was the odd man out, the Italian failing to qualify his Osella after trouble with the Cosworth engines on both his race and spare cars.

RACE

"O Lord," intoned the Rev. Nicholas Hood, "help us keep our lives on the racing line without losing control."

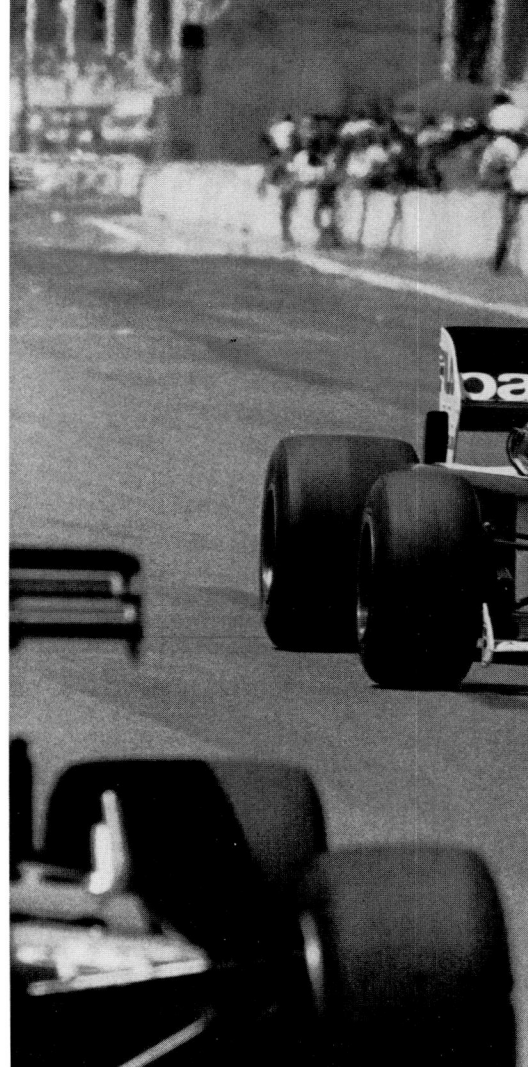

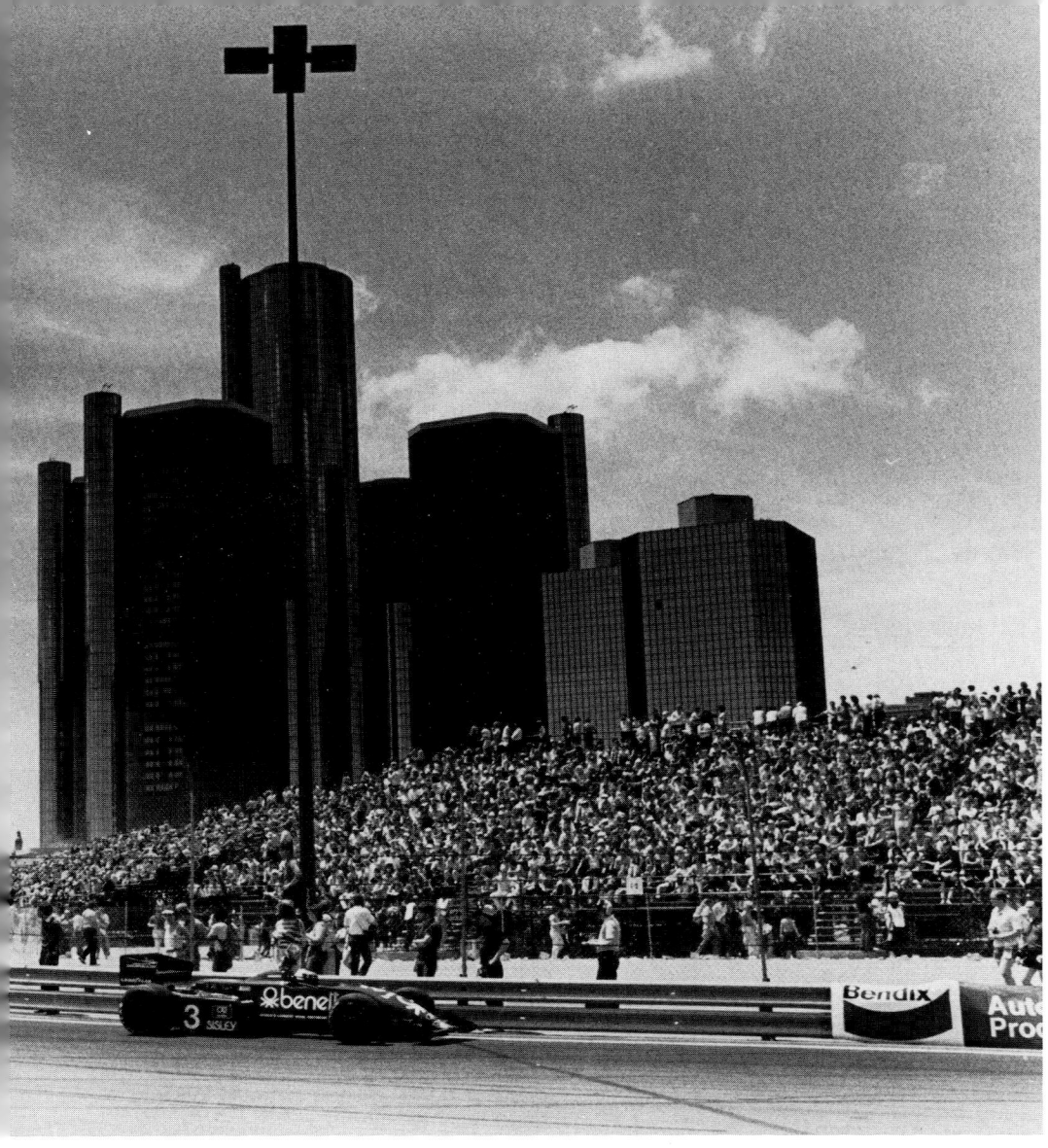

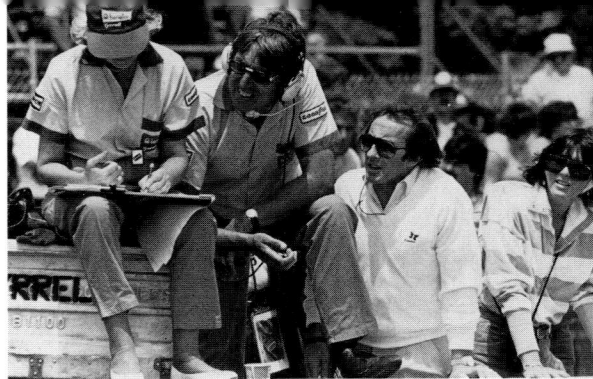

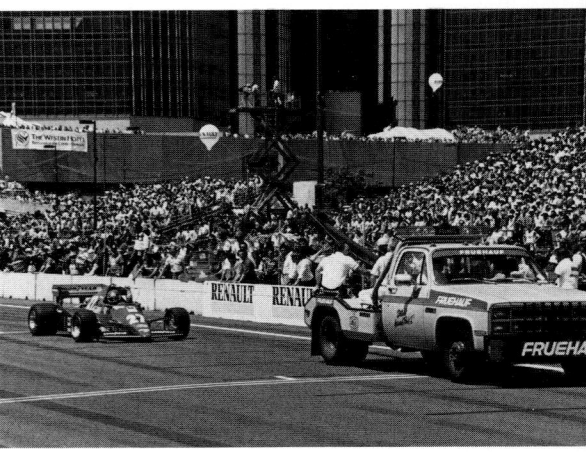

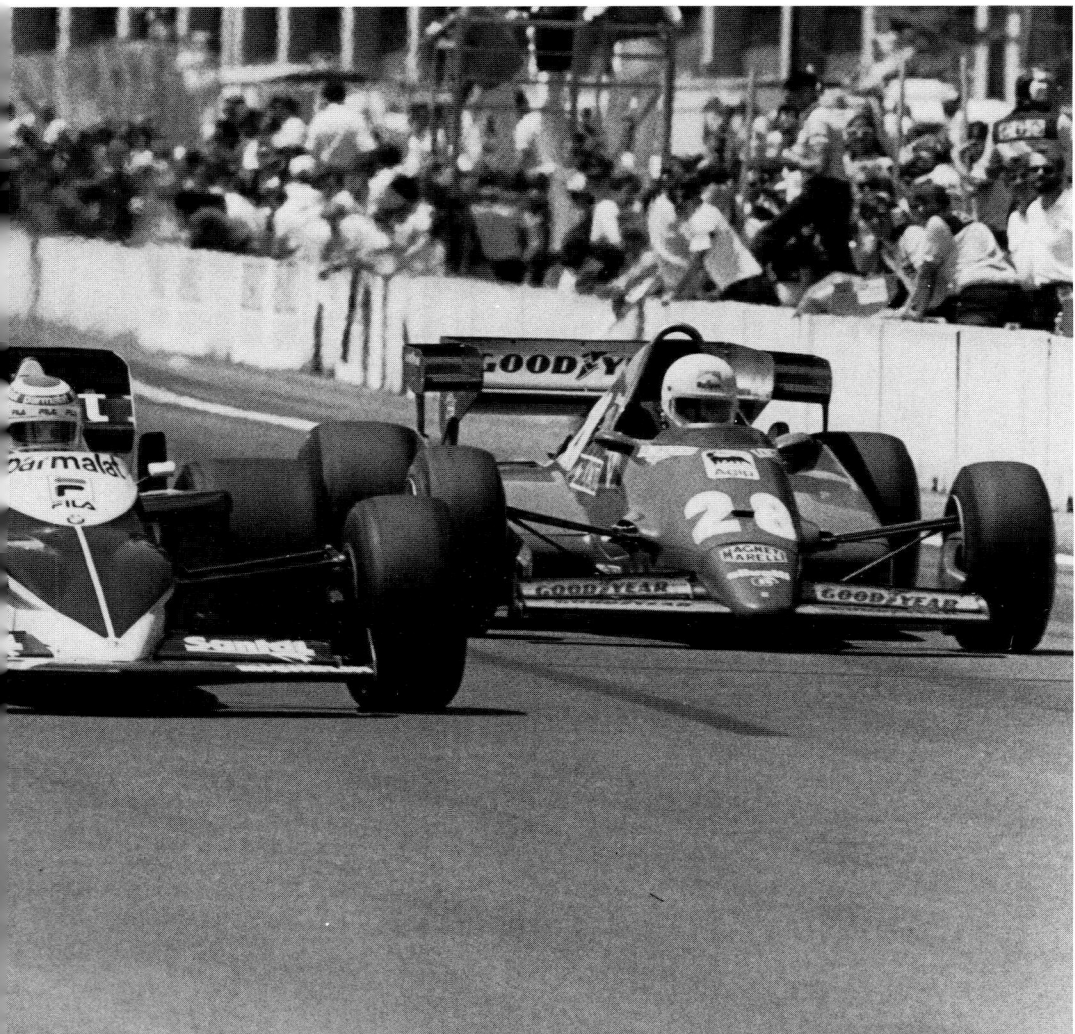

"Norah, listen to this. Stewart's trying to tell me Piquet isn't making a pit stop. Bloody ex-drivers think they know it all. . . ." Ken Tyrrell examines his wife's lap chart while the former World Champion and Tyrrell driver offers encouragement *(top)*.
Tambay stalled his Ferrari at the start and waited to receive a push-start but, instead, officials towed the car out of the race *(above)*.

The words of invocation were entirely appropriate as the teams made final preparations. Decisions normally reserved for practice had been made during the morning warm-up as various compounds were tried in an effort to match tyres to the track conditions of the day. McLaren, for example, tried four different tyres, found a compound and construction which gave the best temperatures they had seen all weekend – but still there was no grip. Tyrrell chose 'B' compound Goodyears for Alboreto, with Sullivan taking the softer 'C'. Arrows reckoned the 'B' compound was quicker than the 'C' while Guerrero, having run on full tanks for the first time, found the 'C' compound to be too soft and had no option but to run 'B' – a tyre which he had not been able to try thanks to none being available in the pits.

The problem lay in the inaccessibility of the garage area. If you did not bring it to the pits at the appointed hour, then you did without. Otherwise you faced a 25-minute walk on foot or, in the case of Brabham, their tyre man took an eight-mile drive down the freeway just to get his truck to the garage while the circuit was in use! Renault, undecided over pit-stops, ran Cheever on half a tank of fuel: Prost with a full tank. It was decided a full load of fuel would be too hard on tyres and brakes and the decision to stop was taken – even though Prost had not run on half tanks. Keeping on the racing line for 61 laps would, indeed, be a problem.

Blazing sunshine put Detroit in a party mood – and the racing dilettante was not stuck for choice. There was The Greatest Grand Prix Party; The World's Largest Pit-Stop Party; Grand Prix Fever; The Grand Prix View Party; A Monte Carlo via Detroit Party. And it was a fair bet that no one knew, let alone cared, that René Arnoux had been fastest during the warm-up.

The Ferrari led the field onto the grid at the end of the parade lap – and there was immediate drama. De Cesaris stalled, the Italian waving his arms in the air before promptly climbing out of his car. Derek Ongaro was faced with the second 'Delayed Start' in as many races, only this time, the field stayed put until instructed to complete one more parade lap, the race distance being reduced by one lap accordingly.

Red light; green light – and then Tambay stalled. This time, of course, there was no going back, the field swerving every which way and, somehow, managing to

leave the grid without incident. Tambay was furious, having heated up his tyres to perfection but, when he revved the engine to 9,500, he said it felt as though the tyres were welded to the track. At the Drivers' Briefing, he had been told that in circumstances such as this, he would receive a push start from officials. The next thing he knew, a tow-truck had hitched up to his roll-over bar and was towing the Ferrari out of the way. By the time Patrick realised what they were doing, it was too late. The man lying third in the championship was out of the race.

The officials had barely managed to remove Tambay's car when the field completed lap one, Piquet leading Arnoux with de Angelis following in third place after the most blatant jump start – a move which gained him little except a penalty. In the event, that too would count for nothing when the Lotus rolled to a halt four laps later with a broken pinion.

In the meantime, the Lotus had opened a gap over de Cesaris's Alfa Romeo with Alboreto holding fifth place ahead of Warwick and Rosberg, the Williams driver having made up ground by running round the outside of Boutsen, Cheever and Surer (held up by Tambay) at the first corner. Prost was 11th and about to lose his right-front nose wing in a brush with Boutsen while Guerrero was comfortably holding down a mid-field position ahead of Mansell, Laffite, Sullivan and Patrese. The rest of the field followed closely with Ghinzani trailed at the rear and about to retire with overheating problems on the Osella. The retirement list grew further when Cheever rolled to a halt, a bolt having broken in the distributor of his Renault.

Piquet and Arnoux had pulled out a 15-second lead over de Cesaris within eight laps and it was clear that the Brabham driver was doing Arnoux a favour by setting a steady pace and not permitting the Frenchman to rush off and destroy his tyres. Arnoux had other ideas and, by lap nine, he was pushing the Brabham hard, the Ferrari driver finding little resistance as he moved into the lead a lap later. But Piquet was not worried. *He* knew he was running with a full tank and had no intention of stopping whereas the Ferrari and, for that matter, the Alfa in third place and the Williams in fourth place, not to mention Warwick's Toleman in fifth position, would all be making planned stops for fuel and tyres.

So Nelson was not bothered when Arnoux pulled out an 18-second gap in the course of the next 10 laps; scarcely concerned when Rosberg closed on the Brabham and moved into second place on lap 20. Of more importance, perhaps, was the progress of Alboreto, now fourth as de Cesaris slipped behind the Tyrrell and Warwick's Toleman.

Although he did not know it at the time, Piquet would have been relieved to hear about Surer's problems. Keen to make up ground after his tardy start, the Swiss had missed his braking and taken to an escape road where a torn piece of paper from a Goodyear advert found its way into the radiator duct. Within a few laps, his water temperature was off the clock with coolant pouring out of the back of the car. Officials mistook this for oil and the Arrows was black-flagged although Surer was intending to stop anyway. The Arrows stopped briefly on lap 11 but any hopes of a place in the points were dashed. Jean-Pierre Jarier never held any such hopes in the first place and he was even more despondent when his Michelins lost their grip within five laps. He made the first of many stops on lap seven and would retire eventually when a wheel nut seized; the time required to free it making a return to the track pointless. Patrese was in the pits on lap eight to attend to brake trouble caused by too much bias to the rear and the Italian (racing the spare Brabham) was destined to retire with no rear brakes on lap 24.

As Patrese climbed from his car, Warwick arrived in the pit lane one lap before he was scheduled to make his stop. The Hart engine had been refusing to pick up cleanly but Derek was unable to get the message across as the mechanics attacked his car, adding fuel and changing tyres. Warwick returned to the track but soon realised there was little to be gained from carrying on and the Toleman retired a lap later before irreparable damage was done.

Lap 29, and Arnoux held a 25-second advantage over Rosberg as the Ferrari rushed into the pits. The mechanics performed faultlessly, the Ferrari accelerating out of the pit lane as Rosberg arrived at the Williams pit. There, things did not run so smoothly, a problem with the right-rear wheel delaying Keke and dropping the Williams to fifth place behind Alboreto and Laffite. Jacques, of course, was due to make a stop but Alboreto was running non-stop although the fresh 'C' Goodyears gave Rosberg a hope of catching the Tyrrell.

At the front, Arnoux had managed to return to the lead with a few seconds to spare over Piquet, so the Brabham team's tactic had not quite paid off. Whether he could have caught and passed the Ferrari became a matter of conjecture two laps later when Arnoux coasted to a halt, an electrical fault putting the Frenchman out of the points once more. Within the space of a few highly charged laps, therefore, Nelson Piquet was leading the race once more with Alboreto a few car lengths behind in second place – and patiently waiting for the Brabham to make its pit stop.

Niki Lauda had made an unplanned pit stop much earlier when he found his Michelin tyres were offering no grip whatsoever. A change of tyres failed to cure the problem and he was to retire later with handling difficulties, shock absorber trouble being mentioned as a possible cause. Watson, on the other hand, had worked his way up the lap chart and, when the race settled down after the pit stops, the Ulsterman found himself in fourth place, within striking distance of Rosberg who, in turn, was 27 seconds behind Alboreto – the man who would shortly take the lead when Piquet made his pit stop – which *must* be due any minute now.

Along the way, Watson had overtaken Winkelhock's ATS with a move which the German driver would have been well advised to follow as he tried to pass Lauda. The result of Manfred's fumbled move was a trip to the outside of the track and instant retirement as a top wishbone broke when the rear of the ATS touched a wall. Danny Sullivan, having run impressively in the mid-field, went missing on lap 31 when a wire came loose and silenced his Ford-Cosworth while Roberto Guerrero's encouraging drive was halted by gear-selection trouble. As the mechanics attempted to carry out repairs, it was noticed that an engine mount had broken. Things became busy in the Theodore pit ten laps later when Cecotto arrived from the back of the field to complain about gear selection trouble. In his case, the problem was incurable and an engine mount was taken from the Venezuelan's car and fitted to Guerrero's, the Theodore rejoining about 20 laps behind the field!

De Cesaris made his scheduled stop on lap 29 but the Italian was to retire a few laps later when he took a trip up an escape road while trying to pass Boutsen's Arrows and claw his way back up the field. The Alfa Romeo did manage to rejoin eventually but stopped at the pits with what was later classified as 'turbo trouble'.

Boutsen was running as hard as he was able considering his hard Goodyears were giving no grip, to such an extent that the Belgian driver barely survived a big moment, his left-rear wheel touching the wall as he made a spectacular exit from the chicane. Towards the end, he had an additional problem, his ill-fitting seat causing much discomfort and Boutsen was powerless to resist a strong challenge from Mansell, the Lotus moving into sixth place on lap 39.

By now, the Tyrrell team's worst suspicions were being confirmed by the lap; Piquet was running non-stop. The gap between the Brabham and the Tyrrell varied between one and four seconds but it was obvious that Alboreto had little chance of finding a way past Piquet. Rosberg was busy watching the red and white McLaren fill his mirrors but, as Watson sat in the Williams slipstream, his tyres went off and he was forced to drop back slightly. Laffite was a comfortable fifth and Mansell was about to be lapped by the leaders. Boutsen was next with Prost an unhappy eighth, well clear of Giacomelli as the Italian struggled to bring his smoking Toleman to the finish. Boesel had an unenviable struggle with Michelins which had been hopeless from the start, the Brazilian realising there was little point in stopping since his team-mate had kindly used up the team's supply of tyres!

Brabham, of course, had plenty of Michelins and they had no intention of using them. At least, not until lap 51. Going into the right-hander behind the pits, Piquet suddenly felt the back of the car go loose; a left-rear had punctured. Alboreto was onto the Brabham in a flash and into the lead a few corners later while Piquet made his way back to the pits. The team changed all four tyres and quickly sloshed in a few gallons of fuel, Piquet returning in fourth place. He wound up the boost and set after Watson but a pit signal a few laps later showing a 20-second gap meant a conservative run to the flag would be more advisable.

Watson made one final charge, setting fastest lap as he did so, but the final order remained the same, Ford-Cosworth cars filling the first three places. Ken Tyrrell stood on the pit wall and gave his man a triumphant wave while Rosberg deserved his points for second, fifth place for Laffite helping move Williams into second place in the Constructors' Championship, just four points behind Renault. Mansell took sixth place and the single point, he said, meant as much as winning a Grand Prix. It had been a struggle, an electrical short under his seat causing considerable pain in the closing laps.

There was considerable pain in the Brabham pit as Gordon Murray attempted to console his Chief Mechanic. "We lost Long Beach and Imola," said Murray. "And now this." Then a pause. "Never mind. Well done; the car finished." Just another case of good old-fashioned gratitude and diplomacy.

May:

Tom Sneva (March-Cosworth DFX 83C) wins Indy 500 from Penske-Cosworth DFX PC11s of Al Unser Snr and Rick Mears.

June:

Gerard Ducarouge joins John Player Team Lotus as Chief Engineer.

New York Grand Prix, scheduled for September 25, cancelled due to legal and political problems.

FOCA announce plans to set up permanent Information Centre in Los Angeles to improve communications in the USA.

FOLLOWING THE CONFUSION AT SPA-FRANCORCHAMPS two weeks previously, it was no surprise to find the Brabham team firmly placing a protest with the Detroit organisers over the revised exhaust systems used by Renault.

Renault insisted that the exhaust pipes had been rerouted to exit below the car's underwings to avoid the excessive tyre temperatures caused by the former location of the exhausts at the top of the side-pods.

Gordon Murray, on the other hand, had claimed from the outset that Renault were using exhaust gases to energise the boundary layer of the underwing and thereby reduce turbulence. They were therefore using the engine and turbocharger as moving aerodynamic parts and that, according to the vague regulations, was illegal.

Murray said he was protesting simply to find out if the system was legal since there was a considerable benefit to be had – a fact Brabham had discovered many years before during private testing. But at least the protest had been placed at a race where the alleged offender had not finished in the points (Prost was eighth; Cheever had failed to finish).

Renault, in turn, protested the rear wing which was found to be a fraction too high on one side of Piquet's Brabham. However, the amount in question was so small that the scrutineers, on rechecking the height, were unable to verify the protest.

Both protests were subsequently rejected and Brabham indicated they would appeal to the FISA.

Wheel of fortune. A loose electrical wire on René Arnoux's Ferrari cost the Frenchman the lead.
Photo: John Townsend

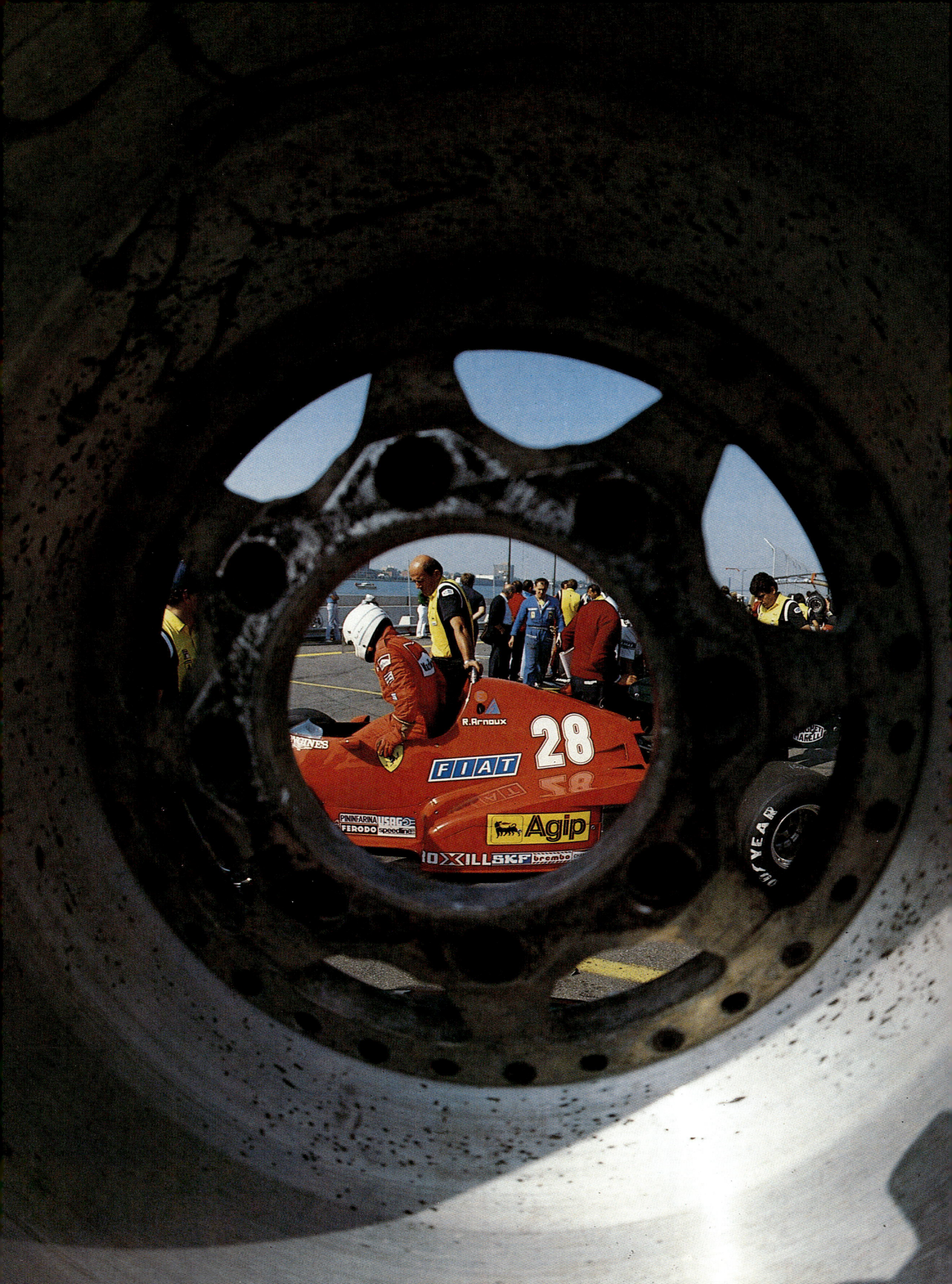

Entries and practice times

No.	Driver	Nat	Car	Tyre	Engine	Entrant	Practice 1	Practice 2
1	Keke Rosberg	SF	Saudia WILLIAMS FW08C	G	Ford Cosworth DFV	TAG Williams Team	2m 06·382s	**1m 47·728s**
2	Jacques Laffite	F	Saudia WILLIAMS FW08C	G	Ford Cosworth DFV	TAG Williams Team	2m 13·080s	**1m 49·245s**
3	Michele Alboreto	I	Benetton TYRRELL 011	G	Ford Cosworth DFV/DFY	Benetton Tyrrell Team	2m 08·198s	**1m 47·013s**
4	Danny Sullivan	USA	Benetton TYRRELL 011	G	Ford Cosworth DFV/DFY	Benetton Tyrrell Team	2m 18·758s	**1m 48·648s**
5	Nelson Piquet	BR	Parmalat BRABHAM BT52	M	BMW M12/13	Fila Sport	2m 11·506s	**1m 44·933s**
6	Riccardo Patrese	I	Parmalat BRABHAM BT52	M	BMW M12/13	Fila Sport	2m 17·489s	**1m 48·537s**
7	John Watson	GB	Marlboro McLAREN MP4/1C	M	Ford Cosworth DFV/DFY	Marlboro McLaren International	2m 10·632s	**1m 49·250s**
8	Niki Lauda	A	Marlboro McLAREN MP4/1C	M	Ford Cosworth DFV/DFY	Marlboro McLaren International	2m 09·019s	**1m 48·992s**
9	Manfred Winkelhock	D	ATS D6	G	BMW M12/13	Team ATS	2m 12·092s	**1m 49·466s**
11	Elio de Angelis	I	John Player Special LOTUS 93T	P	Renault EF1	John Player Team Lotus	2m 09·601s	**1m 46·258s**
12	Nigel Mansell	GB	John Player Special LOTUS 92	P	Ford Cosworth DFV/DFY	John Player Team Lotus	2m 07·792s	**1m 48·395s**
15	Alain Prost	F	Elf RENAULT RE40	M	Renault EF1	Equipe Renault Elf	2m 15·731s	**1m 47·855s**
16	Eddie Cheever	USA	Elf RENAULT RE40	M	Renault EF1	Equipe Renault Elf	2m 08·418s	**1m 47·334s**
22	Andrea de Cesaris	I	Marlboro ALFA ROMEO 183T	M	Alfa Romeo 183T	Marlboro Team Alfa Romeo	2m 08·034s	**1m 47·453s**
23	Mauro Baldi	I	Marlboro ALFA ROMEO 183T	M	Alfa Romeo 183T	Marlboro Team Alfa Romeo	2m 11·169s	**1m 49·916s**
25	Jean-Pierre Jarier	F	Gitanes LIGIER JS21	M	Ford Cosworth DFV	Equipe Ligier Gitanes	2m 07·652s	**1m 48·994s**
26	Raul Boesel	BR	Gitanes LIGIER JS21	M	Ford Cosworth DFV	Equipe Ligier Gitanes	2m 12·164s	**1m 49·540s**
27	Patrick Tambay	F	Fiat FERRARI 126C2/B	G	Ferrari 126C	Scuderia Ferrari SpA SEFAC	2m 10·994s	**1m 45·991s**
28	René Arnoux	F	Fiat FERRARI 126C2/B	G	Ferrari 126C	Scuderia Ferrari SpA SEFAC	2m 08·851s	**1m 44·734s**
29	Marc Surer	CH	ARROWS A6	G	Ford Cosworth DFV	Arrows Racing Team	2m 09·292s	**1m 46·745s**
30	Thierry Boutsen	B	ARROWS A6	G	Ford Cosworth DFV	Arrows Racing Team	2m 11·107s	**1m 47·586s**
31	Corrado Fabi	I	OSELLA FA1D	M	Ford Cosworth DFV	Osella Squadra Corse	2m 15·085s	**1m 53·516s**
32	Piercarlo Ghinzani	I	OSELLA FA1E	M	Alfa Romeo 1260	Osella Squadra Corse	2m 15·556s	**1m 49·885s**
33	Roberto Guerrero	COL	THEODORE N183	G	Ford Cosworth DFV	Theodore Racing Team	2m 08·496s	**1m 47·701s**
34	Johnny Cecotto	YV	THEODORE N183	G	Ford Cosworth DFV	Theodore Racing Team	2m 14·547s	**1m 51·709s**
35	Derek Warwick	GB	Candy TOLEMAN TG183B	P	Hart 415T	Candy Toleman Motorsport		**1m 47·534s**
36	Bruno Giacomelli	I	Candy TOLEMAN TG183B	P	Hart 415T	Candy Toleman Motorsport	2m 13·205s	**1m 48·785s**

Friday morning and Saturday morning practice sessions not officially recorded.

G – Goodyear, M – Michelin, P – Pirelli.

Fri pm Wet, cool
Sat pm Dry, warm

Starting grid

28 ARNOUX (1m 44·734s)
Ferrari

5 PIQUET (1m 44·933s)
Brabham

27 TAMBAY (1m 45·991s)
Ferrari

11 DE ANGELIS (1m 46·258s)
Lotus

29 SURER (1m 46·745s)
Arrows

3 ALBORETO (1m 47·013s)
Tyrrell

16 CHEEVER (1m 47·334s)
Renault

22 DE CESARIS (1m 47·453s)
Alfa Romeo

35 WARWICK (1m 47·534s)
Toleman

30 BOUTSEN (1m 47·586s)
Arrows

33 GUERRERO (1m 47·701s)
Theodore

1 ROSBERG (1m 47·728s)
Williams

15 PROST (1m 47·855s)
Renault

12 MANSELL (1m 48·395s)
Lotus

6 PATRESE (1m 48·537s)
Brabham

4 SULLIVAN (1m 48·648s)
Tyrrell

36 GIACOMELLI (1m 48·785s)
Toleman

8 LAUDA (1m 48·992s)
McLaren

25 JARIER (1m 48·994s)
Ligier

2 LAFFITE (1m 49·245s)
Williams

7 WATSON (1m 49·250s)
McLaren

9 WINKELHOCK (1m 49·466s)
ATS

26 BOESEL (1m 49·540s)
Ligier

32 GHINZANI (1m 49·885s)
Osella

23 BALDI (1m 49·916s)
Alfa Romeo

34 CECOTTO (1m 51·709s)
Theodore

Did not start:
31 Fabi (Osella), 1m 53·516s, did not qualify

Results and retirements

Place	Driver	Car	Laps	Time and Speed (mph/km/h)/Retirement	
1	Michele Alboreto	Tyrrell-Cosworth V8	60	1h 50m 53·669s	81·158/130·611
2	Keke Rosberg	Williams-Cosworth V8	60	1h 51m 01·371s	81·1/130·517
3	John Watson	McLaren-Cosworth V8	60	1h 51m 02·952s	81·0/130·357
4	Nelson Piquet	Brabham-BMW t/c 4	60	1h 52m 05·854s	80·3/129·230
5	Jacques Laffite	Williams-Cosworth V8	60	1h 52m 26·272s	80·0/128·747
6	Nigel Mansell	Lotus-Cosworth V8	59		
7	Thierry Boutsen	Arrows-Cosworth V8	59		
8	Alain Prost	Renault t/c V6	59		
9	Bruno Giacomelli	Toleman-Hart t/c 4	59		
10	Raul Boesel	Ligier-Cosworth V8	58		
11	Marc Surer	Arrows-Cosworth V8	58		
12	Mauro Baldi	Alfa Romeo t/c V8	56		
	Niki Lauda	McLaren-Cosworth V8	49	Shock absorber	
	Roberto Guerrero	Theodore-Cosworth V8	38	Running, not classified	
	Johnny Cecotto	Theodore-Cosworth V8	34	Gear linkage	
	Andrea de Cesaris	Alfa Romeo t/c V8	33	Turbo	
	René Arnoux	Ferrari t/c V6	31	Electrics	
	Danny Sullivan	Tyrrell-Cosworth V8	30	Electrics	
	Jean-Pierre Jarier	Ligier-Cosworth V8	29	Seized wheel nut	
	Manfred Winkelhock	ATS-BMW t/c 4	26	Accident	
	Derek Warwick	Toleman-Hart t/c 4	25	Engine/water leak	
	Riccardo Patrese	Brabham-BMW t/c 4	24	Brakes	
	Elio de Angelis	Lotus-Renault t/c V6	5	Transmission/pinion	
	Eddie Cheever	Renault t/c V6	4	Distributor	
	Piercarlo Ghinzani	Osella-Alfa Romeo V12	4	Overheating	
	Patrick Tambay	Ferrari t/c V6	0	Stalled at start	

Fastest lap (revised circuit): Watson on lap 55, 1m 47·668s, 83·5902mph/134·525km/h (record).
Previous lap record (2·493 mile circuit): Alain Prost (F1 Renault RE30B t/c V6), 1m 50·438s, 81·276mph/130·801km/h (1982).

Past winners

Year	Driver	Nat	Car	Circuit	Distance miles/km	Speed mph/km/h
1982	John Watson	GB	3·0 McLaren MP4B-Ford	Detroit	154·57/248·75	78·20/128·85
1983	Michele Alboreto	I	3·0 Tyrrell 011-Ford	Detroit	150·00/241·40	81·16/130·61

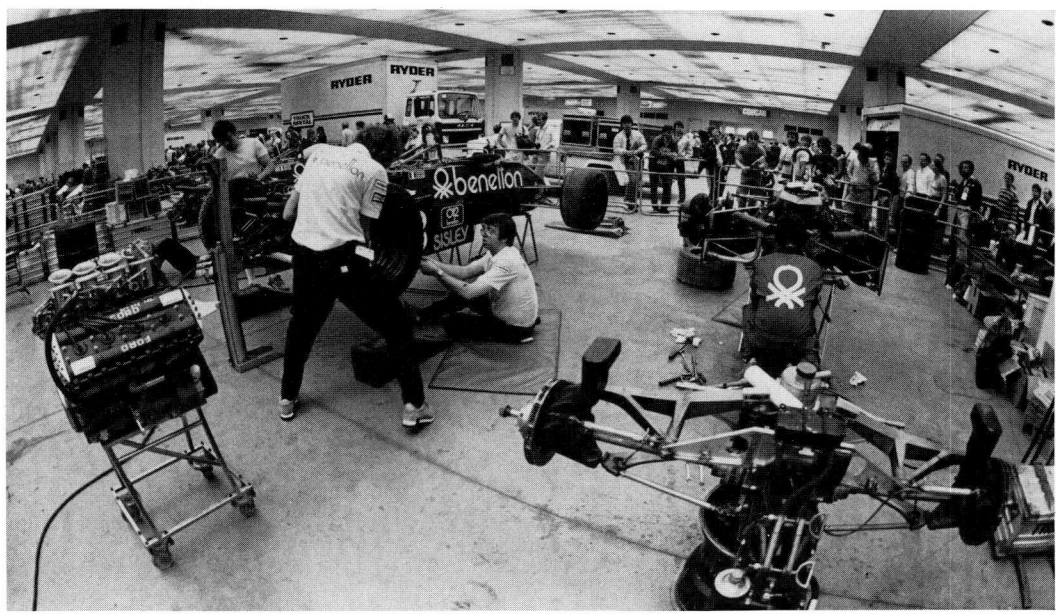

The vast garage at Cobo Hall may have been more than adequate, but the location, half a mile from the pits, left a lot to be desired. The Tyrrell mechanics prepare the winning car.

Circuit data

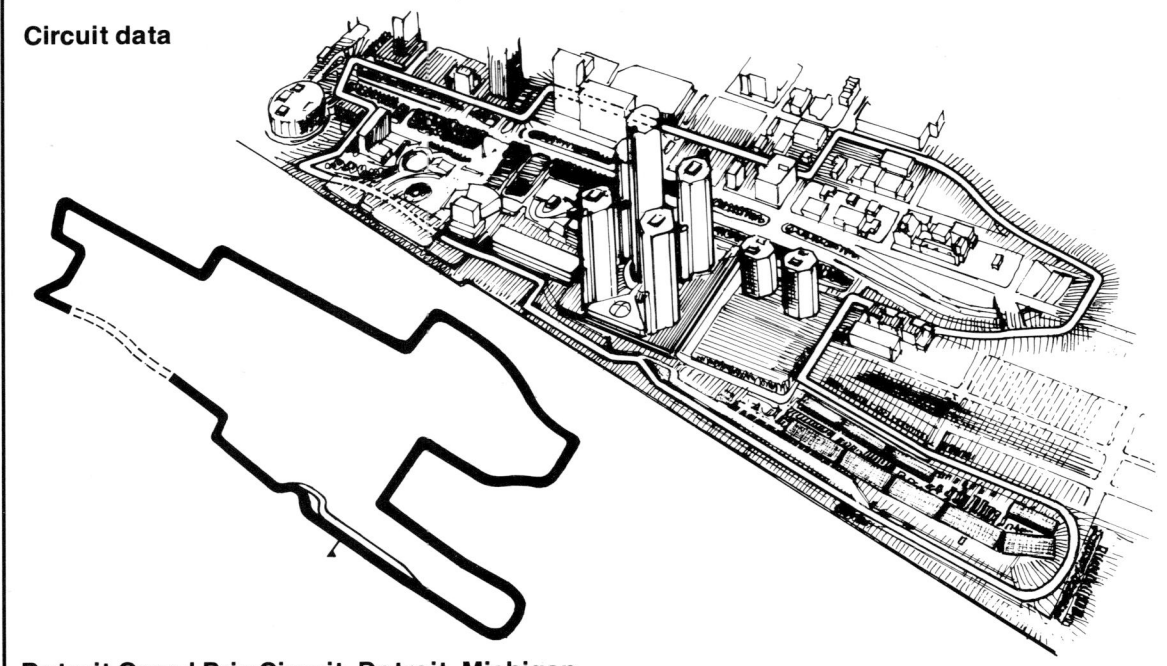

Detroit Grand Prix Circuit, Detroit, Michigan
Circuit length: 2·50 miles/4·0233 km
Race distance: 60 laps, 150 miles/241·401 km
Race weather: Warm, dry.

Fastest laps

Driver	Time	Lap
John Watson	1m 47·668s	55
Keke Rosberg	1m 47·969s	55
Nelson Piquet	1m 48·332s	46
Michele Alboreto	1m 48·443s	54
René Arnoux	1m 48·934s	23
Jacques Laffite	1m 49·252s	28
Jean-Pierre Jarier	1m 49·340s	21
Derek Warwick	1m 49·351s	20
Andrea de Cesaris	1m 49·423s	27
Marc Surer	1m 49·809s	57
Nigel Mansell	1m 50·029s	36
Danny Sullivan	1m 50·088s	26
Bruno Giacomelli	1m 50·150s	41
Thierry Boutsen	1m 50·296s	21
Roberto Guerrero	1m 50·351s	36
Alain Prost	1m 50·555s	29
Niki Lauda	1m 51·318s	17
Johnny Cecotto	1m 51·768s	34
Raul Boesel	1m 51·804s	56
Riccardo Patrese	1m 52·031s	6
Manfred Winkelhock	1m 52·093s	19
Elio de Angelis	1m 52·584s	4
Mauro Baldi	1m 53·198s	44
Eddie Cheever	1m 53·926s	3
Piercarlo Ghinzani	1m 55·000s	4

Points

WORLD CHAMPIONSHIP OF DRIVERS

1	Alain Prost	28 pts
2	Nelson Piquet	27
3	Patrick Tambay	23
4	Keke Rosberg	22
5	John Watson	15
6 =	Niki Lauda	10
6 =	Jacques Laffite	10
8	Michele Alboreto	9
9 =	René Arnoux	8
9 =	Eddie Cheever	8
11	Marc Surer	4
12	Danny Sullivan	2
13 =	Johnny Cecotto	1
13 =	Mauro Baldi	1
13 =	Nigel Mansell	1

CONSTRUCTORS' CUP

1	Renault	36 pts
2	Williams	32
3	Ferrari	31
4	Brabham	27
5	McLaren	25
6	Tyrrell	11
7	Arrows	4
8 =	Theodore	1
8 =	Alfa Romeo	1
8 =	Lotus	1

Lap chart

Laps 1–37 (circled positions shown in parentheses)

No	Driver	Positions lap 1 → 37
5	N. Piquet	5 5 5 5 5 5 5 5 5 23 28 28 28 28 28 28 28 28 28 28 28 28 28 28 28 28 28 28 (28) 28 28 5 5 5 5 5 5
28	R. Arnoux	28 28 28 28 28 28 28 28 28 5 5 5 5 5 5 5 5 5 5 1 1 1 1 1 1 1 1 1 (1) 5 5 3 3 3 3 3 3
11	E. De Angelis	11 11 11 11 11 22 22 22 22 22 1 1 1 1 1 1 1 1 1 5 5 5 5 5 5 5 5 3 3 (2) 1 1 1 1 1 1
22	A. De Cesaris	22 22 22 22 22 3 3 1 1 1 22 22 22 3 3 3 3 3 3 3 3 3 3 3 3 3 3 3 2 2 1 7 7 7 7 7 7
3	M. Alboreto	3 3 3 3 3 1 1 3 3 3 3 3 3 22 35 35 35 35 35 35 35 35 35 35 22 22 22 22 2 1 1 7 2 2 2 2 2
35	D. Warwick	35 35 35 1 1 35 35 35 35 35 35 35 35 22 22 22 22 22 22 22 22 22 22 22 2 2 2 2 (22) 7 7 30 30 30 30 30 30
1	K. Rosberg	1 1 1 35 35 15 15 15 15 15 15 15 15 15 15 2 2 2 2 2 2 2 2 2 (35) 4 7 7 7 7 4 30 12 12 12 12 12
16	E. Cheever	16 16 16 16 16 30 30 30 30 30 30 30 2 2 2 15 15 15 (15) 30 30 30 4 4 4 7 4 4 4 30 (22) 15 15 15 15 15 15
30	T. Boutsen	30 30 30 15 30 6 6 33 33 2 2 2 30 30 30 30 30 30 33 33 4 7 7 7 30 30 30 30 22 12 34 34 (34) 36 36 36
29	M. Surer	29 15 15 30 29 33 33 2 2 33 33 33 33 33 33 33 33 33 33 4 4 7 30 30 30 12 12 12 12 15 36 36 36 36 26 26 26
15	A. Prost	15 29 29 29 6 2 2 4 4 4 4 4 4 4 4 4 4 4 4 7 7 (33) 12 12 12 (35) 15 15 15 15 34 22 22 26 (34) 29 29
33	R. Guerrero	33 33 33 33 33 4 4 8 8 8 8 8 8 7 7 7 7 7 7 12 12 12 9 9 9 9 34 34 34 34 (36) 26 26 (22) 29 8 23
12	N. Mansell	12 2 2 6 2 12 12 12 29 29 (29) 7 7 7 (8) 12 12 12 12 9 9 9 36 36 36 36 36 36 36 26 29 29 29 29 8 23 8
2	J. Laffite	2 6 6 2 4 8 8 29 12 12 9 9 9 9 9 9 9 9 9 15 15 15 15 15 15 9 26 26 26 29 8 8 8 8 23 33 33
4	D. Sullivan	4 4 4 4 12 29 29 (6) 9 9 9 7 12 12 12 34 36 36 36 36 36 34 34 34 34 26 25 25 (25) 8 23 23 23 33
6	R. Patrese	6 12 12 12 8 25 9 9 7 7 12 34 34 34 34 36 34 34 34 34 34 34 6 6 (6) 26 25 25 29 29 29 23 33 33 33
8	N. Lauda	8 8 8 8 25 9 36 36 36 36 36 36 36 36 36 6 6 6 6 6 6 6 6 26 26 26 8 8 8 8 8 33
25	J. P. Jarier	25 25 25 25 9 36 7 7 34 34 34 6 6 6 6 8 8 8 8 8 8 (8) 8 8 25 29 23 23 23
9	M. Winkelhock	9 9 9 9 36 7 34 34 6 6 6 26 25 25 25 (25) 26 26 26 26 26 26 (25) 25 25 29 23 33 33 33
36	B. Giacomelli	36 36 36 36 7 34 23 23 23 26 26 25 25 26 26 26 23 (23) 25 25 25 25 29 29 29 23 33
7	J. Watson	7 7 7 7 34 23 26 26 26 23 23 23 23 23 23 25 25 25 29 29 29 29 23 23 23 33
23	M. Baldi	23 23 23 23 23 (25) 25 25 25 25 29 29 29 29 29 29 23 23 23 23 23 33 33 33
32	P. Ghinzani	32 34 34 34 26
34	J. Cecotto	34 32 26 26 (32)
26	R. Boesel	26 26 32 32

Laps 38–60

Positions lap 38 → 60
5 5 5 5 5 5 5 5 5 5 5 5 5 3 3 3 3 3 3 3 3 3 3
3 3 3 3 3 3 3 3 3 3 3 3 3 1 1 1 1 1 1 1 1 1 1
1 1 1 1 1 1 1 1 1 1 1 1 1 7 7 7 7 7 7 7 7 7 7
7 7 7 7 7 7 7 7 7 7 7 7 7 (5) 5 5 5 5 5 5 5 5 5
2 2 2 2 2 2 2 2 2 2 2 2 2 2 2 2 2 2 2 2 2 2 2
30 12 12 12 12 12 12 12 12 12 12 12 12 12 12 12 12 12 12 12
12 30 30 30 30 30 30 30 30 30 30 30 30 30 30 30 30 30 30 30
15 15 15 15 15 15 15 15 15 15 15 15 15 15 15 15 15 15 15 15
36 36 36 36 36 36 36 36 36 36 36 36 36 36 36 36 (36) 36 36
26 26 26 26 26 26 26 26 26 26 26 26 26 26 26 26 26 26 26
29 29 29 29 29 29 29 29 29 29 29 29 29 29 29 29 29 29
23 23 23 23 23 23 23 23 23 23 23 23 23 23 23 23 23
8 8 8 8 8 8 8 8 8 8 8 8 8 8 8 8 (8)
33

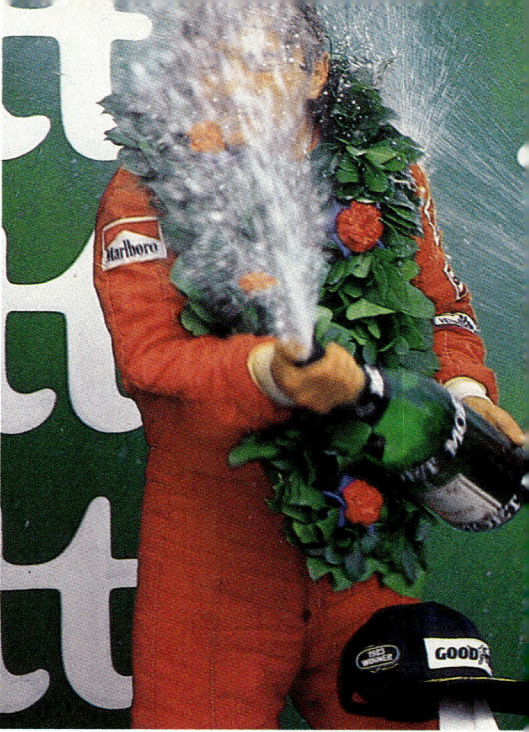

After concentrating hard for 70 laps, Patrick Tambay lets go on the rostrum after finishing third. The Ferrari driver sprays Moet over his victorious team-mate.
Photo: John Townsend and Paul Henri Cahier

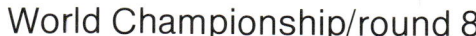

World Championship/round 8

GRAND PRIX LABATT DU CANADA

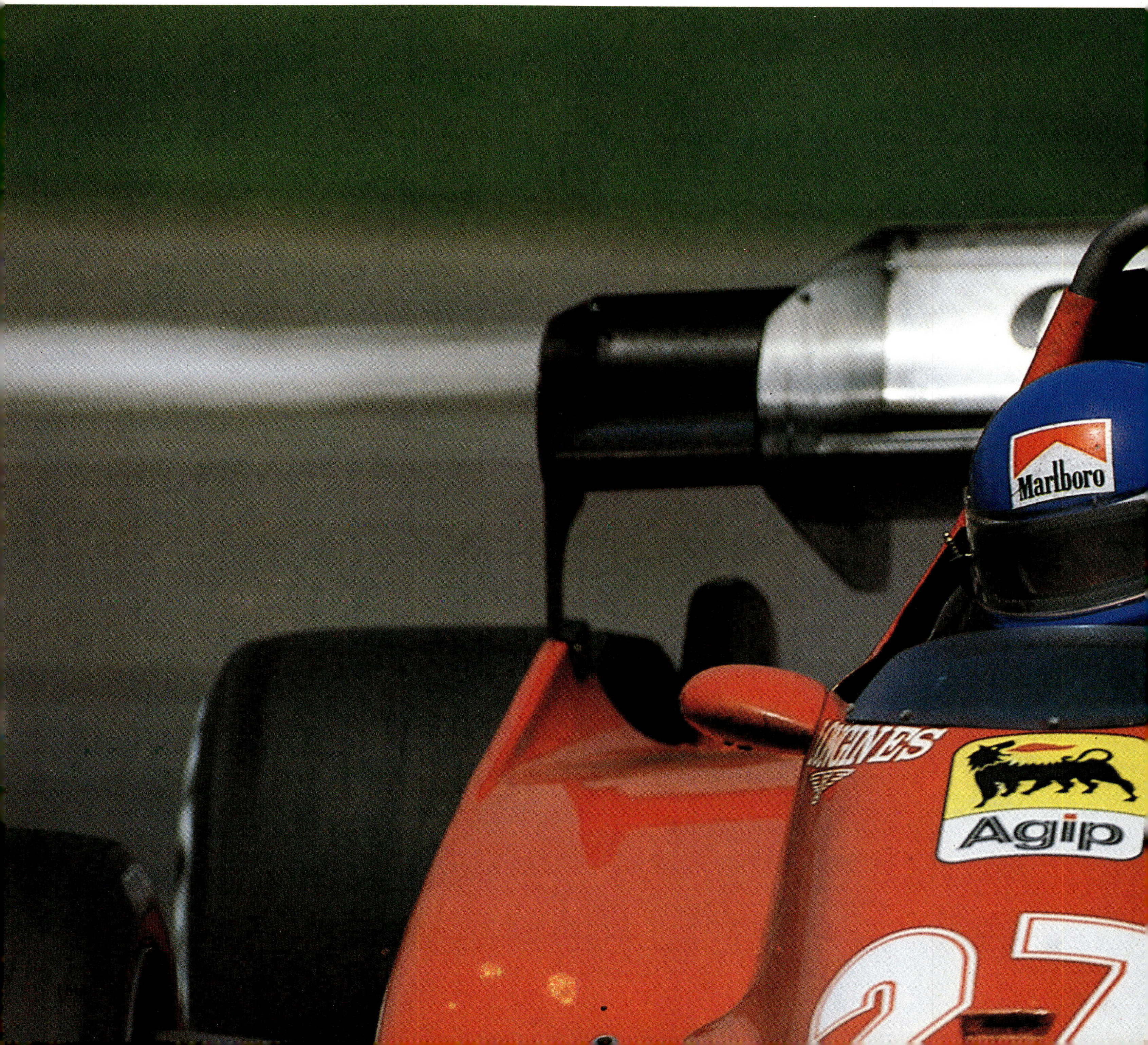

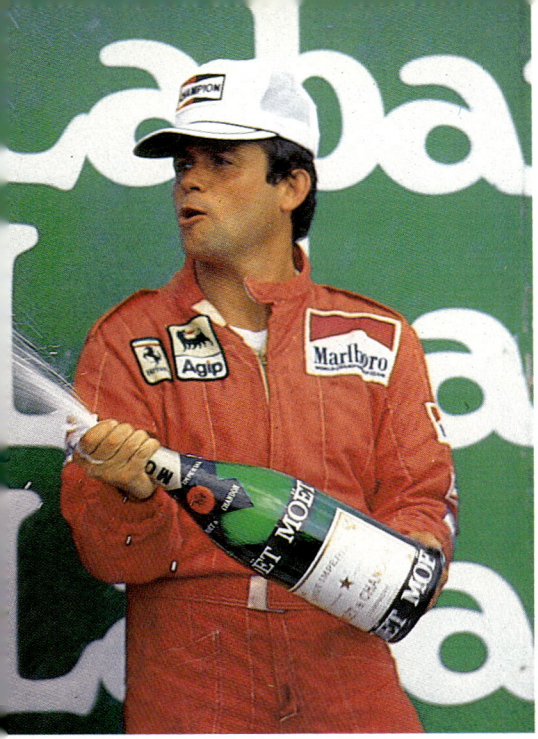

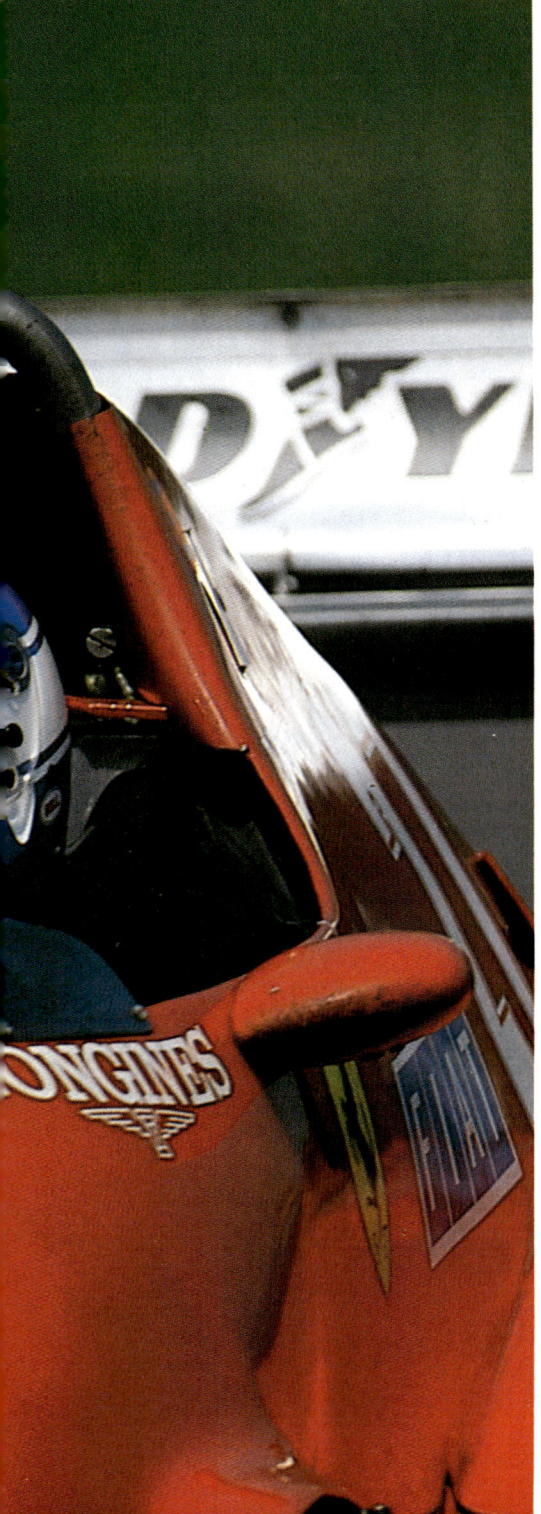

René Arnoux had good reason to phone home. At last, after three pole positions and 94 laps in the lead for Ferrari, the Frenchman had taken the chequered flag for the first time since the start of the season. It was a faultless win, Arnoux leading until his pit-stop and resuming where he had left off a few laps later. It was something to be proud of after such a miserable season; small wonder the champagne-soaked little man kept his laurels on while telephoning the good news to Italy.

René had finished 42 seconds clear of Eddie Cheever, the Renault driver, like Arnoux, at last enjoying a decent race and giving the championship an interesting twist at the half-way mark in the season.

Fifteen points shared between Arnoux and Cheever meant little change at the top of the championship — which suited Nelson Piquet just fine. The Brabham-BMW had retired from third place with a broken throttle cable on lap 16 but, fortunately for Piquet, Alain Prost, the championship leader, had only managed to collect two points for fifth place, the Renault suffering from a down-on-power engine and a puncture.

Prost now held a narrow three point lead over Piquet while Patrick Tambay joined the Brazilian in second place after a fuel vaporisation problem kept the Ferrari out of serious contention and in a distant third place. Tambay had been unable to match the pace of either his team-mate or Riccardo Patrese, the Italian recovering from a practice accident to make a good start and hold second place before retiring his Brabham-BMW with gearbox trouble.

The same fate befell Jacques Laffite but, fighting to keep the turbos in sight, the indefatigable Keke Rosberg brought his Williams home in fourth place. The Finn was a mere five points behind Prost; a remarkable tribute to Rosberg's determination and the reliability of his car.

The final point went to John Watson, the McLaren driver celebrating his MBE by working hard for sixth place in the face of a strong challenge from Thierry Boutsen in the closing stages. Watson, as usual, had started from the back of the grid and his failing carbon fibre brakes meant a wheel-to-wheel scrap with the Arrows which resulted in the two making contact.

Boutsen recovered to finish seventh ahead of Michele Alboreto, the Detroit winner having an unhappy weekend with a car which had no grip and would not handle. Into the bargain, he had blown two of the latest Ford-Cosworth DFYs, one of them the V8 which had given such good service in Detroit seven days before. Fortunes in Grand Prix racing change rapidly. It pays to wear your laurels while you can.

ENTRY AND PRACTICE

With just one week between Detroit and the Canadian Grand Prix, it was not surprising to find few changes to the cars as the teams carried out their preparation in the garages by the Olympic rowing lake of Ile Notre-Dame. Looking for a hook to hang their previews on, the local papers concentrated their attention on Jacques Villeneuve, the French-Canadian making another attempt to qualify for a Grand Prix at the circuit named after his revered brother. This time, Jacques had reached a deal with the RAM March team and John Macdonald, having missed Detroit, flew his car to Toronto to allow Villeneuve the opportunity of a test session at Mosport.

That was the circuit where Gilles Villeneuve made his race debut for Ferrari in 1977 and, had he been alive and driving for Ferrari in 1983, then it would have been a fair bet that Gilles would have taken pole position for his home Grand Prix. René Arnoux and Patrick Tambay dominated all four practice sessions although it was Arnoux who set the fastest time when it mattered most, the Frenchman taking his 17th pole position on Saturday afternoon. René had no major problems to speak of and his main preoccupation appeared to be baulking other drivers, Arnoux incurring the wrath of Cheever and de Angelis. At least it gave the papers something to write about. . . .

While it was no surprise to find Arnoux on pole, the handling of the Ferrari had not looked *that* good through the fast, bumpy curves after the pits. Tambay's car was bouncing so badly on Friday that he tried stiffer springs the following day but that turned out to be a mistake, the car showing little improvement. The change was to be academic, in any case, since Tambay's car suffered a turbo breakage during his run on his first set of qualifiers on Saturday. He switched to the T-car but chose the softer qualifying tyre — which turned out to be another mistake, Tambay managing just one quick lap before the tyres went off. In the end, he had to settle for Friday's time, just under three-tenths slower than Arnoux.

Filling that gap were Alain Prost and Nelson Piquet as the two battled it out for a place on the front row, Prost taking the credit with a single, precise lap on his last set of qualifiers. He did it using his spare car, a chassis he found to his liking after a massive engine failure forced the Frenchman to vacate his regular car on Friday. Although the spare chassis was less rigid, it felt better and Prost decided to use it for the race from the front row with his old enemy. Indeed, the animosity between the two was such that Eddie Cheever was convinced Arnoux thought it was Prost when he blocked the American on Friday. Cheever had no mechanical problems during practice but was disappointed with sixth place.

Piquet, maintaining the calm, philosophical manner evident throughout the season, was not bothered about being pushed off the front row. The Brabham had minor revisions to the aerodynamics but the team were becoming concerned over the growing number of pinion-bearing failures. On Friday, Nelson felt an electrical problem was affecting the low-speed pick-up and he used the T-car in the timed session. His race car was checked and found to be in order, which left the spare chassis for Riccardo Patrese, the Italian using it on Friday after damaging the two left-hand corners of his car. There had been a brief shower half way through the timed session and Patrese had crashed after running off line and understeering into the barrier. The car was repaired in time for the final session but Riccardo was back in the T-car once more when the BMW tightened – but not before he had set fifth fastest time.

The turbo trio, Ferrari, Renault and Brabham-BMW, filled the first three rows and, more significantly, they were over one second clear of the next car, the ATS-BMW of Manfred Winkelhock. There were

two chassis to choose from, the spare carrying the mechanical revisions seen in Detroit, Winkelhock alternating between the two before settling on the older car with the longer side-pods and familiar plumbing to the turbo. The yellow and black ATS looked extremely stable through the fast corners but vicious understeer at the hairpin was costing valuable tenths.

Similarly, the Alfa Romeo of Andrea de Cesaris was impressive through the right-hander after the pits although it became clear that most of the attention was being lavished on his car when team-mate Mauro Baldi just made the grid in 26th place. De Cesaris had a turbo failure on Friday afternoon, the Alfa Romeo creeping into the pit lane amid clouds of thick smoke. It so happened that the computer had just selected the car for weighing and, mindful of his dismissal for not stopping when requested in Brazil, de Cesaris duly swung into the enclosure just as the back of the Alfa caught alight! He was hurriedly persuaded that it would be in order if he was not weighed this time, thank you very much.

Three-tenths of a second saved de Cesaris the embarrassment of being beaten by the Cosworth of Keke Rosberg, the World Champion quite pleased to be in the top ten in the increasingly competitive world of the turbo. Understeer, as in Detroit, was the main problem with the FW08C, Jacques Laffite suffering from the same complaint while struggling unsuccessfully to improve on Friday's time during the second session. None the less, he was 13th, the second fastest Cosworth.

Splitting the Williams were the Tolemans and the Lotus-Renault of Elio de Angelis. Bruno Giacomelli turned out to be the faster of the three, the Italian coping with the understeer on the Toleman much better than his team-mate. Rather than throw the car into the hairpin, Warwick took the slower, smoother route and found he had to dip the clutch on the way. His troubles were made worse by a turbo failure on Saturday and he set his time in the spare car. Elio de Angelis, on the other hand, complained of understeer through the fast corners and no traction out of the hairpin, a problem which was partially solved by a change to softer springs on Saturday. Nigel Mansell had rather more serious alterations to his car on Friday when the Lotus mechanics grafted on the complete rear end from the spare car after the English driver broke a pinion during the morning session. Unfortunately, the two sections did not link precisely and Mansell had traction problems. His race car was back to normal the next day but a mysterious loss of revs in the afternoon meant Mansell was unable to equal a time set in the unofficial session and had to make do with 18th place.

Once again, the Arrows were impressive in every department and Dave Wass and his drivers were able to concentrate on achieving a reasonable race set-up. Both Marc Surer and Thierry Boutsen were extremely smooth through the fast corners and a fresh engine for the Swiss driver on Saturday allowed Surer to save face by qualifying .036sec quicker than his more inexperienced team-mate. Jean-Pierre Jarier got down to work straight away on Saturday afternoon and made a considerable improvement to take 16th place in the Ligier. The handling of the French cars through the right-hander after the pits was terrifying to watch and Raul Boesel was not helped by a fire which forced the Brazilian to use the spare car on Friday.

The competitiveness enjoyed by Michele Alboreto at Detroit seemed a long way off as he struggled to sort the handling on the Tyrrell. The Ford-Cosworth DFY was rather less suited to the longer gearing required at Montreal and the Italian suffered an engine failure into the bargain on Saturday morning. A quick change had Michele back on the track for the timed session – and the fresh DFY promptly blew within a few laps. Alboreto shaved a few tenths off his Friday best by using the spare car fitted with a standard DFV. Danny Sullivan, complaining of a lack of grip, was 22nd fastest, five places behind his team-mate.

On Saturday morning, the McLaren mechanics added the letters MBE to John Watson's name on the flanks of the MP4/1C but the Ulsterman was unable to celebrate his latest honour with a shattering performance on the track. The previous day he had stopped out on the circuit with transmission problems and his progress was disrupted on Saturday by a blown DFY,

Watson climbing into the T-car but failing to improve on 20th place, a fraction slower than Niki Lauda. It was the old story, of course, the McLaren/Michelin combination failing to provide grip and Roberto Guerrero was in similar trouble with the Goodyear qualifiers on his Theodore. Unfortunately for the Colombian, there was no spare car to fall back on when he broke a half-shaft on Friday afternoon and he was delayed further when another engine mounting plate broke on Saturday morning. Guerrero was 21st, his team-mate, Johnny Cecotto, 23rd.

An Osella qualified once more, this time it was the turn of Corrado Fabi in the Cosworth car while Piercarlo Ghinzani failed to make the grid when, among other things, he had clutch trouble with the Alfa Romeo car on Saturday. Jacques Villeneuve joined Ghinzani at the bottom of the time-sheet but it was not for the want of trying on the French Canadian's part. Searching desperately for working temperatures in the Pirellis, the RAM March team softened the car for Saturday and ran more wing, but Villeneuve's inability to go to work for one banzai lap on qualifiers meant he was unable to reproduce the time set in the unofficial session; a time which would have been good enough for the grid.

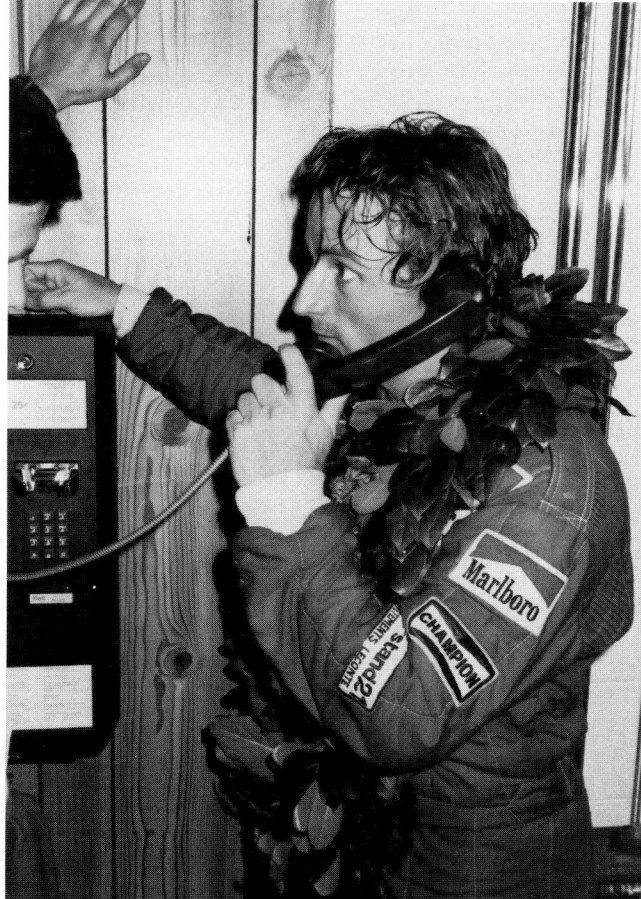

René Arnoux phones the good news after leading from pole and never being challenged throughout *(left)*.
Arnoux leads Patrese, Prost, Piquet and Tambay during the early laps. The Brabham-BMWs retired and Prost finished fifth with a down-on-power engine *(above right)*.
"Look Wattie, it's no good. We can't have the mechanics bowing in front of the car every time you come into the pits." John Watson's McLaren shows evidence of his latest honour. Alan Jenkins confers with the Ulsterman while Watson's mechanic, Tony Van-Dongen, adjusts the front wing angle. After an appalling practice, Watson ran strongly to finish sixth in spite of severe brake trouble *(right)*.
Thierry Boutsen continued to impress, the Arrows driver failing to score his first championship point after a brush with Watson during the final laps *(far right)*.
Alain Prost switched to the spare Renault after finding the less rigid chassis to be preferable. Prost maintained a narrow lead in the championship by taking two points *(below)*.

RACE

At 7 o'clock in the morning, the roads were wet, the sky menacing, and it seemed the forecast of rain in the afternoon would be correct. Happily, this was not to be the case and, by the time the warm-up had been completed, jackets and sweaters had been discarded under a hot sun which would remain for the rest of the afternoon. High temperatures in the pit lane, however, were being caused by more than simply the weather; the warm-up session had provided considerable work for the mechanics.

Roberto Guerrero's Theodore was towed back to the pit lane after the oil light had come on. Fearing a fresh engine was about to blow up, the team were relieved to find the trouble was nothing more than a faulty switch. Warwick had missed his braking point and understeered off, the trip across the grass damaging the underbody of the Toleman while, next door, the mechanics mended a broken bellhousing joint on Giacomelli's car. The metering unit had broken on de Angelis' car and, as a result, the turbine bearing had

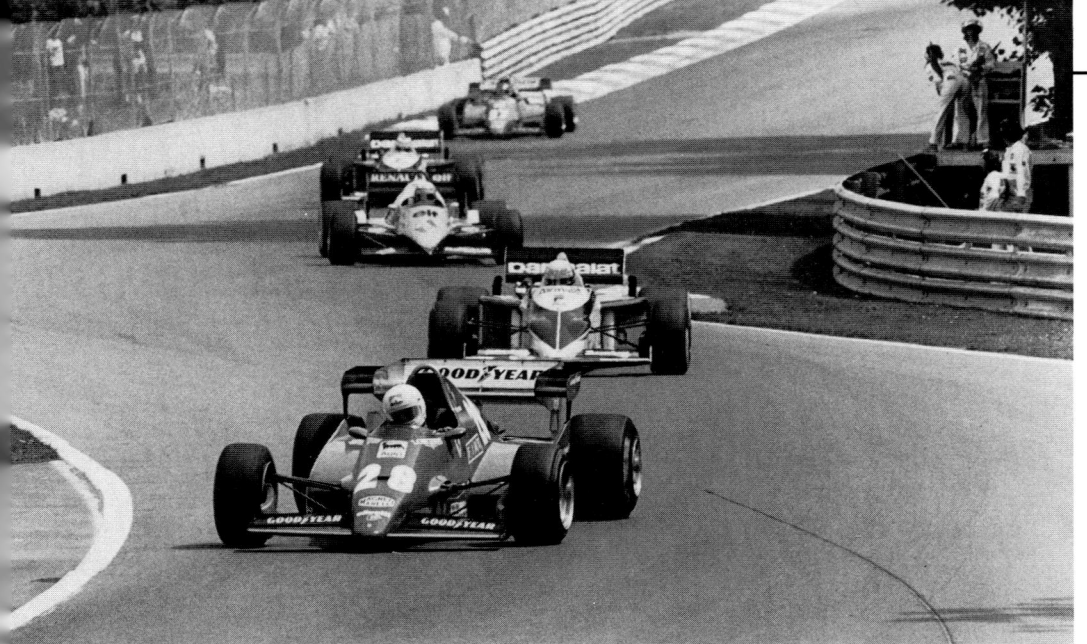

June:
Brands Hatch to host a second Grand Prix in Britain on September 25 in place of cancelled New York date.

John Watson awarded MBE in the Queen's Birthday Honours List.

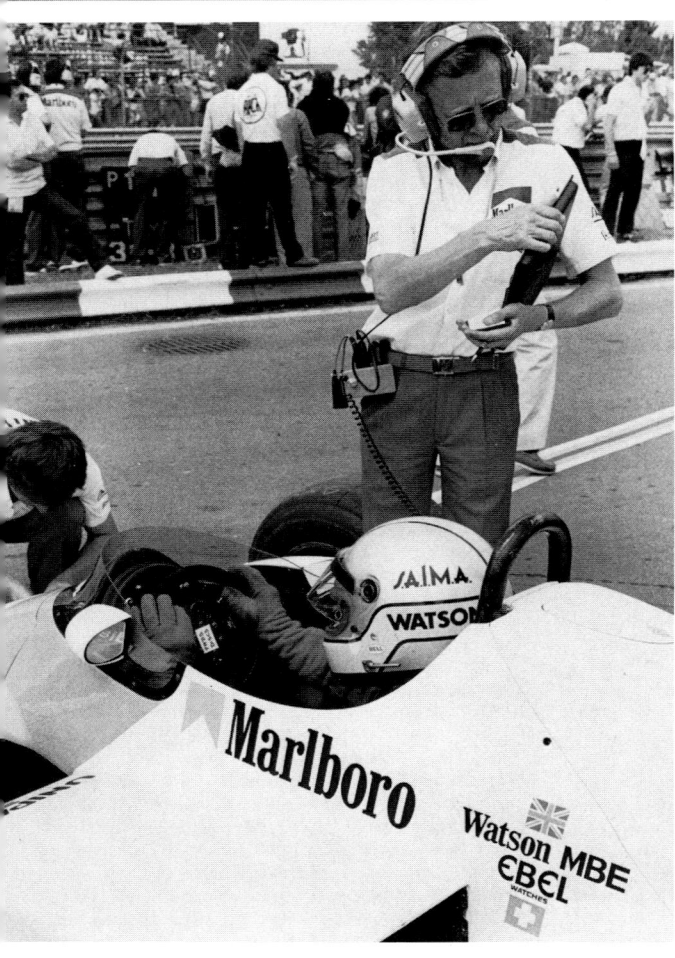

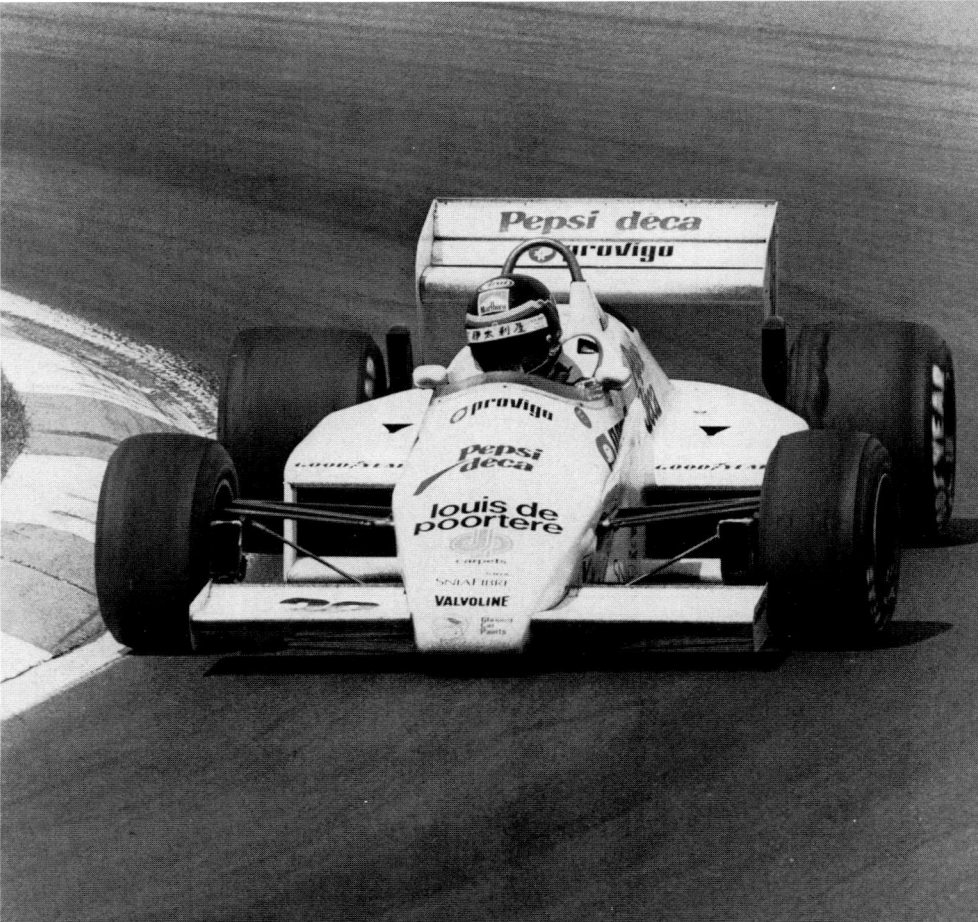

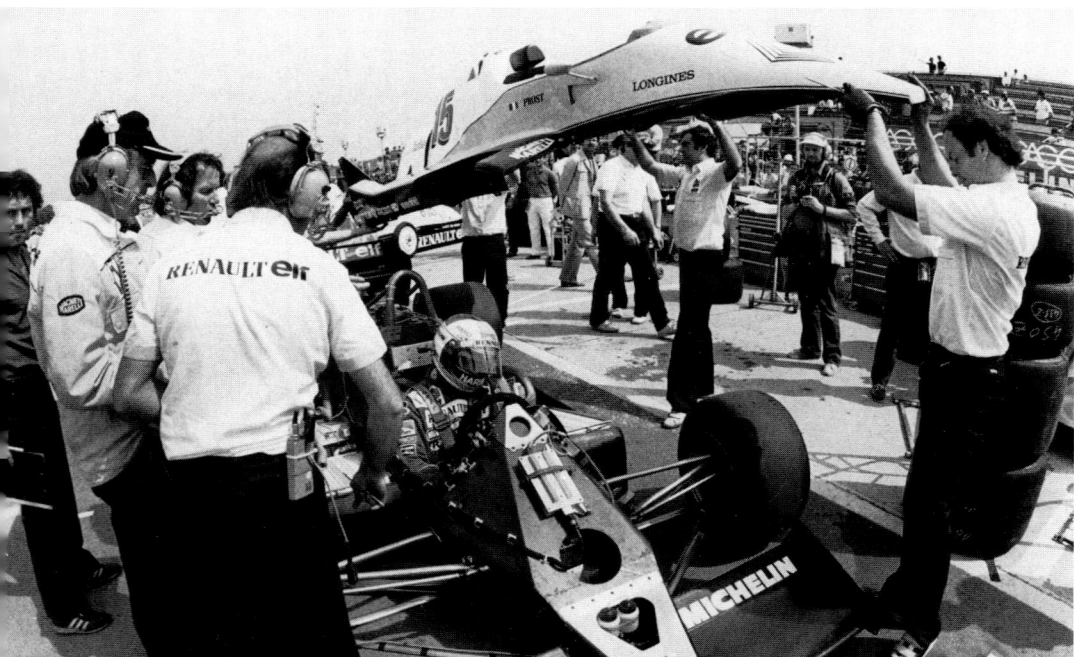

Half-way facts

WITH EIGHT OF THE 15 GRANDS PRIX COMPLETED, the statistics made interesting reading. Prost had won two races while Piquet, Watson, Tambay, Rosberg, Alboreto and Arnoux had taken one each. Five points separated the top four drivers in the championship while Renault and Ferrari were tied at the head of the Constructors' Cup. Ford-Cosworth cars had won three races and the honours in the tyre war were split evenly between Michelin and Goodyear with Arnoux giving the American company their 150th victory in Montreal. Perhaps the most striking feature, however, was the fact that Keke Rosberg, driving a Cosworth-powered Williams, would have been leading the championship had he not been disqualified from second place in Brazil.

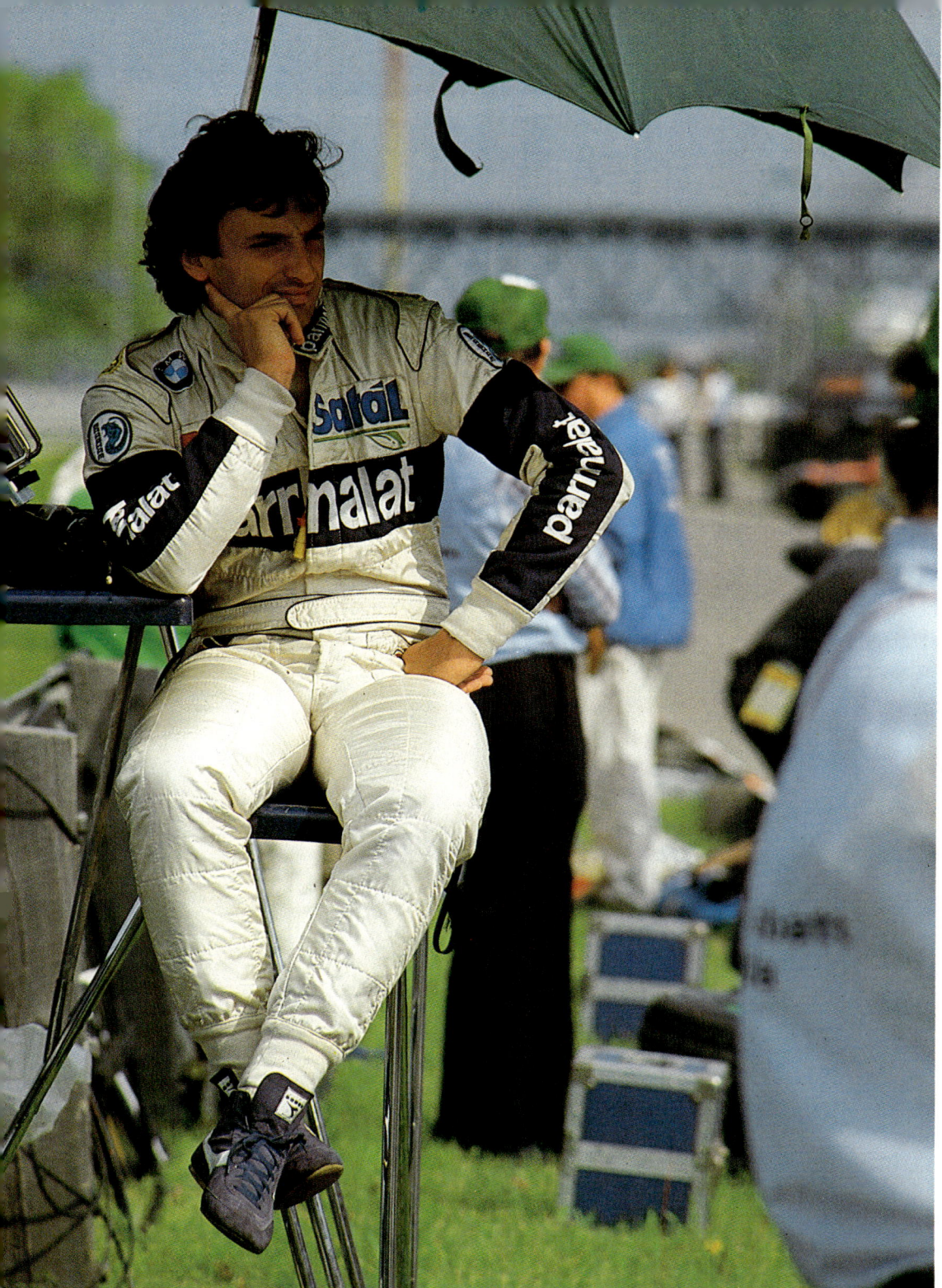

On the sidelines again. Riccardo Patrese held second place in his Brabham-BMW until the gearbox broke.
Photo: Bernard Asset

minutes, later, Nigel Mansell visited the Lotus pit for the first of several stops to change tyres. The Englishman found his car almost undriveable after last minute changes, found to be successful on de Angelis's 93T, clearly did not work on the 92-Cosworth. Mansell would eventually give up the unequal task when the supply of Pirellis ran out.

The race soon established the anticipated pattern as the Ferraris, Renaults and Brabhams pulled away from the rest of the field while Cosworth runners such as Rosberg and Watson made spectacular progress up the lap chart. Arnoux was under no threat as Patrese controlled the remaining four cars in the leading group and the first sign of a down-on-power engine for Prost came when Piquet out-gunned the Renault and took third place on lap five. Tambay and Cheever followed closely but already there was a 12-second gap to the Alfa Romeo of de Cesaris, the Italian gradually losing revs from an overheating engine. Rosberg, having dealt with Winkelhock and Giacomelli, was soon looking for a way past the Alfa but, engine trouble or not, the turbo managed to keep the Williams at bay on the straight. The result was some spectacular attempts at outbraking as the pair reached the hairpin, de Cesaris holding his line cleanly, Rosberg never giving up.

Giacomelli's early charge ended as he slipped down the field allowing Winkelhock to take ninth place ahead of Laffite. Warwick was next but soon to come under pressure from Watson while the McLaren of Lauda engaged in a battle for 14th place with the Arrows of Boutsen. Then, a gap to Alboreto, Guerrero, Sullivan and Cecotto with a further pause before Boesel, Baldi and Fabi came by.

There was to be considerable activity in the mid-field around lap 11 when, first of all, Rosberg made a lunge at the inside of de Cesaris under braking for the hairpin but did not quite make it, the two cars touching and the Williams losing two places to Winkelhock and Laffite. Watson moved ahead of Warwick; Boutsen took 13th place from Giacomelli but an attempt at a similar move by Lauda ended when the McLaren spun while trying to outbrake the Toleman. Lauda, unable to restart his engine, became the fourth retirement.

To add to Prost's problems with a down-on-power engine, his rear tyres started to go off and the Renault lost fourth place to Tambay on lap 12 with Cheever taking his team-mate not long after. All three were to benefit, however, when Nelson Piquet crawled into the pits at the end of lap 16, the Brabham's throttle cable having broken. Arnoux continued to stretch the gap over Patrese but, with Piquet's unfortunate retirement, Tambay now had a clear run at the Italian's Brabham. No sooner had he caught Patrese, and attempted one run down the inside at the hairpin, than an engine misfire – caused by fuel vaporization due, possibly, to overheating on the grid – took the competitive edge off Tambay's charge.

Nevertheless, the Ferrari was clear of Cheever, the Renault driver finding difficulty coping with Michelins which he had not used before. The car, he was to report later, was difficult to balance and was turning in too well, but Eddie had little difficulty pulling away from his team-mate in fifth place. Following the incident at the hairpin, Rosberg was soon on the attack, taking just seven laps to move ahead of Laffite, de Cesaris and Winkelhock. The ATS was soon to make a stop for tyres and Laffite finally got past the Alfa Romeo to take what had become seventh place. Watson was ninth, 10 seconds behind the Alfa Romeo, with Warwick leading a tight group consisting of Boutsen, Giacomelli, Alboreto, Guerrero, Sullivan and Cecotto. That battle was to break up when Sullivan stopped for repairs to his rear wing mounting and Cecotto pulled in on lap 18 to retire with a broken

been damaged necessitating a change of the turbos. Mansell's engine had been smoking badly and the Lotus team tackled an engine change while, of more importance perhaps, was a similar change on the Ferrari of the pole position man. Arnoux stood quietly to one side as the Italians stood shoulder to shoulder, working with extraordinary speed and confidence. The work done, the V6 was fired up, Arnoux climbed aboard and set off towards the starting grid. There was not the slightest hint of panic.

The Ferrari team had taken the surprising decision to fit both their cars with the softer 'C' compound Goodyears on the assumption that the large rear wings would prevent the cars sliding around excessively, wearing out their tyres in the process. Williams, for example, were on 'B' and, with Watson setting the second fastest Cosworth time in the warm-up, an interesting race was in prospect.

For 45 minutes, it seemed there might not be a race at all. A power failure affected the PA system, the computerised timing and the starting lights, the 26 cars sitting silently on the grid while the electricians went to work. The effect of the sun beating down on the grid was to play a part in the outcome of the race –

particularly for Tambay and Prost.

Forty minutes behind schedule, the cars completed their final parade lap, a tardy marshal's failure to remove his marker-board on the grid causing a further delay before the green light finally came on. Arnoux broke with his usual tradition and made an excellent start but Patrese made an even better one from the third row, the Brabham slotting into third place through the first corner before outbraking Prost going into the chicane. He could make no impression on Arnoux, however, and it was immediately apparent that, barring mechanical misfortune and the incorrect treatment of his tyres, the Frenchman was going to dominate the eighth round of the championship.

Certainly, any problems he might have with backmarkers was eased from the start when Jarier stripped first gear on the line. The Ligier then lost 3rd and 5th as the Frenchman crept into the pit lane just ahead of Marc Surer, the Arrows limping round the first lap with a broken output flange between the differential and a constant velocity joint. Both were retired on the spot. Not long after, they were joined by Elio de Angelis, a broken throttle linkage ending the Italian's race. That was at the end of lap two and, seven

crown wheel and pinion. Boesel had been lapped but the Ligier was a safe distance in front of Baldi, Fabi and, of course, the struggling Mansell, due to make his second stop for tyres at the end of lap 19. The rear of the field thinned out further when Fabi and Guerrero retired with engine problems and Boesel's run came to a halt out on the circuit when a rear wheel bearing failed.

Tambay's continuing misfire meant he lost third place to Cheever on lap 30 and the sight of the Renault disappearing into the distance caused Tambay to give serious thought to the misfire. At first, he was convinced it was caused by the electronic injection and it did not occur to the Frenchman to try fiddling with a device which had been placed in the cockpit to bleed the system in the event of a vapour lock. With nothing better to do, he adjusted the control – and the misfire stopped. Furious with himself for not having tried it sooner, Tambay began to pull away from Prost as the Renault driver began to entertain serious thoughts about taking back fourth place.

The routine pit stops began on lap 32, de Cesaris and Warwick coming in together followed a lap later by Prost with Laffite making his stop on lap 34. The main interest, of course, centred on the leaders and Arnoux pulled in at the end of his 35th lap. Apart from a slight delay while a mechanic moved the front jack out of the way, the stop went smoothly, René rejoining in fourth place. Patrese now led for three laps before making his stop, the Brabham mechanics working to perfection and getting their man away in under 12 seconds. Tambay's tenure at the front was brief, the Ferrari coming in at the end of the next lap and, by the time the race had settled down again, Arnoux held a 12-second lead over Patrese with Cheever a few car lengths behind the Brabham. Tambay was a further 7.4 seconds in arrears but some fast lappery by the Ferrari driver soon closed the gap and, by lap 48, Patrese, Cheever and Tambay were running nose to tail. Cheever was enjoying more consistent handling from his second set of tyres and an interesting battle was spoiled when Patrese began to slow with gearbox trouble, the Brabham driver's luck running out again as he dropped out of the top six before staggering into the pits at the end of his 57th lap.

Tambay could make no impression on Cheever since his early burst of speed had ruined his rear tyres and the Frenchman, realising Piquet was out and Prost was struggling, decided to settle for third place and safe championship points. For Arnoux, nothing less than a win would do and he continued to pull away from Cheever. Prost, his gearbox jumping out of fifth, was about to consider himself fortunate to be in fourth place when his left-front tyre punctured and he made a quick stop with 15 laps to go. That dropped the Renault to fifth place behind Rosberg while Watson was now sixth following the retirement of Jacques Laffite with a stripped third gear. Boutsen was seventh and Michele Alboreto had moved into eighth place when the Tolemans fell by the wayside with turbo and engine problems. Sullivan, two laps behind, was running strongly and the Tyrrell driver set eighth fastest lap even though he was under no threat from Winkelhock in 10th place.

The final battle of the afternoon was for one point as Boutsen closed on Watson, the McLaren driver struggling with a locking front brake, the result of his pads on the left-hand side having worn away completely. Driving with great speed and accuracy after such a tiring race, Boutsen attacked Watson with a confidence which belied his lack of experience but an attempt at outbraking into the first chicane resulted in the Arrows losing its left-front nose-wing against the McLaren's right rear wheel. Afterwards Watson said his car had been weaving unpredictably under braking

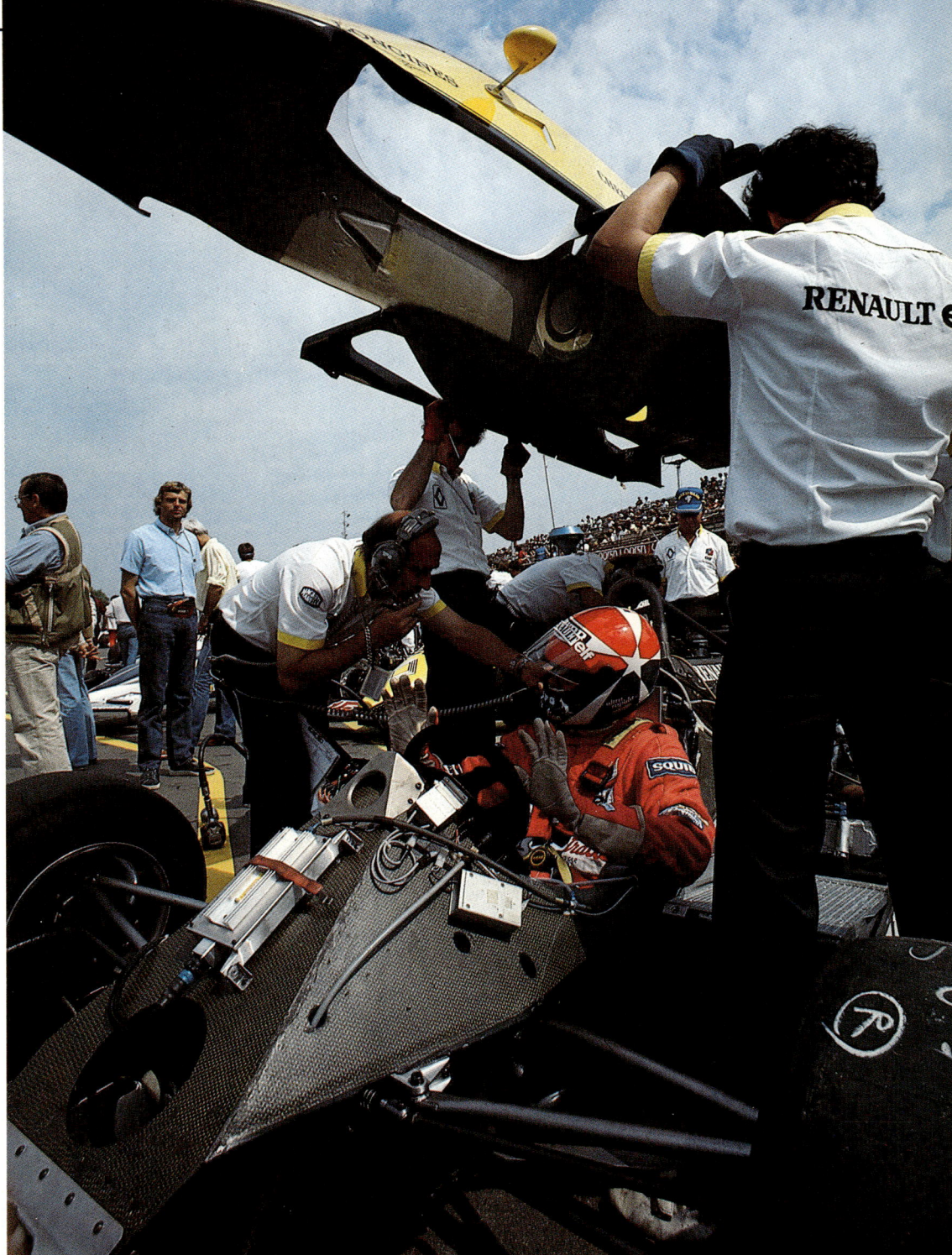

although Boutsen shook his head and commented dryly, "he won't do that to me again."

We expected a certain amount of ill-feeling when Keke Rosberg was questioned about his dice with de Cesaris, bearing in mind previous confrontations between the two in 1982. But Rosberg had no complaints: "He never moved an inch off his line, and the door was open in every corner. I simply didn't have the guts – or the brakes – to take advantage of it. His car braked better than mine. The kid was driving absolutely clean – but very hard." As he spoke, Rosberg took the weight off his right foot after experiencing pains similar to those which afflicted him in Las Vegas the previous year. He did not know what caused the problem but it made the brake and throttle pedals feel as though they were red hot. Fourth place, therefore, was an excellent result for the Williams driver and kept Rosberg in contention for the championship.

The contrast between Rosberg and Arnoux was noticeable as the sweat-soaked World Champion hobbled off. Arnoux looked as calm and composed as his drive had been, although he took on a bedraggled appearance on the rostrum when Tambay sprayed the

contents of his champagne bottle in René's direction.

On a sadder note, a small wreath, placed at the side of the grid by the Osella team in memory of Riccardo Paletti, acted as a reminder of the Canadian Grand Prix's unfortunate history. This year, the race had been incident free and, indeed, the only injuries had occurred to Bruno Giacomelli when he fell off Rosberg's Williams after hitching a ride back to the pits at the end of the race!

The Italian was treated for bruising while the mechanics began dismantling the cars for the journey back to Europe. The Tyrrell team reluctantly accepted Danny Sullivan's disqualification from eighth place when his car was found to be underweight. An exhaust pipe had fallen off during the race but, even when this was placed on the car, a complete loss of water from the cooling system meant the Tyrrell was 4 kilos under. With topping up strictly forbidden, that was that.

As the sun continued to beat down, the rest of the teams took stock. Ferrari were soon to unveil their 126C3, an altogether more competitive proposition than the cars which had just finished first and third. It was a disquieting thought – but one which made the winner's call home all the sweeter.

Entries and practice times

No.	Driver	Nat	Car	Tyre	Engine	Entrant	Practice 1	Practice 2
1	Keke Rosberg	SF	Saudia WILLIAMS FW08C	G	Ford Cosworth DFV	TAG Williams Team	1m 31·583s	**1m 31·480s**
2	Jacques Laffite	F	Saudia WILLIAMS FW08C	G	Ford Cosworth DFV	TAG Williams Team	**1m 32·185s**	1m 32·632s
3	Michele Alboreto	I	Benetton TYRRELL 011	G	Ford Cosworth DFV/DFY	Benetton Tyrrell Team	1m 33·664s	**1m 33·175s**
4	Danny Sullivan	USA	Benetton TYRRELL 011	G	Ford Cosworth DFV/DFY	Benetton Tyrrell Team	1m 34·680s	**1m 33·791s**
5	Nelson Piquet	BR	Parmalat BRABHAM BT52	M	BMW M12/13	Fila Sport	1m 30·366s	**1m 28·887s**
6	Riccardo Patrese	I	Parmalat BRABHAM BT52	M	BMW M12/13	Fila Sport	1m 31·227s	**1m 29·549s**
7	John Watson	GB	Marlboro McLAREN MP4/1C	M	Ford Cosworth DFV/DFY	Marlboro McLaren International	1m 34·008s	**1m 33·705s**
8	Niki Lauda	A	Marlboro McLAREN MP4/1C	M	Ford Cosworth DFV/DFY	Marlboro McLaren International	1m 34·452s	**1m 33·671s**
9	Manfred Winkelhock	D	ATS D6	G	BMW M12/13	Team ATS	1m 31·756s	**1m 30·966s**
11	Elio de Angelis	I	John Player Special LOTUS 93T	P	Renault EF1	John Player Team Lotus	1m 33·231s	**1m 31·822s**
12	Nigel Mansell	GB	John Player Special LOTUS 92	P	Ford Cosworth DFV/DFY	John Player Team Lotus	**1m 33·588s**	1m 34·010s
15	Alain Prost	F	Elf RENAULT RE40	M	Renault EF1	Equipe Renault Elf	1m 29·942s	**1m 28·830s**
16	Eddie Cheever	USA	Elf RENAULT RE40	M	Renault EF1	Equipe Renault Elf	1m 30·255s	**1m 29·863s**
17	Jacques Villeneuve	CDN	MARCH-RAM 01	P	Ford Cosworth DFV	RAM Automotive Team March	1m 37·858s	**1m 35·133s**
22	Andrea de Cesaris	I	Marlboro ALFA ROMEO 183T	M	Alfa Romeo 183T	Marlboro Team Alfa Romeo	1m 31·813s	**1m 31·173s**
23	Mauro Baldi	I	Marlboro ALFA ROMEO 183T	M	Alfa Romeo 183T	Marlboro Team Alfa Romeo	1m 34·988s	**1m 34·755s**
25	Jean-Pierre Jarier	F	Gitanes LIGIER JS21	M	Ford Cosworth DFV	Equipe Ligier Gitanes	1m 34·403s	**1m 32·642s**
26	Raul Boesel	BR	Gitanes LIGIER JS21	M	Ford Cosworth DFV	Equipe Ligier Gitanes	1m 34·967s	**1m 34·486s**
27	Patrick Tambay	F	Fiat FERRARI 126C2/B	G	Ferrari 126C	Scuderia Ferrari SpA SEFAC	**1m 28·992s**	1m 29·658s
28	René Arnoux	F	Fiat FERRARI 126C2/B	G	Ferrari 126C	Scuderia Ferrari SpA SEFAC	1m 28·984s	**1m 28·729s**
29	Marc Surer	CH	ARROWS A6	G	Ford Cosworth DFV	Arrows Racing Team	1m 32·931s	**1m 32·540s**
30	Thierry Boutsen	B	ARROWS A6	G	Ford Cosworth DFV	Arrows Racing Team	1m 32·643s	**1m 32·576s**
31	Corrado Fabi	I	OSELLA FA1D	M	Ford Cosworth DFV	Osella Squadra Corse	1m 35·554s	**1m 34·544s**
32	Piercarlo Ghinzani	I	OSELLA FA1E	M	Alfa Romeo 1260	Osella Squadra Corse	1m 35·493s	**1m 35·171s**
33	Roberto Guerrero	COL	THEODORE N183	G	Ford Cosworth DFV	Theodore Racing Team	1m 35·283s	**1m 33·721s**
34	Johnny Cecotto	YV	THEODORE N183	G	Ford Cosworth DFV	Theodore Racing Team	1m 36·260s	**1m 34·314s**
35	Derek Warwick	GB	Candy TOLEMAN TG183B	P	Hart 415T	Candy Toleman Motorsport	1m 32·351s	**1m 32·116s**
36	Bruno Giacomelli	I	Candy TOLEMAN TG183B	P	Hart 415T	Candy Toleman Motorsport	1m 32·208s	**1m 31·586s**

Friday morning and Saturday morning practice sessions not officially recorded.

G – Goodyear, M – Michelin, P – Pirelli.

Fri pm — Cool, dry
Sat pm — Hot, dry

Starting grid

	28 ARNOUX (1m 28·729s) Ferrari
15 PROST (1m 28·830s) Renault	
	5 PIQUET (1m 28·887s) Brabham
27 TAMBAY (1m 28·992s) Ferrari	
	6 PATRESE (1m 29·549s) Brabham
16 CHEEVER (1m 29·863s) Renault	
	9 WINKELHOCK (1m 30·966s) ATS
22 DE CESARIS (1m 31·173s) Alfa Romeo	
	1 ROSBERG (1m 31·480s) Williams
36 GIACOMELLI (1m 31·586s) Toleman	
	11 DE ANGELIS (1m 31·822s) Lotus
35 WARWICK (1m 32·116s) Toleman	
	2 LAFFITE (1m 32·185s) Williams
29 SURER (1m 32·540s) Arrows	
	30 BOUTSEN (1m 32·576s) Arrows
25 JARIER (1m 32·642s) Ligier	
	3 ALBORETO (1m 33·175s) Tyrrell
12 MANSELL (1m 33·588s) Lotus	
	8 LAUDA (1m 33·671s) McLaren
7 WATSON (1m 33·705s) McLaren	
	33 GUERRERO (1m 33·721s) Theodore
4 SULLIVAN (1m 33·791s) Tyrrell	
	34 CECOTTO (1m 34·314s) Theodore
25 BOESEL (1m 34·486s) Ligier	
	31 FABI (1m 34·544s) Osella
23 BALDI (1m 34·755s) Alfa Romeo	

Did not start:
17 Villeneuve (March-RAM), 1m 35·133s, did not qualify
32 Ghinzani (Osella), 1m 35·171s, did not qualify

Results and retirements

Place	Driver	Car	Laps	Time and Speed (mph/km/h)/Retirement	
1	René Arnoux	Ferrari t/c V6	70	1h 48m 31·838s	106·044/170·661
2	Eddie Cheever	Renault t/c V6	70	1h 49m 13·867s	105·384/169·6
3	Patrick Tambay	Ferrari t/c V6	70	1h 49m 24·448s	105·198/169·3
4	Keke Rosberg	Williams-Cosworth V8	70	1h 49m 48·886s	104·825/168·7
5	Alain Prost	Renault t/c V6	69		
6	John Watson	McLaren-Cosworth V8	69		
7	Thierry Boutsen	Arrows-Cosworth V8	69		
8	Michele Alboreto	Tyrrell-Cosworth V8	68		
*	Danny Sullivan	Tyrrell-Cosworth V8	68		
9	Manfred Winkelhock	ATS-BMW t/c 4	67		
10	Mauro Baldi	Alfa Romeo t/c V8	67		
	Riccardo Patrese	Brabham-BMW t/c 4	57	Gearbox	
	Derek Warwick	Toleman-Hart t/c 4	47		
	Bruno Giacomelli	Toleman-Hart t/c 4	43	Handling/tyres	
	Nigel Mansell	Lotus-Cosworth V8	43	Engine	
	Andrea de Cesaris	Alfa Romeo t/c V8	43	Engine	
	Jacques Laffite	Williams-Cosworth V8	38	Gearbox	
	Raul Boesel	Ligier-Cosworth V8	32	Wheel bearing	
	Roberto Guerrero	Theodore-Cosworth V8	27	Engine	
	Corrado Fabi	Osella-Cosworth V8	27	Engine	
	Johnny Cecotto	Theodore-Cosworth V8	18	Crown wheel & pinion	
	Nelson Piquet	Brabham-BMW t/c 4	16	Throttle cable	
	Niki Lauda	McLaren-Cosworth V8	11	Spun, could not restart	
	Elio de Angelis	Lotus-Renault t/c V6	2	Throttle linkage	
	Jean-Pierre Jarier	Ligier-Cosworth V8	1	Gearbox	
	Marc Surer	Arrows-Cosworth V8	1	Transmission	

* Disqualified

Fastest lap: Tambay, on lap 42, 1m 30·851s, 108·583mph/174·747km/h.
Lap record: Didier Pironi (F1 Ferrari 126C2 t/c V6), 1m 28·323s, 111·691mph/179·749km/h (1982).

Past winners

Year	Driver	Nat	Car	Circuit	Distance miles/km	Speed mph/km/h
1961*	Pete Ryan	CDN	2·5 Lotus 19-Climax	Mosport Park	245·90/395·74	88·38/142·23
1962*	Masten Gregory	USA	2·5 Lotus 19-Climax	Mosport Park	245·90/395·74	88·52/142·46
1963*	Pedro Rodriguez	MEX	3·0 Ferrari 250P	Mosport Park	245·90/395·74	91·55/147·34
1964*	Pedro Rodriguez	MEX	4·0 Ferrari 330P	Mosport Park	245·90/395·74	94·36/151·86
1965*	Jim Hall	USA	5·4 Chaparral 2B-Chevrolet	Mosport Park	245·90/395·74	93·78/150·92
1966*	Mark Donohue	USA	6·0 Lola T70 Mk 2-Chevrolet	Mosport Park	209·02/336·38	101·87/163·94
1967	Jack Brabham	AUS	3·0 Brabham BT24-Repco	Mosport Park	221·31/356·16	82·99/133·56
1968	Denny Hulme	NZ	3·0 McLaren M7A-Ford	St Jovite	238·50/383·83	97·22/156·47
1969	Jacky Ickx	B	3·0 Brabham BT26A-Ford	Mosport Park	221·31/356·16	111·19/179·93
1970	Jacky Ickx	B	3·0 Ferrari 312B/70	St Jovite	238·50/383·83	101·27/162·98
1971	Jackie Stewart	GB	3·0 Tyrrell 003-Ford	Mosport Park	157·38/253·27	81·96/131·90
1972	Jackie Stewart	GB	3·0 Tyrrell 005-Ford	Mosport Park	196·72/316·59	114·28/183·92
1973	Peter Revson	USA	3·0 McLaren M23-Ford	Mosport Park	196·72/316·59	99·13/159·53
1974	Emerson Fittipaldi	BR	3·0 McLaren M23-Ford	Mosport Park	196·72/316·59	117·52/189·13
1976	James Hunt	GB	3·0 McLaren M23-Ford	Mosport Park	196·72/316·59	117·84/189·65
1977	Jody Scheckter	ZA	3·0 Wolf WR1-Ford	Mosport Park	196·72/316·59	118·03/189·95
1978	Gilles Villeneuve	CDN	3·0 Ferrari 312T-3/78	Ile Notre-Dame	195·72/314·98	99·67/160·40
1979	Alan Jones	AUS	3·0 Williams FW07-Ford	Ile Notre-Dame	197·28/317·52	105·35/169·54
1980	Alan Jones	AUS	3·0 Williams FW07B-Ford	Ile Notre-Dame	191·82/308·70	110·00/177·03
1981	Jacques Laffite	F	3·0 Ligier JS17-Matra	Ile Notre-Dame	172·62/277·83	85·31/137·29
1982	Nelsort Piquet	BR	1·5 Brabham BT50-BMW t/c	Ile Notre-Dame	191·82/308·70	107·93/173·70
1983	René Arnoux	F	1·5 Ferrari 126C2/B t/c	Ile Notre-Dame	191·82/308·70	106·04/170·66

* Non-championship (sports cars)

Lap chart

No	Driver	1	2	3	4	5	6	7	8	9	10	11	12	13	14	15	16	17	18	19	20	21	22	23	24	25	26	27	28	29	30	31	32	33	34	35	36	37
28	R. Arnoux	28	28	28	28	28	28	28	28	28	28	28	28	28	28	28	28	28	28	28	28	28	28	28	28	28	28	28	28	28	28	28	28	28	28	(28)	6	6
6	R. Patrese	6	6	6	6	6	6	6	6	6	6	6	6	6	6	6	6	6	6	6	6	6	6	6	6	6	6	6	6	6	6	6	6	6	6	6	(16)	27
15	A. Prost	15	15	15	15	5	5	5	5	5	5	5	5	5	5	5	5	5	27	27	27	27	27	27	27	27	27	27	16	16	16	16	16	16	16	16	16	16
5	N. Piquet	5	5	5	5	15	15	15	15	15	15	15	15	15	27	27	27	27	16	16	16	16	16	16	16	16	16	16	27	27	27	27	27	27	28	28	28	16
27	P. Tambay	27	27	27	27	27	27	27	27	27	27	27	15	15	16	16	15	15	15	15	15	15	15	15	15	15	15	15	15	15	15	(15)	15	15	15	15		
16	E. Cheever	16	16	16	16	16	16	16	16	16	16	16	16	15	15	(5)	9	1	1	1	1	1	1	1	1	1	1	1	1	1	1	1	1	1	1	1	1	1
22	A. De Cesaris	22	22	22	22	22	22	22	22	22	22	22	22	22	9	1	9	2	2	2	2	2	2	2	2	2	2	2	2	2	2	2	2	2	(2)	2	2	2
36	B. Giacomelli	36	36	36	36	1	1	1	1	1	1	2	9	9	22	1	2	2	22	22	22	22	22	22	22	22	22	22	22	7	7	7	7	7	7	7	7	7
9	M. Winkelhock	9	9	1	1	9	9	9	9	9	9	9	2	2	1	1	22	22	22	(9)	7	7	7	7	7	7	7	7	7	7	7	22	(22)	30	30	30	30	30
1	K. Rosberg	1	1	9	9	2	2	2	2	2	2	1	1	1	2	2	7	7	35	35	35	35	35	35	35	35	35	35	35	(35)	36	36	36	36	36			
11	E. De Angelis	11	30	30	2	36	36	36	35	35	35	7	7	7	7	7	35	35	35	30	30	30	30	30	30	30	30	30	30	3	3	3	3	3				
30	T. Boutsen	30	2	2	30	30	35	35	7	7	7	35	35	35	35	35	30	30	30	36	36	36	36	36	36	36	36	36	36	22	22	22	22	22				
2	J. Laffite	2	35	35	35	35	30	7	36	36	30	30	30	30	30	30	36	36	36	3	3	3	3	3	3	3	3	3	3	35	35	35	35	35				
35	D. Warwick	35	8	8	8	8	7	30	30	30	36	36	36	36	36	36	3	3	3	33	33	33	33	33	33	(33)	9	9	9	9	9	9	9	9	9			
8	N. Lauda	8	12	7	7	7	8	8	8	8	8	(8)	3	3	3	3	3	33	33	33	9	9	9	9	9	9	26	26	26	(26)	23	23	23	23	23			
12	N. Mansell	12	7	12	12	12	3	3	3	3	3	33	33	33	33	33	34	26	26	26	26	26	26	26	23	23	23	23	23	4	4	4	4					
3	M. Alboreto	3	3	3	3	3	33	33	33	33	33	33	4	4	4	4	4	(4)	23	23	23	23	23	23	23	23	4	4	4	4	(12)	12	12	12	(12)			
7	J. Watson	7	33	33	33	33	4	4	4	4	4	34	34	34	34	34	26	(34)	31	31	31	31	31	31	(31)	4	4	12	12	12	12	12						
33	R. Guerrero	33	4	4	4	4	34	34	34	34	34	26	26	26	26	26	23	31	4	4	4	4	4	4	12	(12)												
4	D. Sullivan	4	34	34	34	34	26	26	26	26	26	23	23	23	23	31	12	(12)	12	12	12	12	12	12	31	(31)												
26	R. Boesel	26	26	26	26	26	23	23	23	23	23	31	31	31	31	12	4																					
34	J. Cecotto	34	23	23	23	23	(12)	31	31	31	31	31	12	12	12	12	12																					
23	M. Baldi	23	31	31	31	31	31	12	12	12	12	12																										
31	C. Fabi	31	(11)																																			
25	J. P. Jarier	(25)																																				
29	M. Surer	(29)																																				

38	39	40	41	42	43	44	45	46	47	48	49	50	51	52	53	54	55	56	57	58	59	60	61	62	63	64	65	66	67	68	69	70
(6)	28	28	28	28	28	28	28	28	28	28	28	28	28	28	28	28	28	28	28	28	28	28	28	28	28	28	28	28	28	28	28	28
27	(27)	6	6	6	6	6	6	6	6	16	16	16	16	16	16	16	16	16	16	16	16	16	16	16	16	16	16	16	16	16	16	16
28	6	16	16	16	16	16	16	16	16	27	27	27	27	27	27	27	27	27	27	27	27	27	27	27	27	27	27	27	27	27	27	27
16	16	27	27	27	27	27	27	27	27	(15)	1	1	1	1	1	1	1	1	1	1	1	1	1	1	1	1	1	1	1	1	1	1
15	15	15	15	15	15	15	15	15	15	15	15	15	15	15	6	6	15	15	15	15	15	15	15	15	15	15	15	15	15			
1	1	1	1	1	1	1	1	1	1	1	1	1	1	1	1	1	15	7	7	7	7	7	7	7	7	7	7	7	7			
7	7	7	7	7	7	7	7	7	7	7	7	7	7	7	7	7	7	(6)	30	30	30	30	30	30	30	30	30	30	30			
30	30	30	30	30	30	30	30	30	30	30	30	30	30	30	30	30	30	3	3	3	3	3	3	3	3	3	3					
(2)	3	3	3	3	3	3	3	3	3	3	3	3	3	3	3	4	4	4	4	4	4	4	4	4	4	4						
(36)	22	22	22	22	35	35	35	(35)	9	9	9	9	9	9	9	4	4	9	9	9	9	9	9	9	9	9						
3	36	35	35	35	(36)	9	9	9	9	4	4	4	4	4	4	(9)	9	9	23	23	23	23	23	23	23	23						
22	35	36	36	36	(22)	4	4	4	23	23	23	23	23	23	23	23	23															
35	9	9	9	9	23	23	23	23																								
9	4	4	4	4	4	(12)																										
4	23	23	23	23	23																											
(23)	12	12	12	(12)	12																											
12																																

Points

WORLD CHAMPIONSHIP OF DRIVERS

1	Alain Prost	30 pts
2 =	Nelson Piquet	27
2 =	Patrick Tambay	27
4	Keke Rosberg	25
5	René Arnoux	17
6	John Watson	16
7	Eddie Cheever	14
8 =	Niki Lauda	10
8 =	Jacques Laffite	10
10	Michele Alboreto	9
11	Marc Surer	4
12	Danny Sullivan	2
13 =	Johnny Cecotto	1
13 =	Mauro Baldi	1
13 =	Nigel Mansell	1

CONSTRUCTORS' CUP

1 =	Renault	44 pts
1 =	Ferrari	44
3	Williams	35
4	Brabham	27
5	McLaren	26
6	Tyrrell	11
7	Arrows	4
8 =	Theodore	1
8 =	Alfa Romeo	1
8 =	Lotus	1

Circuit data
Circuit Gilles Villeneuve, Ile Notre-Dame, Montreal, Quebec
Circuit length: 2·74 miles/4·41 km
Race distance: 70 laps, 191·82 miles/308·70 km
Race weather: Hot, dry.

Almost unnoticed, Alain Prost mingled with the crowd surrounding the Ferraris on the front of the grid and examined the tyres selected by René Arnoux and Patrick Tambay. Then he stood, hands on hips, for a few seconds before wandering back to his car on the second row. If he was to have any chance of winning, he would need to attack the red cars fairly quickly; unsettle them; force them to push their Goodyears to the limit. Prost's Michelins, he was sure, were up to the job and he knew that, but for an engine misfire, the Renault could have taken a place on the front row. For the time being, however, the second rank was good enough.

As usual, 'Professor' Prost's calculations proved correct. The Ferraris set off at what would literally be a blistering pace and, within 10 laps, the Goodyears had lost their edge, oversteer on the red cars through the Woodcote chicane and better braking on the Renault giving Prost the opportunity to pick them off one-by-one into Copse. By lap 20, he was in the lead.

Underlining the Michelin superiority, Nelson Piquet moved in to challenge the Ferraris but it took the Brabham-BMW driver longer to work his way through. By lap 31, he was in second place but Prost was already 12 seconds to the good. The pit stops would be critical.

Piquet duly took the lead as the Renault dived into the pits five laps later but, unfortunately for the Brazilian, he lost valuable time lapping one or two hectic battles among the back-markers. He lost even more time behind Boesel's Ligier while leaving the pit lane after his stop, but at least the Brabham felt good and Nelson prepared to attack Prost's lead.

To do that, he needed to be informed by his pit of the gap to the leader. But none came. Gordon Murray was already astride his Suzuki Katana and making his way home; Bernie Ecclestone was sure Nelson knew how he was placed. But he didn't and, not being able to see the Renault, Piquet wound down the boost and settled for second place.

Tambay finished third and Arnoux slipped to fifth place but, splitting the Ferraris and making a dull race interesting, Nigel Mansell hauled his new Lotus

World Championship/round 9

Marlboro BRITISH GRAND PRIX

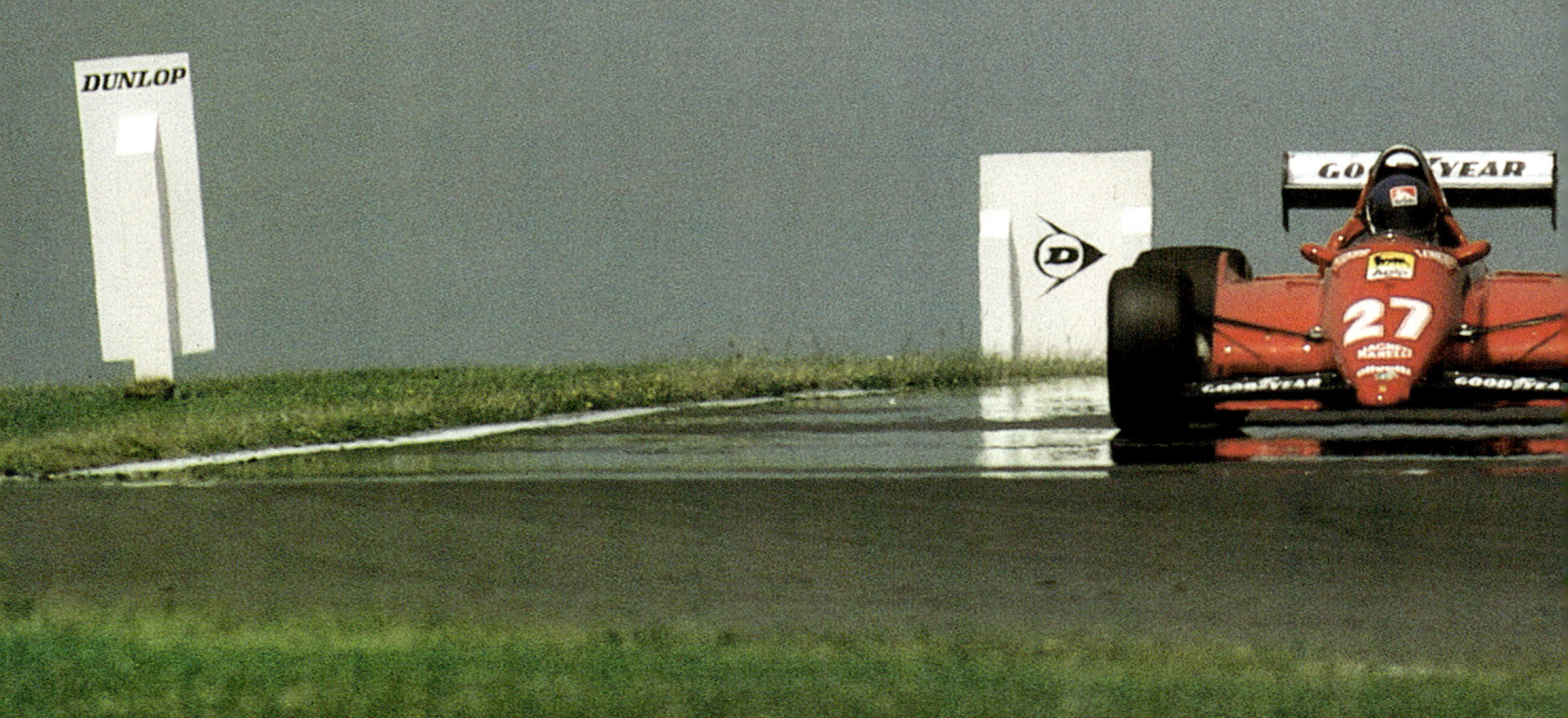

94T-Renault into fourth position after two days of practice dramas to end all practice dramas. The driving force of Gerard Ducarouge had ensured that the new cars had been completed in five weeks and the beleaguered team were given a rewarding boost when Elio de Angelis put his car on the second row of the grid.

The car was clearly competitive although Mansell was unable to vouch for that, a persistent electrical problem keeping him in the pits. By working through the night, a small electrical company in Norfolk produced a new loom which was rushed to the circuit where the car was rewired in time for the warm-up on race morning. Fortunes then switched dramatically as de Angelis retired on the second lap of the race and Mansell, revelling in the power and the handling, slashed through the field to quadruple the Lotus team's championship points at a stroke.

The introduction of a pit stop to the McLaren team's race strategy appeared to revitalise Niki Lauda's interest in going motor racing with a Ford-Cosworth. Considering McLaren had no opportunity to test their routine, the pit stops went surprisingly well and Lauda drove strongly to finish sixth and take a point for the first time since Long Beach. John Watson finished ninth, more than a lap behind, a similar humiliation befalling Keke Rosberg as he struggled with a Goodyear/Cosworth package which was outclassed at Silverstone, the World Champion finishing out of the points for the first time in seven races.

The ninth round of the championship produced a low retirement rate, the most notable being Eddie Cheever's Renault (head gasket) and the Brabham-BMW of Riccardo Patrese (turbo). The Tolemans, for once, had enjoyed a trouble-free practice and were set to score points but Derek Warwick and Bruno Giacomelli were destined to retire once more.

Victory for Prost meant the Renault driver was the first Frenchman to win the British Grand Prix since Robert Benoist in 1927. But Alain cared little about that as he mounted the podium. He had won, sure enough, but joining him on the rostrum were Piquet and Tambay, his principal championship rivals; Prost now led by six points but Tambay and Piquet were keeping in touch.

Alain Prost edges closer to Patrick Tambay's Ferrari and the lead.
Photo: Nigel Snowdon

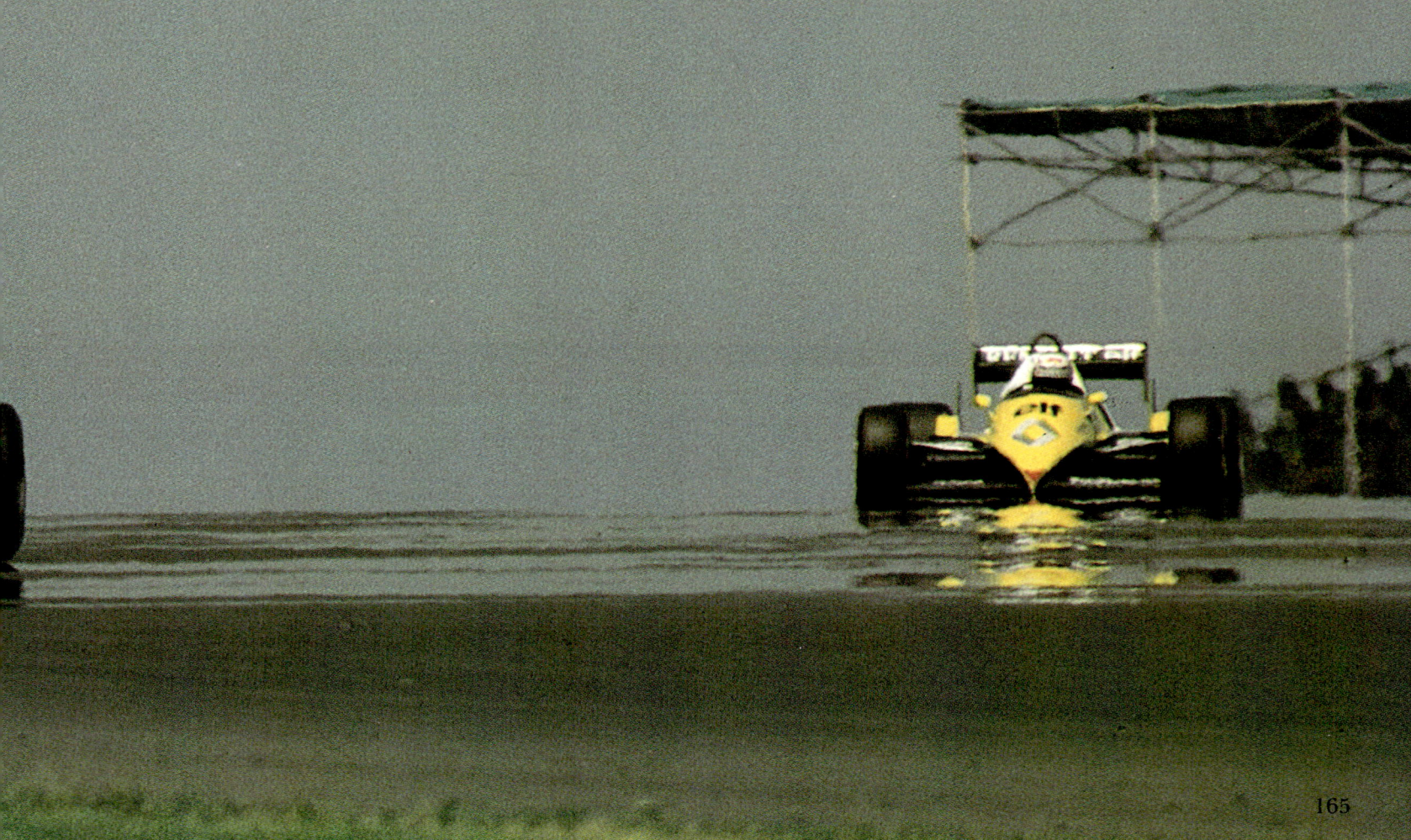

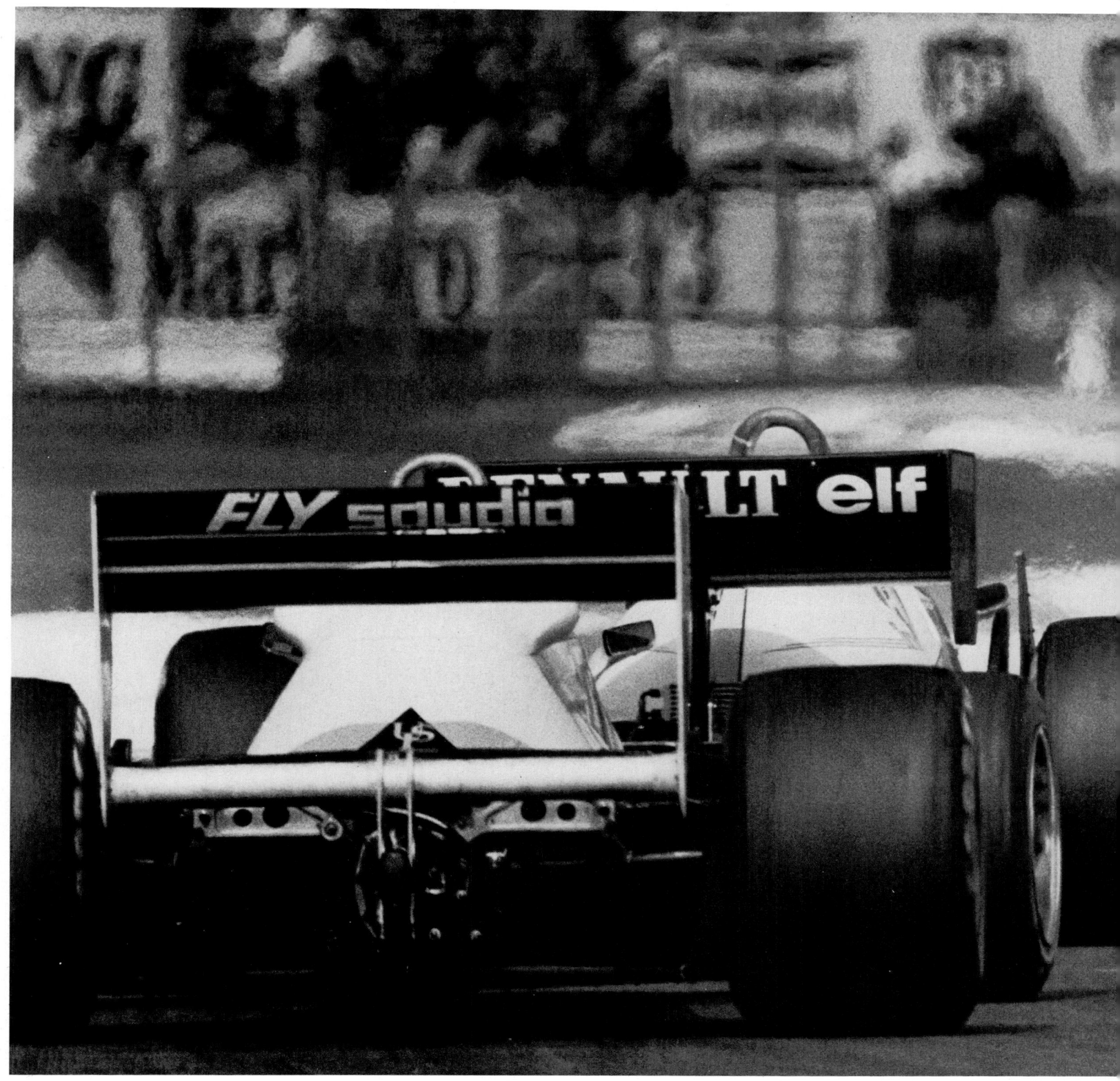

ENTRY AND PRACTICE

The cancellation of the Swiss Grand Prix, scheduled for July 9 at Dijon, gave the teams a break of five weeks and, as might be expected, they had not been idle. There had been testing in England, Germany and Austria and, inbetween, busy development programmes at the factories. Ferrari produced their latest car, the C3, one which had shown an improvement over the C2/B during tyre testing at Silverstone. The latest development meant better braking and turn-in to the fast corners and, more important, less wear on the tyres. Looking like a smoothed-down version of its predecessor, the C3 had done away with the need for body panels around the cockpit, the carbon fibre/ Kevlar construction doubling for bodywork and chassis in a manner similar to the latest ATS. Ferrari had brought two C2 chassis as spares and, as a result of excessive engine temperatures found during testing, it had been decided to fit C2 side-pods to the new chassis

even though it meant a slight weight penalty.

Tambay had need of a spare car on Thursday when fuel feed problems kept his C3 in the garage for most of practice. As a result, the race car was not set up until Friday and that, coupled with a mistake on his quick lap, meant Patrick had to give best to his team-mate in the final session. None the less, Tambay found time to enjoy a joke at Marco Piccinini's expense during official practice. In a masterpiece of collusion with the FISA stewards, Tambay arranged to receive two pieces of paper when his car was weighed; one to give the correct weight, the other to show a figure two kilogrammes under the 540kg limit. Palming the true weight, Tambay rolled to a halt in the Ferrari pit waving the unofficial paper above his head. Piccinini seized it and, at once, his eyes popped out like chapel hat-pegs. Forghieri was summoned immediately but the Ferrari engineer refused to believe it. He frowned at the agitated Piccinini – and then Tambay's laughing eyes inside the blue Bell helmet told the story . . .

Up to that point, Tambay held pole and looked like maintaining it since the Brabhams and the Renaults had failed to improve on the time. As Tambay stood in the garage receiving congratulations from all and sundry, Arnoux fired up his car in the garage next door. With a few minutes of the session remaining, René took to the track and produced a stunning lap; a speciality which earned his 17th pole position and a lap in excess of 150mph. Tambay kept smiling. Just.

Alain Prost, however, found it difficult to disguise his disappointment. Renault had produced two new chassis for their drivers and Prost had tuned his to a fine degree. However, a frustrating misfire would occur for about half a lap each time he ran qualifiers on Friday and, into the bargain, it was felt Goodyear had the edge. Even so, Prost's time from Thursday was good enough to keep him in third place overall. Eddie Cheever was seventh, unable to improve his time and rather unhappy to be that far back, the American saying his car was not bad – but it was not good either.

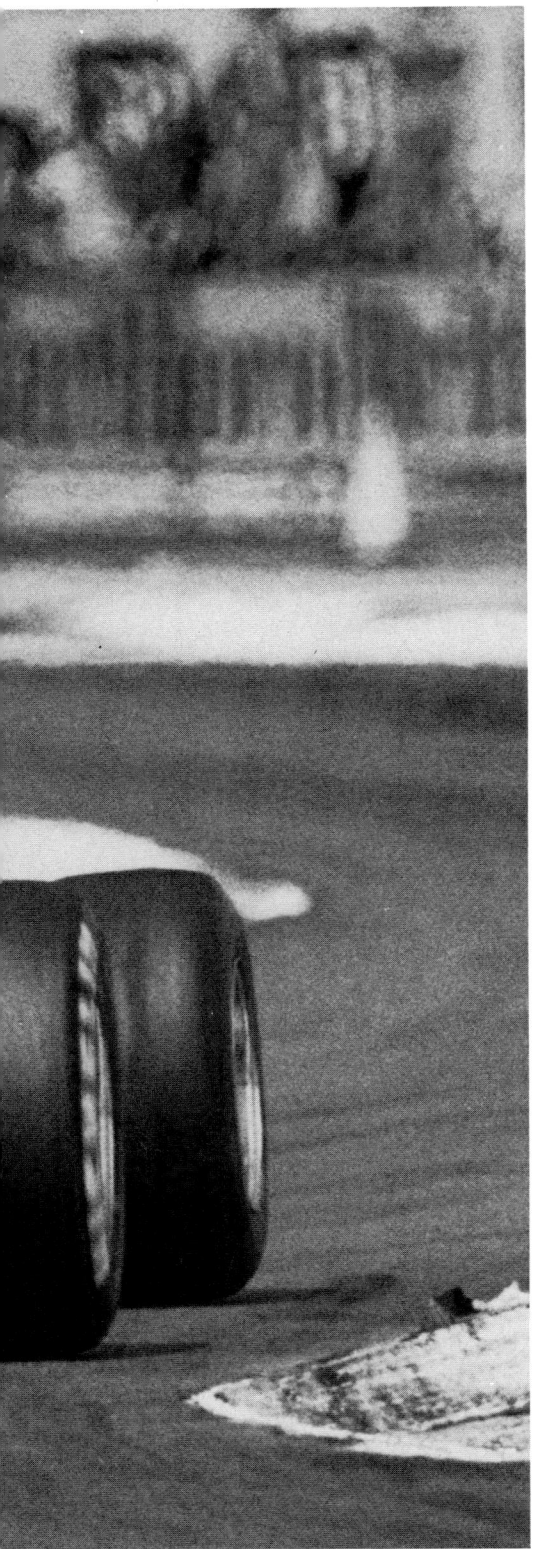

Elio de Angelis, on the other hand, hardly expected his 94T to be perfect. The car had not been finished until the beginning of the week and there had been just enough time for a shake-down at Donington. The team's delight can be imagined when Elio promptly went out and set the fastest time in the first unofficial session. He was just as competitive in the afternoon and, but for a wrong choice of qualifying tyre, he might have improved on Friday and taken a place on the front row.

Gerard Ducarouge had joined Lotus at the beginning of June, the Frenchman realising immediately that the lumbering 93T was of no value and he began work without delay on the 94T. Using the monocoque from the Lotus 91 and incorporating rocker-arm front suspension (against the current fashion of pull rod/push rod designs), Ducarouge penned a striking car which was considerably lighter than its predecessor. Weight distribution had been to the forefront of his thinking and this, coupled with Pirelli tyres which reverted to the stiffer side-walls used in 1982, gave de Angelis a package which roused his enthusiasm to heights not seen since winning the Austrian Grand Prix the previous year. He had even spoken with confidence about pole position and few doubted his words about the excellence of the car.

Nigel Mansell, however, was unable to share his team-mate's optimism. His car had been completed the day before practice began and, from the outset, the Lotus was plagued by an electrical short-circuit. The engine and ancillary components were changed overnight, the mechanics finishing their work at 6 a.m. on Friday. Mansell, who was sleeping with his family in a caravan at the circuit, was roused from his bed and, by 7 a.m., the entire camp site was awake as the Lotus blasted up and down the paddock. The engine ran sweetly enough but, within one lap at racing speeds later in the morning, Mansell and his mechanics were sliding into the depths of despair; the misfire was still there.

Mansell took to the spare 93T in the afternoon and set a time good enough for 18th place on the grid. By now the mechanics had changed everything that could be changed and it was reasoned that the wiring loom was at fault. An order was placed on Friday afternoon with a small company at Diss in Norfolk and a new loom was put into production that evening. De Angelis's car, meanwhile, had not missed a beat. . . .

The value of days and days of testing was thrown into doubt, not only by the speed of the Lotus 'straight out of the box', but also by the unexpectedly poor performance of Nelson Piquet and the Brabham team who knew their way around the Northamptonshire circuit better than most. Riccardo Patrese had come away with the fastest time overall during the tyre testing but the Italian was to play a part in the team's confusion during official practice. Tests at Hockenheim had found a new, shorter nose configuration to be more effective and both race cars were so equipped for Silverstone. In addition, the BT52 had been developed to 'B' specification thanks to suspension modifications, a general tidy-up and smoother bodywork which now carried a revised colour scheme, Bernie Ecclestone having decided on a reversal of the blue and white Parmalat markings.

From the outset, Piquet was unable to balance his car, the Brazilian complaining of understeer. Patrese added to the confusion by complaining of oversteer and the team were in such disarray that thought was given to fetching the test car which had recorded the competitive times a few weeks before. In the end, a problem with his race car meant Piquet had to use the spare chassis – and suddenly he was happy again. The car was easier to drive; it still had the original long nose configuration. Having paid the price for running a modification during practice which had not been testing at that particular circuit, Piquet was soon back on the pace but there was not enough time to allow an improvement on sixth place and Nelson was a little peeved to find himself one tenth slower than Patrese.

ATS produced a new car featuring the revised exhaust layout first seen in Detroit and blown turbos meant Manfred Winkelhock made good use of both the cars at his disposal. But, whereas Ferrari had fitted a neater and more conventional rear wing for Silverstone, ATS were persisting with their enormous rear aerofoil, a device so large that wire struts were required to keep it together. After a disrupted practice on Thursday, the German pushed the yellow and black car onto the fourth row ahead of the Alfa Romeos.

This was a disappointing performance from Andrea de Cesaris since his new and heavily revised 183T was unable to approach the times set during testing with the older chassis. The new cars had smaller fuel tanks and, as a result, a lower monocoque to help smooth the passage of air to the rear wing. De Cesaris said he needed more time to test the new set-up and achieve a better balance and the two Alfas were split by Derek Warwick in the Toleman-Hart.

It was on Toleman's advice and testing that Pirelli had adopted a stiffer sidewall and a narrower tread for Silverstone. Alex Hawkridge was rather upset, therefore, to find Lotus stepping in and reaping Toleman's rewards but, none the less, Toleman were pleased with Warwick's practice performance. For once, nothing had gone wrong and the Englishman had actually managed to complete over 35 laps during the unofficial session on Thursday. It was Warwick's time that afternoon which would determine his grid position since a slight engine misfire ruined his efforts in the final session. Warwick had a new chassis at his disposal incorporating a narrower nose section in the interests of straight-line speed. All three cars present now had twin-plug Hart turbos but Bruno Giacomelli was almost one second slower, having lost much of the first day due to a piston failure.

The Italian was the 12th fastest turbo on a circuit where normally aspirated engines were almost a waste of time. It was galling for a driver of Rosberg's calibre to give away over 100bhp and his spirited handling of the Williams could not begin to bridge the gap. The team tried fairings on the edge of the front nose wing but soon abandoned them and ran almost no wing angle at the rear in a bid to wring out every last mile-per-hour on the straight. The result, of course, made spectacular viewing as Rosberg slid through the corners and onto the kerbs. Realising their efforts on Thursday represented the maximum in qualifying trim, Williams withdrew Rosberg from official practice on Friday and concentrated instead on working on a race set-up. It was to prove a wise move for Rosberg was to remain the fastest Cosworth by taking 13th place. Jacques Laffite was an unhappy 20th after

The top and bottom of Formula 1 at Silverstone; turbos and Michelin left Cosworth and Goodyear standing.

The Brabham team send Nelson Piquet on his way after another exemplary pit stop. The BT52, uprated to 'B' specification in the five-week lull since Canada, gave handling problems during practice as the team experimented with a short nose configuration but, for the race, the car was perfect. Had it not been for a communications lapse between team and driver, Piquet might have been able to challenge Prost for the lead.

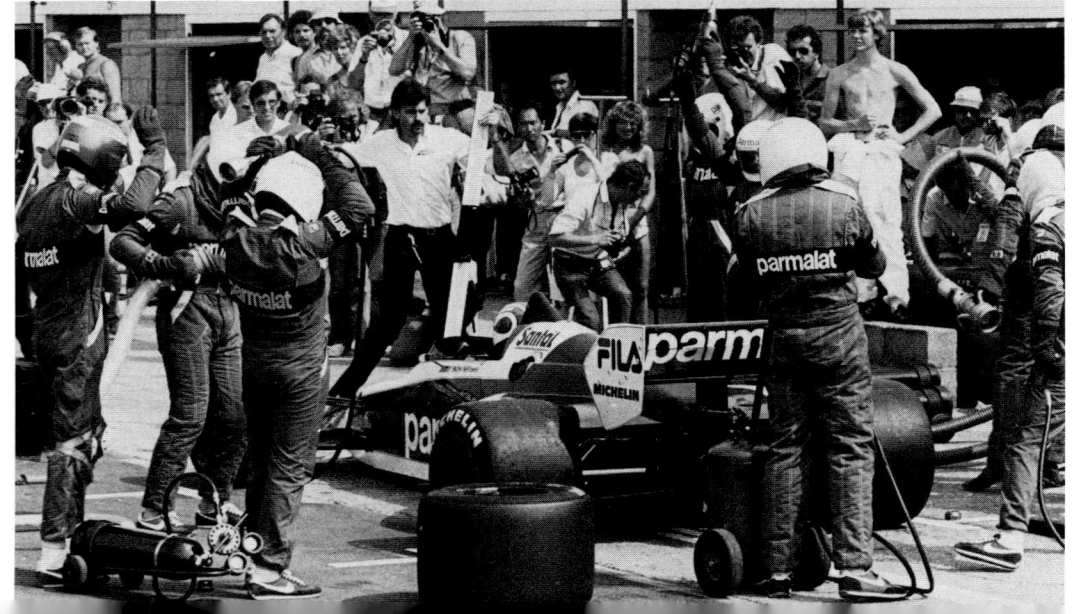

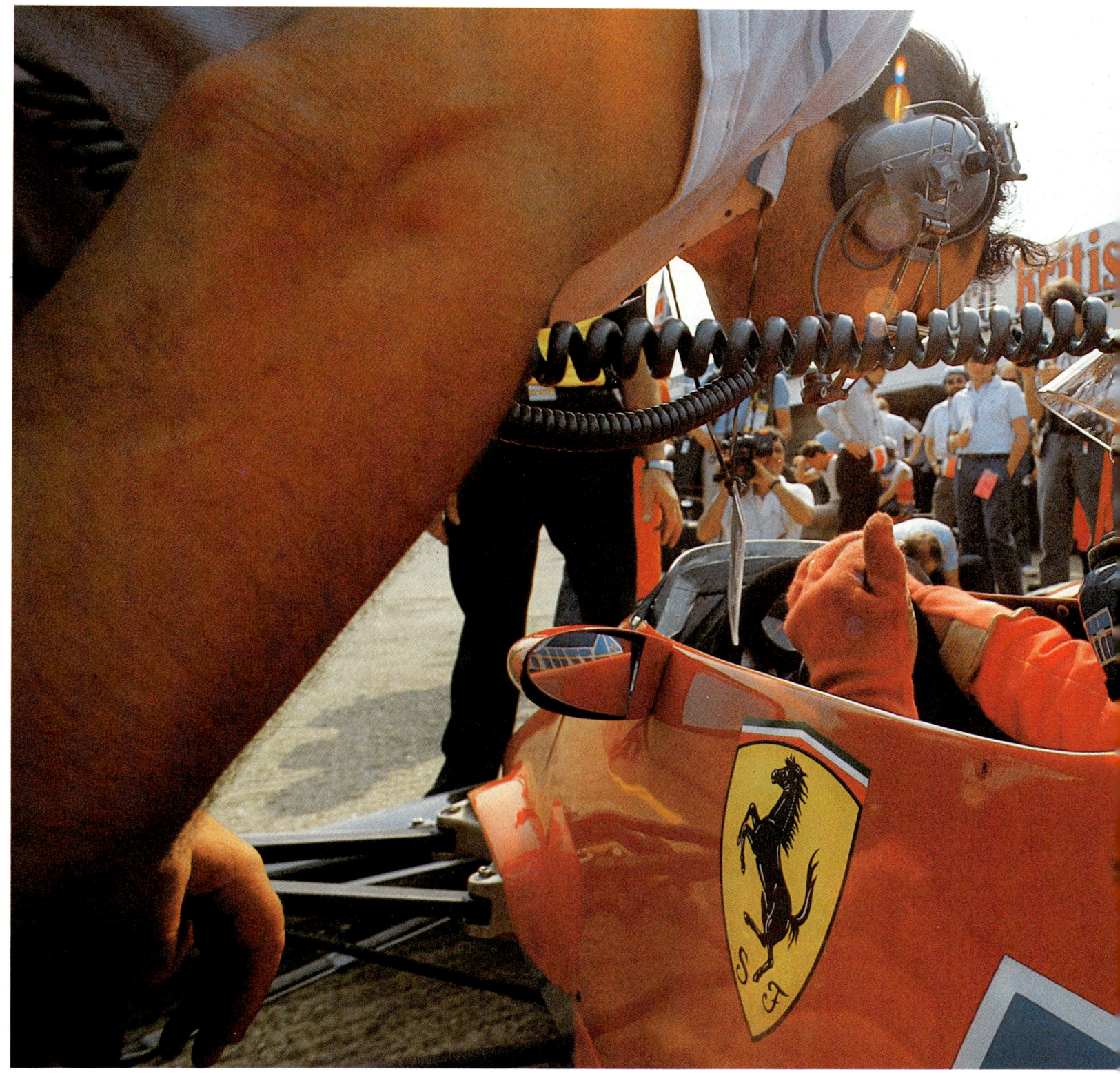

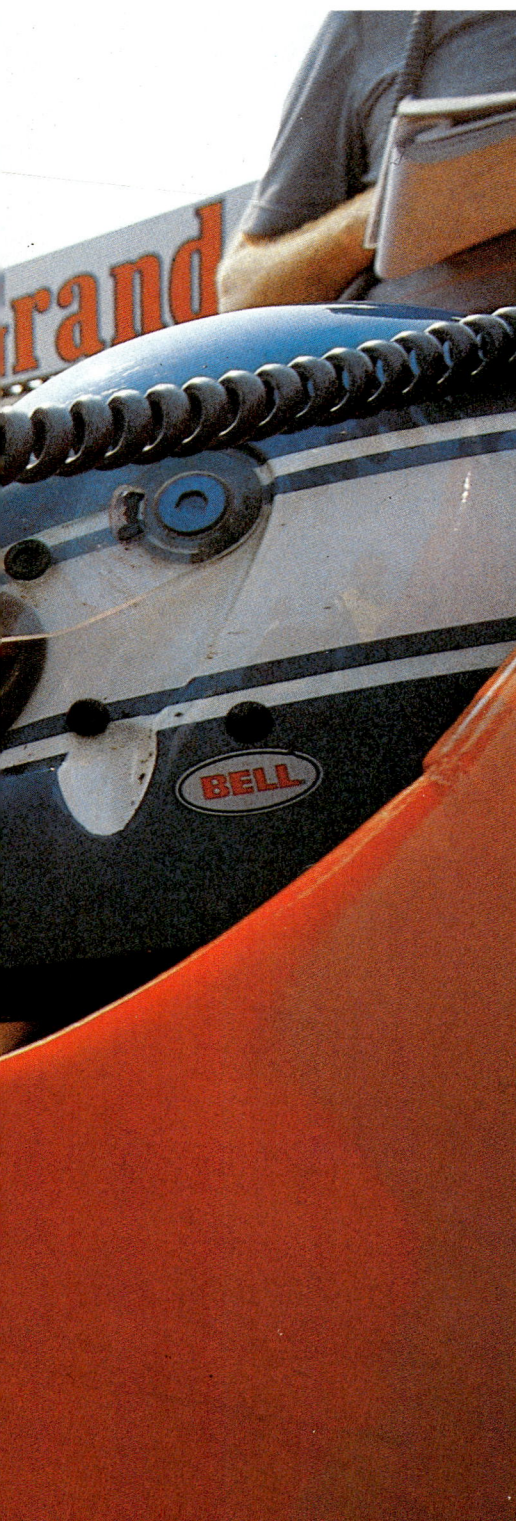

struggling with a tyre growth problem on Thursday.

The British Grand Prix was notable for the serious return of Honda to Formula 1. The Japanese turbo had made its debut at the Race of Champions earlier in the year and, since then, the Spirit team had committed themselves to a busy test programme with the V6 mounted in their converted Formula 2 chassis. A new, lighter car was made ready for Silverstone but the handicap of a heavy power unit remained and the package weighed in at 580 kilos; the original car – now the spare – was another 30 kilos heavier!

It is fair to say the team anticipated problems and, indeed, they were to have their fair share. On Thursday, fuel-feed trouble put Stefan Johansson into the T-car; then he ran out of fuel and a confrontation with a marshal as he prevented him from refuelling out on the circuit did nothing to calm the impatient Swede. Then the handling had a tendency to go from understeer to oversteer and, into the bargain, the engine on the spare car was found to be stronger than the fresh unit installed in the race car for Friday thanks to a continuation of the misfire. Wisely, the team had chosen to run one set of qualifiers and one set of the more durable 'C' compound Goodyears in the final session. The qualifiers were wasted when Johansson, now in the spare car, turned up the boost and discovered that it brought a misfire. Thus he was left to go for a time on low boost and on race rubber – in the heavier car. To qualify 14th was a magnificent achievement by any standards.

Johansson's time put him alongside Niki Lauda after the Austrian had been unable to improve his time from the previous day, an oversteer problem hampering his smooth style. John Watson's progress was interrupted by no fewer than three engine changes and the winner of the last Grand Prix at Silverstone, forced to use his spare car in the final session, was relegated to the back of the grid. Apart from the late addition of refuelling equipment, there was little new on the McLarens.

Similarly, the Tyrrells of Michele Alboreto and Danny Sullivan were as before although a broken fuel line and the subsequent fire modified the equipment on top of Alboreto's DFY on Thursday morning. Neither driver was able to improve on Friday, Alboreto qualifying just ahead of Thierry Boutsen who had the benefit of a new Arrows monocoque. Marc Surer was two places behind his team-mate in 19th position, the Swiss correcting nervous handling by stiffening the front roll bar but, otherwise, there was little else to be done with the Cosworth/Goodyear combination – except watch the turbos steam by on the straights.

A sign of the tight financial restraint placed on Theodore was the fact that neither Roberto Guerrero nor Johnny Cecotto had been able to take part in tyre testing at Silverstone – a circuit not an hour's drive from the team's Midlands base. As a result, Guerrero spent valuable time setting his car up and the Colombian did not get the chance to run with a full tank. But at least he qualified which was more than could be said for an unhappy Cecotto, the Venezuelan running a different set-up to his team-mate and losing his place on the grid to Piercarlo Ghinzani who put the new Tony Southgate designed Osella Alfa Romeo V12 into the race. The Italian team had completed one car in time for a brief test at Monza while the other was

finished off in the Silverstone paddock. Ghinzani qualified in spite of fuel system bothers while Corrado Fabi, new to the car, failed to make the grid when a throttle cable broke on Thursday afternoon and a mechanical fuel pump seized during the final session.

Ligier had decided that the hydraulic suspension was the best bet for Silverstone, the spare car remaining on steel springs. Jean-Pierre Jarier had a DFY fail on Thursday to add to his problems with the handling and his time in the afternoon was disallowed due to a misunderstanding when the Frenchman failed to stop for weighing. His time on Friday was good enough for the back row while Raul Boesel took the spare car on the first day after his race car had fuel metering trouble. Eliseo Salazar, short of sponsorship, was on hand to watch Kenny Acheson attempt to qualify for his first Grand Prix in the RAM March which now featured shorter side-pods and repositioned water radiators. It was a combination of inexperience and a lack of tyre temperature in the rock hard Pirellis which would keep the Ulsterman out of the race, but at least he had tried hard and kept out of everyone's way in the process.

RACE

Those spectators fortunate enough to be inside the Silverstone perimeter fence and away from the traffic jams fuming in the Northamptonshire lanes were able to witness Elio de Angelis set the fastest time in the warm-up at noon. It was another boost for the Lotus team as they crossed their fingers and watched Nigel Mansell complete several troublefree laps in his 94T; indeed, it was the first opportunity he had to learn about the car.

Renault, on the other hand, were into fine tuning and the making of final decisions about tyres. After running soft Michelins all round, Prost opted for a harder compound on the left while Piquet and Brabham felt they could get away with soft rubber all round. An engine was changed on Patrese's car and Johansson reluctantly prepared to race the older Spirit when the misfire continued in the engine bolted to the lighter chassis. Down at the opposite end of the pit lane, the Ferrari mechanics wheeled Tambay's car into the garage and set about an engine change. Their work was completed without panic and the V6 burst into life at the stroke of two o'clock as the first car left the pit lane.

Just 25 drivers took their place on the grid, Ghinzani climbing into Fabi's car in readiness for a start from the pit lane after his own Osella had stopped out on the circuit with an electrical problem. Elsewhere, there was little drama and Derek Ongaro gave the green light to a tidy start but, within the first few hundred yards, several drivers were already attempting to stamp their authority on the proceedings.

Arnoux got away cleanly but Tambay sat it out with his team-mate, braking later into Copse and holding the outside line to take the advantage through the left-hander at Maggots. Cheever made an excellent start, slotting into fifth place behind Prost and Patrese while de Angelis had made a slow get away and was in seventh place behind Piquet. Prost had a violent sideways moment as he powered through Maggots but the Frenchman recovered, as did Rosberg after sliding onto the grass on the exit from Becketts. There was plenty of activity at the back of the field as well, Mansell

Patrick Tambay found time to play a joke on Mauro Forghieri during practice. Tambay was not so amused during the race when his Goodyears failed to match the pace shown by the Ferrari team during practice.
Photo: Bernard Asset

Another impressive practice performance from Manfred Winkelhock ended in retirement for the ATS-BMW during the race.
Photo: John Townsend

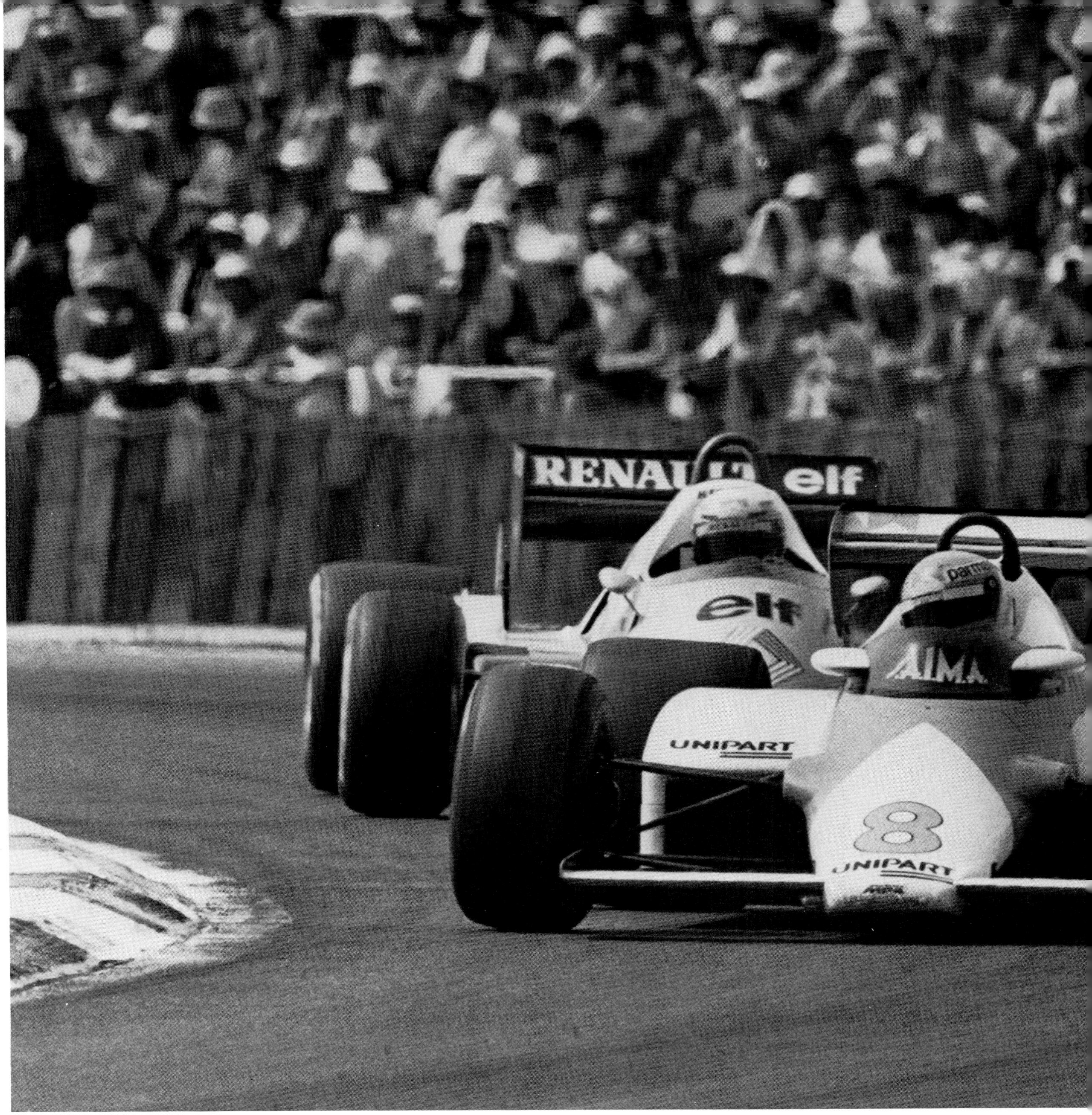

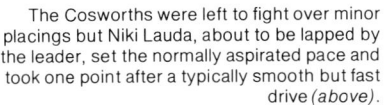

The Cosworths were left to fight over minor placings but Niki Lauda, about to be lapped by the leader, set the normally aspirated pace and took one point after a typically smooth but fast drive *(above)*.

The Ferrari team provided the battle for pole position, the honour falling eventually to René Arnoux with a dramatic last-minute lap. Mechanics cool his tyres in a bid to squeeze another lap out of the Goodyear qualifiers.

Keke Rosberg was out of the points for the first time in seven races, the Williams-Cosworth, no match for the turbos at Silverstone, finishing a distant 11th.

Honda made an official return to Grand Prix racing with a V6 turbo mounted in the back of a Spirit chassis. Stefan Johansson qualified in the middle of the grid in spite of a host of problems but the Swede's race was short-lived, a component rubbing on the fuel pump belt and causing retirement *(far right)*.

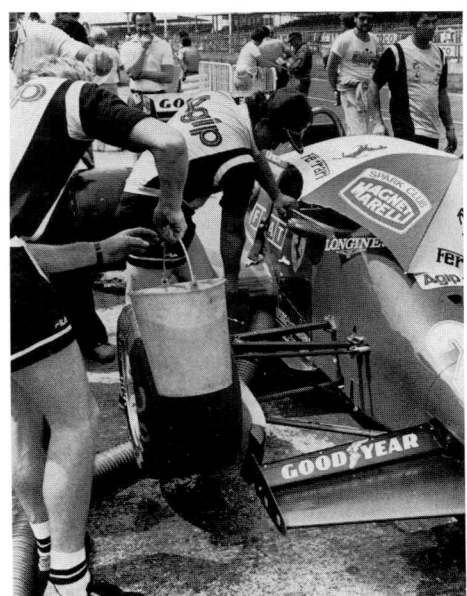

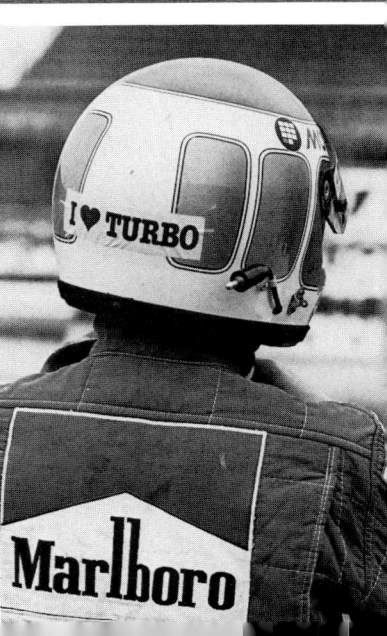

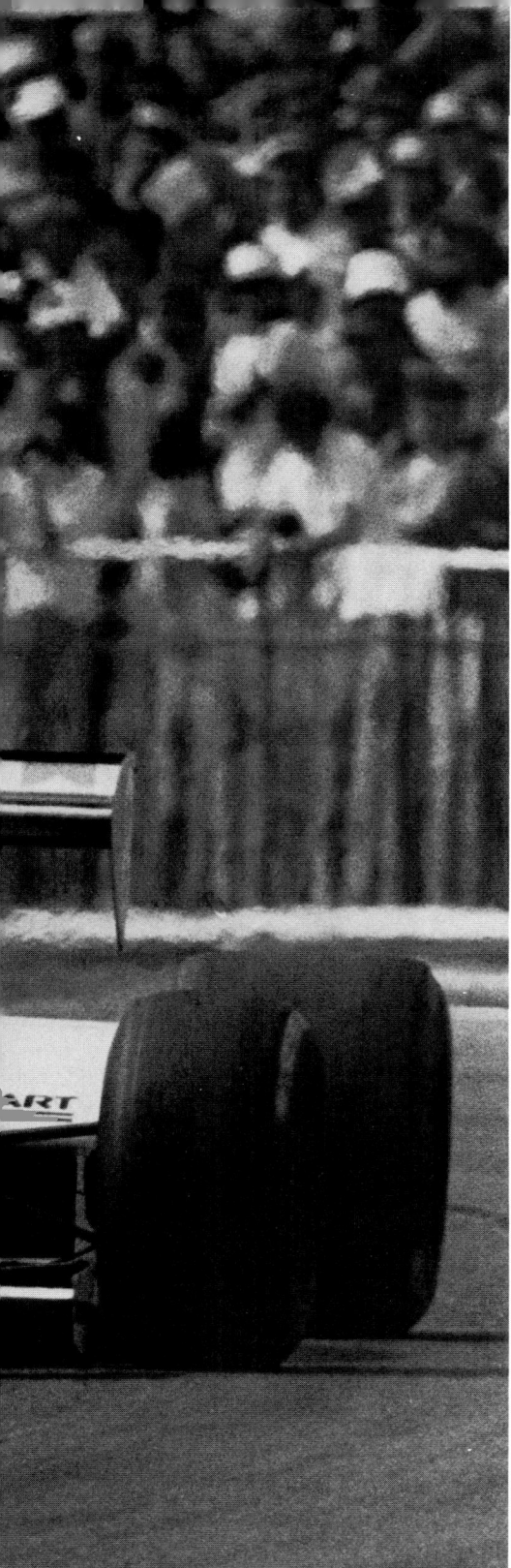

galloping through the field with Watson, running with half a tank of fuel for the first time, making immediate progress from the back of the grid.

De Angelis took sixth place from Piquet at the end of the first lap but a keenly anticipated race from the Italian was to end two corners later when the Lotus pulled off at Becketts with flames belching from the turbochargers. The first indications were that the turbo had failed but, after the race, it was announced that the distributor had gone awry, upset the timing and caused the flame-out. (A few weeks later, however, it was suggested that de Angelis had accidentally flicked a switch in the cockpit as he negotiated Copse, the resulting surge of fuel causing what appeared to be a serious fire at the back of the car. Either way, the engine was unharmed, de Angelis using it during practice for the German Grand Prix.)

Under a blazing sun, the reliability of the turbo runners became suspect when Giacomelli retired with turbo failure and Cheever came into the pits with a blown head gasket at the end of lap three. Two laps later and Johansson was in the pits with a broken belt to the fuel pump. This was replaced and the Spirit rejoined, only to have the the problem occur once more, the failures having been caused by a component rubbing on the belt – an installation problem which the team could write off to inexperience.

It was six years since Renault had taken their first faltering steps along the turbocharged path at Silverstone and, judging by Prost's progress, he had every confidence in his car and tyres. As Tambay opened a small gap over Arnoux, Prost began to attack his former team-mate, the shrewd Renault driver formulating a plan to suit the conditions. By running less wing and using superior power, the Ferrari was able to pull away on the straights but, through the corners it was a different matter as the Goodyears began to lose grip, a problem exacerbated by the vicious circle of too much sliding and too little wing. Prost, continually harrying Arnoux, knew it was simply a matter of time.

Patrese was a few yards behind in fourth place with Piquet gradually reeling in his team-mate. Then a gap to de Cesaris and Winkelhock followed by Warwick and . . . Mansell. From 18th on the grid, the Lotus had gained eight places during the first lap and he closed rapidly on Warwick, challenging the Toleman on lap five. His progress was interrupted, however, when a 40gm balance-weight flew off the front-left tyre and immediately transformed the handling to give Mansell severe oversteer which, in turn, wore his Pirellis. Mansell gave serious consideration to making an early pit-stop but decided against it considering his healthy position on the lap chart.

At least Mansell was comfortably clear of Lauda who, in turn was gradually pulling away from Baldi. Rosberg was 12th but soon to lose the place to Watson, the Ulsterman's charge ending when the power of the Alfa Romeo turbo was to prove an insurmountable object for the Cosworth to deal with. Jarier was 14th with Alboreto next, busily fending off Laffite's Williams, Sullivan's Tyrrell and the Ligier of Boesel. Boutsen was struggling with poor handling thanks to the choice of too soft a tyre and Guerrero was in similar trouble, blistered rear Goodyears and massive oversteer helping the Theodore driver drop to 20th place. Bringing up the rear were Surer (tyre trouble) and

Ghinzani.

At the end of lap nine, Patrese made his way slowly to the pits, a trail of smoke from the rear of the Brabham announcing a turbo failure; nine races and nine retirements for the Italian. It was the sort of disaster which constantly seemed to strike Prost during 1982 but that was in the past. This year, his Renault was showing a remarkable run of reliability or, at least, enough to get him to the finish in every race held so far. And now, his car never felt better although Arnoux was proving difficult to pass. Clearly, he would have to catch the Ferrari driver unaware; outbrake him when he was least expecting it. Prost chose his moment at Copse on lap 14.

With a beautifully precise and confident move, Alain pulled out of the Ferrari's slipstream at the last moment and used the Renault's superior braking to take the inside line. It was so sudden and unexpected that Arnoux had taken his normal line and left plenty of room. He was utterly helpless as his rival made off with second place.

There was further trading of places down the field as Laffite outbraked Alboreto (now struggling with a blistered right-front tyre) and Boesel nipped past Sullivan. But that was essentially the battle in "Division Two" and had no connection with the turbo race at the front of the field.

Prost set off in pursuit of Tambay; Piquet closed on

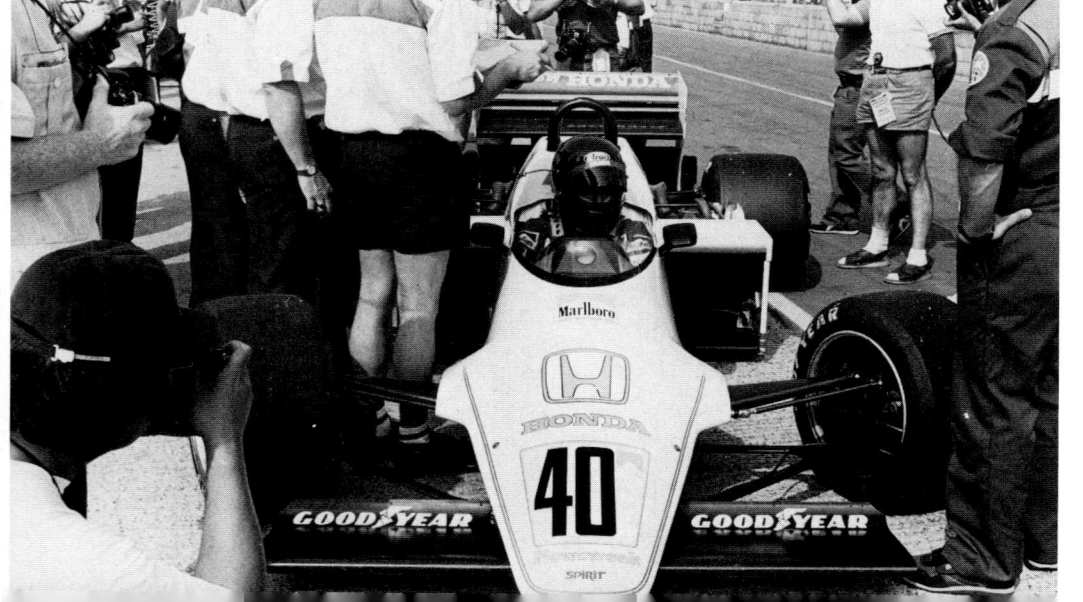

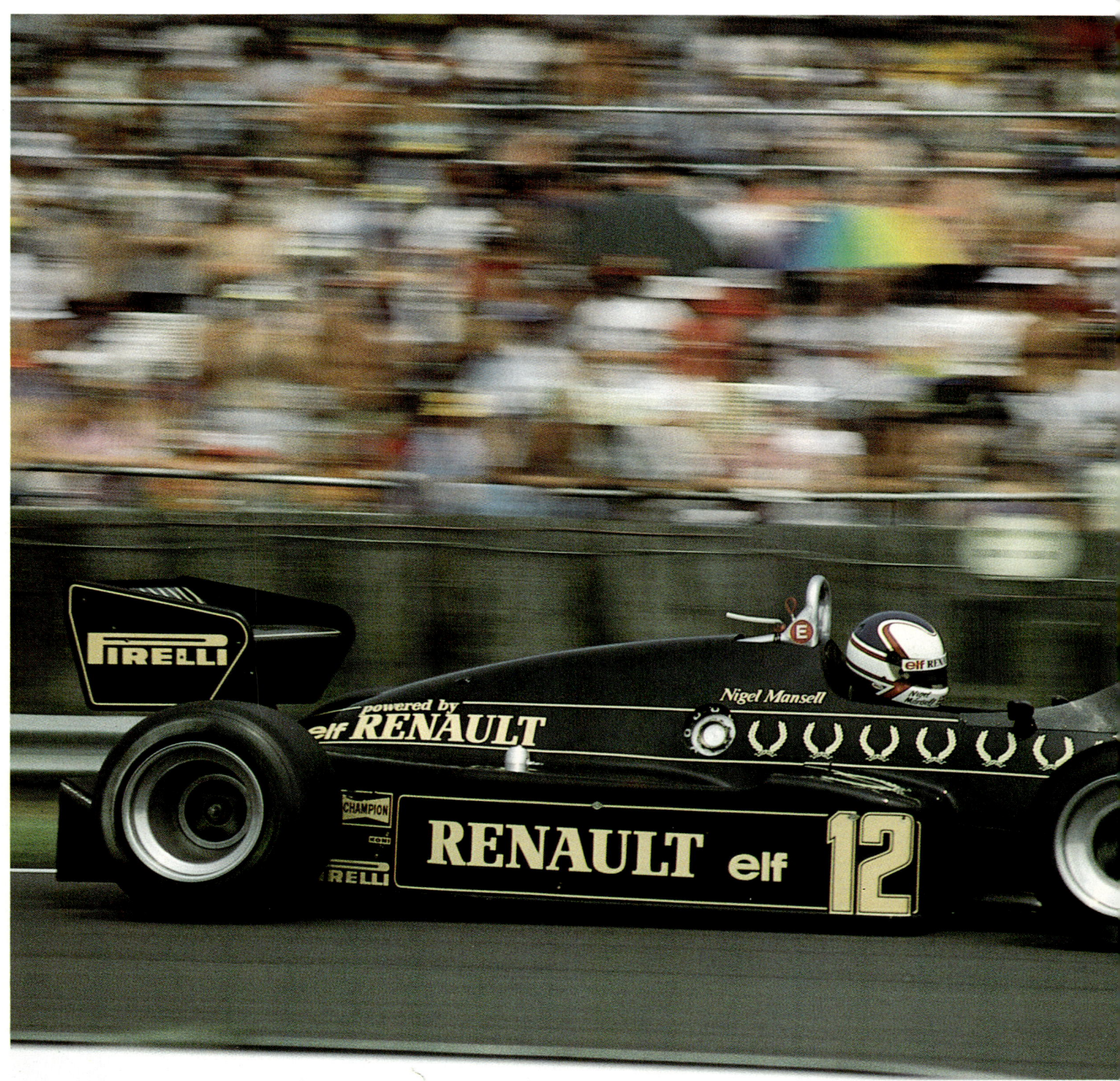

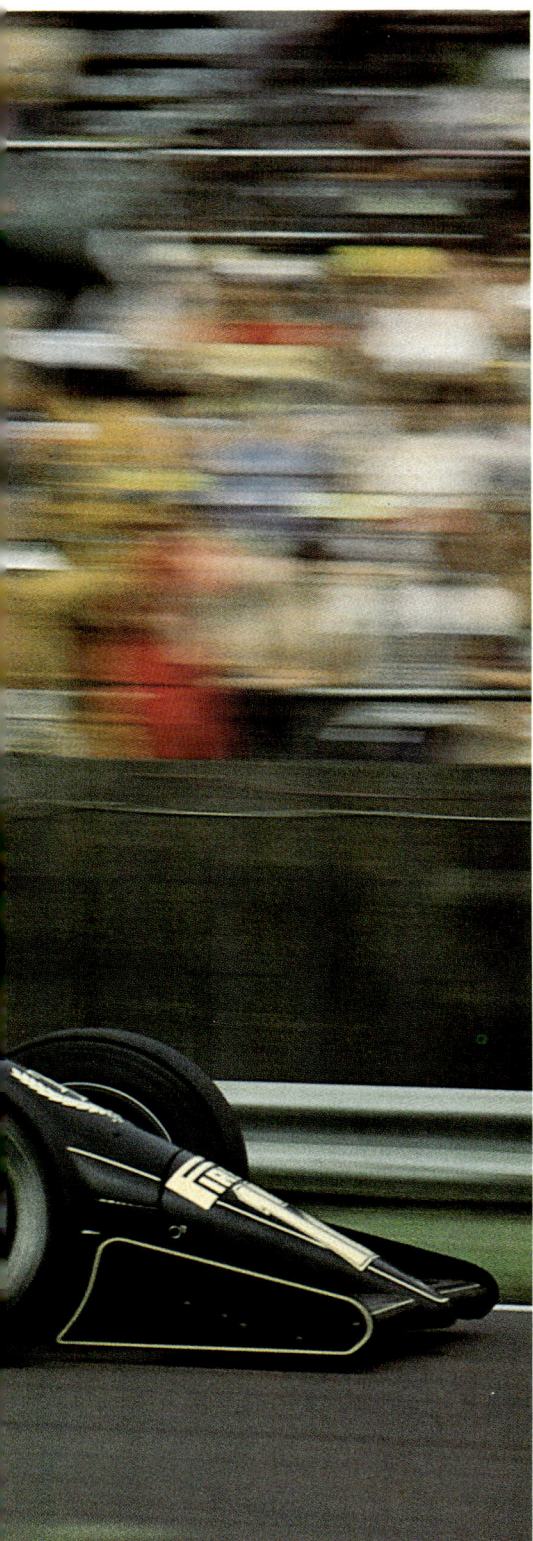

Arnoux while Mansell had another look at Warwick, the Lotus taking seventh place behind Winkelhock and de Cesaris on lap 17. Two laps later and Piquet at last found a way through Arnoux's defences after the two had a frought moment when Nelson tried unsuccessfully to block René behind a back-marker. Prost was now on Tambay's tail and he took the lead from the Ferrari with another incisive move at Copse on lap 20. Piquet was now just 3.5 seconds behind Tambay but it was to take the Brabham driver a considerable time to find his way into second place – and that, more or less, would decide the outcome of the race. Prost was now running free.

The pit stops began earlier than anticipated when Warwick came in at the end of lap 27. The mechanics were ready but it soon became apparent that the Toleman needed more than fuel and tyres, the deranged internals of the gearbox spelling retirement for Toleman – again. Winkelhock lost his excellent sixth position when he made his stop on lap 29, a move which would lead to his eventual retirement several laps later after the engine had overheated while in the pits and damaged the head gasket and exhaust. Watson brought his McLaren in for the team's first planned stop and everything went well – until the driver found difficulty in selecting first gear when signalled to leave the pits!

Watson returned, having lost a lap to the leaders, and the tension began to mount when Arnoux came in at the end of lap 32. Trouble with his right-rear wheel meant a stop of over 15 seconds and allowed de Cesaris to take fourth place. That was to be short-lived, the Alfa Romeo making its stop on lap 34 but a long delay when the Italian stalled his engine due to clutch trouble meant Andrea had dropped to 12th place by the time he had fired the turbo into life. Two laps later and Prost and Tambay came in together, leaving Piquet to lead the race for the first time. The Renault was dispatched in 14.4 seconds and rejoined in second place, but it was to be five laps before Piquet would make his stop.

During that crucial period, the Brabham driver had to work his way through (for the second time) one or two hectic battles among the Cosworth runners at the back of the field and he failed to make much headway while running on his own at the front. The Brabham mechanics were ready for action when Nelson came in at the end of lap 41, the men in blue doing another faultless job by sending Piquet back to the fray in 12.2 seconds. Unfortunately, the dice appeared to be loaded against the Brazilian on this day for he met the Ligier of Boesel in the pit lane and was forced to follow his fellow countryman onto the track.

Mansell was next, the Lotus mechanics working speedily even though the man with the breather pipe took a few valuable seconds to connect his hose. Once Mansell had rejoined, a look at the lap chart showed Prost to be leading Piquet by 17 seconds. Tambay was a further 10 seconds behind with Arnoux fourth but coming under pressure from Mansell. With a new set of rims, Mansell found the handling of his car a revelation and he quickly caught Arnoux who, once again, had worn out his Goodyears within five laps. The Lotus driver tried the inside at Stowe only to find the Frenchman closing the door rather smartly. The black and gold car handled perfectly through the ultra-quick Club corner and allowed Mansell to have a look at the outside line on the approach to the flat-out Abbey Curve. Arnoux was wise to this and blocked the Lotus but, next time round when he did the same, Mansell suddenly darted left and steamed up the inside causing a startled Arnoux to lift off and concede fourth place at a corner where he least expected it. Mansell then narrowed the gap to Tambay slightly but the canny Frenchman had 18 seconds in hand and his tyres, although lacking grip, were in better shape than those of his team-mate.

A clean, crisp drive from Lauda saw the McLaren driver take sixth place ahead of Baldi while de Cesaris had moved ahead of Watson to take eighth place. Jarier was tenth and Keke Rosberg was perplexed to find himself behind the Ligier having already passed the French car before making his pit stop. With nothing better to do in a car which was nicely balanced – but slow – Rosberg gave chase but eventually resigned himself to a place among the also-rans. His team-mate, meanwhile, was embroiled in a battle with Alboreto but Laffite got it all wrong under braking for the Woodcote chicane and went through the escape road, losing a place in the process. Sullivan, Boutsen, Guerrero (about to finish a race for the first time since the 1982 German Grand Prix) and Surer brought up the rear, Ghinzani having stopped with no fuel pressure and Boesel retiring with a leak in the Ligier's hydraulic suspension system.

Earlier, Boesel's engine cover had blown off and landed in the middle of the pit straight at a spot where there was insufficient time for the marshals to retrieve it. Unfortunately, it was to rule out any outbraking manoeuvres into Copse, a fact which Mansell had discovered when he darted from Arnoux's slipstream and somehow managed to avoid the blue fibreglass at the last moment. Apart from the excitement of seeing a Lotus run competitively at last, there was little else to keep the crowd amused during the second half of the race. Piquet had closed the gap on Prost – or, at least, Prost had allowed the gap to shrink since Nelson was receiving no information on his pit board about the progress of the Renault and, assuming the situation to be hopeless, Piquet wound down the boost and settled for a comfortable second place.

Prost duly completed 67 laps to a fairly muted reception, the crowd reserving their cheers for Mansell as the Lotus came home fourth behind Piquet and Tambay. Arnoux was fifth with Lauda thoroughly deserving his point for sixth place. Baldi was seventh although de Cesaris had closed rapidly on his team-mate, the two cars crossing the line in tandem. Ahead of them on the road was Mansell, the Lotus driver slowing rapidly and catching Baldi unawares. The Italian darted to the right, was confronted by the Ligier bodywork, and moved right again – to bang wheels with de Cesaris who appeared not to have seen the chequered flag. Surprisingly, bearing in mind the carnage at Silverstone two years previously, that was the most serious incident of the entire weekend.

However, the day was to end on an unhappy note when Ken Tyrrell lodged a protest against the water injection used on the Renault and Ferrari engines. The Stewards rejected the protest and Tyrrell lodged an appeal with the FIA. So, for the time being, Prost knew his nine points were safe. It had been an easy race, he said. Easy because of the tyres – just as he figured it might have been at the start.

After a frustrating practice, Nigel Mansell finished fourth in the new JPS Lotus-Renault.
Photo: Charles Knight
A vast crowd at Silverstone; but were they getting value for money?
Photo: John Townsend

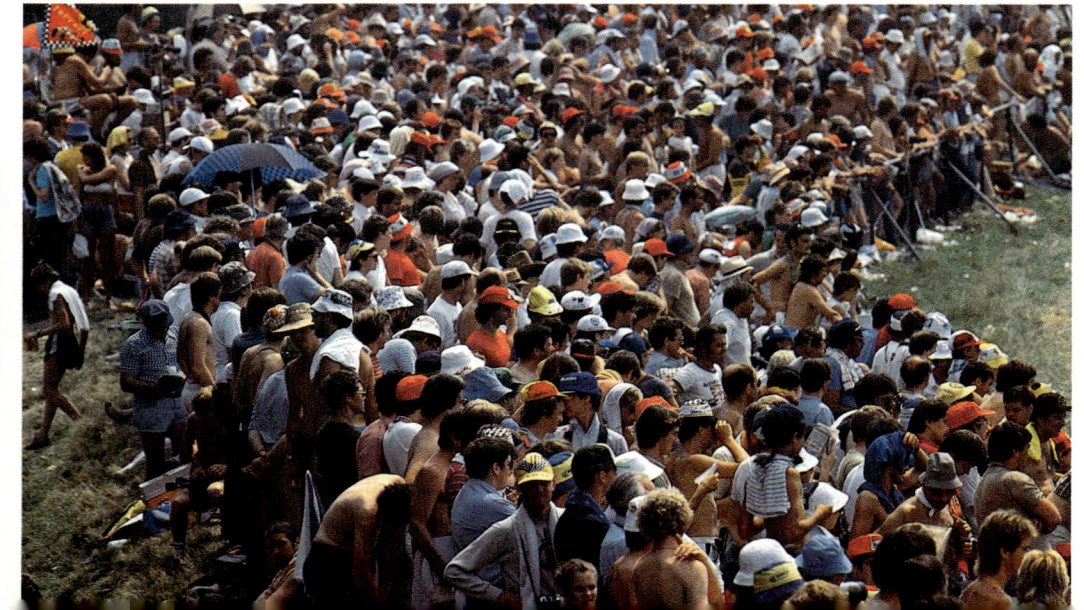

Marlboro British Grand Prix, July 16/statistics

Entries and practice times

No.	Driver	Nat	Car	Tyre	Engine	Entrant	Practice 1	Practice 2
1	Keke Rosberg	SF	Saudia WILLIAMS FW08C	G	Ford Cosworth DFV	TAG Williams Team	1m 13·755s	–
2	Jacques Laffite	F	Saudia WILLIAMS FW08C	G	Ford Cosworth DFV	TAG Williams Team	1m 15·234s	1m 16·762s
3	Michele Alboreto	I	Benetton TYRRELL 011	G	Ford Cosworth DFV/DFY	Benetton Tyrrell Team	1m 14·651s	1m 14·970s
4	Danny Sullivan	USA	Benetton TYRRELL 011	G	Ford Cosworth DFV/DFY	Benetton Tyrrell Team	1m 15·449s	1m 16·347s
5	Nelson Piquet	BR	Parmalat BRABHAM BT52B	M	BMW M12/13	Fila Sport	1m 11·098s	1m 10·933s
6	Riccardo Patrese	I	Parmalat BRABHAM BT52B	M	BMW M12/13	Fila Sport	1m 11·246s	1m 10·881s
7	John Watson	GB	Marlboro McLAREN MP4/1C	M	Ford Cosworth DFV/DFY	Marlboro McLaren International	1m 15·609s	1m 16·091s
8	Niki Lauda	A	Marlboro McLAREN MP4/1C	M	Ford Cosworth DFV/DFY	Marlboro McLaren International	1m 14·267s	1m 15·118s
9	Manfred Winkelhock	D	ATS D6	G	BMW M12/13	Team ATS	1m 13·493s	1m 11·687s
11	Elio de Angelis	I	John Player Special LOTUS 94T	P	Renault EF1	John Player Team Lotus	1m 10·771s	1m 11·114s
12	Nigel Mansell	GB	John Player Special LOTUS 94T	P	Renault EF1	John Player Team Lotus	1m 16·377s	*1m 15·133s
15	Alain Prost	F	Elf RENAULT RE40	M	Renault EF1	Equipe Renault Elf	1m 10·170s	1m 10·808s
16	Eddie Cheever	USA	Elf RENAULT RE40	M	Renault EF1	Equipe Renault Elf	1m 11·055s	1m 11·520s
17	Kenneth Acheson	GB	MARCH-RAM 01	P	Ford Cosworth DFV	RAM Automotive Team March	1m 19·267s	1m 18·103s
22	Andrea de Cesaris	I	Marlboro ALFA ROMEO 183T	M	Alfa Romeo 183T	Marlboro Team Alfa Romeo	1m 13·163s	1m 12·150s
23	Mauro Baldi	I	Marlboro ALFA ROMEO 183T	M	Alfa Romeo 183T	Marlboro Team Alfa Romeo	1m 14·006s	1m 12·860s
25	Jean-Pierre Jarier	F	Gitanes LIGIER JS21	M	Ford Cosworth DFV/DFY	Equipe Ligier Gitanes	† 1m 15·386s	1m 15·767s
26	Raul Boesel	BR	Gitanes LIGIER JS21	M	Ford Cosworth DFV	Equipe Ligier Gitanes	1m 15·386s	1m 16·134s
27	Patrick Tambay	F	Fiat FERRARI 126C3	G	Ferrari 126C	Scuderia Ferrari SpA SEFAC	1m 10·874s	1m 10·104s
28	René Arnoux	F	Fiat FERRARI 126C3	G	Ferrari 126C	Scuderia Ferrari SpA SEFAC	1m 10·436s	1m 09·462s
29	Marc Surer	CH	ARROWS A6	G	Ford Cosworth DFV	Arrows Racing Team	1m 15·135s	1m 15·350s
30	Thierry Boutsen	B	ARROWS A6	G	Ford Cosworth DFV	Arrows Racing Team	1m 14·964s	1m 15·686s
31	Corrado Fabi	I	OSELLA FA1E	M	Alfa Romeo 1260	Osella Squadra Corse	1m 20·400s	1m 17·594s
32	Piercarlo Ghinzani	I	OSELLA FA1E	M	Alfa Romeo 1260	Osella Squadra Corse	1m 17·162s	1m 16·544s
33	Roberto Guerrero	COL	THEODORE N183	G	Ford Cosworth DFV	Theodore Racing Team	1m 15·441s	1m 15·317s
34	Johnny Cecotto	YV	THEODORE N183	G	Ford Cosworth DFV	Theodore Racing Team	1m 16·714s	1m 16·786s
35	Derek Warwick	GB	Candy TOLEMAN TG183B	P	Hart 415T	Candy Toleman Motorsport	1m 12·528s	1m 12·541s
36	Bruno Giacomelli	I	Candy TOLEMAN TG183B	P	Hart 415T	Candy Toleman Motorsport	1m 13·792s	1m 13·422s
40	Stefan Johansson	S	SPIRIT-HONDA 201	G	Honda RA163-E	Spirit Racing	1m 15·535s	1m 13·962s

*Practice time recorded in John Player Special LOTUS 93T

Thursday morning and Friday morning practice sessions not officially recorded.

G – Goodyear, M – Michelin, P – Pirelli.

†Time disallowed

Thur pm	Fri pm
Hot, dry	Hot, dry

Starting grid

	28 ARNOUX (1m 09·462s) Ferrari
27 TAMBAY (1m 10·104s) Ferrari	
	15 PROST (1m 10·170s) Renault
11 DE ANGELIS (1m 10·771s) Lotus	
	6 PATRESE (1m 10·881s) Brabham
5 PIQUET (1m 10·933s) Brabham	
	16 CHEEVER (1m 11·055s) Renault
9 WINKELHOCK (1m 11·687s) ATS	
	22 DE CESARIS (1m 12·150s) Alfa Romeo
35 WARWICK (1m 12·528s) Toleman	
	23 BALDI (1m 12·860s) Alfa Romeo
36 GIACOMELLI (1m 13·422s) Toleman	
	1 ROSBERG (1m 13·755s) Williams
40 JOHANSSON (1m 13·962s) Spirit	
	8 LAUDA (1m 14·267s) McLaren
3 ALBORETO (1m 14·651s) Tyrrell	
	30 BOUTSEN (1m 14·964s) Arrows
12 MANSELL (1m 15·133s) Lotus	
	29 SURER (1m 15·135s) Arrows
2 LAFFITE (1m 15·234s) Williams	
	33 GUERRERO (1m 15·317s) Theodore
26 BOESEL (1m 15·386s) Ligier	
	4 SULLIVAN (1m 15·449s) Tyrrell
7 WATSON (1m 15·609s) McLaren	
	25 JARIER (1m 15·767s) Ligier
*32 GHINZANI (1m 16·544s) Osella	

*Started from pit lane
Did not start:
34 Cecotto (Theodore), 1m 16·714s, did not qualify
32 Fabi (Osella), 1m 17·594s, did not qualify
17 Acheson (RAM March), 1m 18·103s, did not qualify

Results and retirements

Place	Driver	Car	Laps	Time and Speed (mph/km/h)/Retirement	
1	Alain Prost	Renault t/c V6	67	1h 24m 39·780s	139·218/224·049
2	Nelson Piquet	Brabham-BMW t/c 4	67	1h 24m 58·941s	138·7/223·215
3	Patrick Tambay	Ferrari t/c V6	67	1h 25m 06·026s	138·5/222·894
4	Nigel Mansell	Lotus-Renault t/c V6	67	1h 25m 18·732s	138·2/222·411
5	René Arnoux	Ferrari t/c V6	67	1h 25m 38·654s	137·6/221·445
6	Niki Lauda	McLaren-Cosworth V8	66		
7	Mauro Baldi	Alfa Romeo t/c V8	66		
8	Andrea de Cesaris	Alfa Romeo t/c V8	66		
9	John Watson	McLaren-Cosworth V8	66		
10	Jean-Pierre Jarier	Ligier-Cosworth V8	65		
11	Keke Rosberg	Williams-Cosworth V8	65		
12	Jacques Laffite	Williams-Cosworth V8	65		
13	Michele Alboreto	Tyrrell-Cosworth V8	65		
14	Danny Sullivan	Tyrrell-Cosworth V8	65		
15	Thierry Boutsen	Arrows-Cosworth V8	65		
16	Roberto Guerrero	Theodore-Cosworth V8	64		
17	Marc Surer	Arrows-Cosworth V8	64		
	Manfred Winkelhock	ATS-BMW t/c 4	49	Engine/overheating	
	Raul Boesel	Ligier-Cosworth V8	48	Hydraulic suspension leak	
	Piercarlo Ghinzani	Osella-Alfa Romeo V12	46	Fuel pressure	
	Derek Warwick	Toleman-Hart t/c 4	27	Gearbox	
	Riccardo Patrese	Brabham-BMW t/c 4	9	Turbocharger	
	Stefan Johansson	Spirit-Honda t/c V6	5	Fuel pump belt	
	Eddie Cheever	Renault t/c V6	3	Engine/head gasket	
	Bruno Giacomelli	Toleman-Hart t/c 4	3	Turbocharger	
	Elio de Angelis	Lotus-Renault t/c V6	1	Precise reason unknown (see text)	

Fastest lap: Prost, on lap 32, 1m 14·212s, 142·23mph/228·896km/h (record).
Previous lap record: Clay Regazzoni (F1 Williams FW07-Cosworth DFV), 1m 14·40s, 141·87mph/228·32km/h (1979).

Past winners

Year	Driver	Nat	Car	Circuit	Distance miles/km	Speed mph/km/h
1926	Robert Sénéchal/ Louis Wagner	F F	1·5 Delage s/c	Brooklands	287·76/463·10	71·61/115·24
1927	Robert Benoist	F	1·5 Delage s/c	Brooklands	327·00/526·25	85·59/137·74
1935*	Richard Schuttleworth	GB	2·9 Alfa Romeo P3 s/c	Donington	318·88/513·18	63·97/102·95
1936*	Hans Reusch/ Dick Seaman	CH GB	3·8 Alfa Romeo 8C s/c	Donington	306·12/492·65	69·23/111·41
1937*	Bernd Rosemeyer	D	6·1 Auto Union C-type s/c	Donington	250·00/402·34	82·86/133·35
1938*	Tazio Nuvolari	I	3·0 Auto Union D-type s/c	Donington	250·00/402·34	80·49/129·54
1948†	Luigi Villoresi	I	1·5 Maserati 4CLT/48 s/c	Silverstone	238·55/383·91	72·27/116·31
1949	Emmanuel de Graffenried	CH	1·5 Maserati 4CLT/48 s/c	Silverstone	300·00/482·80	77·31/124·41
1950	Giuseppe Farina	I	1·5 Alfa Romeo 158 s/c	Silverstone	202·20/325·41	90·96/146·38
1951	Froilán González	RA	4·5 Ferrari 375	Silverstone	259·97/418·38	96·11/154·67
1952	Alberto Ascari	I	2·0 Ferrari 500	Silverstone	248·80/400·40	90·92/146·32
1953	Alberto Ascari	I	2·0 Ferrari 500	Silverstone	263·43/423·95	92·97/149·62
1954	Froilán González	RA	2·5 Ferrari 625	Silverstone	263·43/423·95	89·69/144·34
1955	Stirling Moss	GB	2·5 Mercedes-Benz W196	Aintree	270·00/434·52	86·47/139·16
1956	Juan Manuel Fangio	RA	2·5 Lancia-Ferrari D50	Silverstone	295·63/475·77	98·65/158·76
1957	Tony Brooks/ Stirling Moss	GB GB	2·5 Vanwall	Aintree	270·00/434·52	86·80/139·69
1958	Peter Collins	GB	2·4 Ferrari Dino 246	Silverstone	219·53/353·30	102·05/164·23
1959	Jack Brabham	AUS	2·5 Cooper T51-Climax	Aintree	225·00/362·10	98·88/159·13
1960	Jack Brabham	AUS	2·5 Cooper T53-Climax	Silverstone	225·00/362·10	108·69/174·92
1961	Wolfgang von Trips	D	1·5 Ferrari Dino 156	Aintree	225·00/362·10	83·91/135·04
1962	Jim Clark	GB	1·5 Lotus 25-Climax	Aintree	225·00/362·10	92·25/148·46
1963	Jim Clark	GB	1·5 Lotus 25-Climax	Silverstone	240·00/386·25	107·75/173·41
1964	Jim Clark	GB	1·5 Lotus 25-Climax	Brands Hatch	212·00/341·18	94·14/151·50
1965	Jim Clark	GB	1·5 Lotus 33-Climax	Silverstone	240·00/386·25	112·02/180·28
1966	Jack Brabham	AUS	3·0 Brabham BT19-Repco	Brands Hatch	212·00/341·18	95·48/153·66
1967	Jim Clark	GB	3·0 Lotus 49-Ford	Silverstone	240·00/386·25	117·64/189·32
1968	Jo Siffert	CH	3·0 Lotus 49B-Ford	Brands Hatch	212·00/341·18	104·83/168·71
1969	Jackie Stewart	GB	3·0 Matra MS80-Ford	Silverstone	245·87/395·69	127·25/204·79
1970	Jochen Rindt	A	3·0 Lotus 72-Ford	Brands Hatch	212·00/341·18	108·69/174·92
1971	Jackie Stewart	GB	3·0 Tyrrell 003-Ford	Silverstone	199·04/320·32	130·48/209·99
1972	Emerson Fittipaldi	BR	3·0 JPS/Lotus 72-Ford	Brands Hatch	201·40/324·12	112·06/180·34
1973	Peter Revson	USA	3·0 McLaren M23-Ford	Silverstone	196·11/315·61	131·75/212·03
1974	Jody Scheckter	ZA	3·0 Tyrrell 007-Ford	Brands Hatch	198·75/319·84	115·74/186·26
1975	Emerson Fittipaldi	BR	3·0 McLaren M23-Ford	Silverstone	164·19/264·24	120·02/193·15
1976	Niki Lauda	A	3·0 Ferrari 312T-2/76	Brands Hatch	198·63/319·67	114·24/183·85
1977	James Hunt	GB	3·0 McLaren M26-Ford	Silverstone	199·38/320·88	130·36/209·79

Circuit data

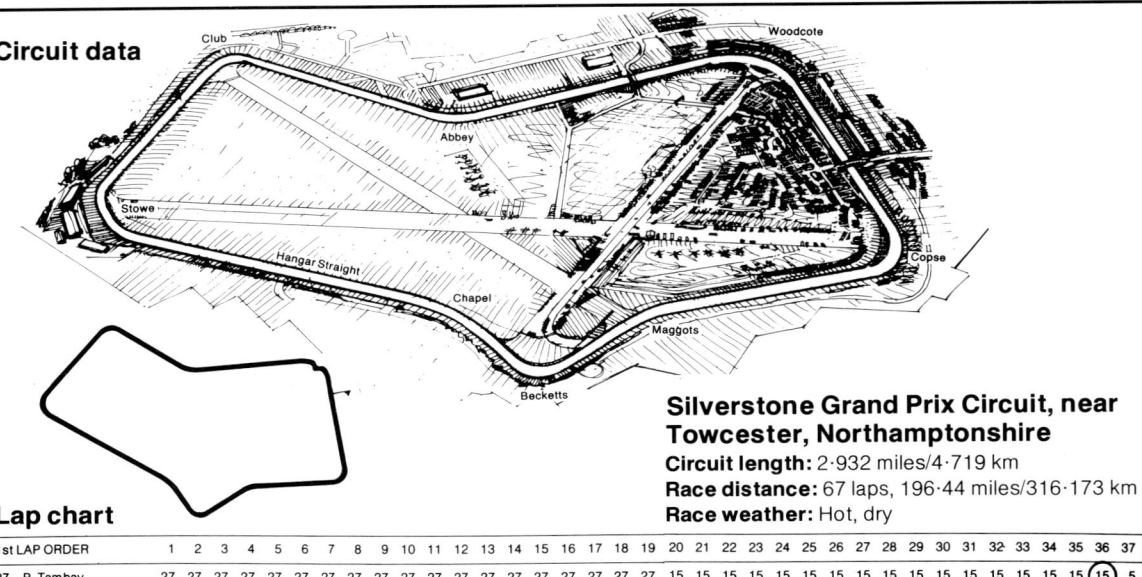

Silverstone Grand Prix Circuit, near Towcester, Northamptonshire
Circuit length: 2·932 miles/4·719 km
Race distance: 67 laps, 196·44 miles/316·173 km
Race weather: Hot, dry

Lap chart

```
1st LAP ORDER        1  2  3  4  5  6  7  8  9 10 11 12 13 14 15 16 17 18 19 20 21 22 23 24 25 26 27 28 29 30 31 32 33 34 35 36 37
27  P. Tambay        27 27 27 27 27 27 27 27 27 27 27 27 27 27 27 27 27 27 27 15 15 15 15 15 15 15 15 15 15 15 15 15 15 15 15(15) 5
28  R. Arnoux        28 28 28 28 28 28 28 28 28 28 28 28 28 15 15 15 15 15 15 27 27 27 27 27 27 27 27 27 27  5  5  5  5  5  5  5 15
15  A. Prost         15 15 15 15 15 15 15 15 15 15 15 15 15 28 28 28 28 28  5  5  5  5  5  5  5  5  5  5  5 27 27 27 27 27(27)12
 6  R. Patrese        6  6  6  6  6  6  6  6  6  5  5  5  5  5  5  5  5  5  5 28 28 28 28 28 28 28 28 28 28 22 12 12 12 27
16  E. Cheever       16 16  5  5  5  5  5  5 22 22 22 22 22 22 22 22 22 22 22 22 22 22 22 22 22 22 22 22 12 12(22) 8 28 28
11  E. De Angelis    11  5 22 22 22 22 22 22  9  9  9  9  9  9  9  9  9  9  9  9  9  9  9  9  9  9 12 12 12(28) 8  8 28 23 23
 5  N. Piquet         5 22  9  9  9  9  9  9 35 35 35 35 35 35 35 12 12 12 12 12 12 12 12 12 12 12 (9) 8  8 28 28 23  9  9
22  A. De Cesaris    22  9 35 35 35 35 35 35 12 12 12 12 12 12 35 35 35 35 35 35 35 35 35  8  8  8 23 23 23 23 23  9  8  8
 9  M. Winkelhock     9 35 12 12 12 12 12  8  8  8  8  8  8  8  8  8  8  8  8  8  8  8  8(35)23 23  7 (7) 9  9  9  1  1  1
35  D. Warwick       35 12 40 40  8  8  8  8 23 23 23 23 23 23 23 23 23 23 23 23 23 23 23 23  7  7  9  9  1  1  1  7  7  7
40  S. Johansson     40 40 23  8 23 23 23 23  1  1  7  7  7  7  7  7  7  7  7  7  7  7  7  7  1  1  1  1 25(25) 7  2  2 22
12  N. Mansell       12 23  8 23  1  1  1  1  7  7  1  1  1  1  1  1  1  1  1  1  1  1  1  1 25 25 25 25  7  7  2 22 22 (2)
23  M. Baldi         23  8  1  1  3  3  7  7 25 25 25 25 25 25 25 25 25 25 25 25 25 25 25  2  2  2  2  2  2 25 25 25 25
 8  N. Lauda          8  1  3  3 25  7 25 25  3  3  3  3  2  2  2  2  2  2  2  2  2  2  2  2  3  3  3  3  3  3  3  3  3  3
 1  K. Rosberg        1  3(16)25  7 25  3  3  4  2  2  2  3  3  3  3  3  3  3  3  3  3  3  3 26 26 26 26 26 26 26 26 26 26
36  B. Giacomelli    36  4 25  7  4  4  4  4  2  4  4  4 26 26 26 26 26 26 26 26 26 26 26  4  4  4  4  4  4  4  4  4  4  4
 3  M. Alboreto       3 33  4  4  2  2  2  2 26 26 26 26  4  4  4  4  4  4  4  4  4  4  4 30 30 30 30 30 30 30 30 30 30 30
 4  D. Sullivan       4 25  7 33 33 26 26 26 30 30 30 30 30 30 30 30 30 30 30 30 30 30 30 33 33 33 33 33 33 33 33 33 33 33
33  R. Guerrero      33 26 33  2 26 30 30 30 33 33 33 33 33 33 33 33 33 33 33 33 33 33 33 29 29 29 29 29 29 29 29 29 29 29
25  J. P. Jarier     25  7 26 30 30 33 33 33 29 29 29 29 29 29 29 29 29 29 29 29 29 29 29 32 32 32 32 32 32 32 32 32 32 32
26  R. Boesel        26  2  2 30 29 29 29 (6)32 32 32 32 32 32 32 32 32 32 32 32 32 32 32
 7  J. Watson         7 30 30 29(40)32 32 32
 2  J. Laffite        2 29 29 32 32
30  T. Boutsen       30 32 32
29  M. Surer         29(36)(36)
32  P. Ghinzani      32
```

```
38 39 40 41 42 43 44 45 46 47 48 49 50 51 52 53 54 55 56 57 58 59 60 61 62 63 64 65 66 67
 5  5  5 (5)15 15 15 15 15 15 15 15 15 15 15 15 15 15 15 15 15 15 15 15 15 15 15 15 15 15
15 15 15 15 12  5  5  5  5  5  5  5  5  5  5  5  5  5  5  5  5  5  5  5  5  5  5  5  5  5
12 12 12 12(12)27 27 27 27 27 27 27 27 27 27 27 27 27 27 27 27 27 27 27 27 27 27 27 27 27
27 27 27 27 27 27 28 28 28 12 12 12 12 12 12 12 12 12 12 12 12 12 12 12 12 12 12 12 12 12
28 28 28 28 28 28 12 12 12 28 28 28 28 28 28 28 28 28 28 28 28 28 28 28 28 28 28 28 28 28
(23) 9  9  9  9  9  9  9  9  8  8  8  8  8  8  8  8  8  8  8  8  8  8  8  8  8  8  8
 9  8  8  8  8  8  8  8  9 23 23 23 23 23 23 23 23 23 23 23 23 23 23 23 23
 8 23 23 23 23 23 23 23  9 22 22 22 22 22 22 22 22 22 22 22 22 22 22 22
 1  1  1  7  7  7  7  7 22 22  7  7  7  7  7  7  7  7  7  7  7  7  7  7
 7  7  7 (1)22 22 22 22 22  7  7 25 25 25 25 25 25 25 25 25 25 25 25 25
22 22 22 22 25 25 25 25 25  1  1  1  1  1  1  1  1  1  1  1  1  1  1  1  1
25 25 25 25  1  1  1  1  1  1  3  3  3  3  3  3  3  3  3  3  3  2  2  2
 3  3  3  3  3  3  3  3  2  2  2  2  2  2  2  2  2  2  2  2  3  3  3
 2  2  2  2  2  2  2  2  3 (9) 4  4  4  4  4  4  4  4  4  4  4
26(26) 4  4  4  4  4  4  4 30 30 30 30 30 30 30 30 30 30 30 30
 4  4 30 30 30 30 30 30 30 33 33 33 33 33 33 33 33 33 33 33
30 30 26 26 26 26 26 26 26(26)33 29 29 29 29 29 29 29 29 29
33 33 33 33 33 33 33 33 29
29 29 29 29 29 29 29 29 29
32 32 32 32 32 32 32(32)
```

Fastest laps

Driver	Time	Lap
Alain Prost	1m 14·212s	32
Nelson Piquet	1m 14·327s	36
Nigel Mansell	1m 14·434s	49
Patrick Tambay	1m 14·805s	62
Riccardo Patrese	1m 14·857s	4
Andrea de Cesaris	1m 15·032s	64
Manfred Winkelhock	1m 15·144s	28
Mauro Baldi	1m 15·207s	65
René Arnoux	1m 15·214s	7
Derek Warwick	1m 15·856s	60
Niki Lauda	1m 15·923s	60
John Watson	1m 16·090s	14
Jacques Laffite	1m 16·228s	36
Eddie Cheever	1m 16·261s	2
Jean-Pierre Jarier	1m 16·477s	53
Keke Rosberg	1m 16·887s	52
Michele Alboreto	1m 17·456s	55
Raul Boesel	1m 17·659s	47
Danny Sullivan	1m 17·858s	60
Thierry Boutsen	1m 17·913s	59
Stefan Johansson	1m 17·934s	3
Roberto Guerrero	1m 18·351s	56
Marc Surer	1m 18·552s	63
Piercarlo Ghinzani	1m 19·920s	37
Elio de Angelis	1m 23·401s	1
Bruno Giacomelli	1m 29·957s	1

Points

WORLD CHAMPIONSHIP OF DRIVERS

1	Alain Prost	39 pts
2	Nelson Piquet	33
3	Patrick Tambay	31
4	Keke Rosberg	25
5	René Arnoux	19
6	John Watson	16
7	Eddie Cheever	14
8	Niki Lauda	11
9	Jacques Laffite	10
10	Michele Alboreto	9
11 =	Marc Surer	4
11 =	Nigel Mansell	4
13	Danny Sullivan	2
14 =	Johnny Cecotto	1
14 =	Mauro Baldi	1

CONSTRUCTORS' CUP

1	Renault	53 pts
2	Ferrari	50
3	Williams	35
4	Brabham	33
5	McLaren	27
6	Tyrrell	11
7 =	Arrows	4
7 =	Lotus	4
9 =	Theodore	1
9 =	Alfa Romeo	1

1978	Carlos Reutemann	RA	3·0 Ferrari 312T-3/78	Brands Hatch	198·63/319·67	116·61/187·66
1979	Clay Regazzoni	CH	3·0 Williams FW07-Ford	Silverstone	199·38/320·88	138·80/223·37
1980	Alan Jones	AUS	3·0 Williams FW07B-Ford	Brands Hatch	198·63/319·67	125·69/202·28
1981	John Watson	GB	3·0 McLaren MP4-Ford	Silverstone	199·38/320·88	137·64/221·51
1982	Niki Lauda	A	3·0 McLaren MP4B-Ford	Brands Hatch	198·63/319·67	124·70/200·68
1983	Alain Prost	F	1·5 Renault RE40 t/c	Silverstone	196·44/316·17	139·22/224·05

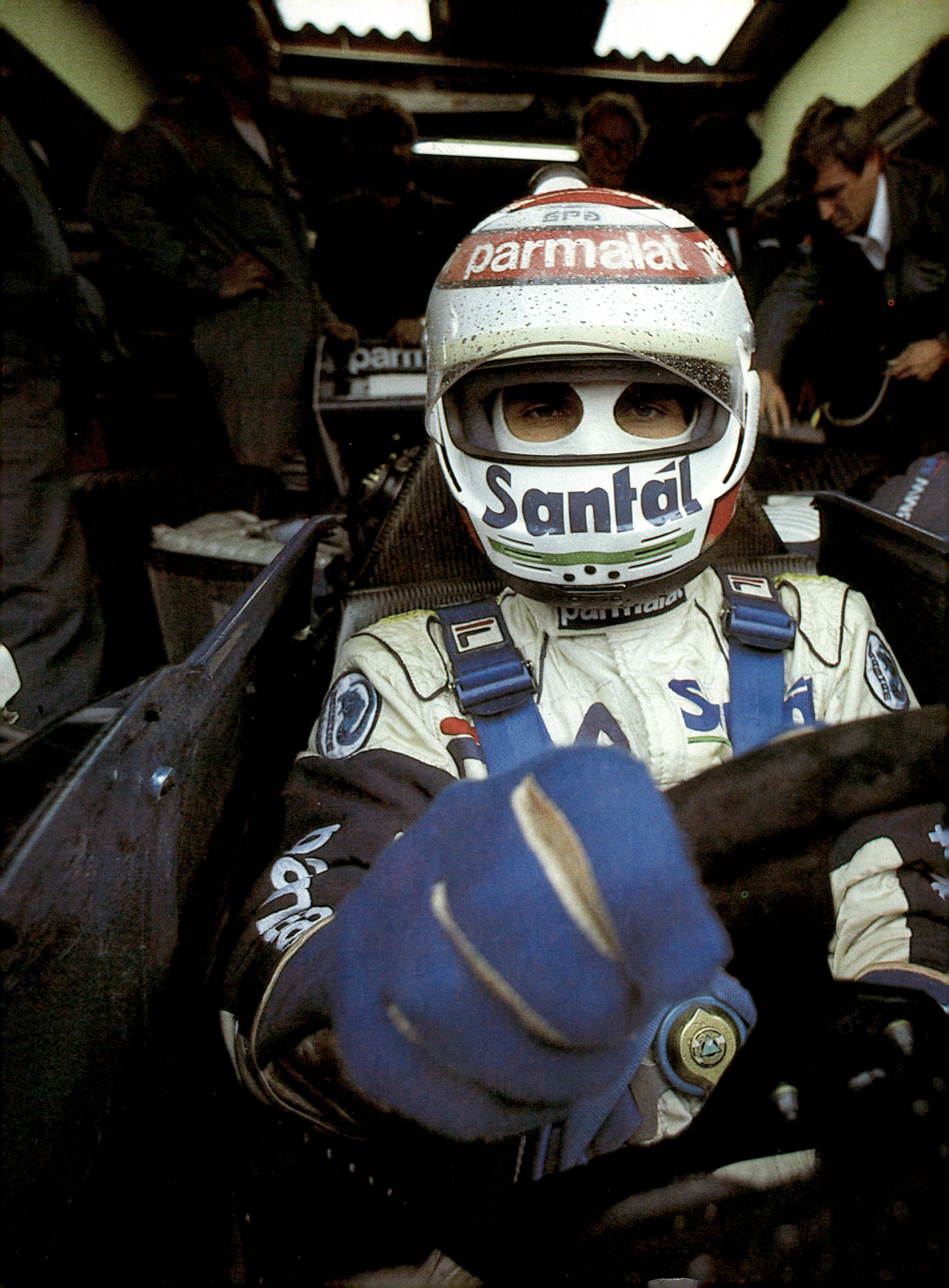

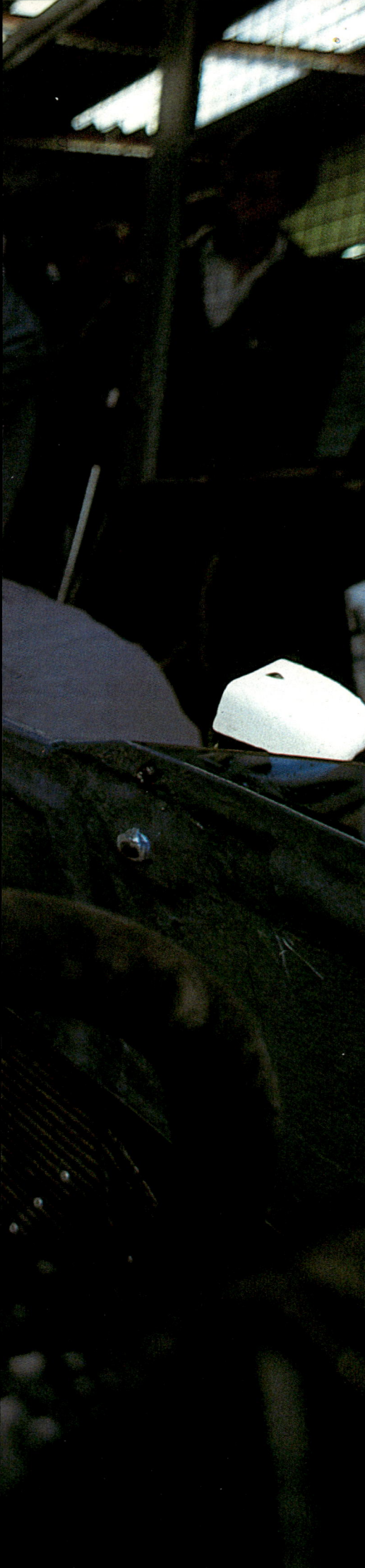

GROSSER PREIS VON DEUTSCHLAND

The Swiss-registered Ferrari Mondial Quattrovalvole edged slowly through the gates on race morning, its driver glancing at the cars already parked in the FOCA paddock. Patrick Tambay climbed out, looked at his watch, and smiled. Forghieri had not arrived. Gathering up his briefcase and blue Goodyear jacket, Tambay walked through the paddock, signing autographs and chatting easily.

Several minutes passed before Mauro Forghieri eased his Lancia into the paddock. He saw Tambay; his jaw dropped. Beaten again.

Tambay laughed heartily as Forghieri strode purposefully across to demand an explanation. When did he arrive? Which route did he take? The Ferrari engineer did not like being beaten on the road any more than his drivers enjoyed a thrashing on the track.

But the mood was good and Tambay was particularly pleased with the course events had taken at a relaxed dinner the previous evening. René Arnoux had agreed, if called upon towards the end of the race, to support his team-mate since Tambay was better placed in the championship. But then Arnoux had made similar concessions before; Alain Prost knew all about that.

And Tambay was to learn at first hand about his 'team-mate' just two laps into the race when Ferrari number 28 outbraked Ferrari number 27 for the lead, leaving Tambay with the option of conceding the corner – or taking them both off. Tambay gave way, as Arnoux knew he would, and Patrick's race was to end nine laps later with engine trouble. But a point had been made.

Arnoux, meanwhile, pulled away, losing his place at the front to Nelson Piquet just once when he stopped for fuel and tyres; that was as close as the Parmalat Brabham driver would get to winning the race.

However, with three laps to go, Piquet seemed secure in second place and the six points would lift the Brazilian closer to the top of the championship table. Then, disaster as a fuel filter housing cracked and petrol ignited on the hot BMW engine as Piquet accelerated towards the first chicane. By the time he had come to a halt, the Brabham was well and truly alight and, as marshals doused the flames, Andrea de Cesaris found himself about to give the Marlboro Alfa Romeo team their best result since returning to Formula 1 in 1979.

De Cesaris was fortunate in more ways than one, Eddie Cheever having stopped his Renault-Elf not long before with a broken fuel pump drive and these retirements allowed Riccardo Patrese to join Arnoux and de Cesaris on the rostrum and score his first points of the season.

With Tambay and Piquet out, the championship remained much as before – which was fortunate for Alain Prost, forced to start in the spare Renault. He had been without fifth gear for much of the race but the good fortune which had smiled on the Frenchman for most of the season continued and Alain found himself taking three more points and extending his lead of the championship.

The Marlboro McLaren team needed more than good luck; they needed a turbo since the Ford-Cosworth proved to be nothing more than an also-ran at Hockenheim. But, continuing the vigour shown at Silverstone, Niki Lauda drove impeccably to finish fifth on the road and completely outpace his normally aspirated rivals.

His only mistake of the weekend was made in the pit lane and it was to prove costly. Overshooting his pit, Lauda reversed his car into position for fuel and tyres but the Stewards later disqualified the Austrian for breaking the regulations. Lauda's loss was Watson's gain, the Ulsterman taking two points with Jacques Laffite finishing sixth in the Saudia Williams.

Three years before, Laffite had won the German Grand Prix to give himself an outside chance of a late run at the championship. Now his fellow-countryman had done the same although it was clear that it was every man for himself within the Ferrari team. The party was over; the joking and *bonhomie* had stopped.

Nelson Piquet vacated the cockpit rather smartly when a split fuel housing caused the rear of his car to catch fire during the closing stages of the race. The Brazilian lost second place as a result.
Photo: Bernard Asset

On his own from here on in. René Arnoux's behaviour at Hockenheim was not quite what Patrick Tambay had expected of his team-mate. Arnoux went on to win his second Grand Prix of the season while Tambay retired with engine failure.
A battle between Riccardo Patrese and Andrea de Cesaris saw the Alfa Romeo overhaul the Brabham-BMW – twice – to give both drivers their best results so far, de Cesaris finishing second, Patrese third *(opposite, top)*.
The ATS team pack up quietly on Saturday after Manfred Winkelhock had failed to qualify for his home Grand Prix.

ENTRY AND PRACTICE

Racing drivers allow little time for superstition and sentiment but few missed the significance of events on Saturday morning at Hockenheim. Ferrari were on the overnight pole, just like the year before. And it was raining, just like the year before. What's more, Didier Pironi had chosen this day to make his return to the Formula 1 paddock, the Ferrari driver still on crutches exactly one year after the horrendous accident which destroyed his championship chances in 1982.

The next day, Patrick Tambay had stepped forward to win the race for Ferrari. In 1983, the fact that, like Pironi, he was on pole and, like Pironi, a strong contender for the championship; the fact that it was raining again as he climbed into his Ferrari; the déjà vu qualities of the circumstances did not escape Tambay. But, in the event, the day was to pass without incident. The rain continued throughout and the grid was established by the times set in the dry on Friday.

The catch-phrase at Hockenheim was 'Goodyear radials.' After successful tests at Fiorano and Daytona earlier in the year, Goodyear at last brought their radial slicks along for Ferrari and Williams to try during practice. But what was good for the tight turns of Daytona and Fiorano did not prove suitable for Hockenheim and Arnoux and Rosberg soon discarded the radials when they found them to be around two seconds slower. Goodyear were still licking their wounds after Silverstone but Ferrari felt they may have been partly to blame by not running the large 'coffee table' rear wing and creating sufficient downforce. Tests had proved that there was little or no drag loss and the Italians duly returned to the large aerofoils. Revisions to the bodywork had pared more weight from the C3 and the team's smooth progress was such that the spare C2Bs were not used.

Tambay set what was to become pole position on his second set of qualifiers and the Frenchman was surprised at the news. The Ferrari has a switch to control the water injection alongside the rev limiter switch and, when Patrick attempted to cut the rev limiter, he inadvertently switched off the water injection. Having discovered after the British Grand Prix that his water injection had failed to work and yet the engine had suffered no loss of power, this latest incident cast doubts on the value of a system which was causing so much trouble in the shape of protests from Ken Tyrrell.

Tambay looked to René Arnoux for his main opposition but René used his first set of qualifiers to set second fastest time and then spent the rest of the session on a set of race tyres. On Saturday, Arnoux was the fastest in the wet, proving conclusively that the Ferrari turbo had the power to drag the large rear wing along the straights. It gave the team cause to wonder just what might have happened had they brought them to Silverstone.

Andrea de Cesaris was in the news in more ways than one. The Marlboro Alfa Romeo driver caused a welcome diversion from the Ferrari, Renault, Brabham monopoly by setting third fastest time with a car which featured revised turbochargers producing an increase in maximum power and top speed. The next day, Andrea hit the headlines by arriving at the circuit without a suitable pass on his car and knocking a policeman over as he tried to barge through a security check. Only a bail bond of DM15,000 enabled the Italian to race on Sunday. His team-mate, Mauro Baldi was rather more circumspect in every respect and qualified in seventh place ahead of Riccardo Patrese.

The Brabham team had a busy weekend one way and another. Nelson Piquet stopped out on the circuit on Friday morning with an electrical problem and then his T-car proceeded to pump out its water thanks to a header tank problem. None the less, Nelson was in

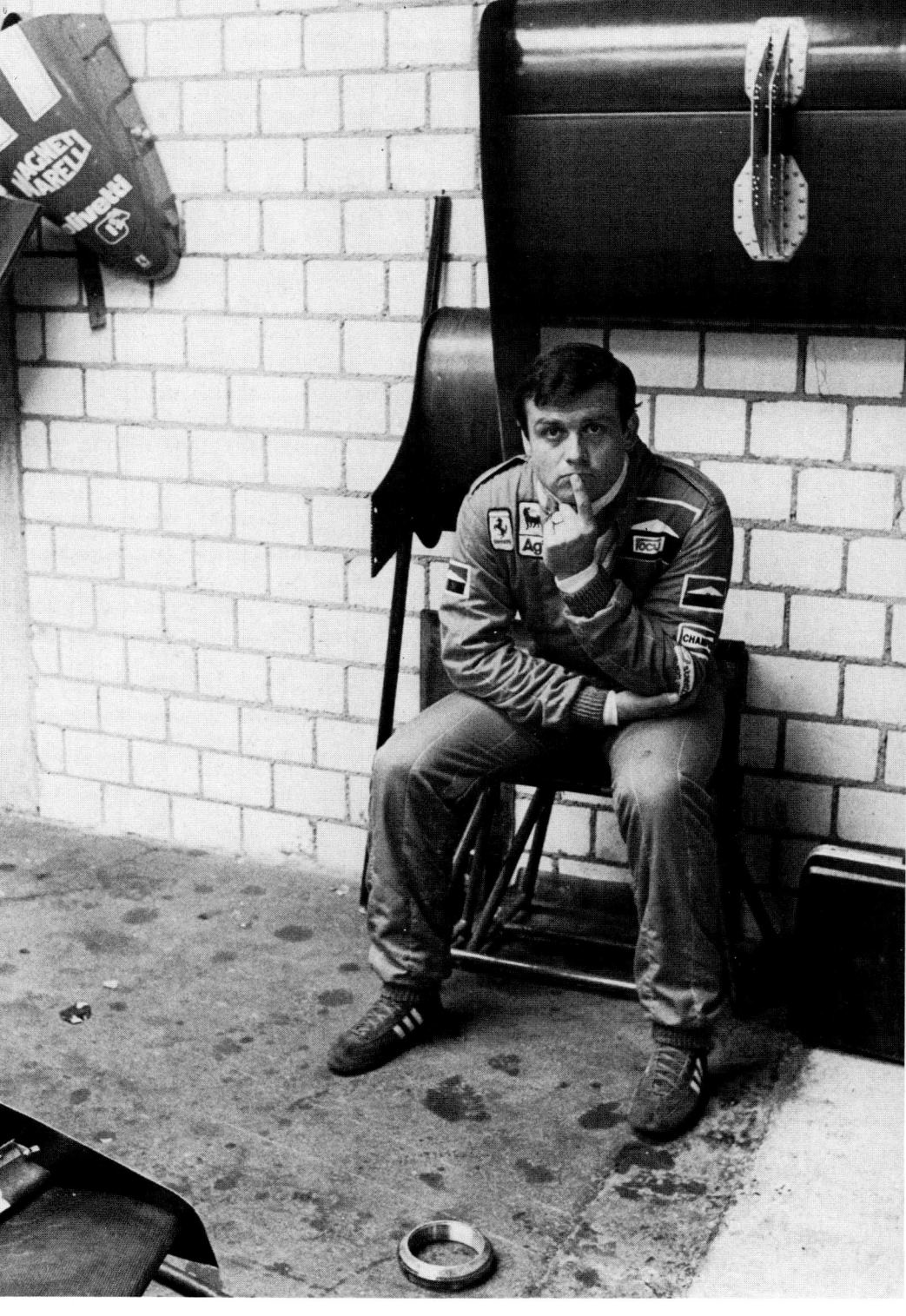

fourth place while Patrese suffered a mysterious loss of power and a broken exhaust on Friday afternoon and he then damaged the nose of his car by slithering off at a chicane on Saturday morning.

It was unusual to see Alain Prost do the same thing, scattering polystyrene blocks marking the chicanes as he went. We were also unaccustomed to finding the championship leader down in fifth place on the grid with a time set in the T-car. The controversial underwing exhaust system on the RE40, protested by Brabham at Detroit, had since been ratified by an Appeal court decision but Renault continued to use the old system at Hockenheim. The most obvious modification was the shortening of the under-bodywork at the rear but, according to Prost, this upset the handling and caused oversteer – hence his preference for the T-car which featured the full length panels. Cheever was three-tenths slower but the American put this down to a loss of power caused, it was thought, by damage to the turbos when the car ran out of fuel while travelling at high speed during the morning session. Nevertheless, Cheever held high hopes for the race and he was equally confident in the wet on Saturday, setting second fastest time with some glorious opposite lock slides.

Derek Warwick was another driver to enjoy driving in the wet although the Englishman had reservations about the safety aspects of ploughing through the ever present blanket of spray which caught Pironi out 12 months previously. Warwick had clutch trouble on Friday morning which meant he had to take to the track on qualifiers without actually having completed a quick lap in his race car. Apart from a misfire, the Candy Toleman handled well enough to give Warwick ninth place, just ahead of his team-mate, Bruno Giacomelli.

Toleman had been helped out by the latest Pirellis with a new front construction to help turn-in and the John Player Lotus team were also looking for an improvement following a successful test session at Hockenheim when Nigel Mansell had come away with a faster time than Prost. Official practice, however, was to be another story for the black and gold cars.

On Friday morning, Elio de Angelis spun in the stadium after a moment of over-enthusiasm on cold tyres. The mechanics set about repairing the damaged steering rack and de Angelis returned to the track with just a few minutes of the timed session remaining. Halfway round his quick lap, the nose section began to droop but the Italian pressed on to set 11th fastest time

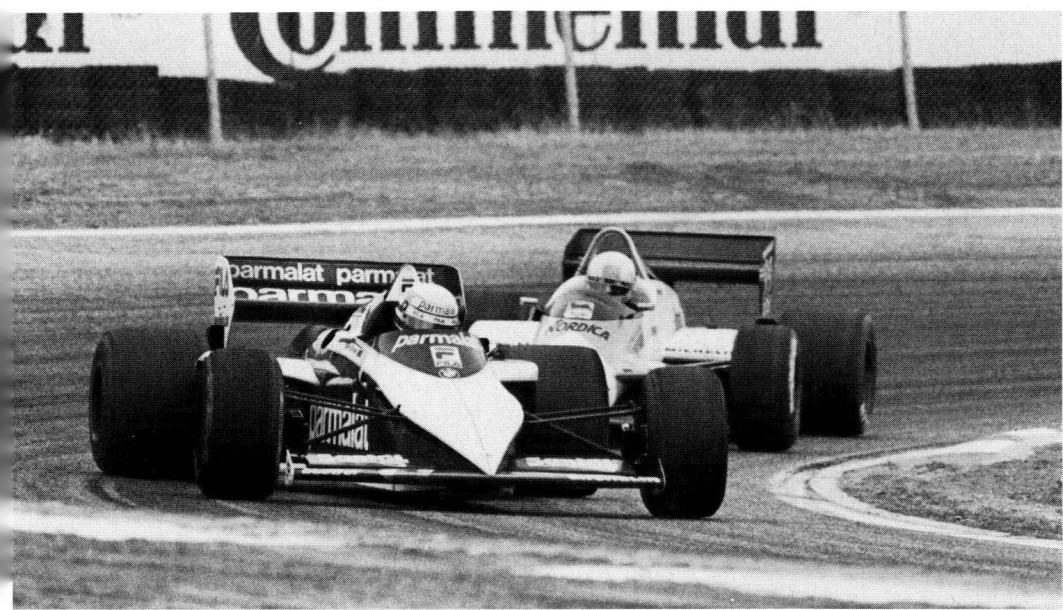

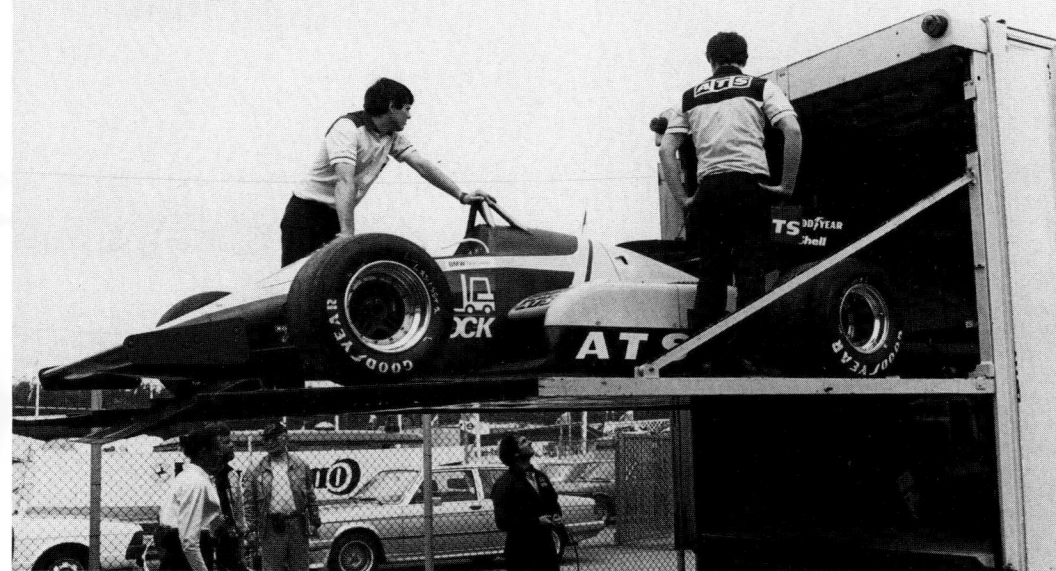

– and it was just as well he did considering the unfavourable weather the next day.

Mansell was in deep trouble too, the Englishman preplexed to find his 94T overheating and refusing to pull more than 6000 revs. A broken water pump drive was thought to be the problem but Mansell managed no more than half-a-lap before the car ground to a halt with a dead engine. There was nothing for it but a return to the unloved 93T spare car and Mansell wrestled the bulky machine into 17th place in the timed session. On Saturday morning, Gerard Ducarouge, Peter Warr, Mansell, a Renault engineer and two mechanics stood around the 94T and scratched their heads as the V6 continued to misfire and overheat; the prospect of having to race the spare car scarcely appealed to Mansell who had come to Hockenheim with firm thoughts about a place in the top three.

Such a notion was the last thing on the minds of the TAG Williams team as they prepared their Ford-Cosworth cars while Patrick Head and Frank Dernie remained at the factory to work on the Honda-powered FW09. A lack of horsepower notwithstanding, the FW08C in wide track configuration did not prove ideal when Keke Rosberg and Jacques Laffite suffered from understeer and were unable to work adequate temperatures into the front tyres. With the aid of a typically flamboyant lap, Rosberg slashed over two seconds off his previous best time to take 12th place, the fastest Cosworth, but the gap of almost six seconds to Tambay was an indication of the magnitude of the problem facing the non-turbo runners. Jacques Laffite, 15th fastest, was over a second slower than his team-mate.

It was even more galling for the Williams team to find their drivers split by Stefan Johansson in the Spirit-Honda; galling because the Swede was bitterly disappointed with his time after a catalogue of problems had afflicted both his cars. A pinion shaft broke during the morning and Stefan took the older, heavier car to bed in brakes while repairs were carried out. Back in his race car again, Johansson discovered that the electrical system could not cope with the high boost and a misfire meant he had to return to the T-car to set a quick time. Had he not been able to complete his one lap of the timed session at under two minutes then the Swede would have been a most disgruntled spectator on Sunday.

Thierry Boutsen continued to impress the establishment by setting the second fastest Cosworth time, one second faster than his Arrows team-mate, Marc Surer. The Swiss driver, however, was saddled with a down-on-power engine while using his first set of qualifiers and switched to the T-car to run his second set. Michele Alboreto continued to use the Benetton Tyrrell 011 while the team worked flat out to prepare the 012 in time for its launch in Austria. The Italian driver had few serious complaints at Hockenheim and took 16th place with Danny Sullivan setting 21st fastest time after his engine had begun to tighten while running his second set of qualifiers.

Niki Lauda went one better and blew a Cosworth on Friday morning, the Austrian setting 18th fastest time while waiting patiently for the arrival of the TAG-Porsche turbo engine in Holland. John Watson was back in 23rd place, unstable braking eroding the Ulsterman's confidence in his Marlboro McLaren MP4/1C.

Raul Boesel's confidence underwent a severe test

THE FIA INTERNATIONAL COURT OF APPEAL REJECTED Gordon Murray's claim that the Renault exhaust system protested by Brabham at Detroit (see Detroit GP), was illegal and details of the court's findings were released at Hockenheim.

The tribunal concluded that the moving parts of the engine and turbocharger did not "*of themselves* (their italics) have an aerodynamic effect on the behaviour of the car" although they did concede that "all constructors tend to use the burnt gases in the best possible conditions" to achieve aerodynamic benefits.

In effect, they came to the conclusion that the exhaust gases were simply the combustion residue from the engine and not developed for an aerodynamic purpose. Renault-type systems were permissable although the wording of the document made it clear that exhaust driven fans and such like would be out of the question.

THE LEGALITY OF THE WATER INJECTION SYSTEM used on the Renault and Ferrari engines, protested at Silverstone by Ken Tyrrell, was questioned again at Hockenheim when Tyrrell and Frank Williams laid a similar portest with the organisers before practice began. As at Silverstone, the protest was swiftly rejected, the organisers preferring the FIA Court of Appeal to sort the matter out.

Tyrrell had gathered a considerable amount of evidence to support his case and he went to great lengths to illustrate his point to anyone who took the trouble to listen. It was Tyrrell's contention that the addition of water to the petrol before it entered the combustion chamber meant the fuel then broke the regulations on four counts:

1) the octane rating exceeded the maximum allowed;
2) the oxygen content exceeded the permissable 2%;
3) the fuel was no longer exclusively made up of hydrocarbons, 2% oxygen and 1% nitrogen by weight as required by the regulations;
4) the fuel contained a power-boosting additive.

Tyrrell emphasised that he did not wish to affect the outcome of the 1983 World Championship. His concern was for 1984 when pit stops would be banned and the fuel capacity reduced from 250 litres to 220 litres. In Tyrrell's opinion, the 'adding of water to the fuel is a blatant mockery of the fuel tank capacity limitations – unless the water tank capacity is added to the petrol tank capacity. The power obtainable from a given quantity of water-petrol fuel is approximately equal to that obtainable using the same quantity of petrol. This clearly circumvents the stated policy of FISA to limit power output by limiting fuel tank capacity.'

The dispute pivoted on the interpretation of the purpose of adding water to the petrol. Renault and Ferrari claimed it was purely for cooling the air intake charge and was therefore not fuel. They showed no outward signs of abandoning their system which, incidentally, differed in approach: Renault adding a fine spray of water into the inlet manifold; Ferrari adding water by means of an emulsifier.

Behind the scenes, however, forces were at work. Elf, who supplied Renault and Tyrrell among others, announced at Hockenheim that they would cut off Tyrrell's fuel supply immediately. They were incensed that Tyrrell should claim their product to be illegal. Tyrrell said this was not the case; he was protesting the actions taken by Renault *after* Elf had supplied the fuel. Elf would not be appeased, and stood by the cancellation of an agreement with Tyrrell which had run for 16 years.

Francois Guiter, Marketing Director of Elf (France), said his engineers and chemists had gone into the question in considerable detail and there was no doubt in his mind that water injection, as they saw it, was quite legal.

Clearly, it was a complicated and highly technical matter which sharply divided opinions in the paddock.

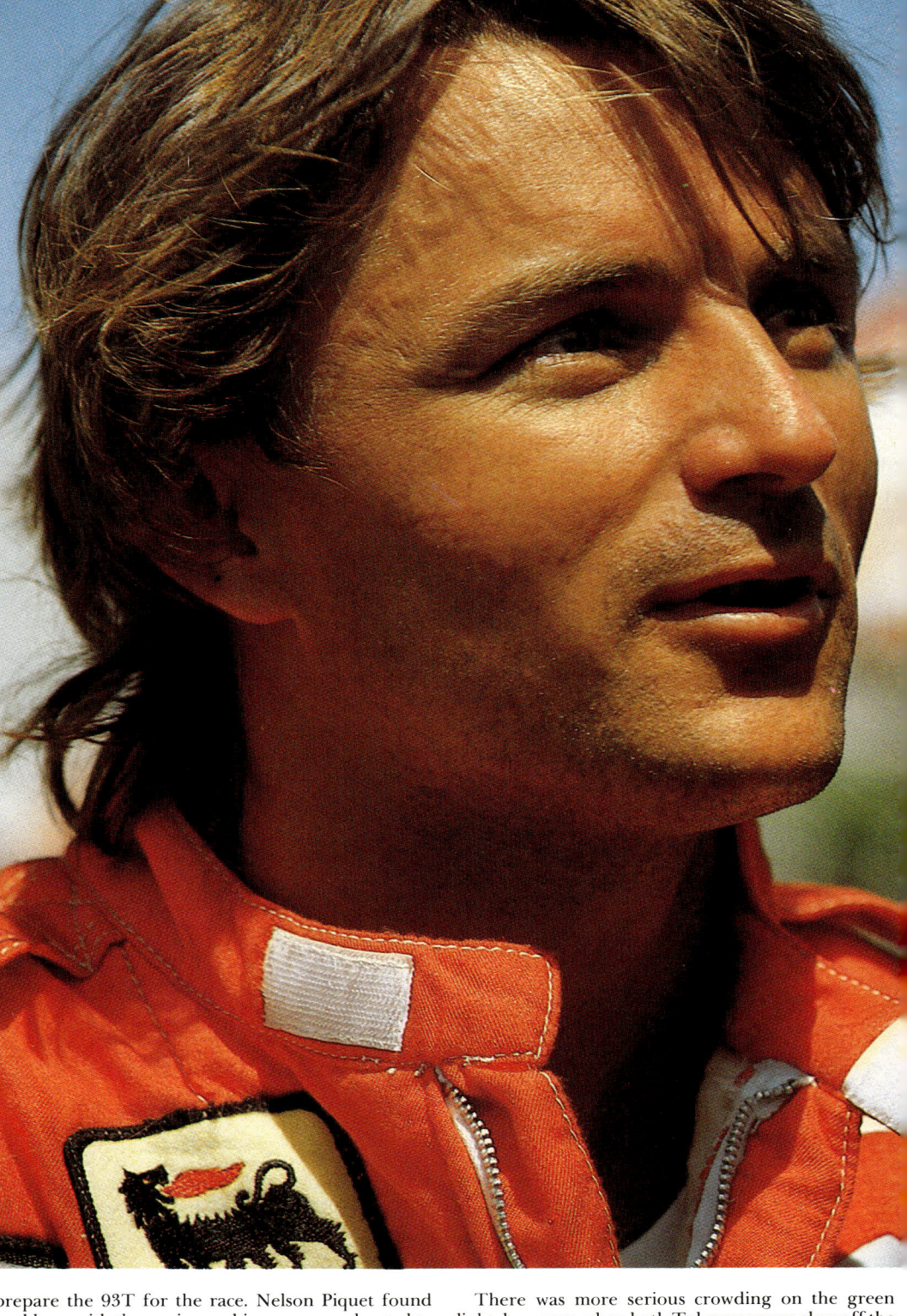

René Arnoux started his late bid for the championship by winning convincingly at Hockenheim.
Photo: DPPI

when the Brazilian crashed heavily at the *Sachskurve* on Friday afternoon. Going for a quick lap, Boesel had ridden over a kerb at the exit of the previous right-hander and the excursion may have damaged a brake pipe. Whatever the reason, Raul found himself with no rear brakes as he hit the pedal in the approach to the second gear *Sachskurve*. The front brakes locked briefly and the Gitanes Ligier ploughed straight on even though the front wheels were on full left lock. The JS21 demolished the catch-fencing and rammed the tyre barrier, making a severe dent in the concrete wall behind it. The front of the car withstood the impact well and the only injury to the driver was a nasty gash inflicted on his neck by a wire from the catch-fencing. After a medical check up, Boesel arrived at the circuit on Saturday wearing a neck collar and insisting he was fit enough to race. His time on his first set of qualifiers had been good enough for 25th place. Alterations to the hydropneumatic suspension meant the ride was too soft for Jean-Pierre Jarier's liking, the Frenchman taking a place on the tenth row.

Running a wide front track and short wheelbase on the Theodore, Roberto Guerrero took 24th place, fractionally slower than his team-mate, Johnny Cecotto. Piercarlo Ghinzani was the final qualifier after his team-mate Corrado Fabi failed to make the cut due to an engine misfire. Kenny Acheson was the first reserve, the Ulsterman kicking himself for having spun at the end of what might have been a lap good enough to make the race. The RAM-March driver's run on his second set of qualifiers was spoiled by a slow-moving car at one of the chicanes and the failure to qualify came as no surprise.

The same could not be said for the ATS team, however, Manfred Winkelhock and team owner, Gunther Schmid, mortified at failing to earn a place on

JULY:
Ayrton Senna da Silva given test drive by Williams at Donington.

Bob Wollek (Porsche 956) wins International German Racing Championship.

Ivan Capelli, Pierluigi Martini and Davy Jones test Brabham-BMW at Brands Hatch. BT52 also driven by Stirling Moss.

Ivan Capelli (Ralt-Alfa Romeo RT3) wins Italian Formula 3 Championship

the grid for their home grand prix after a series of disasters during the all-important hour on Friday afternoon. The continual failure of an oil line to stay attached meant, by the time it was fixed properly, the engine had lost boost and the turbo had suffered serious damage. Switching to the spare car, Manfred found it had an engine misfire and, as a result, he did not complete one flying lap in the first timed session. Winkelhock pounded round to set seventh fastest time in the unofficial session on Saturday morning but the German was thoroughly depressed when the rain continued to fall during the final hour. By then, the irascible Schmid was nowhere to be seen.

THE RACE

A race without the popular German, indeed, the only German, did not deter a large crowd from filling the stadium under a grey sky. An Alfasud race kept them entertained and kept the course officials busy as they reconstructed catch-fences, a job which meant a late start for the Formula 1 warm-up.

Now it was the mechanics' turn to busy themselves as they set about curing the problems caused by the 30-minute session. Mansell continued to have trouble with his 94T and there was nothing for it but to

prepare the 93T for the race. Nelson Piquet found problems with the engine on his race car and opted to run the spare, the Brabham mechanics grafting on the exhaust system and transmission from the race car. Tambay and Prost had engine changes while a controversial incident took place in the Lotus pit. Elio de Angelis had stopped out on the circuit with an electrical problem after just one lap and the Italian driver vented his frustration on *Autocourse* contributor and *Motor Sport* Grand Prix correspondent, Denis Jenkinson, who was chatting to Tony Rudd. De Angelis took exception to strong criticism which had emanated from 'Jenk's' pen and, in attempting to push the bearded journalist out of the garage, the Italian merely succeeded in putting him on his back. It was an unpleasant incident which did nothing for de Angelis's reputation.

As the cars made their way onto the grid, the drama continued as Prost found the temperatures on his new engine to be too high and he pulled into the pits and climbed into the spare Renault. Everything seemed to be in order as the field completed the final parade lap although de Cesaris caused a mild amount of confusion by lining up at the wrong slot on the grid, forcing those behind him to bunch slightly.

There was more serious crowding on the green light, however, when both Tolemans were slow off the mark. Keke Rosberg took to the grass, thumping the bottom of his Williams on the edge of the tarmac as he regained the track in front of Giacomelli while, on the opposite side of the grid, Johansson made a brilliant start and weaved between Mansell and Warwick to take ninth place.

Tambay had staked his claim to this race by beating Arnoux to the first corner and the two Ferraris pulled away from de Cesaris, Piquet and the Renaults of Prost and Cheever. Piquet quickly moved ahead of the Alfa Romeo but de Cesaris, in his anxiety to take the place back, failed to notice an attack by Prost and almost had the Renault on the grass. Cheever, still shadowing his team-mate, was convinced de Cesaris's move was deliberate.

By the time the field had completed the first lap, we were already one car short as Guerrero climbed from his Theodore in the stadium, an engine failure ending his hopes after a good start. Halfway round the second lap and Mansell had pulled off with another engine failure although the Englishman was not sorry to vacate the cockpit of the 93T.

Meanwhile, further on round the circuit, René

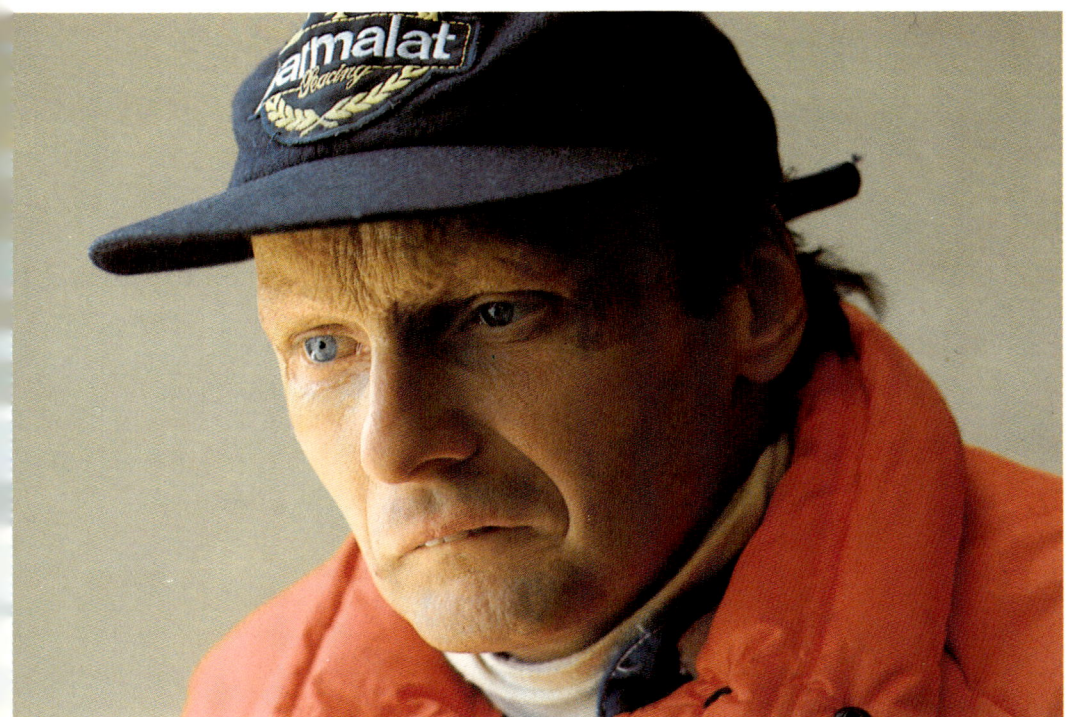

Arnoux was making his views about team tactics known by charging past Tambay and into the lead. Tambay was perplexed since the Ferraris appeared to have the legs of Piquet's Brabham and there was a long way to go. But Arnoux seemed intent on pressing on regardless. Tambay decided to play a waiting game.

Prost was not content to let the Ferraris and the Brabham get away as he sat behind de Cesaris, the Renault taking fourth place and leaving the way clear for his team-mate to have a go at the Alfa. Cheever was alarmed to find himself on the grass as he tried to get alongside and the American took the law into his own hands by banging wheels with de Cesaris in a foolhardy manner as he took fifth place later in the lap.

Lap five and Arnoux had pulled out almost two seconds on Tambay with Piquet and the two Renault another three seconds in arrears. De Cesaris was now sixth, followed closely by Patrese, the Brabham moving ahead a few laps later. Warwick, making up for the slow start, was into ninth place behind Baldi while de Angelis had moved ahead of Johansson as the Swede suffered from the handicap of running the overweight spare Spirit. The two Williams of Rosberg and Laffite were next with the McLaren pair, Lauda and Watson, moving in to challenge. Jarier was on his own in 16th place and Giacomelli split the Arrows of Boutsen and Surer while Sullivan held 20th place in the sole surviving Tyrrell, Alboreto having retired with a broken fuel pump drive.

Although he was not one to admit it, Denis Jenkinson must have felt a small degree of satisfaction as he watched de Angelis make his way into the pits on lap eight. A pressure build-up inside the Renault engine had blown a spark plug out and, by the time the team had changed plugs and sent the Italian on his way, the damage had been done, the Lotus retiring with overheating.

As de Angelis came into the pits for the last time, he passed the Ferrari of Tambay, the Frenchman abandoning his car after a change of spark plugs at the end of the previous lap had failed to cure what was a more serious engine malady. At the same time, Johansson was climbing from his Spirit after stopping at the *Sachskurve* with engine failure; 11 laps and five cars had retired with engine trouble.

Tambay's departure left Arnoux with a 10-second gap to Piquet who was unable to match the Ferrari's straight line speed. The Renaults were another six seconds behind the Brabham and Prost was beginning to find difficulty in keeping his car in fifth gear. Then came Patrese and de Cesaris although seventh place for Warwick would not last long, the Toleman driver missing a gear and contributing to a substantial failure of his Hart engine on lap 17. Giacomelli disappeared not long after with a turbo trouble. The McLarens, by

now, were clear of the Williams pair, Rosberg falling behind his team-mate after his 'C' compound Goodyears had lost their grip and were proving no match for the 'B's used by Laffite. Rosberg was to be given the harder compound during his pit stop but it would make little difference, the World Champion sliding his way into a place at the back of the field for the second race in succession.

The order at the front began to change temporarily when Prost made his pit stop at the end of lap 20. Alain had found difficulty selecting first gear at the start of the race and he had a similar problem while trying to leave his pit and return to the track in sixth place. Arnoux was next, the Ferrari rejoining in second place about 12 seconds behind the new leader, Piquet. Then came Cheever, followed by de Cesaris who had worked his way past Patrese a few laps earlier. The Alfa Romeo crew responded with an uncharacteristically smooth stop but Andrea was dismayed to find a few laps later than a brilliant stop by the Brabham mechanics had Patrese on his way in under 10 seconds – and ahead of the Alfa Romeo once more! With Piquet holding a 10.7 second gap over Arnoux, the Brazilian's stop would be crucial.

Piquet's pit stop, ten laps later than Prost's, had been scheduled for lap 30 since the Brabham team feared the race might be halted if the rain, which had threatened at the start, materialised. In that case, they wanted to be at the head of the field when the flag appeared. It also meant they had to add less fuel at the pit stop. Even so, the Brabham team took slightly longer than usual (by their standards) and Piquet returned to take up second place some 14 seconds behind Arnoux.

Cheever was third but it soon became clear that Prost was in trouble as he slipped from fourth place when overtaken by de Cesaris (back in front of Patrese once more). The Brabham then pushed Prost into sixth place on lap 33 and Alain was unable to respond since fifth gear was now completely inoperative. The rest of the field had been lapped, Lauda setting an impressive pace to lead the Cosworth cars although he blotted his copybook in the pit lane by overshooting his pit and reversing the McLaren into position. Watson was eighth ahead of Laffite and Surer, the Arrows driver suffering from excessive oversteer after deciding to run narrower rear tyres than usual. He was in better shape than his team-mate, however, Boutsen dropping behind Jarier to take 12th place with lack of grip and a lack of brakes. Rosberg continued his unhappy struggle at the back of a field which was down to just 15 runners on lap 34; Baldi, Boesel and Ghinzani having retired with engine problems of one sort or another.

As the race entered the final ten laps, Piquet narrowed the gap on Arnoux from 10.2 to 5.5 seconds

and it seemed the Frenchman might be in trouble. But then a couple of quick laps from René to consolidate his lead showed that he was merely playing with the Brabham driver. Cheever was a further eight seconds in arrears but, on lap 39, the Renault driver went missing, a connecting rod driving the fuel injection pump having broken. The Renault team were perplexed. This sort of failure was highly unusual – just like the head gasket trouble at Silverstone. Once again, however, the unfortunate Cheever was at the receiving end.

Cheever's retirement put de Cesaris into third place, 42 seconds behind Piquet while Patrese, his engine down on power since the pit stop, held an easy fourth place ahead of the struggling Prost. As the leaders passed the pits at the end of lap 42, the Brabham team noticed a trail of liquid spiralling from the rear of Piquet's car. It was either water – or fuel. A few minutes later, their worst fears were confirmed.

As Nelson accelerated towards the first chicane, the fuel warning light came on. By the time he had left the corner, the back of the car was alight, Piquet feeling the heat as he approached the next chicane. By now, the rear of the Brabham was ablaze and the Brazilian did well to bring his car to a halt by the side of the track since the rear brakes had been affected by the fire. Piquet jumped from the car with alacrity, beating his overalls for fear they might be alight. As he did so, a marshal beat the top of his fire extinguisher with little effect as the flames spread. By the time the fire had been doused, enough damage had been done to render the chassis a write-off and Piquet sat down on the barrier to contemplate an easy six points which had gone up in smoke. The fire had been caused by a ruptured fuel filter housing and Patrese wondered if he might suffer the same fate as he passed the smouldering car to take third place.

Marco Piccinini passed on the news of Piquet's mishap by frantically signalling Arnoux to slow his pace and the Ferrari driver cruised home to nine points which would raise the Frenchman's championship hopes. The Alfa Romeo team, meanwhile, waited patiently for Andrea to take second place but their man seemed to take forever to complete his last lap. Worried about strange noises coming from the turbo V8, Andrea crawled across the line to receive a rapturous welcome as the Euroracing team celebrated the best result for Alfa Romeo since they returned to Formula 1 in 1979. Patrese duly finished third whilst Prost, at one point resigned to finishing outside the top six and having his championship lead slashed by Piquet, was amazed to find himself earning three more points and actually *extending* his lead of the championship. If proof were needed that the championship momentum was running with the Renault driver, then this was it.

Lauda crossed the line in fifth place ahead of Watson and Laffite but it was announced later that the Austrian had been disqualified for reversing his car in the pit lane. There had been no protest, merely, as the organisers tactfully put it, a 'hint' from Williams who, no doubt, were still smarting from the heavy justice handed out to Rosberg in Brazil.

Lauda and the McLaren team accepted that the regulations had been broken and chose not to appeal. Over at the Elf motor home, Nelson Piquet bit his fingernails anxiously as he watched a video of his spectacular exit from the race, the extent of the conflagration startling the Brazilian. As befitted Nelson's circumspect attitude in 1983, he merely shrugged his shoulders and accepted it as part and parcel of Grand Prix racing. Over by the Ferrari motor home, however, Tambay climbed into his red Mondial having learnt a lesson about his team-mate's views on the principles of motor racing and the benefits of team-work.

Entries and practice times

No.	Driver	Nat	Car	Tyre	Engine	Entrant	Practice 1	Practice 2
1	Keke Rosberg	SF	Saudia WILLIAMS FW08C	G	Ford Cosworth DFV	TAG Williams Team	**1m 55·289s**	2m 13·337s
2	Jacques Laffite	F	Saudia WILLIAMS FW08C	G	Ford Cosworth DFV	TAG Williams Team	**1m 56·318s**	2m 15·838s
3	Michele Alboreto	I	Benetton TYRRELL 011	G	Ford Cosworth DFV	Benetton Tyrrell Team	**1m 56·398s**	2m 15·547s
4	Danny Sullivan	USA	Benetton TYRRELL 011	G	Ford Cosworth DFV	Benetton Tyrrell Team	**1m 57·426s**	2m 18·376s
5	Nelson Piquet	BR	Parmalat BRABHAM BT52B	M	BMW M12/13	Fila Sport	**1m 51·082s**	2m 16·969s
6	Riccardo Patrese	I	Parmalat BRABHAM BT52B	M	BMW M12/13	Fila Sport	**1m 52·105s**	–
7	John Watson	GB	Marlboro McLAREN MP4/1C	M	Ford Cosworth DFV	Marlboro McLaren International	**1m 57·776s**	–
8	Niki Lauda	A	Marlboro McLAREN MP4/1C	M	Ford Cosworth DFV	Marlboro McLaren International	**1m 56·730s**	–
9	Manfred Winkelhock	D	ATS D6	G	BMW M12/13	Team ATS		
11	Elio de Angelis	I	John Player Special LOTUS 94T	P	Renault EF1	John Player Team Lotus	**1m 54·831s**	2m 14·182s
12	Nigel Mansell	GB	John Player Special LOTUS 94T*	P	Renault EF1	John Player Team Lotus	**1m 56·490s**	–
15	Alain Prost	F	Elf RENAULT RE40	M	Renault EF1	Equipe Renault Elf	**1m 51·228s**	2m 13·620s
16	Eddie Cheever	USA	Elf RENAULT RE40	M	Renault EF1	Equipe Renault Elf	**1m 51·540s**	2m 09·752s
17	Kenneth Acheson	GB	MARCH-RAM 01	P	Ford Cosworth DFV	RAM Automotive Team March	**1m 59·003s**	2m 20·758s
22	Andrea de Cesaris	I	Marlboro ALFA ROMEO 183T	M	Alfa Romeo 183T	Marlboro Team Alfa Romeo	**1m 50·845s**	2m 16·694s
23	Mauro Baldi	I	Marlboro ALFA ROMEO 183T	M	Alfa Romeo 183T	Marlboro Team Alfa Romeo	**1m 51·867s**	2m 15·218s
25	Jean-Pierre Jarier	F	Gitanes LIGIER JS21	M	Ford Cosworth DFV	Equipe Ligier Gitanes	**1m 57·018s**	2m 15·326s
26	Raul Boesel	BR	Gitanes LIGIER JS21	M	Ford Cosworth DFV	Equipe Ligier Gitanes	**1m 58·413s**	–
27	Patrick Tambay	F	Fiat FERRARI 126C3	G	Ferrari 126C	Scuderia Ferrari SpA SEFAC	**1m 49·328s**	2m 10·057s
28	René Arnoux	F	Fiat FERRARI 126C3	G	Ferrari 126C	Scuderia Ferrari SpA SEFAC	**1m 49·435s**	2m 09·594s
29	Marc Surer	CH	ARROWS A6	G	Ford Cosworth DFV	Arrows Racing Team	**1m 57·072s**	–
30	Thierry Boutsen	B	ARROWS A6	G	Ford Cosworth DFV	Arrows Racing Team	**1m 56·015s**	–
31	Corrado Fabi	I	OSELLA FA1E	M	Alfa Romeo 1260	Osella Squadra Corse	**2m 01·113s**	2m 22·859s
32	Piercarlo Ghinzani	I	OSELLA FA1E	M	Alfa Romeo 1260	Osella Squadra Corse	**1m 58·473s**	2m 19·172s
33	Roberto Guerrero	COL	THEODORE N183	G	Ford Cosworth DFV	Theodore Racing Team	**1m 57·790s**	2m 17·479s
34	Johnny Cecotto	YV	THEODORE N183	G	Ford Cosworth DFV	Theodore Racing Team	**1m 57·744s**	2m 15·753s
35	Derek Warwick	GB	Candy TOLEMAN TG183B	P	Hart 415T	Candy Toleman Motorsport	**1m 54·199s**	2m 13·461s
36	Bruno Giacomelli	I	Candy TOLEMAN TG183B	P	Hart 415T	Candy Toleman Motorsport	**1m 54·648s**	–
40	Stefan Johansson	S	SPIRIT-HONDA 201	G	Honda RA163-E	Spirit Racing	**1m 55·870s**	–

*Practice time recorded in John Player Special LOTUS 93T

Friday morning and Saturday morning practice sessions not officially recorded.

G – Goodyear, M – Michelin, P – Pirelli.

Fri pm — Warm, dry
Sat pm — Cool, wet

Starting grid

27 TAMBAY (1m 49·328s) Ferrari

28 ARNOUX (1m 49·435s) Ferrari

22 DE CESARIS (1m 50·845s) Alfa Romeo

5 PIQUET (1m 51·082s) Brabham

15 PROST (1m 51·228s) Renault

16 CHEEVER (1m 51·540s) Renault

23 BALDI (1m 51·867s) Alfa Romeo

6 PATRESE (1m 52·105s) Brabham

35 WARWICK (1m 54·199s) Toleman

36 GIACOMELLI (1m 54·648s) Toleman

11 DE ANGELIS (1m 54·831s) Lotus

1 ROSBERG (1m 55·289s) Williams

40 JOHANSSON (1m 55·870s) Spirit

30 BOUTSEN (1m 56·015s) Arrows

2 LAFFITE (1m 56·318s) Williams

3 ALBORETO (1m 56·398s) Tyrrell

12 MANSELL (1m 56·490s) Lotus

8 LAUDA (1m 56·730s) McLaren

25 JARIER (1m 57·018s) Ligier

29 SURER (1m 57·072s) Arrows

4 SULLIVAN (1m 57·426s) Tyrrell

34 CECOTTO (1m 57·744s) Theodore

7 WATSON (1m 57·776s) McLaren

33 GUERRERO (1m 57·790s) Theodore

26 BOESEL (1m 58·413s) Ligier

*32 GHINZANI (1m 58·473s) Osella

Did not start:
17 Acheson (RAM March), 1m 59·003s, did not qualify
31 Fabi (Osella), 2m 01·113s, did not qualify
9 Winkelhock (ATS), no time recorded, did not qualify

Results and retirements

Place	Driver	Car	Laps	Time and Speed (mph/km/h)/Retirement	
1	René Arnoux	Ferrari t/c V6	45	1h 27m 10·319s	130·813/210·524
2	Andrea de Cesaris	Alfa Romeo t/c V8	45	1h 28m 20·971s	129·058/207·7
3	Riccardo Patrese	Brabham-BMW t/c 4	45	1h 28m 54·412s	128·251/206·4
4	Alain Prost	Renault t/c V6	45	1h 29m 11·069s	127·878/205·8
*	Niki Lauda	McLaren-Cosworth V8	44		
5	John Watson	McLaren-Cosworth V8	44		
6	Jacques Laffite	Williams-Cosworth V8	44		
7	Marc Surer	Arrows-Cosworth V8	44		
8	Jean-Pierre Jarier	Ligier-Cosworth V8	44		
9	Thierry Boutsen	Arrows-Cosworth V8	44		
10	Keke Rosberg	Williams-Cosworth V8	44		
11	Johnny Cecotto	Theodore-Cosworth V8	44		
12	Danny Sullivan	Tyrrell-Cosworth V8	43		
13	Nelson Piquet	Brabham-BMW t/c 4	42	Car on fire/leaking fuel filter	
	Eddie Cheever	Renault t/c V6	38	Fuel injection pump	
	Piercarlo Ghinzani	Osella-Alfa Romeo V12	34	Engine	
	Raul Boesel	Ligier-Cosworth V8	27	Engine	
	Mauro Baldi	Alfa Romeo t/c V8	24	Engine	
	Bruno Giacomelli	Toleman-Hart t/c 4	19	Turbo	
	Derek Warwick	Toleman-Hart t/c 4	17	Engine	
	Stefan Johansson	Spirit-Honda t/c V6	11	Engine	
	Patrick Tambay	Ferrari t/c V6	11	Engine	
	Elio de Angelis	Lotus-Renault t/c V6	10	Overheating	
	Michele Alboreto	Tyrrell-Cosworth V8	4	Fuel pump drive	
	Nigel Mansell	Lotus-Renault t/c V6	1	Engine	
	Roberto Guerrero	Theodore-Cosworth V8	0	Engine	

*Disqualified
Fastest lap: Arnoux, on lap 12, 1m 53·938s, 133·444mph/214·758km/h (record).
Previous lap record: Nelson Piquet (F1 Brabham BT50-BMW t/c 4), 1m 54·035s, 133·331mph/214·576km/h (1982).

Past winners

Year	Driver	Nat	Car	Circuit	Distance miles/km	Speed mph/km/h
1926	Rudi Caracciola	D	2·0 Mercedes s/c	Avus	243·70/392·20	83·95/135·10
1927	Otto Merz	D	6·8 Mercedes-Benz S s/c	Nürburgring Full	316·13/508·77	63·31/101·88
1928	Rudi Caracciola/ Christian Werner	D D	7·0 Mercedes-Benz SS s/c	Nürburgring Full	316·13/508·77	64·43/103·69
1929	Louis Chiron	F	2·0 Bugatti T35C s/c	Nürburgring Full	316·13/508·77	66·30/106·70
1931	Rudi Caracciola	D	7·0 Mercedes-Benz SSKL s/c	Nürburgring North	311·82/501·82	67·26/108·24
1932	Rudi Caracciola	D	2·6 Alfa Romeo P3 s/c	Nürburgring North	354·34/570·25	73·98/119·06
1934	Hans Stuck	D	4·4 Auto Union A-type s/c	Nürburgring North	354·34/570·25	76·38/122·92
1935	Tazio Nuvolari	I	3·2 Alfa Romeo P3 s/c	Nürburgring North	311·82/501·82	75·24/121·09
1936	Bernd Rosemeyer	D	6·0 Auto Union C-type s/c	Nürburgring North	311·82/501·82	81·82/131·68
1937	Rudi Caracciola	D	5·5 Mercedes-Benz W125 s/c	Nürburgring North	311·82/501·82	82·78/133·23
1938	Dick Seaman	GB	3·0 Mercedes-Benz W154 s/c	Nürburgring North	311·82/501·82	80·72/129·91
1939	Rudi Caracciola	D	3·0 Mercedes-Benz W163 s/c	Nürburgring North	311·82/501·82	75·23/121·07
1950*	Alberto Ascari	I	2·0 Ferrari 166	Nürburgring North	266·78/364·96	77·75/125·13
1951	Alberto Ascari	I	4·5 Ferrari 375	Nürburgring North	283·47/456·20	83·76/134·80
1952	Alberto Ascari	I	2·0 Ferrari 500	Nürburgring North	255·12/410·58	82·20/132·29
1953	Giuseppe Farina	I	2·0 Ferrari 500	Nürburgring North	255·12/410·58	83·91/135·04
1954	Juan Manuel Fangio	RA	2·5 Mercedes-Benz W196	Nürburgring North	311·82/501·82	82·87/133·37
1956	Juan Manuel Fangio	RA	2·5 Lancia-Ferrari D50	Nürburgring North	311·82/501·82	85·45/137·52
1957	Juan Manuel Fangio	RA	2·5 Maserati 250F	Nürburgring North	311·82/501·82	88·82/142·94
1958	Tony Brooks	GB	2·5 Vanwall	Nürburgring North	212·60/342·15	90·31/145·34
1959	Tony Brooks	GB	2·4 Ferrari Dino 256	Avus	309·44/498·00	145·35/230·70
1960*	Jo Bonnier	S	1·5 Porsche 718	Nürburgring South	154·04/247·90	80·23/129·12
1961	Stirling Moss	GB	1·5 Lotus 18/21-Climax	Nürburgring North	212·60/342·15	92·30/148·54
1962	Graham Hill	GB	1·5 BRM P57	Nürburgring North	212·60/342·15	80·35/129·31
1963	John Surtees	GB	1·5 Ferrari 156	Nürburgring North	212·60/342·15	95·83/154·22
1964	John Surtees	GB	1·5 Ferrari 158	Nürburgring North	212·60/342·15	96·58/155·43
1965	Jim Clark	GB	1·5 Lotus 33-Climax	Nürburgring North	212·60/342·15	96·76/160·55
1966	Jack Brabham	AUS	3·0 Brabham BT19-Repco	Nürburgring North	212·60/342·15	86·75/139·61
1967	Denny Hulme	NZ	3·0 Brabham BT24-Repco	Nürburgring North	212·60/342·15	101·41/163·20
1968	Jackie Stewart	GB	3·0 Matra MS10-Ford	Nürburgring North	198·65/319·69	85·71/137·94
1969	Jacky Ickx	B	3·0 Brabham BT26A-Ford	Nürburgring North	198·65/319·69	108·43/174·50
1970	Jochen Rindt	A	3·0 Lotus 72-Ford	Hockenheim	210·92/339·44	124·07/199·67
1971	Jackie Stewart	GB	3·0 Tyrrell 003-Ford	Nürburgring North	170·27/274·02	114·45/184·19
1972	Jacky Ickx	B	3·0 Ferrari 312B-2/72	Nürburgring North	198·65/319·69	116·62/187·68
1973	Jackie Stewart	GB	3·0 Tyrrell 006-Ford	Nürburgring North	198·65/319·69	116·79/187·95
1974	Clay Regazzoni	CH	3·0 Ferrari 312B-3/74	Nürburgring North	198·65/319·69	117·33/188·82
1975	Carlos Reutemann	RA	3·0 Brabham BT44B-Ford	Nürburgring North	198·65/319·69	117·73/189·47
1976	James Hunt	GB	3·0 McLaren M23-Ford	Nürburgring North	198·65/319·69	117·18/188·59

Circuit data

Bremskurve 1

Bremskurve 2

Ostkurve

Onkokurve

Sachskurve

Elfkurve

Opelkurve

Hockenheim-Ring, near Heidelberg
Circuit length: 4·2234 miles/6·797 km
Race distance: 45 laps, 190·055 miles/305·865 km
Race weather: Warm, dry

Points

WORLD CHAMPIONSHIP OF DRIVERS

1	Alain Prost	42 pts
2	Nelson Piquet	33
3	Patrick Tambay	31
4	René Arnoux	28
5	Keke Rosberg	25
6	John Watson	18
7	Eddie Cheever	14
8 =	Niki Lauda	11
8 =	Jacques Laffite	11
10	Michele Alboreto	9
11	Andrea de Cesaris	6
12 =	Marc Surer	4
12 =	Nigel Mansell	4
12 =	Riccardo Patrese	4
15	Danny Sullivan	2
16 =	Johnny Cecotto	1
16 =	Mauro Baldi	1

CONSTRUCTORS' CUP

1	Ferrari	59 pts
2	Renault	56
3	Brabham	37
4	Williams	36
5	McLaren	29
6	Tyrrell	11
7	Alfa Romeo	7
8 =	Arrows	4
8 =	Lotus	4
10	Theodore	1

Lap chart

1st LAP ORDER	1	2	3	4	5	6	7	8	9	10	11	12	13	14	15	16	17	18	19	20	21	22	23	24	25	26	27	28	29	30	31	32	33	34	35	36	37	38	39	40	41	42	43	44	45
27 P. Tambay	27	28	28	28	28	28	28	28	28	28	28	28	28	28	28	28	28	28	28	28	5	5	5	5	5	5	28	28	28	28	28	28	28	28	28	28	28	28	28	28	28	28	28	28	28
28 R. Arnoux	28	27	27	27	27	27	27	27	5	5	5	5	5	5	5	5	5	5	5	5	16	28	28	28	28	28	5	5	5	5	5	5	5	5	5	5	5	5	5	5	5	5	22	22	22
5 N. Piquet	5	5	5	5	5	5	5	5	15	15	15	15	15	15	15	15	15	15	16	28	22	6	6	16	16	16	16	16	16	16	16	16	16	16	22	22	22	6	6	6	6	6	6	6	6
22 A. De Cesaris	22	15	15	15	15	15	15	15	16	16	16	16	16	16	16	16	15	6	6	22	22	6	22	16	15	15	15	22	22	22	22	22	6	6	6	6	15	15	15
15 A. Prost	15	16	16	16	16	16	16	16	6	6	6	6	6	6	6	6	6	22	22	6	6	16	15	15	6	6	22	15	6	6	6	6	6	15	15	15	15	8	8
16 E. Cheever	16	22	22	22	22	22	22	6	6	22	22	22	22	22	22	22	22	15	15	15	15	15	22	22	22	6	6	15	15	15	15	15	8	8	8	8	7	7
23 M. Baldi	23	6	6	6	6	6	22	22	35	35	35	35	35	35	35	23	23	23	23	23	23	8	8	8	8	8	8	8	8	8	8	8	8	7	7	7	7	2	2
6 R. Patrese	6	23	23	23	23	35	35	35	23	23	23	23	23	23	8	8	8	8	7	7	7	7	7	7	7	7	7	7	7	7	2	2	2	2	2	2	29	29
40 S. Johansson	40	40	35	35	23	11	23	23	40	40	8	8	8	7	7	7	7	7	2	2	2	2	2	2	2	2	2	2	2	2	29	29	29	25	25
1 K. Rosberg	1	35	40	11	11	11	23	40	8	8	1	1	7	7	7	1	1	2	2	2	2	30	29	29	29	29	29	29	29	29	29	25	25	25	30	30
35 D. Warwick	35	11	11	40	40	40	40	1	8	1	7	7	1	1	2	2	1	25	25	25	29	29	30	30	30	25	25	25	25	25	30	30	30	1	1
11 E. De Angelis	11	1	1	1	1	1	1	8	1	7	7	2	2	2	2	25	25	25	1	30	30	25	25	25	25	25	30	30	30	30	30	1	1	1	1	34	34
2 J. Laffite	2	2	2	2	2	2	7	7	2	25	25	25	25	36	36	30	30	30	29	29	29	1	1	1	1	1	1	1	1	1	1	34	34	34	34	4
30 T. Boutsen	30	36	36	8	8	8	2	25	25	36	36	36	36	36	30	36	36	29	29	1	1	34	34	34	34	34	34	34	34	34	34	4	4	4	4
36 B. Giacomelli	36	30	3	3	7	7	25	36	36	30	30	30	30	29	29	4	4	4	4	34	4	4	4	34	4	4	4	4	4	4	4	4
12 N. Mansell	12	3	30	8	25	25	25	11	36	30	30	29	29	29	4	4	34	34	4	26	26	32	32	32	32	32	32	32	32
3 M. Alboreto	3	25	8	7	30	36	36	30	29	4	4	4	4	34	34	26	26	26	26	26	26	32	32	32
25 J. P. Jarier	25	8	7	30	36	30	30	29	4	4	34	34	34	34	26	26	36	32	32	32	32
8 N. Lauda	8	7	25	25	29	29	29	4	34	34	26	26	26	26	35	32	32	32
7 J. Watson	7	29	29	29	4	4	4	34	26	26	32	32	32	32	32
29 M. Surer	29	4	4	4	34	34	34	26	27	32
4 D. Sullivan	4	34	34	34	26	26	26	32	32	27
34 J. Cecotto	34	32	26	26	32	32	32	11	11
32 P. Ghinzani	32	26	32	32
26 R. Boesel	26

1977	Niki Lauda	A	3·0 Ferrari 312T-2/77	Hockenheim	198·27/319·08	129·57/208·53
1978	Mario Andretti	USA	3·0 JPS Lotus 79-Ford	Hockenheim	189·83/305·51	129·41/208·26
1979	Alan Jones	AUS	3·0 Williams FW07-Ford	Hockenheim	189·83/305·51	134·27/216·09
1980	Jacques Laffite	F	3·0 Ligier JS11/15-Ford	Hockenheim	189·83/305·51	137·22/220·83
1981	Nelson Piquet	BR	3·0 Brabham BT49C-Ford	Hockenheim	189·83/305·51	132·53/213·29
1982	Patrick Tambay	F	1·5 Ferrari 126C2 t/c	Hockenheim	190·05/305·86	130·43/209·90
1983	René Arnoux	F	1·5 Ferrari 126C3 t/c	Hockenheim	190·05/305·86	130·81/210·52

* Non-championship (Formula 2)

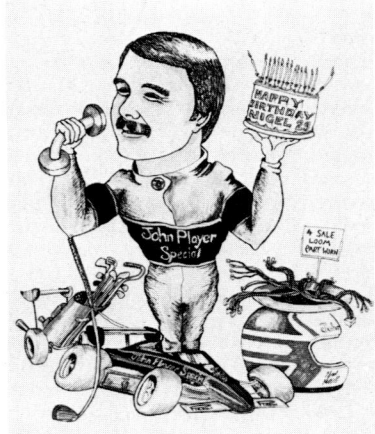

Nigel Mansell, presented with this cartoon by John Player Public Relations man, Tony Jardine, had little to celebrate in Germany. Forced to use the spare 93T, Mansell retired with engine failure on the second lap.

GROSSER PREIS VON ÖSTERREICH

Before Austria, there had been niggling doubts about Prost. Agreed, he was leading the championship but, from time to time, the Renault driver had shown a reluctance to become involved in the cut and thrust for the lead if circumstances were less than perfect. At the Österreichring, however, he not only bolstered his championship chances by opening a lead of 14 points, Prost also won the race in style, leading just six of the 53 laps after choosing his moments carefully and driving with skill and aggression.

René Arnoux was the last to succumb to Prost's advances, the Ferrari driver suffering from gearbox trouble to finish second and move into third place in the championship at the expense of Patrick Tambay who suffered yet another engine failure.

It was not a happy race for Tambay. He had started from pole on the all-Ferrari front row but, apart from watching his team-mate claim priority in the championship struggle within his own team, Tambay had suffered at the hands of Jean-Pierre Jarier when the Ligier driver baulked his fellow-countryman so badly that Arnoux and Nelson Piquet were able to slip by.

Piquet's chances of winning were spoiled by a loss of revs just as the battle with Arnoux and Prost became interesting, but the Brazilian settled for third place and kept remotely in touch with Prost at the top of the championship.

Eddie Cheever, struggling with the wrong choice of tyres, almost caught Piquet on the line and fourth place for the American helped Renault move back in front of Ferrari in the Constructors' Cup. Nigel Mansell's place on the second row came to nought when the Lotus-Renault driver dropped out of contention with tyre trouble and finished a distant fifth. But at least he had scored points during a weekend which had caused nothing but trouble for his team-mate, Elio de Angelis.

A crash and various mechanical problems meant the Italian started from the sixth row but his race lasted no more than 500 metres, the Lotus driver inexplicably losing control and spinning into the barrier. The incident caused the retirement of Bruno Giacomelli, who had started from his best grid position of the season so far, and a further tangling of wheels at the Parmalat chicane (formerly the *Hella Licht*) took out another three cars.

As might be expected, Niki Lauda steered clear of the incidents and went on to set a brilliant standard for the Cosworth runners, the Austrian finishing sixth, albeit two laps behind Prost, the undisputed master of the turbo division – and, it seemed, the championship table. His fourth win of the season was undoubtedly his most impressive.

ENTRY AND PRACTICE

As had become the accepted form during the previous two races, the story of practice was written in the Ferrari pit. No one could approach the red cars in qualifying trim. A rather unsubtle turn or two on the boost control gave them an additional seven mph in straight line speed, René Arnoux breaking the beam on Saturday at 179.055 mph (288.161 km/h); Tambay clocking 178.415 (287.131). Nelson Piquet was next on 175.052 (281.719) and, just to put turbo power in perspective, Keke Rosberg was the fastest Ford-Cosworth at a mere 164.115 (264.118).

For much of the two timed sessions, Arnoux held pole, the Frenchman setting the pace on Friday with a lap which looked fast – if a little untidy. Tambay was about to respond on his second set of qualifiers when the sight of a yellow flag caused him to lift off and he was furious when unable to find any obvious reason for the warning. It later transpired that a deer had appeared from the woods but the animal was soon chased back to safety. Arnoux kicked off on Saturday with a lap which shaved another six-hundredths of a second off his time but then a blown engine put paid to any further improvement with his second set of qualifiers. Tambay had improved his time on his first

set but it was not until late in the session that he set off on an even softer set of qualifiers. In a superbly smooth but dauntingly quick lap, Tambay snatched pole. Yet the lap had been less than perfect to his critical eye – too much understeer through the chicane and the *Boschkurve* – and he allowed the tyres to cool before attempting to squeeze one more lap out of the Goodyears. Everything went well until he reached the *Texaco Schikane* where he slid wide and put a wheel on the grass. In an instant, the Ferrari was spinning across the grass and a chastened Tambay returned to the pits to learn that his previous lap had been good enough for pole.

Ferrari had continued to use their huge rear wings and Lotus brought along the four-layer device last seen flying off the back of Mansell's car at Imola. The mounting had been suitably revised, of course, and both Nigel Mansell and Elio de Angelis found the extra precision in handling to be worth the small trade-off in straight-line speed. After the traumatic practice sessions at Silverstone and Hockenheim, everything fell into place for Mansell in Austria. The Englishman set fourth fastest time on Friday – on race tyres! On Saturday, he used Pirelli qualifiers to improve further and take third place although he was no match for the Ferraris. None the less, Mansell was

enjoying his trouble free practice with the Lotus-Renault 94T thanks to subtle improvements made to the cooling system. By rights, there should have been two black and gold cars on the second row of the grid but, this weekend, it was the turn of Elio de Angelis to suffer from a chapter of disasters. Friday started badly when Elio spun off and damaged the nose of his 94T at the *Texaco Schikane*. As the Lotus mechanics began the repairs, the 93T was wheeled out for the timed session and de Angelis' patience was tested further when the bodywork came adrift and obscured his vision during a quick lap. Everything appeared to be in order on Saturday when de Angelis returned to his 94T and set second fastest lap to Mansell in the unofficial session. But, in the afternoon, the gremlins returned and the highly frustrated Italian found himself two seconds slower than his team-mate after losing engine power.

The Brabham team had been busy building up a spare car following Piquet's fire at Hockenheim and both Nelson and Riccardo Patrese had need of it on Friday. The Italian suffered an engine failure in the unofficial session and Piquet's race car broke an exhaust primary which meant hurried conversion work as the mechanics tailored the spare car to suit both drivers. Back in their race cars on Saturday, both drivers improved as Piquet, the pole position man of

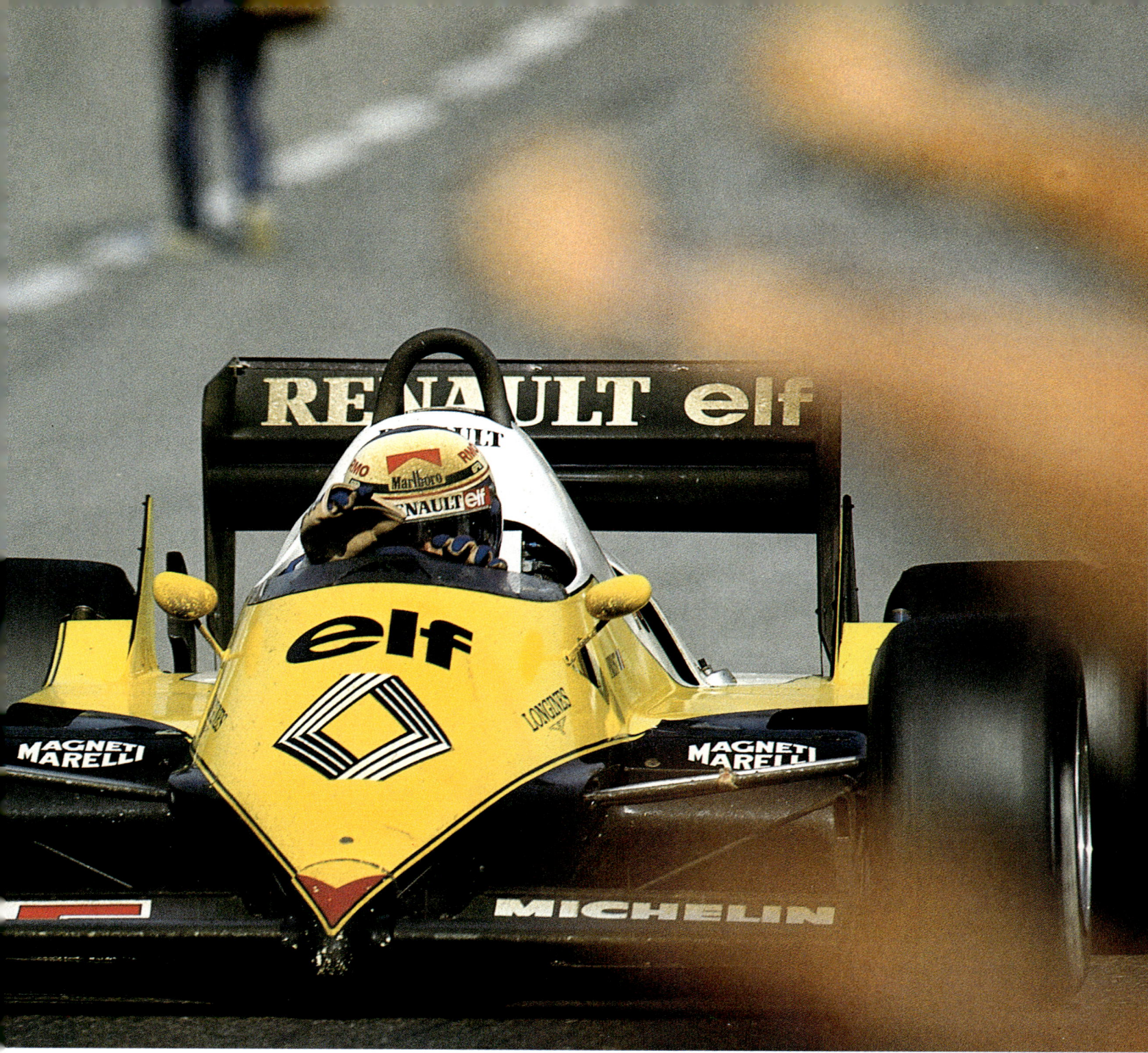

1982, took fourth place to beat the time set by Alain Prost on Friday.

There was little chance of the championship leader responding since he had chosen to spend the final session in his spare car. It was not that he preferred it; simply that the race car, complete with a fresh engine, felt so good and ready for racing in the morning session, that Prost decided to put it away even if he did lose a couple of places on the grid. Besides, the T-car was suffering from the overheating which had bothered Prost at Hockenheim and the team were anxious to get to the bottom of the problem. (Subsequent tests in the garages were to uncover a blockage in the intercooler caused, it was thought, by the water 'furring'.) A cracked heat exchanger was the root of a boost problem for Eddie Cheever on Friday and the American was disappointed when a misfire and a handling problem prevented him from improving during the final session to counter an unexpected challenge from Bruno Giacomelli.

It had been anticipated that Derek Warwick would lead the Toleman attack since the Englishman had at his disposal a development Hart engine with a revised head and a new turbo made by the English company, Holset. Unofficial practice had been very encouraging but, when it came to setting a good time on qualifiers,

Warwick was annoyed to find a drop in boost and a time which was worth no better than 10th place. Giacomelli, meanwhile, was in seventh spot and thoroughly enjoying his new-found status. Similarly, there was a switch in the Alfa Romeo team when Mauro Baldi set ninth fastest time while Andrea de Cesaris was left to languish in 11th position with his Friday time, the Italian sitting out most of the final session while the mechanics changed an engine which had blown at the end of unofficial practice.

Manfred Winkelhock had mixed feelings about his practice; on the one hand, he was happy to have qualified after the débâcle at Hockenheim; on the other, he expected to be much further up the grid than the seventh row. The ATS was quick enough in a straight line – when the BMW was running cleanly. A misfire bothered the team throughout practice and the German driver's progress on Saturday was interrupted by a fire out on the circuit. A turbo had caught alight and Winkelhock, alarmed at the lack of urgency displayed by the marshals, was forced to grab an extinguisher and put the fire out.

Niki Lauda completed just two flying laps on Saturday to underline his opinion that there was no point in flogging round on qualifiers since his time from Friday represented the best he could wring out

AUGUST:
Martin Brundle wins the Austria Grand Prix Formula 3 supporting race with Eddie Jordan Racing Ralt-Toyota RT3. The team's transporter crashes on the return journey to England, killing the chief mechanic, injuring two others and destroying three Ralts.

Deserved applause for Alain Prost as the oil-smudged Renault driver finishes a fine tactical drive by taking his fourth win of the season.
Photo: Bernard Asset

185

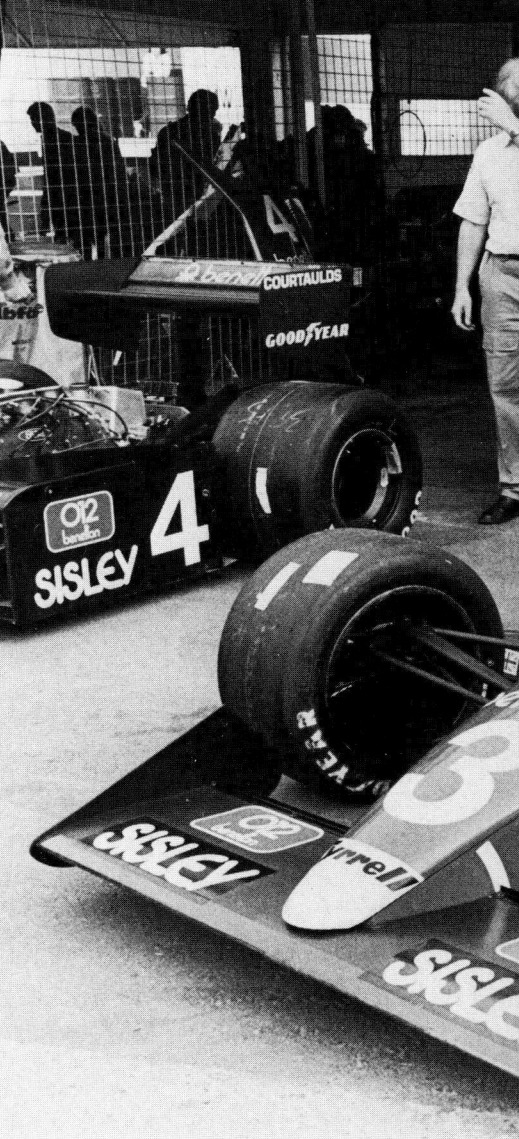

FRANK WILLIAMS CONFIRMED IN AUSTRIA THAT HIS team would be using turbocharged Honda engines in 1984 and 1985. Mr. Nobuhiko Kawamoto, a former mechanic with the Brabham-Honda Formula 2 team in 1966, was present in his capacity as Managing Director of the Honda Motor Company. Mr. Kawamoto confirmed that the engines would be supplied free of charge although he declined to make any comment on the future of his company's association with the Spirit team who had introduced the Japanese V6 to Formula 1 at the British Grand Prix.

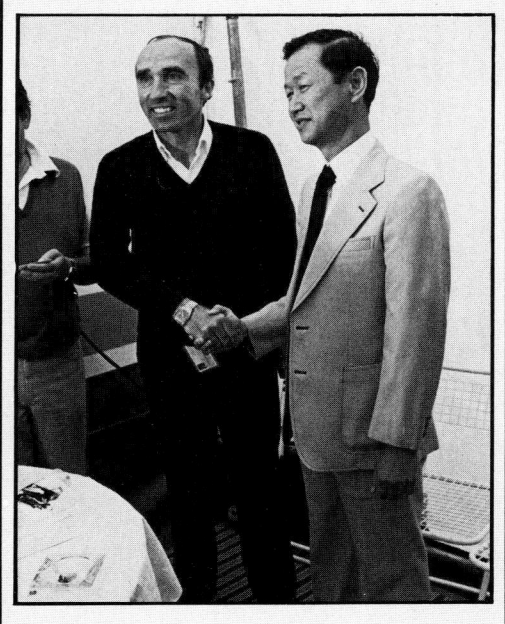

of the McLaren/Cosworth/Michelin combination. Indeed, that one lap on Friday, some 1.5 seconds better than anything which he had done before, represented the best non-turbo time and showed a reawakening of Lauda's interests now that the TAG turbo was nearing completion. John Watson was three places behind his team-mate in 17th place, the Ulsterman unhappy with his car under braking and the team set about removing the carbon fibre discs for the race. The Williams team, meanwhile, had been busy changing engines on Keke Rosberg's car, the World Champion suffering major failures on both days. Rosberg was 15th and 24th place for Jacques Laffite was a surprise since the Frenchman looked both quick and smooth yet his practice time was a disappointment for the man who had enjoyed much success at the Österreichring in the past.

Clearly, a shortage of horsepower was the problem and the Williams team could have made good use of a turbo had one been available. Stefan Johansson *did* have a turbo but the Spirit driver was completely frustrated in his attempts to make the most of it. On Friday, he was stranded out on the circuit with gearbox trouble while, in the afternoon, his Honda V6 failed. The team prayed that it would remain dry on Saturday since the T-car had developed a misfire when the Swede made a vain attempt to qualify in the closing minutes of Friday's practice. With the various problems, Johansson had little time to sort his car and he worked hard for a place alongside Rosberg.

Some hectic last-minute work at Ripley saw the Tyrrell team finish their lastest car, the 012, in time to rush it to Austria. The carbon fibre chassis represented a workmanlike job although the fancy reverse-vee delta wing appeared to be little more than

a publicity gimmick – for the time being at least, Michele Alboreto completing a mandatory few laps with the eye-catching rear wing before reverting to the standard aerofoil. A water leak precluded much development during first practice and it was decided to concentrate on the 011 for the remainder of official practice and the race, Alboreto qualifying in 18th position while Danny Sullivan took 23rd place alongside Laffite.

The Arrows team spent a considerable time searching for a suitable front tyre and a cure for understeer. Thierry Boutsen eclipsing Marc Surer by a couple of tenths in the final session. Jean-Pierre Jarier was the sole Ligier representative when the unfortunate Raul Boesel failed to qualify after receiving less than favourable equipment from the French team. Similarly, Theodore had just one car on the grid when gearbox trouble meant Johnny Cecotto failed to qualify. Roberto Guerrero had no complaints (apart from a serious lack of straight-line speed), the Colombian revelling in the handling of his car on a circuit he enjoyed.

And there were mild celebrations in the Osella camp when both Corrado Fabi and Piercarlo Ghinzani qualified. It had been a close-run thing for Fabi, however, the Italian stopping out on the circuit on Saturday when the throttle cable broke. By effecting his own repairs, he managed to limp back to the pits where the cable was replaced and he returned to the track to discover that the manhandling of his car had dislodged the rear wing. He managed to scrape onto the grid with a few minutes of practice remaining. That left Kenny Acheson at the bottom of the time sheet, the RAM March driver struggling with appalling handling and a straight-line speed some seven mph slower than Rosberg – and 21 mph less than Arnoux's Ferrari!

RACE

The warm-up took on added importance when the sun, which had appeared spasmodically during practice, shone throughout the morning and produced a new dilemma over tyre choice for the race. At the end of the 30 minute session, Alain Prost and Michelin were confident they had the answer, the Renault driver setting the fastest time and declaring himself pleased with his race set-up. He would use a hard compound on the left while Cheever decided to fit the same tyres all round. Ferrari selected a 'B' compound for Tambay and, somewhat surprisingly, 'C' compounds were chosen for Arnoux who was renowned for his harsh treatment of tyres. A turbo was changed on Winkelhock's ATS and de Cesaris's Alfa Romeo received a fresh engine in time for the departure from the pit lane at 2 p.m.

As the cars completed their lap before a capacity crowd drawn, no doubt, from across the Italian border by the Ferrari front row, Johansson found the Honda engine to be misfiring badly. There was worse to come. As he pulled up at the back of the grid, he then discovered that a rear wheel bearing had seized and there was nothing for it but to change to the spare car. As Johansson sprinted down the pit lane, the Spirit mechanics jacked up the rear of his race car and removed it from the grid.

Johannson managed to mobilise the spare car and get onto the track before the pit lane closed and there was no further drama before the cars completed the final parade lap. There was almost a nasty moment on the grid, however, when Prost absent-mindedly began to form on the right instead of the left side. Realising his mistake at the last moment, the Renault driver moved across and had no option but to park his car at an awkward angle as Derek Ongaro prepared to activate the lights.

Assessing the Renault driver's dilemma and reason-

Brian Hart examines the Tyrrell 012, unveiled in Austria. The latest car continued to run the Ford-Cosworth DFY but Hart was more interested in the news that the carbon composite aluminium honeycomb chassis was designed to accept a turbo. The striking rear wing was soon discarded and Alboreto concentrated on the 011 for the race. He crashed while attempting to pass Johansson's Spirit.

The Austrian Grand Prix produced a hectic battle at the front. Tambay leads Arnoux and Piquet into the Boschkurve before retiring with engine trouble. Arnoux and Piquet took turns at the front before Prost (lying fifth behind Mansell) took the lead during the final laps.

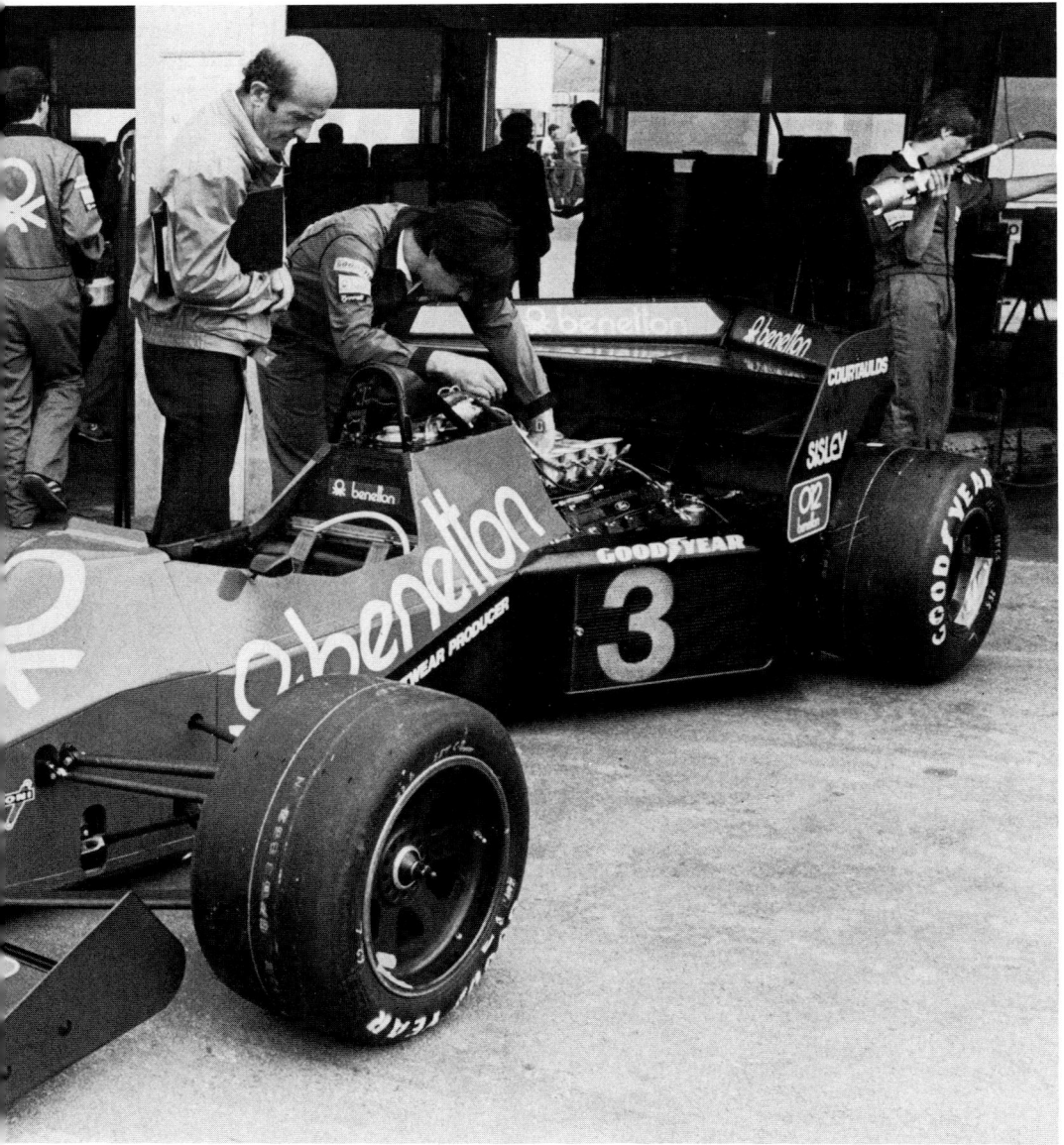

Brabham arrived in Austria with a strengthened fuel filter housing on the BMW following Piquet's fire in Germany.

ing that Prost was not giving rise to a potentially dangerous situation, Ongaro pressed the red and then the green light. Tambay made a perfect start, as did Piquet, the Brabham driver trying to find a way between Arnoux and the pit wall while Mansell was beaten off the line by Prost and Patrese. At first it seemed the start had been a clean one but trouble began as the field began to climb towards the first chicane. De Angelis somehow managed to lose control of his Lotus and spun into the guard rail on the left-hand side of the track. In so doing, he managed to collect Giacomelli (recovering from another slow start) and damage the radiator on the Toleman. The back of the field weaved their way through but the congestion was to cause further trouble at the chicane.

Ghinzani had made up a few places in the confusion and the Osella driver exited the chicane alongside Laffite and Surer. The Williams tangled with the Italian car and was pitched sideways into Surer's Arrows, the Swiss driver spinning to the right and thumping Sullivan's Tyrrell. Meanwhile, Fabi had backed off to avoid the accident – and Watson promptly drove into the back of the Osella and damaged a nose wing on the McLaren. So, within the first 20 seconds, de Angelis, Surer and Sullivan were out; Watson was making his way to the pits for a new nose; Giacomelli was crawling in to retire and Laffite was able to continue although the incident was to take its toll on the Williams.

Had Giacomelli been able to make a reasonable start he would have been clear of the chaos and probably running in eighth place behind Cheever. However, Toleman hopes were upheld by Warwick as he pressed the Renault at the end of the first lap but, when they next appeared, Cheever was on his own. Warwick eventually came into sight, the Toleman making its way into the pit lane to retire with a turbo failure. Warwick climbed from the car and walked quickly away to consider another bleak weekend for the British team.

After seven laps, the leading group of five cars – Tambay, Arnoux, Piquet, Prost and Patrese – had pulled clear of the rest of the field to form an impressive high-speed train. Mansell was dropping back in sixth place, the Lotus driver in trouble already as his Pirellis began to lose their grip. Cheever began to close the gap on Mansell while, several car lengths behind the Renault, de Cesaris had finally managed to move ahead of his Alfa team-mate and, in so doing, Andrea had taken the competitive edge off his tyres. Winkelhock was 10th and pulling away from Johansson who had made another excellent start. However, the weight penalty of running the spare Spirit was beginning to tell and the Swede was soon overhauled by Lauda, the Austrian setting a cracking pace in his McLaren-Cosworth.

The Honda turbo was proving barely capable of holding a Cosworth on the straight and Johansson was soon receiving attention from Alboreto, the Tyrrell driver trying a dubious move at the *Glatzkurve*. The two cars touched with Alboreto spinning across the grass, badly damaging the underside of the Tyrrell as he went. Alboreto's rear wheel had caught the front of the Spirit and Johansson rolled to halt minus a nose cone. Fearing the damage to be much worse, Stefan undid his belts and levered himself out of the cockpit to discover that all four wheels were still attached to the car and pointing in the right direction. With a little assistance, Johansson managed to roll the car down the hill and he brought the V6 back to life and motored back to the pits. The Spirit was checked over, a new nose cone fitted, and Johansson was soon on his way to continue without further hindrance.

Meanwhile, Tambay was controlling the race beautifully; adjusting his driving to cope with understeer at the *Boschkurve* while, at the same time, keeping

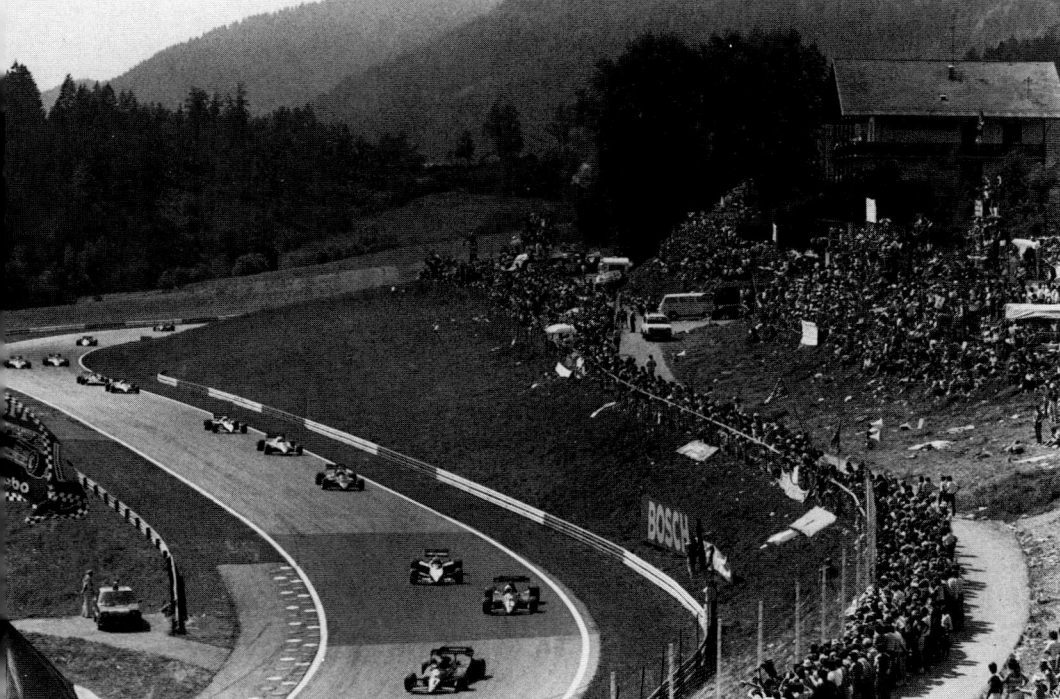

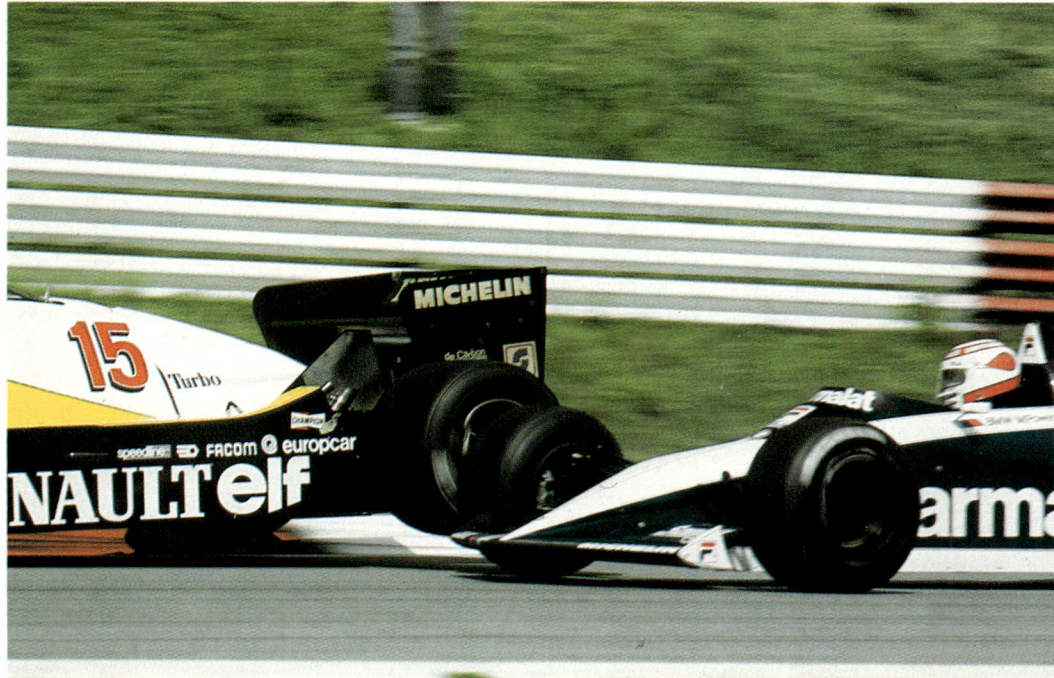

Prost briefly took third place at the chicane from Piquet but the coming together (below) unsettled the Frenchman and Piquet had regained his place by the next corner.
Photo: Bernard Asset

Arnoux at arm's length. Piquet was not far behind in third place and receiving attention from Prost, the Renault driver finding it difficult to run in the turbulence of another car on the straight although he did have the advantage through on the corners.

On lap 15, the leaders lapped Laffite (soon to retire with a vibration caused by a rocker arm bent during the accident on lap one) and Guerrero (beginning to struggle with a disintegrating gearbox which would cause the Theodore driver's retirement on lap 25). Piquet and Prost passed Guerrero on the pit straight and Prost then took the opportunity to have a run at the Brabham under braking for the Parmalat chicane. Prost managed to get alongside as they turned into the corner but Piquet had not left much room and the right-front wheel of the Brabham caught Prost's left-rear. But Prost had the initiative although the incident unsettled the Frenchman and Piquet was able to power back into third place before the next corner. As a result, Patrese had been able to close on his team-mate and the Ferraris had pulled away.

Mansell was now 12 seconds behind in sixth place and the Lotus was coming under continual pressure from Cheever even though the Renault driver was hampered by a lack of grip from his hard Michelins, the sun having retreated to leave the track temperatures lower than Eddie had anticipated. De Cesaris was on his own in eighth place following the retirement of Baldi with a blown turbo on lap 14. Winkelhock was ninth, Lauda 10th and an aggressive drive by Rosberg had moved the Williams through the field following an indifferent start which saw the World Champion at the back of the field at the end of the first lap.

Jarier held 12th place and the Frenchman was to write his name into the race reports with an unseemly series of incidents as the leaders tried to lap the Ligier on lap 22. Tambay, a few lengths ahead of Arnoux, quickly caught Jarier on the approach to *Glatzkurve* and it was clear that Patrick expected the Ligier to move over. Jarier had other ideas and calmly took his line. Then, by driving with scant regard for his mirrors, Jarier proceeded to frustrate Tambay by blocking his every move as they approached the *Boschkurve*. Once again, Jarier took his line into the corner and, by now, Arnoux was glued to his team-mate's tail. Taking a tighter line on the exit,

Arnoux seized an opportunity to trap Tambay behind Jarier since the Ligier was still clinging to the racing line. As Tambay went to pull out of the Ligier's slipstream on the run down to the *Texaco Schikane*, he found Arnoux alongside on his right and Patrick had no option but to lift off. The sudden loss of momentum allowed Piquet to slip through as well and the situation was confused even further as Jarier drifted into the middle of the track to overtake Johansson (who had almost driven off the circuit to get out of the leader's path). Tambay finally got by at the exit of the corner, the Ferrari driver shaking his fist – and not without justification.

Prost might have been able to take advantage of the mayhem caused by Jarier's ignorant behaviour but the Renault driver wisely decided to stay put since he was due to make his pit stop at the end of the lap. Prost was glad of the decision to stop early since his left-front Michelin had picked up rubber from the track and was causing a growing amount of understeer. His mechanics had him back onto the track with a stop of 11.58s and Cheever was the next to come in, four laps later. Similarly, Eddie was happy to stop and take on softer rubber and the American would now lap consistently quicker than he had done during the first 26 laps.

Two laps later and Arnoux lost the lead as he rushed into the pits, leaving Piquet to fend off Tambay. The Ferrari driver really had the bit between his teeth now and a rare mistake by Piquet as he put one wheel on the dirt at the exit of the chicane was all Patrick needed. The Ferrari nosed inside the Brabham as they rushed towards *Glatzkurve*, Tambay taking the lead with a forceful move. As Piquet fell into place behind the Ferrari, he knew it would only be a matter of time before he was back in front one more. The V6 was pumping out a fine haze of oil and, sure enough, Tambay soon began to slow. He trickled into the pits at the end of lap 30 (the lap he was due to stop in any case) and, for the second race in succession, Tambay was out with engine trouble.

At the same time, Patrese went missing on the lap after his pit stop, the Brabham pulling off with no water in the BMW. The block was cracked and the core plug missing and it was difficult to tell which had occurred first. His team-mate, however, was still in the lead although his stop was due at the end of lap 31.

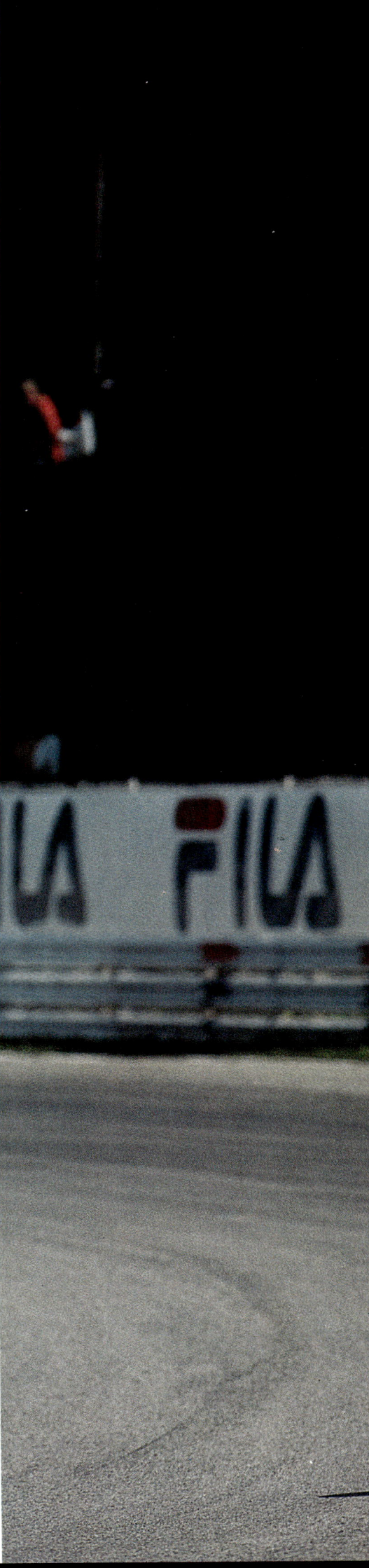

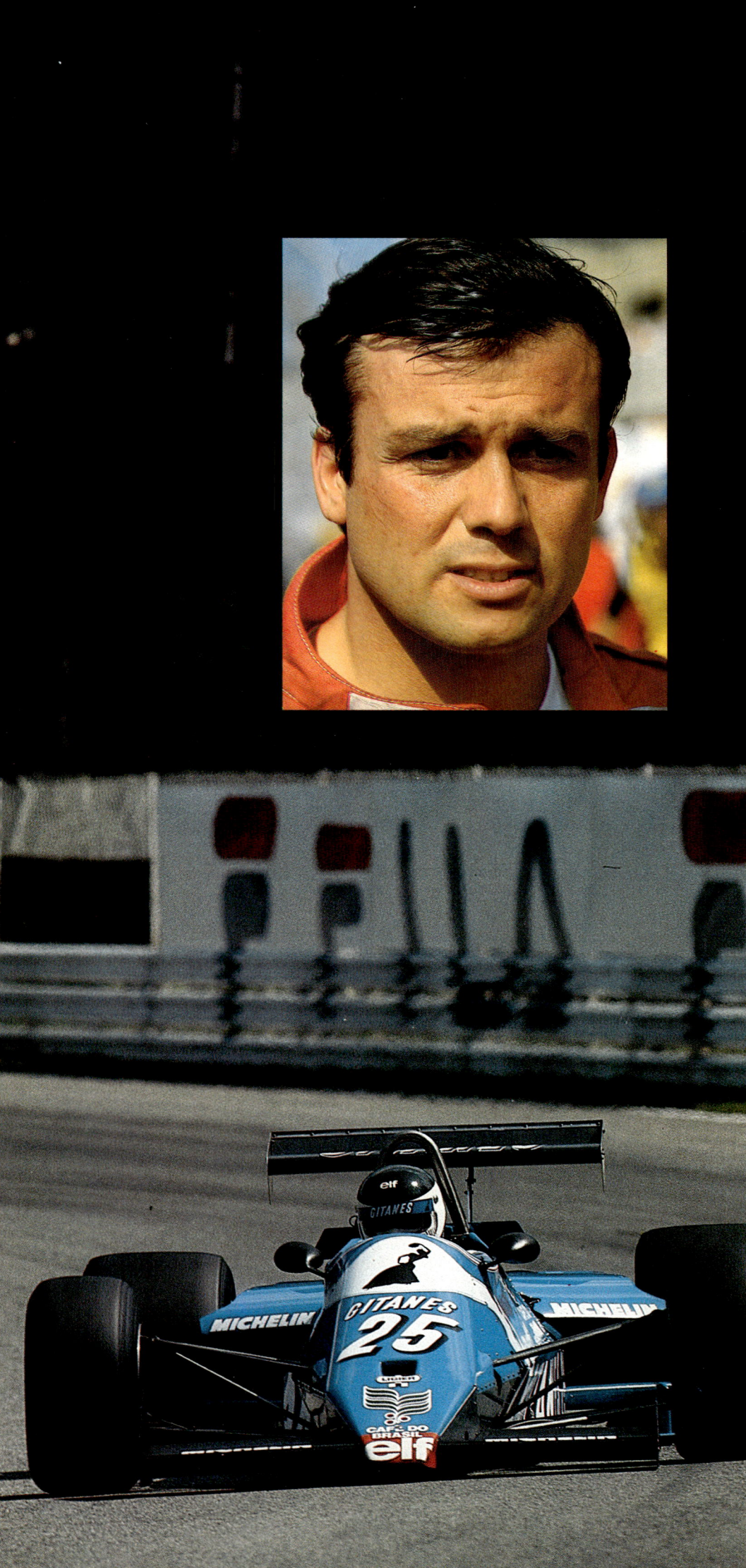

Patrick Tambay retired with engine failure for
the second race in succession but the Ferrari
driver was not impressed by the erratic
behaviour of Jean-Pierre Jarier in the Ligier.
Photos: John Townsend and DPPI (inset)

The Brabham team responded with their customary skill and Nelson accelerated down the pit lane just as Arnoux took fifth gear at the start of the pit straight. This would be crucial. Piquet was clearly at a disadvantage with cold tyres and his rhythm having been broken, whereas Arnoux had been back on the pace for three laps. The Brabham roared up the hill and *just* reached the chicane first. It seemed a matter of time as Arnoux climed all over the Brabham but a cunning piece of driving by Piquet ensured that he held the lead while, at the same time, generating temperature in his tyres as the duo hurtled through *Glatzkurve*. It was a superb piece of driving which allowed Nelson to cross the line ahead of the Ferrari at the end of the lap while, closing on them both, came Prost.

A piece of muddled management by the Alfa Romeo team had lost Andrea de Cesaris his fourth place. The Italian had been instructed to stay out for an extra two laps before making his stop since the pits had become very busy on the lap he was due in. However, the fuel consumption on the engine which had been installed just before the race proved to be much worse than expected and poor de Cesaris ran out of petrol as he approached the pit lane. There was nothing for it but to abandon the car and hand fourth place back to Cheever's Renault. Mansell, the last man to remain unlapped, was a distant fifth while Lauda continued to charge along and move into sixth place. Trouble with third gear meant Rosberg had fallen behind Jarier's Ligier and the retirement of Winkelhock's ATS meant Corrado Fabi was now ninth and running strongly in the Osella. Winkelhock had retired with an engine overheating problem similar to the one which had baffled the team at Silverstone and the various other problems at the back of the field meant Watson was now 10th having dealt with Ghinzani's Osella as the Italian struggled with oversteer caused by the first lap shunt. Bringing up the rear were Johansson and Boutsen, the Arrows driver having lost time in the pits after a spark plug electrode had fallen out.

The battle for the lead was shaping up nicely during the last 15 laps but then Piquet began to lose power, a legacy of the engine overheating while running in close company earlier in the race. Wisely, Piquet decided to turn down the boost and go for a finish and, as he did so the Ferrari and Renault were through in a flash. Now we had an interesting situation. Arnoux was leading and Prost was secure in second place. The six points would be useful to consolidate his championship lead – but could he resist the challenge of having a go at his arch rival? It seemed not, as the Renault closed on the C3 with six laps to go. Prost took a look at the inside under braking for the chicane but thought better of it. Then, leaving the corner and accelerating towards *Glatzkurve*, it was all over. The Ferrari hesitated momentarily as Arnoux struggled to select fourth gear – and Prost was into the lead. The enthralling battles in a superb race were at an end.

Prost, his helmet smothered in oil, took the flag with Arnoux almost seven seconds behind, the Ferrari pulling off not long after when the gearbox broke completely. Piquet just held third place as he struggled across the line ahead of a rapidly advancing Cheever while Mansell was finally lapped to take fifth place – the Lotus driver disappointed to be there after such an encouraging practice. But at least he had scored points. Patrick Tambay sat quietly in the Ferrari motor home and assessed the damage. Six points for Arnoux meant he had overtaken his team-mate and now held third place in the championship. Piquet was still in second place although Prost was now 14 points in the lead. The championship seemed destined to belong to the Frenchman. And after such a clever drive in Austria, no one could doubt that he deserved it.

Entries and practice times

No.	Driver	Nat	Car	Tyre	Engine	Entrant	Practice 1	Practice 2
1	Keke Rosberg	SF	Saudia WILLIAMS FW08C	G	Ford Cosworth DFV	TAG Williams Team	1m 36·136s	**1m 35·380s**
2	Jacques Laffite	F	Saudia WILLIAMS FW08C	G	Ford Cosworth DFV	TAG Williams Team	1m 37·546s	**1m 37·017s**
3	Michele Alboreto	I	Benetton TYRRELL 012	G	Ford Cosworth DFV/DFY	Benetton Tyrrell Team	*1m 36·347s	*1m 36·079s
4	Danny Sullivan	USA	Benetton TYRRELL 011	G	Ford Cosworth DFV	Benetton Tyrrell Team	1m 37·858s	**1m 36·772s**
5	Nelson Piquet	BR	Parmalat BRABHAM BT52B	M	BMW M12/13	Fila Sport	1m 31·912s	**1m 30·566s**
6	Riccardo Patrese	I	Parmalat BRABHAM BT52B	M	BMW M12/13	Fila Sport	1m 31·770s	**1m 31·440s**
7	John Watson	GB	Marlboro McLAREN MP4/1C	M	Ford Cosworth DFV/DFY	Marlboro McLaren International	**1m 36·059s**	1m 36·141s
8	Niki Lauda	A	Marlboro McLAREN MP4/1C	M	Ford Cosworth DFV/DFY	Marlboro McLaren International	**1m 34·518s**	1m 36·604s
9	Manfred Winkelhock	D	ATS D6	G	BMW M12/13	Team ATS	1m 33·754s	**1m 33·211s**
11	Elio de Angelis	I	John Player Special LOTUS 94T	P	Renault EF1	John Player Team Lotus	**1m 34·818s	1m 32·451s
12	Nigel Mansell	GB	John Player Special LOTUS 94T	P	Renault EF1	John Player Team Lotus	1m 31·263s	**1m 30·457s**
15	Alain Prost	F	Elf RENAULT RE40	M	Renault EF1	Equipe Renault Elf	**1m 30·841s**	1m 32·187s
16	Eddie Cheever	USA	Elf RENAULT RE40	M	Renault EF1	Equipe Renault Elf	**1m 31·695s**	1m 31·962s
17	Kenneth Acheson	GB	MARCH-RAM 01	P	Ford Cosworth DFV	RAM Automotive Team March	**1m 38·974s**	1m 39·138s
22	Andrea de Cesaris	I	Marlboro ALFA ROMEO 183T	M	Alfa Romeo 183T	Marlboro Team Alfa Romeo	**1m 32·359s**	1m 32·720s
23	Mauro Baldi	I	Marlboro ALFA ROMEO 183T	M	Alfa Romeo 183T	Marlboro Team Alfa Romeo	1m 31·802s	**1m 31·769s**
25	Jean-Pierre Jarier	F	Gitanes LIGIER JS21	M	Ford Cosworth DFV/DFY	Equipe Ligier Gitanes	**1m 36·435s**	1m 36·437s
26	Raul Boesel	BR	Gitanes LIGIER JS21	M	Ford Cosworth DFV	Equipe Ligier Gitanes	**1m 37·400s**	1m 37·554s
27	Patrick Tambay	F	Fiat FERRARI 126C3	G	Ferrari 126C	Scuderia Ferrari SpA SEFAC	1m 30·358s	**1m 29·871s**
28	René Arnoux	F	Fiat FERRARI 126C3	G	Ferrari 126C	Scuderia Ferrari SpA SEFAC	1m 29·995s	**1m 29·935s**
29	Marc Surer	CH	ARROWS A6	G	Ford Cosworth DFV	Arrows Racing Team	1m 37·175s	**1m 36·619s**
30	Thierry Boutsen	B	ARROWS A6	G	Ford Cosworth DFV	Arrows Racing Team	1m 37·253s	**1m 36·357s**
31	Corrado Fabi	I	OSELLA FA1E	M	Alfa Romeo 1260	Osella Squadra Corse	1m 37·650s	**1m 37·217s**
32	Piercarlo Ghinzani	I	OSELLA FA1E	M	Alfa Romeo 1260	Osella Squadra Corse	1m 38·455s	**1m 37·117s**
33	Roberto Guerrero	COL	THEODORE N183	G	Ford Cosworth DFV	Theodore Racing Team	1m 36·918s	**1m 36·532s**
34	Johnny Cecotto	YV	THEODORE N183	G	Ford Cosworth DFV	Theodore Racing Team	1m 37·677s	**1m 37·497s**
35	Derek Warwick	GB	Candy TOLEMAN TG183B	P	Hart 415T	Candy Toleman Motorsport	1m 32·888s	**1m 31·962s**
36	Bruno Giacomelli	I	Candy TOLEMAN TG183B	P	Hart 415T	Candy Toleman Motorsport	1m 33·333s	**1m 31·693s**
40	Stefan Johansson	S	SPIRIT-HONDA 201	G	Honda RA153-E	Spirit Racing	1m 40·330s	**1m 35·892s**

*Practice times recorded in Benetton TYRRELL 011
**Practice time recorded in John Player Special LOTUS 93T
Friday morning and Saturday morning practice sessions not officially recorded.

G – Goodyear, M – Michelin, P – Pirelli.

Fri pm
Warm, dry,

Sat pm
Warm, dry,

Starting grid

27 TAMBAY (1m 29·871s)
Ferrari

    28 ARNOUX (1m 29·935s)
    Ferrari

12 MANSELL (1m 30·457s)
Lotus

    5 PIQUET (1m 30·566s)
    Brabham

15 PROST (1m 30·841s)
Renault

    6 PATRESE (1m 31·440s)
    Brabham

36 GIACOMELLI (1m 31·693s)
Toleman

    16 CHEEVER (1m 31·695s)
    Renault

23 BALDI (1m 31·769s)
Alfa Romeo

    35 WARWICK (1m 31·962s)
    Toleman

22 DE CESARIS (1m 32·359s)
Alfa Romeo

    11 DE ANGELIS (1m 32·451s)
    Lotus

9 WINKELHOCK (1m 33·211s)
ATS

    8 LAUDA (1m 34·518s)
    McLaren

1 ROSBERG (1m 35·380s)
Williams

    40 JOHANSSON (1m 35·892s)
    Spirit

7 WATSON (1m 36·059s)
McLaren

    3 ALBORETO (1m 36·079s)
    Tyrrell

30 BOUTSEN (1m 36·357s)
Arrows

    25 JARIER (1m 36·435s)
    Ligier

33 GUERRERO (1m 36·532s)
Theodore

    29 SURER (1m 36·619s)
    Arrows

4 SULLIVAN (1m 36·772s)
Tyrrell

    2 LAFFITE (1m 37·017s)
    Williams

32 GHINZANI (1m 37·117s)
Osella

    31 FABI (1m 37·217s)
    Osella

Did not start:
26 Boesel (Ligier), 1m 37·400s, did not qualify
34 Cecotto (Theodore), 1m 37·497s, did not qualify
17 Acheson (RAM March), 1m 38·974s, did not qualify

Results and retirements

Place	Driver	Car	Laps	Time and Speed (mph/km/h)/Retirement	
1	Alain Prost	Renault t/c V6	53	1h 24m 32·745s	138·872/223·494
2	René Arnoux	Ferrari t/c V6	53	1h 24m 39·580s	138·690/223·2
3	Nelson Piquet	Brabham-BMW t/c 4	53	1h 25m 00·404s	138·131/222·3
4	Eddie Cheever	Renault t/c V6	53	1h 25m 01·140s	138·131/222·3
5	Nigel Mansell	Lotus-Renault t/c V6	52		
6	Niki Lauda	McLaren-Cosworth V8	51		
7	Jean-Pierre Jarier	Ligier-Cosworth V8	51		
8	Keke Rosberg	Williams-Cosworth V8	51		
9	John Watson	McLaren-Cosworth V8	51		
10	Corrado Fabi	Osella-Alfa Romeo V12	50		
11	Piercarlo Ghinzani	Osella-Alfa Romeo V12	49		
12	Stefan Johansson	Spirit-Honda t/c V6	48		
13	Thierry Boutsen	Arrows-Cosworth V8	48		
	Manfred Winkelhock	ATS-BMW t/c 4	33	Engine/overheating	
	Andrea de Cesaris	Alfa Romeo t/c V8	31	Out of fuel	
	Patrick Tambay	Ferrari t/c V6	30	Engine/oil union	
	Riccardo Patrese	Brabham-BMW t/c 4	29	Engine/overheating	
	Roberto Guerrero	Theodore-Cosworth V8	25	Gearbox	
	Jacques Laffite	Williams-Cosworth V8	21	Handling/accident damage	
	Mauro Baldi	Alfa Romeo t/c V8	13	Engine	
	Michele Alboreto	Tyrrell-Cosworth V8	8	Accident	
	Derek Warwick	Toleman-Hart t/c 4	2	Turbo	
	Bruno Giacomelli	Toleman-Hart t/c 4	1	Accident damage	
	Danny Sullivan	Tyrrell-Cosworth V8	0	Accident	
	Marc Surer	Arrows-Cosworth V8	0	Accident	
	Elio de Angelis	Lotus-Renault t/c V6	0	Accident	

Fastest lap: Prost, on lap 20, 1m 33·961s, 141·461mph/227·66km/h.
Lap record: René Arnoux (F1 Renault RE t/c V6), 1m 32·53s, 143·659mph/231·197km/h (1980).

Past winners

Year	Driver	Nat	Car	Circuit	Distance miles/km	Speed mph/km/h
1963*	Jack Brabham	AUS	1·5 Brabham BT7-Climax	Zeltweg	159·07/ 256·00	96·34/115·04
1964	Lorenzo Bandini	I	1·5 Ferrari 156	Zeltweg	208·78/ 336·00	99·20/159·65
1965†	Jochen Rindt	A	3·3 Ferrari 250LM	Zeltweg	198·84/ 320·00	97·13/156·32
1966†	Gerhard Mitter/ Hans Herrmann	D	2·0 Porsche 906	Zeltweg	312·18/ 502·40	99·68/160·42
1967†	Paul Hawkins	AUS	4·7 Ford GT40	Zeltweg	312·18/ 502·40	95·29/153·35
1968†	Jo Siffert/	CH	3·0 Porsche 908/02 Spyder	Zeltweg	312·18/ 502·40	106·86/171·97
1969†	Jo Siffert/ Kurt Ahrens	CH D	4·5 Porsche,917	Österreichring	624·40/1004·87	115·78/186·33
1970	Jacky Ickx	B	3·0 Ferrari 312B-1/70	Österreichring	220·38/ 354·67	129·27/208·04
1971	Jo Siffert	CH	3·0 BRM P160	Österreichring	198·34/ 319·20	131·64/211·85
1972	Emerson Fittipaldi	BR	3·0 JPS/Lotus 72-Ford	Österreichring	198·34/ 319·20	133·29/214·51
1973	Ronnie Peterson	S	3·0 JPS/Lotus 72-Ford	Österreichring	198·34/ 319·20	133·99/215·64
1974	Carlos Reutemann	RA	3·0 Brabham BT44-Ford	Österreichring	198·34/ 319·20	134·09/215·80
1975	Vittorio Brambilla	I	3·0 March 751-Ford	Österreichring	106·12/ 170·78	110·30/177·51
1976	John Watson	GB	3·0 Penske PC4-Ford	Österreichring	198·29/ 319·11	132·00/212·41
1977	Alan Jones	AUS	3·0 Shadow DN8-Ford	Österreichring	199·39/ 320·89	122·98/197·91
1978	Ronnie Peterson	S	3·0 JPS/Lotus 79-Ford	Österreichring	199·39/ 320·89	118·03/189·95
1979	Alan Jones	AUS	3·0 Williams FWO7-Ford	Österreichring	199·39/ 320·89	136·52/219·71
1980	Jean-Pierre Jabouille	F	1·5 Renault RS t/c	Österreichring	199·39/ 320·89	138·69/223·20
1981	Jacques Laffite	F	3·0 Ligier JS17-Matra	Österreichring	195·70/ 314·95	134·03/215·70
1982	Elio de Angelis	I	3·0 Lotus 91-Ford	Österreichring	195·70/ 314·95	138·07/222·20
1983	Alain Prost	F	1·5 Renault RE40 t/c	Österreichring	195·70/ 314·95	138·87/223·49

* Non-championship (Formula 1)
† Sports car race

Circuit data

Österreichring, near Knittelfeld

Circuit length: 3·692 miles/5·9424 km
Race distance: 53 laps, 195·699 miles/314·9472 km
Race weather: Hot, dry

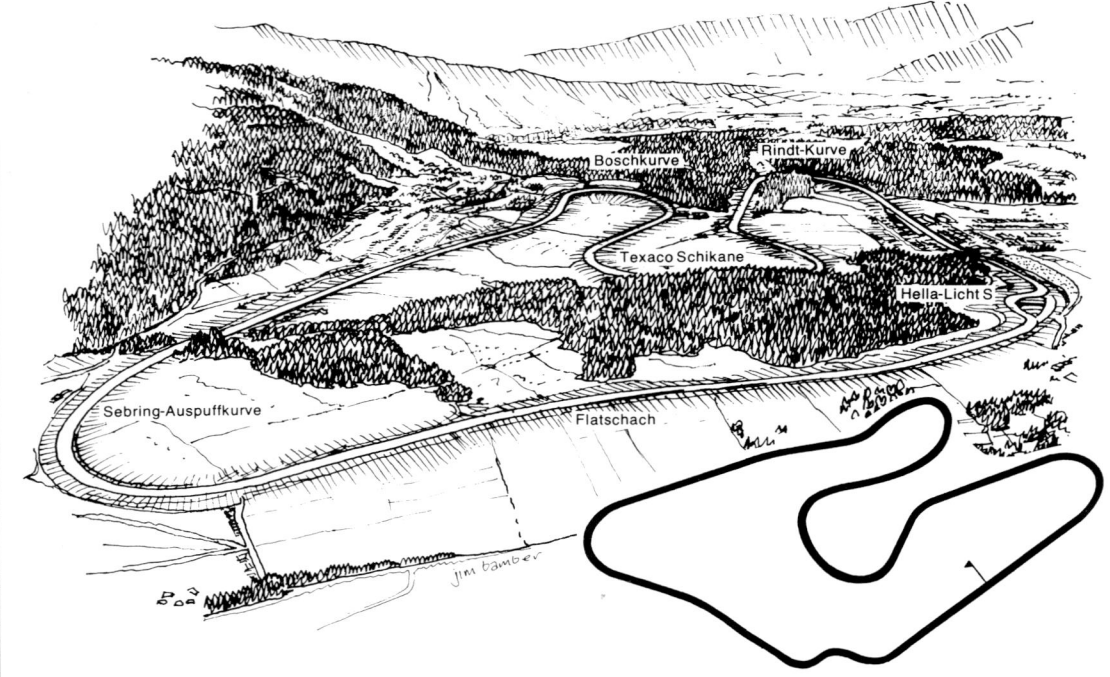

Fastest laps

Driver	Time	Lap
Alain Prost	1m 33·961s	20
Patrick Tambay	1m 34·002s	21
Nelson Piquet	1m 34·004s	18
René Arnoux	1m 34·123s	20
Riccardo Patrese	1m 34·299s	9
Eddie Cheever	1m 34·351s	50
Andrea de Cesaris	1m 34·929s	25
Nigel Mansell	1m 34·976s	8
Mauro Baldi	1m 35·514s	12
Manfred Winkelhock	1m 36·548s	21
Niki Lauda	1m 37·552s	39
John Watson	1m 37·845s	39
Jean-Pierre Jarier	1m 38·074s	45
Keke Rosberg	1m 38·176s	12
Thierry Boutsen	1m 38·586s	45
Michele Alboreto	1m 39·179s	6
Stefan Johansson	1m 39·450s	6
Jacques Laffite	1m 39·952s	10
Roberto Guerrero	1m 40·171s	20
Corrado Fabi	1m 40·341s	44
Piercarlo Ghinzani	1m 42·189s	19
Derek Warwick	1m 46·919s	1
Bruno Giacomelli	2m 20·130s	1

Points

WORLD CHAMPIONSHIP OF DRIVERS

1	Alain Prost	51 pts
2	Nelson Piquet	37
3	René Arnoux	34
4	Patrick Tambay	31
5	Keke Rosberg	25
6	John Watson	18
7	Eddie Cheever	17
8	Niki Lauda	12
9	Jacques Laffite	11
10	Michele Alboreto	9
11 =	Andrea de Cesaris	6
11 =	Nigel Mansell	6
13 =	Marc Surer	4
13 =	Riccardo Patrese	4
15	Danny Sullivan	2
16 =	Johnny Cecotto	1
16 =	Mauro Baldi	1

CONSTRUCTORS' CUP

1	Renault	68 pts
2	Ferrari	65
3	Brabham	41
4	Williams	36
5	McLaren	30
6	Tyrrell	11
7	Alfa Romeo	7
8	Lotus	6
9	Arrows	4
10	Theodore	1

Lap chart

1st LAP ORDER	1	2	3	4	5	6	7	8	9	10	11	12	13	14	15	16	17	18	19	20	21	22	23	24	25	26	27	28	29	30	31	32	33	34	35	36	37	38	39	40	41	42	43	44	45	46	47	48	49	50	51	52	53
27 P. Tambay	27	27	27	27	27	27	27	27	27	27	27	27	27	27	27	27	27	27	27	27	28	28	28	28	28	28	5	5	5	5	5	5	5	5	5	28	28	28	28	28	28	28	28	28	28	15	15	15	15	15	15
28 R. Arnoux	28	28	28	28	28	28	28	28	28	28	28	28	28	28	28	28	28	28	28	28	5	5	5	5	5	5	27	27	27	28	28	28	28	28	28	15	15	15	15	15	15	15	15	15	15	28	28	28	28	28
5 N. Piquet	5	5	5	5	5	5	5	5	5	5	5	5	5	5	5	5	5	5	5	5	27	27	27	27	27	27	28	28	15	15	15	15	15	15	15	5	5	5	5	5	5	5	5	5	5	5	5	5	5	5
15 A. Prost	15	15	15	15	15	15	15	15	15	15	15	15	15	15	15	15	15	15	15	6	6	6	6	6	6	22	22	22	16	16	16	16	16	16	16	16	16	16	16	16	16	16	16	16	16	16
12 N. Mansell	12	6	6	6	6	6	6	6	6	6	6	6	6	6	6	6	6	6	6	15	16	16	16	16	22	22	15	15	16	12	12	12	12	12	12	12	12	12	12	12	12	12	12	12
6 R. Patrese	6	12	12	12	12	12	12	12	12	12	12	12	12	12	12	12	16	16	16	22	22	22	22	15	15	6	16	12	8	8	8	8	8	8	8	8	8	8	8	8	8	8	8
16 E. Cheever	16	16	16	16	16	16	16	16	16	16	16	16	16	16	16	16	12	12	22	15	15	15	15	12	16	16	12	8	9	1	25	25	25	25	25	25	25	25	25	25	25	25	25
35 D. Warwick	35	23	23	23	23	22	22	22	22	22	22	22	22	22	22	22	22	22	12	12	12	12	12	16	12	12	8	9	1	25	1	1	1	1	1	1	1	1	1	1	1	1	1
23 M. Baldi	23	22	22	22	22	23	23	23	23	23	23	23	9	9	9	9	9	9	9	9	9	9	9	9	9	9	9	1	25	31	31	31	31	31	31	31	31	7	7	7	7	7	7
22 A. De Cesaris	22	9	9	9	9	9	9	9	9	9	9	9	8	8	8	8	8	8	8	8	8	8	8	8	8	1	25	31	7	7	7	7	7	7	7	7	7	31	31	31	31	31	31
40 S. Johansson	40	40	40	40	40	40	8	8	8	8	8	8	1	1	1	1	1	1	1	1	1	1	1	1	1	25	31	9	32	32	32	32	32	32	32	32	32	32	32	32
9 M. Winkelhock	9	3	8	8	8	8	40	40	25	25	25	25	1	25	25	25	25	25	25	25	25	25	25	25	25	25	31	7	32	32	40	40	40	40	40	40	40	40	40	40
3 M. Alboreto	3	8	3	3	3	3	3	1	1	1	1	25	30	30	30	30	30	30	30	30	30	30	31	31	31	7	31	7	32	40	30	30	30	30	30	30	30	30	30	30
30 T. Boutsen	30	30	30	25	25	25	25	25	30	30	30	30	33	33	33	33	33	33	33	33	33	31	7	7	7	7	31	7	32	40	30	30
8 N. Lauda	8	25	25	30	30	30	30	1	33	33	33	33	33	2	2	2	2	2	31	31	31	33	33	33	32	32	32	40	30
33 R. Guerreto	33	33	33	33	1	1	1	30	2	2	2	2	2	31	31	31	31	31	2	7	7	7	32	32	40	40	40	30
25 J. P. Jarier	25	1	1	33	33	33	33	31	31	31	31	32	32	32	7	7	7	32	32	40	40	30	30	30
32 P. Ghinzani	32	32	2	2	2	2	32	32	32	32	7	7	7	32	32	32	2	40	40	30	30
2 J. Laffite	2	2	32	31	31	31	31	31	7	7	7	40	40	40	40	40	40	40
1 K. Rosberg	1	31	31	32	32	32	32	40	40	40	40	40
31 C. Fabi	31	35	7	7	7	7	7
36 B. Giacomelli	36	7
7 J. Watson	7

191

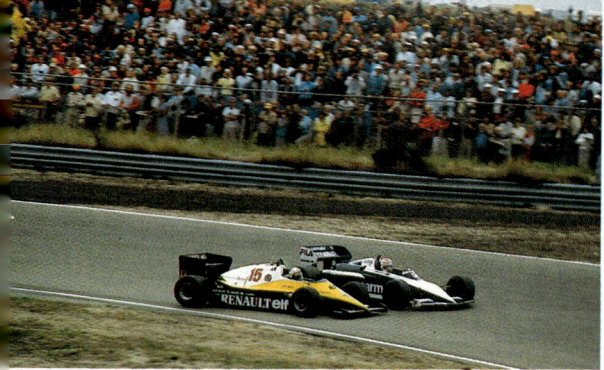

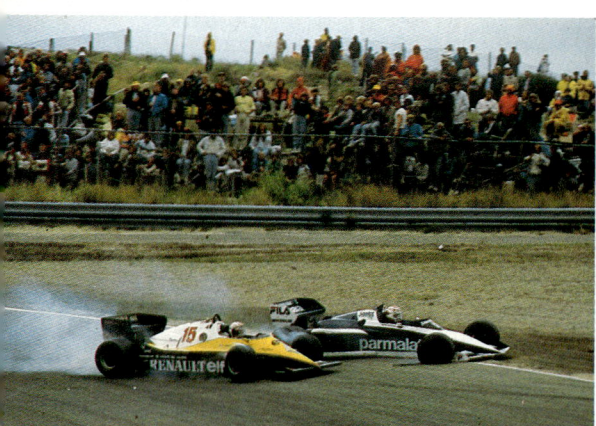

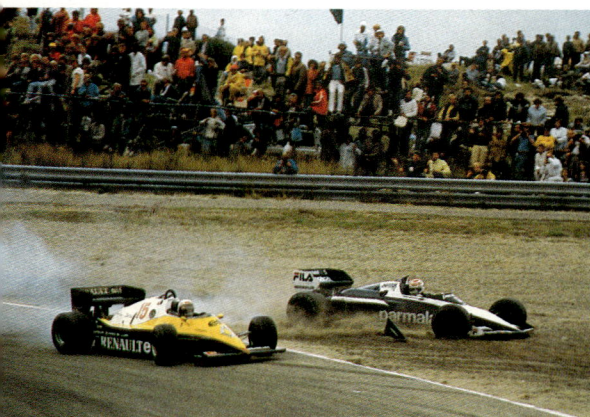

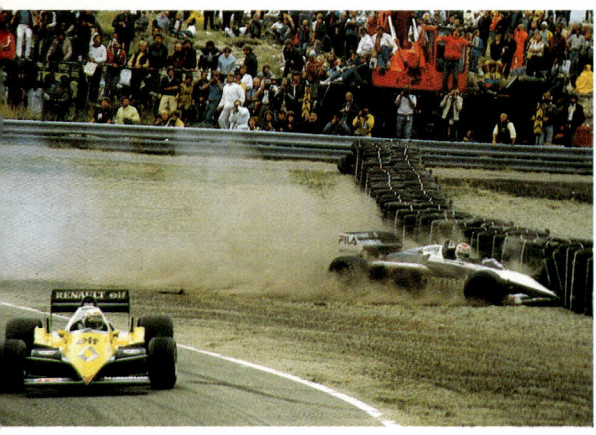

Alain Prost lost control while trying to wrest the lead from Nelson Piquet. Both drivers retired and changed the face of the championship. Photo: Bernard Asset
René Arnoux: an unexpected nine points put the Ferrari driver into serious contention for the championship (right).

GROTE PRIJS VAN NEDERLAND

Under normal circumstances, a Ferrari one-two would have made the headlines. But these were not normal circumstances. For a start, René Arnoux had won the race from 10th place on the grid, the Ferrari driver never having been further back than the third row during the previous 11 races.

Then there was Patrick Tambay. Unlike Arnoux, he had enjoyed a reasonable practice to take a place on the front row alongside Nelson Piquet. Then he made a mess of the start, dropped to 21st place and came through to give Ferrari their first clean sweep since San Marino 1982. That, you might think, was a newsworthy performance. Not so.

The story of the Dutch Grand Prix was the reason *why* they had a clear run to the front and why Arnoux had been allowed to become a serious championship contender overnight. The story of Zandvoort was the incident on lap 42 when Alain Prost, the championship leader, crashed into his closest rival, Nelson Piquet, while disputing the lead. The result: retirement and no points for either Prost or Piquet; nine points for Arnoux. In championship terms, it meant Arnoux was now second, just eight points behind Prost. And Tambay, having taken six points, now held joint third place with Piquet.

That, effectively, was where the championship battle ended. The remainder of the field were looking ahead to 1984 and the Zandvoort paddock was riddled with gossip and speculation. John Watson was a key figure in the seasonal place-swopping but the Ulsterman was receiving cold treatment from McLaren. Apart from being given no indication of his team's plans, Watson had been assigned the Cosworth McLaren while Niki Lauda had the privilege of running the TAG-Porsche turbo car for the first time. It had been a rush job to have the MP4/1E ready but Lauda showed its potential by running strongly until brake trouble intervened.

Watson, meanwhile, was rankled. His casual treatment at the hands of the Marlboro McLaren management fired "Wattie" into an aggressive mood. And it showed in his driving. With a perfectly balanced car, Watson demonstrated what he and a Cosworth were capable of by taking a brilliant third place.

Along the way, he had passed a couple of turbos, including the Candy Toleman-Hart of Derek Warwick but the Englishman was still running at the finish. By taking fourth place, Warwick earned the first championship points for himself and his overjoyed team. Mauro Baldi, driving with an inflamed tendon in his right arm, took fifth place for Marlboro Alfa Romeo and Michele Alboreto scored a point with the new Benetton Tyrrell 012 even though he was a lap down on the winner.

Arnoux said it had been a dull race. But then he had not been watching from the side lines. He had not witnessed the championship table take an interesting twist during a race in which Alain Prost had been poised to put the title almost beyond reach. It had been an uncharacteristic mistake by Prost. But, with so much at stake, these were not normal circumstances.

ENTRY AND PRACTICE

While the McLaren TAG-Porsche may have been the centre of attention in the pit lane, activity on the track underwent a change in the accepted pattern when John Player Team Lotus joined Parmalat Brabham, Ferrari and Renault-Elf in the fight for pole position.

For the first 35 minutes on Friday afternoon, Nigel Mansell's name topped the time sheet, the 94T handling well on fast and slow corners even though the straightline speed could not quite match the pace of its rivals. Mansell's time was eventually bettered by Alain Prost and, ultimately, the pair of them were beaten by Elio de Angelis! The Italian had a new chassis at his disposal but set his quick time with the spare car after his Renault V6 lost its edge. The Lotus drivers had switched to the multi-layer rear wing and were confident of fending off the threat which would surely come from Brabham and Ferrari during the final session.

It was Nelson Piquet who knocked de Angelis off pole but, when the Lotus driver took to the track to answer the challenge, his progress was frustrated by a deflating front tyre while using his first set of qualifiers and a problem with Danny Sullivan's Tyrrell while on his last set of Pirellis. Mansell was also bothered by traffic while making his final run and an improvement on Friday's time was only good enough for fifth place on the grid.

Piquet's improvement, on the other hand, had been considerable. The Brazilian had come to Zandvoort in a confident frame of mind following a series of consistently fast laps during an earlier test session at the circuit. Then, on Friday, nothing went right – particularly with the handling. It was not until Saturday morning that the team discovered a rear shock absorber had not been working properly and Nelson climbed into the T-car to shave one and a half seconds off his time to take pole by a convincing margin.

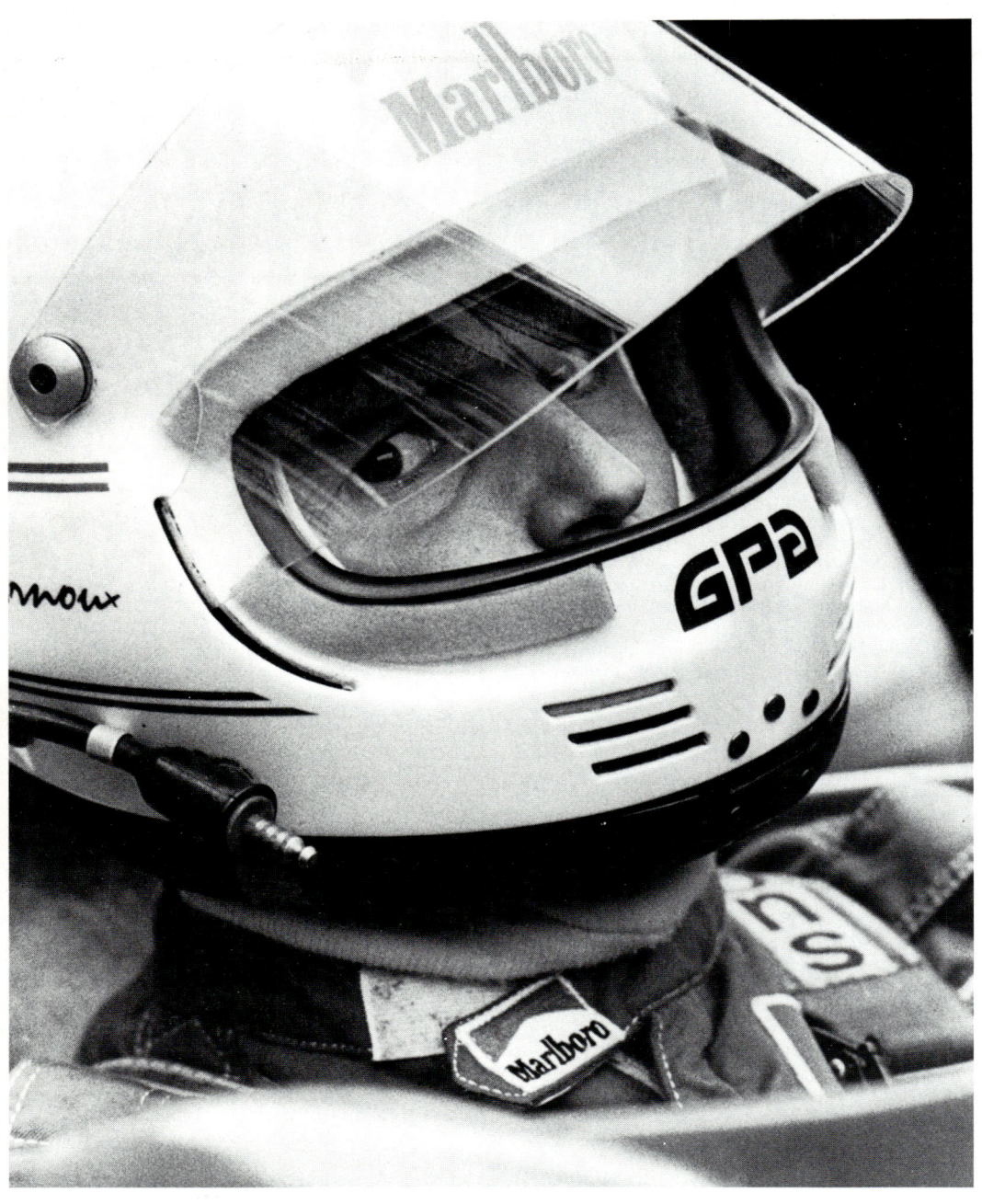

Watching the Brabham's progress with more than a passing interest had been Brian Hart, the engine man having supplied the team with a boost control valve to improve engine response at slow speed. It obviously worked, as did a water spray to cool the air as it entered the intercooler on the spare car and Riccardo Patrese was obviously keen to have a run in this chassis once Nelson had done his work for the day. Unfortunately, Riccardo was to fall foul of Andrea de Cesaris while attempting to improve on sixth fastest time with his second set of qualifiers.

Patrese had just left the pits and was cruising slowly towards *Hugenholtzbocht* when de Cesaris, on a fast lap, arrived on the scene and was caught unawares, the Alfa Romeo narrowly missing the Brabham. What followed was a comic opera display as an angry de Cesaris pulled in front of Patrese and almost came to a standstill. Then, later on, Andrea blocked Riccardo as the Brabham driver attempted his fast lap and the two drivers were to become involved once more before de

Cesaris pulled into the pits. Patrese had one more try at a fast lap before returning to the pits where he found an overexcited Alfa Romeo driver waiting to beat him over the head almost before the Brabham had come to a halt. Patrese, still wearing his helmet of course, was more concerned about failing to improve on his sixth place. . . .

A reflection on the change of status within Ferrari was the fact that the spare C3 had been given to René Arnoux while Patrick Tambay had to make do with the older C2. And, as it turned out, the team had made the correct decision since Arnoux had constant need of his space car during a practice filled with problems. On Friday morning he had a turbo failure and then the spare car developed an injection problem. Things were not much better on Saturday and Arnoux was back in the T-car once more after his race chassis had more turbo trouble. Arnoux managed just five laps, the last one being good enough for 10th place. Tambay, on the other hand, had been able to work on

setting his car up for the circuit since the team had given the earlier tyre test session a miss. Apart from a small handling problem on the slower corners, Tambay was happy with his car and took a place on the front row.

Second fastest on Friday but slipping to fourth place overall, Alain Prost was quite content with his prospects for the race. The Renault team had fitted their spare car with the controversial 'spaghetti' exhaust system now that they had discovered the overheating problems had been caused by the intercoolers and not the exhaust layout. Prost tried the spare car briefly but few conclusions were reached and he concentrated on his usual car for the race. Eddie Cheever was disappointed to be down in 11th place, his progress on Friday interrupted by traffic while, during the final session, he was disturbed to find that the qualifying tyres were dramatically altering the handling of his car for no obvious reason.

Apart from running the Holset turbos once more, the Tolemans of Derek Warwick and Bruno Giacomelli had adjustable boost controls fitted in the cockpit for the first time. Warwick was seventh fastest but felt he should have been faster during the final session. The team made the mistake of failing to try a new construction qualifying tyre on Saturday morning and, when Warwick ran them for the first time in the afternoon, he discovered the Pirellis gave so much grip at the rear that the car understeered too much. Nevertheless, the engines on both cars ran reliably and the team were confident.

De Cesaris's self-inflicted problems with Patrese meant he failed to improve on his time from the first official session and the incident with the Brabham was the final straw in a frustrating day for the Italian. During the unofficial practice on Saturday morning, an engine had been badly damaged when a spark plug broke up and time was lost while repairs were carried out. Andrea retained eighth place while Mauro Baldi did well to take a place alongside Cheever after an inflamed tendon in his right arm had caused considerable pain. Manfred Winkelhock was ninth fastest, the German driver enjoying a reasonably trouble-free practice and it seemed the heavy revisions made by the ATS team to the exhaust and cooling systems on the BMW engine had finally eliminated the overheating problems which had troubled the team.

The fastest Cosworth car belonged to Marc Surer in 14th place, the gap between the Arrows driver and the last man on the grid, Danny Sullivan, being just over one second. However, an indication of the discrepancy between the turbos and the rest was the interval of 1.7 secs between Surer and Giacomelli in 13th place. The Swiss driver did not let that bother him as he rushed round Zandvoort in a series of glorious power slides, his team-mate Thierry Boutsen taking a more circumspect 21st place. John Watson was 15th fastest in the Cosworth McLaren, the Ulsterman switching back to carbon fibre brakes after rejecting them in Austria. Watson had been beaten on the first day by Niki Lauda in the TAG turbo but an otherwise impressive run of reliability was halted on Saturday afternoon by turbo trouble and Lauda had to make do with 19th place. The team's original plan had been to qualify Lauda in the spare Cosworth car and then concentrate on the turbo but that idea was dropped when the team were reminded of de Angelis's problems under similar circumstances in Brazil.

Once again, Stefan Johansson qualified comfortably in spite of the usual niggling problems – engine misfire and throttle lag – with the Spirit-Honda, now painted in a distinctive red, white and blue colour scheme. Jacques Laffite was fractionally slower than the Spirit which meant the Frenchman was in 17th place, three rows ahead of the reigning World Champion. The Williams drivers were having difficulties with the slow

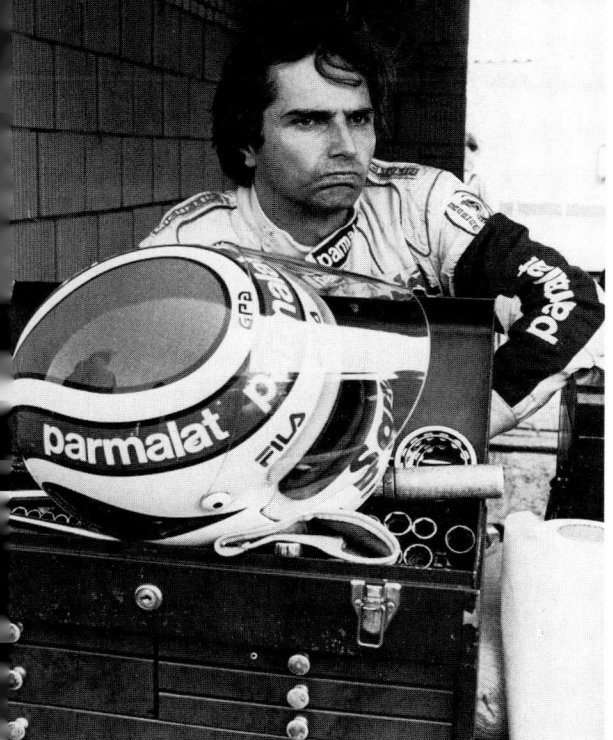

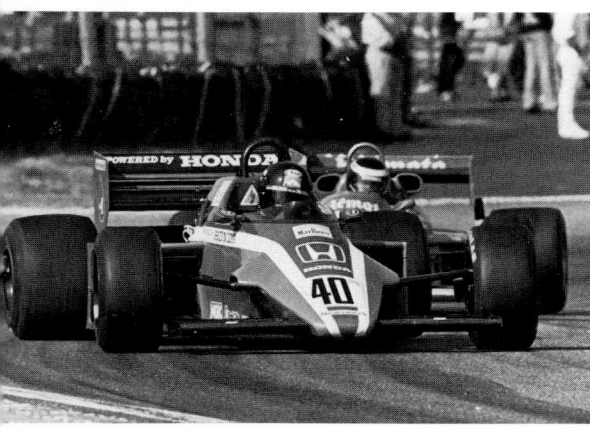

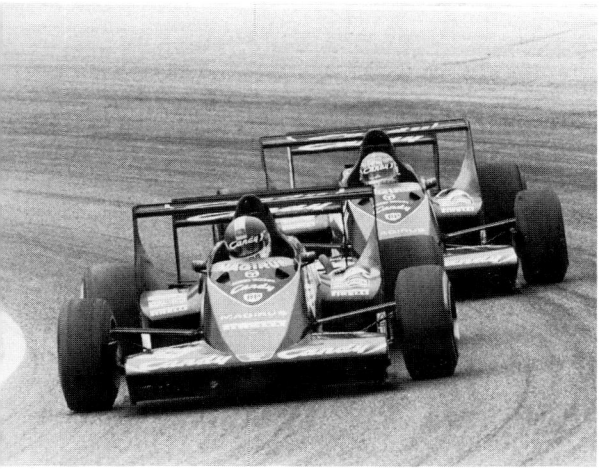

Nelson Piquet took his enforced retirement philosophically. He may have lost the lead and nine points – but so had Alain Prost *(top)*. Exuberant as ever, Stefan Johansson made another storming start in the Spirit-Honda but lost ground with a brief fire while refuelling. The Swedish driver eventually took seventh place. Derek Warwick and the Toleman team scored their first championship points when the Englishman finished fourth. Bruno Giacomelli finished in 13th place with handling problems.

corners but, that aside, Keke Rosberg felt he could have improved considerably had he used a softer qualifying tyre on Saturday. Similarly, the Tyrrell team reckoned they had wasted time by running the wrong tyres, the gap between a good and a not-so-good tyre being worth as much as two seconds. The 012 for Michele Alboreto now had stronger wishbones following signs of weakness which had been shown up during tests at Monza and the team were still ironing out a fuel pick-up problem.

Fortunately for Roberto Guerrero, his practice with the Theodore was free from serious technical problems. The Colombian driver was more or less in charge of setting up his car since both Morris Nunn and Nigel Bennett, not present at Zandvoort, were more concerned with CART racing. Guerrero qualified in 20th place but his team-mate, Johnny Cecotto, failed to make the grid and the Venezuelan was extremely annoyed with Winkelhock after being blocked by the ATS during his struggle to qualify. Ligier had repaired the car damaged by Raul Boesel at Hockenheim and the Brazilian did well to qualify at Zandvoort since he had been given the engine raced by Jean-Pierre Jarier in Austria. Osella did not have the luxury of a spare car and, while Corrado Fabi qualified in 25th place, Piercarlo Ghinzani missed out by a tenth of a second. Trailing at the back came Kenny Acheson, the RAM March driver facing a hopeless struggle with an engine which was useless on the straights. The Ulsterman's frame of mind was not helped by a brake failure on Saturday morning although, fortunately, it occurred at the chicane rather than the end of the main straight.

RACE

At the end of the morning warm-up, Riccardo Patrese headed the time sheet and a quick glance at the various performances in race trim indicated that those with Michelin tyres appeared to have the edge. Even more interesting was the performance of John Watson, the Ulsterman taking fourth place. He may have been using a Cosworth but, clearly, another hard-charging drive was in store. The McLaren mechanics merely made a few small adjustments to his car and then had time for a sandwich before battle commenced in earnest. A few doors along the pit lane, the Brabham team had no time for such luxuries; the mechanics, in their smart white overalls, sweating profusely in the overcast but clammy conditions as they switched engines from the spare chassis to Nelson Piquet's race car. Patrese's car, meanwhile, had sprung an oil leak but that was cured in time for the Italian to join his colleagues on the grid.

Winckelhock's BMW refused to fire as the field started their final parade lap and, by the time the ATS was under way, the leaders were about to reappear at the start of the pit straight. Winkelhock eventually joined them but made the mistake of weaving his way back to his grid position rather than starting from the back as the regulations required. All this took time, of course, and the front row were stationary for quite some time before the red light came on. The delay was beginning to tell on Tambay's clutch and, when the green light appeared, the Ferrari almost stalled. Tambay managed to steer his car to the left and, somehow, the rest of the field missed him as they rushed towards *Tarzan* for the first time.

Piquet, having made a clean start, arrived first, the Brazilian unchallenged as he turned into the corner. Behind him, however, there was the unexpected presence of Eddie Cheever, the Renault driver having made an astonishing start from 11th place on the grid. It had been a brave move, the American committing himself to a high speed run along the pit wall as he squeezed past Warwick and the two Lotus drivers. There was clearly no love lost here as Mansell then

tried to pass de Angelis at the exit of the corner, unsuccessfully as it turned out, but he did manage to run round the outside of his team-mate before running out of road at *Gerlachbocht* and losing four places in the process.

So, by the end of the first lap, Mansell was in tenth place behind Johansson (another good start). Arnoux, anxious to keep in touch with the leaders, had also made up a couple of places and the Ferrari driver was seventh behind de Angelis and de Cesaris although the Alfa Romeo driver's race would last five laps before

AUGUST:

Jonathan Palmer (Ralt-Honda RH6/83H) wins European Formula 2 Championship.

Franz Konrad (Anson SA4) wins German Formula 3 Championship.

Teo Fabi, non-qualifier for the 1982 Dutch Grand Prix in a Toleman-Hart, wins his first CART race driving a March-Cosworth DFX 83C at Pocono.

ending with an expensive-looking engine failure. At the other end of the field, Tambay held 21st place while the unfortunate Guerrero made his way into the pits for a new nose section after an incident with Jarier. Guerrero was able to rejoin a few laps later while the Ligier retired out on the circuit with broken suspension.

As de Cesaris came to a smokey halt in the pits, Prost had moved into second place and Cheever, his engine not picking up cleanly out of the slow corners, was now third and receiving attention from Patrese. Arnoux was fifth and pulling away from Warwick and de Angelis. Mansell took eighth place from Johansson and Watson had dealt with Baldi in an exceptionally precise manner to comfortably lead the normally aspirated section of the field. The McLaren driver had made a reasonable start only to become boxed in at *Tarzan* but, thereafter, he passed one car per lap and now held 11th place. At the end of lap nine, he was ninth having taken the place from Johansson even though the Spirit driver bravely tried to sit it out with the McLaren under braking for *Tarzan*.

After 10 laps, Piquet led Prost by five seconds, both drivers running easily and planning their tactics for later in the race. Cheever had finally given way to Patrese and Arnoux had caught them both. The Frenchman was clearly enjoying the challenge and it was obvious he had not let his problems during practice destroy any hopes he may have held over winning the race. Indeed, he *needed* to win this race if he was to keep his championship hopes alive. There were over 60 laps to go and anything might happen. Prost's Renault might fail; Piquet's turbo could lose boost again. Arnoux put his head down and continued his drive passing, as he did so, de Angelis's Lotus, abandoned after the fuel metering unit had packed up and caused the engine to cut out.

By lap 20, Arnoux had caught Patrese, the powerful BMW keeping the Ferrari at bay on the straights. At the end of the next lap, however, Arnoux pointed the red car at the inside line for *Tarzan* and used the superior braking of the Ferrari to slip inside the Brabham and give Patrese no option but to concede the corner. It was a crisp but breathtaking move; one which Nigel Mansell would have been well advised to follow six laps later while trying to pass Warwick. Or, to be more precise, Mansell would have been better off not trying the move at all.

As he rushed past his pit at the end of lap 26. Mansell was advised that he was due to make his stop at the end of the next lap. Nigel, however, had his sights set on sixth place and, leaving his braking impossibly late, the Lotus driver went careering past the Toleman on the inside, ran wide, spun on the marbles as he tried to pull the car round the outer edge of the corner – and stalled. The crestfallen Englishman was left to climb from the cockpit and return to the pits to offer his excuses. Warwick, meanwhile, continued on his way. Grinning broadly.

Back at the pits, Lauda was taking off his helmet while the McLaren mechanics examined boiling brake fluid on the TAG car. The turbo had run strongly, the Austrian moving quietly and calmly through the field to hold 12th place but the brakes had proved inadequate for the powerful turbo and its inherent lack of engine braking. It was by no means a disgraceful debut, the Porsche-built V6 having run sweetly throughout. Now the team could concentrate their attention on the progress of their Cosworth car, the flying Watson making a mockery of the Hart's turbo power at this circuit by taking sixth place from Warwick just before the Toleman driver made his routine pit stop.

Piquet was now working his way carefully through the back-markers even though Prost was closing the gap gradually, the two cars running together by lap 37. At the end of the next lap, Cheever made his stop and everything seemed to go according to plan until Cheever attempted to accelerate out of the pit lane. The yellow and white car returned to the track very slowly and the American driver managed to coax his car through the next lap before returning to the pits – where he was promptly waved back out again: the team were waiting for Prost. Cheever struggled back onto the track once more but was never seen again, a combination of a faulty electronic box controlling the fuel injection and a damaged turbine wheel causing the V6 to stop out on the circuit.

René Arnoux, meanwhile, had made an excellent stop at the end of lap 39, the Ferrari driver getting away in just over 10 seconds and maintaining his third place in the process. Two laps later and the Renault team were indicating to Prost that he was due to stop but the Frenchman, having caught Piquet easily, was anxious to move ahead and gain valuable seconds on the Brabham before pulling into the pit lane. Rushing into the braking area for *Tarzan*, Prost began a legitimate move as he took to the inside, Piquet allowing him enough room for an attempt at outbraking. Everything went according to plan until the Renault, alongside the Brabham now, suddenly locked its brakes on the dusty track surface. Prost corrected the slide but the car then flicked the other way – and collected the Brabham, pushing it straight off the track and into the tyre barrier.

Piquet was out with a bent front wishbone and a punctured tyre but, miraculously, the impact had deflected Prost back onto his line and the Renault driver selected a gear and continued on his way – unharmed. Or so we thought.

With a complete absence of the hysterics which would have followed such an incident the previous year, Piquet climbed from his car and trotted across the track to sympathetic applause from the crowd. Just as he was ruminating on the injustice of it all and the fact that Prost's nine points, linked with his own retirement, would more or less settle the championship, the commentator announced that Prost had crashed! No points for the Renault driver either! And Arnoux was now leading . . .

The incident had taken its toll on Prost's car. The left-front nose wing had been damaged by the impact and it began to rotate on its axis as Prost made his way through the fast sweepers at the back of the circuit.

THE ARRIVAL OF A NEW CAR CAN BE RELIED ON TO create a fair amount of interest in the pit lane but the first official appearance of the Marlboro McLaren MP4/1E represented one of the most interesting and significant developments of the season.

The normally peaceful McLaren pit was over-run by curious onlookers anxious to see, not the chasis for this was merely a reworked Cosworth monocoque, but the engine which powered it. Another turbo had appeared on the Formula 1 scene and, in deference to *Techniques d'Avant Garde*, the company which wrote the cheques, it had not escaped everyone's attention that the V6 had been designed and engineered by Porsche.

This was not merely a new turbo; it heralded the arrival, albeit indirectly, of another major manufacturer despite the fact that the McLaren management were not keen to have the Porsche name emphasised at the expense of TAG.

It was clear from the start that John Barnard would have preferred not to race the turbo at this stage. He had installed the engine in a 'hack' chassis (MP4/1 – the monocoque crash-tested frequently by Andrea de Cesaris in 1981) and undertaken shake-down tests in July. Barnard's ideal plan would have been to design a completely new package to make the most of the turbo and lessons learnt during testing. But that would have taken until the end of 1983 and certain commercial interests did not allow that sort of time.

The result was another revised chassis which was less than ideal in Barnard's view. The car was hastily completed, the mechanics adding the finishing touches on the cross-channel ferry and in the paddock at Zandvoort. It had been hoped to have two turbo cars ready but the second chassis remained unfinished in the paddock, purely as a source of spares.

McLaren had funded an impressive engine management system built by Bosch and there were surprisingly few problems when Niki Lauda took to the track during the first timed practice session. A straight-line speed in keeping with Ferrari and Brabham indicated that there was no shortage of horsepower although a lack of downforce meant the chassis could not match the power in the corners.

Lauda qualified in 19th place. "It's good for a new car," he admitted. "But there's a lot to be done." He retired from the race with brake trouble, the Cosworth specification discs proving inadequate for the additional weight and speed of the turbo and its inherent lack of engine braking. But it was an impressive debut none the less.

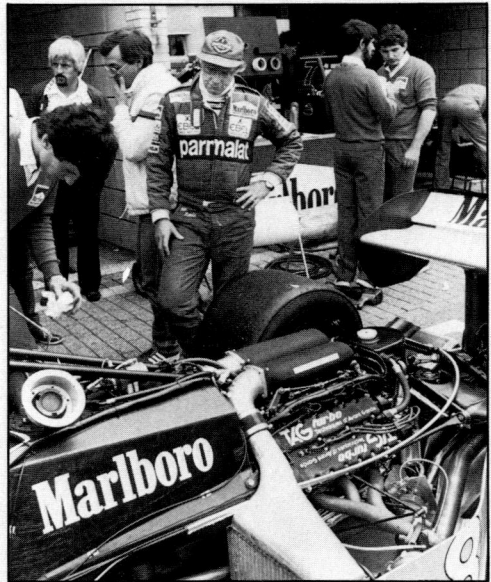

Niki Lauda contemplates the enormous potential of the TAG-Porsche turbo, unveiled at Zandvoort. The McLaren ran impressively before retiring with brake trouble.

Approaching *Bos Uit*, the Renault momentarily lost grip at the front as Prost went over a bump, the car then understeering and locking a front brake as Prost tried desperately to stop the Renault from ploughing straight on. But there was nothing he could do. The Renault thumped the barrier very hard and Prost, no more than half-a-mile from his pit stop, could merely climb from the cockpit and curse his impatience.

During the confusion, Patrese had made his pit stop and the Brabham team were disturbed to note that the turbo inlet shield was missing from the Italian's car. There had been no time to replace it and Patrese returned to the track to take what would become second place when Piquet and Prost disappeared from the lap chart.

Third place now belonged to Tambay, the Frenchman having switched off his rev-limiter early in the race and begun to carve his way through. The Cosworths were easy enough to pass but it took Patrick several laps to work his way in front of Winkelhock and he was frustrated after the race to discover that his delay behind the ATS could have been avoided.

It took the officials no less than 50 laps to decide that Winkelhock should be black-flagged and disqualified for not starting from the back of the grid. When he finally came in and was told of the Stewards' decision, the German was furious. Furthermore, the team's anger was heightened by the fact that their designer, Gustav Brunner, had suffered a broken foot when he stepped into the path of Cheever's Renault while waving the ATS away from its pit stop. The only consolation was that Brunner might have been more seriously injured had Cheever not been hampered by his engine problem.

It was engine trouble which brought the first retirement (for mechanical reasons) of the season for Keke Rosberg, the Williams driver giving up the struggle on lap 53 with a DFV which was misfiring so badly that it was almost impossible to drive. It was discovered later that a fault in the fuel system had caused the problem and the team's weekend was rounded off when Laffite retired with tyre trouble.

With 20 laps to go, Arnoux found himself with a lead of 36 seconds, but Patrese was being caught by Tambay. For the next 15 laps, the gap between the two opened and closed as the power of the BMW kept the Ferrari at bay on the straights while Tambay was able to make up ground through the quick corners and under braking. Then, on lap 67, the BMW lost power and Patrese began a sudden slide down the lap chart.

As Arnoux reeled off the final laps, Boutsen disappeared when his Cosworth broke a valve and Fabi rolled to a halt at *Tarzan* with a blown Alfa V12. With the challenge removed from the race, Arnoux's attention was taken by listening for telltale sounds of failure from his engine and gearbox but the Ferrari ran like clockwork to the flag, the Italian team scarcely able to believe their luck as Tambay finished second to give them a massive lead in the constructor's championship.

Watson was very satisfied with his third place and Baldi did well to bring his Alfa Romeo home in fifth place in spite of his still-painful arm. Alboreto, despite a last-minute stop for fuel, was rewarded with a point for sixth place in the Tyrrell 012 and Johansson, who had lost ground earlier after running wide and picking up dirt on his tyres, was pleased to finish a race and take seventh in Spirit-Honda.

But the happiest place to be was the Toleman pit where the British team celebrated their first championship points as Warwick brought the Hart-powered car home in fourth place. It had taken them 38 races to do it. But Warwick said it had been worth waiting. Meanwhile, Prost sat quietly in the Renault motorhome and doubtless felt it would have been worth waiting for his pit-stop.

Entries and practice times

No.	Driver	Nat	Car	Tyre	Engine	Entrant	Practice 1	Practice 2
1	Keke Rosberg	SF	Saudia WILLIAMS FW08C	G	Ford Cosworth DFV	TAG Williams Team	1m 20·666s	**1m 20·391s**
2	Jacques Laffite	F	Saudia WILLIAMS FW08C	G	Ford Cosworth DFV	TAG Williams Team	1m 21·395s	**1m 19·979s**
3	Michele Alboreto	I	Benetton TYRRELL 012	G	Ford Cosworth DFV/DFY	Benetton Tyrrell Team	**1m 20·149s**	1m 20·282s
4	Danny Sullivan	USA	Benetton TYRRELL 011	G	Ford Cosworth DFV	Benetton Tyrrell Team	1m 20·863s	**1m 20·842s**
5	Nelson Piquet	BR	Parmalat BRABHAM BT52B	M	BMW M12/13	Fila Sport	1m 17·194s	**1m 15·630s**
6	Riccardo Patrese	I	Parmalat BRABHAM BT52B	M	BMW M12/13	Fila Sport	1m 17·544s	**1m 16·940s**
7	John Watson	GB	Marlboro McLAREN MP4/1C	M	Ford Cosworth DFV/DFY	Marlboro McLaren International	1m 21·010s	**1m 19·787s**
8	Niki Lauda	A	Marlboro McLAREN MP4/1E	M	TAG PO1	Marlboro McLaren International	**1m 20·169s**	1m 21·050s
9	Manfred Winkelhock	D	ATS D6	G	BMW M12/13	Team ATS	1m 18·086s	**1m 17·306s**
11	Elio de Angelis	I	John Player Special LOTUS 94T	P	Renault EF1	John Player Team Lotus	**1m 16·411s**	—
12	Nigel Mansell	GB	John Player Special LOTUS 94T	P	Renault EF1	John Player Team Lotus	1m 16·721s	**1m 16·711s**
15	Alain Prost	F	Elf RENAULT RE40	M	Renault EF1	Equipe Renault Elf	**1m 16·611s**	1m 16·642s
16	Eddie Cheever	USA	Elf RENAULT RE40	M	Renault EF1	Equipe Renault Elf	1m 18·067s	**1m 17·676s**
17	Kenneth Acheson	GB	MARCH-RAM 01	P	Ford Cosworth DFV	RAM Automotive Team March	1m 23·425s	**1m 23·093s**
22	Andrea de Cesaris	I	Marlboro ALFA ROMEO 183T	M	Alfa Romeo 183T	Marlboro Team Alfa Romeo	**1m 17·233s**	1m 17·552s
23	Mauro Baldi	I	Marlboro ALFA ROMEO 183T	M	Alfa Romeo 183T	Marlboro Team Alfa Romeo	**1m 17·887s**	1m 18·885s
25	Jean-Pierre Jarier	F	Gitanes LIGIER JS21	M	Ford Cosworth DFV/DFY	Equipe Ligier Gitanes	1m 20·381s	**1m 20·247s**
26	Raul Boesel	BR	Gitanes LIGIER JS21	M	Ford Cosworth DFV	Equipe Ligier Gitanes	1m 21·738s	**1m 20·660s**
27	Patrick Tambay	F	Fiat FERRARI 126C3	G	Ferrari 126C	Scuderia Ferrari SpA SEFAC	1m 16·857s	**1m 16·370s**
28	René Arnoux	F	Fiat FERRARI 126C3	G	Ferrari 126C	Scuderia Ferrari SpA SEFAC	1m 18·202s	**1m 17·397s**
29	Marc Surer	CH	ARROWS A6	G	Ford Cosworth DFV	Arrows Racing Team	1m 20·153s	**1m 19·696s**
30	Thierry Boutsen	B	ARROWS A6	G	Ford Cosworth DFV	Arrows Racing Team	**1m 20·245s**	1m 20·257s
31	Corrado Fabi	I	OSELLA FA1E	M	Alfa Romeo 1260	Osella Squadra Corse	1m 22·047s	**1m 20·815s**
32	Piercarlo Ghinzani	I	OSELLA FA1E	M	Alfa Romeo 1260	Osella Squadra Corse	1m 21·763s	**1m 20·926s**
33	Roberto Guerrero	COL	THEODORE N183	G	Ford Cosworth DFV	Theodore Racing Team	1m 21·592s	**1m 20·190s**
34	Johnny Cecotto	YV	THEODORE N183	G	Ford Cosworth DFV	Theodore Racing Team	1m 21·734s	**1m 20·955s**
35	Derek Warwick	GB	Candy TOLEMAN TG183B	P	Hart 415T	Candy Toleman Motorsport	**1m 17·198s**	1m 17·666s
36	Bruno Giacomelli	I	Candy TOLEMAN TG183B	P	Hart 415T	Candy Toleman Motorsport	1m 18·642s	**1m 17·902s**
40	Stefan Johansson	S	SPIRIT-HONDA 201	G	Honda RA163-E	Spirit Racing	1m 20·447s	**1m 19·966s**

Friday morning and Saturday morning practice sessions not officially recorded.

G – Goodyear, M – Michelin, P – Pirelli.

Fri pm — Warm, dry
Sat pm — Cool, dry

Starting grid

	5 PIQUET (1m 15·630s) Brabham
27 TAMBAY (1m 16·370s) Ferrari	
	11 DE ANGELIS (1m 16·411s) Lotus
15 PROST (1m 16·611s) Renault	
	12 MANSELL (1m 16·711s) Lotus
6 PATRESE (1m 16·940s) Brabham	
	35 WARWICK (1m 17·198s) Toleman
22 DE CESARIS (1m 17·233s) Alfa Romeo	
	9 WINKELHOCK (1m 17·306s) ATS
28 ARNOUX (1m 17·397s) Ferrari	
	16 CHEEVER (1m 17·676s) Renault
23 BALDI (1m 17·887s) Alfa Romeo	
	36 GIACOMELLI (1m 17·902s) Toleman
29 SURER (1m 19·696s) Arrows	
	7 WATSON (1m 19·787s) McLaren
40 JOHANSSON (1m 19·966s) Spirit	
	2 LAFFITE (1m 19·979s) Williams
3 ALBORETO (1m 20·149s) Tyrrell	
	8 LAUDA (1m 20·169s) McLaren
33 GUERRERO (1m 20·190s) Theodore	
	30 BOUTSEN (1m 20·245s) Arrows
25 JARIER (1m 20·247s) Ligier	
	1 ROSBERG (1m 20·391s) Williams
26 BOESEL (1m 20·660s) Ligier	
	31 FABI (1m 20·815s) Osella
4 SULLIVAN (1m 20·842s) Tyrrell	

Did not start:
32 Ghinzani (Osella). 1m 20·926s, did not qualify
34 Cecotto (Theodore), 1m 20·955s, did not qualify
17 Acheson (RAM March), 1m 23·093s, did not qualify

Results and retirements

Place	Driver	Car	Laps	Time and Speed (mph/km/h)/Retirement	
1	René Arnoux	Ferrari t/c V6	72	1h 38m 41·950s	115·640/186·105
2	Patrick Tambay	Ferrari t/c V6	72	1h 39m 02·789s	115·264/185·5
3	John Watson	McLaren-Cosworth V8	72	1h 39m 25·691s	114·767/184·7
4	Derek Warwick	Toleman-Hart t/c 4	72	1h 39m 58·789s	114·146/183·7
5	Mauro Baldi	Alfa Romeo t/c V8	72	1h 40m 06·242s	114·021/183·5
6	Michele Alboreto	Tyrrell-Cosworth V8	71		
7	Stefan Johansson	Spirit-Honda t/c V6	70		
8	Marc Surer	Arrows-Cosworth V8	70		
9	Riccardo Patrese	Brabham-BMW t/c 4	70		
10	Raul Boesel	Ligier-Cosworth V8	70		
11	Corrado Fabi	Osella-Alfa Romeo V12	68	Engine	
12	Roberto Guerrero	Theodore-Cosworth V8	68		
13	Bruno Giacomelli	Toleman-Hart t/c 4	68		
14	Thierry Boutsen	Arrows-Cosworth V8	68	Engine	
	Keke Rosberg	Williams-Cosworth V8	53	Engine/misfire	
	Nelson Piquet	Brabham-BMW t/c 4	41	Accident with Prost	
	Alain Prost	Renault t/c V6	41	Accident damage	
	Eddie Cheever	Renault t/c V6	39	Electrics/turbo	
	Jacques Laffite	Williams-Cosworth V8	37	Tyres	
	Nigel Mansell	Lotus-Renault t/c V6	26	Spun off	
	Niki Lauda	McLaren-TAG t/c V6	25	Brakes	
	Danny Sullivan	Tyrrell-Cosworth V8	20	Engine	
	Elio de Angelis	Lotus-Renault t/c V6	12	Fuel metering unit	
	Andrea de Cesaris	Alfa Romeo t/c V8	5	Engine	
	Jean-Pierre Jarier	Ligier-Cosworth V8	3	Suspension damage	
	*Manfred Winkelhock	ATS-BMW t/c 4	50		

*Disqualified
Fastest lap: Arnoux, on lap 33, 1m 19·863s, 119·097mph/191·668km/h.
Lap record: René Arnoux (F1 Renault RE t/c V6), 1m 19·35s, 119·867mph/192·907km/h (1980).

Past winners

Year	Driver	Nat	Car	Circuit	Distance miles/km	Speed mph/km/h
1949*	Luigi Villoresi	I	1·5 Ferrari 125 GP s/c	Zandvoort	104·22/167·72	77·09/124·06
1950*	Louis Rosier	F	4·5 Lago-Talbot	Zandvoort	234·49/377·37	76·63/123·32
1951*	Louis Rosier	F	4·5 Lago-Talbot	Zandvoort	234·49/377·37	78·45/126·26
1952	Alberto Ascari	I	2·0 Ferrari 500	Zandvoort	234·49/377·37	81·13/130·53
1953	Alberto Ascari	I	2·0 Ferrari 500	Zandvoort	234·49/377·37	81·05/130·43
1955	Juan Manuel Fangio	RA	2·5 Mercedes-Benz W196	Zandvoort	260·54/419·30	89·65/144·27
1958	Stirling Moss	GB	2·5 Vanwall	Zandvoort	195·41/314·48	93·93/151·17
1959	Jo Bonnier	S	2·5 BRM P25	Zandvoort	195·41/314·48	93·46/150·42
1960	Jack Brabham	AUS	2·5 Cooper T53 Climax	Zandvoort	195·41/314·48	96·27/154·93
1961	Wolfgang von Trips	D	1·5 Ferrari Dino 156	Zandvoort	195·41/314·48	96·23/154·83
1962	Graham Hill	GB	1·5 BRM P57	Zandvoort	208·43/335·44	95·44/153·60
1963	Jim Clark	GB	1·5 Lotus 25-Climax	Zandvoort	208·43/335·44	97·53/156·96
1964	Jim Clark	GB	1·5 Lotus 25-Climax	Zandvoort	208·43/335·44	98·02/157·74
1965	Jim Clark	GB	1·5 Lotus 33-Climax	Zandvoort	208·43/335·44	100·87/162·33
1966	Jack Brabham	AUS	3·0 Brabham BT19-Repco	Zandvoort	234·49/377·37	100·10/161·1
1967	Jim Clark	GB	3·0 Lotus 49-Ford	Zandvoort	234·49/377·37	104·45/168·09
1968	Jackie Stewart	GB	3·0 Matra MS10-Ford	Zandvoort	234·49/377·37	84·66/136·25
1969	Jackie Stewart	GB	3·0 Matra MS80-Ford	Zandvoort	234·49/377·37	111·04/178·71
1970	Jochen Rindt	A	3·0 Lotus 72-Ford	Zandvoort	208·43/335·44	112·96/181·78
1971	Jacky Ickx	B	3·0 Ferrari 312B-2/71	Zandvoort	182·38/293·51	94·06/151·38
1973	Jackie Stewart	GB	3·0 Tyrrell 006-Ford	Zandvoort	189·07/304·27	114·35/184·02
1974	Niki Lauda	A	3·0 Ferrari 312B-3/74	Zandvoort	196·94/316·95	114·72/184·62
1975	James Hunt	GB	3·0 Hesketh 308-Ford	Zandvoort	196·94/316·95	100·48/177·80
1976	James Hunt	GB	3·0 McLaren M23-Ford	Zandvoort	196·94/316·95	112·68/181·35
1977	Niki Lauda	A	3·0 Ferrari 312T-2/77	Zandvoort	196·94/316·95	116·12/186·87
1978	Mario Andretti	USA	3·0 JPS/Lotus 79-Ford	Zandvoort	196·94/316·95	116·92/188·16
1979	Alan Jones	AUS	3·0 Williams FW07-Ford	Zandvoort	196·94/316·95	116·62/187·67
1980	Nelson Piquet	BR	3·0 Brabham BT49-Ford	Zandvoort	190·23/306·14	116·19/186·99
1981	Alain Prost	F	1·5 Renault RE t/c	Zandvoort	190·23/306·14	113·71/183·00
1982	Didier Pironi	F	1·5 Ferrari 126C2 t/c	Zandvoort	190·23/306·14	116·38/187·30
1983	René Arnoux	F	1·5 Ferrari 126C3 t/c	Zandvoort	190·23/306·14	115·64/186·10

*Non-championship

Circuit data

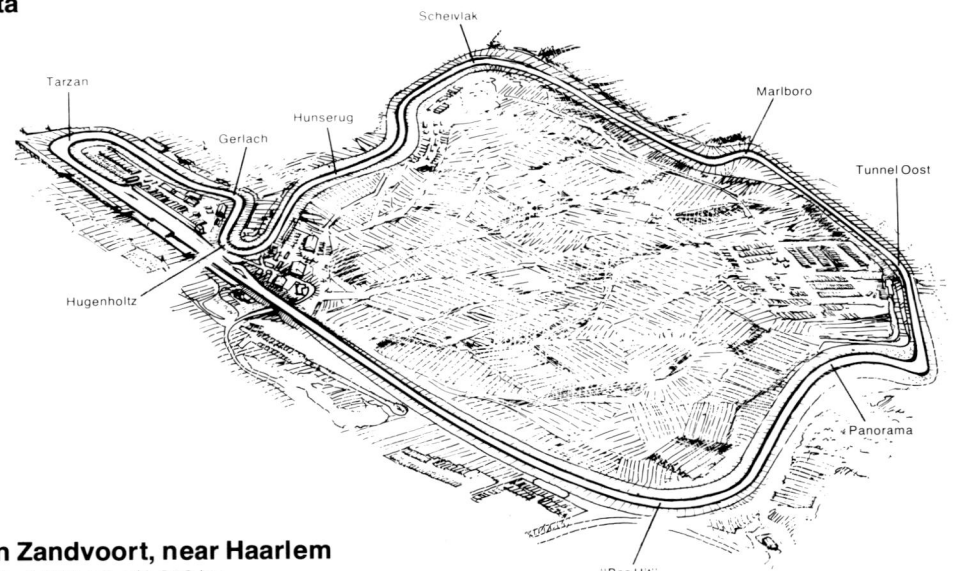

Circuit van Zandvoort, near Haarlem
Circuit length: 2·642 miles/4·252 km
Race distance: 72 laps, 190·228 miles/306·144 km
Race weather: Cool, dry

Fastest laps

Driver	Time	Lap
René Arnoux	1m 19·863s	33
Patrick Tambay	1m 20·020s	37
Nelson Piquet	1m 20·235s	4
Alain Prost	1m 20·331s	33
Riccardo Patrese	1m 20·807s	61
Andrea de Cesaris	1m 20·900s	4
Derek Warwick	1m 21·010s	4
Eddie Cheever	1m 21·153s	4
John Watson	1m 21·185s	54
Mauro Baldi	1m 21·326s	21
Nigel Mansell	1m 21·342s	25
Elio de Angelis	1m 21·733s	10
Michele Alboreto	1m 21·753s	61
Bruno Giacomelli	1m 22·289s	4
Niki Lauda	1m 22·462s	12
Stefan Johansson	1m 22·652s	25
Raul Boesel	1m 23·151s	28
Keke Rosberg	1m 23·205s	14
Thierry Boutsen	1m 23·387s	20
Marc Surer	1m 23·482s	31
Roberto Guerrero	1m 23·527s	62
Jacques Laffite	1m 23·731s	7
Corrado Fabi	1m 24·502s	4
Danny Sullivan	1m 24·638s	5
Jean-Pierre Jarier	1m 25·259s	3

Points

WORLD CHAMPIONSHIP OF DRIVERS

1	Alain Prost	51 pts
2	René Arnoux	43
3 =	Nelson Piquet	37
3 =	Patrick Tambay	37
5	Keke Rosberg	25
6	John Watson	22
7	Eddie Cheever	17
8	Niki Lauda	12
9	Jacques Laffite	11
10	Michele Alboreto	10
11 =	Andrea de Cesaris	6
11 =	Nigel Mansell	6
13 =	Marc Surer	4
13 =	Riccardo Patrese	4
15 =	Mauro Baldi	3
15 =	Derek Warwick	3
17	Danny Sullivan	2
18	Johnny Cecotto	1

CONSTRUCTORS' CUP

1	Ferrari	80 pts
2	Renault	68
3	Brabham	41
4	Williams	36
5	McLaren	34
6	Tyrrell	12
7	Alfa Romeo	9
8	Lotus	6
9	Arrows	4
10	Toleman	3
11	Theodore	1

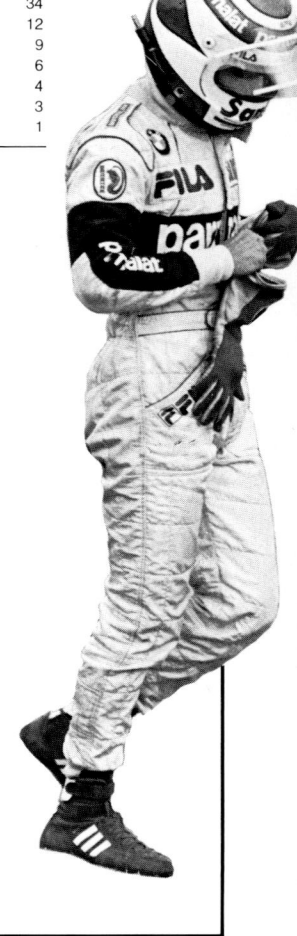

Lap chart

1st LAP ORDER	1	2	3	4	5	6	7	8	9	10	11	12	13	14	15	16	17	18	19	20	21	22	23	24	25	26	27	28	29	30	31	32	33	34	35	36	37	38	39
5 N. Piquet	5	5	5	5	5	5	5	5	5	5	5	5	5	5	5	5	5	5	5	5	5	5	5	5	5	5	5	5	5	5	5	5	5	5	5	5	5	5	5
16 E. Cheever	16	16	16	15	15	15	15	15	15	15	15	15	15	15	15	15	15	15	15	15	15	15	15	15	15	15	15	15	15	15	15	15	15	15	15	15	15	15	15
15 A. Prost	15	15	15	15	16	16	16	6	6	6	6	6	6	6	6	6	6	6	6	6	6	6	6	28	28	28	28	28	28	28	28	28	28	28	28	28	28	28	(28)
6 R. Patrese	6	6	6	6	6	6	6	16	16	16	16	16	16	16	28	28	28	28	28	28	28	6	6	6	6	6	6	6	6	6	16	16	16	16	16	(16)	6		
22 A. De Cesaris	22	22	22	22	28	28	28	28	28	28	28	28	28	16	16	16	16	16	16	16	16	16	16	16	16	16	16	16	6	6	6	6	6	6	6	6	7		
11 E. De Angelis	11	28	28	28	35	35	35	35	35	35	35	35	35	35	35	35	35	35	35	35	35	35	35	35	35	35	35	35	7	7	7	7	7	7	7	27			
28 R. Arnoux	28	11	35	35	11	11	11	11	11	11	11	(11)	12	12	12	12	12	12	12	12	12	12	12	12	12	7	7	7	7	(35)	27	27	27	27	27	16			
35 D. Warwick	35	35	11	11	12	12	12	12	12	12	12	7	7	7	7	7	7	7	7	7	7	7	7	7	23	23	23	23	27	(23)	9	9	9	9	9	(9)			
40 S. Johansson	40	40	12	12	(22)	40	40	40	7	7	7	40	40	23	23	23	23	23	23	23	23	23	23	27	27	27	23	23	9	40	(40)	3	35	35	35				
12 N. Mansell	12	12	40	40	40	7	7	7	7	40	40	40	23	23	9	9	9	9	9	9	9	9	9	9	27	27	9	9	9	9	40	3	3	35	3	3			
23 M. Baldi	23	23	23	23	23	23	23	23	23	23	23	9	27	27	27	27	27	27	27	27	27	9	9	40	40	40	40	40	40	3	35	35	23	23	23				
29 M. Surer	29	29	3	3	7	3	3	3	9	9	9	9	8	27	40	40	40	8	8	8	8	8	40	40	40	3	3	3	3	35	23	23	1	1	1				
3 M. Alboreto	3	3	1	7	3	9	9	9	3	8	8	27	8	8	8	8	8	40	40	40	40	40	8	1	1	1	1	1	1	1	1	1	1	1	1				
1 K. Rosberg	1	1	7	1	1	1	8	8	8	3	27	23	3	3	1	1	1	1	1	1	1	1	1	(8)	1	30	30	30	30	30	30	30	30	29	29				
2 J. Laffite	2	7	9	9	9	8	1	1	1	27	3	3	1	1	1	1	1	1	1	1	1	1	1	1	30	29	29	29	29	29	29	26	26	26	26				
7 J. Watson	7	9	8	8	8	27	27	27	27	1	1	1	36	36	36	36	36	36	36	36	36	36	36	29	31	31	31	26	26	26	26	40	40	40	40				
9 M. Winkelhock	9	8	29	27	27	36	36	36	36	36	36	29	29	29	29	29	29	29	29	29	29	29	29	(36)	26	26	26	31	31	31	31	31	31	31	36				
8 N. Lauda	8	2	2	29	29	29	29	29	29	29	29	30	30	30	30	30	30	30	30	30	30	30	30	(26)	36	36	36	36	36	36	36	36	36	31	31				
30 T. Boutsen	30	25	25	2	36	2	2	2	2	30	30	30	26	26	26	26	26	26	26	26	31	2	2	2	2	2	2	2	2	2	(2)	33	33					
25 J. P. Jarier	25	27	27	30	2	30	30	30	30	26	26	2	2	2	2	2	2	2	2	2	(31)	2	33	33	33	33	33	33	33	33	33	33							
27 P. Tambay	27	30	30	36	30	4	26	26	26	2	2	2	4	4	4	4	4	4	4	4	31	31	31	31	2	33													
4 D. Sullivan	4	4	36	4	4	26	4	4	4	4	4	4	31	31	31	31	31	31	31	33	33	33	33																
36 B. Giacomelli	36	36	4	26	26	31	31	31	31	31	31	31	33	33	33	33	33	33	33																				
26 R. Boesel	26	26	26	31	31	33	33	33	33	33	33	33																											
31 C. Fabi	31	31	31	33	33																																		
33 R. Guerrero	(33)	33	33																																				

40	41	42	43	44	45	46	47	48	49	50	51	52	53	54	55	56	57	58	59	60	61	62	63	64	65	66	67	68	69	70	71	72
5	5	28	28	28	28	28	28	28	28	28	28	28	28	28	28	28	28	28	28	28	28	28	28	28	28	28	28	28	28	28	28	28
15	15	7	(7)	6	6	6	6	6	6	6	6	6	6	6	6	6	6	6	6	6	6	6	6	6	6	6	27	27	27	27	27	27
28	28	(27)	6	27	27	27	27	27	27	27	27	27	27	27	27	27	27	27	27	27	27	27	27	27	27	27	7	7	7	7	7	7
(6)	7	6	27	7	7	7	7	7	7	7	7	7	7	7	7	7	7	7	7	7	7	7	7	7	7	7	6	35	35	35	35	35
7	27	35	35	35	35	35	35	35	35	35	35	35	35	35	35	35	35	35	35	35	35	35	35	35	35	23	23	23	23	23		
27	6	3	3	23	23	23	23	23	23	23	23	23	23	23	23	23	23	23	23	23	23	23	(3)	3	3	6	3	3				
35	35	23	23	3	3	3	3	3	3	3	3	3	3	3	3	3	3	3	3	3	3	(3)	3	3	6	3	6	40	40			
3	3	30	30	9	9	9	9	9	9	30	30	30	30	30	30	30	30	30	30	30	30	30	30	30	29	29	29					
23	23	29	9	30	30	30	30	30	(9)	29	29	29	29	29	29	29	29	29	29	29	29	40	40	40	40	6						
1	1	9	29	29	29	29	29	29	26	26	26	40	40	40	40	40	40	40	40	40	26	26	26	26								
30	30	(1)	26	26	26	26	26	26	40	40	40	26	26	26	26	26	26	26	31	31	31											
29	29	26	1	40	40	40	40	40	36	36	36	36	36	(36)	36	31	31	31	31	31	33	33	33									
9	9	40	40	1	1	36	36	36	36	1	1	(1)	31	31	31	36	36	36	36	36	36	36	36									
26	26	36	36	36	36	1	1	1	1	31	31	33	33	33	33	33	33	33	33	33	36											
40	40	31	31	31	31	31	31	31	31	33	33	33																				
36	36	33	33	33	33	33	33	33	33																							
31	31																															
33	33																																

197

GRAN PREMIO D'ITALIA

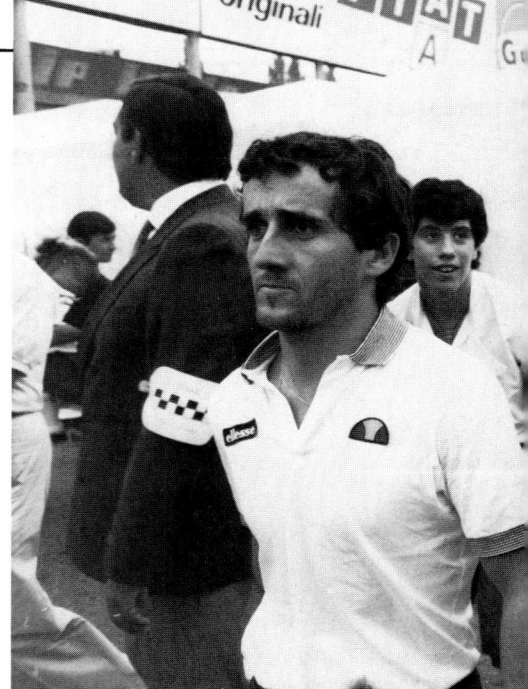

You could learn a lot about the championship from the way the drivers arrived at Monza on race day. Nelson Piquet, third with 37 points, breezed in on a Moto Guzzi, hair blowing in the wind, his girlfriend hanging on behind. René Arnoux, second with 43 points, cruised in at the wheel of a Rolls Royce, the bronze car crammed with trendy friends; Arnoux, wearing sunglasses and a Ferrari tee-shirt, enjoying the enthusiastic applause along the way.

And the championship leader? Alain Prost gave the appearance of being more anxious about his well-being than his 51 points when he arrived by helicopter, the unshaven Renault driver jammed between two bodyguards, each man hefty enough to tackle the unruly Ferrari supporters single-handed. There had been unpleasant scenes during testing when the *tifosi* dropped stones in the Renault's path and made animal noises which appeared to come quite naturally to most of them.

The Renault management insisted Prost was enjoying himself. "He's having fun with the bodyguards," they said. "They're joking all the time. He was under more pressure at Zandvoort than here. We've employed the protection to take the pressure off him."

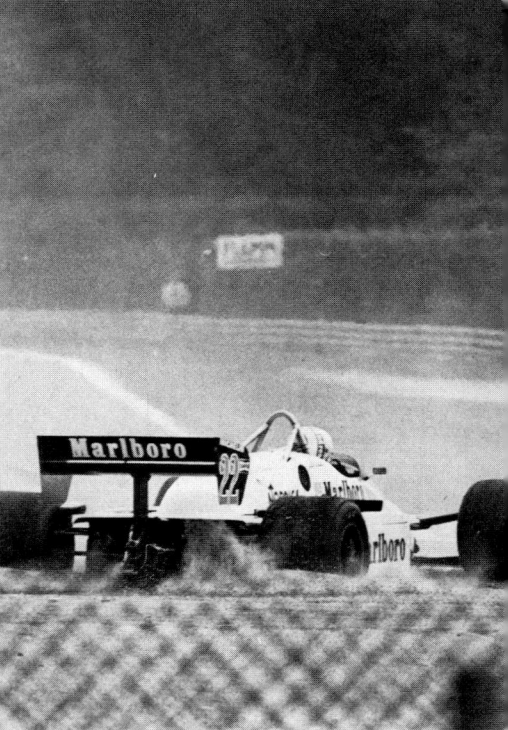

Maybe so, but the little man had a harrassed look about him and it was not to be a happy time if you judged the weekend by his performance on the track. The Renaults lacked grip and neutral handling during practice and Prost's race ended with a turbo failure. Arnoux, short on grip but enjoying better reliability, took second place while Tambay, the fourth member of the championship equation, lost power and finished fourth behind the Renault of Eddie Cheever, the American driver having engaged in a strenuous battle with Arnoux before losing fourth gear.

None of them, however, could match Piquet. Having given best to his team-mate, Riccardo Patrese, who started from pole, Piquet was able to assume the lead when the Italian retired after three laps with a spectacular engine failure. Piquet's car, on the other hand, was perfect and Nelson was able to wind down the boost and dominate from the front. It was the sort of performance which Brabham had threatened ever since Piquet won in Brazil, six months before. Finally they had come good — just at the right time.

As a result of his second win of the season Piquet had closed to within three points of Arnoux who, in turn, was just two points behind Prost. Tambay, 11 points adrift of the Renault driver, had become the outsider.

Simply to score two points by finishing fifth was a landmark in a dismal season for Elio de Angelis, the Lotus-Renault stuttering home minus third and fifth gears. Derek Warwick took another championship point for Toleman with Bruno Giacomelli next up, the Italian having stolen seventh place from Nigel Mansell on the line as the Lotus driver backed off in the face of the *tifosi* flooding onto the track.

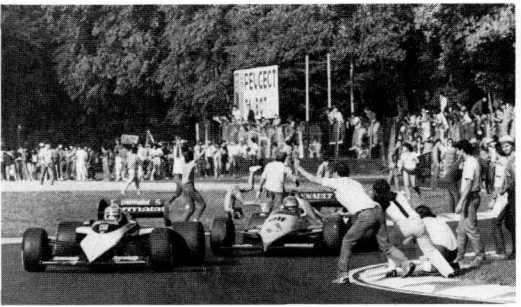

They had little to celebrate — by their standards — since a Ferrari had not won. But at least Arnoux was bidding strongly for the title and Piquet had thrown the championship wide open with an easy win. And it could have been worse for the Italians. Prost could have won — in which case his heavyweight friends would have been fully employed in the midst of shamefully chaotic scenes unique to Monza.

ENTRY AND PRACTICE

It was a surprise to learn that an Italian driver had not taken pole position at Monza since 1953 when Alberto Ascari claimed the honour in his Ferrari. You would be forgiven for thinking, therefore, that Riccardo Patrese's fastest lap on Saturday afternoon would be received with an overwhelming display of patriotism. Not quite.

The Italian driver's abiding handicap was the fact that he was not in a Ferrari when he claimed pole. What's more, he was driving for Bernard Ecclestone, a man who the Italian mob scarcely held dear to their

hearts. Into the bargain, he had just beaten the two Ferraris; the muted reception accorded to Patrese as he returned to the pits made that quite clear.

The Brabhams, running larger turbos, had dominated practice. Patrese had set the pace during the first 30 minutes on Friday and Nelson Piquet then beat his time on his second set of qualifiers. The Brazilian was confident of retaining his pole position on Saturday and it was not until the Ferraris had improved that Piquet made his way to the spare Brabham and set off with about half-an-hour remaining. He was soon back in the pits to complain that the BMW was down-on-power and the team quickly transferred him to his race

car which did not have the benefit of a water spray mounted in front of the intercooler. That was to be of academic interest, however, for the engine blew up before Nelson could get going. By now, Patrese had set his time and the Italian was leaning idly by the pit wall. In a last-ditch attempt, the mechanics strapped Piquet into Riccardo's car and the Brazilian scorched out of the pit lane. Then, just as he powered out of *Curvetta Sud* to start his quick lap, the chequered flag was shown. There were those who suggested that the flag had been waved a few seconds too soon but there was no question that the sixty minutes were up. Patrese was on pole and Nelson, having failed to improve on

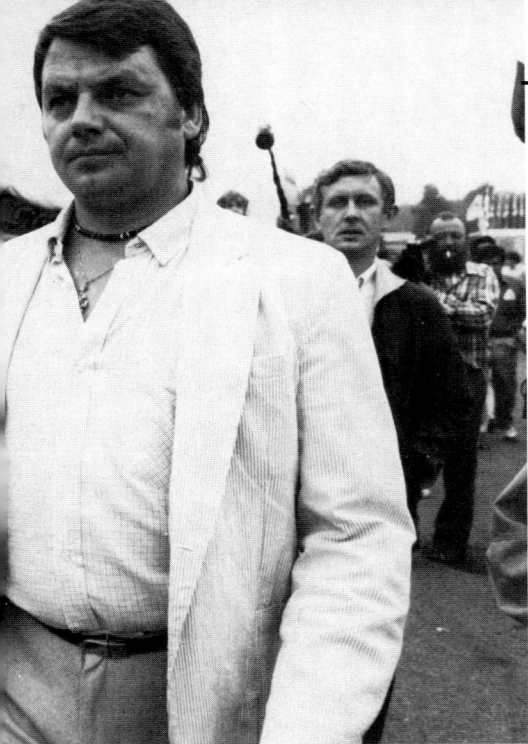

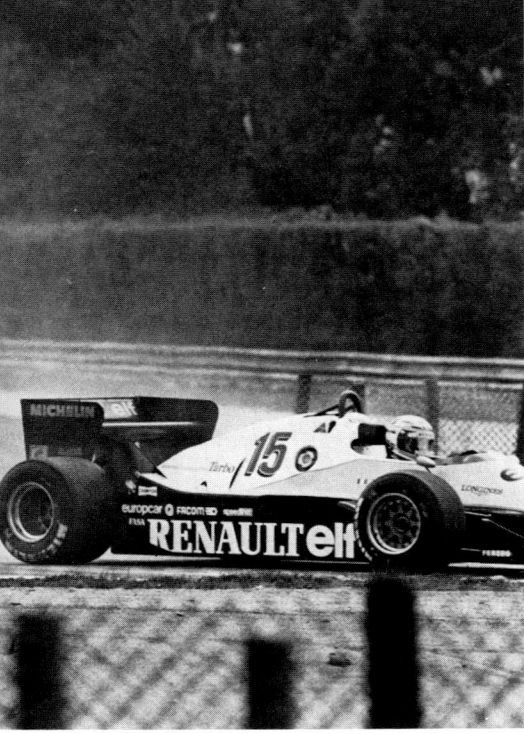

An unshaven and rather forlorn Alain Prost is dwarfed by one of his three bodyguards.
Andrea de Cesaris, thoroughly overexcited after watching Eddie Cheever outbrake Patrick Tambay into the chicane, misjudges his braking and spins the Alfa Romeo into retirement. Alain Prost is forced to flat-spot his tyres in avoidance.
The crowd control was non-existent after the race. Nelson Piquet and Eddie Cheever, first and third respectively after two excellent drives, make their way back to the pits while a member of the public expresses his enthusiasm by doing a handstand on the infield!

SEPTEMBER:
Nimrod Racing Automobiles goes into liquidation.

Keke Rosberg tests Williams FW09 Honda at Donington.

Alain Prost re-signs with Renault.

Morris Nunn resigns from Theodore team.

Michael Andretti (Ralt RT4) wins Formula Mondial North American Cup.

Friday's time, was disappointed to be fourth, behind the Ferraris.

As expected, no expense was spared for Monza and the Ferrari team wheeled out four 126C3s on Friday morning. The latest chassis was given to Tambay and he found it to be slightly quicker than his regular C3. Keeping it for Saturday afternoon, Tambay improved his time on his first run and his attempts at a high-boost answer to Patrese's challenge ended when the turbo began to emit clouds of blue smoke. The quality of the Goodyear qualifiers had presented Ferrari with a problem once René Arnoux had discovered the race compounds to be just as quick during the first session. He hedged his bets during final practice by taking the opportunity to use the race tyres and find a clear lap before claiming third place on the grid.

Every move made by the Ferrari team was watched intently by the occupants of the concrete stand opposite. Earlier in the day, the organisers had received their full approval by stopping practice to retrieve the two Ferraris which had been abandoned out on the circuit. Arnoux's turbo had broken and Tambay had bent a steering arm after losing control while leaving the chicane. Neither car was in a dangerous position but the power of Ferrari at Monza was demonstrated by the organisers not only stopping practice but also returning the cars to the pits against the direction of the circuit! Had the cars been blue and white or, indeed, yellow and white, doubtless they would have been left where they were.

The championship momentum, of course, lay with the yellow and white Renault number 15. And there were those who said the pressure of defending an eight point lead was beginning to tell on Alain Prost. There had been the mistake at Zandvoort; most out of character. Then he arrived in Italy accompanied by three bodyguards (one an ex-Mitterrand chauffeur), the little man looking frail and forlorn as the heavies escorted him everywhere – even to the restaurant at night and then back to his bedroom door. There had been threats against his life and, while the team were taking no chances, it was presumed the threats had been designed to distract Prost from the job in hand.

On top of that, some of Alain's troubles were of his own making. The Frenchman was continuing to vacillate over the signing of his contract with Renault for 1984 and that was having a most unsettling effect on both himself and the team. Then, the final irony; his cars were not running properly.

The team had built a new chassis for the occasion but Prost spent Friday jumping in and out of the spare car in a bid to cure problems with grip and down-on-power engines. The engines in both cars refused to rev properly and, by the end of practice on Friday, Prost was down in seventh place. He was much happier on Saturday, however, Prost having taken the decision to stay with Renault for another year. In the lunch break, the team changed the intercoolers and turbos and, by the time the final session was due to start, Prost found his car to be handling much better and he improved by over a second to take fifth place.

Eddie Cheever, meanwhile, had also improved but the American was unhappy to be in seventh place. Like Prost, Cheever had found his engine to be 400 revs down on Friday and, just as he was going for a flyer in the final session, he was inadvertently blocked by Niki Lauda. Splitting the Renaults was the Alfa Romeo of Andrea de Cesaris, the Italian having set the pace during tyre testing and on Friday morning. Thereafter, however, the team made little progress, de Cesaris commenting that the car handled well but he added that they were short of straightline speed. Then, an engine failed towards the end of the unofficial session on Saturday while, at the same time, Mauro Baldi broke another turbo and was unable to set a quick time in the afternoon, the second Alfa taking 10th place.

The inconsistency of the Pirelli qualifying and race tyres threw the Lotus team into some disarray. Apart from the comparatively narrow rears giving little traction out of the chicanes which dominated Monza, neither Elio de Angelis nor Nigel Mansell could gain much benefit from the qualifiers on Friday. De Angelis tried his spare car on Friday and found it to be such an improvement that he decided to use it for the remainder of the weekend, the Italian improving his time on Saturday and taking eighth place. Nigel Mansell was 11th, the Englishman hampered by a loss

of 2000rpm on Friday. The Renault V6 was changed overnight but the replacement suddenly lost power towards the end of his final run and Mansell parked the car out on the circuit. It was later discovered that the Lotus had run out of fuel . . .

The ATS team were without their talented engineer, Gustav Brunner, recovering from the leg injuries received at Zandvoort. Manfred Winkelhock had his usual catalogue of minor problems compounded by a spin into the sand at one of the chicanes on Friday. The following day, he stripped fifth gear and pulled off the track opposite the pits. Manfred set his quickest time right at the end of the final session after taking the best that was left of his two sets of qualifying tyres and completing a typically brave lap which was good enough for ninth place.

A straightline speed some five to 10 mph slower than the quickest turbos went some way to deflating the euphoria surrounding the Toleman team after Zandvoort. All three cars were fitted with Holset turbos but Derek Warwick and Bruno Giacomelli found the TG183Bs to be lacking in every department, the Englishman taking a disappointing 12th place while Giacomelli prepared to celebrate his 31st birthday by starting from the seventh row, sandwiched by Lauda and Watson.

The Porsche engineers had carried out considerable development work based on the lessons learned in Holland but the McLaren chassis, still without large wings and plenty of downforce since that was not so important at Monza, gave the drivers plenty of work in the corners. In addition, continuing brake trouble meant an early switch from carbon fibre to steel discs and Lauda, recovering from an insect bite on his left foot, whittled down his time gradually. Watson, of course, was driving the TAG turbo in anger for the first time, the Ulsterman commenting that he was adapting to the new driving technique required by the turbo. He used just one set of qualifying tyres on Friday, preferring to run a set of race tyres and gain more experience with the car. On Saturday, he recorded what was to become his grid time on his first set of qualifiers and, just as he was preparing to go out with his final set, fuel pressure problems meant the engine refused to run properly. In fact, Watson's best time of the weekend (1m 33.921s) had been set during the unofficial session on Saturday and, while 15th place on the grid may have appeared acceptable, the gap of 1.3 seconds to Giacomelli in 14th position told the true story.

There was no disguising the fact, however, that the Ford-Cosworths were outclassed once more and Keke Rosberg, the quickest in 'Division Two', ran virtually no rear wing angle as his Williams danced and darted its way into 16th place. More disturbing by far was the failure of Jacques Laffite to qualify for the second time in his lengthy Grand Prix career. The Frenchman had spent the first day running Goodyear radials (with little effect) and, when the change to cross-plies was made on Saturday, Jacques was unable to work his Williams round in a respectable time thanks, in part, to a mismatched set of tyres which produced oversteer, a handling characteristic which Laffite disliked intensely.

Stefan Johansson almost joined Laffite after another two days of problems with the Spirit-Honda. On Friday evening, two engine failures meant he had not qualified. On Saturday, the V6 developed a misfire and, by the time that had cleared, his second set of qualifying tyres had gone off. Then the engine blew! But at least that one lap had been good enough for 17th place. Spirit brought along their first pukka Formula 1 car, the 101, which was finished off in the paddock but the various problems with the two race chassis meant they had no opportunity to run it. Just getting into the race was occupying their full attention . . .

Thierry Boutsen, in 18th place, was the faster of the two Arrows drivers although Marc Surer had been forced to use the T-car after a valve spring had broken in his regular car during the final session. Jean-Pierre Jarier split the two Arrows in his Ligier, the Frenchman running a Ford-Cosworth DFY once again while his team-mate, Raul Boesel, had to make do with a DFV, the Brazilian failing to qualify by just under one tenth of a second. Roberto Guerrero took 21st place and his Theodore team-mate, Johnny Cecotto, would have been alongside the Colombian with a time

199

set during the first unofficial session. However, Cecotto was unable to match that time when it mattered and the Venezuelan took the last place on the grid after failing to improve on Saturday despite the aid of a tow from de Angelis's Lotus. The future of the team had seemed uncertain for some time and rumours gathered strength once more when Morris Nunn, present in the pit lane but playing no part in running Theodore, announced that he had resigned from the company a few days before.

Michele Alboreto was the centre of much stronger speculation over his future although his standing can not have been helped by 24th place on the grid. The 012 Tyrrell featured a revised front suspension but the team wasted valuable time by not generating enough tyre temperature and failing to run qualifiers at the right time. In fact, Alboreto's best lap was set on Friday morning and Danny Sullivan went a tenth of a second quicker in his Tyrrell 010 to take 22nd place.

On Friday evening, Corrado Fabi had failed to qualify but the Italian improved sufficiently during the final session to take a place on the back row. That meant two Osellas on the grid for their home Grand Prix, Piercarlo Ghinzani having qualified comfortably on Friday after taking advantage of a good tow, the Alfa Romeo V12 bouncing off the rev-limiter as he passed the pits. An engine failure on Saturday morning meant he did not take part in the final session and Ghinzani slipped from 17th to 23rd place. That left Kenneth Acheson as the final non-qualifier. The Ulsterman may have been bottom of the list but this time the RAM-March had been more competitive than of late thanks to the use of a Cosworth DFY on loan from McLaren. In addition, Acheson had taken advice from Watson but the lack of a decent qualifier from Pirelli finally told and he failed by 0.16 sec.

RACE

Alain Prost arrived by helicopter shortly after 10 a.m. and, by then, René Arnoux had already been through the ritual of nosing his Rolls Royce between the enthusiastic spectators. They applauded every move he made and René seemed to thrive on the adulation. His mood was not so sunny a few hours later when both Ferrari drivers found their cars to be desperately short of grip in the warm conditions. The handling was good but eighth and tenth places on the time sheet were not what Arnoux and Tambay had expected. In fact, they had both been slower than John Watson in the TAG turbo while the fastest time overall had gone to Prost, much happier now with the handling of his Renault.

Patrese had been second fastest with Piquet fourth and a lively discussion ensued between the two when Nelson tried to establish ground rules for teamwork now that he was in with a chance of winning the championship. Riccardo was, by all accounts, less than interested in the well-being of the Brazilian. This was Monza after all – and it was only the second time in his Grand Prix career that Patrese had taken pole position. However, Patrese's thinking may have been altered slightly when Bernie Ecclestone reminded the Italian that he had yet to sign a contract for 1984 . . .

Riccardo was not about to stand on ceremony at the green light and the pole position Brabham made a perfect start to take a clear lead into the first corner. The Ferraris were slow by comparison, as was Piquet, the Brabham blocking another flying start by Eddie Cheever as he tried to find a way through. Prost, meanwhile, had made a clean getaway and was challenging Arnoux as they approached the braking area for the chicane. Further back, the Tolemans had been slow off the mark and Rosberg swept his Williams to the right to avoid Giacomelli, the World Champion breaking the rules by crossing a white line marking the edge of the track. The organisers, anxious not to have a repeat of the Peterson incident in 1978, had made it clear at the drivers' briefing that the line was to be treated as though it were a stone wall. Rosberg's contempt of the rules was to earn a one minute penalty and a $2000 fine.

By the end of the first lap, Piquet had taken second place and the two Brabhams were pulling clear of the rest; Tambay leading Arnoux, Cheever, de Cesaris and Prost. From the start, Tambay was aware that his engine was not pulling properly and he began to drop back, the Frenchman helpless against the advances of Arnoux on lap two. Cheever then took a run at

Tambay as the pair entered the pit straight, the Renault driver completing a neat piece of outbraking as they reached the chicane. Following hard on their heels was de Cesaris, the Italian becoming thoroughly overexcited by the whole affair and completely misjudging his braking. The Alfa Romeo slewed sideways, clouting the back of Tambay's Ferrari as it did so, before spinning backwards into the sandy run-off area. Prost was forced to lock his brakes in avoidance but both he and Tambay were able to continue while de Cesaris began the task of burying his back wheels with each successive and frustrated attempt to extricate his car. Eventually he was persuaded to give up and the Italian posted the first retirement.

The second retirement followed moments later when a roar from the heartless crowd signalled the sight of Patrese crawling slowly towards the pits with blue smoke issuing from the back of his car. A spark-box malfunction had caused a piston to burn out and the unhappy Italian watched his team-mate rush by and take a lead which he would hold for the rest of the afternoon.

Mauro Baldi was the next to go, the Alfa Romeo causing an even bigger smoke screen thanks to a blown turbo and, as he reached the pits, Baldi found another red and white car, the McLaren-TAG of Niki Lauda, receiving attention. An electrical problem was causing the turbo to run badly and the Austrian would complete several more laps at the back of the field before retiring. His team-mate, meanwhile, was making impressive progress, Watson working his way past Winkelhock and then taking seventh place from Warwick with a move which illustrated clearly that the Porsche-built engine was not short of power.

Ahead of them, Piquet had opened a gap of five seconds to Arnoux who was receiving close attention from Cheever. Then, an eight-second gap to Tambay with Prost and de Angelis a few lengths behind. The Lotus felt good but de Angelis pushed his Pirellis to the limit as he took fifth place from the Renault on lap 10. Then a six-second gap to Watson who was now pulling away from Warwick. The rest of the field were split into small groups, Winkelhock leading Mansell, Giacomelli and Rosberg and then a delay before a tussle between Alboreto and Jarier appeared, followed by the Arrows team running in formation and then a scrap between the Theodores and Danny Sullivan's Tyrrell. Bringing up the rear were the Osellas with Ghinzani a lap behind after stopping to attend to a faulty sparkbox. Missing from the lap chart was the Spirit-Honda, Johansson having stopped out on the circuit with distributor trouble.

The retirement list lengthened when Ghinzani stopped once more, this time with gearbox trouble, and Watson's fine drive came to an end when the turbo faltered as he passed the pits at the end of lap 13. Watson pulled off and explained that the engine had died, the result, he thought, of an electrical problem. Subsequent examination at Weissach was to reveal a very minor malfunction in the valve gear although the team were reluctant to talk about that . . .

As Piquet maintained his lead, Cheever continued to harry Arnoux's Ferrari and the only change to the top of the lap chart occurred on lap 14 when de Angelis powered past Tambay to take fourth place, a sure sign that the Ferrari V6 was not delivering the goods. An equally sure indication that Prost was now losing boost was the fact that the Renault was unable to make any impression on Tambay.

There was stalemate until the pit stops, Cheever and de Angelis coming in together, the Renault getting away in 11.6 seconds while the Lotus team were not so slick, de Angelis being delayed by 14.2 seconds. Added to that, Elio found it took some time to work his Pirellis up to a decent temperature and, once Tambay had made his stop four laps later, the Italian was very unhappy to find himself running behind the Ferrari once more.

But, for the moment, that was of little importance to the crowd. They were still buzzing with excitement after watching Prost make his pit stop at the end of lap 26. The Renault had come in as planned but when Prost raised his visor and two engineers poked their heads into the cockpit, it was clear all was not well. Sure enough, the Renault crawled away from the pits, Prost completing one more lap at a very slow pace before retiring with a broken turbo wheel.

Lauda, still struggling with his engine problem, made one more pit stop and, as he pulled away, the hot turbo stalled – a common failing with the TAG. The McLaren rolled to a halt at the Brabham pit where, Lauda noted, the mechanics were poised, ready for action. The race leader was due at the end of that lap. The fact had not escaped Bernie Ecclestone's attention either and, to everyone's amazement, the Brabham boss leapt over the wall and began to apply his weight to the back of Lauda's car!

The McLaren was removed in time and Piquet's stop, the fastest of the day at 10.15 seconds, went as smoothly as ever, Nelson accelerating back to a comfortable lead of over 20 seconds. During his stop, Piquet had been shown a 'boost' sign by Gordon Murray and Nelson responded by winding down the appropriate knob in the cockpit. As a result, the BMW sounded as though it had cracked an exhaust but the team and Piquet knew better. Barring some terrible misfortune, this race was in the bag.

Arnoux and Cheever resumed where they had left off before their pit stops, the Renault driver poking his nose alongside once or twice during a tremendous duel which, regrettably, was to end when Cheever lost fourth gear with 15 laps to go. There was a mild flurry of excitement when Arnoux was then able to concentrate on closing the gap to Piquet but the Brabham driver simply stepped up his pace to make the result a foregone conclusion.

The back of the field thinned out considerably during the closing stages. Alboreto retired from his battle with Jarier when a clutch plate failed and the second Tyrrell of Sullivan stopped when a defective drive to the fuel pump caused the Cosworth to gradually lose revs. Winkelhock's exhaust broke, Boutsen stopped with a broken valve and Fabi retired when an oil union failed on the Alfa Romeo. During the final three laps, the throttle pedal on Guerrero's Theodore bent but the Colombian driver managed to keep going until the finish.

Any hopes de Angelis may have had of catching Tambay were ruined when he lost third gear. Then, with one lap remaining, the Lotus came past the pits with the Renault V6 bouncing off the rev-limiter; fifth gear had broken as well. Indeed, the only battle of any consequence was shaping up when Giacomelli began to close on Mansell's seventh place. The Toleman driver unlapped himself going into the last lap and this gave him a chance to cut the five-second gap to the Lotus.

Piquet duly took a victory which he thoroughly deserved and, as the Brabham mechanics climbed back over the pit wall, the *tifosi* began pouring over and under the spectator fencing. Arnoux came by in second place, the Ferrari several seconds clear of Cheever's Renault, the American driver flushed after such an exhilarating race. Tambay was fourth and de Angelis managed to complete the lap and take his first points of the season with fifth place. Warwick finished a distant sixth and, by now, over a minute had passed since Piquet had taken the flag.

The mob continued to flood onto the track just as Mansell and Giacomelli rounded the final corner. The sight of a wall of people surging down from the first chicane caused Mansell to back off and Giacomelli, keeping his right foot hard on the throttle, rushed past the Lotus and took seventh place. Mansell crossed the line and then swung the Lotus into the pit lane. He explained that he was not willing to kill anyone for the sake of seventh place – a fair comment considering the circumstances and the Lotus team's previous experiences in the aftermath of tragedy at Monza. Peter Warr was not so charitable towards either the Italians or his driver, the Lotus team manager commenting icily that motor racing was a serious business and adding that Mansell's contract was due for renewal. There was also the small matter of $3000, the difference in prize money between seventh and eighth places . . .

It's likely that Alain Prost did not give a second thought to the money lost when he retired from sixth place. He was more concerned about the latest championship positions; his lead had shrunk from eight points to just two with two races to go. As he sat surrounded by his bodyguards, the championship favourite could only conclude that nothing was safe any more.

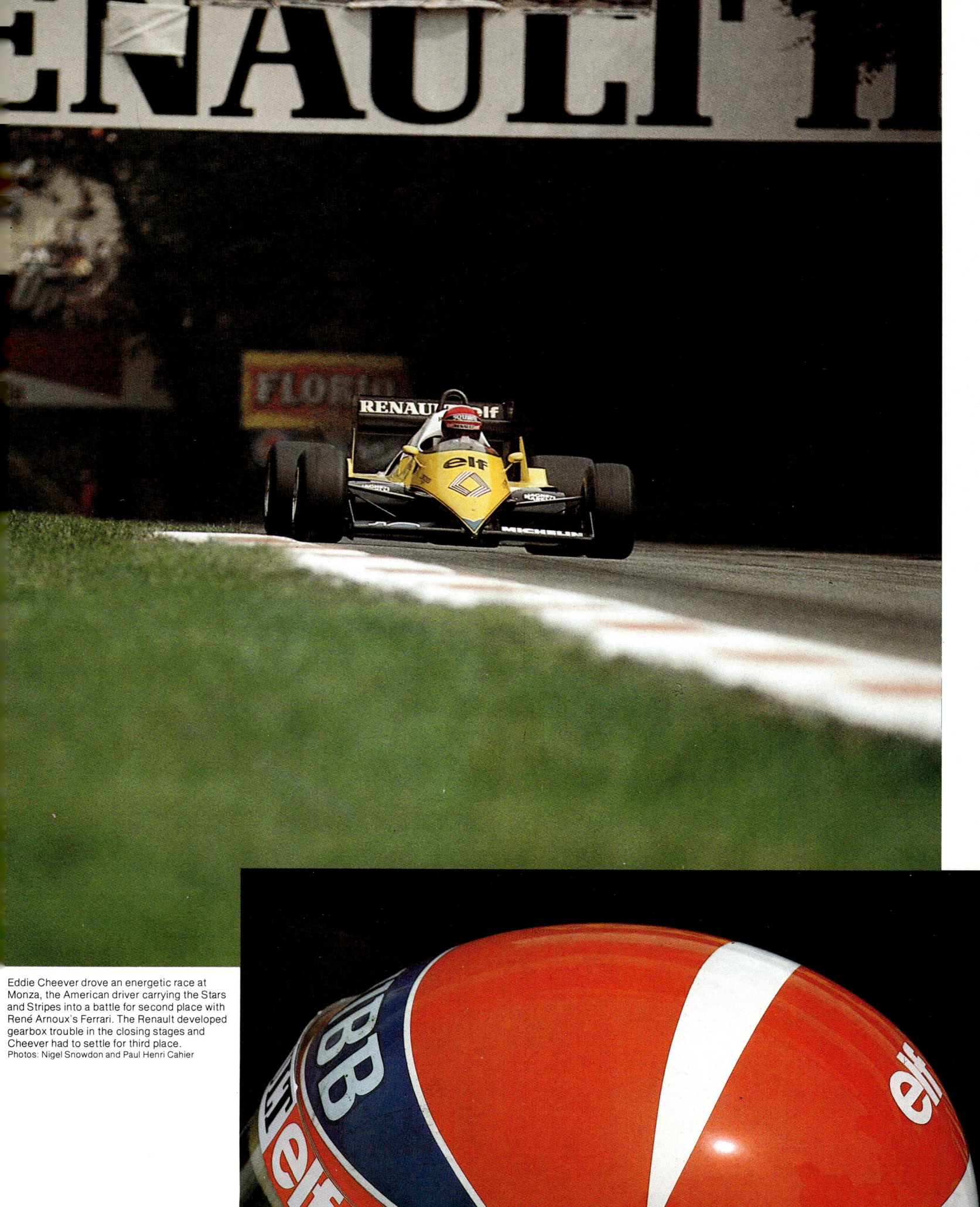

Eddie Cheever drove an energetic race at Monza, the American driver carrying the Stars and Stripes into a battle for second place with René Arnoux's Ferrari. The Renault developed gearbox trouble in the closing stages and Cheever had to settle for third place.
Photos: Nigel Snowdon and Paul Henri Cahier

Gran Premio d'Italia, September 11/statistics

Entries and practice times

No.	Driver	Nat	Car	Tyre	Engine	Entrant	Practice 1	Practice 2
1	Keke Rosberg	SF	Saudia WILLIAMS FW08C	G	Ford Cosworth DFV	TAG Williams Team	1m 36·631s	1m 35·291s
2	Jacques Laffite	F	Saudia WILLIAMS FW08C	G	Ford Cosworth DFV	TAG Williams Team	1m 37·277s	1m 37·245s
3	Michele Alboreto	I	Benetton TYRRELL 012	G	Ford Cosworth DFV/DFY	Benetton Tyrrell Team	1m 36·788s	1m 37·319s
4	Danny Sullivan	USA	Benetton TYRRELL 011	G	Ford Cosworth DFV/DFY	Benetton Tyrrell Team	1m 37·565s	1m 36·644s
5	Nelson Piquet	BR	Parmalat BRABHAM BT52B	M	BMW M12/13	Fila Sport	1m 30·202s	1m 30·475s
6	Riccardo Patrese	I	Parmalat BRABHAM BT52B	M	BMW M12/13	Fila Sport	1m 30·253s	1m 29·122s
7	John Watson	GB	Marlboro McLAREN MP4/1E	M	TAG P01	Marlboro McLaren International	1m 35·928s	1m 34·705s
8	Niki Lauda	A	Marlboro McLAREN MP4/1E	M	TAG P01	Marlboro McLaren International	1m 33·190s	1m 33·133s
9	Manfred Winkelhock	D	ATS D6	G	BMW M12/13	Team ATS	1m 34·161s	1m 31·959s
11	Elio de Angelis	I	John Player Special LOTUS 94T	P	Renault EF1	John Player Team Lotus	1m 32·590s	1m 31·628s
12	Nigel Mansell	GB	John Player Special LOTUS 94T	P	Renault EF1	John Player Team Lotus	1m 34·610s	1m 32·423s
15	Alain Prost	F	Elf RENAULT RE40	M	Renault EF1	Equipe Renault Elf	1m 32·244s	1m 31·144s
16	Eddie Cheever	USA	Elf RENAULT RE40	M	Renault EF1	Equipe Renault Elf	1m 31·613s	1m 31·564s
17	Kenneth Acheson	GB	MARCH-RAM 01	P	Ford Cosworth DFV/DFY	RAM Automotive Team March	1m 37·755s	1m 37·272s
22	Andrea de Cesaris	I	Marlboro ALFA ROMEO 183T	M	Alfa Romeo 183T	Marlboro Team Alfa Romeo	1m 31·295s	1m 31·272s
23	Mauro Baldi	I	Marlboro ALFA ROMEO 183T	M	Alfa Romeo 183T	Marlboro Team Alfa Romeo	1m 32·407s	1m 32·593s
25	Jean-Pierre Jarier	F	Gitanes LIGIER JS21	M	Ford Cosworth DFV/DFY	Equipe Ligier Gitanes	1m 37·270s	1m 36·220s
26	Raul Boesel	BR	Gitanes LIGIER JS21	M	Ford Cosworth DFV	Equipe Ligier Gitanes	1m 37·798s	1m 37·186s
27	Patrick Tambay	F	Fiat FERRARI 126C3	G	Ferrari 126C	Scuderia Ferrari SpA SEFAC	1m 31·036s	1m 29·650s
28	René Arnoux	F	Fiat FERRARI 126C3	G	Ferrari 126C	Scuderia Ferrari SpA SEFAC	1m 30·799s	1m 29·901s
29	Marc Surer	CH	ARROWS A6	G	Ford Cosworth DFV	Arrows Racing Team	1m 36·796s	1m 36·435s
30	Thierry Boutsen	B	ARROWS A6	G	Ford Cosworth DFV	Arrows Racing Team	1m 36·968s	1m 35·624s
31	Corrado Fabi	I	OSELLA FA1E	M	Alfa Romeo 1260	Osella Squadra Corse	1m 38·577s	1m 36·834s
32	Piercarlo Ghinzani	I	OSELLA FA1E	M	Alfa Romeo 1260	Osella Squadra Corse	1m 36·647s	
33	Roberto Guerrero	COL	THEODORE N183	G	Ford Cosworth DFV	Theodore Racing Team	1m 37·677s	1m 36·619s
34	Johnny Cecotto	YV	THEODORE N183	G	Ford Cosworth DFV	Theodore Racing Team	1m 37·105s	1m 37·634s
35	Derek Warwick	GB	Candy TOLEMAN TG183B	P	Hart 415T	Candy Toleman Motorsport	1m 33·738s	1m 32·677s
36	Bruno Giacomelli	I	Candy TOLEMAN TG183B	P	Hart 415T	Candy Toleman Motorsport	1m 35·489s	1m 33·384s
40	Stefan Johansson	S	SPIRIT-HONDA 201	G	Honda RA163-E	Spirit Racing	1m 37·862s	1m 35·483s

Friday morning and Saturday morning practice sessions not officially recorded.

G – Goodyear, M – Michelin, P – Pirelli.

Fri pm — Warm, dry
Sat pm — Warm, dry

Starting grid

6 PATRESE (1m 29·122s)
Brabham

27 TAMBAY (1m 29·650s)
Ferrari

28 ARNOUX (1m 29·901s)
Ferrari

5 PIQUET (1m 30·202s)
Brabham

15 PROST (1m 31·144s)
Renault

22 DE CESARIS (1m 31·272s)
Alfa Romeo

16 CHEEVER (1m 31·564s)
Renault

11 DE ANGELIS (1m 31·628s)
Lotus

9 WINKELHOCK (1m 31·959s)
ATS

23 BALDI (1m 32·407s)
Alfa Romeo

12 MANSELL (1m 32·423s)
Lotus

35 WARWICK (1m 32·677s)
Toleman

8 LAUDA (1m 33·133s)
McLaren

36 GIACOMELLI (1m 33·384s)
Toleman

7 WATSON (1m 34·705s)
McLaren

1 ROSBERG (1m 35·291s)
Williams

40 JOHANSSON (1m 35·483s)
Spirit

30 BOUTSEN (1m 35·624s)
Arrows

25 JARIER (1m 36·220s)
Ligier

29 SURER (1m 36·435s)
Arrows

33 GUERRERO (1m 36·619s)
Theodore

4 SULLIVAN (1m 36·644s)
Tyrrell

32 GHINZANI (1m 36·647s)
Osella

3 ALBORETO (1m 36·788s)
Tyrrell

31 FABI (1m 36·834s)
Osella

34 CECOTTO (1m 37·105s)
Theodore

Did not start:
26 Boesel (Ligier), 1m 37·186s, did not qualify
2 Laffite (Williams), 1m 37·245s, did not qualify
17 Acheson (RAM March), 1m 37·272s, did not qualify

Results and retirements

Place	Driver	Car	Laps	Time and Speed (mph/km/h)/Retirement	
1	Nelson Piquet	Brabham-BMW t/c 4	52	1h 23m 10·880s	135·178/217·548
2	René Arnoux	Ferrari t/c V6	52	1h 23m 21·092s	134·899/217·1
3	Eddie Cheever	Renault t/c V6	52	1h 23m 29·492s	134·651/216·7
4	Patrick Tambay	Ferrari t/c V6	52	1h 23m 39·903s	134·402/216·3
5	Elio de Angelis	Lotus-Renault t/c V6	52	1h 24m 04·560s	133·719/215·2
6	Derek Warwick	Toleman-Hart t/c 4	52	1h 24m 24·228s	133·222/214·4
7	Bruno Giacomelli	Toleman-Hart t/c 4	52	1h 24m 44·802s	132·662/213·5
8	Nigel Mansell	Lotus-Renault t/c V6	52	1h 24m 46·915s	132·600/213·4
9	Jean-Pierre Jarier	Ligier-Cosworth V8	51		
10	Marc Surer	Arrows-Cosworth V8	51		
11	*Keke Rosberg	Williams-Cosworth V8	51		
12	Johnny Cecotto	Theodore-Cosworth V8	50		
13	Roberto Guerrero	Theodore-Cosworth V8	50		
	Corrado Fabi	Osella-Alfa Romeo V12	46	Broken oil union	
	Danny Sullivan	Tyrrell-Cosworth V8	44	Fuel pump drive	
	Thierry Boutsen	Arrows-Cosworth V8	42	Engine	
	Manfred Winkelhock	ATS-BMW t/c 4	35	Broken exhaust	
	Michele Alboreto	Tyrrell-Cosworth V8	29	Clutch	
	Alain Prost	Renault t/c V6	26	Turbo	
	Niki Lauda	McLaren-TAG t/c V6	24	Electrics	
	John Watson	McLaren-TAG t/c V6	13	Engine	
	Piercarlo Ghinzani	Osella-Alfa Romeo V12	10	Gearbox	
	Mauro Baldi	Alfa Romeo t/c V8	5	Turbo	
	Stefan Johansson	Spirit-Honda t/c V6	4	Distributor	
	Riccardo Patrese	Brabham-BMW t/c 4	3	Electrics/engine	
	Andrea de Cesaris	Alfa Romeo t/c V8	2	Spun off	

*Finished 9th on the road but penalised one minute for infringement of rules at start.
Fastest lap: Piquet, on lap 20, 1m 34·431s, 137·393mph/221·113km/h.
Lap record: René Arnoux (F1 Renault RE30B t/c), 1m 33·619s, 138·585mph/223·031km/h (1982).

Past winners

Year	Driver	Nat	Car	Circuit	Distance miles/km	Speed mph/km/h
1921	Jules Goux	F	3·0 Ballot	Brescia	322·49/ 519·00	89·94/144·74
1922	Pietro Bordini	I	2·0 Fiat 804	Monza	497·10/ 800·00	86·90/139·95
1923	Carlo Salamano	I	2·0 Fiat 805 s/c	Monza	497·10/ 800·00	91·03/146·50
1924	Antonio Ascari	I	2·0 Alfa Romeo P2 s/c	Monza	497·10/ 800·00	98·79/158·99
1925	Gastone Brilli-Peri	I	2·0 Alfa Romeo P2 s/c	Monza	497·10/ 800·00	94·82/152·60
1926	Lotus Charavel	F	1·5 Bugatti T39A s/c	Monza	372·82/ 600·00	85·88/138·20
1927	Robert Benoist	F	1·5 Delage s/c	Monza	310·69/ 500·00	89·66/144·30
1928	Louis Chiron	F	2·0 Bugatti T35C s/c	Monza	372·82/ 600·00	99·36/159·90
1931	Giuseppe Campari/ Tazio Nuvolari	I	2·3 Alfa Romeo Monza s/c	Monza	967·94/1557·75	96·79/155·78
1932	Tazio Nuvolari/ Giuseppe Campari	I	2·7 Alfa Romeo ZP3 s/c	Monza	520·46/ 837·61	104·09/167·52
1933	Luigi Fagioli	I	2·7 Alfa Romeo P3 s/c	Monza	310·69/ 500·00	108·58/174·74
1934	Rudi Caracciola/ Luigi Fagioli	D	2·4 Mercedes-Benz W25 s/c	Monza	310·66/ 499·96	65·35/105·18
1935	Hans Stuck	D	5·0 Auto Union B-type s/c	Monza	312·53/ 502·97	85·18/137·08
1936	Bernd Rosemeyer	D	6·0 Auto Union C-type s/c	Monza	313·17/ 504·00	84·10/135·35
1937	Rudi Caracciola	D	5·7 Mercedes-Benz W125 s/c	Leghorn	223·18/ 359·18	81·59/131·31
1938	Tazio Nuvolari	I	3·0 Auto Union D-type s/c	Monza	260·71/ 419·58	96·76/155·73
1947	Carlo Felice Trossi	I	1·5 Alfa Romeo 158 s/c	Milan Park	214·37/ 345·00	70·34/113·19
1948	Jean-Pierre Wimille	F	1·5 Alfa Romeo 158 s/c	Turin	223·69/ 360·00	70·38/113·26
1949	Alberto Ascari	I	1·5 Ferrari 125 s/c	Monza	313·17/ 504·00	105·04/169·04
1950	Giuseppe Farina	I	1·5 Alfa Romeo 158 s/c	Monza	313·17/ 504·00	109·70/176·54
1951	Alberto Ascari	I	4·5 Ferrari 375	Monza	313·17/ 504·00	115·52/185·92
1952	Alberto Ascari	I	2·0 Ferrari 500	Monza	313·17/ 504·00	110·04/177·09
1953	Juan Manuel Fangio	RA	2·0 Maserati A6SSG	Monza	313·17/ 504·00	110·68/178·13
1954	Juan Manuel Fangio	RA	2·5 Mercedes-Benz W196	Monza	313·17/ 504·00	111·98/180·22
1955	Juan Manuel Fangio	RA	2·0 Mercedes-Benz W196	Monza	310·69/ 500·00	128·49/206·79
1956	Stirling Moss	GB	2·5 Maserati 250F	Monza	310·69/ 500·00	129·73/208·79
1957	Stirling Moss	GB	2·5 Vanwall	Monza	310·64/ 500·25	129·73/208·79
1958	Tony Brooks	GB	2·5 Vanwall	Monza	250·10/ 402·50	121·21/195·08
1959	Stirling Moss	GB	2·5 Cooper T45-Climax	Monza	257·55/ 414·00	124·38/200·18
1960	Phil Hill	USA	2·4 Ferrari Dino 246	Monza	310·69/ 500·00	132·06/212·53
1961	Phil Hill	USA	1·5 Ferrari Dino 156	Monza	267·19/ 430·00	130·11/209·39
1962	Graham Hill	GB	1·5 BRM P57	Monza	307·27/ 494·50	123·62/198·94
1963	Jim Clark	GB	1·5 Lotus 25-Climax	Monza	302·27/ 494·50	127·74/205·58
1964	John Surtees	GB	1·5 Ferrari 158	Monza	278·68/ 448·50	127·77/205·63
1965	Jackie Stewart	GB	1·5 BRM P261	Monza	271·54/ 437·00	130·46/209·96
1966	Ludovico Scarfiotti	I	3·0 Ferrari 312/66	Monza	242·96/ 391·00	135·92/218·75

Lap chart

1st LAP ORDER	1	2	3	4	5	6	7	8	9	10	11	12	13	14	15	16	17	18	19	20	21	22	23	24	25	26	27	28	29	30	31	32	33	34	35	36	37
6 R. Patrese	6	6	(6)	5	5	5	5	5	5	5	5	5	5	5	5	5	5	5	5	5	5	5	5	5	5	5	5	5	5	5	5	5	5	5	5	5	5
5 N. Piquet	5	5	28	28	28	28	28	28	28	28	28	28	28	28	28	28	28	28	28	28	28	28	28	(28)	27	27	(27)	28	28	28	28	28	28	28	28	28	28
27 P. Tambay	27	28	16	16	16	16	16	16	16	16	16	16	16	16	16	16	16	16	16	(16)	27	28	28	28	16	16	16	16	16	16	16	16	16	16	16	16	16
28 R. Arnoux	28	27	27	27	27	27	27	27	27	27	27	11	11	11	11	11	11	11	11	11	11	27	15	16	35		11	11	11	11	11	11	11	11	11	11	11
16 E. Cheever	16	16	15	15	15	15	15	15	11	11	11	27	27	27	27	27	27	27	27	27	15	16	35	(35)	11	11	11	11	11	11	11	11	11	11	11	11	11
22 A. De Cesaris	22	22	11	11	11	11	11	11	15	15	15	15	15	15	15	15	15	15	15	15	(11)	35	(15)	11	36	36	(36)	35	35	35	35	35	35	35	35	35	35
15 A. Prost	15	15	23	23	35	35	35	7	7	7	7	7	35	35	35	35	35	35	35	35	35	11	9	35	35	9	9	9	9	12	12	12					
11 E. De Angelis	11	11	12	35	7	7	7	35	35	35	35	35	9	9	9	9	9	9	9	9	9	9	36	(12)	9	9	36	36	12	36	36	36					
12 N. Mansell	12	12	35	7	12	12	9	9	9	9	9	12	12	12	12	12	12	12	36	36	12	(9)	12	9	12	12	12	36	(9)	1	1						
23 M. Baldi	23	23	7	12	9	9	12	12	12	12	12	36	36	36	36	36	36	36	36	12	12	(1)	3	1	1	1	1	1	1	29	29						
35 D. Warwick	35	35	9	9	1	36	36	36	36	36	1	1	1	1	1	1	1	1	1	1	1	3	(3)	29	29	29	29	29	25	25	25						
9 M. Winkelhock	9	7	1	1	36	1	1	1	1	1	3	3	3	3	3	3	3	25	25	25	25	25	(25)	29	30	30	30	25	30	30	30						
7 T. Watson	7	9	36	36	(23)	29	3	3	3	3	25	25	25	25	25	25	23	3	3	30	30	30	30	25	25	25	30	30	34	34							
1 K. Rosberg	1	8	40	40	29	3	25	25	25	25	29	29	29	29	29	29	(29)	29	30	29	29	(15)	25	25	34	34	34	34	34	33	33						
8 N. Lauda	8	1	29	29	30	25	29	29	29	29	30	30	30	30	30	30	30	30	30	30	30	30	25	34	33	33	33	33	33	31							
36 B. Giacomelli	36	36	30	30	3	30	30	30	30	30	30	34	34	34	34	34	34	34	34	34	34	34	33	33	33	31	31	31	31	4							
29 M. Surer	29	40	3	3	25	33	33	33	33	34	34	33	33	33	33	33	33	33	33	33	33	33	31	31	4	4	4	4	4	4							
40 S. Johansson	40	29	25	25	33	34	34	34	34	33	33	4	4	4	4	4	4	31	31	31	31	31	4	4													
30 T. Boutsen	30	30	(8)	33	4	4	4	4	4	4	31	31	31	31	31	4	4	4	4	4	4																
33 R. Guerrero	33	3	33	4	31	31	31	31	31	31	8	8	8	8	8	8	8	8	(8)	(8)																	
3 M. Alboreto	3	25	4	34	(32)	32	32	32	(32)	8	8	8																									
25 J. P. Jarier	25	33	34	32	32	8	8	8	8																												
4 D. Sullivan	4	4	32	31	8																																
34 J. Cecotto	34	34	31	8																																	
32 P. Ghinzani	32	32																																			
31 C. Fabi	31	31																																			

38	39	40	41	42	43	44	45	46	47	48	49	50	51	52
5	5	5	5	5	5	5	5	5	5	5	5	5	5	5
28	28	28	28	28	28	28	28	28	28	28	28	28	28	28
16	16	16	16	16	16	16	16	16	16	16	16	16	16	16
27	27	27	27	27	27	27	27	27	27	27	27	27	27	27
11	11	11	11	11	11	11	11	11	11	11	11	11	11	11
35	35	35	35	35	35	35	35	35	35	35	35	35	35	35
12	12	12	12	12	12	12	12	12	12	12	12	12	12	36
36	36	36	36	36	36	36	36	36	36	36	36	36	36	12
1	1	1	1	1	1	1	1	1	1	1	1	1	1	1
25	25	25	25	25	25	25	25	25	25	25	25	25		
29	29	29	29	29	29	29	29	29	29	29	29	29		
30	30	30	(30)	34	34	34	34	34	34	34	34	34		
34	34	34	34	34	33	33	34	33	33	33	33			
33	33	33	33	33	31	31	(31)							
31	31	31	31	31	4	(4)								
4	4	4	4	(4)										

Circuit data

Autodromo Nazionale di Monza, near Milan

Circuit length: 3·6039 miles/5·80 km

Race distance: 52 laps, 187·403 miles/301·600 km

Race weather: Warm, dry

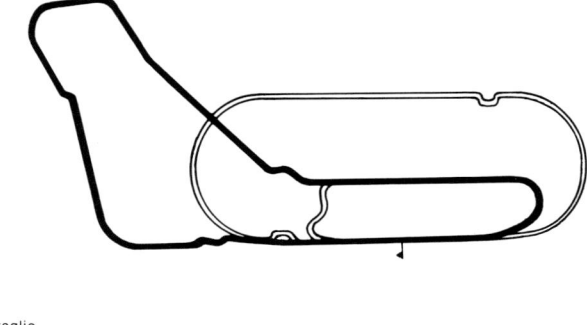

Curve di Lesmo
Curva del Serraglio
Variante Cariplo
Variante Ascari
Curva Grande
Variante Goodyear
Curvetta

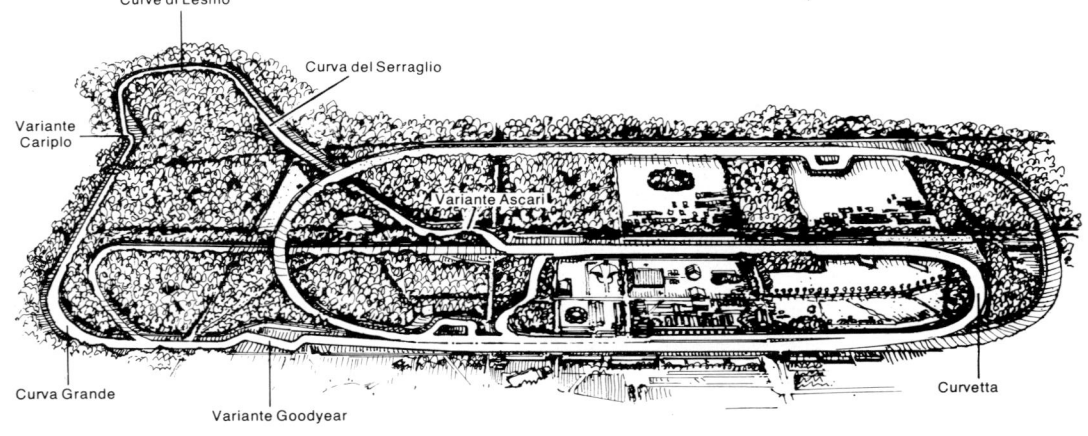

Fastest laps

Driver	Time	Lap
Nelson Piquet	1m 34·431s	20
René Arnoux	1m 34·592s	15
Eddie Cheever	1m 34·644s	9
Elio de Angelis	1m 34·735s	11
Alain Prost	1m 34·871s	24
Patrick Tambay	1m 34·886s	25
John Watson	1m 35·022s	13
Nigel Mansell	1m 35·035s	43
Bruno Giacomelli	1m 35·130s	51
Derek Warwick	1m 35·588s	17
Manfred Winkelhock	1m 35·853s	18
Mauro Baldi	1m 36·398s	4
Jean-Pierre Jarier	1m 36·567s	41
Keke Rosberg	1m 36·987s	43
Niki Lauda	1m 37·132s	8
Marc Surer	1m 37·585s	41
Michele Alboreto	1m 37·828s	16
Stefan Johansson	1m 37·965s	3
Johnny Cecotto	1m 38·412s	40
Roberto Guerrero	1m 38·444s	42
Thierry Boutsen	1m 38·476s	26
Corrado Fabi	1m 39·334s	55
Danny Sullivan	1m 39·516s	34
Piercarlo Ghinzani	1m 40·271s	4
Riccardo Patrese	2m 59·185s	1
Andrea de Cesaris	3m 04·569s	2

Points

WORLD CHAMPIONSHIP OF DRIVERS

1	Alain Prost	51 pts
2	René Arnoux	49
3	Nelson Piquet	46
4	Patrick Tambay	40
5	Keke Rosberg	25
6	John Watson	22
7	Eddie Cheever	21
8	Niki Lauda	12
9	Jacques Laffite	11
10	Michele Alboreto	10
11 =	Andrea de Cesaris	6
11 =	Nigel Mansell	6
13 =	Marc Surer	4
13 =	Riccardo Patrese	4
13 =	Derek Warwick	4
16	Mauro Baldi	3
17 =	Danny Sullivan	2
17 =	Elio de Angelis	2
19	Johnny Cecotto	1

CONSTRUCTORS' CUP

1	Ferrari	89 pts
2	Renault	72
3	Brabham	50
4	Williams	36
5	McLaren	34
6	Tyrrell	12
7	Alfa Romeo	9
8	Lotus	8
9 =	Arrows	4
9 =	Toleman	4
11	Theodore	1

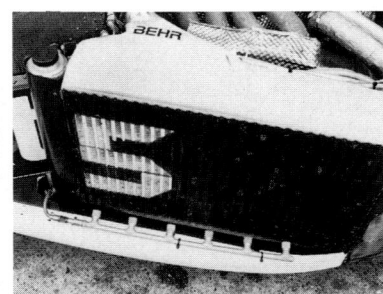

By spraying water at the intercooler, the Brabham team were able to lower the intake temperatures during qualifying. "It's like holding a wet hand out of the window of a moving automobile," was how Paul Rosche, Managing Director of engineering at BMW described this latest tweak. "The hand becomes cooler in the head wind than it would if it were dry."

1967	John Surtees	GB	3·9 Honda RA300	Monza	242·96/ 391·00	140·50/226·12
1968	Denny Hulme	NZ	3·0 McLaren M7A-Ford	Monza	242·96/ 391·00	145·41/234·02
1969	Jackie Stewart	GB	3·0 Matra MS80-Ford	Monza	242·96/ 391·00	146·97/236·52
1970	Clay Regazzoni	CH	3·0 Ferrari 312B-1/70	Monza	242·96/ 391·00	147·08/236·67
1971	Peter Gethin	GB	3·0 BRM P160	Monza	196·51/ 316·25	150·75/242·62
1972	Emerson Fittipaldi	BR	3·0 JPS/Lotus 72-Ford	Monza	197·36/ 317·63	131·61/211·81
1973	Ronnie Peterson	S	3·0 JPS/Lotus 72-Ford	Monza	197·36/ 317·63	132·63/213·45
1974	Ronnie Peterson	S	3·0 JPS/Lotus 72-Ford	Monza	186·76/ 300·56	135·10/217·42
1975	Clay Regazzoni	CH	3·0 Ferrari 312T/75	Monza	186·76/ 300·56	135·48/218·03
1976	Ronnie Peterson	S	3·0 March 761-Ford	Monza	187·41/ 301·60	124·12/199·75
1977	Mario Andretti	USA	3·0 JPS/Lotus 78-Ford	Monza	187·41/ 301·60	128·01/206·02
1978	Niki Lauda	A	3·0 Brabham BT46-Alfa Romeo	Monza	144·16/ 232·00	128·95/207·53
1979	Jody Scheckter	ZA	3·0 Ferrari 312T-4	Monza	180·20/ 290·00	131·85/212·18
1980	Nelson Piquet	BR	3·0 Brabham BT49-Ford	Imola	186·41/ 300·00	113·98/183·44
1981	Alain Prost	F	1·5 Renault RE30 t/c	Monza	187·40/ 301·60	129·87/209·00
1982	René Arnoux	F	1·5 Renault RE30B t/c	Monza	187·40/ 301·60	136·39/219·50
1983	Nelson Piquet	BR	1·5 Brabham BT52B-BMW t/c	Monza	187·40/ 301·60	135·18/217·55

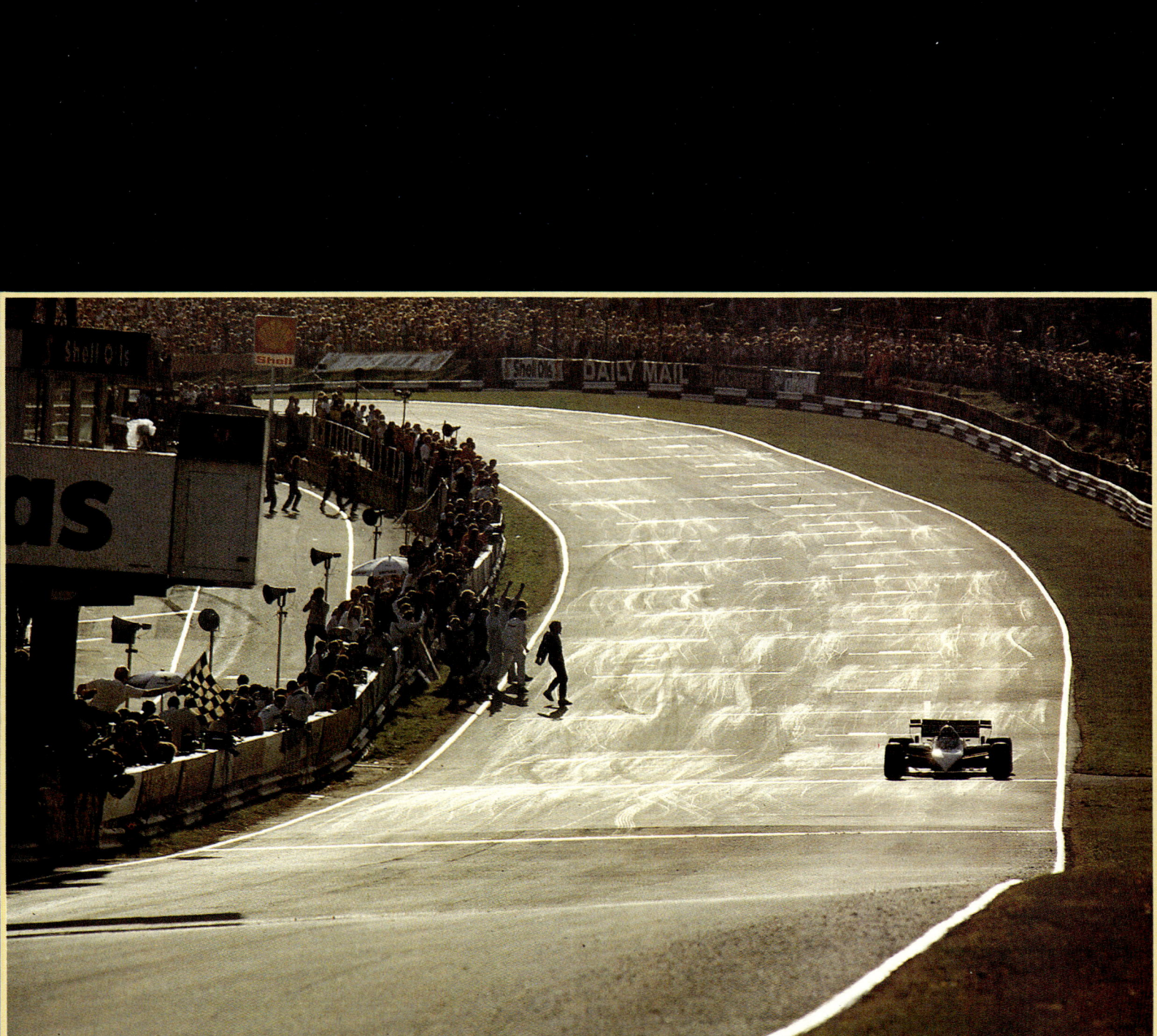

JOHN PLAYER GRAND PRIX OF EUROPE

Nelson Piquet crosses the Brands Hatch starting grid for the final time to take his second win in succession and strengthen his challenge for the championship (opposite).
Photo: Nigel Snowdon

Cadwell Park, Donington, Mallory Park, Thruxton, Oulton Park, Silverstone Grand Prix, Brands Hatch Club, Silverstone Club, Snetterton; Nelson Piquet had won races on them all. But there was nothing quite so satisfying as bringing his Parmalat Brabham-BMW across the grid on the Brands Hatch Grand Prix circuit for the 76th and final time on September 25. Now his record was complete; he had won races at every major British circuit but, more important, he had taken his championship tally to within two points of Alain Prost.

The Renault-Elf driver, finishing second, had done all that he could. There was no answer to Piquet's speed at Brands Hatch and Prost was pleased with this result at a circuit which, hitherto, had confounded the French team. Prost was also pleased to see Piquet rather than René Arnoux levering himself from the winning car. Had it been the man Alain loved to hate, then Arnoux would have been leading the championship by one point. But Arnoux's challenge for the honour of being the first French World Champion had been weakened considerably by a spin early in the race. The Ferrari finished in ninth place leaving René eight points behind Prost and very much the outsider with just one race to run.

Indeed, Ferrari's seemingly insurmountable lead in the Constructors' Championship had been whittled down, not so much by Prost's second place, but by the failure of the red cars to score any points for the first time since Detroit. Apart from Arnoux's worst result in seven races, Patrick Tambay's slim chances of winning the championship had ended against the bank at Druids when brake trouble cost the Frenchman fourth place.

Initially, the championship battle had been confused by the performance of Elio de Angelis and Riccardo Patrese. The JPS Lotus driver had taken his first pole position with a car and tyre combination which worked perfectly. Patrese's Brabham was alongside but the two Italians came to grief when de Angelis challenged for the lead and the two cars collided. Both spun, de Angelis retiring eventually with engine failure and Patrese dropping to an eventual seventh place.

Nevertheless, John Player, sponsors of the event, were heartened by the performance of Nigel Mansell as the Englishman repeated his drive at Silverstone, this time working his way into third place and taking fastest lap. Andrea de Cesaris had a trouble-free race to finish fourth in the Marlboro Alfa Romeo but the Italian might have been forced to defend his position had the fire extinguisher not gone off in the cockpit of Derek Warwick's Candy Toleman-Hart 20 laps from the finish. Warwick persevered to finish fifth with Bruno Giacomelli following his team mate to take his first point of the season.

The race, taking the convenient title of 'Grand Prix of Europe', replaced the proposed New York Grand Prix, cancelled due to political and planning problems. The RAC Motor Sports Association and Brands Hatch gambled heavily but their excellent organisation was rewarded by glorious weather and a healthy crowd.

The second half of the race may have lacked excitement but the result ensured the championship would remain on a knife-edge. Piquet's win was the second in succession for the Brazilian and just as convincing as his victory at Monza two weeks before. In fact, it had been much more strenuous for the Brabham driver, the switch-back nature making him work hard for nine vital points and the completion of a personal ambition.

ENTRY AND PRACTICE

For the sponsors, it was a dream come true. There, up on the rostrum, was Elio de Angelis, celebrating his first pole position, enthusing over the handling of his Lotus-Renault and speaking with emotion about Colin Chapman. The media, tiring of discussions over the championship, plunged into print.

"It's a pity the old man is not here," said Elio. "He would have loved this – both for myself and for him, especially after the problems we have had this year."

Those problems seemed very much in the past as de Angelis dominated proceedings from the moment practice began in warm and dry conditions on Friday morning. The Italian driver was fastest in three of the four sessions, the combination of the 94T, Renault power and Pirelli tyres working well on a circuit which required high downforce above all else. Elio set the fastest time on Friday afternoon even though his engine was misfiring slightly at peak revs and he prepared to defend his position the following day.

Saturday dawned damp and grey and the track was wet for the first 40 minutes of the unofficial session. It was during this period that de Angelis was caught out as he put two wheels on the grass at Druids, lost control of the Lotus and came to a halt in the catch-fencing. Fortunately, he was in the spare car at the time, the incident having damaged the front suspension pick-up points, and he returned to the pits to take over his race car. Running his first set of qualifiers later in the day, de Angelis improved his time and then waited for the anticipated challenge from Brabham. It never came. The closest anyone got was when Patrese worked his Brabham round in 1m 12.458s, but even that was not as quick as de Angelis had managed on Friday. Elio never did use his second set of qualifiers . . .

Patrese's time, however, had edged Nigel Mansell off the front row and the Englishman was unable to respond. One of the first to leave the pits when practice got under way, Mansell had a moment at Paddock which more or less finished his chances on the first set of qualifiers. Then, just as he was in the middle of his flying lap on the second set, the Lotus arrived at Surtees to find the track strewn with debris following a spin a few seconds before by Nelson Piquet. As a result, Mansell failed to improve his time although he did manage to retain third place overall – thanks, mainly, to Piquet's aforementioned spin.

The fact that he did spin was scarcely surprising since the Brabham, on full qualifying boost, was terrifying to behold as Nelson twitched his way along Cooper Straight. And this was in spite of the addition of Ferrari-type rear wings. During tests at Snetterton, Brabham had found the extra downforce generated by the wings worth the small trade-off in drag although it took most of Friday's practice at Brands to rid the car of the resulting understeer. Because of the spin, therefore, Piquet did not improve his time although he remained fourth on the grid and, more important perhaps, the leading championship contender.

Indeed, Piquet was more interested in the progress made by his three rivals and, at the end of practice, the Ferraris filled row three with Prost and Cheever on row four. Arnoux was the quicker of the two Italian cars, René complaining that there was not as much grip, while Tambay, who had taken part in the test session at Brands Hatch with a C2B, said the C3 offered little improvement. Apart from having understeer and losing boost on Friday, Tambay had to survive a potentially hazardous moment during the final session. Both Ferrari drivers had complained of a temperature imbalance with the Goodyear qualifiers and Tambay was adjusting his roll bar to suit the rapidly changing handling as the front and rear tyres reached their peak at different times. As he crossed the bump at the start-and-finish line, Tambay's left hand slipped off the adjuster and accidentally triggered the fire extinguisher which, in turn, cut the electrics. Thus, the Ferrari driver found himself coasting trowards Paddock Bend at 170 mph while being sprayed with extinguisher fluid! Somehow he managed to get the car round the corner before pulling off and quickly evacuating the cockpit. After that, he deserved sixth place on the grid.

Tambay had been delighted with the handling of his car while running slicks on the damp but drying track during the morning session. Eddie Cheever felt much the same about the handling of his Renault when comparing it with the struggle he was having with the car in the dry. To add to his problems, he suffered a turbo failure on Saturday afternoon although, by then, he had improved to take seventh place on his first set of qualifiers.

Alain Prost had the additional hassle of dealing with

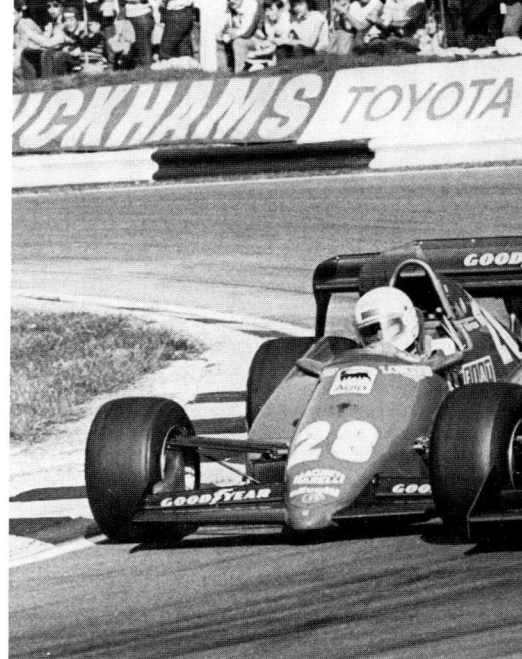

No love lost here as Arnoux and Cheever dispute fourth place not long before the Ferrari driver spun off. Cheever lost what might have been third place when a stud broke on his helmet visor (right).

the pressures accorded to the leader of the World Championship and the little Frenchman arrived at Brands Hatch to find he was at the centre of a controversy over an interview published in *L'Equipe*. Alain had made some rather pointed remarks about René Arnoux, but he went to the trouble of holding a press conference to explain that his conversation with the journalist in question had been 'off the record' and he did not expect to see what was supposed to have been light-hearted remarks appear in print. Prost agreed he had little time for Arnoux as a person but added that he would never criticise René's driving in the manner implied in the story. All very plausable – but scarcely the sort of worry Prost needed at this stage in the championship.

As it was, he had enough on his plate coping with the RE40, now fitted with a large rear wing similar to Ferrari – and Brabham. Alain was back in chassis number 05 (the one crashed at Zandvoort) since he preferred the feel of this car to the new chassis produced for Monza. Given the team's poor record at Brands Hatch, Prost was relieved to be no further back than the fourth row after failing to improve his time during the final session.

Manfred Winkelhock also failed to improve on Saturday after experiencing a misfire on his BMW. The ATS team had modified the exhaust system and fitted very large front wings and the German driver

> **SEPTEMBER:**
> *Michele Alboreto signs for Ferrari; Tambay axed.*

made spectacular viewing while the going was wet on Saturday morning. Niki Lauda was one of the few drivers to spin while coping with turbo power in the tricky conditions and the Austrian had to give best to his team-mate after almost losing control on a Brands Hatch bump while running his final set of qualifiers. Once again, there had been several revisions to the exhaust, turbo and radiator installations and Lauda had the added complication of suffering an engine problem on Friday morning and then losing time while mechanics completed the lengthy change to a fresh unit. John Watson had engine problems of a different kind when his TAG turbo refused to start while warm on Saturday afternoon. None the less, the Ulsterman gradually worked his times down to a respectable lap worth 10th place on the grid ahead of Derek Warwick's Toleman-Hart.

To say that Warwick was disappointed to be that far back would be understating the case. Flushed by a fine win in the endurance race at Brands Hatch the week before and confident that the Toleman/Pirelli combination would show well on one of his favourite circuits, Warwick had talked confidently about taking a place on the front three rows of the grid. Those plans received a considerable setback when the team discovered that the Pirelli qualifiers were no better than the race tyres – on their chassis. Warwick's mood darkened when he discovered that Lotus, on the other hand, were gaining two seconds a lap when running qualifiers. On Friday, Warwick tried a set of qualifiers but, after just three corners at racing speeds, the rubber had gone off. He set his fastest times using race rubber on both days and it was little consolation to learn that he had been the quickest driver while the track was wet on Saturday morning. Bruno Giacomelli was a tenth of a second slower in 12th place.

The Alfa Romeo team also arrived at Brands Hatch in a confident mood following a successful run during the test session when the 183T displayed good balance and grip. Further modifications to the waste gates should have reduced the throttle lag but, from the

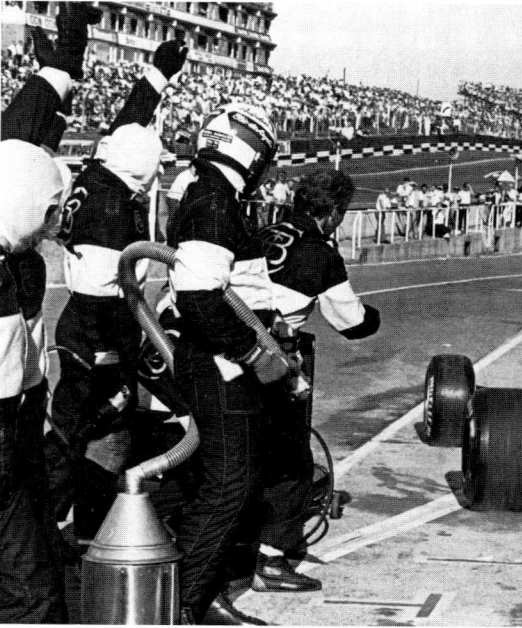

start of practice, Andrea de Cesaris was unhappy with the handling. He was even more unhappy with himself on Friday afternoon when he lost control at Westfield, the Alfa Romeo flying off the road and damaging the left-rear corner. The car was repaired in time for the final session but de Cesaris found the engine to be so poor that he switched to the T-car. In the end, his best lap was the one just before he crashed and Andrea had to make do with 14th place, a couple of tenths quicker than his team-mate, Mauro Baldi.

Encouraging tests with the Williams-Honda lent weight to stories that the team might bring one along to Brands Hatch but, in the event, a shortage of spares meant Williams made do with their Cosworth cars for the last time. Since that successful chapter in the Williams history was about to close, Keke Rosberg made an arrangement with Frank to buy an FW08C-Cosworth. They agreed on a price for chassis number nine – and then Keke promptly dumped it into the catch-fencing at Dingle Dell! As usual, the Finn had been running on the limit when he put a wheel off line and he walked back to check on the terms of the purchase with Frank! It was the first time Rosberg had crashed in over a year and he took over the team's spare car to become the fastest Cosworth on the grid. That meant 16th place, a suitable indication of the progress made by the turbos in 15 months since Keke had taken pole at Brands Hatch for the 1982 British Grand Prix.

Rosberg's shunt was the last thing the team needed since they had their hands full with a three-car entry for this race. As a token of gratitude for Jonathan Palmer's services as test driver, Williams had entered the 1983 Formula 2 Champion in the hope that it might help him earn a permanent Formula 1 drive with another team for 1984. Jonathan was entrusted with chassis number six, last used by Rosberg in the Race of Champions, and the team produced the tub from chassis number two and built it up as a spare following Keke's visit to the catch-fencing. Unfortunately, it was not ready in time for Jacques Laffite to use following an engine failure on Friday morning. That was to be the start of a bad weekend for the Frenchman since the final session would be a complete disaster; his first set of qualifiers spoiled by leaking safety bolts on one rim and Jacques had difficulty warming up the second set, the rear tyres having gone off by the time he had worked his fronts to the correct temperature. The net result was 29th place on the time sheet and the second failure to qualify in succession . . .

And Jacques's frustration was to be compounded by the fact that Palmer managed to qualify in 25th place, a fine achievement considering the young Englishman had no experience of getting the most out of the brief competitive life in his qualifiers.

Sporting yet another change of wardrobe to suit their latest sponsor, the MacConnal-Mason art gallery, Arrows arrived at Brands with few alterations to their cars. Running as large a rear wing as they dared, Arrows managed to keep Marc Surer competitive with the Cosworth yardstick, Rosberg's Williams, the Swiss taking 17th place with Thierry Boutsen fractionally slower. This was a most creditable performance from the Belgian driver who had never seen the long circuit at Brands Hatch before. His previous experience had been limited to racing Formula Ford on the Club circuit and, since the back section was tricky and difficult to learn, his ability to adapt to the circuit quickly was another indication of his exceptional promise. Spirit brought along their latest car, the 101, but just a few laps on Friday morning told the team that the engine installation was in need of some fundamental changes and the car was put away for the rest of the weekend, Stefan Johansson returning to his usual brace of Formula 2-based chassis. The Swede's enthusiasm for driving racing cars bubbled out of the

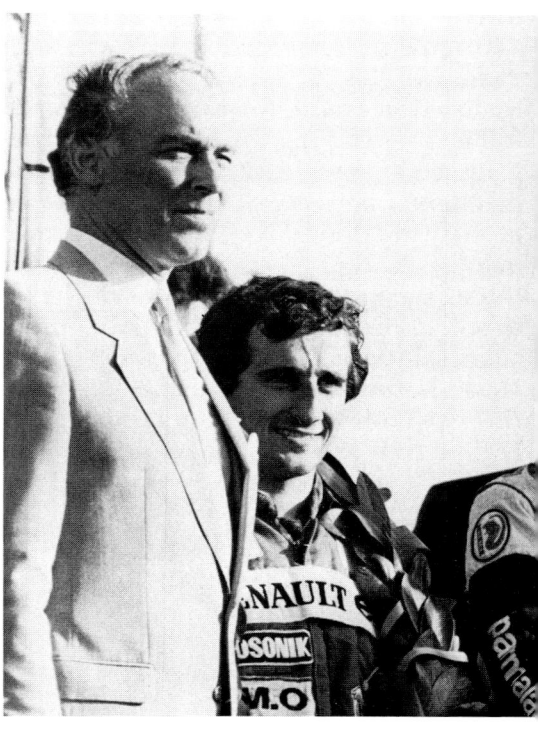

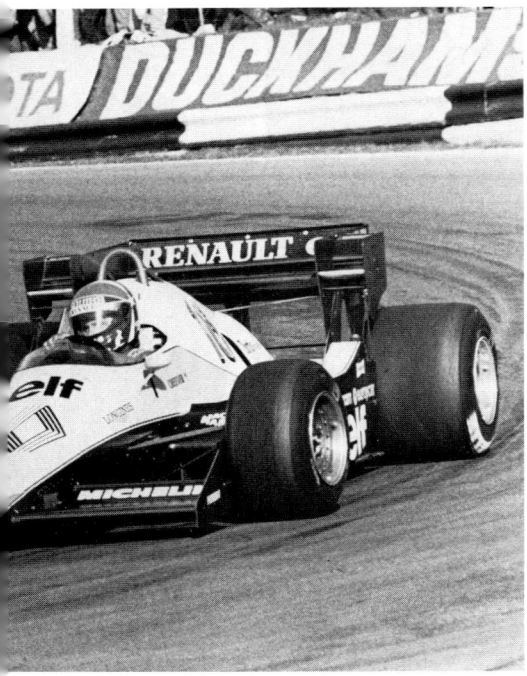

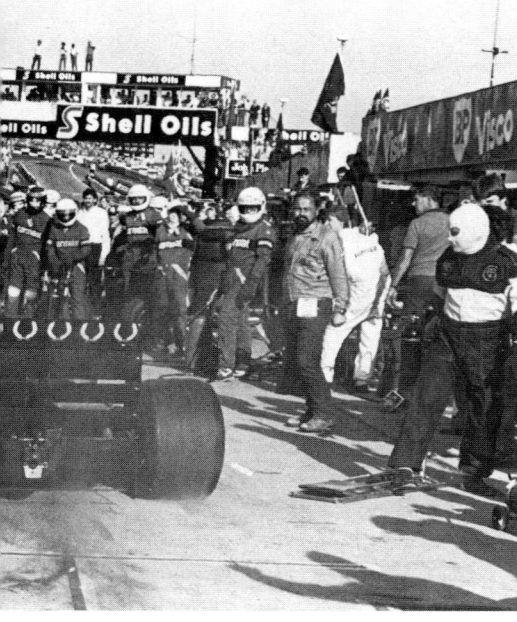

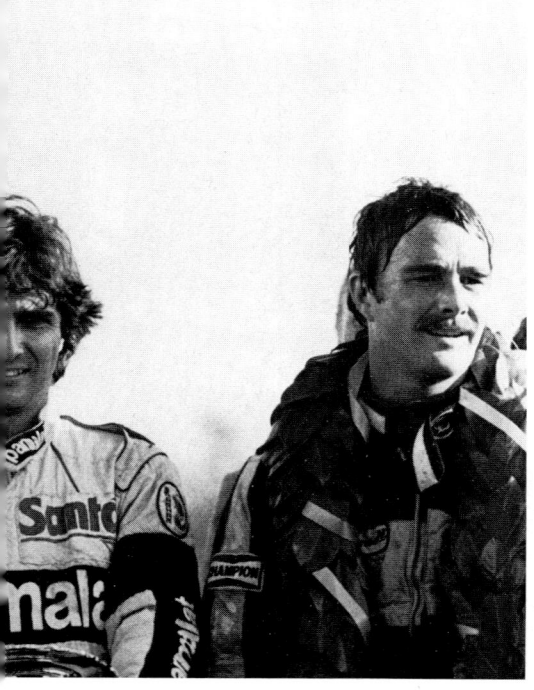

Nigel Mansell blasts away from the pits after the Lotus mechanics had turned in a brilliant performance by dealing with their man in under 10 seconds (below left).

Three men looking pleased with life: Prost, happy to have finished second at a circuit which had defeated Renault in the past; Piquet, content with nine points and the completion of an impressive tally of victories at British circuits; Mansell, satisfied with third place and a hardworking drive on his second set of tyres (bottom).

cockpit as he flung the Spirit around the circuit during the wet session on Saturday but, when the serious business got under way, Stefan's sense of humour was put to the test when the Honda began to misfire once more. Doubts over the team's future with Honda were not helped when news filtered through that Williams had not experienced any misfire problems with their turbo during testing although history had shown that running a car in testing and during the heat of a Grand Prix qualifying session were two entirely different propositions.

Testing was the last thing on the Tyrrell team's mind when they rushed through their second 012 chassis for Danny Sullivan. The new car had not turned a wheel before practice started and yet the American was running strongly throughout, his only problem being a blown DFY on Friday morning. Danny took 20th place while, for a couple of tense minutes during the final session, it seemed that the much vaunted Michele Alboreto might not qualify. The young Italian, of course, was the centre of speculation over a drive with Ferrari for 1984 but, for the time being, he was fully occupied with trying to discover why his car was nearly *three* seconds slower than it had been during testing. Alboreto even resorted to trying his team-mate's car briefly on Saturday and, in the end, his time from Friday was just good enough for last place on the grid. Roberto Guerrero, in 21st place, was the sole Theodore representative when Johnny Cecotto's entry was withdrawn at the last minute. There was talk of the Venezuelan driver refusing to pay his fine for arriving late at the drivers' briefing at Monza and another source mentioned the fact that he was having difficulty with sponsorship money. Either way, Cecotto was present in the pit lane and not looking unduly worried about his role as spectator.

Both Ligiers qualified, Raul Boesel being just three-tenths slower than Jean-Pierre Jarier who, as usual, had the use of the team's DFY. Piercarlo Ghinzani managed to qualify his Osella-Alfa Romeo after running an additional rear wing but his team-mate, Corrado Fabi, failed to make the cut. First reserve was Kenny Acheson, the Ulsterman continuing to improve in the RAM March although inconsistent Pirellis and appalling handling meant Acheson faced a difficult task and, having qualified on Friday, he was unable to improve the next day and suffered the anguish of watching his place being taken by Ghinzani.

RACE

Had the race been run a week earlier, on the date allocated for the 1000-kilometre endurance race, then we would have had the first wet race of the year with a minimal crowd. But the sun shone on Brands Hatch and the RAC with a most unseasonal display of brilliance and the crowd, while perhaps not the massive turn-out seen the previous July, was by no means short of the number needed to turn the event into a profitable venture.

The warm-up was scheduled for 10.30 a.m., thus giving the teams nearly four hours to make final preparations. Tambay was concerned about a drop in boost while Arnoux had a slight electrical misfire. Similarly, Eddie Cheever took over the spare car while his mechanics ripped the wiring apart on his usual chassis in an attempt to trace a minor fault. Prost, meanwhile, was perfectly happy with his car and set the fastest lap of the session, pole position man de Angelis not far behind. But there was trouble for his front row partner when Patrese came in to report a misfire at high revs and the Brabham mechanics set about replacing various electrical parts. Alboreto had switched to Sullivan's car, Winkelhock broke a turbo and the McLaren mechanics wasted valuable time trying to coax Watson's engine back to life.

The Brabham team had finished their work on

Patrese's car by the time the track was officially opened once more but the Italian was soon back in the pits to say that the misfire was as bad as ever. The spare car, tailored for Piquet, was hurriedly wheeled out and Patrese set off to take his place on the grid. During the 20-minute wait for the final count-down, Riccardo stood patiently by the car while his mechanics adjusted the pedals and the seat to suit the Italian.

Twenty-six cars completed the final lap but only 25 took the green light, Jean-Pierre Jarier's Ligier not making the race after a shaft running between the engine and gearbox had broken. Although de Angelis had pole, he did have the traditional Brands Hatch disadvantage of starting on a slight slope and, as the back of the car stepped out of line, Patrese made a perfect start and led into Paddock. For the first few yards, Mansell seemed to be out of control as the Lotus waltzed across from right to left but the Englishman kept up the momentum and was looking for a way inside his team-mate under braking for Druids – only to have de Angelis shut the door rather smartly.

Cheever had made another dazzling start, this time from the fourth row, the Renault rocketing between the Ferraris and actually looking for a way around the outside of Piquet as they approached Druids. The Brabham driver locked his right-front wheel as he saw what he thought was going to be a large accident between the Lotus drivers. The pack bunched dramatically, Piquet almost ramming the back of Mansell's car. For a moment it looked as though Cheever would actually take fourth place from Piquet but the Brabham had regained control as they swept along Cooper Straight, Nelson even thinking about depriving Mansell of third spot.

All this activity had allowed Patrese and de Angelis to pull away and, at the end of the lap, there was a gap of two or three car lengths to Mansell, who appeared to be holding the rest at bay. Indeed, the Lotus driver was fast realising that his set of Pirellis were less than perfect and this was confirmed when Piquet took third place as they reached Hawthorn for the second time. Cheever passed the Lotus in a determined move going into Dingle Dell Corner and, by the end of lap three, Mansell had fallen behind Prost and Arnoux.

That gave Prost a clear road to catch Cheever and the two Renaults circulated nose-to-tail for a couple of laps, Prost making it clear that he wanted by, Cheever making it equally clear that he was in no mood to step aside having made such a good start. Prost eventually took fourth place going into Paddock at the beginning of lap nine and attention then shifted to a battle which had been growing more intense at the front.

Initially, de Angelis had been content to sit behind Patrese since the Brabham had superior straight line speed. Elio changed his mind, however, when Piquet began to close and the Lotus made a couple of attempts at nosing inside the Brabham under braking. The Lotus driver had driven with commendable smoothness but, on lap 11, he lost that composure when he tried to slip inside Patrese under braking for Surtees. Considering it was a tricky corner leading onto a long straight, it was not a wise place to carry out such a move and, in any case, Patrese predictably shut the door. The two cars touched and spun, Patrese losing a place to his team-mate while de Angelis revved furiously as he slithered across the grass and regained the track to take sixth place. Two laps later and the pole position man's race was run, the Lotus pulling into the pits with its engine cooked. De Angelis was to say that he knew it was about to fail before he became involved with Patrese but the more cynical observers were to suggest that the V6 did not take kindly to the harsh treatment as de Angelis vented his frustration on the throttle and the Brands Hatch grass . . .

Piquet could not have asked for more. Into the bargain, he had Patrese in second place keeping Prost at bay although the Renault was to move ahead four

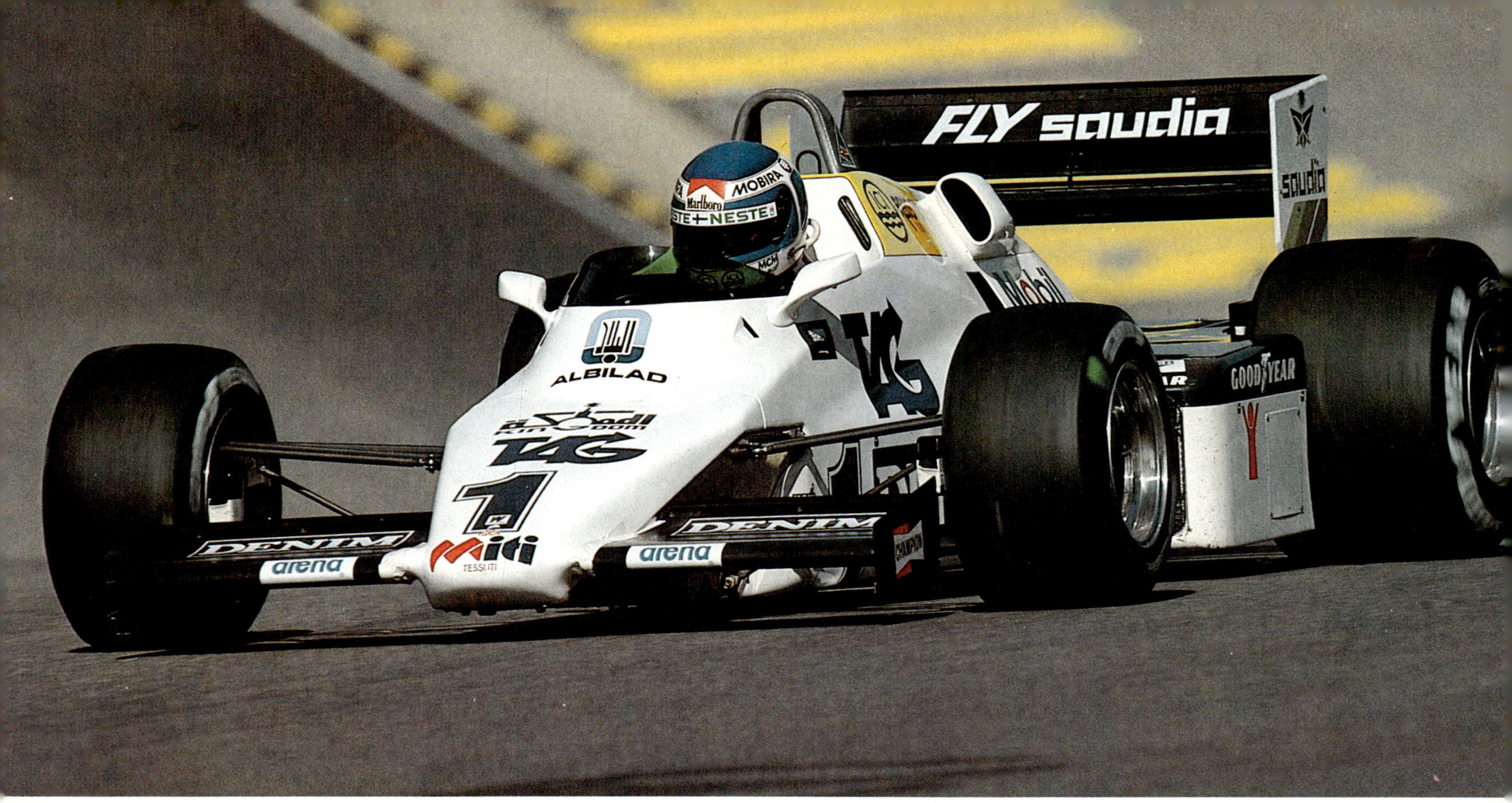
FLY saudia
saudia
ALBILAD
TAG
1
DENIM
arena
GOODYEAR
Mobil

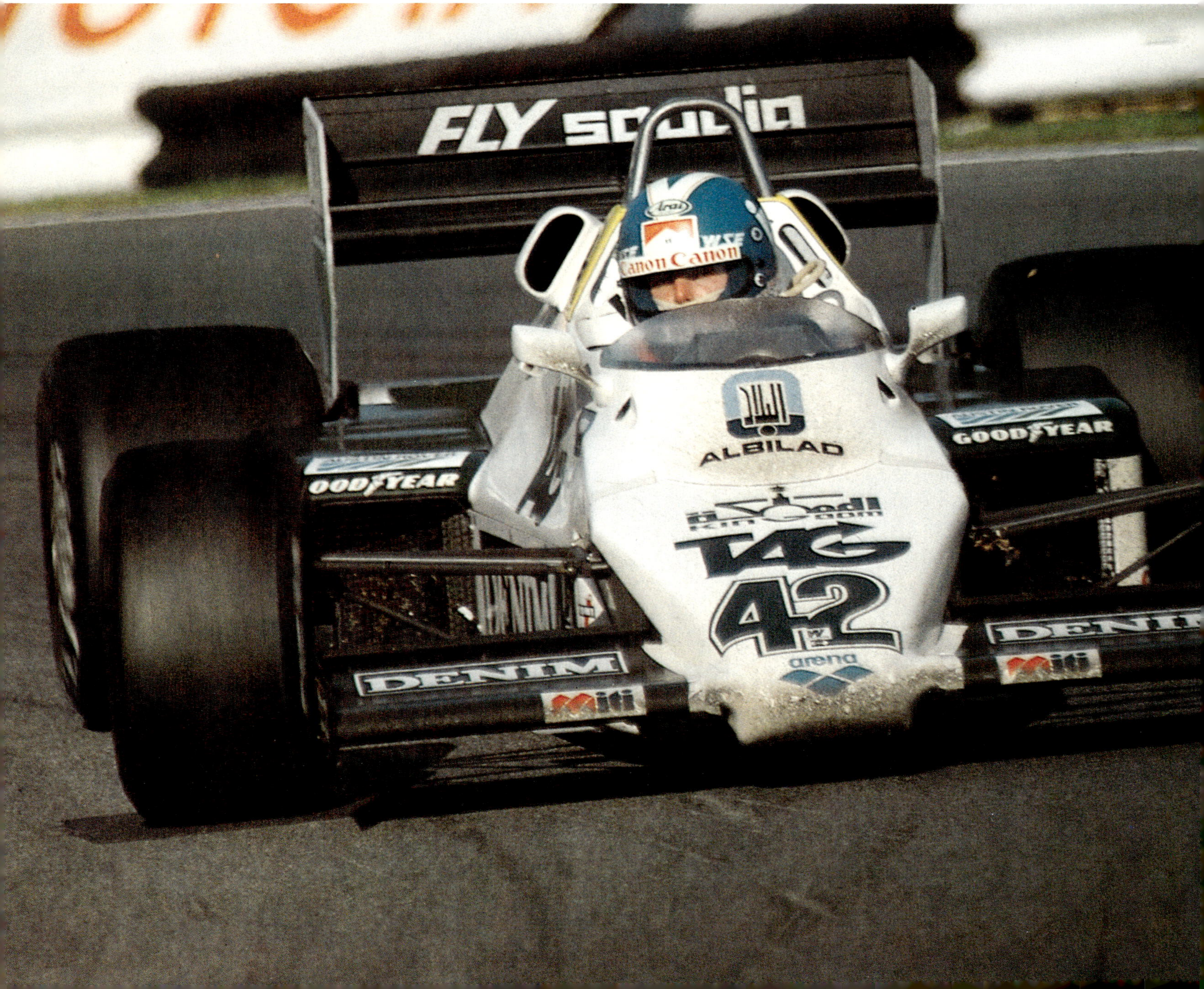
FLY saudia
ALBILAD
TAG
42
GOODYEAR
DENIM
Canon Canon
arena

laps later. The gap to Piquet was just over 10 seconds but Nelson put the hammer down and reeled off a string of quick laps which matched anything Prost had to offer. Patrese, lapping over a second slower than the leaders, fell into the clutches of Cheever who, in turn, had been caught by Arnoux. After 15 laps, however, the Ferrari driver's tyres lost their edge and his brake pedal began to give trouble. Then, on lap 20, a disastrous mistake by the Frenchman.

Going into Surtees, the Ferrari got away from Arnoux and he rolled backwards across the kerb on the outside of the corner. Although he had not hit anything, Arnoux came to rest straddling the kerb, the rear wheels spinning in the dirt, the fronts raised slightly off the ground as the car rocked gently on the edge of the concrete. Arnoux called for help and was pushed onto the track to resume in 19th place. That move, of course, raised the question of receiving outside help but, since Arnoux was to finish out of the points, it did not really matter. Besides, there was no question that the Ferrari had come to halt in a dangerous position and he had managed to keep the engine running.

Thus, after 20 laps, Piquet was maintaining a gap of around 11 seconds over Prost with Patrese, his Brabham suffering from slight damage to the rear suspension as a result of the earlier incident, running ahead of Cheever and Mansell. They had been joined by Tambay (whose Goodyears were also losing grip), Winkelhock, de Cesaris, Warwick, Watson, Lauda and Rosberg (the Williams in a different league to the remaining Cosworth runners), the 10 cars running in a high-speed train although, with so few overtaking opportunities at Brands Hatch, the order was to remain much the same for the next few laps.

There had been surprisingly few retirements but Lauda added his name to the list at the end of his 26th lap when he came in with engine failure, the Austrian having just passed his team-mate. Watson was having trouble with his rear wing, the side-piece which received support from the top of the sidepod, having come adrift. When Watson made his pit stop, John Barnard was on hand to rip the offending wing section off the car but that left the main side-plate with inadequate support. The plan was to send Watson back out while the team prepared a new wing but Watson never got that far, the aerofoil finally breaking up and depositing the McLaren into the catch-fencing at Hawthorn – at very high speed. A visibly shaken Watson stepped from his car and spent the remainder of his 150th Grand Prix sitting quietly at the marshals' post.

Several laps earlier, Danny Sullivan had made an equally spectacular exit when an oil line supplying the pressure guage in the cockpit of his Tyrrell broke – just as he was approaching Paddock. The oil found its way onto the rear tyres and Sullivan spun harmlessly on the exit of the corner. Along the way, however, he had crossed a kerb and a combination of sparks and a hot exhaust set the oil alight. Unaware of the blaze at the back of his car, Sullivan selected a gear and set off for Druids where, once again, the back of the Tyrrell began to slide wildly, Sullivan now realising something was amiss. With smoke and flames billowing from the car, the American calmly pulled off at the back of the paddock where marshals well and truly coated the car with extinguisher powder. Prior to this, Sullivan had been running in company with his team-mate and Stefan Johansson although the Spirit driver was to have a lucky escape when Watson's McLaren, which had rejoined in front of Johansson, lost its wing and sent a section of aerofoil spinning through the air to smash the windscreen on the Swede's car.

The pit stops began in earnest when Cheever came in at the end of lap 35. A battle for third place between Patrese and Mansell broke up when the Brabham came in a few laps later and, similarly, a fight for fifth between Tambay and de Cesaris ended when the Alfa Romeo came into a busy pit lane on the same lap as Arnoux. Everything went according to plan, particularly for the Lotus team who had Mansell away in 9.62s. By fitting pre-heated Pirellis, the Englishman was able to keep Eddie Cheever at bay on his first lap back on the track but the dispute became academic when the Renault dashed into the pits once more at the end of lap 45. A screw holding his visor in place had broken and it took Eddie some time to get the message across and even longer for the mechanics to slap some tape on the side of his helmet.

The Ferrari team had taken the opportunity of revising their tyre choice during the pit stops, Tambay leaving with a more suitable combination of the softer 'C' all round with a harder 'B' on the left rear. With everything to gain and little to lose on Arnoux's car, they gambled on 'Cs' all round but René had soon worked his way through that lot and was back in 14 laps later for more rubber, his race and, perhaps, his championship chances in tatters.

As ever, the Brabham team kept Piquet running until as late as possible, the leader coming in at the end of lap 44. The small amount of fuel was quickly added but a problem with the air gun used on the left-rear tyre meant Nelson was delayed by 19 seconds, some 10 seconds longer than the team would have liked. Fortunately, his lead was such that Piquet was able to rejoin with Prost still about 12 seconds in arrears. The Renault team had fitted a softer set which gave Prost understeer and, in addition, the stop in the pits brought a slight engine misfire which precluded any hopes the Frenchman may have had of catching Piquet. Besides, his second place was secure since Tambay was a further 22 seconds behind and suffering from brake trouble as Mansell, very happy with the balance from his second set of tyres, moved in to attack.

Tambay could offer no resistance as the Lotus moved ahead under braking for Paddock and, a few laps later, Tambay's right front brake was to lock completely at Druids and send the Ferrari into the barrier and retirement. Tambay was uninjured but he climbed from his car in the knowledge that his run at the championship was at an end.

De Cesaris, who had been challenging the Ferrari at the time, was happy to accept fourth place and the Italian was equally relieved to note that Warwick had dropped back after closing to within a few seconds of the Alfa Romeo. The Toleman driver had been occupied for most of lap 56 by the fire extinguisher which had gone off in the cockpit. Apart from being unable to see where he was going for a while, Warwick then had to cope with the fact that his right hand and part of his right thigh had been frozen by the fluid! Gradually the feel came back but, by then, de Cesaris had pulled away. At least the Toleman was running strongly and, backing that up in sixth place, came Bruno Giacomelli, about to score a point for the first time since the 1982 German Grand Prix. Patrese, the last driver to remain unlapped, had slipped to seventh while Manfred Winkelhock was the first Goodyear runner home, the ATS taking eighth place ahead of Arnoux and Cheever. An impressive drive by Alboreto, considering he had lost fourth gear on the third lap, came to an end when his engine failed with 11 laps to go. Rosberg had also retired with engine failure but Palmer, driving steadily, had moved ahead of Ghinzani and Boesel during the opening stages of the race. Ghinzani then stopped three times to attend to a sticking throttle, but not before he had covered Palmer's car with oil to such an extent that the Englishman's mirrors were useless. He behaved impeccably, however, when shown the blue flag.

Piquet, in fact, had lapped the Williams twice by the time he took the chequered flag to signal a superb win. Prost was the first person to congratulate the Brazilian when he stepped from his car, the Frenchman playfully flicking water at Nelson as he added up the championship score. Two points between them with one race to go and, while that may not have been cause for wild celebration, the Renault team produced a rich, creamy cake in the shape of a racing car. Mansell, after such a hard drive, was slightly put out at receiving nothing more than a bunch of flowers. Piquet, on the other hand, had an impressive trophy to complete his 'British Collection'.

The 'silly season' of rumour and gossip was in full swing, indeed, almost out of control, at Brands Hatch. Alain Prost's signature on a Renault contract had done nothing to ease speculation and attention was fixed on the future of Michele Alboreto – and just about anyone else with an international licence. Here is a sample of the stories bouncing from motor home to motor home:

Alan Jones figured in the future plans of the Ligier-Renault team although no one had seen or heard from the Australian driver for quite some time. Originally, Jones had been linked with McLaren but that story had been forgotten even though the plans for John Watson's future remained in doubt, the Ulsterman as much in the dark about McLaren's intentions as the word-hundry media.

Judging by Renault's reluctance to agree to Eddie Cheever's terms for another year, the American was seen as a likely candidate for the Ligier-Renault team. On the other hand, he was friendly with Mansour Ojjeh of TAG and he was now associated with McLaren . . .

As for the Renault Number Two seat, it seemed just about every driver on the grid was talking to the French team. Watson had made it clear he might be available – as had Jarier, Surer and Formula 2's Philippe Strieff. But Renault, it was said, were more interested in Derek Warwick – and Patrick Tambay, once the news broke that the Frenchman had been axed by Ferrari. His replacement at Maranello would be Michele Alboreto (and this, finally, laid to rest stories that Ferrari might run a 'B' team with outside sponsorship).

Thus Tyrrell had a vacancy – maybe two – and Corrado Fabi's Italian connection would be useful if Ken wished to hang on to his Benetton sponsorship. De Angelis, for reasons best known to Lotus, had done enough (5th place at Monza and pole position at Brands Hatch no less) to warrant his signature on a contract for another year but a wordy statement from Hethel more or less made it clear that Nigel Mansell might be unemployed in 1984. Quite where he would go was not certain and the rumour machine had few answers to that.

However, there was strong speculation that Patrese would no longer be required at Brabham; Tambay and Cecotto being mentioned as possible replacements. The Theodore team's Formula 1 future was in doubt and, besides, Guerrero's name had been linked with both Lotus and Renault. Warwick was said to be talking to Lotus as well although there was the chance that he might remain with Toleman if they either found enough money to develop Brian Hart's engine further or switched completely and run a BMW engine.

Then there was Manfred Winkelhock. He had a BMW engine to put on the table during discussions with Toleman, Tyrrell and Arrows. It was said that Al Unser Jnr had turned down the offer of a drive with Brabham while Jonathan Palmer, in discussion with every team in the paddock, would have liked the opportunity to even *consider* turning down a drive. Frank Williams had re-signed Keke Rosberg while Jacques Laffite had another year to run on his contract. Frank said he was very happy about that – but if Jacques wanted to go, then that would be fine too. Mansell was said to be a likely replacement if the Frenchman went back to Ligier provided, of course, the French team had not signed Carlos Reutemann!

Yes, the Argentinian's name had surfaced and it seemed only a matter of time before Jackie Stewart and James Hunt would be capturing the headlines with stories of how they had reluctantly turned down massive offers from a team whose name they could not disclose for fear of spoiling another good 'silly season' story.

The Williams team, sponsored by Saudia Airlines, set the pace in the Cosworth race at Brands Hatch. Jonathan Palmer did all that was asked of him by qualifying for his first Grand Prix. Palmer takes the oil-smeared car through Druids during the closing stages of a steady drive.
Photos: Paul Henri Cahier & John Colley

John Player Grand Prix of Europe, September 25/statistics

Entries and practice times

No.	Driver	Nat	Car	Tyre	Engine	Entrant	Practice 1	Practice 2
1	Keke Rosberg	SF	Saudia WILLIAMS FW08C	G	Ford Cosworth DFV	TAG Williams Team	**1m 14·917s**	1m 15·252s
2	Jacques Laffite	F	Saudia WILLIAMS FW08C	G	Ford Cosworth DFV	TAG Williams Team	1m 18·467s	**1m 18·261s**
3	Michele Alboreto	I	Benetton TYRRELL 012	G	Ford Cosworth DFY	Benetton Tyrrell Team	**1m 17·456s**	1m 17·936s
4	Danny Sullivan	USA	Benetton TYRRELL 012	G	Ford Cosworth DFY	Benetton Tyrrell Team	1m 17·134s	**1m 16·640s**
5	Nelson Piquet	BR	Parmalat BRABHAM BT52B	M	BMW M12/13	Fila Sport	**1m 12·724s**	1m 13·095s
6	Riccardo Patrese	I	Parmalat BRABHAM BT52B	M	BMW M12/13	Fila Sport	1m 13·475s	**1m 12·458s**
7	John Watson	GB	Marlboro McLAREN MP4/1E	M	TAG P01 (TTE P01)	Marlboro McLaren International	1m 14·296s	**1m 13·783s**
8	Niki Lauda	A	Marlboro McLAREN MP4/1E	M	TAG P01 (TTE P01)	Marlboro McLaren International	1m 15·266s	**1m 13·972s**
9	Manfred Winkelhock	D	ATS D6	G	BMW M12/13	Team ATS	**1m 13·679s**	1m 14·750s
11	Elio de Angelis	I	John Player Special LOTUS 94T	P	Renault EF1	John Player Team Lotus	**1m 12·623s**	1m 13·089s
12	Nigel Mansell	GB	John Player Special LOTUS 94T	P	Renault EF1	John Player Team Lotus	1m 12·342s	**1m 12·092s**
15	Alain Prost	F	Elf RENAULT RE40	M	Renault EF1	Equipe Renault Elf	**1m 13·342s**	1m 13·526s
16	Eddie Cheever	USA	Elf RENAULT RE40	M	Renault EF1	Equipe Renault Elf	1m 13·592s	**1m 13·253s**
17	Kenneth Acheson	GB	MARCH-RAM 01	P	Ford Cosworth DFV/DFY	RAM Automotive Team March	**1m 17·577s**	1m 18·069s
22	Andrea de Cesaris	I	Marlboro ALFA ROMEO 183T	M	Alfa Romeo 183T	Marlboro Team Alfa Romeo	**1m 14·403s**	1m 15·440s
23	Mauro Baldi	I	Marlboro ALFA ROMEO 183T	M	Alfa Romeo 183T	Marlboro Team Alfa Romeo	**1m 14·727s**	1m 15·174s
25	Jean-Pierre Jarier	F	Gitanes LIGIER JS21	M	Ford Cosworth DFV/DFY	Equipe Ligier Gitanes	1m 17·141s	**1m 16·880s**
26	Raul Boesel	BR	Gitanes LIGIER JS21	M	Ford Cosworth DFV	Equipe Ligier Gitanes	**1m 17·177s**	1m 17·593s
27	Patrick Tambay	F	Fiat FERRARI 126C3	G	Ferrari 126C	Scuderia Ferrari SpA SEFAC	1m 13·898s	**1m 13·157s**
28	René Arnoux	F	Fiat FERRARI 126C3	G	Ferrari 126C	Scuderia Ferrari SpA SEFAC	1m 13·596s	**1m 13·113s**
29	Marc Surer	CH	ARROWS A6	G	Ford Cosworth DFV	Arrows Racing Team	**1m 15·346s**	1m 15·501s
30	Thierry Boutsen	B	ARROWS A6	G	Ford Cosworth DFV	Arrows Racing Team	1m 16·094s	**1m 15·428s**
31	Corrado Fabi	I	OSELLA FA1E	M	Alfa Romeo 1260	Osella Squadra Corse	1m 19·087s	**1m 17·816s**
32	Piercarlo Ghinzani	I	OSELLA FA1E	M	Alfa Romeo 1260	Osella Squadra Corse	1m 17·850s	**1m 17·408s**
33	Roberto Guerrero	COL	THEODORE N183	G	Ford Cosworth DFV	Theodore Racing Team	**1m 16·769s**	1m 17·454s
34	Johnny Cecotto	YV	THEODORE N183	G	Ford Cosworth DFV	Theodore Racing Team		Entry withdrawn
35	Derek Warwick	GB	Candy TOLEMAN TG183B	P	Hart 415T	Candy Toleman Motorsport	1m 14·411s	**1m 13·855s**
36	Bruno Giacomelli	I	Candy TOLEMAN TG183B	P	Hart 415T	Candy Toleman Motorsport	1m 15·521s	**1m 13·949s**
40	Stefan Johansson	S	SPIRIT-HONDA 201	G	Honda RA163-E	Spirit Racing	1m 16·525s	**1m 15·912s**
42	Jonathan Palmer	GB	Saudia WILLIAMS FW08C	G	Ford Cosworth DFV	TAG Williams Team	**1m 17·432s**	1m 17·524s

Friday morning and Saturday morning practice sessions not officially recorded.

G – Goodyear, M – Michelin, P – Pirelli.

Fri pm
Warm, dry

Sat pm
Warm, dry

Starting grid

	11 DE ANGELIS (1m 12·092s) Lotus
6 PATRESE (1m 12·458s) Brabham	
	12 MANSELL (1m 12·623s) Lotus
5 PIQUET (1m 12·724s) Brabham	
	28 ARNOUX (1m 13·113s) Ferrari
27 TAMBAY (1m 13·157s) Ferrari	
	16 CHEEVER (1m 13·253s) Renault
15 PROST (1m 13·342s) Renault	
	9 WINKELHOCK (1m 13·679s) ATS
7 WATSON (1m 13·783s) McLaren	
	35 WARWICK (1m 13·855s) Toleman
36 GIACOMELLI (1m 13·949s) Toleman	
	8 LAUDA (1m 13·972s) McLaren
22 DE CESARIS (1m 14·403s) Alfa Romeo	
	23 BALDI (1m 14·727s) Alfa Romeo
1 ROSBERG (1m 14·917s) Williams	
	29 SURER (1m 15·346s) Arrows
30 BOUTSEN (1m 15·428s) Arrows	
	40 JOHANSSON (1m 15·912s) Spirit
4 SULLIVAN (1m 16·640s) Tyrrell	
	33 GUERRERO (1m 16·769s) Theodore
*25 JARIER (1m 16·880s) Ligier	
	26 BOESEL (1m 17·177s) Ligier
32 GHINZANI (1m 17·408s) Osella	
	42 PALMER (1m 17·432s) Williams
3 ALBORETO (1m 17·456s) Tyrrell	

Did not start:
17 Acheson (RAM March), 1m 17·577s, did not qualify
31 Fabi (Osella), 1m 17·816s, did not qualify
2 Laffite (Williams), 1m 18·261s, did not qualify
*25 Jarier (Ligier), mechanical failure on start-line

Results and retirements

Place	Driver	Car	Laps	Time and Speed (mph/km/h)/Retirement	
1	Nelson Piquet	Brabham-BMW t/c 4	76	1h 36m 45·865s	123·165/198·214
2	Alain Prost	Renault t/c V6	76	1h 36m 52·436s	123·0/197·949
3	Nigel Mansell	Lotus-Renault t/c V6	76	1h 37m 16·180s	122·5/197·144
4	Andrea de Cesaris	Alfa Romeo t/c V8	76	1h 37m 20·261s	122·4/196·983
5	Derek Warwick	Toleman-Hart t/c 4	76	1h 37m 30·780s	122·2/196·661
6	Bruno Giacomelli	Toleman-Hart t/c 4	76	1h 37m 38·055s	122·1/196·500
7	Riccardo Patrese	Brabham-BMW t/c 4	76	1h 37m 58·549s	121·6/195·696
8	Manfred Winkelhock	ATS-BMW t/c 4	75		
9	René Arnoux	Ferrari t/c V6	75		
10	Eddie Cheever	Renault t/c V6	75		
11	Thierry Boutsen	Arrows-Cosworth V8	75		
12	Roberto Guerrero	Theodore-Cosworth V8	75		
13	Jonathan Palmer	Williams-Cosworth V8	74		
14	Stefan Johansson	Spirit-Honda t/c V6	74		
15	Raul Boesel	Ligier-Cosworth V8	73		
	Patrick Tambay	Ferrari t/c V6	67	Accident/lost brake fluid	
	Michele Alboreto	Tyrrell-Cosworth V8	65	Engine	
	Piercarlo Ghinzani	Osella-Alfa Romeo V12	63	Running, not classified	
	Marc Surer	Arrows-Cosworth V8	51	Engine	
	Keke Rosberg	Williams-Cosworth V8	43	Engine	
	Mauro Baldi	Alfa Romeo t/c V8	39	Clutch	
	John Watson	McLaren-TAG t/c V8	36	Accident/rear wing failure	
	Danny Sullivan	Tyrrell-Cosworth V8	27	Fire/broken oil line	
	Niki Lauda	McLaren-TAG t/c V6	26	Engine	
	Elio de Angelis	Lotus-Renault t/c V6	13	Engine	
	Jean-Pierre Jarier	Ligier-Cosworth V8	0	Transmission, did not start	

Fastest lap: Mansell, on lap 70, 1m 14·342s, 126·563mph/203·683km/h.
Lap record: Didier Pironi (F1 Ligier JS11/15-Cosworth DFV), 1m 12·368, 130·015mph/209·239km/h (1980).

Past winners

1983	Nelson Piquet	BR	1·5 Brabham BT52B-BMW t/c	Brands Hatch	198·63/319·67	123·16/198·21

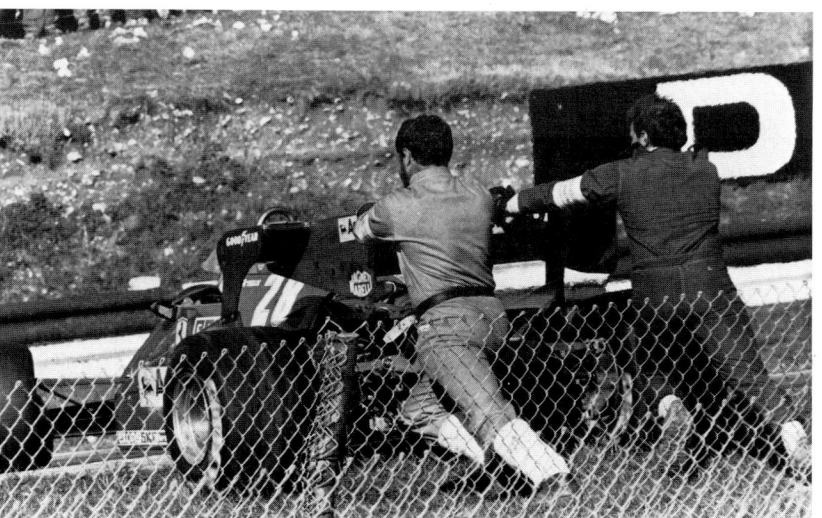

René Arnoux is pushed back onto the track after spinning away his chances in the race and, possibly, the championship.

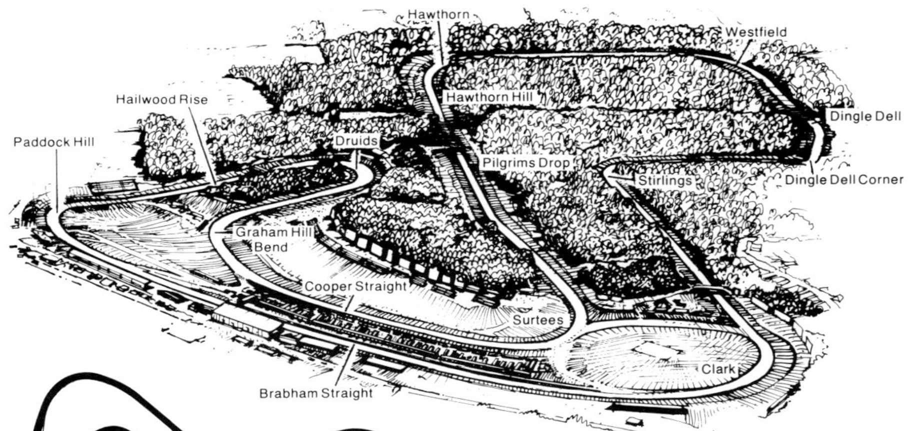

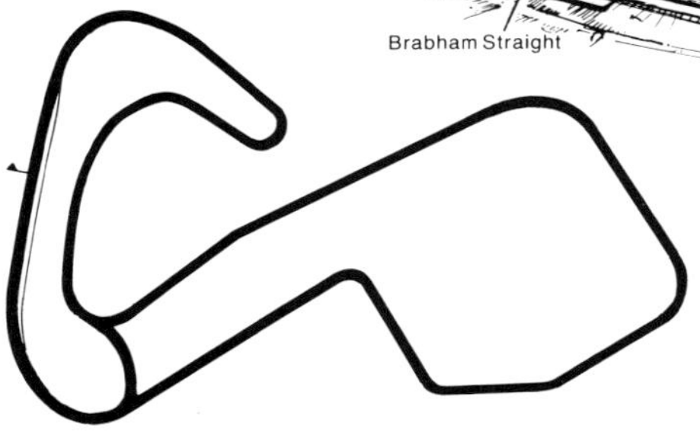

Circuit data

Brands Hatch Grand Prix Circuit, Fawkham, Kent
Circuit length: 2·6136 miles/4·206 km
Race distance: 76 laps, 198·63 miles/319·67 km
Race weather: Hot, dry

Lap chart

1st LAP ORDER		1	2	3	4	5	6	7	8	9	10	11	12	13	14	15	16	17	18	19	20	21	22	23	24	25	26	27	28	29	30	31	32	33	34	35	36	37
6	R. Patrese	6	6	6	6	6	6	6	6	6	6	5	5	5	5	5	5	5	5	5	5	5	5	5	5	5	5	5	5	5	5	5	5	5	5	5	5	5
11	E. De Angelis	11	11	11	11	11	11	11	11	11	11	6	6	6	6	15	15	15	15	15	15	15	15	15	15	15	15	15	15	15	15	15	15	15	15	15	15	15
12	N. Mansell	12	5	5	5	5	5	5	5	5	5	15	15	15	15	6	6	6	6	6	6	6	6	6	6	6	6	6	6	6	6	6	6	6	6	6	6	6
5	N. Piquet	5	16	16	16	16	16	16	16	15	15	16	16	16	16	16	16	16	16	16	16	16	16	16	16	16	16	16	16	16	16	16	16	16	16	12	12	12
16	E. Cheever	16	12	15	15	15	15	15	15	16	16	28	28	28	28	28	28	28	28	28	12	12	12	12	12	12	12	12	12	12	12	12	12	12	12	27	27	27
9	M. Winkelhock	9	15	28	28	28	28	28	28	28	28	11	11	12	12	12	12	12	12	12	27	27	27	27	27	27	27	27	27	27	27	27	27	27	27	22	22	22
28	R. Arnoux	28	28	12	12	12	12	12	12	12	12	12	12	9	27	27	27	27	27	27	9	9	9	22	22	22	22	22	22	22	22	22	22	22	22	(16)	9	35
15	A. Prost	15	9	9	9	9	9	9	9	9	9	9	9	27	9	9	9	9	9	9	22	22	22	9	9	9	9	9	9	9	9	9	9	9	9	9	35	1
27	P. Tambay	27	27	27	27	27	27	27	27	27	27	27	27	22	22	22	22	22	22	22	35	35	35	35	35	35	35	35	35	35	35	35	35	35	35	35	1	36
35	D. Warwick	35	35	22	35	35	22	22	22	22	22	22	22	35	35	35	35	35	35	35	7	7	7	8	8	8	7	7	7	7	7	7	7	1	1	1	36	(9)
22	A. De Cesaris	22	22	35	22	22	35	35	35	35	35	35	35	7	7	7	7	7	7	7	8	8	8	7	7	7	1	1	1	1	1	1	1	36	36	36	16	16
8	N. Lauda	8	8	8	8	8	7	7	7	7	7	7	7	8	8	8	8	8	8	8	1	1	1	1	1	1	36	36	36	36	36	36	36	(7)	28	28	28	28
23	M. Baldi	23	23	7	7	7	8	23	23	23	1	8	8	1	1	1	1	1	1	1	36	36	36	36	36	36	23	23	23	23	23	23	23	23	23	(23)	29	29
7	J. Watson	7	7	36	23	23	23	8	1	1	8	1	1	(11)	23	23	23	23	23	36	23	23	23	23	23	23	28	28	28	28	28	28	28	28	29	29	3	3
36	B. Giacomelli	36	36	23	36	36	36	1	8	8	23	23	23	23	36	36	36	36	36	23	29	29	29	29	29	29	29	29	29	29	29	29	29	29	3	3	7	40
29	M. Surer	29	1	1	1	1	1	36	36	36	36	36	36	36	29	29	29	29	29	29	40	40	40	28	28	28	(8)	40	40	3	3	3	3	3	7	7	40	30
40	S. Johansson	40	29	29	29	29	29	29	29	29	29	29	29	29	40	40	40	40	40	40	3	3	3	40	40	40	40	3	3	40	40	40	40	40	40	40	30	33
1	K. Rosberg	1	40	40	40	40	40	40	40	40	40	40	40	40	4	3	3	3	3	3	4	4	28	3	3	3	3	4	30	30	30	30	30	30	30	30	33	42
33	R. Guerrero	33	33	33	40	4	4	4	4	4	4	4	4	4	3	4	4	4	4	4	28	28	4	4	4	4	4	30	33	33	33	33	33	33	33	33	42	23
4	D. Sullivan	4	4	4	33	3	3	3	3	3	3	3	3	3	33	33	33	33	33	33	33	33	33	30	30	30	30	33	42	42	42	42	42	42	42	42	23	26
32	P. Ghinzani	32	30	30	4	33	33	33	33	33	33	33	33	33	30	30	30	30	30	30	30	30	30	33	33	33	33	42	26	26	26	26	26	26	26	26	26	32
3	M. Alboreto	3	3	3	3	30	30	30	30	30	30	30	30	30	42	42	42	42	42	42	42	42	42	42	42	42	42	26	32	32	32	32	32	32	32	32	32	
26	R. Boesel	26	26	26	26	26	26	26	26	26	42	42	42	42	26	26	26	26	26	26	26	26	26	26	26	26	26	32										
30	T. Boutsen	30	32	32	32	32	32	32	32	42	26	26	26	26	32	32	32	32	32	32	32	32	32	32	32	32	32											
42	J. Palmer	42	42	42	42	42	42	42	42	32	32	32	32	32																								

38	39	40	41	42	43	44	45	46	47	48	49	50	51	52	53	54	55	56	57	58	59	60	61	62	63	64	65	66	67	68	69	70	71	72	73	74	75	76
5	5	5	5	5	5	(5)	5	5	5	5	5	5	5	5	5	5	5	5	5	5	5	5	5	5	5	5	5	5	5	5	5	5	5	5	5	5	5	5
15	15	15	(15)	27	(27)	15	15	15	15	15	15	15	15	15	15	15	15	15	15	15	15	15	15	15	15	15	15	15	15	15	15	15	15	15	15	15	15	15
6	12	12	12	(12)	15	27	27	27	27	27	27	27	27	27	27	27	27	27	27	27	27	27	27	27	27	27	27	12	12	12	12	12	12	12	12	12	12	12
12	27	27	27	15	(36)	12	12	12	12	12	12	12	12	12	12	12	12	12	12	12	12	12	12	12	12	12	12	27	27	22	22	22	22	22	22	22	22	22
27	35	36	36	36	12	16	22	22	22	22	22	22	22	22	22	22	22	22	22	22	22	22	22	22	22	22	22	22	22	35	35	35	35	35	35	35	35	35
(22)	1	(1)	16	16	16	22	(16)	35	35	35	35	35	35	35	35	35	35	35	35	35	35	35	35	35	35	35	35	35	35	36	36	36	36	36	36	36	36	36
35	36	(35)	22	22	22	35	35	36	36	36	36	36	36	36	36	36	36	36	36	36	36	36	36	36	36	36	36	36	36	6	6	6	6	6	6	6	6	6
1	16	16	35	35	35	36	36	6	6	6	6	6	6	6	6	6	6	6	6	6	6	6	6	6	6	6	6	6	6	9	9	9	9	9	9	9	9	
36	22	22	1	1	1	6	6	9	9	9	9	9	9	9	9	9	9	9	9	9	9	9	9	9	9	9	9	9	9	16	16	16	16	16	16	28	28	
16	(6)	6	6	6	6	9	9	28	28	28	28	28	28	(28)	3	3	3	3	16	16	16	16	16	16	16	16	16	16	16	28	28	28	28	28	28	16	16	
(28)	9	9	9	9	9	28	28	29	29	29	29	3	3	3	16	16	16	16	3	3	28	28	28	28	28	28	28	28	28	30	30	30	30	30	30	30	30	
9	28	28	28	28	28	29	29	3	3	3	3	29	16	16	30	30	30	30	30	28	3	3	3	30	30	30	30	30	30	33	33	33	33	33	33	33	33	
29	29	29	29	29	29	3	3	30	30	30	30	16	30	30	28	28	28	28	28	30	30	30	30	3	3	3	33	33	33	42	42	42	42	42	42	42		
3	3	3	3	3	3	30	30	16	16	16	16	30	29	33	33	33	33	33	33	33	33	33	33	33	33	33	(3)	42	42	40	40	40	40	40	40	40		
30	30	30	30	30	30	33	33	33	33	33	33	33	33	42	42	42	42	42	42	42	42	42	42	42	42	42	42	40	40	26	26	26	26	26	26			
(40)	33	33	33	33	33	42	42	42	42	42	42	42	42	40	40	40	40	40	40	40	40	40	40	40	40	40	40	26	26									
33	42	42	42	42	(42)	40	40	40	40	40	40	40	40	26	26	26	26	26	26	26	26	26	26	26	26	26	26											
42	40	40	40	40	40	26	26	26	26	26	26	26	26	(32)	32	32	32	32	32	32	32	32	(32)	32	32													
23	26	26	26	26	26	32	32	(32)	32	32	32	32	32																									
26	32	32	32	32	32																																	
32	(23)																																					

The designation 'European Grand Prix' first awarded to the Italian Grand Prix in 1923 was no more than a courtesy title. It became an arbitary decision taken each year by the FIA and granted to an existing Grand Prix as a token of the race's stature. The European Grand Prix gradually lost its significance during the Fifties and disappeared altogether in the Sixties.

However, the revival of the European Grand Prix in 1983 was a different matter and, while the title may have been a convenient one for the Brands Hatch race, it nevertheless marked the beginning of what appears to be a regular event in its own right. We have not listed the winners of the European Grand Prix in its previous guise since they appear elsewhere in Autocourse.

Fastest laps

Driver	Time	Lap
Nigel Mansell	1m 14·342s	70
Alain Prost	1m 14·616s	73
Derek Warwick	1m 14·732s	39
Nelson Piquet	1m 14·778s	38
Bruno Giacomelli	1m 14·877s	64
Andrea de Cesaris	1m 14·905s	72
René Arnoux	1m 14·924s	56
Patrick Tambay	1m 14·933s	48
Riccardo Patrese	1m 15·107s	56
Eddie Cheever	1m 15·161s	65
Keke Rosberg	1m 15·260s	36
Michele Alboreto	1m 15·599s	55
Elio de Angelis	1m 15·601s	6
Manfred Winkelhock	1m 15·710s	35
John Watson	1m 15·800s	30
Niki Lauda	1m 15·957s	22
Thierry Boutsen	1m 16·050s	4
Roberto Guerrero	1m 16·279s	59
Mauro Baldi	1m 16·392s	25
Jonathan Palmer	1m 16·794s	26
Marc Surer	1m 17·039s	35
Stefan Johansson	1m 17·042s	32
Danny Sullivan	1m 17·222s	27
Piercarlo Ghinzani	1m 18·406s	60
Raul Boesel	1m 18·698s	53

Points

WORLD CHAMPIONSHIP OF DRIVERS

1	Alain Prost	57 pts
2	Nelson Piquet	55
3	René Arnoux	49
4	Patrick Tambay	40
5	Keke Rosberg	25
6	John Watson	22
7	Eddie Cheever	21
8	Niki Lauda	12
9	Jacques Laffite	11
10=	Michele Alboreto	10
10=	Nigel Mansell	10
12	Andrea de Cesaris	9
13	Derek Warwick	6
14=	Marc Surer	4
14=	Riccardo Patrese	4
16	Mauro Baldi	3
17=	Danny Sullivan	2
17=	Elio de Angelis	2
19=	Johnny Cecotto	1
19=	Bruno Giacomelli	1

CONSTRUCTORS' CUP

1	Ferrari	89 pts
2	Renault	78
3	Brabham	59
4	Williams	36
5	McLaren	34
6=	Tyrrell	12
6=	Alfa Romeo	12
6=	Lotus	12
9	Toleman	7
10	Arrows	4
11	Theodore	1

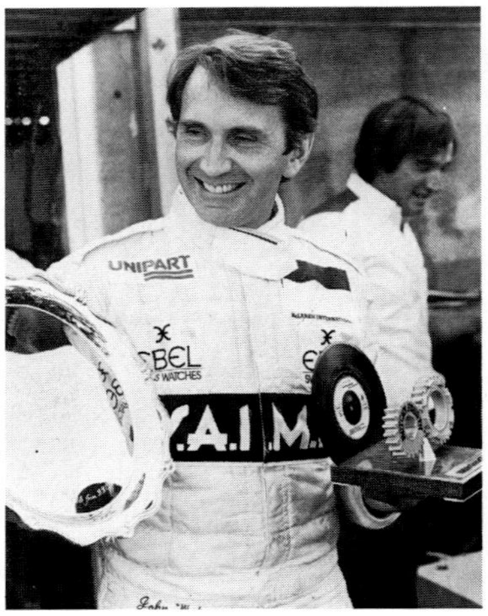

The BBC presented John Watson (or John McLaren, as Murray Walker called him) with a silver salver to commemorate his 150th Grand Prix. Watson's mechanics did not let the occasion slip by without giving their man a momento of his 'record' appearance; two gearbox dog-rings representing a 'notchy fourth', Watson's favourite and most regular complaint when he could find little else wrong with his car. Watson's race was to end in the catch-fencing when the rear wing broke.

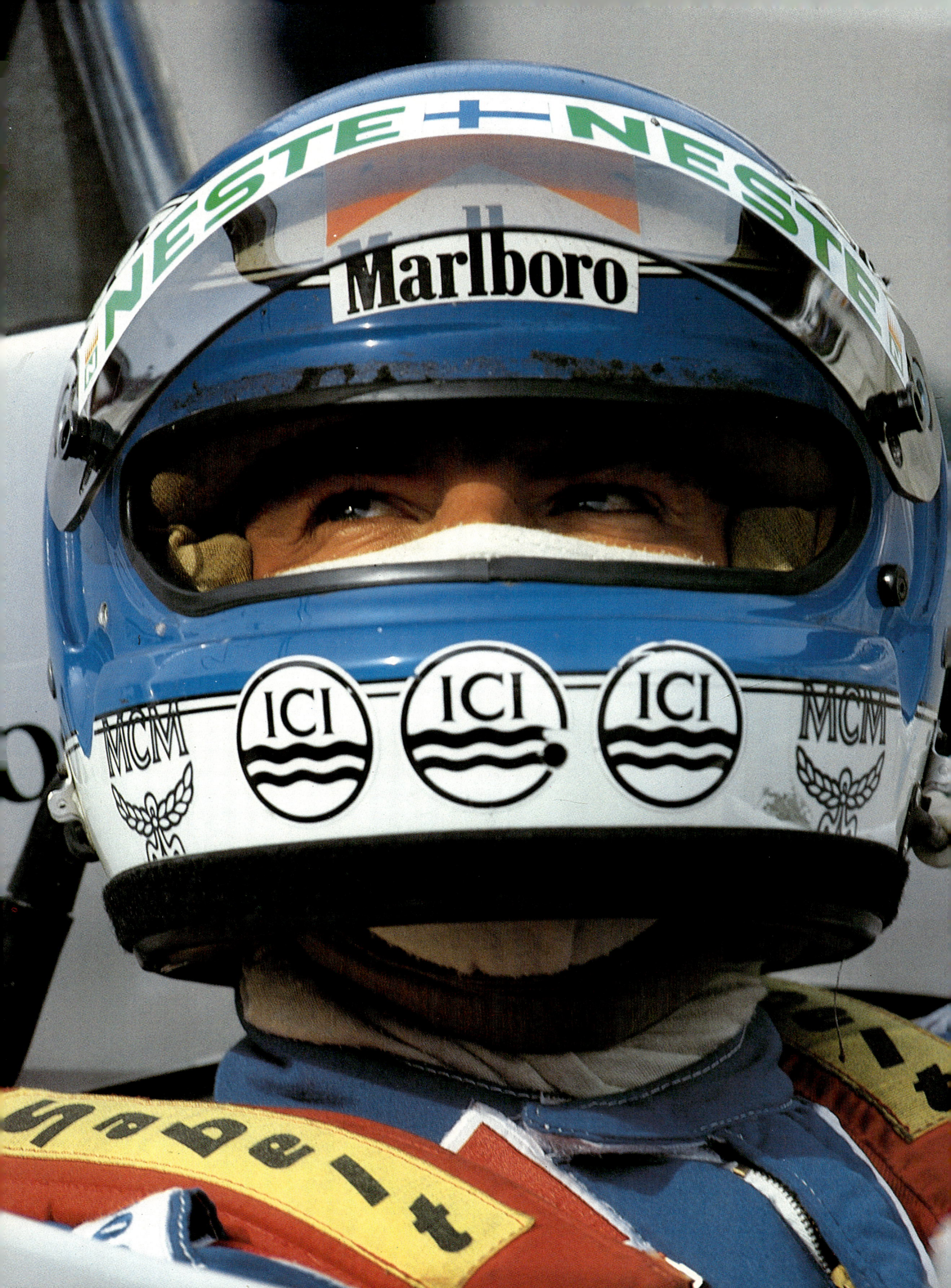

The Brabham team's stop-watches told them the championship, barring misfortune, was in the bag. Then, when Nelson Piquet drove close to the pit wall a few laps before his scheduled stop, they knew he felt the same way.

Here was the signal for a change to hard tyres all round at the pit stop; a conservative choice if ever there was one and a sure indication that Piquet was going to stroke home. Given his devastating performance in the opening laps, he could afford to.

Although the Brazilian was two points behind Alain Prost when they arrived at Kyalami for the final confrontation, the run of play during testing and practice indicated that the advantages were held by Piquet. The Parmalat Brabham-BMW had superior top speed and excellent traction onto the long straight. Moreover, Nelson had won the championship before and, outwardly at least, his relaxed approach contrasted with the controlled tension within the Renault-Elf camp as they edged closer and closer to the dream of moulding a French World Champion.

Piquet then scored more psychological points when he took a place on the front row alongside Patrick Tambay's pole position Ferrari. Prost, happy with the handling of his car, was back on row three. In between were Riccardo Patrese — keen to help his team-mate since contracts were beckoning — and Arnoux, still shooting for the championship. To make absolutely sure of the title, all three contenders needed to go for a win.

Brabham then hatched a clever plan to give Piquet victory while, at the same time, pushing the opposition to breaking point. Instead of stopping Nelson late in the race, as had been their wont, it was decided to start his car with a small amount of fuel and make an early pit stop. That way, he could not only run in the cool air at the front, but he would also force Renault and Ferrari to over-extend themselves as they tried to keep up. The plan, devised initially by Bernie Ecclestone, worked perfectly.

Piquet's times during the first ten laps simply destroyed the opposition. By lap 12, he was as many seconds in front and, even better, Patrese held second place while Prost was engaged in a fight for third with Niki Lauda's Marlboro McLaren. By the time Piquet made his pit stop on lap 28, the championship battle was almost won.

Arnoux, never higher than seventh, had retired with engine trouble and Tambay, down in sixth place, was barely able to keep in touch with the Marlboro Alfa Romeo of Andrea de Cesaris. Prost, meanwhile, was in fourth place but the Frenchman's hopes were sagging as his throttle lag increased, a sure sign that the turbo was failing. When he came in to make his routine stop on lap 35, the mechanics pounced on the car — and Prost simply undid his belts, climbed out and walked away. He still had his two-point advantage, of course, and the championship now rested on the reliability of the Brabham-BMW.

Once he had received the news of Prost's demise, the same thought occurred to Piquet. His lap times dropped by two seconds; the boost was wound down even further. Fourth place would be good enough and Nelson was not worried when Patrese took the lead on lap 59; he was scarcely bothered when Lauda took second place 10 laps later.

A superb charge from 12th place on the grid ended when an electrical fault caused the TAG turbo to cut out six laps from the end and Piquet, cool as you like, let de Cesaris into second place. With Derek Warwick's Candy Toleman a lap behind in fourth place, Nelson had it made. The outgoing World Champion, Keke Rosberg, was running in fifth place during a very impressive debut for the Honda-powered Williams and Eddie Cheever was about to present the disconsolate Renault team with one point for sixth place. That would ensure that Ferrari had captured the Constructors' Cup for the second year in succession.

Patrese duly scored his first win of the season, the Brabham mechanics waiting on the track to welcome Piquet home to his second World Championship. Two years previously, he had won the title almost by default. In 1983, however, he had been the outstanding driver of the year, his speed and self-assurance at Kyalami proving that beyond doubt.

Racing a Honda-powered Williams FW09 for the first time, Keke Rosberg, a member of the ICI Fibre Record Sportswear Team, not only qualified well but finished in a very competitive fifth place.
Photo: Don Morley

SOUTHERN SUN HOTELS GRAND PRIX OF SOUTH AFRICA

ENTRY AND PRACTICE

At first, the Kyalami organisers had been very unhappy about having their race moved from one end of the calendar to the other simply to suit the sudden rule change brought into force at the end of 1982. There was every chance the championship might have been settled before the teams made the long trek to South Africa, since it seemed unlikely that the fight for the title would run until the final race for the third year in succession. In the event, those fears were to prove unfounded and, furthermore, the three-way fight for the championship could not have been closer. Whichever way you looked at the points, Alain Prost, Nelson Piquet and René Arnoux had to go for a win; racking up a few points for fourth or fifth place might not be good enough.

The South African Grand Prix had been deferred since it was felt the teams would not have been able to produce the new flat-bottomed cars in time for the original date. It was 21 months since the Grand Prix cars had last raced at Kyalami and the teams were granted two days of testing at the beginning of the week. Patrick Tambay ended each day with the fastest time and the Ferrari driver continued the theme throughout the two days of practice. The organisers were delighted. Not only did they have the championship to boost their race, they also gathered a fair amount of publicity thanks to Tambay's defiant two-fingered gesture at Ferrari's decision to dismiss the Frenchman from the team. Tambay, of course, was as tactful and polite as ever when discussing Mr. Ferrari's decision and he simply let his performance on the track do the talking. Quite simply, no one could touch him – although Nelson Piquet tried hard enough.

Having got over a problem with a sticking exhaust valve on Thursday morning, Tambay set off with his fresh engine and took pole with his second set of qualifiers. Piquet then beat that time by a tenth of a second and the Ferrari team set about fitting Tambay's car with a mixture of the best of the remaining qualifying tyres from the first two runs. They figured there was perhaps one lap left in the rubber. Tambay duly proved them correct by shaving another two tenths off Piquet's time with a stunning lap on a clear track. On Friday, he went out and established a reasonable time on his first set of qualifiers and then sat in his car, waiting patiently for someone to beat the previous day's time. He never did use his second set.

Tambay gave the $3,000 prize for pole position to his mechanics who made no secret of the fact that they would like to see their man win his last race with the team. All this, of course, merely served to heighten an already tense atmosphere within the team. Marco Piccinini's decision to help Enzo Ferrari make up his mind that Tambay, rather than Arnoux, should leave did not receive an enthusiastic reception within the team. Now there was the question of helping Arnoux win the championship. Would Tambay play a part? "No," came the reply. "I don't think I should be asked to make another sacrifice for the team, do you?"

Arnoux, meanwhile, had other problems on his mind. Apart from being unable to match Tambay's pace, René found his car coasting to a halt with an electrical problem as he prepared himself for his second run on qualifiers during the first timed session. The Ferrari came to rest in a dangerous position and, after persuading the marshals that it should be moved, Arnoux was caught unawares when the rear wheel of the C3 ran over his right foot. René made it back to the pits where he plunged his foot into a bucket of cold water. Nothing was broken but, judging by the swelling, his hopes of taking part in the race were in jeopardy. The next day, Arnoux was at least able to wear his driving shoe and he completed many laps in the unofficial session even though his foot was giving pain. In a brave effort, so typical of this gutsy driver, Arnoux managed to shave a tenth off his previous best time in the afternoon to take fourth place. At least he

had beaten Prost in the process . . .

Splitting the two Ferraris were the pair of smartly turned out blue and white Brabhams, Piquet beating Riccardo Patrese by a couple of tenths of a second. Apart from minor revisions to the oil cooling, there were few changes and both cars carried the Ferrari-type rear wings first seen at Brands Hatch. Thus, both Brabhams had excellent traction out of Leeukop and yet they were not short of straight-line speed either, Piquet crossing the timing line at 185mph (298km/h) on Thursday, easily the fastest car at that point.

Practice had started badly when both drivers suffered engine failures during the first unofficial session and it seemed BMW might need most of the 13 engines brought to Kyalami. Once they had been finely tuned to the conditions, however, there were few problems although Patrese lost a turbo just as he was coming to the end of his fastest lap on Thursday. That meant the Italian was down in 12th place and, with his contract for 1984 far from settled, Patrese was keen to create the right impression. To that end, he put in an exceptionally ragged lap during the final session and improved to third place. Piquet had his moments too, the Brazilian spinning as he made a vain and final attempt to dislodge Tambay from pole. In the meantime, a place on the front row was good enough – particularly as Prost had finished practice back in fifth place . . .

Prost, though, was not unduly worried. He had expected the Ferraris and Brabhams, with their qualifying boost, to set the pace on the long straight and a seven mph shortfall in straight-line speed merely confirmed the fact. Renault were taking no chances and they brought four cars, Prost having the pick of 06 (new at Monza) and his favourite 05. He used the latter on Thursday, putting it away for the final practice safe in the knowledge that the handling was perfect and he had frequently started races from the third row. Austria was a good example of that – and everyone knew what happened there. Besides, Prost had not been helped by a wrong choice of qualifying tyre on Friday and Eddie Cheever was even worse off, the American starting his last race for Renault from 14th place. A turbo had failed on Thursday morning and the replacement cost him 400 revs in the official session. Apart from that, the handling was poor even though he had similar settings to his team-mate and it was a mightly disgruntled Cheever who stalked around the Renault garage on Friday evening.

The most remarkable performance of practice came from the Williams team as the Honda turbo engines, making their first public appearance in the back of the new FW09 chassis, scarcely missed a beat throughout the two days. With turbo power at his disposal for the first time, Rosberg was back where he belonged, the World Champion taking sixth place with a time set on Thursday. And that was without the luxury of qualifying boost, the Honda engine not taking kindly to that at this stage of its development. Rosberg had a long moment on the grass at the exit of Sunset while running race tyres during the final session. Not long after, while turning in a more prudent lap on qualifiers, he inadvertently blocked Manfred Winkelhock. The ATS driver was so incensed that the two cars banged wheels and almost came to a standstill as they approached Clubhouse – blocking the way for an even more irate John Watson.

Rosberg's only problem had been a misfire caused by a wastegate sticking during the morning, which is why he ran on race tyres first thing in the afternoon. Jacques Laffite had a similar problem on Thursday afternoon and he used Rosberg's car to set what would become 10th fastest time. Jacques was unable to improve when the handling became inconsistent in the final session – but anything was better than failing to qualify.

Nigel Mansell made the biggest improvement on Friday by jumping 10 places from 17th position. The JPS Lotus driver had experienced a frustrating day on Thursday when the boost fell away as he used his first set of qualifiers. Switching to the spare car, Mansell found the engine in that chassis had a misfire and things did not look much brighter the following morning when the replacement Renault V6 in his race car refused to pull properly. Fortunately that was fixed in time for the final hour and, by selecting the correct set of Pirellis and in Mansell's words, "giving it the gun", he vaulted from row eight to row four. Elio de Angelis, on the other hand, slipped from eighth to 11th place in the last session thanks to making the wrong choice of qualifier. This was the final straw. Elio had started out with high hopes having been second fastest to Tambay during the test sessions earlier in the week. Then, when they ran more boost during official practice – he merely succeeded in going slower! Part of the problem was traced to a split intercooler on Thursday evening.

That was the sort of problem which usually afflicted Manfred Winkelhock but the German driver had a relatively trouble-free practice, the ATS being one of the quickest cars through the speed trap on Thursday. Andrea de Cesaris, on the other hand, was some 10mph slower than the ATS during the first day's practice thanks to a failing turbo. The Italian had to use the spare Marlboro Alfa Romeo for the rest of the session and he was determined to improve on 15th place the following afternoon. To say he tried hard would be understating the case somewhat. He was absolutely terrifying to behold. Watching him fling the 183T through the corners without lifting, you felt he would either crash or take pole position – assuming he reached the timing line. Remarkably, he completed the final session without incident and took ninth place, a fraction slower than Winkelhock. Mauro Baldi, just as spectacular, was not as effective, the Italian being one second slower than his team-mate.

> **OCTOBER:**
> *Richard Noble, driving Thrust 2, creates new World Land Speed Record of 633.468 mph at Black Rock Desert, USA.*
>
> *David Hobbs (Chevrolet Camaro) wins SCCA TransAm Championship.*
>
> *Jacques Villeneuve (Frissbee-Chevrolet GR3) wins SCCA CanAm Championship.*
>
> AFTER FINISHING FIFTH IN THE SOUTH AFRICAN Grand Prix, Keke Rosberg announced that his doctor had ordered a complete rest for five weeks. Rosberg had felt unwell since Monaco, a liver complaint caused a lack of energy and constant tiredness. Tests for hepatitis had proved negative and, when the symptoms persisted, Rosberg returned to his doctor who ordered a break from driving as well as business and leisure activities as soon as the season had ended.

Niki Lauda took 12th place in the Marlboro McLaren, the Austrian reporting few problems with the TAG turbo which featured revised intercooling. It was John Watson who bore the brunt of the team's problems thanks, in part, to overheating causing a poor pick-up. On Friday, he came across the Rosberg/Winkelhock incident and lost the use of one set of qualifiers "thanks to those two idiots conducting their argument in the middle of the track". Then, an engine misfire kept him in the pits for the rest of the session and he had to make do with 15th place earned the previous day.

When Rory Byrne stepped off the South African Airways 747 in Johannesburg on Wednesday morning, his baggage was bulging with bits of Toleman TG183B. The team's designer had received urgent calls from Kyalami following eventful testing when Bruno Giacomelli's car suffered a broken pick-up point for a wishbone and Derek Warwick crashed his car heavily at Clubhouse after the rear brakes had mysteriously locked. The Candy Toleman team worked wonders by repairing both tubs and Warwick was disappointed at being unable to repay their efforts with a decent grid position. The English driver, suffering from a mild virus infection, made a slight mistake during his final lap on Thursday and he could not coax the Toleman-Hart beyond 13th place the following day. Giacomelli, a couple of tenths slower, was three places behind Warwick.

Now that Williams had switched to turbo engines, it left just four teams using the Ford-Cosworth and the altitude at Kyalami merely underlined the demise of the ubiquitous DFV. Michele Alboreto, the fastest of the normally aspirated brigade, was 2.5 secs slower than Baldi's Alfa Romeo and 4.5 secs behind Tambay's Ferrari. Unlike Brands Hatch, the higher track temperatures meant the Benetton Tyrrell team had few problems generating warmth in their Goodyears although, in the final session, Alboreto felt his engine was losing power after he had failed to take advantage of a tow from Danny Sullivan. Alboreto then commandeered his team-mate's car but was unable to improve on his time from Thursday. Sullivan, on the other hand, did improve slightly but it made little difference to his grid position.

The two Tyrrells would start ahead of Thierry Boutsen's Arrows and, for all his efforts on Friday, Marc Surer was unable to beat either his team-mate or the Gitanes Ligier of Jean-Pierre Jarier. Raul Boesel put his Ligier in 23rd place and Kenny Acheson was guaranteed a start in his first Grand Prix when only 26 cars took part in practice – Theodore and Spirit having decided against making the trip to South Africa. Acheson, running a Williams DFV in his RAM March, took a creditable 24th place, the Ulsterman sitting out the final session while the mechanics changed a crown-wheel and pinion. The Kelemata Osellas, meanwhile, thrashed round and round but neither Corrado Fabi nor Piercarlo Ghinzani could approach Acheson's time. In fact, they were so slow that, officially, they failed to make the race once the 110% rule had been applied but it seemed unfair to deny them the opportunity of racing after travelling such a long way and the rest of the teams duly signed a piece of paper agreeing to let the Italian cars take their places at the back of the grid.

RACE

A clear blue sky and the promise of high track temperatures on race day brought disappointment for Tambay and Arnoux. During similar conditions the previous day, Tambay had put in several hard laps in the company of Piquet and soon found that, under the circumstances, his Goodyears were no match for the Michelins. The times set during the warm-up confirmed his worst fears; Ferrari number 27 was in sixth place, number 28 in tenth. Piquet was third, Prost fourth but, topping the list was none other than Niki Lauda with a lap of 1m 09.504s, a very respectable time indeed. Clearly, this was another variable for the championship contenders to consider.

Piquet had tried his spare car briefly but decided to stick with his regular chassis even though there had been minor brake trouble. Other than that, there were few problems and the Brabham mechanics had time for a leisurely lunch.

Down in the Williams garage, however, it was all hands to the pumps as they set about making the first Honda engine change against the clock. After just a few laps of the warm-up, Rosberg had brought his FW09 back to the pits with bits of Honda engine dribbling out of an exhaust pipe. With no spare car available, there was no alternative but to set about an engine change. Ninety-five minutes later, the new turbo was fired up with the minimum of fuss.

Earlier, there had been anything but a calm and orderly atmosphere in the pit lane. Mindful that the narrow facilities were hardly conducive to rapid pit stops, the organisers had taken the wise decision to implement a ban on everyone bar essential personnel in the pit lane. Unfortunately, they decided to bring the rule into operation during the warm-up. Even more unfortunate was the fact that they declined to warn people accustomed to being in the pits during this period. As a result, there were one or two ugly scenes as officials tried to throw out important people such as François Guiter of Elf and the heated arguments in the Renault pit did nothing to help keep the team calm during this most important day.

Indeed, sitting in a Formula 1 car was probably the safest place to be and Prost had no major problems to report. By opting for softer Michelins on the right, Prost had come to the same conclusion as Piquet but Lauda had decided to gamble on the soft compound all round. An engine misfire on de Angelis's Lotus saw the Italian switch to the T-car for the race while Kenny Acheson, preparing for his first Grand Prix, became accustomed to running the March with a full tank for the first time!

As the mechanics warmed the engines, Piquet found time to nip into the Renault garage and slap a 'Nelson Piquet Fan Club' sticker on the side of Prost's car. Alain eventually peeled it off and then sat on the pit counter and amused the photographers by sticking it on the

front of his overalls. By 1 p.m., however, the joking was at an end as the cars left the pits for the last time.

Watson had not been able to complete a single flying lap during the warm-up due to an engine misfire and a change of components failed to cure the problem, as he soon discovered when he made his way towards the grid. The spare McLaren, available for the first time, had been prepared just in case and Watson dived into the pits once more and made a last-minute switch. Then, to his total frustration, that car refused to start when he was given the signal to complete the final parade lap. Watson eventually got going and had caught the field by the time they had reached Sunset. Watson gradually worked his way towards his grid position but, in so doing, he was contravening the rule which required him to start from the back of the grid – despite the fact that he was safely in position by the time the field trickled onto the main straight. Watson should have known better, however, and the move would earn disqualification after 19 laps.

Derek Ongaro held the field on the red light for just over four seconds and, on the green, the two Brabhams made perfect starts while the Ferraris were slow to get away. Mansell raised plenty of dust as he moved to his left but the ride across the dirt got him nowhere and merely left a space for de Cesaris to come storming through from the fifth row. Cheever had made another of his rapid starts but, this time he had left himself too much to do by starting from the seventh row and his way was soon barred by Lauda's McLaren.

As they completed the first lap, Piquet had pulled out a lead of two seconds over his team-mate while it was clear that Tambay had been holding up de Cesaris and Prost as they rushed past the Ferrari on the way towards Crowthorne. Rosberg, Arnoux and Lauda were next but, behind them, all hell was about to break loose as Cheever and Laffite ran side-by-side down the straight. The Williams driver found himself being edged towards the dirt on the left and he had no option but to hit the brakes while his left wheels were on the grass. The result was a high-speed spin and retirement in the catch-fencing. Laffite was unhurt but furious. That brought the retirements to three since Winkelhock and Ghinzani had retired with engine trouble.

During the next 10 laps, Piquet simply destroyed the opposition. The plan had been to start with a minimal amount of fuel and pull out such a lead that he would be able to make an early stop and yet return to the front. To that end, the plan was working perfectly, Nelson setting his fastest lap on his sixth tour and pulling out a lead of ten seconds over Patrese. The main interest, of course, lay with the progress of Prost, and a battle for third place with de Cesaris meant the Renault was consistently lapping one second slower than Piquet. The sight of the blue and white Brabham disappearing into the distance can have done nothing for Prost's peace of mind. Then, to make matters worse, he felt the throttle lag deteriorating; a sure sign that a turbo was giving trouble.

That apart, the progress of Lauda's McLaren was worth watching as he passed de Angelis, Arnoux and Rosberg and began to challenge Tambay for fifth place, the Austrian moving ahead under braking at Crowthorne on lap nine. Tambay had been literally powerless to respond, the Ferrari suffering a boost problem as well as struggling on hard tyres which gave poor traction at the rear. Arnoux, meanwhile, was coping with a deflating front tyre and, on the same lap, he knew his championship hopes were at an end when the engine, having lost most of its water, spluttered and coughed as the Frenchman made his way slowly to the pits. Now the title fight was down to two.

The field was down to 21 cars now that Mauro Baldi had retired his Alfa Romeo after the V8 had lost its water and Elio de Angelis's Lotus sounded far from healthy as he struggled through another lap after the mechanics had unsuccessfully tried to cure the problem during a lengthy pit stop. Mansell held 12th place but he would lose that on lap 13 when he stopped to have a broken gear linkage attended to and the rest of his afternoon would be spent struggling on tyres which would require two further pit stops.

It had taken Prost several laps to deal with de Cesaris, the Renault driver setting his fastest lap as he pulled out of the Alfa Romeo's slipstream and took third place on lap nine. Now he had a clear run at cutting back the four-second gap to Patrese but the Frenchman's lap times, if anything, increased and he was gradually reeled in by Lauda's McLaren. On lap 17, the Austrian dealt with the Renault in a typically clean and precise manner and he immediately set after Patrese's second place. Clearly, Prost was in trouble as he lapped around the high 1m 11s mark while Piquet continued to cut laps of 1m 10s with contemptuous ease.

Now, the only hurdle left for Brabham to overcome was the pit stop and, as ever, the mechanics performed with exemplary precision, sending Nelson on his way in 11.8 seconds (and not the 9.2s given by the official bulletin). At Piquet's request, they had fitted hard tyres all round for, on this occasion, Nelson was leaving nothing to chance. His lead was such that he rejoined, still in the lead, with a four-second advantage over Patrese, who had Lauda's McLaren snapping at his heels. The BMW power was proving too much for the TAG to cope with on the straights and Lauda had been trying unsuccessfully to find a way by for several laps.

The Brabham team immediately began to relay the gap to Piquet and Nelson, refusing to believe that he could *still* be in the lead, felt sure the 'plus' signs on his pit board were a mistake and really ought to read 'minus'. He stepped up his effort. As it was, his first lap

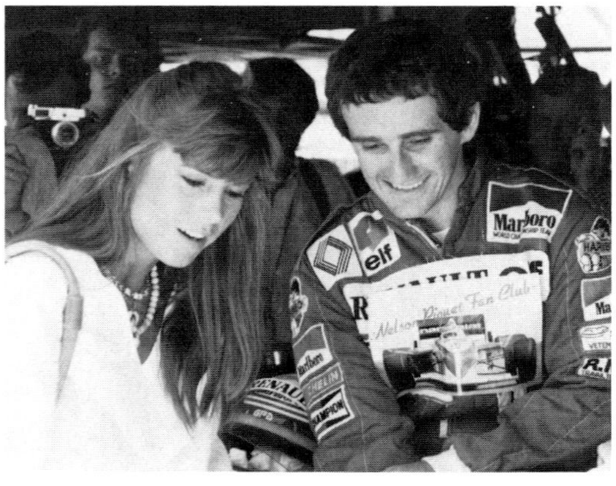

Alain Prost kept everyone amused during the final count-down to the race by wearing the fan club sticker which Nelson Piquet had slapped on the Frenchman's car. Prost shares the joke with Piquet's number one supporter, Sylvia Tamsma.

with a full tank (the race, don't forget, had only run one-third distance) had been an astonishing 1m 11.263. To put that in perspective, the next four drivers, Patrese, Lauda and Prost, were all running in the 1m 12s (with considerably less fuel) and Nelson reeled off the next four laps as follows: 1m 11.415s; 1m 11.501s; 1m 11.771s and 1m 11.974s. That took him to the end of lap 34. The race, and the championship, were about to take a dramatic turn.

At the end of lap 35, Prost brought his Renault into the pits and the mechanics immediately set to work. As they did so, Prost had a few words with Michel Tetu and then undid his belts and began to climb from the car. A turbo wheel had been damaged and there seemed little point in continuing. The mechanics were dumb struck and stood around for a few seconds, not knowing what to do. There was no option but to place the old tyres back on the car and push it away since Cheever was due to stop two laps later.

Eddie's stop went smoothly enough but the same could not be said for Lauda after the Austrian had made his stop a few laps earlier. A problem with the right-rear wheel meant Niki was delayed by 23 seconds and, when the race settled down, he still held third place but had lost considerable ground to Patrese. Rosberg's pit stop had taken longer than usual since the FW09, which the team, originally, did not intend to race until 1984, was not designed with refuelling in mind. Nevertheless, Rosberg took the opportunity to fit softer Goodyears and his lap times dropped dramatically after the stop.

With 30 laps remaining, Piquet led from Patrese, Lauda, de Cesaris, Tambay and Warwick. The Toleman driver, after making a good start and passing the two Lotuses and Cheever's Renault, had a quiet race although, for a while, it looked as though Rosberg, in seventh place, might threaten the Toleman. Thanks to the high track temperatures, a considerable amount of rubber had been scattered across the circuit and much of it found its way into the intercooler and radiator ducts on the Williams. As a result, the Honda began to misfire as the temperatures rose and Keke was forced to cut his revs and briefly concede his place to Cheever before stepping up his pace once more and repassing the Renault with little difficulty.

The two Tyrrells of Alboreto and Sullivan were ninth and 10th but the Italian was to lose the place when his DFY failed on lap 60. Fabi had already retired for similar reasons and Giacomelli had lost his place in front of the Tyrrells when his turbo caught fire and set the back of the Toleman alight. Tambay was forced to park his Ferrari when the turbo finally gave up and Prost's last hope of winning the championship was that a similar failure should befall Piquet's Brabham.

Once Nelson had seen the specially prepared sign which signalled Prost's departure, his lap times dropped immediately. Winding down the boost, Piquet began to cruise and only increased his pace when the temperatures began to rise. It made little difference and he decided it would be better to drive slowly once more. Fortunately, the temperature gauge stopped climbing . . .

By now, Patrese had caught his team-mate and Nelson offered no resistance as the Italian took the lead on lap 60. However, he did react by returning to the 1m 11s mark when Lauda closed on the Brabham but Niki was in no mood to stand on ceremony and he took second place on lap 69. Then de Cesaris approached the Brabham and Nelson knew it would be in order to let the Alfa Romeo through as well since fourth place would be good enough to win the championship and Warwick, currently holding fifth place, was too far behind to be a threat. However, the matter was to resolve itself not long after de Cesaris moved into third place when they all moved up one position as Lauda pulled off suddenly at Clubhouse, the electrics having failed. A brilliant drive, admittedly on the right tyres for the occasion, was over.

Thus Warwick, his Hart engine not missing a beat once again, was heading for fourth place while the Williams team and Keke Rosberg deserved the praise heaped upon them for such an exceptional debut and fifth place with the FW09/Honda combination. Cheever was a disconsolate sixth, his engine down-on-power almost from the start of the race; Sullivan had driven energetically to take seventh while the two Arrows of Surer and Boutsen had run steadily to finish eighth and ninth ahead of Jarier's Ligier. Lauda was to be classified 11th while Kenny Acheson, lapped six times, had nevertheless persevered with his single set of Pirellis and cramp in his right foot to bring the March home in 12th place – and in one piece. Mansell, running strongly enough to set third fastest lap, was too far behind to be classified at the end of a miserable race for Lotus.

Brabham, on the other hand, could not have asked for more. As Patrese took the flag, we had to remind ourselves that this was just the third time he had managed to finish a race this season. De Cesaris thoroughly deserved his second place, the Italian never having given up with a car which was not easy to drive, but the applause was reserved for Piquet in third place, the Brabham driver taking the title by two points.

Not only had Renault lost the Drivers' Championship, they had also failed to take the Constructors' Cup which, in the end, was won by Ferrari even though neither of the red cars had finished. While the Brabham team celebrated, the mood in the French pit was understandably glum. The Renault and Brabham mechanics exchanged shirts (much to the agitation of Gerard Larrousse) and the Williams team presented Gordon Murray with the numbers '1' and '2' as a token of their new status as reigning champions.

It had been made possible thanks to a combination of Murray's genius, BMW's increase in competitiveness and Piquet's extraordinary display of speed and ice-cool confidence. Nelson declared that he would get drunk that evening – although he was not sure how since he had never done it before. The mechanics, of course, offered their assistance. It would be the only occasion during the weekend when Nelson Piquet would have little or no control over his destiny.

Entries and practice times

No.	Driver	Nat	Car	Tyre	Engine	Entrant	Practice 1	Practice 2
1	Keke Rosberg	SF	Saudia WILLIAMS FW09	G	Honda RA163-E	TAG Williams Team	**1m 07·256s**	1m 07·344s
2	Jacques Laffite	F	Saudia WILLIAMS FW09	G	Honda RA163-E	TAG Williams Team	**1m 07·931s**	1m 08·652s
3	Michele Alboreto	I	Benetton TYRRELL 012	G	Ford Cosworth DFY	Benetton Tyrrell Team	**1m 11·096s**	1m 11·284s
4	Danny Sullivan	USA	Benetton TYRRELL 012	G	Ford Cosworth DFY	Benetton Tyrrell Team	1m 11·750s	**1m 11·382s**
5	Nelson Piquet	BR	Parmalat BRABHAM BT52B	M	BMW M12/13	Fila Sport	**1m 06·792s**	1m 06·821s
6	Riccardo Patrese	I	Parmalat BRABHAM BT52B	M	BMW M12/13	Fila Sport	1m 08·181s	**1m 07·001s**
7	John Watson	GB	Marlboro McLAREN MP4/1E	M	TAG P01 (TTE P01)	Marlboro McLaren International	**1m 08·328s**	1m 10·635s
8	Niki Lauda	A	Marlboro McLAREN MP4/1E	M	TAG P01 (TTE P01)	Marlboro McLaren International	**1m 07·974s**	1m 08·587s
9	Manfred Winkelhock	D	ATS D6	M	BMW M12/13	Team ATS	1m 07·726s	**1m 07·682s**
11	Elio de Angelis	I	John Player Special LOTUS 94T	P	Renault EF1	John Player Team Lotus	**1m 07·937s**	1m 07·980s
12	Nigel Mansell	GB	John Player Special LOTUS 94T	P	Renault EF1	John Player Team Lotus	1m 09·443s	**1m 07·643s**
15	Alain Prost	F	Elf RENAULT RE40	M	Renault EF1	Equipe Renault Elf	**1m 07·186s**	1m 08·136s
16	Eddie Cheever	USA	Elf RENAULT RE40	M	Renault EF1	Equipe Renault Elf	**1m 08·069s**	1m 08·360s
17	Kenneth Acheson	GB	MARCH-RAM 01	P	Ford Cosworth DFV	RAM Automotive Team March	**1m 13·352s**	
22	Andrea de Cesaris	I	Marlboro ALFA ROMEO 183T	M	Alfa Romeo 183T	Marlboro Team Alfa Romeo	1m 08·970s	**1m 07·759s**
23	Mauro Baldi	I	Marlboro ALFA ROMEO 183T	M	Alfa Romeo 183T	Marlboro Team Alfa Romeo	1m 09·364s	**1m 08·628s**
25	Jean-Pierre Jarier	F	Gitanes LIGIER JS21	M	Ford Cosworth DFV/DFY	Equipe Ligier Gitanes	**1m 12·017s**	1m 12·538s
26	Raul Boesel	BR	Gitanes LIGIER JS21	M	Ford Cosworth DFV	Equipe Ligier Gitanes	**1m 12·745s**	1m 13·330s
27	Patrick Tambay	F	Fiat FERRARI 126C3	G	Ferrari 126C	Scuderia Ferrari SpA SEFAC	**1m 06·554s**	1m 07·029s
28	René Arnoux	F	Fiat FERRARI 126C3	G	Ferrari 126C	Scuderia Ferrari SpA SEFAC	1m 07·222s	**1m 07·105s**
29	Marc Surer	CH	ARROWS A6	G	Ford Cosworth DFV	Arrows Racing Team	1m 12·309s	**1m 12·049s**
30	Thierry Boutsen	B	ARROWS A6	G	Ford Cosworth DFV	Arrows Racing Team	1m 11·988s	**1m 11·658s**
31	Corrado Fabi	I	OSELLA FA1E	M	Alfa Romeo 1260	Osella Squadra Corse	1m 14·483s	**1m 13·656s**
32	Piercarlo Ghinzani	I	OSELLA FA1E	M	Alfa Romeo 1260	Osella Squadra Corse	**1m 14·903s**	1m 15·503s
35	Derek Warwick	GB	Candy TOLEMAN TG183B	P	Hart 415T	Candy Toleman Motorsport	**1m 08·061s**	1m 08·301s
36	Bruno Giacomelli	I	Candy TOLEMAN TG183B	P	Hart 415T	Candy Toleman Motorsport	**1m 08·350s**	1m 08·439s

Thursday morning and Friday morning practice sessions not officially recorded.

G – Goodyear, M – Michelin, P – Pirelli.

Thur pm	Fri pm
Hot, dry	Hot, dry

Starting grid

27 TAMBAY (1m 06·554s)
Ferrari

　　5 PIQUET (1m 06·792s)
　　Brabham

6 PATRESE (1m 07·001s)
Brabham

　　28 ARNOUX (1m 07·105s)
　　Ferrari

15 PROST (1m 07·186s)
Renault

　　1 ROSBERG (1m 07·256s)
　　Williams

12 MANSELL (1m 07·643s)
Lotus

　　9 WINKELHOCK (1m 07·682s)
　　ATS

22 DE CESARIS (1m 07·759s)
Alfa Romeo

　　2 LAFFITE (1m 07·931s)
　　Williams

11 DE ANGELIS (1m 07·937s)
Lotus

　　8 LAUDA (1m 07·974s)
　　McLaren

35 WARWICK (1m 08·061s)
Toleman

　　16 CHEEVER (1m 08·069s)
　　Renault

7 WATSON (1m 08·328s)
McLaren

　　36 GIACOMELLI (1m 08·350s)
　　Toleman

23 BALDI (1m 08·628s)
Alfa Romeo

　　3 ALBORETO (1m 11·096s)
　　Tyrrell

4 SULLIVAN (1m 11·382s)
Tyrrell

　　30 BOUTSEN (1m 11·658s)
　　Arrows

25 JARIER (1m 12·017s)
Ligier

　　29 SURER (1m 12·049s)
　　Arrows

26 BOESEL (1m 12·745s)
Ligier

　　17 ACHESON (1m 13·352s)
　　RAM March

31 FABI (1m 13·656s)
Osella

　　32 GHINZANI (1m 14·903s)
　　Osella

Results and retirements

Place	Driver	Car	Laps	Time and Speed (mph/km/h)/Retirement	
1	Riccardo Patrese	Brabham-BMW t/c 4	77	1h 33m 25·708s	126·100/202·939
2	Andrea de Cesaris	Alfa Romeo t/c V8	77	1h 33m 35·027s	125·889/202·6
3	Nelson Piquet	Brabham-BMW t/c 4	77	1h 33m 47·677s	125·579/202·1
4	Derek Warwick	Toleman-Hart t/c 4	76		
5	Keke Rosberg	Williams-Honda t/c V6	76		
6	Eddie Cheever	Renault t/c V6	76		
7	Danny Sullivan	Tyrrell-Cosworth V8	75		
8	Marc Surer	Arrows-Cosworth V8	75		
9	Thierry Boutsen	Arrows-Cosworth V8	74		
10	Jean-Pierre Jarier	Ligier-Cosworth V8	73		
11	Niki Lauda	McLaren-TAG t/c V6	71	Electrics	
12	Kenneth Acheson	RAM March-Cosworth V8	71		
	Nigel Mansell	Lotus-Renault t/c V6	68	Running, not classified	
	Raul Boesel	Ligier-Cosworth V8	66	Running, not classified	
	Michele Alboreto	Tyrrell-Cosworth V8	60	Engine	
	Patrick Tambay	Ferrari t/c V6	56	Turbo	
	Bruno Giacomelli	Toleman-Hart t/c 4	56	Turbo/fire	
	Alain Prost	Renault t/c V6	35	Turbo	
	Corrado Fabi	Osella-Alfa Romeo V12	28	Engine	
	Elio de Angelis	Lotus-Renault t/c V6	20	Engine/misfire	
	John Watson	McLaren-TAG t/c V6	18	Disqualified	
	René Arnoux	Ferrari t/c V6	9	Engine	
	Mauro Baldi	Alfa Romeo t/c V8	5	Engine	
	Piercarlo Ghinzani	Osella-Alfa Romeo V12	1	Engine	
	Manfred Winkelhock	ATS-BMW t/c 4	1	Engine	
	Jacques Laffite	Williams-Honda t/c V6	1	Accident	

Fastest lap: Piquet, on lap 6, 1m 09·948s, 131·245mph/211·219km/h.
Lap record: Alain Prost (F1 Renault RE 30B t/c V6), 1m 08·278, 134·455mph/216·385km/h (1982).

Past winners

Year	Driver	Nat	Car	Circuit	Distance miles/km	Speed mph/km/h
1934	Whitney Straight	GB	2·9 Maserati 8CM s/c	Prince George	91·20/146·77	95·68/153·98
1936	'Mario' Massacurati	I	2·0 Bugatti T35B s/c	Prince George	198·54/319·52	87·43/140·70
1937	Pat Fairfield	ZA	1·0 ERA A-type s/c	Prince George	198·54/319·52	89·17/143·50
1938	Buller Meyer	ZA	1·5 Riley	Prince George	198·54/319·52	86·53/139·26
1939	Luigi Villoresi	I	1·5 Maserati 4CM	Prince George	198·54/319·52	99·67/160·40
1960*	Paul Frère	B	1·5 Cooper T45-Climax	East London	145·80/234·64	84·88/136·60
1960*	Stirling Moss	GB	1·5 Porsche 718	East London	194·40/312·86	89·24/143·62
1961*	Jim Clark	GB	1·5 Lotus 21-Climax	East London	194·40/312·86	92·20/148·38
1962	Graham Hill	GB	1·5 BRM P57	East London	199·26/320·68	93·57/150·59
1963	Jim Clark	GB	1·5 Lotus 25-Climax	East London	206·55/332·41	95·10/153·05
1965	Jim Clark	GB	1·5 Lotus 25-Climax	East London	206·55/332·41	97·97/157·68
1966*	Mike Spence	GB	2·0 Lotus 33-Climax	East London	145·80/234·64	97·75/157·31
1967	Pedro Rodriguez	MEX	3·0 Cooper T81-Maserati	Kyalami	203·52/327·53	97·09/156·25
1968	Jim Clark	GB	3·0 Lotus 49-Ford	Kyalami	204·00/328·31	107·42/172·88
1969	Jackie Stewart	GB	3·0 Matra MS10-Ford	Kyalami	204·00/328·31	110·62/178·03
1970	Jack Brabham	AUS	3·0 Brabham BT33-Ford	Kyalami	204·00/328·31	111·70/179·76
1971	Mario Andretti	USA	3·0 Ferrari 312B-1/71	Kyalami	201·45/324·20	112·36/180·83
1972	Denny Hulme	NZ	3·0 McLaren M19A-Ford	Kyalami	201·41/324·20	114·23/183·83
1973	Jackie Stewart	GB	3·0 Tyrrell 006-Ford	Kyalami	201·45/324·20	117·14/188·52
1974	Carlos Reutemann	RA	3·0 Brabham BT44-Ford	Kyalami	198·90/320·10	116·22/187·04
1975	Jody Scheckter	ZA	3·0 Tyrrell 007-Ford	Kyalami	198·90/320·10	115·55/185·96
1976	Niki Lauda	A	3·0 Ferrari 312T/76	Kyalami	198·90/320·10	116·65/187·73
1977	Niki Lauda	A	3·0 Ferrari 312T-2/77	Kyalami	198·90/320·10	116·59/187·63
1978	Ronnie Peterson	S	3·0 JPS/Lotus 78-Ford	Kyalami	198·90/320·10	116·70/187·81
1979	Gilles Villeneuve	CDN	3·0 Ferrari 312T-4	Kyalami	198·90/320·10	117·19/188·60
1980	René Arnoux	F	1·5 Renault RE t/c	Kyalami	198·90/320·10	123·19/198·25
1981*	Carlos Reutemann	RA	3·0 Williams FWO7B-Ford	Kyalami	196·35/315·99	112·31/180·75
1982	Alain Prost	F	1·5 Renault RE 30B t/c	Kyalami	196·35/315·99	127·82/205·70
1983	Riccardo Patrese	I	1·5 Brabham-BMW BT52B t/c	Kyalami	196·35/315·99	126·10/202·94

*Non-championship

Circuit data

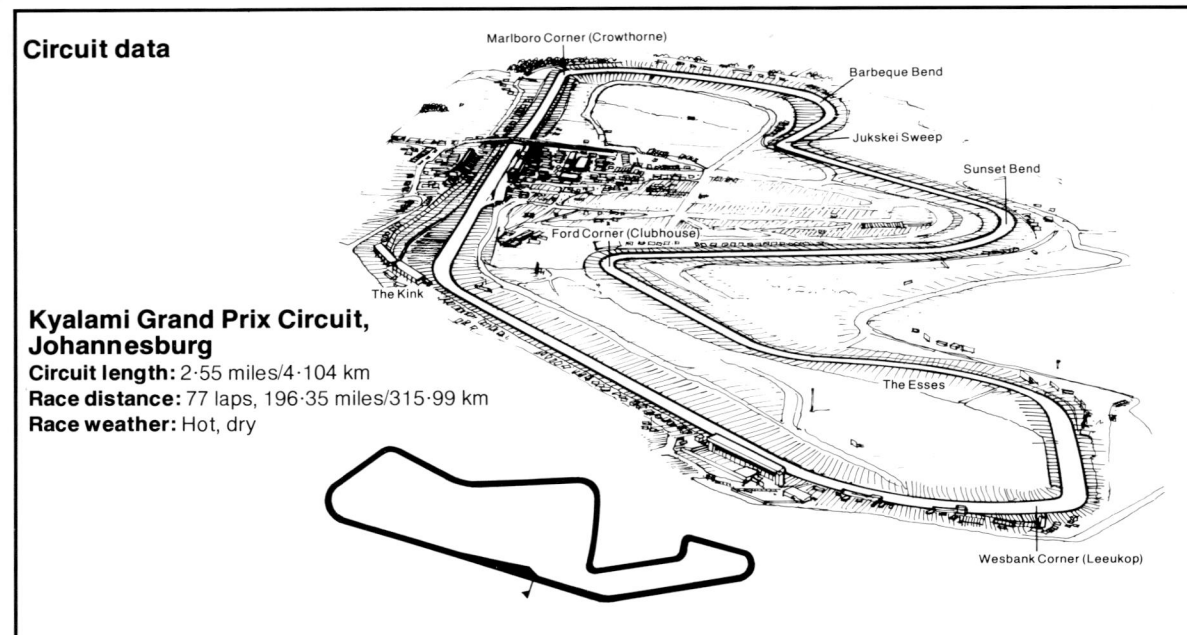

Kyalami Grand Prix Circuit, Johannesburg

Circuit length: 2·55 miles/4·104 km
Race distance: 77 laps, 196·35 miles/315·99 km
Race weather: Hot, dry

Marlboro Corner (Crowthorne)
Barbeque Bend
Jukskei Sweep
Sunset Bend
Ford Corner (Clubhouse)
The Kink
The Esses
Wesbank Corner (Leeukop)

Fastest laps

Driver	Time	Lap
Nelson Piquet	1m 09·948s	6
Niki Lauda	1m 10·634s	17
Nigel Mansell	1m 10·825s	60
Riccardo Patrese	1m 10·848s	8
Alain Prost	1m 11·166s	9
Patrick Tambay	1m 11·267s	7
Andrea de Cesaris	1m 11·401s	5
Keke Rosberg	1m 11·656s	51
Eddie Cheever	1m 11·953s	6
Bruno Giacomelli	1m 12·058s	51
Derek Warwick	1m 12·102s	11
René Arnoux	1m 12·183s	6
Mauro Baldi	1m 12·686s	4
Elio de Angelis	1m 12·709s	16
John Watson	1m 13·194s	17
Danny Sullivan	1m 13·494s	70
Michele Alboreto	1m 13·507s	50
Marc Surer	1m 14·489s	60
Thierry Boutsen	1m 15·100s	47
Jean-Pierre Jarier	1m 15·144s	18
Raul Boesel	1m 15·886s	5
Corrado Fabi	1m 17·153s	8
Kenneth Acheson	1m 17·212s	7
Manfred Winkelhock	1m 23·427s	1
Jaques Laffite	1m 24·689s	1
Piercarlo Ghinzani	1m 29·776s	1

Points

WORLD CHAMPIONSHIP OF DRIVERS

1	Nelson Piquet	59 pts
2	Alain Prost	57
3	René Arnoux	49
4	Patrick Tambay	40
5	Keke Rosberg	27
6 =	John Watson	22
6 =	Eddie Cheever	22
8	Andrea de Cesaris	15
9	Riccardo Patrese	13
10	Niki Lauda	12
11	Jacques Laffite	11
12 =	Michele Alboreto	10
12 =	Nigel Mansell	10
14	Derek Warwick	9
15	Marc Surer	4
16	Mauro Baldi	3
17 =	Danny Sullivan	2
17 =	Elio de Angelis	2
19 =	Johnny Cecotto	1
19 =	Bruno Giacomelli	1

CONSTRUCTORS' CUP

1	Ferrari	89 pts
2	Renault	79
3	Brabham	72
4	Williams	38
5	McLaren	34
6	Alfa Romeo	18
7 =	Tyrrell	12
7 =	Lotus	12
9	Toleman	10
10	Arrows	4
11	Theodore	1

Lap chart

1st LAP ORDER	1	2	3	4	5	6	7	8	9	10	11	12	13	14	15	16	17	18	19	20	21	22	23	24	25	26	27	28	29	30	31	32	33	34	35	36	37
5 N. Piquet	5	5	5	5	5	5	5	5	5	5	5	5	5	5	5	5	5	5	5	5	5	5	5	5	5	5	5	(5)	5	5	5	5	5	5	5	5	5
6 R. Patrese	6	6	6	6	6	6	6	6	6	6	6	6	6	6	6	6	6	6	6	6	6	6	6	6	6	6	6	6	6	6	6	6	6	6	6	6	6
27 P. Tambay	27	22	22	22	22	22	22	22	15	15	15	15	15	15	15	15	15	8	8	8	8	8	8	8	8	8	8	8	8	(8)	15	(15)	22	22			
22 A. de Cesaris	22	15	15	15	15	15	15	15	22	22	22	8	8	8	8	8	15	15	15	15	15	15	15	15	15	15	15	15	15	15	15	22	22	27	27		
15 A. Prost	15	27	27	27	27	27	27	27	8	8	8	22	22	22	22	22	22	22	22	22	22	22	22	22	22	22	22	22	22	22	22	27	27	8	8		
1 K. Rosberg	1	1	1	1	1	8	8	8	27	27	27	27	27	27	27	27	27	27	27	27	27	27	27	27	27	27	27	27	27	27	27	16	16	16	(16)		
28 R. Arnoux	28	28	28	28	8	1	1	1	1	1	1	1	1	1	1	1	1	1	1	1	1	1	1	1	1	1	1	1	1	1	1	(1)	8	8	35	35	
11 E. De Angelis	11	11	8	8	28	28	28	28	16	16	16	16	16	35	35	35	35	35	35	35	35	35	35	35	35	35	35	35	(35)	16	16	35	35	36	1		
9 M. Winkelhock	9	8	16	16	16	16	16	16	35	35	35	35	35	16	16	16	16	16	16	16	16	16	16	16	16	16	16	16	16	35	35	36	36	1	36		
8 N. Lauda	8	16	11	11	23	35	35	35	12	12	12	(12)	36	36	36	36	36	36	36	36	36	36	36	36	36	36	36	36	36	36	36	1	1	3	3		
35 D. Warwick	35	35	35	35	35	12	12	12	36	36	36	36	7	7	7	7	7	(7)	3	3	3	3	3	3	3	3	3	3	3	3	3	3	3	4	4		
2 J. Laffite	2	12	12	23	11	7	7	36	7	7	7	3	3	3	3	3	4	4	4	4	4	4	4	4	4	4	4	4	4	4	4	4	4	29	29		
16 E. Cheever	16	7	23	12	12	36	36	7	3	3	3	(12)	4	4	4	4	29	29	29	29	29	29	29	29	29	29	29	29	29	29	29	30	30	30	30		
12 N. Mansell	12	23	7	7	3	3	3	29	29	29	4	4	29	29	29	29	30	30	30	30	30	30	30	30	30	30	30	30	30	30	30	25	25				
7 J. Watson	7	36	36	36	36	(11)	25	25	4	4	4	29	30	30	30	30	26	25	25	25	25	25	25	25	25	25	25	25	25	25	25	17	17				
23 M. Baldi	23	3	3	3	3	25	29	29	25	30	30	30	30	26	26	26	26	25	17	17	17	17	17	17	17	17	17	17	17	17	17	26	26				
36 B. Giacomelli	36	29	25	25	25	29	4	4	30	25	26	26	26	17	17	17	17	17	31	31	31	31	31	31	31	31	26	26	26	26	26	12	12				
3 M. Alboreto	3	25	29	29	29	4	30	30	(28)	26	17	17	17	31	31	31	31	31	26	26	26	26	26	26	26	12	12	12	12	12	12						
29 M. Surer	29	30	30	30	30	30	26	26	17	31	31	31	25	25	25	25	12	12	12	12	12	12	12	12	(12)												
25 J.-P. Jarier	25	4	4	4	4	26	17	17	31	25	25	25	12	12	12	12	11	(11)																			
30 T. Boutsen	30	26	26	26	26	17	31	31	11	11	11	11	11	11	11	11																					
32 P. Ghinzani	32	17	17	17	17	31	11	11	11																												
26 R. Boesel	26	31	31	31	31																																
4 D. Sullivan	4																																				
17 K. Acheson	17																																				

	38	39	40	41	42	43	44	45	46	47	48	49	50	51	52	53	54	55	56	57	58	59	60	61	62	63	64	65	66	67	68	69	70	71	72	73	74	75	76	77
	5	5	5	5	5	5	5	5	5	5	5	5	5	5	5	5	5	5	5	5	5	5	6	6	6	6	6	6	6	6	6	6	6	6	6	6	6	6	6	6
	6	6	6	6	6	6	6	6	(6)	6	6	6	6	6	6	6	6	6	6	6	6	5	5	5	5	5	5	5	5	8	8	8	5	5	5	22	22	22		
	22	22	22	27	27	27	27	(27)	8	8	8	8	8	8	8	8	8	8	8	8	8	8	8	8	8	8	8	8	5	5	5	22	22	22	5	5	5			
	27	27	27	(22)	8	8	8	8	22	22	22	22	22	22	22	22	22	22	22	22	22	22	22	22	22	22	22	22	22	22	22	35	35	35	35	35				
	8	8	8	8	22	22	22	22	27	27	27	27	27	27	27	27	35	35	35	35	35	35	35	35	35	35	35	35	35	35	35	16	16	1	1	1				
	35	35	35	35	35	35	35	35	35	35	35	35	35	35	35	35	1	1	1	1	1	1	1	16	16	16	16	16	1	1	16	16	16							
	1	1	1	1	1	1	1	1	1	1	1	1	16	1	27	16	16	16	16	16	16	16	16	1	1	1	1	1	4	4	4	4								
	36	16	16	16	16	16	16	16	16	16	16	16	16	1	16	3	3	3	4	4	4	4	4	4	4	4	4	4	29	29	29	29								
	16	36	36	36	36	(36)	3	3	3	3	3	3	3	3	3	4	4	4	(3)	29	29	29	29	29	29	29	29	29	30	30	30									
	3	3	3	3	3	4	4	4	4	4	4	4	29	29	29	30	30	30	30	30	30	30	30	30	25	25														
	4	4	4	4	4	36	29	29	29	29	29	29	29	30	30	25	25	25	25	25	25	25	25	25																
	29	29	29	29	29	30	30	30	30	30	30	30	36	36	36	25	17	17	17	17	17	17	17	17																
	30	30	30	30	30	30	36	36	36	36	36	30	30	30	30	17	17	17	17	12	12	12	12	12																
	17	17	17	17	17	17	17	17	17	17	17	17	17	17	17	12	12	12	12	26	26	26	26	26																
	26	26	26	26	26	26	26	12	12	12	12	12	12	12	12	26	26	26	26																					
	12	12	12	12	12	12	12	26	26	26	26	26	26	26	26																									

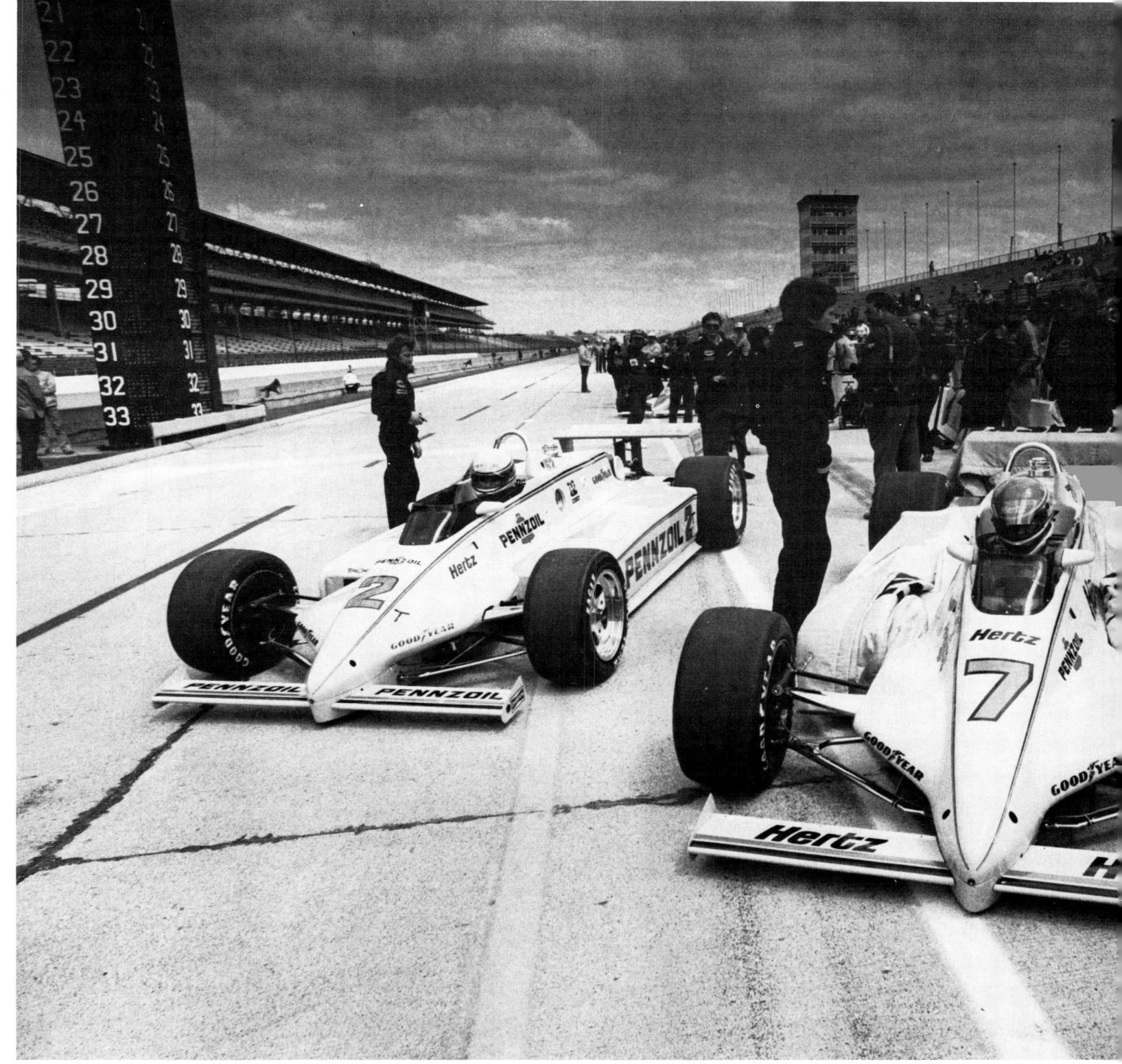

The Old Order changeth

American Review by Gordon Kirby

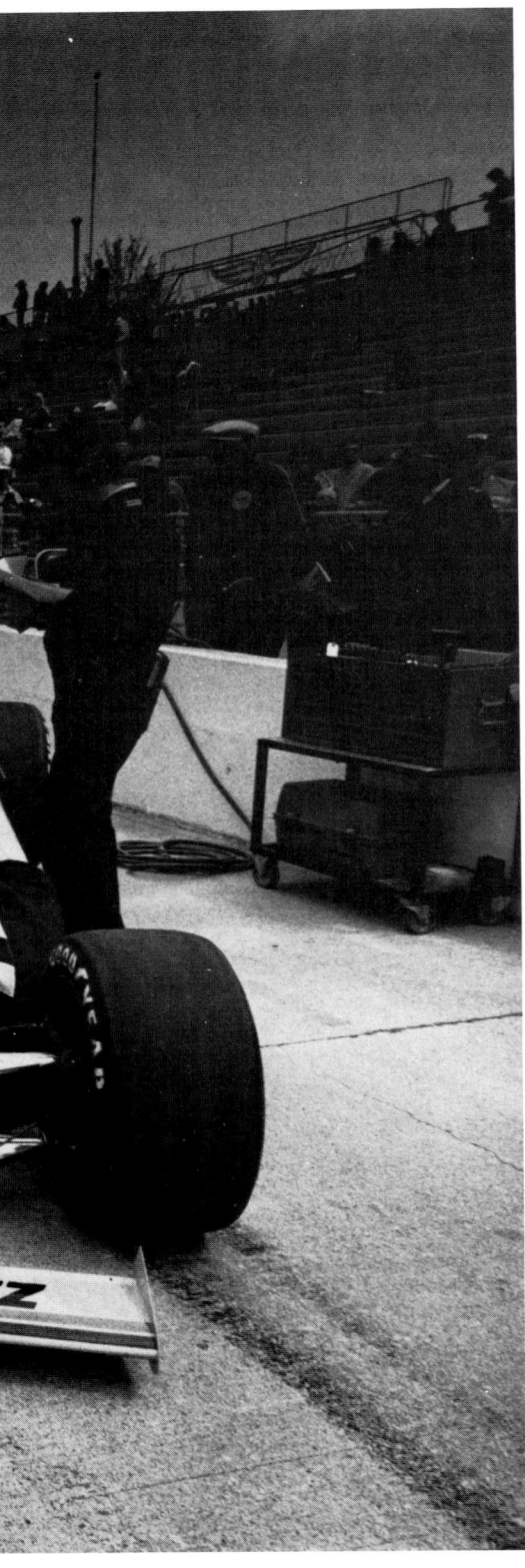

The Penske PC11s of Rick Mears (left) and Al Unser began to lose ground to the Marches at mid-season and the team raced revised versions of the 1982 PC10 before paying March the ultimate accolade by buying an 83C. Unser's position at the top of the championship during the first half of the season was due to Al completing every lap and never falling below the top three during the first six races.

After two years of steady growth America's native national championship – known in contemporary terms as the CART/PPG Indy Car World Series – really came to life in 1983. Backed by CART's aggressive business and promotional methods the once-dormant Indycar fields bristled with energy, youth and sharp competition last summer. Eight different drivers won the first ten races of the year. Rookies Teo Fabi, John Paul Jr and Al Unser Jr established themselves as major contenders and racewinners. As the season wore on the hitherto all-conquering Penske team found themselves struggling to qualify among the top ten and everywhere you looked in an Indycar garage there were new or revitalised teams and best of all, eager young faces buckling themselves into place and frequently outrunning the likes of Unser, Andretti, Mears, Sneva, Johncock and Rutherford.

The rebirth of the American national driving championship under the aegis of CART and nom de plume "Indy Car World Series" began in the winter of 1978-79 when CART (Championship Auto Racing Teams) broke away from USAC (United States Auto Club). Staged for the first time in 1916 by the AAA (American Automobile Association) the American national championship traces it's beginnings back to 1909 and was passed into the hands of USAC in 1955 after that year's Le Mans tragedy compelled the AAA to withdraw from automobile race organising. Through the 'sixties in particular, the USAC Championship boomed thanks largely to money and equipment from the likes of Ford, Firestone and Goodyear. When Ford and Firestone withdrew however, USAC fell into a spider's web of problems which saw the championship debilitate steadily.

Formed in June of '78 as an entrants' association aimed at pressuring USAC into making drastically-needed changes, the original CART coterie included Roger Penske, Pat Patrick, Dan Gurney, Tyler Alexander, Jim Hall, Jerry O'Connell and Bob Fletcher. Also deeply involved in CART's early formation and subsequent breakaway were most of the leading drivers such as Bobby and Al Unser, Johnny Rutherford, Gordon Johncock, Wally Dallenbach and Rick Mears. Mario Andretti was embroiled in Formula 1 at the time while then-USAC champion Tom Sneva was more a maverick than an "aligned" driver. A more spectacular and voluble maverick was of course, A. J. Foyt who was one of the original motivators of CART before jumping ship in his usual unpredictable manner in January of 1979.

Through that year and 1980 Foyt ran only in USAC-sanctioned races and there is no doubt his presence in what was otherwise a distinctly lacklustre series managed to keep the leaky USAC ship afloat and the CART-USAC war alive through the middle of 1981. That was the year of the six-month dispute over racewinner Bobby Unser's yellow flag passing manoeuvre in the Indianapolis 500 and by the end of 1981 USAC had finally fallen into public ridicule. Indianapolis 500 aside, the old club was by then out of the championship car-race organising business.

Meanwhile the shape and style of the dinosaur-riddled championship has changed rapidly and in the past two seasons in particular, CART's PPG Industries-sponsored Indy Car World Series has undergone a genuine transformation. A three-year television contract with NBC, a brace of new venues and steady improvements in prize money has attracted a steady stream of new teams and new drivers and in 1983 the newcomers really began to make their presence felt. F1 refugee Teo Fabi, young IMSA GT champion John Paul Jr and precociously-talented CanAm champion Al Unser Jr proved themselves capable of leading and winning races, each of the three rookies driving for teams new to the business of Indycar racing. 1982 Rookie-of-the-Year Bobby Rahal and his CanAm/road racing-backgrounded team continued to win races and be a major contender while other contenders included road-racing trained drivers like Kevin Cogan, Geoff Brabham, Derek Daly, Josele Garza and Chip Ganassi.

Of the old guard only Al Unser Sr and Mario Andretti enjoyed good years with Unser Sr, in his first year with five-time champions Penske Racing, leading the championship for most of the season. Older brother Bobby had retired reluctantly the previous winter while Gordon Johncock and Johnny

Rutherford spent most of the year on the sidelines after respective leg-breaking crashes. Wally Dallenbach retired four years ago and has been CART's chief steward since 1981 while supremely fast speedway racer Tom Sneva finally won the Indy 500 in 1983 after ten years of trying. Mears, a fresh face in 1978, continues in his prime, a three-time CART champion.

As for Foyt he appeared only at Indianapolis in 1983 and was an early retirement after running near the back of the field. In September problems with his back, a legacy of a series of heavy crashes in both Indy and stock cars in recent years, forced Foyt into hospital. At the same time he released a new co-authored biography about himself wherein the four-time Indy winner emerged as a fallen hero of the most profane kind – an arrogant, bitter-minded man with no love for anything connected with the changing times. . . .

In the middle of all this, road racing has become more and more a part of the Indycar season. Six of the past year's thirteen Indycar races were run on "road courses" and at presstime as many as nine of 1984's projected races were to take place on some type of road circuit/city street/airfield venue. In fact, the clearest indicator of the rejuvenation of the American national championship was the appearance in October of Indycars in preference to Formula One on a five-turn, 1.25-mile irregular oval laid-out in Caesar's Palace downtown Las Vegas parking lot and more importantly, the switch at Long Beach in 1984 from F1 to Indycars. While those changes were taking shape CART Chairman John Frasco and F1 dealmaker Bernie Ecclestone aimed arrows at each other in an apparent fight over places to race in the USA which was too bad because in a more perfect world the two outwardly similar series of automobile races would surely serve as a complement to each other.

It was of course economics which made Long Beach and Las Vegas change from F1 to Indy cars and it must therefore be noted that because of the rapid recent growth of Indycar racing, the only real-world difference between the two forms of racing is that the American derivative is considerably cheaper. There are of course, numerous subtle and not so subtle differences in content, style and attitudes but there can be no denying that CART's overall "package" of promotion, rules management/enforcement and cost-controlling is much more in check than F1's FISA-fogged, non-package. Certainly the budget of multiple Indycar champions Penske Racing is about one-tenth that of Ferrari but it must also be remembered that it was poor overall management, rulemaking and cost-controlling on the part of USAC which almost killed Indycar racing in the 'seventies and that CART was founded as an association of independant, self-governing team owners, devoid of and not terribly interested in factory support.

That opinion continues to prevail in all corners of the organisation and was reflected in September's four-year rule package (1984-87) which freezes the existing engine/aerodynamic rules and puts firm limits on the use of all types of electronic controls. After much debate the engine rules have been stabilised much as they were in '83. For the next four years CART's rules cater exclusively to turbocharged engines restricted to 48 ins Hg manifold pressure (1.65 atmospheres). There is an eight-cylinder maximum and two types of engine are permitted; 2.65 litre (161 cubic inch) overhead camshaft engines and 3.4 litre (209 cubic inch) American, "production-based" engines. A "grandfather" clause allows teams who raced regularly with normally-aspirated 5.8 litre (355 cubic inches) Chevrolet V8s in 1982 and '83 to continue using that type of engine.

As well as setting these engine rules for four years it is also CART's intention to maintain the current chassis/aerodynamic regulations over the four-year period. That means Indycars will continue to be sidepodded, "tunnel" cars with bodywork fixed one inch above the chassis baseline. There were to be some refinements of the footbox and front suspension construction regulations which would be announced after our deadline but otherwise the chassis/ aerodynamic prescriptions will remain unchanged.

New under CART's 1984-87 rules is a restriction on electronic controls for both chassis and engines. This restriction applies to things like "active" suspension systems and new fuel and ignition systems, all of which

Bobby Rahal, a leading contender in his Truesports March 83C, took his first win of the season by beating Teo Fabi at Riverside *(right)*.
Photo: Robert Harmeyer

Bobby Allison put himself in contention for his first NASCAR Championship by winning three races in a row in the middle of a hot, dry summer in the South *(below)*.
Photo: Mark Clifford

Carl Haas commissioned a Lola Indycar and Mario Andretti drove the T700 to victory at Elkhart Lake during a troubled season for the Haas/Paul Newman partnership *(bottom)*.
Photo: Robert Harmeyer

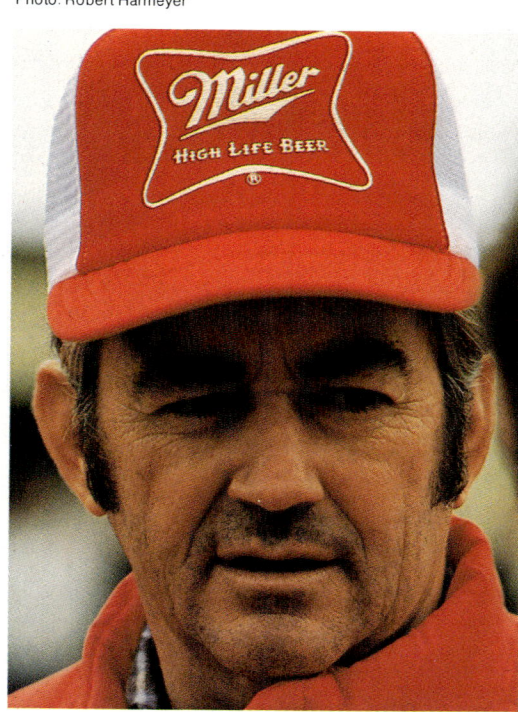

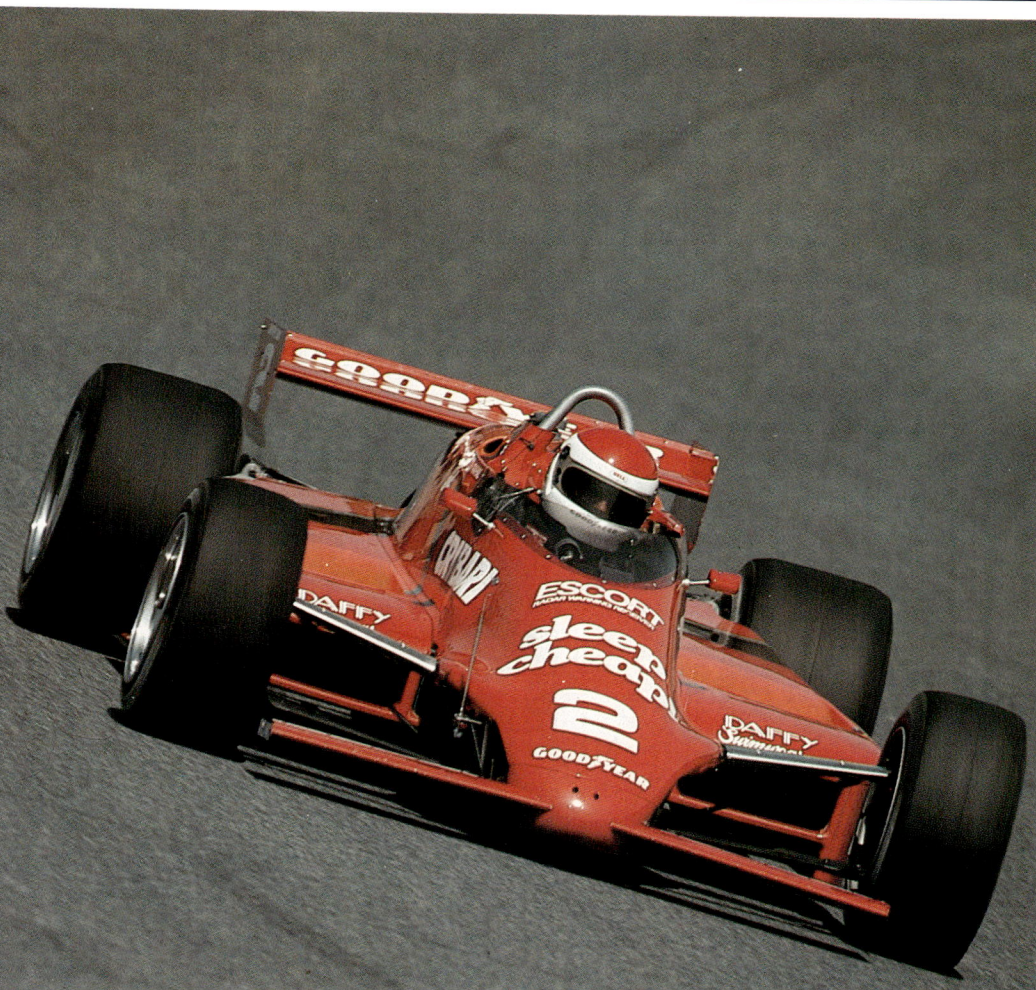

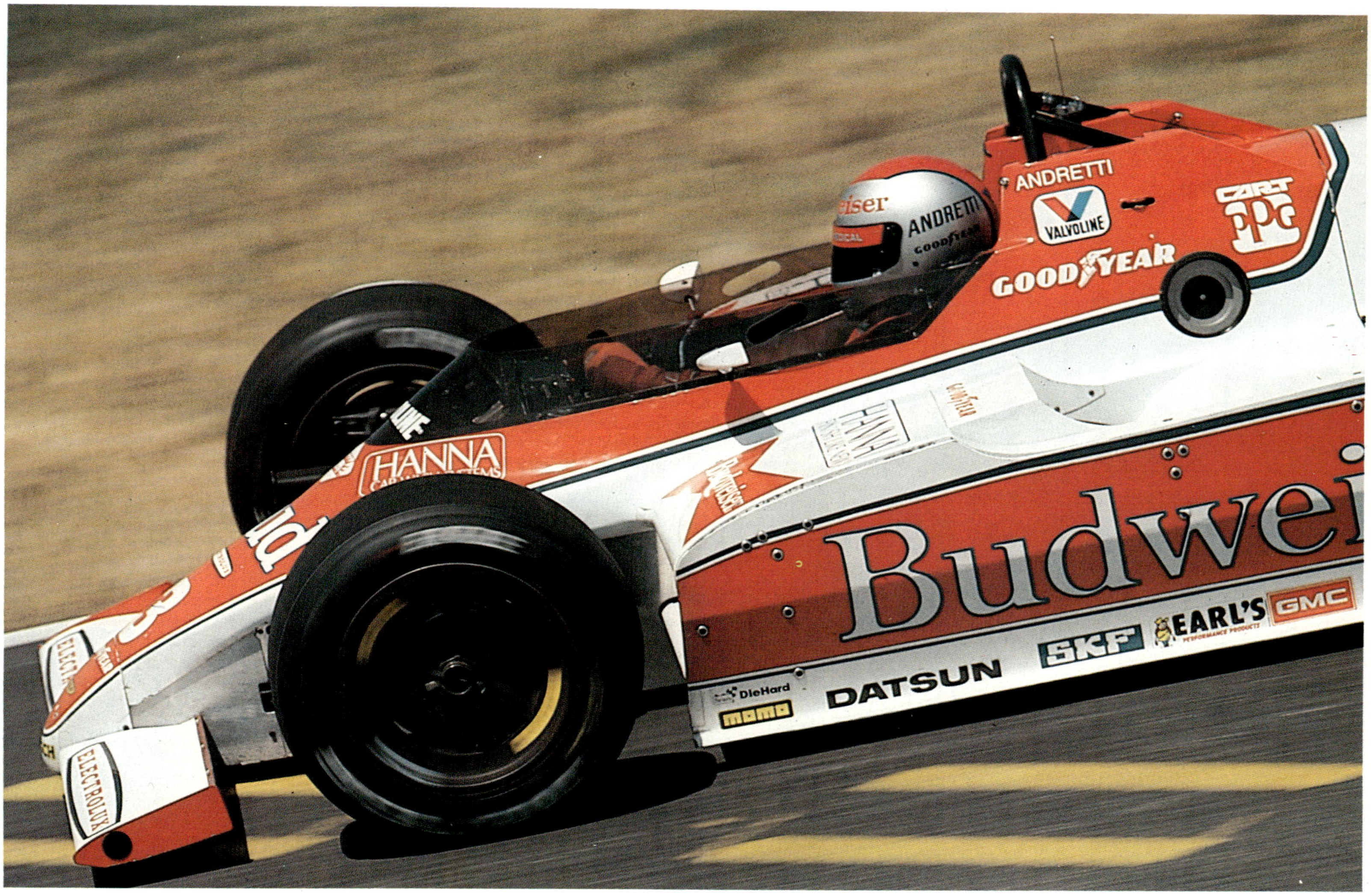

Team VDS switched to CART racing with considerable success. John Paul Jnr (below) won the Michigan 500 and ran competitively in the team's Penske PC10. The American broke his leg during practice at Indianapolis and was temporarily replaced by Geoff Brabham who finished fourth at the Brickyard. Team VDS' thriving engine shop supplied engines to the Newman/Haas and Truesports teams.
Photos: Robert Harmeyer, David Hutson and John Townsend

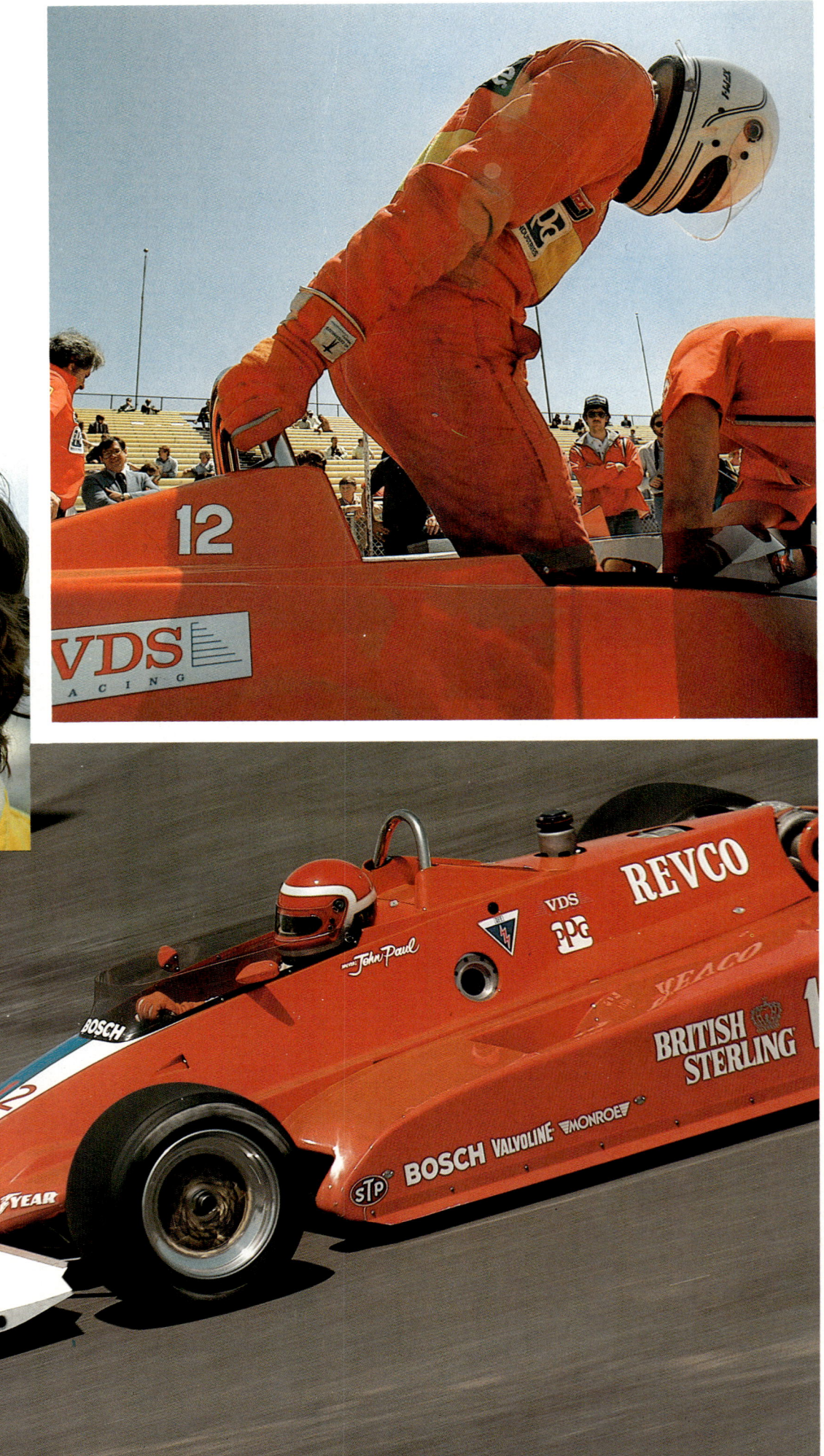

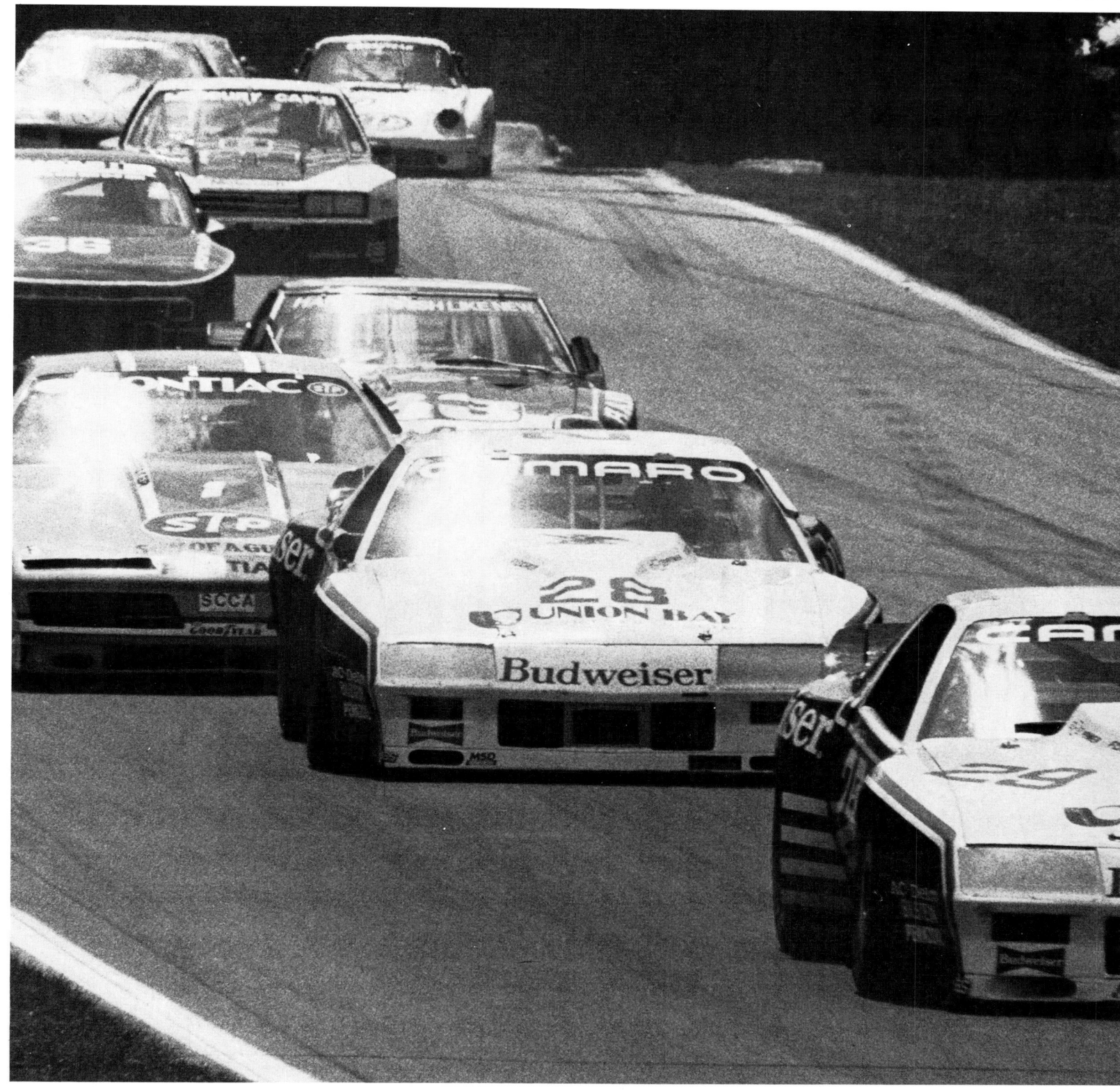

David Hobbs won the Elkart Lake TransAm race in his Camaro (No. 29) and fought for the championship with Tom Gloy's Mercury Capri (lying fifth behind Ribbs, Forbes-Robinson and Newman).

. . . with big fields and lots of noise it was too bad the SCCA's non-business attitude failed to draw many spectators . . .

After a dismal season in Formula 1 with Toleman, Teo Fabi switched to CART racing with the Forsythe Racing March. The Italian shook the Indy Establishment by taking pole with a record lap at 207.395 mph. Fabi led until his fuel tank sprang a leak but he went on to take more pole positions and finally led from start to finish at Pocono.

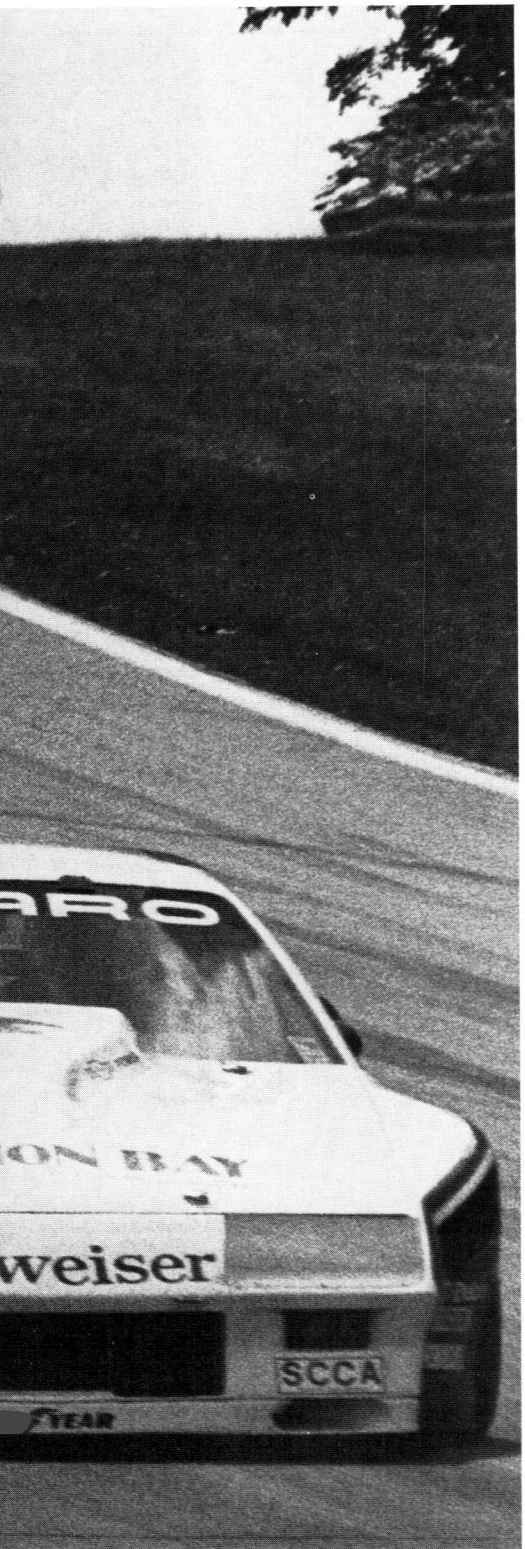

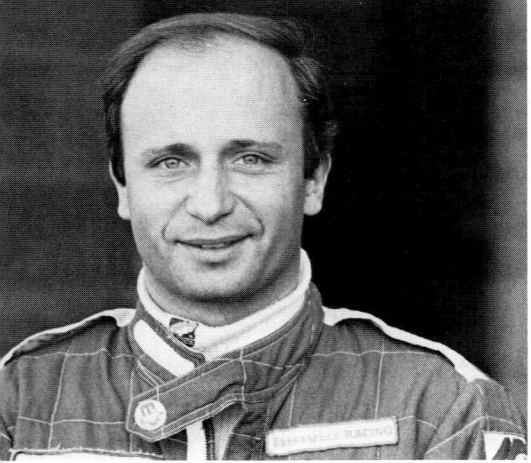

will be permitted only on a basis of "function, availability and cost". In other words, exotic and expensive "factory-team-only" electronic systems will not be allowed. In the same vein (restricting cost and complexity) CART's 1984-87 rules ban engine intake intercooling (viz.: "devices designed to reduce the inlet charge below the temperature differential obtained by the evaporation of fuel.")

ABOARD

The 1983 CART Board (elections held annually after the last race of the season) comprised chairman John Frasco, Roger Penske, Pat Patrick, Jim Trueman (owner of the Truesports/Bobby Rahal team), privateer Bill Alsup, Pancho Carter (drivers' representative), Johnny Capels (mechanics' representative) and Art Groenevelt (chairman of Provimi Veal Inc and entrant of a two-car team of Marches). Of the original founders only Penske and Patrick remain although Tyler Alexander and partner Teddy Mayer are returning with a new team next season. Two other important influences on CART's early growth were Jim Hall and Bobby Hilin both of whom saw their Indycar teams come and go in the first four year's of CART's existence. Initial CART "White paper" author Dan Gurney continued to build cars in 1983 although his team was inactive.

Chairman Frasco is a lawyer who won an injunction on behalf of the original CART Board, allowing them to enter the 1979 Indianapolis 500 after USAC had barred them from the race. In the autumn of 1980 Frasco was elected chairman and as well as presiding over the organisation's meetings he handles all the financial and contractual aspects of the Indycar series. The real force behind CART however is Technical and Operations Director Kirk Russell. Universally acknowledged among the teams as a fair and tireless man, Russell was trained as a chemical engineer and worked as a technical inspector for both USAC and the SCCA before taking over as CART's technical chief during the organisation's formative days.

It must also be noted incidentally that a good portion of CART's current strength has come about as a result of the steady decline in recent years of the SCCA's CanAm series and of sports car racing in general in the USA. Teams, drivers and racetracks which in a different time might have disdained Championship Car racing are now an integral part of the refurbished Indycar scene and the fact of the matter is that after years of squabbling among the SCCA, USAC and IMSA, the newly-invented CART organisation – run by the competitors themselves and happily unaffiliated with the FISA – has quickly supplanted those other organisations as if they were relics of a bygone age.

MARCH Vs. PENSKE

Much as in 1982, the Indycar championship was again dominated by a fight between Penske Racing and the latest from March Engineering although this time the Marches were faster, more plentiful – a magnificent customer racing car. In the hands of people like Tom Sneva, Teo Fabi and Bobby Rahal the third generation March Indycar – the 83C – proved itself to be an extremely effective weapon on all types of tracks, to the point that Penske bought an 83C toward the end of the season and then ordered a couple of 84Cs!

Driving a March prepared by Bignotti-Cotter Racing and sponsored by Texaco, Tom Sneva scored a fine win in the Indianapolis 500. Sneva's first win at Indy was also the first Memorial Day Classic for constructor March while rookie Teo Fabi did Mr. Herd's company proud by qualifying on the pole with a new record and later emerging as the strongest championship threat to Penske Racing.

With five championships in the previous six years to their credit Penske Racing moved confidently into the new season with a developed version of 1982's highly-successful PC10, this new car called the PC11. Replacing Kevin Cogan in the "second" car alongside defending champion Rick Mears was 44-year-old Al Unser Sr. A three-time Indy 500 winner otherwise ranked second only to Foyt on the Indycar winners' list (36 wins going into the '83 season, compared to Foyt's 67), Unser quickly found a home in the Penske team. After finishing a fighting second to Tom Sneva at Indianapolis and replaying the battle at Milwaukee two weeks later, the canny, persistent Unser took firm

hold of the top of the point table with a good win in a heat and humidity-soaked 500 km race on an airfield in downtown Cleveland on July 3rd.

Through the first six races, Unser's PC11 completed every lap, never out of the top three. By that point in the summer however it was clear the Penskes were losing ground to the Marches and in August the team began to race rebuilt versions of the previous year's PC10s. While Mears sorted-out the new 10s, Unser stuck with his 11 for a couple of races and had a terrible time, finishing a distant eleventh after a stop to replace a sparkbox in the Pocono 500 and then dropping out of the Riverside 500 kms two weeks later because of a jammed gearbox.

For the last five races both Unser and Mears had PC10Bs to drive as well as a Chevy-engined PC11. There was also a March 83C which Mears tested for the first time the day after he had won the tenth round of the thirteen-race schedule. Mears' win in the mid-September 200-miler at Michigan was his first win in thirteen months and it pushed him back into the championship stakes as we went to press, close behind Teo Fabi, the latter continuing to edge closer to Unser Sr's strong but by no means impregnable lead.

Fabi had first raced in America two years earlier, driving a March in the CanAm for Paul Newman's team. After a dismal season of F1 with a Toleman in 1982, Fabi found more work in the USA for the new season where he was reunited with the crew of mechanics who had run his car in the CanAm and were now working for a new Chicago-based team run by power system leasors and manufacturers, Jerry and John Forsythe. The ambitious Forsythe brothers were quick to put a new operation together for their third year of Indycar racing with team manager Barry Green and mechanics from the defunct Newman CanAm team and Fabi in the cockpit. The Forsythes had originally tried to hire Johnny Rutherford and had tested the ex-McLaren/Chaparral driver in an early March 83C which Fabi stepped into in January for a solid round of pre-season testing.

After dropping out of the Atlanta season-opener while running third Fabi really found form at Indianapolis. Before the Italian rookie started practising at the Brickyard, an announcement was made that the Forsythe March would be a Skoal Bandit-sponsored car for the balance of the season and Fabi gave the tobacco company a perfect start to their Indycar programme by going steadily faster and after the first weekend of qualifying was rained-off, emerging to steal the coveted pole in grand style with a new track record (2 mins 53.582 secs, 207.395 mph for the four laps).

Fabi continued his performance into the race, leading strongly until his fuel tank sprang a leak during his second refuelling stop, just short of one-quarter distance. Two weeks later Fabi underlined his ability by qualifying on the pole at the tight, flat Milwaukee mile, this time making the flag for the first time after engine and neck problems dropped him down to fourth, a lap behind at the end of the 150-mile sprint race. At the Cleveland 500 kms airfield race Fabi again ran near the front only to lose time in the closing stages with spongey brakes, making it home a lap down in third.

At the Michigan 500 Fabi took his third pole of the year but after losing his clutch and then spinning he finally dropped out of the race when he stopped in the wrong pit and had a small refuelling fire. At the Elkhart Lake road race two weeks later, Fabi was nosed off the pole by Mario Andretti and after running at the front in the early laps he spun off and stalled, losing four laps before he could get restarted.

Everything finally came good for Fabi and the Forsythe operation at the mid-August Pocono 500 however as the little Italian ran at the front all the way, leading more than half the race and beating Al Unser Jr to the flag by four and a half seconds. It was the first time in seventeen years that a European had won an Indycar race (that being Graham Hill's 1966 Indy 500 triumph) and it began a series of good results for Fabi.

At Riverside he took his fifth pole of the year, lead much of the race and finished second to Bobby Rahal after a jack broke during a pitstop as well as a disputed "stop-and-go" penalty for driving over an air hose in Rahal's pit. At Mid-Ohio two weeks later Fabi started second, slipped to fourth and then came back to win his second race of the season after the three cars in

The immaculate Group 44 Jaguar XJR-5 GTP car, driven by Bob Tullius, Bill Adam and Doc Bundy, won a number of races in the IMSA Camel GT series and was a serious contender for the championship until mid-season
Photos: Mark Clifford

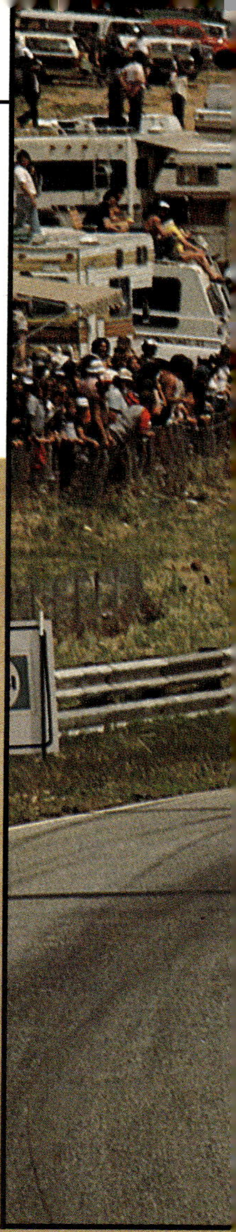

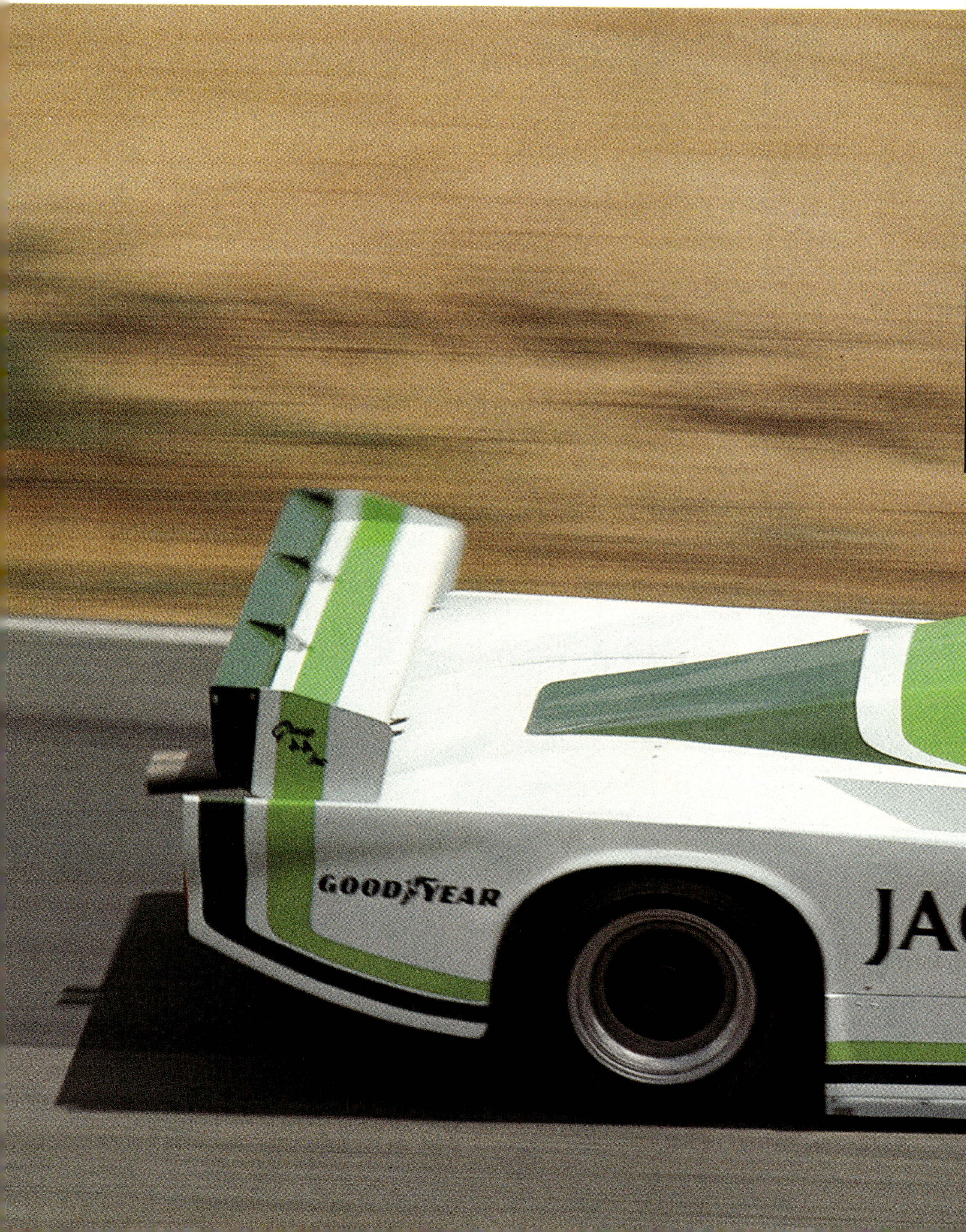

GOOD$YEAR

JAGUA

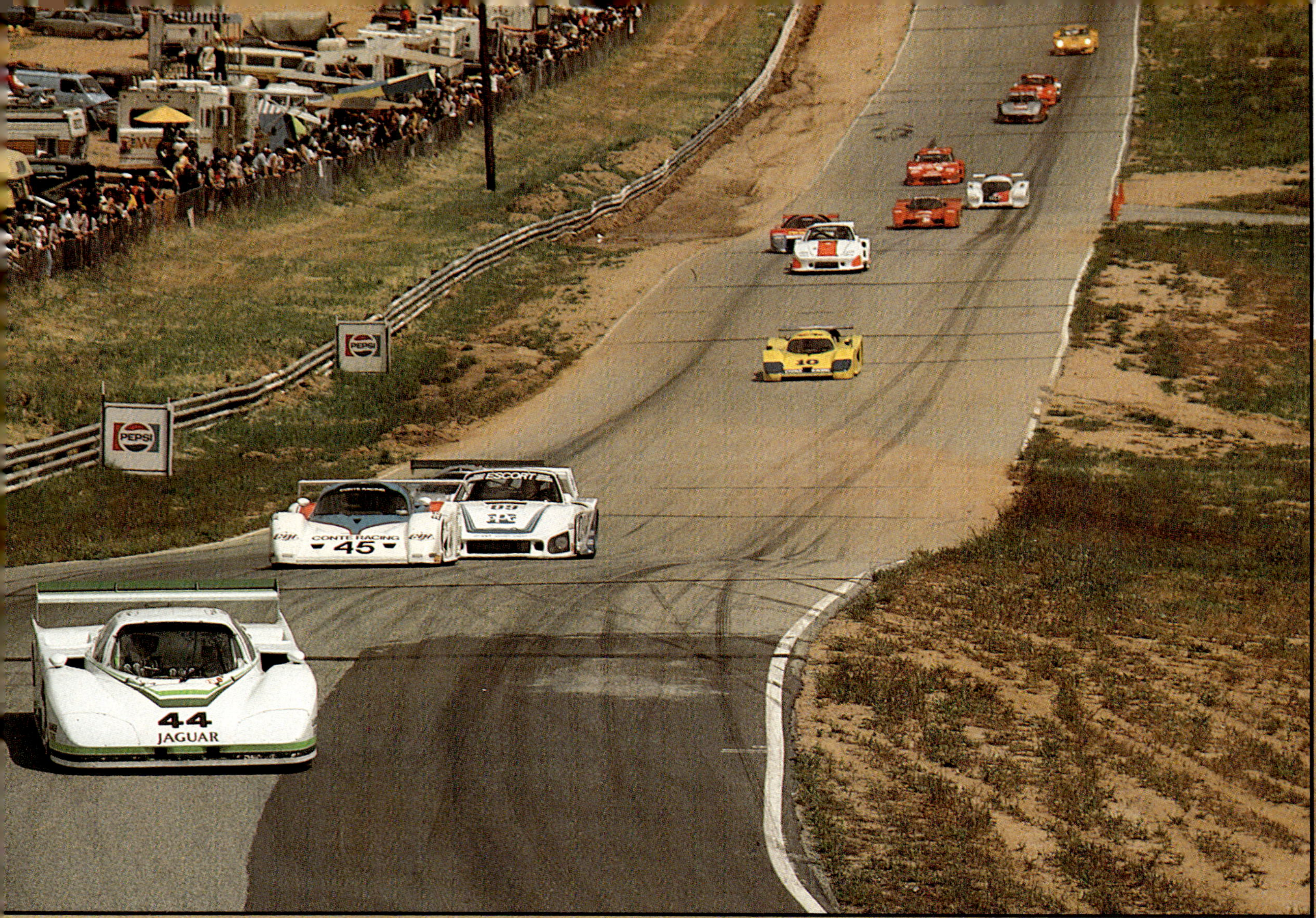
PEPSI
PEPSI
CONTE RACING
45
ESCORT
44
JAGUAR

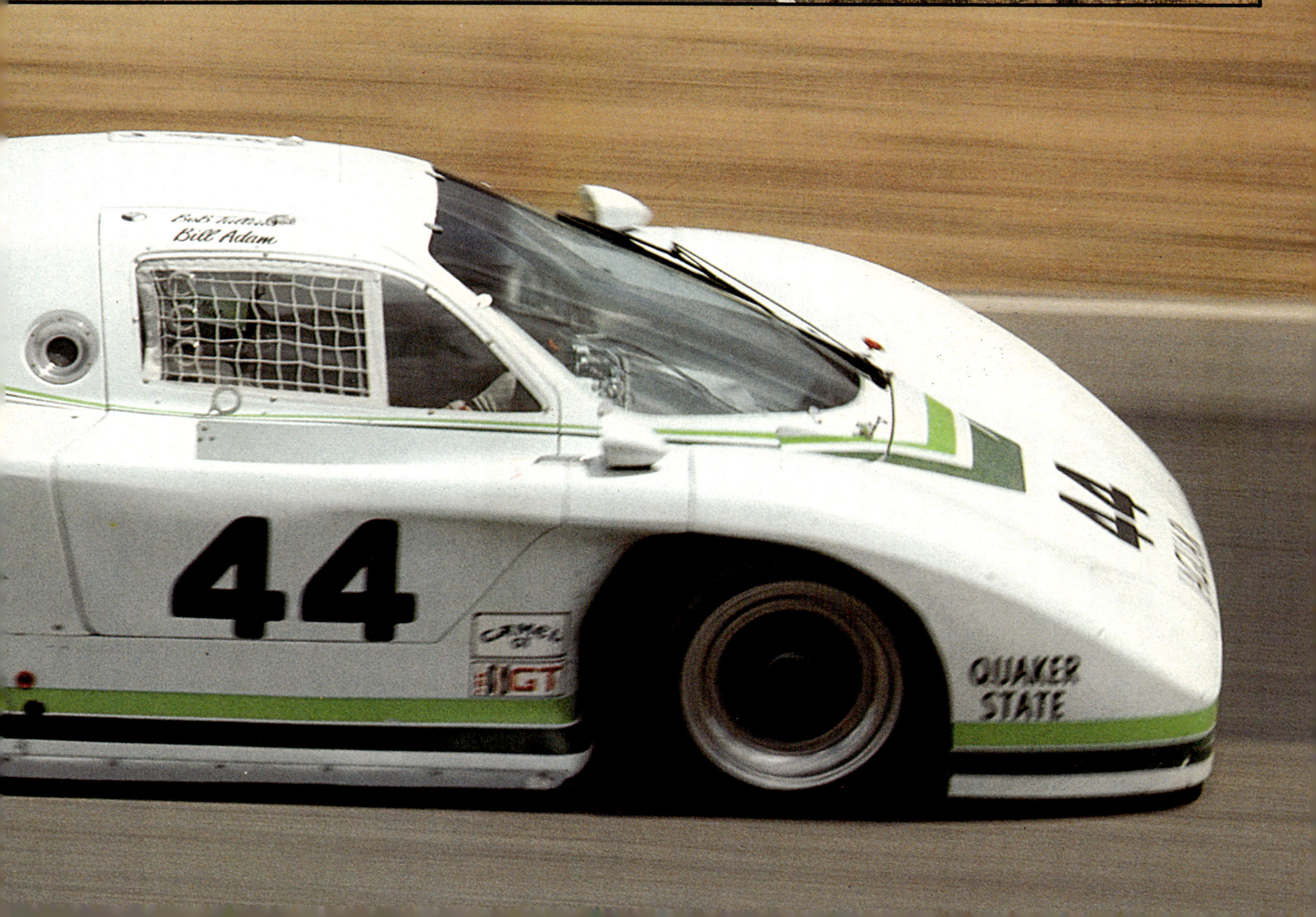
Bob Tullius
Bill Adam
44
44
CAMEL
GT
QUAKER
STATE

front of him (Rahal, Unser Jr and Paul Jr) all ran into problems. The last race run before our deadline was a 200-miler at Michigan where Fabi finished third, never being able to match the pace of the fastest cars. Nevertheless he finished two places and one lap ahead of point leader Al Unser Sr and therefore continued to edge closer with three races remaining . . .

TOM TERRIFIC AND THE MASTER MECHANIC

In addition to Fabi's Forsythe 83C there were eight or nine other Marches on the line for most races last year. Eighteen March products were in the 33-car field at Indianapolis and the company's first win at the Brickyard came with Tom Sneva and George Bignotti, the fast-but-volatile combination of driver and old-style chief mechanic who have nevertheless done more than anyone else to properly establish the March marque in Indycar circles.

Sneva and Bignotti first got together for the 1981 season with hardware store distribution king Dan Cotter partnering the 67-year-old Bignotti's latest venture. Along with the Whittington brothers, Bignotti-Cotter Racing were the earliest March customers and the fearsomely-fast Sneva won two races for Mr. Herd's product in 1981 as well as leading more laps than any other driver. Speedway ace Sneva added two more wins in 1982 but like the previous year both wins came on short, one-mile tracks (Milwaukee and Phoenix) while comparatively poor engine reliability ruined Sneva's chances in most longer races.

Right from the start Sneva and Bignotti had been at odds over budgets and a lack of testing and as the wins came and sponsorship from Texaco followed, the debate continued between driver and chief mechanic (Bignotti being the winningest man on Indycar turf incidentally, with 82 racewinners to his credit going into the '83 season). Dissatisfied with his position with March, Bignotti also struck a deal for '83 with Teddy Yip to bolster his pair of new Marches with a couple of new Theodore chassis. With the first Theodore arriving in late April, the short-staffed, overworked Bignotti mechanics were also mired in engine problems, Sneva and teammate Kevin Cogan losing a dozen engines over the two weeks of practice!

Despite minimal track time Sneva qualified fourth and amazed everyone by going the distance in the 500 and winning after a fine, late-race battle with Al Unser Sr. Sneva again beat Unser at Milwaukee two weeks later although his car was subsequently disqualified when it failed to pass the post-race skirt height check. Five weeks later an appeals court reversed the decision, re-installing Sneva as the winner although by that time things were already going downhill for the team and Sneva was looking hard for a new seat for 1984.

In the road races that followed over the second half of the season the two Bignotti-Cotter cars (the Theodores making a couple of starts) were often all over the road, their handling giving Sneva and Cogan some vivid moments. On the ovals both men were usually fast but unreliable. Sneva led both the Michigan and Pocono 500s but was elimianted at Michigan in an incident with a slower car and then had a gearbox failure at Pocono. For a while Tom hung on, picking-up points here and there, but when an oil leak put him out of the Michigan 200 in September his remote chance of regaining his 1977 & '78 title disappeared altogether. Cogan meanwhile found himself a number two drive of the worst kind and rarely finished although he continued to show considerable speed and seemed to mature in the face of adversity. At presstime his only real result of the year had been a fifth at Indianapolis.

The other leading March contender in 1983 was Bobby Rahal, apparently settling into a longterm relationship with Red Roof Inns hotel chain owner and amateur/IMSA GT racer Jim Trueman. Fielding Marches as they had in 1982, the Truesports team were even more competitive in their second year of Indycar racing although a series of small problems and incidents contrived to keep Rahal from having any untroubled races until late August when he beat Fabi home in the mid-summer desert heat at Riverside.

At Mid-Ohio two weeks later Rahal qualified a specially-built, Chevy-powered 83C "road racer" on the pole and ran off with the race before fuel feed problems dropped him to third at the finish. As we closed for press Rahal had inched his way into remote,

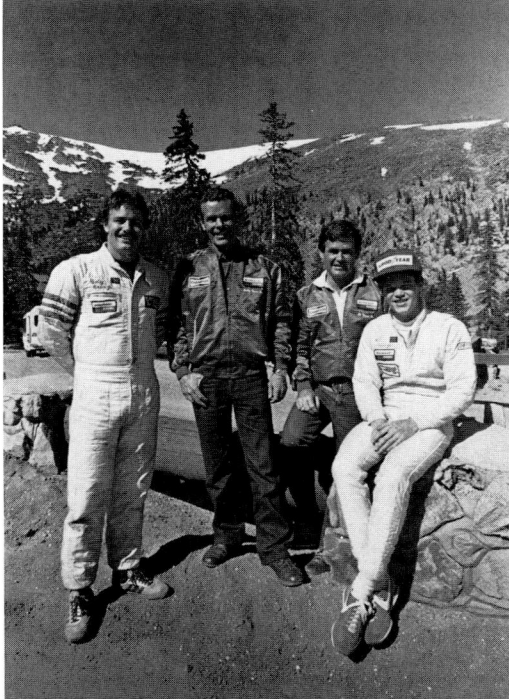

late-season championship contention by qualifying on the pole for the Michigan 200 and finishing a close second to Rick Mears in a race that averaged 182.325 mph – the fastest Indycar race in history.

Other regular March runners last year included Mike Mosley, Pancho Carter, Howdy Holmes, Danny Ongais and Tony Bettenhausen although none of them produced any exceptional results, aside from Mosley being in the middle of the front row at Indy. A. J. Foyt and old buddy George Snider drove Foyt's pair of new Marches at Indianapolis and both were early retirements after the Texan spent most of the month at the bedside of his dying father.

After a couple of seasons driving Wildcats for Pat Patrick's team, Mario Andretti moved into a new operation for 1983. The team was run from the Chicago shop of seven-time F5000/CanAm champion entrant Carl Haas who commissioned a new Lola Indycar – the T700 – from Eric Broadley and struck a partnership with part-time racer and former CanAm team owner Paul Newman, the actor bringing Budweiser Beer sponsorship with him. A late start and a long list of teething troubles were complicated by a crash during practice for the season-opener and another crash during the race at Indianapolis when Johnny Parsons spun while passing Andretti.

With steady aerodynamic improvements the T700 got better however, and Andretti was able to win the mid-season Elkhart Lake road race and run competitively on all types of tracks in most late-season races, the former Grand Prix driver taking a victory at Las Vegas.

TWO SHARP ROOKIES

The leading Eagle runner last year was 21-year-old CanAm champion Al Unser Jr who moved into Indycars with automobile dealer Rick Galles' new team. Galles had run young Unser's successful assaults on the Super Vee (in 1981) and CanAm championships (1982) and the rookie team acquitted themselves well despite some confusion over the development of the Eagle. "Little Al" was fast everywhere and as the season wore on he began to show exceptional speed and maturity although a series of minor problems kept him out of the winner's circle. Unser Jr had led six of the ten races run at presstime and scored his best result in the Pocono 500, finishing a fighting second to Fabi in one of two appearances in a March. For 1984, Unser Jr has turned-down an offer to drive Formula 1 for Brabham in favour of another season of Indycar racing for Rick Galles.

Unser Jr joined Fabi and John Paul Jr as the leading newcomers to Indycar racing last year. The 22-year-old Paul was IMSA GT champion in 1982 and moved into Indycars with Team VDS, Count van der Straten's team quitting the CanAm after seven years of

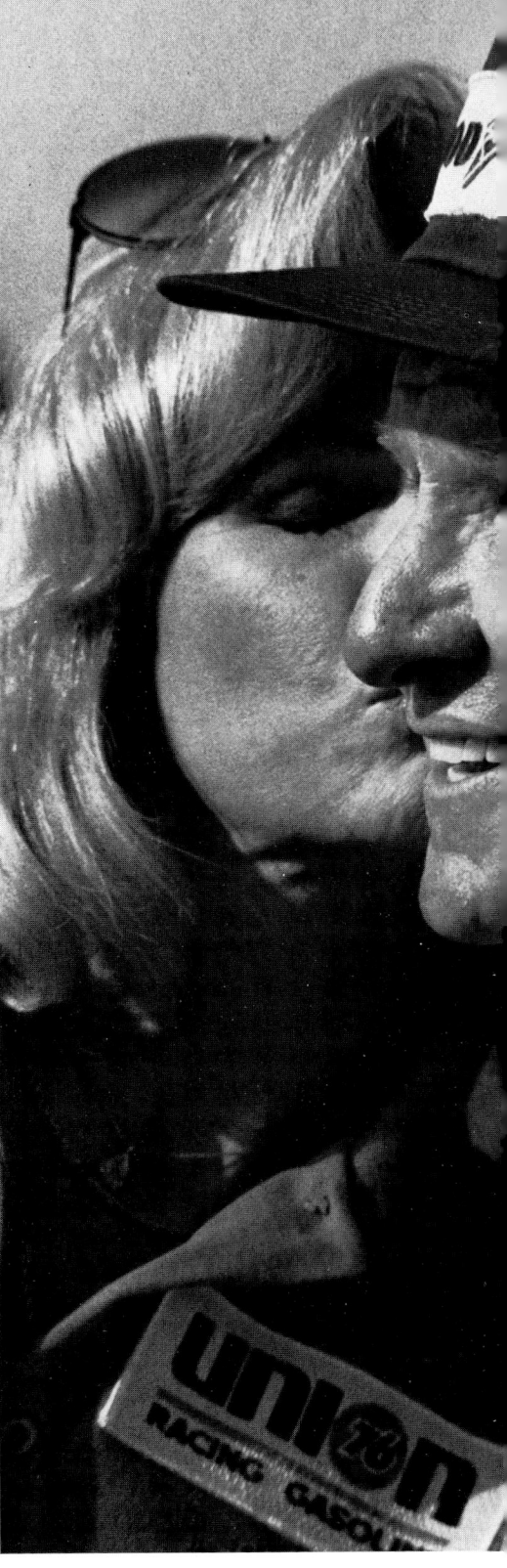

Keeping the talent in the family. With Bobby Unser retired from active racing, his son Bobby Jnr (left) made his mark in SuperVee. Al Jnr (right) continued to show exceptional speed in CART while his father led the series for most of the season. The talented Unsers are pictured at Pike's Peak hillclimb. Al Jnr won in 1983 and set a new course record, returning 'The Peak' to the family once more.
Cale Yarborough won the Daytona 500 but the NASCAR championship was disputed by Darrell Waltrip and Bobby Allison.

F5000/CanAm racing to go Indycar racing with a pair of Penske PC10s. From the start young Paul was able to go fast but a run of early-season crashes, including a leg-breaking meeting with the wall during practice at Indianapolis, cast a pall over the first part of his year.

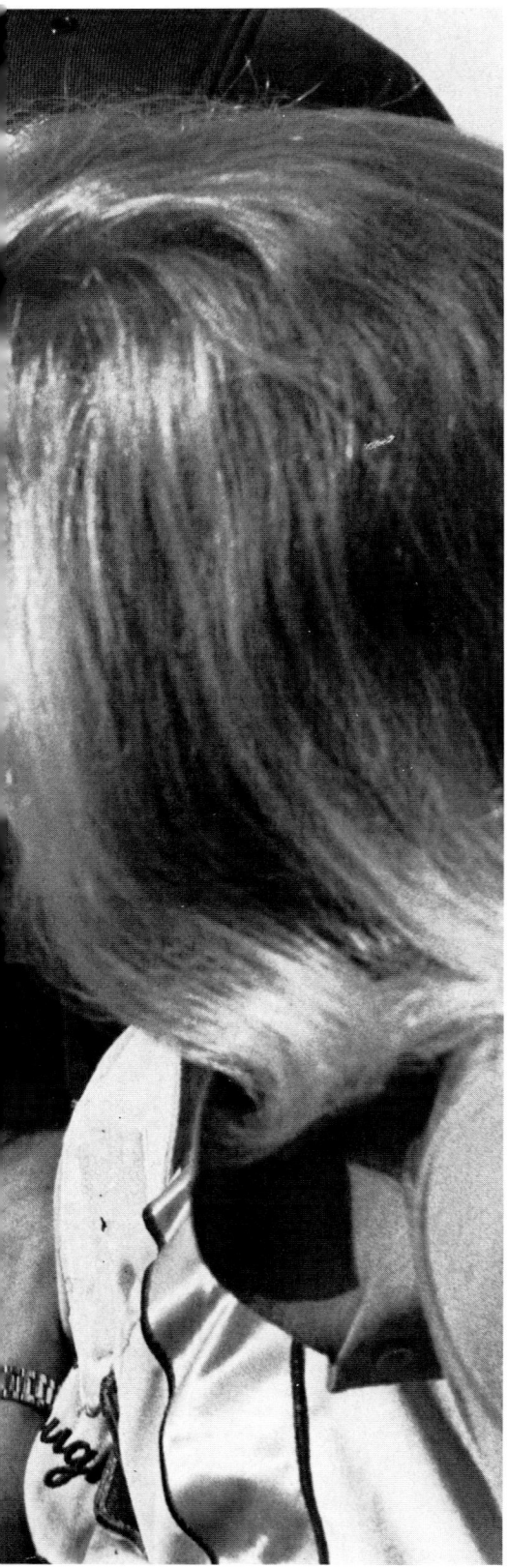

good second in the Cleveland 500Ks.

A terrible 1983 season was had by oil wildcatter Pat Patrick's team. After winning the Indy 500 in 1982 with Gordon Johncock the Patrick team produced all-new Wildcat mk 9s for 1983 and Johnny Rutherford replaced a retiring Bobby Unser in the second car with up-and-coming FF/FSVee graduate Chip Ganassi added as an occasional third driver. Johncock and Rutherford qualified and ran up front in the season-opener on Atlanta's high banks with Johncock winning after Mears, Sneva, Rahal and Fabi had problems. At Indianapolis however the new Wildcats were terrible, proving a real handful to turn-in on the smooth, barely-banked, ultra-fast, four-cornered speedway. Rutherford crashed twice in the space of ten days, breaking his right ankle and putting himself out of action for three months. Johncock qualified tenth, just short of 200 mph after more than 1,300 miles of practice and hung in there for four hundred miles before his gearbox gave out. Out of the limelight, Ganassi did a very workmanlike job as he was to do all season, qualifying in the middle of the field and finishing eighth, five laps behind winner Sneva.

After Indy, Patrick quickly formed an alliance with a financially-strapped Danny Ongais for the Patrick team to use Ongais' pair of March 83Cs and by the middle of the season the first of a March-bodied-and-podded Wildcat was out and running. While Rutherford recovered, Johncock and Ongais raced the latter's Marches but Johncock crashed heavily when a rear wishbone broke while he was running at the front of the Michigan 500. Johncock's right leg and ankle were very badly broken in the crash and although he was soon up and about, visiting the races on crutches as a radio/TV commentator, he was not expected to be able to drive until the spring of 1984.

Rutherford returned to work at the Pocono 500 and ran with the leaders until a suspension breakage put him into the wall, thankfully without injury. A shortage of cars and engines meant Rutherford didn't appear again until the Michigan 200 in September by which point it looked as if Patrick Racing would become a March customer for 1984. . . .

Other drivers to have a few moments to savour from the '83 Indycar season included Geoff Brabham and Derek Daly. CanAm champion with Team VDS in '81 and number two at Bignotti-Cotter in '82, Brabham was without a regular drive last year although he filled-in for John Paul Jr at Indianapolis after Paul broke his leg in the second week of practice and finished a strong fourth behind Sneva and the two works Penskes. Had it not been for stalling while leaving the pits on one occasion, Brabham could have been right in the hunt at the end.

After losing his job in the Williams Grand Prix team, Irishman Daly decided to try Indycar racing and showed he was up to the job despite making only irregular appearances. Daly ran well at Indianapolis but lost his drive after a series of disagreements with amateur team owner Rose Wysard. Later in the season he found a home with the fledgling Provimi Veal team and impressed everyone during the season's last three races in one of their Marches.

WHISTLIN' DIXIE

Down in the southland, through one of the hottest, driest summers in American history, NASCAR's Winston Cup Grand National championship quickly focussed itself, as it had for the two previous years, into a one-on-one duel between defending champion Darrell Waltrip and challenger Bobby Allison. Two-time champion Waltrip continued with Junior Johnson's cars – Chevrolet Monte Carlos in '83 – while veteran Allison continued to chase a hitherto elusive title driving for Waltrip's old team Di Gard Racing, in Chevrolet-powered chassis fitted with Buick Regal sheetmetal.

The 45-year-old Allison had finished second in the championship five times since 1970 – twice to Waltrip in the previous two years but over the middle of the summer of '83 he began to take control of the championship and as we closed for press he had put himself in a very strong position by winning three races in a row. With six of 30 races to go Allison had an 80-point lead over Waltrip, about half the 170 points awarded for a win. Even so the 36-year old Waltrip was

still in contention for his third successive title . . .

The overall picture of Grand National racing continued healthy as ever with more sponsors, more competitors, rebuilding racetracks and an unchallenged spectacle following. Even though Allison and Waltrip dominated the points table they rarely looked like sure-fire racewinners. At presstime Allison had won six races and Waltrip had won five times. Others to have won races were Cale Yarborough (4), Richard Petty (2), Dale Earnhardt (2) and one apiece for Harry Gant, Neil Bonnett, Ricky Rudd, Buddy Baker and Tim Richmond.

General Motors' products continued to dominate the show with Allison in Buicks, Waltrip in Chevrolets, Yarborough also in a Chevy, Petty aboard Pontiacs, Gant (Buick), Bonett (Chevrolet), Rudd (Chevrolet) and Richmond (Pontiac) also in GM cars. 1980 champion Earnhardt continued as the strongest Ford driver in Bud Moore's cars while Buddy Baker and Bill Elliott were the only other top Ford runners.

DECLINE OF THE AMERICAN SPORTS CAR?

While stock car racing and most forms of oval track racing continue to live healthy American lives, the world of big-time road racing is clearly floundering in North America. Long blinded to the needs of professional racing, the SCCA found themselves with an all-but-irrelevant CanAm in 1983, alongside a competitive, interesting but ineptly-promoted TransAm and a Formula Atlantic series (now called Formula Mondial) which the club had always viewed with disdain.

There were only six CanAm races last year with Jacques Villeneuve (Frissbee-Chevrolet) fighting for the title with Jim Crawford (Ensign-Cosworth). Michael Roe (VDS-Chevy) was fast but fragile while John Fitzpatrick made a few races in a Porsche 956.

The TransAm featured a couple of well-developed Budweiser/Chevrolet Camaros driven aggressively by David Hobbs and Willy T. Ribbs who traded wins back and forth throughout the year. Other contenders included Tom Gloy (Mercury Capri), Elliott Forbes-Robinson (Pontiac TransAm) and Gene Felton (Pontiac Firebird). With big fields and lots of noise it was too bad the SCCA's non-business attitude failed to draw many spectators to the races.

The ill-conceived Formula Mondial series floundered from race-to-race, lacking any real management or direction from the CASC who must have finally realised they had bitten off more than they could chew. A handful of eager youngsters kept the series alive with 21-year-old Michael Andretti taking the title in Brian Robertson's Ralt American team before making his Indycar debut at Las Vegas in October. Andretti's major rival was a shoestring-budgeted Roberto Moreno. Others to win races included Josele Garza and Mark Moore.

Although sanctioned by the SCCA, most Super Vee races took place with CART events in 1983. Primary championship protagonists were Ed Pimm and Price Cobb, the former driving Ansons and Ralts for the Red Roof/Truesports teams and the latter making a strong comeback despite losing his sponsor in mid-season. Other frontrunners included Roger Penske Jr, Chip Robinson and Lugwig Heimrath Jr, all of them Ralt-mounted.

IMSA's seventeen round Camel GT championship lacked topline entries in 1983 although the series continued as a strong amateur stomping ground. LeMans winner Al Holbert dominated the championship driving two March 83Gs, one powered by a normally-aspirated 5.8 litre Chevy and the other by a turbocharged Porsche 934 engine. Co-driving with various drivers including Jim Trueman and Doc Bundy, Christian Holbert won six races and sewed-up the title by the end of July.

The only threat to Holbert was veteran Bob Tullius who kept the pressure on Holbert in many races with his beautifully-crafted Jaguar V12-engined Group 44 GTP car. Tullius won three races with the car but like Holbert, he didn't do the complete championship. Appearing for the first time at Elkhart Lake in late August were the much-anticipated, front-engined Ford Mustang GTP cars and lo and behold, following the demise of the few, fast cars, the Fords scored a miraculous debut victory! Klaus Ludwig/Tim Coconis drove the winner with Bobby Rahal/Geoff Brabham surviving a pit fire and other delays to finish third.

Also, Paul's father (World Endurance Champion in 1982) was arrested on an attempted murder charge but the tall, soft-spoken youngster from Georgia put it all behind him and came back to win the mid-summer Michigan 500. In only his fourth Indycar start, Paul drove a magnificent race, stealing the lead from Rick Mears on the last lap moments before Mears crashed while trying to match the rookie! Incidentally, Team VDS' thriving engine shop also supplied engines last year to the Newman/Haas and Truesports teams.

In addition to VDS a handful of other teams ran Penske PC10s last year. The Machinists' Union continued their Indycar team for a fourth year with Roger Mears and Josele Garza in the cockpits, the young Mexican showing well on four or five occasions. Also PC10-mounted was Pete Halsmer who drove for veteran entrant Frank Arciero's team and finished a

The Canon Racing 956, driven regularly by
Jonathan Palmer, Jan Lammers and Richard
Lloyd, finished eighth at Le Mans *(right)*.
Photo: Nigel Snowdon
Jochen Mass led Stefan Bellof initially in the
77-mile 'sprint' at the Norisring but Bellof, very
much the young star of endurance racing in
1983, took the lead from his more experienced
team-mate and gave the works Rothmans
Porsche team a one-two finish *(below)*.
Photo: International Press Agency

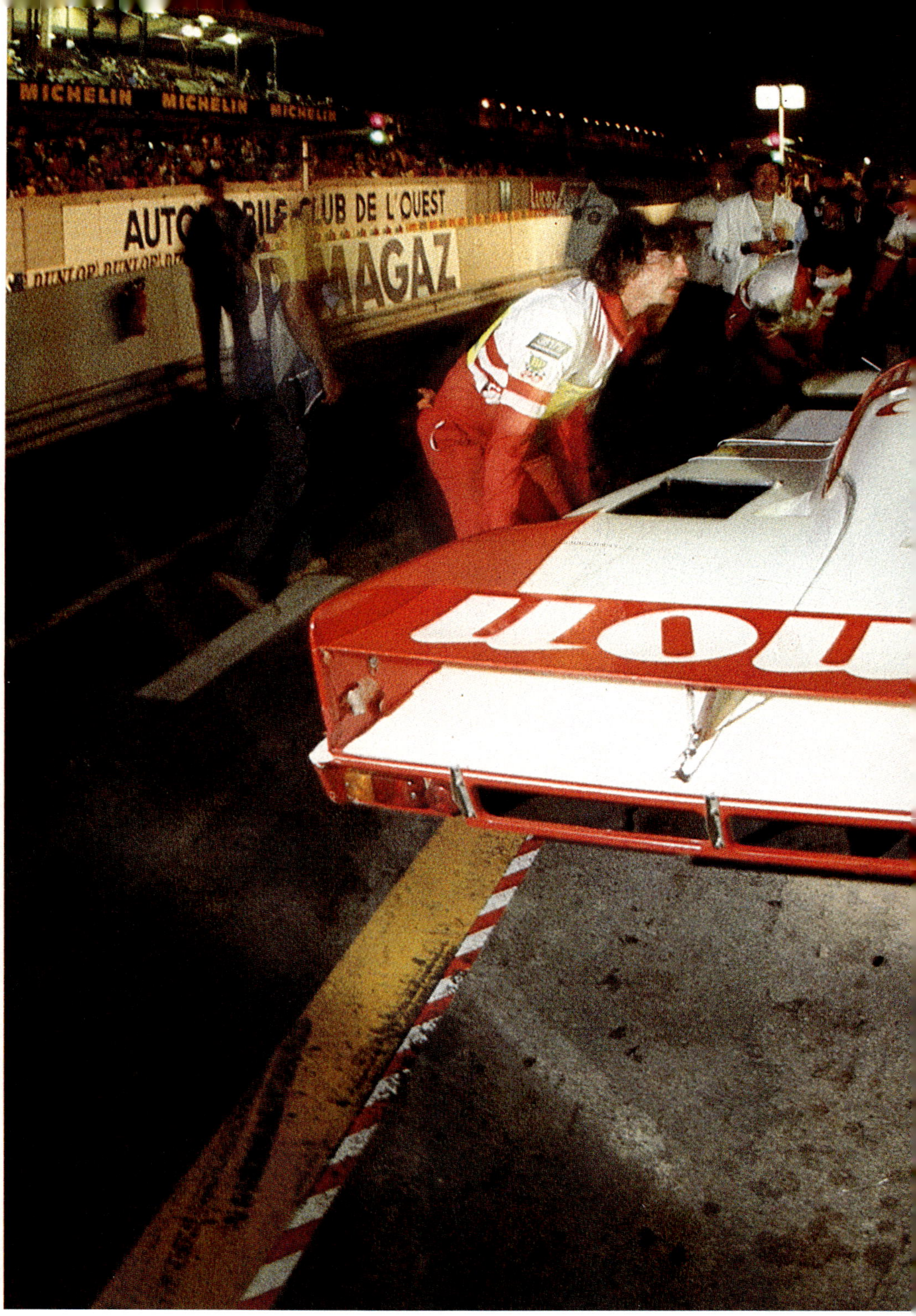

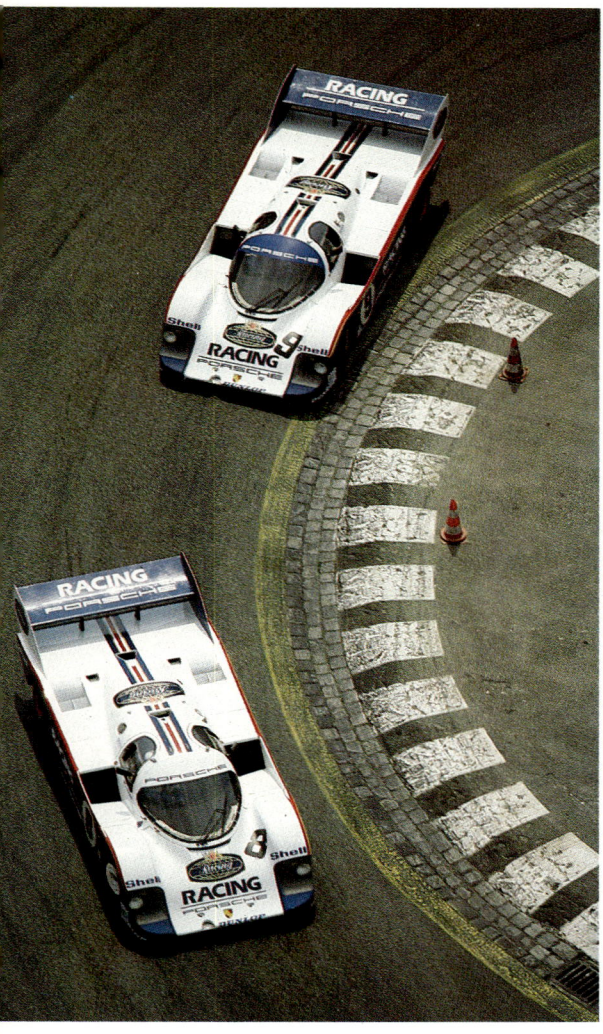

Vern Schuppan shared a Kremer 956 with Alan
Jones to finish fourth at Silverstone *(right)*.
Photo: Nigel Snowdon
Joest Racing ran two Porsches, the most
successful being the Marlboro-backed 956
driven by Bob Wollek and Stefan Johansson.
Thierry Boutsen took the Swedish driver's place
at Monza where the privately run Porsche
stunned the works team by winning the opening
race of the season *(far right)*.
Photo: Michael Keppel

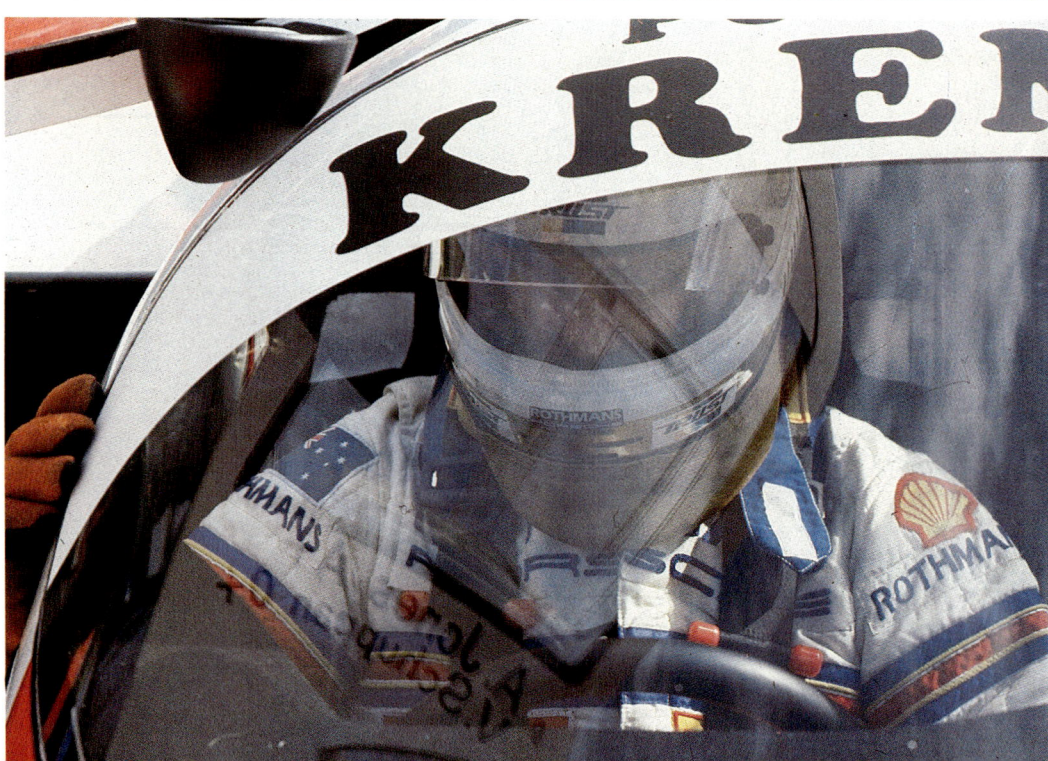

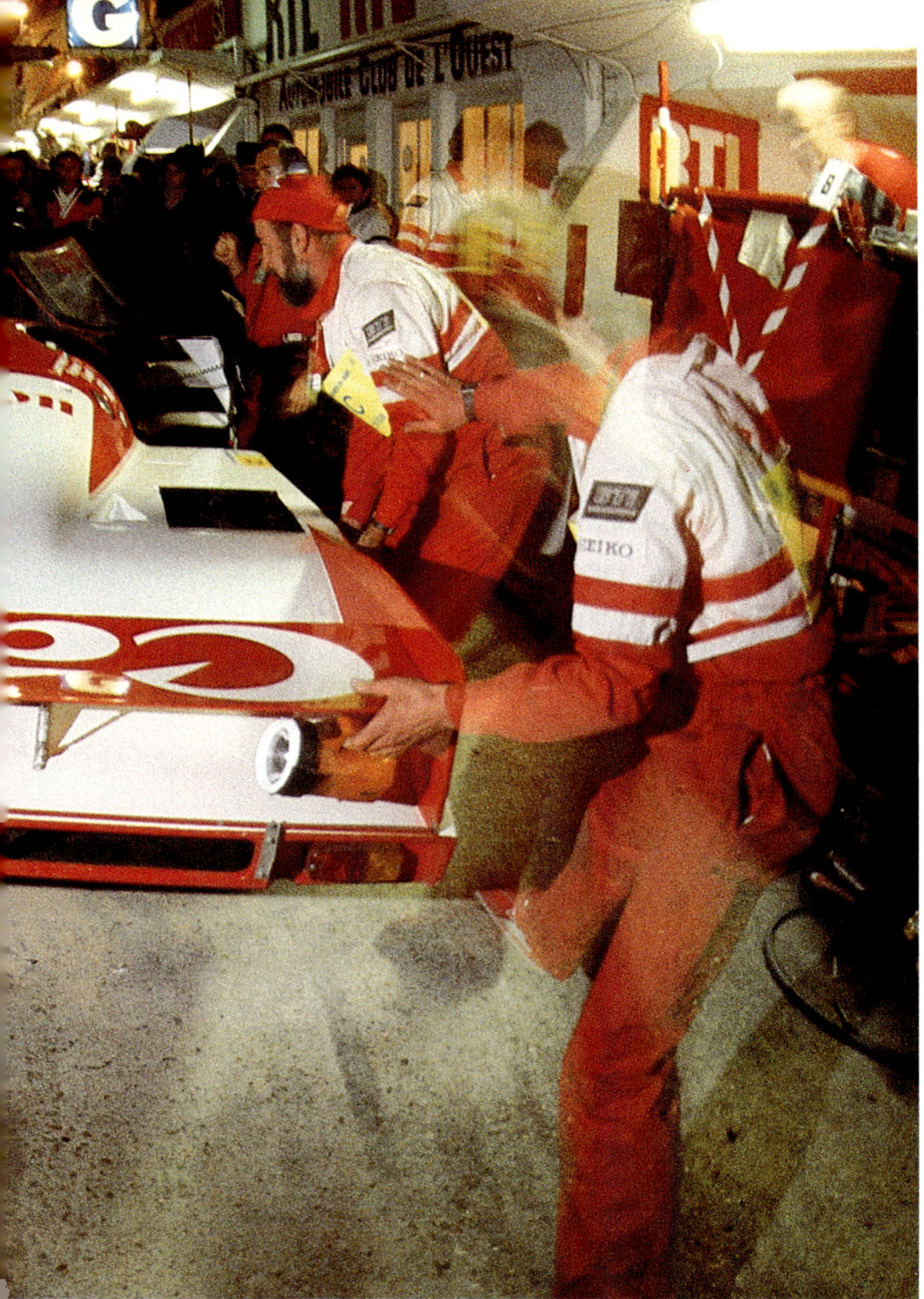

No contest

Endurance Sports Car
Racing Review 1983
by Quentin Spurring,
Editor, *Autosport*

Were an international sporting promotions consultant to be given a free hand, and asked to design a motor racing class capable of challenging Formula 1 for worldwide attention, then what criteria would be set for the cars, the events and the drivers?

The class would certainly be for sports cars sensational in appearance, and the consultant would demand that they would be the fastest road racing cars in the world. He would also insist that over 50 of them would be made available to event promoters. Their designers would be able to use any engine they liked, of any size, so that a large variety of chassis and engines would be raced.

There would be active participation by at least half a dozen of the world's best known motor manufacturers, and other industry support in the form of several major tyre companies. Sponsorship would come from many household-name international corporations.

The schedule would include a number of established classics, and it would send the cars to several different countries on at least three continents.

In order to guarantee the prestige of the series, the promotions consultant would suggest that the cars should be driven not only by all the top specialist professionals, but also by about a third of the current crop of Grand Prix aces.

Impossible? Not at all. Indeed, this description already fits exactly the FIA World Endurance Championships for Group C sports cars, which completed the second season of its existence in 1983.

The C-cars are, indeed, sensational in appearance and performance, the fastest road racing cars in the world at up to 230mph (370kmh). No fewer than 58 of these machines were raced in the Group C class alone. And there were 26 different chassis, and 15 different engines.

Although the series, alas, lost Ford, official factory participation came from Porsche, Lancia, Mazda, Nissan, Toyota and Aston Martin. Eight tyre manufacturers – Avon, Bridgestone, Dunlop, Firestone, Goodyear, Michelin, Pirelli and Yokohama – produced tyres. And international companies sponsoring cars included such as Rothmans and Marlboro, Martini and Coca Cola, Canon and Nikon, Esso and Shell.

The schedule included the events at Monza, Silverstone, Nürburgring, Le Mans, Spa-Francorchamps, Fuji and Kyalami, in seven countries on three continents (although sadly there was again no US fixture).

The established sports car experts such as Bell, Fitzpatrick, Ickx, Mass, Wollek and the rest were opposed by Formula 1 stars like Rosberg, Patrese, Warwick, Alboreto, Ghinzani, Johansson and Boutsen, not to mention Indycar names like Andretti and Fabi, and rising Formula 2 hotshoes like Palmer and Bellof.

And yet ... Still sports car racing lags behind Formula 1, which takes the lion's share of raceday crowds, media coverage and sponsorship. The biggest single reason for this is simple: as things stand, it is possible to bring a truly impressive number of these cars and drivers together only once in each season, at Le Mans. The promoters of all the other races struggle to assemble more than 20 fully fledged C-cars, a third of the machines available.

The three problem areas in Group C racing can be defined as expense, exposure and expectation.

The expense of a full 1983 race programme was daunting: over £600,000 to run a 'privateer' Porsche 956. Here was a racing car costing £158,000 on its

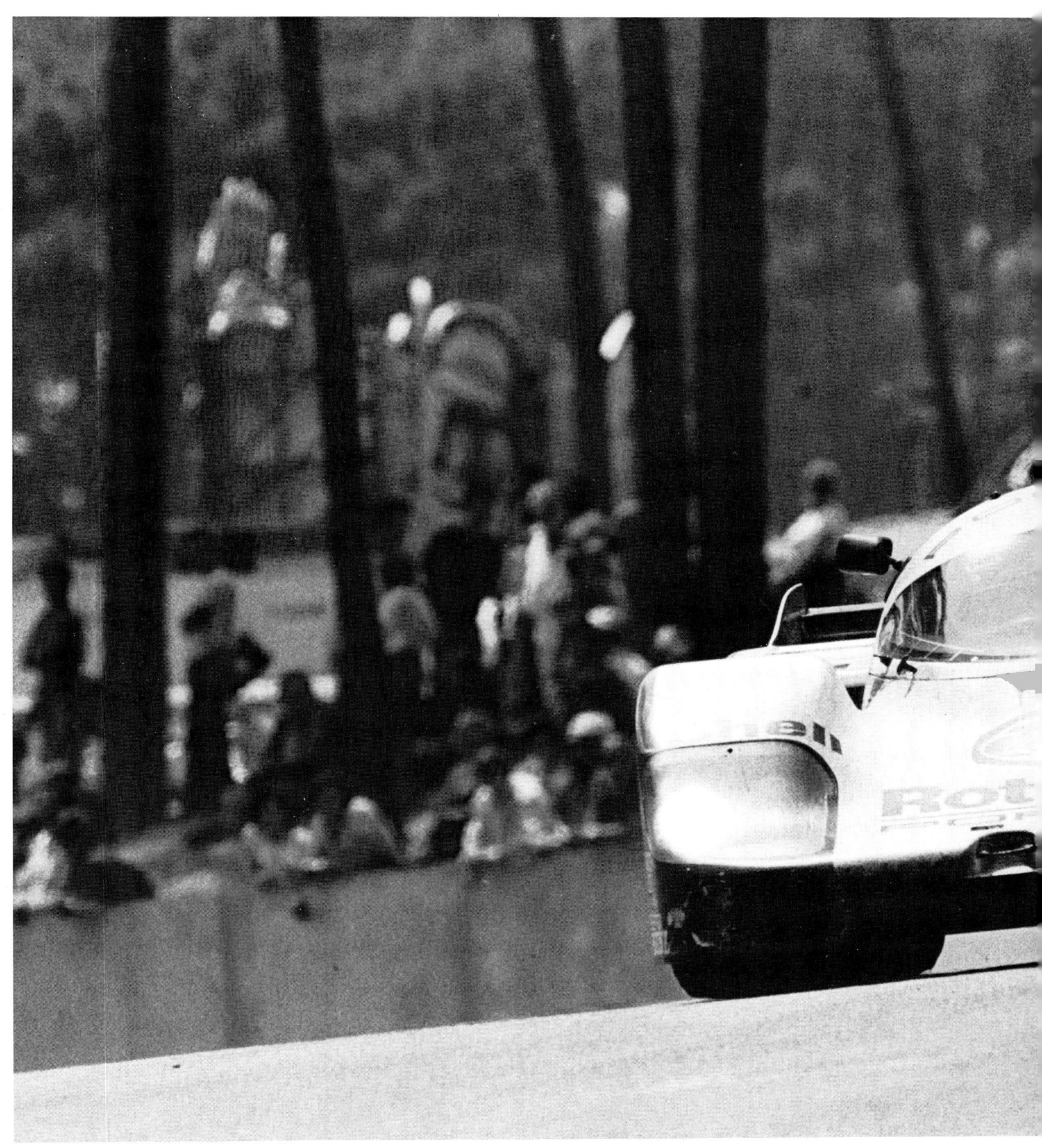

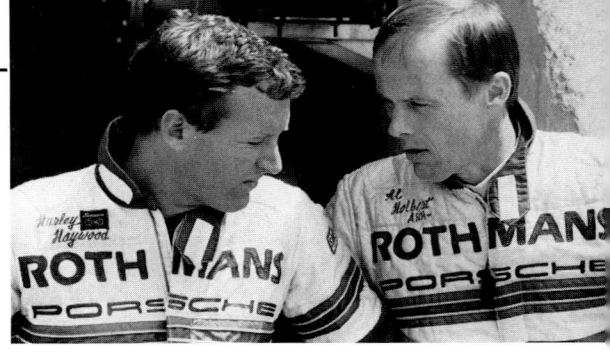

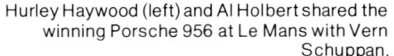
Hurley Haywood (left) and Al Holbert shared the winning Porsche 956 at Le Mans with Vern Schuppan.

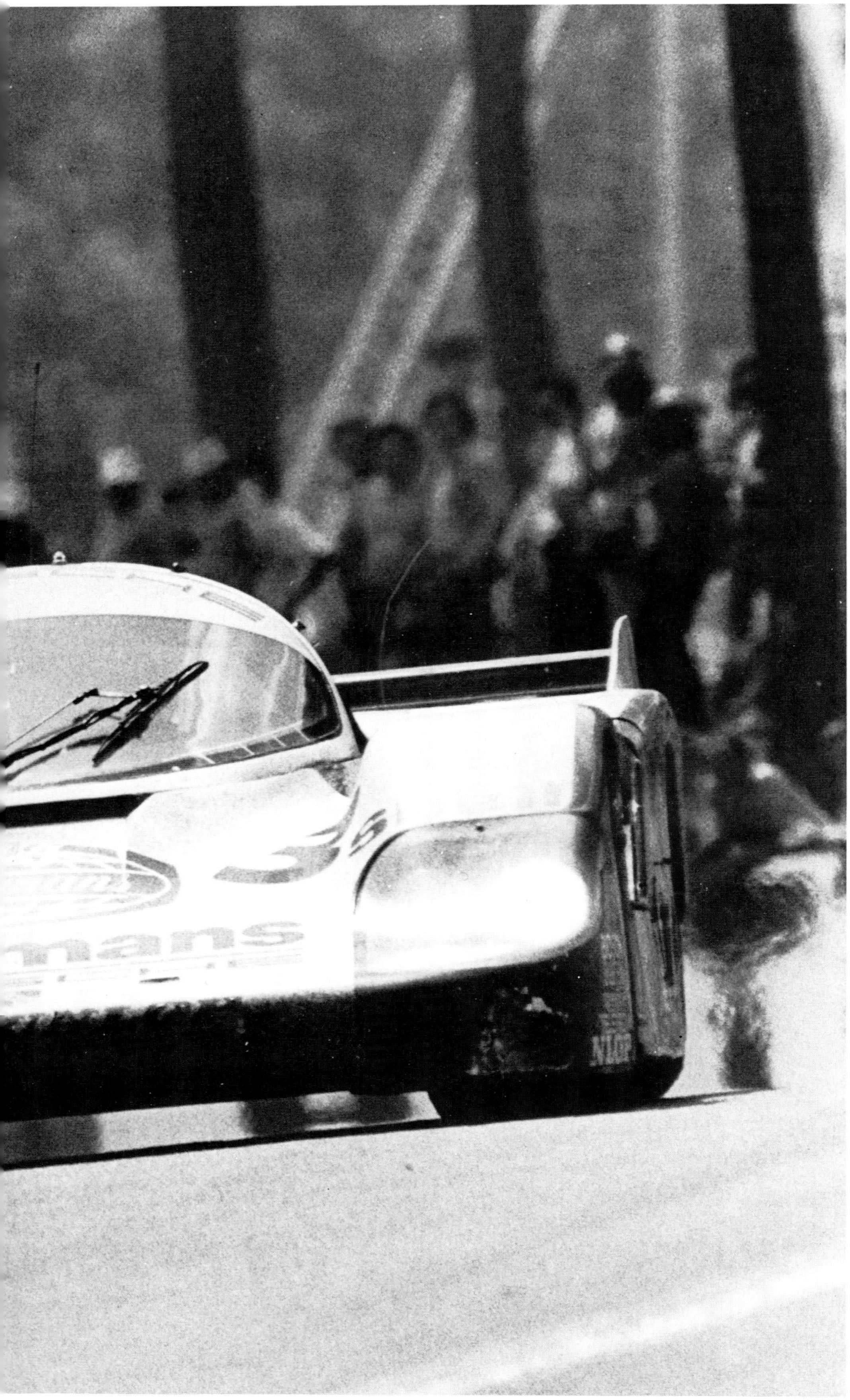

own. The engine, complete with turbos and intercoolers, cost £38,750; the gearbox £10,000; a longtail body kit £7,500. Add to all the vehicle costs the administrative, workshop, staff and travelling expenses, plus driver retainers and fuel and tyre bills, and you begin to see where the money went. Few teams could afford to run one of these off-the-shelf Porsches, let alone develop new cars and engines. The event promoters did not pay start money and the prize funds were low: the highest race-winning purse was the £11,650 at Le Mans, a sum with no meaning in terms of the overall costs. Thus the teams were reliant on big sponsorship. To gain it, strong media coverage was essential.

But the exposure in the media fell short of most predictions, because there remained a stunning lack of understanding of sports car racing among the media (although television coverage did show a definite improvement). This was one of the factors which made genuinely effective sponsorship hard to come by, the other being the crushing domination of the race results by a single marque.

The expectations of all the rival teams were limited by the vastly superior performance of the Porsche 956, and in particular the team of factory entered cars. Although this works team itself was beaten during the year, Porsches won every race without serious challenge. In fact, the German company's tenth Manufacturers title was clinched as early as June, when nine of its products finished in the first ten at Le Mans.

Yet even some of the private Porsche owners had sponsorship problems, and the situation was drastically more serious for the teams campaigning any other type of car.

These three problem areas all contributed to a general shortage of money, so that precious few teams could participate in a full season. In fact, fewer than 20 Group C cars took part in more than two World Championship races. Not only that, but the only regular contenders were the works and private Porsches and the latest Lancias . . .

The Porsche 956 retained the same basic characteristics first seen in 1982: monocoque chassis (the first such Porsche), twin ground-effect air tunnels, a 2.6-litre, twin-turbo version of the so-familiar flat-six engine producing up to 640bhp on the race boost pressures. The works cars, however, were built to a more advanced specification than the customer cars. This included a lighter chassis which reduced the vehicle weight to around 810 kgs, the customer models being some 30 kgs heavier; revised steering geometry which made the works cars easier to drive; a high-downforce nose section which eliminated the understeer plaguing the privateers until some of them copied it late in the season; and, most significantly, higher-compression engines governed by the Bosch Motronic management systems, controlling electronically such functions as revs, boost pressure, oil and water temperatures, and battery voltage output. With the 'works' Dunlop contract, the works team also enjoyed a near-monopoly of the latest Denloc boltless tyres, which made a small but useful improvement to stability and handling.

The customer cars were built more or less to the 1982 works specification and their lower compression engines featured the standard mechanical controls, and thus were less fuel-efficient. Porsche constructed 12 of these, although one was retained by the company's R&D division and used as a mobile testbed for the TAG turbo Formula 1 engine.

Two were run out of Germany by Joest Racing, sponsored by Marlboro and New Man fashion, while two more were run out of Britain by the J David backed John Fitzpatrick Racing team (one of these being used occasionally for CanAm events in the USA). The rest of the first batch went to American Preston Henn, whose car was also based at JFR; to

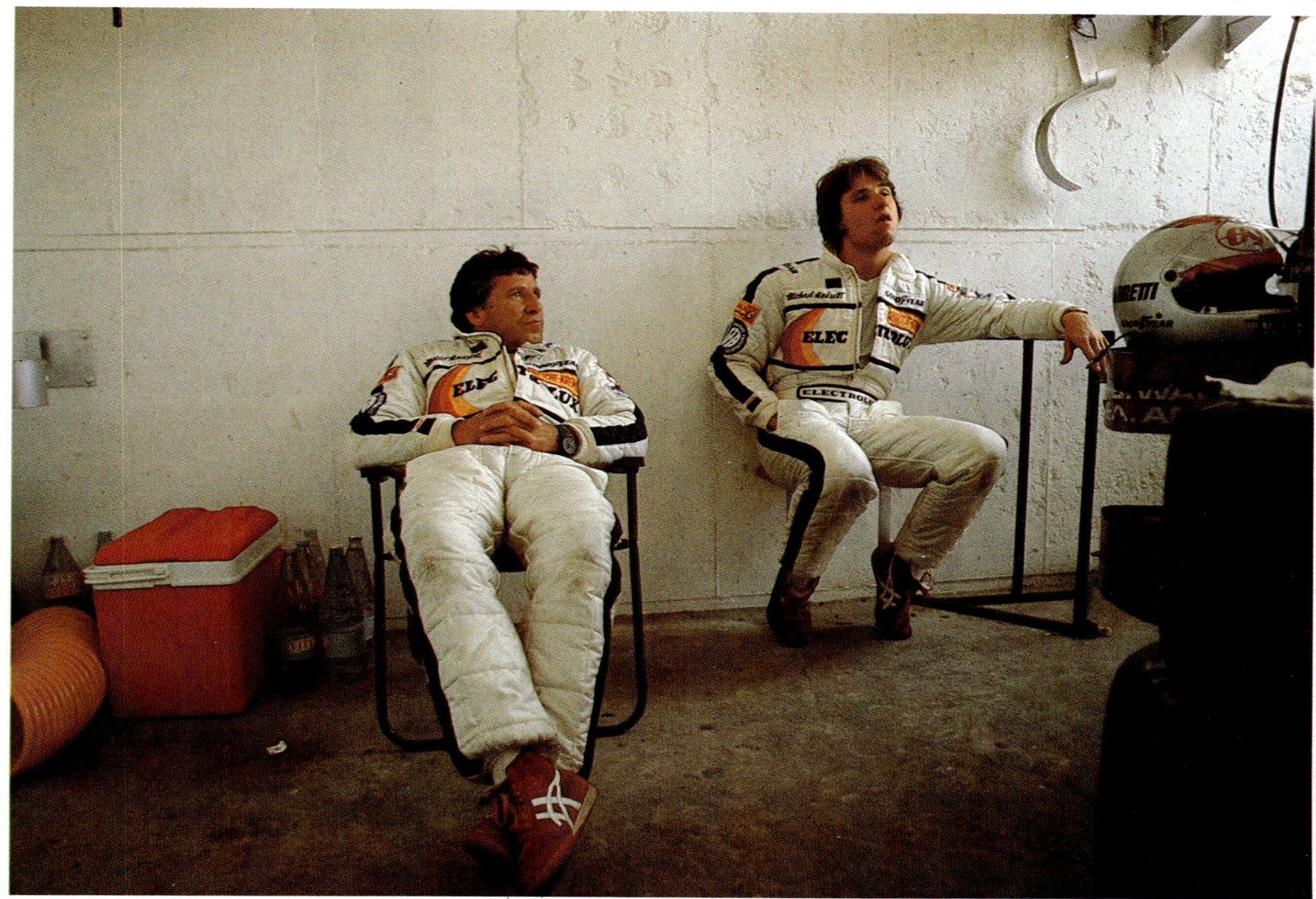

Reinhold Obermaier's Boss fashion sponsored German team; to Richard Lloyd's Canon Racing organisation in Britain; to the Kremer brothers in Germany, who had to use their initiative to gain race-to-race sponsorship; and to the Japanese Team Trust, whose car was raced only in national championship events but was successful in the World series race at Fuji.

Towards the end of the season, two cars which had been destined for use in a new John Frankenheimer film (subsequently postponed), were instead sold to the Swiss Walter Brun and to another Japanese entrant, Yoshiho Matsuda.

Of the 11 customer Porsches which raced during 1983, the regular contenders were the two Joest cars, one of the JFR entries, and those of the Canon, Kremer and Obermaier teams.

Given the relatively advanced specification of the factory team cars, it came as a shock to everyone when Joest Racing's Marlboro 956 beat them in the opening round at Monza. The works team was running its new 8:1 compression engines, and rumours abounded that somehow the Joest team had contrived to replace its customer-standard 7.5:1 unit with a similar power plant. Whatever, the defeat sent the works team into a short crash programme of extra development, honing the latest engine so that both power and fuel efficiency were improved. At Silverstone, Nürburgring and Le Mans, mechanical and driver failings aside, the works Rothmans-Porsche cars were in a class of their own.

These three races produced a clamour of discontent from Porsche's customers, some of whose sponsors were beginning to ask awkward questions. The privateers demanded that they should be given the opportunity to buy the higher-compression engines. The factory bowed to this pressure, and the better financed teams were equipped with the 8:1 power units for the next event, which was the big-money, non-championship race at the Norisring in Germany, a sprint event.

To their dismay, however, the privateers were yet again crushed by the works cars, and there was increased dissatisfaction when it was discovered that the works team now not only had the option of fitting big or small turbocharger units, but had also come up with another better engine, with a compression ratio of 8.5:1.

The private JFR team enjoyed a moment of glory by beating the works cars in the Euro round at Brands Hatch, a victory gained by technical ingenuity. But in the World series races at Spa and Fuji, the performance gap, although increasingly contentious, remained and might even have broadened. At Fuji, the winning Rothmans-Porsche not only finished a fast race six laps ahead of the best privately entered car, but was also very remarkably fuel-efficient, consuming only 525 litres of the 600-litre allowance.

Lancia, in their first season with the new LC2 design, were in no position to compete with this impressive display by Porsche. The decision to build a C-car had been taken relatively late, and Cesare Fiorio's Italian team had to complete the project in about six months. The new car was built around a new 2.6-litre V8 engine commissioned from Ferrari, with twin turbos and horsepower to match the Porsche. Like the 956, the LC2 featured twin air tunnels and a five-speed gearbox, and the engine had similar electronic controls by Magneti Marelli, with Weber electronic fuel injection. It was an advanced project, completed too quickly, and the works cars, sponsored by Martini aperitif and MS cigarettes, proved to be very fast but very fragile.

The team's most serious difficulty arose straight away, at Monza. The Pirelli tyres were not up to the job. Efforts were made to resolve this problem but, ultimately, Fiorio and chief engineer Gianni Tonti were compelled to switch to Dunlops. But the entire suspension geometry of the LC2 had been designed for the Italian radials – and no amount of testing could make the cars handle on the British crossplies.

Initially the cars were mechanically unreliable, too.

There was a series of electrical failures, and then the Ferrari 268C engine was found to have porous cylinder heads. Although the cars were on the pace of the works Porsches during qualifying, and could outrun most of the privateers in the races, the first four events for the two-car works team resulted in only one finish. A third LC2, sold to the private Mirabella team, fared no better.

Fiorio worked hard during the 11-week mid-season break after Le Mans, and with scrupulous attention to detail, in order to improve reliability, and indeed all three of these cars did finish the next race, at Spa. By now, however, Fiorio's thoughts centred on a long winter of development prior to a renewed attack in 1984. However, the Lancias, with interim suspension modifications, did come good at last in the final Euro races in Italy.

After Porsche and Lancia came very little. Before the start of the season, Ford shelved a promising new Group C project which was to have replaced the C100s. This not only led Cosworth Engineering to shelve development of the proposed DFL turbo, but also left that company with no real endurance racing customers, for Cosworth's 1982 teams – Rondeau, Lola, Grid and Sauber SHS among them – were in various financial difficulties with their Group C programmes.

Only three new designs were built to take the 3.9-litre normal induction DFL which had been so numerous the season before. Predictably, the 4-series Rondeau 'wing-car' was off the pace: three were entered for Le Mans but none finished. After this disaster, constructor Jean Rondeau reduced his operation and set his sights lower. Chuck Graemiger's neat Cheetah G-603 might have potential, but competed irregularly due to financial restraints. Finally, the Japanese Dome organisation constructed an impressive new chassis which raised a few eyebrows at Fuji.

Andretti and son. Mario and Mike Andretti, driving a Kremer Porsche 956, might have won Le Mans had the race been another lap longer (left).
Photo: Diana Burnett

The Lancia team, sponsored by Martini, took the late decision to build a Group C car around a new 2.6-litre V8 engine commissioned from Ferrari. These advanced cars, driven mainly by Michele Alboreto, Riccardo Patrese, Piercarlo Ghinzani and Teo Fabi, finally came good at Imola, late in the season.
Photos: Nigel Snowdon

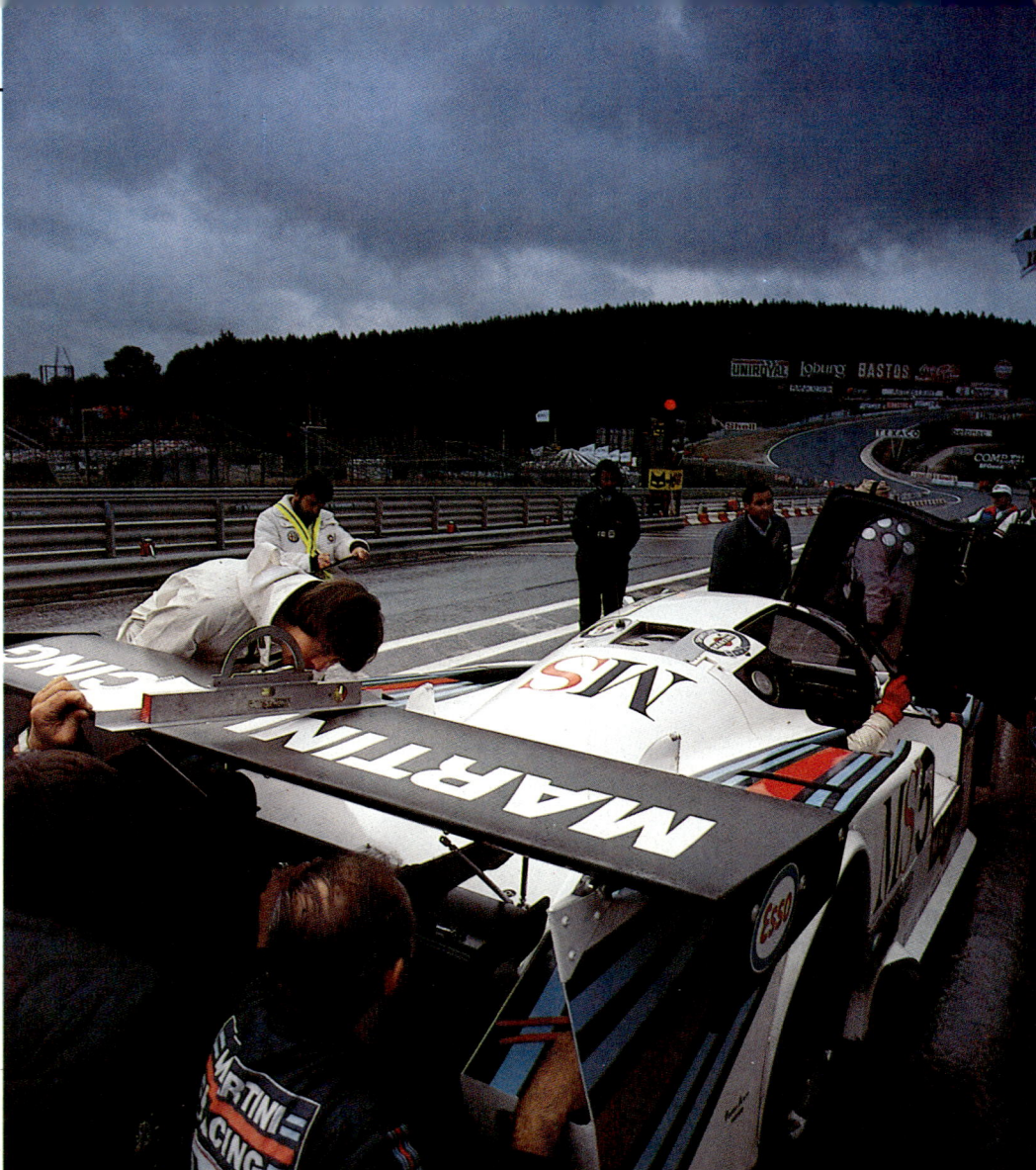

BMW, intent on Formula 1, still could not align themselves with the Group C fuel consumption formula as defined, although their engines were used in a number of cars. Notable among these was the new Sauber C-7 which was the only non-Porsche in the top ten at Le Mans, and which also finished Fuji, contesting only these two races. The Sauber's engine was the underpowered 3.5-litre BMW straight-six, and a 3.2-litre version of this unit, with turbocharging, appeared in one of Walter Brun's new Sehcars. The Swiss, who had taken over the Sauber SHS organisation, gave himself an uphill struggle with updated cars, financed and constructed by the Seger & Hoffmann aeronautics company. The BMW powered Sehcar was promising, but Brun himself destroyed it at the 'Ring on its debut. He escaped with bruising and came to Le Mans with a new Porsche engined chassis which was in an unready state. Unwilling to persevere in the face of a variety of problems, Brun then took the easy way out and became a Porsche 956 owner.

Aston Martin Tickford sank some £100,000 into modifying the stock-block 5.3-litre normal induction V8 so that it was smaller, lighter and a little more powerful than its predecessor, and could be employed as a stressed chassis member in the new EMKA. This car, commissioned by Steve O'Rourke, was designed by Len Bailey and built in Britain by Michael Cane Racing. It was an interesting project, and the car finished Le Mans, but yet again the programme was curtailed by money problems.

The Aston Martin engine also ran in Viscount Downe's Nimrod C2B, a heavily modified 1982 car which had been redesigned by Ray Mallock. This Bovis sponsored team did several races and the car was clearly quicker than before, but race finishes were

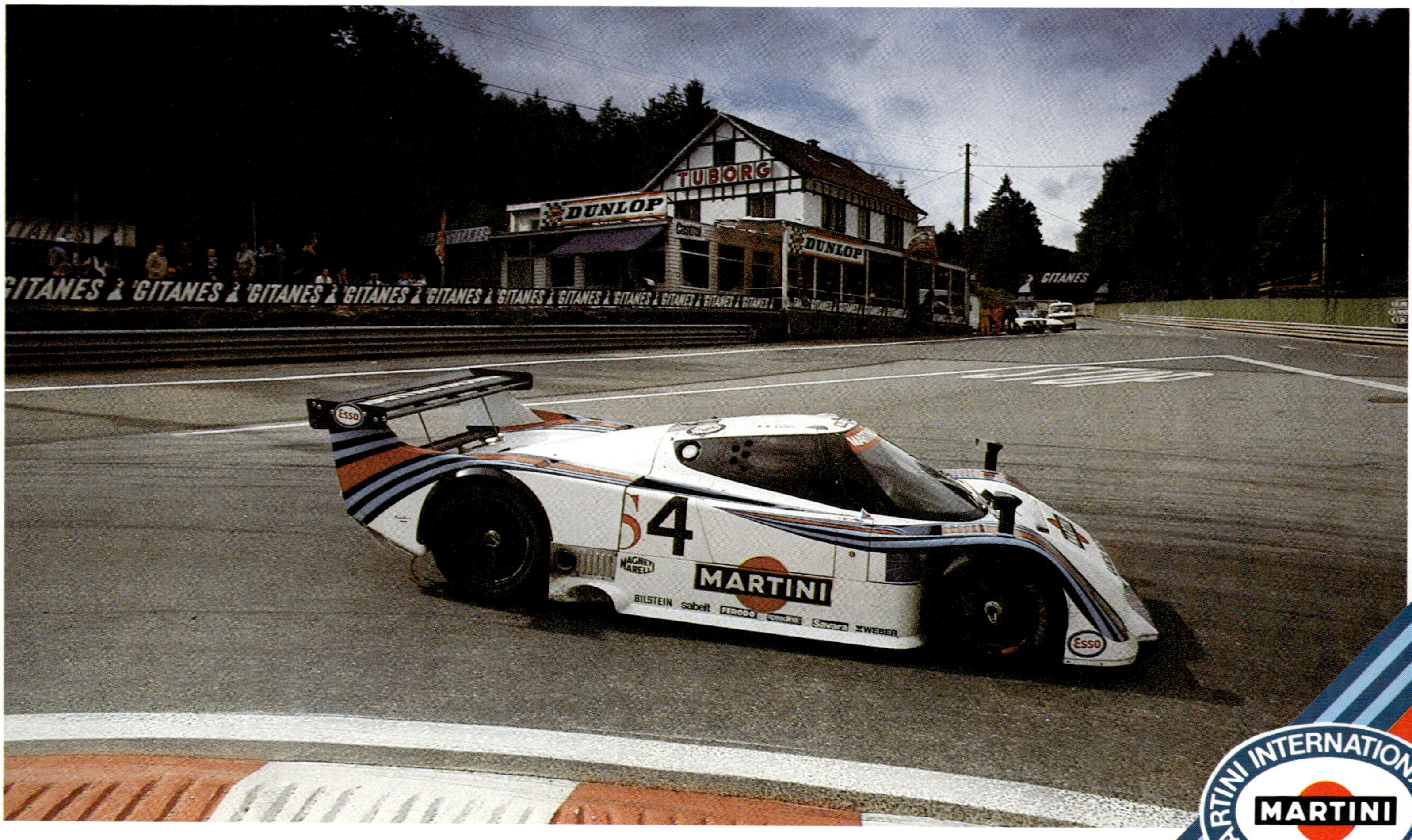

Vern Schuppan brings the third works Porsche into the pits at Le Mans after the 956 had lost a door on the Mulsanne Straight. This was to disrupt the cooling air flow to the cylinder head water radiator and the engine overheated and seized as the car entered the final lap. Al Holbert managed to coax the Porsche across the line in first place.

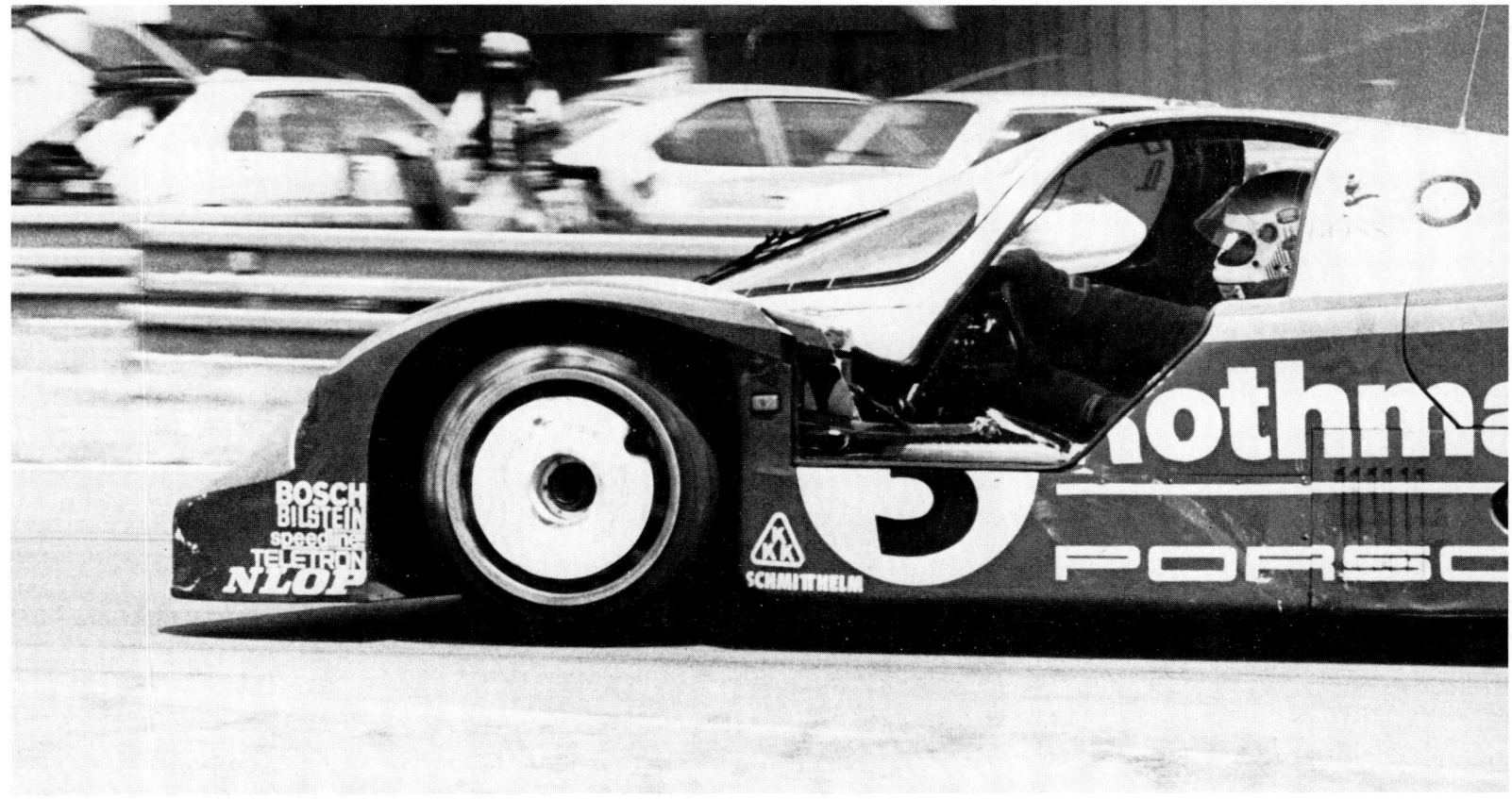

hard to come by. The works Nimrod team did not participate after an early foray into IMSA racing in the USA, and the intriguing new Andrew Thorby design never did see the light of day.

Another big stock-block V8, the Chevrolet, powered the Tiga GC83, but this ungainly car did not appear until the end of the season.

At the other end of the scale, the 1.4-litre single-turbo Lancia engine powered Eugenio Bersini's Lancia LC1 cars, the 1982 works Group 6 chassis converted to Group C by Guglielmo Bellasi. This team secured a fifth place at the 'Ring, but later reduced operations when the money ran out.

With most of the endurance racing season strewn with stories like these – stories of interesting and in some cases promising projects, curtailed by shortage of development funds – it was uplifting to find the active manufacturer interest which abounded in Japan. Mazda, Nissan and Toyota are apparently committed to contesting the World series in the future.

Mazda had run the all-new 717C cars at Le Mans, achieving a one-two in C Junior despite handling characteristics which alarmed the drivers. The team's new rotary engine, which will be turbocharged, was not ready for Fuji, but Nissan and Toyota both had interim Group C engines (2.1-litre turbo four-cylinders) pending the completion of their own more powerful units for 1984.

The Nissan engine was impressive in Kazuyoshi Hoshino's March 83G and in Haruhito Yanagida's very effective Fairlady Z, while the less powerful Toyota also went well in one of the excellent new chassis of the Dome team.

There is the possibility that Porsche's domination will be challenged in 1984 by Lancia and perhaps by other European teams. But Fuji left those who made the trip with the impression that the sun of increased competition in Group C might well be rising in the east.

GROUP C JUNIOR

The new class was not a success, for the only regular contender was the Giorgio Stirano designed Alba, the world's first (and so far only) carbonfibre chassis sports-racing car. The car was powered by a new 1.8-litre turbo four-cylinder built by the Carma organisation of Carlo Facetti and Martino Finotto, which was homologated under a paperwork agreement with Giannini.

The Alba was clearly the fastest Junior and it won the class when it finished, except at Fuji where it was delayed and victory went to a locally entered, converted March 75S. The other Junior class winner, at Spa, was the Mazda rotary engined Harrier built by Lester Ray and run by the British Mann's team.

GROUP B

FISA's production inspired class does not look set to become successful until 1985, when a number of teams will be racing the very interesting new version of the Porsche 911 Turbo and the promised Ferrari GTO. For the moment, with Group B development concentrated on rallying, the endurance racing promoters relied on rehomologated Group 4 cars, the Porsche 930 (the conventional 911 Turbo) and the BMW M1.

The BMW's 3.5-litre six-cylinder was about 100 bhp more powerful than the Porsche's 3.3. turbo, and the M1s dominated the class, notably Jens Winther's Team Castrol entry which was usually co-driven by David Mercer and Frank Jelinski. The prestige result – at Le Mans – was however claimed by the Porsche of the Charles Ivey Racing team, which had won Group 5 at Le Mans in 1981-82.

THE RULES

Following the debut season of Group C in 1982, FISA kept rule revisions to a minimum, persevering with the original concept of a free-engine sports car racing formula with an 800 kgs minimum weight limit, and the practical restrictions on engine power outputs applied by means of a maximum fuel allowance, rather than by predetermined engine capacity.

The cars were again restricted to maximum fuel tankage of 100 litres, and could refuel only five times in the 1000kms events.

However, the anomaly which spoiled some of the 1982 races was removed, in that six-hour duration events were banned. Silverstone and Fuji in the World series had to fall into line by staging 1000kms distance events, and Le Mans was the only duration race.

The Group C Junior class was introduced, the cars having a 55-litre tankage and a minimum weight of 700kgs, but the same free-engine vehicle regulations. The Juniors competed for a separate FIA trophy, as did the Group B cars.

For 1984, the Group C cars will be restricted to 85-litre tankage, although the team managers will be able to refuel as many times as they wish. The C Junior rules will remain unaltered.

Alongside the 1983 World Endurance Championship of Makes, FISA again ran the concurrent Drivers series, which is becoming increasingly prestigious. In addition, the governing body instituted the 1983 European Endurance Championship of Drivers, which shared some of the races with the World series. The opening races at Monza, Silverstone, Nürburgring, Le Mans and Spa-Francorchamps counted towards both the World and the European titles. The remaining World races were at Fuji and Kyalami, while the Euro series went its separate way, to Brands Hatch, Imola and Mugello.

The format of the schedule was not auspiciously successful, serving largely to confuse spectators and media, and excluding once more an American race. The many efforts to resolve the disagreements over the vehicle rules, which have soured the relationship between FISA in Europe and IMSA in the USA, were unsuccessful, although there are signs that the USA (and Canada) will return to the World Championship in 1984.

The Rothmans-Porsche factory team, directed by Peter Falk and managed by Norbert Singer, took a little time to establish its superiority, and not even for the works drivers was it a season free of incident, and sometimes pure drama.

For a start, Monza produced that shock defeat at the hand of Joest Racing's Marlboro 956, driven by Bob Wollek and Thierry Boutsen (deputising for Stefan Johansson who had a clashing Formula 1 commitment). Try as they did, neither Jacky Ickx nor Derek Bell could drop Wollek during the first stints – and then the Marlboro car showed that it could go further between refuelling halts. From then on, the works cars, co-driven respectively by Jochen Mass and Al Holbert (standing in for Stefan Bellof), fought a losing battle. At the end, the Ickx/Mass car was 73 seconds behind. The Bell/Holbert entry lost a dozen laps in the pits due to a seized rear wheel bearing, and finished seventh.

The late Rolf Stommelen, sharing Joest Racing's New Man 956 with Hans Heyer and Clemens Schickentanz, came in three laps down in third place, making Monza a fine start for Reinhold Joest's team.

The Obermaier-Boss 956, in which Jurgen Barth joined regulars Axel Plankenhorn/Jurgen Lassig, ran the first of a somehow depressing series of circumspect races and was rewarded with fourth place, ten laps behind. John Fitzpatrick/David Hobbs, delayed after Fitz was forced off the road by a backmarker, recovered to finish fifth narrowly ahead of Jan Lammers/Tiff Needell/Richard Lloyd (Canon 956), also delayed.

Piercarlo Ghinzani had claimed a fine pole position for the debutant Lancia Martini, and led eight laps before a rear tyre blew. Later this car went out with overheating, but team mates Riccardo Patrese/Michele Alboreto survived a difficult race with tyres to finish ninth, behind one of the converted Lancia LC1 cars of the Sivama-Grifone team.

Silverstone was notable for the stunning arrival on the Group C scene of Stefan Bellof, who somehow produced an incredible pole lap at 144mph. He and Bell won the race, too, although challenged strongly all the way by Wollek/Johansson in the Marlboro 956 which finished only 50 seconds behind. Mass, though, had the first Rothmans-Porsche accident of the season when he went off on a wet track in trying to wrest back second place from Johansson. Lammers/Boutsen (Canon 956) were third ahead of the steady Boss 956, and the new Kremer 956 driven by Alan Jones and Vern Schuppan.

Jones had led the race early on with his car on intermediate tyres on a drying track. On wet tyres, the initial leading had been done by the two works Lancias, but both were retired with overheating. The New Man 956 went out with ignition failure, and the new Henn 956 with a blown engine. The JDavid 956 was eighth, after electrical problems.

The last World Championship race ever to be held on the epic Nürburgring North Circuit resulted in another Rothmans-Porsche victory, but it was even harder won. Bellof's pole was again untouchable (126mph), but in the race he had a massive accident at Pflanzgarten, all but somersaulting the car which nevertheless was wrecked. The Ickx/Mass car was almost four minutes in the lead when the race was stopped soon

after half-distance, due to the accident which befell Walter Brun's Sehcar-BMW. In the restart, Mass suffered a rear suspension breakage, but the works mechanics did a fine job and the car continued to win from Wollek/Johansson, whose Marlboro 956 might have won if both turbos had been working instead of only one. Lammers in the Canon 956 was joined by World Champion Keke Rosberg and Jonathan Palmer, and the car finished third ahead of the reliable Boss 956. The JDavid 956 also suffered a suspension failure and dropped to sixth place behind one of the Lancia LC1s.

Lancia Martini ran only one LC2, and Patrese/Alboreto went out with transmission failure. A similar fate befell the debutant Mirabella LC2, in which Ghinzani was loaned to join Giorgio Francia/Paulo Barilla, the team's regulars.

Thus far, Monza had featured 12 Group C entries, Silverstone 19, the 'Ring 13. Thirty-eight of them came to Le Mans, where Rothmans-Porsche scored a thrillingly dramatic victory. First, the Mass/Bellof works car was retired with engine trouble. Then, the Ickx/Bell car was delayed by electrical problems, after losing time in a lap two collision with the Canon 956. Finally, the third works entry, driven by Al Holbert/Hurley Haywood/Vern Schuppan, lost one of its doors. This disrupted the cooling air flow to the cylinder head water radiator, and the engine overheated. It terrified Holbert by seizing solid as he entered his final lap. Miraculously, it restarted, and somehow it got Holbert to the finish line. All the while, Bell was closing fast in the recovering sister car, which was only 64 seconds behind at the end, and running out of fuel . . .

One more lap, and the race might have been won by Mario Andretti and his son Michael, sharing the Kremer 956 with Philippe Alliot.

There were six more Porsche in the top ten, all survivors of the various delays which are inescapable at Le Mans. They finished in the order New Man, JDavid (the team's second car, backed by Skoal Bandit), Marlboro, Boss, Canon and Henn. Splitting them in ninth place came the reliable Sauber C-7, making its race debut in some style.

Apart from the Mass/Bellof works car, the only Porsche non-finish occured when the other JDavid entry broke its fuel pump. None of the Lancia LC2 cars was among the 21 survivors, Alboreto/Teo Fabi retiring with transmission failure, Ghinzani/Hans Heyer with a broken turbo, and Barilla/Alessandro Nannini/Jean-Claude Andruet with engine failure in the third works entry. The Rondeau-Cosworth and WM-Peugeot challenges never materialised and, of these five cars, only one of the WMs finished.

Rothmans-Porsche and the other teams had 11 weeks in which to recover their composure after the breathless Le Mans, and most of the 956 teams took in the non-championship Norisring 200 Miles before resuming the World series at Spa-Francorchamps. Bellof triumphed after a long fight with Mass, and behind the works team's one-two came Wollek (Marlboro), Fitzpatrick (JDavid) and Rosberg, this time in the Kremer car. Walter Brun's new 956 made its debut but Harald Grohs was

stopped by gearbox failure; Hobb's JDavid car leaked out its water, the Canon car stranded Lammers with a blown engine, and Hans Heyer's fast run in the solo Lancia Martini ended when a driveshaft broke.

As at Le Mans, Ickx claimed the pole at Spa, where the works team had a less dramatic race. He and Mass won, but only after the Bell/Bellof car, leading, had been delayed by a braking problem. Third on this occasion and the privateer 'class' winner was the Fitzpatrick/Hobbs JDavid 956, with the new Brun 956 fourth crewed by Grohs and Hans Stuck Jnr, who enjoyed his first ever race in a Porsche. The Boss 956 droned round to finish fifth. The reworked Lancia LC2s of Francia/Barilla (Mirabella) and Patrese/Fabi (Martini) were sixth and seventh, and the Ghinzani/Alboreto works car 11th after a long delay with an obscure electrical problem.

The Canon 956 misfired all day and Lammers/Boutsen were ninth, but neither of the Joest entries even made it to the finish. Johansson's Marlboro 956 was punted into retirement by Patrese's Lancia, and later the suspension failed on the New Man 956. Trying to keep his Drivers championship hopes alive, Wollek had moved across to this car to join Heyer and Volkert Merl. He had led the series until this point, but now Ickx moved ahead of him, and he had Mass and Bell tapping on his shoulder.

Before jetting off to Japan, the top teams contested the first European Championship only event, at Brands Hatch. Here Rothmans-Porsche were defeated for a second time, on this occasion by the technical ingenuity of the JDavid team. On all the Porsches, there are vents in the underbody to feed cooling air to the cylinder block; the British team instead ran fans off the turbo piping to cool the block, which enabled them to close off the vents, thus increasing ground-effect downforce. On a dry track, the power loss (caused by driving the fans) was detrimental to performance, but not in the rain, and that was how the race began. The team had recruited Derek Warwick, who had been impressive at Spa in the Kremer 956 until co-driver Franz Konrad had blown the engine. Warwick drove brilliantly on the wet circuit and, when the track dried out, he and Fitzpatrick had built up an unassailable lead. Now with a bigger power advantage than ever, the works cars came back at the privateer, but Bellof's late challenge was thwarted when he flat-spotted a tyre in avoiding a backmarker. Warwick/Fitzpatrick held on to win by 45 seconds from Ickx/Mass, with Bell/Bellof third.

Lancia Martini's best result of the season this far came when Patrese/Alboreto finished fourth, the car having been very competitive in the rain, but a turbo failure stopped Nannini/Beppe Gabbiani, and Barilla's Mirabella entry was pushed off by a backmarker.

Two busted distributor drivebelts dropped Wollek/Johansson to sixth in the Marlboro 956, while an electrical problem delayed the Canon 956 and Lammers/Palmer finished ninth. The Boss 956 was again reliably fifth, but the Henn team's attempt to follow Obermaier's example of consistency failed when the car, co-driven by its owner and Divina Galica, was crashed out of the race by David Sutherland.

Wollek's hopes of the World

Endurance Championship of Drivers finally died at Fuji, where the Rothmans-Porsches were totally in command even though they did not win without more drama. The Bell/Bellof car had a puncture, and Ickx/Mass seemed to have it sewn up when Mass suffered a blowout at 180mph. The result of a mechanic's mistake, in fitting two right-side rear tyres during the previous pitstop, the incident produced a fine piece of reflex car control by Mass, but Bell/Bellof were through once more, and held off the repaired Ickx/Mass entry by 50 seconds.

Fuji saw the World series debuts of the Team Trust and Matsuda Porsches, and they marked it by finishing third and fourth, driven respectively by Schuppan/Naohiro Fujita and Henri Pescarolo/Boutsen. The Matsuda 956 was race-managed by the JDavid team mechanics, whose own car had been seriously damaged in a practice accident. The solo Joest entry, the New Man 956, suffered three mid-race collisions and finished down in fifth place, ending Wollek's title bid.

The Kremer 956 was also damaged before the race, but was miraculously repaired in time for the start, although Johansson/Alliot retired early with an oil leak. The Henn 956 went out with front body damage, but its sister Advan sponsored entry for this race, the Brun 956, held on to finish sixth. All the Lancias and the Canon 956 were absent, being saved for the final Euro rounds at Imola and Mugello, and the World finale at Kyalami.

By now, Rothmans-Porsche had repeated the treble achieved in 1982, having not only won Le Mans and clinched the Makes title, but also with the Drivers crown in the bag. With the one round to go, the only drivers still in contention were the works team's Jacky Ickx and Derek Bell, and Ickx had only to protect an 11-point lead to claim the title for the second successive year.

Kyalami, unfortunately, took place too late to be included in this review, but first the Euro championship came to its close in Italy. At Imola, the works Lancias finally came good and, in the absence of the Rothmans Porsches, defeated all the privateers. Teo Fabi/Hans Heyer won the race for the Martini team, and Nannini/Gabbiani were running second when stopped by a gearbox breakage. Fitzpatrick/Hobbs inherited the place with the JDavid 956 and Wollek/Johansson (Marlboro 956) were third. Bell arranged to share the Canon 956 with Palmer so as to remain hopeful of the Euro title, but Palmer collided with the barriers and the pair finished no higher than fourth. The Boss 956 was fifth and the New Man 956 sixth, after a busted gear linkage had stopped the Mirabella Lancia.

Bell urgently sought another Group C seat for the finale at Mugello and secured another ride in the Canon Porsche. The car started from pole position but was slowed on race day by a down-on-power engine, so Bell/Palmer, co-driving with rally star Henri Toivonen, finished third behind the sole-surviving Lancia of Patrese/Nannini. Because he had to drop his lowest score (only the best six results counted), Wollek could only claim the title if he and Johansson won the race, and that is just what they did, leaving the runners-up, Ickx and Bell, to fight out the World crown at Kyalami.

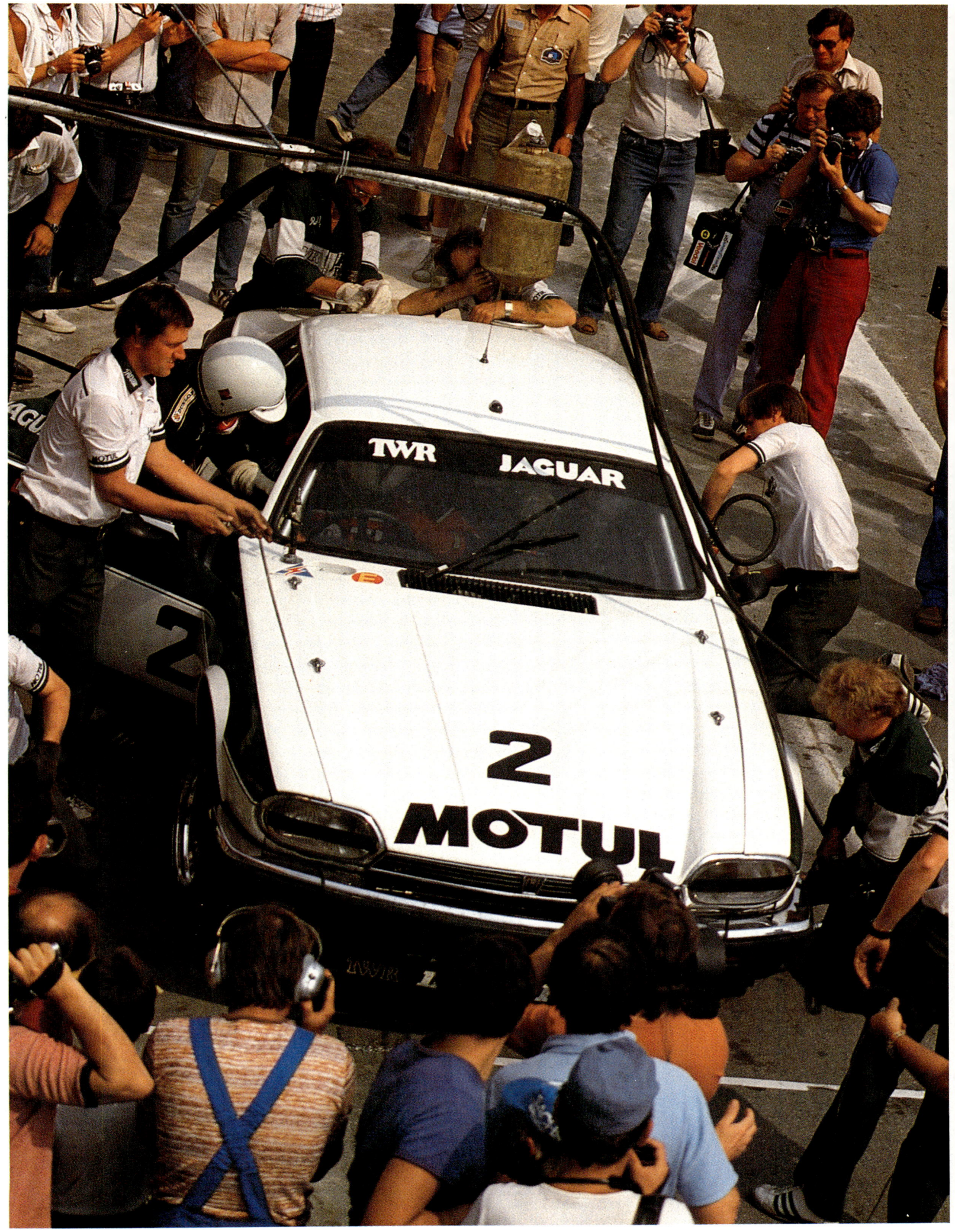

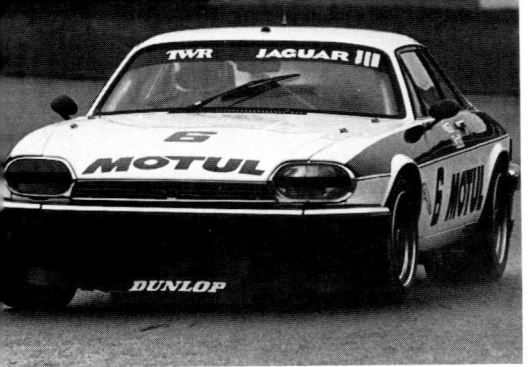

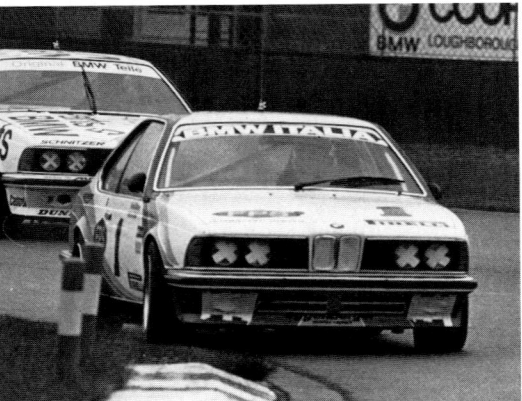

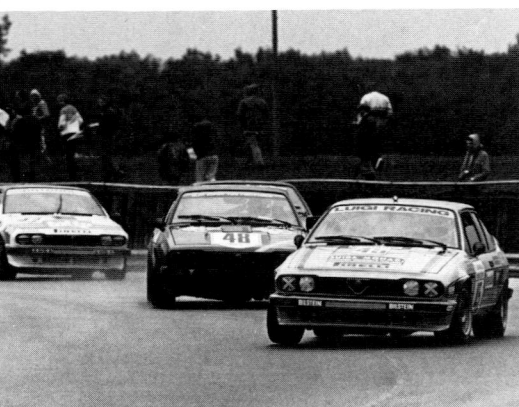

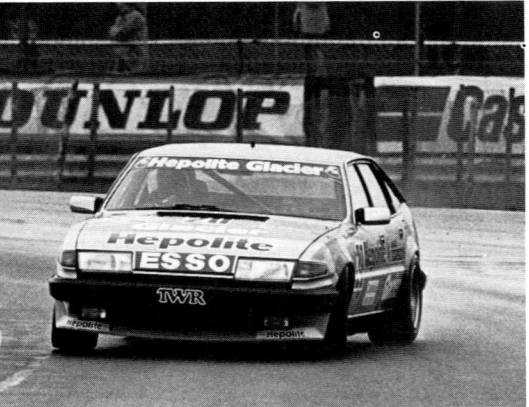

Chuck Nicholson hands over the leading Jaguar XJ-S to Tom Walkinshaw at Bruno. After the sixth race of the championship, Walkinshaw held a one-point lead over Dieter Quester *(left)*. Photo: Andrew Whyte

A revitalized 'formula' and an exciting season's racing from some of the world's major manufacturers *(above)*.

Britain's TT – the RAC Tourist Trophy race – is the world's oldest motor race, bar none.

Its original intention has not always been maintained. Early in the century (it began in 1905, on the Isle of Man) it was for genuine touring cars, basically of the type you could buy, with regulations taking weight and fuel consumption into specific account. Over the years, the connection between 'TT' and 'touring' often disappeared; but the introduction of 'Group A' to Europe in 1982 brought the spirit of the old idea to life again. Now, after a second season, the new 'formula' is claiming the engineering and the promotional attention of some of the world's major manufacturers.

Post-war production-car racing began at Silverstone in 1949 when sports and saloon cars ran together. The idea caught on, to the extent that, from 1952, the BRDC began running separate races for both types at its Silverstone internationals.

Those races were sprints, however, and it was in Germany that the first long-distance race for modern saloons was organised in 1961 – the Nürburgring 6-hour. This was followed by a 12-hour event on the same circuit, and inspired Britain to hold a couple of 6-hour races of its own, at Brands Hatch in 1962 and 1963.

It was in 1963 that the Saar section of the ADAC, organisers of the Nürburgring 6-hour, enlisted the aid of other national clubs throughout Europe in creating a new championship. Twenty-one seasons on, the series is alive and well. It had started healthily as a driver-only championship, and was adopted quickly by the FIA – but it lost its way by going to Group 5 in the late Sixties. With some stirring BMW v Ford battles in the Group 2 series of the early Seventies, when Alfa Romeo's GTA also starred for a while, the series seemed to recover. Then interest waned. BMW's CSL was a fabulous car, but in 'Batmobile' form it became the only serious contender in racing – and so unreal that road-going versions were sold with their aerodynamic aids wrapped up in the boot. Meanwhile the BMWs raced on, with few challengers.

Now Group A has changed all that. True, the wording of the regulations is as loose in any language as it probably has to be, leading to extremes of interpretation from all the leading contenders. This, they argue, is what regulations are for; it is a pity, therefore, that there have been several inter-team arguments. Interested manufacturers stand aside, while chief European series co-ordinator Pierre Aumonier looks to the future; as the 1983 season came to an end, he was determined to find an expert from a non-manufacturing nation to act as technical officer – above all to establish an interpretation of the regulations deemed fair by all, to all. A dream? – maybe; but surely a step in the right direction?

What a cracking season 1983 has been, though. The racing has risen above the wrangles and resulted in a cliff-hanging finish – the two leading contenders drawing clear for the final at Zolder. To be sure of taking the championship for BMW, veteran Dieter Quester simply had to beat Scotland's Tom Walkinshaw, architect of Britain's first serious assault on European touring car racing since the Sixties. The Jaguar driver's task was a little harder: he had to beat Quester *and* finish in the top four overall . . . and all this in the twelfth race of the season.

While BMW and Jaguar have been the main marques contending victory (they came to Zolder with five wins each), others have come to the fore, too, and shared in the success. A few years ago, the name of Rover was totally dissociated from the sport. It's greatest victory had been the TT of 1907. Now it is the leading marque in British racing and, after making unsuccessful appearances at Donington and the Nürburgring, it showed Austin-Rover's clear intentions for 1984 by taking 3rd place at Spa and winning the TT convincingly – the Vitesse is now a serious contender for outright victory in the long-distance continental races.

Another name to watch in Division 3 (over 2500cc) is Volvo, whose 240 was homologated with more powerful turbo and larger intercooler just before the TT, and went like a rocket – while it went. Ford may be out of things officially, but they are never far away, and there have been impressive Mustang performances. Alfa Romeo are strongest in the 2.5-litre section (Div.2) but have not had things completely their own way; they have been sufficiently dominant to take the manufacturers' title, which is based on class performance alone. Close behind were VW, the Belgian-entered Sciroccos normally taking Div.3 honours – Audi (a different marque in ETC terms) being the strongest rival. Future interest is likely to open up these classes, and therefore the manufacturers' title fight. Rumours were rife by the season's end. After Jaguar, who next? Perhaps even cautious, clever Daimler-Benz?

Meanwhile, the drivers' championship was developing into a tussle. First of all, it was between the reigning champions Helmut Kelleners and Umberto Grano (Eggenberger BMW 635CSi) and the Schnitzer BMW drivers including the ever-enthusiastic and still-brilliant Hans-Joachim Stuck; but by the mid-way point last year's runner-up Tom Walkinshaw had established a miniscule one-point lead over thrice-champion Dieter Quester.

Up to that point, it had been largely a case of ten or a dozen 635s versus two Jaguars, the latter having more power but, as specified, by Group A rules, weighing over 200kg more. Any advantage the Jaguars might have on performance was pretty equally balanced by their need for an extra pitstop, normally two to the BMWs' one, for both makes are limited to 120 litres' fuel capacity.

The Rovers, which like the Jaguars were prepared by TWR (although run quite separately), made their presence felt in 'Part Two'. Tom Walkinshaw is Britain's most experienced touring car racer, having been close to Ford and BMW and won for them in their heydays; his companies were a natural choice to organise the British assault. The ironic side is the Jaguar and Rover, once forced together by BL, are clearly rivals now. At TWR they are prepared on opposite sides of the road.

It was fitting, then, that two established names should come to the final neck and neck. At Silverstone it was Rover's day; Quester ran a good steady race to 5th; Jaguar were in tyre and other kinds of trouble, but Walkinshaw still picked up a couple of useful points.

And, at Zolder, Quester made sure of the title by finishing fourth while Walkinshaw was classified eighth – a slightly misleading result on paper for what had been a tense and dramatic race; an appropriate finish to a championship which has come to life.

A Championship comes to life

European Championships for FIA 'Group A' touring cars by Andrew Whyte

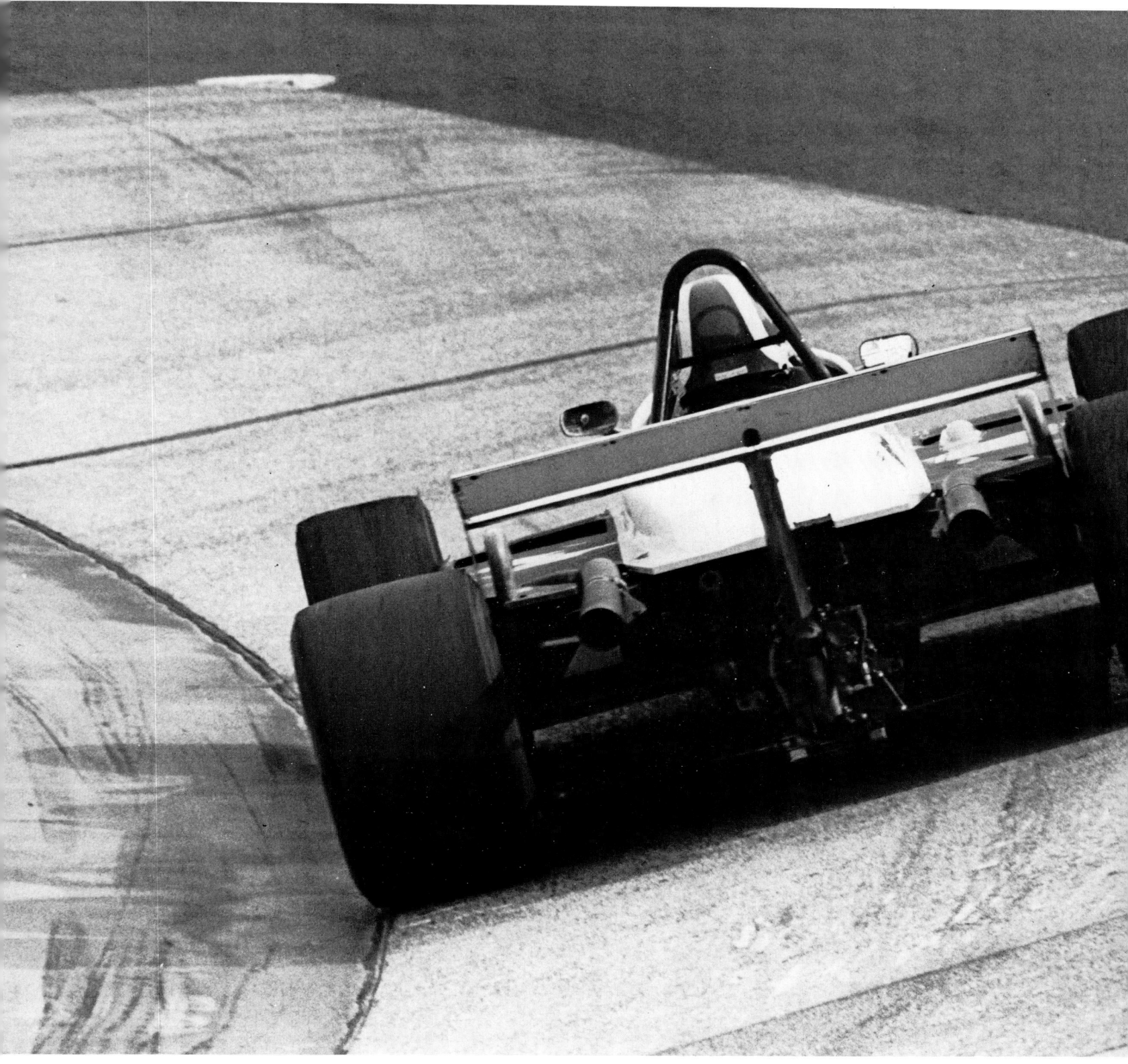

Palmer's perfection

by Ian Phillips, Formula 2 Correspondent *Autosport*

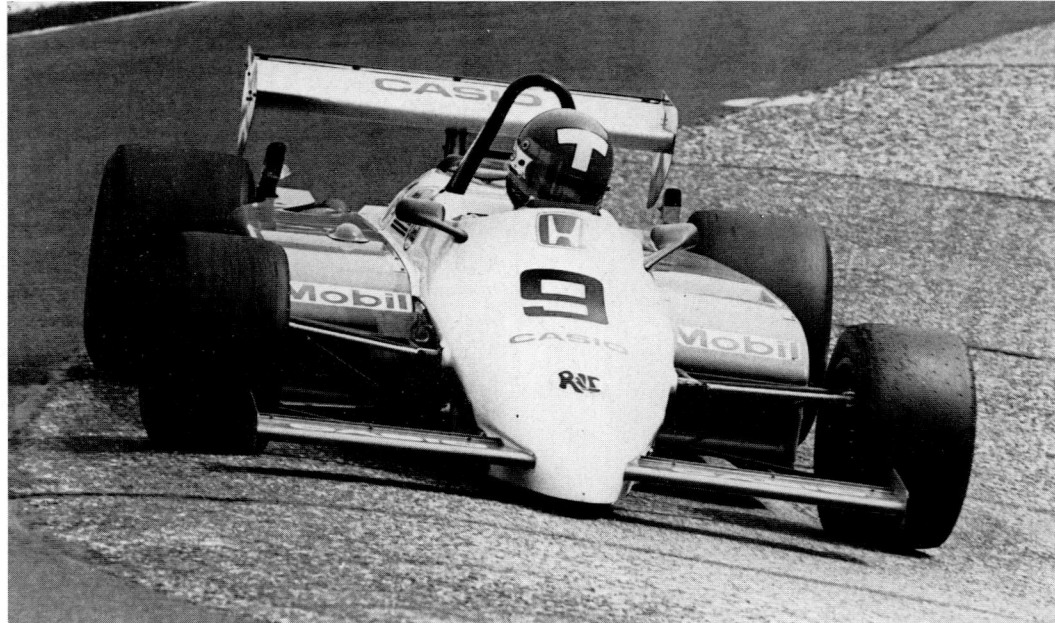

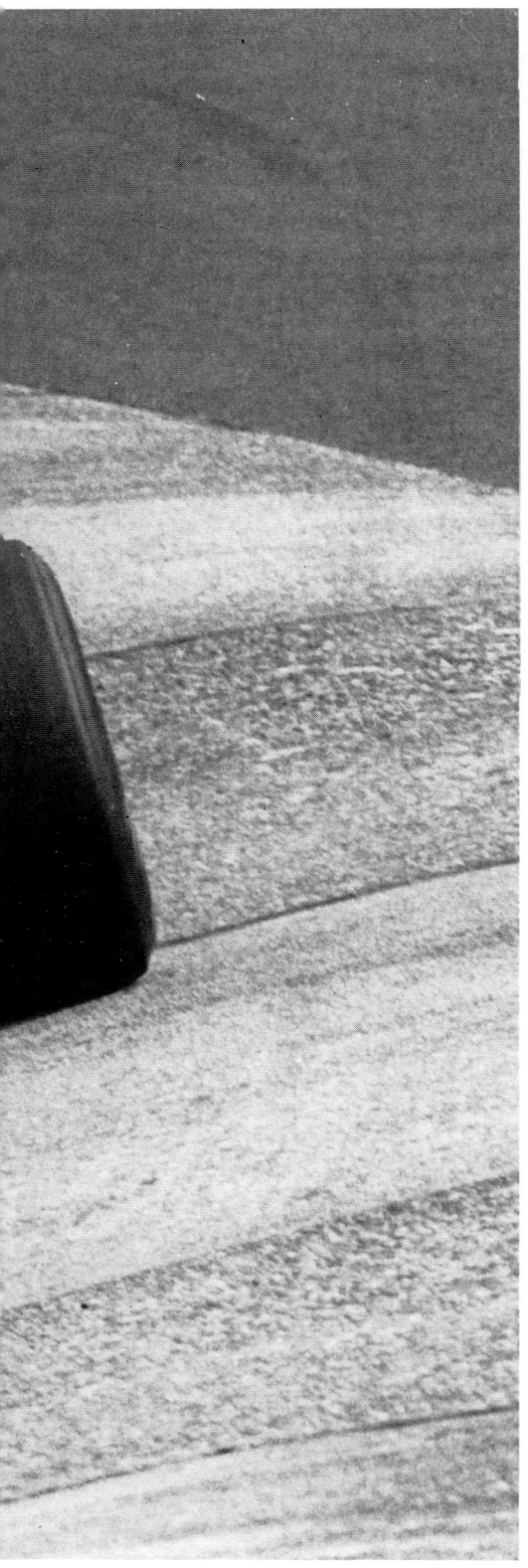

A clear-cut one-two for the Ralt-Hondas of Ron Tauranac. Jonathan Palmer *(above)* taking the championship with team-mate Mike Thackwall *(above right)*.

With a record-breaking run of five successive Championship wins in the last five races, Jonathan Palmer conclusively wrapped up the European Formula 2 Championship title. His teammate Mike Thackwell started the sequence of six Ralt-Honda successes at the start of the second half of the season and the statistics will always show that the clear-cut one two for Ron Tauranac's team was a steam roller affair.

Early in the season though it had looked a very different affair. The March-BMW combination looked as if they were carrying on where they had left off in their triumphant 1982 season with Beppe Gabbiani winning four of the first five races for the Onyx Race Engineering run team.

At the sixth of the 12-round series, at rain affected Pau, Gabbiani and Thackwell were in a class of their own but neither driver scored points. The Honda hierarchy didn't accept that showing as proof that their cars were now fully competitive as well as ultra reliable and in a very matter-of-fact manner they told Tauranac it wasn't good enough. It was really unjustified pressure, illustrating the difficulties of working with a culture which has so little understanding of European racing, but the picture did change and the Honda whitewash, anticipated for two years, finally materialized.

The bare facts of the matter are that Ralt-Hondas won seven races, took seven fastest laps, six pole positions, 20 point scoring places from 24 starts and three 1-2 results. It was an impressive display of strength of a well organised, well prepared team.

But beneath the welter of glorious statistics it wasn't really a good season overall. The racing itself was rarely good; regulation wrangles destroyed the spirit of the formula mid-season and the quality of the grids was not up to the recent high standard. The last remark should not be interpreted as meaning the Formula was struggling. If this was to be the season when F2 was hit by the European economic depression then it survived well for, with the exception of the last race (after the championship had been settled), each grid contained at least 20 brand new proprietary 1983 chassis. Yes, money was tight but if that was to be the worst year, then the formula survived very well.

The campaign opened at the traditionally wet and cold Silverstone in mid-March and it looked as if little had changed except for Beppe Gabbiani's luck. The Italian had been an F2 fast man since his debut in 1979 but he'd never had the luck to win. March perhaps gambled in installing him as team leader in the works team which had been farmed out to Mike Earle's Onyx team. But at the age of 26 Gabbiani, tutored by the experienced Peter Gethin, added maturity to his unquestioned flair. He won that race from flag to flag and followed it up a fortnight later with a cool win from eighth on the grid at Thruxton.

In those opening two races Mike Thackwell, still only 21 but back in full time employment for the first time in 18 months, led the Ralt-Honda challenge.

Having qualified second at Silverstone, he took pole at Thruxton and was the only man to lead either race other than Gabbiani. Jonathan Palmer started the season still bounding with enthusiasm and energy after the disaster of 1982. When a speck of dirt in the fuel system put him out of Silverstone he must have felt nothing had changed. But Thruxton gave him his first of 11 successive finishes with third place behind Gabbiani and Thackwell. At Hockenheim he scored his long awaited first F2 win with a convincing display from flag to flag.

It seemed that the jinx had been cracked but at the Nürburgring, the Ralt team floundered as they had throughout 1982. Palmer still finished in the points though and it was to be the only off-weekend of the year. Gabbiani won again as he did at Vallelunga two weeks later, this time from pole position. But underneath the euphoria of the Onyx March success lurked the quietly improving Honda-powered Ralts. Other than Palmer's non-finish at Silverstone, they'd finished every race and, except at Nürburgring, they had been Gabbiani's only challengers. It was now a package which was working efficiently; satisfied of that Tauranac embarked on a serious weight saving campaign to enable the chassis to maximise the 30 bhp power advantage of the V6 engine of which he had exclusive use.

At Pau either Gabbiani or Thackwell could have won by a lap but a combination of team and driver errors provided the only non-Ralt or works March win of the year. At Jarama the Ralt transformation was complete and as a team they ran 1-2 for almost the entire race until a misfire dropped Palmer back to third. However, the satisfaction of the day was lost in a welter of protest from the March teams. They objected to the dual springing systems used by Ralt, Maurer and AGS (who filled the first five places in Spain) as being devices which permitted the cars to run lower than the statutory 4 cms ground clearance which the rule book said must be adhered to "at all times". It looked horribly like sour grapes for this was the first race that no March was competitive. That impression though was false for the Ralt system had been questioned as early as Nürburgring. It became a behind closed doors dispute at Vallelunga, then more open at Pau where Tauranac put on single springs after discussions over a cup of coffee with fellow Australian, March engineer Ralph Bellamy who was the prime mover in the objections. At Jarama both Ralts were fitted with the controversial system and the long-threatened protest materialised.

It was a messy affair which highlighted not only the poorly written rules but the inability of the Stewards to act. FISA issued a clarification the day after the event and the following Thursday, after unofficial practice at Donington, the Ralts and AGS were excluded from the Jarama results. Tauranac appealed the decision and won but while AGS and Maurer continued to use dual springs they were never seen on a Ralt again – and they won all the remaining races.

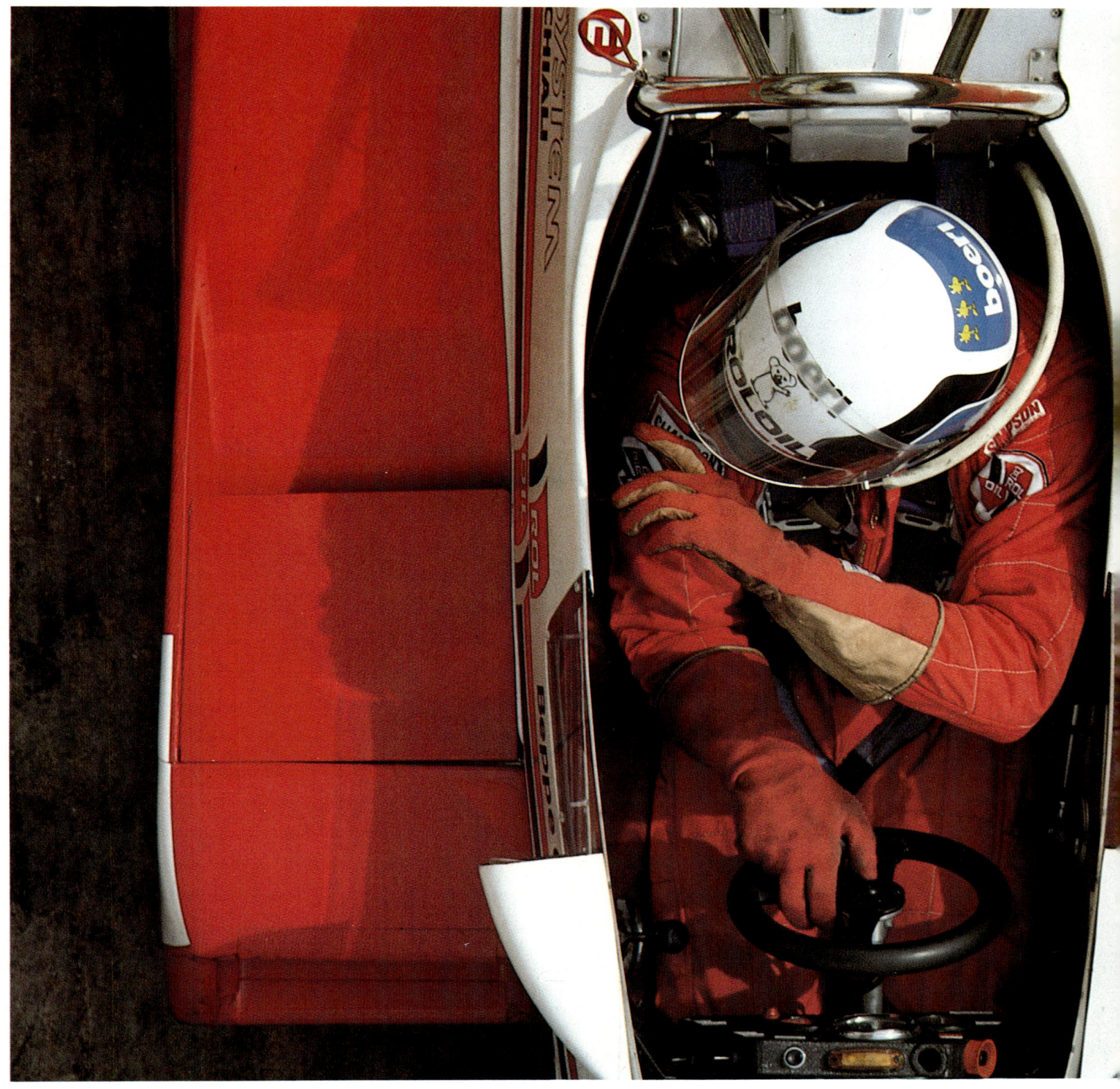

. . . drive like an Italian, think like an Englishman was the motto hammered home to Gabbiani

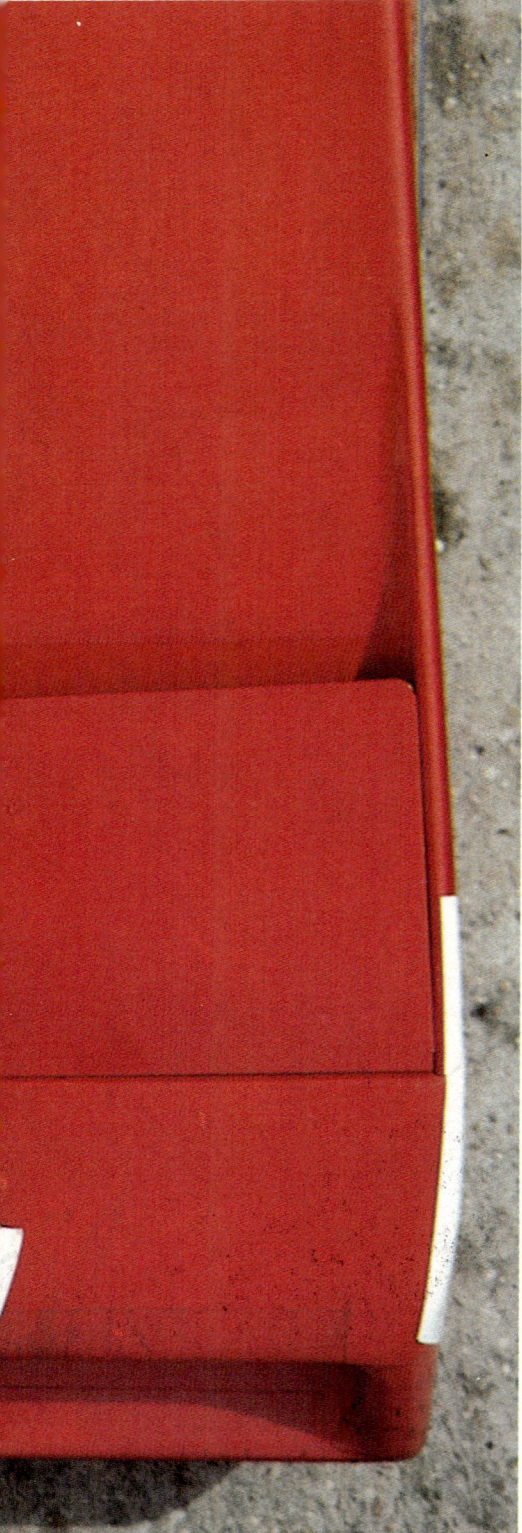

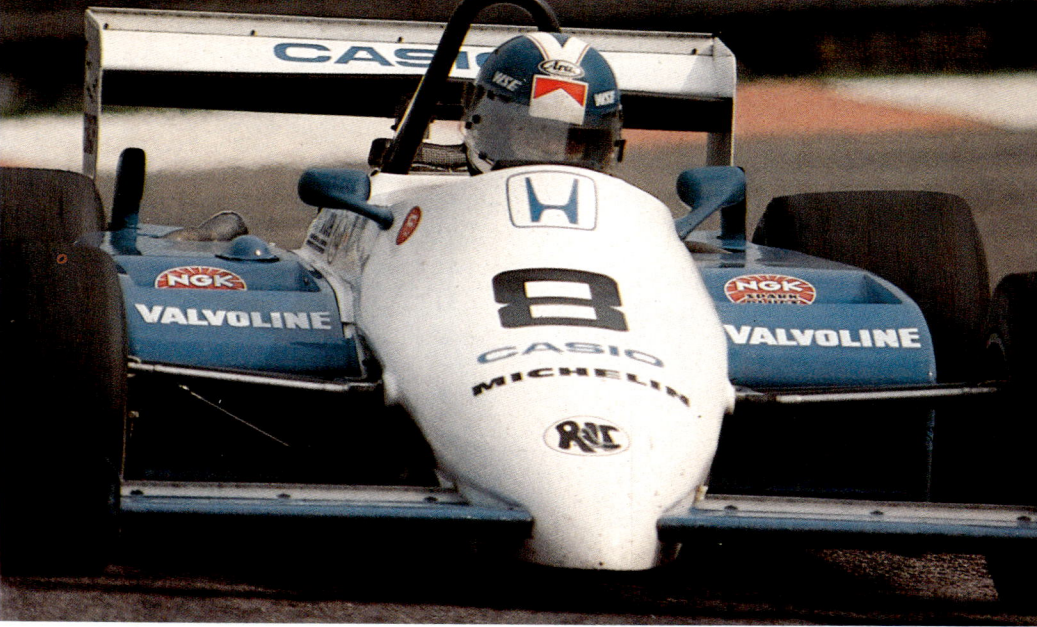

Despite the overturning of the decision by the appeal court, which was more on a point of law rather than a vindication of the car, the rules were never satisfactory although no further protesting was done. In fact, which ever way you look at it, Tauranac came out on top for while he was able to stall the protest for four races, the subject became an effective red herring for everyone to chase while he got on with the business of turning his cars into winners.

At Donington, running strictly within the letter and spirit of the law, Palmer and Thackwell qualified and finished first and second. Gabbiani kept them in sight until a oil line fell off but that was the last time he was competitive throughout a meeting.

Going into the Donington race – presuming all previous on the road results stood – Gabbiani still led the series with 36 points to the 29 of Palmer and Thackwell. With his two cars filling the front row for the first time – Palmer on pole by over a second – Tauranac heard his two drivers planning to race each other to the flag over the final 20 laps if they had dispensed with the opposition. Sensing that his and Honda's dream of the Championship might be at stake, he struck a deal with Thackwell there and then that Palmer was to win the series. It was a justifiable decision as Tauranac was acknowledging Palmer's tremendous personal perseverance and enthusiasm in the quest for improved performance and the Championship title. With age very much on his side Thackwell was able to accept the deal.

As it turned out, such an agreement was probably unnecessary as Palmer, sensing his goal, drove with supreme confidence in the final races to score five successive wins, equalling Ronnie Peterson's 1971 record (two of which were non-championship events). There was very much a pattern to Palmer's racing. He'd usually set the time to beat early on in qualifying and then dedicated the rest of his time to fine-tuning his car. At the end of the day it might not have changed much from the original settings but at least he knew how it would be if race conditions changed and this served him well. He prepared himself with a combination of answers to theoretical questions; it was a well-thoughtout plan of attack which gave him the edge as those less dedicated and prepared were left searching for excuses in his wake.

His rivals Gabbiani, Thackwell, Philippe Streiff and Stefan Bellof could all match him for speed and ability but not the obsessive dedication to the task of making life easier for themselves by striving for car perfection. It was that quality which won Palmer the crown and made the Ralt-Honda combination so effective.

To eliminate one of the advantages which March had in their championship stampede of the previous year, Tauranac switched to Michelin tyres for 1983, the French company expanding their involvement to cover 14 cars. A new regulation, restricting each car to just 14 tyres for official practice and the race was introduced at the start of the season which caused a few headaches initially but ultimately worked well.

Beppe Gabbiani matured into a confident, fast driver, the Italian surprising the pundits by taking four wins in his March-BMW at the beginning of the season *(left)*
Photo: Keith Sutton
Jonathan Palmer won the European Formula 2 Championship by a persistent search for perfection. The Englishman built up a rapport with Ron Tauranac and converted the Honda-powered Ralt into an unbeatable combination by the end of the season *(above)*.
Photo: John Townsend

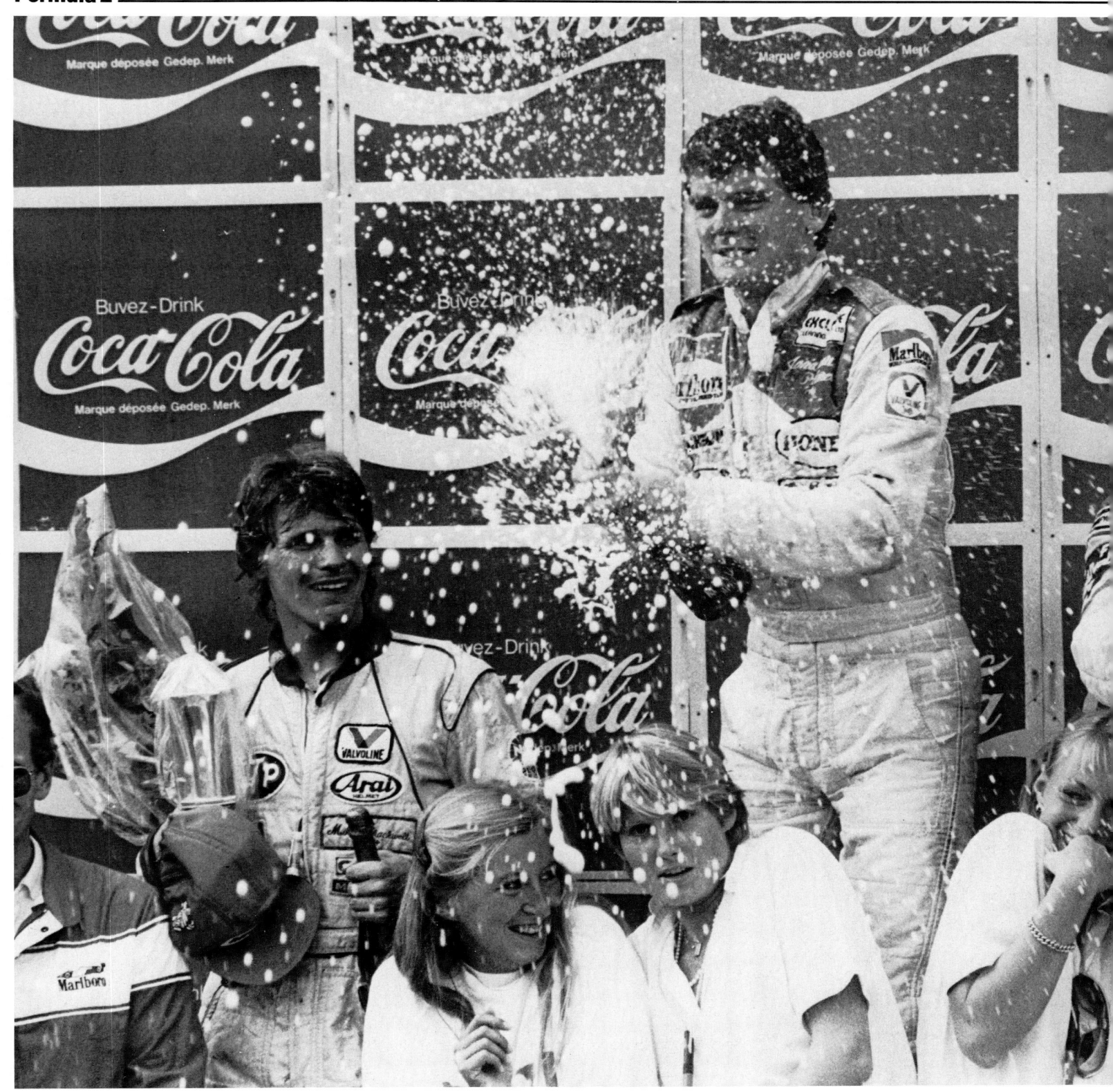

**. . . he struck a deal
with Thackwell there
and then that Palmer
was to win the series**

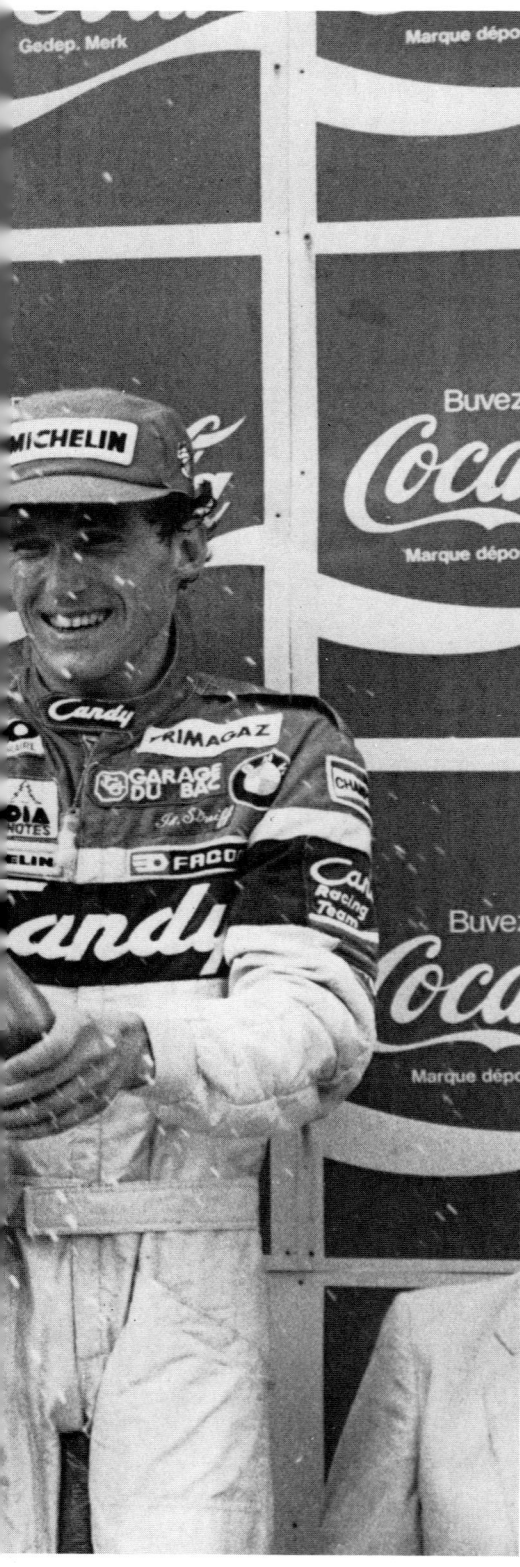

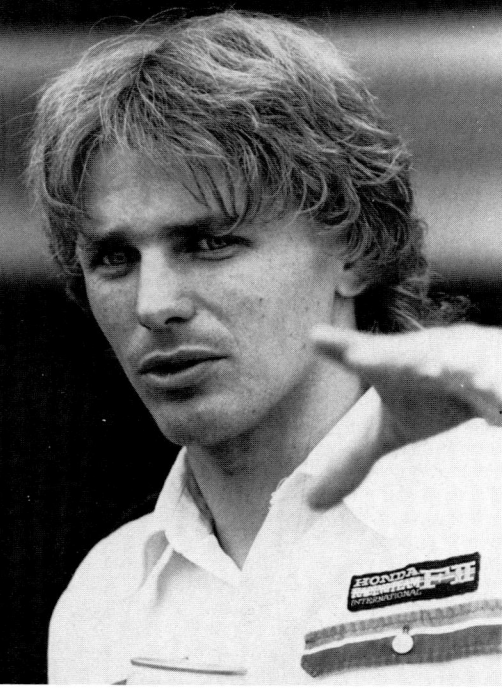

That, plus a communication problem, meant that it wasn't until mid-season that the Ralt team got the best out of the tyres. A healthy rumour that Ralt might switch back to Bridgestone mid-season conjured up an official Michelin interpreter and the dieted Casio-backed cars were suddenly able to run the same rubber as their rivals and, such was the relationship at the end of the year, Tauranac was able to get his own codings to confuse everyone else.

Like Palmer, Thackwell only had one non-finish all season caused by a non-attributable accident at Misano. Having had just half a dozen races in a private March in 1982, in which he convinced Tauranac he had fully recovered from the near fatal accident he had in the 1981 Ralt-Honda, he rejoined the team for this season thankful of the opportunity to re-establish himself but well aware of his lack of competitive mileage. A couple of pre-season testing accidents served as reminders but front row grid positions and two successive second places in the opening races brought back the old confidence and flair. It was at Vallelunga in the raceday warm-up that he added aggression and his rehabilitation was complete. He opened up and matured as a person. Perhaps his biggest fault was a reliance on his ability to drive around a problem rather than work at solving it. His drives at Pau with a bent rear wing and at Jarama without a nose or front wings proved the point.

If anyone had suggested at the start of the season that Beppe Gabbiani would walk away with the championship there would have been derision. There was no question that he was fast but too often he had been wild with it. Only March's Robin Herd was insistent that he was the man to defend Corrado Fabi's title in the Roloil March. Drive like an Italian, think like an Englishman was the motto which was hammered home to Gabbiani and how well he responded. Such was the ease in which he drove to score his Silverstone, Thruxton and Nürburgring wins, he was able to run a grade softer tyre than even his team mates. At Vallelunga Christian Danner ran the same set-up on the second Onyx car but still Gabbiani was able to use them better and won again. It was only in the third race at Hockenheim that he made a silly mistake under frustrating circumstances. If he had won at Pau, surely the championship would have been his. And he could have won that race.

Having changed to slicks he spun on the still damp track and broke a driveshaft rejoining, still in the lead. But in the truck was sitting a stronger set specially designed for the tortuous street circuit. It was perhaps that combination of circumstances which lost the championship. He drove his heart out in all the remaining races but the advantage had been handed to Ralt and was never reclaimed. For all his casual exterior, Gabbiani is deadly serious about his racing now and should have convincingly buried any doubts.

Jonathan Palmer celebrates his championship with a win at Zolder. The Ralt-Honda driver was ably supported throughout the year by Mike Thackwell *(left and above right)* who proved beyond doubt that he had overcome the setbacks suffered earlier in his career. Philippe Streiff *(right)* reached his peak during the second half of the season, the AGS driver usually finishing in the top three.

He is no test driver but given a car that is good there are few that are quicker.

It has always been said that Formula 2 is a two year programme for a driver and like Palmer, Philippe Streiff peaked beautifully in the second half of his second year. He'd shown considerable promise the year before in the little French AGS team. Sadly they lost all their faithful backers during the winter and so started the year with a wholly unsponsored 'B' specification of the previous year's car. The financial situation put unreasonable constraints on Streiff's driving but the team's prayers were answered in the form of Italian amateur Fulvio Balablio and his Topolino comic books backing after Nürburgring. With £100,000 for the two cars, Henri Julien's team were in comparative clover. The only time Streiff finished out of the top three in the last five races was at Misano when his engine went while he was leading. Aerodynamic revisions to the neatly made and, latterly, on the weight limit car made it effective everywhere and the very talented Streiff was the only man capable of challenging the Ralts in the final races where he was able to prove that the four cylinder BMW engine was also still a very competitive proposition.

In the first half of the season Germans Stefan Bellof and Christian Danner were strong contenders. The Maurer team were never able to provide a reliable car to suit the explosive ability of Bellof while Danner shouldered the burden of developing the new March 832 well, in only his third season of single seater racing, and perhaps lacked only in racecraft, impetuosity clouding a normally intelligent and lucid approach.

Alessandro Nannini's results were overall disappointing in the beautifully made but not entirely competitive new Minardi. In the old car he drove magnificiently at Nürburgring, hounding Gabbiani every inch of the way. His potential is enormous but still very raw and might have blossomed earlier in a controlled English environment.

Austrian Jo Gartner won his first race in F2 at Pau courtesy of the superior Bridgestone tyres in the conditions. The choice of one of the ex-works Spirit cars converted to take a BMW engine might not have been entirely practical for a private team without direct factory support or endless funds but, in the circumstances, he did a fine job. Newcomer Alain Ferté was the most exciting newcomer of the year and won on the road at Pau only to be disqualified for running underweight. He showed well everywhere when the constrictions of being a Maurer driver allowed but he dropped out mid-season after a contractual dispute with the German. Belgian Thierry Tassin was another who was beginning to get to grips with the Formula before he had to vacate his Onyx March due to money problems. Dave Scott, who started his F2 career with pole position in his first race at Silverstone, replaced Tassin and in the final two races won himself a lot of admirers with quick and intelligent drives. His former F3 sparring partner Quique Mansilla began and ended the year well but had worrying money problems between times. His early season James Gresham Racing March teammate, Lamberto Leoni, took pole at Hockenheim and threatened to add to his 1977 Misano win before he too fell foul of sponsorship problems.

The French Martini team returned to F2 for the first time since their 1977 Championship year with René Arnoux. Their Marlboro backed car was simple in concept although under-developed at the start of the season. Driver Philippe Alliot showed signs of being excitable initially and after a horrendous Nürburgring meeting they missed Vallelunga to rebuild and test. From then on both car and driver were always competitive, especially at Misano, and lacked only reliability.

It wasn't a vintage year by any means, but perhaps we'd been spoiled and expected too much. A new F2 Association steering committee was appointed towards the end of the season to first protect and secondly enhance the formula's position. One only has to look at the 1980s "exports" to Grand Prix racing, Derek Warwick, Andrea de Cesaris, Michele Alboreto, Stefan Johansson and Thierry Boutsen, to realise that the Formula has an important role to play and on a pound-for-pound basis, it is as inexpensive as any comparable forms of racing, none of which can provide the same 'real racing' environment.

I t began as a monotony, stayed that way for what seemed like an eternity and then suddenly exploded into a series of dramatic confrontations that made previous Marlboro Formula 3 Championships pale in comparison.

This year's national stepping stone formula was all about personalities. Two of them. Ayrton Senna and Martin Brundle. Favourite and underdog.

The Brazilian began his year with a change of name. Prior to 1983 he'd been happy to be known as Ayrton Senna da Silva but the latter title didn't quite fit his self-image in what he clearly saw as his most important season of motor racing to date. Allied to New Zealander Dick Bennett's brilliantly run West Surrey Racing team, which had taken Dr Jonathan Palmer to title success in 1981 and Quique Mansilla to a close second last year (Bennetts also masterminded Stefan Johansson's 1980 championship), Senna hit the scene with all the predictability of Hurricane Hetty. Like Roberto Moreno, a fellow Brazilian, he was much feared even before he sat in an F3 car for the first time. A swift look at his record from lesser formulae shows why. In FF2000 in 1982 Senna was in a class of his own, challenged only by Calvin Fish. When race one of the 1983 Marlboro British F3 series rolled round at Silverstone in March few doubted that the much heralded South American would wipe the floor with his opposition.

He did. Scot David Leslie took the pole, much to Senna and Bennetts' undisguised disgust, but the race belonged to Aryton and so did the extra point for fastest lap. The Brazilian had indulged in a quick spin on cold tyres at Becketts during the first practice session, but from that point on he made no mistakes during a run of dominance hitherto unseen in the formula. Thruxton, Silverstone (both Club and Grand Prix), Donington and Brands Hatch yielded up victories to the man whom everyone confidently predicted would be in a Grand Prix car before the end of the year. And on all but one occasion Brundle dutifully followed home second. Sometimes the Englishman, spurned by Dave Price and BP at the end of 1982 after developing into the practice pacemaker, would get his Eddie Jordan Racing Ralt's nose in front, but each time Senna would duly put him in his place and eke out just enough of a cushion to win without *too* much pressure. Without fail after each race, Brundle would praise his rival's talent, but with each race his own determination increased. Far from settling for second best, Brundle set aim on being top dog. Ayrton Senna was to be the making of him.

The first signs that the Marlboro British series was not dead as a spectacle came at Silverstone, season mid-point and the combined Marlboro/European round. Ironically, neither Brundle nor Senna raced on the mandatory Marlboro Avons, electing instead to seek Euro points on Yokohama rubber. From a comfortable pole Brundle led from start to finish, leaving Senna trailing in his wake, and incredibly it was the Brazilian who cracked under the pressure. With graining tyres he simply tried too hard, spun at Club and then repeated the manoeuvre terminally at

Woodcote in full view of a press corps that had come to respect his talent enormously but only barely tolerate his accusations that others weren't playing fair on the occasions on which Ayrton's temperament got the better of him.

Brundle's win signalled the start of the excitement. At Cadwell Park for the next round the duo traded pole position through practice but although Senna eventually took the honour he did not take the start, suffering a huge but mercifully injury-free shunt at the Mountain which wrecked his newly built Ralt. Now that the pressure was really on, and Senna's will to win at all costs was tested to the limit, it was not to be the last chassis Bennetts and his crew would have to rebuild . . .

The great confrontation finally came at Snetterton, Brundle's home track, in early July. Here, for the first time on Marlboro rubber, the 'new' Brundle and Senna would fight it out. From pole the Englishman took a narrow advantage, but the dice ended in controversy when the two cars made contact on the Revitt Straight heading for the Esses. Each driver was quick to protest *his* innocence but the upshot was that Senna retired as Brundle continued to victory and a post-race hearing which ultimately failed to apportion blame. Whatever, the damage was done and relations between the two rivals became, to be diplomatic, somewhat strained.

Senna's revenge came when he beat Brundle again in front of the F1 team managers at the British GP

supporting race at Silverstone, but Brundle got his own back at Donington later in the month, beating Senna fair and square on a circuit in which the Brazilian had only recently been highly impressive in his first F1 drive in a Williams FW08C. Brundle then dominated Oulton Park before Senna tried an over-ambitious overtaking manoeuvre at Fosters which put them both out, going on to win the non-championship support race to the Austrian Grand Prix. Tragedy stalked the Jordan team, however, for on its return from Austria its transporter crashed over a cliff, killing Brundle's friend and chief mechanic, Rob Bowden. A much respected figure, Rob was instrumental in establishing the '83 Jordan equipe as one to fear and it was a determined but confused team that regrouped for the next Marlboro race at Silverstone. There Brundle was again put away by Senna, his car's legality subsequently protested by Senna and Bennetts after it failed a check on skirt heights.

Regardless, Brundle maintained his spirit and wiped up the next three races – Oulton (where Senna crashed in a rash overtaking attempt on the outside of Druids), Thruxton (where Senna trailed before retiring with engine damage) and Silverstone (where Senna had to settle for second). Brundle had thus hauled himself into a one point lead in the series, something few would have predicted after Senna's incredible opening. In truth, however, the English-man was still three points in arrears, for while Senna

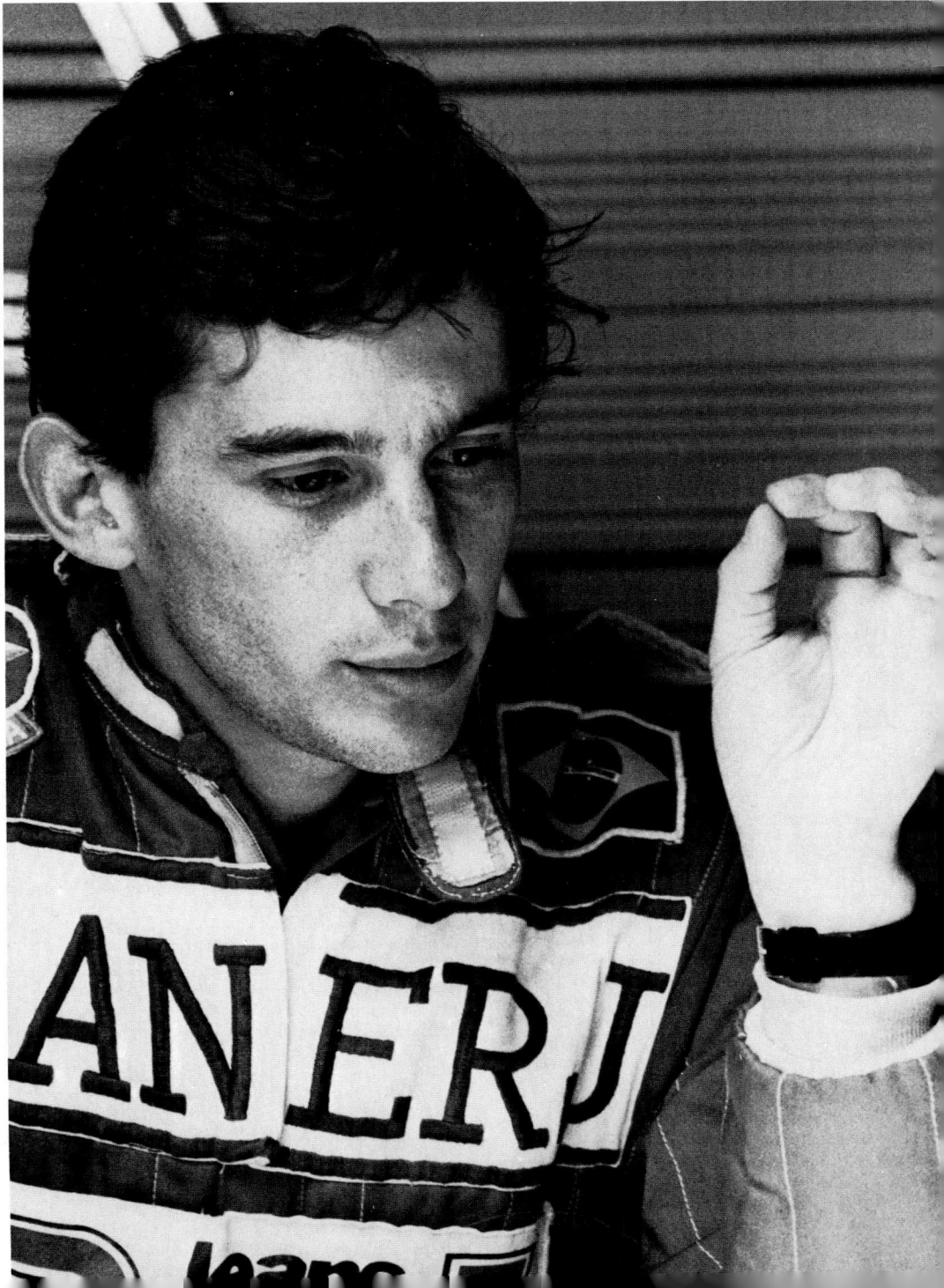

Tale of two Tigers

by David Tremayne, Editor, *Motoring News*

had already dropped three scores, as dictated by the rules, Brundle had dropped only two and had still to discard his lowest result – third at Silverstone in late April. Thus, just as last season, the outcome of the series depended on the final race at Thruxton, with the odds against Brundle who had to win and take fastest lap to make sure of the title. In the event, victory went to Senna but the truth is that either man was deserving of the spoils.

Without doubt, Aryton Senna is one of the most exciting drivers to appear on the scene for many years and his progress in Formula 1 will be very closely monitored. Such driving talent is not seen every day and if Ayrton can only bring a little more calm to some of his decisions made on the track few doubt he will develop into World Championship material. Interestingly, whenever the Brazilian had to play second fiddle he would always run very much closer to Brundle than the latter would when following Senna. But the flipside of that particular coin was that Brundle never damaged his car in a racing situation, save at Monaco. At one stage it appeared Senna might take the Piquet-style route to stardom, with Brundle playing the Warwick role, but Martin's latter-half season form showed him to be a mature, intelligent and quick driver fully deserving of F1 consideration.

Not surprisingly, the Senna/Brundle duo stole the limelight in the domestic series, with only Canadian Allen Berg and Briton Calvin Fish managing to take the victor's laurels (Berg when Senna and Brundle ran

to European specification at Silverstone in June and Fish when they tangled at Oulton in August). But of the other drivers, American Davy Jones showed the most potential. The young New Yorker first drove for Murray Taylor Racing in 1982, the year Taylor's team won the title with Tommy Byrne, and his initial flair continued into 1983. Unfortunately, however, Davy's talent failed to mature, despite Taylor's seasoned guidance, and he always looked like a driver defeating himself. This was never clearer than at Oulton Park in August when he lost ground to Fish, made it up, then lost it in a rash overtaking manoeuvre, time and again. On that occasion Fish took the overall win, but Jones could have enjoyed those nine points had he used his head more.

While Jones showed the speed if not quite the coolness to win, Fish proved a major disappointment throughout the season. The one man to challenge Senna in FF2000 in 1982, much was expected of him when he signed for Dave Price's BP-backed equipe. Rumour suggests he alienated his bosses at an early stage and through the year it seemed he received little moral support from his team. For all that he drove well on occasion but never looked likely to make the big breakthrough without the help of his principal rivals tangling. Berg, Pacific champion down under during last winter, found the initial adaptation from Atlantic to F3 spec Ralts difficult but once he had parted company with Neil Trundle Racing early in the year he seemed to settle down, revealing an aggressive flair as

Brundle's team-mate.

Others to make their mark were David Leslie and Johnny Dumfries. The Scot showed he has lost none of his sadly overlooked talent by putting John Robinson's pretty Magnum 833 on pole for the first round but unhappily a third at Oulton in September proved his best result after a season in which Lady Luck clearly envied his new bride, Jane. With Ron Tauranac's Ralt RT3 at its development limit, the Magnum might just manage to leapfrog into a position of dominance next year, if Robinson and his family team can raise the money for a full development programme. Dumfries, ironically, made his best showings in European races, despite being a regular Marlboro runner. Starting the year with Associated Motor Racing's ex-Brundle/Price Ralt-VW, he showed plenty of car control and bags of flair but a combination of circumstances, some his fault, kept him down to a lowly points score. In the combined European/Marlboro race at Silverstone in June, however, he ran behind Brundle and showed a great deal more cool than Senna, while he again trailed Brundle at Donington in October before an unfortunate spin. In the right team he is a potential F3 champion for 1984.

On the European front, F3 proved as popular as ever, to the point where several Marlboro teams were at one stage making noises about upping roots and joining the continental circus. At the start of the year Emanuele Pirro, team-mate to 1982 Euro champion Oscar Larrauri, made the running before 1982 Marlboro champion Tommy Byrne, in a Jordan Ralt, leapt into the limelight. Both, however, fell into bad patches and once Michelin had produced a taller front tyre to combat Yokohama's latest rubber Dane John Nielsen moved to the fore with his Ralt-VW. Just as it seemed *he* had made the break from his pursuers, however, Italy's Pierluigi Martini hit a winning streak and despite rib injuries sustained in a practice shunt at Donington in October and subsequent defeat by Brundle at that venue he hauled himself within two points of the Dane with only the Croix-en-Ternois finale remaining. Following that Senna/Brundle-like encounter, Martini emerged the worthy victor.

While its continental strength seems unquestionable, F3 showed definite signs of weakness on the home front, with several poorly supported races and few full-budget teams. However, late-season proposals formed by the BRDC and the BARC suggest that 1984 could see a dramatic improvement. At last the number of championship rounds has been cut from 20 to 17 and a separate class has been established for year-old cars, along European series lines. Furthermore, international grade C licence holders will be eligible for the first time, so hopefully grids will expand significantly.

It is likely that we have been privileged to see a really vintage year of domestic F3 racing, along the lines of the Piquet/Warwick confrontations of 1978, and that only serves once again to underline the formula's importance to aspiring Grand Prix drivers. Yet again, it has put the European Formula Two Championship into the shade.

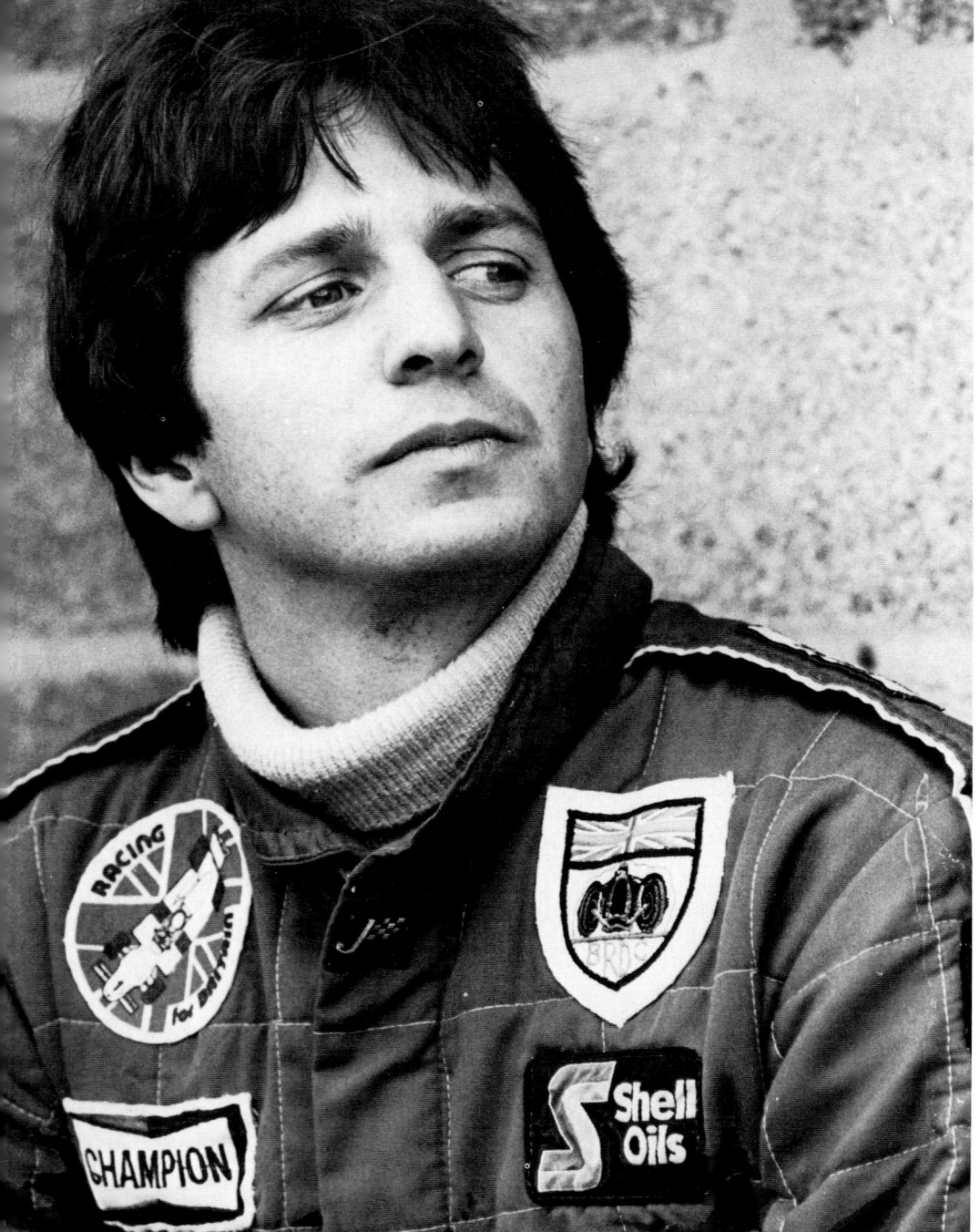

Marlboro RACE OF CHAMPIONS

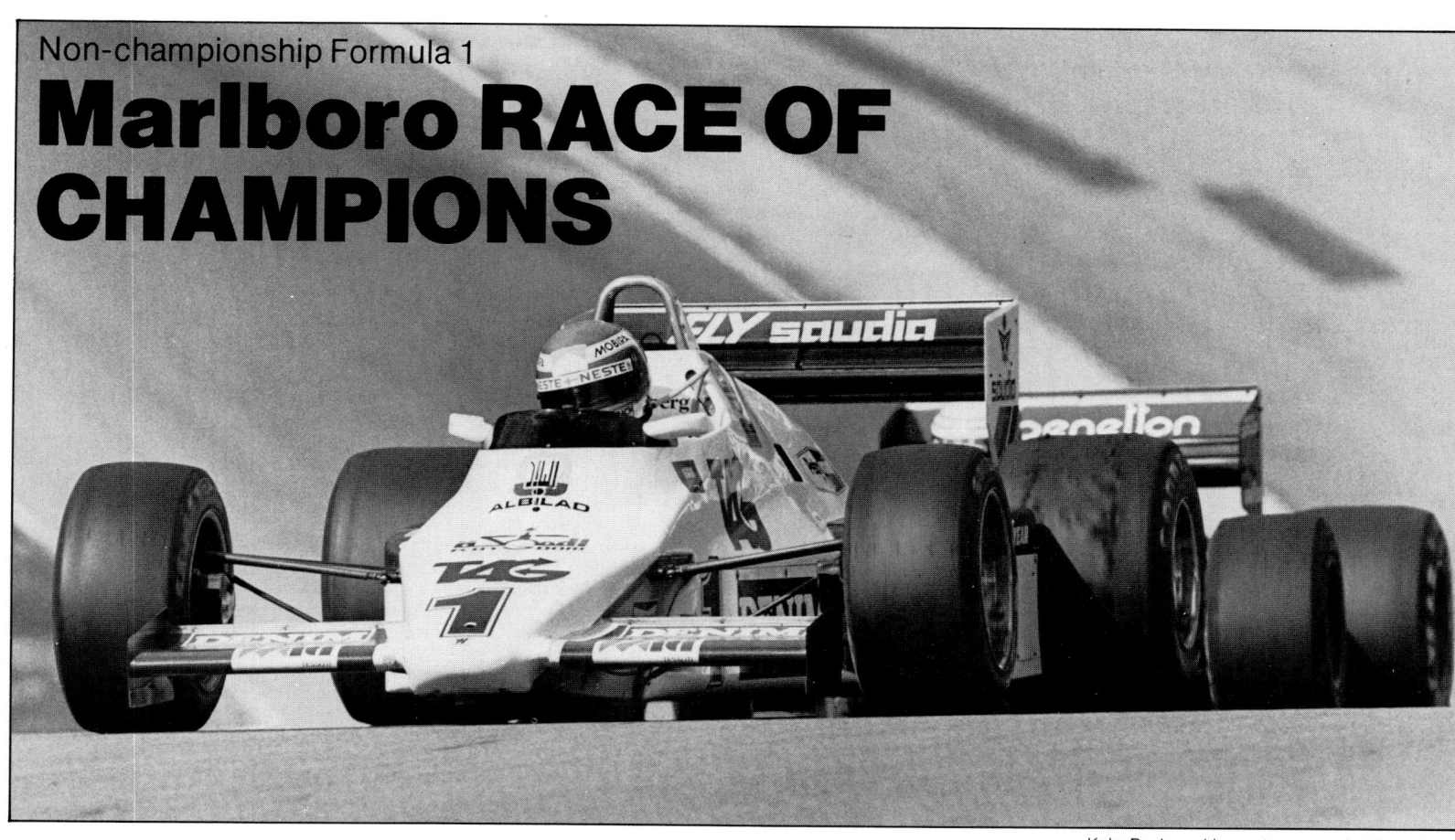

Marlboro Race of Champions, Brands Hatch, April 10/statistics

Keke Rosberg, his rear tyre severely blistered, holds off Danny Sullivan's determined challenge for the lead. The quality of this duel made up for what the non-championship race lacked in quantity.

Entries and practice times

No.	Driver	Nat	Car	Tyre	Engine	Entrant	Practice 1	Practice 2
1	Keke Rosberg	SF	Saudia WILLIAMS FW08C	G	Ford Cosworth DFV	TAG Williams Team	1m 16·583s	**1m 15·766s**
4	Danny Sullivan	USA	Benetton TYRRELL 011	G	Ford Cosworth DFV	Benetton Tyrrell Team	1m 18·860s	**1m 18·446s**
5	Hector Rebaque	MEX	Parmalat BRABHAM BT52	M	BMW M12/13	Fila Sport	**1m 19·592s**	1m 19·996s
7	John Watson	GB	Marlboro McLAREN MP4/1C	M	Ford Cosworth DFV	Marlboro McLaren International	1m 22·073s	**1m 18·062s**
12	Nigel Mansell	GB	John Player Special LOTUS 93T	P	Renault EF1	John Player Team Lotus	1m 21·736s	**1m 18·894s**
17	Jean-Louis Schlesser	F	MARCH-RAM 01	P	Ford Cosworth DFV	RAM Automotive Team March	–	–
26	Raul Boesel	BR	Gitanes LIGIER JS21	M	Ford Cosworth DFV	Equipe Ligier Gitanes	1m 20·132s	**1m 19·236s**
28	René Arnoux	F	Fiat FERRARI 126C2B	G	Ferrari 126C	Scuderia Ferrari SpA SEFAC	1m 17·682s	**1m 15·839s**
29	Chico Serra	BR	ARROWS A6	G	Ford Cosworth DFV	Arrows Racing Team	**1m 22·402s**	–
30	Alan Jones	AUS	ARROWS A6	G	Ford Cosworth DFV	Arrows Racing Team	1m 18·862s	**1m 17·501s**
33	Roberto Guerrero	COL	THEODORE N183	G	Ford Cosworth DFV	Theodore Racing Team	**1m 18·862s**	1m 19·065s
34	Brian Henton	GB	THEODORE N183	G	Ford Cosworth DFV	Theodore Racing Team	1m 19·406s	**1m 18·549s**
40	Stefan Johansson	S	SPIRIT-HONDA 201	G	Honda RA163-E	Spirit Racing	–	**1m 35·500s**

Friday morning and Saturday morning practice sessions not officially recorded.

G – Goodyear, M – Michelin, P – Pirelli.

	Fri pm	Sat pm
	Dry, cool	Dry, cool

Starting grid

	1 ROSBERG (1m 15·766s) Williams
28 ARNOUX (1m 15·839s) Ferrari	
	30 JONES (1m 17·501s) Arrows
7 WATSON (1m 18·062s) McLaren	
	4 SULLIVAN (1m 18·446s) Tyrrell
34 HENTON (1m 18·549s) Theodore	
	33 GUERRERO (1m 18·862s) Theodore
12 MANSELL (1m 18·894s) Lotus	
	26 BOESEL (1m 19·236s) Ligier
5 REBAQUE (1m 19·592s) Brabham	
	29 SERRA (1m 22·402s) Arrows
40 JOHANSSON (1m 35·500s) Spirit	
	17 SCHLESSER (No time recorded) RAM March

Results and retirements

Place	Driver	Car	Laps	Time and Speed (mph/km/h)/Retirement	
1	Keke Rosberg	Williams-Cosworth V8	40	53m 15·253s	117·886/189·719
2	Danny Sullivan	Tyrrell-Cosworth V8	40	53m 15·743s	117·8/189·580
3	Alan Jones	Arrows-Cosworth V8	40	53m 43·895s	116·7/187·810
4	Brian Henton	Theodore-Cosworth V8	40	53m 55·773s	116·3/187·166
5	Raul Boesel	Ligier-Cosworth V8	40	53m 56·224s	116·3/187·166
6	John-Louis Schlesser	RAM March-Cosworth V8	39		
7	Roberto Guerrero	Theodore-Cosworth V8	39		
	Chico Serra	Arrows-Cosworth V8	30	Gear linkage	
	René Arnoux	Ferrari t/c V6	23	Tyres	
	Hector Rebaque	Brabham-BMW t/c 4	14	Tyres/suspension damaged during pit stop	
	John Watson	McLaren-Cosworth V8	8	Transmission	
	Nigel Mansell	Lotus-Renault t/c V6	6	Handling	
	Stefan Johansson	Spirit-Honda t/c V6	4	Engine	

Fastest lap: Arnoux, on lap 18, 1m 17·826s, 120·897mph/194·564km/h.
Lap record: Didier Pironi (F1 Ligier JS11/15-Cosworth DFV), 1m 12·368s, 130·015mph/209·239km/h (1980).

Circuit data

Brands Hatch Grand Prix Circuit, Fawkham, Kent
Circuit length: 2·6136 miles/4·206 km
Race distance: 40 laps, 104·544 miles/168·24 km
Race weather: Warm, dry

Fastest laps

Driver	Time	Lap
René Arnoux	1m 17·826s	18
Raul Boesel	1m 18·123s	37
Keke Rosberg	1m 18·628s	4
Danny Sullivan	1m 18·728s	10
Chico Serra	1m 18·906s	28
Alan Jones	1m 19·205s	25
Roberto Guerrero	1m 19·278s	36
Brian Henton	1m 19·314s	39
John Watson	1m 19·375s	5
Hector Rebaque	1m 19·874s	11
Jean-Louis Schlesser	1m 20·896s	36
Stefan Johansson	1m 21·850s	4
Nigel Mansell	1m 23·764s	4

1983 RESULTS A detailed summary of the season

Formula 2

MARLBORO/DAILY EXPRESS INTERNATIONAL TROPHY, Silverstone Grand Prix Circuit, Great Britain, March 20. European Formula 2 Championship, round 1. 47 laps of the 2·932-mile/4·719-km circuit, 137·80 miles/221·79 km.
1 Beppe Gabbiani, I (March 832-BMW), 1h 08m 30·71s, 120·68 mph/194·22 km/h.
2 Mike Thackwell, NZ (Ralt RH6/83-Honda), 1h 08m 57·31s.
3 Christian Danner, D (March 832-BMW), 1h 09m 40·25s.
4 Stefan Bellof, D (Maurer MM83-BMW), 46 laps (DNF, throttle cable).
5 Philippe Streiff, F (AGS JH19B-BMW), 46.
6 Lamberto Leoni, I (March 832-BMW), 46.
7 Oscar Larrauri, RA (Minardi 283-BMW), 46; **8** Pierre Petit, F (Maurer MM83-BMW), 45; **9** Emilio de Villota, E (March 832-BMW), 44.
Fastest lap: Bellof, 1m 19·93s, 132·06 mph/212·53 km/h.
Retired: Guido Dacco, I (Merzario M28-BMW), 0 laps, accident; Tomas Kaiser, S (Maurer MM82-BMW), 1, accident; Alessandro Nannini, I (Minardi 283-BMW), 3, gearbox; Philippe Alliot, F (Martini 001-BMW), 3, accident; Kenny Acheson, GB (Maurer MM83-BMW), 5, accident; Roberto Del Castello, I (March 832-BMW), 7, accident; Thierry Tassin, B (March 832-BMW), 10, accident; Jonathan Palmer, GB (Ralt RH6/83-Honda), 12, fuel pressure relief valve; Fulvio Ballabio, I (Merzario M28-BMW), 12, accident; Enrique Mansilla, RA (March 832-BMW), 13, accident; Pierre Chauvet, A (Spirit 201-BMW), 15, accident; Frank Jelinski, D (Maurer MM82-BMW), 15, accident; Jo Gartner, A (Spirit 201-BMW), 23, accident; Alain Ferte, F (Maurer MM83-BMW), 26, accident; Dave Scott, GB (March 832-BMW), 30, engine.
Championship points: 1 Gabbiani, 9; **2** Thackwell, 6; **3** Danner, 4; **4** Bellof, 3; **5** Streiff, 2; **6** Leoni, 1.

P & O FERRIES/JOCHEN RINDT TROPHY, Thruxton Circuit, Great Britain, April 4. European Formula 2 Championship, round 2. 55 laps of the 2·356-mile/3·792-km circuit, 129·58 miles/208·54 km.
1 Beppe Gabbiani, I (March 832-BMW), 1h 03m 54·06s, 121·67 mph/195·81 km/h.
2 Mike Thackwell, NZ (Ralt RH6/83-Honda), 1h 04m 01·91s.
3 Jonathan Palmer, GB (Ralt RH6/83-Honda), 1h 04m 08·57s.
4 Thierry Tassin, B (March 832-BMW), 1h 04m 24·64s.
5 Philippe Alliot, F (Martini 001-BMW), 1h 04m 42·34s.
6 Frank Jelinski, D (Maurer MM82-BMW), 54 laps.
7 Enrique Mansilla, RA (March 832-BMW), 54; **8** Philippe Streiff, F (AGS JH19B-BMW), 54; **9** Alessandro Nannini, I (Minardi 283-BMW), 54; **10** Kenny Acheson, GB (Maurer MM83-BMW), 54; **11** Lamberto Leoni, I (March 832-BMW), 54; **12** Pierre Petit, F (Maurer MM83-BMW), 53; **13** Christian Danner, D (March 832-BMW), 51.
Disqualified: Alain Ferte, F (Maurer MM83-BMW), disqualified for using unmarked tyres.
Fastest lap: Thackwell, 1m 07·70s, 125·28 mph/201·62 km/h.
Retired: Fulvio Ballabio, I (Merzario M28-BMW), 0 laps, electrics; Guido Dacco, I (Merzario M28-BMW), 1, accident; Pierre Chauvet, A (Spirit 201-BMW), 4, engine; Roberto Del Castello, I (March 832-BMW), 13, electrics; Oscar Larrauri, RA (Minardi 283-BMW), 16, engine; Jo Gartner, A (Spirit 201-BMW), 16, suspension; Stefan Bellof, D (Maurer MM83-BMW), 23, ignition; Dave Scott, GB (March 832-BMW), 29, suspension; Tomas Kaiser, S (Maurer MM82-BMW), 46, driveshaft.
Championship points: 1 Gabbiani, 18; **2** Thackwell, 12; **3** Danner and Palmer, 4; **5** Bellof and Tassin, 3.

JIM CLARK RENNEN, Hockenheim-Ring, German Federal Republic, April 10. European Formula 2 Championship, round 3. 30 laps of the 4·223-mile/6·797-km circuit, 126·69 miles/203·91 km.
1 Jonathan Palmer, GB (Ralt RH6/83-Honda), 1h 02m 25·22s, 121·78 mph/195·99 km/h.
2 Christian Danner, D (March 832-BMW), 1h 02m 47·52s.
3 Mike Thackwell, NZ (Ralt RH6/83-Honda), 1h 03m 15·02s.
4 Jo Gartner, A (Spirit 201-BMW), 1h 03m 20·50s.
5 Alessandro Nannini, I (Minardi 283-BMW), 1h 03m 53·14s.
6 Thierry Tassin, B (March 832-BMW), 1h 03m 56·36s.
7 Lamberto Leoni, I (March 832-BMW), 1h 03m 58·82s; **8** Philippe Alliot, F (Martini 001-BMW), 1h 04m 03·20s; **9** Rolf Biland, CH (March 832-BMW), 1h 04m 06·34s; **10** Kenny Acheson, GB (Maurer MM83-BMW), 29 laps; **11** Barti Stadler, A (Maurer MM82-BMW), 29; **12** Alain Ferte, F (Maurer MM83-BMW), 29; **13** Aldo Bertuzzi, I (Toleman TG280-Hart), 28; **14** Fulvio Ballabio, I (Merzario M28-BMW), 28; **15** Guido Dacco, I (Merzario M28-BMW), **27** (DNF, gear selectors).
Fastest lap: Palmer, 2m 03·76s, 122·84 mph/197·69 km/h (record).
Retired: Tomas Kaiser, S (Maurer MM82-BMW), 1 lap, engine; Philippe Streiff, F (AGS JH19B-BMW), 1, engine; Roberto Del Castello, I (March 832-BMW), 4, engine; Pierre Petit, F (Maurer MM83-BMW), 5, engine; Peter Sturtz, D (March 802-BMW), 8, engine; Beppe Gabbiani, I (March 832-BMW), 8, accident; Pierre Chauvet, A (Spirit 201-BMW), 13, engine.
Did not start: Oscar Larrauri, RA (Minardi 283-BMW), accident on warm up; Dave Scott, GB (March 832-BMW), gearbox; Stefan Bellof, D (Maurer MM83-BMW), gearbox.
Championship points: 1 Gabbiani, 18; **2** Thackwell, 16; **3** Palmer, 13; **4** Danner, 10; **5** Tassin, 4; **6** Bellof and Gartner, 3.

EIFELRENNEN, Nurburgring Nordschleife, German Federal Republic, April 24. European Formula 2 Championship, round 4. 9 laps of the 12·94-mile/20·83-km circuit, 116·46 miles/187·47 km.
1 Beppe Gabbiani, I (March 832-BMW), 58m 46·44s, 118·93 mph/191·40 km/h.
2 Alessandro Nannini, I (Minardi FLY281B-BMW), 58m 53·41s.
3 Christian Danner, D (March 832-BMW), 58m 58·26s.
4 Jonathan Palmer, GB (Ralt RH6/83-Honda), 59m 34·28s.
5 Alain Ferte, F (Maurer MM83-BMW), 59m 39·53s.
6 Thierry Tassin, B (March 832-BMW), 59m 40·64s.
7 Mike Thackwell, NZ (Ralt RH6/83-Honda), 59m 42·22s; **8** Frank Jelinski, D (Maurer MM82-BMW), 1h 00m 02·10s; **9** Kenny Acheson, GB (Maurer MM83-BMW), 1h 00m 04·21s; **10** Pierre Petit, F (Maurer MM83-BMW), 1h 00m 31·05s; **11** Dave Scott, GB (March 832-BMW), 1h 00m 32·79s; **12** Rolf Biland, CH (March 832-BMW), 1h 01m 04·70s; **13** Aldo Bertuzzi, I (Toleman TG280-Hart), 1h 03m 43·03s; **14** Jo Gartner, A (Spirit 201-BMW), 6 laps (DNF, wheel bearing).
Fastest lap: Danner, 6m 28·03s, 120·09 mph/193·27 km/h (record).
Retired: Fulvio Ballabio, I (Merzario M28-BMW), 0 laps, accident; Guido Dacco, I (Toleman T850-BMW), 0, accident; Richard Dallest, F (Merzario M28-BMW), 1, electrics; Stefan Bellof, D (Maurer MM83-BMW), 1, throttle cable; Philippe Streiff, F (AGS JH19B-BMW), 2, suspension; Lamberto Leoni, I (March 832-BMW), 3, suspension; Tomas Kaiser, S (Maurer MM82-BMW), 4, overheating.
Did not start: Enrique Mansilla, RA (March 832-BMW), accident in practice; Philippe Alliot, F (Martini 001-BMW), accident in practice.
Championship points: 1 Gabbiani, 27; **2** Palmer and Thackwell, 16; **4** Danner, 14; **5** Nannini, 8; **6** Tassin, 5.

33 GRAN PREMIO ROMA, Autodromo di Vallelunga, Italy, May 8. European Formula 2 Championship, round 5. 65 laps of the 1·988-mile/3·200-km circuit, 129·22 miles/208·00 km.
1 Beppe Gabbiani, I (March 832-BMW), 1h 14m 59·60s, 103·41 mph/166·42 km/h.
2 Jonathan Palmer, GB (Ralt RH6/83-Honda), 1h 15m 09·85s.
3 Mike Thackwell, NZ (Ralt RH6/83-Honda), 1h 15m 28·87s.
4 Thierry Tassin, B (March 832-BMW), 1h 15m 29·34s.
5 Philippe Streiff, F (AGS JH19B-BMW), 1h 15m 43·82s.
6 Guido Dacco, I (Toleman T850-BMW), 64 laps.
7 Alessandro Nannini, I (Minardi 283-BMW), 64; **8** Tomas Kaiser, S (Maurer MM82-BMW), 64; **9** Lamberto Leoni, I (March 832-BMW), 64; **10** Christian Danner, D (March 832-BMW), 63 (DNF, accident); **11** Kenny Acheson, GB (Maurer MM83-BMW), 63; **12** Pierre Petit, F (Maurer MM83-BMW), 63; **13** Aldo Bertuzzi, I (March 832-BMW), 62; **14** Alain Ferte, F (Maurer MM83-BMW), 60.
Fastest lap: Gabbiani, 1m 08·14s, 105·05 mph/169·06 km/h (record).
Retired: Fulvio Ballabio, I (AGS JH19-BMW), 9 laps, accident; Richard Dallest, F (Merzario M28-BMW), 25, electrics; Jo Gartner, A (Spirit 201-BMW), 36, engine; Pierre Chauvet, A (Spirit 201-BMW), 41, wheel bearing; Enrique Mansilla, RA (March 832-BMW), 42, fuel pressure.
Did not start: Roberto Del Castello, I (March 832-BMW), engine on warm up lap; Dave Scott, GB (March 832-BMW), cwp on grid.
Championship points: 1 Gabbiani, 36; **2** Palmer, 22; **3** Thackwell, 20; **4** Danner, 14; **5** Nannini and Tassin, 8.

43 GRAND PRIX DE PAU, Circuit de Pau, France, May 22. European Formula 2 Championship, round 6. 73 laps of the 1·715-mile/2·760-km circuit, 125·19 miles/201·48 km.
1 Jo Gartner, A (Spirit 201-BMW), 1h 45m 18·65s, 72·45 mph/116·60 km/h.
2 Kenny Acheson, GB (Maurer MM83-BMW), 1h 45m 44·56s.
3 Jonathan Palmer, GB (Ralt RH6/83-Honda), 1h 46m 12·61s.
4 Thierry Tassin, B (March 832-BMW), 1h 46m 24·58s.
5 Christian Danner, D (March 832-BMW), 1h 46m 24·89s.
6 Rolf Biland, CH (March 832-BMW), 69 laps.
7 Fulvio Ballabio, I (AGS JH19B-BMW), 67; **8** Mike Thackwell, NZ (Ralt RH6/83-Honda), 67; **9** Tomas Kaiser, S (Maurer MM82-BMW), 66; **10** Philippe Streiff, F (AGS JH19B-BMW), 63.
Disqualified: Alain Ferte, F (Maurer MM83-BMW), finished 1st on the road but disqualified due weight infringement; Stefan Bellof, D (Maurer MM83-BMW), finished 3rd on the road but disqualified due weight infringement.
Fastest lap: Bellof, 1m 13·12s, 84·44 mph/135·89 km/h.
Retired: Alessandro Nannini, I (Minardi FLY281B-BMW), 0 laps, accident; Pierre Petit, F (Maurer MM83-BMW), 18, accident; Pierre Chauvet, A (Spirit 201-BMW), 24, accident; Richard Dallest, F (Merzario M28-BMW), 28, accident; Lamberto Leoni, I (March 832-BMW), 28, accident; Beppe Gabbiani, I (March 832-BMW), 29, driveshaft; Guido Dacco, I (Toleman TG280-BMW), 30, accident; Philippe Alliot, F (Martini 001-BMW), 59, engine.
Did not start: Roberto Del Castello, I (March 832-BMW), did not qualify; Aido Bertuzzi, I (March 832-BMW), did not qualify; Michel Ferte, F (Martini 001-BMW), did not qualify; Dave Scott, GB (March 832-BMW), did not qualify.
Championship points: 1 Gabbiani, 36; **2** Palmer, 26; **3** Thackwell, 20; **4** Danner, 16; **5** Gartner, 12; **6** Tassin, 11.

EUROPEAN FORMULA 2 CHAMPIONSHIP RACE, Circuito Permanente del Jarama, Spain, June 12. European Formula 2 Championship, round 7. 65 laps of the 2·058-mile/3·312-km circuit, 133·77 miles/215·28 km.
1 Mike Thackwell, NZ (Ralt RH6/83-Honda), 1h 28m 50·80s, 90·29 mph/145·31 km/h.
2 Stefan Bellof, D (Maurer MM83-BMW), 1h 28m 53·16s.
3 Jonathan Palmer, GB (Ralt RH6/83-Honda), 1h 29m 06·29s.
4 Philippe Streiff, F (AGS JH19B-BMW), 1h 29m 25·62s.
5 Alain Ferte, F (Maurer MM83-BMW), 1h 29m 29·99s
6 Enrique Mansilla, RA (March 832-BMW), 1h 29m 43·15s.
7 Beppe Gabbiani, I (March 832-BMW), 1h 29m 59·20s; **8** Richard Dallest, F (Merzario M28-BMW), 1h 30m 06·30s; **9** Christian Danner, D (March 832-BMW), 1h 30m 13·77s; **10** Rolf Biland, CH (March 832-BMW), 64 laps; **11** Roberto Del Castello, I (March 832-BMW), 63; **12** Fulvio Ballabio, I (AGS JH19-BMW), 63; **13** Emilio de Villota, E (Minardi 283-BMW), 63 (DNF, accident); **14** Patrick Neve, B (March 832-BMW), 62; **15** Aldo Bertuzzi, I (March 832-BMW), 62; **16** Dave Scott, GB (March 832-BMW), 60 (DNF, engine); **17** Jo Gartner, A (Spirit 201-BMW), 58.
Fastest lap: Thackwell, 1m 20·02s, 92·59 mph/149·01 km/h (record).
Retired: Philippe Alliot, F (Martini 001-BMW), 11 laps, accident; Alessandro Nannini, I (Minardi 283-BMW), 25, throttle; Kenny Acheson, GB (Maurer MM83-BMW), 27, accident; Pierre Petit, F (Maurer MM83-BMW), 37, accident; Pierre Chauvet, A (Spirit 201-BMW), 47, accident; Guido Dacco, I (March 832-BMW), 56, engine.
Championship points: 1 Gabbiani, 36; **2** Palmer, 30; **3** Thackwell, 29; **4** Danner, 16; **5** Gartner, 12; **6** Tassin, 11.

EUROPEAN FORMULA 2 CHAMPIONSHIP RACE, Donington Park Circuit, Great Britain, June 25. European Formula 2 Championship, round 8. 70 laps of the 1·9573-mile/3·150-km circuit, 137·01 miles/220·50 km.
1 Jonathan Palmer, GB (Ralt RH6/83-Honda), 1h 16m 39·02s, 107·25 mph/172·60 km/h.
2 Mike Thackwell, NZ (Ralt RH6/83-Honda), 1h 16m 57·39s.
3 Philippe Streiff, F (AGS JH19B-BMW), 1h 17m 18·12s.
4 Kazuyoshi Hoshino, J (March 832-BMW), 1h 17m 23·96s.
5 Christian Danner, D ((March 832-BMW), 1h 17m 35·50s.
6 Dave Scott, GB (March 832-BMW), 69 laps.
7 Stefan Bellof, D (Maurer MM83-BMW), 69; **8** Kenny Acheson, GB (Maurer MM83-BMW), 69; **9** Derek Daly, IRL (March 832-Hart), 69; **10** Enrique Mansilla, RA (March 832-BMW), 69; **11** Roberto Del Castello, I (March 832-BMW), 68; **12** Michel Ferte, F (Martini 001-BMW), 67; **12** Pierre Chauvet, A (Spirit 201-BMW), 66.
Fastest lap: Thackwell, 1m 04·69s, 108·92 mph/175·29 km/h.
Retired: Aldo Bertuzzi, I (March 832-BMW), 0 laps, accident; Guido Dacco, I (March 832-BMW), 0, accident; Beat Jans, CH (March 832-BMW), 0, accident; Alain Ferte, F (Maurer MM83-BMW), 0, accident; Alessandro Nannini, I (Minardi 283-BMW), 2, pinion, Jo Gartner, A (Spirit 201-BMW), 4, engine; Pierre Petit, F (Maurer MM83-BMW), 14, gear linkage; Beppe Gabbiani, I (March 832-BMW), 14, engine; Philippe Alliot, F (Martini 001-BMW), 15, gear linkage; Tomas Kaiser, S (Maurer MM82-BMW), 22, broken upright.
Did not start: Fulvio Ballabio, I (AGS JH19-BMW), driver unwell.
Championship points: 1 Palmer, 39; **2** Gabbiani, 36; **3** Thackwell, 35; **4** Danner, 18; **5** Gartner, 12; **6** Streiff and Tassin, 11.

TROFEO RICCARDO PALETTI, Autodromo Santamonica, Misano, Italy, July 24. European Formula 2 Championship, round 9. 58 laps of the 2·167-mile/3·488-km circuit, 125·69 miles/202·30 km.
1 Jonathan Palmer, GB (Ralt RH6/83-Honda), 1h 09m 37·74s, 108·32 mph/174·32 km/h.
2 Pier Luigi Martini, I (Minardi 283-BMW), 1h 10m 41·61s.
3 Roberto Del Castello, I (March 832-BMW), 1h 10m 50·60s.
4 Guido Dacco, I (March 832-BMW), 57 laps.
5 Fulvio Ballabio, I (AGS JH19B-BMW), 57.
6 Fredy Lienhard, CH (March 832-BMW), 55.
7 Richard Dallest, F (Merzario M28-BMW), 54. No other finishers.
Fastest lap: Philippe Alliot, F (Martini 001-BMW), 1m 10·95s, 109·97 mph/176·98 km/h (record).
Retired: Dave Scott, GB (March 832-BMW), 2 laps, accident; Enrique Mansilla, RA (March 832-BMW), 3, accident; Michel Ferte, F (Martini 001-BMW), 4, accident; Christian Danner, D (March 832-BMW), 7, accident; Mike Thackwell, NZ (Ralt RH6/83-Honda), 7, accident; Philippe Streiff, F (AGS JH19B-BMW), 16, engine; Alessandro Nannini, I (Minardi 283-BMW), 20, brakes; Alliot, 20, suspension; Pierre Chauvet, A (Spirit 201-BMW), 21, engine; Jo Gartner, A (Spirit 201-BMW), 23, wheel bearing; Beppe Gabbiani, I (March 832-BMW), 32, suspension; Aldo Bertuzzi, I (March 832-BMW), 44, engine.

Did not start: Stefan Bellof, D (Maurer MM83-BMW), disqualified: Pierre Petit, F (Maurer MM83-BMW), withdrawn.
Championship points: 1 Palmer, 48; **2** Gabbiani, 36; **3** Thackwell, 35; **4** Danner, 18; **5** Gartner, 12; **6** Streiff and Tassin, 11.

21 GRAN PREMIO DEL MEDITERRANEO, Ente Autodromo di Pergusa, Sicily, July 31. European Formula 2 Championship, round 10. 45 laps of the 3·076-mile/4·950-km circuit, 138·42 miles/222·75 km.
1 Jonathan Palmer, GB (Ralt RH6/83-Honda), 1h 10m 11·30s, 118·32 mph/190·42 km/h.
2 Philippe Streiff, F (AGS JH19B-BMW), 1h 10m 18·07s.
3 Mike Thackwell, NZ (Ralt RH6/83-Honda), 1h 10m 24·63s.
4 Beppe Gabbiani, I (March 832-BMW), 1h 10m 45·71s.
5 Jo Gartner, A (Spirit 201-BMW), 1h 10m 58·19s.
6 Michel Ferte, F (Martini 001-BMW;, 1h 10m 59·94s.
7 Christian Danner, D (March 832-BMW), 1h 11m 21·50s, **8** Enzo Coloni, I (Minardi 283-BMW), 43 laps: **9** Fulvia Ballabio, I (AGS JH19-BMW), 43; **10** Fredy Lienhard, CH (March 832-BMW), 43; **11** Alessandro Nannini, I (Minardi 283-BMW), 41 (DNF, accident); **12** Philippe Alliot, F (Martini 001-BMW), 41 (DNF, suspension); **13** Roberto Del Castello, I (March 832-BMW), 40.
Fastest lap: Nannini, 1m 31·37s, 120·92 mph/194·62 km/h.
Retired: Enrique Mansilla, RA (March 832-BMW), 5, engine; Richard Dallest, F (Merzario M28-BMW), 5, gearbox; Stefan Bellof, D (Maurer MM83-BMW), 10, accident; Pierre Petit, F (Maurer MM83-BMW), 12, brakes; Guido Dacco, I (March 832-BMW), 30, accident; Dave Scott, GB (March 832-BMW), 34, spun and stalled.
Did not start: Aldo Bertuzzi, I (March 832-BMW), transmission in warm up.
Championship points: 1 Palmer, 57; **2** Gabbiani and Thackwell, 39; **4** Danner, 18; **5** Streiff, 17; **6** Gartner, 14.

GRAND PRIX de FORMULE 2, Omloop van Zolder, Belgium, August 21. European Formula 2 Championship, round 11. 46 laps of the 2·648-mile/4·262-km circuit, 121·81 miles/196·05 km.
1 Jonathan Palmer, GB (Ralt RH6/83-Honda), 1h 06m 12·03s, 110·41 mph/177·68 km/h.
2 Mike Thackwell, NZ (Ralt RH6/83-Honda), 1h 06m 22·86s.
3 Philippe Streiff, F (AGS JH19B-BMW), 1h 06m 55·98s.
4 Christian Danner, D (March 832-BMW), 1h 06m 57·41s.
5 Philippe Alliott, F (Martini 001-BMW), 1h 07m 06·03s.
6 Enrique Mansilla, RA (March 832-BMW), 1h 07m 26·92s.
7 Stefan Bellof, D (Maurer MM83-BMW), 1h 07m 38·36s; **8** Pierre Petit, F (Maurer MM83-BMW), 45 laps; **9** Didier Theys, B (Martini 001-BMW), 45; **10** Roberto Del Castello, I (March 832-BMW), 45; **11** Rolf Biland, CH (March 832-BMW), 45; **12** Pierre Chauvet, A (Spirit 201-BMW), 44; **13** Aldo Bertuzzi, I (March 832-BMW), 41.
Fastest lap: Palmer, 1m 25·09s, 112·03 mph/180·29 km/h (record).
Retired: Guido Dacco, I (March 832-BMW), 0 laps, accident; Dave Scott, GB (March 832-BMW), 0, accident; Tomas Kaiser, S (Maurer MM82-BMW), 0, driveshaft; Frank Jelinski, D (Maurer MM83-BMW), 12, ignition; Beppe Gabbiani, I (March 832-BMW), 12, accident; Alessandro Nannini, I (Minardi 283-BMW), 13, accident; Jo Gartner, A (Spirit 201-BMW), 23, engine; Fulvio Ballabio, I (AGS JH19-BMW), 25, still running but not classified; Paolo Barilla, I (Minardi 283-BMW), 33, ignition.
Championship points: 1 Palmer, 66; **2** Thackwell, 45; **3** Gabbiani, 39; **4** Danner and Streiff, 21; **6** Gartner, 14.

EUROPEAN FORMULA 2 CHAMPIONSHIP RACE, Autodromo Internazionale del Mugello, Italy, September 4. European Formula 2 Championship, round 12. 42 laps of the 3·259-mile/5·245-km circuit, 136·88 miles/220·29 km.
1 Jonathan Palmer, GB (Ralt RH6/83-Honda), 1h 14m 58·38s, 109·54 mph/176·29 km/h.
2 Mike Thackwell, NZ (Ralt RH6/83-Honda), 1h 14m 58·70s.
3 Philippe Streiff, F (AGS JH19B-BMW), 1h 16m 06·00s
4 Alessandro Nannini, I (Minardi 283-BMW), 1h 16m 27·42s.
5 Dave Scott, GB (March 832-BMW), 1h 16m 32·69s.
6 Fulvio Ballabio, I (AGS JH19-BMW), 41 laps.
7 Jo Gartner, A (Spirit 201-BMW), 41; **8** Richard Dallest, F (Merzario M28-BMW), 41; **9** Beppe Gabbiani, I (March 832-BMW), 41; **10** Christian Danner, D (March 832-BMW), 40.
Fastest lap: Palmer, 1m 45·69s, 111·01 mph/178·65 km/h.
Retired: Guido Dacco, I (March 832-BMW), 13 laps, misfire: Pierre Chauvet, A (Spirit 201-BMW), 22, engine; Philippe Alliott, F (Martini 001-BMW), 25, engine; Enrique Mansilla, RA (March 832-BMW), 34, accident; Oscar Laurrauri, RA (Minardi 283-BMW), 34, electrics.
Did not start: Roberto Del Castello, I (March 832-BMW), engine in warm up.

Final Championship points:

1 Jonathan Palmer, GB	68 (75)
2 Mike Thackwell, NZ	51
3 Beppe Gabbiani, I	39
4 Philippe Streiff, F	25
5 Christian Danner, D	21
6 Jo Gartner, A	14

7 Thierry Tassin, B and Alessandro Nannini, I, 11; **9** Stefan Bellof, D, 9; **10** Pier Luigi Martini, I and Kenny Acheson, GB, 6; **12** Philippe Alliot, F, Alain Ferte, F, Guido Dacco, I and Roberto Del Castello, I, 4; **16** Kazuyoshi Hoshino, J, Dave Scott, GB and Fulvio Ballabio, I, 3; **19** Enrique Mansilla, RA, 2; **20** Lamberto Leoni, I, Frank Jelinski, D, Fredy Lienhard, CH, Rolf Biland, CH and Michel Ferte, F, 1.

Formula 3

MARLBORO CHAMPIONSHIP RACE, Silverstone Short Circuit, Great Britain, March 6. Marlboro British Formula 3 Championship, round 1. 20 laps of the 1·608-mile/2·588-km circuit, 32·16 miles/51·76 km.
1 Ayrton Senna da Silva, BR (Ralt RT3/83-Toyota), 18m 07·14s, 106·50 mph/171·39 km/h.
2 Martin Brundle, GB (Ralt RT3/83-Toyota), 18m 13·57s.
3 Davy Jones, USA (Ralt RT3/83-VW), 18m 14·40s.
4 Calvin Fish, GB (Ralt RT3/83-VW), 18m 15·78s.
5 Mario Hytten, CH (Ralt RT3/82-Toyota), 18m 22·40s.
6 Johnny Dumfries, GB (Ralt RT3/82-VW), 18m 23·59s.
7 David Leslie, GB (Magnum 833-Toyota), 18m 23·94s; **8** Tony Trevor, GB (Ralt RT3/82-Toyota), 18m 29·00s; **9** Tim Lee-Davey, GB (Ralt RT3/82-Toyota), 18m 30·80s; **10** Allen Berg, CDN (Ralt RT3/82-Toyota), 18m 42·45s.
Fastest lap: Senna da Silva, 53·84s, 107·51 mph/173·02 km/h (record).
Marlboro Championship points: 1 Senna da Silva, 10; **2** Brundle, 6; **3** Jones, 4; **4** Fish, 3; **5** Hytten, 2; **6** Dumfries, 1.

MARLBORO CHAMPIONSHIP RACE, Thruxton Circuit, Great Britain, March 13. Marlboro British Formula 3 Championship, round 2. 20 laps of the 2·356-mile/3·792-km circuit, 47·12 miles/75·84 km.
1 Ayrton Senna da Silva, BR (Ralt RT3/83-Toyota), 26m 26·31s, 106·27 mph/171·02 km/h.
2 Martin Brundle, GB (Ralt RT3/83-Toyota), 26m 27·14s.
3 Mario Hytten, CH (Ralt RT3/82-Toyota), 27m 14·25s.
4 David Leslie, GB (Magnum 833-Toyota), 27m 16·16s.
5 Johnny Dumfries, GB (Ralt RT3/82-VW), 27m 17·17s.
6 Tim Lee-Davey, GB (Ralt RT3/82-Toyota), 27m 25·52s.

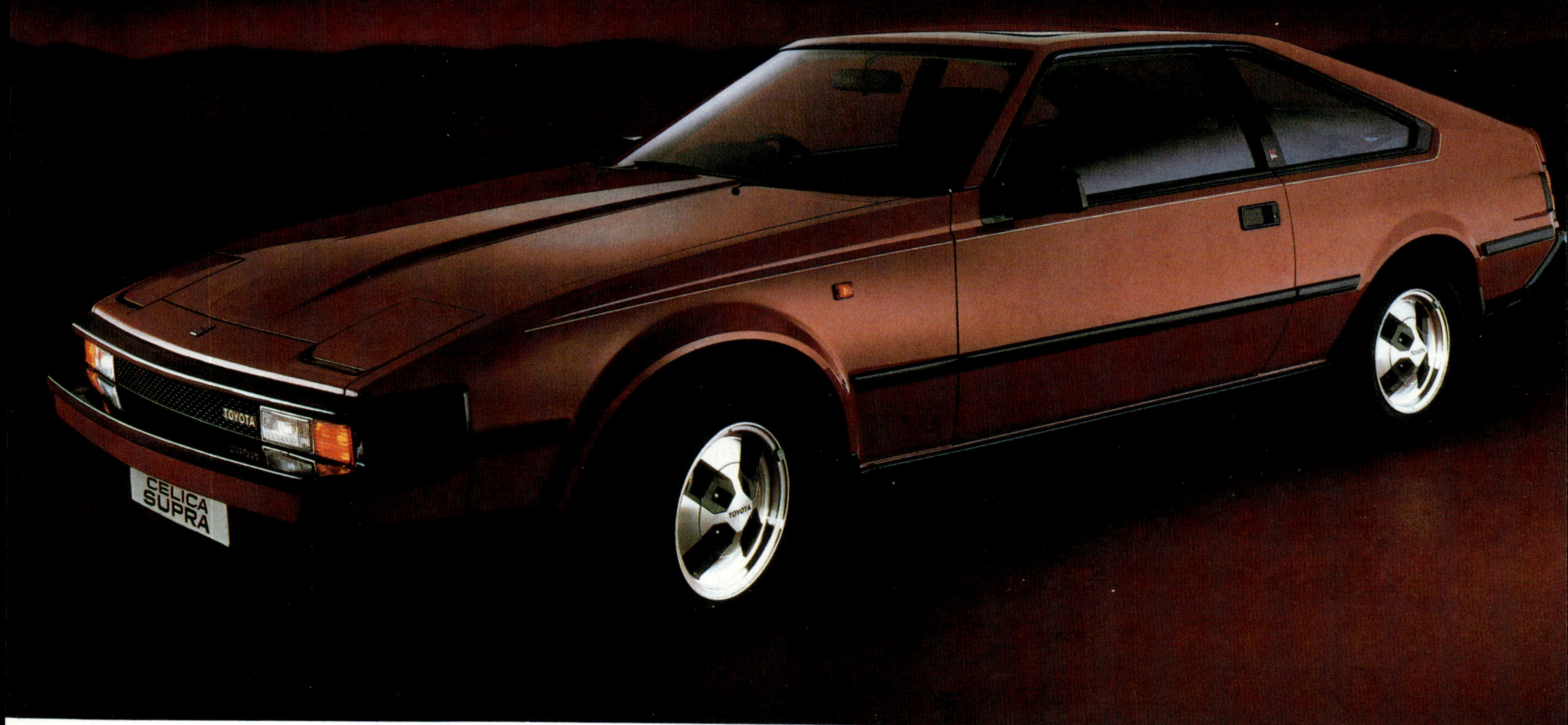

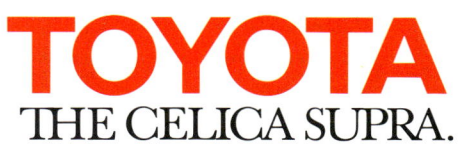

The Celica Supra. Rarer than a Ferrari, less common than a Porsche.

No more than a few hundred Celica Supras will be on the road this year – so if you ever see one, it'll be a fleeting glimpse.

Zero to 60mph in 8.3 seconds* from a 2.8 twin-cam, fuel injection engine capable of 168bhp at 5600rpm and over 135mph.*

A slick five-speed gearbox. Rack and pinion steering with variable power assistance, and tilt adjustable column. All round independent suspension with disc brakes front and rear. High-speed Michelin XDX tyres on alloy wheels. Foglamps and electric retractable headlamps.

Open her up and she performs like a true luxury sports car.

Air conditioning, electric sun-roof, electric windows, a three-band stereo radio/cassette unit with electric aerial and five speakers.

A rally-bred driver's seat that's eight ways adjustable – including a pneumatic lumbar support and full instrumentation including cruise control.

The Celica Supra is a rare Toyota.

The price: £10,593·32.**

TOYOTA
THE CELICA SUPRA.

7 Tommy Grunnah, USA (Ralt RT3/81-Toyota), 27m 52·83s; **8** Allen Berg, CDN (Ralt RT3/82-Toyota), 27m 56·59s; **9** Martin Wood, GB (Ralt RT3/82-Toyota), 19 laps; **10** Bill Burley, GB (March 813B-Toyota), 19 (Including 1 min penalty).
Fastest lap: Brundle, 1m 18·95s, 107·43 mph/172·89 km/h.
Marlboro Championship points: 1 Senna da Silva, 19; **2** Brundle, 13; **3** Hytten, 6; **4** Jones, 4; **5** Fish, Dumfries and Leslie, 3.

EUROPEAN FORMULA 3 CHAMPIONSHIP RACE, Autodromo di Vallelunga, Italy, March 13. European Formula 3 Championship, round 1. 30 laps of the 1·988-mile/3·200-km circuit, 59·64 miles/96·00 km.
1 Emanuele Pirro, I (Ralt RT3-Alfa Romeo), 36m 55·26s; 96·40 mph/155·14 km/h.
2 John Nielsen, DK (Ralt RT3-VW), 36m 55·71s.
3 Pier-Luigi Martini, I (Ralt RT3-Alfa Romeo), 36m 56·56s.
4 Enzo Coloni, I (Ralt RT3- Alfa Romeo), 37m 06·89s.
5 Ruggero Melgrati, I (Ralt RT3-Alfa Romeo), 37m 07·32s.
6 Pascal Fabre, F (Martini MK39-Alfa Romeo), 37m 20·67s.
7 Enzo Sabastiani, I (Ralt RT3-Alfa Romeo), 37m 21·96s; **8** Ivan Capelli, I (Ralt RT3-Alfa Romeo), 37m 24·87s; **9** Jakob Bordoli, CH (Ralt RT3-Toyota), 37m 39·00s; **10** Stefano Livio, I (Dallara 382-Alfa Romeo), 37m 41·66s.
Fastest lap: Martini, 1m 13·16s, 97·84 mph/157·46 km/h.
Heat winners. Heat 1: Roberto Ravaglia, I (Ralt RT3-Toyota). **Heat 2:** Pirro.
European Championship points: 1 Pirro, 9; **2** Nielsen, 6; **3** Martini, 4; **4** Coloni, 3; **5** Melgrati, 2; **6** Fabre, 1.

MARLBORO CHAMPIONSHIP RACE, Silverstone Grand Prix Circuit, Great Britain, March 20. Marlboro British Formula 3 Championship, round 3. Aggregate of two 6 lap heats of the 2·932-mile/4·719-km circuit, 12 laps, 35·18 miles/56·63 km.
1 Ayrton Senna da Silva, BR (Ralt RT3/83-Toyota), 19m 36·51s, 107·66 mph/173·26 km/h.
2 Martin Brundle, GB (Ralt RT3/83-Toyota), 19m 38·47s.
3 Calvin Fish, GB (Ralt RT3/83-VW), 19m 43·52s.
4 Davy Jones, USA (Ralt RT3/83-VW), 20m 08·93s.
5 David Leslie, GB (Magnum 833-Toyota), 20m 13·48s.
6 Tony Trevor, GB (Ralt RT3/82-Toyota), 20m 14·73s.
7 Allen Berg, CDN (Ralt RT3/83-Toyota), 20m 25·61s; **8** Martin Wood, GB (Ralt RT3/82-Toyota), 20m 46·98s; **9** Gerry Amato, GB (Ralt RT3/80-Toyota), 21m 02·86s; **10** Greg Atkinson, GB (March 793-Toyota), 21m 03·86s.
Fastest lap: Senna da Silva, 1m 36·28s, 109·63 mph/176·43 km/h.
Marlboro Championship points: 1 Senna da Silva, 29; **2** Brundle, 19; **3** Jones and Fish, 7; **5** Hytten, 6; **6** Leslie, 5.

MARLBORO CHAMPIONSHIP RACE, Donington Park Circuit, Great Britain, March 27. Marlboro British Formula 3 Championship, round 4. 20 laps of the 1·9573-mile/3·150-km circuit, 39·15 miles/63·00 km.
1 Ayrton Senna da Silva, BR (Ralt RT3/83-Toyota), 23m 23·35s, 100·42 mph/161·61 km/h.
2 Martin Brundle, GB (Ralt RT3/83-Toyota), 23m 28·98s.
3 Davy Jones, USA (Ralt RT3/83-VW), 23m 29·71s.
4 Mario Hytten, CH (Ralt RT3/83-Toyota), 24m 00·61s.
5 Richard Trott, GB (Ralt RT3/83-Toyota), 24m 03·28s.
6 David Leslie, GB (Magnum 833-Toyota), 24m 05·32s.
7 Martin Wood, GB (Ralt RT3/82-Toyota), 24m 34·00s; **8** Johnny Dumfries, GB (Ralt RT3/82-VW), 24m 36·58s; **9** Greg Atkinson, GB (March 793-Toyota), 19 laps. No other finishers.
Fastest lap: Senna da Silva and Jones, 1m 09·52s, 101·36 mph/163·12 km/h (record).
Marlboro Championship points: 1 Senna da Silva, 39; **2** Brundle, 25; **3** Jones, 12; **4** Hytten, 9; **5** Fish, 7; **6** Leslie, 6.

MARLBORO CHAMPIONSHIP RACE, Thruxton Circuit, Great Britain, April 4. Marlboro British Formula 3 Championship, round 5. 20 laps of the 2·356-mile/3·792-km circuit, 47·12 miles/75·84 km.
1 Ayrton Senna da Silva, BR (Ralt RT3/83-Toyota), 25m 03·29s, 112·84 mph/181·60 km/h.
2 Martin Brundle, GB (Ralt RT3/83-Toyota), 25m 04·53s.
3 Calvin Fish, GB (Ralt RT3/83-VW), 25m 25·33s.
4 Mario Hytten, CH (Ralt RT3/83-Toyota), 25m 28·27s.
5 Allen Berg, CDN (Ralt RT3/83-Toyota), 25m 29·11s.
6 Tim Lee-Davey, GB (Ralt RT3/82-Toyota), 25m 34·30s.
7 Johnny Dumfries, GB (Ralt RT3/82-VW), 25m 36·55s; **8** Tony Trevor, GB (Ralt RT3/82-Toyota), 25m 39·83s; **9** Tommy Grunnah, USA (Ralt RT3/83-Toyota), 25m 40·09s; **10** Eric Lang, USA (Ralt RT3/83-VW), 25m 52·04s.
Fastest lap: Brundle, 1m 14·52s, 113·82 mph/183·18 km/h.
Marlboro Championship points: 1 Senna da Silva, 48; **2** Brundle, 32; **3** Jones and Hytten, 12; **5** Fish, 11; **6** Leslie, 6.

EUROPEAN FORMULA 3 CHAMPIONSHIP RACE, Omloop van Zolder, Belgium, April 17. European Formula 3 Championship, round 2. 22 laps of the 2·648-mile/4·262-km circuit, 58·26 miles/93·76 km.
1 Emanuele Pirro, I (Ralt RT3-Alfa Romeo), 34m 09·1s, 102·36 mph/164·73 km/h.
2 Didier Theys, B (Ralt RT3- Alfa Romeo), 34m 12·2s.
3 Gerhard Berger, A (Ralt RT3-Alfa Romeo), 34m 12·8s.
4 Tommy Byrne, IRL (Ralt RT3-VW), 34m 23·1s.
5 Pascal Fabre, F (Martini MK39-Alfa Romeo), 34m 34·5s.
6 Roberto Ravaglia, I (Ralt RT3-Toyota), 34m 37·8s.
7 Jakob Bordoli, CH (Ralt RT3-Toyota), 34m 49·5s; **8** Jo Zeller, CH (Ralt RT3-Toyota), 34m 49·6s; **9** John Bosch, NL (Ralt RT3-Toyota), 34m 52·2s; **10** Nils-Kristian Nissen, DK (Anson SA4-VW), 34m 56·2s.
Fastest lap: Berger, 1m 31·9s, 103·74 mph/166·95 km/h.
European Championship points: 1 Pirro, 18; **2** Nielsen and Theys, 6; **4** Martini and Berger, 4; **6** Coloni, Fabre and Byrne, 3.

MARLBORO CHAMPIONSHIP RACE, Silverstone Short Circuit, Great Britain, April 24. Marlboro British Formula 3 Championship, round 6. 25 laps of the 1·608-mile/2·588-km circuit, 40·20 miles/64·70 km.
1 Ayrton Senna da Silva, BR (Ralt RT3/83-Toyota), 22m 33·59s, 106·92 mph/172·07 km/h.
2 Davy Jones, USA (Ralt RT3/83-VW), 22m 38·73s.
3 Martin Brundle, GB (Ralt RT3/83-Toyota), 22m 39·00s.
4 Calvin Fish, GB (Ralt RT3/83-VW), 22m 49·70s.
5 Johnny Dumfries, GB (Ralt RT3/83-VW), 22m 50·24s.
6 David Leslie, GB (Magnum 833-Toyota), 22m 53·13s.
7 Allen Berg, CDN (Ralt RT3/83-Toyota), 23m 01·72s; **8** Mario Hytten, CH (Ralt RT3/83-Toyota), 23m 03·99s; **9** Tony Trevor, GB (Ralt RT3/82-Toyota), 23m 08·93s; **10** Tim Lee-Davey, GB (Ralt RT3/82-Toyota), 23m 10·44s.
Fastest lap: Senna da Silva, 53·58s; 108·04 mph/173·87 km/h (record).
Marlboro Championship points: 1 Senna da Silva, 58; **2** Brundle, 36; **3** Jones, 18; **4** Fish, 14; **5** Hytten, 12; **6** Leslie, 7.

EUROPEAN FORMULA 3 CHAMPIONSHIP RACE, Magny-Cours, France, May 1. European Formula 3 Championship, round 3. 26 laps of the 2·392-mile/3·848-km circuit, 62·19 miles/100·05 km.
1 John Nielsen, DK (Ralt RT3-VW), 38m 07·64s, 97·87 mph/157·51 km/h.
2 Francois Hesnault, F (Ralt RT3-VW), 38m 17·71s.
3 Michel Ferte, F (Martini MK39-Alfa Romeo), 38m 24·75s.
4 Nils-Kristian Nissen, DK (Anson SA4-VW), 38m 25·14s.
5 Tommy Byrne, IRL (Ralt RT3-Toyota), 38m 25·22s.
6 Gerhard Berger, A (Ralt RT3-Alfa Romeo), 38m 30·05s.
7 Cathy Muller, F (Ralt RT3-VW), 38m 59·20s; **8** Jo Zeller, CH (Ralt RT3-Toyota), 39m 01·03s; **9** Oscar Pedersoli, I (Anson SA4-Alfa Romeo), 39m 15·77s; **10** Jose-Louis Llobell, E (Avidesa-Toyota), 39m 21·59s.
Fastest lap: Zeller, 1m 24·72s; 100·23 mph/161·30 km/h.
European Championship points: 1 Pirro, 22; **2** Nielsen, 15; **3** Theys and Hesnault, 6; **5** Byrne and Berger, 5.

MARLBORO CHAMPIONSHIP RACE, Thruxton Circuit, Great Britain, May 2. Marlboro British Formula 3 Championship, round 7. 20 laps of the 2·356-mile/3·792-km circuit, 47·12 miles/75·84 km.
1 Ayrton Senna da Silva, BR (Ralt RT3/83-Toyota), 24m 51·88s; 113·70 mph/182·98 km/h.
2 Martin Brundle, GB (Ralt RT3/83-Toyota), 24m 55·28s.
3 Davy Jones, USA (Ralt RT3/83-VW), 24m 55·95s.
4 Mario Hytten, CH (Ralt RT3/83-Toyota), 25m 15·09s.
5 David Leslie, GB (Magnum 833-Toyota), 25m 18·45s.
6 Allen Berg, CDN (Ralt RT3/83-Toyota), 25m 20·43s.
7 Tim Lee-Davey, GB (Ralt RT3/82-Toyota), 25m 27·61s; **8** Tony Trevor, GB (Ralt RT3/82-Toyota), 25m 29·41s; **9** Eric Lang, USA (Ralt RT3/83-VW), 25m 29·60s; **10** Mike Blanchet, GB (March 813B-Toyota), 25m 39·39s.
Fastest lap: Senna da Silva, 1m 14·0s; 114·55 mph/184·35 km/h.
Marlboro Championship points: 1 Senna da Silva, 68; **2** Brundle, 42; **3** Jones, 22; **4** Hytten, 15; **5** Fish, 14; **6** Leslie, 9.

MARLBORO CHAMPIONSHIP RACE, Brands Hatch Indy Circuit, Great Britain, May 8. Marlboro British Formula 3 Championship, round 8. 20 laps of the 1·2036-mile/1·937-km circuit, 24·07 miles/38·74 km.
1 Ayrton Senna da Silva, BR (Ralt RT3/83-Toyota), 17m 21·6s, 83·20 mph/133·90 km/h.
2 Martin Brundle, GB (Ralt RT3/83-Toyota), 17m 24·0s.
3 Davy Jones, USA (Ralt RT3/83-VW), 17m 31·3s.
4 Calvin Fish, GB (Ralt RT3/83-VW), 17m 36·0s.
5 Allen Berg, CDN (Ralt RT3/83-Toyota), 17m 53·7s.
6 David Leslie, GB (Magnum 833-Toyota), 17m 55·3s.
7 Tim Lee-Davey, GB (Ralt RT3/82-Toyota), 18m 04·3s; **8** Tony Trevor, GB (Ralt RT3/82-Toyota), 18m 11·2s; **9** Mike Blanchet, GB (March 813-Toyota), 19 laps; **10** Carlton Tingling, JA (Ralt RT3/83-VW), 19.
Fastest lap: Senna da Silva, 50·7s, 83·46 mph/134·32 km/h.
Marlboro Championship points: 1 Senna da Silva, 78; **2** Brundle, 48; **3** Jones, 26; **4** Fish, 17; **5** Hytten, 15; **6** Leslie, 10.

25 GRAND PRIX DE MONACO F3, Monte Carlo, May 14. 24 laps of the 2·058-mile/3·312-km circuit, 49·39 miles/79·49 km.
1 Michel Ferte, F (Martini MK39-Alfa Romeo), 38m 18·709s, 77·41 mph/124·58 km/h.
2 John Nielsen, DK (Ralt RT3/83-VW), 38m 22·069s.
3 Tommy Byrne, IRL (Ralt RT3/83-Toyota), 38m 37·634s.
4 Pier Luigi Martini, I (Ralt RT3/83-Alfa Romeo), 38m 38·583s.
5 Didier Theys, B (Ralt RT3/83-Alfa Romeo), 38m 47·806s.
6 Roberto Ravaglia, I (Ralt RT3/83-Toyota), 38m 48·612s.
7 Francois Hesnault, F (Ralt RT3/83-VW), 38m 59·810s; **8** Pascal Fabre, F (Martini MK39-Alfa Romeo), 39m 01·027s; **9** Claudio Langes, I (Anson SA4-Alfa Romeo), 39m 01·832s; **10** Fernando Cazzaniga, I (Anson SA4-Alfa Romeo), 39m 02·443s.
Fastest lap: Ferte, 1m 34·90s; 78·035 mph/125·58 km/h.

EUROPEAN FORMULA 3 CHAMPIONSHIP RACE, Osterreichring, Austria, May 22. European Formula 3 Championship, round 4. 16 laps of the 3·692-mile/5·942-km circuit, 59·07 miles/95·07 km.
1 Tommy Byrne, IRL (Ralt RT3-Toyota), 29m 42·13s, 119·344 mph/192·049 km/h.
2 Gerhard Berger, A (Ralt RT3-Alfa Romeo), 29m 44·03s.
3 Emanuele Pirro, I (Ralt RT3-Alfa Romeo), 29m 45·79s.
4 Pier Luigi Martini, I (Ralt RT3-Alfa Romeo), 29m 46·40s.
5 Didier Theys, B (Ralt RT3-Alfa Romeo), 29m 46·47s.
6 Pascal Fabre, F (Martini MK39-Alfa Romeo), 30m 03·07s.
7 Cathy Muller, F (Ralt RT3-VW), 30m 03·55s; **8** Jo Zeller, CH (Ralt RT3-Toyota), 30m 02·18s; **9** Ruggero Melgrati, I (Ralt RT3-Alfa Romeo), 30m 07·54s; **10** Harri Kangas, A (Ralt RT3-Toyota), 30m 07·63s.
Fastest lap: Martini, 1m 50·14s, 120·69 mph/194·23 km/h.
European Championship points: 1 Pirro, 22; **2** Nielsen, 15; **3** Byrne, 14; **4** Berger, 11; **5** Theys, 8; **6** Martini, 7.

MARLBORO CHAMPIONSHIP RACE, Silverstone Short Circuit, Great Britain, May 30. Marlboro British Formula 3 Championship, round 9. 30 laps of the 1·608-mile/2·588-km circuit, 48·24 miles/77·64 km.
1 Ayrton Senna de Silva, BR (Ralt RT3/83-Toyota), 27m 00·98s, 107·14 mph/172·42 km/h.
2 Martin Brundle, GB (Ralt RT3/83-Toyota), 27m 11·08s.
3 Allen Berg, CDN (Ralt RT3/83-Toyota), 27m 23·47s.
4 Calvin Fish, GB (Ralt RT3/83-VW), 27m 25·65s.
5 Davy Jones, USA (Ralt RT3/83-VW), 27m 27·60s.
6 Richard Trott, GB (Ralt RT3/83-Toyota), 27m 38·23s.
7 Mario Hytten, CH (Ralt RT3/83-Toyota), 27m 41·46s; **8** Eric Lang, USA (Ralt RT3/83-VW), 27m 43·28s; **9** Tony Trevor, GB (Ralt RT3/82-Toyota), 27m 51·04s; **10** Carlton Tingling, JA (Ralt RT3/82-VW), 29 laps.
Fastest lap: Senna da Silva, 53·70s, 107·80 mph/173·49 km/h.
Marlboro Championship points: 1 Senna da Silva, 88; **2** Brundle, 54; **3** Jones, 28; **4** Fish, 20; **5** Hytten, 15; **6** Leslie, 10.

EUROPEAN FORMULA 3 CHAMPIONSHIP RACE, La Charte Circuit, France, June 5. European Formula 3 Championship, round 5. 40 laps of the 1·445-mile/2·325-km circuit, 57·80 miles/93·00 km.
1 Roberto Ravaglia, I (Ralt RT3-Toyota), 43m 16·00s, 80·14 mph/128·97 km/h.
2 Didier Theys, B (Ralt RT3-Alfa Romeo), 43m 23·09s.
3 Pascal Fabre, F (Martini MK39-Alfa Romeo), 43m 30·02s.
4 Claudio Langes, I (Anson SA4-Alfa Romeo), 43m 56·65s.
5 Michel Ferte, F (Martini MK39-Alfa Romeo), 44m 03·03s.
6 Max Busslinger, CH (Ralt RT3-Toyota), 44m 11·82s.
7 Ruggero Melgrati, I (Ralt RT3- Alfa Romeo), 44m 15·61s; **8** Enrique Benamo, RA (Ralt RT3-Alfa Romeo), 44m 17·45s; **9** Philippe Huart, F (Anson SA4-Toyota), 44m 18·20s; **10** James Weaver, GB (Anson SA4-Alfa Romeo), 44m 21·00s.
Fastest lap: Ravaglia, 1m 03·58s; 81·80 mph/131·64 km/h.
Heat winners. Heat 1; Theys. **Heat 2:** Ravaglia.
European Championship points: 1 Pirro, 22; **2** Nielsen, 15; **3** Byrne and Theys, 14; **5** Berger, 11; **6** Ravaglia, 10.

MARLBORO EUROPEAN F3 TROPHY, Silverstone Grand Prix Circuit, Great Britain, June 12. European Formula 3 Championship, round 6. Marlboro British Formula 3 Championship, round 10. 20 laps of the 2·932-mile/4·719-km circuit, 58·64 miles/94·38 km.
1 Martin Brundle, GB (Ralt RT3/83-Toyota), 28m 44·71s, 122·40 mph/196·98 km/h.
2 Tommy Byrne, IRL (Ralt RT3/83-Toyota), 29m 00·55s.
3 Didier Theys, B (Ralt RT3/83-Alfa Romeo), 29m 03·15s.
4 Roberto Ravaglia, I (Ralt RT3/83-Toyota), 29m 03·55s.
5 Carlos Abella, E (Ralt RT3/83-Toyota), 29m 08·00s
6 Nils-Kristian Nissen, DK (Anson SA4-VW), 29m 08·47s.
7 John Nielsen, DK (Ralt RT3/83-VW), 29m 08·96s; **8** Bernard Santal, F (Ralt RT3/83-Toyota), 29m 18·86s; **9** Ruggero Melgrati, I (Ralt RT3/83-Alfa Romeo), 29m 26·67s; **10** Allen Berg, CDN (Ralt RT3/83-Toyota), 29m 29·72s.
Overall fastest lap: Johnny Dumfries, GB (Ralt RT3/83-VW), 1m 24·52s, 124·88 mph/200·97 km/h (record).
Marlboro fastest lap: Davy Jones, USA (Ralt RT3/83-VW), 1m 26·69s, 121·76 mph/195·95 km/h.
European Championship points: 1 Pirro, 22; **2** Byrne, 20; **3** Theys, 18; **4** Nielsen, 15; **5** Ravaglia, 13; **6** Berger, 11.
Marlboro Championship points: 1 Senna da Silva, 88; **2** Brundle, 54; **3** Jones, 35; **4** Fish, 24; **5** Berg, 18; **6** Hytten, 15.

MARLBORO CHAMPIONSHIP RACE, Cadwell Park Circuit, Great Britain, June 19. Marlboro British Formula 3 Championship, round 11. 20 laps of the 2·250-mile/3·621-km circuit, 45·00 miles/72·42 km.
1 Martin Brundle, GB (Ralt RT3/83-Toyota), 28m 13·43s, 95·66 mph/153·95 km/h.
2 Calvin Fish, GB (Ralt RT3/83-VW), 28m 28·77s.
3 Davy Jones, USA (Ralt RT3/83-VW), 28m 31·82s.
4 Eric Lang, USA (Ralt RT3/83-VW), 28m 52·03s.
5 Mario Hytten, CH (Ralt RT3/83-Toyota), 28m 56·02s.
6 Tony Trevor, GB (Ralt RT3/82-Toyota), 29m 21·17s.
No other finishers.
Fastest lap: Brundle, 1m 24·01s, 96·42 mph/155·17 km/h.
Marlboro Championship points: 1 Senna da Silva, 88; **2** Brundle, 64; **3** Jones, 39; **4** Fish, 30; **5** Berg, 18; **6** Hytten, 17.

EUROPEAN FORMULA 3 CHAMPIONSHIP RACE, Autodromo Nazionale di Monza, Italy. June 26 European Formula 3 Championship , round 7. 17 laps of the 3·604-mile/5·800-km circuit, 61·27 miles/98·60 km.
1 John Nielsen, DK (Ralt RT3/83-VW), 31m 36·62s, 116·29 mph/187·15 km/h.
2 Roberto Ravaglia, I (Ralt RT3/83-Toyota), 31m 37·28s.
3 Tommy Byrne, IRL (Ralt RT3/83-Toyota), 31m 46·69s.
4 Enzo Coloni, I (Ralt RT3/83-Alfa Romeo), 31m 48·69s.
5 Pier-Luigi Martini, I (Ralt RT3/83-Alfa Romeo), 31m 49·16s.
6 Emanuele Pirro, I (Ralt RT3/83-Alfa Romeo), 31m 49·36s.
7 Ruggero Melgrati, I (Ralt RT3/83-Alfa Romeo), 32m 15·57s, **8** Pascal Fabre, F (Martini MK39-Alfa Romeo), 32m 19·29s; **9** Adrian Campos, E (Avidesa 383-Alfa Romeo), 32m 42·43s; **10** Max Busslinger, CH (Ralt RT3/83-Toyota), 32m 44·35s.
Fastest lap: Martini, 1m 50·10s, 117·84 mph/169·64 km/h.
European Championship points: 1 Nielsen and Byrne, 24; **3** Pirro, 23; **4** Ravaglia, 19; **5** Theys, 18; **6** Berger, 11.

MARLBORO CHAMPIONSHIP RACE, Snetterton Circuit, Great Britain, July 3. Marlboro British Formula 3 Championship, round 12. 25 laps of the 1·917-mile/3·085-km circuit, 47·93 miles/77·13 km.
1 Martin Brundle, GB (Ralt RT3/83-Toyota), 26m 07·15s, 110·09 mph/177·17 km/h.
2 Davy Jones, USA (Ralt RT3/83-VW), 26m 08·18s.
3 Calvin Fish, GB (Ralt RT3/83-VW), 26m 11·72s.
4 Tony Trevor, GB (Ralt RT3/83-Toyota), 26m 39·67s.
5 Mario Hytten, CH (Ralt RT3/83-Toyota), 26m 44·31s.
6 Eric Lang, USA (Ralt RT3/83-VW), 26m 56·20s.
7 Martin Wood, GB (Ralt RT3/82-Toyota), 27m 06·96s, **8** Ronnie Grant, GB (Ralt RT3/83-VW), 24 laps. No other finishers.
Fastest lap: Aryton Senna da Silva, 1m 02·16s, 111·02 mph/178·67 km/h.
Marlboro Championship points: 1 Senna da Silva, 89; **2** Brundle, 73; **3** Jones, 45; **4** Fish, 34; **5** Hytten, 19; **6** Berg, 18.

EUROPEAN FORMULA 3 CHAMPIONSHIP RACE, Autodromo Santamonica, Misano, Italy, July 10. European Formula 3 Championship, round 8. 26 laps of the 2·167-mile/3·488-km circuit, 56·34 miles/90·69 km.
1 Tommy Byrne, IRL (Ralt RT3-Toyota), 33m 08·86s, 102·00 mph/164·15 km/h.
2 Pier Luigi Martini, I (Ralt RT3-Alfa Romeo), 33m 10·34s.
3 Roberto Ravaglia, I (Ralt RT3-Alfa Romeo), 33m 16·76s.
4 Nils-Kristian Nissen, DK (Anson SA4-Alfa Romeo), 33m 24·51s.
5 John Bosch, NL (Ralt RT3-Toyota), 33m 30·63s.
6 Claudio Langes, I (Ralt RT3-Toyota), 33m 35·46s.
7 Gerhard Berger, A (Ralt RT3-Alfa Romeo), 33m 37·50s; **8** Jose-Louis Llobell, E (Avidesa 383-Alfa Romeo), 33m 37·90s; **9** Pascal Fabre, F (Martini MK39-Alfa-Romeo), 33m 40·28s; **10** Jo Zeller, CH (Ralt RT3-Toyota), 33m 40·60s.
Fastest lap: Byrne, 1m 15·84s, 102·88 mph/165·57 km/h.
European Championship points: 1 Byrne, 33; **2** Nielsen, 24; **3** Pirro and Ravaglia, 23; **5** Theys, 18; **6** Martini, 15.

MARLBORO CHAMPIONSHIP RACE, Silverstone Grand Prix Circuit, Great Britain, July 16. Marlboro British Formula 3 Championship, round 13. 20 laps of the 2·932-mile/4·719-km circuit, 58·64 miles/94·38 km.
1 Ayrton Senna da Silva, BR (Ralt RT3/83-Toyota), 28m 59·55s, 121·36 mph/195·31 km/h.
2 Martin Brundle, GB (Ralt RT3/83-Toyota), 29m 01·16s.
3 Calvin Fish, GB (Ralt RT3/83-VW), 29m 18·58s.
4 Allen Berg, CDN (Ralt RT3/83-Toyota), 29m 18·74s.
5 Johnny Dumfries, GB (Ralt RT3/82-VW), 29m 20·98s.
6 Mario Hytten, CH (Ralt RT3/83-VW), 29m 33·39s.
7 Davy Jones, USA (Ralt RT3/83-VW), 29m 39·46s; **8** David Leslie, GB (Magnum 833-Toyota), 29m 43·42s; **9** Eric Lang, USA (Ralt RT3/83-VW), 29m 43·73s; **10** Tim Lee-Davey, GB (Ralt RT3/83-Toyota), 29m 53·45s.
Fastest lap: Senna da Silva, 1m 26·32s; 122·28 mph/196·79 km/h.
Marlboro Championship points: 1 Senna da Silva, 99; **2** Brundle, 79; **3** Jones, 45; **4** Fish, 38; **5** Berg, 21; **6** Hytten, 20.

MARLBORO CHAMPIONSHIP RACE, Donington Park Circuit, Great Britain, July 24. Marlboro British Formula 3 Championship, round 14. 30 laps of the 1·9573-mile/3·1500-km circuit, 58·72 miles/94·50 km.
1 Martin Brundle, GB (Ralt RT3/83-Toyota), 35m 09·21s, 100·22 mph/161·29 km/h.
2 Aryton Senna da Silva, BR (Ralt RT3/83-Toyota), 35m 09·61s.
3 Davy Jones, USA (Ralt RT3/83-VW), 35m 12·38s.
4 Calvin Fish, GB (Ralt RT3/83-VW), 35m 30·03s.
5 Richard Trott, GB (Ralt RT3/83-Toyota), 35m 45·21s.
6 David Leslie, GB (Magnum 833-Toyota), 35m 59·90s.
7 Eric Lang, USA (Ralt RT3/83-VW), 36m 02·43s; **8** Tony Trevor, GB (Ralt RT3/82-Toyota), 36m 11·18s; **9** Mario Hytten, CH (Ralt RT3/83-Toyota), 36m 14·66s; **10** Carlton Tingling, JA (Ralt RT3/82-VW), 29 laps.
Fastest lap: Senna da Silva, 1m 09·76s; 101·01 mph/162·56 km/h.
Marlboro Championship points: 1 Senna da Silva, 106; **2** Brundle, 88; **3** Jones 49; **4** Fish, 41; **5** Berg, 21; **6** Hytten, 20.

EUROPEAN FORMULA 3 CHAMPIONSHIP RACE, Circuit van Zandvoort, Holland, July 31. European Formula 3 Championship, round 9. 22 laps of the 2·642-mile/4·252-km circuit, 58·12 miles/93·54 km.
1 John Nielsen, DK (Ralt RT3/VW), 34m 18·14s, 101·67 mph/163·62 km/h.
2 Pier Luigi Martini, I (Ralt RT3-Alfa Romeo), 34m 21·22s.
3 Emanuele Pirro, I (Ralt RT3-Alfa Romeo), 34m 27·79s.
4 Didier Theys, B (Ralt RT3-Alfa Romeo), 34m 35·99s.
5 Roberto Ravaglia, I (Ralt RT3-Toyota), 34m 36·62s.
6 Kurt Thiim, DK (Ralt RT3-Alfa Romeo), 34m 40·99s.
7 Tommy Byrne, IRL (Ralt RT3-Toyota), 34m 46·48s; **8** Cor Euser, NL (Martini MK34-Toyota), 34m 50·97s; **9** Jo Zeller, CH (Ralt RT3-Toyota), 34m 51·86s; **10** Pascal Fabre, F (Martini MK39-Alfa Romeo), 34m 52·03s.
Fastest lap: Nielsen, 1m 32·25s, 103·33 mph/166·29 km/h.
European Championship points: 1 Nielsen and Byrne, 33; **3** Pirro, 27; **4** Ravaglia, 25; **5** Theys and Martini, 21.

MARLBORO CHAMPIONSHIP RACE, Oulton Park Circuit, Great Britain, August 6. Marlboro British Formula 3 Championship, round 15. 35 laps of the 1·654-mile/2·662-km circuit, 57·89 miles/93·17 km.
1 Calvin Fish, GB (Ralt RT3/83-VW), 34m 17·14s, 101·31 mph/163·04 km/h.
2 Davy Jones, USA (Ralt RT3/83-VW), 34m 18·01s.
3 Allen Berg, CDN (Ralt RT3/83-Toyota), 34m 21·97s.
4 David Leslie, GB (Magnum 833-Toyota), 34m 33·41s.
5 Tony Trevor, GB (Ralt RT3/82-Toyota), 34m 56·62s.
6 Carlton Tingling, JA (Ralt RT3/82-VW), 34 laps.
No other finishers.

Fastest lap: Ayrton Senna da Silva, BR (Ralt RT3/83-Toyota), 57·49s, 103·57 mph/166·68 km/h.
Marlboro Championship points: 1 Senna da Silva, 107; **2** Brundle, 88; **3** Jones, 55; **4** Fish, 50; **5** Berg, 25; **6** Hytten, 20.

EUROPEAN FORMULA 3 CHAMPIONSHIP RACE, Ring Knutstorp, Sweden, August 7. European Formula 3 Championship, round 10. 45 laps of the 1·292-mile/2·079-km circuit, 58·14 miles/93·56 km.
1 John Nielsen, DK (Ralt RT3-VW), 43m 14·53s, 80·66 mph/129·81 km/h.
2 Gerhard Berger, A (Ralt RT3-Alfa Romeo), 43m 29·97s.
3 Emanuele Pirro, I (Ralt RT3-Alfa Romeo), 43m 33·29s.
4 Pier Luigi Martini, I (Ralt RT3-Alfa Romeo), 43m 34·48s.
5 Didier Theys, B (Ralt RT3-Alfa Romeo), 43m 36·22s.
6 Roberto Ravaglia, I (Ralt RT3-Toyota), 43m 43·22s.
7 Pascal Fabre, F (Martini MK39-Alfa Romeo), 44m 03·50s; **8** Tommy Byrne, IRL (Ralt RT3-Toyota), 44m 10·28s; **9** Jo Zeller, CH (Ralt RT3-Toyota), 44m 10·48s; **10** Ruggero Melgrati, I (Ralt RT3-Alfa Romeo), 45m 07·67s (Including 1 min penalty).
Fastest lap: Not given.
European Championship points: 1 Nielsen, 42; **2** Byrne, 33; **3** Pirro, 31; **4** Ravaglia, 26; **5** Martini, 24; **6** Theys, 23.

OSTERREICHRING FORMULA 3 RACE, Osterreichring, Austria, August 13. 16 laps of the 3·6924-mile/5·9424-km circuit, 59·08 miles/95·08 km.
1 Martin Brundle, GB (Ralt RT3-Toyota), 29m 45·487s, 119·09 mph/191·66 km/h.
2 Bernard Santal, F (Ralt RT3-Toyota), 30m 03·152s.
3 Jacob Bordoli, CH (Ralt RT3-Toyota), 30m 06·377s.
4 Gerhard Berger, A (Ralt RT3-Alfa Romeo), 30m 06·590s.
5 Urs Duddler, CH (Ralt RT3-Toyota), 30m 07·933s.
6 Franz Konrad, A (Anson SA4-VW), 30m 17·472s.
7 Hans-Peter Kaufmann, CH (Ralt RT3-Toyota), 30m 39·587s; **8** Niki Nufer, D (Ralt RT3-Toyota), 30m 44·602s; **9** Karl-Christian Lueck, D (Ralt RT3-VW), 30m 44·737s; **10** Thomas von Loewis of Menar, D (Anson SA4-Toyota), 30m 45·011s.
Fastest lap: Brundle, 1m 50·26s, 120·55 mph/194·01 km/h (record).

MARLBORO CHAMPIONSHIP RACE, Silverstone Short Circuit, Great Britain, August 29. Marlboro British Formula 3 Championship, round 16. 30 laps of the 1·608-mile/2·588-km circuit, 48·24 miles/77·64 km.
1 Ayrton Senna da Silva, BR (Ralt RT3/83-Toyota), 27m 02·45s, 107·04 mph/172·26 km/h.
2 Martin Brundle, GB (Ralt RT3/83-Toyota), 27m 03·89s.
3 Davy Jones, USA (Ralt RT3/83-VW), 27m 05·28s.
4 Allen Berg, CDN (Ralt RT3/83-Toyota), 27m 15·20s.
5 Calvin Fish, GB (Ralt RT3/83-VW), 27m 20·69s.
6 Johnny Dumfries, GB (Ralt RT3/83-Toyota), 27m 34·55s.
7 Tony Trevor, GB (Ralt RT3/82-Toyota), 27m 33·16s; **8** Tim Lee-Davey, GB (Ralt RT3/82-Toyota), 27m 37·73s; **9** David Hunt, GB (Ralt RT3/83-Toyota), 27m 45·82s; **10** Paul Jackson, GB (Sparton SE420-VW), 27m 48·69s.
Fastest lap: Jones, 53·57s, 108·06 mph/173·91 km/h (record).
Marlboro Championship points: 1 Senna da Silva, 116; **2** Brundle, 94; **3** Jones, 60; **4** Fish, 52; **5** Berg, 28; **6** Hytten, 20.

EUROPEAN FORMULA 3 CHAMPIONSHIP RACE, Circuit Automobile Paul Armagnac Nogaro, France, September 4. European Formula 3 Championship, round 11. 30 laps of the 1·939-mile/3·120-km circuit, 58·17 miles/93·60 km.
1 Pier Luigi Martini, I (Ralt RT3-Alfa Romeo), 37m 59·97s, 91·83 mph/147·79 km/h.
2 Emanuele Pirro, I (Ralt RT3-Alfa Romeo), 38m 01·88s.
3 John Nielsen, DK (Ralt RT3/-VW), 38m 03·68s.
4 Bernard Santal, F (Ralt RT3-Alfa Romeo), 38m 15·28s.
5 Tommy Byrne, IRL (Ralt RT3-Toyota), 38m 26·90s.
6 Didier Theys, B (Ralt RT3-Alfa Romeo), 38m 27·96s.
7 Nils-Kristian Nissen, DK (Anson SA4-VW), 38m 28·40s; **8** Roberto Ravaglia, I (Ralt RT3-Toyota), 38m 28·66s; **9** Cathy Muller, F (Ralt RT3-VW), 38m 29·63s; **10** Patrick Gonin, F (Ralt RT3-VW), 38m 51·54s.
Fastest lap: Nielsen, 1m 14·78s, 93·33 mph/150·20 km/h.
European Championship points: 1 Nielsen, 46; **2** Pirro, 37; **3** Byrne, 35; **4** Martini, 33; **5** Ravaglia, 26; **6** Theys, 24.

MARLBORO CHAMPIONSHIP RACE, Oulton Park Circuit, Great Britain, September 11. Marlboro British Formula 3 Championship, round 17. 20 laps of the 1·654-mile/2·662-km circuit, 33·08 miles/53·24 km.
1 Martin Brundle, GB (Ralt RT3/83-Toyota), 19m 26·68s, 101·07 mph/162·66 km/h.
2 Calvin Fish, GB (Ralt RT3/83-VW), 19m 47·77s.
3 David Leslie, GB (Magnum 833-Toyota), 19m 50·37s.
4 Richard Trott, GB (Ralt RT3/83-Toyota), 19m 51·67s.
5 Allen Berg, CDN (Ralt RT3/83-Toyota), 19m 53·98s.
6 Eric Lang, USA (Ralt RT3/83-VW), 20m 08·14s.
7 Tony Trevor, GB (Ralt RT3/82-Toyota), 20m 08·18s; **8** Carlton Tingling, JA (Ralt RT3/82-VW), 20m 08·23s; **9** David Hunt, GB (Ralt RT3/83-Toyota), 20m 09·58s; **10** Leo Andersson, S (Ralt RT3/82-Toyota), 19 laps.
Fastest lap: Davy Jones, USA (Ralt RT3/83-VW), 57·18s, 104·13 mph/167·58 km/h (record).
Marlboro Championship points: 1 Senna da Silva, 116; **2** Brundle, 103; **3** Jones, 61; **4** Fish, 58; **5** Berg, 30; **6** Hytten, 20.

EUROPEAN FORMULA 3 CHAMPIONSHIP RACE, Circuito Permanente del Jarama, Spain, September 11. European Formula 3 Championship, round 12. 30 laps of the 2·058-mile/3·312-km circuit, 61·74 miles/99·36 km.
1 Pier Luigi Martini, I (Ralt RT3/83-Alfa Romeo), 42m 35·41s, 86·98 mph/139·98 km/h.
2 Emanuele Pirro, I (Ralt RT3/83-Alfa Romeo), 42m 41·49s.
3 John Nielsen, DK (Ralt RT3/83-VW), 42m 44·84s.
4 Claudio Langes, I (Anson SA4-Alfa Romeo), 42m 53·15s.
5 Roberto Ravaglia, I (Ralt RT3/83-Toyota), 42m 53·61s.
6 Didier Theys, B (Ralt RT3/83-Alfa Romeo), 42m 57·09s.
7 Adrian Campos, E (Avidesa 383-Alfa Romeo), 43m 00·32s; **8** Ruggero Melgrati, I (Ralt RT3/83-Alfa Romeo), 43m 04·41s; **9** Cathy Muller, F (Ralt RT3/83-VW), 43m 15·93s; **10** Bernard Santal, F (Ralt RT3/83-Toyota), 43m 19·18s.
Fastest lap: Martini, 1m 24·58s, 87·59 mph/140·97 km/h.
European Championship points: 1 Nielsen, 50; **2** Pirro, 43; **3** Martini, 42; **4** Byrne, 35; **5** Ravaglia, 28; **6** Theys, 25.

MARLBORO CHAMPIONSHIP RACE, Thruxton Circuit, Great Britain, September 18. Marlboro British Formula 3 Championship, round 18. 20 laps of the 2·356-mile/3·792-km circuit, 47·12 miles/75·84 km.
1 Martin Brundle, GB (Ralt RT3/83-Toyota), 25m 11·69s, 112·21 mph/180·58 km/h.
2 Davy Jones, USA (Ralt RT3/83-VW), 25m 13·93s.
3 Calvin Fish, GB (Ralt RT3/83-VW), 25m 20·10s.
4 David Leslie, GB (Magnum 833-Toyota), 25m 31·07s.
5 David Hunt, GB (Ralt RT3/83-Toyota), 25m 41·78s.
6 Eric Lang, USA (Ralt RT3/83-VW), 25m 50·07s.
7 Carlton Tingling, JA (Ralt RT3/82-VW), 26m 27·23s; **8** Ronnie Grant, GB (Ralt RT3/82-VW), 19 laps. No other finishers.
Fastest lap: Brundle, 1m 14·87s, 113·28 mph/182·31 km/h.
Marlboro Championship points: 1 Senna da Silva, 116; **2** Brundle, 113; **3** Jones, 67; **4** Fish, 62; **5** Berg, 30; **6** Leslie, 21.

EUROPEAN FORMULA 3 CHAMPIONSHIP RACE, Autodromo Dino Ferrari, Imola, Italy, September 25. European Formula 3 Championship, round 13. 18 laps of the 3·132-mile/5·040-km circuit, 56·38 miles/90·72 km.
1 Pier Luigi Martini, I (Ralt RT3/83-Alfa Romeo), 32m 34·17s, 103·84 mph/167·11 km/h.
2 John Nielsen, DK (Ralt RT3/83-VW), 32m 34·80s.
3 Ivan Capelli, I (Ralt RT3/83-Alfa Romeo), 32m 45·56s.
4 Emanuele Pirro, I (Ralt RT3/83-Alfa Romeo), 32m 45·58s.
5 Claudio Langes, I (Anson SA4-Alfa Romeo), 32m 46·44s.
6 Gerhard Berger, A (Ralt RT3/83-Alfa Romeo), 32m 50·87s.
7 Franco Forini, I (Dellara 383-Toyota), 32m 51·04s; **8** Didier Theys, B (Ralt RT3/83-Alfa Romeo), 33m 06·30s; **9** Kurt Thiim, DK (Ralt RT3/83-Alfa Romeo), 33m 08·61s; **10** Cathy Muller, F (Ralt RT3/83-VW), 33m 09·04s.
Fastest lap: Nielsen, 1m 47·16s, 105·21 mph/169·32 km/h.
European Championship points: 1 Nielsen, 56; **2** Martini, 51; **3** Pirro, 46; **4** Byrne, 35; **5** Ravaglia, 28; **6** Theys, 25.

MARLBORO CHAMPIONSHIP RACE, Silverstone Grand Prix Circuit, Great Britain, October 2. Marlboro British Formula 3 Championship, round 19. 20 lps of the 2·932-mile/4·719-km circuit, 58·64 miles/94·38 km.
1 Martin Brundle, GB (Ralt RT3/83-Toyota), 28m 55·23s, 121·65 mph/195·78 km/h.
2 Ayrton Senna da Silva, BR (Ralt RT3/83-Toyota), 28m 55·87s.
3 Davy Jones, USA (Ralt RT3/83-VW), 29m 12·39s.
4 Calvin Fish, GB (Ralt RT3/83-VW), 29m 24·08s.
5 Allen Berg, CDN (Ralt RT3/83-Toyota), 29m 30·94s.
6 David Leslie, GB (Magnum 833-Toyota), 29m 41·52s.
7 Mario Hytten, CH (Ralt RT3/.83-Toyota), 29m 49·02s; **8** Carlos Abella, E (Ralt RT3/83-Toyota), 30m 01·80s; **9** Paul Jackson, GB (Sparton SE420-VW), 30m 10·68s; **10** Mike Blanchet, GB (Ralt RT3/81-82-Toyota), 30m 13·11s.
Fastest lap: Brundle, 1m 26·02s, 122·80 mph/197·63 km/h.
Marlboro Championship points: 1 Brundle, 123; **2** Senna da Silva, 122; **3** Jones, 71; **4** Fish, 65; **5** Berg, 32; **6** Leslie, 22.

EUROPEAN FORMULA 3 CHAMPIONSHIP RACE, Donington Park Circuit, Great Britain, October 9. European Formula 3 Championship, round 14. 30 laps of the 1·9573-mile/3·1500-km circuit, 58·72 miles/94·50 km.
1 Martin Brundle, GB (Ralt RT3/83-Toyota), 37m 47·09s, 93·24 mph/150·05 km/h.
2 Pier Luigi Martini, I (Ralt RT3/83-Alfa Romeo), 38m 02·03s.
3 James Weaver, GB (Ralt RT3/83-VW), 38m 03·77s.
4 John Nielsen, DK (Ralt RT3/83-VW), 38m 05·59s.
5 Claudio Langes, I (Anson SA4-Alfa Romeo), 38m 05·60s.
6 Carlos Abella, E (Ralt RT3/83-Toyota), 38m 07·41s.
7 Ruggero Melgrati, I (Ralt RT3/83-Alfa Romeo), 38m 15·06s; **8** Didier Theys, B (Ralt RT3/83-Alfa Romeo), 38m 21·79s; **9** Emanuele Pirro, I (Ralt RT3/83-Alfa Romeo), 38m 22·14s; **10** Kurt Thiim, DK (Ralt RT3/83-Alfa Romeo), 38m 22·74s.
Fastest lap: Melgrati, 1m 12·21s, 97·58 mph/157·04 km/h.
European Championship points: 1 Nielsen, 59; **2** Martini, 57; **3** Pirro, 46; **4** Byrne, 35; **5** Ravaglia, 28; **6** Theys, 25.

MARLBORO CHAMPIONSHIP RACE, Thruxton Circuit, Great Britain, October 23. Marlboro British Formula 3 Championship, round 20. 15 laps of the 2·356-mile/3·792-km circuit, 35·34 miles/56·88 km.
1 Ayrton Senna da Silva, BR (Ralt RT3/83-Toyota), 18m 39·78s, 113·61 mph/182·84 km/h.
2 Davy Jones, USA (Ralt RT3/83-VW), 18m 45·21s.
3 Martin Brundle, GB (Ralt RT3/83-Toyota), 18m 48·31s.
4 Mario Hytten, CH (Sparton SE420-VW), 19m 01·01s.
5 Calvin Fish, GB (Ralt RT3/83-VW), 19m 01·63s.
6 Eric Lang, USA (Ralt RT3/83-VW), 19m 02·76s.
7 David Hunt, GB (Ralt RT3/83-Toyota), 19m 09·25s; **8** Mike Blanchet, GB (Ralt RT3/82-Toyota), 19m 17·35s; **9** Cartlton Tingling, JA (Ralt RT3/82-VW), 19m 22·66s. No other finishers.
Fastest lap: Senna da Silva, 1m 13·87s, 114·98 mph/185·04 km/h.

Final Marlboro Championship points:

1 Aryton Senna da Silva, BR	132
2 Martin Brundle, GB	123 (127)
3 Davy Jones, USA	77
4 Calvin Fish, GB	67
5 Allen Berg, CDN	32
6 Mario Hytten, CH	23

7 David Leslie, GB, 22; **8** Tony Trevor, GB, 9; **9** Johnny Dumfries, GB and Richard Trott, GB, 8; **11** Tim Lee-Davey, GB and David Hunt, GB, 2; **13** Mike Blanchet, GB and Carlton Tingling, JA, 1.

EUROPEAN FORMULA 3 CHAMPIONSHIP RACE, Croix-En-Ternois, France, October 23. European Formula 3 Championship, round 15. 48 laps of the 1·181-mile/1·900-km circuit, 56·69 miles/91·20 km.
1 Pier Luigi Martini, I (Ralt RT3/83-Alfa Romeo), 42m 40·75s, 79·66 mph/128·20 km/h.
2 Emanuele Pirro, I (Ralt RT3/83-Alfa Romeo), 42m 44·91s.
3 Roberto Ravaglia, I (Ralt RT3/83-Toyota), 42m 45·13s.
4 John Nielson, DK (Ralt RT3/83-VW), 42m 50·98s.
5 Ruggero Melgrati, I (Ralt RT3/83-Alfa Romeo), 43m 12·38s.
6 Ivan Capelli, I (Ralt RT3/83-Alfa Romeo), 43m 13·17s.
7 Didier Theys, B (Ralt RT3/83-Alfa Romeo), 43m 21·75s; **8** Patrick Gonin, F (Ralt RT3/83-VW), 43m 24·35s; **9** Cathy Muller, F (Ralt RT3/83-VW), 43m 26·03s; **10** Kurt Thiim, DK (Ralt RT3/83-Alfa Romeo), 43m 26·61s.
Fastest lap: Martini, 52·72s, 80·62 mph/129·74 km/h.

Final European Championship points:

1 Pier Luigi Martini, I	66
2 John Nielsen, DK	62
3 Emanuele Pirro, I	52
4 Tommy Byrne, IRL	35
5 Roberto Ravaglia, I	32
6 Didier Theys, B	25

7 Gerhard Berger, A and Martin Brundle, GB, 18; **9** Claudio Langes, I, 11; **10** Pascal Fabre, F, 8; **11** Nils-Kristian Nissen, DK, 7; **12** Enzo Coloni, I, Francois Hesnault, F and Michel Ferte, F, 6; **15** Ivan Capelli, I, 5; **16** Ruggero Melgrati, I and James Weaver, GB, 4; **18** Carlos Abella, E and Bernard Santal, F, 3; **20** John Bosch, NL, 2; **21** Max Busslinger, CH and Kurt Thiim, DK, 1.

World Endurance Championship/European Endurance Championship

MONZA 1000 KM/TROFEO FILIPPO CARACCIOLO, Autodromo Nazionale di Monza, Italy, April 10. World Endurance Championship, round 1. European Endurance Championship, round 1. 173 laps of the 3·604-mile/5·800-km circuit, 623·49 miles/1003·40 km.
1 Bob Wollek/Thierry Boutsen, F/B (2·6 t/c Porsche 956), 5h 12m 06·9s, 119·86 mph/192·90 km/h (1st Group C).
2 Jacky Ickx/Jochen Mass, B/D (2·6 t/c Porsche 956), 5h 13m 19·8s.
3 Rolf Stommelen/Hans Heyer/Clemens Schickentanz, D/D/D (2·6 t/c Porsche 956), 170 laps.
4 Axel Plankenhorn/Jurgen Barth/Jurgen Lassig, D/D/D (2·6 t/c Porsche 956), 163.
5 John Fitzpatrick/David Hobbs, GB/GB (2·6 t/c Porsche 956), 161.
6 Jan Lammers/Tiff Needell/Richard Lloyd, NL/GB/GB (2·6 t/c Porsche 956), 161.
7 Derek Bell/Al Holbert, GB/USA (2·6 t/c Porsche 956), 161; **8** Dullio Truffo/Roberto Sigala, I/I (1·4 t/c Lancia LC1), 154; **9** Riccardo Patrese/Michele Alboreto, I/I (2·6 t/c Lancia Martini LC2), 151; **10** Edgar Doren/Christian Jurgensson, D/D (3·5 BMW M1), 145 (1st Group B).
Fastest lap: Fitzpatrick, 1m 40·4s, 129·23 mph/207·98 km/h (record).
Championship points. World and European Drivers: 1 Wollek and Boutsen, 20; **3** Ickx and Mass, 15; **5** Stommelen, Heyer and Schickentanz, 12.
World Manufacturers: 1 Porsche, 20; **2** Lancia, 3; **3** BMW, 1.

GRAND PRIX INTERNATIONAL 1000 KMS, Silverstone Grand Prix Circuit, Great Britain, May 8. World Endurance Championship, round 2. European Endurance Championship, round 2. 212 laps of the 2·932 mile/4·719-km circuit, 621·58 miles/1000·43 km.
1 Derek Bell/Stefan Bellof, GB/D (2·6 t/c Porsche 956), 5h 02m 42·93s, 123·20 mph/198·27 km/h (1st Group C).
2 Bob Wollek/Stefan Johansson, F/S (2·6 t/c Porsche 956), 5h 03m 36·14s.
3 Jan Lammers/Thierry Boutsen, NL/B (2·6 t/c Porsche 956), 205 laps.
4 Jurgen Lassig/Axel Plankenhorn/Harald Grohs, D/D/D (2·6 t/c Porsche 956), 201.
5 Alan Jones/Vern Schuppan, AUS/AUS (2·6 t/c Porsche 956), 201.
6 Tony Dron/Richard Cleare, GB/GB (3·0 t/c Kramer-Porsche C-K5), 197.
7 Ray Mallock/Mike Salmon, GB/GB (5·4 Nimrod-Aston Martin C2), 184;
8 John Fitzpatrick/David Hobbs, GB/GB (2·6 Porsche 956), 180; **9** Martino Finotto/Carlo Facetti, I/I (1·8 t/c Alba-Giannini), 172 (1st Junior Group C); **10** Jens Winther/David Mercer/Wolfgang Braun, D/GB/D (3·5 BMW M1), 169 (1st Group B).
Fastest lap: Riccardo Patrese, I (2·6 t/c Lancia Martini LC2), 1m 18·39s, 135·65 mph/218·31 km/h (record).
Championship points. World and European Drivers: 1 Wollek, 35; **2** Boutsen, 32; **3** Bell, 24; **4** Plankenhorn, Lassig and Bellof, 20.
World Manufacturers: 1 Porsche, 40; **2** Nimrod, 4; **3** Lancia, 3; **4** Alba and BMW, 2.

ADAC BITBURGER 1000 KMS, Nurburgring Nordschleife, German Federal Republic, May 29. World Endurance Championship, round 3. European Endurance Championship, round 3. 44 laps of the 12·94-mile/20·83-km circuit, 569·36 miles/916·52 km.
1 Jochen Mass/Jacky Ickx, D/B (2·6 t/c Porsche 956), 5h 26m 34·63s, 104·64 mph/168·40 km/h (1st Group C).
2 Bob Wollek/Stefan Johansson, F/S (2·6 t/c Porsche 956), 5h 30m 34·99s.
3 Keke Rosberg/Jan Lammers/Jonathan Palmer, SF/NL/GB (2·6 t/c Porsche 956), 43 laps.
4 Hans Heyer/Axel Plankenhorn/Jurgen Lassig, D/D/D (2·6 t/c Porsche 956), 42.
5 Oscar Larrauri/Massimo Sigala, RA/I (1·4 t/c Lancia LC1), 40.
6 John Fitzpatrick/David Hobbs, GB/GB (2·6 t/c Porsche 956), 39.
7 Edgar Doren/Helmut Gall/Jurgen Hamelmann, D/D/D (3·3 t/c Porsche 930), 37 (1st Group B); **8** Claude Haldi/Klaus Utz, CH/D (2·0 t/c Porsche 924GTS), 37; **9** Franz-Josef Brohling/Axel Felder/Jochen Felder, D/D/D (1·6 Ford Escort RS), 36; **10** Georg Memminger/Heinz Kuhn-Weiss/Gunther Steckkoning, D/D/D (3·3 t/c Porsche 930), 36.
Fastest lap: Stefan Bellof, D (2·6 t/c Porsche 956), 6m 25·91s, 120·75 mph/194·33 km/h (record).
Championship points. World and European Drivers: 1 Wollek, 50; **2** Ickx and Mass, 35; **4** Boutsen, 32; **5** Johansson, Lammers, Plankenhorn and Lassig, 30.
World Manufacturers: 1 Porsche, 60; **2** Lancia, 11; **3** Nimrod, 4; **4** Alba, Ford and BMW, 2.

TROPEE DINERS CLUB/SPA 1000 KMS, Spa-Francorchamps, Belgium, September 4. World Endurance Championship, round 5. European Endurance Championship, round 5. 144 laps of the 4·332-mile/6·972-km circuit, 623·81 miles/1003·97 km.
1 Jacky Ickx/Jochen Mass, B/D (2·6 t/c Porsche 956), 5h 44m 33·52s, 108·63 mph/174·82 km/h (1st Group C).
2 Derek Bell/Stefan Bellof, GB/D (2.6 t/c Porsche 956), 5h 45m 36·54s.
3 John Fitzpatrick/David Hobbs, GB/GB (2.6 t/c Porsche 956), 139 laps.
4 Hans Stuck/Harald Grohs/Walter Brun, D/D/CH (2.6 t/c Porsche 956), 138.
5 Jurgen Lassig/Axel Plankenhorn/Herve Regout, D/D/B (2.6 t/c Porsche 956), 136.
6 Giorgio Francia/Paolo Barilla, I/I (2.6 t/c Lancia LC2), 134.
7 Riccardo Patrese/Teo Fabi, I/I (2.6 t/c Lancia LC2), 132; **8** Dieter Schornstein/Jean-Michel Martin/"John Winter", D/B/D (2.7 t/c Porsche 936C), 127; **9** Jan Lammers/Thierry Boutsen, NL/B (2.6 t/c Porsche 956), 127; **10** Bruno Sotty/Valentin Bertapelle/Gerard Cuynet, F/F/F (3.5 URD C 82-BMW), 121.
Fastest lap: Bellof, 2m 14·11s, 116·02 mph/186·72 km/h.
Championship points. World and European Drivers: 1 Ickx, 70; **2** Wollek, 56; **3** Mass, 55; **4** Bell, 54; **5** Lassig and Plankenhorn, 42.
World Manufacturers: 1 Porsche, 100; **2** Lancia, 17; **3** Nimrod, 4; **4** Sauber, Alba, Ford and BMW, 2; **8** URD, 1.

GRAND PRIX INTERNATIONAL 1000 KMS, Brands Hatch Grand Prix Circuit, Great Britain, September 18. European Endurance Championship, round 6. 232 laps of the 2·6136-mile/4·2060-km circuit, 606·36 miles/975·79 km (shortened to 6 hours due rain).
1 Derek Warwick/John Fitzpatrick, GB/GB (2.6 t/c Porsche 956), 6h 01m 01·74s, 100·77 mph/162·17 km/h (1st Group C).
2 Jacky Ickx/Jochen Mass, B/D (2.6 t/c Porsche 956), 231 laps.
3 Derek Bell/Stefan Bellof, GB/D (2.6 t/c Porsche 956), 231.
4 Riccardo Patrese/Michele Alboreto, I/I (2.6 t/c Lancia LC2-83), 226.
5 Jurgen Lassig/Axel Plankenhorn/Herve Regout, D/D/B (2.6 t/c Porsche 956), 216.
6 Bob Wollek/Stefan Johansson, F/S (2.6 t/c Porsche 956), 210.
7 Hans Heyer/Dieter Schornstein/Volkert Merl, D/D/D (2.8 t/c Porsche 936C), 207; **8** Emilio de Villota/Dudley Wood/Skeeter McKitterick, E/GB/USA (3.9 Grid S 1-Cosworth DFL), 204; **9** Jonathan Palmer/Jan Lammers, GB/NL (2.6 t/c Porsche 956), 201; **10** Carlo Facetti/Martino Finotto, I/I (1.8 t/c Alba-Giannini), 200 (1st Junior Group C).
Fastest lap: Bellof, 1m 19·88s, 117·78 mph/189·55 km/h.
Championship points. European Drivers: 1 Ickx, 85; **2** Mass, 70; **3** Bell, 66; **4** Wollek, 62; **5** Lassig and Plankenhorn, 50.

FUJI 1000 KMS, Fuji International Speedway, Japan, October 2. World Endurance Championship, round 6. 225 laps of the 2·7067-mile/2·3560-km circuit, 609·01 miles/980·10 km.
1 Derek Bell/Stefan Bellof, GB/D (2.6 t/c Porsche 956), 4h 57m 06·36s, 122·99 mph/197·933 km/h (1st Group C).
2 Jacky Ickx/Jochen Mass, B/D (2.6 t/c Porsche 956), 4h 57m 56·29s.
3 Vern Schuppan/Naohiro Fumita, AUS/J (2.6 t/c Porsche 956), 219 laps.
4 Henri Pescarolo/Thierry Boutsen, F/B (2.6 t/c Porsche 956), 218.
5 Bob Wollek/Hans Heyer, F/D (2.6 t/c Porsche 956), 209.
6 Kenji Takahashi/Clemens Schickentanz, J/D (2.6 t/c Porsche 956), 203.
7 Kazuyoshi Hoshino/Akira Hagiwara, J/J (2.1 t/c March 83G-Nissan), 198;
8 Kiyoshi Misaki/Masakazu Nakamura, J/J (2.1 March 75S/C-Toyota), 198 (1st Junior Group C); **9** Keiji Matsumoto/Kaoru Hoshino/Masanori Sekiya, J/J/J (2.1 t/c Dome 83C-Toyota), 196; **10** Fulvio Ballabio/Max Welti, I/CH (3.5 Sauber C 7-BMW), 196.
Fastest lap: Not given.
Championship points. World Drivers: 1 Ickx, 85; **2** Mass, 70; **3** Wollek and Bell, 64; **5** Boutsen, 44; **6** Lassig and Plankenhorn, 42.
World Manufacturers: 1 Porsche, 120; **2** Lancia, 17; **3** March and Nimrod, 4; **5** Sauber, 3; **6** Dome, Alba, Ford and BMW, 2; **10** URD, 1.

1000 KMS di IMOLA, Autodromo Dino Ferrari, Imola, Italy, October 16. European Endurance Championship, round 7. 191 laps of the 3·132-mile/5·040-km circuit, 598·21 miles/962·64 km (race shortened to 6 hours due rain).
1 Teo Fabi/Hans Heyer, I/D (2.6 t/c Lancia LC2/83), 6h 00m 13·76s, 99·574 mph/160·248 km/h (1st Group C).
2 John Fitzpatrick/David Hobbs, GB/GB (2.6 t/c Porsche 956), 190 laps.
3 Bob Wollek/Stefan Johansson, F/S (2.6 t/c Porsche 956), 188.
4 Derek Bell/Jonathan Palmer, GB/GB (2.6 t/c Porsche 956), 180.
5 Jurgen Lassig/Axel Plankenhorn/Herve Regout, D/D/B (2.6 t/c Porsche 956), 180.
6 Dieter Schronstein/Volkert Merl, D/D (2.6 t/c Porsche 956), 179.
7 Neil Crang/Gordon Spice, AUS/GB (5.0 Tiga GC83-Chevrolet), 173; **8** "Gimax"/Oscar Larrauri, I/RA (1.4 t/c Lancia LC1); **9** Loris Kessel/Laurant Ferrier/Rolf Biland, CH/CH/CH (3.3 Cheetah G603-Cosworth DFL), 159; **10** Edgar Doren/Helmut Gall, D/D (3.5 BMW M1), 158 (1st Group B).
Fastest lap: Alessandro Nannini, I (2.6 t/c Lancia LC2/83), 1m 40·90s, 111·735 mph/179·820 km/h.
Championship points. European Drivers: 1 Ickx, 85; **2** Bell, 76; **3** Wollek, 74; **4** Mass, 70; **5** Fitzpatrick, 64; **6** Lassig and Plankenhorn, 58.

1000 KMS di MUGELLO, Autodromo Internazionale Mugello, Italy, October 23. European Endurance Championship, round 8. 187 laps of the 3·259-mile/5·245-km circuit, 609·43 miles/980·82 km (race stopped at 6 hour mark).
1 Bob Wollek/Stefan Johansson, F/S (2.6 t/c Porsche 956) 6h 00m 00·35s, 101·58 mph/163·48 km/h (1st Group C).
2 Riccardo Patrese/Alessandro Nannini, I/I (2.6 t/c Lancia LC2-83), 184 laps.
3 Derek Bell/Jonathan Palmer/Henri Toivonen, GB/GB/SF (2.6 t/c Porsche 956), 180.
4 John Fitzpatrick/David Hobbs/Thierry Boutsen, GB/GB/B (2.6 t/c Porsche 956), 179.
5 Jurgen Lassig/Axel Plankenhorn/Herve Regout, D/D/B (2.6 t/c Porsche 956), 179.
6 Volkert Merl/Dieter Schornstein/Gianpiero Moretti, D/D/I (2.6 t/c Porsche 956), 177.
7 Oscar Larrauri/"Gimax", RA/I (1.4 t/c Lancia LC1), 169; **8** Loris Kessel/Laurent Ferrier, CH/CH (3.3 Cheetah G603-Cosworth DFL), 165; **9** Mario Galiceti/Eduardo Covoni, I/I (1.4 t/c Lancia LC1), 157; **10** Yves Courage/Aldo Bertuzzi/Gianni Giudici, F/I/I (3.3 Cougar C01B-Cosworth DFL), 157.
Fastest lap: Hobbs, 1m 47·72s, 108·92 mph/175·29 km/h (record).

Final European Endurance Championship points:

1 Bob Wollek, F	88 (94)
2 Jacky Ickx, B	85
3 Derek Bell, GB	84 (88)
4 Stefan Johansson, S	74
5 John Fitzpatrick, GB	71
6 Jochen Mass, D	70

7 Han Heyer, D, 56; **8** David Hobbs, GB, Jurgen Lassig, D and Axel Plankenhorn, D, 54; **10** Stefan Bellof, D, 47; **12** Thierry Boutsen, B, 44; **13** Jonathan Palmer, GB, 39; **14** Jan Lammers, NL, 37; **15** Herve Regout, B, 36.

Final World Endurance Championship results will be given in Autocourse 1984/85.

Le Mans 24 Hours

51 GRAND PRIX D'ENDURANCE, LES 24 HEURES DU MANS, Circuit de la Sarthe, Le Mans, France, June 18/19. World Endurance Championship, round 4. European Endurance Championship round 4. 370 laps of the 8·467-mile/13·626-km circuit, 3132·79 miles/5041·62 km.
1 Vern Schuppan/Hurley Haywood/Al Holbert, AUS/USA/USA (2.6 t/c Porsche 956) 370 laps, 130·53 mph/210·07 km/h. (1st Group C).
2 Jacky Ickx/Derek Bell, B/GB (2.6 t/c Porsche 956), 370 laps.
3 Mario Andretti/Mike Andretti/Philippe Alliot, USA/USA/F (2.6 t/c Porsche 956), 364.
4 Volkert Merl/Clemens Schickentanz/Maurizio DeNarvaez, D/D/COL (2.6 t/c Porsche 956), 361.
5 John Fitzpatrick/Guy Edwards/Rupert Keegan, GB/GB/GB (2.6 t/c Porsche 956), 358.
6 Klaus Ludwig/Stefan Johansson/Bob Wollek, D/S/F (2.6 t/c Porsche 956), 354.
7 Axel Plankenhorn/Desire Wilson/Jurgen Lassig, D/ZA/D (2.6 t/c Porsche 956), 347; **8** Jonathan Palmer/Richard Lloyd/Jan Lammers, GB/GB/NL (2.6 t/c Porsche 956), 339. **9** Diego Montoya/Tony Garcia/Albert Naon, USA/USA/USA (3.5 Sauber C7-BMW), 338; **10** Preston Henn/Claude Ballot-Lena/Jean-Louis Schlesser, USA/F/F (2.6 t/c Porsche 956), 327; **11** John Cooper/Paul Smith/David Ovey, GB/GB/GB (3.3 t/c Porsche 930), 303 (1st Group B); **12** Takashi Yorino/Yoshini Katayama/Yojiro Terada, J/J/J (1.3 Mazda 717C), 302 (1st Group C Junior); **13** Heinz Kuhn-Weiss/Georg Memminger/Fritz Muller, D/D/D (3.3 t/c Porsche 930), 299; **14** Bruno Sotty/Gerard Cuynet, F/F (3.5 URD C81-BMW), 292; **15** Jacques Almeras/Jean-Marie Almeras/Jacques Guillot, F/F/F (3.3 t/c Porsche 930), 279; **16** Roger Dorchy/Alain Couderc/Pascal Fabre, F/F/F (2.8 t/c WM P83-Peugeot), 278; **17** Tiff Needell/Nick Faure/Steve O'Rourke, GB/GB/GB (5.3 EMKA-Aston Martin), 275; **18** Steve Soper/Jeff Allam/James Weaver, GB/GB/GB (1.3 Mazda 717C), 267; **19** Lucien Guitteny/Pierre Yver/Bernard de Dryver, F/F/B (3.3 Rondeau M382-Cosworth DFL), 266; **20** Daniel Herregods/Pascal Witmeur/Jean-Paul Liberti, B/B/B (3.3 Rondeau M382-Cosworth DFL), 265; **21** Raymond Touroul/Michel Lateste/ Michel Bienvault, F/F/F (3.3 t/c Porsche 930), 264.
Running but not classified: Raymond Boutinard/Alain le Page/Patrick Gonin, F/F/F (4.7 Porsche 928S), 234; Francois Hesnault/Thierry Perrier/Bernard Salem, F/F/F (1.4 t/c Lancia LC1), 232; Claude Haldi/Gunther Steckkonig/Bernd Schiller, CH/D/D (3.3 t/c Porsche 930), 217; Oscar Larrauri/Massimo Sigala/Max Cohen-Olivar, RA/I/MOR (1.4 t/c Lancia LC1), 217; John Sheldon/Francois Duret/Ian Harrower, GB/F/GB (3.0 De Cadanet Lola MM-Cosworth DFV), 214.
Fastest lap: Ickx, 3m 29·7s, 145·35 mph/233·92 km/h (record).
Retired: Jochen Mass/Stefan Bellof, D/D (2.6 t/c Porsche 956), 281, engine; Ray Mallock/Mike Salmon/Steve Earle, GB/GB/GB (5.3 Nimrod NRA-C2-Aston Martin), 218, engine; Leopold von Beyern/Angelo Pallavicini/Jens Winther, D/CH/DK (3.5 BMW M1), 180, gearbox; Carlo Facetti/Martino Finotto/Marco Vanoli, I/I/CH (1.8 t/c Alba-Giannini), 158, engine; Hubert Streibig/Jacques Heuclin/Noel del Bello, F/F/F (2.2 Sthemo-BMW), 71, engine; Thierry Boutsen/Henri Pescarlo, B/F (3.9 Rondeau M482-Cosworth DFL), 174, engine; Paolo Barilla/Alessandro Nannini/Jean-Claude Andruet, I/I/F (2.6 t/c Lancia LC2), 135, engine; Alain Ferte/Michel Ferte/Jean Rondeau, F/F/F (3.9 Rondeau M482-Cosworth DFL), 90, engine; Ralph Kent-Cooke/Jim Adams/Francois Servanin, USA/USA/F (3.9 Lola T610-Cosworth DFL), 165, overheating; Piercarlo Ghinzani/Hans Heyer, I/D (2.6 t/c Lancia LC2), 121, turbo; Jean-Daniel Raulet/Marcel Pignard/Didier Theys, F/F/B (2.8 t/c WM P83-Peugeot), 102, engine; Alain de Cadanet/Yves Courage/Michel Dubois, GB/F/F (3.3 Cougar C01B-Cosworth DFL), 86, engine; Vic Elford/Anny-Charlotte Verney/Joel Gouhier, GB/F/F (3.0 Rondeau M379-Cosworth DFV), 136, engine; John Fitzpatrick/David Hobbs/Dieter Quester, GB/GB/A (2.6 t/c Porsche 956), 135, fuel pump; Francois Migault/David Kennedy/Martin Birrane, F/IRL/GB (3.3 Ford C100-Cosworth DFL), 16, out of fuel; Eliseo Salazar/Chris Craft/.Nick Mason, RCH/GB/GB (3.3 Dome C-Cosworth DFL), 75, gearbox; Jacques Villeneuve/Ludwig Heimrath Jnr/David Deacon, CDN/CDN/CDN (3.9 Sehcar-Cosworth DFL), 68, exhaust; Derek Warwick/Frank Jelinski/Patrick Gaillard, GB/D/F (3.0 t/c Kramer C-K5-Porsche), 76, headgasket; Fred Stiff/Dudley Wood/Ray Ratcliff, USA/GB/USA (3.9 Grid S1-Cosworth DFL), 69, engine; Dany Snobeck/Xavier Lapeyre/Alain Cudini, F/F/F (3.3 Rondeau M382-Cosworth DFL), 31, engine; Tony Dron/Richard Cleare/Richard Jones, GB/GB/GB (3.0 t/c Kramer C-K5-Porsche), 8, battery; Michele Alboreto/Teo Fabi, I/I (2.6 t/c Lancia LC2), 27, transmission; Jean-Pierre Jaussaud/Philippe Streiff, F/F (3.9 Rondeau M482-Cosworth DFL), 12, oil leak; Jean-Michel Martin/Philippe Martin/Marc Duez, B/B/B (2.8 t/c Porsche 936C), 9, fuel pump; Alexandre Yvon/Jean-Marie Lemerle/Michael Krankenberg, F/F/D (3.3 t/c Porsche 930), 7, gearbox.
Championship points. World and European Drivers: 1 Wollek, 56; **2** Ickx, 50; **3** Bell, 39; **4** Johansson, 36; **5** Mass, 35; **6** Plankenhorn and Lassig, 34.
World Manufacturers: 1 Porsche, 80; **2** Lancia, 11; **3** Nimrod, 4; **4** Sauber, Alba, Ford and BMW, 2.

European Touring Car Championship

500 KM di MONZA, Autodromo Nazionale di Monza, Italy, March 20. European Touring Car Championship, round 1. 87 laps of the 3·604-mile/5·800-km circuit, 313·55 miles/504·60 km.
1 Dieter Quester/Carlo Rossi, A/I (3.5 BMW 635 CSi), 3h 07m 54·6s, 100·11 mph/161·11 km/h (1st over 2500cc class).
2 Tom Walkinshaw/Chuck Nicholson, GB/GB (5.3 Jaguar XJ-S), 3h 07m 58·1s.
3 Hans Heyer/Amin Hahne, D/D (3.5 BMW 635 CSi), 3h 08m 08·7s.
4 Thierry Boutsen, B (3.5 BMW 635 CSi), 3h 08m 16·4s.
5 Hans Stuck/Walter Brun, D/CH (3.5 BMW 635 CSi), 86 laps.
6 Helmut Kelleners/Umberto Grano, D/I (3.5 BMW 635 CSi), 86.
7 Michel Delcourt/Dany Swyssen/Jean-Marie Baert, B/B/B (3.5 BMW 635 CSi), 85; **8** Marco Vanoli/Martino Finotto, I/I (3.5 BMW 635 CSi), 85; **9** Guiseppe Briozzo/Hans Stalder/Georges Bosshard, I/D/D (3.5 BMW 635 CSi), 84; **10** Michel de Deyne/Marc Duez, B/B (5.7 Chevrolet Camaro), 83.
Fastest lap: Walkinshaw, 2m 05·5s, 103·38 mph/166·37 km/h.
Other class winners. 1601cc-2500cc: Lella Lombardi/Giancarlo Naddeo, I/I (2.5 Alfa Romeo GTV6), 82. **Up to 1600 cc:** Pierre Fermine/Simon de Liedekerke, B/B (1.6 VW Golf GTI), 77.
Championship points. Drivers: 1 Quester and Rossi, 29; **3** Walkinshaw and Nicholson, 21; **5** Lombardi, Naddeo, Fermine and de Liedekerke, 20.
Manufacturers: 1 Alfa Romeo, VW and BMW, 20; **4** Jaguar, 15; **5** Opel, 12.

500 KM di VALLELUNGA, Autodromo di Vallelunga, Italy, April 10. European Touring Car Championship, round 2. 157 laps of the 1·988-mile/3·200-km circuit, 312·12 miles/502·40 km.
1 Helmut Kelleners/Umberto Grano, D/I (3.5 BMW 635 CSi), 3h 51m 41·94s, 80·84 mph/130·10 km/h. (1st over 2500cc class).
2 Manfred Winkelhock/Dieter Quester, D/A (3.5 BMW 635 CSi), 3h 51m 50·87s.
3 Chuck Nicholson/Pierre Dieudonne/Tom Walkinshaw, GB/B/GB (5.3 Jaguar XJ-S), 156 laps.
4 Michel Delcourt/Dany Swyssen, B/B (3.5 BMW 635 CSi), 155.
5 Armin Hahne/Jean Xhenceval, D/B (3.5 BMW 635 CSi), 155.
6 Hans Stuck/Walter Brun, D/CH (3.5 BMW 635 CSi), 154.
7 Zdenek Vojtech/Bretislav Enge, CS/CS (3.5 BMW 635 CSi), 154; **8** Marco Vanoli/Georges Bosshard, I/D (3.5 BMW 635 CSi), 153; **9** Urs Knecht/Giuseppe Briozzo/Hans Stalder, D/I/D (3.5 BMW 635 CSi), 152; **10** Maurizio Micangeli/Fritz Muller, I/D (2.8 BMW 528i), 152.
Fastest lap: Walkinshaw, 1m 25·91s, 83·33 mph/134·11 km/h.
Other class winners. 1601cc-2500cc: Roberto Marazzi/Dagmar Suster/Giancarlo Naddeo, I/I/I (2.5 Alfa Romeo GTV6), 147. **Up to 1600cc:** Peter Siekel/.Lothar Schorg, D/D (1.6 Audi 80), 147.
Championship points. Drivers: 1 Quester, 50; **2** Kelleners and Grano, 36; **4** Fermine and de Liedekerke, 30; **6** Manage, Thibaut, Herregods and Bergmeister, 27.
Manufacturers: 1 BMW and Alfa Romeo, 40; **3** VW, 35; **4** Jaguar, 27; **5** Audi, 20; **6** Opel, 12.

DONINGTON 500 KMS, Donington Park Circuit, Great Britain, May 1. European Touring Car Championship, round 3. 160 laps of the 1·9573-mile/3·150-km circuit, 313·17 miles/504·00 km.
1 John Fitzpatrick/Enzo Calderari/Martin Brundle, GB/I/GB (5.3 Jaguar XJ-S), 4h 23m 24·49s, 71·33 mph/114·79 km/h (1st over 2500cc class).
2 Hans Heyer/Dieter Quester, D/A (3.5 BMW 635 CSi), 4h 23m 44·95s.
3 Walter Brun/Hans Stuck, D/CH (3.5 BMW 635 CSi), 4h 24m 40·60s.
4 Zdenek Vojtech/Bretislav Enge, CS/CS (3.5 BMW 635 CSi), 157 laps.
5 Tom Walkinshaw/Chuck Nicholson, GB/GB (5.3 Jaguar XJ-S), 156.
6 Carlo Rossi/Marco Vanoli, I/CH (3.5 BMW 635 CSi), 155.
7 Thomas Lindstrom/Stanley Dickens, S/S (2.1 t/c Volvo 240 Turbo), 153; **8** Dany Swyssen/Michel Delcourt, B/B (3.5 BMW 635 CSi), 153; **9** Steve Soper/Jeff Allam, GB/GB (3.5 Rover Vitesse), 153; **10** Philippe Menage/Alain Thibaut, B/B (1.6 VW Scirocco), 153 (1st up to 1600cc class).
Fastest lap: Helmut Kelleners, D (BMW 635 CSi), 1m 32·02s, 76·57 mph/123·23 km/h.
Other class winners. 1601cc-2500cc; Giorgio Francia/Marco Micangeli, I/I (2.5 Alfa Romeo GTV6), 151.
Championship points. Drivers: 1 Quester, 71; **2** Menage and Thaibaut, 47; **4** Fermine and de Liedekerke, 40; **6** Heyer, 37.
Manufacturers: 1 Alfa Romeo, 60; **2** VW and BMW, 55; **4** Jaguar, 47; **5** Audi, 35; **6** Opel, 12.

ENNA-PERGUSA 500 KMS, Ente Autodromo di Pergusa, Enna, Sicily, May 15. European Touring Car Championship, round 4. 102 laps of the 3·076-mile/4·950-km circuit, 313·75 miles/504·90 km.
1 Tom Walkinshaw/Chuck Nicholson, GB/GB (5.3 Jaguar XJ-S), 3h 16m 50·08s, 95·63 mph/153·90 km/h (1st over 2500cc class).
2 Helmut Kelleners/Umberto Grano, D/I (3.5 BMW 635 CSi), 3h 17m 46·61s.
3 Marco Vanoli/Rene Hollinger, I/D (3.5 BMW 635 CSi), 101 laps.
4 Hans Stuck/Walter Brun, D/CH (3.5 BMW 635 CSi), 101.
5 Giorgio Francia/Marco Micangeli, I/I (2.5 Alfa Romeo GTV 6), 99 (1st 1601cc-2500cc class).
6 Renato Drovandi/Gianfranco Brancatelli, I/I (2.5 Alfa Romeo GTV6), 99.
7 Dominique Fornage/Philippe Haezebrouck, F/B (3.5 BMW 635 CSi), 98; **8** Giuseppe Briozzo/Hans Stalder/Georges Bosshard, I/D/D (3.5 BMW 635 CSi), 98; **9** Toni Fischaber/Manfred Trint, D/D (2.5 Alfa Romeo GTV6), 97; **10** Robert Schumacher/Hermann Tilke, D/D (2.0 Opel Kadett GT/E), 96.
Fastest lap: Not available.
Other class winners. Up to 1600cc: Peter Seikel/Lothar Schorg, D/D (1.6 Audi 80), 94.
Championship points. Drivers: 1 Quester, 71; **2** Walkinshaw, 60; **3** Menage and Thibaut, 59; **5** Kelleners and Grano, 57.
Manufacturers: 1 Alfa Romeo, 80; **2** VW and BMW, 70; **4** Jaguar, 67; **5** Audi, 55; **6** Opel, 22.

MUGELLO 500 KMS, Autodromo Internazionale del Mugello, Italy, May 22. European Touring Car Championship, round 5. 96 laps of the 3·259-mile/5·245-km circuit, 312·86 miles/503·52 km.
1 Helmut Kelleners/Umberto Grano, D/I (3.5 BMW 635 CSi), 3h 40m 54·09s, 84·98 mph/136·76 km/h (1st over 2500cc class).
2 Zdenek Vojtech/Bretislav Enge, CS/CS (3.5 BMW 635 CSi), 3h 41m 15·77s.
3 Tom Walkinshaw/John Fitzpatrick, GB/GB (5.3 Jaguar XJ-S), 3h 41m 48·37s.
4 Hans Stuck/Walter Brun, D/CH (3.5 BMW 635 CSi), 3h 42m 09·87s.
5 Dieter Quester/Hans Heyer, A/D (3.5 BMW 635 CSi), 3h 42m 15·12s.
6 Marco Vanoli/Martino Finotto, I/I (3.5 BMW 635 CSi), 95 laps.
7 Michel Delcourt/Dany Swyssen, B/B (3.5 BMW 635 CSi), 95; **8** Jean-Louis Bos/Christian Duby, F/F (3.5 BMW 635 CSi), 95; **9** Giorgio Francia/Marco Micangeli, I/I (2.5 Alfa Romeo GTV6), 94 (1st 1601cc-2500cc class); **10** "Davit"/Francois-Xavier Boucher, B/B (2.8 BMW 528 i), 95.
Fastest lap: Kelleners/Grano, 2m 14·86s, 87·00 mph/140·01 km/h.
Other Class winners: Up to 1600cc: Philippe Menage/Alain Thibaut, B/B (1.6 VW Scirocco), 89.
Championship points. Drivers: 1 Kelleners and Grano, 86; **3** Quester, 81; **4** Menage and Thibaut, 79; **6** Walkinshaw, 76.
Manufacturers: 1 Alfa Romeo, 100; **2** VW and BMW, 90; **4** Jaguar, 79; **5** Audi, 70; **6** Opel, 26.

EUROPEAN TOURING CAR CHAMPIONSHIP RACE, Brno, Czechoslovakia, June 12. European Touring Car Championship, round 6. 56 laps of the 6·788-mile/10·925-km circuit, 380·13 miles/611·80 km.
1 Tom Walkinshaw/Chuck Nicholson, GB/GB (5.3 Jaguar XJ-S), 3h 31m 14·23s, 107·92 mph/173·68 km/h (1st over 2500cc class).
2 Dieter Quester/Hans Heyer, A/D (3.5 BMW 635 CSi), 55 laps.
3 Hans Stuck/Walter Brun, D/CH (3.5 BMW 635 CSi), 55.
4 Michel Delcourt/Dany Swyssen, B/B (3.5 BMW 635 CSi), 55.
5 Walter Nussbaumer/Herbert Hartge, D/D (3.5 BMW 635 CSi), 55.
6 Enzo Calderari/Pierre Dieudonne, I/B (5.3 Jaguar XJ-S), 55.
7 Marco Vanoli/Rene Hollinger, I/D (3.5 BMW 635 CSi), 54; **8** Jean-Louis Bos/Christian Duby/Jean Krucker, F/F/CH (3.5 BMW 635 CSi), 54; **9** Dominique Fornage/Christian Dorche, F/F (3.5 BMW 635 CSi), 54; **10** Giuseppe Briozzo/Hans-Jurgen Durig/Urs Knecht, I/D/D (3.5 BMW 635 CSi), 53.
Fastest lap: Nicholson, 3m 39·18s, 111·49 mph/179·43 km/h.
Other class winners: Up to 1600cc: Axel Huweler/Alfons Hohenester, D/D (1.6 VW Golf GTI), 51. **1601cc-2500cc:** Giorgio Francia/Marco Micangeli, I/I (2.5 Alfa Romeo GTV6), 52.
Championship points. Drivers: 1 Walkinshaw, 105; **2** Quester, 102; **3** Kelleners and Grano, 86; **5** Seikel and Schorg, 82.
Manufacturers: 1 Alfa Romeo, 120; **2** VW, 110; **3** BMW, 105; **4** Jaguar, 99; **5** Audi, 82; **6** Opel, 38.

EUROPEAN TOURING CAR CHAMPIONSHIP RACE, Osterreichring, Austria, June 26. European Touring Car Championship, round 7. 96 laps of the 3·692-mile/5·942-km circuit, 354·43 miles/570·43 km.
1 Tom Walkinshaw/Martin Brundle, GB/GB (5.3 Jaguar XJ-S), 3h 30m 33·75s, 101·01 mph/162·56 km/h (1st over 2500cc class).
2 Enzo Calderari/Pierre Dieudonne, I/B (5.3 Jaguar XJ-S), 3h 30m 53·96s.
3 Hans Stuck/Walter Brun, D/CH (3.5 BMW 635 CSi), 3h 30m 58·10s.
4 Michel Delcourt/Dany Swyssen, B/B (3.5 BMW 635 CSi), 95 laps.
5 Marco Vanoli/Rene Hollinger, I/D (3.5 BMW 635 CSi), 94.
6 Dominique Fornage/Johannes Wollstad, F/A (3.5 BMW 635 CSi), 92.
7 Jean-Louis Bos/Christian Duby, F/F (3.5 BMW 635 CSi), 91; **8** Winni Vogt/Joachim Winkelhock, D/D (2.3 BMW 323i), 90 (1st 1601cc-2500cc class); **9** Lella Lombardi/Giancarlo Naddeo, I/I (2.5 Alfa Romeo GTV6), 90; **10** "Davit"/Francois-Xavier Boucher, B/B (2.8 BMW 528i), 90.
Fastest lap: Zdenek Vojtech, CS (3.5 BMW 635 CSi), 2m 08·35s, 103·57 mph/166·68 km/h.
Other class winners: Up to 1600cc: Alain Thibaut/Philippe Menage, B/B (1.6 VW Scirocco GTI), 88.
Championship points. Drivers: 1 Walkinshaw, 134; **2** Quester, 102; **3** Menage and Thibaut, 99; **5** Seikel and Schorg, 97.
Manufacturers: 1 Alfa Romeo, 135; **2** VW, 130; **3** Jaguar, 119; **4** BMW, 117; **5** Audi, 97; **6** Opel, 46.

NURBURGRING 6 HOURS, Nurburgring Nordschleife, German Federal Republic, July 10. European Touring Car Championship, round 8. 44 laps of the 12·94-mile/20·83-km circuit, 569·36 miles/916·52 km.
1 Dieter Quester/Manfred Winkelhock, A/D (3.5 BMW 635 CSi), 6h 06m 06·47s, 93·34 mph/150·22 km/h (1st over 2500cc class).
2 Helmut Kelleners/Umberto Grano, D/I (3.5 BMW 635 CSi), 43 laps.
3 Marco Vanoli/Christian Danner, CH/D (3.5 BMW 635 CSi), 43.
4 Jean-Louis Bos/Christian Duby/Jean Krucker, F/F/CH (3.5 BMW 635 CSi), 42.
5 Dominique Fornage/Philippe Haezebrouck/Dieter Gartmann, F/F/D (3.5 BMW 635 CSi), 42.
6 Herbert Hartge/Walter Nussbaumer/Jorg van Omman, D/CH/D (3.5 BMW 635 CSi), 42.
7 Jurgen Fritzsche/Roland Asche, D/D (2.0 Opel Kadett GT/E), 41 (1st 1601cc-2500cc class); **8** Hans Stuck/Walter Brun, D/CH (3.5 BMW 635 CSi), 41; **9** Willi Bergmeister/Daniel Herregods, D/B (1.6 VW Scirocco GTI), 41 (1st up to 1600cc class); **10** Thomas Lindstrom/Anders Olofsson, S/S (2.0 Volvo 240 Turbo), 41.
Fastest lap: Tom Walkinshaw, GB (5.3 Jaguar XJ-S), 8m 02·44s, 96·59 mph/155·45 km/h.
Championship points. Drivers: 1 Walkinshaw, 134; **2** Quester, 131; **3** Menage and Thibaut, 114; **5** Kelleners and Grano, 107.
Manufacturers: 1 Alfa Romeo and VW, 150; **3** BMW, 137; **4** Jaguar, 119; **5** Audi, 101; **6** Opel, 66.

EUROPEAN TOURING CAR CHAMPIONSHIP RACE, Salzburgring, Austria, July 17. European Touring Car Championship, round 9. 137 laps of the 2·635-mile/4·241-km circuit, 361·00 miles/581·02 km.
1 Tom Walkinshaw/Chuck Nicholson, GB/GB (5.3 Jaguar XJ-S), 3h 30m 58·31s, 102·67 mph/165·23 km/h (1st over 2500cc class).
2 Hans Stuck/Walter Brun, D/CH (3.5 BMW 635 CSi), 3h 31m 49·28s.
3 Dieter Quester/Manfred Winkelhock, A/D (3.5 BMW 635 CSi), 3h 32m 04·19s.
4 Helmut Kelleners/Umberto Grano, D/I (3.5 BMW 635 CSi), 136 laps.
5 Walter Nussbaumer/Jacques Isler, CH/CH (3.5 BMW 635 CSi), 133.
6 Marco Vanoli/Ed Kofel, CH/A (3.5 BMW 635 CSi), 132.
7 Fritz Muller/Heinz Kuhn-Weiss, D/D (3.5 BMW 635 CSi), 132; **8** Gianfranco Brancatelli/Rinaldo Drovandi, I/I (2.5 Alfa Romeo GTV6), 132 (1st 1601cc-2500cc class); **9** Maurizio Macangeli/Georges Cremer, I/A (2.5 Alfa Romeo GTV6), 129; **10** Toni Fischaber/Mario Ketterer, D/D (2.5 Alfa Romeo GTV6), 129.
Fastest lap: Walkinshaw, 1m 30·16s, 105·21 mph/169·32 km/h.
Other class winners: Up to 1600cc; Philippe Menage/Alain Thibaut, B/B (1.6 VW Scirocco GTI), 126.
Championship points. Drivers: 1 Walkinshaw, 163; **2** Quester, 147; **3** Menage and Thibaut, 134; **5** Kelleners and Grano, 120.
Manufacturers: 1 Alfa Romeo and VW 170; **3** BMW, 152; **4** Jaguar, 139; **5** Audi, 107; **6** Opel, 66.

SPA 24 HOURS, Spa-Francorchamps, Belgium, July 30/31. European Touring Car Championship, round 10. 480 laps of the 4·332-mile/6·972-km circuit, 2079·36 miles/3346·56 km.
1 Thierry Tassin/Hans Heyer/Armin Hahne, B/A/D (3.5 BMW 635 CSi), 24h 01m 05·27s, 86·29 mph/138·87 km/h (1st over 2500cc class).
2 Dieter Quester/Manfred Winkelhock/Carlo Rossi, A/D/I (3.5 BMW 635 CSi), 472 laps.
3 Jeff Allam/Peter Lovett/Steve Soper, GB/GB/GB (3.5 Rover Vitesse), 469.
4 Alain Semoulin/Bernard de Dryver/Guy Pirenne, B//B/B (3.0 Ford Capri), 465.
5 Marcello Cipriani/Daniele Toffoli/Massimo Sienna, I/I/I (3.5 BMW 635 CSi), 450.
6 Gianfranco Brancatelli/Rinaldo Drovandi/Emilio Zapico, I/I/E (2.5 Alfa Romeo GTV6), 447 (1st 1601cc-250cc class).
7 "Davit"/Francois Boucher/Philippe Hoebake, B/B/B (2.8 BMW 528 i), 439; **8** Antonio Palma/Dagmar Suster/Bigliazzi, I/YU/I (2.5 Alfa Romeo GTV6), 436; **9** Philippe van der Velde/Robert Hanon, B/B (3.0 Ford Capri), 434; **10** Francois Hesnault/Pierre-Francois Rousselot/Dermagne, F/F/F (3.5 BMW 635 CSi), 431.
Fastest lap: Helmut Kelleners, D (3.5 BMW 635 CSi), 2m 47·88s, 92·59 mph/149·01 km/h.
Other class winners: Up to 1600cc: Claude Holvoet/Pierre van Hourck/Jean-Pierre Jacquemin, B/B/B (1.6 Toyota Corolla).
Championship points. Drivers: 1 Quester, 168; **2** Walkinshaw, 163; **3** Menage and Thibaut, 144; **5** Kelleners and Grano, 120.

Manufacturers: 1 Alfa Romeo, 175 (190); **2** VW, 170 (182); **3** BMW, 160 (172); **4** Jaguar, 139; **5** Audi, 107; **6** Opel, 66.

CANON TOURIST TROPHY, Silverstone Grand Prix Circuit, Great Britain, September 11. European Touring Car Championship, round 11. 107 laps of the 2·932-mile/4·719-km circuit, 313·72 miles/504·93 km.
1 Rene Metge/Steve Soper, F/GB (3.5 Rover Vitesse), 3h 09m 31·73s, 99·31 mph/159·82 km/h (1st over 2500cc class).
2 Jonathan Palmer/James Weaver, GB/GB (3.5 BMW 635 CSi), 3h 09m 48·93s.
3 Zdenek Vojtech/Bretislav Enge, CS/CS (3.5 BMW 635 CSi), 3h 10m 38·41s.
4 Michel Delcourt/Barrie Williams, B/GB (3.5 BMW 635 CSi), 106 laps.
5 Dieter Quester/Hans Heyer/Walter Brun, A/D/CH (3.5 BMW 635 CSi), 106.
6 Helmut Kelleners/Umberto Grano, D/I (3.5 BMW 635 CSi), 106.
7 Marco Vanoli/Rene Hollinger, CH/CH (3.5 BMW 635 CSi), 106; **8** Zdenek Vojtech/Herbert Hartge, CS/D (3.5 BMW 635 CSi), 106; **9** Tom Walkinshaw/Pierre Dieudonne, GB/B (5.3 Jaguar XJ-S), 105; **10** Frank Sytner/Brian Muir, GB/AUS (3.5 BMW 635 CSi), 104.
Fastest lap: Soper, 1m 40·19s, 105·35 mph/169·54 km/h (record).
Other class winners: Up to 1600cc: Richard Longman/Rex Greenslade, GB/GB (1.6 Ford Escort 1600i), 98. **1601cc-2500cc:** Rinaldo Drovandi/Emilio Zapico, I/E (2.5 Alfa Romeo GTV6), 102.
Championship points. Drivers: 1 Quester, 178; **2** Walkinshaw, 165; **3** Thibaut and Menege, 144; **5** Kelleners and Grano, 127.
Manufacturers: 1 Alfa Romeo, 180 (210); **2** VW, 170 (197); **3** BMW, 157 (187); **4** Jaguar, 141; **5** Audi, 107; **6** Opel, 66.

EUROPEAN TOURING CAR CHAMPIONSHIP RACE, Omloop van Zolder, Belgium, September 25. European Touring Car Championship, round 12. 111 laps of the 2·648-mile/4·262-km circuit, 292·93 miles/473·08 km.
1 Helmut Kelleners/Umberto Grano, D/I (3.5 BMW 635 CSi), 3h 30m 26·6s.
2 Marc Duez/Michel de Deyne, B/B (3.5 BMW 635 CSi), 3h 31m 46·5s.
3 Michel Delcourt/"Davit"/Guy Trigaux, B/B/B (3.5 BMW 635 CSi), 3h 32m 11·1s.
4 Hans Stuck/Dieter Quester, D/A (3.5 BMW 635 CSi), 110 laps.
5 Marco Vanoli/Jacques Isler, CH/CH (3.5 BMW 635 CSi), 110.
6 Fritz Muller/Heniz Kuhn-Weiss, D/D (3.5 BMW 635 CSi), 109.
7 George Bosshard/Philippe Haezebrouck, D/B (3.5 BMW 635 CSi), 109; **8** Tom Walkinshaw/Win Percy/Martin Brundle, GB/GB/GB (5.3 Jaguar XJ-S), 109; **9** Rinaldo Drovandi/Emilio Zapico, I/E (2.5 Alfa Romeo GTV6), 108 (1st 1600cc-2500cc class); **10** Lella Lombardi/Giancarlo Naddeo, I/I (2.5 Alfa Romeo GTV6), 107.
Fastest lap: Not given.
Other class winners: Up to 1600cc: Peter Seikel/Andre Hardy, D/B (1.6 Audi 80), 105.

Final Championship points. Drivers:

1 Dieter Quester, A	181 (193)
2 Tom Walkinshaw, GB	168
3 Helmut Kelleners, D	156
Umberto Grano, I	156
5 Philippe Menage, B	144
Alain Thibaut, B	144

7 Hans Stuck, D and Daniel Herregods, B, 125; **9** Peter Seikel, D, 117; **10** Walter Brun, CH, 116.
Manufacturers:

1 Alfa Romeo	180 (230)
2 VW	170 (212)
3 BMW	165 (207)
4 Jaguar	142 (144)
5 Audi	127
6 Opel	66

Robert Bosch/VW Super Vee

1982 results

The final round of the 1982 Robert Bosch/VW Super Vee Championship was run after Autocourse 1982/83 went to press.

ROBERT BOSCH/VW SUPER VEE RACE, Phoenix International Raceway, Arizona, United States of America, November 6. Robert Bosch/VW Super Vee Championship, round 11. 60 laps of the 1·000-mile/1·609-km circuit, 60·00 miles/96·54 km.
1 Mike Andretti, USA (Ralt RT5-VW), 33m 21·0s, 107·946 mph/173·722 km/h.
2 Ed Pimm, USA (Ralt RT5-VW), 33m 25·0s.
3 Mike Miller, USA (Ralt RT5-VW), 60 laps.
4 Don Roberts, USA (Ralt RT5-VW), 60.
5 Rich Vogler, USA (Ralt RT5-VW), 60.
6 Davy Jones, USA (Ralt RT5- VW), 60.
7 Roger Penske Jnr, USA (Ralt RT5-VW), 59; **8** Rick Talbot, USA (Ralt RT5-VW), 59; **9** Bob Cicconi, USA (Anson SA3C-VW), 58; **10** Ben Gustafson, USA (Ralt RT5-VW), 58.
Fastest lap: Andretti, 27·32s, 131·772 mph/212·066 km/h (record).
Final Championship points:

1 Mike Andretti, USA	152
2 Ed Pimm, USA	116
3 Davy Jones, USA	107
4 Mike Miller, USA	99
5 Rick Talbot, USA	77
6 Greg Atwell, USA	65

7 Mike Rosen, USA, 63; **8** Brad Murphy, USA, 61; **9** Jerrill Rice, USA, 58; **10** Stan Fox, USA, 57; **11** Don Roberts, USA, 56; **12** Bob Cicconi, USA, 44; **13** Roger Penske Jnr, USA, 42; **14** Jerry Knapp, USA, 39; **15** Tim Evans, USA, 38; **16** Peter Moodie, JAM, 32; **17** Brad Hulings, USA, 28; **18** Ben Gustafson, USA, 27; **19** Oma Kimbrough, USA, 23; **20** John Timken, USA, 21.

1983 results

ROBERT BOSCH/VW SUPER VEE RACE, Long Beach Grand Prix Circuit, California, United States of America, March 26. Robert Bosch/VW Super Vee Championship, round 1. 30 laps of the 2·035-mile/3·275-km circuit, 61·05 miles/98·25 km.
1 Mike Andretti, USA (Ralt RT5-VW), 50m 01·908s, 73·21 mph/117·82 km/h.
2 Hubert Phipps, USA (Ralt RT5-VW), 50m 13·018s.
3 Jerrill Rice, USA (Ralt RT5-VW), 30 laps.
4 Chip Robinson, USA (Ralt RT5-VW), 30.
5 Ed Jones, GB (Shannon AJ82V-VW), 30.
6 Mike Rosen, USA (Ralt RT5-VW), 30.
7 Ludwig Heimrath Jnr, CDN (Ralt RT5-VW), 30; **8** Roger Penske Jnr, USA (Ralt RT5-VW), 30; **9** Ed Pimm, USA (Ralt RT5-VW), 30; **10** Don Roberts, USA (Ralt RT5-VW), 30.
Fastest lap: Andretti, 1m 37·819s, 74·89 mph/120·52 km/h.
Championship points: 1 Andretti, 20; **2** Phipps, 16; **3** Rice, 14; **4** Robinson, 12; **5** Jones, 11; **6** Rosen, 10.

ROBERT BOSCH/VW SUPER VEE RACE, Mosport Park Circuit, Ontario, Canada, June 5. Robert Bosch/VW Super Vee Championship, round 2. 24 laps of the 2·459-mile/3·957-km circuit, 59·02 miles/94·97 km.
1 Price Cobb, USA (Ralt RT5-VW), 32m 21·110s, 109·452 mph/176·145 km/h.
2 Ludwig Heimrath Jnr, CDN (Ralt RT5-VW), 32m 22·774s.
3 Chip Robinson, USA (Ralt RT5-VW), 24 laps.
4 Ed Pimm, USA (Anson SA4-VW), 24.
5 Roger Penske Jnr, USA (Ralt RT5-VW), 24.
6 John Stephanus, USA (Ralt RT5-VW), 24.
7 John Timken Jnr, USA (Ralt RT5-VW), 24; **8** Don Roberts, USA (Ralt RT5-VW), 24; **9** John Andretti, USA (Ralt RT5-VW), 24; **10** Kim Campbell, USA (Ralt RT5-VW), 23.
Fastest lap: Heimrath Jnr, 1m 20·002s, 110·65 mph/178·07 km/h.
Championship points: 1 Robinson, 26; **2** Heimrath Jnr, 25; **3** Cobb and M. Andretti, 20; **5** Penske Jnr and Pimm, 19.

ROBERT BOSCH/VW SUPER VEE RACE, Wisconsin State Fair Park Speedway, Milwaukee, United States of America, June 12. Robert Bosch/VW Super Vee Championship, round 3. 62 laps of the 1·000-mile/1·609-km circuit, 62·00 miles/99·76 km.
1 Ed Pimm, USA (Anson SA4-VW), 37m 15·13s, 99·86 mph/160·71 km/h.
2 Roger Penske Jnr, USA (Ralt RT5-VW), 62 laps.
3 Stan Fox, USA (Ralt RT5-VW), 62.
4 Price Cobb, USA (Ralt RT5-VW), 62.
5 Ben Gustafson, USA (Ralt RT5-VW), 62.
6 Chip Robinson, USA (Ralt RT5-VW), 62.
7 Ludwig Heimrath Jnr, CDN (Ralt RT5-VW), 62; **8** Don Roberts, USA (Ralt RT5-VW), 61; **9** Kim Campbell, USA (Ralt RT5-VW), 61; **10** John Stephanus, USA (Ralt RT5-VW), 61.
Fastest lap: Not available.
Championship points: 1 Pimm, 39; **2** Robinson, 36; **3** Penske Jnr, 35; **4** Heimrath Jnr, 34; **5** Cobb, 32; **6** Roberts, 22.

ROBERT BOSCH/VW SUPER VEE RACE, Burke Lakefront Airport Circuit, Cleveland, Ohio, United States of America, July 3. Robert Bosch/VW Super Vee Championship, round 4. 24 laps of the 2·48-mile/3·99-km circuit, 59·52 miles/95·76 km.
1 Price Cobb, USA (Ralt RT5-VW), 34m 15·44s, 95·559 mph/153·787 km/h.
2 Chip Robinson, USA (Ralt RT5-VW), 34m 23·43s.
3 Ed Pimm, USA (Anson SA4-VW), 24 laps.
4 Arie Luyendijk, NL (Anson SA4-VW), 24.
5 Peter Moodie, JA (Vector GR002-VW), 24.
6 Ludwig Heimrath Jnr, CDN (Ralt RT5-VW), 24.
7 Ed Jones, GB (Shannon-VW), 24; **8** Stan Fox, USA (Ralt RT5-VW), 24; **9** Roger Penske Jnr, USA (Ralt RT5-VW), 24; **10** Paul Barnhart, USA (Anson SA4-VW), 24.
Fastest lap: Not available.
Championship points: 1 Pimm, 53; **2** Cobb and Robinson, 52; **4** Heimrath Jnr, 44; **5** Penske Jnr, 42; **6** Jones and Fox, 26.

ROBERT BOSCH/VW SUPER VEE RACE, Road America, Elkhart Lake, Wisconsin, United States of America, July 31. Robert Bosch/VW Super Vee Championship, round 5. 15 laps of the 4·000-mile/6·437-km circuit, 60·00 miles/96·56 km.
1 Price Cobb, USA (Ralt RT5-VW), 33m 47·15s, 106·554 mph/171·482 km/h.
2 Mike Rosen, USA (Ralt RT5-VW), 33m 58·99s.
3 Roger Penske Jnr, USA (Ralt RT5-VW), 15 laps.
4 Don Roberts, USA (Ralt RT5-VW), 15.
5 Ted Prappas, USA (Ralt RT5-VW), 15.
6 Paul Barnhart Jnr, USA (Anson SA4-VW), 15.
7 John Timken, USA (Ralt RT5-VW), 15; **8** Doug Clark, USA (Ralt RT5-VW), 15; **9** Chip Robinson, USA (Ralt RT5-VW), 15; **10** Ed Jones, GB (Shannon-VW), 15.
Fastest lap: Ed Pimm, USA (Anson SA4-VW), 2m 13·64s, 102·95 mph/165·68 km/h.
Championship points: 1 Cobb, 72; **2** Robinson, 59; **3** Penske Jnr, 56; **4** Pimm, 53; **5** Heimrath Jnr, 44; **6** Roberts, 34.

ROBERT BOSCH/VW SUPER VEE RACE, Pocono International Raceway, Pennsylvania, United States of America, August 13. Robert Bosch/VW Super Vee Championship, round 6. 25 laps of the 2·500-mile/4·023-km circuit, 62·50 miles/100·58 km.
1 Ed Pimm, USA (Ralt RT5-VW), 29m 25·019s, 127·477 mph/205·154 km/h.
2 Price Cobb, USA (Ralt RT5-VW), 29m 26·239s.
3 Stan Fox, USA (Ralt RT5-VW), 25 laps.
4 Roger Penske Jnr, USA (Ralt RT5-VW), 25.
5 Mike Rosen, USA (Ralt RT5-VW), 25.
6 Ludwig Heimrath Jnr, CDN (Ralt RT5-VW), 25.
7 Ben Gustafson, USA (Ralt RT5-VW), 25; **8** Don Roberts, USA (Ralt RT5-VW), 25; **9** John Fergus, USA (Ralt RT5-VW), 25; **10** Doug Clark, USA (Ralt RT5-VW), 25.
Fastest lap: Not given.
Championship points: 1 Cobb, 88; **2** Pimm, 73; **3** Penske Jnr, 68; **4** Robinson, 59; **5** Heimrath Jnr, 54; **6** Roberts, 42.

ROBERT BOSCH/VW SUPER VEE RACE, Mid-Ohio Sports Car Course, Lexington, Ohio, United States of America, September 11. Robert Bosch/VW Super Vee Championship, round 7. 25 laps of the 2·400-mile/3·862-km circuit, 60·00 miles/96·55 km.
1 Ed Pimm, USA (Anson SA4-VW), 37m 27·07s, 96·125 mph/154·698 km/h.
2 Mike Rosen, USA (Ralt RT5-VW), 37m 27·39s.
3 Chip Robinson, USA (Ralt RT5-VW), 25 laps.
4 Price Cobb, USA (Ralt RT5-VW), 25.
5 Ludwig Heimrath Jnr, CDN (Ralt RT5-VW), 25.
6 Roger Penske Jnr, USA (Ralt RT5-VW), 25.
7 Mark Austin Dismore, USA (Ralt RT5-VW), 25; **8** John Fergus, USA (Ralt RT5-VW), 25; **9** Don Roberts, USA (Ralt RT5-VW), 25; **10** Bob Schader, USA (Van Dieman RF83-VW), 25.
Fastest lap: Rosen, 1m 28·06s, 98·115 mph/157·90 km/h.
Championship points: 1 Cobb, 100; **2** Pimm, 93; **3** Penske Jnr, 78; **4** Robinson, 73; **5** Heimrath Jnr, 65; **6** Rosen, 53.

ROBERT BOSCH/VW SUPER VEE RACE, Michigan International Raceway, Brooklyn, Michigan, United States of America, September 18. Robert Bosch/VW Super Vee Championship, round 8. 30 laps of the 2·000-mile/3·219-km circuit, 60·00 miles/96·57 km.
1 Ed Pimm, USA (Ralt RT5-VW), 22m 33·8s, 159·55 mph/256·77 km/h.
2 Ludwig Heimrath Jnr, CDN (Ralt RT5-VW), 22m 34·9s.
3 Don Roberts, USA (Ralt RT5-VW), 30 laps.
4 Price Cobb, USA (Ralt RT5-VW), 30.
5 Roger Penske Jnr, USA (Ralt RT5-VW), 30.
6 Ben Gustafson, USA (Ralt RT5-VW), 30.
7 Stan Fox, USA (Ralt RT5-VW), 30; **8** Chip Robinson, USA (Ralt RT5-VW), 30; **9** John Fergus, USA (Ralt RT5-VW), 30; **10** Stuart Moore, USA (Anson SA4-VW), 30.
Fastest lap: Heimrath Jnr and Pimm, 44·5s, 161·798 mph/260·388 km/h.
Championship points: 1 Pimm, 113; **2** Cobb, 112; **3** Penske Jnr, 89; **4** Robinson and Heimrath Jnr, 81; **6** Roberts, 77.

ROBERT BOSCH/VW SUPER VEE RACE, Riverside International Raceway, California, United States of America, September 25. Robert Bosch/VW Super Vee Championship, round 9. 24 laps of the 2·547-mile/4·099-km circuit, 61·13 miles/98·38 km.
1 Ed Pimm, USA (Ralt RT5-VW), 35m 35·581s, 112·530 mph/181·099 km/h.
2 Chip Robinson, USA (Ralt RT5-VW), 35m 36·423s.
3 Ludwig Heimrath Jnr, CDN (Ralt RT5-VW), 24 laps.
4 Ted Prappas, USA (Ralt RT5-VW), 24.
5 Roger Penske Jnr, USA (Ralt RT5-VW), 24.
6 Bob Earl, USA (Ralt RT5-VW), 24.
7 Don Roberts, USA (Ralt RT5-VW), 24; **8** Dominic Dobson, USA (Ralt RT5-VW), 24; **9** Mike Rosen, USA (Ralt RT5-VW), 24; **10** Peter Moodie, JA (Anson SA4-VW), 24.
Fastest lap: Prappas, 1m 20·153s, 113·49 mph/182·64 km/h.
Championship points: 1 Pimm, 133; **2** Cobb, 112; **3** Penske Jnr, 100; **4** Robinson, 97; **5** Heimrath Jnr, 95; **6** Roberts, 72.

ROBERT BOSCH/VW SUPER VEE RACE, Laguna Seca Raceway, California, United States of America, October 23. Robert Bosch/VW Super Vee Championship, round 10. 32 laps of the 1·900-mile/3·056-km circuit, 60·80 miles/97·79 km.
1 Price Cobb, USA (Ralt RT5-VW), 33m 47·21s, 107·971 mph/173·762 km/h.
2 Chip Robinson, USA (Ralt RT5-VW), 33m 48·20s.
3 Roger Penske Jnr, USA (Ralt RT5-VW), 32 laps.
4 Ted Prappas, USA (Ralt RT5-VW), 32.
5 Bob Earl, USA (Anson SA4-VW), 32.
6 Ed Pimm, USA (Anson SA4-VW), 32.
7 Peter Moodie, JA (Anson SA4-VW), 32; **8** Dennis Vitollo, USA (Ralt RT5-VW), 32; **9** Jeff Lee, USA (Ralt RT5-VW), 32; **10** Mike Hopper, USA (Ralt RT5-VW), 31.
Fastest lap: Ludwig Heimrath Jnr, CDN (Ralt RT5-VW), 1m 02·50s, 109·44 mph/176·13 km/h.
Championship points: 1 Pimm, 143; **2** Cobb, 132; **3** Penske Jnr, 114; **4** Robinson, 113; **5** Heimrath Jnr, 95; **6** Roberts, 71.

ROBERT BOSCH/VW SUPER VEE RACE, Phoenix International Raceway, Arizona, United States of America, October 30. Robert Bosch/VW Super VEE Championship, round 11. 60 laps of the 1·000-mile/1·609-km circuit, 60·00 miles/94·64 km.
1 Ludwig Heimrath, Jnr, CDN (Ralt RT5-VW), 32m 28·96s, 110·828 mph/178·360 km/h.
2 Ben Gustafson, USA (Ralt RT5-VW), 32m 36·20s.
3 Ted Prappas, USA (Ralt RT5-VW), 60 laps.
4 Roger Penske Jnr, USA (Ralt RT5-VW), 60.
5 Price Cobb, USA (Ralt RT5-VW), 60.
6 Chip Robinson, USA (Ralt RT5-VW), 60.
7 Stan Fox, USA (Ralt RT5-VW), 59; **8** Ed Pimm, USA (Ralt RT5-VW), 59; **9** Arie Luyendyk, NL (Anson SA4-VW), 59; **10** John Timken, USA (Ralt RT5-VW), 59.
Fastest lap: Not given.

Final Championship points:

1 Ed Pimm, USA	151
2 Price Cobb, USA	143
3 Roger Penske Jnr, USA	126
4 Chip Robinson, USA	123
5 Ludwig Heimrath Jnr, CDN	115
6 Don Roberts, USA	71

7 Ted Prappas, USA, 62; **8** Mike Rosen, USA, 60; **9** Stan Fox, USA, 58; **10** Ben Gustafson, USA, 49.

Indianapolis 500

INDIANAPOLIS 500, indianapolis Motor Speedway, Indiana, United States of America, May 29. CART PPG Indy Car World Series, round 2. 200 laps of the 2·500-mile/4·023-km circuit, 500·00 miles/804·57 km.
1 Tom Sneva, USA (March 83C-Cosworth DFX), 3h 05m 03·066s, 162·117 mph/260·901 km/h.
2 Al Unser, USA (Penske PC11-Cosworth DFX), 3h 05m 14·240s.
3 Rick Mears, USA (Penske PC11-Cosworth DFX), 3h 05m 24·928s.
4 Geoff Brabham, AUS (Penske PC10-Cosworth DFX), 199 laps.
5 Kevin Cogan, USA (March 83C-Cosworth DFX), 198.
6 Howdy Holmes, USA (March 83C-Cosworth DFX), 198.
7 Pancho Carter, USA (March 83C-Cosworth DFX), 197; **8** Chip Ganassi, USA (Wildcat Mk9-Cosworth DFX), 195; **9** Scott Brayton, USA (March 83C-Cosworth DFX), 195; **10** Al Unser Jnr, USA (Eagle 83-Cosworth DFX), 192 (Including 2 lap penalty for passing under yellow flag); **11** Steve Chassey, USA (Eagle 82-Chevrolet), 192; **12** Chris Kneifel, USA (Primus-Cosworth DFX), 191; **13** Mike Mosley, USA (March 83C-Cosworth DFX), 169 (DNF, accident); **14** Gordon Johncock, USA (Wildcat Mk9-Cosworth DFX), 163 (DNF, gearbox); **15** Dick Simon, USA (March 83C-Cosworth DFX), 161; **16** Mike Chandler, USA (Rattlesnake-Cosworth DFX), 153 (DNF, gearbox); **17** Tony Bettenhausen, USA (March 83C-Cosworth DFX), 153 (DNF, cv joint); **18** Bill Whittington, USA(March 82/83C-Cosworth DFX), 144 (DNF, gearbox); **19** Derek Daly, IRL (March 83C-Cosworth DFX), 126 (DNF, engine); **20** Bobby Rahal, USA (March 83C-Cosworth DFX), 110 (DNF, radiator); **21** Danny Ongais, USA (March 83C-Cosworth DFX), 101 (DNF, vibration); **22** Johnny Parsons, USA (Penske PC10-Cosworth DFX), 80 (DNF, accident); **23** Mario Andretti, USA (Lola T700-Cosworth DFX), 79 (DNF, accident); **24** Dennis Firestone, USA (March 82C-Cosworth DFX), 77 (DNF, oil leak); **25** Josele Garza, MEX (Penske PC10-Cosworth DFX), 64 (DNF, oil leak); **26** Teo Fabi, I (March 83C-Cosworth DFX), 47 (DNF, fuel leak); **27** Don Whittington, USA (March 81/83C-Cosworth DFX), 44 (DNF, electrics); **28** Roger Mears, USA (Penske PC10-Cosworth DFX), 43 (DNF, accident); **29** Steve Krisiloff, USA (Lola T700-Cosworth DFX), 42 (DNF, driveshaft); **30** Pat Bedard, USA (March 83C-Cosworth DFX), 25 (DNF, accident); **31** A. J. Foyt, USA (March 83C-Cosworth DFX), 24 (DNF, gear linkage); **32** George Snider, USA (March 83C-Cosworth DFX), 22 (DNF, ignition); **33** Chet Fillip, USA (Eagle 83-Cosworth DFX), 11 (DNF, black flagged).
Fastest Qualifier: Fabi, 2m 53·582s, 207·395 mph/333·769 km/h (4 laps).
Fastest lap: Fabi, 45·568s, 197·507 mph/317·856 km/h.
Championship points: 1 Unser, 32; **2** Mears and Sneva, 21; **4** Johncock, 20; **5** Paul Jnr, 14; **6** Holmes and Brabham, 12.

SCCA Budweiser Can-Am Challenge

SCCA BUDWEISER CAN-AM CHALLENGE RACE, Mosport Park Circuit, Ontario, Canada, June 5. SCCA Budweiser Can-Am Challenge, round 1. 60 laps of the 2·459-mile/3·957-km circuit, 147·54 miles/237·42 km.
1 Jacques Villeneuve, CDN (5.0 Frissbee GR3-Chevrolet), 1h 19m 19·314s, 111·78 mph/179·89 km/h.
2 Jim Crawford, GB (3.3 Ensign 180B-Cosworth DFL), 59 laps.
3 Michael Roe, IRL (5.0 Lola T333-Chevrolet), 59.
4 Hurley Haywood, USA (5.8 March 83G-Chevrolet), 57.
5 Horst Kroll, CDN (5.0 Frissbee-Chevrolet), 57.
6 Charles Monk, CDN (5.0 Frissbee-Chevrolet), 56.
7 Roman Pechmann, CDN (2.0 Lola T290-Ford), 55; **8** Paul Wheatley, CDN (5.0 Lola T333CS-Chevrolet), 53; **9** Al Holbert, USA (3.0 t/c March 83G-Porsche), 52 (DNF, turbo); **10** Bob Roy, CDN (2.0 Lola T294-Ford), 48.
Fastest lap: Villeneuve, 1m 12·600s, 121·93 mph/196·23 km/h.
Championship points: 1 Villeneuve, 20; **2** Crawford, 16; **3** Roe, 14; **4** Haywood, 12; **5** Kroll, 11; **6** Monk, 10.

SCCA BUDWEISTEER CAN-AM CHALLENGE RACE, Lime Rock Park, Connecticut, United States of America, July 3. SCCA Budweiser Can-Am Challenge, round 2. 80 laps of the 1·53-mile/2·46-km circuit, 122·40 miles/196·80 km.
1 Jim Crawford, GB (3.3 Ensign 180B-Cosworth DFL), 1h 08m 20·945s, 107·448 mph/172·920 km/h.
2 Michael Roe, IRL (5.0 VDS 002-Chevrolet), 78 laps.
3 Bertil Roos, S (2.0 Scandia B3-Hart), 78.
4 Charles Monk, CDN (5.0 Frissbee-Chevrolet), 75.
5 Horst Kroll, CDN (5.0 Frissbee-Chevrolet), 73.
6 E. B. Lunken, USA (2.0 Invader-BMW), 73.
7 Bob Meyer, USA (5.0 Lola T333CS-Chevrolet), 72; **8** Marzio Romano, CH (2.0 Ralt RT2-Hart), 69 (DNF, body damage); **9** Roman Pechmann, CDN (2.0 Lola T290-Hart), 69; **10** Jeremy Hill, CDN (2.0 March 75S-BMW), 59 (DNF, engine).
Fastest lap: Jacques Villeneuve, CDN (5.0 Frissbee GR3-Chevrolet), 46·930s, 117·366 mph/188·882 km/h.
Championship points: 1 Crawford, 36; **2** Roe, 30; **3** Villeneuve, 24; **4** Kroll and Monk, 22; **6** Roos, 19.

SCCA BUDWEISER CAN-AM CHALLENGE RACE, Road America, Elkhart Lake, Wisconsin, United States of America, July 18. SCCA Budweiser Can-Am Challenge, round 3. 40 laps of the 4·000-mile/6·437-km circuit, 160·00 miles/257·48 km.
1 John Fitzpatrick, GB (2.6 t/c Porsche 956), 1h 28m 24·84s, 108·58 mph/174·74 km/h.
2 Jacques Villeneuve, CDN (5.0 Frissbee GR2-Chevrolet), 1h 28m 36·45s.
3 Charles Monk, CDN (5.0 Frissbee-Chevrolet), 40 laps.
4 Bertil Roos, S (2.0 Scandia B3-Hart), 40.
5 Marzio Romano, CH (2.0 Ralt RT2-Hart), 40.
6 Eddie Wachs, USA (2.0 Toleman TG280-Hart), 39.
7 Wally Dallenbach Jnr, USA (2.0 Ralt RT2-Hart), 39; **8** Walt Bohren, USA (5.0 Escort-Chevrolet), 37; **9** Gerald Molnar, USA (2.0 Invader-Ford), 35; **10** John Macaluso, USA (2.0 Brabert FWH 001-Hart), 34.
Fastest lap: Villeneuve, 2m 02·960s, 117·111 mph/188·471 km/h.
Championship points: 1 Crawford, 41; **2** Villeneuve, 40; **3** Monk, 36; **4** Roe, 32; **5** Roos, 31; **6** Kroll, 23.

SCCA BUDWEISER CAN-AM CHALLENGE RACE, Trois-Rivieres, Quebec, Canada, September 4. SCCA Budweiser Can-Am Challenge, round 4. 60 laps of the 2·100-mile/3·380-km circuit, 126·00 miles/202·80 km.
1 Jacques Villeneuve, CDN (5.0 Frissbee GR2-Chevrolet), 1h 26m 39·210s, 87·244 mph/140·405 km/h.
2 Jim Crawford, GB (3.3 Ensign 180B-Cosworth DFL), 59 laps.
3 Marzio Romano, CH (2.0 Ralt RT2-Hart), 58.
4 Horst Kroll, CDN (5.0 Frissbee-Chevrolet), 58.
5 Bertil Roos, S (2.0 Scandia B3-Hart), 57.
6 Eddie Wachs, USA (2.0 Toleman TG280-Hart), 56.
7 Charles Monk, CDN (5.0 Frissbee-Chevrolet), 55; **8** Rob Meyer, USA (5.0 Lola T333CS-Chevrolet), 53; **9** Roman Pechmann, CDN (2.0 Lola T290-Hart), 52; **10** Cliff Dawson, CDN (2.0 Ralt RT1-Hart), 49.
Fastest lap: Villeneuve, 1m 26·056s, 87·222 mph/140·370 km/h.
Championship points: 1 Villeneuve, 60; **2** Crawford, 57; **3** Monk, 44; **4** Roos, 42; **5** Kroll, 35; **6** Romano, 33.

SCCA BUDWEISER CAN-AM CHALLENGE RACE, Mosport Park, Ontario, Canada, September 11. SCCA Budweiser Can-Am Challenge, round 5. 60 laps of the 2·459-mile/3·957-km circuit, 147·54 miles/237·42 km.
1 Jim Crawford, GB (3.3 Ensign 180B-Cosworth DFL), 1h 16m 06·814s, 116·31 mph/187·18 km/h.
2 Jacques Villeneuve, CDN (5.0 Frissbee GR2-Chevrolet), 1h 16m 08·561s.
3 John Fitzpatrick, GB (2.6 t/c Porsche 956), 58 laps.
4 Marzio Romano, CH (2.0 Ralt RT2-Hart), 57.
5 Eddie Wachs, USA (2.0 Toleman TG280-Hart), 56.
6 Bertil Roos, S (2.0 Scandia B3-Hart), 55.
7 Gerald Molnar, USA (2.0 Invader-Hart), 55; **8** Horst Kroll, CDN (5.0 Frissbee-Chevrolet), 54; **9** Robert Meyer, USA (5.0 Lola T333CS-Chevrolet), 53; **10** Rupert Bragg-Smith, CDN (5.0 Chevron B24-Chevrolet), 52.
Fastest lap: Michael Roe, IRL (5.0 VDS 002-Chevrolet), 1m 12·234s, 122·55 mph/197·22 km/h.
Championship points: 1 Crawford, 77; **2** Villeneuve, 76; **3** Roos, 52; **4** Romano and Monk, 45; **6** Kroll, 43.

SCCA BUDWEISER CAN-AM CHALLENGE RACE, Sears Point International Raceway, Sonoma, California, United States of America, October 9. SCCA Budweiser Can-Am Challenge, round 6. 50 laps of the 2·523-mile/4·060-km circuit, 126·15 miles/203·00 km.
1 Jacques Villeneuve, CDN (5.0 Frissbee GR3-Chevrolet), 1h 14m 22·702s, 101·76 mph/163·77 km/h.
2 Jim Crawford, GB (3.3 Ensign 180B-Cosworth DFL), 1h 14m 24·27s.
3 Michael Roe, IRL (5.0 VDS 002-Chevrolet), 49 laps.
4 Horst Kroll, CDN (5.0 Frissbee-Chevrolet), 47.
5 Bertil Roos, S (2.0 Scandia B3-Hart), 47.
6 Charles Monk, CDN (5.0 Frissbee-Chevrolet), 46.
7 Frank Joyce, USA (5.0 CAC 2-Chevrolet), 45; **8** Gary Gove, USA (2.0 Ralt RT4-Hart), 45; **9** Clive Bush, USA (5.0 Conquest B2-Chevrolet), 45; **10** Walt Bohren, USA (5.0 Escort-Chevrolet), 43.
Fastest lap: Villeneuve, 1m 25·81s, 105·85 mph/170·35 km/h.

Final Championship points:

1 Jacques Villeneuve, CDN	96
2 Jim Crawford, GB	93
3 Bertil Roos, S	63
4 Charles Monk, CDN	55
5 Horst Kroll, CDN	55
6 Marzio Romano, CH	48

7 Michael Roe, IRL, 46; **8** Eddie Wachs, USA, 34; **9** John Fitzpatrick, GB, 34; **10** Rob Meyer, USA, 28; **11** Roman Pechmann, CDN, 23; **12** Gerard Molnar, USA, 20; **13** Walt Bohren, USA, 14; **14** Randy Zimmer, USA, 13; **15** Hurley Haywood, USA, 12.

SCCA Budweiser Trans-Am Championship

SCCA BUDWEISER TRANS-AM CHAMPIONSHIP RACE, Moroso Motorsports Park, Florida, United States of America, May 1. SCCA Budweiser Trans-Am Championship, round 1. 45 laps of the 2·250-mile/3·621-km circuit, 101·25 miles/162·95 km.
1 Gene Felton, USA (Pontiac Trans-Am), 1h 11m 12·692s, 85·309 mph/137·291 km/h.
2 David Hobbs, GB (Chevrolet Camaro), 1h 11m 13·410s.
3 Greg Pickett, USA (Chevrolet Corvette), 45 laps.
4 Frank Leary, USA (Pontiac Trans-Am), 45.
5 Willy T. Ribbs, USA (Chevrolet Camaro), 44.
6 Ludwig Heimrath, CDN (Porsche 930), 44.
7 Phil Currin, USA (Chevrolet Corvette), 44; **8** Brad Murphy, USA (Ford Mustang), 44; **9** Paul DePirro, USA (Chevrolet Camaro), 43 (DNF, igniton), **10** Paul Newman, USA (Datsun XZ Turbo), 43.
Fastest Qualifier: Tom Gloy, USA (Ford Mustang), 1m 21·931s, 98·864 mph/159·106 km/h.
Fastest lap: Ribbs, 1m 21·561s, 99·312 mph/159·827 km/h.
Championship points. Drivers: 1 Felton, 20; **2** Hobbs, 16; **3** Pickett, 14; **4** Leary, 12; **5** Ribbs, 11; **6** Heimrath, 10.
Manufacturers: 1 Pontiac, 9; **2** Chevrolet, 6; **3** Porsche, 1.

SCCA BUDWEISER TRANS-AM CHAMPIONSHIP RACE, Summit Point International Raceway, West Virginia, United States of America, May 15. SCCA Budweiser Trans-Am Championship, round 2. 50 laps of the 2·00-mile/3·22-km circuit, 100·00 miles/161·00 km.
1 David Hobbs, GB (Chevrolet Camaro), 1h 08m 36·695s, 87·449 mph/140·735 km/h.
2 Tom Gloy, USA (Mercury Capri), 1h 08m 57·064s.
3 Paul Newman, USA (Datsun ZX Turbo), 50 laps.
4 Phil Currin, USA (Chevrolet Corvette), 49.
5 Paul Miller, USA (Porsche Carrera Turbo), 49.
6 Dave Watson, USA (Pontiac Firebird), 49.
7 Greg Pickett, USA (Chevrolet Corvette), 49; **8** Lyn St. James, USA (Mercury Capri), 48; **9** Bill Craine, USA (Chevrolet Corvette), 48; **10** Frank Search, USA (Chevrolet Corvette), 47.
Fastest Qualifier: Gloy, 1m 16·04s, 94·679 mph/152·371 km/h.
Fastest lap: Willy T. Ribbs, USA (Chevrolet Camaro), 1m 15·566s, 94·036 mph/151·336 km/h.
Championship points. Drivers: 1 Hobbs, 36; **2** Pickett, 23; **3** Currin, 21; **4** Felton, 20; **5** Newman, 20; **6** Gloy, 18.
Manufacturers: 1 Chevrolet, 15; **2** Pontiac, 10; **3** Mercury, 6; **4** Datsun, 4; **5** Porsche, 3.

SCCA BUDWEISER TRANS-AM CHAMPIONSHIP RACE, Sears Point International Raceway, Sonoma, California, United States of America, June 5. SCCA Budweiser Trans-Am Championship, round 3. 40 laps of the 2·523-mile/4·060-km circuit, 100·92 miles/162·40 km.
1 David Hobbs, GB (Chevrolet Camaro), 1h 12m 42·560s, 82·28 mph/132·42 km/h.
2 Gene Felton, USA (Pontiac Trans-Am), 1h 13m 08·58s.
3 Tom Gloy, USA (Mercury Capri), 40 laps.
4 Elliott Forbes-Robinson, USA (Pontiac Trans-Am), 40.
5 Vern Smith, USA (Mercury Capri), 40.
6 Steve Saleen, USA (Pontiac Trans-Am), 39.
7 Willy T. Ribbs, USA (Chevrolet Camaro), 39; **8** Frank Emmett, USA (Chevrolet Corvette), 39; **9** Les Lindley, USA (Chevrolet Camaro), 39; **10** Rob McFarlin, USA (Ford Mustang), 39.
Fastest Qualifier: Greg Pickett, USA (Chevrolet Corvette), 1m 40·709s, 90·081 mph/144·971 km/h.
Fastest lap: Hobbs, 1m 42·390s, 88·608 mph/142·600 km/h.
Championship points. Drivers: 1 Hobbs, 56; **2** Felton, 36; **3** Gloy, 32; **4** Pickett, 25; **5** Ribbs, 22; **6** Currin, 21.
Manufacturers: 1 Chevrolet, 24; **2** Pontiac, 16; **3** Mercury, 10; **4** Datsun, 4; **5** Porsche, 3.

SCCA BUDWEISER TRANS-AM CHAMPIONSHIP RACE, Portland International Raceway, Oregon, United States of America, June 12. SCCA Budweiser Trans-Am Championship, round 4. 52 laps of the 1·915-mile/3·082-km circuit, 99·58 miles/160·26 km.
1 Willy T. Ribbs, USA (Chevrolet Camaro), 1h 06m 45·398s, 89·501 mph/144·038 km/h.
2 Greg Pickett, USA (Chevrolet Corvette), 1h 06m 45·998s.
3 Tom Gloy, USA (Mercury Capri), 52 laps.
4 David Hobbs, GB (Chevrolet Camaro), 52.
5 Gene Felton, USA (Pontiac Trans-Am), 52.
6 Frank Leary, USA (Pontiac Trans-Am), 52.
7 Karl Durkheimer, USA (Porsche 911SC), 51; **8** Bill Craine, USA (Chevrolet Corvette), 51; **9** Frank Search, USA (Chevrolet Corvette), 51; **10** Jim Derhaag, USA (Pontiac Firebird), 51.
Fastest Qualifier: Pickett, 1m 09·47s, 99·23 mph/159·69 km/h (record).
Fastest lap: Hobbs, 1m 10·81s, 97·36 mph/156·69 km/h.
Championship points. Drivers: 1 Hobbs, 68; **2** Felton, 49; **3** Gloy, 46; **4** Ribbs, 42; **5** Pickett, 41; **6** Leary, 41.
Manufacturers: 1 Chevrolet, 33; **2** Pontiac, 18; **3** Mercury, 14; **4** Datsun, 4; **5** Porsche, 3.

SCCA BUDWEISER TRANS-AM CHAMPIONSHIP RACE, Seattle International Raceway, Washington, United States of America, June 26. SCCA Budweiser Trans-Am Championship, round 5. 42 laps of the 2·250-mile/3·621-km circuit, 94·50 miles/152·08 km.
1 Elliott Forbes-Robinson, USA (Pontiac Trans-Am), 1h 06m 17·76s, 85·525 mph/137·64 km/h.
2 Paul Miller, USA (Porsche 924 Turbo), 1h 06m 21·05s.
3 Tom Gloy, USA (Mercury Capri), 42 laps.
4 Lyn St. James, USA (Mercury Capri), 42.
5 Frank Leary, USA (Pontiac Trans-Am), 42.
6 Larry Park, USA (Chevrolet Corvette), 42.
7 David Schroeder, USA (Porsche 911SC), 42; **8** Steve Saleen, USA (Pontiac Trans-Am), 42; **9** Jim Derhaag, USA (Pontiac Trans-Am), 41; **10** Bill Craine, USA (Chevrolet Corvette), 41.
Fastest Qualifier: Miller, 1m 24·02s, 96·41 mph/155·16 km/h (record).
Fastest lap: Willy T. Ribbs, USA (Pontiac Trans-Am), 1m 25·31s, 94·95 mph/152·81 km/h.
Championship points. Drivers: 1 Hobbs, 68; **2** Gloy, 60; **3** Felton, 49; **4** Ribbs, 42; **5** Pickett, 41; **6** Leary, 33.
Manufacturers: 1 Chevrolet, 34; **2** Pontiac, 27; **3** Mercury, 18; **4** Porsche, 9; **5** Datsun, 4.

SCCA BUDWEISER TRANS-AM CHAMPIONSHIP RACE, Mid-Ohio Sports Car Course, Lexington, Ohio, United States of America, July 17. SCCA Budweiser Trans-Am Championship, round 6. 42 laps of the 2·400-mile/3·862-km circuit, 100·80 miles/162·20 km.
1 Willy T. Ribbs, USA (Chevrolet Camaro), 1h 09m 06·330s, 87·518 mph/140·846 km/h.
2 David Hobbs, GB (Chevrolet Camaro), 1h 09m 18·730s.
3 Tom Gloy, USA (Mercury Capri), 42 laps.
4 Darin Brassfield, USA (Chevrolet Corvette), 42.
5 Elliott Forbes-Robinson, USA (Pontiac Trans-Am), 42.
6 Steve Saleen, USA (Pontiac Trans-Am), 42.
7 Paul Newman, USA (Datsun 280ZX Turbo), 41; **8** Paul DePirro, USA (Chevrolet Camaro), 41; **9** Jim Derhaag, USA (Pontiac Firebird), 40; **10** Craig Shafer, USA (Chevrolet Camaro), 39.
Fastest Qualifier: Forbes-Robinson, 1m 33·056s, 92·84 mph/149·41 km/h.
Fastest lap: Ribbs, 1m 35·11s, 90·842 mph/146·196 km/h (record).
Championship points. Drivers: 1 Hobbs, 84; **2** Gloy, 74; **3** Ribbs, 62; **4** Felton, 49; **5** Forbes-Robinson, 45; **6** Pickett, 41.
Manufacturers: 1 Chevrolet, 43; **2** Pontiac, 29; **3** Mercury, 22; **4** Porsche, 9; **5** Datsun, 4.

SCCA BUDWEISER TRANS-AM CHAMPIONSHIP RACE, Road America, Elkhart Lake, Wisconsin, United States of America, July 31. SCCA Budweiser Trans-Am Championship, round 7. 25 laps of the 4·000-mile/6·437-km circuit, 100·00 miles/160·93 km.
1 David Hobbs, GB (Chevrolet Camaro), 1h 04m 01·37s, 93·72 mph/150·83 km/h.
2 Elliott Forbes-Robinson, USA (Pontiac Trans-Am), 1h 04m 05·97s.
3 Tom Gloy, USA (Mercury Capri), 25 laps.
4 Ludwig Heimrath, CDN (Porsche 930), 25.
5 Jerry Hansen, USA (Pontiac Trans-Am), 25.
6 Paul DePirro, USA (Chevrolet Camaro), 25.
7 Dave Watson, USA (Pontiac Firebird), 25; **8** Tim Evans, USA (Pontiac Trans-Am), 25; **9** Lyn St. James, USA (Mercury Capri), 25; **10** Rick Dittman, USA (Chevrolet Corvette), 25.
Fastest Qualifier: Hobbs, 2m 17·233s, 104·93 mph/168·87 km/h (record).
Fastest lap: Hobbs, 2m 21·01s, 102·12 mph/164·35 km/h.
Championship points. Drivers: 1 Hobbs, 106; **2** Gloy, 88; **3** Ribbs, 62; **4** Forbes-Robinson, 61; **5** Felton, 49; **6** Pickett, 41.
Manufacturers: 1 Chevrolet, 52; **2** Pontiac, 35; **3** Mercury, 26; **4** Porsche, 12; **5** Datsun, 4.

SCCA BUDWEISER TRANS-AM CHAMPIONSHIP RACE, Brainerd International Raceway, Minnesota, United States of America, August 8. SCCA Budweiser Trans-Am Championship, round 8. 33 laps of the 3·000-mile/4·828-km circuit, 99·00 miles/159·32 km.
1 Willy T. Ribbs, USA (Chevrolet Camaro), 58m 58·57s, 100·72 mph/162·09 km/h.
2 David Hobbs, GB (Chevrolet Camaro), 59m 00·37s.
3 Tom Gloy, USA (Mercury Capri), 33 laps.
4 Elliott Forbes-Robinson, USA (Pontiac Trans-Am), 33.
5 Paul DePirro, USA (Chevrolet Camaro), 33.
6 Gene Felton, USA (Pontiac Trans-Am), 33.
7 Frank Leary, USA (Pontiac Trans-Am), 33; **8** Jim Derhaag, USA (Pontiac Firebird), 33; **9** Jerry Hansen, USA (Pontiac Firebird), 33; **10** Vern Smith, USA (Mercury Capri), 32.
Fastest Qualifier: Ribbs, 1m 37·953s, 110·26 mph/177·45 km/h (record).
Fastest lap: Ribbs, 1m 40·420s, 107·55 mph/173·08 km/h (record).
Championship points. Drivers: 1 Hobbs, 122; **2** Gloy, 102; **3** Ribbs, 84; **4** Forbes-Robinson, 73; **5** Felton, 59; **6** Leary, 47.
Manufacturers: 1 Chevrolet, 61; **2** Pontiac, 38; **3** Mercury, 30; **4** Porsche, 12; **5** Datsun, 4.

SCCA BUDWEISER TRANS-AM CHAMPIONSHIP RACE, Trois-Rivieres, Quebec, Canada, September 4. SCCA Budweiser Trans-Am Championship, round 9. 35 laps of the 2·100-mile/3·380-km circuit, 73·50 miles/118·30 km.
1 John Paul Jnr, USA (Chevrolet Camaro), 56m 27·893s, 78·102 mph/125·693 km/h.
2 Richard Spenard, CDN (Pontiac Trans-Am), 57m 24·155s.
3 Elliott Forbes-Robinson, USA (Pontiac Trans-Am), 35 laps.
4 Dave Watson, USA (Pontiac Firebird), 34.
5 Tom Gloy, USA (Mercury Capri), 34.
6 Paul Miller, USA (Porsche Carrera Turbo), 33.
7 Rob McFarlin, USA (Ford Mustang), 33; **8** Jim Derhaag, USA (Pontiac Trans-Am), 33; **9** R. J. Valentine, USA (Pontiac Firebird), 33; **10** Vern Smith, USA (Mercury Capri), 33.
Fastest Qualifier: Spenard, 1m 34·317s, 80·155 mph/128·997 km/h (record).
Fastest lap: Paul Jnr, 1m 35·109s, 79·488 mph/127·923 km/h (record).
Championship points. Drivers: 1 Hobbs, 122; **2** Gloy, 113; **3** Ribbs, 90; **4** Forbes-Robinson, 87; **5** Felton, 59; **6** Derhaag, 48.
Manufacturers: 1 Chevrolet, 70; **2** Pontiac, 44; **3** Mercury, 32; **4** Porsche, 13; **5** Datsun, 4.

SCCA BUDWEISER TRANS-AM CHAMPIONSHIP RACE, Sears Point International Raceway, Sonoma, California, United States of America, September 18. SCCA Budweiser Trans-Am Championship, round 10. 40 laps of the 2·523-mile/4·060-km circuit, 100·92 miles/162·40 km.
1 Willy T. Ribbs, USA (Chevrolet Camaro), 1h 13m 40·6s, 82·186 mph/132·265 km/h.
2 Tom Gloy, USA (Mercury Capri), 1h 13m 49·3s.
3 Frank Leary, USA (Pontiac Firebird), 40 laps.
4 Dave Watson, USA (Pontiac Firebird), 40.
5 Elliott Forbes-Robinson, USA (Pontiac Firebird), 40.
6 Jerry Brassfield, USA (Chevrolet Camaro), 40.
7 Jim Derhaag, USA (Pontiac Firebird), 40; **8** Paul Newman, USA (Datsun ZX Turbo); 39; **9** Larry Park, USA (Chevrolet Corvette), 39; **10** Richard Wall, USA (Chevrolet Camaro), 39.
Fastest Qualifier: David Hobbs, GB (Chevrolet Camaro), 1m 39·824s, 90·986 mph/146·427 km/h.
Fastest lap: Hobbs, 1m 40·47s, 90·403 mph/145·489 km/h.
Championship points. Drivers: 1 Gloy, 129; **2** Hobbs, 124; **3** Ribbs, 110; **4** Forbes-Robinson, 98; **5** Felton, 59; **6** Derhaag, 57.
Manufacturers: 1 Chevrolet, 79; **2** Pontiac, 48; **3** Mercury, 38; **4** Porsche, 13; **5** Datsun, 4.

SCCA BUDWEISER TRANS-AM CHAMPIONSHIP RACE, Riverside International Raceway, California, United States of America, September 25. SCCA Budweiser Trans-Am Championship, round 11. 40 laps of the 2·547-mile/4·099-km circuit, 101·88 miles/163·69 km.
1 David Hobbs, GB (Chevrolet Camaro), 1h 00m 37·6s, 102·078 mph/164·278 km/h.
2 Willy T. Ribbs, USA (Chevrolet Camaro), 1h 00m 48·8s.
3 Paul Newman, USA (Datson ZX Turbo), 40 laps.
4 Frank Leary, USA (Pontiac Trans-Am), 40.
5 Wally Dallenbach Jnr, USA (Pontiac Trans-Am), 40.
6 Jim Derhaag, USA (Pontiac Firebird), 40.
7 Jerry Brassfield, USA (Chevrolet Camaro), 40; **8** Bob Hagestad, USA (Porsche 926), 40; **9** Mark Wolocatiuk, USA (Chevrolet Corvette), 40; **10** Les Lindley, USA (Chevrolet Camaro), 40.
Fastest Qualifier: Hobbs, 1m 22·581s, 111·832 mph/179·976 km/h.
Fastest lap: Ribbs, 1m 24·021s, 107·940 mph/173·712 km/h.
Championship points. Drivers: 1 Hobbs, 146; **2** Gloy, 129; **3** Ribbs, 126; **4** Forbes-Robinson, 98; **5** Leary, 73; **6** Derhaag, 67.
Manufacturers: 1 Chevrolet, 88; **2** Pontiac, 51; **3** Mercury, 38; **4** Porsche, 13; **5** Datsun, 8.

SCCA BUDWEISER TRANS-AM CHAMPIONSHIP RACE, Caesars Palace Indy Circuit, Nevada, United States of America, October 8. SCCA Budweiser Trans-Am Championship, round 12. 89 laps of the 1·125-mile/1·811-km circuit, 100·13 miles/161·18 km.
1 Willy T. Ribbs, USA (Chevrolet Camaro), 1h 12m 53s, 82·323 mph/132·486 km/h.
2 Dave Watson, USA (Pontiac Firebird), 1h 12m 56s.
3 Tom Gloy, USA (Mercury Capri), 89 laps.
4 David Hobbs, GB (Chevrolet Camaro), 89.
5 Wally Dallenbach Jnr, USA (Pontiac Trans-Am), 89.
6 Jerry Brassfield, USA (Chevrolet Camaro), 89.
7 Jim Derhaag, USA (Pontiac Firebird), 89; **8** Craig Carter, USA (Chevrolet Camaro), 88; **9** Andy Porterfield, USA (Chevrolet Camaro), 88; **10** Frank Leary, USA (Pontiac Firebird), 87.
Fastest Qualifier: Ribbs, 40·912s, 99·479 mph/160·096 km/h.
Fastest lap: Gloy, 41·338s, 97·973 mph/157·672 km/h.

Final Championship points. Drivers:

1 David Hobbs, GB	158
2 Willy T. Ribbs, USA	148
3 Tom Gloy, USA	143
4 Elliott Forbes-Robinson, USA	102
5 Frank Leary, USA	79
6 Jim Derhaag, USA	76

7 Gene Felton, USA, 59; **8** Dave Watson, USA, 59; **9** Paul Newman, USA, 51; **10** Lyn St. James, USA, 45; **11** Paul Miller, USA, 43; **12** Greg Pickett, USA, 41; **13** Paul DePirro, USA, 36; **14** Vern Smith, USA, 29; **15** Jerry Brassfield, USA, 29.

Manufacturers:

1 Chevrolet	97
2 Pontiac	57
3 Mercury	42
4 Porsche	13
5 Datsun	8

CART PPG Indy
1982 results

The final round of the 1982 CART PPG Indy Car World Series was run after Autocourse 1982/83 went to press.

MILLER HIGH LIFE 150, Phoenix International Raceway, Arizona, United States of America, November 6. CART PPG Indy Car World Series, round 11. 150 laps of the 1·000-mile/1·609-km circuit, 150·00 miles/241·40 km.
1 Tom Sneva, USA (March 82C-Cosworth DFX), 1h 21m 05s, 110·997 mph/178·632 km/h.
2 Rick Mears, USA (Penske PC10-Cosworth DFX), 1h 21m 11s.
3 Mario Andretti, USA (Wildcat Mk8B-Cosworth DFX), 150 laps.
4 Kevin Cogan, USA (Penske PC10-Cosworth DFX), 148.
5 Bobby Rahal, USA (March 82C-Cosworth DFX), 148.
6 Tony Bettenhausen, USA (March 82C-Cosworth DFX), 147.
7 Roger Mears, USA (Penske PC10-Cosworth DFX), 147; **8** Bill Alsup, USA (Penske PC9C-Cosworth DFX), 146; **9** Gary Bettenhausen, USA (March 82C-Cosworth DFX), 146; **10** Howdy Holmes, USA (March 82C-Cosworth DFX), 145; **11** Pancho Carter, USA (March 82C-Cosworth DFX), 145 (including 1 lap penalty for passing under yellow flag), **12** Mike Mosley, USA (March 82C-Cosworth DFX), 145.
Fastest Qualifier: Rick Mears, 23·881s, 150·747 mph/242·603 km/h.
Final Championship points:

1 Rick Mears, USA	294
2 Bobby Rahal, USA	242
3 Mario Andretti, USA	188
4 Gordon Johncock, USA	186
5 Tom Sneva, USA	144
6 Kevin Cogan, USA	136

7 Al Unser, USA, 125; **8** Geoff Brabham, AUS, 110; **9** Roger Mears, USA, 103; **10** Tony Bettenhausen, USA, 80; **11** Bill Alsup, USA, 70; **12** Johnny Rutherford, USA, 62; **13** Josele Garza, MEX and Howdy Holmes, USA, 56; **15** Hector Rebaque, MEX and Gary Bettenhausen, USA, 48; **17** Pancho Carter, USA, 47; **18** Johnny Parsons, USA, 41; **19** Mike Mosley, USA, 37; **20** Tom Bigelow, USA, 32.

1983 results

KRACO DIXIE 200, Atlanta International Raceway, Georgia, United States of America, April 17. CART PPG Indy Car World Series, round 1. 132 laps of the 1·522-mile/2·449-km circuit, 200·904 miles/323·268 km.
1 Gordon Johncock, USA (Wildcat Mk9C-Cosworth DFX), 1h 22m 29·295s, 146·133 mph/235·178 km/h.
2 Al Unser, USA (Penske PC11-Cosworth DFX), 1h 23m 01·2s.
3 John Paul Jnr, USA (Penske PC10-Cosworth DFX), 131 laps.
4 Pete Halsmer, USA (Penske PC10-Cosworth DFX), 130.
5 Mario Andretti, USA (Lola T700-Cosworth DFX), 128.
6 Al Unser Jnr, USA (Eagle 82-Cosworth DFX), 127.
7 Roger Mears, USA (Penske PC10-Cosworth DFX), 127; **8** Rick Mears, USA (Penske PC11-Cosworth DFX), 126; **9** Howdy Holmes, USA (March 83C-Cosworth DFX), 126; **10** Tony Bettenhausen, USA (March 82C-Cosworth DFX), 126; **11** Jim McElreath, USA (Penske PC7-Cosworth DFX), 125; **12** Doug Heveron, USA (Wildcat Mk8B-Cosworth DFX), 121.
Fastest Qualifier: Rick Mears, 26·730s, 204·983 mph/329·887 km/h.
Championship points: 1 Johncock, 20; **2** Unser, 16; **3** Paul Jnr, 14; **4** Halsmer, 12; **5** Andretti, 10; **6** Unser Jnr, 8.

DANA-REX MAYS 150, Wisconsin State Fair Park Speedway, Milwaukee, Wisconsin, United States of America, June 12. CART PPG Indy Car World Series, round 3. 150 laps of the 1·000-mile/1·609-km circuit, 150·00 miles/241·40 km.
1 Tom Sneva, USA (March 83C-Cosworth DFX), 1h 17m 31s, 116·10 mph/186·84 km/h.
2 Al Unser, USA (Penske PC11-Cosworth DFX), 1h 17m 32s.
3 Rick Mears, USA (Penske PC11-Cosworth DFX), 150 laps.
4 Teo Fabi, I (March 83C-Cosworth DFX), 149.
5 Mike Mosley, USA (March 82C-Cosworth DFX), 148.
6 Bobby Rahal, USA (March 83C-Cosworth DFX), 147 (including 1 lap penalty).
7 Howdy Holmes, USA (March 83C-Cosworth DFX), 147; **8** Roger Mears, USA (Penske PC10-Cosworth DFX), 147; **9** Pete Halsmer, USA (Penske PC10-Cosworth DFX), 146; **10** Tony Bettenhausen, USA (March 83C-Cosworth DFX), 145; **11** Dick Simon, USA (March 83C-Cosworth DFX), 144; **12** Danny Ongais, USA (Wildcat Mk9-Cosworth DFX), 144.
Fastest Qualifier: Fabi, 26·259s, 137·096 mph/220·634 km/h.
Championship points: 1 Unser, 48; **2** Sneva, 41; **3** Mears, 35; **4** Johncock, 20; **5** Holmes, 18; **6** Halsmer, 16.

BUDWEISER CLEVELAND 500, Burke Lakefront Airport Circuit, Cleveland, Ohio, United States of America, July 3. CART PPG Indy Car World Series, round 4. 125 laps of the 2·485-mile/3·999-km circuit, 310·63 miles/499·88 km.
1 Al Unser, USA (Penske PC11-Cosworth DFX), 2h 51m 54s, 108·202 mph/174·134 km/h.
2 Pete Halsmer, USA (Penske PC10-Cosworth DFX), 2h 52m 26s.
3 Teo Fabi, I (March 83C-Cosworth DFX), 124 laps.
4 Mike Mosley, USA (March 83C-Cosworth DFX), 124.
5 Tom Sneva, USA (March 83C-Cosworth DFX), 123.
6 Roger Mears, USA (Penske PC10-Cosworth DFX), 121.
7 Rick Mears, USA (Penske PC11-Cosworth DFX), 120; **8** Pancho Carter, USA (March 82C-Cosworth DFX), 119; **9** Al Unser Jnr, USA (Eagle 83-Cosworth DFX), 119; **10** Desire Wilson, ZA (March 83C-Cosworth DFX), 117; **11** Phil Kruger, USA (Penske PC9-Cosworth DFX), 109; **12** Howdy Holmes, USA (March 83C-Cosworth DFX), 95.
Fastest Qualifier: Mario Andretti, USA (Lola T700-Cosworth DFX), 1m 13·516s, 121·688 mph/195·837 km/h.
Championship points: 1 Unser, 69; **2** Sneva, 52; **3** Mears, 41; **4** Halsmer, 32; **5** Fabi, 29; **6** Mosley, 22.

NORTON MICHIGAN 500, Michigan International Speedway, Brooklyn, United States of America, July 17. CART PPG Indy Car World Series, round 5. 250 laps of the 2·000-mile/3·219-km circuit, 500·00 miles/804·75 km.
1 John Paul Jnr, USA (Penske PC10-Cosworth DFX), 3h 42m 27s, 134·862 mph/217·039 km/h.
2 Al Unser, USA (Penske PC11-Cosworth DFX), 3h 42m 42s.
3 Mario Andretti, USA (Lola T700-Cosworth DFX), 250 laps.
4 Rick Mears, USA (Penske PC11-Cosworth DFX), 249 (DNF, accident).
5 Bobby Rahal, USA (March 83C-Cosworth DFX), 249.
6 Pancho Carter, USA (March 82C-Cosworth DFX), 248.
7 Al Unser Jnr, USA (Eagle 83-Cosworth DFX), 248; **8** Chip Ganassi, USA (Wildcat Mk9-Cosworth DFX), 248; **9** Chris Kneifel, USA (Primus-Cosworth DFX), 242; **10** Steve Chassey, USA (Eagle 82-Chevrolet), 241; **11** Dick Ferguson, USA (March 81C-Cosworth DFX), 235; **12** Scott Brayton, USA (March 83C-Cosworth DFX), 235.
Fastest Qualifier: Teo Fabi, I (March 83C-Cosworth DFX), 35·621s, 202·128 mph/325·293 km/h.
Championship points: 1 Unser, 85; **2** Mears, 53; **3** Sneva, 52; **4** Paul Jnr, 35; **5** Halsmer, 32; **6** Fabi, 29.

PROVIMI VEAL 200, Road America, Elkhart Lake, Wisconsin, United States of America, July 31. CART PPG Indy Car World Series, round 6. 50 laps of the 4·000-mile/6·437-km circuit, 200·00 miles/257·48 km.
1 Mario Andretti, USA (Lola T700-Cosworth DFX), 2h 00m 42·75s, 99·410 mph/159·984 km/h.
2 Al Unser Jnr, USA (Eagle 83-Cosworth DFX), 2h 00m 58·73s.
3 Al Unser, USA (Penske PC11-Cosworth DFX), 50 laps.
4 Tom Sneva, USA (Theodore-Cosworth DFX), 49.
5 John Paul Jnr, USA (Penske PC10-Cosworth DFX), 49.
6 Steve Chassey, USA (Eagle 82-Chevrolet), 49.
7 Pancho Carter, USA (March 82C-Cosworth DFX), 49; **8** Roger Mears, USA (Penske PC10-Cosworth DFX), 48; **9** Derek Daly, IRL (March 83C-Cosworth DFX), 47 (DNF, spun off); **10** Bobby Rahal, USA (March 83C-Cosworth DFX), 47 (DNF, out of fuel); **11** Josele Garza, MEX (Penske PC10-Cosworth DFX), 47 (DNF, out of fuel); **12** Tony Bettenhausen, USA (March 83C-Cosworth DFX), 46 (DNF, out of fuel).
Fastest Qualifier: Andretti, 1m 58·898s, 121·112 mph/194·910 km/h.
Championship points: 1 Unser, 99; **2** Sneva, 64; **3** Mears, 53; **4** Andretti, 46; **5** Paul Jnr, 45; **6** Unser Jnr, 37.

DOMINO'S PIZZA 500, Pocono International Raceway, Pennsylvania, United States of America, August 14. CART PPG Indy Car World Series, round 7. 200 laps of the 2·500-mile/4·023-km circuit, 500·00 miles/804·60 km.
1 Teo Fabi, I (March 83C-Cosworth DFX), 3h 42m 28s, 134·852 mph/217·023 km/h.
2 Al Unser Jnr, USA (March 83C-Cosworth DFX), 3h 42m 32s.
3 Rick Mears, USA (Penske PC10B-Cosworth DFX), 200 laps.
4 Mike Mosley, USA (March 83C-Cosworth DFX), 199.
5 Bobby Rahal, USA (March 83C-Cosworth DFX), 199.
6 Pancho Carter, USA (March 82C-Cosworth DFX), 199.
7 Mario Andretti, USA (Lola T700-Cosworth DFX), 197; **8** Chris Kneifel, USA (Primus-Cosworth DFX), 196; **9** Josele Garza, MEX (Penske PC10-Cosworth DFX), 195; **10** Tony Bettenhausen, USA (March 83C-Cosworth DFX), 194; **11** Al Unser, USA (Penske PC11-Cosworth DFX), 191; **12** Tom Sneva, USA (March 83C-Cosworth DFX), 153 (DNF, transmission).
Fastest Qualifier: Sneva, 46·912s, 191·849 mph/308·750 km/h.
Championship points: 1 Unser, 101; **2** Mears, 67; **3** Sneva, 66; **4** Unser Jnr, 53; **5** Andretti, 52; **6** Fabi, 50.

LOS ANGELES TIMES/BUDWEISER 500, Riverside International Raceway, California, United States of America, August 28. CART PPG Indy Car World Series, round 8. 95 laps of the 3·30-mile/5·31-km circuit, 313·50 miles/504·45 km.
1 Bobby Rahal, USA (March 83C-Cosworth DFX), 2h 45m 28s, 113·678 mph/182·947 km/h.
2 Teo Fabi, I (March 83C-Cosworth DFX), 2h 45m 56s.
3 John Paul Jnr, USA (Penske PC10-Cosworth DFX), 95 laps.
4 Al Unser Jnr, USA (Eagle 83-Cosworth DFX), 94.
5 Tom Sneva, USA (March 83C-Cosworth DFX), 93.
6 Tom Klauser, USA (Schkee DB6-Chevrolet), 90.
7 Pancho Carter, USA (March 82C-Cosworth DFX), 89; **8** Tony Bettenhausen, USA (March 83C-Cosworth DFX), 88; **9** Roger Mears, USA (Penske PC10-Cosworth DFX), 84; **10** Danny Ongais, USA (March 83C-Cosworth DFX), 76 (DNF, engine); **11** Al Unser, USA (Penske PC11-Cosworth DFX), 75 (DNF, transmission); **12** Jerry Karl, USA (Penske PC9-Cosworth DX), 74.
Fastest Qualifier: Fabi, 1m 30·887s, 130·712 mph/210·360 km/h.
Championship points: 1 Unser, 103; **2** Sneva, 76; **3** Mears and Fabi, 67; **5** Unser Jnr, 66; **6** Paul Jnr, 59.

ESCORT RADAR WARNING 200, Mid-Ohio Sports Car Course, Lexington, Ohio, United States of America, September 11. CART PPG Indy Car World Series, round 9. 84 laps of the 2·400-mile/3·862-km circuit, 201·60 miles/324·41 km.
1 Teo Fabi, I (March 83C-Cosworth DFX), 2h 01m 49·0s, 99·297 mph/159·80 km/h.
2 Mario Andretti, USA (Lola T700-Cosworth DFX), 2h 02m 15·0s.
3 Bobby Rahal, USA (March 83C-Chevrolet), 84 laps.
4 Al Unser, USA (Penske PC10B-Cosworth DFX), 83.
5 Danny Ongais, USA (March 83C-Cosworth DFX), 83.
6 Kevin Cogan, USA (Theodore-Cosworth DFX), 83.
7 Tom Sneva, USA (March 83C-Cosworth DFX), 83; **8** Howdy Holmes, USA (March 83C-Cosworth DFX), 82; **9** Rick Mears, USA (Penske PC10B-Cosworth DFX), 81 (DNF, accident); **10** Pancho Carter, USA (March 82C-Cosworth DFX), 80; **11** Greg Leffler, USA (Eagle 82-Chevrolet), 78; **12** Roger Mears, USA (Penske PC10-Cosworth DFX), 78.
Fastest Qualifier: Rahal, 1m 21·364s, 106·189 mph/170·894 km/h.
Championship points: 1 Unser, 115; **2** Fabi, 88; **3** Sneva, 82; **4** Mears, 71; **5** Andretti, 68; **6** Rahal, 67.

DETROIT NEWS GRAND PRIX 200, Michigan International Speedway, Brooklyn, Michigan, United States of America, September 18. CART PPG Indy Car World Series, round 10. 100 laps of the 2·000-mile/3·219-km circuit, 200·00 miles/321·90 km.
1 Rick Mears, USA (Penske PC10B-Cosworth DFX), 1h 05m 49·0s, 182·325 mph/293·423 km/h.
2 Bobby Rahal, USA (March 83C-Cosworth DFX), 1h 05m 57·0s.
3 Teo Fabi, I (March 83C-Cosworth DFX), 99 laps.
4 Mario Andretti, USA (Lola T700-Cosworth DFX), 99.
5 Al Unser, USA (Penske PC10B-Cosworth DFX), 98.
6 Chip Ganassi, USA (Wildcat Mk9B-Cosworth DFX), 98.
7 John Paul Jnr, USA (Penske PC10-Cosworth DFX), 98; **8** Howdy Holmes, USA (March 83C-Cosworth DFX), 97; **9** Tony Bettenhausen, USA (March 83C-Cosworth DFX), 97; **10** Al Unser, Jnr, USA (Eagle 83-Cosworth DFX), 96; **11** Mike Mosley, USA (March 83C-Cosworth DFX), 96; **12** Geoff Brabham, AUS (March 83C-Cosworth DFX), 96.
Fastest Qualifier: Rahal, 35·075s, 205·274 mph/330·356 km/h.
Championship points: 1 Unser, 125; **2** Fabi, 102; **3** Mears, 92; **4** Rahal, 84; **5** Sneva, 82; **6** Andretti, 80.

CAESARS PALACE 200, Las Vegas Indy Circuit, Nevada, United States of America, October 9. CART PPG Indy Car World Series, round 11. 178 laps of the 1·125-mile/1·811-km circuit, 200·25 miles/322·36 km.
1 Mario Andretti, USA (Lola T700-Cosworth DFX), 2h 17m 48s, 87·192 mph/140·322 km/h.
2 John Paul Jnr, USA (Penske PC10-Cosworth DFX), 2h 17m 49·26s.
3 Chip Ganassi, USA (Wildcat Mk9B-Cosworth DFX), 177 laps.
4 Al Unser, USA (Penske PC10B-Cosworth DFX), 177.
5 Pete Halsmer, USA (Penske PC10-Cosworth DFX), 177.
6 Pancho Carter, USA (March 82C-Cosworth DFX), 176.
7 Roger Mears, USA (Penske PC10-Cosworth DFX), 175; **8** Chris Kneifel, USA (Primus-Cosworth DFX), 175; **9** Bobby Rahal, USA (March 83C-Chevrolet), 173; **10** Al Unser Jnr, USA (Eagle 83-Cosworth DFX), 171 (DNF, accident); **11** Josele Garza, MEX (Penske PC10-Cosworth DFX), 170; **12** Steve Chassey, USA (Eagle 82-Chevrolet), 168.
Fastest Qualifier: Paul Jnr, 34·888s, 116·086 mph/186·822 km/h.
Championship points: 1 Unser, 137; **2** Fabi, 102; **3** Andretti, 101; **4** Mears, 92; **5** Rahal, 88; **6** Sneva and Paul Jnr, 82.

CRIBARI WINES 300 KMS, Laguna Seca Raceway, California, United States of America, October 23. CART PPG Indy Car World Series, round 12. 98 laps of the 1·900-mile/3·056-km circuit, 186·20 miles/299·49 km.
1 Teo Fabi, I (March 83C-Cosworth DFX), 1h 44m 28·0s, 106·943 mph/172·108 km/h.
2 Mario Andretti, USA (Lola T700-Cosworth DFX), 1h 44m 49·7s.
3 Chip Ganassi, USA (Wildcat Mk9B-Cosworth DFX), 98 laps.
4 Al Unser Jnr, USA (Eagle 83-Cosworth DFX), 98.
5 Howdy Holmes, USA (March 83C-Cosworth DFX), 96.
6 Roger Mears, USA (Penske PC10-Cosworth DFX), 94.
7 Bobby Rahal, USA (March 83C-Chevrolet), 93; **8** Jeff Wood, USA (Eagle 83-Chevrolet), 92; **9** Chris Kneifel, USA (Primus-Cosworth DFX), 91 (DNF, accident); **10** Steve Chassey, USA (Eagle 83-Chevrolet), 88; **11** Al Unser, USA (Penske PC10B-Cosworth DFX), 87; **12** Josele Garza, MEX (Penske PC10-Cosworth DFX), 85.
Fastest Qualifier: Fabi, 56·920s, 120·169 mph/193·393 km/h.
Championship points: 1 Unser, 139; **2** Fabi, 124; **3** Andretti, 117; **4** Rahal, 94; **5** Mears, 92; **6** Unser Jnr, 84.

MILLER HIGH LIFE 150, Phoenix International Raceway, Arizona, United States of America, October 30. CART PPG Indy Car World Series, round 13. 150 laps of the 1·000-mile/1·609-km circuit, 150·00 miles/241·40 km.
1 Teo Fabi, I (March 83C-Cosworth DFX), 1h 11m 03s, 126·671 mph/203·857 km/h.
2 Mario Andretti, USA (Lola T700-Cosworth DFX), 1h 11m 12s.
3 Tom Sneva, USA (March 83C-Cosworth DFX), 149 laps.
4 Al Unser, USA (Penske PC10B-Cosworth DFX), 148.
5 Chip Ganassi, USA (Wildcat Mk9B-Cosworth DFX), 148.
6 Kevin Cogan, USA (March 83C-Cosworth DFX), 148.
7 Pete Halsmer, USA (Penske PC10-Cosworth DFX), 147; **8** Al Unser Jnr, USA (Eagle 83-Cosworth DFX), 147; **9** Mike Andretti, USA (March 83C-Cosworth DFX), 147; **10** Pancho Carter, USA (March 82C-Cosworth DFX), 146; **11** John Paul Jnr, USA (Penske PC10-Cosworth DFX), 145; **12** Tony Bettenhausen, USA (March 83C-Cosworth DFX), 143.
Fastest Qualifier: Fabi, 24·947s, 144·306 mph/232·237 km/h.

Final Championship points:

1 Al Unser, USA	151
2 Teo Fabi, I	146
3 Mario Andretti, USA	133
4 Tom Sneva, USA	96
5 Bobby Rahal, USA	94
6 Rick Mears, USA	92

7 Al Unser Jnr, USA, 89; **8** John Paul Jnr, USA, 84; **9** Chip Ganassi, USA, 56; **10** Pancho Carter, USA, 53; **11** Pete Halsmer, USA, 48; **12** Roger Mears, USA, 43; **13** Howdy Holmes, USA, 39; **14** Mike Mosley, USA, 36; **15** Kevin Cogan, USA, 26.

NASCAR Winston Cup Grand National
1982 results

The final rounds of the 1982 NASCAR Winston Cup Grand National series were run after Autocourse 1982/83 went to press.

AMERICAN 500, North Carolina Motor Speedway, Rockingham, North Carolina, United States of America, October 31. NASCAR Winston Cup Grand National, round 28·492 laps of the 1·017-mile/1·637-km circuit, 500·36 miles/805·26 km.
1 Darrell Waltrip, USA (Buick), 4h 20m 47s, 115·122 mph/185·270 km/h.
2 Bobby Allison, USA (Chevrolet), 4h 20m 56·5s.
3 Neil Bonnet, USA (Ford), 492 laps.
4 Terry Labonte, USA (Buick), 491.
5 Morgan Shepherd, USA (Buick), 491.
6 Richard Petty, USA (Pontiac), 491.
7 Buddy Baker, USA (Pontiac), 488; **8** Ron Bouchard, USA (Buick), 486; **9** Lennie Pond, USA (Chevrolet), 479; **10** D. K. Ulrich, USA (Buick), 471.
Fastest Qualifier: Cale Yarborough, USA (Buick), 25·562s, 143·228 mph/230·503 km/h.
Championship points. Drivers: 1 Waltrip, 4149; **2** B. Allison, 4112; **3** Labonte, 3987; **4** R. Petty, 3621; **5** Gant, 3612; **6** Arrington, 3463.
Manufacturers: 1 Buick, 225; **2** Pontiac, 87; **3** Chevrolet, 77; **4** Ford, 76; **5** Chrysler, 1.

ATLANTA JOURNAL 500, Atlanta International Raceway, Georgia, United States of America, November 6. NASCAR Winston Cup Grand National, round 29. 328 laps of the 1·522-mile/2·449-km circuit, 499·22 miles/803·41 km.
1 Bobby Allison, USA (Buick), 3h 48m 51s, 130·884 mph/210·637 km/h.
2 Harry Gant, USA (Buick), 3h 48m 51·5s.
3 Darrell Waltrip, USA (Buick), 328 laps.
4 Tim Richmond, USA (Buick), 328.
5 Joe Ruttmann, USA (Buick), 327.
6 Dave Marcis, USA (Buick), 327.
7 Ricky Rudd, USA (Pontiac), 326; **8** Terry Labonte, USA (Buick), 326; **9** Rodney Combs, USA (Buick), 326; **10** Mark Martin, USA (Buick), 325.
Fastest Qualifier: Morgan Shepherd, USA (Buick), 32·853s, 166·779 mph/268·404 km/h.
Championship points. Drivers: 1 Waltrip, 4319; **2** B. Allison, 4297; **3** Labonte, 4129; **4** Gant, 3787; **5** R. Petty, 3744; **6** Marcis, 3590.
Manufacturers: 1 Buick, 234; **2** Pontiac, 87; **3** Chevrolet, 77; **4** Ford, 76; **5** Chrysler, 1.

WINSTON WESTERN 500, Riverside International Raceway, California, United States of America, November 21. NASCAR Winston Cup Grand National, round 30. 119 laps of the 2·620-mile/4·216-km circuit, 311·78 miles/501·76 km.
1 Tim Richmond, USA (Buick), 3h 07m 24s, 99·823 mph/160·649 km/h.
2 Ricky Rudd, USA (Pontiac), 3h 07m 31s.
3 Darrell Waltrip USA (Buick), 119 laps.
4 Neil Bonnet, USA (Ford), 119.
5 Mark Martin, USA (Buick), 118.
6 Ron Bouchard, USA (Buick), 117.
7 Benny Parsons, USA (Buick), 117; **8** Morgan Shepherd, USA (Buick), 116; **9** Jody Ridley, USA (Ford), 115; **10** Jim Bown, USA (Buick), 115.
Fastest Qualifier: Waltrip, 1m 22·021s, 114·995 mph/185·066 km/h (record).
Final Championship points. Drivers:

1 Darrell Waltrip, USA	4489
2 Bobby Allison, USA	4417
3 Terry Labonte, USA	4211
4 Harry Gant, USA	3877
5 Richard Petty, USA	3814
6 Dave Marcis, USA	3666

7 Buddy Arrington, USA, 3642; **8** Ron Bouchard, USA, 3545; **9** Ricky Rudd, USA, 3537; **10** Morgan Shepherd, USA, 3451; **11** Jimmy Means, USA, 3423; **12** Dale Earnhardt, USA, 3402; **13** Jody Ridley, USA, 3333; **14** Mark Martin, USA, 3042; **15** Kyle Petty, USA, 3024; **16** Joe Ruttman, USA, 3021; **17** Neil Bonnett, USA, 2966; **18** Benny Parsons, USA, 2892; **19** J. D. McDuffie, USA, 2886; **20** Lake Speed, USA, 2850.
Manufacturers:

1 Buick	243
2 Pontiac	93
3 Ford	79
4 Chevrolet	77
5 Chrysler	1

1983 results

DAYTONA 500, Daytona International Speedway, Florida, United States of America, February 20. NASCAR Winston Cup Grand National, round 1. 200 laps of the 2·500-mile/4·023-km circuit, 500·miles/804·67 km.
1 Cale Yarborough, USA (Pontiac), 3h 12m 20s, 155·979 mph/251·023 km/h.
2 Bill Elliott, USA (Ford), 3h 12m 20s (Yarborough won by 1 car length).
3 Buddy Baker, USA (Ford), 200 laps.
4 Joe Ruttmann, USA (Chevrolet), 200.
5 Dick Brooks, USA (Ford), 199.
6 Terry Labonte, USA (Chevrolet), 199.
7 Tom Sneva, USA (Chevrolet), 199; **8** David Pearson, USA (Chevrolet), 198; **9** Bobby Allison, USA (Chevrolet), 198; **10** Jody Ridley, USA (Buick), 197.
Fastest Qualifier: Ricky Rudd, USA (Chevrolet), 45·257s, 198·864 mph/320·040 km/h.
Championship points. Drivers: 1 Yarborough, 180; **2** Elliott, 175; **3** Baker and Ruttman, 170; **5** Labonte, 150; **6** Sneva, 146.
Manufacturers: 1 Pontiac, 9; **2** Ford, 6; **3** Chevrolet, 3.

RICHMOND 400, Richmond Fairgrounds Raceway, Virginia, United States of America, February 27. NASCAR Winston Cup Grand National, round 2. 400 laps of the 0·542-mile/0·872-km circuit, 216·80 miles/348·80 km.
1 Bobby Allison, USA (Chevrolet), 2h 43m 45s, 79·584 mph/128·078 km/h.
2 Dale Earnhardt, USA (Ford), 2h 43m 45s (Allison won by 4 car lengths).
3 Neil Bonnet, USA (Chevrolet), 400 laps.
4 Geoff Bodine, USA (Pontiac), 399.
5 Harry Gant, USA (Buick), 399.
6 Bill Elliott, USA (Ford), 398.
7 Joe Ruttmann, USA (Buick), 398; **8** Richard Petty, USA (Pontiac), 398; **9** Dave Marcis, USA (Chevrolet), 397; **10** Buddy Baker, USA (Ford), 396.
Fastest Qualifier: Richy Rudd, USA (Chevrolet), 20·882s, 93·439 mph/150·375 km/h.
Championship points. Drivers: 1 Ruttmann, 326; **2** Elliott, 325; **3** Allison, 318; **4** Baker, 304; **5** Bonnett, 272; **6** Labonte, 247.
Manufactrurers: 1 Pontiac, Ford and Chevrolet, 12; **4** Buick, 2.

WARNER W HODGDON CAROLINA 500, North Carolina Motor Speedway, North Carolina, United States of America, March 13. NASCAR Winston Cup Grand National, round 3. 492 laps of the 1·017-mile/1·637-km circuit, 500·36 miles/805·26 km.
1 Richard Petty, USA (Pontiac), 4h 25m 30s, 113·055 mph/181·944 km/h.
2 Bill Elliott, USA (Ford), 4h 25m 30s (Petty won by ½ car length).
3 Darrell Waltrip, USA (Chevrolet), 492 laps.
4 Lake Speed, USA (Chevrolet), 490.
5 Harry Gant, USA (Buick), 489.
6 Ricky Rudd, USA (Chevrolet), 489.
7 Tim Richmond, USA (Pontiac), 488; **8** Dick Brooks, USA (Ford), 486; **9** Cale Yarborough, USA (Chevrolet), 486; **10** Bobby Allison, USA (Chevrolet), 484.
Fastest Qualifier: Rudd, 25·529s, 143·413 mph/230·800 km/h.
Championship points. Drivers: 1 Elliott, 500; **2** Allison, 457; **3** Bonnett, 404; **4** Ruttman, 402; **5** Petty, 376; **6** Baker, 371.
Manufacturers: 1 Pontiac, 21; **2** Ford, 18; **3** Chevrolet, 16; **4** Buick, 4.

COCA COLA 500, Atlanta International Raceway, Georgia, United States of America, March 27. NASCAR Winston Cup Grand National, round 4. 328 laps of the 1·522-mile/2·449-km circuit, 499·22 miles/803·27 km.
1 Cale Yarborough, USA (Chevrolet), 4h 01m 27s, 124·055 mph/199·65 km/h.
2 Neil Bonnet, USA (Chevrolet), 4h 01m 29s.
3 Buddy Baker, USA (Ford), 328 laps.
4 Joe Ruttman, USA (Buick), 328.
5 Richard Petty, USA (Pontiac), 328.
6 Dick Brooks, USA (Ford), 328.
7 Mark Martin, USA (Buick), 328; **8** Terry Labonte, USA (Chevrolet), 328; **9** Tim Richmond, USA (Pontiac), 327; **10** Ricky Rudd, USA (Chevrolet), 326.
Fastest Qualifier: Geoff Bodine, USA (Pontiac), 32·672s, 167·703 mph/269·891 km/h.
Championship points. Drivers: 1 Bonnett, 584; **2** Elliott, 573; **3** Ruttman, 567; **4** Allison, 545; **5** Baker, 536; **6** Petty, 536.
Manufacturers: 1 Chevrolet, 25; **2** Pontiac, 23; **3** Ford, 22; **4** Buick, 7.

TRANSOUTH 500, Darlington International Raceway, South Carolina, United States of America, April 10. NASCAR Winston Cup Grand National, round 5. 367 laps of the 1·366-mile/2·198-km circuit, 501·32 miles/806·67 km.
1 Harry Gant, USA (Buick), 3h 50m 05·0s, 130·406 mph/209·87 km/h.
2 Darrell Waltrip, USA (Chevrolet), 3h 50m 05·5s.
3 Mark Martin, USA (Buick), 367 laps.
4 Ricky Rudd, USA (Chevrolet), 366.
5 Bill Elliott, USA (Ford), 365.
6 Cale Yarborough, USA (Chevrolet), 365.
7 Neil Bonnet, USA (Chevrolet), 363; **8** Bobby Allison, USA (Buick), 359; **9** Geoff Bodine, USA (Pontiac), 353; **10** D. K. Ulrich, USA (Buick), 353.
Fastest Qualifier: Tim Richmond, USA (Pontiac), 31·160s, 157·818 mph/253·98 km/h.
Championship points. Drivers: 1 Bonnet, 735; **2** Elliott, 728; **3** Allison, 692; **4** Gant, 677; **5** Ruttman, 675; **6** Yarborough, 658.
Manufacturers: 1 Chevrolet, 31; **2** Ford, 24; **3** Pontiac, 23; **4** Buick, 16.

NORTHWESTERN BANK 400, North Wilksboro Speedway, North Carolina, United States of America, April 17. NASCAR Winston Cup Grand National, round 6. 400 laps of the 0.625-mile/1·006-km circuit, 250·00 miles/402·34 km.
1 Darrell Waltrip, USA (Chevrolet), 2h 44m 03s, 91·436 mph/147·152 km/h.
2 Bobby Allison, USA (Buick), 2h 44m 11s.
3 Harry Gant, USA (Buick), 400 laps.
4 Neil Bonnett, USA (Chevrolet), 400.
5 Geoff Bodine, USA (Pontiac), 400.
6 Terry Labonte, USA (Chevrolet), 399.
7 Joe Ruttman, USA (Buick), 399; **8** Lake Speed, USA (Chevrolet), 398; **9** Dave Marcis, USA (Chevrolet), 398; **10** Richard Petty, USA (Pontiac), 398.
Fastest Qualifier: Bonnet, 40·060s, 112·332 mph/180·780 km/h (2 laps).
Championship points. Drivers: 1 Bonnett, 900; **2** Allison, 867; **3** Gant, 847; **4** Elliott, 833; **5** Ruttman, 821; **6** Brooks, 795.
Manufactrurers: 1 Chevrolet, 40; **2** Pontiac, 25; **3** Ford, 24; **4** Buick, 22.

VIRGINIA NATIONAL BANK 500, Martinsville Speedway, Virginia, United States of America, April 24. NASCAR Winston Cup Grand National, round 7. 500 laps of the 0·525-mile/0·845-km circuit, 262·50 miles/422·45 km.
1 Darrell Waltrip, USA (Chevrolet), 3h 57m 14s, 66·460 mph/106·957 km/h.
2 Harry Gant, USA (Buick), 3h 57m 14·5s.
3 Bobby Allison, USA (Buick), 500 laps.
4 Joe Ruttman, USA (Buick), 500.
5 Ricky Rudd, USA (Chevrolet), 500.
6 Terry Labonte, USA (Chevrolet), 499.
7 Ron Bouchard, USA (Buick), 497; **8** Dick Brooks, USA (Ford), 495; **9** Buddy Arrington, USA (Dodge), 493; **10** Jimmy Means, USA (Chevrolet), 491.
Fastest Qualifier: Rudd, 21·021s, 89·910 mph/144·706 km/h.
Championship points. Drivers: 1 Allison, 1037; **2** Gant, 1022; **3** Bonnett, 1015; **4** Ruttman, 981; **5** Brooks, 937; **6** Elliott, 933.
Manufacturers: 1 Chevrolet, 49; **2** Buick, 28; **3** Pontiac, 25; **4** Ford, 24.

WINSTON 500, Alabama International Motor Speedway, Talladega, Alabama, United States of America, May 1. NASCAR Winston Cup Grand National, round 8. 188 laps of the 2·660-mile/4·281-km circuit, 500·08 miles/804·80 km.
1 Richard Petty, USA (Pontiac), 3h 14m 55s, 153·936 mph/247·735 km/h.
2 Benny Parsons, USA (Buick), 3h 14m 55s (Petty won by one car length).
3 Lake Speed, USA (Chevrolet), 188 laps.
4 Harry Gant, USA (Buick), 188.
5 Bill Elliott, USA (Ford), 188.
6 Terry Labonte, USA (Chevrolet), 188.
7 Jimmy Means, USA (Buick), 188; **8** Ricky Rudd, USA (Chevrolet), 187; **9** Dave Marcis, USA (Chevrolet), 187; **10** Bobby Allison, USA (Buick), 186.
Fastest Qualifier: Cale Yarborough, USA (Chevrolet), 47·254s, 202·650 mph/326·133 km/h (record).
Championship points. Drivers: 1 Gant, 1187; **2** Allison, 1171; **3** Bonnett, 1133; **4** Ruttman, 1116; **5** Elliott, 1093; **6** Petty, 1060.
Manufacturers: 1 Chevrolet, 53; **2** Pontiac, 34; **3** Buick, 34; **4** Ford, 26.

MARTY ROBBINS 420, Nashville International Raceway, Tennessee, United States of America, May 7. NASCAR Winston Cup Grand National, Round 9. 420 laps of the 0·596-mile/0·959-km circuit, 250·32 miles/402·78 km.
1 Darrell Waltrip, USA (Chevrolet), 3h 32m 23s, 70·717 mph/113·808 km/h.
2 Bobby Allison, USA (Buick), 419 laps.
3 Harry Gant, USA (Buick), 419.
4 Morgan Shepherd, USA (Buick), 418.
5 Bill Elliott, USA (Ford), 416.
6 Richard Petty, USA (Pontiac), 415.
7 Joe Ruttman, USA (Buick), 415; **8** Terry Labonte, USA (Chevrolet), 414; **9** Ron Bouchard, USA (Buick), 414; **10** Tim Richmond, USA (Pontiac), 412.
Fastest Qualifier: Waltrip, 20·807s, 103·119 mph/165·954 km/h.
Championship points. Drivers: 1 Gant, 1352; **2** Allison, 1346; **3** Ruttman, 1262; **4** Bonnett, 1257; **5** Elliott, 1248; **6** Petty, 1210.
Manufacturers: 1 Chevrolet, 62; **2** Buick, 40; **3** Pontiac, 35; **4** Ford, 28.

MASON-DIXON 500, Dover Downs International Speedway, Delaware, United States of America, May 15. NASCAR Winston Cup Grand National, round 10. 500 laps of the 1·000-mile/1·604-km circuit, 500·00 miles/804·67 km.
1 Bobby Allison, USA (Buick), 4h 21m 13s, 114·847 mph/184·828 km/h.
2 Darrell Waltrip, USA (Chevrolet), 4h 21m 15s.
3 Joe Ruttman, USA (Buick), 499 laps.
4 Bill Elliott, USA (Ford), 498.
5 Buddy Baker, USA (Ford), 497.
6 Morgan Shepherd, USA (Buick), 493.
7 Richard Petty, USA (Pontiac), 493; **8** Dale Earnhardt, USA (Ford), 491; **9** Harry Gant, USA (Buick), 490; **10** Sterling Martin, USA (Pontiac), 483.
Fastest Qualifier: Ruttman, 25·785s, 139·616 mph/224·690 km/h (record).
Championship points. Drivers: 1 Allison, 1531; **2** Gant, 1490; **3** Ruttman, 1432; **4** Elliott, 1413; **5** Petty, 1361; **6** Bonnett, 1336.
Manufacturers: 1 Chevrolet, 68; **2** Buick, 49; **3** Pontiac, 35; **4** Ford, 31.

VALLEYDALE 500, Bristol International Raceway, Tennessee, United States of America, May 21. NASCAR Winston Cup Grand National, round 11. 500 laps of the 0·533-mile/0·858-km circuit, 266·50 miles/428·89 km.
1 Darrell Waltrip, USA (Chevrolet), 2h 51m 07s, 93·445 mph/150·385 km/h.
2 Bobby Allison, USA (Buick), 2h 51m 09s.
3 Morgan Shepherd, USA (Buick), 499 laps.
4 Neil Bonnet, USA (Chevrolet), 499.
5 Richard Petty, USA (Pontiac), 498.
6 Terry Labonte, USA (Chevrolet), 498.
7 Ron Bouchard, USA (Buick), 498; **8** Bill Elliott, USA (Ford), 495; **9** Dale Earnhardt, USA (Ford), 495; **10** Tim Richmond, USA (Pontiac), 494.
Fastest Qualifier: Bonnett, 17·399s, 110·409 mph/177·686 km/h.
Championship points. Drivers: 1 Allison 1706; **2** Gant, 1572; **3** Elliott, 1555; **4** Ruttman, 1526; **5** Petty, 1516; **6** Bonnett, 1501.
Manufacturers: 1 Chevrolet, 77; **2** Buick, 55; **3** Pontiac, 37; **4** Ford, 31.

WORLD 600, Charlotte Motor Speedway, North Carolina, United States of America, May 29. NASCAR Winston Cup Grand National, round 12. 400 laps of the 1·500-mile/2·414-km circuit, 600·00 miles/965·80 km.
1 Neil Bonnett, USA (Chevrolet), 4h 15m 51s, 140·707 mph/226·445 km/h.
2 Richard Petty, USA (Pontiac), 4h 15m 52s.
3 Bobby Allison, USA (Buick), 400 laps.
4 Darrell Waltrip, USA (Chevrolet), 399.
5 Dale Earnhardt, USA (Ford), 399.
6 Lake Speed, USA (Chevrolet), 398.
7 Buddy Baker, USA (Ford), 398; **8** Kyle Petty, USA (Pontiac), 395; **9** Morgan Shepherd, USA (Buick), 392; **10** Dave Marcis, USA (Chevrolet), 390.
Fastest Qualifier: Baker, 2m 12·645s, 162·841 mph/262·067 km/h (4 laps).
Championship points. Drivers: 1 Allison, 1881; **2** Petty, 1691; **3** Bonnett, 1681; **4** Elliott, 1675; **5** Gant, 1665; **6** Waltrip, 1658.
Manufacturers: 1 Chevrolet, 86; **2** Buick, 59; **3** Pontiac, 43; **4** Ford, 33.

BUDWEISER 400, Riverside International Raceway, California, United States of America, June 5. NASCAR Winston Cup Grand National, round 13. 95 laps of the 2·620-mile/4·216-km circuit, 248·90 miles/400·56 km.
1 Ricky Rudd, USA (Chevrolet), 2h 49m 35s, 88·063 mph/141·723 km/h.
2 Bill Elliott, USA (Ford), 2h 49m 42s.
3 Harry Gant, USA (Buick), 95 laps.
4 Dale Earnhardt, USA (Ford), 95.
5 Dick Brooks, USA (Ford), 95.
6 Kyle Petty, USA (Pontiac), 95.
7 Darrell Waltrip, USA (Chevrolet), 95; **8** Morgan Shepherd, USA (Buick), 95; **9** Bill Schmitt, USA (Chevrolet), 94; **10** Richard Petty, USA (Pontiac), 93.
Fastest Qualifier: Waltrip, 1m 21·016s, 116·421 mph/187·361 km/h (record).
Championship points. Drivers: 1 Allison, 1978; **2** Elliott, 1845; **3** Gant, 1835; **4** Petty, 1830; **5** Waltrip, 1809; **6** Bonnett, 1805.
Manufacturers: 1 Chevrolet, 95; **2** Buick, 63; **3** Pontiac, 44; **4** Ford, 39.

VAN SCOY DIAMOND MINE 500, Pocono International Raceway, Pennsylvania, United States of America, June 12. NASCAR Winston Cup Grand National, round 14. 200 laps of the 2·500-mile/4·023-km circuit, 500·00 miles/804·57 km.
1 Bobby Allison, USA (Buick), 3h 53m 13s, 128·636 mph/207·019 km/h.
2 Darrell Waltrip, USA (Chevrolet), 3h 53m 22s.
3 Richard Petty, USA (Pontiac), 200 laps.
4 Tim Richmond, USA (Pontiac), 199.
5 Benny Parsons, USA (Buick), 199.
6 Bill Elliott, USA (Ford), 199.
7 Neil Bonnett, USA (Chevrolet), 199; **8** Dale Earnhardt, USA (Ford), 199; **9** Terry Labonte, USA (Chevrolet), 199; **10** Joe Ruttmann, USA (Pontiac), 198.
Fastest Qualifier: Waltrip, 59·088s, 152·315 mph/245·127 km/h (record).
Championship points. Drivers: 1 Allison, 2163; **2** Elliott and Petty, 2000; **4** Waltrip, 1984; **5** Bonnett, 1956; **6** Gant, 1949.
Manufacturers: 1 Chevrolet, 101; **2** Buick, 72; **3** Pontiac, 48; **4** Ford, 40.

GABRIEL 400, Michigan International Speedway, Brooklyn, Michigan, United States of America, June 19. NASCAR Winston Cup Grand National, round 15. 200 laps of the 2·000-mile/3·219-km circuit, 400·00 miles/643·80 km.
1 Cale Yarborough, USA (Chevrolet), 2h 53m 00·00s, 138·728 mph/223·261 km/h.
2 Bobby Allison, USA (Buick), 2h 53m 01·01s.
3 Tim Richmond, USA (Pontiac), 200 laps.
4 Darrell Waltrip, USA (Chevrolet), 200.
5 Terry Labonte, USA (Chevrolet), 200.
6 Ricky Rudd, USA (Chevrolet), 200.
7 Buddy Baker, USA (Ford), 200; **8** Harry Gant, USA (Buick), 200; **9** Geoff Bodine, USA (Pontiac), 200; **10** Morgan Shepherd, USA (Buick), 200.
Fastest Qualifier: Labonte, 44·454s, 161·965 mph/260·657 km/h.
Championship points. Drivers: 1 Allison, 2338; **2** Waltrip, 2149; **3** Petty, 2130; **4** Gant, 2091; **5** Elliott, 2088; **6** Bonnett, 2026.
Manufacturers: 1 Chevrolet, 110; **2** Buick, 78; **3** Pontiac, 52; **4** Ford, 40.

FIRECRACKER 400, Daytona International Speedway, Florida, United States of America, July 4. NASCAR Winston Cup Grand National, round 16. 160 laps of the 2·500-mile/4·023-km circuit, 400·00 miles/643·68 km.
1 Buddy Baker, USA (Ford), 2h 23m 20s, 167·442 mph/269·471 km/h.
2 Morgan Shepherd, USA (Buick), 2h 23m 49s.
3 David Pearson, USA (Chevrolet), 160 laps.
4 Ron Bouchard, USA (Buick), 160.
5 Terry Labonte, USA (Chevrolet), 160.
6 Geoff Bodine, USA (Pontiac), 159.
7 Bill Elliott, USA (Ford), 159; **8** Jody Ridley, USA (Buick), 159; **9** Dale Earnhardt, USA (Ford), 158; **10** Lennie Pond, USA (Buick), 157.
Fastest Qualifier: Cale Yarborough, USA (Chevrolet), 45·770s, 196·635 mph/316·453 km/h.
Championship points. Drivers: 1 Allison, 2464; **2** Waltrip, 2252; **3** Elliott, 2234; **4** Gant, 2221; **5** Petty, 2194; **6** Bonnett, 2105.
Manufacturers: 1 Chevrolet, 114; **2** Buick, 84; **3** Pontiac, 53; **4** Ford, 49.

BUSCH NASHVILLE 420, Nashville International Raceway, Nashville, Tennessee, United States of America, July 16. NASCAR Winston Cup Grand National, round 17. 420 laps of the 0·596-mile/0·959-km circuit, 250·32 miles/402·78 km.
1 Dale Earnhardt, USA (Ford), 2h 55m 12s, 85·726 mph/137·962 km/h.
2 Darrell Waltrip, USA (Chevrolet), 2h 55m 23s.
3 Tim Richmond, USA (Pontiac), 419 laps.
4 Bobby Allison, USA (Buick), 419.
5 Ricky Rudd, USA (Chevrolet), 417.
6 Neil Bonnett, USA (Chevrolet), 417.
7 Bill Elliott, USA (Ford), 416; **8** Harry Gant, USA (Buick), 416; **9** Dave Marcis, USA (Chevrolet), 416; **10** Morgan Shepherd, USA (Buick), 414.
Fastest Qualifier: Ron Bouchard, USA (Buick), 20·827s, 103·020 mph/165·794 km/h.
Championship points. Drivers: 1 Allison, 2629; **2** Waltrip, 2427; **3** Elliott, 2380; **4** Gant, 2363; **5** Petty, 2300; **6** Bonnett, 2260.
Manufacturers: 1 Chevrolet, 120; **2** Buick, 87; **3** Ford, 58; **4** Pontiac, 57.

LIKE COLA 500, Pocono International Raceway, Pennsylvania, United States of America, July 24. NASCAR Winston Cup Grand National, round 18. 200 laps of the 2·500-mile/4·023-km circuit, 500·00 miles/804·60 km.
1 Tim Richmond, USA (Pontiac), 4h 21m 17s, 114·818 mph/184·781 km/h.
2 Darrell Waltrip, USA (Chevrolet), 4h 21m 19s.
3 Bobby Allison, USA (Buick), 200 laps.
4 Neil Bonnett, USA (Chevrolet), 200.
5 Harry Gant, USA (Buick), 200.
6 Bill Elliott, USA (Ford), 200.
7 Ricky Rudd, USA (Chevrolet), 200; **8** Dave Marcis, USA (Chevrolet), 200; **9** Joe Ruttman, USA (Buick), 200; **10** Richard Petty, USA (Pontiac), 200.
Fastest Qualifier: Richmond, 59·218s, 151·981 mph/244·589 km/h.
Championship points. Drivers: 1 Allison, 2804; **2** Waltrip, 2602; **3** Elliott, 2535; **4** Gant, 2523; **5** Petty, 2434; **6** Bonnett, 2425.
Manufacturers: 1 Chevrolet, 126; **2** Buick, 91; **3** Pontiac, 66; **4** Ford, 59.

TALLADEGA 500, Alabama International Motor Speedway, Talladega, Alabama, United States of America, July 31. NASCAR Winston Cup Grand National, round 19. 188 laps of the 2·660-mile/4·281-km circuit, 500·08 miles/804·83 km.
1 Dale Earnhardt, USA (Ford), 2h 55m 52s, 170·611 mph/274·571 km/h.
2 Darrell Waltrip, USA (Chevrolet), 2h 55m 52s (Earnhardt won by ½ car length).
3 Tim Richmond, USA (Pontiac), 188 laps.
4 Richard Petty, USA (Pontiac), 188.
5 Harry Gant, USA (Buick), 188.
6 Geoff Bodine, USA (Pontiac), 188.
7 Dick Brooks, USA (Ford), 187; **8** Bill Elliott, USA (Ford), 187; **9** Bobby Allison, USA (Buick), 186; **10** Mark Martin, USA (Chevrolet), 186.
Fastest Qualifier: Cale Yarborough, USA (Chevrolet), 47·460s, 201·744 mph/324·675 km/h.
Championship points. Drivers: 1 Allison, 2947; **2** Waltrip, 2777; **3** Gant, 2678; **4** Elliott, 2677; **5** Petty, 2599; **6** Bonnett, 2483.
Manufacturers: 1 Chevrolet, 132; **2** Buick, 93; **3** Pontiac, 70; **4** Ford, 68.

CHAMPION SPARK PLUG 400, Michigan International Speedway, Brooklyn, Michigan, United States of America, August 21. NASCAR Winston Cup Grand National, round 20. 200 laps of the 2·000-mile/3·219-km circuit, 400·00 miles/643·80 km.
1 Cale Yarborough, USA (Chevrolet), 2h 42m 42s, 147·511 mph/237·395 km/h.
2 Darrell Waltrip, USA (Chevrolet), 2h 42m 42·5s.
3 Bill Elliott, USA (Ford), 200 laps.
4 Terry Labonte, USA (Chevrolet), 200.
5 Tim Richmond, USA (Pontiac), 200.
6 Richard Petty, USA (Pontiac), 200.
7 Dale Earnhardt, USA (Ford), 200; **8** Lake Speed, USA (Chevrolet), 199; **9** David Pearson, USA (Chevrolet), 199; **10** Buddy Baker, USA (Ford), 199.
Fastest Qualifier: Labonte, 44·325s, 162·437 mph/261·416 km/h.
Championship points. Drivers: 1 Allison, 3013; **2** Waltrip, 2952; **3** Elliott, 2847; **4** Petty, 2754; **5** Gant, 2751; **6** Bonnett, 2541.
Manufacturers: 1 Chevrolet, 141; **2** Buick, 93; **4** Pontiac and Ford, 72.

BUSCH 500, Bristol International Raceway, Tennessee, United States of America, August 27. NASCAR Winston Cup Grand National, round 21. 419 laps of the 0·533-mile/0·858-km circuit, 223·33 miles/359·50 km (race stopped due rain).
1 Darrell Waltrip, USA (Chevrolet), 2h 29m 50s, 89·430 mph/143·923 km/h.
2 Dale Earnhardt, USA (Ford), 2h 29m 50s (Waltrip won by 1 car length).
3 Bobby Allison, USA (Buick), 419 laps.
4 Geoff Bodine, USA (Pontiac), 418.
5 Terry Labonte, USA (Chevrolet), 418.
6 Harry Gant, USA (Buick), 418.
7 Ron Bouchard, USA (Buick), 418; **8** Morgan Shepherd, USA (Buick), 410; **9** Richard Petty, USA (Pontiac), 407; **10** Neil Bonnett, USA (Chevrolet), 405.
Fastest Qualifier: Joe Ruttman, USA (Pontiac), 17·144s, 111·923 mph/180·122 km/h.

Championship points. Drivers: 1 Allison, 3178; **2** Waltrip, 3137; **3** Elliott, 2929; **4** Gant, 2906; **5** Petty, 2897; **6** Bonnett, 2675.
Manufacturers: 1 Chevrolet, 150; **2** Buick, 97; **3** Ford, 78; **4** Pontiac, 75.

SOUTHERN 500, Darlington International Raceway, South Carolina, United States of America, September 5. NASCAR Winston Cup Grand National, round 22. 367 laps of the 1·366-mile/2·198-km circuit, 500·00 miles/804·67 km.
1 Bobby Allison, USA (Buick), 4h 03m 52s, 123·343 mph/198·501 km/h.
2 Bill Elliott, USA (Ford), 4h 03m 59s.
3 Darrell Waltrip, USA (Chevrolet), 367 laps.
4 Neil Bonnett, USA (Chevrolet), 367.
5 Terry Labonte, USA (Chevrolet), 367.
6 Buddy Baker, USA (Ford), 366.
7 Cale Yarborough, USA (Chevrolet), 366; **8** Benny Parsons, USA (Buick), 366; **9** Morgan Shepherd, USA (Buick), 364; **10** David Pearson, USA (Chevrolet), 363.
Fastest Qualifier: Bonnett, 31·285s, 157·187 mph/252·967 km/h.
Championship points. Drivers: 1 Allison, 3363; **2** Waltrip, 3307; **3** Elliott, 3104; **4** Petty, 3024; **5** Gant, 3003; **6** Bonnett, 2840.
Manufacturers: 1 Chevrolet, 154; **2** Buick, 106; **3** Ford, 84; **4** Pontiac, 75.

WRANGLER SANFORSET 400, Richmond Fairgrounds Raceway, Virginia, United States of America, September 11. NASCAR Winston Cup Grand National, round 23. 400 laps of the 0·542-mile/0·972-km circuit, 216·80 miles/348·90 km.
1 Bobby Allison, USA (Buick), 2h 43m 08s, 79·381 mph/127·751 km/h.
2 Ricky Rudd, USA (Chevrolet), 2h 43m 10s.
3 Darrell Waltrip, USA (Chevrolet), 399 laps.
4 Bill Elliott, USA (Ford), 399.
5 Terry Labonte, USA (Chevrolet), 398.
6 Richard Petty, USA (Pontiac), 396.
7 Buddy Baker, USA (Ford), 396; **8** Neil Bonnett, USA (Chevrolet), 396; **9** Trevor Boys, USA (Chevrolet), 392; **10** D. K. Ulrich, USA (Buick), 384.
Fastest Qualifier: Waltrip, 20·965s, 96·069 mph/154·608 km/h.
Championship points. Drivers: 1 Allison, 3548; **2** Waltrip, 3477; **3** Elliott, 3266; **4** Petty, 3174; **5** Gant, 3106; **6** Bonnett, 2987.
Manufacturers: 1 Chevrolet, 160; **2** Buick, 115; **3** Ford, 87; **4** Pontiac, 76.

BUDWEISER 500, Dover Downs International Speedway, Delaware, United States of America, September 18. NASCAR Winston Cup Grand National, round 24. 500 laps of the 1·000-mile/1·609-km circuit, 500·00 miles/804·67 km.
1 Bobby Allison, USA (Buick), 4h 18m 45s.
2 Geoff Bodine, USA (Pontiac), 4h 18m 45s (Allison won by 1 car length).
3 Tim Richmond, USA (Pontiac), 500 laps.
4 Terry Labonte, USA (Chevrolet), 499.
5 Darrell Waltrip, USA (Chevrolet), 499.
6 Morgan Shepherd, USA (Buick), 499.
7 Neil Bonnett, USA (Chevrolet), 493; **8** Bill Elliott, USA (Ford), 491; **9** Richard Petty, USA (Pontiac), 491; **10** Clark Dwyer, USA (Chevrolet), 480.
Fastest Qualifier: Labonte, 25·793s, 139·573 mph/224·620 km/h.
Championship points. Drivers: 1 Allison, 3733; **2** Waltrip, 3632; **3** Elliott, 3411; **4** Petty, 3317; **5** Gant, 3218; **6** Bonnett, 3138.
Manufacturers: 1 Chevrolet, 163; **2** Buick, 124; **3** Ford, 87; **4** Pontiac, 82.

GOODY'S 500, Martinsville Speedway, Virginia, United States of America, September 25. NASCAR Winston Cup Grand National, round 25. 500 laps of the 0·525-mile/0·845-km circuit, 262·50 miles/422·25 km.
1 Ricky Rudd, USA (Chevrolet), 3h 27m 16s, 76·134 mph/122·525 km/h.
2 Bobby Allison, USA (Buick), 3h 27m 20s.
3 Darrell Waltrip, USA (Chevrolet), 500 laps.
4 Dale Earnhardt, USA (Ford), 499.
5 Geoff Bodine, USA (Pontiac), 499.
6 Neil Bonnett, USA (Chevrolet), 499.
7 Joe Ruttman, USA (Buick), 499; **8** Harry Gant, USA (Buick), 498; **9** Richard Petty, USA (Pontiac), 489; **10** Buddy Arrington, USA (Dodge), 487.
Fastest Qualifier: Waltrip, 21·195s, 89·342 mph/143·782 km/h.
Championship points. Drivers: 1 Allison, 3908; **2** Waltrip, 3802; **3** Elliott, 3537; **4** Petty, 3455; **5** Gant, 3360; **6** Bonnett, 3288.
Manufacturers: 1 Chevrolet, 172; **2** Buick, 130; **3** Ford, 90; **4** Pontiac, 84.

HOLLY FARMS 400, North Wilkesboro Speedway, North Carolina, United States of America, October 2. NASCAR Winston Cup Grand National, round 26. 400 laps of the 0·265-mile/1·006-km circuit, 250·00 miles/402·34 km.
1 Darrell Waltrip, USA (Chevrolet), 2h 28m 56s, 100·716 mph/162·086 km/h.
2 Dale Earnhardt, USA (Ford), 2h 28m 59s.
3 Bobby Allison, USA (Buick), 400 laps.
4 Bill Elliott, USA (Ford), 400.
5 Terry Labonte, USA (Chevrolet), 399.
6 Ricky Rudd, USA (Chevrolet), 399.
7 Ron Bouchard, USA (Buick), 398; **8** Morgan Shepherd, USA (Buick), 398; **9** Harry Gant, USA (Buick), 398; **10** Tim Richmond, USA (Pontiac), 398.
Fastest Qualifier: Waltrip, 19·644s, 114·539 mph/184·332 km/h.
Championship points. Drivers: 1 Allison, 4078; **2** Waltrip, 3987; **3** Elliott, 3702; **4** Petty, 3582; **5** Gant, 3498; **6** Bonnett, 3412.
Manufacturers: 1 Chevrolet, 181; **2** Buick, 134; **3** Ford, 96; **4** Pontiac, 84.

MILLER HIGH LIFE 500, Charlotte Motor Speedway, North Carolina, United States of America, October 9. NASCAR Winston Cup Grand National, round 27. 334 laps of the 1·500-mile/2·414-km circuit, 501·00 miles/806·28 km.
1 Richard Petty, USA (Pontiac), 3h 34m 43s, 139·998 mph/255·304 km/h.
2 Darrell Waltrip, USA (Chevrolet), 3h 34m 47s.
3 Benny Parsons, USA (Chevrolet), 334 laps.
4 Terry Labonte, USA (Chevrolet), 334.
5 Tim Richmond, USA (Pontiac), 334.
6 Buddy Baker, USA (Ford), 334.
7 Bobby Allison, USA (Buick), 334; **8** Bill Elliott, USA (Ford), 334; **9** Ricky Rudd, USA (Chevrolet), 334; **10** Cale Yarborough, USA (Chevrolet), 333.
Fastest Qualifier: Richmond, 2m 12·456s, 163·073 mph/262·440 km/h (4 lap average).

Championship points (prior to final 3 rounds).
Drivers:

1 Bobby Allison, USA	4229
2 Darrell Waltrip, USA	4162
3 Bill Elliott, USA	3849
4 Richard Petty, USA	3658
5 Harry Gant, USA	3574
6 Terry Labonte, USA	3513

7 Neil Bonnett, USA, 3497; **8** Dale Earnhardt, USA, 3381; **9** Ricky Rudd, USA, 3381; **10** Tim Richmond, USA, 3176; **11** Joe Ruttman, USA, 3151; **12** Dick Brooks, USA, 2985; **13** Dave Marcis, USA, 2959; **14** Geoff Bodine, USA, 2955; **15** Kyle Petty, USA, 2943.

Manufacturers:

1 Chevrolet	187
2 Buick	134
3 Ford	97
4 Pontiac	93

Final results will be given in Autocourse 1984/85.

IMSA Camel GT and Endurance Championship

1982 results

The final round of the 1982 IMSA Camel GT and Endurance Championship was run after Autocourse 1982/83 went to press.

DAYTONA IMSA CAMEL GT 3 HOURS, Daytona International Speedway, Florida, United States of America, November 28. IMSA CAMEL Endurance Championship, round 10. IMSA CAMEL GT Championship, round 18. 84 laps of the 3·840-mile/6·180-km circuit, 322·56 miles/519·12 km.
1 Danny Ongais/Ted Field, USA/USA (5·9 Lola T600-Chevrolet), 3h 01m 25·684s, 106·673 mph/171·673 km/h.
2 John Fitzpatrick/Bob Wollek, GB/F (3·0 t/c Porsche 935), 3h 02m 06·537s.
3 Derek Bell/Randy Lanier, GB/USA (3·0 t/c Porsche 935), 83 laps.
4 Al Holbert/Preston Henn/Doc Bundy, USA/USA/USA (3·0 t/c Porsche 935), 83.
5 Billy Hagen/Gene Felton, USA/USA (5·9 Chevrolet Camaro), 82 (1st over 2500 cc GT class).
6 Don Devendorf/Tony Adamowicz, USA/USA (2·8 t/c Datsun ZX Turbo), 82.
7 Chip Mead/John Paul Snr, USA/USA (5·7 Pontiac Firebird), 81; **8** Chet Vincentz/Wayne Baker, USA/USA (3·0 t/c Porsche 934), 80; **9** Terry Wolters/M. L. Speer, USA/USA (3·0 t/c Porsche 935), 79; **10** Diego Montoya/Roberto Guerrero, USA/COL (3·5 BMW M1), 79. 1st up to 2500 cc GT class: Jim Downing/John Maffucci, USA/USA (Mazda RX-7), 78.
Fastest Qualifier: Wollek, 1m 42·476s, 134·900 mph/217·100 km/h (record).
Fastest lap: Ongais, 1m 45·36s, 131·207 mph/211·157 km/h (record).
Final Championship Points. Endurance:

1 John Paul Snr, USA	146
2 M. L. Speer, USA	140
Terry Wolters, USA	140
4 John Paul Jnr, USA	138
5 Bob Akin, USA	111
6 Derek Bell, GB	94
Jim Downing, USA	94
John Maffucci, USA	94

9 Roger Manderville, USA, 80; **10** Amos Johnson, USA, 80.
GT Championship. Overall:

1 John Paul Jnr, USA	235
2 Ted Field, USA	167
3 John Paul Snr, USA	125
John Fitzpatrick, GB	125
5 Danny Ongais, USA	111
6 Terry Wolters, USA	92

7 M. L. Speer, USA, 77; **8** Bob Akin, USA, 71; **9** Derek Bell, GB, 61; **10** Dave Cowart, USA and Kenper Miller, USA, 54.
GT Championship. Over 2500 cc GT class:

1 Don Devendorf, USA	154
2 Rene Rodriguez, USA	124
3 Tico Almeida, USA	111
4 Chester Vincentz, USA	84
5 Gene Felton, USA	77
6 Wayne Baker, USA	65

GT Championship. Up to 2500 cc GT class:

1 Jim Downing, USA	212
2 Roger Manderville, USA	200
3 Joe Varde, USA	157
4 Logan Blackburn, USA	144
5 George Alderman, USA	130
6 John Maffucci, USA	110

1983 results

22 PEPSI DAYTONA 24 HOURS, Daytona International Speedway, Florida, United States of America, February 5/6. IMSA CAMEL GT Championship, round 1. 618 laps of the 3·840-mile/6·180-km circuit, 2373·12 miles/3819·16 km.
1 Preston Henn/Bob Wollek/Claude Ballot-Lena/A. J. Foyt, USA/F/F/USA (3·2 t/c Porsche 935), 24h 01m 27·025s, 98·781 mph/158·972 km/h.
2 Randy Lanier/Terry Wolters/Marty Hinze, USA/USA/USA (5·8 March 83G-Chevrolet), 612 laps.
3 Pete Halsmer/Robert Reed/Rick Knoop, USA/USA/USA (2·6 Mazda RX-7), 598 (1st over 2500 cc GT class).
4 M. L. Speer/Ken Madren/Ray Ratcliff, USA/USA/USA (3·2 t/c Porsche 935), 578.
5 Diego Febles/Kikos Fonseca/Roy Valverde, PR/USA/USA (3·0 Porsche Carrera), 568.
6 Ralph Kent-Cooke/Jim Adams/John Bright, USA/USA/GB (5·8 Lola T600-Chevrolet), 563.
7 Tico Almeida/Ernesto Soto/Miguel Morejon, USA/YV/USA (3·0 Porsche Carrera), 561; **8** Pierre Honegger/Walt Bohren/David Palmer, USA/USA/GB (2·6 Mazda GTP), 553; **9** Wayne Baker/Jim Mullen/Bob Garretson, USA/USA/USA (3·0 t/c Porsche 934), 551; **10** Paul Gilgan/Al Leon/Wayne Pickering, USA/USA/USA (3·0 Porsche Carrera), 547.
1st up to 2500 cc GT class: Lee Mueller/Terry Visgar/Hugh McDonough, USA/USA/USA (2·3 Mazda RX-7), 544.
Fastest Qualifier: Wollek, 1m 42·155s, 135·324 mph/217·782 km/h (record).
Fastest lap: Wollek, 1m 49·220s, 126·570 mph/203·694 km/h.
Championship points. Overall: 1 Wollek, 20; **2** Hinze, Lanier and Wolters, 16; **5** Speer, Madren and Ratcliff, 12. **GT over 2500 cc: 1** Halsmer and Knoop, 20; **3** Febles and Fonseca, 16. **GT up to 2500 cc: 1** Mueller, Visger and McDonough, 20.

BUDWEISTER GRAND PRIX OF MIAMI CAMEL GT, Miami, Florida, United States of America, February 27. IMSA CAMEL GT Championship, round 2. 27 laps of the 1·85-mile/2·98-km circuit, 49·95 miles/80·46 km (Race shortened due rain).
1 Al Holbert, USA (5·8 March 83G-Chevrolet), 1h 00m 00s, 51·072 mph/82·192 km/h.
2 John Paul Jnr, USA (5·8 Lola T600-Chevrolet), 27 laps.
3 Klaus Ludwig, D (1·9 t/c Ford Mustang), 27.
4 John Fitzpatrick, GB (3·2 t/c Porsche 935), 27.
5 Bob Tullius, USA (5·3 Jaguar XJR-5), 27.
6 Don Whittington, USA (3·2 t/c Porsche 935), 27.
7 Tony Garcia, USA (3·3 Mirage M12-Cosworth DFL), 27; **8** Jochen Mass, D (3·2 t/c Porsche 935), 27; **9** Bob Wollek, F (3·2 t/c Porsche 935), 27; **10** Marty Hinze, USA (5·8 March 83G-Chevrolet), 26.
Fastest Qualifier: Paul Jnr, 1m 24·646s, 78·681 mph/126·624 km/h.
Fastest lap: Danny Ongais, USA (5·8 Lola T600-Chevrolet), 1m 40·140s, 66·507 mph/107·032 km/h.

BUDWEISER GRAND PRIX OF MIAMI CAMEL GTO, Miami, Florida, United States of America, February 27. 34 laps of the 1·85-mile/2·98-km circuit, 62·90 miles/101·32 km.
1 Gene Felton, USA (5·8 Chevrolet Camaro), 1h 03m 15·205s, 59·665 mph/96·021 km/.h.
2 Ludwig Heimrath, CDN (3·0 t/c Porsche 934), 1h 03m 31·692s.
3 Robert Overby, USA (5·8 Chevrolet Camaro), 34 laps.
4 "Jamsel", ES (3·0 Porsche Carrera), 33.
5 Kikos Fonseca, USA (3·0 Porsche Carrera), 33.
6 Ernesto Soto, YV (3·0 Porsche Carrera), 33.
7 Doug Lutz, USA (3·0 Porsche Carrera), 33; **8** Lloyd Frink, USA (5·8 Chevrolet Corvette), 33; **9** Bob Lee, USA (5·7 Buick Skyhawk), 32; **10** Tico Almeida, USA (5·0 Ford Mustang), 32.
Fastest lap: Diego Montoya, USA (3·5 BMW M1), 1m 45·770s, 62·967 mph/101·335 km/h.
2500 cc race winner, February 26: Roger Manderville, USA (Mazda RX-7), 34 laps, 62·90 miles/101·32 km in 54m 45·597s, 68·919 mph/110·914 km/h.
Championship points. Overall: 1 Holbert, 24; **2** Wollek, 22; **3** Paul Jnr, 18; **4** Hinze, 16; **5** Lanier and Wolters, 15. **GT over 2500 cc: 1** Fonseca, 23; **2** Halsmer, Knoop and Felton, 20. **GT up to 2500 cc: 1** Manderville, 30; **2** Mueller, 21; **3** Visger and McDonough, 20.

31 COCA-COLA 12 HOURS OF SEBRING CAMEL GT, Sebring International Raceway, Florida, United States of America, March 19. IMSA CAMEL GT Championship, round 3. 231 laps of the 4·850-mile/7·805-km circuit, 1120·35 miles/1802·96 km.
1 Wayne Baker/Jim Mullen/Kees Nierop, USA/USA/CDN (3·0 t/c Porsche 934), 12h 01m 17·745s, 93·195 mph/149·982 km/h (1st over 2500 cc GT class).
2 Bob Akin/Dale Whittington/John O'Steen, USA/USA/USA (3·2 t/c Porsche 935), 12h 02m 52·547s.
3 Hurley Haywood/Al Holbert, USA/USA (3·2 t/c Porsche 935), 229 laps.
4 Don Courtney/Luis Sereix/Brent O'Neill, USA/USA/USA (5·9 Chevrolet Monza), 227.
5 Reggie Smith/Lyn St. James/Drake Olsen, USA/USA/USA (5·3 Nimrod-Aston Martin NRA C2), 224.
6 Jack Dunham/Jeff Kline/Jon Compton, USA/USA (2·3 Mazda RX-7), 224 (1st up to 2500 cc GT class).
7 Luis Gordillo/Manuel Prieto/Chiqui Soldevila, PR/PR/PR (3·0 Porsche Carrera), 224; **8** Joe Varde/Jack Baldwin/John Casey, USA/USA/USA (2·3 Mazda RX-7), 223; **9** John Morton/Tom Klauser, USA/USA (5·0 Ford Mustang), 222; **10** Al Leon/Paul Gilgan/Wayne Pickering, USA/CDN/USA (3·0 Porsche Carrera), 222.
Fastest Qualifier: John Paul Snr, USA (3·2 t/c Porsche 935), 2m 23·965s, 121·279 mph/195·179 km/h (record).
Fastest lap: Bill Whittington, USA (3·2 t/c Porsche 935), 2m 22·750s, 122·312 mph/196·842 km/h (record).
Championship points. Overall: 1 Holbert, 39; **2** Wollek, 22; **3** Akin, Whittington, O'Steen, Cooke-Kent and Adams, 20; **GT over 2500 cc: 1** Baker, 30; **2** Fonseca, Halsmer and Knoop, 23. **GT up to 2500 cc: 1** Dunham, 32; **2** Manderville, 30; **3** Mueller, 29.

NISSAN-DATSUN CAMEL GT, Road Atlanta, Georgia, United States of America, April 10. IMSA CAMEL GT Championship, round 4. 124 laps of the 2·520-mile/4·055-km circuit, 312·48 miles/502·82 km.
1 Bob Tullius/Bill Adam, USA/CDN (5·3 Jaguar XJR-5), 3h 17m 43·509s, 94·823 mph/152·60 km/h.
2 Emory Donaldson/Bill Whittington, USA/USA (5·8 March 83G-Chevrolet), 3h 18m 01·500s.
3 Gianpiero Moretti/Sarel van de Merwe, I/ZA (3·2 t/c Porsche 935), 122 laps.
4 Skeeter McKitterick/Tom Sneva, USA/USA (3·3 Grid Plaza S1-Cosworth DFV), 119.
5 Dave Cowart/Kenper Miller, USA/USA (3·0 t/c March 82G-Porsche), 119.
6 John Paul Jnr/Rene Rodriguez, USA/USA (3·2 t/c Porsche 935), 119.
7 Pepe Romero/Doc Bundy, USA/USA (5·8 March 83G-Chevrolet), 118; **8** Wayne Baker/Jim Mullen, USA/USA (3·0 t/c Porsche 934), 117 (1st over 2500 cc GT class). **9** John Carusso/Phil Currin, USA/USA (5·8 Chevrolet Corvette), 117; **10** John Gunn, USA (5·8 Phoenix JG1-Chevrolet), 115.
1st up to 2500 cc GT class: George Alderman, USA (2·5 Datsun ZX), 114.
Fastest Qualifier: Bundy, 1m 23·053s, 109·231 mph/175·79 km/h.
Fastest lap: Whittington, 1m 19·490s, 114·128 mph/183·67 km/h (record).
Championship points. Overall: 1 Holbert, 39; **2** Tullius, 28; **3** Paul Jnr, 24; **4** Wollek, 22; **5** Akin, O'Steen, Kent-Cooke and Dale Whittington, 20. **GT over 2500 cc: 1** Baker and Mullen, 50; **3** Fonseca, 31. **GT up to 2500 cc: 1** Dunham, 47; **2** Kline, 35; **3** Manderville and Downing, 32.

LOS ANGELES TIMES/DATSUN GRAND PRIX OF ENDURANCE, Riverside International Raceway, California, United States of America, April 24. IMSA CAMEL GT Championship, round 5. 196 laps of the 3·25-mile/5·23-km circuit, 637·00 miles/1025·08 km.
1 John Fitzpatrick/David Hobbs/Derek Bell, GB/GB/GB (3·2 t/c Porsche 935), 6h 00m 29·890s, 108·020 mph/173·841 km/h.
2 Al Holbert/Jim Trueman, USA/USA (5·8 March 83G-Chevrolet), 195 laps.
3 Mauricio DeNarvaez/Bob Wollek, COL/F (3·2 t/c Porsche 935), 192.
4 Ralph Kent-Cooke/Harald Grohs, USA/D (5·8 Lola T600-Chevrolet), 191.
5 Wayne Baker/Jim Mullen/Kees Nierop, USA/USA/CDN (3·0 t/c Porsche 934), 181 (1st over 2500 cc GT class).
6 Billy Hagen/Gene Felton, USA/USA (5·9 Chevrolet Camaro), 177.
7 Bob Akin/Dale Whittington, USA/USA (3·2 t/c Porsche 935), 176; **8** Chuck Kendall/Jim Cook, USA/USA (3·5 BMW M1), 176; **9** Bruce Leven/Hurley Haywood, USA/USA (3·0 t/c Lola T600-Porsche), 172; **10** Wally Dallenbach Jnr/Whitnay Ganz/Dennis Aase, USA/USA/USA (2·0 Toyota Celica), 171 (1st up to 2500 cc GT class).
Fastest Qualifier: Holbert, 1m 36·284s, 121·516 mph/195·5461 km/h (record).
Fastest lap: Jim Adams, USA (5·8 Lola T600-Chevrolet), 1m 40·050s, 116·942 mph/188·199 km/h.
Championship points. Overall: 1 Holbert, 54; **2** Wollek, 34; **3** Kent-Cooke, 30; **4** Tullius, 28; **5** Paul Jnr, Akin and Whittington, 24. **GT over 2500 cc: 1** Baker and Mullen, 70; **3** Felton, 41. **GT up to 2500 cc: 1** Dunham, 47; **2** Ganz and Kline, 35.

MONTEREY TRIPLE CROWN CAMEL GT, Laguna Seca Raceway, California, United States of America, May 1. IMSA CAMEL GT Championship, round 6. 53 laps of the 1·900-mile/3·058-km circuit, 100·70 miles/162·07 km.
1 Al Holbert, USA (5·8 March 83G-Chevrolet), 56m 31·498s, 106·891 mph/172·024 km/h.
2 Bob Tullius, USA (5·3 Jaguar XJR-5), 57m 39·502s.
3 Bobby Rahal, USA (1·9 t/c Ford Mustang Turbo), 52 laps.
4 Hurley Haywood, USA (3·0 t/c Lola T600-Porsche), 51.
5 Diego Montoya, USA (3·5 BMW M1), 49 (1st over 2500 cc GT class).
6 Don Devendorf, USA (2·8 t/c Datsun ZX Turbo), 49.
7 Roberto Moreno, BR (2·0 Toyota Celica), 48; **8** Billy Hagen, USA (5·9 Chevrolet Camaro), 48; **9** Wayne Baker, USA (3·0 t/c Porsche 934), 47; **10** Bruno Beilcke, USA (3·5 BMW M1), 47.
Fastest Qualifier: Holbert, 1m 00·258s, 113·512 mph/182·679 km/h.
Fastest lap: Holbert, 1m 01·420s, 111·364 mph/179·223 km/h (record).
2500 cc race winner: Boy Hayje, NL (2·0 BMW 320), 39 laps, 74·10 miles/119·26 km in 46m 20·261s, 95·948 mph/154·413 km/h.
Championship points. Overall: 1 Holbert, 74; **2** Tullius, 43; **3** Haywood, 35; **4** Wollek, 34; **5** Fizpatrick and Kent-Cooke, 30. **GT over 2500 cc: 1** Baker, 78; **2** Mullen, 70; **3** Felton, 41. **GT up to 2500 cc: 1** Dunham, 50; **2** Manderville, 47; **3** Ganz and Kline, 35.

CHARLOTTE CAMEL GT 500 KM RACE, Charlotte Motor Speedway, North Carolina, United States of America, May 15. IMSA CAMEL GT Championship, round 7. 138 laps of the 2·250-mile/3·621-km circuit, 310·50 miles/499·70 km.
1 Al Holbert/Jim Trueman, USA/USA (3·0 t/c March 83G-Porsche), 3h 02m 17·138s, 102·202 mph/.164·478 km/h.
2 Dave Cowart/Kenper Miller, USA/USA (3·0 t/c March 82G-Porsche), 136 laps.
3 Bob Tullius/Bill Adam, USA/CDN (5·3 Jaguar XJR-5), 135.
4 Ken Madren/M. L. Speer, USA/USA (3·2 t/c Porsche 935), 134.
5 Wayne Baker/Jim Mullen, USA/USA (3·0 t/c Porsche 934), 133 (1st over 2500 cc GT class).
6 Diego Montoya/"Fomfor", USA/ES (3·5 BMW M1), 133.
7 Rick Knoop/John Morton, USA/USA (2·3 Mazda RX-7), 132 (1st up to 2500 cc GT class); **8** Chester Vincentz/Dave White, USA/USA (3·0 t/c Porsche 934), 132; **9** Boy Hayje/Wally Dallenbach Jnr, NL/USA (2·0 Toyota Celica), 132; **10** Jim Downing/John Maffucci, USA/USA (2·3 Mazda RX-7), 132.
Fastest Qualifier: Holbert, 1m 08·051s, 119·028 mph/191·557 km/h.
Fastest lap: Holbert, 1m 10·530s, 114·845 mph/184·825 km/h.
Championship points. Overall: 1 Holbert, 94; **2** Tullius, 55; **3**-Whittington, 36; **4** Haywood and Trueman, 35; **6** Wollek, 34. **GT over 2500 cc: 1** Baker, 98; **2** Mullen, 70; **3** Montoya, 48. **GT up to 2500 cc: 1** Manderville, 57; **2** Hayje, 52; **3** Dunham, 50.

COCA-COLA 500 CAMEL GT 3 HOUR RACE, Lime Rock Park, Connecticut, United States of America, May 30. IMSA CAMEL GT Championship, round 8. 174 laps of the 1·53-mile/2·46-km circuit, 266·22 miles/428·04 km.
1 Bob Tullius/Bill Adam, USA/CDN (5·3 Jaguar XJR-5), 3h 01m 56·933s, 87·216 mph/140·360 km/h.
2 Bob Akin/John O'Steen, USA/USA (3.2 t/c Porsche 935), 173 laps.
3 Diego Montoya, USA (3.5 BMW M1), 169 (1st over 2500cc GT class).
4 Al Holbert/Doc Bundy, USA/USA (3.0 t/c March 83G-Porsche), 169.
5 Wayne Baker/Jim Mullen, USA/USA (3.0 t/c Porsche 934), 168.
6 Rick Knoop/John Morton, USA/USA (2.6 Mazda RX-7), 165.
7 Bob Leitzinger/Logan Blackburn, USA/USA (2.5 Datsun ZX), 163 (1st up to 2500cc GT class); **8** Jim Downing/John Maffucci, USA/USA (2.3 Mazda RX-7), 163; **9** Roger Manderville/Amos Johnson, USA/USA (2.3 Mazda RX-7), 160; **10** George Drolson/John Qates, USA/USA (2.0 t/c Porsche 924 Carrera), 160.
Fastest Qualifier: Holbert, 49·779s, 109·926 mph/176·908 km/h.
Fastest lap: Tullius, 51·060s, 107·168 mph/172·470 km/h.
Championship points. Overall: 1 Holbert, 106; **2** Tullius, 75; **3** Adam, 52; **4** Akin, 43; **5** Whittington, 36; **6** Trueman, Haywood and O'Steen, 35. **GT over 2500cc: 1** Baker, 113; **2** Mullen, 105; **3** Montoya, 68. **GT up to 2500cc: 1** Manderville, 69; **2** Downing, 62; **3** Maffucci, 56.

LUMBERMENS 6 HOUR CAMEL GT, Mid-Ohio Sports Car Course, Ohio, United States of America, June 19. IMSA CAMEL GT Championship, round 9. 212 laps of the 2·400-mile/3·862-km circuit, 508·80 miles/818·74 km.
1 Jim Trueman/Doc Bundy/Bobby Rahal, USA/USA/USA (5.8 March 83G-Chevrolet), 6h 00m 47·516s, 84·614 mph/136·173 km/h.
2 Bob Akin/John O'Steen, USA/USA (3.0 t/c Porsche 935), 201 laps.
3 Billy Hagan/Gene Felton, USA/USA (5.9 Chevrolet Camaro), 201 (1st over 2500cc GT class).
4 Chester Vincentz/Dave White, USA/USA (3.0 t/c Porsche 934), 199.
5 Joe Varde/Jack Baldwin, USA/USA (2.3 Mazda RX-7), 196 (1st up to 2500cc GT class).
6 Gianpiero Moretti/Sarel van der Merwe, I/ZA (3.0 t/c Porsche 935), 196.
7 Jim Downing/John Maffucci, USA/USA (2.3 Mazda RX-7), 194; **8** Roger Manderville/Amos Johnson, USA/USA (2.3 Mazda RX-7), 193; **9** Ken Madren/M. L. Speer, USA/USA (3.0 t/c Porsche 935), 193; **10** Don Courtney/Brent O'Neill, USA/USA (5.8 Chevrolet Monza), 191.
Fastest Qualifier: Rahal, 1m 24·643s, 102·076 mph/164·275 km/h (record).
Fastest lap: Bob Tullius, USA (5.3 Jaguar XJR-5), 1m 30·680s, 94·683 mph/152·377 km/h (record).
Championship points. Overall: 1 Holbert, 106; **2** Tullius, 75; **3** Akin, 58; **4** Adam, 52; **5** O'Steen, 50; **6** Whittington, 36. **GT over 2500cc: 1** Baker, 116; **2** Mullen, 108; **3** Montoya, 68. **GT up to 2500cc: 1** Manderville, 81; **2** Downing, 77; **3** Maffucci, 71.

PAUL REVERE 250 CAMEL GT, Daytona International Speedway, Florida, United States of America, July 3. IMSA CAMEL GT Championship, round 10. 654 laps of the 3·840-mile/6·180-km circuit, 249·60 miles/401·70 km.
1 Hurley Haywood/A. J. Foyt, USA/USA (3.2 t/c Porsche 935), 2h 05m 53·110s, 118·966 mph/191·457 km/h.
2 Marty Hinze/Don Whittington, USA/USA (5.8 March 83G-Chevrolet), 2h 07m 21·770s.
3 Bob Akin/John O'Steen, USA/USA (3.2 t/c Porsche 935), 64 laps.
4 Billy Hagen/Gene Felton, USA/USA (5.9 Chevrolet Camaro), 63 (1st over 2500cc GT class).
5 M. L. Speer/Wayne Pickering, USA/USA (3.2 t/c Porsche 935), 63.
6 John Gunn/Ricardo Londono, USA/USA (5.8 Phoenix-JG1-Chevrolet), 63.
7 Tico Almeida/Ernesto Soto, USA/USA (5.0 Ford Mustang), 62; **8** Diego Montoya/"Fomfor", USA/ES (3.5 BMW M1), 61; **9** Jim Downing, USA (2.3 Mazda RX-7), 60 (1st up to 2500cc GT class); **10** Roger Manderville, USA (2.3 Mazda RX-7), 60.
Fastest Qualifier: Haywood, 1m 48·336s, 127·603 mph/205·357 km/h.
Fastest lap: Haywood, 1m 48·655s, 127·228 mph/294·753 km/h.
Championship points. Overall: 1 Holbert, 106; **2** Tullius, 75; **3** Akin, 70; **4** O'Steen, 62; **5** Haywood, 55; **6** Speer, 53. **GT over 2500cc: 1** Baker, 121; **2** Mullen, 113; **3** Felton, 85. **GT up to 2500cc: 1** Downing, 97; **2** Manderville, 96; **3** Maffucci, 71.

PEPSI GRAND PRIX 500 KM CAMEL GT, Brainerd International Raceway, Minnesota, United States of America, July 10. IMSA CAMEL GT Championship, round 11. 104 laps of the 3·000-mile/4·828-km circuit, 312·00 miles/502·112 km.
1 Al Holbert/Jim Trueman, USA/USA (3.0 t/c March 83G-Porsche), 3h 10m 06·340s, 98·472 mph/158·475 km/h.
2 David Cowart/Kenper Miller, USA/USA (5.8 March 83G-Chevrolet), 103 laps.
3 John Kalagian/John Mills, USA/USA (5.8 Lola T600-Chevrolet), 103.
4 Bob Akin/Dannis Aase, USA/USA (3.2 t/c Porsche 935), 102.
5 Don Devendorf/Tony Adamowicz, USA/USA (2.8 t/c Datsun ZX), 101 (1st over 2500 cc GT class).
6 "Fomfor", ES (3.5 BMW M1), 99.
7 Roger Manderville/Amos Johnson, USA/USA (2.3 Mazda RX-7), 97 (1st up to 2500cc GT class); **8** Jim Downing/John Maffucci, USA/USA (2.3 Mazda RX-7), 95; **9** Joe Varde/Jack Baldwin, USA/USA (2.3 Mazda RX-7), 95; **10** Wayne Baker/Bob Raub, USA/USA (5.9 Pontiac Firebird), 95.
Fastest Qualifier: Holbert, 1m 31·543, 117·977 mph/189·865 km/h.
Fastest lap: Holbert, 1m 33·780s, 115·160 mph/185·332 km/h.
Championship points. Overall: 1 Holbert, 126; **2** Akin, 80; **3** Tullius, 75; **4** O'Steen, 62; **5** Trueman and Haywood, 55. **GT over 2500cc: 1** Baker, 132; **2** Mullen, 112; **3** Felton, 91. **GT up to 2500cc: 1** Manderville, 116; **2** Downing, 112; **3** Maffucci, 86.

SEARS POINT 3 HOUR CAMEL GT, Sears Point International Raceway, Sonoma, California, United States of America, July 24. IMSA CAMEL GT Championship, round 12. 106 laps of the 2·523-mile/4·060-km circuit, 267·44 miles/430·36 km.
1 Al Holbert/Jim Trueman, USA/USA (3.0 t/c March 83G-Porsche), 3h 00m 31·230s, 88·079 mph/141·749 km/h.
2 John Morton/Bob Lobenberg, USA/USA (5.9 Lola T600-Chevrolet), 3h 02m 18·000s.
3 John Kalagian/Rex Ramsey, USA/USA (5.9 Lola T600-Chevrolet), 105 laps.
4 David Cowart/Kenper Miller, USA/USA (5.9 March 83G-Chevrolet), 105.
5 Don Devendorf/Tony Adamowicz, USA/USA (2.8 t/c Datsun ZX), 102 (1st over 2500cc GT class).
6 Pete Halsmer/Rick Knoop, USA/USA (2.6 Mazda RX-7), 101.
7 Gianpiero Moretti/Sarel van der Merwe, I/ZA (3.2 t/c Porsche 935), 100; **8** Wayne Baker/Jim Mullen, USA/USA (3.0 t/c Porsche 934), 99; **9** Joe Varde/Jack Baldwin, USA/USA (2.3 Mazda RX-7), 99 (1st up to 2500cc GT class); **10** Billy Hagen/Gene Felton, USA/USA (5.9 Chevrolet Camaro), 99.
Fastest Qualifier: Lobenberg, 1m 30·638s, 99·296 mph/159·801 km/h.
Fastest lap: Bill Adam, CDN (5.3 Jaguar XJR-5), 1m 34·480s, 95·528 mph/153·737 km/h.
Championship points. Overall: 1 Holbert, 146; **2** Akin, 80; **3** Tullius, 77; **4** Trueman, 75; **5** O'Steen, 62; **6** Haywood, 55. **GT over 2500cc: 1** Baker, 144; **2** Mullen, 124; **3** Felton, 101. **GT up to 2500cc: 1** Manderville, 131; **2** Downing, 124; **3** Varde and Baldwin, 102.

G. I. JOE'S GRAN PRIX 3 HOUR CAMEL GT, Portland International Raceway, Portland, Oregon, United States of America, July 31. IMSA CAMEL GT Championship, round 13. 152 laps of the 1·915-mile/3·082-km circuit, 291·08 miles/468·46 km.
1 Al Holbert, USA (3.0 t/c March 83G-Porsche), 3h 00m 12·310s, 96·916 mph/155·971 km/h.
2 John Morton/Bob Lobenberg, USA/USA (5.9 Lola T600-Chevrolet), 3h 01m 07·460s.
3 Don Devendorf/Tony Adamowicz, USA/USA (2.8 t/c Datsun ZX), 146 laps (1st over 2500cc GT class).
4 "Fomfor"/Diego Montoya, ES/USA (3.5 BMW M1), 145.
5 Wayne Baker/Jim Mullen, USA/USA (3.0 t/c Porsche 934), 141.
6 Roger Manderville/Amos Johnson, USA/USA (2.3 Mazda RX-7), 139 (1st up to 2500cc GT class).
7 Tom Winters/Bob Bergstrom, USA/USA (2.0 Porsche 924 Carrera), 138; **8** John Chamberlain/Jerry Pillar, USA/USA (5.9 Chevrolet Corvette), 138; **9** Bob Leitzinger, USA (2.5 Datsun ZX), 138; **10** Jim Downing/John Maffucci, USA/USA (2.3 Mazda RX-7), 135.
Fastest Qualifier: Bob Tullius, USA (5.3 Jaguar XJR-5), 1m 04·554s, 106·794 mph/171·868 km/h.
Fastest lap: Tullius, 1m 05·840s, 104·708 mph/168·511 km/h.
Championship points. Overall: 1 Holbert, 166; **2** Tullius, 81; **3** Akin, 80; **4** Trueman, 75; **5** Haywood, 63; **6** O'Steen, 62. **GT over 2500cc: 1** Baker, 156; **2** Mullen, 136; **3** Felton, 101. **GT up to 2500cc: 1** Manderville, 151; **2** Downing, 134; **3** Maffucci, 108.

LABATT'S GT 6 HOUR CAMEL GT, Mosport Park Circuit, Ontario, Canada, August 8. IMSA CAMEL GT Championship, round 14. 224 laps of the 2·459-mile/3·957-km circuit, 550·82 miles/886·37 km.
1 Bob Tullius/Bill Adam, USA/CDN (5.3 Jaguar XJR-5), 6h 00m 16·429s, 91·770 mph/147·689 km/h.
2 David Cowart/Kenper Miller, USA/USA (5.9 March 83G-Chevrolet), 6h 01m 25·633s.
3 Rick Knoop/John Morton, USA/USA (2.6 Mazda RX-7), 212 laps (1st over 2500cc GT class).
4 Craigh Allen/George Schwartz, CDN/CDN (5.9 Pontiac Firebird), 206.
5 Roger Manderville/Amos Johnson, USA/USA (2.3 Mazda RX-7), 206 (1st up to 2500cc GT class).
6 Jim Downing/John Maffucci, USA/USA (2.3 Mazda RX-7), 204.
7 Al Holbert/Jim Trueman, USA/USA (3.0 t/c March 83G-Porsche), 201; **8** Tim Selby/Earl Roe, CDN/CDN (2.0 Porsche 914/6), 200; **9** Ken Madren/M. L. Speer/Wayne Pickering, USA/USA/USA (3.0 t/c Porsche 935), 199; **10** John Graham/Hurley Haywood/Eddie Wachs, CDN/USA/USA (3.0 t/c Porsche 935), 196.
Fastest Qualifier: Holbert, 1m 17·190s, 114·730 mph/184·640 km/h (record).
Fastest lap: Holbert, 1m 19·080s, 111·988 mph/180·227 km/h (record).
Championship points. Overall: 1 Holbert, 178; **2** Tullius, 101; **3** Trueman, 87; **4** Akin, 86; **5** Adam, 78; **6** Haywood, 71. **GT over 2500cc: 1** Baker, 166; **2** Mullen, 136; **3** Felton, 113. **GT up to 2500cc: 1** Manderville, 171; **2** Downing, 149; **3** Maffucci, 123.

BUDWEISER 500 CAMEL GT, Road America, Elkhart Lake, Wisconsin, United States of America, August 21. IMSA CAMEL GT Championship, round 15. 115 laps of the 4·000-mile/6·437-km circuit, 460·00 miles/740·26 km.
1 Klaus Ludwig/Tim Coconis, D/USA (1.7 t/c Ford Mustang GTP), 4h 48m 38·330s, 95·621 mph/153·89 km/h.
2 Don Devendorf/Tony Adamowicz, USA/USA (2.8 t/c Datsun ZX), 113 laps (1st over 250cc GT class).
3 Bobby Rahal/Geoff Brabham, USA/AUS (1.7 t/c Ford Mustang GTP), 113.
4 Paul Canary/Eppie Wietzes, USA/CDN (5.9 Pontiac Firebird), 108.
5 Roger Manderville/Amos John son, USA/USA (2.3 Mazda RX-7), 107 (1st up to 2500cc GT class);.
6 Rob Dyson/Ken Slagle, USA/USA (5.9 Pontiac Firebird), 107.
7 Jim Downing/John Maffucci, USA/USA (2.3 Mazda RX-7), 107; **8** John Morton/Bob Lobenberg, USA/USA (5.9 Lola T600-Chevrolet), 107; **9** Joe Varde/Jeff Kline, USA/USA (2.3 Mazda RX-7), 107; **10** John Kalagian/John Mills, USA/USA (5.9 Lola T600-Chevrolet), 106.
Fastest Qualifier: Al Holbert, USA (3.0 t/c March 83G-Porsche), 2m 09·949s, 110·813 mph/178·336 km/h.
Fastest lap: Lobenberg, 2m 11·590s, 109·431 mph/176·112 km/h.
Championship points. Overall: 1 Holbert, 184; **2** Tullius, 101; **3** Trueman, 93; **4** Akin, 86; **5** Adam, 78; **6** Haywood, 71. **GT over 2500cc: 1** Baker, 174; **2** Mullen, 144; **3** Felton, 113. **GT up to 2500cc: 1** Manderville, 191; **2** Downing, 164; **3** Johnson, 141.

POCONO CAMEL GT 500, Pocono International Raceway, Pennsylvania, United States of America, September 11. IMSA CAMEL GT Championship, round 16. 179 laps of the 2·800-mile/4·506-km circuit, 501·20 miles/806·57 km.
1 Bob Tullius/Doc Bundy, USA/USA (5.3 Jaguar XJR-5), 4h 52m 01·537s, 102·977 mph/165·725 km/h.
2 Gianpiero Moretti/Sarel van der Merwe, I/ZA (3.2 t/c Porsche 935), 176 laps.
3 Billy Hagen/Gene Felton, USA/USA /5.9 Chevrolet Camaro), 172 (1st over 2500cc GT class).
4 Bob Akin/John O'Steen, USA/USA (3.2 t/c Porsche 935), 171.
5 "Fomfor"/Drake Olsen, ES/USA (3.5 BMW M1), 169.
6 Jim Downing/John Maffucci, USA/USA (2.3 Mazda RX-7), 163 (1st up to 2500cc GT class).
7 Tom Winters/Bob Bergstrom, USA/USA (2.0 Porsche 924 Carrera), 162; **8** George Alderman/Carson Baird, USA/USA (2.5 Datsun ZX), 162; **9** Don Devendorf/Tony Adamowicz, USA/USA (2.8 t/c Datsun ZX), 160; **10** Chester Vincentz/Jim Mullen, USA/USA (3.0 t/c Porsche 934), 159.
Fastest qualifier: Tullius, 1m 24·832s, 118·823 mph/191·227 km/h.
Fastest lap: Bob Holbert, USA (3.0 t/c March 83G-Porsche), 1m 27·110s, 115·716 mph/186·226 km/h.

Championship points (prior to final round at Daytona on November 27)
Overall:

1 Al Holbert, USA	184 (Champion)
2 Bob Tullius, USA	121
3 Bob Akin, USA	98
4 Jim Trueman, USA	93
5 John O'Steen, USA	80
6 Bill Adam, CDN	78

7 Hurley Haywood, USA, 71; **8** Kenper Miller, USA and David Cowart, USA, 63; **10** M. L. Speer, USA, 53; **11** Bobby Rahal, USA and Gianpiero Moretti, I, 47; **13** John Kalagian, USA, John Morton, USA and Bob Lobenberg, USA, 44. **GT over 2500cc: 1** Wayne Baker, USA, 174; **2** Jim Mullen, USA, 154; **3** Gene Felton, USA, 134; **4** Billy Hagen, USA, 126; **5** Don Devendorf, USA, 115; **6** Diego Montoya, USA, 105. **GT up to 2500cc: 1** Roger Manderville, USA, 201; **2** Jim Downing, USA, 184; **3** John Maffucci, USA, 158; **4** Amos Johnson, USA, 151; **5** Joe Varde, USA, 124; **6** Jack Baldwin, USA, 102.
Final results will be given in Autocourse 1984/85